THE SULTAN PARDONS SCHEHERAZADE.

# ARABIAN NIGHTS

The Text Revised and Emendated throughout by

H. W. DULCKEN, Ph.D.

WITH UPWARDS OF TWO HUNDRED ILLUSTRATIONS BY EMINENT ARTISTS.

CASTLE

ISBN 0-89009-800-X

Manufactured in the United States of America



84 85 86 87 3 2 1 0 9 8 7 6 5 4 3 2 1

CONTENTS.

*Contents.*

ILLUSTRATIONS.

## *List of Illustrations.*

*List of Illustrations.*

ILLUSTRATED

ARABIAN NIGHTS'

Entertainments

"The lives of former generations are a lesson to posterity; that a man may review the remarkable events which have happened to others, and be admonished; and may consider the history of people of preceding ages, and of all that hath befallen them, and be restrained. . . . . Such are the Tales of a Thousand and One Nights with their romantic Stories and their Fables."—LANE.

# THE ARABIAN NIGHTS

HE chronicles of the ancient Kings of Persia, who extended their empire into the Indies, and as far as China, tell of a powerful king of that family, who dying, left two sons. The eldest, Shahriar, inherited the bulk of his empire; the younger, Shahzenan, who like his brother Shahriar was a virtuous prince, well beloved by his subjects, became King of Samarcande.

After they had been separated ten years, Shahriar resolved to send his vizier to his brother to invite him to his court. Setting out with a retinue answerable to his dignity, that officer made all possible haste to Samarcande. Shahzenan received the ambassador with the greatest demonstrations of joy. The vizier then gave him an account of his embassy. Shahzenan answered thus:—"Sage vizier, the Sultan does me too much honour; I long as passionately to see him, as he does to see me. My kingdom is in peace, and I desire no more than ten days to get myself ready to go with you; there is no necessity that you should enter the city for so short a time: I pray you to pitch your tents here, and I will order provisions in abundance for yourself and your company."

At the end of ten days, the King took his leave of his Queen, and went out of town in the evening with his retinue, pitched his royal pavilion near the vizier's tent, and discoursed with that ambassador till midnight. But willing once more to embrace the Queen, whom he loved entirely, he returned alone to his palace, and went straight to her apartment.

The King entered without any noise, and pleased himself to think how he should surprise his wife, whose affection for him he never doubted. Great was his surprise, when by the lights in the royal chamber, he saw a male slave in the Queen's apartment! He could scarcely believe his own eyes. "How!" said he to himself, "I am scarce gone from Samarcande, and they dare thus disgrace me!" And he drew his scimitar, and killed them both; and quitting the town privately, set forth on his journey.

When he drew near the capital of the Indies, the Sultan Shahriar and all the court came out to meet him: the princes, overjoyed at meeting, embraced, and entered the city together, amid the acclamations of the people; and the Sultan conducted his brother to the palace he had provided for him.

But the remembrance of his wife's disloyalty made such an impression upon the countenance of Shahzenan, that the Sultan could not but notice it. Shahriar endeavoured to divert his brother every day, by new schemes of pleasure, and the most splendid entertainments; but all his efforts only increased the King's sorrow.

One day, Shahriar had started on a great hunting match, about two days' journey from his capital; but Shahzenan, pleading ill health, was left behind. He shut himself up in his apartment, and sat down at a window that looked into the garden.

Suddenly a secret gate of the palace opened, and there came out of it twenty women, in the midst of whom walked the Sultaness. The persons who accompanied the Sultaness threw off their veils and long robes, and Shahzenan was greatly surprised when he saw that ten of them were black slaves, each of whom chose a female companion.

THE MEETING OF THE BROTHERS.

The Sultaness clapped her hands, and called: "Masoud, Masoud!" and immediately a black came running to her; and they all remained conversing familiarly together.

When Shahzenan saw this he cried: "How little reason had I, to think that no one was so unfortunate as myself!"—So, from that moment he forbore to repine. He ate and drank, and he continued in very good humour; and when the Sultan returned, he went to meet him with a shining countenance.

Shahriar was overjoyed to see his brother so cheerful; and spoke thus: "Dear brother, ever since you came to my court I have seen you afflicted with a deep melancholy; but now you are in the highest spirits. Pray tell me why you were so melancholy, and why you are now cheerful?"

Upon this, the King of Tartary continued for some time as if he had been meditating, and contriving what he should answer; but at last replied as follows: "You are my Sultan and master; but excuse me, I beseech you, from answering your question."—"No, dear brother," said the Sultan, "you must answer me; I will take no denial." Shahzenan for a time hesitated to reply; but not being able to withstand his brother's importunity, told him the story of the Queen of Samarcande's treachery: "This," said he, "was the cause of my grief; judge, whether I had not reason enough to give myself up to it."

Then Shahriar said: "I cease now to wonder at your melancholy. But, bless Allah, who has comforted you; let me know what your comfort is, and conceal nothing from me." Obliged again to yield to the Sultan's pressing instances, Shahzenan gave him the particulars of all that he had seen from his window. Then Shahriar spoke thus: "I must see this with my own eyes; the matter is so important, that I must be satisfied of it myself." "Dear brother," answered Shahzenan, "that you may without much difficulty. Appoint another hunting match; and after our departure you and I will return alone to my apartments; the next day you will see what I saw." The Sultan, approving the stratagem, immediately appointed a new hunting match; and that same day the tents were set up at the place appointed.

Next day the two princes set out, and stayed for some time at the place of encampment. They then returned in disguise to the city, and went to Shahzenan's apartment. They had scarce placed themselves in the window, when the secret gate opened, the Sultaness and her ladies entered the garden with the blacks. Again she called Masoud; and the Sultan saw that his brother had spoken truth.

"O heavens!" cried he, "what an indignity! Alas! my brother, let us abandon our dominions and go into foreign countries, where we may lead an obscure life, and conceal our misfortune." "Dear brother," replied Shahzenan, "I am ready to follow; but promise me that you will return when we meet any one more unhappy than ourselves." So they secretly left the place. They travelled as long as it was day, and passed the first night under some trees. Next morning they went on till they came to a fair meadow on the sea-shore, and sat down under a large tree to refresh themselves.

Soon they heard a terrible noise; the sea opened, and there arose out of it a great black column, ascending towards the clouds. Then they were seized with fear, and climbed up into the tree to hide themselves. And the dark column advanced towards the shore, and there came forth from it a black genie, of prodigious stature, who carried on his head a great glass box, shut with four locks of fine steel. He came into the meadow and laid down his burden at the foot of the tree in which the two princes were hidden. The genie opened the box with four keys that he had at his girdle, and there came out a lady magnificently apparelled, and of great beauty. Then the genie said: "O lady, whom I carried off on your wedding day, let me sleep a few moments." Having spoken thus, he laid his head upon her knee and fell asleep.

The lady looking up at the tree, saw the two princes, and made a sign to them to come down without making any noise. But they were afraid of the genie, and would fain have been excused. Upon this she laid the monster's head softly on the ground, and ordered them to come down, saying, "If you hesitate, I will wake up this genie, and he shall kill you." So the princes came down to her. And when she had remained with them for some time, she pulled out a string of rings, of all sorts, which she showed them, and said: "These are the rings of all the men with whom I have conversed, as with you. There are full fourscore and eighteen of them, and I ask yours to make up the hundred. This wicked genie never leaves me. But he may lock me up in this glass box, and hide me in the bottom of the sea: I find a way to cheat his care. You may see by this, that when a woman has formed a project, no one can hinder her from putting it into execution." Then said the two kings: "This monster is more unfortunate than we." So they returned to the camp, and thence to the city.

Then Shahriar ordered that the Sultaness should be strangled; and he beheaded all her women with his own hand. After this he resolved to marry a virgin every day, and to have her killed the next morning. And thus every day a maiden was married, and every day a wife was sacrificed.

THE SLEEPING GENIE AND THE LADY.

The report of this unexampled cruelty spread consternation through the city. And at length, the people who had once loaded their monarch with praise and blessings, raised one universal outcry against him.

The grand vizier, who was the unwilling agent of this horrid injustice, had two daughters, the eldest called Sheherazade, and the youngest Dinarzade. The latter was a lady of very great merit; but the elder had courage, wit, and penetration in a remarkable degree. She studied much, and had such a tenacious memory, that she never forgot any thing she had once read. She had successfully applied herself to philosophy, physic, history, and the liberal arts; and made verses that surpassed those of the best poets of her time. Besides this, she was a perfect beauty; all her great qualifications were crowned by solid virtue; and the vizier passionately loved a daughter so worthy of his affection.

One day, as they were discoursing together, she said to him, "Father, I have one favour to beg of you, and most humbly pray you to grant it me."—"I will not refuse it," he answered, "provided it be just and reasonable."—"I have a design," resumed she, "to stop the course of that barbarity which the Sultan exercises upon the families of this city."—"Your design, daughter," replied the vizier, "is very commendable; but how do you intend to effect it?"—"Father," said Sheherazade, "since by your means the Sultan celebrates a new marriage, I conjure you to procure me the honour of being his bride."

This proposal filled the vizier with horror. "O heavens," replied he, "have you lost your senses, daughter, that you make such a dangerous request to me? You know the Sultan has sworn by his soul that he will never be married for two days to the same woman; and would you have me propose you to him?"—"Dear father," said the daughter, "I know the risk I run; but that does not frighten me. If I perish, at least my death will be glorious; and if I succeed, I shall do my country an important piece of service."—"No, no," said the vizier, "whatever you can represent to induce me to let you throw yourself into that horrible danger, do not think that I will agree to it. When the Sultan shall order me to strike my dagger into your heart, alas! I must obey him; what a horrible office for a father!"—"Once more, father," said Sheherazade, "grant me the favour I beg."—"Your stubbornness"—replied the vizier—"will make me angry; why will you run headlong to your ruin? I am afraid the same thing will happen to you that happened to the ass, who was well off, and could not keep so." "What happened to the ass?" asked Sheherazade.—"I will tell you," said the vizier.

## THE STORY OF THE ASS, THE OX, AND THE LABOURER.

A very rich merchant had the gift of understanding the languages of beasts; but with this condition, that, on pain of death, he should reveal to nobody what they said;—and this hindered him from communicating to others the knowledge he thus acquired.

He had in the same stall an ox and an ass; and one day, as he sat near them, he heard the ox say to the ass,—"Oh! how happy do I think you, when I consider the ease you enjoy and the little labour that is required of you! Your greatest business is to carry our master when he has a short journey to make; and were it not for that, you would be perfectly idle. I am treated in quite a different manner, and my condition is as miserable as yours is pleasant. It is scarce daylight when I am fastened to a plough, and the labourer, who is always behind me, beats me continually: and after having toiled from morning to night, when I am brought in, they give me nothing to eat but dry beans; and when I have satisfied my hunger with this trash, I am forced to lie all night upon filthy straw; so that you see I have reason to envy your lot."

The ass answered,—"They do not lie who call you a foolish beast. You kill yourself for the ease, profit, and pleasure of those who give you no thanks for so doing. But they would not treat you so if you had as much courage as strength. When they come to fasten you to your stall, why do you not strike them with your horns? Nature has furnished you with the means to procure for yourself respect, but you do not make use of them. They bring you only sorry beans and bad straw; eat none of these, only smell at and leave them. If you follow the advice I give you, you will quickly find a change in your condition, for which you will thank me."

The ox took the ass's advice in very good part, and professed himself much obliged for the good counsel. After this discourse, of which the merchant lost not a word, they held their peace.

Next morning the labourer fastened the ox to the plough, and led him off to his usual work. The ox was very troublesome all that day; and in the evening, when the labourer brought him back to the stall, the vicious beast was restive, and ran at the labourer, as if he would have pushed him with his horns. In a word, he did all that the ass advised him to do. Next day the labourer finding the manger still full of beans, and the ox lying on the ground with his legs stretched out, and panting in a strange manner, believed the beast was sick, and, pitying him, acquainted the merchant with the fact. The merchant perceiving that the ox had followed the mischievous advice of the ass, ordered the labourer to go and put the ass in the ox's place, and to be sure to work him hard. The labourer did so; the ass was forced to draw the plough all that day; besides, he was so soundly beaten, that he could scarcely stand when he came back.

Meanwhile the ox was very well satisfied. He ate up all that was in his stall, and rested the whole day; and did not fail to compliment the ass for his advice when he came back. The ass answered not one word, so angry was he at the treatment he had received; but he said within himself,—"By my own imprudence I have brought this misfortune upon myself; and if I cannot contrive some way to get out of it, I am certainly undone;"—and as he spoke thus, his strength was so much exhausted, that he fell down in his stall, half dead.

The merchant was curious to know what passed between the ass and the ox; therefore he went out and sat down by them, and his wife was with him. When he arrived, he heard the ass say to the ox,—"Comrade, tell me, I pray you, what you intend to do to-morrow, when the labourer brings you meat?" "What shall I do!" said the ox; I shall continue to do as you taught me." "Beware of that," replied the ass, "it will ruin you; for as I came home this evening, I heard the merchant, our master, say to the labourer,—'Since the ox does not eat, and is not able to work, I will have him killed to-morrow; therefore, do not fail to send for the butcher.' This is what I had to tell you,"—said the ass. "The concern I have for your safety, and my friendship for you, obliged me to let you know it, and to give you new advice. As soon as they bring you your bran and straw, rise up, and eat heartily. Our master will by this think you are cured, and, no doubt, will recall his orders for killing you; whereas, if you do otherwise, you are certainly gone."

This discourse had the effect which the ass designed. The merchant, who had listened very attentively, burst into such a fit of laughter, that his wife was surprised at it, and said, "Pray, husband, tell me what you laugh at so heartily, that I may laugh with you." "Wife," said he, "I only laugh at what our ass just now said to our ox. The matter is a secret, which I am not allowed to reveal." "And what hinders you from revealing the secret?" asked she. "If I tell it it you," replied he, "it will cost me my life." "If you do not tell me what the ox and the ass said to one another," cried his wife, "I swear by heaven that you and I shall never live together again."

Having spoken thus, she went into the house in great anger, and sitting down in a corner, she cried there all night. Her husband, finding next morning that she continued in the same humour, told her she was a very foolish woman to afflict herself in that manner. "I shall never cease weeping," said she,' 'till you have satisfied my curiosity." "But I tell you very seriously," replied he, "that it will cost me my life, if I yield to your indiscretion." "Let what will happen," said she, "I insist upon knowing this matter." "I perceive," said the merchant, "that it is impossible to bring you to reason; and since I foresee that you will procure your own death by your obstinacy, I will call in your children, that they may see you before you die." Accordingly, he called for them, and sent for her father and mother, and other relations. When they heard the reason of their being called for, they did all they could to convince her that she was in the wrong; but she told them that she would rather die than yield that point to her husband. The merchant was like a man out of his senses, and almost ready to risk his own life to save that of his wife, whom he loved dearly.

Now this merchant had fifty hens and a cock, with a dog, that gave good heed to all that passed; and while the merchant was considering what he should do, he saw his dog run towards the cock, who was crowing lustily, and heard him speak thus: "You, cock, I am sure, will not be allowed to live long; are you not ashamed to be so merry to-day?" "And why," said the cock, "should I not be merry to-day as well as on other days?" "If you do not know," replied the dog, "then I will tell you, that this day our master is in great affliction; his wife would have him reveal a secret, which is of such a nature that its discovery will cost him his life."

The cock answered the dog thus: "What, has our master so little sense? He has but one wife, and cannot govern her! and though I have fifty, I make them all do what I please. Let him make use of his reason; he will speedily find a way to rid himself of his trouble."—"How?" asked the dog; "what would you have him do?"—"Let him

THE VIZIER AND HIS DAUGHTER.

go into the room where his wife is," replied the cock, "lock the door, and take a good stick and beat her well; and, I will answer for it, that will bring her to her senses, and make her forbear asking him any more to reveal what he ought not to tell her." The merchant had no sooner heard what the cock said, than he took up a good stick, went to his wife, whom he found still crying, and, shutting the door, belaboured her so soundly, that she cried out, "It is enough, husband, it is enough; let me alone, and I will never ask the question more." "Daughter," added the grand vizier, "you deserve to be treated as the merchant treated his wife."

"Father," replied Sheherazade, "I beg you will not take it ill that I persist in my opinion. I am in no way moved by the story of that woman." In short, the father, overcome by the resolution of his daughter, yielded to her importunity; and though he was very much grieved that he could not divert her from her fatal resolution, he went that minute to inform the Sultan that next night he would bring him Sheherazade.

SHEHERAZADE RELATING HER FIRST STORY TO THE SULTAN.

The Sultan was much surprised at the sacrifice which the grand vizier proposed making. "How could you resolve," said he, "to bring me your own daughter?"—"Sir," answered the vizier, "it is her own offer." "But do not deceive yourself, vizier," said the Sultan: "to-morrow when I put Sheherazade into your hands, I expect you will take away her life; and if you fail, I swear that you shall die."

Sheherazade now set about preparing to appear before the Sultan: but before she went, she took her sister Dinarzade apart, and said to her, "My dear sister, I have need of your help in a matter of very great importance, and must pray you not to deny it me. As soon as I come to the Sultan, I will beg him to allow you to be in the bride-chamber, that I may enjoy your company for the last time. If I obtain this favour, as I hope to do, remember to awaken me to-morrow an hour before day, and to address me in words like these: 'My sister, if you be not asleep, I pray you that, till day-break, you will relate one of the delightful stories of which you have read so many.' Immediately I will begin to tell you one; and I hope, by this means, to deliver the city from the consternation it is in." Dinarzade answered that she would fulfil her sister's wishes.

When the hour for retiring came, the grand vizier conducted Sheherazade to the palace, and took his leave. As soon as the Sultan was left alone with her, he ordered her to uncover her face, and found it so beautiful, that he was charmed with her; but, perceiving her to be in tears, he asked her the reason. "Sir," answered Sheherazade, "I have a sister who loves me tenderly, and whom I love; and I could wish that she might be allowed to pass the night in this chamber, that I might see her, and bid her farewell. Will you be pleased to grant me the comfort of giving her this last testimony of my affection?" Shahriar having consented, Dinarzade was sent for, and came with all diligence. The Sultan passed the night with Sheherazade upon an elevated couch, and Dinarzade slept on a mattress prepared for her near the foot of the bed.

An hour before day, Dinarzade awoke, and failed not to speak as her sister had ordered her.

Sheherazade, instead of answering her sister, asked leave of the Sultan to grant Dinarzade's request. Shahriar consented. And, desiring her sister to attend, and addressing herself to the Sultan, Sheherazade began as follows:—

## THE STORY OF THE MERCHANT AND THE GENIE.

IR, there was formerly a merchant who had a great estate in lands. goods, and money. He had numbers of deputies, factors, and slaves, One day, being under the necessity of going a long journey, he mounted his horse, and put a wallet behind him with some biscuits and dates, because he had to pass over a great desert, where he could procure no provisions. He arrived without accident at the end of his journey; and, having despatched his business, took horse again, in order to return home.

"On the fourth day of his journey, being in want of refreshment, he alighted from his horse, and sitting down by a fountain, took some biscuits and dates out of his wallet; and, as he ate his dates, he threw the stones about on all sides. When he had done eating, being a good Mussulman, he washed his hands, his face, and his feet, and said his prayers. He was still on his knees, when he saw a Genie appear, white with age, and of enormous stature. The monster advanced towards him, scimitar in hand, and spoke to him in a terrible voice, thus: 'Rise up, that I may kill thee, as thou hast killed my son.' The merchant, frightened at the hideous shape of the giant, answered: 'How can I have slain thy son? I do not know him, nor have I ever seen him.' 'What!' replied the Genie, 'didst not thou take dates out of thy wallet, and after eating them, didst not thou throw the shells on all sides?' 'I do not deny it,' answered the merchant. 'Then,' said the Genie, 'I tell thee thou hast killed my son; and the way was thus: When thou threwest the date stones, my son was passing by, and one of them was flung into his eye, and killed him; therefore I must kill thee." 'Ah! my lord, pardon me,' cried the merchant; 'for, if I have killed thy son, it was accidentally; therefore suffer me to live.' 'No, no,' said the Genie, 'I must kill thee, since thou hast killed my son.' The Genie then threw the merchant upon the ground, and lifted up the scimitar to cut off his head."

When Sheherazade spoke these words, she perceived it was day; and knowing that the Sultan rose betimes in the morning, she held her peace. " Oh sister," said Dinarzade, " what a wonderful story is this !" " The remainder of it," said Sheherazade, " is more surprising ; and you will be of my mind, if the Sultan will let me live this day, and permit me to continue the story to-night." Shahriar, who had listened to Sheherazade with pleasure, said to himself, " I will stay till to-morrow, for I can at any time put her to death, when she has made an end of her story."—So, having resolved to defer her death till the following day, he arose, and having prayed, went to the council.

The grand vizier, in the mean time, was in a state of cruel suspense. Unable to sleep, he passed the night in lamenting the approaching fate of his daughter, whose executioner he was destined to be. How great was his surprise when the Sultan entered the council chamber, without giving him the horrible order he expected.

The Sultan spent the day, as usual, in regulating the affairs of his kingdom ; and on the approach of night, retired with Sheherazade to his apartment. The next morning, before the day appeared, Dinarzade did not fail to address her sister : " My dear sister," she said, " if you are not asleep, I entreat you, before the morning breaks, to continue your story." The Sultan did not wait for Sheherazade to ask permission, but said, " Finish the tale of the Genie and the Merchant : I am curious to hear the end of it." Sheherazade immediately went on as follows :

" Sir, when the merchant perceived that the Genie was about to slay him, he cried, 'One word more, I entreat thee ; have the goodness to grant me a little delay ; give me only time to go and take leave of my wife and children, and divide my estate among them, as I have not yet made my will ;—and when I have set my house in order, I promise to return to this spot, and submit myself to thee.' 'But if I grant thee the respite thou askest,' replied the Genie, 'I fear thou wilt not return.' 'I swear by the God of heaven and earth, that I will not fail to repair hither.' 'What length of time requirest thou ?' said the Genie : 'It will take me a full year to arrange every thing. But I promise thee, that after twelve months have passed thou shalt find me under these trees, waiting to deliver myself into thy hands.' On this, the Genie left him near the fountain, and immediately disappeared.

" The merchant, having recovered from his fright, mounted his horse, and continued his journey. But if, on the one hand, he rejoiced at escaping for the moment from a great present peril, he was, on the other, much distressed, when he recollected the fatal oath he had taken. On his arrival at home, his wife and family received him with signs of the greatest joy ; but instead of returning their embraces, he wept so bitterly, that they supposed something very extraordinary had happened. His wife inquired the cause of his tears, and of his violent grief. 'We were rejoicing,' she said, 'at your return, and you alarm us all by the state of mind we see you in ; I entreat you to explain the cause of your sorrow.' 'Alas !' he replied, 'How should I feel cheerful, when I have only a year to live ?' He then related to them what had passed, and that he had given his word to return, and at the end of a year, to submit to his death.

" When they heard this melancholy tale, they were in despair. The wife uttered the most lamentable groans, tearing her hair, and beating her breast ; the children made the house resound with their grief ; while the father mingled his tears with theirs.

" The next day, the merchant began to settle his affairs, and first of all to pay his debts. He made many presents to his different friends, and large donations to the poor. He set at liberty many of his slaves of both sexes ; divided his property among his children ; appointed guardians for those of tender age ; to his wife he returned all the fortune she brought him, and added as much more as the law would permit.

" The year soon passed away, and he was compelled to depart. He took in his wallet his graveclothes ; but when he attempted to take leave of his wife and children, his grief quite overcame him. They could not bear his loss, and almost resolved to accompany him, and all perish together. Compelled at length to tear himself away, he addressed them in these words :—'In leaving you, my children, I obey the command of God ; imitate me, and submit with fortitude to this necessity. Remember, that to die is the inevitable destiny of man.' Having said this, he snatched himself away from them, and set out. He arrived at the destined spot on the very day he had promised. He got off his horse, and, seating himself by the side of the fountain, with such sorrowful sensations as may easily be imagined, waited the arrival of the Genie.

"While he was kept in this cruel suspense, there appeared an old man leading a hind, who came near to him. When they had saluted each other, the old man said, 'May I ask of you, brother, what brought you to this desert place, which is so full of evil genii, that there is no safety? From the appearance of these trees, one might suppose this spot was inhabited; but it is, in fact, a solitude, where to tarry is dangerous.'

"The merchant satisfied the old man's curiosity, and related his adventure. The old man listened with astonishment to the account, and when it was ended, he said, 'Surely nothing in the world can be more surprising; and you have kept your oath inviolate! In truth I should like to be a witness to your interview with the Genie.' Having said this, he sat down near the merchant, and while they were talking, another old man followed by two black dogs, appeared. As soon as he was near enough, he saluted them, and inquired the reason of their stay in that place. The first old man related the adventure of the merchant, exactly as the other had told it; and added, that this was the appointed day, and therefore he was determined to remain, to see the event.

"The second old man, who also thought it very curious, resolved to stay likewise; and sitting down, joined in the conversation. He was hardly seated, when a third arrived, and addressing himself to the other two, asked why the merchant, who was with them, appeared so melancholy. They related the cause, which seemed to the new comer so wonderful, that he also resolved to be witness to what passed between the Genie and the merchant. He therefore sat down with them for this purpose.

"They quickly perceived, towards the plain, a thick vapour or smoke, like a column of dust, raised by the wind. This vapour approached them; and on its sudden disappearance, they saw the Genie, who, without noticing them, went towards the merchant, with his scimitar in his hand; and taking him by the arm, cried, 'Get up, that I may kill thee, as thou hast slain my son.' The merchant and the three old men were so horrified that they began to weep, and filled the air with their lamentations.

"When the old man, who led the hind, saw the Genie lay hold of the merchant, and about to murder him without mercy, he threw himself at the monster's feet, and kissing them, said, 'Prince of the Genii, I humbly entreat you to abate your rage, and do me the favour to listen to me. I wish to relate my own history, and that of the hind, which you see here! and if you find it more wonderful and surprising than the adventure of this merchant, whose life you wish to take, may I not hope, that you will at least remit a third part of the punishment of this unfortunate man?"—After meditating for some time, the Genie answered, 'Good, I agree to it.'"

### The History of the First Old Man and the Hind.

"I am now going," said he, "to begin my tale, and I request your attention. The hind, that you see here, is my cousin; nay more, she is my wife. When I married her, she was only twelve years old; and she ought therefore to look upon me not only as her relation and husband, but even as her father.

"We lived together thirty years, without having any children; this, however, did not decrease my kindness and regard for her. Still my desire for an heir was so great, that I purchased a female slave, who bore me a son of great promise and beauty. Soon afterwards my wife was seized with jealousy, and consequently took a great aversion to both mother and child; yet she so well concealed her feelings that I, alas! never had a suspicion of them till too late.

"In the meantime my son grew up; and he was about ten years old when I was obliged to make a journey. Before my departure, I recommended both the slave and the child to my wife, whom I trusted implicitly, and begged her to take care of them during my absence, which would last not less than a year. Now was the time she endeavoured to gratify her hatred. She applied herself to the study of magic; and

THE MERCHANT AND THE GENIE.

when she was sufficiently skilled in that diabolical art to execute the horrible design she meditated, the wretch carried my son to a distant place. There, by her enchantments, she changed him into a calf; and giving the creature to my steward, told him it was a purchase of hers, and ordered him to rear it. Not satisfied even with this infamous action, she changed the slave into a cow, which she also sent to my steward.

"Immediately on my return I inquired after my child and his mother. 'Your slave is dead,' said she, 'and it is now more than two months since I have beheld your son; nor do I know what is become of him.' I was deeply affected at the death of the slave; but as my son had only disappeared, I consoled myself with the hope that he would soon be found. Eight months however passed, and he did not return; nor could I learn any tidings of him. The festival of the great Bairam was approaching; to celebrate it, I ordered my steward to bring me the fattest cow I had, for a sacrifice. He obeyed my commands; and the cow he brought me was my own slave, the unfortunate mother of my son. Having bound her, I was about to offer her up; but she lowed most sorrowfully, and tears even fell from her eyes. This seemed to me so extraordinary, that I could not but feel compassion for her; and I was unable to strike the fatal blow. I therefore ordered that she should be taken away, and another cow brought.

"My wife, who was present, seemed angry at my compassion, and resisted an order which defeated her malice. 'What are you about, husband?' said she. 'Why not sacrifice this cow? Your steward has not a more beautiful one, nor one more proper for the purpose.' Wishing to oblige my wife, I again approached the cow; and struggling with the pity that held my hand, I was again going to give the mortal blow, when the victim a second time disarmed me by her renewed tears and moanings. I then delivered the instruments into the hands of my steward. 'Take them,' I cried, 'and perform the sacrifice yourself, for the lamentations and tears of the animal have overcome me.'

"The steward was less compassionate than I; he sacrificed her. On taking off her skin we found her greatly emaciated, though she had appeared very fat. 'Take her away,' said I, to the steward, greatly mortified. 'I give her to you to do as you please with; feast upon her with any friend you choose; and if you have a very fat calf, bring it in her place.' I did not inquire what he did with the cow, but he had not been gone long before a remarkably fine calf was brought out. Although I was ignorant that this calf was my own son, yet I felt a sensation of pity arise in my breast at the first sight of him. As soon as he perceived me, he made so great an effort to come to me, that he broke his cord. He lay down at my feet, with his head on the ground, as if he endeavoured to seek my compassion, and would beg me not to have the cruelty to take away his life. He was striving in this manner to make me understand that he was my son.

"I was still more surprised and affected by this action, than I had been by the tears of the cow. I felt a kind of tender pity, and a great interest for him; or, to speak more correctly, nature guided me to what was my duty. 'Go back,' I cried, 'and take all possible care of this calf, and in its stead bring me another directly.'

"So soon as my wife heard this, she exclaimed, 'What are you about, husband? Do not, I pray you, sacrifice any calf but this.' 'Wife,' answered I, 'I will not sacrifice him; I wish to preserve him, therefore do not oppose it.' This wicked woman, however, did not agree to my wish. She hated my son too much to suffer him to remain alive; and she continued to demand his death so obstinately, that I was compelled to yield. I bound the calf; and, taking the fatal knife, was going to bury it in the throat of my son, when he turned his tearful eyes so persuasively upon me, that I had no power to execute my intention. The knife fell from my hand, and I told my wife I was determined to have another calf brought. She tried every means to induce me to alter my mind. I continued firm, however, in my resolution, in spite of all she could say; promising, in order to appease her, to sacrifice this calf at the feast of Bairam on the following year.

"The next morning my steward desired to speak with me in private. 'I am come,' said he, 'to give you some information, which, I trust, will afford you pleasure. I have a daughter, who has some little knowledge of magic; and yesterday, as I was bringing back the calf which you were unwilling to sacrifice, I observed that she smiled on seeing it, and the next moment began to weep. I inquired of her the cause of two such contrary emotions. 'My dear father,' she answered, 'that calf, which you bring back, is the son of our master; I smiled with joy at seeing him still alive, and wept at the recollection of his mother, who was yesterday sacrificed in the shape of a cow. These two metamorphoses have been contrived by the enchantments of our master's wife, who hated both the mother and the child.' This,' continued the steward, 'is what my daughter said, and I come to report it to you.' Imagine, O Genie, my surprise at hearing these words: I immediately went with my steward, to speak to his daughter myself. I went first to the stable, where the calf had been placed; he could not return my caresses; but he received them in a way which convinced me that he was really my son.

"When the daughter of the steward made her appearance, I asked her if she could restore the poor creature to his former shape.—'Yes,' replied she, 'I can.' 'Ah!' exclaimed I, 'if you can perform such a miracle, I will make you the mistress of all I possess.' She then answered with a smile, 'You are our master, and I know how much we are bound to you; but I must mention, that I can restore your son to his own form, only on two conditions: firstly, that you bestow him upon me for my husband; and secondly, that I may be permitted to punish her who changed him into a calf.' 'To the first condition,' I replied, 'I agree with all my heart; I will do still more, I will give you, for your own separate use, a considerable sum of money, independent of what I destine for my son. You shall perceive that I properly value the important service you do me. I agree also to the stipulation concerning my wife; for a horrible crime like this is worthy of punishment. I abandon her to you. Do what you please with her; I only entreat you to spare her life.' 'I will treat her then,' she said, 'as she has treated your son.' To this I gave my consent, provided she first restored me my son.

"The damsel then took a vessel full of water; and pronouncing over it some words I did not understand, she thus addressed the calf: 'O calf, if thou hast been created as thou now appearest, by the all-powerful Sovereign of the world, retain that form; but, if thou art a man, and hast been changed by enchantment into a calf, reassume thy natural figure!' As she said this, she threw the water over him, and he instantly regained his own form.

"'My child! my dear child!' I exclaimed; 'it is Allah, who hath sent this damsel to us, to destroy the horrible charm with which you were enthralled, and to avenge the evil that has been done to you and your mother. I am sure your gratitude will lead you to accept her for a wife, as I have already promised for you.' He joyfully consented; but before they were united the damsel changed my wife into this hind, which you see here. I wished her to have this form in preference to any other, that we might see her, without repugnance, in our family.

"Since that time my son has become a widower, and is now travelling. Many years have passed since I have heard any thing of him; I have therefore now set out with a view to gain some information; and as I did not like to trust my wife to the care of any one, during my absence, I thought proper to carry her with me. This is the history of myself and the hind. Can any thing be more wonderful?" "I agree with you," said the Genie, "and in consequence, I remit to this merchant a third part of his penalty."

"As soon as the first old man had finished his history," continued Sheherazade, "the second, who led the two black dogs, said to the Genie, 'I will tell you what has happened to me, and to these two dogs, which you see here; and I am sure you will find my history still more astonishing than that which you have heard. But when I have told it, will you forgive this merchant another third of his penalty?' 'Yes,' answered the Genie, 'provided your history surpass that of the hind.'" This being settled, the second old man began as follows:—

### The History of the Old Man and the Two Black Dogs.

"Great Prince of the Genii, you must know, that these two black dogs, which you see here, and myself, are three brothers. Our father left us, when he died, one thousand sequins each. With this sum we all embarked in the same calling; namely, as merchants. Soon after we had opened our warehouse, my eldest brother, who is now one of these dogs, resolved to travel, and carry on his business in foreign countries. With this view he sold all his goods, and bought such kind of merchandize as was adapted to the different lands he proposed visiting.

"He departed, and was absent a whole year. At the end of that time, a poor man who seemed to me to be asking charity, presented himself at my warehouse.—'God help you,' said I. 'And you also,' answered he: 'is it possible you do not know me?' On looking attentively at him, I recognized my brother. 'Ah! my brother,' I cried, embracing him, 'how should I possibly know you in the state you are in?' I made him come in directly, and enquired concerning his health and the success of his voyage. 'Do not ask me;' he replied, 'you behold in me a token of my fate. To enter into a detail of all the misfortunes that I have suffered in the last year, and which have reduced me to the state you see, would only be to renew my affliction.'

"I instantly shut up my shop; and putting aside all my own affairs, I took him to the bath, and dressed him in the best apparel my wardrobe afforded. I examined the state of my business; and finding by my accounts, that I had just doubled my capital, and that I was now worth two thousand sequins, I presented him with half my fortune. 'Let this, my brother,' I said, 'make you forget your losses.' He joyfully accepted the thousand sequins; again settled his affairs; and we lived together as we had done before.

"Some time after this, my second brother, the other of these black dogs, wished also to dispose of his property. Both his elder brother and myself tried every means in our power to dissuade him from his intention, but in vain. He sold all, and with the money he bought such merchandize as he considered proper for his journey. He took his departure, and joined a caravan. At the end of a year he also returned, as destitute as his brother had been. I furnished him with clothes; and as I had gained another thousand sequins, I gave them to him. He directly bought a shop, and continued to carry on his business.

"One day both my brothers came to me, and proposed that I should make a voyage with them, for the purpose of traffic. At first I opposed their scheme. 'You have travelled,' said I, 'and what have you gained?—Who will ensure that I shall be more fortunate than you?' In vain did they use every argument they thought could induce me to try my fortune. I still refused to consent to their design. They returned, however, so often to the subject, that, after withstanding their solicitations for five years, I at length yielded.

"When it became necessary to prepare for the voyage, and we were consulting on the sort of merchandize to be bought, I discovered that they had consumed their capital, and that nothing remained of the thousand sequins I had given to each. I did not, however, reproach them. On the contrary, as my fortune had increased to six thousand sequins, I divided the half with them, saying, 'We must, my brothers, risk only three thousand sequins, and endeavour to conceal the rest in some secure place; so that, if our voyage be not more successful than the ventures you have already made, we shall be able to console ourselves with what we have left, and resume our former profession. I will give one thousand sequins to each of you, and keep one thousand myself; and I will conceal the other three thousand in a corner of my house.' We purchased our goods, embarked in a vessel, which we ourselves freighted, and set sail with a favourable wind. After sailing about a month, we arrived, without any accident, at a port, where we landed, and disposed of our merchandize with great advantage. I, in particular, sold mine so well, that I gained ten sequins for one. We then purchased the produce of the country we were in, in order to traffic with it in our own.

"About the time when we were ready to embark for our return, I accidentally met on the sea-shore a woman, very handsome, but poorly dressed. She accosted me by kissing my hand;—entreated me most earnestly to permit her to go with me, and besought me

THE MEETING ON THE SEA SHORE.

to take her for my wife. I pleaded many difficulties against such a plan; but at length she said so much to persuade me, urging that I ought not to regard her poverty, and assuring me I should be well satisfied with her conduct, that I was entirely overcome. I directly procured proper dresses for her; and when I had married her in due form, she embarked with me, and we set sail.

"During our voyage, I found my wife possessed of so many good qualities, that I loved her every day more and more. In the meantime my two brothers, who had not traded so advantageously as myself, and who were jealous of my prosperity, began to feel exceedingly envious. They even went so far as to conspire against my life; and one night, while my wife and I were asleep, they threw us into the sea.

"My wife proved to be a fairy; consequently, she possessed supernatural power. You may therefore imagine she was not hurt. As for me, I should certainly have perished but for her aid. I had hardly, however, fallen into the water before she took me up, and transported me to an island. As soon as it was day the fairy thus addressed me: 'You may observe, my husband, that in saving your life, I have not badly rewarded the good you have done me. You must know that I am a fairy; I saw you upon the shore, when you were about to sail, and felt a great regard for you. I wished to try the goodness of your heart, and therefore I presented myself before you in the disguise you saw. You acted most generously; and I am delighted to find an opportunity of showing my gratitude. But I am angry with your brothers; nor shall I be satisfied till I have taken their lives.'

"I listened with astonishment to the words of the fairy, and thanked her, as well as I could, for the great obligation she had conferred on me. 'But, lady,' said I to her, 'I must entreat you to pardon my brothers; for although I have the greatest reason to complain of their conduct, yet I am not so cruel as to wish their ruin.' I elated to her what I had done for each of them, and my story only increased her anger. 'I must instantly fly after these ungrateful wretches,' cried she, 'and bring them to a just punishment; I will destroy their vessel, and sink them to the bottom of the sea.' 'No, beautiful lady,' replied I, 'for Heaven's sake moderate your indignation, and do not execute so dreadful a design; remember they are still my brothers, and that we are bound to return good for evil.'

"I appeased the fairy by these words; and so soon as I had pronounced them, she transported me in an instant from the island, where we were, to the top of my own house, which was terraced. She then disappeared. I descended, opened the doors, and dug up the three thousand sequins which I had hidden. I afterwards repaired to my shop, opened it, and received the congratulations of the merchants in the neighbourhood on my safe return. When I went home I perceived these two black dogs, which came towards me, fawning. I could not imagine what this meant; but the fairy, who soon appeared, satisfied my curiosity. 'My dear husband,' said she, 'be not surprised at seeing these two dogs in your house; they are your brothers.' My blood ran cold on hearing this, and I inquired by what power they had been transformed into their present shape. 'It is I,' replied the fairy, 'who have done it; at least it is one of my sisters, to whom I gave the commission; and she has also sunk their ship. You will lose the merchandize it contained, but I shall recompense you in some way; as to your brothers, I have condemned them to remain under this form for ten years, as a punishment for their perfidy.' Then, after informing me where I might hear of her, she disappeared.

"The ten years are now completed, and I am travelling in search of her. As I was passing this way I met this merchant, and the good old man, who is leading his hind, and here I tarried. This, O Prince of the Genii, is my history; does it not appear to you most marvellous?" "Yes," replied the Genie, "I confess it is wonderful, and therefore I remit the second third of the merchant's punishment."

When the second old man had finished his story the third began, by asking the Genie, as the others had done, if he would forgive the remaining third of the merchant's crime, provided this third history surpassed the other two, in the singularity and marvellousness of its events: the Genie repeated his former promise.

"The third old man related his history to the Genie, but as it has not yet come to my knowledge, I cannot repeat it; but I know it was so much beyond the others, in the variety of wonderful adventures it contained, that the Genie was astonished. He had no sooner heard the conclusion than he said, 'I grant thee the remaining third part of the merchant's pardon; and he ought to be greatly obliged to you all for having, by telling your histories, freed him from his dangerous position; but for this aid he would not now have been in this world.' Having said this, he disappeared, to the great joy of the whole party.

"The merchant did not omit to bestow many thanks upon his liberators. They rejoiced with him at his safety, and then bidding him adieu, each went his separate way. The merchant returned home to his wife and children, and spent the remainder of his days with them in peace. But, sir," added Sheherazade, "however wonderful those tales which I have related to your Majesty may be, they are not equal to that of the fisherman." Dinarzade, observing that the Sultan made no answer, said, "Since there is still some time, my sister, pray tell this history; the Sultan, I hope, will not object to it." Shahriar consented to the proposal, and Sheherazade went on as follows:—

## THE HISTORY OF THE FISHERMAN.

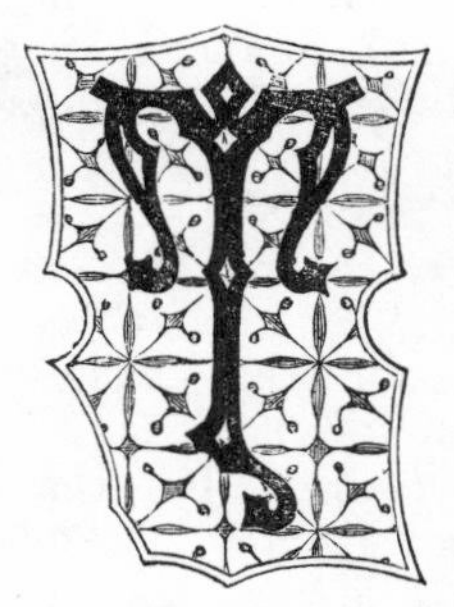

HERE once lived, sir, a fisherman, who was old and feeble, and so poor, that he could barely obtain food for himself, and for the wife and three children who made up his family. He went out very early every morning to his work; and he made it an absolute rule that he would throw his nets only four times a day.

"One morning he set out before the moon had set: when he had got to the sea-shore, he undressed himself and threw his nets. In drawing them to land, he felt them drag heavily; and began to imagine he should have an excellent haul; at which he was much pleased. But, on pulling up the nets, he found that instead of fish he had only caught the carcass of an ass; and he was much vexed and afflicted at having made so bad a haul. When he had mended his nets, which the weight of the ass had torn in many places, he cast them a second time into the sea. He again found considerable resistance in drawing them up, and again he thought they were filled with fish; but great was his disappointment, when he discovered only a large basket, filled with sand and mud. 'O Fortune!' he exclaimed, with a melancholy voice, and in the greatest distress, 'cease to be angry with me. Persecute not an unfortunate being, who supplicates thee to spare him. I came from home to seek for life, and thou threatenest me with death. I have no other trade, by which I can subsist, and even with all my toil, I can hardly supply the most pressing wants of my family; but I am wrong to complain of thee, that takest a pleasure in deluding the virtuous, and leavest good men in obscurity, while thou favourest the wicked, and exaltest those who possess no virtue to recommend them.'

"Having thus vented his complaints, he angrily threw the basket aside and washing his nets from mud and slime, he threw them a third time. He brought up only stones, shells, and filth. It is impossible to describe his despair, which now almost deprived him of his senses. But the day now began to break, and like a good Mussulman, he did not neglect his prayers, to which he added the following supplication: 'Thou knowest, O Lord, that I throw my nets only four times a day; three times have I thrown them into the sea, without any profit for my labour. One more cast alone remains; and I entreat thee to render the sea favourable, as thou formerly didst to Moses.'

"When the fisherman had finished his prayer, he threw his nets for the fourth time. Again he supposed he had caught a great quantity of fish, as they were just as heavy as before. He nevertheless found none; but discovered a vase of yellow copper, which seemed, from its weight, to be filled with something; and he observed that it was shut up and stoppered with lead, on which there was the impression of a seal. 'I will sell this to a founder,' said he, joyfully, 'and with the money I shall get for it, I will purchase a measure of corn.'

"He had examined the vase on all sides; he now shook it, to judge of its contents by the sound. He could hear nothing; and this, together with the impression of the seal on the lead, made him think it was filled with something valuable. To decide the question, he took his knife, and cut it open without much difficulty. He directly turned the top downwards, and was much surprised to find nothing come out: he set it down before him, and while he watched it closely, there issued from it so thick a smoke, that he was obliged to step back a few paces. This smoke by degrees rose almost to the clouds, and spread itself over sea and land, appearing like a thick fog. The fisherman, as may easily be imagined, was much surprised at this sight. When the smoke had all come out from the vase, it again collected itself, and became a solid body, taking the shape of a Genie, twice as large as any of the giants. At the appearance of this huge monster, the fisherman wished to run away; but his fear was so great, he was unable to move.

"'Solomon, Solomon,' cried the Genie, 'great prophet of Allah, pardon, I beseech thee. I will never more oppose thy will; but will obey all thy commands.'

"The fisherman had no sooner heard these words spoken by the Genie, than he regained his courage, and said, 'Proud spirit, what is this thou sayest? Solomon, the prophet of the Most High has been dead more than eighteen hundred years. Tell me, then, thy history, and wherefore thou hast been shut up in this vase?'

"To this speech the Genie, looking disdainfully at the fisherman, answered, 'Speak more civilly; thou art very bold to call me a proud spirit.' 'Perhaps, then,' returned the fisherman, 'it will be more civil to call thee a bird of good omen.' 'I tell thee,' said the Genie, 'speak to me more civilly, before I kill thee.' 'And for what reason, pray, wouldst thou kill me?' asked the fisherman. 'Hast thou already forgotten that I have set thee at liberty?' 'I remember it very well,' returned the Genie, 'but that shall not prevent my destroying thee; and I will only grant thee one favour.' 'And what is that?' asked the fisherman. 'It is,' replied the Genie, 'to permit thee to choose the manner of thy death.' 'But in what,' resumed the other, 'have I offended thee? Is it thus thou dost recompense me for the good service I have done thee?' 'I cannot treat thee otherwise,' said the Genie; 'and to convince thee of it, attend to my history.'

"'I am one of those spirits who rebelled against the sovereignty of Allah. All the other Genii acknowledged the great Solomon, the prophet of God, and submitted to him. Sacar and myself were the only ones who disdained to humble ourselves. In revenge for my contumacy, this powerful monarch charged Assaf, the son of Barakhia, his first minister, to come and seize me. This was done; and Assaf captured me, and brought me by force before the throne of the king, his master.

"'Solomon, the son of David, commanded me to quit my mode of life, acknowledge his authority, and submit to his laws. I haughtily refused to obey him; and exposed myself to his resentment rather than take the oath of fidelity and submission which he required of me. In order, therefore, to punish me, he confined me in this copper vase; and to prevent my forcing my way out he put upon the leaden cover the impression of his seal, on which the great name of Allah is engraven. Thereupon he gave the vase to one of those Genii who obeyed him, and ordered the spirit to throw me into the sea; which, to my great sorrow, was done directly.

"'During the first period of my captivity, I swore, that if any man delivered me before the first hundred years were passed, I would make him rich, even after his death. The time elapsed, and no one released me. During the second century I swore, that if any one set me free, I would discover to him all the treasures of the earth; still no help came. During the third, I promised to make my deliverer a most powerful monarch, to be always at his command, and to grant him every day any three requests he chose to make. This age, like the former, passed away, and I remained in bondage. Enraged at last, to be so long a prisoner, I swore that I would without mercy kill the person who should release me; and that the only favour I would grant him, should be the choice of what manner of death he preferred. Since, therefore, thou hast come here to-day, and hast delivered me, fix upon whatever kind of death thou wilt.'

"The fisherman was much grieved at this speech. 'How unfortunate,' he exclaimed,

THE FISHERMAN AND THE GENIE.

'am I to come here and render so great a service to such an ungrateful creature! Consider, I entreat thee, thy injustice; and revoke thine unreasonable oath. Pardon me, and Allah will, in like manner, pardon thee. If thou wilt generously suffer me to live, he will defend thee from all attempts that will be made against thy life.' 'No,' answered the Genie, 'thy death is inevitable; determine only how I shall kill thee.' The fisherman was in great distress, at finding the Genie thus resolved on his death; not so much on his own account, as on that of his three children; for he anticipated with anguish the wretched state to which his death would reduce them. He still endeavoured to appease the Genie. 'Alas!' he cried, 'have pity on me, in consideration of what I have done for thee.' 'I have already told thee,' replied the Genie, 'that it is for that very reason I am obliged to take thy life.' 'It is very strange,' cried the fisherman, 'that thou art determined to return evil for good. The proverb says, that he who does good to him that does not deserve it, is always ill rewarded. I did think, I own, that it was false, because nothing is more contrary to reason, and the rights of society: yet I find it too cruelly true.' 'Let us lose no time,' cried the Genie, 'thy arguments will not alter my resolution. Make haste, and tell me how thou wilt die.'

"Necessity is the spur to invention; and the fisherman thought of a stratagem. 'Since, then,' said he, 'I cannot escape death, I submit to the will of God; but before I choose the manner of my death, I conjure thee, by the great name of Allah, which is graven upon the seal of the prophet Solomon, the son of David, to answer me truly a question I am going to put to thee.' When the Genie found that he should be compelled to answer positively, he trembled, and said to the fisherman, 'Ask what thou wilt, and make haste.'

"So soon as the Genie had promised to speak the truth, the fisherman said to him, 'I wish to know whether thou really wert in that vase; darest thou swear it by the great name of Allah?' 'Yes,' answered the Genie, 'I do swear by the great name of Allah, that I most certainly was there.' 'In truth,' replied the fisherman, 'I cannot believe thee. This vase cannot contain one of thy feet; how then can it hold thy whole body?' 'I swear to thee, notwithstanding,' replied the monster, 'that I was there just as thou seest me. Wilt thou not believe me after the solemn oath I have taken?' 'No, truly,' retorted the fisherman, 'I shall not believe thee unless I see it.'

"Immediately the form of the Genie began to change into smoke, and to extend itself as before over both the shore and the sea; and then, collecting itself, it began to enter the vase, and continued to do so with a slow and equal motion, till nothing remained without. A voice immediately issued forth, saying, 'Now,—thou unbelieving fisherman,—art thou convinced now, that I am in the vase?' But instead of answering the Genie, the fisherman immediately took the leaden cover, and clapped it on the vase. 'Genie,' he cried, 'it is now thy turn to ask pardon, and choose what sort of death is most agreeable to thee. But no; it is better that I should throw thee again into the sea; and I will build on the very spot where thou art cast, a house upon the shore, in which I will live, to warn all fishermen that shall come and throw their nets, not to fish up so wicked a Genie as thou art, that takest an oath to kill him who shall set thee at liberty.'

"At this insulting speech, the enraged Genie tried his utmost to get out of the vase, but in vain; for the impression of the seal of Solomon the prophet, the son of David, prevented him. Knowing then, that the fisherman had the advantage over him, he began to conceal his rage. 'Take heed,' said he in a softened tone, 'take heed what thou doest, O fisherman. Whatever I said was merely in jest, and thou shouldst not take it seriously.' 'O Genie,' answered the fisherman, 'thou, who wert a moment ago the greatest of all the genii, art now the most insignificant; and suppose not that thy flattering speeches will avail thee anything. Thou shalt assuredly return to the sea; and if thou hast passed so much time there as thou hast asserted, thou mayest as well remain till the day of judgment. I entreated thee in the name of God not to take my life, and as thou hast rejected my prayers, I ought to reject thine likewise.'

"The Genie tried every argument to move the fisherman's pity, but in vain. 'I conjure thee to open the vase,' said he;—'if thou givest me my liberty again, thou shalt have reason to be satisfied with my gratitude.' 'Thou art too treacherous for me,—I will not trust thee;' returned the fisherman: 'I should deserve to lose my life, were I so foolish as to put it in thy power a second time. For thou wouldst probably treat me as the Greek King treated Douban, the physician. I will tell thee the story:"—

## The History of the Greek King, and Douban, the Physician.

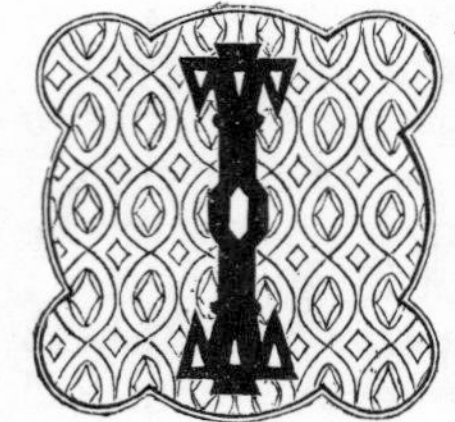

N the country of Zouman, in Persia, there lived a King, whose subjects were of Greek origin. This King was sorely afflicted with a leprosy, and his physicians had unsuccessfully tried every remedy they knew, when a very learned physician, called Douban, arrived at the court.

"He had acquired his profound learning by studying different authors in the Greek, Latin, Persian, Arabic, Turkish, Syriac, and Hebrew languages; and besides having a consummate knowledge of philosophy, he was also well acquainted with the good and bad properties of all kinds of plants and drugs.

"As soon as he was informed of the King's illness, and heard that the physicians had given their master up, he dressed himself as neatly as possible, and obtained an audience of the King. 'Sir,' said he, 'I know that all the physicians who have attended your Majesty, have been unable to remove your leprosy; but if you will do me the honour to accept of my services, I will engage to cure you without medicines or ointments.' The King, pleased with this proposal, replied, 'If thou art really so skilful as thou pretendest, I promise to shower wealth on thee and thy posterity; and in addition to the presents thou shalt have, thou shalt be my first favourite; but dost thou tell me in earnest, that thou wilt remove my leprosy without making me swallow any potion or applying any remedy externally?' 'Yes, sir,' replied the physician, 'I flatter myself I shall succeed, with the help of God; and to-morrow I will begin my cure.'

"Douban returned to his house, and made a sort of racket or bat, with a hollow in the handle to admit the drug he meant to use; that being done, he also prepared a sort of round ball, or bowl, in the manner that seemed best; and the following day he presented himself before the King, and prostrating himself at the monarch's feet, kissed the ground before him.

"Douban then arose, and having made a profound reverence, told the King that he must ride on horseback to the place where he was accustomed to play at bowls. The King did as he was recommended; and when he had reached the bowling-green the physician approached him, and putting into his hand the bat, which had been prepared, said, 'O King, exercise yourself with striking yonder ball with this bat, till you find yourself in a profuse perspiration. When the remedy I have enclosed in the handle of the bat is warmed by your hand, it will penetrate through your whole body; you may then leave off playing, for the drug will have taken effect; and when you return to your palace get into a warm bath, and be well rubbed and washed; then go to bed, and to-morrow you will be quite cured.'

"The King took the bat, and spurred his horse after the ball till he struck it. It was sent back to him by the officers who were playing with him, and he struck it again; and thus the game continued for a considerable time, till he found his hand as well as his whole body thoroughly heated, and the remedy in the bat began to operate as the physician had prophesied; the King then ceased playing, returned to the palace, bathed, and observed very punctually all the directions that had been given him.

"He soon found the good effects of the prescription; for when he arose the next morning he perceived with equal surprise and joy, that his leprosy was entirely cured, and that his body was as clear, as if he had never been attacked by that malady. As soon as he was dressed he went into the audience-chamber, where he mounted his throne and received the congratulations of all his courtiers, who had assembled on that day, partly to gratify their curiosity, and partly to testify their joy at their master's recovery.

"Douban entered, and went to prostrate himself at the foot of the throne, with his face towards the ground. The King when he saw him, called to him, and made him sit by his side; and pointing him out to the assembly, gave him in that public way all the praise the physician so well deserved. Nor did the King stop here, for at a grand entertainment at court on that day, he placed the physician at his own table to dine with him alone.

"The Greek King," continued the fisherman, "was not satisfied with admitting the physician to his own table; towards evening, when the courtiers were about to depart, he caused him to be dressed in a long rich robe resembling that which the courtiers usually wore in the King's presence; and in addition, made him a present cf two thousand sequins. For the next few days he did nothing but caress his new favourite; in short, this Prince, thinking he could never repay the obligations he owed to the skilful physician, was continually conferring on him some fresh proof of his gratitude.

"The King had a grand vizier, who was avaricious, envious, and prone by nature to every species of crime. This man observed with malicious fury the presents which had been bestowed upon the physician, whose great character and merit he was determined to lessen and destroy in the mind of the King. To accomplish this purpose, he went to the monarch, and said in private, that he had some intelligence of the greatest moment to communicate. The King asked him what it was. 'Sir,' replied he, 'it is very dangerous for a monarch to place confidence in a man, of whose fidelity he is not assured. While you overwhelm the physician Douban with your favours, and bestow all this kindness and regard upon him, you are ignorant that he is a traitor, who has introduced himself into the court, in order to assassinate you.' 'What is this you dare tell me?' cried the King,—'Recollect to whom you speak, and that you advance an assertion, which I shall not easily believe.'—'O King,' resumed the vizier, I am accurately informed of what I have the honour to represent to you; do not therefore continue to repose such a dangerous confidence in Douban. If your Majesty is, as it were, in a dream, it is time to awake; for I repeat, that the physician Douban has travelled from the farthest part of Greece, his own country, solely to carry out the horrible design I have mentioned.'

"'No, no, vizier,' interrupted the King, 'I am sure this man, whom you consider a hypocrite and a traitor, is one of the most virtuous and best of men; there is no one in the world whom I respect so much. You know by what remedy, or rather by what miracle, he cured me of my leprosy; and if he had sought my life, why did he thus save it? Cease then from endeavouring to instil unjust suspicions into my mind, for instead of listening to them, I now inform you, that from this very day I bestow upon him a pension of one thousand sequins a month, for the rest of his life. And were I to share all my riches, and even my kingdoms with him, I could never sufficiently repay what he has done for me. I see the reason of this. His virtue excites your envy; but do not suppose that I shall suffer myself to be prejudiced against him. I well remember what a vizier said to King Sindbad, his master, to prevent the King's giving orders for the death of his son.'

"This speech very much excited the curiosity of the vizier. 'I beg your Majesty will pardon me, if I have the boldness to ask you what it was that the vizier of King Sindbad said to his master, to avert the death of his son.' The Greek King had the complaisance to satisfy his questioner. 'This vizier,' said he, 'first represented to King Sindbad, that he ought to hesitate to do a thing, which was founded on the suggestion of a mother-in-law, lest she should repent her advice,'—and he related the following story":—

### The History of the Husband and the Parrot.

HERE lived once a good man who had a beautiful wife, of whom he was so passionately fond, that he could scarcely bear to have her out of his sight. One day, when some particular business obliged him to leave her, he went to a place where they sold all sorts of birds. He purchased a parrot, which was not only highly accomplished in the art of talking, but also possessed the rare gift of telling everything that was done in its presence. The husband took it home in a cage to his wife, and begged of her to keep it in her chamber, and to take great care of it during his absence; and thereupon he set out on his journey.

"On his return he did not fail to question the parrot as to what had passed while he was away; and the bird very quickly related a few circumstances, which occasioned the husband to reprimand his wife. She supposed that some of her slaves had betrayed her; but they all assured her they were faithful, and agreed in charging the parrot with the crime. Anxious to discover the truth of this matter, the wife devised a method of quieting the suspicions of her husband, and at the same time of revenging herself on the parrot, if he were the culprit. The next time the husband was absent, during the night she ordered one of her slaves to turn a handmill under the bird's cage, and another to sprinkle water like rain over the cage, and a third to wave a looking-glass before the parrot so as to flash the light of a candle in its face. The slaves were employed the greater part of the night in obeying their mistress's orders, and they succeeded to her satisfaction.

THE HUSBAND PRESENTS THE PARROT TO HIS WIFE.

"The following day, when the husband returned, he again applied to the parrot to be informed of what had taken place. The bird replied, 'My dear master, the lightning, the thunder and the rain so disturbed me the whole night, that I cannot tell you how much I have suffered.' The husband, who knew there had been no storm that night, became convinced that the parrot did not always tell truth; and that having lied with respect to the weather the bird had also deceived him concerning his wife. Extremely enraged at the parrot's supposed duplicity, he took the bird out of the cage, and, dashing it on the floor, killed it: he, however, afterwards learnt from his neighbours, that the poor parrot had not deceived him concerning the conduct of his wife; and he repented of having destroyed it."

"'When the Greek King,' said the fisherman to the Genie, 'had finished the story of the parrot, he added, 'You vizier, through envy of Douban, who has done you no evil, wish me to order his death; but I will take good care, lest, like the husband who killed his parrot, I should afterwards repent.'

"The vizier was too desirous of the death of Douban, to let the matter rest where it was. 'O King,' replied he, 'the loss of the parrot was of little importance; nor do I think his master could long have regretted it. It is not envy that makes me hostile to him, it is the interest alone that I take in your Majesty's preservation; it is my zeal which induces me to give my advice in this important matter. If my information is false, I deserve the same punishment that a certain vizier once underwent.' 'What had that vizier done worthy of chastisement?' asked the Greek King. 'I will tell your Majesty,' answered the vizier, 'if you will have the goodness to listen.'"

### The History of the Vizier, who was Punished.

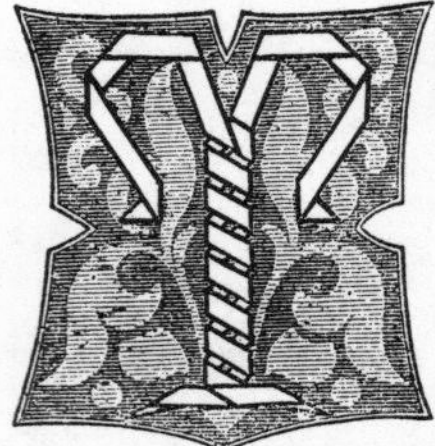

HERE was once a King, whose son was passionately fond of hunting. His father, therefore, often indulged him in this diversion; but at the same time gave positive orders to his grand vizier always to accompany the Prince, and never to lose sight of him.

"One hunting morning, the hunters roused a stag, and the Prince set off in pursuit, thinking the vizier was following him. He galloped so long, and his eagerness carried him so far, that at last he found himself quite alone. He immediately stopped, and observing that he had lost his way, endeavoured to retrace his steps, in order to join the vizier, who had not been sufficiently prompt in following him. He was, however, unable to find the track; and riding to and fro without getting into the right path, he by chance met a lady of somewhat attractive mien, who was weeping most bitterly. The Prince immediately checked his horse, and inquired of her who she was, what she did alone in that place, and whether he could assist her?—'I am,' she answered, 'the daughter of an Indian king. In riding out into the country, I was overcome with sleep, and fell from my horse. He has run away, and I know not what has become of him.' The young Prince was sorry for her misfortune, and proposed to take her up behind him; an offer which she accepted.

"As they passed by an old ruined building, the lady made some excuse to alight; the Prince therefore stopped, and suffered her to dismount. He also alighted, and walked towards the building, holding his horse by the bridle. Imagine, then, what was his astonishment when he heard the lady pronounce these words within the walls: '*Rejoice, my children, I have brought you a very nice fat youth.*' And directly afterwards other voices answered, '*Where is he, mother? Let us eat him instantly, for we are very hungry!*'

"The Prince had heard enough to convince him of the danger he was in: he plainly perceived that the woman who represented herself as the daughter of an Indian king, was in reality the wife of one of those savage demons, called Ogres, who live in desert places,* and make use of a thousand wiles to surprise and devour unfortunate travellers. He trembled with fear, and instantly mounted his horse.

"The pretended Princess at that moment made her appearance; and finding she had failed in her scheme, she cried, 'Do not be afraid, but tell me who you are, and what you seek?'—'I have lost my way,' he replied, 'and am endeavouring to find it.'—'If you are lost,' she said, 'recommend yourself to Allah, and he will deliver you from your difficulty.'

"The young Prince could not believe that she spoke sincerely, but judged that she considered him already in her power; he lifted up his hands, therefore, towards heaven,

* The belief in Genii was prevalent throughout the East long before the time of Mahomet. They were supposed to haunt solitary places, particularly toward nightfall; a superstition congenial to the habits and notions of the inhabitants of lonely and desert countries. The Arabs supposed every valley and barren waste to have its tribe of genii, who were subject to a dominant spirit, and roamed forth at night to beset the pilgrim and the traveller. Whenever, therefore, they entered a lonely valley toward the close of the evening, they used to supplicate the presiding spirit, or lord of the place, to protect them from the evil genii under his command. Those columns of dust raised by whirling eddies of wind, and which sweep across the desert, are supposed to be caused by some evil genius or sprite of gigantic size.

and said 'Cast thine eyes upon me, O all-powerful Lord, and deliver me from this mine enemy!' At this prayer, the Ogress went back into the ruin, and the Prince rode off as fast as possible. He fortunately discovered the right road; and arriving safely at home, related to his father, word for word, the great danger he had encountered through the neglect of the grand vizier. The King was so enraged at that minister, that he ordered him to be instantly strangled."

"'O King,' continued the vizier of the Greek King, 'I speak of the physician Douban; if you do not take care, the confidence you place in him will be betrayed. I know well that he is a spy, sent by your enemies to attempt your Majesty's life. He has cured you, you say,—but who can tell that? He has, perhaps, only cured you in appearance, and not in truth; and who can tell whether this remedy, in the end, will not produce the most pernicious effects?'

"The Greek King was naturally rather weak, and had neither penetration enough to discover the wicked intention of his vizier, nor firmness to persist in his first opinion. This conversation filled him with strange doubts. 'You are right, vizier,' said he, 'he may have come for the express purpose of taking my life—an object he can easily accomplish, even by the mere smell of some of his drugs. We must consider what is to be done in this difficulty!'

"When the vizier perceived the King in the disposition he wished to produce, he said to him, 'The best and most certain means, great King, to ensure your repose, and put your person in safety, is instantly to send to Douban, and on his appearance, to cause him to be beheaded.' 'Indeed,' replied the King, 'I think I ought to prevent his designs.' Having said this, he called one of his officers, and ordered him to summon the physician. The latter, quite unsuspicious of the King's design, hastened to the palace.

"'Knowest thou,' said the King, as soon as he saw him, 'why I sent for thee?' 'No, Sir,' answered Douban, 'and I wait, till your Majesty pleases to instruct me.' 'I have ordered thee to come,' replied the King, 'that I may free myself from thy snares, by taking thy life.'

"It is impossible to express the astonishment of Douban, when he heard himself thus addressed. 'For what reason, O King,' replied he, 'does your Majesty condemn me to death? What crime have I committed?'—'I have been credibly informed,' said the King, 'that thou art a spy, and that thou hast come to my court to take away my life; but to prevent that, I will now deprive thee of thine. Strike!' added he to an officer who was present, 'and deliver me from a treacherous wretch who has introduced himself here only to assassinate me.'

"On hearing this, the physician began to think that the honours and riches which had been heaped upon him, had excited some enemies against him, and that the King, through weakness, had suffered himself to be guided by these; and indeed, this was the case. He began to repent having cured the King; but this repentance came too late. 'Is it thus,' he cried, 'that you repay the good I have done you?' The King, however, paid no attention to his remonstrances, and a second time desired the officer to execute his orders. The physician had then recourse to prayers. 'Ah! sir,' he cried, 'if you prolong my life, God will prolong yours; do not kill me, lest God should treat you in the same manner.'

"'You see then,' said the fisherman, interrupting hinself in his narrative, and addressing himself to the Genie, 'that what has passed between the Greek King and the physician Douban is exactly similar to what has happened between us.'

"'The Greek King, however,' he continued, 'instead of regarding the entreaties of the physician, who conjured him in the name of God to relent, exclaimed, 'No, no, you must die, or you will take away my life more mysteriously even than you have cured me.' Douban, in the meantime, complained bitterly and with many tears, at finding his important services so ill requited; and at last prepared for death. The officer then put a bandage over the prisoner's eyes, tied Douban's hands, and was going to draw his scimitar. But the courtiers who were present, felt so much for the physician, that they entreated the King to pardon him, assuring his Majesty he was not guilty, and that they would answer for his innocence. But the King was inflexible, and spoke so peremptorily, that they dared not reply.

"On his knees, his eyes bandaged, and ready to receive the stroke that was to terminate his existence, the physician once more addressed the King in these words: 'Since your Majesty refuses to revoke the order for my death, I entreat you at least to give me leave to return home, to arrange my funeral, take a last farewell of my family, bestow some money in charity, and leave my books to those who will know how to make a good use of them. There is one among them, which I wish to present to your Majesty. It is a very rare and curious work, and worthy of being kept even in your treasury with the greatest care.' 'What book can there be,' replied the King, 'so valuable as to deserve such honour?' 'Sir,' answered the physician, 'it contains powers of the most curious nature; and one of the principal effects it can produce is, that when my head shall be cut off, if your Majesty will take the trouble to open the book at the sixth leaf, and read the third line on the left-hand page, my head will answer every question you wish to ask.' The King was so desirous of seeing such a wonderful thing, that he put off the physician's death till the next day, and sent him home under a strong guard.

"The unfortunate prisoner then arranged all his affairs; and as the news got abroad that an unheard-of prodigy was to happen after his execution, the viziers, emirs, officers of the guard, in short all the court flocked the next day to the hall of audience, to witness the extraordinary event.

"Douban the physician appeared presently, and advanced to the foot of the throne with a very large volume in his hand. He then placed the book on a vase, and unfolding the cover in which the book was wrapped, presented it to the monarch, and thus addressed him: 'May it please your Majesty to receive this book; and directly my head shall have been struck off, order one of your officers to place the head on the vase upon the cover of the book. As soon as it is there the blood will cease to flow; then open the book, and my head shall answer all your questions. But, sir,' added Douban, 'permit me once more to implore your mercy. Consider, I beg of you, in the name of Allah, that I protest to you I am innocent.' 'Thy prayers,' answered the King, 'are useless; and were it only to hear thy head speak after thy death, I would wish for thy execution.' So saying, he took the book from the hands of the physician, and ordered the headsman to do his duty.

"The head was so cleverly cut off, that it fell into the vase; and it had hardly been on the cover an instant before the blood ceased to run. Then, to the astonishment of the King and of all the spectators, it opened its eyes, and said, 'Will your Majesty now open the book?' The King did so; and finding that the first leaf stuck to the second, put his finger to his mouth, and moistened it, in order to turn over the leaves more easily. He turned them over, one by one, till he came to the sixth leaf; and observing nothing written upon the appointed page, he said to the head, 'Physician, there is no writing.' 'Turn over a few more leaves,' replied the head. The King continued turning them over, still putting his finger frequently to his mouth, till the poison, in which each leaf had been dipped, began to produce its effect. The monarch then felt himself suddenly agitated in a most extraordinary manner; his sight failed him, and he rolled to the foot of the throne in strong convulsions.

"When the physician Douban, or rather his head, saw that the poison had begun to work, and the King had only a few moments to live, he exclaimed, 'Tyrant, behold how those princes are treated, who abuse their power, and sacrifice the innocent! Sooner or later, Allah punishes their injustice and their cruelty.' As soon as the head had finished these words, the King expired; and at the same moment the small remnant of life, that remained in the head itself, flickered away.

"Such, my Lord," continued Sheherazade, "was the end of the Greek King and the physician Douban. I shall now return to the fisherman and the Genie.

"When the fisherman had finished the history of the Greek King and the physician Douban, he applied it to the Genie, whom he still kept confined in the vase. 'If,' said he,

THE PRINCE AND THE OGRESS.

'the Greek King had permitted Douban to live, Allah would have bestowed the same benefit on the King: but he rejected the humble prayers of the physician, and Allah punished him. This, O Genie, is the case with thee. If I had been able to make thee relent, and could have obtained the favour I asked of thee, I should have pitied the state in which thou now art: but as thou didst persist in thy determination to kill me, in spite of the great service I did thee in setting thee at liberty, I ought, in my turn, to show no mercy. By leaving thee within this vase, and casting thee into the sea, I shall deprive thee of the use of thy being till the end of time.'

"'Once more, my good friend,'" replied the Genie, 'I entreat thee not to be guilty of so cruel an act. Remember that revenge is not a part of virtue; on the contrary, it is praiseworthy to return good for evil. Do not then serve me as Imma of old treated Ateca.' 'And how was that?' asked the fisherman. 'If thou wishest to be informed, open this vase,' answered the Genie: 'dost thou think that I am in the humour, confined in this narrow prison, to relate stories? I will tell thee as many as thou wilt, when thou hast let me out.' 'No, no,' said the fisherman, 'I will not release thee; it is better for me to cast thee to the bottom of the sea.' 'One word more, fisherman,' cried the Genie: 'I will teach thee how to become rich beyond thy imagining.'

"The hope of escaping from poverty and want at once disarmed the fisherman. 'I would listen to thee,' he cried, 'if I had the least ground to believe thee; swear to me by the great name of Allah that thou wilt faithfully observe thy promise, and I will open the vase. I do not believe that thou wilt dare to violate such an oath.' The Genie took the oath; the fisherman immediately removed the covering of the vase, and the smoke instantly poured from it. The first thing the Genie did, after he had re-assumed his usual form, was to kick the vase into the sea. This action rather alarmed the fisherman. 'What dost thou mean, O Genie, by this?' he cried, 'dost thou not intend to keep the oath thou hast taken? Or must I address the same words to thee which the physician Douban did to the Greek King? *Suffer me to live, and Allah will prolong thy days.*'

"The fear expressed by the fisherman made the Genie laugh; 'Be of good cheer, fisherman,' answered he, 'I have thrown the vase into the sea only in jest, and to see whether thou wouldst be alarmed: but to show I intend to keep my word, take thy nets and follow me.' So they went out, and passed by the city and crossed the summit of a mountain, from whence they descended into a vast plain, which led them to a lake, situated between four small hills.

"When they had arrived on the borders of the lake, the Genie said to the fisherman, 'Throw thy nets, and catch fish.' The fisherman did not doubt that he should take some, for he saw a great quantity in the lake; but he was greatly surprised to notice that they were of four different colours; white, red, blue, and yellow. He threw his nets and caught four fish, one of each colour. 'Carry these fish to the palace,' said the Genie, 'and offer them to the Sultan, and he will give thee more money than thou hast seen in thy life. Come thou every day and fish in this lake; but be careful to throw thy nets only once each day; if you neglect my warning, some evil will befall you, therefore take care.' Having said this, he struck his foot against the ground; the earth opened and he disappeared, the ground closing over him.*

"The fisherman resolved to observe the advice and instructions of the Genie, in every point, and to take care never to throw his nets a second time. He went back to the town very well satisfied with his success, and reflecting on his adventure. He went directly and presented himself with his fish at the Sultan's palace.

"Your Majesty may imagine how much the Sultan was surprised, when he saw the four fish brought him by the fisherman. He took them up one by one, examined them very attentively, and after admiring them a long time he said to his first vizier: 'Take these fish, and carry them to that excellent cook, whom the Emperor of the Greeks sent me; I think they must be as delicious as they are beautiful.'

"The vizier took them, and delivered them himself into the hands of the cook. Here are four fish,' said he, 'which have been presented to the Sultan; he commands

* Moslem legends pretend that the earth was originally peopled by these Genii, but they rebelled against the Most High, and usurped terrestrial dominion, which they maintained for two thousand years. At length, Azazil, or Lucifer, was sent against them and defeated them, overthrowing their mighty king Gian ben Gian, the founder of the pyramids, whose magic buckler of talismanic virtue fell subsequently into the hands of King Solomon the Wise, giving him power over the spells and charms of magicians and evil genii. The rebel spirits, defeated and humiliated, were driven into an obscure corner of the earth. Then it was that God created man, with less dangerous faculties and powers, and gave him the world for a habitation.

you to dress them.' He then returned to the Sultan, his master, who desired him to give the fisherman four hundred pieces of gold; a command which the vizier punctually obeyed. The fisherman, who had never before beheld so large a sum of money at once, could not conceal his joy; and thought the whole adventure a dream. He soon, however, proved it to be a reality, and applied the gold to a good purpose in relieving the wants of his family.

"We must now, my Lord," continued Sheherazade, "give some account of what passed in the Sultan's kitchen, where we shall find great confusion and difficulty. As soon as the cook had cleaned the fish, which the vizier had brought, she put them to fry over the fire in a vessel with some oil. When she thought they were sufficiently done on one side, she turned them. She had hardly done so, when the wall of the kitchen appeared to separate, and a beautiful and majestic young damsel came out of the opening. She was dressed in a satin robe, embroidered with flowers after the Egyptian manner, and adorned with ear-rings and a necklace of large pearls, and gold bracelets, set with rubies; she held a rod of myrtle in her hand. To the great astonishment of the cook, who stood motionless with amazement, she approached the pan, and striking one of the fish with her rod, she said, 'Fish, fish, art thou doing thy duty?' The fish answered not a word. She repeated the question, when the four fishes all raised themselves up and said very distinctly, 'Yes, yes—if you reckon, we reckon; if you pay your debts, we pay ours; if you fly, we conquer, and are content.' As soon as they had spoken these words, the damsel overturned the vessel, and went back through the wall, which immediately closed up, and was as if it had never been disturbed.

"When the cook, who was greatly alarmed at all these wonders, had in some measure recovered from her fright, she went to take up the fish, which had fallen upon the hot ashes; but she found them blacker and more burnt than the coals themselves, and not at all in a fit state to be put before the Sultan. At this she was greatly distressed, and began to weep and lament bitterly. 'Alas!' said she, 'what will become of me? I am sure, when I relate to the Sultan what I have seen, he will not believe me. And how his anger will be excited against me!'

"While she was in this distress, the grand vizier entered, and asked if the fish were ready. The cook then related all that had taken place, at which the vizier was greatly astonished: but without telling the Sultan anything about the matter, he invented some excuse for the non-appearance of the fish, which satisfied his master. He then sent directly for the fisherman; on whose arrival he said, 'Bring me four more fish, like those you brought before; for an accident has happened, which prevents their being served up to the Sultan.' The fisherman did not tell the vizier of the injunction laid upon him by the Genie, but pleaded the length of the way as an excuse for not being able to procure any more fish that day; he promised, however, to bring some the next morning.

"The fisherman, in order to be in time, set out before it was day, and went to the lake. He threw his nets, and upon drawing them out, found four more fishes, like those he had taken the day before, each of a different colour. He returned directly, and brought them to the grand vizier at the appointed time. The vizier took them, and carried them into the kitchen, where he shut himself up with only the cook, who prepared to dress them in his presence. She put them on the fire as she had done with the others on the preceding day. When they were dressed on one side, she turned them; and immediately the wall of the kitchen opened, and the same damsel appeared, with her myrtle wand in her hand. She approached the pan, in which the fish were, and striking one of them, repeated the words she had used on the preceding day; and all the fish raised their heads, and made the same answer. The damsel overturned the vessel with her rod, as she had done before, and went away through the opening in the wall, by which she had entered. The grand vizier witnessed all that passed. 'This is very surprising,' he cried, 'and too extraordinary to be kept secret from the Sultan's ears. I will myself go and inform him of this prodigy.' Accordingly he went directly, and gave an exact account of all that had passed.

"The Sultan was much astonished, and became very anxious to see this wonderful sight. For this purpose, he again sent for the fisherman. 'Friend,' said he to him, 'canst thou not bring me four more fish of different colours?' 'If your Majesty,' answered the fisherman, 'will grant me three days, I can promise to do so.' He obtained the time he wished, and went again, for the third time, to the lake. Not less successful than before, he caught four fishes of different colours, the first time he threw his nets. The fisherman hastened to carry them to the Sultan, who was the more pleased at seeing them, as he did not expect them so soon: and he ordered four hundred pieces of money to be given to the man.

"As soon as the Sultan had obtained the fish, he had them brought into his own cabinet, together with the different things that were necessary for preparing them. He shut himself up with the grand vizier, who began to cook the fish, and put them on the fire in a proper vessel. As soon as they were done on one side, he turned them on the other. The wall of the cabinet immediately opened; but instead of the beautiful damsel, there appeared a negro, in the dress of a slave. This negro was of gigantic stature, and held a large green rod in his hand. He advanced towards the vessel, and touching one of the fish with his rod, he cried out in a terrible tone: 'Fish, fish, art thou doing thy duty?' At these words, the fish lifted up their heads and answered, 'Yes, yes, we are; if you reckon, we reckon; if you pay your debts, we pay ours: if you fly, we conquer, and are content.' The fish had scarcely said this, when the negro overturned the vessel into the middle of the cabinet, and reduced the fish to cinders. Having done this, he haughtily retired through the opening in the wall, which instantly closed, and appeared as perfect as before.

"'After what I have seen,' said the Sultan to his grand vizier, 'I cannot think of letting this matter rest. It is certain that these fish signify something very extraordinary, and I must discover what it is. He sent for the fisherman, and when the man arrived, the Sultan said to him: 'The fish thou hast brought me have caused great uneasiness; where dost thou catch them?' 'I caught them, O Sultan,' answered he, 'in a lake, which is situated in the midst of four small hills, beyond the mountain you may see from hence.' 'Do you know that lake?' said the Sultan to the vizier. 'No, my Lord,' answered he, 'I have never even heard it mentioned, though I have hunted in the vicinity of the mountain, and beyond it, for nearly sixty years.' The Sultan asked the fisherman about what distance the lake was from the palace; he replied, that it was not more than three hours' journey. On hearing this, as there was still time to arrive there before night, the Sultan ordered his whole court to accompany him, while the fisherman served as a guide.

"They all ascended the mountain; and on going down on the other side, they were much surprised at the appearance of a large plain, which no one had ever before remarked. They at length arrived at the lake, which they found situated exactly among four hills, as the fisherman had reported. Its water was so transparent, that they could see that all the fish were of the same colours as those the fisherman had brought to the palace.

"The Sultan halted at the side of the lake; and after contemplating the fish with looks of great admiration, he inquired of his emirs and all his courtiers, if it could be possible that they had never seen this lake, which was so close to the city? They all said they had never even heard it mentioned. 'Since you all agree, then,' said he, 'that you have never heard it spoken of, and since I am not less astonished than yourselves at this novelty, I am resolved not to return to my palace till I have discovered for what reason this lake is now placed here, and why there are fish of only four colours in it.' Thereupon he ordered them to encamp around; his own pavilion, and the tents of his immediate household were pitched on the borders of the lake.

"When the day closed the Sultan retired to his pavilion, and began an important conversation with his vizier. 'My mind,' said he, 'is much disturbed; this lake suddenly placed here, this black who appeared to us in my cabinet, these fish too, which we heard speak; all this so much excites my curiosity, that I am determined to be satisfied. Therefore I have made up my mind to execute the design I meditate. I shall

THE SULTAN AND HIS COURT AT THE FISH-POND.

go quite alone from my camp, and order you to keep my departure a profound secret. Remain in my pavilion, and when my emirs and courtiers present themselves at the entrance to-morrow morning, send them away and say I am somewhat indisposed, and wish to remain alone. You will continue to do so every day till my return.'

"The grand vizier endeavoured by many arguments to dissuade the Sultan from carrying out his design. He represented the great danger to which his master exposed himself, and the unnecessary trouble and difficulties he might thus encounter, and probably without result. But all his eloquence was exhausted to no effect; the Sultan did not listen to him, but prepared to set out. He put on a dress proper for walking, and armed himself with a sabre; and as soon as he found that everything in the camp was quiet, he departed quite alone.

"The Sultan bent his course towards one of the small hills, which he ascended without much difficulty; and the descent on the other side was still easier. He then pursued his way over a plain, till the sun rose. He now perceived before him, in the distance, a large building, the sight of which filled him with joy; for he now hoped to gain some intelligence of what he wished to know. When he came near he remarked that the building was a magnificent palace, or rather a strong castle, built of polished black marble, and covered with fine steel, so bright, that it shone like a mirror. Delighted to have so soon met with something, at least, worth investigation, he stopped opposite the front of the castle, and examined it with much attention; he then advanced towards the folding doors, one of which was open. Though he might have entered, he thought it better to knock. At first he knocked gently, and waited some time; but finding that no one answered his summons, he thought it might not have been heard; he therefore knocked a second time, much louder than before; still no one came. He redoubled his efforts, but in vain. At this he was much astonished, for he could not imagine that a castle so well built could be deserted. 'If there is no person there,' said the Sultan to himself, 'I have nothing to fear; and if any one comes, I have arms to defend myself with.'

"At last he entered, and pausing in the vestibule, he called out, 'Is there no one here to receive a stranger, who is in want of refreshment on his journey?'—He repeated this call two or three times, as loudly as he could; still there was no answer. This silence increased his astonishment. He passed on to a very spacious court, and looking on every side, he could not discover a living creature. He then entered, and passed through some large halls, in which were spread carpets of silk, while the recesses were full of sofas entirely covered with the stuffs of Mecca; the curtains hung before the doors were of the richest manufactures of India, embroidered with gold and silver. The Sultan went on, and came to a most splendid saloon, in the midst of which there was a large reservoir, with a lion of massive gold at each corner. Streams of water issued from the mouths of the four lions, and in falling, appeared to break into a thousand diamonds and pearls, which formed a goodly addition to a fountain that sprang from the middle of the basin, rising almost to the top of a dome, beautifully painted in the arabesque style.

The castle was surrounded on three sides by a garden, radiant with all kinds of flowers, with fountains, groves, and many other beauties; but what more than all else rendered this spot enchanting, was the multitude of birds, which filled the air with their sweetest notes. This was their constant habitation; for nets were thrown entirely over the trees, which prevented escape of the beautiful songsters.

"The Sultan continued a long time walking from one apartment to another; and everything around him was grand and magnificent. Being somewhat fatigued, he sat down in an open cabinet, which looked into the garden. Here he sat meditating upon all he had seen, and anticipating future marvels; and was reflecting on the different objects around, when suddenly a plaintive voice, uttering the most heart-rending cries, struck his ear. He listened attentively, and distinctly heard these melancholy words: 'O Fortune, thou hast not suffered me long to enjoy my happy lot, but hast rendered me the most wretched of men; cease, I entreat thee, thus to persecute me, and rather by a speedy death put an end to my sufferings! Alas, is it possible I can still exist, after all the torments I have suffered?'

"The Sultan, much affected by these lamentable complaints, immediately rose and went towards the spot whence they issued. He came to the entrance of a large hall. Drawing the curtain aside, he saw a young man seated upon a sort of throne, raised a little from the ground. This man was handsome to behold, and was very richly dressed. A look of sorrow was impressed on his countenance. The Sultan approached and saluted the stranger. The youth returned the compliment by a deep bending of his head, but did not rise. 'Certainly,' said he to the Sultan, 'I ought to rise to receive you, and show you all possible respect,—but a most powerful reason prevents me; you will not, I trust, take it amiss.' 'I feel myself highly honoured, sir,' replied the Sultan, 'by the good opinion you express of me. Whatever may be your motive for not rising, I willingly receive your apologies. Attracted by your complaints, and hoping to relieve your sufferings, I come to offer you my assistance. I trust I shall be permitted to afford some consolation to you in your misfortunes, and I will use all my endeavours to do so. I flatter myself you will not object to relate the history of your sorrows to me. But, in the first place, I beg you to inform me, what is the meaning of that lake in which there are fish of four different colours: tell me also how this castle came here and how you came to be in it thus alone?'

"Instead of answering these questions, the young man began to weep most bitterly. 'How inconstant is Fortune!' he cried. 'She delights in hurling down those whom she has raised up. Who can say he has ever enjoyed from her a life of calm and pure happiness?'

"The Sultan, touched with compassion at the youth's condition, again requested him to relate the cause of such sorrow: 'Alas, my lord,' answered the youth, 'can I be otherwise than sorrowful, or can these eyes ever cease from shedding tears?' With these words he lifted up his robe, and the Sultan perceived he was a man only to his waist, and that from thence to his feet he had been changed into black marble.

"The Sultan's surprise may be readily imagined, when he saw the deplorable state of the young man. 'What you show me,' said he to him, 'fills me with horror, but at the same time excites my interest; I am impatient to learn your history, which must no doubt be very singular; and I am convinced that the lake and the fish have some connection with it. I entreat you, therefore, to relate your story; and indeed you may find consolation in doing so; for the unhappy often experience some relief in imparting the tale of their sorrows.' 'I will not refuse you this satisfaction,' replied the young man, 'although I cannot relate my history without renewing the most dreadful grief; but I must forewarn you to prepare your ears and your mind, nay even your eyes, for something that passes all belief.'

## The History of the Young King of the Black Isles.

MUST first inform you," began the young man, "that my father, who was named Mahmoud, was the King of this State. It is the kingdom of the Black Isles, and takes its name from four small neighbouring mountains, that were formerly islands; and the capital, in which my father dwelt, was situated on the spot which is now occupied by yonder lake. You will hear how these changes took place, as I proceed with my history.

"The King, my father, died at the age of seventy years. Immediately upon mounting his throne I married, and the person whom I chose as the partner of my state, was my cousin. I had every reason to be satisfied with the proofs of affection I received from her;—and I returned her regard with equal tenderness. Our union produced unmixed happiness for five years; but at the end of that time I began to perceive that the Queen, my cousin, no longer loved me.

"One day after dinner, when she had gone to bathe, I felt inclined to sleep, and threw myself on a sofa; two of the Queen's women, who happened to be in the room, seated themselves, one at my head the other at my feet to fan me, as much to refresh me with the cool air, as to keep off the flies, which might have disturbed my slumbers. These two women, supposing me asleep, began to talk in whispers; but my eyes were only closed, and I overheard their whole conversation.

"'Is it not a pity,' said one of them to the other, 'that the Queen does not love our King, who is such an amiable prince?' 'Surely it is;' replied the other, 'and I cannot conceive why she goes out every night and leaves him; does he not perceive it?' 'How should he perceive it?' resumed the first; 'every night she mixes in his drink the juice of a certain herb, which makes him sleep all night so profoundly, that she has time to go wherever she likes; and when at break of day she returns to him, she awakes him by passing a particular scent under his nose.'

"You may judge my astonishment at this speech, and how I felt when I heard it! Nevertheless I had sufficient command over myself to suppress my emotions; I pretended to awake, and gave no sign of having heard anything.

"Presently the Queen returned from the bath; we supped together, and before we went to bed she presented me with the cup of water, which it was usual for me to take; but instead of drinking it, I approached a window that was open, and threw it out unperceived by her. I then returned the cup into her hands, that she might suppose I had drunk the contents. We soon retired to rest; and shortly afterwards, supposing that I was asleep, she got up with very little precaution, and even said aloud: 'Sleep, and I would thou mightest never wake more.' She dressed herself quickly, and left the chamber.

"So soon as the Queen was gone I rose up and threw on my clothes as quickly as possible; and taking my scimitar, I followed her so closely, that I heard her footsteps just before me. I regulated my steps by hers, walking softly for fear of being heard. She passed through several doors, which opened by virtue of some magic words she pronounced; the last she opened was that of the garden, which she entered. I stopped at this door that she might not see me, while she crossed a lawn; and following her with my eyes, as well as the obscurity of the night would permit, I remarked that she went into a little wood, which was bounded by a thick hedge. I repaired thither by another way; and hiding myself behind the hedge that skirted one of the paths, I perceived that she was walking with a man.

"I did not fail to listen attentively to their discourse, when I heard what follows: 'I do not,' said the Queen to her companion, 'deserve your reproaches for my want of diligence; you well know the reason of it; but if all the tokens of love which I have hitherto given you are not sufficient to persuade you of my sincerity, I am ready to give you still more convincing proofs; you have only to command, you know my power. I will if you wish it, before the sun rises, change this great city and this beautiful palace into frightful ruins, which shall be inhabited only by wolves, and owls, and ravens. Shall I transport all the stones, with which these walls are so strongly built, beyond Mount Caucasus, and farther than the boundaries of the habitable world? You have only to speak, and all this place shall be transformed.'

"As the Queen finished this speech, she and her lover reached the end of the walk, and turning to enter another, passed before me. I had already drawn my scimitar, and as the man walked past me, I struck him on the neck, and he fell. I believed I had killed him; and satisfied such was the case, I retired precipitately, without discovering myself to the Queen, whom I wished to spare, as she was my cousin.

"Although her lover's wound was mortal, she yet contrived by her magic art to preserve in him a kind of existence, which can be called neither death nor life. As I traversed the garden to return to the palace, I heard the Queen weeping bitterly; and judging of her grief by her cries, I was not sorry to have left him alive. When I reached my chamber I returned to bed; and satisfied with the punishment I had inflicted on the wretch who had offended me, I fell asleep. On waking the next morning, I found the Queen by my side; I cannot say whether she was in a real or a feigned sleep, but I got up without disturbing her, and retired to my closet, where I finished dressing. I afterwards attended the council; and, on my return, the Queen, dressed in mourning, with her hair dishevelled and torn, presented herself before me. 'My Lord,' said she, 'I come to entreat your Majesty not to be displeased at the state in which you now see me. I have just received intelligence of three events, which occasion the grief I so strongly feel, that I can scarcely express it.' 'What are these events, madam?' I inquired. 'The death of the Queen my beloved mother,' replied she; 'that of the King, my father, who was killed in battle; and of my brother, who fell down a precipice.'

"I was not sorry that she had invented this pretext to conceal the true cause of her affliction; and I concluded that she did not suspect me of having been the murderer of her lover. 'Madam,' said I, 'I do not blame your sorrow; on the contrary, I assure you that I sympathize in the cause. I should be much surprised if you were not affected by such a loss; weep, for your tears are an undoubted proof of the kindness of your heart. I hope, nevertheless, that time and philosophy will restore to you your wonted cheerfulness.'

"She retired to her apartments, and, abandoning herself to her grief, she passed a whole year there, weeping and bewailing the death of her lover. At the expiration of that time, she requested my permission to build for herself, in the centre of the palace, a mausoleum, in which, she said, she designed to pass the remainder of her days. I did

THE YOUNG KING HEARS A CONVERSATION.

not refuse; and she erected a magnificent palace, with a dome, which may be seen from this place; and she called it the Palace of Tears.

"When it was completed, she had her lover removed, and brought to this mausoleum, from the place whither she had transported him on the night I wounded him. She had till that period preserved his life by giving him certain potions, which she administered herself, and continued to give him daily after his removal to the Palace of Tears.

"All her enchantments, however, did not avail much; for he was not only unable to walk or stand, but had also lost the use of his speech, and gave no signs of life, but by looks. Although the Queen had only the consolation of seeing him and saying to him all the tender things that her love inspired, yet she constantly paid him two long visits every day. I was well acquainted with this circumstance, but I pretended to be ignorant of it.

"Moved by curiosity, I went one day to the Palace of Tears, to know how the Queen passed her time there; and concealing myself in a place where I could see and hear what passed, I heard her speak these words to her lover: 'Oh, what a heavy affliction to me to see you in this state! I share with you all the agonies you endure. But, dearest Life, I am always speaking to you, and yet you return no answer; how long will this distressing silence continue? Speak but once, and I am satisfied. Alas! these moments, that I pass with you, endeavouring to mitigate your sufferings, are the happiest of my life. I cannot exist away from you, and I should prefer the pleasure of seeing you continually to the empire of the whole universe.'

"This speech, which was frequently interrupted by tears and sobs, at length exhausted my patience. I could no longer remain in concealment; but approaching her, exclaimed, 'Madam, you have wept enough; it is now time to have done with a grief which dishonours us both; you forget what you owe to me, as well as what you owe to yourself.' 'Sir,' replied she, 'if you still retain any regard for me, I entreat you to leave me to my sorrows, which time can neither diminish nor relieve.'

"I endeavoured, but in vain, to bring her to a sense of her duty; finding that all my arguments only increased her obstinacy, I at last desisted and left her. She continued to visit her lover every day; and for two years she was inconsolable.

"I went a second time to the Palace of Tears while she was there. I hid myself as before, and heard her say: 'It is now three years since you have spoken to me; nor do you return the tokens of affection and fondness which I offer you in my complaints and sighs. Is it from insensibility or disdain? Hast thou, O Tomb, destroyed that excess of tenderness which he bore me? Hast thou closed for ever those dear eyes, which beamed with love, and were all my delight? Ah, no, I cannot think it; rather let me say, thou art become the depository of the rarest treasure the world ever saw.'

"I confess to you, my Lord, that I was enraged at these words; and indeed this cherished lover, this adored mortal, was not the kind of man you would imagine. He was a black Indian, one of the original inhabitants of this country. I was, as I have said, so enraged at this speech, that I suddenly showed myself; and apostrophizing the tomb as my wife had done, I said, 'Why dost thou not, O Tomb, swallow up this monster, who is disgusting to human nature? Or rather, why dost thou not consume both the lover and his mistress?'

"So soon as I had spoken these words, the Queen, who was seated near the Black, started up like a fury. 'Ah, wretch!' cried she to me, 'it is you who have been the cause of my grief; think not that I am ignorant of your doings. I have already dissembled too long. It was your barbarous hand which reduced the object of my affection to the miserable state he now is in. And have you the cruelty to come and insult my despair?' 'Yes,' exclaimed I, confronting her, transported with anger; 'I have chastised the monster as he deserved, and I ought to treat thee in the same manner. I repent that I have not already done it, for thou hast too long abused my goodness.' As I said this I drew my scimitar, and raised my arm to punish her. 'Moderate thy rage,' said she to me, with a disdainful smile; she looked upon me with an air of indifference. After a moment she pronounced some words, which I did not understand, and added, 'By virtue of my enchantments, I command thee, from this moment, to become half marble, and half man.' Immediately, my Lord, I was changed to what you see, already dead among the living, and still living among the dead.

"As soon as this cruel enchantress—for she is unworthy of the title of Queen—had thus transformed me, and by means of her magic had conveyed me to this apartment, she destroyed my capital, which had been flourishing and well inhabited; she annihilated the palaces, public places, and markets; turned the whole region into a lake or pond, and rendered the country, as you may perceive, quite a desert. The four sorts of fish, which are in the lake, are four different classes of inhabitants, who professed different religions, and inhabited the capital. The white were Mussulmen; the red, Persians and fire-worshippers; the blue, Christians; and the yellow, Jews. The four little hills were four islands, which originally gave the kingdom its name. I was informed of all this by the enchantress, who herself related to me the effects of her rage. Nor was even this all. Her fury is not satiated by the destruction of my empire, and the enchantment of myself; for she comes every day and gives me a hundred blows upon my shoulders, with a thong made of a bull's hide, drawing blood at every stroke. As soon as she has finished this punishment, she covers me with a coarse stuff, made of goat's hair, and puts a robe of rich brocade over it, not for the sake of honouring me, but to mock my despair."—As he said this, the young King of the Black Isles could not refrain from tears; and the Sultan's heart was so oppressed, he could offer him no consolation. The young King then, lifting up his eyes towards heaven, exclaimed, 'I submit, O powerful Creator of all things, to thy judgments, and to the decrees of thy providence. Since it is thy pleasure, I patiently suffer every evil; yet I trust thy infinite goodness will one day recompense me.'

"The Sultan was much affected by the recital of this strange story, and felt eager to revenge the unfortunate King's injuries. 'Inform me,' cried he, 'where this perfidious enchantress resides; and also where is this infamous paramour, whom she has entombed before his death.' 'My Lord,' answered the Prince, 'he, as I have before mentioned, is at the Palace of Tears in a tomb, formed like a dome; and the building has a communication with the castle, in the direction of the entrance. I cannot exactly tell you to what spot the enchantress has retired; but she visits her lover every day at sunrise, after having inflicted on me the cruel punishment I have described; and you may easily judge, that I cannot defend myself from such inhumanity. She always brings with her a sort of liquor, which is the only thing that can keep him alive; and she never ceases to complain of the silence which he has kept unbroken since he was wounded.'

"'No one, Prince,' replied the Sultan, 'deserves greater commiseration than yourself; nor can any one sympathize more in your misfortune than I do. A more extraordinary fate never happened to any man; and they, who may hereafter compose your history, will be able to relate an event more surprising than anything yet recorded. One thing only is wanting to complete it, and that is your revenge; nor will I leave anything untried to accomplish this end.' The Sultan having first informed the Prince of his own name and rank, and of the reason of his entering the castle, consulted with him on the best means of accomplishing a just revenge; and a plan occurred to the Sultan, which he directly communicated. They agreed upon the steps it was necessary to take, in order to ensure success; and they deferred the execution of the plan till the following day. In the meantime, as the night was far advanced, the Sultan took some repose. The young Prince, as usual, passed his time in continued wakefulness, for he had been unable to sleep since his enchantment; but now the hopes, however slight, which he cherished of being soon relieved from his sufferings, constantly occupied his thoughts.

"The Sultan rose as soon as it was day; and, concealing in his chamber his robe and external dress, which might have encumbered him, he went to the Palace of Tears. He found it illuminated by a multitude of torches of white wax, and became conscious of a delicious perfume, issuing from various beautiful golden vases, regularly arranged. As soon as he perceived the bed on which the wounded man was lying, he drew his sabre, and destroyed, without resistance, the little life that remained in the wretch. He then dragged the body into the court of the castle, and threw it into a well. Having done this, he returned, and lay down in the Indian's place, hiding his sabre under the coverlid, and there he watched to complete the revenge he meditated. The enchantress arrived soon after. Her first business was to go into the apartment in which she had immured her husband, the King of the Black Isles. She directly stripped him, and, began with horrible barbarity, to inflict upon his shoulders the accustomed number of blows. The poor prince filled the whole building with his cries, and conjured her in the most pathetic manner to have pity on him; the cruel enchantress, however, ceased not to beat him till she had completed the hundred stripes. 'Thou hadst no compassion on my lover;' said she, 'therefore expect none from me.' As soon as she had finished her cruel work, she threw over him the coarse garment made of goat-skin, covering this with the robe of brocade. She next went to the Palace of Tears; and, on entering, began to renew her lamentations. When she approached the couch, where she thought to find her lover, she exclaimed, 'Alas! what cruelty to have thus destroyed the tranquil joy of so tender and fond a mistress as I am! Merciless Prince, thou reproachest me with being inhuman, when I make thee feel the effects of my resentment,—and has not thy barbarity far exceeded my revenge? Hast thou not, traitor, in destroying almost the existence of this adorable object, equally destroyed mine? Alas!' added she, addressing herself to the Sultan, whom she took for her lover, 'will you always, Light of my life, thus keep silence? Are you resolved to let me die without the consolation of hearing you again declare you love me? Utter at least one word, I conjure you.'

"Then the Sultan, pretending to awake from a profound sleep, and imitating the language of the Indians, answered the Queen in a solemn tone. 'There is no strength or power,' he said, 'but in Allah alone, who is all powerful.' At these words the enchantress, who never expected to hear her lover speak, gave a violent scream, for very joy. 'My dear Lord,' she exclaimed, 'do you deceive me, is what I hear true? Is it really you who speak?' 'Wretched woman,' replied the Sultan, 'are you worthy of an answer?' 'What!' cried the Queen, 'do you reproach me?' 'The cries, the tears, the groans of thy husband,' answered the supposed Indian, 'whom you every day torture with so much barbarity, continually disturb my rest. I should have been cured long since, and should have recovered the use of my tongue, if you had disenchanted him. This, and this only, is the cause of my silence, of which you so bitterly complain.' 'Then,' said the enchantress, 'to satisfy you I am ready to do what you command—do you wish him to be restored to his former shape?' 'Yes,' replied the Sultan, 'and hasten to set him free, that I may no longer be disturbed by his cries.'

"The Queen immediately went out from the Palace of Tears; and taking a vessel of water, she pronounced over it some words, which caused it instantly to boil, as if it had been placed on a fire. She proceeded to the apartment where the young King, her husband, was. 'If the Creator of all things,' said she, throwing the water over him, 'hath formed thee, as thou now art, or if he is angry with thee, be not changed; but if thou art in this state by virtue of my enchantment, take back thy natural form, and become as thou wert before.' She had hardly concluded, when the Prince, recovering his first shape, rose up with all possible joy, and returned thanks to God. 'Go,' said the enchantress, addressing him, 'hasten from this castle, and never return, lest it should cost you your life!' The young King yielded to necessity, and left the Queen without uttering a word. He concealed himself in a secure spot, where he impatiently waited the completion of the Sultan's design, the commencement of which had been so successful.

"The enchantress then returned to the Palace of Tears; and on entering, said to the Sultan, whom she still mistook for the Indian: 'I have done, my love, what you ordered me; nothing, therefore, now prevents your getting up, and affording me the satisfaction I have so long been deprived of.' The Sultan, still imitating the language of the Blacks, answered in a somewhat severe tone: 'What you have yet done is not sufficient for my cure. You have destroyed only a part of the evil: but you must strike at the root.' 'What do you mean by those words, my charming friend?' asked she. 'What can I mean,' he cried, 'but the city and its inhabitants, and the four isles, which you have destroyed by your magic?—Every day towards midnight the fish raise their heads out of the pond, and cry for vengeance against us both. This is the real cause why my recovery is so long delayed. Go quickly and re-establish everything in its former state; and on your return I will give you my hand, and you shall assist me in rising.'

"The Queen, exulting in the expectations these words produced, joyfully exclaimed: 'You shall soon then, my life, recover your health; for I will instantly go and do what you have commanded.' In fact she went that very instant, and when she arrived on the border of the pond, she took a little water in her hand and scattered it about. So soon as she had done this, and pronounced certain words over the fish and the pond, the city re-appeared. The fish became men, women, and children; all arose as Mahometans, Christians, Persians, and Jews; freemen came forth, and slaves; in short, each took his former shape. The houses and shops became filled with inhabitants, who found all things in the same situation and order in which they had been previous to the change effected by the Queen's enchantment. The officers and attendants of the Sultan, who had happened to encamp upon the site of the great square, were astonished at finding themselves on a sudden in the midst of a large, well-built, and populous city.

THE PRINCE OF THE BLACK ISLES FREED FROM HIS ENEMY.

"But to return to the enchantress. As soon as she had completed this change she hastened back to the Palace of Tears to enjoy the reward of her labours. 'My dear lord,' she cried on entering, 'I have returned to participate in the pleasure of your renewed health, for I have done all you have required of me; arise, and give me your hand.' 'Come near, then—,' said the Sultan, still imitating the manner of the Indian. She did so. 'Nearer still!' he cried. She obeyed. Then raising himself up, he seized her so suddenly by the arms that she had no opportunity of perceiving how she had been deceived; and with one stroke of his sabre he separated her body into two parts, which fell on each side of him. Having done this, he left the corpse where it fell, and went to seek the Prince of the Black Isles, who was waiting with the greatest impatience for him. 'Rejoice, Prince,' said he, embracing him, 'you have nothing more to fear, for your cruel enemy exists no longer.'

"The young Prince thanked the Sultan in a way which proved that his heart was truly penetrated with gratitude; and wished his deliverer, as a reward for the important service he had rendered him, a long life and the greatest prosperity. 'May you too live happily and at peace in your capital!' replied the Sultan, 'and should you hereafter have a wish to visit mine, which is so near, I shall receive you with the truest pleasure, and you shall be as highly honoured and respected as in your own.' 'Powerful monarch,' answered the Prince, 'to whom I am so much indebted, do you think you are very near your capital!'—'Certainly,' replied the Sultan; 'I presume, at least, that I am not more than four or five hours' journey from thence.' 'It is a whole year's journey,' said the Prince, 'although I believe you might come here in the time you mention, because my city was enchanted; but since it has been restored all this is altered. This, however, shall not prevent my following you, were it necessary to go to the very ends of the earth. You are my liberator; and to show you every mark of my gratitude as long as I live, I shall freely accompany you, and resign my kingdom without regret.'

"The Sultan was extremely surprised to find that he was so distant from his dominions, and could not comprehend how it had happened; but the young King of the Black Isles convinced him so fully of the fact, that he no longer doubted it. 'It matters not,' resumed the Sultan. 'The trouble of returning to my dominions will be sufficiently recompensed by the satisfaction of having assisted you, and of having gained a son in you; for, as you will do me the honour me to accompany me, I shall look upon you as my son; and, as I am childless, I from this moment make you my heir and successor.' This interview between the Sultan and the King of the Black Isles was terminated by the most affectionate embraces; and the young Prince at once prepared for his journey. In three weeks he was ready to depart, greatly regretted by his Court and subjects, who received at his hands a near relation of his own as their King.

"At length the Sultan and the Prince set out, with a hundred camels laden with inestimable riches, which had been selected from the treasury of the young King, who was, moreover, accompanied by fifty handsome nobles, well mounted and equipped. Their journey was a pleasant one; and when the Sultan, who had despatched couriers to give notice of his arrival, and explain the reason of his delay, drew near to his capital, the principal officers, whom he had left there, came to receive him, and to assure him that his long absence had not occasioned any change in his empire. The inhabitants also, crowded to meet him, and welcomed him with acclamations, and every demonstration of joy; and the rejoicings were continued for several days.

"The day after his arrival, the Sultan assembled his courtiers, and gave them an ample detail of the occurrences, which, contrary to his wishes, had delayed his return: he then declared to them his intention of adopting the King of the Four Black Isles, who had left a large kingdom to accompany and live with him; and lastly, to reward the fidelity with which they served him, he bestowed presents on all, according to each man's rank and station.

"With regard to the fisherman, as he had been the first cause of the deliverance of the young Prince, the Sultan overwhelmed him with rewards, and made him and his family happy and prosperous for the rest of their days.'

## THE HISTORY OF THREE CALENDERS, SONS OF KINGS, AND OF FIVE LADIES OF BAGDAD.

URING the reign of the Caliph Haroun Alraschid, there lived at Bagdad, a porter, who, notwithstanding that his profession was mean and laborious, was nevertheless a man of wit and humour. One morning, as he was standing with a large basket before him, in a place where he usually waited for employment, a young lady of a fine figure, with her face hidden by a large muslin veil, came up to him, and said with a pleasing air:—'Porter, take up your basket, and follow me.' The porter, delighted to hear these words, pronounced in so agreeable a manner, put his pannier on his head and went after the lady, saying, 'O happy day! O happy meeting!'

"The lady stopped at a closed door, and knocked. A venerable Christian with a long white beard opened it, and she put some money into his hands without saying a single word; but the Christian, who knew what she wanted, went in, and very soon brought out a large jar of excellent wine. 'Take this jar,' said the lady to the porter, 'and put it in the basket.' When this was done, she desired him to follow her and walked on; the porter still exclaiming, 'O day of happiness! O day of agreeable surprise and joy!'

"The lady stopped at the shop of a seller of fruits and flowers, where she chose various sorts of apples, apricots, peaches, lemons, citrons, oranges, myrtles, sweet basil, lilies, jessamine, and many other sweet-scented flowers and plants. She told the porter to put all those things in his basket, and follow her. Passing by a butcher's shop, she ordered five-and-twenty pounds' weight of his finest meat to be weighed, and this likewise was put into the porter's basket.

"At another shop she bought some capers, tarragon, small cucumbers, parsley, and other herbs, pickled in vinegar: at another, some pistachios, walnuts, hazelnuts, almonds, kernels of the pine, and similar fruits; elsewhere she purchased all sorts of almond patties. The porter, as he put all these things into his basket, which began to fill it, said, 'My good lady, you should have told me that you intended making so many purchases, and I would have provided a horse, or rather a camel, to carry them. I shall have more than I can lift, if you add much to what is already here.' The lady laughed at this speech, and again desired him to follow her.

"She then went into a druggist's, where she provided herself with all sorts of sweet-scented waters, with cloves, nutmeg, pepper, ginger, and a large piece of ambergris and several other Indian spices, which completely filled the porter's basket; still she ordered him to follow her. He did so, till they arrived at a magnificent house, the front ornamented with handsome columns; and at the entrance was a door of ivory. Here they stopped, and the lady gave a gentle knock. While they waited for the door to be opened, the porter's mind was filled with a thousand different thoughts. He was surprised that a lady, dressed like this one, should perform the office of housekeeper; for he conceived it impossible that she should be a slave. Her air was so noble, that he supposed her free, if not a person of distinction. He was wishing to ask her some questions concerning her quality and position; but just as he was preparing to speak, another female, who opened the door, appeared to him so beautiful, that he was silent with astonishment, or rather he was so struck by the brilliancy of her charms, that he very nearly let his basket and all that was in it fall; so much did this fair object engross his attention. He thought he had never seen any beauty in his whole life to equal hers, who was before him. The lady, who had brought the porter, observed the disturbed state of his mind, and divined the cause of it. This discovery amused her; and she took so much pleasure in examining the countenance of the porter, that she forgot the door was open. 'Come in, sister—,' said the beautiful portress. 'What do you wait for? Don't you see, that this poor man is so heavily laden, he can hardly bear his load?'

"As soon as the first lady and the porter had come in, the second, who opened the door, shut it; and all three, passing through a handsome vestibule, crossed a very spacious court, surrounded by an open gallery, or corridor, which communicated with many magnificent apartments, all on the same floor. At the end of this court there was a sort of cabinet, richly furnished, with a throne of amber in the middle, supported by four ebony pillars, enriched with diamonds and pearls of extraordinary size, and covered with red satin, relieved by a bordering of Indian gold, of admirable workmanship. In the middle of the court there was a large basin lined with white marble, and full of the clearest transparent water, which rushed from the mouth of a lion of gilt bronze.

"Although the porter was heavily laden, this did not prevent him from admiring the magnificence of the house, and the neatness and regularity with which everything in it was arranged; but his attention was particularly attracted by a third lady, who appeared still more beautiful than the second, and who was seated on the amber throne. As soon as she perceived the other two females, she came down from the throne, and advanced towards them. The porter conjectured from the looks and behaviour of the first two ladies, that this third was the principal personage; and he was not mistaken. This last lady was called Zobeidè; she, who opened the door, was called Safiè · and the name of the one who had been out for the provisions, was Aminè.

"'You do not, my dear sisters,' said Zobeidè, accosting the other two, 'perceive that this man is almost fainting under his load. Why do you not discharge him?' Aminè and Safiè then took the basket, one standing at each side; Zobeidè also assisted, and all three put it on the ground. They then began to empty it; and when they had done so, the agreeable Aminè took out her purse, and rewarded the porter very liberally. He was well satisfied with what he received, and was taking up his basket to go, but could not muster sufficient resolution; so much was he delighted by the sight of three such rare beauties, all of whom appeared to him equally charming; for Aminè had also taken off her veil, and he found her quite as handsome as the others. The thing that puzzled him most, was that there did not seem to be any man in the house; and yet a great part of the provisions he brought, such as the dried fruits, cakes, and sweetmeats, were most suitable for persons who wish to drink much and to feast.

"Zobeidè at first thought the porter was waiting to get breath; but observing he remained a long time, she asked him what he waited for, and whether he was sufficiently paid. 'Give him something more,' added she, speaking to Aminè, 'and let him be satisfied.' 'Madam,' answered the porter, 'it is not that which detains me; I am already but too well paid for my trouble. I know very well that I am guilty of an incivility in staying where I ought not; but I hope you will have the goodness to pardon it, and ascribe it to the astonishment I experience in seeing no man among three ladies of such uncommon beauty. A party of ladies without men is as melancholy and stupid as a party of men without ladies.' To this he added some pleasantries in proof of what he advanced. He did not forget to repeat what they say at Bagdad, that there was no comfort at table unless there were four; and he concluded by saying, that as the ladies were three, they had the greatest want of a fourth.

"The ladies laughed heartily at the reasoning of the porter. Zobeidè, however, then addressed him in a serious manner. 'You carry your fooleries, my friend, a little too far; but though you do not deserve that I should enter into any explanation with you, I will at once inform you, that we are three sisters, who arrange all our affairs so secretly, that no one knows anything of them. The great reason we have to fear a discovery, forbids us to make our arrangements public: and an author of repute, whom we have read, says, *Keep thy own secret, and tell it to no one; for he who reveals a secret, is no longer master of it. If thine own breast cannot contain thy secret, how can the breast of him, to whom thou entrustest it?*

"'Ladies,' replied the porter, 'from your appearance alone I thought you possessed a singular degree of merit; and I perceive that I am not mistaken. Although fortune has not been so propitious to me, as to provide me with a better profession than the one I follow, yet I have cultivated my mind as much as I was able, by reading books of science and history; and permit me, I entreat, to say, that I also have read in another a maxim, which I have always happily practised. *Conceal your secret,* says the writer, *only from such as are known to be indiscreet, and who will abuse your confidence; but make no difficulty in discovering it to prudent men, because they know how to keep it.* The secret, then, with me is as safe as if it were locked up in a cabinet, the key of which is lost, and the door sealed.

"Zobeidè saw that the porter was not deficient in cleverness; but thinking that he was desirous of being at the entertainment they were going to have, she jestingly replied, 'You know that we are preparing to regale ourselves, and you must also know

THE THREE LADIES AND THE PORTER.

we cannot do this, but at a considerable expense; and it would not be just that you should partake of the feast without bearing part of the cost.' The beautiful Safiè was of her sister's opinion. 'My friend,' she said to the porter, 'have you never heard the common saying, "If thou bringest something, thou shalt return with something, if thou bringest nothing, thou shalt carry nothing away."'

"The porter would have been obliged to retire in confusion, in spite of his rhetoric, had it not been for Aminè, who took his part very strongly. 'My dear sisters,' she said to Zobeidè and Safiè, 'I entreat you to permit him to remain with us. I need not tell you he will divert us, for you must see he is a witty man. I assure you, that had it not been for his readiness, quickness, and courage in following me, I should not have executed my many commissions in so short a time. Besides, if I were to repeat to you all the amusing things he said to me on the way, you would not be much surprised that I am become his advocate.'

"At this speech of Aminè's, the porter, in a transport of joy, fell on his knees and kissed the ground at the feet of this charming woman. 'My dear lady,' said he, as he rose, 'you have begun my happiness, and placed it almost at its summit by this generous advocacy, for which I can never sufficiently express my gratitude. In short, ladies,' added he, addressing the three sisters at once, 'do not suppose because you have done me so great an honour, that I will abuse it; or that I consider myself as a man, who is worthy of it; on the contrary, I shall ever regard myself as the humblest of your slaves.' Saying this, he wished to return the money he had received; but the grave Zobeidè ordered him to keep it. 'What we have once given,' she said, 'as a recompense to those who have rendered us any service, we never take back. But in agreeing that you should remain with us, we not only make the condition, that you keep the secret we are going to entrust you with, but we also require, that you shall strictly observe the rules of propriety and decorum.' While her sister was speaking, the beautiful Aminè took off her walking dress, and fastening her robe to her girdle, to be more at liberty in preparing the table, she placed on it various kinds of meat, and put some bottles of wine, and several golden cups upon a sideboard. Hereupon the ladies seated themselves round the table, and made the porter place himself by their side. He, for his part, was delighted beyond measure, at seeing himself at table with three persons of such extraordinary beauty.

"They had scarcely begun to eat, when Aminè, who had placed herself near the sideboard, took a bottle and goblet, and poured out some wine for herself. Having drunk the first glass, according to the Arabian custom, she then poured out one for each of her sisters, who drank one after the other. Then filling the goblet for the fourth time, she presented it to the porter, who, as he took it, kissed her hand; and before he drank it he sung a song, the purport of which was, that as the wind carried with it the odour of any perfumed spot over which it passed, so the wine which he was about to drink, coming from her hand, acquired a more exquisite flavour than it naturally possessed. This song pleased the ladies very much, and they too sang, each in her turn. In short, the company were in most excellent spirits during the repast, which lasted a long time, and was accompanied by everything that could render it agreeable.

"The day began to close, when Safiè, in the name of her sisters, said to the porter, 'Arise, and go; it is time to retire.' To this, the porter, who had not the heart to quit them, answered, 'Ah, ladies, where would you command me to go in the state I am in? I am almost beside myself from gazing on you, and from the good cheer you have given me; and I shall never find the way to my own house. Allow me the night to recover myself in; I will pass it wherever you please; but no shorter time will restore me to the state I was in when I came here; and even then I fear I shall leave the better part of myself behind.'

"Aminè again took the part of the porter: 'He is right, my sister,' she exclaimed; 'I am convinced of the propriety of his demand. He has sufficiently amused us; and if you will believe me, or rather if you love me, I am sure you will suffer him to pass the evening with us.' 'We cannot refuse any request of yours, sister,' replied Zobeidè. 'Porter,' she added, addressing herself to the man; 'we are willing to grant you even this favour, but we must impose a fresh condition: whatever we may do in your presence, with respect to yourself or anything else, beware of asking us any questions; for in questioning us about things that do not at all concern you, you may hear what will not please you. Take care, therefore, and be not too curious in attempting to discover the motives of our actions.'

"'Madam,' replied the porter, 'I promise to observe the conditions with so much exactitude, that you shall have no reason to reproach me with having infringed them, still less to punish my indiscretion. My tongue shall be motionless; and my eyes shall be like a mirror, that preserves none of the objects whose image it receives.' 'To let you see,' said Zobeidè, with a serious air, 'that what we require of you is not newly established among us, observe what is written over the door, on the inside.' The porter went and read these words, which were written in large letters of gold: WHOEVER TALKS ABOUT WHAT DOES NOT CONCERN HIM, OFTEN HEARS WHAT DOES NOT PLEASE HIM! He came back directly and said to the three sisters, 'I swear to you, ladies, that you shall not hear me speak a word concerning anything which does not regard me, and in which you have any interest.'

"This matter being settled, Aminè brought supper; and when she had lighted up the hall with numerous candles, prepared with aloes and ambergris, which scattered a very agreeable perfume, and cast a brilliant radiance around, she seated herself at the table with her sisters and the porter. They began to eat, drink, sing, and recite verses. The ladies took pleasure in making the porter intoxicated, under the pretence of calling upon him to drink to their health. Wit and repartee were not wanting. The company were at length all in the best humour, when they heard a knocking at the gate. They instantly got up, and all ran to open it; but Safiè, to whom this office more particularly belonged, was the most active. The other two, seeing her before them, stopped, and waited till she came back to tell them who it was that could have any business with them at so late an hour. Safiè soon returned, and spoke thus: 'Sisters, here is a charming opportunity to spend part of the night very pleasantly; and if you are of my opinion we will not let it escape us. There are three calenders at the door; at least they appear by their dress to be calenders; but what will doubtless surprise you is, that they are all three blind of the right eye, and have their heads, beards, and eyebrows shaved. They say they have only just arrived at Bagdad, where they have never been before; and as it is dark, and they knew not where to lodge, they knocked at our door by chance; and entreat us for the love of God, to have the charity to take them in. They care not where we put them, provided they are under cover, and will be satisfied even with a stable. They are young and comely, and seem to be men of some spirit; but I cannot without laughing, think of their amusing and uniform appearance.' Safiè could not indeed refrain from laughing most heartily, nor could either her sisters or the porter keep from joining in her mirth. 'Shall we,' said she, 'let them come in? It is impossible but that with such men as these, we shall finish the day even better than we began it. They will amuse us very much, and they will be no expense to us, since they only ask a lodging for one night, and it is their intention to leave us as soon as it is day.'

"Zobeidè and Aminè made some difficulty in agreeing to the request of Safiè; and she herself well knew the reason of their reluctance; but she expressed so great a desire to have her way, that they could not refuse her. 'Go,' said Zobeidè to her, 'and let them come in; but do not fail to caution them not to speak about what does not concern them, and make them read the inscription over the inside of the door.' At these words, Safiè joyfully ran to open the door, and soon returned, accompanied by the three calenders.

"On entering they made a low bow to the sisters, who had risen to receive them, and who obligingly told them they were welcome; and they professed themselves happy in being able to oblige them, and contribute towards lessening the fatigue of their journey. They then invited their new guests to sit down with them. The magnificence of the place and the kindness of the ladies gave the calenders a very high idea of the beautiful hostess and her sisters; but before they took their places, chancing to cast their eyes towards the porter, and observing that he was dressed very like other calenders, from whom they differed in many points of discipline, as for instance, in having their beards and eye-brows shaven, one of them said: 'This man appears to be one of our Arabian brethren, who revolted.'

"The porter, half asleep, and heated with the wine he had drunk, was much disturbed at these words; and without rising he said to the calender who had spoken, casting at the same time a fierce look at the three, 'Seat yourselves, and meddle not with what does not concern you. Have you not read the inscription over the door? Do not pretend then to make the world live after your fashion; but live according to ours.'—'My good friend,' replied the calender, who had been the cause of this outbreak, 'do not be angry, for we should be very sorry to give you any cause; on the contrary, we are ready to receive your commands.' The quarrel would not have ended here had not the ladies interfered, and pacified the disputants.

"When the calenders were seated, the sisters helped them to meat and drink, and the delighted Safiè in particular took care to supply them with wine. When they had both eaten and drunk as much as they wished, they intimated that they should be happy to give their entertainers some music, if the ladies had any instruments, and would order them to be brought. The ladies accepted the offer with pleasure; and the beautiful Safiè immediately got up to procure some instruments, and returning the next moment, offered the calenders a native flute, another used in Persia, and a tambourine. Each calender received from her hand the instrument he liked best, and they all began to play a little air. The ladies were acquainted with the words, which were very lively, and accompanied the air with their voices: frequently interrupting each other with fits of laughter caused by the nature of the words.

"In the midst of this entertainment, and when the party were in high good humour, they heard a knock at the door. Safiè immediately left off singing, and went to see who was there."

"But I must now inform you, my Lord," said Sheherazade to the Sultan, "that it is proper for your Majesty to know, how any one came to knock so late at the door of this house. The caliph Haroun Alraschid made it a frequent practice to go through the city in disguise during the night, in order to discover whether every thing was quiet and orderly. On this evening, therefore, the caliph had set out from his palace, at his accustomed hour, accompanied by Giafar, his grand vizier, and Mesrour, chief of the eunuchs; all three were disguised as merchants. In passing through the street where these ladies lived, the Prince heard the sound of the instruments, interspersed with laughter, and said to his vizier, 'Go and knock at the door of that house, where I hear so much noise; I wish to gain admittance, and learn the cause of it.' The vizier endeavoured to persuade the caliph that they were only women, who were making merry that evening, and that the wine seemed to have exhilarated their spirits; and that the caliph ought not to expose himself where it was probable he might meet with some insult; besides, the time, he said, was improper, and it was useless to disturb the amusements of the people. 'Nevertheless,' said the caliph, 'knock, as I order you.'

"It was, then, the grand vizier Giafar, who had knocked at the door by order of the caliph, who wished not to be known. Safiè opened it, and the vizier observed by the light of a candle she carried, that she was very beautiful. He played his part very well. He first made a profound reverence, and then with a most respectful air, he said, 'Madam, we are three merchants of Moussoul; we arrived here about ten days ago, with some very rich merchandize; which we have deposited in a khan, where we have taken up our lodging. We have been to spend the day with a merchant of this city, who had invited us to go to see him. He entertained us very sumptuously; and as the wine we drank put us into a very good humour, he sent for a company of dancers. The night was already far advanced, and while we were playing on our instruments, the company was dancing, and all were making a great noise, the watch happened to pass by, and obliged us to open the door. Some of the guests were arrested: we, however, were so fortunate as to escape, by getting over a wall. But,' added the vizier, 'as we are strangers, and have taken perhaps rather more wine than we ought, we are afraid of meeting with a second party of the watch, or perhaps with the officers from whom

ZOBEIDÈ PREPARES TO WHIP THE DOGS.

we escaped, before we arrive at our khan, which is still a long way off. And even if we reached the khan in safety, the gate would be shut, and whoever may come will not be admitted till morning. This is the reason, madam, that in passing by, when we heard the sound of instruments and voices, we thought all those who belonged to the house had not yet gone to rest; and we took the liberty to knock, to beg you to afford us a retreat till the morning. If we appear to you worthy of taking a part in your amusements, we will endeavour, as far as we are able, to contribute to the enjoyment of the evening, and thus to make amends for the interruption we have caused; if we appear unworthy, grant us at least that we may pass the night under the shelter of your vestibule.'

"During the speech of Giafar, the beautiful Safiè had an opportunity of examining the vizier and his companions, whom he called merchants like himself; and judging from their countenances, that they were not common men, she said, that she was not mistress, but if they would be patient for a moment, she would return and bring an answer. Safiè went and related all to her sisters, who hesitated some time as to what they ought to do. But they were naturally kind; and as they had shown the same favour to the three calenders, they resolved to permit these merchants also to come in. The caliph, the grand vizier, and the chief of the eunuchs, being introduced by the beautiful Safiè, saluted the ladies and the calenders with great civility. They, supposing their visitors to be merchants, returned their salute in the same manner; and Zobeidè, as the principal person, said with that grave and serious air which well suited her: 'You are welcome;—but in the first place, do not take it ill if we ask of you one favour.' 'What favour,' cried the vizier, 'can we refuse to such beautiful ladies?' 'It is,' replied Zobeidè, 'to have eyes, but no tongues; to forbear to ask questions about what you may see, or to strive to learn the cause; and to be silent about what does not concern you, lest you should hear what will not be pleasant to you.' 'You shall be obeyed, madam;' replied the vizier, 'for we are neither censurers, nor indiscreet, inquisitive persons. It is enough for us to attend to our own business, without meddling with what does not regard us.' After this they all seated themselves, and the conversation became general; and they drank to the health of the new guests.

"While the vizier Giafar entertained them with his conversation, the caliph could not refrain from admiring the extraordinary beauty, the great elegance, the lively disposition and agreeable spirit of the ladies; while the appearance of the three calenders, who were all blind of the right eye, surprised him very much. He wished to learn the cause of this peculiarity, but the conditions the ladies had imposed upon him and his companions, prevented any inquiry. Moreover, when he reflected upon the richness of the appointments and furniture, and the regularity and arrangement everywhere apparent, he could hardly persuade himself the whole scene was not the effect of enchantment.

"The conversation having fallen upon the various sorts of amusement, and the different modes of enjoying life, the calenders got up and danced in their peculiar way; and their skill, while it greatly increased the good opinion the ladies had already conceived of them, attracted also the applause and approbation of the caliph and his company. As soon as the calenders had finished their dance, Zobeidè got up, and taking Aminè by the hand, said to her, 'Come, sister, the company shall not think that we will put them under any restraint; nor shall their presence prevent us from doing, as we have always been accustomed to do.' Aminè, who perfectly understood what her sister meant, rose and took away the dishes, tables, bottles, and glasses, and the instruments on which the calenders had played. Nor did Safiè remain idle; she swept the hall, put everything in its proper place, snuffed the candles, and added more aloe wood and ambergris. Having done this, she requested the three calenders to sit on a sofa on one side and the caliph and his companions to take their places on the other. 'Get up,' said she, then, turning to the porter, 'and be ready to assist us in whatever we want you to do; a man like you, as strong as a house, ought never to remain idle.' The porter had slept, till he was somewhat sobered; he got up therefore very quickly, and fastening his cloak to his girdle, cried, 'I am ready to do anything you please.' 'That is well,' answered Safiè, 'and you shall not remain long with your arms crossed.' A little while after Aminè came in with a sort of seat, which she placed in the middle of the room. She then went to the door of a closet, and having opened it, she made a sign to the porter to approach. 'Come and assist me,' she cried. He did so; and quitting the room with her, returned a moment after, followed by two black dogs, each of which he led by a chain fastened to its collar. These dogs, which appeared to have been very ill-used and severely beaten with a whip, he brought into the middle of the room.

"Zobeidè, who was sitting between the calenders and the caliph, then got up, and approaching the porter, said, in a very grave manner, and with a deep sigh, 'We must do our duty.' She then turned up her sleeves, so as to uncover her arms to the elbow, and taking a whip, which Safiè presented to her, said, 'Porter, lead one of these dogs to my sister Aminè, and then come to me with the other.' The porter did as he was ordered; as he approached Zobeidè, the dog, which he held, began to howl, and turning towards her, lifted up its head in a most supplicating manner. But she, without regarding the distressful gestures of the dog, which must have excited pity, or its cries, which filled the whole house, flogged it, till she was out of breath; and when she had not strength left to beat it any more, she threw away the whip; then taking the chain from the porter, she took up the dog by the forepaws, and looking at each other with a melancholy air, they mingled their tears together. Zobeidè hereupon took out her handkerchief, wiped the tears from the dog's eyes, and kissed it; then returning the chain to the porter, she desired him to lead that dog back from whence he had taken it, and bring her the other.

"The porter carried the one that had been beaten back to the closet. Returning, he took the other from the hands of Aminè, and presented it to Zobeidè, who was waiting for it. 'Hold it, as you did the first,' said she; then taking the whip, she served this dog as she had served the other. She then wept with it, dried its tears, kissed it, and returned it to the porter, who was saved the trouble of leading it back to the closet by the agreeable Aminè, who took it herself.

"The three calenders, with the caliph and his party, were all much astonished at this ceremony. They could not comprehend why Zobeidè, after having so violently whipped the two dogs, which, according to the tenets of the Mussulman religion, are impure animals, should afterwards weep with them, kiss them, and dry their tears. The guests conversed together about it, and the caliph in particular was very desirous of knowing the reason of an action, which appeared to him very singular. He made signs to the vizier to inquire, but that officer turned his head the other way, till at last, importuned by repeated signs, he answered by a very respectful gesture, intimating, that it was not yet time to satisfy his master's curiosity.

"Zobeidè remained for some time in the middle of the room, as if to rest from the fatigue of beating the two dogs. 'My dear sister,' said the beautiful Safiè, 'will you not return to your place, that I also may perform my part?' 'Yes,' replied Zobeidè; and she seated herself on the sofa, with the caliph, Giafar, and Mesrour on her right hand, and the three calenders and the porter on the left.

"The company continued for some time silent: at length Safiè, who had placed herself on the seat in the middle of the room, said to Aminè, 'Sister, arise; you understand what I mean.' Aminè rose and went into a different closet from that whence the dogs had been brought; she returned with a case, covered with yellow satin, and richly ornamented with embroidery of green and gold. She opened it, and took out a lute, which she presented to her sister. Safiè took it, and after having tuned it, began to play upon the lute, accompanying it with her voice: she sang an air on the grief of absence, in so agreeable a style, that the caliph and the rest of the company were enchanted. When she had finished, as she had sung with a great deal of action as well as passion, she offered the lute to Aminè, saying, 'Sister, my voice fails me; do you take it, and oblige the company by playing and singing instead of me.'

"Aminè played a little prelude, to hear that the instrument was in tune; then she sang for some time on the same subject, but became so affected by the words she uttered, that she had not power to finish the air. Zobeidè began to praise her sister: 'You have done wonders,' said she; 'it is easy to perceive, that you feel the griefs you express.' Aminè had not time to reply to this speech; she felt herself so oppressed at that moment, that she could think of nothing but giving herself air; and opening her robe, she exposed a bosom, not white as one would suppose the beautiful Aminè's neck to be, but so covered with scars, as to create a species of horror in the spectators. But the relief thus obtained, was of no service to her, for she fainted away.

"Whilst Zobeidè and Safiè ran to assist their sister, one of the calenders exclaimed, 'I would rather have slept in the open air, than have come here to witness such a spectacle.'

"The caliph, who heard this speech, approached him, and inquired what all this meant. 'We know no more than you,' replied the calender. 'What!' resumed the caliph, 'do not you belong to the house? Cannot you inform me about these two black dogs, and this lady, who appears to have been so ill-treated?' 'Sir,' said the calender, 'we never were in this house before now, and entered it only a few minutes sooner than you.' This increased the astonishment of the caliph. 'Perhaps,' said he, 'the man who is with you can give us some information.' The calender made signs to the porter to draw near, and asked him if he knew why the black dogs had been beaten, and why Aminè's bosom was so scarred? 'Sir,' replied the porter, 'I swear by the great name of Allah, that if you know nothing of the matter, we are all equally ignorant. It is true that I live in this city, but till to-day I never entered this house; and if you are surprised to see me here, I am not less astonished at being in such company. What increases my surprise,' added he, 'is to see these ladies living without any man in the house.'

"The caliph and his party, as well as the calenders, had thought that the porter belonged to the family, and that he would have been able to tell them what they wished so much to know. The caliph resolved to satisfy his curiosity, and risk the consequences. 'Attend to me,' he said to the rest; 'we are seven men, and here are only three women. Let us then compel them to give us the information we request; and if they refuse to comply with a good grace, we can force them to obey.' The grand vizier, Giafar, opposed this plan; and explained the consequences of it to the caliph, without discovering to the calenders who his companion was; for he always addressed him like a merchant. 'Consider, sir, I beg,' said he, 'that we have our reputation to preserve. You know on what condition these ladies suffered us to become their guests; and we accepted the terms. What will they say to us, if we break the compact? And we should have only ourselves to blame, if any misfortune happened to us in consequence of our curiosity. It is not to be supposed, that these ladies would require such a promise from us, if they were not able to make us repent any breach of our agreement.'

"The vizier now drew the caliph a little aside, and spoke to him in a low voice. 'My Lord,' he said, 'the night will not last long. If your Majesty will but have a little patience, I will come in the morning and bring these women before you, when you are on your throne; and you may learn from them whatever you wish to know.' Although this advice was very judicious, the caliph rejected it, and desired the vizier to be silent, declaring he would not wait so long, but would that instant have the information he wished. The next question was, who should make the inquiry. The caliph endeavoured to persuade the calenders to speak first, but they excused themselves. At last they all agreed that the porter should be spokesman. He was preparing to ask the fatal question, when Zobeidè approached them. She had been assisting Aminè, who had recovered from her fainting. As she had heard them speak in rather a loud and warm manner, she said to them, 'What are you talking of? What is your contest about?'

"The porter then addressed her as follows: 'These gentlemen, madam, entreat you to have the goodness to explain to them, why you wept with those dogs, after having treated them so ill, and what is the reason that the lady who fainted has her bosom covered with scars. This, madam, is what I have been required by them to ask of you.'

"At these words Zobeidè turned with a haughty and menacing gesture to the caliph and the calenders. 'Is it true, strangers,' she asked, 'that you have commissioned this man to require this information of me?' They all allowed it to be the case, except the vizier Giafar, who did not open his lips. Upon this she replied to them in a tone, which showed how much she was offended. 'We granted you the favour you requested of us; and in order to prevent any cause of discontent or dissatisfaction on your part, as we were alone, we made our permission to you to stay, subject to one positive condition—that you should not speak about what does not concern you, lest you should hear what would not please you. After we have received you and entertained you as well as we possibly could, you do not scruple to break your word. This probably arises from the readiness with which we granted your request; but that surely is no excuse for you; and your conduct, therefore, cannot be considered as honourable.' So saying, she struck the floor with her foot; and clapping her hands three times, she called out, 'Enter quickly!' A door immediately opened, and seven strong powerful black slaves rushed in, with scimitars in their hands; and each seized one of the guests. They threw the

THE SLAVES ABOUT TO DESTROY THE GUESTS OF ZOBEIDÈ.

astonished men on the ground, drew them into the middle of the hall, and prepared to cut off their heads.

"The alarm of the caliph may be easily imagined. Too late, he repented his disregard of the advice of his vizier. The unfortunate caliph, Giafar, Mesrour, the porter, and the three calenders, were about to pay with their lives for their indiscreet curiosity; but before they received the fatal stroke, one of the slaves said to Zobeidè and her sisters, 'High, mighty, and revered mistresses, do you command us to cut their throats?' 'Stop,' answered Zobeidè, 'it is necessary that we first question them.' 'Madam,' cried the affrighted porter, 'in the name of Allah do not make me die for the crime of another. I am innocent, and they alone are guilty. Alas!' he continued, weeping, 'we were passing the time so agreeably! These one-eyed calenders are the cause of this misfortune. Such ill-favoured fellows would be enough to ruin a whole city. I entreat you, madam. not to confound the innocent with the guilty; and remember, it is much more commendable to pardon a miserable wretch like me, who has never a friend, than to overwhelm him with your power, and sacrifice him to your resentment.'

"Zobeidè, in spite of her anger, could not help laughing inwardly at the lamentations of the porter. But without seeming to pay any attention to him, she addressed herself again to the others. 'Answer me,' said she, 'and tell me who you are! If you fail, you have only an instant to live. I cannot believe that you are honourable men, or persons of authority or distinction in whatever country you call your own; for if that had been the case, you would have paid more attention to our condition and more respect to us.'

"The caliph, who was naturally impatient, suffered infinitely more than the rest, at finding that his life depended upon the commands of an offended and justly irritated woman but he began to perceive there were some hopes for him and the rest, when he found that she wished to know who they all were; as he imagined she would by no means take away his life, when she should be informed of his rank. Therefore he whispered to his vizier, who was near him, instantly to declare who he was. But this wise and prudent minister, wishing to preserve the honour of his master, and unwilling to make public the great affront the caliph had brought upon himself, answered, 'We suffer only what we deserve.' When, however, in obedience to the caliph, he wished to speak, Zobeidè would not give him time. She immediately addressed herself to the three calenders, and observing that they were all three blind with one eye, she asked if they were brothers. 'No, madam,' answered one of them for the rest, 'we are not brothers by blood, but only brethren in so far as we are all calenders; that is, in pursuing and observing the same kind of life.' 'Have you,' said she, addressing one of them in particular, 'been deprived of one eye from your birth?' 'No, indeed, madam,' he answered, 'I became so through a most surprising adventure, from the recital or perusal of which, were it written, every one must derive advantage. After this misfortune had happened to me, I shaved my beard and eyebrows, and adopting the habit I wear, became a calender.'

"Zobeidè put the same question to the other, who returned the same answer as the first. But the last, who spoke, added, 'That you may know, madam, we are not common persons, and to inspire you with some pity for us, we must tell you, that we are all the sons of kings. Although we have never met until this evening, we have had sufficient time to inform each other of this circumstance; and I can assure you, that the kings who gave us birth, have made some noise in the world!'

"During this speech Zobeidè became less angry, and told the slaves to set the prisoners at liberty, but at the same time to remain in the room. 'They,' said she, 'who shall relate their history to me, and explain the motives which brought them to this house, shall suffer no harm, but shall have permission to go where they please; but none that refuse to give us this satisfaction shall be spared.' So the three calenders, the caliph, the grand vizier Giafar, the eunuch Mesrour, and the porter, all remained on the carpet in the middle of the hall before the three ladies, who sat on a sofa, with the slaves behind them, ready to execute any orders they might receive.

"The porter, understanding that he had only to relate his history in order to be free from the great danger that threatened him, spoke first. 'You are already acquainted, madam,' he said, 'with my history, and with the circumstance that brought me to your house. What I have to relate therefore will soon be finished. Your sister engaged me this morning at the place where I take my stand in my calling as a porter, by which I endeavour to gain a living. I followed her to a wine-merchant's, to a herb-seller's, to an orange merchant's, and to shops where are sold almonds, nuts, and other dried fruits. We then went to a confectioner's, and to a druggist's; and from thence with my basket on my head, as full as it well could be, I came here, where you have the goodness to suffer me to remain till now—a favour I shall never forget. This is the whole of my history.'

"When the porter had concluded, Zobeidè, very well satisfied with him, said, 'Arise, and begone, nor ever let us see thee again.' 'I beg of you, madam,' replied he, 'to let me remain a little longer. It would be unfair that I should not hear the histories of these men, after they had the pleasure of hearing mine.' Saying this he took his place at the end of the sofa, truly delighted at finding himself free from a danger which had greatly alarmed him. One of the calenders next spoke, and addressing himself to Zobeidè as the principal person who had commanded them to give an account of themselves, he began his history as follows:

### The History of the First Calender, the Son of a King.

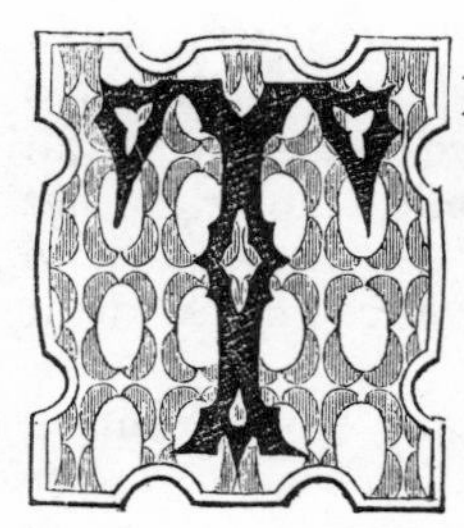

HAT you may know, madam, how I lost my right eye, and the reason why I have been obliged to take the habit of a calender, I must begin by telling you, that I am the son of a King. My father had a brother, who, like himself, was a monarch, and this brother ruled over a neighbouring state. He had two children, a son and a daughter; the former of whom was about my age.

"When I had finished my education, and the King, my father, had allowed me a proper degree of liberty, I went regularly every year to see my uncle, and passed a month or two at his court, after which I returned home. These visits produced the most intimate friendship between the Prince, my cousin, and myself. The last time I saw him he received me with demonstrations of the greatest joy and tenderness; indeed he was more affectionate than he had ever yet been; and wishing one day to amuse me by a great entertainment, he made extraordinary preparations for it. We remained a long time at table; and after we had both supped, he said to me, 'My dear cousin, you can never imagine what has occupied my thoughts since your last journey. I have employed a great number of workmen in carrying out the design I meditated. I have erected a building, which is just finished, and we shall soon be able to lodge there: you will not be sorry to see it; but you must first take an oath, that you will be both secret and faithful: these two things I must require of you.'

"The friendship and familiarity in which we lived, forbade me to refuse him any thing; without hesitation, therefore, I took the oath he required. 'Wait for me in this place,' he cried, 'and I will be with you in a moment.' He did not in fact detain me long, but returned bringing with him a lady of very great beauty, and most magnificently dressed. He did not tell me who she was, nor did I think it right to inquire. We again sat down to the table with the lady, and remained there some time, talking of different things, and emptying goblets to each other's health. The Prince then said to me: 'We have no time to lose; oblige me by taking this lady with you, and conducting her by yonder path to a place, where you will see a tomb, newly erected, in the shape of a dome. You will easily know it, as the door is open. Enter there together, and wait for me; I will join you directly.'

"Faithful to my oath, I did not seek to know more. I offered my hand to the lady; and following the instructions which the Prince my cousin had given me, I conducted her safely to our destination by the light of the moon. We had scarcely arrived at the tomb, when we saw the Prince, who had followed us, and who appeared with a vessel full of water, a shovel or spade, and a small sack, in which there was some mortar. With the spade he destroyed the empty sarcophagus, which was in the middle of the tomb; he took the stones away, one by one, and placed them in a corner. When he had taken them all away, he made a hole in the ground, and I perceived a trap-door in the pavement. He lifted it up, and disclosed the beginning of a winding staircase. Then addressing himself to the lady, my cousin said, 'This is the way, madam, that leads to the place I have mentioned to you.' At these words the lady approached and descended the stairs. The Prince prepared to follow her; but first turning to me, he said, 'I am infinitely obliged to you, cousin, for the trouble you have had; receive my best thanks for it, and farewell.' 'My dear cousin,' I cried, 'what does all this mean?' 'That is no matter,' he answered, 'you may return by the way by which you came.'

"Unable to learn anything more from him, I was obliged to bid him farewell. As I returned to my uncle's palace, the fumes of the wine I had taken began to affect my head. I nevertheless reached my apartment, and retired to rest. On waking the next morning, I made many reflections on the occurrences of the night before, and recalled all the circumstances to my recollection of so singular an adventure. The whole appeared to me to be a dream. I was so much persuaded of its unreality, that I sent to know if the Prince, my cousin, had risen. But when they brought me word, that he had not slept at home, and that they knew not what was become of him, and were very much distressed at his absence, I concluded that the strange adventure of the tomb was too true. This afflicted me very much; and shunning the gaze of all, I went secretly to the public cemetery, or burial-place, where there were a great many tombs similar to that which I had before seen. I passed the day in examining them all, but was unable to discover the one I sought. I spent four days in the endeavour, but without success.

"It is necessary for me to inform you that the King, my uncle, was absent during the whole of this time. He had been away for some time on a hunting party. I was very unwilling to wait for his coming back, and having requested his ministers to apologize for my departure, I set out on my return to my father's court, from which I was not accustomed to make so long a stay. I left my uncle's ministers very much distressed at the unaccountable disappearance of the Prince; but as I could not violate the oath I had taken to keep the secret, I dared not lessen their anxiety, by revealing to them any part of what I knew.

"I arrived in my father's capital, and contrary to the usual custom, I discovered at the gate of the palace a numerous guard, by whom I was immediately surrounded. I demanded the reason of this; when an officer answered, 'The army, Prince, has acknowledged the grand vizier as King, in the room of your father, who is dead; and I arrest you as a prisoner, in the name of the new monarch.' At these words, the guards seized me, and led me into the usurper's presence. Judge, madam, what was my surprise and grief!

"This rebellious vizier had conceived a strong hatred against me, and had for a long time cherished it. The cause of his hostility was as follows: When I was very young, I was fond of shooting with a cross-bow. One day I carried my weapon to the upper part of the palace, and amused myself with it on the terrace. A bird happened to fly up before me; I shot at it, but missed; and the arrow, by chance, struck the vizier on the eye, and destroyed the sight, as he was taking the air on the terrace of his own house. As soon as I was informed of this accident, I went and made my apologies to him in person. Nevertheless he cherished a strong resentment against me, and gave me proofs of his ill-will on every opportunity. Now that he found me in his power, he evinced his hatred in the most barbarous manner. As soon as he saw me, he ran towards me with looks of fury, and digging his fingers into my right eye, he tore it from the socket. And thus did I become half blind.

"But the usurper did not confine his cruelty to this despicable action. He ordered that I should be imprisoned in a sort of cage, and carried in this manner to some distant place, where the executioner was to cut off my head and to leave my body to be devoured by birds of prey. Accompanied by another man, the executioner mounted his horse, and carried me with him. He did not stop till he came to a place suited for the fulfilment of his design. I managed, however, to excite his compassion, by entreaties, prayers, and tears. 'Go,' said he to me, 'depart instantly out of the kingdom, and take care never to return; if you do, you will only encounter certain destruction, and will be the cause of mine.' I thanked him for the mercy he showed me: and when I found myself alone, I consoled myself for the loss of my eye, with the reflection that I had just escaped a greater misfortune.

"In the condition to which I was reduced, I could not travel very fast. During the

THE KING DISCOVERS THE DEAD BODY OF HIS SON.

day, I concealed myself in unfrequented and secret places, and journeyed by night as far as my strength would permit me. At length I arrived in the country belonging to the King, my uncle; and I proceeded directly to the capital.

"I gave him full particulars of the dreadful cause of my return, and explained the miserable state in which he saw me. 'Alas!' cried he, 'was it not sufficient that I have lost my son; but must I also learn the death of a brother, whom I dearly loved; and find you in the deplorable state in which I see you now!' He informed me of the distress he had suffered, from his failure to obtain any tidings of his son, in spite of all the inquiries he had made, and all the diligence he had used. The tears ran from the eyes of this unfortunate father as he gave me this account; and he appeared to me so much afflicted, that I could not resist his grief; nor could I keep the oath I had taken to my cousin. In short, I related to the King everything that had occurred.

"He listened to me with some appearance of consolation, and when I had finished, he said, 'Dear nephew, the story you have told me, affords me some little hope. I well know that my son built such a tomb, and I know very nearly on what spot it was erected. With the recollection which you may have preserved, I flatter myself we shall be able to discover it. But since he has done all this so secretly, and required you also not to reveal the fact, I am of opinion that we two only should make the search, that the circumstance may not be generally known and talked of.' The King had also another reason, which he hid from me, for wishing to keep this a secret. This reason, as the conclusion of my history will show, was a very important one.

"We disguised ourselves, and went out by a garden gate, which opened into the fields. We were fortunate enough very soon to discover the object of our search. I immediately recognized the tomb, and was the more rejoiced, as I had once so long and so vainly endeavoured to find it. We entered, and found the iron trap-door shut down upon the opening to the stairs. We had great difficulty in lifting it up, because the Prince had cemented it down with the lime and the water he carried with him when I saw him last: at length, however, we raised it. My uncle was the first who descended; and I followed. About fifty steps brought us to the bottom of the stairs, to a sort of ante-room, which was full of a thick smoke, very unpleasant to the smell, and which obscured the light thrown from a very brilliant lamp.

"From this ante-chamber we passed on to one much larger, the roof of which was supported by large columns, and illuminated by many lights. In the middle of the apartment, there was a cistern, and on each side we observed various sorts of provisions. We were much surprised to find no one here. Opposite to us, there was a raised sofa with an ascent of some steps, and beyond this there appeared a very large bed, the curtains of which were closely drawn. The King went up to the bed, and opening the curtains revealed the Prince, his son, reclining upon it with the lady; but both were burnt, and charred black, as if they had been thrown on to an immense fire, and had been taken off before their bodies were consumed. What surprised me even more than this sight itself was, that my uncle did not evince any sorrow or regret at seeing that his son had thus lamentably perished. He spat on the dead face, and cried in an angry voice: 'Such is thy punishment in this world!—but thy doom in the next will be eternal!' Not satisfied with this terrible speech, he pulled off his slipper, and struck his son an angry blow on the cheek.

"I cannot express the astonishment I felt at seeing the King, my uncle, treat his dead son in that manner. 'Sir,' said I to him, 'however violent my grief may be at beholding this heartrending sight, yet I cannot yield to it without first inquiring of your Majesty, what crime the Prince, my cousin, can have committed, to deserve that his lifeless corpse should be insulted thus?' The King replied: 'Nephew, I must inform you, that my unworthy son loved his sister from his earliest years, and was equally beloved by her. I rather encouraged their rising friendship, because I did not foresee the danger that was to ensue. And who could have foreseen it? This affection increased with their years, and reached such a pitch, that I dreaded the consequences. I applied the only remedy then in my power. I severely reprimanded my son for his conduct, and represented to him the horrors that would arise, if he persisted in it; and the eternal shame he would bring upon our family.

"'I talked to his sister in the same manner, and shut her up, that she should have no further communication with her brother. But the unhappy girl had tasted of the poison; and all the obstacles that my prudence suggested, only irritated her passion, and that of her brother.

"'My son, convinced that his sister continued to love him, prepared this subterranean asylum, under pretence of building a tomb, hoping some day to find an opportunity of getting access to the object of his flame, and concealing her in this place. He chose the moment of my absence to force his way into the retreat of his sister, which is a circumstance that my honour will not allow me to publish. After this criminal proceeding he shut himself up with her in this building, which he furnished, as you perceive, with all sorts of provisions. But Allah would not suffer such an abominable crime to remain unchastised; and has justly punished both of them.' He wept bitterly as he said these words, and I mingled my tears with his.

"After a pause, he cast his eyes on me; 'Dear nephew,' resumed he, embracing me, 'If I lose an unworthy son, I may find in you a happy amends for my loss.' The reflections which this speech called forth, on the untimely end of the Prince and the Princess, again drew tears from us both.

"We reascended the same staircase, and quitted this dismal abode. We put the iron trap-door in its place, and covered it with earth and the rubbish of the building; to conceal, as much as possible, this dreadful example of the Divine anger.

"We returned to the palace before our absence had been observed, and shortly after we heard a confused noise of trumpets, cymbals, drums, and other warlike instruments. A thick dust, which obscured the air, soon informed us of the cause, and announced the arrival of a formidable army. The same vizier who had dethroned my father, and had taken possession of his dominions, now came with a large number of troops, to seize my uncle's territory.

"The King, who had only his usual guard, could not resist so many enemies. They invested the city, and as the gates were opened to them without resistance, they soon took possession of it. They had not much difficulty in penetrating to the palace of the King, who attempted to defend himself; but he fell, selling his life dearly. For my part, I fought for some time; but seeing that I must surrender if I continued to resist, I retreated, and had the good fortune to escape, taking refuge in the house of an officer of the King, on whose fidelity I could depend.

"Overcome with grief, and persecuted by fortune, I had recourse to a stratagem, as a last resource to preserve my life. I shaved my beard and my eyebrows, and put on the habit of a calender; and thus disguised left the city without being recognized. After that, it was no difficult matter for me to quit the dominions of the King my uncle, by unfrequented roads. I avoided the towns, till I arrived in the empire of the powerful Sovereign of all true Believers, the glorious and renowned caliph Haroun Alraschid, when I ceased to fear. I considered what plan I should adopt, and I resolved to come to Bagdad, and throw myself at the feet of this great monarch, whose generosity is everywhere admired. I shall move his compassion, thought I, by the recital of my eventful history; he will no doubt commiserate the fate of an unhappy Prince, and I shall not implore his assistance in vain.

"At length, after a journey of several months, I arrived to-day at the gates of the city: when the evening came on, I entered the gates, and after I had rested a little time to recover my spirits, and settle which way I should turn my steps, this other calender, who is sitting next me, arrived also. He saluted me, and I returned the compliment. 'You appear,' said I, 'a stranger like myself.' 'You are not mistaken,' replied he. At the very moment he made this answer, the third calender, whom you see now, came towards us. He greeted us, and stated that he, too, was a stranger, and had just arrived at Bagdad. Like brothers we united, and resolved never to separate.

"But it was late, and we did not know where to seek a lodging in a city where we never had been before. Our good fortune brought us to your door, and we took the liberty of knocking; you have received us with so much benevolence and charity, that we cannot sufficiently thank you. This, madam, is what you desired me to relate;

thus it was that I lost my right eye; this is the reason I have my beard and my eye-brows shaved, and why I am at this moment in your company.

"Enough," said Zobeidè, "we thank you, and you may retire, whenever you please. The calender excused himself from obeying this last request, and entreated the lady to allow him to stay, and hear the history of his two companions, whom he could not well abandon; he also begged to hear the adventures of the three other persons of the party.

"The history of the first calender appeared very surprising to the whole company, and particularly to the caliph. The presence of the slaves, armed with their scimitars, did not prevent him from saying in a whisper to the vizier, 'As long as I can remember, I never heard any thing to compare with this history of the calender, though I have been all my life in the habit of hearing similar narratives.' The second calender now began to tell his history; and addressing himself to Zobeidé, spoke as follows:—

## The History of the Second Calender, the son of a King.

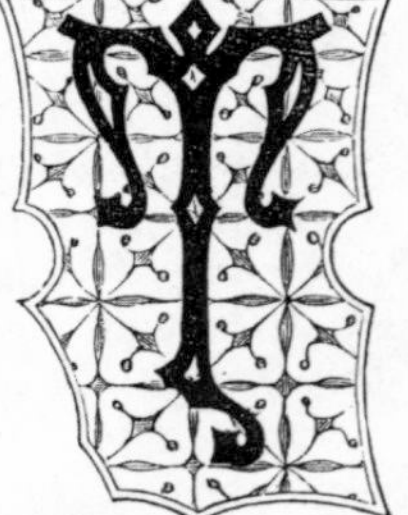

O obey your commands, lady, and that you may understand the strange adventure by which I lost my right eye, I must give you an account of my whole life.

"I too am a Prince by birth. I was scarcely more than an infant, when the King, my father, observing that I possessed great quickness of intellect, began to devote great pains to my education. He summoned from every part of his dominions, the men most famous in science, and for their knowledge of the fine arts, that they might instruct me. I no sooner knew how to read and write, than I learnt by heart the whole of the Koran, that admirable book, in which we find the basis, the precepts, and regulations of our religion. That my knowledge might not be shallow and superficial, I perused the works of the most approved authors who have written on that subject, and who have explained and illustrated the Koran by their commentaries. To this study I added an acquaintance with all the traditions received from the mouth of our prophet, by those illustrious men who were his contemporaries. Not satisfied with possessing a deep and extensive knowledge of our religion, I made a particular study of our histories, and became master of polite literature, of poetry and versification. I then applied myself to geography and chronology, and was anxious to attain a knowledge of our own language in its greatest purity; and all this I effected without neglecting the manly exercises in which a Prince should be proficient. It was in caligraphy however that I most delighted, and at length I excelled in forming the characters of our Arabic language; I surpassed all the writing masters of our kingdom, even those who had acquired the greatest reputation.

"Fame bestowed upon me even more honour than I deserved. She was not satisfied with spreading a report of my talents throughout the dominions of the King, my father, but even carried the account of them to the court of the Indies, whose powerful monarch became so curious to see me, that he sent an ambassador bearing the richest presents to my father, with the request that I would visit him. This embassy, for many reasons, delighted my father. He felt assured that it was the best possible thing for a Prince of my age to travel to foreign courts; and he was very well pleased with the opportunity of forming a friendship with the Sultan of India. I set out with the ambassador; but I had very few attendants, and little baggage, on account of the length and difficulties of the way.

"We had been about a month on our journey, when we saw in the distance an immense cloud of dust; and soon afterwards we discovered fifty horsemen, well armed. They were robbers, and approached us at full speed. As we had ten horses laden with our baggage, and the presents which I was to make to the Sultan in my father's name, and as our party consisted but of very few persons, you may easily imagine that the robbers attacked us without hesitation. Unable to repel force by force, we told them we were the ambassadors of the Sultan of India, and that we hoped they would do

THE YOUNG PRINCE MAKES HIS ESCAPE.

nothing contrary to the respect they owed to him. By this appeal we thought we should preserve both our equipage and our lives; but the robbers insolently answered, 'Why do you suppose we shall respect the Sultan your master? We are not his subjects, nor even within his realm.' Having said this, they immediately surrounded and attacked us on all sides. I defended myself as long as I could; bnt finding that I was wounded, and seeing the ambassador and all our attendants overthrown, I took advantage of the remains of strength in my horse, which was also wounded, and escaped from them. I pushed the poor creature on as far as he would carry me; he then suddenly fell under my weight, quite dead from fatigue, and loss of blood. I disentangled myself from the fallen steed as fast as possible; and finding that no one pursued me, I supposed the robbers had their attention engrossed by the plunder they had seized.

"Thus I was left alone, wounded, destitute of every help, in a country where I was an entire stranger. I was afraid to return to the high road, from the dread of falling once more into the hands of the robbers. I bound up my wound, which was not dangerous, and walked on for the rest of the day; in the evening I arrived at the entrance of a cave. I went in, ate some fruits which I had gathered as I came along, and passed the night in the cave quite unmolested.

"For some days I continued my journey, without coming to any place where I could rest; but at the end of about a month I arrived at a very large city, populous, and most delightfully and advantageously situated; for several rivers flowed round it, and the climate was like a perpetual spring. The number of agreeable objects which presented themselves to my eyes, excited in my bosom so great a joy, that it stifled for the moment the bitter regret I felt at my miserable position. My whole face, my hands and my feet were of a brown tawny colour, for the sun had quite burnt me: and my slippers were so completely worn out by walking, that I was obliged to travel barefoot; besides this, my clothes were all in rags.

"I entered the town in order to hear the language spoken, and thence to find out where I was. I addressed myself to a tailor, who was at work in his shop. Struck by my youth, and by a certain manner about me, which intimated that my rank was higher than my appearance betokened, he made me sit down near him. He asked me who I was, whence I came, and what had brought me to that place? I concealed nothing from him, but informed him of every circumstance that had happened to me, and did not even hesitate to reveal my name. The tailor listened to me very attentively; but, when I had finished my narration, instead of giving me any consolation, he increased my anxieties. 'Beware,' said he to me, 'how you impart to any one else the information you have given me; for the Prince, who reigns in this kingdom, is the greatest enemy of the King your father; and if he should be informed of your arrival in this city, I doubt not but he will inflict some evil upon you. I readily believed that the tailor spoke sincerely when he told me the name of the Prince; but as the enmity between my father and that King has no connection with my adventures, I shall not enter into any detail of it.

"I thanked the tailor for the advice he had given me; and told him that I placed implicit faith in his good counsel, and should never forget the favour he had shown me. As he supposed I must be hungry, he brought me something to eat, and even offered me an apartment at his house; and I accepted his hospitality.

"Some days after my arrival, the tailor, remarking that I was tolerably recovered from the effects of my long and painful journey, and knowing that most of the Princes of our religion take the precaution to make themselves acquainted with some art or trade, that they may be prepared in case of a reverse of fortune to guard against want, asked me if I knew any thing by which I could earn a livelihood, without being chargeable to any one. I told him that I was well versed in the science of laws, both human and divine, that I was a grammarian, a poet, and above all, that I wrote remarkably well. 'With all this,' he replied, 'you will not in this country procure a morsel of bread; this kind of knowledge here is entirely valueless. If you choose to follow my advice,' he added, 'you will procure a short jacket; and as you are strong and hardy, you may go into the neighbouring forest, and cut wood for fuel. You may then go and offer it for sale in the market; and I assure you that you may gain a comfortable little income, that shall keep you independent of every one. By these means you will be enabled to wait, till Heaven shall become favourable to you; and till the cloud of bad fortune, which hangs over you, and obliges you to conceal your birth, shall have blown over. I will furnish you with a cord and a hatchet.'

"The fear of being known, and the necessity of supporting myself, determined me to pursue this plan, in spite of the degradation and labour it involved.

"The next day the tailor brought me a hatchet and a cord, and also a short jacket, and recommending me to some poor people who obtained their livelihood in the same manner, he begged that I might be allowed to go with them. They led me to the forest; and from that day I regularly brought back upon my head a large bundle of wood, which I sold for a small gold coin, current in that country; for although the forest was not far off, wood was nevertheless dear in that city, because there were few men who gave themselves the trouble of going to cut it. I soon acquired a considerable sum, and was enabled to repay the tailor what he had expended on my account.

"I had earned my livelihood thus for more than a year; when happening one day to go deeper into the forest than usual, I came to a very pleasant spot, where I began to cut my wood. In cutting up the root of a tree, I discovered an iron ring fastened to a trap-door of the same metal. I immediately cleared away the earth that covered the door, and on lifting it up, I perceived a staircase, by which I descended with my hatchet, in my hand. When I came to the bottom of the stairs, I found myself in a vast palace, which struck me very much by the great brilliancy with which it was illuminated; indeed it was as light, as if it had been built on the most open spot above ground. I went forward along a gallery supported on columns of jasper, with bases and capitals of massive gold; but I stopped suddenly on beholding a lady who appeared to have so noble and graceful an air, and to possess such extraordinary beauty, that my attention was removed from every other object, and my eyes fixed on her alone.

"That this beautiful lady might not have the trouble of coming to me, I made haste to approach her; and while I was making a most respectful obeisance, she said to me, 'What are you, a man or a Genie?' 'I am a man, madam,' I answered, rising, 'nor have I any commerce with genii.' 'By what chance,' she asked, with a deep sigh, 'do you come here? I have remained here more than twenty-five years, and during the whole of that time I have seen no man but yourself.'

"Her great beauty, which had already made a deep impression on me, together with the mildness and good humour with which she received me, gave me courage to say, 'Before, madam, I have the honour of satisfying your curiosity, permit me to tell you, that I feel highly delighted at this unexpected interview, which offers me the means both of consoling myself under my own affliction, and perhaps of making you happier than you now are.' I then faithfully related to her my strange adventures, assured her that she saw in me the son of a King, told why I appeared to her in that condition, and explained how accident had discovered to me the entrance into the magnificent prison in which I found her, and of which to all appearance she was heartily tired. 'Alas, Prince!' she replied, again sighing, 'you may truly call this rich and superb prison unpleasing and wearisome. The most enchanting spots cannot afford delight when we are detained in them against our will. Is it possible you have never heard any one speak of the great Epitimarus, King of the Ebony Isle, a place so called from the great quantity of that precious wood which it produces? I am the Princess, his daughter.

"The King, my father, had chosen for my husband a Prince who was my cousin; but on the very night of our nuptials, in the midst of the rejoicings held by the court in the capital of the Isle of Ebony, and before I had been given to my husband, a Genie carried me away. I fainted almost at the moment when he seized me, and lost all recollection, and when I recovered my senses, I found myself in this place. For a long time I was inconsolable; but habit and necessity have reconciled me to the sight and company of the Genie. Twenty-five years have passed, as I have already told you, since I was brought to this place, in which I must own that the bare expression of a wish procures me not only everything necessary for life, but whatever can satisfy a Princess who is fond of decoration and dress.

"'Every ten days,' continued the Princess, 'the Genie comes and passes the night here; he never sleeps here oftener, and gives as a reason that he is married to another lady, who would be jealous of the infidelity of which he was guilty, should it come to her knowledge. In the meantime, if I have wish for his presence, I have only to touch a talisman, which is placed at the entrance of my chamber, and he comes. It is now four days since he was here, and I have therefore to wait six days more before he again makes his apparance. You may thus remain five days with me, and keep me company if it be agreeable to you; and I will endeavour to regale and entertain you as befits your merit and quality.'

"I should have thought myself but too happy to obtain so great a favour by asking it; the more unhesitatingly did I therefore accept the hospitality thus obligingly offered. The Princess then conducted me to the most elegant, convenient, and sumptuous bath you can possibly imagine. When I came out I found, instead of my own dress, a very rich suit, which I put on, less for its magnificence than to render myself more worthy of my hostess's notice.

"We seated ourselves on a sofa, covered with superb drapery, and cushions of the richest Indian brocade. The Princess then set before me a variety of the most delicate and rare dishes. We ate together, and passed our time very agreeably in one another's company.

"Anxious to devise every method of entertaining me, she produced next day at dinner a flask of very old wine, the finest I ever tasted; and to please me, she drank several glasses with me. So soon as my head became heated with this agreeable liquor, I said, 'Beautiful Princess, you have been buried here alive much too long; follow me, and go and enjoy the brightness of the genuine day, of which for so many years you have been deprived. Abandon this false, glaring light that surrounds you here.' She answered, smiling, 'Prince, let us talk no further on this subject. I value not the most beautiful day in the world, if you will pass nine with me here, and give up the tenth to the Genie.' 'Princess,' I replied, 'I see very well, that it is the dread you have of the Genie which makes you speak in this fashion. As for myself, I fear him so little, that I am determined to break his talisman in pieces, with the magic spell, that is inscribed upon it. Let him then come; I will confront him; and however brave, however formidable he may be, I will make him feel the weight of my arm. I have taken an oath to exterminate all the genii in the world, and he shall be the first to feel my vengeance.' The Princess, who knew the consequence of this conduct, conjured me not to touch the talisman. 'It will be the means,' she said, 'of destroying both you and myself. I am better acquainted with the nature of genii than you can be.' But the wine I had drunk prevented me from understanding the propriety of her reasons; I kicked down the talisman, and broke it in pieces.

"This was no sooner done than the whole palace shook, as if ready to fall to atoms. This earthquake was accompanied by a most dreadful noise like thunder, and by flashes of lightning, which deepened the intermediate darkness. The terrible appearances in a moment dissipated the fumes of the wine from my brain, and made me own, though too late, the fault I had committed. 'Princess,' I exclaimed, 'what does all this mean?' Without thinking of her own peril, and fearful only for me, she answered in great alarm, 'Alas! you are undone, unless you save yourself by flight.'

"I followed her advice; and my fear was so great, that I forgot my hatchet and my cord. I had hardly gained the staircase, by which I descended, when the enchanted palace opened, and the Genie entered. 'What has happened to you, and why have you called me?' he demanded of the Princess, in an angry tone. She replied hastily: 'A violent pain obliged me to search for the bottle you see; I drank two or three glasses, and unfortunately making a false step I fell against the talisman, which I thus broke. This is the whole matter.' At this answer the Genie, in the utmost rage, exclaimed: 'Shameless and deceitful woman, how then came this hatchet and this cord here?' 'I have never seen them,' replied she, 'till this instant. Perhaps, in the haste and impetuosity with which you came, you have taken them up in passing through some place, and have brought them here, without being aware of it.'

The Genie replied only by reproaches, and by blows, of which I could plainly distinguish the sound. It distressed me beyond measure to hear the cries and sobs of the

THE GENIE BRINGS THE HATCHET AND CORD.

Princess, who was being thus cruelly used. I had already taken off the habit which she had made me put on, and resumed my own, which I had carried to the staircase the day before, after I had been in the bath. I proceeded up the stairs, and felt the more penetrated with grief and compassion, as I considered myself the cause of this misfortune: and felt as if I were the most criminal and ungrateful of men, and that I had sacrificed the most beautiful Princess on earth to the barbarity of an implacable Genie. 'It is true,' said I to myself, 'that she has been a prisoner for-five-and twenty years; but, excepting liberty, she had everything to make her happy. My conduct has put an end to her peace, and raised against her the cruel hatred of a merciless demon. I then shut down the trap-door, covered it over with the earth, and returned to the city with a load of wood, which I collected, without even knowing what I was about, so much was I unnerved and afflicted at what had happened.

"My host, the tailor, expressed great joy at my return. 'Your absence,' said he, 'has caused me much uneasiness on account of the secret of your birth, with which you have entrusted me. I knew not what to think, and began to fear some one might have recognized you. God be praised that you are come back!' I thanked him much for his sympathy and affection, but did not inform him of anything that had happened; nor did I tell the reason why I returned without my hatchet and cord. I retired to my chamber, where I reproached myself a thousand times for my great imprudence. 'Nothing,' I cried, 'could have equalled the mutual happiness of the Princess and myself, if I had been satisfied, and had not broken the talisman.'

"While I was abandoning myself to these afflicting thoughts, the tailor entered my apartment and said that an old man, a stranger, had brought my hatchet and cord, which he had found on his way. 'Your companions,' added the tailor, 'who went to cut wood with you, have told him that you live here. Come and speak to him, as he wishes to deliver the hatchet and cord into your own hands.' At this speech I changed colour, and trembled from head to foot. The tailor inquired the cause of my emotion. I was about to reply, when suddenly the floor of my chamber opened. The old man, who had not the patience to wait, appeared, and presented himself to us with the hatchet and cord. This old man was in fact the Genie, who had carried off the beautiful Princess of the Isle of Ebony, and who had thus come in disguise, after having treated her with the greatest barbarity. 'I am a Genie,' he said to us, 'a son of the daughter of Eblis, Prince of the Genii. Is not this thy hatchet?' added he, addressing me, 'and is not this thy cord?'

"The Genie gave me no time to answer these questions; nor indeed should I have been able to reply, as his dreadful appearance took away all my presence of mind. He seized me by the middle of my body, and carrying me out of the chamber, sprang into the air, and rose me up towards the clouds with such rushing velocity, that I seemed to feel the great height to which I ascended, before I was aware of the distance I had travelled in a very short space of time. He then descended towards the earth; and having caused it to open, by striking his foot against it, he sank into it, and I instantly found myself in the enchanted palace, and in the presence of the beautiful Princess of the Isle of Ebony. But alas! what a sight! It pierced my very inmost heart. This Princess was covered with blood, and lay prostrate on the ground more dead than alive, with her face bathed in tears.

"Perfidious wretch,' said the Genie, holding me up to her, 'is not this thy lover?' She cast her languid eyes upon me, and in a sorrowful tone answered, 'I know him not, nor have I ever seen him till this instant.' 'What!' cried the Genie, 'dare you affirm you do not know him, although he is the cause of your being punished as I have justly chastised you?' 'If he is a stranger to me,' she replied, 'do you wish me to utter a falsehood, which would prove his destruction?' 'Well then,' exclaimed the Genie, drawing his scimitar, and offering it to the Princess, 'if you have never seen him, take this scimitar, and cut off his head.' Alas!' she answered, 'how can I do what you require of me? My strength is so exhausted, that I cannot lift up my arm; and even were I able, do you think I could put to death an innocent person, whom I do not know?' 'This refusal, then,' added the Genie, 'completely proves to me your crime.' And then turning to me, he said, 'Are you too acquainted with her?'

"I should have been the most ungrateful and most perfidious of men, if I had not preserved the same fidelity towards her which she had shown towards me; I therefore said, 'How should I know her, when this is the first time I have ever set eyes upon her? 'If that is true,' he replied, 'take the scimitar and cut off her head. It is the price I set on your liberty, and the only way to convince me you have never seen her before, as you affirm.' 'With all my heart!' I answered, and took the scimitar in my hand. Do not, however, imagine, that I approached the beautiful Princess of the Isle of Ebony, for the purpose of becoming the instrument of the Genie's barbarity. I did it only to show her by my actions, as well as I could, that as she had the courage to sacrifice her life from love of me, I could not refuse to give my own life to save hers. The Princess understood my meaning; and in spite of her pain and suffering gave me to understand by her looks, that she should willingly die, and was well satisfied to know that I was equally ready. I then drew back, and throwing the scimitar on the ground, said to the Genie, 'I should be eternally condemned by all men, if I had the cowardice to murder, not only a person whom I do not know, but a lady, like the one I now see before me, ready to expire. You may treat me as you please, for I am in your power; but I will never obey your barbarous commands.'

"'I am well aware,' said the Genie, 'that both of you brave my rage, and insult my jealousy; but you shall find what I can do by the manner in which I shall treat you.' At these words, the monster took up the scimitar, and cut off one of the hands of the Princess, who had barely time to bid me an eternal farewell with the other, before the great loss of blood from her former wounds, increased by this last outrage, extinguished her life, not two moments after the perpetration of this last cruelty; at the sight of which I fainted.

"When I recovered my senses, I complained to the Genie, for allowing me to remain in expectation of death. 'Strike!' I cried, 'I am ready to receive the mortal wound, and expect it from you as the greatest favour you can bestow.' Instead, however, of complying with my request, he said, 'You have now seen how Genii treat women, whom they suspect of infidelity. She received you here; and if I were convinced that she had done me any farther wrong, I would this instant annihilate you; but I shall content myself with changing you into a dog, an ass, a lion, or a bird. Make your choice; I wish not to control you.' These words gave me some hopes of softening him; I said, 'Moderate, O powerful Genie, your wrath, and since you have decided to spare my life, grant it me in a generous manner. If you pardon me, I shall always remember your clemency; and you will act like as one of the best of men pardoned his neighbour, that bore him a most deadly envy.' The Genie asked me what had happened between these two neighbours? I told him, if he would have the patience to listen to me, I would relate the history.

## The History of the Envious Man, and of him who was Envied.

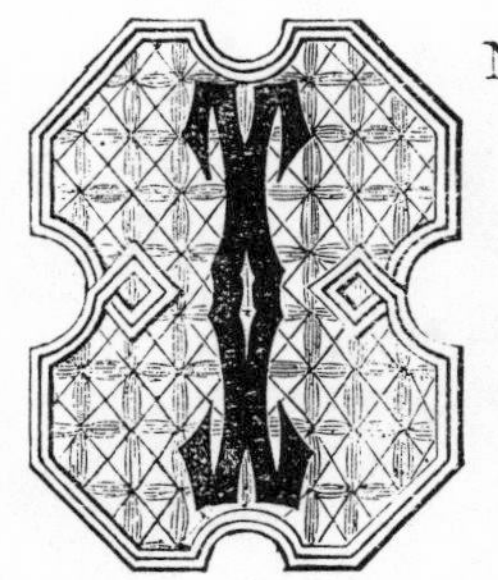

IN a town of some importance, there were two men, who lived next door to each other. One of them was so manifestly envious of the other, that the latter resolved to change his abode, and go and reside at some distance from him. He supposed that nearness of residence alone was the cause of his neighbour's animosity; and perceived that although he was continually doing his envious neighbour some friendly office, that he was not the less hated. He therefore sold his house, and the small estate attached to it, and went to the capital of the kingdom, which was at no great distance, and bought a small piece of ground about half a league from the town, on which there stood a very convenient dwelling. He had also a good garden, and a court of moderate size, in which there was a deep cistern, that was not now used.

"The good man having made this purchase, put on the habit of a dervise, in order to pass his life in peace; and arranged many cells in his house, where he soon established a small community of dervises. The report of his virtue was soon generally spread abroad, and failed not to attract the attention and visits of great numbers of the principal inhabitants, as well as of the common people. At length he was honoured and respected by almost every one. Men came from a great distance to request him to offer up prayers for them; and all who remained in retirement with him, published abroad the report of the blessings they thought they received from Heaven through his means.

"The great reputation of this man at length reached the town from whence he had come; and the envious man hearing of it, was so vexed, that he left his house and all his affairs, with the determination to go and destroy his former neighbour. For this purpose, he went to the hospital of dervises, whose charitable founder received him with every possible mark of friendship. The envious man told him that he had come with the express design of communicating an affair of great importance to him; but that he must speak to him in private. 'In short,' said he, 'in order that no one may hear us, let us, I pray you, walk in your court; and when night comes on, order all the dervises to their cells.' The chief of the dervises did as he requested.

"When the envious man found himself alone with the good dervise, he began to relate to him whatever came into his thoughts, while they walked from one end of the court to the other; till observing they were just at the edge of the well, he gave him a push, and thrust him into it; and there was no one by to witness this wicked act. Then he went away directly to the gate of the house, and passing out unseen, returned home well satisfied with his journey, and highly pleased to think that the object of his envy was no more. In this idea, however, he was deceived.

"It was a most fortunate thing for the dervise that this well was inhabited by fairies and genii, who were ready to assist him. They caught and supported him in their arms in such a way, that he received not the least injury. He naturally supposed there was something very extraordinary in his having sustained, without injury, a fall that would under ordinary circumstances have cost him his life; and yet he could not perceive anything to account for his safety. He soon, however, heard a voice say, 'Do you know anything of this man, to whom we have been so serviceable?' and some other voices answered, 'No.' The first then resumed, 'I will tell you. This man, with the most charitable and benevolent intentions in the world, left the town where he lived, and came to settle in this place, with the hope of being able to cure one of his neighbours of the envy and hatred the latter had conceived against him. He soon became so universally esteemed, that the envious man could not endure the thought, and determined, therefore, to put an end to his late neighbour's existence. This design he would have executed, had it not been for the assistance we afforded this good man, whose reputation is so great, that the Sultan, who resides in the neighbouring town, was coming to visit him to-morrow, in order to recommend the Princess, his daughter, to the holy dervises.'

"Another voice then asked what occasion the Princess had for the prayers of the dervise; and the first answered, 'Are you ignorant then, that she is possessed by the power of the Genie Maimoun, the son of Dimdim, who has fallen in love with her? But I know how this good dervise can cure her. The thing is by no means difficult, as you shall hear. In his hospital there is a black cat, which has a white spot at the end of her tail, about the size of a small coin. Let him only pull out seven hairs from this white spot, and burn them; and then with the smoke perfume the head of the Princess. The moment she feels the smoke, she will be so thoroughly cured and free from Maimoun, the son of Dimdim, that he will never again be able to come near her.'

"The chief of the dervises did not lose a single syllable of this conversation between the fairies and genii, who afterwards remained silent the whole night. The next morning as soon as the day began to break, and the different objects became visible, the dervise perceived, as the well was decayed in many places, that he could climb out without any difficulty.

"The other dervises who were seeking for him were delighted at his appearance. He related to them in a few words, the cunning and wicked attempt of the guest

THE ENVIOUS MAN PLUCKS THE HAIRS OUT OF THE CAT'S TAIL.

he had entertained the day before;—and then retired to his cell. Presently the black cat, which had been mentioned in the discourse of the fairies and genii, came to him to be taken notice of as usual. He took it up, and plucked out seven hairs from the white spot in its tail; these he put aside, to use whenever he should have occasion for them.

"The sun had not long risen above the horizon, when the Sultan, who wished to neglect no means which he thought gave any chance of curing the Princess, arrived at the gate. He ordered his guards to wait, and went in accompanied by the principal officers. The dervises received him with the greatest respect. The Sultan directly took the chief aside, and said to him, 'Worthy sheikh, you are perhaps already acquainted with the cause of my visit?' The dervise answered modestly, 'My lord, if I do not deceive myself, it is the illness of the Princess, that has been the occasion of my seeing you; an honour of which I am unworthy.'—'You are right,' replied the Sultan, 'and you will restore almost my life to me if, by means of your prayers I obtain the recovery of my daughter's health.'—'If your Majesty,' answered the worthy man, 'will have the goodness to suffer the Princess to come here, I flatter myself that, with the help and favour of God, she shall return in perfect health.'

"The Prince, rejoiced at the idea of his daughter's cure, immediately sent for the Princess, who soon appeared, accompanied by a numerous train of female slaves and eunuchs, and veiled in such a manner, that her face could not be seen. The chief of the dervises made the slaves hold a shovel over the head of the Princess; and so soon as he threw the seven white hairs upon some burning coals, which by his direction had been brought in the shovel, the Genie Maimoun, the son of Dimdim, uttered a violent scream, and left the Princess quite at liberty. The first thing she did was to put her hand to the veil which covered her face, and lift it up to see where she was. 'Where am I?' she cried; 'who has brought me here?'—At these words the Sultan could not conceal his joy. He embraced his daughter; he kissed her eyes; and then took the hand of the dervise and kissed it. 'Do ye judge!' said he to his officers; 'What return does he deserve, who has cured my daughter?' They all answered, that he was worthy of her hand. 'This is the very reward I was meditating for him!' the Sultan cried; 'and from this moment I proclaim him my son-in-law.'

"Soon after this the first vizier died, and the Sultan immediately advanced the dervise to the vacant post; and when the Sultan himself soon afterwards died without any male issue, this excellent man was proclaimed his successor, by the general voice of the different religious and military orders.

"One day, as he was walking with his courtiers, the good dervise who was thus raised to the throne of his father-in-law observed the envious man among the crowd in the road. He called one of the viziers who accompanied him, telling him in a whisper to bring that man, whom he pointed out, and to be sure not to alarm him. The vizier obeyed; and when the envious man was in the presence of the Sultan, the latter addressed him in these words: 'I am very happy, my friend, to see you; go directly,' said he, speaking to an officer, 'and count out from my treasury a thousand pieces of gold; nay more, deliver to him twenty bales of the most valuable merchandise my magazines contain, and let a sufficient guard escort him home.' After having given the officer this commission, he dismissed the envious man, and continued his walk.

"When I had told this history to the Genie who had assassinated the Princess of the Isle of Ebony, I applied the moral to myself. 'O Genie,' I said, 'you may observe how this benevolent monarch acted towards the envious man, and was not only ready to forget that he had attempted his life, but even sent him back laden with the benefits I have mentioned.' In short, I employed all my eloquence to persuade him to imitate so excellent an example, and to pardon me. But I found it impossible to alter his resolution.

"'All that I can do for you,' he said, 'is to spare your life; yet do not flatter yourself that I shall suffer you to depart safe and well. I must at least make you feel what I can do by my enchantments.' At these words he violently seized me, and carrying me through the vaulted roof of the subterranean palace, which opened at his approach, he soared up with me so high, that the earth appeared to me only like a small white cloud. From this height he again descended as quick as lightning, and alighted on the top of a mountain. On this spot he took up a handful of earth, and pronouncing, or rather muttering certain words, of which I could not understand the meaning, threw it over me: 'Quit the figure of a man,' he cried, 'and assume that of an ape.' He immediately disappeared, and I remained quite alone, changed into an ape, overwhelmed with grief, in an unknown country, and ignorant whether I was near the dominions of the King, my father.

"I descended the mountain, and came to a flat, level region, the extremity of which I did not reach till I had travelled a month; at length I arrived at the seacoast. There was at this time a profound calm, and I perceived a vessel about half a league from the shore. Taking advantage of this fortunate circumstance, I broke off a large branch from a tree, and dragged it to the beach. I then got astride it, with a stick in each hand to serve for oars. In this manner I rowed myself along towards the vessel, and when I was sufficiently near to be seen, I presented a most extraordinary sight to the sailors and passengers who were upon deck. They looked at me with admiration and astonishment. In due time I got alongside, and taking hold of a rope I climbed up to the deck. But as I could not speak I found myself in the greatest embarrassment. In fact, the danger I now ran was not less imminent than that I had before experienced when I was in the power of the Genie.

"The merchants who were on board were both scrupulous and superstitious, and thought that I should be the cause of some misfortune to them during their voyage, if they received me. 'I will kill him,' cried one, 'with a blow of this handspike.' 'Let me shoot an arrow through his body,' exclaimed another;—'And then let us throw his body into the sea,' said a third. They would not have failed to execute their different threats, if I had not run to the captain, and thrown myself at his feet. In this supplicating posture I laid hold of the hem of his garment; and he was so struck with this action, as well as with the tears that fell from my eyes, that he took me under his protection, declaring that if any one did me the slightest injury he would make him repent it. He even caressed and encouraged me. In spite of the loss of my speech, I showed him by means of signs how much I was obliged to him.

"The wind which succeeded this calm was not a strong one, but it was favourable. It did not change for fifty days, and it carried us safely into the harbour of a large city, commercial, well-built, and populous. Here we cast anchor. This city was of considerable importance, as it was the capital of a powerful kingdom. Our vessel was immediately surrounded by a multitude of small boats, filled with people, who came either to congratulate their friends on their arrival, or to get tidings from them as to what they had seen in the country they had come from; while some came from mere curiosity to see a ship which had arrived from a distance.

"Among the rest some officers stepped on board, and desired, in the name of the Sultan, to speak to the merchants who were with us. 'The Sultan, our sovereign,' said one of them to the merchants, who immediately appeared, 'has charged us to express to you the pleasure your arrival gives him, and entreats each of you to take the trouble of writing a few lines upon this roll of paper. That you may understand his motive for this, I must inform you, he had a first vizier who, besides showing great ability in the management of affairs, wrote in the most perfect style. This minister died a few days since. The Sultan is very much afflicted at his loss, and, as he values proficiency in writing beyond everything, he has taken a solemn oath to appoint as his vizier that person who shall write as well as the last vizier did. Many have presented specimens of their abilities, but he has not yet found any one throughout the empire whom he has thought worthy to occupy the vizier's place.'

"Each of those merchants who thought they could write well enough to aspire to this high dignity, wrote whatever they thought proper. When they had done, I advanced and took the paper from the hands of him who held it. Everybody, and particularly the merchants who had written, cried out in alarm, thinking, that I meant either to destroy it or throw it into the water; but they were soon undeceived, when they saw me hold the paper very properly, and make a sign that I also wished to write in my turn.

Their fears were now changed to astonishment. Yet, as they had never seen an ape that could write, and as they could not believe I was more skilful than other animals of my species, they wished to take the roll from my hands; but the captain still continued to take my part. 'Suffer him to try,' he said;—'let him write; if he only blots the paper, I promise you I will instantly punish him: but if on the contrary he writes well, as I hope he will, for I have never seen any ape more clever and ingenious, nor one who seemed so well to understand every thing, I declare that I will adopt him as my son. I once had a son, who did not possess half so much ability as I find in this ape.'

"As they now all ceased to oppose my design, I took the pen, and did not leave off writing till I had given an example of six different sorts of characters used in Arabia. Each specimen contained either a distich, or an impromptu stanza of four lines, in praise of the Sultan. My writing not only excelled that of the merchants, but I dare say they had never seen any so beautiful in that whole country. When I had finished, the officers took the roll and carried it to the Sultan.

"The monarch paid no attention to any of the specimens of writing except mine, which pleased him so much, that he said to the officers: 'Take the finest and most richly caparisoned horse from my stable, and the most magnificent robe of brocade you can find, to adorn the person of him who has written these six varieties of character, and bring him to me.' At this order of the Sultan's, the officers could not forbear laughing.

"This conduct irritated him so much that he would have punished them, had they not said, 'We entreat your Majesty to pardon us; these words were not written by a man, but by an ape.'—'What do you say?' cried the Sultan; 'Are not these wonderful specimens of writing from the hand of man?'—'No, sire,' answered one of the officers; 'we assure your Majesty that we saw an ape write them.' This matter appeared so wonderful to the Sultan, that he felt very desirous of seeing me. 'Do as I command you,' said he to the officer, 'and hasten to bring me this extraordinary ape.'

"The officers returned to the vessel, and showed their order to the captain, who said the Sultan should be obeyed. They immediately dressed me in a robe of very rich brocade, and carried me on shore, where they set me on a horse, and brought me to the Sultan, who was waiting in his palace for me, with a considerable number of people belonging to the court, whom he had assembled to do me honour. The march commenced; while the gate, the streets, public buildings, windows, and terraces of palaces and houses were filled with an immense number of persons of every age and sex, whom curiosity had drawn together from all quarters of the town to see me; for the report had got abroad in an instant that the Sultan had chosen an ape for his grand vizier. After having afforded a very uncommon sight to all these people, who ceased not to express their surprise by loud and repeated shouts, I arrived at the Sultan's palace.

"I found the Prince seated on his throne, amidst the nobles of his court. I made him three low bows, and at the last reverence, I prostrated myself, and kissed the earth by his feet. I then rose, and seated myself exactly like an ape. None of the assembly could withhold their admiration; nor did they comprehend how it was possible for an ape to be so well acquainted with the form and respect attached to sovereigns; nor was the Sultan less astonished than the courtiers. The whole ceremony of audience would have been complete if I had only been able to add speech to my actions; but apes never speak, and the advantage of having once been a man, could not in that respect assist me.

"The Sultan dismissed the courtiers, and there remained with him only the chief of his eunuchs, a little slave, and myself. He went from the hall of audience into his own apartment, where he ordered a repast to be served up. While he was at table, he made me a sign to come and eat with him. As a mark of my obedience, I got up, kissed the ground, and then seated myself at table; I ate, however, with much modesty and moderation.

"Before the table was cleared, I perceived a writing-desk, and requested by signs that it might be brought to me. As soon as I had it, I wrote upon a large peach some lines of my own composition, setting forth my gratitude to the Sultan. His astonishment at reading them, after I presented the peach to him, was greater than ever. When the dishes were taken away, the servants brought a particular sort of wine, of which he desired them to give me a glass. I drank it, and then wrote some fresh verses, which explained the state in which I now found myself, after my numerous sufferings. The Sultan, having read these also, exclaimed: 'A man who could be capable of acting thus, would be one of the greatest men that ever lived.' The Prince then ordered a chess-board to be brought, and asked me, by a sign, if I could play, and would engage with him? I kissed the ground, and putting my hand on my head, I showed him I was ready to receive that honour. He won the first game, but the second and third ended in my favour. Perceiving that this somewhat disconcerted him, I wrote a stanza to amuse him, and presented it to him. The verse set forth how two powerful armed bodies fought the whole day with the greatest ardour, but made peace in the evening, and passed the night together very tranquilly upon the field of battle.

THE SULTAN'S DAUGHTER IN THE PRESENCE OF THE APE.

"All these circumstances appearing to the Sultan greatly to exceed what he had ever seen or heard of the address and ingenuity of apes, he wished to have more witnesses of these prodigies. He had a daughter, who was called the Queen of Beauty; he therefore desired the chief of the eunuchs to bring her. 'Go,' said he to that officer, 'and bring your lady here; I wish her to partake of the pleasure I enjoy.' The chief of the eunuchs went, and brought back the Princess with him. When she entered her face was uncovered, but she was no sooner fairly within the apartment than she instantly drew her veil about her, and said to the Sultan, 'Your Majesty must have forgotten yourself. I am surprised that you order me to appear before men.'—'What is this, daughter?' answered the Sultan. 'It seems that you are the person who has forgotten herself. There is no one here but the little slave, the eunuch, and myself; and we are always at liberty to see your face. Why, then, do you hide your face in your veil, and assert that I have done wrong in ordering you to come here?'—'Sir,' replied the Princess, 'your Majesty will be convinced I am not mistaken. The ape, or rather the creature which you see there under that form, is not an ape, but a young Prince, the son of a great King. He has been changed into an ape by enchantment. A Genie, the son of the daughter of Eblis, has been guilty of this malicious action, after he had cruelly killed the Princess of the Isle of Ebony, daughter of King Epitimarus.'

"The Sultan was astonished at this speech, and turning to me, asked, but not now by signs, whether what his daughter said was true?—As I could not speak, I put my hand upon my head to show that she had spoken the truth. 'How came you to know, daughter,' said the King, 'that the Prince had been transformed into an ape by means of enchantment?'—'Sir,' replied the Princess, 'your Majesty may recollect that when I was a child, I had an old woman as one of my attendants. She was very well skilled in magic, and taught me seventy rules of that science, by virtue of which I could instantly cause your capital to be transported to the middle of the ocean—nay, beyond Mount Caucasus. By means of this science I know all persons who have been enchanted the moment I behold them; not only who they are, but by whom also they were enchanted. Be not therefore surprised that I have at first sight discovered this Prince, in spite of the charm which prevented him from appearing in your eyes what he really is.'—'My dear daughter!' exclaimed the Sultan, 'I did not think you were so skilful.'—'Sir,' added the Princess, 'these things are curious, and worthy of being studied; but I do not think it becomes me to boast of my knowledge.'—'Since this is the case,' replied the Sultan, 'you can dissolve the enchantment under which this Prince suffers.'—'I can, sir,' said she, 'and restore him to his own form.'—'Do so, then,' said the Sultan. 'You could not do me a greater favour, as I wish to have him for my grand vizier, and bestow you upon him for a wife.'—'I am ready, sir,' answered the Princess, 'to obey you in all things you may please to command.'

"The Queen of Beauty then went to her apartment, and returned with a knife, which had some Hebrew characters engraved upon the blade. She desired the Sultan, the chief of the eunuchs, the little slave, and myself, to go down into a secret court of the palace; and then leaving us under a gallery which surrounded the court, she went into the middle of it, where she described a large circle, and traced several words, both in the ancient Arabic characters and in those which are called the characters of Cleopatra.

"When she had done this, and prepared the circle as she required it to be, she went and placed herself in the midst of it, where she began her incantations, and repeated several verses from the Koran. By degrees the air was darkened, as if night was coming on, and the whole world seemed vanishing. We were seized with the greatest fear, and this was the more increased when we saw the Genie, the son of the daughter of Eblis, suddenly appear, in the shape of a huge, terrible lion.

"So soon as the Princess perceived this monster, she said to it, 'Dog, how darest thou, instead of cringing before me, present thyself under this horrible form, thinking to alarm me?'—'And how darest thou, replied the lion, 'break the treaty, which we have made and confirmed by a solemn oath, not to injure each other?'—'Wretch!' cried the Princess, 'thou art he whom I have to reproach on that account.'—'Thou shalt pay dearly,' interrupted the lion, 'for the trouble thou hast given me in coming here.' In saying this, he opened his dreadful jaws, and advanced to devour her. But she, being on her guard, sprang back, and had just time to pluck out a hair from her head; and pronouncing two or three words, she changed it into a sharp scythe, with which she immediately cut the lion in two pieces through the middle.

"The two parts of the lion directly disappeared, and the head only remained, which changed into a large scorpion. The Princess then took the form of a serpent, and began a fierce combat with the scorpion, which, finding itself in danger of being defeated, changed into an eagle, and flew away. But the serpent then became another eagle, black and more powerful, and went in pursuit of it. We now lost sight of them for some time.

"Shortly after they had disappeared, the earth opened before us, and a black and white cat appeared. The hairs of this creature stood quite on end, and it mewed and cried in a horrible manner. A black wolf closely followed it, and gave it no respite. The cat, being hard pressed, changed into a worm, and finding itself near a pomegranate, which had fallen by accident from a tree that grew upon the bank of a deep but narrow canal, instantly made a hole in the fruit, and concealed itself there. The pomegranate at once began to swell, and became as large as a gourd, which rose up as high as the gallery, and rolled backwards and forwards there several times; it then fell down to the bottom of the court, and broke into a thousand pieces.

"The wolf in the meantime transformed itself into a cock, and running to the seeds of the pomegranate, began swallowing them one after the other as fast as possible. When it had eaten all it could see, it came to us with its wings extended, and crowed loudly, as if to inquire of us whether there were any more seeds. There was one lying on the border of the canal, which the cock, on returning, perceived. He ran towards it as quickly as possible; but at the very instant when his beak was upon it, the seed rolled into the canal, and changed into a small fish. The cock then flew into the canal, and, changing to a pike, pursued the little fish. They were both two hours under water, and we knew not what was become of them; when suddenly we heard some horrible cries that made us tremble. Soon after we saw the Genie and the Princess all on fire. They darted flames against each other with their breath, and at last came to a close attack. Then the fire increased, and everything about was encompassed with smoke and flame, which rose to a great height. We were afraid, and not without reason, that the whole palace would be burnt; but we soon had a much stronger cause for terror; for the Genie having disengaged himself from the Princess, came towards the gallery where we stood, and blew his flames all over us. This would have destroyed us, if the Princess, running to our assistance, had not compelled him by her cries, to retreat to a distance, and defend himself against her. In spite, however, of all the haste she made, she could not prevent the Sultan from having his head singed and his face scorched; the chief of the eunuchs, too, was killed on the spot, and a spark flew into my right eye and blinded me. Both the Sultan and I expected to perish, when we suddenly heard the cry of 'Victory, victory!' and the Princess immediately appeared to us in her own form, while the Genie lay at our feet reduced to a heap of ashes.

"The Princess approached us; and then immediately asked for a cup of water, which was brought by the young slave, whom the fire had not injured. She took it, and after pronouncing some words over it, she threw some of the water upon me, and said, 'If thou art an ape by enchantment, change thy form, and take that of a man, which thou hadst before.' She had hardly concluded, when I again became a man, as I had been before I was changed, except that I had lost one eye.

"I was preparing to thank the Princess, but she did not give me time. Turning to the Sultan, her father, she said, 'Sire, I have gained the victory over the Genie, as your Majesty may see, but it is a victory which has cost me dear. I have but a few moments to live, and you will not have the satisfaction of carrying out the marriage you intended. In this dreadful combat the fire has penetrated my body, and I feel that it will soon consume me. This would not have happened if I had perceived the last seed of the pomegranate when I was in the shape of a cock, and had swallowed it as I did the others. The Genie had taken that form as a last resource, and on that depended the success of the combat, which would then have been fortunate, and without danger to me, had I perceived my enemy's stratagem. I did not perceive it; and this omission obliged me to have recourse to fire, and fight with that powerful weapon, between heaven and earth, as you saw me do. In spite of his dreadful power and experience, I convinced him that my knowledge and art were greater than his. I have at length conquered and reduced him to ashes; but I cannot escape the death which I feel approaching.'

"When the Princess had finished this account of the battle, the Sultan, in a tone which showed how much he was agitated by the recital, answered, 'You see, my daughter, the state to which your father is reduced. Alas! I am only astonished that I still live. The eunuch, your governor, is dead, and the Prince, whom you have delivered from enchantment, has lost an eye.' He could say no more, for his tears and sobs stopped his utterance. Both his daughter and myself were extremely affected at his sufferings, and mingled our tears with his.

"While we were abandoning ourselves to the expression of our sorrow, the Princess suddenly exclaimed, 'I burn! I inwardly burn!' The fire which had been consuming her, had at last seized her whole body, and she did not cease to call out, 'I burn!' till death put an end to her almost insupportable sufferings. The effect of this fire was so extraordinary, that in a few minutes she was reduced, like the Genie, to a heap of ashes.

"I need not say how much this dreadful and melancholy sight dismayed and grieved us. I would rather have continued an ape, or a dog, my whole life, than have seen my benefactress perish in such a horrid manner. The Sultan, too, on his part, was beyond measure afflicted. He uttered the most lamentable cries, violently beating his head and breast, till at last, yielding to despair, he fainted, and I feared even his life would fall a sacrifice to his excessive sorrow.

"The cries of the Sultan brought the eunuchs and officers to his assistance, and they found great difficulty in restoring him to consciousness. There was no occasion for either the monarch or myself to give them a very long detail of this adventure to convince them of the propriety of our sorrow; the two heaps of ashes, to which the Princess and the Genie had been reduced, were quite sufficient proof. As the Sultan could scarcely support himself, he was obliged to lean upon two officers to get to his apartment.

"As soon as the knowledge of the late tragical event was spread through the palace and the city, every one lamented the melancholy fate of the Princess, surnamed the Queen of Beauty, and sympathized in the grief of the Sultan. All put on mourning for seven days, and performed many ceremonies. The ashes of the Genie they scattered in the wind, but collected those of the Princess in a costly vase, and preserved them. This vase was then deposited in a superb mausoleum, which was erected on the very spot where the ashes had been found.

"The grief which preyed upon the Sultan for the loss of his daughter brought on a disease that confined him to his bed for a whole month. He had not quite recovered his health when he called me to him, and said: 'Listen, Prince, and attend to the order which I am going to give you; if you fail to execute it, your life will be the forfeit.' I assured him I would obey. Then he proceeded thus: 'I have always lived in a state of the greatest happiness, nor had any unfortunate event ever occurred under my rule. Your arrival has destroyed my peace. My daughter is dead; her governor is no more; and I have escaped with my life only by a miracle. You are the cause of all these misfortunes, for which I can find no consolation. These are the reasons which induce me to desire you will leave me unmolested; but go immediately, for if you remain here any longer, it will be the cause of my death also, since I am persuaded your presence is productive only of misfortune. This is all that I have to say to you. Go, and beware how you appear again in my kingdom. If you disobey me, no consideration shall prevent my making you repent it.' I wished to speak, but he prevented me by some angry words; and I was obliged to leave his palace.

"Driven to and fro, rejected and abandoned by every one, I knew not what was to become of me. Before I left the city I went to a bath, had my beard and eyebrows shaved, and put on the dress of a calender. I then began my journey, lamenting less my own miserable condition than the death of the two beautiful Princesses, which I had occasioned. I travelled through many countries without making myself known. At last I resolved to visit Bagdad, in hopes of being able to present myself to the Commander of the Faithful, and excite his compassion by the recital of my strange history. I arrived

THE TRANSFORMATION.

here this evening, and the first person I met was the calender, my brother, who has already related his life. You know, madam, what happened afterwards, and how I came to have the honour of being at your house."

When the second calender had finished his history, Zobeidè, to whom he had addressed himself, said, "You have done well, and I give you leave to go whenever you please." But instead of taking his departure, he entreated her to grant him the same favour she had vouchsafed to the other calender, near whom he took his place. Then the third calender, knowing it was his turn to speak, addressed himself, like the others, to Zobeidè, and began his history as follows:—

## The History of the Third Calender, the Son of a King.

HAT I am going to relate, most honourable lady, is of a very different nature from that of the stories you have already heard. Each of the two Princes, who have recited their histories, has lost an eye, as it were by the power of destiny, while I have lost mine in consequence of my own fault. I have sought out my misfortune, as you will find by what I am going to tell.

"I am called Agib, and am the son of a King, whose name was Cassib. After his death I took possession of his throne, and established my residence in the same city which he had made his capital. This city, which is situated on the sea coast, has a remarkably handsome and safe harbour, with an arsenal sufficiently extensive to supply an armament of a hundred and fifty vessels of war, always lying ready for service on any occasion, and to equip fifty merchantmen, and as many sloops and yachts, for the purposes of amusement and pleasure on the water. My kingdom was composed of many beautiful provinces, and also contained a number of considerable islands, almost all of which were situated within sight of my capital.

"The first thing I did was to visit the provinces; I then made them arm, had my whole fleet equipped, and went round to all my islands in order to conciliate the affections of my subjects, and to confirm them in their duty and allegiance. After I had been at home some time, I set out again; and these voyages, by giving me some slight knowledge of navigation, infused such a taste for it into my mind, that I resolved to go on a voyage of discovery beyond my islands. For this purpose I equipped only ten ships; and embarking in one of them, we set sail.

"During forty days our voyage was prosperous, but on the night of the forty-first the wind became adverse, and so violent, that we were driven at the mercy of the tempest, and thought we should have been lost. At break of day, however, the storm abated, the clouds dispersed, and the rising sun brought fine weather with it. We now landed on an island, where we remained two days, to take in provisions. Having done this, we again put to sea. After ten days' sail we began to hope to see land; for since the night of the storm I had altered my intention, and determined to return to my kingdom—but I then discovered that my pilot knew not where we were. In fact, on the tenth day, a sailor who was ordered to the mast-head for the purpose of scanning the horizon reported that to the right and left he could perceive only the sky and sea, but that straight before him he observed a great blackness.

"At this intelligence the pilot changed colour; and throwing his turban on the deck with one hand, he struck his face with the other, and cried out, 'Ah, my lord, we are lost! Not one of us can possibly escape the danger which threatens us, and with all my experience, it is not in my power to ensure the safety of any one of you. Speaking thus, he began to weep like one who thought his destruction inevitable; and his despair spread alarm and fear through the whole vessel. I asked him what reason he had for this outburst of grief. 'Alas!' he answered, 'the tempest we have experienced has so driven us from our track, that by midday to-morrow we shall find ourselves near yonder dark object, which is a black mountain, consisting entirely of a mass of loadstone, that will soon attract our fleet, on account of the bolts and nails in the ships. To-morrow, when we shall have come within a certain distance, the power of the loadstone will be so great, that all the nails will be drawn out of the keels, and attach themselves to the mountain; our ships will then fall in pieces and sink. As it is the property of a loadstone to attract iron, and as its own power increases by this attraction, the mountain towards the sea is entirely covered with the nails that belonged to the immense number of ships which it has destroyed; and this mass of iron fragments, at the same time, preserves and augments the virtue of attraction in the loadstone.

"'This mountain,' continued the pilot, 'is very steep, and on the summit there is a large dome, made of fine bronze, and supported upon columns of the same metal. At the top of the dome there is also a bronze horse, with the figure of a man upon it. The rider's breast is covered by a leaden breastplate, upon which some talismanic characters are engraven; and there is a tradition that this statue is the principal cause of the loss of the many vessels and men who have been drowned in this place; and that it will never cease from being destructive to all who shall have the misfortune to approach it, until it is overthrown.' When the pilot had finished his speech, he wept anew, and his tears excited the grief of the whole crew. As for myself, I did not doubt that I was now approaching the end of my days. Every man began to think of his own preservation, and to try every possible means to save himself; and during this period of uncertainty, we all agreed to make the survivors, if any should be saved, the heirs of the rest.

"The next morning we distinctly perceived the black mountain, and the idea we had formed of it made it appear still more dreadful and rugged than it really was. About midday we found ourselves so near it that we began to experience what the pilot had foretold. We saw the nails, and every other piece of iron belonging to the vessel, fly towards the mountain, against which they struck with a horrible noise, impelled by the violence of the magnetic attraction. The vessels then immediately fell to pieces, and sank to the bottom of the sea, which was so deep in this place that we could never discover the bottom by sounding. All my people perished; but Allah had pity upon me, and suffered me to save myself by clinging to a plank, which was driven by the wind directly to the foot of the mountain. I did not sustain the least injury, and had the good fortune to land near a flight of steps, which led to the summit of the mountain. I was much rejoiced at sight of these steps, for there was not the least vestige of land, either to the right or left, upon which I could have set my foot to save my life. I returned thanks to Allah, and invoking his holy name, began to ascend the mountain. The path was narrow, and so steep and difficult, that had the wind been at all violent I must have been blown into the sea. At last I reached the summit without any accident; and entering the dome, I prostrated myself on the ground, and offered my thanks to Heaven for the favour it had shown me.

"I passed the night under this dome, and while I was asleep, a venerable old man appeared to me, and said: 'Agib, attend! When you wake, dig up the earth under your feet, and you will find a brazen bow with three leaden arrows, manufactured under certain stars to deliver mankind from many evils, which continually menace them. Shoot these three arrows at the statue; the man will be precipitated into the sea, and the horse will fall at your feet. You must bury the horse in the same spot from whence you take the bow and arrows. When you have done this the sea will begin to be agitated, and will rise as high as the foot of the dome at the top of the mountain. When it shall have risen thus high, you will see a boat come towards the shore, with only one man in it, holding an oar in each hand. This man will be of brass, but different from the statue that was overthrown. Embark with him without pronouncing the name of Allah, and let him be your guide. In ten days he will have carried you into another sea, where you will find the means of returning to your own country in safety; provided, as I have already said, you forbear from mentioning the name of Allah during the whole of your voyage.'

"Thus spake the old man. As soon as I was awake, I got up much consoled by this vision, and did not fail to do as the old man had directed me. I disinterred the bow and the arrows, and shot at the statue. With the third arrow I overthrew the rider, who fell into the sea, while the horse came crashing down to my feet. I buried it in the place where I had found the bow and arrows; and while I was doing this, the sea rose by degrees, till it reached the foot of the dome on the summit of the mountain. I perceived a boat at a distance, coming towards me. I offered my thankful prayers to Allah at thus seeing my dream in every respect fulfilled. The vessel at length approached the land, and I saw in it a man made of brass, as had been described. I embarked, and took particular care not to pronounce the name of Allah. I did not even utter a single word. When I had taken my seat, the brazen figure began to row from the mountain. He continued to work without intermission till the ninth day, when I saw some islands, which made me hope I should soon be free from every danger. The excess of my joy made me forget the direction the old man had given me in my dream: 'Blessed be Allah!' I cried out—'Allah be praised!'

I had hardly pronounced these words, when the boat and the brazen man sank to the bottom of the sea. I remained in the water, and swam during the rest of the day towards the nearest island. The night which came on was exceedingly dark; and as I no longer knew where I was, I continued swimming at a venture. My strength was at last quite exhausted, and I began to despair of being able to save myself. The wind had much increased, and a mountainous wave threw me upon a flat, shallow shore, and retiring, left me there. I immediately made haste to get farther on land, for fear another wave should come and carry me back. The first thing I then did was to undress and wring the water out of my clothes; and I spread them upon the sand, which was still warm from the heat of the preceding day.

"The next morning, as soon as the sun had quite dried my garment, I put it on, and began to wander on the shore, trying to discover where I was. I had not walked far before I found my place of refuge to be a small desert island, very pleasant to look upon, and containing many sorts of fruit-trees, as well as others; but I observed that it was at a considerable distance from the mainland; and this rather lessened the joy I felt at having escaped from the sea. I nevertheless trusted in Heaven to dispose of my fate according to its will. Soon afterwards I discovered a very small vessel, which seemed to come full-sail directly from the mainland, with her prow towards the island where I was. As I had no doubt the crew were coming to anchor here, and as I knew not what sort of people they might be, whether friends or enemies, I determined not to show myself at first. I therefore climbed into a very thick tree, from whence I could examine the new-comers in safety. The vessel soon sailed up a small creek or bay, where ten slaves landed, with a spade and other implements in their hands, for digging up the earth. They went towards the middle of the island, where I observed them stop, and turn up the earth for some time; and, judging by their movements, I concluded they were lifting up a trap-door. They immediately returned to the vessel, from which they landed many sorts of provisions and furniture; and each taking a load, they carried them to the place where they had before dug up the ground. They then seemed to descend, and I conjectured there was a subterraneous building. I saw them once more go to the vessel and come back with an old man, who brought with him a youth of comely appearance, about fourteen or fifteen years old. They all descended at the spot where the trap-door had been lifted up. When they came out again they shut down the door, and covered it with earth as before; then they returned to the creek where their vessel lay; but I observed that the young man did not come back with them. From this I concluded that they had left him in the subterraneous dwelling. This circumstance very much excited my astonishment.

"The old man and the slaves then embarked, and hoisting the sails, bore away for the mainland. When I found the vessel so far distant that I could not be perceived by the crew, I came down from the tree, and went directly to the place where I had seen the men dig away the earth. I now worked as they had done, and at last discovered a stone, two or three feet square. I lifted it up, and found that it concealed the entrance to a flight of stone stairs. I descended, and found myself in a large chamber, the floor of which was covered with a carpet. Here were also a sofa and some cushions covered with a rich stuff, and on the sofa sat a young man with a fan in his hand. I perceived all these things by the light of two torches, and also noticed fruits and pots of flowers,

AGIB ASCENDING THE LOADSTONE ROCK.

which were near him. At the sight of me the young man was much alarmed, but to give him courage, I said to him on entering, 'Whoever you are, fear nothing. A King, and the son of a King, I have no intention of doing you any injury. On the contrary, you may esteem it a most fortunate circumstance that I am come here to deliver you from this tomb, where you seem to me to have been buried alive, though I am at a loss to conjecture the reason. What, however, most embarrasses me—for I will not deny that I have witnessed everything that has happened since you landed on this island—and what I cannot understand is, why you have suffered yourself to have been buried here, without making any resistance.'

"The young man was much encouraged by this speech; and with a polite gesture requested that I would take a seat near him. As soon as I had complied with his invitation, he said, 'Prince, I am about to inform you of a circumstance, whose singular nature will very much surprise you.

"'My father is a jeweller; and by his industry and skill in his profession, he has amassed a very large fortune. He has a great number of slaves and factors, who make many voyages for him in his own vessels. He has also correspondents in many courts, who are his customers, and purchase of him precious stones and jewels. He had been married a long time without having any children, when one night he dreamed that he should have a son, whose life however would be but short. When he awoke, the remembrance of this dream gave him much uneasiness. Some time after this, my mother informed him that she was about to give him an heir. In due time I was born, to the great joy of all the family. My father observed with the greatest exactness the moment of my birth, and consulted the astrologers concerning my destiny. The wise men answered: "Your son shall live without any accident or misfortune till he is fifteen; but he will then run a great risk of losing his life, and will not escape this danger without much difficulty. Should he be fortunate enough to come safely out of this peril, his life will be preserved for many years. About this time, too," they added, "the equestrian statue of brass, which stands on the top of the loadstone mountain, will be overthrown by Prince Agib, the son of King Cassib, and will fall into the sea; and the stars also show that fiftv days afterwards your son will be killed by that Prince."

"'As this prediction agreed with my father's dream, it caused him great anxiety and sorrow. Still he did not omit to bestow every care on my education, and continued to do so till now, when I am in the fifteenth year of my age. He was yesterday informed that ten days ago the brazen figure was overthrown by the Prince, whom I mentioned to you; and this intelligence gave him such alarm, and cost him so many tears, that he hardly looks like the man he was before.

"'Since first he heard this prediction of the astrologers, my father has tried every means to frustrate my horoscope, and preserve my life. Long since he took the precaution to have this habitation built, in order to conceal me for the fifty days, directly he should learn that the statue had been overthrown. . . . It was on this account that, as soon as he knew what had happened ten days since, he came here for the purpose of concealing me during the forty days that remain; and he has promised, at the expiration of that time, to come and take me back. As for myself,' added the youth, 'I have the greatest hopes; for I do not believe that Prince Agib will come and look for me underground, in the midst of a desert island. This, my lord, is all I have to tell you.'

"While the son of the jeweller was relating his history to me, I inwardly laughed at those astrologers, who had predicted that I should take away his life; and I felt myself so very unlikely to verify their prediction, that directly he had finished speaking, I exclaimed with transport: 'Oh, dear youth, put thy trust in the goodness of Allah, and fear nothing. Esteem this confinement only as a debt you had to pay, and from which from this hour you are free. I am delighted at my own good fortune in being cast away here, after suffering shipwreck, that I may guard you against those who would attempt your life. I will not quit you for a moment during the forty days which the vain and absurd conjectures of the astrologers have caused to appear as a time of peril. During this time, I will render you every service in my power, and afterwards I will, with your father's permission and yours, take the opportunity of embarking in your vessel, in order to return to the continent; and when I am at home in my own kingdom, I shall never forget the obligation I am under to you, and will endeavour to prove my gratitude by every means in my power.'

"I encouraged him by this discourse, and thus gained his confidence. Fearful of alarming him, I took care to conceal from him the fact that I was the very person whom he dreaded; nor did I give him the least suspicion of the truth. We conversed about various things till night; and I easily discovered that the young man possessed a sensible and well-informed mind. We ate together of his store of provisions, which was so abundant that it would have lasted more than the forty days had there been other guests beside myself. We continued to converse together for some time after supper, and then retired to rest.

"When the youth got up the next morning, I presented him with a basin and some water. He washed himself, while I prepared the dinner, which I served up at the proper time. After our repast, I invented a sort of game, which was to amuse us, not only during the day, but for those that followed. I prepared the supper in the same way I had done the dinner; we then supped and retired to rest, as on the preceding day.

"We had sufficient opportunity to contract a friendship for each other. I perceived that he had an inclination for me; and on my side, the regard I felt for him was so strong, that I often said to myself, 'The astrologers, who have predicted to the father that his son should be slain by my hands, were impostors, for it is impossible I can ever commit so horrid a crime.' In short, we passed thirty-nine days in the pleasantest manner possible in this subterraneous habitation.

"At length, the fortieth morning arrived. The youth, when he was getting up, said to me, in a transport of joy which he could not restrain: 'Behold me now, Prince, on the fortieth day; and, thanks to Allah and your good company, I am not dead. My father will not fail very soon to acknowledge his obligation, and furnish you with every means and opportunity that you may return to your kingdom. But while we are waiting,' added he, 'I beg of you to have the goodness to warm some water, that I may enjoy a thorough bath. I wish to prepare myself and change my dress, in order to receive my father with the greater respect.' I put the water on the fire, and when it was sufficiently warm, I filled the bath. The youth stepped in: I washed and rubbed him myself. He then got out, and went into the bed I had prepared for him, and I threw the cover over him. After he had reposed himself, and slept for some time, he said to me: 'O Prince, do me the favour to bring me a melon and some sugar; I want to eat something to refresh me.'

"I chose one of the melons which remained, and put it on a plate; and as I could not find a knife to cut it, I asked the youth if he knew where I should look for one. 'There is one,' he replied, 'upon the cornice over my head.' I looked up and perceived one there, but I over-reached myself in endeavouring to get it; and at the very moment I had it in my hand, my foot by some means got so entangled in the covering of the bed, that I unfortunately fell down on the young man, and pierced him to the heart with the knife. In an instant he was dead.

"At this sight I wept most bitterly. I beat my head and breast, I tore my habit, and threw myself on the ground in grief and despair. 'Alas!' I cried, 'only a few hours more, and he would have been free from the danger against which he sought an asylum; and at the very moment when I thought the peril past, I am become the assassin, and have myself fulfilled the prediction. But I ask thy pardon, O Lord,' I added, raising my head and hands towards heaven; 'and if I am guilty of his death, I desire to live no longer.'

"After this misfortune, death would have been very acceptable to me, and I should have met it without dread. But we are seldom afflicted with evil, or blessed with good fortune, at the very moment we may desire either.

"Remembering after a time that all my tears and sorrow could not restore the youth to life, and that, as the forty days were now concluded, I should be surprised by the father, I went out of the subterraneous dwelling, and ascended to the top of the stairs.

I replaced the large stone over the entrance, and covered it with earth. Scarcely had I finished my task when, looking towards the mainland, I perceived the vessel which was coming for the young man. Meditating what plan I should pursue, I said to myself: 'If I let them see me, the old man will probably seize me, and order his slaves to kill me, when he discovers that his son has been murdered. Whatever I could allege in my own justification would never persuade him of my innocence. It is surely better, then, to withdraw myself from his sight, while I have the power, rather than expose myself to his resentment.'

"Near the subterraneous cavern there was a large tree, the thick foliage of which seemed to me to offer a secure retreat. I immediately climbed into this tree, and had hardly placed myself so as not to be seen, when I observed the vessel come to land in the same place where it had before anchored. The old man and the slaves instantly came on shore, and approached the subterraneous dwelling in a manner that showed they had some hopes of a good result. But when they saw that the ground had been lately disturbed, they changed colour, especially the old man. They then lifted up the stone, and descended the stairs. They called the young man by his name, but no answer was returned. This redoubled their anxiety. They sought him, and at last found him stretched on his couch with the knife through his heart, for I had not had the courage to draw it out. At this mournful sight, they uttered such lamentable cries that my tears flowed afresh. The old man fainted with horror. The slaves brought him out in their arms that he might feel the air, and placed him at the foot of the very tree in which I was. Notwithstanding all their efforts to recover him, the unfortunate father remained so long in an insensible state, that they more than once despaired of his life.

"He at length recovered from this long fainting-fit. The slaves then went down and brought up the body of his son, clothed in the poor youth's finest garments; and as soon as the grave which they made was ready, they put the body in. Supported by two slaves, with his face bathed in tears, the old man threw in the first piece of earth, and then the slaves filled up the grave. This melancholy duty done, the furniture and remainder of the provisions were put on board the vessel. The old man, overcome with sorrow, and unable to walk alone, was carried to the vessel in a sort of litter by the slaves; and they immediately put to sea. They were soon at a considerable distance from the island, and I lost sight of them.

"I now remained alone in the island, and passed the following night in the subterraneous dwelling, which had not been again shut up; and the next day I took a survey of the whole island, resting in the pleasantest spots whenever I felt weary. I passed a whole month in this solitary manner. At the end of that time I perceived that the sea retired considerably, that the island appeared to become larger, and that the distance from the mainland visibly decreased. In truth, the water narrowed so much that there was now only a small channel between me and the continent, and I passed over to the mainland without going deeper than the middle of my leg. I then walked so far on the flat sand, that I was greatly fatigued. At last I reached firmer ground, and had left the sea at a considerable distance behind me, when I saw in the distance something that appeared like a large fire. At this I was much rejoiced; 'for here,' said I to myself, 'I shall certainly find some people, as a fire cannot light itself.' But as I came nearer I found myself mistaken in my conjecture, and discovered that what I had taken for a fire was a sort of castle of red copper, from which the rays of the sun were reflected in such a manner that it seemed all flames.

"I stopped near this castle, and sat down—partly to admire the beauty of the building, and partly to rest myself. I had not yet become tired of contemplating this magnificent house, when I perceived ten handsome young men, who came out, as it appeared to me, for the purpose of walking; but it struck me as a very surprising circumstance, that they were all blind of the right eye. An old man, of rather tall stature and very venerable appearance, accompanied them.

"I was very much astonished at meeting, at one time, so many people who were all not only blind of one but the same eye. While I was endeavouring to conjecture, in my own mind, for what purpose or by what accident they were thus collected together, they accosted me, and showed signs of great joy at my appearance. After the first greetings had passed, they inquired of me what brought me there: I told them that my history was rather long, but added that, if they would take the trouble to sit down, I would afford them the satisfaction they wished, by telling my adventures. They seated themselves, and I related to them everything that had happened to me, from the moment I had left my own kingdom till that instant. This narration greatly excited their surprise. When I had finished my story, they entreated me to come with them into the castle. I accepted their offer, and we entered the building together. After passing

AGIB CONTEMPLATING THE CASTLE OF COPPER.

through a long suite of halls, antechambers, saloons, and cabinets, all very handsomely furnished, we came at length to a large and magnificent apartment, where there were ten small blue sofas, placed in a circle, but separate from each other. These served both as seats for repose during the day, and also as beds to sleep upon in the night. In the midst of this circle there was another sofa, less raised than the others, but of the same colour, upon which sat the old man of whom I have spoken, while the young men seated themselves upon the surrounding ten. As each sofa held only one person, one of the young men said to me, 'Friend, sit down upon the carpet in the centre of this room, and seek not to know anything that regards us, nor the reason why we are all blind of the right eye; be satisfied with what you see, and do not seek to gratify any curiosity you may feel.' The old man did not remain long seated;

he rose presently and went out, but very soon returned, bringing with him a supper for the ten young men, to each of whom he distributed a certain portion. He gave me mine in the same way, and, like the rest, I ate my share apart. As soon as this repast was finished, the old man presented to each of us a cup of wine.

"My history appeared to these men so extraordinary, that they made me repeat it when supper was over. This afterwards led to a conversation, which lasted the greater part of the night. One of the young men now observed that it was late, and said to the old one, 'You see that it is time to retire to rest, and yet you do not bring us what we require for the discharge of our duty.' At this the old man got up and went into a cabinet, from whence he brought upon his head, one after the other, ten basins, all covered with blue stuff; he placed one of these, with a torch, before each of the young men. They uncovered their basins, which contained some ashes, some charcoal in powder, and some lampblack. They mixed all these ingredients together, and began to rub them over their faces and smear their countenances, until their appearance was very frightful. After they had blacked themselves over in this manner, they began to weep, to make great lamentations, and to beat themselves on the head and breast, while they cried out continually: 'Behold the consequences of our idleness and debauchery!'

"They passed almost the whole night in this strange occupation; at last they ceased their lamentations, and the old man brought them some water, in which they washed their faces and hands. They then took off their dresses, which were much torn, and put on others, and no one would have supposed they had been engaged in the extraordinary proceedings which I had witnessed. Judge what were my feelings during all this period. I was tempted a thousand times to break the silence which they had imposed upon me, and to ask them questions; and very amazement prevented me from getting any rest during the remainder of the night.

"The following morning, as soon as we were up, we went out to take the air, and I then said to my companions, 'I must inform you, gentlemen, that I retract the promise you extorted from me last night, as I can no longer observe it. You are wise men, and you have given me sufficient reason to believe that you possess an enlarged understanding; yet, at the same time, I have seen you do things which none but madmen would be guilty of. Whatever misfortune my inquiry may bring upon me, I cannot refrain from asking for what reason you daubed your faces with ashes, charcoal, and black paint, and how you have each lost an eye. There must be some very singular cause for all this; I entreat you, therefore, to satisfy my curiosity.' Notwithstanding the urgency of my request, they only answered that I was inquiring about things that did not concern me, that I had no interest in their actions, and that I must remain content. We passed the day in converse upon different subjects, and, when night approached, we supped separately, as before. The old man again brought the blue basins, with the contents of which the others anointed themselves; they then wept, beat themselves, and exclaimed, 'Behold the consequences of our idleness and debauchery!' The next night, and on the third also, they did the same thing.

"I could at last no longer resist my curiosity, and I very seriously entreated them to satisfy me, or to inform me by what road I could return to my kingdom; for I told them it was impossible that I could remain any longer with them, and every night be witness to the extraordinary sight I beheld, if I was not permitted to know the causes that produced it. One of the young men thus answered me, in the name of the rest: 'Do not be astonished at what we do in your presence; if we have not hitherto yielded to your entreaties, it has been entirely out of friendship for you, and to spare you the anguish of being yourself reduced to the state in which you see us. If you wish to share our unhappy fate you have only to speak, and we will tell you what you wish to know.' I told them I was determined to be satisfied at all risks. 'Once more,' resumed the same young man who had before spoken, 'we advise you to restrain your curiosity; for it will cost you the sight of your right eye.' 'I care not,' I answered; 'and I declare to you, that if this misfortune does happen, I shall not consider you as the cause of it, but shall lay the blame entirely on myself.' Again he represented to me that, when I should have lost my eye, I must not expect to remain with them, even if I had thought of doing so; for their number was complete, and could not be increased. I told them that it would be a satisfaction to me to continue to dwell among such agreeable men as they appeared to be; but still, if a separation were necessary, I would submit to it; since, whatever might be the consequence, I was determined that my curiosity should be gratified.

"The ten young men, seeing that I was not to be shaken in my resolution, took a sheep and killed it: after they had taken off the skin, they gave me the knife they had made use of, and said, 'Take this knife: it will serve you for an occasion that will presently arise. We are going to sew you up in this skin, in which you must be entirely concealed. We shall then retire, and leave you in this place. Soon afterwards a bird of most enormous size, which they call a roc, will appear in the air; and, taking you for a sheep, it will swoop down upon you, and lift you up to the clouds: but let not this alarm you. The bird will soon return with his prey towards the earth, and will lay you down on the top of a mountain. As soon as you feel yourself upon the ground, rip open the skin with the knife, and set yourself free. On seeing you the roc will be alarmed, and fly away, leaving you at liberty. Tarry not in that place, but go on until you arrive at a castle of enormous magnitude, entirely covered with plates of gold, set with large emeralds and other precious stones. Go to the gate, which is always open, and enter. All of us who are here have been in that castle; but we will tell you nothing of what we saw, nor will we relate what happened to us there, as you will learn everything yourself. The only thing we can tell you of is, that our sojourn in that palace cost each of us a right eye, and that the penance you have seen us perform we are obliged to undergo in consequence of our having been there. The particular history of each of us is full of wonderful adventures; it would make a large book—but we cannot now tell you more.'

"When the young man had finished speaking, I wrapped myself up in the sheep-skin, and took the knife which they gave me. After they had taken the trouble to sew me up in the skin they left me, and retired into their apartment. It was not long before the roc which they had mentioned made its appearance. It swooped down upon me, took me up in its talons as if I were a sheep, and carried me to the summit of a mountain. When I perceived that I was upon the ground, I did not fail to make use of my knife. I ripped open the skin, threw it off, and appeared before the roc, which flew away the instant it saw me. This roc is a white bird, of enormous size. Its strength is such, that it can lift up elephants from the ground and carry them to the top of mountains, where it devours them.

"My impatience to arrive at the castle was such, that I lost not an instant in proceeding thither. Indeed, I made so much haste that I reached it in less than half a day; and I may add, that I found it much more magnificent than it had been described. The gate was open, and I entered a square court of vast extent. It contained ninety-nine doors, made of sandalwood and that of the aloe-tree, and one (the hundredth) door was of gold. Besides all these, there were entrances to many magnificent staircases, which led to the upper apartments, and some others which I did not then see. The hundred doors I have mentioned formed the entrances either into gardens, or into storerooms filled with riches, or into some other apartments which contained objects most surprising to behold.

"Opposite to me I saw an open door, through which I entered into a large saloon, where forty young ladies were sitting. Their beauty was so perfect that the imagination cannot conceive anything beyond it. They were all very magnificently dressed; and as soon as they perceived me they rose, and without waiting for my salutation they called out, with an appearance of joy, 'Welcome, my brave lord, you are welcome!' And one of them, speaking for the rest, said, 'We have a long time expected a person like you. Your manner sufficiently shows that you possess all the good qualities we could wish; and we hope that you will not find our company disagreeable or unworthy of you.' After much resistance on my part, they persuaded me to sit down on a seat more raised than those on which they sat; and when I showed embarrassment at this distinction, they said, 'It is your right: from this moment you are our lord, our master, and our judge; we are your slaves, and ready to obey your commands.' Nothing in the world could have astonished me more than the desire and eagerness these ladies professed to render me every possible service. One brought me warm water to wash my feet; another poured perfumed water over my hands; some came with a complete change of apparel for me: some of the ladies served up a delicious repast, while others stood before me with glasses in their hands, ready to pour out the most delicious wine. Everything was done without confusion, and in such admirable order and such a pleasant way, that I was quite charmed. I ate and drank; and when I had finished, all the ladies placed themselves around me, and asked me to relate the circumstances of my journey. I gave them so full an account of my adventures that my story lasted till nightfall. Then some of the forty ladies who were seated nearest to me stayed to converse with me, while others, observing it was night, went out to seek for lights. They returned with a prodigious number, that produced almost the brilliance of day; but they were arranged with so much symmetry and taste, that we could hardly wish for the return of daylight.

"Some of the ladies covered the tables with dried fruits and sweetmeats of every kind; they also furnished the sideboard with many sorts of wine and sherbet, while others of the ladies came with several musical instruments. When everything was ready, they invited me to sit down to table; the ladies bore me company, and we remained there a considerable time. Those who entertained us with music sang to the sound of their instruments, thus producing a delightful concert. The rest began to dance, moving in pairs, one after the other, in the most graceful and elegant manner possible. It was past midnight before all these amusements were concluded. One of the ladies then, addressing me, said, 'You are fatigued with the distance you have come to-day, and it is time you should take some repose. Your apartment is prepared.' and they conducted me to a magnificent apartment. The other ladies then left me there and retired.

"I had hardly finished dressing myself in the morning, before the ladies came to my apartment. They were as splendidly adorned as on the preceeding day. They saluted me, and conducted me to a bath, but in a different manner; and when I had bathed, they brought me another dress, still more magnificent than the first. In short, Madam, not to tire you by repeating the same thing over again, I may tell you at once that I passed a whole year with these forty ladies, and that during the whole of the time the pleasures of the life I led were not marred by the least uneasiness or disquietude.

"I was therefore greatly surprised when, at the end of the year, the forty ladies, instead of presenting themselves to me in their accustomed good spirits, one morning entered my apartment with their countenances bathed in tears. Each of them came and embraced me, and said, 'Adieu, dear prince, adieu; we are now compelled to leave you!'

"Their tears affected me deeply. I entreated to know the cause of their grief, and why they were obliged to leave me. 'In the name of Allah, ye beautiful ladies,' I exclaimed, 'tell me, I beseech you, is it in my power to console you, or will my aid and assistance prove useless?' Instead of answering my question directly, they said, 'Would to God we had never seen or known you! Many men have done us the honour of visiting us before you came; but no one possessed the elegance, the gentleness, the power of pleasing, the merit we find in you; nor do we know how we shall be able to live without you.' And as they said this their tears flowed afresh. 'Amiable ladies,' I cried, 'do not, I beg of you, keep me any longer in suspense, but tell me the cause of your sorrow?' 'Alas!' answered they, 'what can it be that afflicts us but the necessity of separating from you? Perhaps we shall never meet again. Yet still, if you really wish it, and have sufficient command over yourself to observe the conditions, it is not absolutely impossible we may return to you.' 'In truth, ladies,' I replied, 'I do not at all understand what you mean; I conjure you to speak more openly!' 'Well, then, said one of them, 'to satisfy you, we must inform you we are all Princesses, and the daughters of Kings. You have seen what manner of life we lead here; but at the end of each year we are compelled to absent ourselves for forty days, to fulfil some duties which may not be left undone, but the nature of which we are not at liberty to reveal; after this period we again return to this castle. Yesterday the year ended, and to-day we must leave you. This is the great cause of our affliction. Before we go, we will give you the keys of the whole palace, and particularly of the hundred doors, within which you will find ample room to gratify your curiosity and amuse your solitude during our absence. But, for your own sake, and for our particular interest, we entreat you to keep away from the golden door. If you open it we shall never see you again; and the fear we are in lest you should, increases our sorrow. We hope you will profit by the advice we have given you. Your repose, your happiness, nay your life, depends upon it; therefore be careful. If you indiscreetly yield to your curiosity, you will also do us much injury. We conjure you, therefore, not to be guilty of this fault, but to let us have the

AGIB.—"LEFT ALONE."

joy of finding you here at the end of the forty days. We would take the key of the golden door with us, but it would be an offence to a prince like yourself to doubt your circumspection and discretion.'

"At this speech I was greatly affected. I made them understand that their absence would cause me much pain, and thanked them very much for the good advice they gave me. I assured them I would profit by it, and would perform things much more difficult, if any sacrifice might procure me the happiness of passing the remainder of my life with ladies of such rare and extraordinary merit. We took a most tender leave of one another. I embraced them all; and they departed from the castle, in which I remained quite alone.

"The delight of their company, our sumptuous mode of life, and the concerts and various amusements with which the ladies had enlivened my stay, had so entirely engrossed my time during the year, that I had not had the least opportunity, nor indeed inclination, to examine the wonders of this enchanted palace. I had not even paid any attention to the multitude of extraordinary objects which were continually before my eyes; so much had I been enchanted by the charms and accomplishments of the ladies, and the pleasure I felt at finding them always employed in endeavouring to amuse me. I was very sorrowful at their departure; and although their absence was to last only forty days, the time during which I was to be deprived of their society, seemed to me an age.

"I determined, in my own mind, to observe the advice they had given me, not to open the golden door; but as I was permitted, with that one exception, to satisfy my curiosity, I took the keys belonging to the other apartments, which were regularly arranged, and opened the first door. I entered a fruit garden, to which I thought nothing in the world was comparable; not even that Paradise of which our religion promises us the enjoyment after death. The admirable order and arrangement, in which the trees were disposed, the abundance and variety of the fruits, many of which were of kinds unknown to me, together with their freshness aud beauty, and the elegant neatness apparent in every spot, filled me with astonishment. Nor must I neglect to inform you, that this delightful garden was watered in a most singular manner: small channels, cut out with great art and regularity, and of different sizes, conveyed the water in great abundance to the roots of some trees which required a liberal supply to make them send forth their first leaves and flowers: while others, whose fruits were already set, received a smaller quantity of moisture; those whose fruit was much swelled had still less, while a fourth sort, on which the fruit had come to maturity, had just what was sufficient to ripen them. The size also, which all the fruits attained very much exceeded what we are accustomed to observe in our gardens. These channels that conducted the water to the trees on which the fruit was ripe, had barely enough water to preserve it in the same state without decaying it.

"I could not grow weary of examining and admiring this beautiful spot; I should never have left it if I had not, from this beginning, conceived a still higher idea of the things which I had not yet seen. I returned with my mind full of the wonders I had beheld. I then closed the first door, and opened the next.

"Instead of a fruit garden I now discovered a flower garden, which was not in its kind less singular. It contained a spacious parterre, not watered so abundantly as the first garden, but with greater skill and management, for each flower received just the amount of irrigation it required. The rose, the jessamine, the violet, the narcissus, the hyacinth, the anemone, the tulip, the ranunculus, the carnation, the lily, and an infinity of other flowers, which in other places bloom at various times, came all into flower at once in this spot; and nothing could be softer than the air in this garden.

"On opening the third door, I discovered a very large aviary. It was paved with marble of different colours, and of the finest and rarest sort. The cages were of sandal wood and aloes, and contained a great number of nightingales, goldfinches, canaries, larks, and other birds, whose notes were sweeter and more melodious than any I had ever heard. The vases which contained their food and water were of jasper, or of the most valuable agate. This aviary also was kept with the greatest neatness; and from its vast extent, I conceive that not less than a hundred persons would be necessary to maintain it in the perfection in which it appeared; and yet I could see no one, either here or in the other gardens, nor did I observe a single noxious weed, nor the least superfluous thing that could offend the sight.

"The sun had already set; and I retired much delighted with the warbling of the multitude of birds, which were flying about in search of commodious resting places where to perch and enjoy the repose of the night. I went back to my apartment, and determined to open all the other doors, except the hundredth, on the succeeding days. The next day I did not fail to go to the fourth door, and open it. But if the sights which I had seen on the foregoing days had surprised me, what I now beheld put me in ecstacy. I first entered a large court, surrounded by a building of a very singular sort of architecture, of which, to avoid being very prolix, I will not give you a description.

"This building had forty doors, all open. Each door was an entrance into a sort of treasury, containing more riches than many kingdoms. In the first room I found large quantities of pearls; and, what is almost incredible, the most valuable, which were as large as pigeons' eggs, were more numerous than the smaller. The second was filled with diamonds, carbuncles, and rubies; the third with emeralds; the fourth contained gold in ingots; the fifth gold in money; the sixth ingots of silver; and the two following coined silver. The rest were filled with amethysts, chrysolites, topazes, opals, turquoises, jacinths, and every other sort of precious stone we are acquainted with—not to mention agate, jasper, cornelian, and coral, in branches and whole trees, with which one apartment was entirely filled. Struck with surprise and admiration at the sight of all these riches, I exclaimed, 'It is impossible that all the treasures of every potentate in the universe, if they were collected in the same spot, can equal these! How happy am I in possessing all these treasures, and in sharing them with such amiable Princesses!'

"I will not detain you, Madam, by giving you an account of all the wonderful and valuable things which I saw on the following days; I will only inform you, that I spent nine and thirty days in opening the ninety-nine doors, and in admiring everything the rooms thus disclosed contained. There now remained only the hundredth door, which I was forbidden to touch. The fortieth day since the departure of the charming Princesses now arrived. If only for that one day, I had maintained the power over myself I ought to have had, I should have been the happiest instead of the most miserable of men. The Princesses would have returned the next day; and the pleasure I should have experienced in receiving them ought to have acted as a restraint upon my curiosity; but through a weakness, which I shall never cease to lament, I yielded to the temptation of some demon, who did not suffer me to rest till I had subjected myself to the pain and punishment I have since experienced.

"Though I had promised to restrain my curiosity, I opened the fatal door. Before I even set my foot within this room, a very agreeable odour struck me, but it was so powerful, it made me faint. I soon, however, recovered; but instead of profiting by the warning, instantly shutting the door, and giving up all idea of satisfying my curiosity, I persevered and entered—having first waited till the odour was lessened and dispersed through the air. I then felt no inconvenience from it. I found a very large vaulted room, the floor of which was strewn with saffron. It was illuminated by torches made of aloe-wood and ambergris, and placed on golden stands: these torches exhaled a strong perfume. The brightness caused by them was still further heightened by many lamps of silver and gold, which were filled with oil composed of many perfumes.

"Among the numerous objects which attracted my attention was a black horse, the best shaped and most beautiful that ever was seen. I went close to it, to observe it more attentively. It had a saddle and bridle of massive gold, richly worked. On one side of its manger there was clean barley and sesame, and the other was filled with rosewater. I took hold of the horse's bridle, and led it towards the light, to examine it the better. I mounted it, and endeavoured to make it go; but as it would not move I struck it with a switch, which I had found in its magnificent stable. So soon as it had felt the stroke the horse began to neigh in a most dreadful manner; then spreading its wings, which I had not till that moment perceived, it rose so high in the air, that I lost sight of the ground. I now thought only of holding fast on its back; nor did I experience any injury, except the great terror with which I was seized. At length my steed began to descend towards the earth, and lighted upon the terraced roof of a castle; then, without giving me time to get down, it shook me so violently that I fell off behind, and with a blow of its tail it struck out my right eye.

"In this way I became blind; and the prediction of the ten young lords was now instantly brought to my recollection. The horse itself immediately spread its wings, took flight, and disappeared. I rose up, much afflicted at the misfortune which I had thus voluntarily brought upon myself. I traversed the whole terrace, keeping my hand up to my eye, as I felt very considerable pain from the stroke. I then went down, and came to a saloon, which I immediately recognized from observing ten sofas disposed in a circle, and a single one, less elevated, in the middle: it was, in fact, in the very castle whence I had been carried up by the roc.

"The ten young lords were not in the castle. I, however, waited, and it was not long before they came, accompanied by the old man. They did not seem at all astonished at seeing me, nor at observing that I had lost my right eye. 'We are very sorry,' they said, 'we cannot congratulate you, on your return, in the manner we could have wished; but you know we were not the cause of your misfortune.' 'It would be,' I replied, 'very wrong in me to accuse you of it: I brought it entirely upon myself, and the fault lies with me alone.' 'If thy misfortune,' answered they, 'can derive any consolation from knowing that others are in the same situation, we can afford thee that satisfaction. Whatever may have happened to you, be assured we have experienced the same. Like yourself, we have enjoyed every species of pleasure for a whole year; and we should have continued in the enjoyment of the same happiness if we had not opened the golden door during the absence of the Princesses. You have not been more prudent than we were, and you have experienced the same punishment that has fallen upon us. We wish we could receive you into our society, to undergo the same penance we are performing, and of which we know not the duration; but we have before informed you of the circumstances which prevent us. You must, therefore, take your departure, and go to the Court of Bagdad, where you will meet with the person who will be able to decide your fate.' They pointed out the road I was to follow; I then took my leave and departed.

"During my journey I shaved my beard and eyebrows, and put on the habit of a calender. I was a long time on the road, and it was only this evening that I arrived in this city. At one of the gates I encountered these two calenders, my brethren, who were equally strangers with myself. On thus accidentally meeting, we were all much surprised at the singular circumstance, that each of us had lost his right eye. We had not, however, much leisure to converse on the subject of our mutual misfortune. We had only time, Madam, to implore your assistance, which you have generously afforded us.

"When the third calender had finished the recital of his history, Zobeidè, addressing herself both to him and his brethren, said, 'Depart! You are all three at liberty to go wherever you please.' But one of the calenders answered, 'We beg of you, Madam, to pardon our curiosity, and permit us to stay and hear the adventures of these guests, who have not yet spoken. The lady then turned to the side where sat the caliph, the vizier Giafar, and Mesrour, of whose real condition and character she was still ignorant, and desired each of them to relate his history.

"The grand vizier, Giafar, who was always prepared to speak, immediately answered Zobeidè. 'We obey, Madam,' said he; 'but we have only to repeat to you what we already related before we entered. We are merchants of Moussoul, and we are come to Bagdad for the purpose of disposing of our merchandise, which we have placed in the warehouses belonging to the khan where we live. We dined to-day together, with many others of our profession, at a merchant's of this city. Our host treated us with the most delicate viands and finest wines, and had moreover provided a company of male and female dancers, and a set of musicians, to sing and play. The great noise and uproar which we all made attracted the notice of the watch, who came and arrested many of the guests; but we had the good fortune to escape. As, however, it was very late, and the door of our khan would be shut, we knew not whither to go. It happened, accidentally, that we passed through your street; and as we heard the sounds of pleasure and gaiety within your walls, we determined to knock at the door. This is the only history we have to tell, and we have done according to your commands.'

"After listening to this narration, Zobeidè seemed to hesitate as to what she should say. The three calenders, observing her indecision, entreated her to be equally generous to the three pretended merchants of Moussoul as she had been to them. 'Well then,'

AGIB LOSES HIS EYE.

she cried, 'I will comply. I wish all of you to be under the same obligation to me. I will therefore do you this favour, but it is only on condition that you instantly quit this house, and go wherever you please.' Zobeidè gave this order in a tone of voice that showed she meant to be obeyed: the caliph, the vizier, Mesrour, the three calenders, and the porter, therefore, went away without answering a word; for the presence of the seven armed slaves served to make them very respectful. So soon as they had left the house and the door had been closed behind them, the caliph said to the three calenders, without letting them know who he was, 'Ye are strangers, and but just arrived in this city; what do you intend to do, and which way do you think of going, as it is not yet daylight?' And they answered, 'This very thing, sir, embarrasses us.' 'Follow us then,' returned the caliph, 'and we will relieve you from this difficulty.' He then whispered his vizier, and ordered him to conduct them to his own house, and bring them to the palace in the morning. 'I wish,' added he, 'to have their adventures written; for they are worthy of a place in the annals of my reign.'

"The vizier Giafar took the three calenders home; the porter went to his own house, and the caliph, accompanied by Mesrour, returned to his palace. He retired to his couch; but his mind was so entirely occupied by all the extraordinary things he had seen and heard, that he was unable to close his eyes. He was particularly anxious to know who Zobeidè was, and the motives she could possibly have for treating the two black dogs so ill, and also the reason that Aminè's bosom was so covered with scars. The morning at length broke, while he was still engaged with these reflections. He immediately rose, and went into the council-chamber of the palace; he then gave audience, and seated himself on his throne.

"It was not long before the grand vizier arrived, and hastened to perform the customary obeisances. 'Vizier,' said the caliph to him, 'the business which is now before us is not very pressing; that of the three ladies and the two black dogs is of more consequence; and my mind will not be at rest till I am fully informed of everything that has caused me so much astonishment. Go, and order these ladies to attend; and at the same time bring back the three calenders with you. Hasten, and remember I am impatient for your return.'

"The vizier, who was well acquainted with the hasty and passionate disposition of his master, hurried to obey him. He arrived at the house of the ladies, and, with as much politeness as possible, informed them of the orders he had received to conduct them to the caliph; but he made no reference to the events of the night before.

"The ladies immediately put on their veils, and went with the vizier, who, as he passed his own door, called for the calenders. They had just learnt that they had already seen the caliph, and had even spoken to him without even knowing it was he. The vizier brought them all to the palace; he had executed his commission with so much diligence that his master was perfectly satisfied. The caliph ordered the ladies to stand behind the doorway which led to his own apartment, that he might preserve a certain decorum before the officers of his household. He kept the three calenders near him; and these men made it sufficiently apparent, by their respectful behaviour, that they were not ignorant in whose presence they had the honour to appear.

"When the ladies were seated, the caliph turned towards them and said, 'When I inform you, ladies, that I introduced myself to you last night, disguised as a merchant, I shall, without doubt, cause you some alarm. You are afraid, probably, that you offended me, and you think, perhaps, that I have ordered you to come here—only to show you some marks of my resentment; but be of good courage, be assured that I have forgotten what is past, and that I am even very well satisfied with your conduct. I wish that all the ladies of Bagdad possessed as much sense as I have observed in you. I shall always remember the moderation with which you behaved after the incivility we were guilty of towards you. I was then only a merchant of Moussoul, but I am now Haroun Alraschid, the Seventh Caliph of the glorious House of Abbas, which holds the place of our Great Prophet. I have ordered you to appear here, only that I may be informed who you are, and to learn the reason why one of you, after having ill-treated the two black dogs, wept with them: nor am I less curious to hear how the bosom of another became so covered with scars.'

"Though the caliph pronounced these words very distinctly, and the three ladies understood them very well, the vizier Giafar did not fail to repeat them, according to custom. The prince had no sooner encouraged Zobeidè by this speech, which he addressed to her, than she gave him the satisfaction he required, beginning her history in the following manner: —

### The History of Zobeide.

"Commander of the Faithful! —The history, which I am going to relate to your Majesty, is probably one of the most surprising you have ever heard. The two black dogs and myself are three sisters, daughters of the same mother and father; and I shall, in the course of my narration, inform you by what strange accident my two sisters have been transformed into dogs. The two ladies, who live with me, and who are now here, are also my sisters, by the same father, but by a different mother. She whose bosom is covered with scars is called Aminè; the name of the other is Safiè, and I am called Zobeidè.

"After the death of our father, the estate which he left was equally divided amongst us. When my two half-sisters had received their share, they went and lived with their mother; my other two sisters and I remained with ours, who was still alive, and who, when she died, left a thousand sequins to each of us. When we had received our property, my two elder sisters (for they are both older than I) married. They went, of course, to live with their husbands, and left me alone. Not long after their marriage, the husband of my eldest sister sold everything he possessed, both in land and moveables; and with the money he thus got together, and with what he had received with my sister, they both went over to Africa. My sister's husband there squandered away, in good cheer and dissipation, not only all his own fortune, but also that which my sister brought him. At length, finding himself reduced to the greatest distress, he found out some pretext for a divorce, and drove her from him.

"She returned to Bagdad, after suffering almost incredible evils during the long journey. She came to seek a refuge at my house, in so miserable a state, that she would have excited pity even in the most obdurate hearts. I received her with every mark of affection she could expect from me. I inquired of her how she came to be in so wretched a condition; she informed me, with tears in her eyes, of the bad conduct of her husband, and of the unworthy treatment she had experienced from him. I was moved at her misfortunes, and mingled my tears with hers. I then made her go the bath, and supplied her with clothes from my own stores; this being done, I addressed these words to her: 'You are my elder sister, and I shall always look upon you as a mother. During your absence, God has caused the little fortune which has fallen to my portion to prosper; and the occupation I have followed has been that of breeding and bringing up silk-worms. Be assured, that everything I possess is equally yours, and that you have the same power that I possess of disposing of it.

"From this time we lived together in the same house, for many months, in perfect harmony. We often talked about our other sister, and were much surprised at never hearing anything of her. At last, she unexpectedly came and her appearance was as miserable, on her arrival, as that of the eldest had been. Her husband had likewise ill-treated her, and I received her with the same kindness that I had shown to her sister.

"Some time after this, both my sisters, under the pretence, as they said, that they were a considerable burden to me, informed me that they had thoughts of marrying again. I told them, that if the only reason for this intention was the idea that they were an expense to me, I begged they would continue to live with me, without thinking of that, as my income was sufficient to maintain us all three to live in the style and manner suitable to our condition; but I added, 'I rather think you really wish to marry again. If that is the fact, I am very much astonished at it. How can you, after the experience you have had of the small degree of satisfaction and comfort attached to the married state, ever think of entering it a second time? You must be very well aware, that it is not common to meet with a virtuous and good husband. Believe me, it is better and much more agreeable that we should continue to live together.'

"All my remonstrances were thrown away upon them. They had determined in their own minds to marry, and they executed their intentions. But at the end of a few months they came again to me, and made a thousand excuses for not having followed my advice. 'You are, it is true, our youngest sister,' they said, 'but you possess more sense than we. If you will once more receive us into your house, and only consider us as your slaves, we will never again be guilty of the folly we have committed.' 'My dear sisters,' answered I, 'my regard for you is not changed since last we parted. Return, and enjoy with me whatever I possess.' I embraced them, and we lived together as before.

"A year passed, and we continued on the best terms. Observing that Allah had blessed my small fortune, I determined to make a sea-voyage, and risk some part of my property in a commercial speculation. With this view I went with my two sisters to Balsora, where I purchased a vessel ready for sea, and loaded it with the merchandize I had brought with me from Bagdad. We set sail with a favourable wind, and soon reached the Persian Gulf. When we were in the open sea, we steered directly for India; and after twenty days' sail, we came in sight of the shore. The first land that appeared was a very high mountain, at the foot of which we perceived a town of considerable beauty and magnitude. As the wind was fresh, we soon arrived in the harbour, where we cast anchor.

"I was too impatient to go ashore to wait till my sisters were ready to accompany me; I therefore disembarked by myself, and went directly to the gate of the town. I observed rather a numerous guard. Most of the men were sitting down, while others who were standing, held clubs in their hands, and the aspect of them all was so hideous, that it frightened me. I saw, however, that they did not stir, and that even their eyes were motionless. This gave me courage; and on approaching still nearer to them, I perceived they were all petrified. I then entered the town and passed through several streets, in all of which I observed men in every attitude, but they were, like statues, absolutely turned to stone. In the quarter of the town where the merchants resided, I found many shops shut up; and in some that were open I perceived men who were petrified like the rest. I looked up towards the chimneys, and, as I perceived no smoke, I concluded that the people in the houses were as lifeless and motionless as every one in the streets, and that all the inhabitants were changed into stone.

"In a large open place, in the middle of the town, I discovered a great gate, covered with plates of gold, the two folding-doors of which were open; a silk curtain was drawn before it, and I could perceive a lamp suspended from the inside of the gate. After contemplating this building for some time, I decided it must be the palace of the Prince to whom this country belonged. Having been much astonished at not meeting with any one living person, I went into the building in the hope of discovering some one. I drew aside the curtain; and my astonisment was much increased when I saw in the vestibule a number of porters, or guards—some standing, others sitting, and every one of them petrified.

"I passed on to a large court, where there were many people: some seemed in the very act of going out, and others of coming in; nevertheless, they all remained where they stood, since they also were turned to stone, in the same manner as those whom I had before seen. I passed on to a second court, and from thence to a third; but both were deserted, and a horrid silence reigned throughout the place. Advancing to a fourth court, I saw opposite to me a very beautiful building, the windows of which were furnished with a trellis of massive gold. I concluded that this was the apartment of the Queen. I entered, and, going into a large hall, I saw many black petrified ennuchs. I immediately passed on, and went into a chamber very richly decorated, in which I perceived a lady, also transformed into stone: I knew that this was the Queen, by a crown of gold which she had upon her head, and by her necklace of pearls, each jewel in it as large and round as a small nut. I examined these gems very closely, and thought I had never seen any more beautiful.

"I continued to admire, for some time, the riches and magnificence of this apartment, and above all the carpet, the cushions, and a sofa, which was covered with Indian

ZOBEIDÈ DISCOVERS THE YOUNG MAN RECITING THE KORAN.

stuff of cloth-of-gold, upon which there were figures of men and of animals, in silver, of very superior workmanship. From the chamber of the petrified queen I passed on, through many other magnificent apartments of various descriptions, until I came to one of an immense size, in which there was a throne of massive gold, enriched with large emeralds, and raised a few steps above the floor. Upon the throne was a bed covered with very rich stuff, bordered with pearls; but what surprised me more than all the rest was a very brilliant light, which seemed to issue from above the bed. I was curious to discover the cause of this light; I accordingly mounted the throne, and leaning my head forward, I perceived, upon a small stool, a diamond as large as an ostrich's egg, and so perfect that I could discover no defect in it. This diamond sparkled so rarely, that I could scarcely support the brilliancy of it when I looked at it by daylight.

"There was a bolster at each end of the bed, and a large lighted torch, the use of which I did not understand. The presence of these torches, however, led me to conclude that there was some one alive in this superb palace; for I could not suppose that the torches would contiuue burning of themselves. Many other remarkable objects struck my attention in this chamber; but the diamond alone, which I have just mentioned, was of inestimable value.

"As all the doors were either wide open or only half closed, I passed through more apartments as beautiful as those I had before seen. I then went to the offices and store rooms, which were filled with innumerable articles of immense worth; and I was so much engaged in observing all these wonders, that I absolutely forgot myself. I thought neither of my vessel, nor of my sisters, but was anxious only to satisfy my curiosity. In the meantime night came on, and its approach warned me to retire. I then wished to go back as I had come; but it was no easy matter to find my way. I wandered about through the apartments, and finding myself in the large chamber in which stood the throne, the bed, the large diamond, and the lighted torches, I resolved to pass the night there, and early the next morning to go back to my vessel. I threw myself upon the bed, though not without some fear at the reflection that I was alone in this deserted place; and doubtless it was this fear which prevented me from sleeping.

"It was about midnight when I heard a voice like that of a man reading the Koran, in the same manner and tone in which it was the custom to read it in our temples. This gave me great joy. I immediately got up, and, taking a torch to light my footsteps, I went on from one chamber to another on that side whence I heard the voice. I stopped at the door of a cabinet, from which I was sure the voice issued. Laying down the torch on the ground, I looked through a small opening into what appeared to me an apartment dedicated to religion. I perceived within it, as in our temples, a sort of niche, which pointed out the direction in which the Faithful should turn when they say their prayers. There were also some lamps suspended, and also two chandeliers containing large candles, made of white wax, all of which were lighted.

"I perceived, also, a small carpet, spread out in the same manner as those which we are accustomed to kneel upon when we pray. A young man, of a pleasant countenance, was seated upon this carpet, reading aloud, with great attention, from the Koran, which lay before him upon a small desk. Astonished and delighted at this sight, I endeavoured to account to myself for the astonishing fact that he was the only person alive in a town where everyone else was petrified, and I felt sure that there was something very extraordinary in this.

"As the door was scarcely shut, I entered, and, placing myself before the niche, I prayed aloud in the following words:—

"'Praise be to Allah, who hath granted us a prosperous voyage: may He continue to favour us with His protection till we arrive in our own country. Listen to me, O Lord, and grant my prayer!' The young man then cast his eyes upon me, and said: 'I entreat you, good lady, to tell me who you are, and what has brought you to this desolate city? I will inform you, in return, who I am, what has happened to me, and for what reason the inhabitants of this city are reduced to the condition you have seen, and how it happens, also, that I alone am safe, and have escaped the dreadful disaster that has befallen them.'

"I related to him, in a few words, whence I came, what had induced me to make this voyage, and how I had fortunately arrived at this port, after twenty days' sail. I entreated him, in his turn, to fulfil the promise he had made me; and I remarked to him that I had been greatly struck by the frightful desolation which I had observed in all places of the city through which I had passed.

"'Dear lady,' replied the young man, 'have a moment's patience.' With these words he shut the Koran, put it into a rich case, and laid it in the niche. I took this opportunity to observe him very accurately, and I perceived so much grace and beauty in his countenance, that I felt an emotion to which I had been a stranger till then. He made me sit down near him, and before he began his history I could not refrain from saying to him, with an air by which he might perceive the sentiments he had inspired: 'It is impossible for any one to wait with more impatience than with which I await the explanation of the many surprising things which have struck my sight from the moment when I first entered this town; nor can my curiosity be too soon gratified: speak, I conjure you, dear object of my soul; tell me by what miracle you alone are alive amidst a multitude who seem to have died in such an uncommon manner.'

"The young man answered thus: 'You have made it very apparent, madam, by the prayer you have addressed to Allah, that you are not ignorant of the true God. I am now about to inform you of a remarkable instance of His greatness and power. You must know that this city was the capital of a very powerful kingdom, under the rule and government of the King, my father. This Prince, with all his court, the inhabitants of this city, and also all his other subjects, were of the religion of the Magi, idolaters of fire, and of Nardoun, the ancient King of the Giants, who rebelled against Allah.

"'Although both my father and mother were idolaters, I had in my infancy the good fortune to have a preceptress, or nurse, who was of the true religion: she was thoroughly acquainted with the Koran, could repeat it by heart, and explain it perfectly well. 'My Prince,' she would often say to me, 'there is only one true God; beware how you acknowledge and adore any other.' She taught me also to read the Arabic language; and the book which she gave me for this purpose was the Koran. So soon as I was capable of understanding it, she explained to me all the particular points of that admirable book, and made me enter thoroughly into the spirit of it; this she did entirely unknown to my father, and every one besides. She at length died; but not before she had given me all the instruction that was necessary to convince me most completely of the truth of the Mohammedan religion. After her death I remained constant and firm in the sentiments and opinions she had instilled into me; and I felt a perfect abhorrence of the god Nardoun, and the worship of fire.

"'About three years and a few months ago, a voice, like thunder, was heard on a sudden all over the town, so very distinctly that no inhabitant lost a single word. The words spoken were these: 'O PEOPLE! ABANDON THE WORSHIP OF NARDOUN, AND OF FIRE; AND ADORE THE ONLY GOD, WHO SHOWS MERCY.'

"'The same voice was heard three successive years, yet not one person was converted. On the last day of the third year, between three and four o'clock in the morning, every one of the inhabitants was, in an instant, transformed into stone; each remaining in the very posture and spot he then happened to be in. The King my father experienced the same fate: he was changed into the black stone you may behold in a part of the palace; and the Queen my mother experienced a similar transformation.

"'I am the only person on whom Allah has not inflicted this terrible punishment. I have continued to serve him with greater zeal than ever, and I am well persuaded, dear lady, that he has sent you hither for my consolation and comfort. How much do I thank Him for His great mercies! for I own to you, that this solitude was becoming very distressing to me.'

"This narrative, and more particularly the latter part, still further increased my attachment to the Prince. I said to him, 'I can no longer doubt that Providence has conducted me to your country for the express purpose of enabling you to leave this melancholy spot. The vessel in which I arrived may lead you to conclude that I am of some consequence in Bagdad, where I have left property as valuable as that which I have brought. I can venture to offer you a safe retreat there till the powerful Commander of the Faithful, the Vicar of our great Prophet, of whom you must have heard, shall have bestowed upon you all the honours you so well deserve. This illustrious Prince resides at Bagdad; and be assured that directly he is informed of your arrival in his capital, you will acknowledge you have not sought his assistance in vain. It is not possible for you to live any longer in a city where every object you behold is a monument of grief. My vessel is at your service, and you may dispose of it at your pleasure.' He joyfully accepted my offer, and we passed the rest of the night in talking of our voyage.

"As soon as the morning appeared we departed from the palace, and went towards the harbour; where we found my sisters, the captain, and my slaves, all in great alarm for my safety. I introduced my sisters to the Prince, and informed them of the reason that had prevented my return on the preceding day; I related to them also my adventures, told them how I met the young Prince, related his history, and explained the cause of the desolation which reigned over the whole of the beautiful city.

"The sailors were many days engaged in landing the merchandize which I had brought with me, and in shipping in the place of it the most valuable and precious things in silver, gold, and jewels, we could find in the palace. We left behind us all the furniture, and a multitude of articles worked in gold, for want of space to stow them in. Many vessels would have been necessary had we attempted to transport to Bagdad all the riches we saw in this city

"After we had filled the ship with whatever we wished to carry away, we set sail with as favourable a wind as we could desire; having first taken in such a supply of provisions and water as we judged sufficient for our voyage. Of food, indeed, there yet remained a considerable quantity, which we had brought from Bagdad.

"At the commencement of our voyage the young Prince, my sisters, and myself, passed our time together very agreeably every day: but alas! this harmony and good humour did not last long. My sisters became jealous of the good understanding which they could see existed between the Prince and myself; and in a malicious manner asked me what I intended to do with him when we arrived at Bagdad. I was very well aware that they put this question to me only for the purpose of discovering my sentiments. I therefore pretended to give the matter a pleasant turn, and jestingly told them I intended to make him my husband; then turning directly to the Prince, I said to him, 'I entreat you, Prince, to accede to my plan. As soon as we arrive at Bagdad, it is my intention to offer myself to you as the humblest of your slaves, to render you every service in my power, and to acknowledge you as absolute master over my actions.'

"'Lady,' replied the Prince, 'I know not whether you say this in jest or not; but, with respect to myself, I declare most seriously before these ladies, your sisters, that I most willingly accept from this instant the offer you have now made me; not, indeed, that I consider you in the light of my slave, but as my benefactress and wife, and I here claim no power whatever over your actions.'" At this speech my sisters instantly changed colour; and, from this moment, I observed that they no longer continued to have their former regard for me.

"We had already reached the Persian Gulf, and were very near Balsora: if the wind proved strong and favourable I hoped to arrive in that city on the following day. But in the night, while I was fast asleep, my sisters seized the opportunity to throw me into the sea. They treated the Prince in the same manner; and he was unfortunately drowned. For some moments I supported myself on the surface of the water; and by good fortune, or rather by a miracle, I felt firm ground beneath my feet. I waded onwards towards a dark object before me, which, from what the obscurity would suffer me to distinguish, I conjectured to be land. I happily gained the shore; and when the day appeared, I found that I was in a small desert island, about twenty miles from the town of Balsora. I immediately dried my clothes in the sun, and, in walking about, I discovered many sorts of fruit, and also a spring of fresh water. From these helps I had great hopes of being able to preserve my life.

"I then went and rested myself in the shade; and reposing there, I observed a very large and long serpent with wings. It advanced towards me, first moving to one side and then to the other, with its tongue hanging out of its mouth. From this I conjectured it had received some injury. I immediately got up, and perceived that this snake was pursued by another serpent still larger, which held it fast by the end of its tail, and was endeavouring to devour it. The distress of the first serpent excited my compassion; and, instead of running away, I had the boldness and courage to take up a stone which I accidentally found near me, and to let it fall with all my strength on the larger serpent. I struck the monster on its head, and crushed it to pieces. The other, finding itself at

ZOBEIDÈ ON THE ISLAND.

liberty, immediately opened its wings and flew away. I continued to look for some time at this extraordinary animal; and when I lost sight of it, I again seated myself in the shade in another spot, and fell asleep.

"What was my astonishment, when I awoke, to find close by my side a negro woman, of a lively and agreeable expression of countenance, holding by a chain two black dogs. I immediately sat up, and asked her who she was. 'I am,' she replied, 'that serpent which you delivered not long since from its most cruel enemy. I imagined I could not better repay the important services you had rendered me than by the deed I have just now performed. I was well acquainted with the treachery of your sisters; and to avenge the wrong they had done you, as soon as I was delivered by your generous assistance, I collected together a great many of my companions, who are fairies like myself: we immediately transported all the lading of your vessel to your warehouses at Bagdad; and we then sunk the ship. These two black dogs which you see here are your sisters: I have transformed them thus; but this punishment will not be sufficient, and I wish you to treat them in the manner I am going to point out.'

"As she spoke thus, the fairy took the two black dogs and myself in her arms, and transported us to Bagdad, where I found laid up in my warehouse all the riches with which my vessel had been laden. Before the fairy left me she delivered to me the two black dogs, and spoke as follows: 'By order of Him who can dry the seas, and under the penalty of being transformed as these women have been, I command you to inflict upon each of your sisters, every night, one hundred lashes with a whip, as a punishment for the crime they have been guilty of towards you and towards the young Prince whom they have drowned.' I felt myself compelled to promise to execute what she required.

"Every evening from that time I have, though unwillingly, treated them in the manner your Majesty witnessed last night. I endeavour to express to them, by my tears, with what repugnance and grief I fulfil my cruel duty; and in all this you may plainly perceive that I am rather to be pitied than blamed. If there be anything else that regards me, and of which you may wish to be informed, my sister Aminè, by the recital of her history, will afford you every explanation."

The caliph, who had listened with admiration and astonishment to the adventures of Zobeidè, desired his grand vizier Giafar to request the agreeable Aminè to explain by what means she became so covered with scars. Addressing herself to the caliph, that lady began her history in the following manner:—

## THE HISTORY OF AMINÈ.

OMMANDER of the Faithful! That I may not repeat those things which your majesty has already been informed of by my sister, I will only mention that my mother, after taking a house in which she might pass her widowhood in private, bestowed me in marriage on the heir of one of the richest men in this city.

"I had not been married quite a year, when my husband died. I thus became a widow, and was in possession of all his property, which amounted to above ninety thousand sequins. The interest only of this sum would have been quite sufficient to maintain me during the remainder of my life with ease and reputation. As soon as the first six months of my mourning were over, I ordered ten different dresses to be made up, which were so very magnificent that each cost me a thousund sequins; and when my year of mourning was finished I began to wear them.

"I was one day quite alone, and employed about my domestic affairs, when my slaves came and told me that a lady wanted to speak with me. I desired them to let her come in. She appeared to be very far advanced in years. On entering, she saluted me by kissing the ground, and then rising on her knees, she said, 'I entreat you, good lady, to excuse the liberty which I have taken, in coming to importune you; but the assurance I have received of your charitable disposition is the cause of my boldness. I must inform you, most honourable lady, that I have an orphan daughter, who is to be married to-day; we are both strangers, and have not the least acquaintance with any one in this city. This causes us great anxiety and disquietude; because we are loth that the numerous family with which we are going to be connected should imagine that we are altogether unknown, and of no respectability and credit. It is for this reason, most charitable lady, that you would lay us under an infinite obligation, if you would honour the nuptials with your presence. For if you grant us this favour, our own countrywomen will know that we are not looked upon here as poor wretches, when they perceive that a person of your rank has had the condescension to do us so great an honour. But if, alas! you reject our petition, how great will our mortification be! and we know not to whom else to address ourselves!'

"The poor lady was in tears as she delivered this speech, which very much excited my compassion. 'My good mother,' replied I, 'do not distress yourself any more; I shall be very happy to oblige you in the way you wish. Tell me where I must come; I only wish for sufficient time to dress myself properly for such an occasion.' The old woman was so overjoyed at this answer that she would have fallen at my feet and kissed them, if I had not prevented her. 'My dear good lady,' she cried, as she rose, 'Allah will recompense you for the goodness you have shown to those who will always consider themselves as your servants; He will make your bosom overflow with joy from the reflection of your having been the cause of so much joy to us. I will not give you the trouble of remembering the house, but only request that you will have the goodness to go with me in the evening at the time I shall come and call for you. Farewell, lady, till I have the honour of seeing you again.'

"She had no sooner left me, than I went and selected the dress I liked best; I also brought out a necklace of large pearls, a pair of bracelets, some rings, both for the fingers and ears, of the finest and most brilliant diamonds; for I seemed to have a presentiment that something remarkable would happen to me.

"The evening began to close, when the old lady, with a countenance that expressed great joy, arrived at my house. She kissed my hand, and said, 'The parents and relations of my son-in-law have all arrived, and they are ladies of the first consequence in this city. You may now come, whenever it is agreeable to you; and I am ready to serve as your guide. We immediately set out. She walked before to show me the way. I followed with a number of my female slaves, all properly dressed for the occasion. In a wide street, that had been fresh swept and watered, we stopped at a large door, lighted by a lamp, by the help of which I could distinguish this inscription written over the door in letters of gold: 'THIS IS THE CONTINUAL ABODE OF PLEASURES AND OF JOY.' The old lady knocked, and the door instantly opened. My guide conducted me through a court into a large hall, where I was received by a young lady of incomparable beauty. She immediately came towards me; and, after embracing me, she made me sit next to her on a sofa, over which there was a sort of throne, or canopy, formed of precious wood enriched with diamonds. 'You have come here, lady,' she said to me, 'to be present at some nuptials; but I trust we shall have other persons married than those you expect. I have a brother, who is one of the handsomest and most accomplished of men. He is so charmed with the description which he has heard of your beauty that his fate absolutely depends upon you; and he will be most unfortunate and wretched if you do not have pity upon him. He is well acquainted with the position you hold in the world, and I can assure you that he is not unworthy of your alliance. If my prayers can have any weight with you, I readily join them to his, and entreat you not to reject the offer of marriage which he makes you.'

"Since the death of my husband the idea of a second marriage had never come into my head; but I did not posses sufficient resolution to refuse so beautiful a supplicant. I had no sooner given my assent to her prayer by my silence, and a blush which suffused my cheek, than the young lady clapped her hands; a young man immediately entered with so majestic an air, and so much grace, that I thought myself fortunate in having made so excellent a conquest. He seated himself near me; and I discovered, by the conversation that passed between us, that his merit was still greater than his sister had declared it to be.

"When she found that we were very well satisfied with each other, she clapped her hands a second time, and the cadi immediately entered. He drew up a contract for our marriage, signed it, and had it also witnessed by four persons, whom he brought with him for that purpose. My new husband required of me one condition, and it was the only one; this was, that I should neither see nor speak to any other man than himself. He then took an oath that if I observed these terms, I should have every reason to be satisfied with him. Our marriage was then solemnized; and thus I became a principal person where I only thought of being a spectator and a guest.

"About a month after our marriage, having occasion to purchase some silk stuff, I asked leave of my husband to go out and dispatch this business. He immediately granted my request; and I took with me, by way of companion, the old woman of whom I have already spoken, and who lived in the house. Two of my female slaves likewise accompanied me.

"When we had come to that street in which the merchants reside, the old woman said to me, 'Since you are come, my good mistress, to look for silk stuff, I will take you to a young merchant here with whom I am very well acquainted; he has some of every sort; and I assure you that at his warehouse you will find whatever you may want, without fatiguing yourself by running from shop to shop.' I suffered her to conduct me; and we entered a shop where there was a young merchant, comely to look upon. I sat down and requested the old woman to speak for me, and ask him to show me some of the most beautiful silk stuffs he had. The old woman wished me to make the request myself; but I told her that one of the conditions of my marriage was that I should not speak to any man but my husband, and that I did not intend to infringe it.

"The merchant showed me a variety of silks; one of them pleased me more than the rest, and I desired the old woman to ask the price of it. In answer to her he said, 'I will sell it to her for neither silver nor gold; but I will make her a present of it, if she will have the condescension to permit me to kiss her cheek.' I desired the old woman to tell him that his proposal was very rude and impertinent. But, instead of doing as I ordered, she told me she thought that what the merchant required was a matter of no importance; that he did not ask me to speak, but I had only to present my cheek to him, a civility I could show in a moment. My desire to possess the silk was so great that I foolishly followed the old woman's advice. She and my slaves immediately stood up before me, that no person might observe me. I then drew aside my veil, but, instead of kissing me, the merchant gave me such a bite that the blood flowed from the wound.

"The surprise and pain were so great, that I fainted and fell down. I remained so long insensible that the merchant had sufficient opportunity to shut up his shop and make his escape. When I came to myself, I perceived my cheek entirely covered with blood. The old lady and my women had taken the precaution from the first to cover my face with my veil, so that when the people collected to see what was the matter, they could perceive nothing; but believed my fainting fit arose only from a sudden weakness that had seized me.

"The old woman who accompanied me, and who was extremely chagrined at the accident which had happened, endeavoured, nevertheless, to give me courage. 'Indeed, my good mistress,' she said to me, 'I sincerely ask your pardon. I alone am the cause of this misfortune. I brought you to this merchant because he was my countryman, and I could never have thought he would have been guilty of the great wickedness he has committed. But be not downcast; let us lose no time in returning to your house; I will give you a remedy which shall make so perfect a cure in three days that not the least mark or scar shall remain on your cheek.' My fainting had rendered me so weak that I could scarcely walk; I contrived to get home, but on entering my chamber I again fainted. In the meantime the old woman applied the remedy she had promised me; I recovered from the fit, and went immediately to bed.

"Night came, and with it my husband. He perceived that my head was closely muffled, and asked me the reason of it. I told him that I had a bad head-ache, hoping this answer would satisfy him; but he took up a taper, and observing that I had a wound on my cheek, he cried, 'How did this happen?' Now although I had not been guilty of a very great fault, I could not make up my mind to discover the whole affair to him; moreover, I considered it indelicate to enter into details on such a subject. I told him, that as I went that day to purchase the silk I wanted, and which he had given me permission to buy, a porter carrying a bundle of wood had passed so close to me at the corner of a very narrow street that one of the sticks had grazed my cheek; but added that the hurt was a mere trifle.

"On hearing this my husband became exceedingly angry. 'This act,' he cried, 'shall not remain unpunished. I will to-morrow give an order to the officer of the police, to

AMINÈ AND THE LADY.

arrest all these brutes of porters, and hang every one of them.' Fearful of occasioning the death of so many innocent people, I exclaimed, 'Beware, my lord, of committing such an act of injustice: I should be very sorry to be the cause of your doing this; and if I were to be guilty of such a crime, I should think myself unworthy of pardon.' 'Tell me then sincerely,' he said, 'how did you receive your wound?'

"I then asserted that it had been done by a seller of brooms, who came riding by me on his ass with his head turned on one side; and the ass, I said, pushed by me so violently, that I fell down and cut my cheek against a piece of glass.' 'Then,' exclaimed my husband, 'the sun shall not have risen to-morrow morning, before the grand vizier Giafar shall be informed of this insolence. He shall order the death of every broom-seller in the city.' 'In the name of God, dear husband,' I cried, interrupting him, 'I entreat you to pardon those poor men: they are not to blame.' 'What, then, madam,' said he, 'am I to believe? Speak! I insist on hearing the strict truth from your lips.' 'My lord,' I replied, 'I was seized with a giddiness, and fell down; this is the whole matter.'

"My husband lost all patience at these words. 'I have already listened too long to your falsehoods,' he cried; then he clapped his hands, and three slaves immediately came in. 'Drag her from the bed,' he exclaimed, 'and lay her down in the middle of the chamber.' This order was instantly executed by the slaves. One of them held me by the head, another by the feet, and he commanded the third to fetch a sabre. As soon as my husband saw the slave return with his weapon, he cried out: 'Strike! cut her body in two, and throw it into the Tigris, and let it become food for the fishes. This is the punishment I inflict on those upon whom I have bestowed my affections, and who cannot preserve their fidelity to me.' As he observed that the slave hesitated to obey the cruel order, 'Strike,' he cried again; 'why do you stop? what do you wait for?'

"'Lady,' said the slave to me, 'the last moment of your existence is at hand; recollect if there be anything you wish to dispose of before your death.' I requested permission to speak a few words. This prayer was granted. I raised my head, and casting a tender look at my husband, I said, 'Alas! to what a state am I reduced! Must I die in the very prime of my life?' I wished to say more, but my tears and sighs choked my utterance. This appeal had no effect on my husband. On the contrary, he began to reproach me so bitterly, that it would have been useless for me to answer him. I then had recourse to prayers; but, heedless of my entreaties, he ordered the slave to do his duty. At this moment the old woman appeared who had been my husband's nurse, and throwing herself at his feet, endeavoured to appease him. 'My son,' she cried, 'as a reward for having nursed and brought you up, I conjure you to grant me her pardon. Remember that he who slays shall be slain; and that by your present cruelty you will tarnish your reputation, and lower yourself in the estimation of society. What will people not say if you carry out your cruel, inhuman purpose?' She uttered these words in so affecting a manner, and accompanied her entreaties with so many tears, that they made a very strong impression on my husband.

"'Be it so,' he said to his nurse; 'out of regard to you I will spare her life; but I am determined she shall carry some marks to make her remember her crime.' And by his order one of the slaves gave me so many blows with a small pliant cane on my sides and bosom, that the skin and flesh were fearfully torn, and I remained quite senseless. After this the same slaves who had executed his cruel sentence carried me into another house, where I was taken all possible care of by the old woman. I was obliged to keep my bed for four months: at length I was cured; but the scars which I could not prevent you from seeing yesterday have always remained. As soon as I was able to go out, I wished to return to the house which my first husband had bequeathed to me; but I could only discover the place where it had stood, for in the excess of his fury my second husband had not only caused it to be pulled down, but had had the whole street where it stood razed to the ground. This, no doubt, was a most unjustifiable and unheard-of revenge; but against whom could I lodge my complaint? Its author had taken such measures to conceal himself, that I could not discover him. Besides, if I could even find him, I might easily conjecture, from the manner in which he had treated me, that his power was almost absolute. How then was I to complain?

"Entirely desolate, and deprived of every succour, I had recourse to my dear sister Zobeidè, who has already related her history to your majesty. I informed her of my misfortune. She received me with her accustomed goodness, and exhorted me to bear my afflictions with patience. 'Such is the world,' she said: 'it generally deprives us either of our fortunes, our friends, or our lovers, and sometimes even of all.' To prove the truth of her assertion, she gave me an account of the death of the young prince, which had been occasioned by the jealousy of her two sisters. She then informed me in what manner they had been transformed into dogs, and after giving me a thousand proofs of her friendship and regard, she presented to me my youngest sister, who after the death of her mother had come to live with her.

"We gave hearty thanks to Allah for having thus again united us; and we resolved for the future to remain at liberty and never again to separate. We have for a long time continued to pass this tranquil kind of life, and as I have the whole management of the house, I take a pleasure in sometimes going out myself, to purchase the provisions we may have occasion for. This was my errand yesterday. The porter whom I employed to carry home my purchases proved to be possessed of some wit and humour; and we detained him that he might divert us. The three calenders arrived about the beginning of the evening, and requested us to give them shelter till the morning. We received them upon one express condition, which they agreed to: we placed them at our own table, and they amused us with some music in a manner peculiar to themselvės. Then it was that we heard a knock at our gate; and we saw standing there three merchants of Moussoul, of a good handsome appearance, who requested of us the same favour which the calenders had already received; and we granted it them on the same condition, but not one of them observed his promise. Although we had the power to punish them, and might have done so with the greatest justice, we were satisfied with only requiring the recital of each man's history; and we confined our revenge to the act of immediately dismissing them, and thus depriving them of the retreat they had requested.

"The Caliph Haroun Alraschid was very well satisfied with the account he thus received of the circumstances that had excited his curiosity; and he publicly expressed the pleasure and astonishment which these narratives had afforded him. When the caliph had heard what he wished to learn, he wished to give some proofs of his generosity and magnificence to the calenders, who were princes; and also to make the three ladies feel the largeness of his bounty. Without therefore employing the intervention of his grand vizier, he himself said to Zobeidè, 'Has not that fairy whom you first beheld under the form of a serpent, and who has imposed upon you the rigorous law of which you spoke, given you any information where she lives; or rather, has she not promised to see you again, and suffer the two dogs to reassume their natural form?'

"'I ought not to have forgotten, Commander of the Faithful,' replied Zobeidè, 'to have informed you, that the fairy put a small packet of hair into my hands. When she gave it to me, she declared that I should one day have occasion for her presence; that in such a case, if I only burnt two single hairs, she would instantly be with me, although she should happen to be beyond Mount Caucasus.' 'O lady, where is this packet of hair?' asked the caliph. Zobeidè replied that she had always carried it about with her very carefully. She then took it out of her pocket, and opening the lid of the box in which she kept it, showed it to the caliph, who immediately exclaimed, 'Let us make the fairy appear now; you cannot call her more opportunely.'

"Zobeidè consented, some fire was brought, and she directly put the contents of the packet upon it. Immediately the whole palace shook; and the fairy, in the shape of a lady most magnificently dressed, appeared before the caliph. 'Commander of the Faithful,' said she to the prince, 'you see me here, ready to receive your commands. The lady who has called me hither at your desire once rendered me a very important service; to give her a proof of my gratitude, I have punished the perfidy of her sisters by transforming them into dogs, but if your majesty desires it, I will restore them to their natural shape.'

"'Beautiful fairy,' answered the caliph, 'you cannot afford me a greater pleasure than by granting me that favour. I will then find some means of consoling them for so severe a punishment; but in the first place, I have another request to make to you in behalf of the lady who has been so ill treated by her husband. As you are acquainted with almost everything, I do not believe you can be ignorant of that man's name and position. And you will oblige me very much if you mention the name of the cruel wretch who was not satisfied with punishing her so barbarously, but even most unjustly deprived her of all the fortune which belonged to her. I am astonished that so criminal and inhuman an act, a crime committed in open defiance of my power and authority, has never come to my knowledge.'

"'That I may oblige your majesty,' replied the fairy, 'I will restore the two dogs to their original form; I will cure the lady of all her scars so perfectly that no one shall be able to tell she has ever been wounded; and I will then inform you of the name of him who has treated her so ill.'

"The caliph instantly sent to Zobeidè's house for the two dogs. When they appeared, the fairy asked for a cup of water, which was given to her. She pronounced some words over it which the spectators did not understand, and then threw some of the water over Aminè and the two dogs. The latter were immediately changed into two women of most extraordinary beauty, and the scars of the former disappeared. The fairy then addressed the caliph as follows: 'I have, O Commander of the Faithful, only now to discover to you the name of the unknown husband. He is very nearly related to you, for he is no other than Prince Amin, your eldest son, and brother to Prince Mamoun. Enamoured of this lady, from the description he had heard of her beauty, he made use of the pretext you have heard related to get her into his power, and married her. With regard to the blows she received by his order, he is in some measure to be excused. His wife allowed herself to be too easily persuaded; and the different excuses she invented were enough to make him think her much more criminal than she really was. This is all that I can tell you for your satisfaction.' Having concluded this speech, the fairy saluted the caliph, and disappeared.

"Then it was that this great caliph, filled with wonder and astonishment, and well satisfied at the alterations and changes that he had been the means of effecting, performed some actions which will be eternally spoken of. He first of all summoned before him his son, Prince Amin, told him he was acquainted with the secret of his marriage, and informed him of the cause of the wound in Aminè's cheek. The prince did not wait for his father's command to reinstate his wife—he immediately became reconciled to her.

"The caliph next declared that he bestowed his heart and hand upon Zobeidè, and proposed her other three sisters to the calenders, the sons of kings, who joyfully accepted them for their wives. The caliph then assigned to each of the calender-princes a most magnificent palace in the city of Bagdad; he raised them to the first offices of the empire, and admitted them into his council. The principal cadi of Bagdad was summoned, and, with proper witnesses, drew up the forms of marriage; and in bestowing happiness on a number of persons who had experienced incredible misfortunes, the illustrious and magnificent Caliph Haroun Alraschid earned for himself a thousand benedictions."

## THE HISTORY OF SINDBAD THE SAILOR.

IN the reign of the same caliph, Haroun Alraschid, whom I mentioned in my last story, there lived in Bagdad a poor porter, who was named Hindbad. One day, during the most violent heat of summer, he was carrying a heavy load from one extremity of the city to the other. Much fatigued by the length of the way he had already come, and with much ground yet to traverse, he arrived in a street where the pavement was sprinkled with rose-water, and a grateful coolness refreshed the air. Delighted with this mild and pleasant situation, he placed his load on the ground, and took his station near a large mansion. The delicious scent of aloes and frankincense which issued from the windows, and, mixing with the fragrance of the rose-water, perfumed the air; the sound of a charming concert issuing from within the house accompanied by the melody of the nightingales, and other birds peculiar to the climate of Bagdad; all this, added to the smell of different sorts of viands, led Hindbad to suppose that some grand feast was in progress here. He wished to know to whom this house belonged; for, not having frequent occasion to pass that way, he was unacquainted with the names of the inhabitants. To satisfy his curiosity, therefore, he appoached some magnificently-dressed servants who were standing at the door, and inquired who was the master of that mansion. 'What,' replied the servant, 'are you an inhabitant of Bagdad, and do not know that this is the residence of Sindbad the sailor, that famous voyager who has roamed over all the seas under the sun?' The porter, who had heard of the immense riches of Sindbad, could not help comparing the situation of this man,

THE SERVANT INVITES HINDBAD TO THE HOUSE.

whose lot appeared so enviable, with his own deplorable position; and distressed by the reflection, he raised his eyes to heaven, and exclaimed in a loud voice, 'Almighty Creator of all things, deign to consider the difference that there is between Sindbad and myself. I suffer daily a thousand ills, and have the greatest difficulty in supplying my wretched family with bad barley bread, whilst the fortunate Sindbad lavishes his riches in profusion, and enjoys every pleasure. What has he done to obtain so happy a destiny, or what crime has been mine to merit a fate so rigorous?' As he said this he struck the ground with his foot, like a man entirely abandoned to despair. He was still musing on his fate, when a servant came towards him from the house, and taking hold of his arm, said, 'Come, follow me; my master Sindbad wishes to speak with you.'

"Hindbad was not a little surprised at the compliment thus paid him. Remembering the words he had just uttered, he began to fear that Sindbad sent for him to reprimand him, and therefore he tried to excuse himself from going. He declared that he could not leave his load in the middle of the street. But the servant assured him that it should be taken care of, and pressed him so much to go that the porter could no longer refuse.

"His conductor led him into a spacious room, where a number of persons were seated round a table, which was covered with all kinds of delicate viands. In the principal seat sat a grave and venerable personage, whose long white beard hung down to his breast; and behind him stood a crowd of officers and servants ready to wait on him. This person was Sindbad. Quite confused by the number of the company and the magnificence of the entertainment, the porter made his obeisance with fear and trembling. Sindbad desired him to approach, and seating him at his right hand, helped him himself to the choicest dishes, and made him drink some of the excellent wine with which the sideboard was plentifully supplied.

"Towards the end of the the repast, Sindbad, who perceived that his guests had done eating, began to speak; and addressing Hindbad by the title 'my brother,' the common salutation amongst the Arabians when they converse familiarly, he inquired the name and profession of his guest. 'Sir,' replied the porter, 'my name is Hindbad.' 'I am happy to see you,' said Sindbad, 'and can answer for the pleasure the rest of the company also feel at your presence; but I wish to know from your own lips what it was you said just now in the street:' for Sindbad, before he went to dinner, had heard from the window every word of Hindbad's ejaculation, which was the reason of his sending for him. At this request, Hindbad, full of confusion, hung down his head, and replied, 'Sir, I must confess to you that, put out of humour by weariness and exhaustion, I uttered some indiscreet words, which I entreat you to pardon.' 'Oh,' resumed Sindbad, 'do not imagine that I am so unjust as to have any resentment on that account. I feel for your situation, and instead of reproaching you, I pity you heartily; but I must undeceive you on one point respecting my own history, in which you seem to be in error. You appear to suppose that the riches and comforts I enjoy have been obtained without any labour or trouble. In this you are mistaken. Before attaining my present position, I have endured for many years the greatest mental and bodily sufferings that you can possibly conceive. Yes, gentlemen,' continued the venerable host, addressing himself to the whole company, 'I assure you that my sufferings have been so acute that they might deprive the greatest miser of his love of riches. Perhaps you have heard only a confused account of my adventures in the seven voyages I have made on different seas; and as an opportunity now offers, I will, with your leave, relate the dangers I have encountered; and I think the story will not be uninteresting to you.'

"As Sindbad was going to relate his history chiefly on the porter's account, he gave orders, before he began it, to have his guest's burden, which had been left in the street, brought in, and placed where Hindbad should wish. When this matter had been adjusted, he spoke in these words:—

## The First Voyage of Sindbad the Sailor.

SQUANDERED the greater part of my paternal inheritance in youthful dissipation; but at length I saw my folly, and became convinced that riches were not of much use, when applied to such purposes as those to which I had devoted them; and I reflected that the time I spent in dissipation was of still greater value than gold, and that nothing could be more truly deplorable than poverty in old age. I recollected the words of the wise Solomon, which my father had often repeated to me,—that it is better to be in the grave than poor. Feeling the truth of this reflection, I resolved to collect the small remains of my patrimony and to sell my goods by auction. I then formed connections with some merchants who trafficked by sea, and consulted those who appeared best able to give me advice. In short, I determined to employ to some profit the small sum I had remaining; and no sooner was this resolution formed than I put it into execution. I repaired to Balsora, where I embarked with several merchants in a vessel which had been equipped at our united expense.

"We set sail, and steered towards the East Indies by the Persian Gulf, which is formed by the coast of Arabia Felix on the right, and the Persian shore on the left. It is commonly supposed to be seventy leagues in breadth in the widest part. Beyond this gulf, the Western Sea or Indian Ocean is very spacious, and is bounded by the coast of Abyssinia, extending in length four thousand five hundred leagues to the island of Vakvak. I was at first troubled with the sickness that attacks voyagers by sea; but I soon recovered my health, and I have never afterwards been subject to that malady. In the course of our voyage we touched at several islands, and sold or exchanged our merchandise. One day, when our vessel was in full sail, we were unexpectedly becalmed before a small island which appeared just above the water, and in its verdure resembled a beautiful meadow. The captain ordered the sails to be lowered, and gave permission to those passengers who wished it to go ashore, and of this number I formed one. But while we were regaling ourselves with eating and drinking, and enjoying ourselves after the fatigues we had endured at sea, the island suddenly trembled, and we felt a severe shock.

"The people who had remained in the ship perceived the earthquake in the island, and immediately called us to re-embark as soon as possible, or we should all perish; for that what we supposed to be an island was nothing but the back of a whale. The most active of the party jumped into the boat, whilst others threw themselves into the water, to swim to the ship; as for me, I was still on the island, or, more properly speaking, on the whale, when it dived below the surface; and I had only time to seize a piece of wood which had been brought to make a fire with, when the monster disappeared beneath the waves. Meantime the captain, willing to avail himself of a fair breeze, which had sprung up, set sail with those who had reached his vessel, and left me to the mercy of the waves. I remained in this deplorable situation the whole of that day and the following night. On the return of morning, I had neither strength nor hope left; but a breaker happily threw me on an island. The shore was high and steep, and I should have found great difficulty in landing, had not some roots of trees, which fortune seemed to have furnished for my preservation, assisted me. I threw myself on the ground, where I continued lying more than half dead till the sun rose.

"Though extremely enfeebled by the fatigues I had undergone, I still tried to creep about in search of some herb or fruit that might satisfy my hunger. I found some, and had also the good luck to meet with a stream of excellent water, which contributed not a little to my recovery. Having in a great measure regained my strength, I began to explore the island, and entered a beautiful plain, where I perceived a horse grazing. I bent my steps towards it, trembling between fear and joy, for I could not ascertain whether I was advancing to safety or perdition. I remarked, as I approached, that the creature was a mare tied to a stake; her beauty attracted my attention; but whilst I was admiring her I heard from underground the voice of a man, who shortly after appeared, and, coming to me, asked me who I was. I related my adventure to him; whereupon he took me by the hand, and led me into a cave, where I found some other persons, who were not less astonished to see me than I was to meet them there.

"I ate some food which they offered me; and upon my asking them what they did in a place which appeared so barren, they replied that they were grooms to King Mihragè, who was the sovereign of that isle; and that they came hither every year, about this season, with some mares belonging to the king, for the purpose of having a breed between them and a sea-horse which came on shore at that spot. They tied up the mares as I had seen, because they were obliged almost immediately, by their cries, to drive back the sea-horse, which otherwise began to tear the mares in pieces. As soon as the mares were with foal they carried them back, and the colts were called sea-colts, and set apart for the king's use. They told me that the morrow was the day fixed for their departure, and if I had been one day later I must certainly have perished; because they lived so far off that it was impossible to reach their habitations without a guide.

"Whilst they were talking to me, the horse rose out of the sea, as they had described, and immediately attacked the mares. He would have torn them to pieces; but the grooms began to make such a noise that he let go his prey, and again plunged into the ocean.

"The following day they returned, with the mares, to the capital of the island, whither I accompanied them. On our arrival, King Mihragè, to whom I was presented, asked me who I was, and by what chance I had reached his dominions; and when I had satisfied his curiosity, he expressed pity at my misfortune. At the same time, he gave orders that I should be taken care of, and be supplied with everything I might want. These orders were executed in a manner that proved alike the king's generosity and the exactness of his officers.

"As I was a merchant, I associated with persons of my own profession. I sought, in particular, such as were foreigners, partly to hear some intelligence of Bagdad, and partly in the hope of meeting some one with whom I could return; for the capital of King Mihragè is situated on the sea-coast, and has a beautiful port, where vessels from all parts of the world daily arrive. I also sought the society of the Indian sages, and found great pleasure in their conversation; but this did not prevent me from attending at court very regularly, nor from conversing with the governors of provinces, and some less powerful kings, tributaries of Mihragè, who were about his person. They asked me a thousand questions about my country; and I was not less inquisitive about the laws and customs of their different states, or whatever particulars appeared to merit my curiosity.

"In the dominions of King Mihragè there is an island, called Cassel. I had been told that in that island there was heard every night the sound of cymbals, and this had given rise to the sailors' opinion that Degial had chosen that spot for his residence. I felt a great desire to witness these wonders. During my voyage, I also saw some fish of one and two hundred cubits in length, which occasion much fear, but do no harm: they are so timid that men frighten them away by beating on a board. I remarked also some other fish that were not above a cubit long, and whose heads resembled that of an owl.

"After I returned, as I was standing one day near the port, I saw a ship come towards the land. When the crew had cast anchor, they began to unload its goods, and the merchants to whom the cargo belonged took it away to their warehouses. Happening to cast my eyes on some of the packages, I saw my name written thereon, and, having attentively examined them, I recognised them as the same which I had embarked in the ship in which I left Balsora. I also recollected the captain; but as I felt assured that he thought me dead, I went up to him, and asked him to whom those parcels belonged. 'I had on board with me,' replied he, 'a merchant of Bagdad, named Sindbad. One day, when we were near an island, or at least what appeared to be one, he went ashore, with some other passengers, on this supposed island, which was nothing but an enormous whale that had fallen asleep on the surface of the water. The fish no sooner felt the heat of a fire they lighted on its back to cook their provisions, than it began to move and flounce about in the sea. Most of the persons who were on it were drowned, and the unfortunate Sindbad was one of the number. These parcels belonged to him; and I have resolved to sell them, that if I meet with any of his family I may be able to pay over to them the profit I shall have made on the principal.' 'Captain,' said I then, 'I am that Sindbad, whom you supposed dead, but who is still alive; and these parcels are my property and merchandise.'

"When the captain of the vessel heard me speak thus, he exclaimed, 'Great God! whom shall I trust? There is no longer truth in man! With my own eyes I saw Sindbad perish; the passengers I had on board were also witnesses of his death; and you have the assurance to say that you are that same Sindbad? What impudence is this! At first sight you appeared a man of probity and honour; yet you assert an

SINDBAD IN THE TUB.

impious falsity, to possess yourself of some merchandise which does not belong to you.' 'Have patience,' replied I, 'and do me the favour to listen to what I have to say.' 'Well,' cried he, 'what can you have to say? Speak, and I will hear.' I then related in what manner I had been saved, and by what accident I had met with King Mihragè's grooms, who had brought me to his court.

"The captain was rather staggered at my discourse, but was soon convinced that I was not an impostor; for some people who arrived from his ship knew me, and began to congratulate me on my fortunate escape. At last he recollected me himself, and embracing me, exclaimed, 'Heaven be praised that you have happily escaped from that great peril. I cannot express the pleasure I feel at your safety. Here are your goods; take them, for they are yours, and do with them what you like.' I thanked him, and praised his honourable conduct, and, by way of acknowledgment, I begged him to accept part of the merchandise; but he refused to take anything.

"I selected the most precious and valuable things in my bales as presents for King Mihragè. As this prince had been informed of my misfortunes, he asked me where I had obtained such rare curiosities. I related to him the manner in which I had recovered my property, and he had the condescension to express his joy at my good fortune. He accepted my presents, and gave me others of far greater value. Hereupon I took my leave of him, and re-embarked in the same vessel in which I had come; having first exchanged what merchandise remained for products of the country, consisting of aloes and sandal wood, camphor, nutmegs, cloves, pepper, and ginger. We touched at several islands, and at last landed at Balsora, from whence I came here, having realised about a hundred thousand sequins. I returned to my family, and was received by them with the joy of true and sincere friendship. I purchased slaves of both sexes, and bought a magnificent house and grounds. Thus I established myself, determined to forget the hardships I had endured, and to enjoy the pleasures of life."

Thus Sindbad concluded the story of his first voyage; and he ordered the musicians to go on with their concert, which he had interrupted by the recital of his history. The company continued to feast till night approached; and when it was time to separate, Sindbad ordered a purse containing a hundred sequins to be brought to him, and gave it to the porter, with these words: "Take this, Hindbad; return to your home, and come again to-morrow, to hear the continuation of my history." The porter retired quite confused by the honour conferred on him, and the present he had received. The account he gave of his adventure to his wife and children rejoiced them greatly, and they did not fail to return thanks to Providence for the bounties bestowed by means of Sindbad.

"Hindbad dressed himself in his best clothes on the following day, and betook himself to the house of his liberal patron, who received him with smiling looks and a friendly air. As soon as the guests all had arrived the feast was served, and they sat down to eat. When the repast was over, Sindbad thus addressed his guests. 'My friends, I request you to have the kindness to listen to me while I relate the adventures of my second voyage. They are more worthy of your attention than were those of my first.' The company were silent, and Sindbad began to speak as follows:"

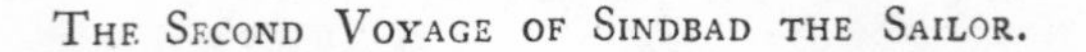

## The Second Voyage of Sindbad the Sailor.

S I had the honour to tell you yesterday, I had resolved, after my first voyage, to pass the rest of my days in tranquillity at Bagdad. But I soon grew weary of an idle life; the desire of seeing foreign countries and carrying on some traffic by sea returned. I bought merchandise which I thought likely to answer in the enterprise I meditated; and I set off a second time with some merchants whose probity I could rely on. We embarked in a good vessel, and recommending ourselves to the care of Allah, we began our voyage.

"We went from island to island, and bartered our goods very profitably. One day we landed on one which was covered with a variety of fruit trees, but so desert that we could not discover any habitation, or the trace of a human being. We walked in the meadows, and along the brooks that watered them; and whilst some of my companions were amusing themselves with gathering fruits and flowers, I took out some of the wine and provisions I had brought with me, and seated myself by a little stream under some trees, which afforded a delightful shade. I made a good meal of what I had with me; and when I had satisfied my hunger, sleep gradually stole over my senses. I cannot say how long I slept, but when I awoke the ship was no longer in view. I was much surprised at this circumstance, and rose to look for my companions, but they were all gone; and I could only just descry the vessel in full sail, at such a distance that I soon lost sight of it.

"You may imagine what were my reflections when I found myself in this dismal state. I thought I should have died with grief; I groaned and shrieked aloud; I beat my head and threw myself on the ground, where I remained a long time, overwhelmed by a rushing current of thoughts, each more distressing than the last. I reproached myself a thousand times for my folly in not being contented with my first voyage, which ought to have satisfied my craving for adventure; but all my regrets were of no avail, and my repentance came too late. At length I resigned myself to the will of Heaven; and not knowing what would become of me, I ascended a high tree, from whence I looked on all sides, to try if I could not discover some object to inspire me with hope. Casting my eyes towards the sea, I could discern only water and sky; but perceiving on the land side a white spot, I descended from the tree, and taking up the remainder of my provisions, I walked towards the object, which was so distant that at first I could not distinguish what it was. As I approached, I perceived it to be a ball of prodigious size, and when I got near enough to touch it, I found it was soft. I walked round it to see if there was an opening, but could find none; and the ball appeared so smooth that any attempt to climb it would have been fruitless. Its circumference might be about fifty paces.

"The sun was then near setting; the air grew suddenly dark, as if obscured by a thick cloud. I was surprised at this change, but how much did my amazement increase, when I perceived it to be occasioned by a bird of most extraordinary size, which was flying towards me. I recollected having heard sailors speak of a bird called a roc; and I concluded that the great white ball which had drawn my attention must be the egg of this bird. I was not mistaken; for shortly afterwards it lighted on the white ball, and placed itself as if to sit upon it. When I saw this huge fowl coming I drew near to the egg, so that I had one of the claws of the bird just before me; this claw was as big as the trunk of a large tree. I tied myself to the claw with the linen of my turban, in hopes that the roc, when it took its flight the next morning, would carry me with it out of that desert island. My project succeeded; for at break of day the roc flew away, and bore me to such a height that I could no longer distinguish the earth; then it descended with such rapidity that I almost lost my senses. When the roc had alighted, I quickly untied the knot that bound me to its foot, and had scarcely released myself when it darted on a serpent of immeasurable length, and seizing the snake in its beak, flew away.

"The place in which the roc left me was a very deep valley, surrounded on all sides by mountains of such height that their summits were lost in the clouds, and so steep that there was no possibility of climbing them. This was a fresh embarrassment; for I had no reason to rejoice at my change of situation, when I compared it with the island I had left.

"As I walked along this valley, I remarked that it was strewn with diamonds, some of which were of astonishing size. I amused myself for some time by examining them, but soon perceived from afar some objects which destroyed my pleasure, and created in me great fear. These were a great number of serpents, so long and large that the smallest of them would have swallowed an elephant with ease. During the daytime they hid themselves in caves from the roc, their mortal enemy, and only came out when it was dark. I passed the day in walking about the valley, resting myself occasionally when an opportunity offered; and when the sun set I retired into a small cave, where I thought I should be in safety. I closed the entrance, which was low and narrow, with a stone large enough to protect me from the serpents, but which yet allowed a little light to pass into the cave. I supped on part of my provisions, and could plainly hear the serpents which began to make their appearance. Their tremendous hissings caused me great fear, and, as you may suppose, I did not pass a very quiet night. When the day appeared the serpents retired. I left my cave with trembling, and may truly say that I walked a long time on diamonds, without feeling the least desire to possess them. At last I sat down, and notwithstanding my agitation, after making another meal off my provisions I fell asleep, for I had not once closed my eyes during all the previous night. I had scarcely began to doze, when something falling near me, with a great noise, awoke me. It was a large piece of fresh meat, and at the same moment I saw a number of other pieces rolling down the rocks from above.

"I had always supposed the account to be fictitious which I had heard related by seamen and others, of the Valley of Diamonds, and of the means by which merchants procured these precious gems. I now knew it to be true. The method of proceeding is this: The merchants go to the mountains which surround the valley about the time that the eagles hatch their young. They cut large pieces of meat, and throw them into the valley; and the diamonds on which the lumps of meat fall stick to them. The eagles, which are larger and stronger in that country than in any other, seize these pieces of meet, to carry to their young at the top of the rocks. The merchants then run to the eagles' nests, and by various noises oblige the birds to retreat, and then take the diamonds that have stuck to the pieces of meat. This is the method they employ to procure the diamonds from the valley, which is inaccessible on every side. I had supposed it impossible ever to leave this valley, and began to look on it as my tomb; but now I changed my opinion, and turned my thoughts to the preservation of my life. I began by collecting the largest diamonds I could find, and with these I filled my leather bag in which I had carried my provisions. I then took one of the largest pieces of meat, and tied it tight round me with the linen of my turban: in this state I laid myself on the ground, tightly securing my leather bag round me.

"I had not been long in this position before the eagles began to descend, and each seized a piece of meat, with which it flew away. One of the strongest darted on the piece to which I was attached, and carried me up with it to its nest. The merchants then began their cries to frighten away the eagles; and when they had obliged the birds to quit their prey, one of them approached, but was much surprised and alarmed on seeing me. He soon, however, recovered from his fear; and instead of inquiring by what means I came there, began to quarrel with me for trespassing on what he called his property. 'You will speak to me with pity instead of anger,' said I, 'when you learn by what means I reached this place. Console yourself; for I have diamonds for you as well as for myself; and my diamonds are more valuable than those of all the other merchants added together. I have myself chosen some of the finest at the bottom of the valley, and have them in this bag.' Saying this, I showed him my store. I had scarcely finished speaking, when the other merchants perceiving me, flocked round me with great astonishment, and their wonder was still greater when I related my history. They were less surprised at the stratagem I had employed to save myself than at my courage in attempting to put it in execution.

"They conducted me to the place where they lived together, and on seeing my diamonds they all expressed their admiration, and declared they had never seen any to equal them in size or quality. The nest into which I had been transported belonged to one of these merchants, for each merchant has his own; I entreated him, therefore, to choose for himself from my stock as many as he pleased. He contented himself with taking only one, and that too was the smallest I had, and as I pressed him to take more, without fear of wronging me, he refused. 'No,' he said, 'I am very well satisfied with this, which is sufficiently valuable to spare me the trouble of making any more voyages to complete my little fortune.'

"I passed the night with these merchants, to whom I recounted my history a second time, for the satisfaction of those who had not heard it before. I could scarcely contain

SINDBAD IN THE VALLEY OF DIAMONDS.

myself for joy, when I reflected on the perils that I had gone through; it appeared as if my present state was but a dream, and I could not believe that I had nothing more to fear.

"The merchants had been for some days in that spot, and as they now appeared to be contented with the diamonds they had collected, we set off all together on the following day, and travelled over high mountains, which were infested by prodigious serpents; but we had the good fortune to escape them. We reached the nearest port in safety, and from thence embarked for the Isle of Roha, where the tree grows from which camphor is extracted. This tree is so large and thick that a hundred men may easily take shelter under it. The juice of which the camphor is formed runs out at an incision made at the top of the tree, and is received in a vessel, where it remains till it acquires a proper consistency, and becomes what is called camphor. After the juice has been extracted the tree withers and dies.

"The rhinoceros is a native of this island: it is a smaller animal than the elephant, yet larger than the buffalo. It has a horn on its nose about a cubit in length; this horn is solid, and cut through the middle from one extremity to the other; and on it are several white lines, which represent the figure of a man. The rhinoceros fights with the elephant, and piercing his enemy's body with its horn, carries him off on his head; but as the fat and blood of the elephant run down on his eyes and blind him, he falls on the ground; and what is more wonderful than all, the roc comes and seizes them both in its claws, and flies away with them to feed its young.

"I will pass over several other peculiarities of this island, lest I should tire you. I exchanged some of my diamonds for valuable merchandise. We set sail for other islands; and at last, after having touched at several ports, we reached Balsora, from which place I returned to Bagdad. The first thing I did was to distribute a great deal of money amongst the poor; and I enjoyed with credit and honour the remainder of my immense riches, which I had acquired with much labour and fatigue."

Here Sindbad closed the relation of his second voyage. He again ordered a hundred sequins to be given to Hindbad, whom he invited to come on the morrow to hear the history of the third.

The guests returned home: and the following day repaired at the usual hour to the house of Sindbad; where the porter, who had almost forgotten his poverty, also made his appearance. They sat down to table; and when the repast was ended, Sindbad requested the company to attend to him, and he began to tell the story of his third voyage.

## The Third Voyage of Sindbad the Sailor.

HE agreeable life I led in my prosperity soon obliterated the remembrance of the dangers I had encountered in my two voyages; but as I was in the prime of life, I grew tired of passing my days in slothful repose; and banishing all thoughts of the perils I might have to face, I set off from Bagdad with some rich merchandise of the country, which I carried with me to Balsora. There I again embarked with other merchants. We made a long voyage, and touched at several ports, and by these means carried on a very profitable commerce.

"One day, as we were sailing in the open sea, we were overtaken by a violent tempest, which made us lose our reckoning. The storm continued for several days, and drove us near an island, which the captain would gladly have avoided approaching, but we were under the necessity of casting anchor there. When the sails were furled, the captain told us that this region and some of the neighbouring isles were inhabited by hairy savages, who would come to attack us. He further declared that although they were only dwarfs, we must not attempt to make any resistance; for as their number was inconceivable, if we should happen to kill one they would pour upon us like locusts, and destroy us. This account put the whole crew in a terrible consternation, and we were too soon convinced that the captain had spoken the truth. We saw coming towards us an innumerable multitude of hideous savages, entirely covered with red hair, and about two feet high. They threw themselves into the sea, and swam to the ship, which they soon completely surrounded. They spoke to us as they approached, but we could not understand their language. They began to climb the sides and ropes of the vessel with so much swiftness and agility that their feet scarcely seemed to touch them, and soon came swarming upon the deck.

"You may imagine the situation we were in, not daring to defend ourselves, nor even to speak to these intruders, to endeavour to avert the impending danger. They unfurled the sails, cut the cable from the anchor, and after dragging the ship ashore, obliged us to disembark; then they conveyed us to another island, from whence they had come. All voyagers carefully avoided this island, for the dismal reason you are going to hear; but our misfortune had led us there, and we were obliged to submit to our fate.

"We left the shore, and penetrating farther into the island, we found some fruits and herbs, which we ate to prolong our lives as much as possible; for we all expected to be sacrificed. As we walked, we perceived at some distance a large building, towards which we bent our steps. It was a large and lofty palace, with folding gates of ebony, which opened as we pushed them. We entered the court-yard, and saw facing us a vast apartment, with a vestibule, on one side of which was a large heap of human bones, while on the opposite side appeared a number of spits for roasting. We trembled at this spectacle; and as we were fatigued with walking, our legs failed us, and we fell on the earth, where we remained a considerable time, paralysed by fear and unable to move.

"The sun was setting; and while we were in the piteous state I have described, the door of the apartment suddenly opened with a loud noise, and there entered a black man of frightful aspect, and as tall as a large palm-tree. In the middle of his forehead gleamed a single eye, red and fiery as a burning coal; his front teeth were long and sharp, and projected from his mouth, which was as wide as that of a horse, with the under lip hanging on his breast; his ears resembled those of an elephant, and covered his shoulders, and his long and curved nails were like the talons of an immense bird. At the sight of this hideous giant we all fainted, and remained a long time like dead men.

"At last our senses returned, and we saw him seated under the vestibule, glaring at us with his piercing eye. When he had scanned us well, he advanced towards us, and stretching forth his hand to seize me, took me up by the poll, and turned me round every way, as a butcher would handle the head of a sheep. After having well examined me, finding me meagre, and little more than skin and bone, he released me. He took up each of my companions in their turn, and examined them in the same manner, and as the captain was the fattest of the party, he held him in one hand as I should hold a sparrow, and with the other ran a spit through his body; then kindling a large fire he roasted him, and ate him for his supper in the inner apartment to which he retired. When he had finished his repast, he returned to the vestibule, where he lay down to sleep, and snored louder than thunder. He did not wake till the next morning; but we passed the night in the most agonising suspense. When daylight returned the giant awoke, and went abroad, leaving us in the palace.

"When we supposed him at some distance, we began to give vent to our lamentations; for the fear of disturbing the giant had kept us silent during the night. The palace resounded with our groans. Although there were many of us, and we had but one common enemy, the idea of delivering ourselves by his death never occurred to any one of us. But however difficult of accomplishment such an enterprise might have been, we ought to have made the attempt at once.

"We deliberated on various methods of action, but could not determine on any; and submitting ourselves to the will of Allah, we passed the day in walking over the island, and eating what plants and fruit we could meet with, as we had done the preceding day. Towards evening we sought for some shelter in which to pass the night, but finding none we were obliged to return to the palace.

"The giant duly returned to sup on one of our companions. After his hideous meal he fell asleep and snored till day-break, when he arose and went out as before. Our situation appeared to be so hopeless that some of my comrades were on the point of throwing themselves into the sea, rather than be sacrificed by the horrible monster; and they advised the rest to follow their example; but one of the company thus addressed them: 'We are forbidden to kill ourselves; and even were such an act permitted, would it not be more rational to endeavour to destroy the barbarous giant, who has destined us to such a cruel death?'

"As I had already formed a project of that nature, I now communicated it to my fellow-sufferers, who approved of my design. 'My friends,' said I then, 'you know that there is a great deal of wood on the sea shore. If you will take my advice, we can make some rafts, and when they are finished we will leave them in a proper place till we can find an opportunity to make use of them. In the meantime we can put in execution the design I propose to you to rid ourselves of the giant. If my stratagem succeeds, we may wait here with patience till some vessel passes, by means of which we may quit this fatal isle; if, on the contrary, we fail, we shall have recourse to our rafts, and put to sea. I own that, in exposing ourselves to the fury of the waves on such fragile barks, we run a great hazard of losing our lives; but if we are destined to perish, is it not preferable to be swallowed up by the sea than to be buried in the entrails of that monster, who has already devoured two of our companions?' My advice was approved by all; and we immediately built some rafts, each large enough to support three persons.

"We returned to the palace towards evening, and the giant arrived a short time after us. Again one of our party was sacrificed to his inhuman appetite. But we were soon revenged on him for his cruelty. After he had finished his horrible meal, he laid himself down as usual to sleep. As soon as we heard him snore, nine of the most courageous amongst us, and myself, took each a spit, and heating the points red hot, thrust them into his eye, and blinded him.

"The pain which the giant suffered made him groan hideously. He suddenly raised himself, and threw his arms about on all sides, to seize some one, and sacrifice him to his rage; but fortunately we had time to get at some distance from him, and to throw ourselves on the ground in places where he could not set his feet on us. After having sought us in vain, he at last found the door, and went out, bellowing with pain.

"We quitted the palace immediately after the giant, and repaired to that part of the shore where our rafts lay. We set them afloat, and waited till daybreak before embarking on them, in case we should see the giant approach, with some guide to lead him to us; but we hoped that if he did not make his appearance by that time, and if his cries and groans, which now resounded through the air, ceased, we might suppose him dead; and in that case we proposed remaining in the island till we could obtain some safer mode of transport. But the sun had scarcely risen above the horizon, when we perceived our cruel enemy, accompanied by too giants nearly as huge as himself, who led him, and a great number of others, who walked very rapidly before him.

"At this sight we immediately ran to our rafts and rowed away as fast as possible. The giants seeing this, provided themselves with large stones, hastened to the shore, and even ventured to their waists into the sea, to hurl the stones at us, which they did so adroitly that they sunk all the rafts excepting that I was upon. Thus I and two companions were the only men who escaped, the others being all drowned.

"As we rowed with all our strength, we were soon beyond reach of the stones.

"When we had gained the open sea, we were tossed about at the mercy of the winds and waves, and we passed that day and night in the most cruel suspense; but on the morrow we had the good fortune to be thrown on an island, where we landed with great joy. We found some excellent fruit, which soon recruited our exhausted strength.

"When night came on we went to sleep on the sea shore; but were soon awakened by the noise made on the ground by the scales of an immense serpent, long as a palm tree. It was so near to us that it devoured one of my companions, notwithstanding the efforts he made to extricate himself from its deadly grasp; for the serpent shook him several times, and then crushing him on the earth, quickly swallowed him.

"My other comrade and myself immediately took to flight; and although we had fled some distance, we heard a noise which made us suppose that the serpent was crushing the bones of the unhappy man it had destroyed. On the following day we perceived our suspicions had been well founded. 'O Allah!' I then exclaimed, 'what a horrible fate

AFTER SUPPER.

will be ours! Yesterday we were rejoicing at our escape from the cruelty of a giant and the fury of the waves, and to-day we are again terrified by a peril not less dreadful.'

"As we walked along, we remarked a large and high tree, on which we proposed to pass the following night, hoping we might there be in safety. We ate some fruit as we had done on the preceding day, and at the approach of night we climbed the tree. We soon heard the serpent which came hissing to the foot of the tree; it raised itself against the trunk, and meeting with my companion, who had not climbed so high as I, it swallowed him and retired.

"I remained on the tree till daybreak, when I came down, more dead than alive: indeed I could only anticipate the same fate. This idea chilled me with horror, and I advanced some paces to throw myself into the sea; but as life is sweet as long as it will last, I resisted this impulse of despair, and submitted myself to the will of Allah, who disposes of our lives as is best for us.

"I collected a great quantity of small wood and furze; and tying it in faggots, put it round the tree in a large circle, and tied some across to cover my head. I enclosed myself within this circle when the evening came on, and sat down with the dismal consolation that I had done all in my power to preserve my life. The serpent returned with the intention of devouring me, but he could not succeed, being prevented by the rampart I had formed. The whole night he was watching me as a cat watches a mouse; at last day returned, and the serpent retired; but I did not venture out of my fortress, till the sun shone.

"I was so fatigued with watching, as well as with the exertion of forming my retreat, and had suffered so much from the enemey's pestilential breath, that death appeared preferable to a repetition of such horror. I again ran towards the sea with the intention of putting an end to my existence: but Allah pitied my condition; and at the moment that I was going to throw myself into the sea, I descried a vessel at a great distance. I cried out with all my strength, and unfolded and waved my linen turban, to attract the attention of those on board. This had the desired effect: all the crew saw me, and the captain sent a boat to bring me off.

"As soon as I was on board, the merchants and seamen were eager to learn by what chance I had reached that desert island; and after I had related to them all that had happened, the oldest of them told me that they had often heard of the giants who lived in that island; that they were cannibals, and that they devoured men raw as well as roasted. With regard to the serpents, they added that there were many in the island, which hid themselves in the day, and roamed forth for prey at night.

"They expressed their joy at my fortunate escape from so many perils; then as they supposed I must be in want of something to eat, they pressed upon me the best they had; and the captain, observing that my clothes were much torn, had the generosity to give me some of his.

"We remained a considerable time at sea, and touched at several islands; at length we landed on the Isle of Salahat, where the sandal wood is cultivated which is much used in medicine. We entered the port, and cast anchor, and the merchants began to unload their goods to sell or exchange them. One day, the captain called me to him, and said, 'Brother, I have in my possession some goods which belonged to a merchant who was for some time on board my ship. As this merchant is dead, I am going to have them valued, that I may render an account of them to his heirs, should I ever meet them.' The bales of which he spoke were already upon deck. He showed them to me, saying, 'These are the goods; I wish you to take charge of them, and traffic with them, and you shall receive for your trouble what is usually given in such cases.' I consented, and thanked him for the opportunity he afforded me of employing myself.

"The clerk of the ship registered all the bales with the names of the merchants to whom they belonged; when he asked the captain in what name he should register those destined for my charge, the captain replied, 'In the name of Sindbad the sailor.' I could not hear my own name without emotion; and looking at the captain, I recognised in him the very same person who in my second voyage had left me on the island where I had fallen asleep by the side of a brook, and who had put to sea without waiting for me. I did not at first recollect him, so much was he changed in appearance since the time when I last saw him. As he thought me dead, it is not to be wondered at that he did not recognise me. 'Captain,' said I to him, 'was the merchant to whom these things belonged called Sindbad?' 'Yes,' returned he, 'that was his name; he was from Bagdad, and embarked on board my vessel at Balsora. One day, when he went ashore on an island for fresh water, he was left behind; I know not through what mistake. None of the crew noticed his absence till four hours after, when the wind blew so fresh against us that it was impossible to return.' 'You believe him to be dead?' said I. 'Most assuredly,' replied the captain. 'Then open your eyes,' cried I, 'and convince yourself that the same Sindbad whom you left in the desert island is now before you. I fell asleep on the banks of a little stream, and when I awoke I found that the ship was gone.'

"At these words the captain fixed his eyes on me, and after scrutinising me very attentively, at last recollected me. 'God be praised!' cried he, embracing me; 'I am delighted that fortune has given me an opportunity of repairing my fault. Here are your goods, which I have preserved with care, and always had valued at every port I stopped at. I return them to you with the profit I have made on them.' I received them with the gratitude due to such honesty.

"From the Island of Salahat we went to another, where I provided myself with cloves, cinnamon, and other spices. When we had sailed some distance, we perceived an immense tortoise, twenty cubits in length and the same in breadth. We also saw a fish that had milk like a cow; its skin is so hard that bucklers are frequently made of it. I saw another fish that was of the shape and colour of a camel. At length, after a long voyage, we arrived at Balsora, from whence I came to Bagdad with so much wealth that I did not know the amount of it. I gave a great deal to the poor, and bought a considerable quantity of land."

Sindbad thus finished the history of his third voyage. Again he gave Hindbad a hundred sequins, inviting him to the usual repast on the morrow, and promising he should hear the account of the fourth voyage. Hindbad and the other guests retired, and on the following day returned at the same hour. When dinner was over, Sindbad continued the relation of his adventures.

## The Fourth Voyage of Sindbad the Sailor.

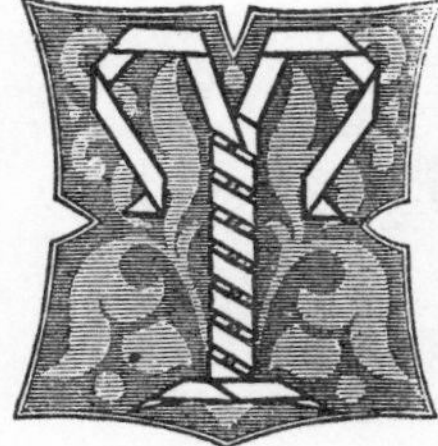

HE pleasures and amusements in which I indulged, after my third voyage, had not charms sufficiently powerful to deter me from venturing on the sea again. I gave way to my love for traffic and adventure. I settled my affairs, and furnished myself with the merchandise suited to the places I intended to visit, and set out, and travelled towards Persia, some of the provinces of which I traversed, till I at last reached a port, where I embarked. We set sail, and touched at several ports of the mainland, and at some of the Oriental islands; but one day, while tacking ship, we were surprised by a sudden squall of wind, which obliged the captain to lower the sails. He gave the necessary orders for encountering the danger which threatened us, but all our precautions were fruitless. The squall burst upon us; our sails were torn in a thousand pieces; and the vessel, becoming ungovernable, was driven on a sand bank and went to pieces. A great number of the crew perished, and the cargo was swallowed up by the waves.

"With some other merchants and seamen I had the good fortune to get hold of a plank; we were all drawn by the strength of the current towards an island that lay before us. We found some fruits and fresh water, which recruited our strength, and we lay down to sleep in the spot where the waves had thrown us, without seeking to explore the land on which we had been cast; the grief we felt at our misfortune rendered us careless as to our fate. The next morning, when the sun was risen, we left the shore, and advancing into the island, perceived some habitations, towards which we bent our steps. When we drew near, a great number of blacks came forward, and, surrounding us, made us prisoners. They seemed to divide us among themselves, and then led us away to their houses.

"Five of my comrades and myself were taken into the same place. Our captors made us sit down, and then offered us a certain herb, inviting us by signs to eat of it. My companions, without considering that the people who offered it to us did not eat of it themselves, only consulted their hunger and devoured it greedily. I had a sort of presentiment that this herb was given us for no good purpose, and refused even to taste it; and it was well I did so, for a short time after I perceived that my companions soon lost all sense of their position, and did not know what they said. The blacks then served us with some rice dressed with the oil of the cocoa-nut; and my comrades, not being sensible of what they did, ate ravenously of this mess. I likewise partook of it, but fed sparingly.

"The blacks had given us the herb first to turn our brains, and thus banish the sorrow which our miserable situation would create, and the rice was given to fatten us. As these men were anthropophagi, they designed to feast on us when we were in good condition. My poor companions fell victims to the barbarous custom of these wretches, because they had lost their senses, and could not foresee their destiny. As for me, instead of fattening as the others had done, I grew thinner every day. The fear of death, which constantly haunted me, poisoned the food I took, and I fell into a state of languor, which was in the end very beneficial to me; for when the blacks had devoured my comrades, they were content to let me remain till I should be worth eating.

"In the meantime I was allowed a great deal of liberty, and my actions were scarcely observed. This afforded me the opportunity one day of quitting the habitation of the blacks, and escaping. An old man, who watched me, and guessed my intention, called me to return; but I only quickened my pace, and soon got out of his sight. This old man was the only person in the neighbourhood; all the other blacks had absented themselves, as was their frequent custom, and were not to return till night. Being therefore certain that they would be too late to come in search of me when they returned home, I continued my flight till evening, and then stopped to take a little rest and satisfy my hunger. I soon set out again, and walked for seven days, taking care to avoid those places continually which appeared inhabited, and living on cocoa-nuts, which afforded me both drink and food.

"On the eighth day I came to the sea shore; here I saw some white people employed in gathering pepper, which grew very plentifully in that place. Their occupation was a good omen to me, and I approached them without fear of danger. They came towards me as soon as they perceived me, and asked me in Arabic from whence I came.

"Delighted to hear my native language once more, I readily satisfied their curiosity, and related to them the manner in which I had been shipwrecked, and how I had come to that island, where I had fallen into the hands of the blacks. 'But these blacks are cannibals,' said they; 'by what miracle did you escape their cruelty?' I gave them the same account which you have just heard, and they were very much surprised.

"I remained with them until they had collected as much pepper as they chose to gather. They made me embark with them in the vessel which had conveyed them, and we soon reached another island, from whence they had come. My deliverers presented me to their king, who was a good prince. He had the patience to listen to the recital of my adventures, which astonished him; and he ordered me some new clothes, and desired I might be taken care of. This island was very populous, and abounded in all sorts of articles for commerce, which was carried on to a great extent in the town where the king resided. The pleasantness of my new quarters began to console me for my misfortunes, and the kindness of this generous prince made me completely happy. Indeed, I appeared to be his greatest favourite; consequently all ranks of people endeavoured to please me, so that I was soon considered more as a native than a stranger.

"I remarked one thing which appeared to me very singular; every one, the king not excepted, rode on horseback without saddle, bridle, or stirrups. I one day took the liberty to ask his majesty why such things were not used in his city; he replied that he had never heard of the things of which I spoke.

"I immediately went to a workman, and gave him a model from which to make the tree of a saddle. When he had executed his task, I myself covered the saddle-tree with leather, richly embroidered in gold, and stuffed it with hair. I then applied to a locksmith, who made me a bit and some stirrups also, according to the patterns I gave him.

"When these articles were completed, I presented them to the king, and tried them on one of his horses: the prince then mounted his steed, and was so pleased with its

SINDBAD MAKES A SADDLE FOR THE KING.

accoutrements, that he testified his approbation by making me considerable presents. I was then obliged to make several saddles for his ministers and the principal officers of his household, who all rewarded me with very rich and handsome gifts. I also made some for the wealthiest inhabitants of the town, by which I gained great reputation and credit.

"As I constantly attended at court, the king said to me one day, 'Sindbad, I love you; and I know that all my subjects who have any knowledge of you think with me, and entertain a high regard for you. I have one request to make, which you must not deny me.' 'O king,' replied I, 'there is nothing your majesty can command which I will not perform, to prove my obedience to your orders. Your power over me is absolute.' 'I wish you to marry,' resumed the prince, 'that you may have a tender tie to attach you to my dominions, and prevent your returning to your native country.' As I did not dare to refuse the king's offer, he bestowed on me in marriage a lady of his court who was noble, beautiful, rich, and accomplished. After the ceremony of the nuptials I took up my abode in the house of my wife, and lived with her for some time in perfect harmony. Nevertheless I was discontented with my situation, and designed to make my escape at the first convenient opportunity, and return to Bagdad, for the splendid establishment I possessed in this new country could not obliterate my native city from my mind.

"While I was thus meditating an escape, the wife of one of my neighbours, with whom I was very intimate, fell sick and died. I went to console the widower, and finding him in the deepest affliction, I said to him, 'May God preserve you, and grant you a long life.' 'Alas!' replied he, 'how can I obtain what you wish me? I have only one hour to live.' 'Oh,' resumed I, 'do not suffer such dismal ideas to take possession of your mind; I hope that I shall enjoy your friendship for many years.' 'I wish with all my heart,' said he, 'that your life may be of long duration. As for me, the die is cast, and this day I shall be buried with my wife: such is the custom which our ancestors have established in this island, and which is still inviolably observed; the husband is interred alive with his dead wife, and the living wife with the dead husband. Nothing can save me, and every one submits to this law.'

"Whilst he was relating to me this singularly barbarous custom, the bare idea of which filled me with terror, his relations, friends, and neighbours came to make arrangements for the funeral. They dressed the corpse of the woman in the richest attire, as on the day of her nuptials, and decorated her with all her jewels. They then placed her on an open bier, and the procession set out. The husband, dressed in mourning, went immediately after the body of his wife, and the relations followed. They bent their course towards a high mountain, and when they had reached the summit, a large stone was raised which covered a deep pit, and the body was let down into the pit in all its sumptuous apparel and ornaments. Thereupon the husband took his leave of his relations and friends, and without making any resistance suffered himself to be placed on a bier, with a jug of water and seven small loaves by his side; he was then let down into the pit as his wife had been. This mountain extended to a great distance, reaching even to the sea-shore, and the pit was very deep. When the ceremony was ended the stone was replaced, and the company retired. I need scarcely tell you that I was particularly affected by this ceremony. All the others who were present did not appear to feel it deeply, for they had become habituated to see the same kind of scene. I could not avoid telling the king my sentiments on this subject. 'O king,' said I, 'I cannot express my astonishment at the strange custom which exists in your dominions, of interring the living with the dead; I have visited many nations, but in the whole course of my travels I never heard of so cruel a decree.' 'What can I do, Sindbad?' replied the king, 'it is a law common to all ranks, and even I submit to it. I shall be interred alive with the queen my consort, if she happens to die first.' 'Will your majesty allow me to ask', resumed I, 'if strangers are obliged to conform to this custom?' 'Certainly,' said the king, smiling at the obvious motive of my question, 'they are not exempt when they marry in the island.'

"I returned home thoughtful and sad. The fear that my wife might die before me, and that I must be interred with her, distressed me beyond measure. Yet how could I remedy this evil? I must have patience, and submit to the will of God. Nevertheless I trembled at the slightest indisposition of my wife, and, alas! I soon had good reason to fear: she was taken dangerously ill and died in a few days. To be buried alive appeared to me as horrible a fate as being devoured by the anthropophagi; yet I was obliged to submit. The king, accompanied by his whole court, proposed to honour the procession with his presence; and the principal inhabitants of the city also, out of respect to me, were present at my interment.

"When all was in readiness for the ceremony, the corpse of my wife, decorated with her jewels, and dressed in her most magnificent clothes, was placed on a bier, and the procession set out. As the chief mourner in this dreadful tragedy, I followed the body of my wife, my eyes full of tears, and deploring my miserable destiny. Before we arrived at the mountain I made an appeal to the compassion of the spectators. I first addressed myself to the king, then to the courtiers who were near me, and bowing to the ground to kiss the hem of their garments, I entreated them to have pity on me. 'Consider,' said I, 'that I am a stranger, who ought not to be subject to your rigorous law, and that I have another wife and children in my own country.' I pronounced these words in a heartrending tone, but no one seemed moved; on the contrary, the spectators hastened to deposit the corpse in the pit, and soon after I was let down also on another bier, with a jug of water and seven loaves. At last, this fatal ceremony being completed, they replaced the stone over the mouth of the cave, notwithstanding my paroxysms of grief and my piteous lamentation.

"As I approached the bottom of the pit, I discovered by the little light that shone from above the nature of this subterranean abode. It was a vast cavern, and might be about fifty cubits deep. I soon smelt an insupportable stench, which arose from the mouldering corpses that were strewed around. I even fancied I heard the last sighs of some miserable wretches who had lately fallen victims to this inhuman law. So soon as the bier stopped at the bottom of the cave I stepped from it to the ground, and stopping my nostrils, went to a distance from the dead bodies. I threw myself on the ground, where I remained a long time bathed in tears, and with a number of useless exclamations of regret and despair I made the cavern re-echo. I beat my head and breast, and gave way to the most violent grief. Nevertheless, I did not call on death to release me from this habitation of horror; the love of life still glowed within me, and induced me to seek to prolong my days. I felt my way to the bier on which I had been placed; and notwithstanding the intense darkness which prevailed, I found my bread and water, and ate and drank of it. The cave now appeared to be more spacious, and to contain more bodies than I had at first supposed. I lived for some days on my provisions, but as soon as they were exhausted I prepared to die. I had become resigned to my fate, when suddenly I heard the stone above me raised. A corpse and a living person were let down. The deceased was a man. It is natural to have recourse to violent means to preserve life when a man is reduced to the last extremity. While the woman was descending, I approached the spot where her bier was to be placed, and when I perceived that the aperture by which she had been lowered was closed, I gave the unhappy creature two or three heavy blows on the head with a large bone. She was stunned, or, to say the truth, I killed her, committing this inhuman action to obtain the bread and water which had been allowed her. I had now provisions for some days. At the end of that time a dead woman and her living husband were let down into the pit. I killed the man as I had slain the woman; and as at that time there happened, fortunately for me, to be a great mortality in the city, I was not in want of food, always obtaining my supplies by the same cruel means.

"One day, when I had just put an end to an unfortunate woman, I heard footsteps, and a sound like breathing. I advanced in the direction from whence the sound proceeded. I heard a louder breathing at my approach, and I fancied I saw something fleeing from me. I followed this flying shadow, which occasionally stopped and then again retreated panting as I drew near. I pursued it so long, and went so far, that at last I perceived a small speck of light resembling a star. I continued to walk towards this light, sometimes losing it as obstacles intervened in my path, but always seeing it again after a time, till I arrived at an opening in the rock large enough to allow me to pass.

"At this discovery I stopped for some time to recover from the violent emotion occasioned by my rapid chase; then passing through the crevice, I found myself on the sea shore. You may imagine the excess of my joy; it was so great, I could scarcely persuade myself that my imagination did not deceive me. When I became convinced that it was a reality, and that my senses did not play me false, I perceived that the thing which I had heard pant, and which I had followed, was an animal that lived in the sea, and was accustomed to go into that cave to devour the dead bodies.

"I returned to the cave to collect from the different biers all the diamonds, rubies, pearls, golden bracelets, in short, everything of value on which I could lay my hands in the dark, and I brought all my plunder to the shore. I tied it up in several packets with the cords which had served to let down the biers, of which there were many lying around. I left my goods in a convenient place, till a proper opportunity should offer for conveying them away. I had no fear of their being spoiled by the rain, for it was not the season for wet weather.

"At the end of two or three days I perceived a vessel just sailing out of the harbour, and passing by the spot where I was. I made signals with my linen turban, and cried aloud with all my strength. They heard me on board, and despatched the boat to fetch me. When the sailors inquired by what misfortune I had got in that place, I replied, that I had been wrecked two days since on that shore, with all my merchandise. Fortunately for me, these people did not stop to consider whether my story was probable, but, satisfied with my answer, they took me into the boat with my bales.

"When we had reached the vessel the captain, who was glad to be the instrument of my safety, and who was moreover occupied with the management of the ship, never thought of doubting the tale of the wreck; to remove any scruples he might feel, I offered him some precious stones, but he refused them.

"We passed several islands; amongst others, the Island of Bells, distant about ten days' sail from that of Serendib, sailing with a fair wind, and six days from the Isle of Kela, where we landed. Here we found lead mines, some Indian canes, and excellent camphor.

"The king of the Isle of Kela is very rich and powerful. His authority extends over the Island of Bells, which is two days' journey in extent; the inhabitants are still so uncivilized as to eat human flesh. After we had made an advantageous traffic in this Island, we again set sail, and touched at several ports. At length I arrived happily at Bagdad, with immense riches, which I need not describe to you in detail. To show my gratitude to Heaven for the mercies shown me, I spent a great deal in charity, giving money for the support of the mosques and for the relief of the poor. I then entirely gave myself up to the society of my relations and friends, and passed my time in feasting and entertainments."

"Sindbad here concluded the relation of his fourth voyage, which occasioned still more surprise in his audience than had been excited by the three preceding accounts. He repeated his present of a hundred sequins to Hindbad, whom he requested, with the rest of the company, to return on the following day to dine, and hear the story of his fifth voyage. Hindbad and the others took their leave and retired. The next day, when all were assembled, they sat down to table; and at the conclusion of the repast, Sindbad began the account of his fifth voyage in the following words:—

### The Fifth Voyage of Sindbad the Sailor.

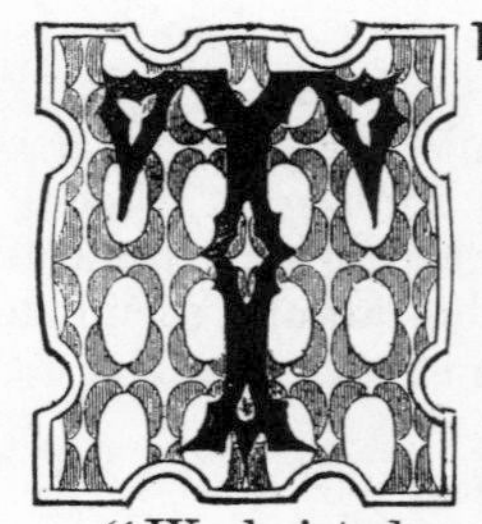

HE pleasures I enjoyed soon made me forget the perils I had endured; yet these delights were not sufficiently attractive to prevent my forming the resolution of venturing a fifth time on the sea. I again provided myself with merchandise, packed it up, and sent it overland to the nearest seaport. Unwilling to trust again to a captain, and wishing to have a vessel of my own, I built and equipped one at my own expense. As soon as it was ready I loaded it and embarked; and as I had not sufficient cargo of my own to fill it, I received on board several merchants of different nations, with their goods.

"We hoisted our sails to the first fair wind, and put to sea. After sailing for a considerable time, the first place we stopped at was a desert island, where we found the egg of a roc, as large as that of which I spoke on a former occasion: it contained a small

SINDBAD KILLS THE OLD MAN OF THE SEA.

roc, almost hatched; for its beak had begun to pierce through the shell. The merchants who were with me broke the egg with hatchets, cut out the young roc piece by piece, and roasted it. I had seriously advised them not to touch the egg, but they would not attend to me.

"They had scarcely finished their meal, when two immense clouds appeared in the air at a considerable distance from us. The captain whom I had engaged to navigate the vessel knew by experience what it was, and cried out that the father and mother of the young roc were coming. He warned us to re-embark as quickly as possible, to escape the danger which threatened us. We took his advice, and set sail immediately.

"The two rocs approached, uttering the most terrible screams, which they redoubled on finding their egg broken and their young one destroyed. Designing to revenge themselves they flew away towards the mountains from whence they came, and disappeared for some time, while we used all diligence to sail away, and prevent what nevertheless befel us.

"They soon returned, and we perceived that each had an enormous piece of rock in its claws. When they were exactly over our ship they stopped, and, suspending themselves in the air, one of them let fall the piece of rock he held. The skill of the pilot, who suddenly turned the vessel, prevented our being crushed by its fall, but the stone fell close to us into the sea, in which it made such a chasm that we could almost see the bottom. The other bird, unfortunately for us, let his piece of rock fall so directly on the ship that it broke and split our vessel into a thousand pieces. The sailors and passengers were all crushed to death or drowned. I myself was under water for some time; but rising again to the surface, I had the good fortune to seize a piece of the wreck. Swimming sometimes with one hand and sometimes with the other, still clutching the plank I had seized, and with the wind and current both in my favour, I at length reached an island where the shore was very steep. But I contrived to clamber up the beach, and got on land.

"I seated myself on the grass to recover from my fatigue. When I had rested I rose, and advanced into the island, to reconnoitre the ground. This region seemed to me like a delicious garden. Wherever I turned my eyes I saw beautiful trees, some loaded with green, others with ripe fruits, and transparent streams meandering between them. I ate of the fruits, which I found excellent, and quenched my thirst at the inviting brooks.

"When night came, I lay down on the grass in a convenient spot. But I did not sleep an hour at a time; my rest was continually interrupted by my fear at being alone in such a desert place; and I passed the greater part of the night in lamenting my fate, and reproaching myself for the imprudence of venturing from home, where I had possessed everything that could make me comfortable. These reflections led me so far, that I meditated the idea of taking my own life; but day returned with its cheerful light, and dissipated my gloomy thoughts. I rose, and walked amongst the trees, though not without some degree of trepidation.

"When I had advanced a little way into the island, I perceived an old man, who appeared very decrepit. He was seated on the bank of a little rivulet. At first I supposed he might be a shipwrecked mariner like myself. I approached and saluted him: he replied only by a slight inclination of the head. I asked him what he was doing, but instead of answering, he made signs to me to take him on my shoulders, and cross the brook, making me understand that he wanted to gather some fruit.

"I supposed he wished me to render him this piece of service; and taking him on my back, I waded through the stream. When I had reached the other side, I stooped, and desired him to alight; instead of complying (I cannot help laughing whenever I think of it), this old man, who appeared to me so decrepit, nimbly threw his legs, which I now saw were covered with a skin like a cow's, over my neck, and seated himself fast on my shoulders, at the same time squeezing my throat so violently that I expected to be strangled; this alarmed me so much that I fainted away.

"Notwithstanding my condition, the old man kept his place on my neck, and only loosened his hold sufficiently to allow me to breathe. When I had somewhat recovered, he pushed one of his feet against my stomach, and kicking my side with the other, obliged me to get up. He then made me walk under some trees, and forced me to gather and eat the fruit we found. He never quitted his hold during the day; and when I wished to rest at night, he laid himself on the ground with me, always clinging to my neck. He never failed to awaken me with a push in the morning, and then he made me get up and walk, kicking me all the time. Imagine how miserable it was to me to bear this burden, without the possibility of getting rid of it.

"One day I chanced to find on the ground several dried gourds, which had fallen from the tree that bore them. I took a large one, and after having cleared it well, I squeezed into it the juice of several bunches of grapes, which the island produced in great abundance. When I had filled the gourd, I placed it in a particular spot, and some days after returned with the old man. On tasting the contents, I found the juice converted into excellent wine, which for a little time made me forget the ills that weighed upon me. The drink gave me new vigour, and raised my spirits so high that I began to sing and dance as I went along.

"Perceiving the effect this beverage had taken on my spirits, the old man made signs to me to let him taste it; I gave him the gourd, and the liquor pleased his taste so well that he drank it to the last drop. There was enough to inebriate him, and the fumes of the wine very soon rose into his head; he then began to sing after his own manner, and to sway to and fro on my shoulders. The blows he gave himself made him feel very much disturbed, and his legs loosened by degrees; so that, finding he no longer held me tight, I threw him on the ground, where he lay motionless. I then took a large stone and crushed him to death.

"I was much rejoiced at having got rid of this old man; and I walked towards the sea shore, where I met some people, who belonged to a vessel which had anchored there to get fresh water. They were very much astonished at seeing me and hearing the account of my adventure. 'You had fallen,' said they, 'into the hands of the Old Man of the Sea, and you are the first of his captives whom he has not strangled. This island is famous for the number of persons he has killed. The sailors and merchants who land here never dare approach except in a strong body.'

"After giving me this information, they took me to their ship, whose captain received me with the greatest politeness, when he heard what had befallen me. He set sail, and in a few days we anchored in the harbour of a large city, where the houses were built of stone.

"One of the merchants of the ship had contracted a friendship for me. He entreated me to accompany him, and conducted me to the quarters set apart for foreign merchants. He gave me a large sack, and then introduced me to some people belonging to the city, who were also furnished with sacks. He requested them to take me with them to gather cocoa, and said to me, 'Go, follow them, and do as they do; and do not stray from them, for your life will be in danger if you leave them.' He gave me provisions for the day, and I set off with my new friends.

"We arrived at a large forest of tall straight trees, the trunks of which were so smooth that it was impossible to climb up to the branches where the fruit grew. These were all cocoa trees; and we proposed to knock down the fruit and fill our sacks. On entering the forest, we saw a great number of monkeys of all sizes, who fled at our approach, and ran up the trees with surprising agility. The merchants who were with me collected stones, and threw them with great force at the monkeys, who had reached some of the highest branches. I did the same, and soon perceived that these animals were aware of our proceedings. They gathered the cocoa nuts, and threw them down at us with gestures which plainly showed their anger and spite. We picked up the cocoa-nuts, and at intervals threw up stones, to irritate the monkeys. By this contrivance we obtained nuts enough to fill our sacks: a thing utterly impracticable by any other method.

"When we had collected a sufficient quantity, we returned to the city, where the merchant who had sent me to the forest gave me the value of the cocoa-nuts I had brought. At last I had collected such a quantity of cocoa-nuts, that I sold them for a considerable sum.

"The vessel in which I came had sailed with the merchants, who had loaded it with the cocoa-nuts they had purchased. I waited for the arrival of another, which shortly after came into harbour to take in a cargo of the same description. I sent on board all the cocoa-nuts which belonged to me; and when the ship was ready to sail I took leave of the merchant to whom I was under so much obligation. As he had not yet settled his affairs, he could not embark with me.

"We set sail, and steered towards the island where pepper grows in such abundance. From thence we made the Island of Comari, where the best species of the aloe is found, and whose inhabitants bind themselves by a law not to drink wine or suffer any kind of debauchery to exist among them. In these two islands I exchanged all my cocoa-nuts for pepper and aloe-wood; and I then, like the other merchants, engaged on my own account in a pearl fishery, in which I employed many divers. I had soon collected by these means a great number of very large and perfect gems, with which I joyfully put to sea, and arrived safely at Balsora, from whence I returned to Bagdad. Here I sold for a large sum the pepper, aloes, and pearls which I had brought with me. I bestowed a tenth part of my profit in charity, as I had done on my return from every former voyage, and endeavoured by all kinds of relaxation to recover from my fatigues."

"When he had concluded his narrative, Sindbad gave a hundred sequins to Hindbad, who retired with all the other guests. The same party returned to the rich Sindbad's house the next day; and after their host had regaled them in as sumptuous a manner as on the preceding days, he requested silence, and began the account of his sixth voyage.

## The Sixth Voyage of Sindbad the Sailor.

I FEEL convinced, my friends, that you all wonder how I could be tempted again to expose myself to the caprice of fortune, after I had undergone so many perils in my other voyages. I am astonished myself when I think of it. It was fate alone that impelled me, at the expiration of a year, to venture a sixth time on the changeful sea, notwithstanding the tears and entreaties of my relations and friends, who did all in their power to persuade me to stay at home.

"Instead of taking the route of the Persian Gulf, I passed through some of the provinces of Persia and the Indies, and arrived at a seaport, where I embarked in a good ship, with a captain who was determined to make a long voyage. Long indeed it proved, but at the same time unfortunate; for the captain and pilot lost their way, and did not know how to steer. They at length found out where we were; but we had no reason to rejoice at the discovery, for the captain astonished us all by suddenly quitting his post, and uttering the most lamentable cries. He threw his turban on the deck, tore his beard, and beat his head, like a man distraught. We asked the reason of this violent grief, and he replied, 'I am obliged to announce to you that we are in the greatest peril. A rapid current is hurrying the ship along, and we shall all perish in less than a quarter of an hour. Pray Allah to deliver us from this dreadful danger, for nothing can save us unless he takes pity on us.' He then gave orders for setting the sails; but the ropes broke in the attempt, and the ship became entirely unmanageable, and was dashed by the current against the foot of a rock, where it split and went to pieces. Nevertheless we had time to disembark our provisions, as well as the most valuable part of the cargo.

"When we were assembled on the shore the captain said, 'God's will be done. Here we may dig our graves, and bid each other an eternal farewell; for we are in a place so desolate that no one who ever was cast on this shore returned to his own home.' This speech increased our distress, and we embraced each other with tears in our eyes, deploring our wretched fate.

"The mountain, at the foot of which we were, formed one side of a large and long island. The coast was covered with the remains of vessels which had been wrecked on it; and the scattered heaps of bones, which lay strewn about in every direction, convinced us of the dreadful fact that many lives had been lost in this spot. Almost incredible quantities of merchandise of every sort were heaped up on the shore.

"In every other region it is common for a number of small rivers to discharge themselves into the sea; but here a large river of fresh water takes its course from the sea, and runs along the coast through a dark cave, the entrance to which is extremely high and wide. The most remarkable feature in this place is, that the mountain is composed of rubies, crystals, and other precious stones. Here, too, a kind of pitch, or bitumen, distils from the rock into the sea, and the fishes which eat it return it in the form of ambergris, which the waves leave on the shore. The majority of the trees are aloes, and are equal in beauty to those of Comari.

"To complete the description of this place, from which no vessel ever returns, I have only to mention that it is impossible for a ship to avoid being dragged thither, if it comes within a certain distance. If a sea breeze blows, the wind assists the current, and there

SINDBAD SLEEPS ON THE RAFT.

is no remedy; and if the wind comes from land, the high mountain impedes its effect, and causes a calm, which allows the current full force, and then it whirls the ship against the coast, and dashes it to pieces as it shattered ours. In addition to this, the mountain is so steep that it is impossible to reach the summit, or indeed to escape by any means.

"We remained on the shore, quite heart-broken, expecting to die. We had divided our provisions equally, so that each person lived a longer or a shorter time according to the manner in which he husbanded his portion.

"Those who died first were interred by the others. I had the dismal office of burying my last companion; for, besides managing my share of provisions with more care than the rest had shown in the consumption of theirs, I had also a store which I kept concealed from my comrades. Nevertheless, when I buried the last of them, I had so little food left that I imagined I must soon follow him; so I dug a grave and resolved to throw myself into it, since no one remained to perform this last office for me. I must confess that whilst I was thus employed, I could not avoid reproaching myself as the sole cause of my misfortune, and most heartily did I repent this last voyage. Nor was I satisfied with reproaching myself, but I bit my hands in my despair, and had nearly put an end to my existence.

"But Allah still had pity on me, and inspired me with the thought of going to the river which lost itself in the recesses of the cave. I examined the stream with great attention; and it occurred to me that, as the river ran under ground, it must in its course come out to daylight again. I therefore conjectured that if I constructed a raft, and placed myself on it, the current of the water might perhaps bring me to some inhabited country. If I perished, it was but altering the manner of my death; but if, on the contrary, I got safely out of this fatal place, I should not only escape the cruel death by which my companions perished, but might also meet with some fresh opportunity of enriching myself.

"These reflections made me work at my raft with fresh vigour. I made it of thick pieces of wood and great cables, of which there was abundance on the coast: I tied them closely together, and formed a strong framework. When it was completed, I placed on it a cargo of rubies, emeralds, ambergris, crystal, and also some gold and silver stuffs. When I had stowed all these things so as to balance the raft, and fastened them to the planks, I embarked on my vessel, guiding it with two little oars which I had provided; and driving along with the current, I resigned myself to the will of God.

"As soon as I was under the vault of the cavern I lost the light of day; the current carried me on, but I was unable to discern its course. I rowed for some days in this obscurity without ever perceiving the least ray of light. At one time the vault of the cavern was so low that my head almost struck against it; and this rendered me very attentive to avoid the danger when it recurred. During this time I consumed no more of my provisious than was absolutely necessary to sustain nature: but, frugal as I was, they came to an end. I then fell into a sweet sleep. I cannot tell whether I slept long; but when I awoke I was surprised to find myself in an open country, near a bank of the river, to which my raft was fastened, and in the midst of a large concourse of blacks. I rose and saluted them; they spoke to me, but I could not understand them.

"At this moment I felt so transported with joy that I could scarcely believe myself awake. Being at length convinced that my deliverance was not a dream, I pronounced aloud these Arabic words, 'Invoke the Almighty, and he will come to thy assistance; thou needst not care for aught besides. Close thine eyes, and while thou sleepest Allah will change thy fortune from evil to good.'

"One of the blacks, who understood Arabic, hearing me speak thus, advanced towards me, and spoke as follows: 'Brother, be not surprised at seeing us; we live in this country, and we came hither to-day to this river, which flows from the neighbouring mountain, to water our fields by cutting canals to admit the water. We observed that the current bore something along, and we immediately ran to the bank to see what it was, and perceived this raft; one of us instantly swam to it, and guided it to shore. We fastened it as you see, and were waiting for you to wake. We entreat you to relate to us your history, which must be very extraordinary; tell us how you could venture on this river, and from whence you came.' I requested him first to give me some food, and promised to satisfy their curiosity when I had eaten.

"They produced several kinds of meat, and when I had satisfied my hunger I related to them all that had happened to me. They appeared to listen to my story with great admiration. As soon as I had finished my history, their interpreter told me that I had astonished them with my relation, and I must go myself to the king, to recount my adventures; for they were of too extraordinary a nature to be repeated by any one but by the person himself to whom they had happened. I replied that I was ready to do anything they wished. The blacks then sent for a horse, which arrived shortly after; they placed me on it, and while some walked by my side to show me the way, certain stalwart fellows hauled the raft out of the water, and followed me, carrying it on their shoulders, with the bales of rubies.

"We went together to the city in Serendid, for this was the name of the island; and the blacks presented me to their king. I approached the throne on which he was seated, and saluted him in the manner adopted towards sovereigns in India, namely, by prostrating myself at his feet and kissing the earth. The prince made me rise; and receiving me with an affable air, he seated me by his side. He first asked me my name; I replied that I was called Sindbad, surnamed the Sailor, from having made several voyages; and ended, that I was a citizen of Bagdad. 'How then,' said the monarch, 'came you into my dominions, and from whence have you arrived?'

"I concealed nothing from the king, but related to him all you have heard me tell; he was so pleased with it that he ordered the history of my adventures to be written in letters of gold, that it might be preserved amongst the archives of his kingdom. The raft was then produced, and the bales were opened in his presence. He admired the aloe-wood and ambergris, but above all the rubies and emeralds, as he had none in his treasury equal to them in value.

"Perceiving that he examined my valuables with pleasure, and that he looked repeatedly at the rarest of them, I prostrated myself before him, and took the liberty of saying, 'O king, not only am I your servant, but the cargo of my raft also is at your disposal, if your majesty will do me the honour of accepting it.' The king smiled, and replied that he did not desire to possess anything which belonged to me; that as God had given me these things, I ought not to be deprived of them; that instead of diminishing my riches, he should add to them; and that when I left his dominions I should carry with me proofs of his liberality. I could only reply to this by praying for his prosperity and by praising his generosity.

"He ordered one of his officers to attend me, and placed some of his own servants at my disposal. The officers faithfully fulfilled the charge with which they were entrusted and conveyed all the bales to the place appointed for my lodging. I went every day at certain hours to pay my court to the king, and employed the rest of my time in seeing the city and whatever was most worthy of my attention.

"The island of Serendid is situated exactly under the equinoctial line, so that the days and nights are of equal length. It is eighty parasangs long, and as many in breath. The principal town is situated at the extremity of a beautiful valley, formed by a mountain which is in the middle of the island, and which is by far the highest in the world: it is discernible at sea at a distance of three days' sail. Rubies and many sorts of minerals are found there, and most of the rocks are formed of emery, which is a sort of metallic rock used for cutting precious stones.

"All kinds of rare and curious plants and trees, particularly the cedar and cocoa tree, grow here in great abundance, and there are pearl fisheries on the coast, at the mouth of the rivers; some of the valleys also contain diamonds. I made a devotional journey up the mountain, to the spot where Adam was placed on his banishment from Paradise; and I had the curiosity to ascend to the summit.

"When I came back to the city I entreated the king to grant me permission to return to my native country, and he acceeded to my request in the most obliging and honourable manner. He commanded me to receive a rich present from his treasury; and when I went to take my leave, he placed in my hands another gift, still more considerable than the first, and at the same time gave me a letter for the Commander of the Believers, our sovereign lord, saying, 'I request you to deliver for me this letter and this present to the Caliph Haroun Alraschid, and to assure him of my friendship. I took the present and the letter with the greatest respect, and promised his majesty that I would most punctually execute the orders with which he was pleased to honour me. Before I embarked, the king sent for the captain and the merchants with whom I was to sail, and charged them to pay me all possible attention.

"The letter of the King of Serendid was written on the skin of a certain animal, highly prized in that country on account of its rareness. It is of a yellowish colour.

The letter itself was in characters of azure, and it contained the following words in the Indian language:—

"'THE KING OF THE INDIES, WHO IS PRECEDED BY A THOUSAND ELEPHANTS; WHO LIVES IN A PALACE, THE ROOF OF WHICH GLITTERS WITH THE LUSTRE OF AN HUNDRED THOUSAND RUBIES, AND WHO POSSESSES IN HIS TREASURY TWENTY THOUSAND CROWNS ENRICHED WITH DIAMONDS, TO THE CALIPH HAROUN ALRASCHID.

"'Although the present that we send you be inconsiderable, yet receive it as a brother and a friend, in consideration of the friendship we bear you in our heart. We feel happy in having an opportunity of testifying this friendship to you. We ask the same share in your affections, as we hope we deserve it, being of a rank equal to that you hold. We salute you as a brother. Farewell.'

"The present comprised, firstly, a vase made of one single ruby, pierced and worked into a cup of half a foot in height and an inch thick, filled with fine round pearls, all weighing half a drachm each; secondly, the skin of a serpent, which had scales as large as an ordinary coin, and which possessed the peculiar virtue of preserving those who lay on it from all disease; thirdly, fifty thousand drachms of the most exquisite aloe-wood, together with thirty pieces of camphor as large as pistachio-nuts; and lastly, a female slave of the most enchanting beauty, whose clothes were covered with jewels.

"The ship set sail, and, after a long but fortunate voyage, we landed at Balsora, from whence I returned to Bagdad. The first thing I did after my arrival was to execute the commission I had been intrusted with. I took the letter of the King of Serendid, and presented myself at the gate of the Commander of the Faithful, followed by the beautiful slave, and some of my family, who carried the presents which had been committed to my care. I mentioned the reason of my appearance there, and was immediately conducted to the throne of the caliph. I prostrated myself at his feet, explained my errand, and gave him the letter and the present. When he read the contents, he inquired of me whether it was true that the King of Serendid was as rich and powerful as he reported himself to be in his letter.

"I prostrated myself a second time, and when I arose, replied, 'Commander of the Faithful, I can assure your majesty that the King of Serendid does not exaggerate his riches and grandeur: I have seen his wealth and magnificence. The splendour of his palace cannot fail to excite admiration. When this prince wishes to appear in public, a throne is prepared for him on the back of an elephant; on this he sits, and proceeds between two rows, composed of his ministers, favourites, and others belonging to the court. Before him, on the same elephant, sits an officer with a golden lance in his hand, and behind the throne another stands with a pillar of gold, on the top of which is placed an emerald about half a foot long and an inch thick. The king is preceded by a guard of a thousand men habited in silk and gold stuffs, and mounted on elephants richly caparisoned.

"'While the king is on his march, the officer who sits before him on the elephant proclaims from time to time with a loud voice: 'This is the great monarch, the powerful and tremendous Sultan of the Indies, whose palace is covered with a hundred thousand rubies, and who possesses twenty thousand diamond crowns. This is the crowned monarch, greater than ever was Solima, or the great Mihragè.'

"'After he has pronounced these words, the officer who stands behind the throne cries, in his turn: 'This monarch, who is so great and powerful, must die, must die, must die!' The first officer then resumes: 'Glory be to him who lives and dies not.'

"'The King of Serendid is so just that there are no judges in his capital, nor in any other part of his dominions; his people do not want them. They know and observe with exactness the true principles of justice, and never deviate from their duty; therefore tribunals and magistrates would be useless among them.'

"The caliph was satisfied with my discourse, and said: 'The wisdom of this king appears in his letter; and after what you have told me, I must confess that such wisdom is worthy of such subjects, and such subjects worthy of their ruler.' With these words he dismissed me with a rich present."

"Sindbad here finished his discourse, and his visitors retired; but Hindbad, as usual, received his hundred sequins. The guests and the porter returned on the following day, and Sindbad began the relation of his seventh and last voyage in these terms:—

### The Seventh and last Voyage of Sindbad the Sailor.

"On my return from my sixth voyage, I absolutely relinquished all thoughts of ever venturing again on the seas. I was past the prime of life, and at an age which

SINDBAD IS FREED FROM THE ELEPHANTS.

required rest; and besides this I had sworn never more to expose myself to the perils I had so often experienced. I prepared therefore to enjoy my life in quiet and repose.

"One day when I was regaling a number of friends, one of my servants came to tell me that an officer of the caliph wanted to speak to me. I left the table, and went to him. 'The caliph,' said he, 'has ordered me to acquaint you that he wishes to see you.' I followed the officer to the palace, and he presented me to the prince, whom I saluted by prostrating myself at his feet. 'Sindbad,' said the caliph, 'I want you to do me a service. You must go once more to the King of Serendid with my answer and presents; it is but right that I should make him a proper return for the civility he has shown me."

"This order of the caliph's was a thunderbolt to me. 'Commander of the Faithful,' replied I, 'I am ready to execute anything with which your majesty may desire to entrust me; but I humbly entreat you to consider, that I am worn down with the unspeakable fatigues I have undergone. I have even made a vow never to leave Bagdad.' I then took occasion to relate the long history of my adventures, which he had the patience to listen to attentively. When I had done speaking, the caliph said, 'I confess that these are extraordinary adventures; nevertheless they must not prevent your making the voyage I propose, for my sake: it is only to the island of Serendid. Execute the commission I entrust you with, and then you will be at liberty to return. But you must go; for you must be sensible that it would be highly indecorous, as well as derogatory to my dignity, if I remained under obligation to the king of that island.'

"As I plainly saw that the caliph had resolved on my going, I signified to him that I was ready to obey his commands. He seemed much pleased, and ordered me a thousand sequins to pay the expenses of the voyage.

"In a few days I was prepared for my departure; and as soon as I had received the presents from the caliph, together with a letter written with his own hand, I set off and took the route of Balsora, from whence I embarked. After a pleasant voyage, I arrived at the island of Serendid. I immediately acquainted the ministers with the commission I had come to execute, and begged them to procure me an audience as soon as possible.

"The monarch immediately recollected me, and evinced great joy at my visit. 'Welcome, Sindbad,' said he; 'I assure you I have often thought of you since your departure. Blessed be this day in which I see you again.' I made a suitable reply to this compliment; and after thanking the king for his kindness, I delivered the letter and present of the caliph, which he received with every mark of satisfaction and pleasure.

"The caliph sent him a complete bed of gold tissue, estimated at a thousand sequins, fifty robes of a very rare stuff, a hundred more of white linen, the finest that could be procured from Cairo, Suez, Cufa, and Alexandria; a bed of crimson, and another of a different pattern and colour. Besides this, he sent a vase of agate, greater in width than in depth, of the thickness of a finger—on the sides there was sculptured in bas-relief a man kneeling on the ground, and in his hand a bow and arrow, with which he was going to shoot at a lion; and a richly ornamented table, which was supposed from tradition to have belonged to the great Solomon. The letter of the caliph ran thus:—

"'HEALTH, IN THE NAME OF THE SOVEREIGN GUIDE OF THE RIGHT ROAD, TO THE POWERFUL AND HAPPY SULTAN, FROM THE PART OF ABDALLA HAROUN ALRASCHID, WHOM GOD HAS PLACED ON THE THRONE OF HONOUR, AFTER HIS ANCESTORS OF HAPPY MEMORY.

"'We have received your letter with joy; and we send you this, proceeding from our council, the garden of superior minds. We hope that in casting your eyes over it you will perceive our good intention, and think it agreeable. Farewell.'

"The King of Serendid was rejoiced to find that the caliph reciprocated his own feelings of friendship. Soon after this audience I requested another, that I might ask leave to depart, which I had some difficulty to obtain. At length I succeeded, and the king at my departure ordered me a very handsome present. I re-embarked immediately, intending to return to Bagdad; but had not the good fortune to arrive so soon as I expected, for Allah had disposed it otherwise.

"Three or four days after we had set sail we were attacked by corsairs, who easily made themselves masters of our vessel, as we were not in a state for defence. Some persons in the ship attempted to make resistance, but their boldness cost them ther lives. I and all those who had the prudence to submit quietly to the corsairs were made slaves. After they had stripped us, and clothed us in rags instead of our own garments, they bent their course towards a distant island, where they sold us.

"I was purchased by a rich merchant, who brought me to his house, gave me food to eat, and clothed me as a slave. Some days after, as he was not well informed who I was, he asked me if I knew any trade. I replied that I was not an artisan, but a merchant by profession, and that the corsairs who had sold me had taken from me all I possessed. 'But tell me,' said he, "do you think you could shoot with a bow and arrow?' I replied, that I had practised that sport in my youth, and that I had not entirely lost my skill. He then gave me a bow and some arrows, and making me mount behind him on an elephant, he took me to a vast forest at the distance of some hours' journey from the city. We went a great way into the forest, till the merchant came to a spot where he wished to stop, and made me alight. Then he showed me a large tree. 'Get up in that tree,' said he, 'and shoot at the elephants that pass under it; for there are many of those animals in this forest: if one should fall, come and let me know.' Thereupon he left me some provisions, and returned to the city. I remained in the tree on the watch the whole night.

"During the first night no elephants came; but the next day, as soon as the sun had risen, a great number made their appearance. I shot many arrows at them, and at last one fell. The others immediately retired, and left me at liberty to go and inform my master of the success I had met with. To reward me for this good intelligence, he regaled me with an excellent repast, and praised my address. We then returned together to the forest, where we dug a pit to bury the elephant I had killed. It was my master's intention to let the carcase rot in the earth, and then to take possession of the teeth.

"I continued my new occupation for two months; and not a day passed in which I did not kill an elephant. I did not always place myself on the same tree; sometimes I ascended one, sometimes another. One morning, when I was waiting for some elephants to pass, I perceived, to my great astonishment, that instead of traversing the forest as usual, they stopped and came towards me with a terrible noise, and in such numbers that the ground was covered with them and trembled under their footsteps. They approached the tree in which I had stationed myself, and surrounded it with their trunks extended, and their eyes all fixed upon me. At this surprising spectacle I remained motionless, and was so unnerved that my bow and arrows fell from my hands.

"My terror was not groundless. After the elephants had viewed me for some time, one of the largest twisted his trunk round the body of the tree, and shook it with so much violence, that he tore it up by the roots and threw it on the ground. I fell with the tree; but the animal took me up with his trunk, and placed me on his shoulders, where I lay extended more dead than alive. The huge beast now put himself at the head of his companions, who followed him in a troop, and he carried me to a retired spot, where he set me down, and then went away with the rest. I thought it a dream.

"At length, after I had waited some time, seeing no other elephants, I arose, and perceived that I was on a little hill of some extent, entirely covered with bones and teeth of elephants. I now felt certain that this was their cemetery or place of burial; and that they had brought me hither to show it me, that I might desist from destroying them, as I took their lives merely for the sake of possessing their teeth. I did not stay long on the hill, but turned my steps towards the city, and, after walking for a day and a night, at last arrived at my master's. I did not meet any elephant. They had gone farther into the forest, to leave me an unobstructed passage from the hill.

"As soon as my master saw me, he exclaimed, 'Ah, poor Sindbad! I was anxious to know what could have become of you. I have been to the forest, and found a tree newly torn up by the roots, and your bow and arrows on the ground; after seeking you everywhere in vain, I despaired of ever seeing you again. Pray tell me what has happened to you, and by what fortunate chance you are still alive.' I satisfied his curiosity; and the following day he accompanied me to the hill, and with great joy convinced himself of the truth of my history. We loaded the elephant on which we had come with as many teeth as it could carry, and when we returned my master thus addressed me:—'Brother—for I will no longer treat you as a slave, after the discovery you have imparted to me, and which cannot fail to enrich me—may God pour on you all sorts of blessings and prosperity! Before him I give you your liberty. I had concealed from you what I am now going to relate. The elephants of our forest destroy annually a great number of slaves, whom we send in search of ivory. Whatever advice we give them, they are sure, sooner or later, to lose their lives by the wiles of these animals. Providence has delivered you from their fury, and has conferred this mercy on you alone. It is a sign that you are especially protected, and that you are required in this world to be of use to mankind. You have procured me a surprising advantage: we have not hitherto been able to get ivory without risking the lives of our slaves, and now our whole city will be enriched by your means. I intend to give you considerable presents. I might easily move the whole city to join me in making your fortune, but that is a pleasure I will keep for myself alone.'

"To this obliging discourse I replied:—'Master, may Allah preserve you! The liberty you grant me acquits you of all obligation towards me; and the only recompense I desire for the service I have had the good fortune to perform for you and the inhabitants of your city, is permission to return to my country.' 'Well,' he replied, 'the monsoon will soon bring us vessels, which come to be laden with ivory. I will then send you away, with a sufficient sum to pay your expenses home.' I again thanked him for the liberty he had given me, and for the good-will he showed me. I remained with him till the season for the monsoon, and during this interval we made frequent excursions to the hill, and filled his magazines with ivory. All the other merchants in the city filled their warehouses likewise, for my discovery did not long remain a secret.

"The ships at length arrived, and my master having chosen the one in which I was to embark, loaded it with ivory, making over half the cargo to me. He did not omit an abundance of provisions for my voyage, and he also obliged me to accept some rare curiosities of his country. After I had thanked him as much as possible for all the obligations he had conferred on me, I embarked.

"We touched at several islands to procure supplies. Our vessel having originally sailed from a port of the mainland of India, we touched there; and, fearful of the dangers of the sea to Balsora, I took out of the ship the ivory which belonged to me, and resolved to continue my journey by land. I sold my share of the cargo for a large sum of money, and purchased a variety of curious things for presents: when I had finished my preparations, I joined a caravan of merchants. I remained a long time on the road, and suffered a great deal; but I bore all with patience, when I reflected that I had to fear neither tempests nor corsairs, serpents, nor any other peril that I had before encountered.

"All these fatigues being at last surmounted, I arrived happily at Bagdad. I went immediately and presented myself to the caliph, and gave him an account of my embassy. The caliph told me that my long absence had occasioned him some uneasiness, but that he always hoped that Allah would not forsake me.

"When I related the adventure of the elephants he appeared much surprised, and would scarcely have believed it had not my truthfulness been well known to him. He thought this, as well as the other histories I had detailed to him, so curious that he ordered one of his secretaries to write it in letters of gold, for preservation in his treasury. I retired well satisfied with the presents and honours he conferred on me; and then resigned myself entirely to my family, my relations, and friends."

"Sindbad thus concluded the recital of his seventh and last voyage; and, addressing himself to Hindbad, added: 'Well, my friend, have you ever heard of one who has suffered more than I have, or been in so many trying situations? Is it not just, that after so many troubles I should enjoy an agreeable and quiet life?' As he finished these words, Hindbad approaching him, kissed his hand, and said, 'I must confess that you have encountered frightful perils; my afflictions are not to be compared with yours. If my troubles weigh heavily upon me at the time I suffer them, I can still enjoy the small profit my labours produce. You not only deserve a quiet life, but are worthy of all the riches you possess, since you make so good a use of them, and are so generous. May you continue to live happily till the hour of your death!'

"Sindbad caused Hindbad to receive another hundred sequins. He admitted him to his friendship, told him to quit the calling of a porter, and to continue to eat at his table, that he might all his life have reason to remember Sindbad the Sailor."

THE FISHERMAN DRAWING HIS NET.

## THE THREE APPLES.

"Sir," said Scheherazade, "the Caliph Haroun Alraschid one day desired his grand vizier Giafar to be with him on the following morning. 'I wish,' said he, 'to visit all parts of the city, and to ascertain in what esteem my officers of justice are held. If there be any of whom just complaints are made, we will discharge them, and put others in their places who will give greater satisfaction. If, on the contrary, there be any who are praised, we will reward them according to their deserts.'

"The grand vizier repaired to the palace at the appointed time. The caliph, Giafar, and Mesrour the chief of the eunuchs, disguised themselves, that they might not be known, and set out together.

"They passed through several squares and many market-places; and as they came into a small street they perceived, by the light of the moon, a man with a white beard, and of tall stature, carrying nets on his head. He had on his arm a basket made of palm-leaves, and in his hand a stick. 'To judge by this old man's appearance,' said the caliph, 'I should not suppose him rich; let us address him, and question him concerning his lot.' 'Good man,' said the vizier, 'what art thou?' 'My lord,' replied the old man, 'I am a fisherman, but the poorest and most miserable of my trade. I went out at noon to go and fish, and from that time till now I have caught nothing; and yet I have a wife and young children, but have nothing wherewith to feed them.'

"The caliph, touched with compassion, said to the fisherman, 'Wilt thou return, and cast thy nets once more? We will give thee an hundred sequins for what thou bringest up.' The fisherman, taking the caliph at his word, and forgetting all the troubles of the past day, returned towards the Tigris, in company with him, Giafar, and Mesrour.

"They arrived on the banks of the river. The fisherman cast his nets, and drew out a chest, closely shut and very heavy. The caliph immediately ordered the vizier to count out a hundred sequins to the fisherman, whom he then dismissed. Mesrour took the chest on his shoulders by order of his master, who, anxious to know what it could contain, returned immediately to the palace. On opening the chest, they found a large basket made of palm-leaves, the upper part sewn together with a bit of red worsted. To satisfy the impatience of the caliph, they cut the worsted with a knife, and drew out of the basket a parcel wrapped in a piece of old carpet, and tied with cord. The cord was soon untied and the packet undone, and then they saw, to their horror, the body of a young lady, whiter than snow, and cut into pieces. The caliph's astonishment at this dismal spectacle cannot be described; but his surprise was quickly changed to anger; and, casting a furious look at the vizier, he cried, 'Wretch! is this the way you inspect the actions of my people? Murder is committed with impunity under your administration, and my subjects are thrown into the Tigris, that they may rise in vengeance against me on the day of judgment! If you do not speedily revenge the death of this woman by the execution of her murderer, I swear by the holy name of God that I will have you hanged, with forty of your relations.' 'Commander of the Faithful,' replied the grand vizier, 'I entreat your majesty to grant me time to make proper investigation.' 'I give you three days,' returned the caliph; 'look to it.'

"The vizier Giafar returned home in the greatest distress. 'Alas!' thought he, 'how is it possible, in so large and vast a city as Bagdad, to discover a murderer, who no doubt has committed this crime secretly and alone, and has now in all probability fled from the city? Another man in my place might perhaps take any wretch out of prison, and have him executed, to satisfy the caliph; but I will not load my conscience with such a deed; I will rather die than save my life by such means.'

"He ordered the officers of police and justice who were under his command to make strict search for the criminal. They sent out their underlings, and exerted themselves personally in this affair, which concerned them almost as much as the vizier. But all their diligence was fruitless; they could discover no traces that might lead to the murderer's capture, and the vizier concluded that, unless Heaven interposed in his favour, his death was inevitable.

"On the third day, an officer of the sultan came to the house of the unhappy minister, and summoned him to his master. The vizier obeyed, and when the caliph demanded of him the murderer, he replied, with tears in his eyes, 'O Commander of the Faithful, I have found no one who could give me any intelligence concerning him.'

The caliph reproached Giafar in the bitterest words, and commanded that he should be hanged before the gates of the palace, together with forty of the Barmecides.

"Whilst the executioners were preparing the gibbets, and the officers went to seize the forty Barmecides at their different houses, a public crier was ordered by the caliph to proclaim, in all the quarters of the city, that whoever wished to have the satisfaction of seeing the execution of the grand vizier Giafar, and forty of his family, the Barmecides, was to repair to the square before the palace.

"When everything was ready, the judge, accompanied by a great number of attendants and guards belonging to the palace, placed the grand vizier and the forty Barmecides each under the gibbet that was destined for him; and a cord was fastened round the neck of each of the prisoners. The people who crowded the square could not behold such a spectacle without feeling pity and shedding tears; for the vizier Giafar and his relations the Barmecides were much beloved for their probity, liberality, and disinterestedness, not only at Bagdad, but throughout the whole empire of the caliph.

"Everything was ready for the execution of the caliph's cruel order, and the next moment would have seen the death of some of the worthiest inhabitants of the city, when a young man, of comely appearance, and well dressed, pressed through the crowd till he reached the grand vizier. He kissed the captive Giafar's hand, and exclaimed, 'Sovereign vizier, chief of the emirs of this court, the refuge of the poor! you are not guilty of the crime for which you are going to suffer; let me expiate the death of the lady who was thrown into the Tigris; I am her murderer: I alone ought to be punished.'

"Although this speech created great joy in the vizier, he nevertheless felt pity for a youth, whose countenance, far from expressing guilt, indicated nobility of soul. He was going to reply, when a tall man of advanced age, who had also pushed through the crowd, came up, and said to the vizier, 'My lord, do not believe what this young man says to you. I alone am the person that killed the lady who was found in the chest; I alone am worthy of punishment. In the name of God, I conjure you not to confound the innocent with the guilty.' 'O my master,' interrupted the young man, addressing himself to the vizier, 'I assure you that it was I who committed this wicked action, and that no person in the world is my accomplice.' 'Alas! my son,' resumed the old man, 'despair has led you hither, and you wish to anticipate your destiny; as for me, I have lived for a long time in this world, and ought to quit it without regret; let me sacrifice my life to save yours. My lord,' continued he, addressing the vizier, 'I repeat it—I am the criminal; sentence me to death, and let justice be done.'

"The contest between the old man and the youth obliged the vizier Giafar to bring them before the caliph, with the permission of the commanding officer of justice, who was happy to have an opportunity of obliging him.

"When he came into the presence of the sovereign, he kissed the ground seven times, and then spoke these words: 'Commander of the Faithful, I bring to you this old man and this youth, each of whom accuses himself as the murderer of the lady.' The caliph then asked the two men which of them had murdered the lady in so cruel a manner, and then thrown her into the Tigris. The youth assured him that he had committed the deed; the old man maintained that the crime was his. 'Go,' said the caliph to the vizier, 'give orders that both of them be hanged.' 'But, Commander of the Faithful,' replied the vizier, 'if one only is guilty, it would be unjust to execute the other.'

"At these words the young man cried out, 'I swear by the great God who has built up the heavens to where they now are, that it is I who killed the lady, who cut her in pieces, and then threw her into the Tigris four days since. As I hope for mercy on the day of judgment, what I say is true; therefore I am the person who is to be punished.' The caliph was surprised at this solemn oath, which he was inclined to believe, as the old man made no reply. Therefore, turning to the youth, he exclaimed, 'Unhappy wretch! for what reason hast thou committed this detestable crime? What motive canst thou have for coming to offer thyself for execution?' 'Commander of the Faithful,' returned the young man, 'if all that has passed between this lady and myself could be written, it would form a history which might be serviceable to mankind.' 'Then I command thee to relate it,' said the caliph. Obedient to the order the young man began his story in these words :—

### The History of the Lady who was Murdered, and of the Young Man her Husband.

OVEREIGN of the Believers, I must acquaint your majesty that the murdered lady was my wife, and daughter to this old man whom you see, who is my uncle on my father's side. She was only twelve years of age when he bestowed her on me in marriage; and eleven years have passed since that period. She has borne me three sons, who are still alive, and I must do her the justice to say, that she never gave me the least cause for displeasure. She was prudent and virtuous; and her greatest pleasure was to make me happy. In return I loved her with the truest affection, and anticipated all her wishes, instead of thwarting them.

"About two months since she fell sick: I treated her with all possible care, and spared no pains to effect her cure. At the expiration of a month she grew better, and wished to go to the bath. Before she went out of the house she said to me, 'Cousin,' for so she used familiarly to call me, 'I wish to eat some apples: you would oblige me very much if you could procure me some. I have had this desire for a long time, and I must confess that it has now increased to such a degree, that if I am not gratified I fear some misfortune will happen.' I replied, 'I will do all in my power to content you.'

"I immediately went into all the markets and shops I could think of in quest of apples; but I could not obtain one, although I offered to pay a sequin for each. I returned home much vexed at having taken so much trouble to no purpose. As for my wife, when she came back from the bath, and did not see any apples, she was so chagrined that she could not sleep all night. I rose early the next morning and went into all the gardens, but could not succeed in my purpose. I only met with an old gardener, who told me that, whatever pains I might take, I should not find any apples excepting in your majesty's gardens at Balsora.

"As I was passionately fond of my wife, and could not bear the thought of neglecting any means to satisfy her longing, I put on the dress of a traveller, and, having informed her of my intention, I set out for Balsora. I travelled with such despatch that I reached my home at the end of a fortnight. I brought with me three apples, which had cost me a sequin apiece. They were the last in the garden, and the gardener would not sell them at a lower price. When I arrived I presented them to my wife; but her longing was then over, so she received in silence, and only placed them by her side. But her sickness continued, and I did not know what remedy to apply for her disorder.

"A few days after my return, as I sat in my shop in the public square, where all sorts of fine stuffs are sold, I saw a tall black slave enter, holding an apple in his hand, which I knew to be one of those I had brought from Balsora. I could have no doubt on the subject, for I knew that there were none in Bagdad, nor in any of the gardens in the environs. I called the slave, and said, 'My good slave, pray tell me where you got that apple.' He replied, laughing, 'It is a present from my mistress. I have been to see her to-day, and found her unwell. I saw three apples by her side, and asked her where she had got them; and she told me, that her foolish husband had been a fortnight's journey on purpose to get them for her. We breakfasted together, and when I came away I brought this with me.'

"This intelligence enraged me beyond measure. I rose and then shut up my shop; I ran hastily home, and went into the chamber of my wife. I looked for the apples;

and seeing but two, I inquired what was become of the third. My wife, turning her head towards the side where the apples were, and perceiving that there were only two, replied coldly, 'I do not know what is become of it, cousin.' This answer convinced me that the slave had spoken truth. Transported by a fit of jealousy, I drew a knife which hung from my girdle, and plunged it in the breast of my unhappy wife. I then cut off her head, and hewed her body into pieces. I tied up these pieces in a bundle, which I concealed in a folding basket, and after sewing up the opening of the basket with some red worsted, I enclosed it in a chest, and as soon as it was night carried it on my shoulders to the Tigris, and threw it in.

"My two youngest children were in bed and asleep, and the third was from

THE BLACK MAN STEALS THE APPLE.

home. On my return I found him sitting at the door, weeping bitterly. I asked him the reason of his tears. 'Father,' said he, 'this morning I took away from my mother, without her knowledge, one of the three apples you brought her. I kept it for some time, but as I was playing with it in the street, with my little brothers, a great black slave who was passing snatched it out of my hand, and took it away with him. I ran after him, asking him for it; I told him that it belonged to my mother, who was ill, and that you had been a fortnight's journey to procure it for her. All my entreaties were useless, for he would not return it; and as I followed him, crying, he turned back and beat me, and then ran off as fast as he could through so many winding streets that I lost sight of him. Since then I have been walking about the city waiting for your return. I was staying here for you, my father, to beg that you will not tell my mother, lest it should make her worse.' And when he had finished speaking he wept anew.

"This story of my son's plunged me into the deepest affliction. I now saw the enormity of my crime, and repented, too late, my credulous belief of the story of the wicked slave. My uncle, who is now present, arrived at that moment. He came to see his daughter; but instead of finding her alive he learnt from my lips that she was no more, for I disguised nothing from him, and without waiting for his condemnation I denounced myself as the most criminal of men. Nevertheless, instead of pouring forth the reproaches I justly deserved, this good man mingled his tears with mine, and we wept together three whole days; he for the loss of a daughter he had always tenderly loved, I for that of a wife who was dear to me, and of whom I had miserably deprived myself by giving credit to the false statement of a lying slave.

"This, Sovereign of the Faithful, is the sincere confession which your majesty required of me: you know the extent of my crime, and I humbly supplicate you to give orders for my punishment; however rigorous it may be, I shall not murmur at it, but esteem it too light."

"At this the caliph was in great astonishment; but this equitable prince, finding that the youth was more to be pitied than blamed, began to take his part. 'The action of this young man,' said he, 'is excusable in the sight of God, and may be pardoned by man. The wicked slave is the sole cause of this murder: he is the only one who ought to be punished; therefore,' continued he, addressing the vizier, 'I give you three days to find him: if you do not produce him within that time your life shall be the forfeit instead of his.'

"The unhappy Giafar, who had congratulated himself on his safety, was again overwhelmed with despair on hearing this new decree of the caliph; but as he did not dare to argue with his sovereign, with whose disposition he was well acquainted, he went out of his master's presence, and returned to his own house with his eyes bathed in tears, fully persuaded that he had only three days to live. He was so convinced of the impossibility of finding the slave, that he did not even seek him. 'It is not to be believed,' cried he, 'that in such a city as Bagdad, where there are vast numbers of black slaves, I should ever be able to discover the man the caliph requires. If Allah do not reveal him to me as he revealed the murderer, nothing can possibly save me.'

"He passed the two first days in weeping with his family, who could not help murmuring at the rigour of the caliph. On the third day he prepared for death with firmness, and like a minister who had ever acted with integrity, and had done nothing of which he was ashamed. He sent for the cadi and other witnesses, who signed the will he made in their presence. Then he embraced his wife and children, and bade them a last farewell. All his family melted into tears—never was there a more affecting spectacle. At length an officer of the palace arrived, with the news that the caliph was much displeased at not having heard from him about the black slave whom he had commanded the vizier to discover. 'I am ordered,' continued he, 'to bring you to the foot of the throne.' The miserable vizier prepared to follow the officer; but as he was going, his youngest daughter was brought to him. She was five or six years old, and the women who had the care of her were bringing her to take leave of her father.

"As he was particularly fond of this daughter, he entreated the officer to allow him a few minutes to speak to her. He approached the child, and, taking her in his arms, kissed her several times. In kissing her he perceived she had something large and fragrant in her bosom. 'My dear little girl,' said he, 'what have you in your bosom?' 'My dear father,' replied she, 'it is an apple, on which is written the name of the caliph, our lord and master. Rihan our slave sold it me for two sequins.'

"At these words the grand vizier Giafar cried aloud with surprise and joy, and immediately took the apple from the child's bosom. He ordered the slave to be called, and exclaimed, when the black was brought into his presence, 'Rascal! where didst thou get this apple?' 'My lord,' replied the slave, 'I swear to you, that I have not stolen it either from your garden or from that of the Commander of the Faithful.

"'The other day I passed through a street where there were three or four children at play. One of them had this apple in his hand, and I took it away from him. The child ran after me, saying that the apple did not belong to him, but to his mother, who was ill; that his father, to gratify her longing, had gone to a great distance to procure it, and had brought her three; that this was one which he had taken without his mother's knowledge. He entreated me to return it, but I would not attend to him, and brought the apple home; after which I sold it to the little lady, your daughter, for two sequins. This is all I have to say.'

"Giafar could not help marvelling how the roguery of a slave had caused the death of an innocent woman, and nearly deprived himself of life. He took the slave with him, and when he reached the palace he related to the caliph what the slave had confessed, and the chance by which he discovered the crime.

"The astonishment of the caliph was beyond all bounds; he could not contain himself, and burst into violent fits of laughter. At last, having regained his composure, he said to the vizier, that since his slave had occasioned all this distress he merited an exemplary punishment. 'Commander of the Faithful,' replied the vizier, 'I cannot deny it; yet his crime is not unpardonable. I know a history, far more surprising, of a vizier of Cairo, called Noureddin Ali, and of Bedreddin Hassan, of Balsora. As your majesty takes pleasure in hearing such stories, I am ready to relate it to you; provided that if you find it more wonderful than the circumstance which occasions me to tell it, you will remit the punishment of my slave.' 'Let it be so,' returned the caliph; 'but you have undertaken a great enterprise, and I do not think you can save your slave, for the story of the apples is very marvellous.' Giafar then began his story in these words:—

## The History of Noureddin Ali and Bedreddin Hassan.

OMMANDER of the Faithful, there was once a sultan in Egypt who was a great observer of justice. He was merciful, beneficent, and liberal, and his valour made him the terror of the neighbouring states. He provided for the poor, and patronised men of learning, whom he raised to the first offices in the state. The vizier of this sultan was a prudent, wise, and discerning man, skilled in literature and all the sciences. This minister had two sons, handsome in person, and resembling their father in talents. The eldest was named Schemseddin Mohammed, and the youngest Noureddin Ali. The latter in particular possessed as much merit as can fall to the lot of any man. On the death of the vizier, their father, the sultan sent for them, and having put on each the dress of an ordinary vizier, spoke thus: 'I regret your father's death, and feel sincerely for your loss; and as I wish to prove my sympathy to you, I invest each of you with equal dignity; for I know you live together, and are perfectly united. Go and imitate your father.'

"The two new viziers thanked the sultan for the favour he had conferred on them, and returned home to order their father's funeral. When a month had expired they made their appearance in public, and went for the first time to the council of the sultan, after which they continued to attend regularly every day that it assembled. Whenever the sultan went out to hunt one of the brothers accompanied him, and this honour was accorded to them alternately. One evening, when the eldest brother was to accompany the sultan to the chase on the morrow, the brothers were talking after supper on different subjects, Schemseddin Mohammed said to Noureddin Ali, 'Brother, as we are not yet married, and live in such harmony, a thought has occurred to me. Let us both marry on the same day, and wed two sisters, whom we will choose out of some family whose rank is equal to our own. What think you of this proposal?' 'I think, brother,' replied Noureddin Ali, 'it is worthy of the friendship that unites us. You could not have proposed a better plan, and I am ready to do whatever you wish in this matter.' 'Oh,' resumed the eldest, 'this is not all; my design goes much farther. In the event that our marriage is blessed with offspring, and that your wife brings you a son, while mine presents me with a daughter, we will unite the two when they are of a proper age.' 'Ah!' exclaimed his brother, 'this is indeed an admirable project. This marriage will complete our union, and I readily give my consent. But, brother,' added he, "if this marriage is indeed to take place, should you expect my son to settle a fortune on your daughter?' 'In that there is no difficulty,' replied the other, 'and I am persuaded that besides the usual agreements in a marriage contract, you would not object to give in your son's name at least three thousand sequins, three good estates, and three slaves.' 'That I cannot agree to,' returned Noureddin Ali. 'Are not we brothers and colleagues, each invested with the same dignity and title? and do not we both know what is just? Inasmuch as the man is more noble than the woman, ought not you to bestow a handsome marriage portion on your daughter? I perceive you are a man who wishes to enrich himself at the expense of others.'

"Although Noureddin Ali spoke these words in jest, his brother, who was of a fiery temper, was highly offended. 'Woe to thy son!' said he, angrily, 'since you dare to prefer him to my daughter. I am surprised that you should have the audacity even to suppose him worthy of her. You must be mad, that you thus proclaim yourself my equal, by saying that we are colleagues. Know that after such insolence I would not marry my daughter to your son, even if you were to give her more riches than you possess.' This strange quarrel between the brothers about the marriage of their children, who were not yet born, did not cease here. Schemseddin Mohammed went so far as to threaten his brother. 'If I were not obliged,' said he, 'to accompany the sultan to-morrow, I would treat you as you deserve; but on my return you shall learn that it does not become the younger brother to treat the elder with the insolence you have shown towards me.' With these words he retired to his apartment, and his brother followed his example.

"Schemseddin Mohammed rose very early the next morning, and repaired to the palace; from whence he went out with the sultan, who extended his journey beyond Cairo, towards the pyramids. As for Noureddin Ali, he passed the night in great distress; and having well considered that it was not possible for him to remain any longer with a brother who treated him with such contempt, he formed the resolution of quitting his home. He caused a good mule to be caparisoned, provided himself with money, precious stones, and some eatables; and having told his people that he was going on a journey of three or four days, and that he wished to be alone, he departed.

"On leaving Cairo, he went over the desert towards Arabia; but his mule became lame on the road, and he was obliged to continue his journey on foot. He had the good fortune to be overtaken by a messenger who was going to Balsora, and who took him up behind him on his camel. When they were arrived at Balsora, Noureddin Ali alighted, thanking the messenger for his assistance. As he walked along the streets, seeking for a lodging, he saw a person of high rank coming towards him, accompanied by a numerous train; and all the inhabitants paid great respect to this personage, waiting to let him pass; and Noureddin Ali stopped like the rest. It was the grand vizier of the Sultan of Balsora, parading the city to enforce peace and good order by his presence.

"This minister chanced to cast his eyes on the young man, and was struck with his engaging countenance: he looked on Noureddin Ali with favour, and as he passed near him, perceiving that the stranger wore a traveller's garb, he stopped to ask him who he was, and from whence he came. 'My lord,' replied Noureddin Ali, 'I come from Egypt, and am a native of Cairo. I have quitted my country on account of a quarrel with one of my relations, and I have resolved to travel over the whole world, and to die rather than return home.' When the grand vizier, who was a venerable old man, heard these words, he replied, 'My son, do not persevere in the project you have formed. In this world there is nothing but misery, and you little think what hardships you will have to endure. Come rather with me, and perhaps I can make you forget the cause which has induced you to quit your country.'

NOUREDDIN ALI ON HIS JOURNEY TOWARDS ARABIA.

"Noureddin Ali followed the grand vizier of Balsora, who soon became acquainted with his good qualities, and conceived a great affection for him; so that one day when they were alone together, the old man thus addressed him: 'My son, I am, as you see, so far advanced in years that there is no prospect of my living much longer. Heaven has given me an only daughter as handsome as yourself, and she is now of a marriageable age. Many of the most powerful lords of this court have already demanded her of me for their sons, but I never could bring myself to part with her. Now, I love you, and think you so worthy of being allied to my family that I am willing to accept you as my son-in-law in preference to all who have offered themselves. If this proposal pleases you, I will inform the sultan my master that I have adopted you by this marriage, and I will entreat him to permit me to bestow upon you my appointment as grand vizier of Balsora; and as I require rest from business in my old age, I will resign to you all my possessions, with the administration of the affairs of state.'

"On hearing this speech, which showed the kindness and generosity of the speaker, Noureddin Ali threw himself at the grand vizier's feet, and in terms which evinced the joy and gratitude that flowed from his heart, declared himself ready to do anything his patron should dictate. The grand vizier then called together the principal officers of his household, and ordered them to prepare the great hall in his house for a grand entertainment. He sent invitations to all the nobles of the court, and to the great men of the city, to summon them to the feast. Noureddin Ali had made him acquainted with his rank, and when they were all assembled he thus addressed them: 'My friends, I am happy to inform you of a circumstance which I have hitherto kept secret. I have a brother who is grand vizier of the Sultan of Egypt, as I have the happiness to be grand vizier to the sultan of these dominions. This brother of mine has an only son, whom he would not marry at the court of Egypt, and he has sent him here to be united to my daughter, that the two branches of our family might be thus joined together. This young nobleman whom you see here, and whom I recognised as my nephew on his arrival, I am going to make my son-in-law. I trust you will do him the honour of being present at the nuptials, which I intend shall be solemnised this day.' The grand vizier spoke thus because he thought that no one could be offended at his preferring his nephew to all those noblemen who had offered their alliance; and indeed, they replied that he did right to conclude this marriage, that they would willingly be present at the ceremony, and that they hoped Allah would bless both uncle and nephew many years with the fruits of this happy union. When they had thus expressed their approbation of the marriage of the vizier's daughter with Noureddin Ali, they sat down to table, and feasted for a considerable time. Towards the end of the repast the confectionery was served, and when, according to custom, each guest had taken as much as he wished to carry away, the cadis entered with the marriage contract in their hands. The chief among the noblemen signed it, and the whole company retired.

"When all the guests were gone, the grand vizier desired the attendants who had the care of the bath to conduct Noureddin Ali thither. He found provided for him new linen of a beautiful fineness and whiteness, as well as every other necessary. When the bridegroom had enjoyed his bath he was going to resume his own dress, but another of the greatest magnificence was presented to him in its place. Thus adorned, and perfumed with the most exquisite odours, he returned to the grand vizier, his father-in-law, who was charmed with his appearance, and placed him by his side, saying, 'My son, you have disclosed to me who you are and the rank you held at the Egyptian court; you have also told me that you had a quarrel with your brother, and that this caused you to leave your country; I entreat you to relate to me the nature of this quarrel, for you must now trust me entirely and conceal nothing from me.'

"Noureddin Ali related all the circumstances connected with his dispute with his brother. The grand vizier could not refrain from laughing very heartily. 'This is indeed,' said he, 'the strangest thing I ever heard of! Is it possible that your quarrel was carried to such lengths merely for an imaginary wedding? I am sorry that you quarrelled with your elder brother for such a trifle; however, I perceive that he was in the wrong to be offended with what you said merely in jest, and I ought to be thankful to Heaven that this strife between two brothers has been the means of procuring me a son-in-law such as you. But,' continued the old man, 'the night is advancing, and it is time for you to retire. Go, my daughter is expecting your arrival. To-morrow I will present you to the sultan, and I flatter myself he will receive you in a way that shall satisfy us both.'

"Noureddin Ali left his father-in-law to repair to the chamber of his bride. And it is a very remarkable thing that on the same day that these nuptials were celebrated at Balsora, Schemseddin Mohammed was married at Cairo in the following manner:—

"After Noureddin Ali had left Cairo with the intention never to return, Schemseddin Mohammed, his elder brother, who was absent with the sultan on the hunting party, returned at the end of a month. The sultan was passionately fond of hunting, or they would not have been away so long. Schemseddin Mohammed at once ran into the apartment of Noureddin Ali; but great was his surprise on being informed that his brother had left Cairo, under pretence of making a journey of four or five days; that he set off on a mule on the very day of the sultan's departure; and that since that time he had never been seen or heard of. Schemseddin Mohammed was the more chagrined at this intelligence as he accused himself of having caused his brother's flight by the harsh words he had used towards him. He despatched a courier who passed through Damascus and went on to Aleppo; but Noureddin Ali was at that time at Balsora. When the messenger returned without bringing any tidings of him, Schemseddin Mohammed determined to send in other directions to seek for Noureddin Ali, but in the meantime he formed the design of marrying. He made choice of the daughter of one of the most powerful nobles of Cairo, and was united to her on the same day that his brother married the daughter of the grand vizier of Balsora.

"But this is not all," continued Giafar; "I will now tell you, Commander of the Faithful, what happened afterwards. At the expiration of nine months the wife of Schemseddin Mohammed brought her husband a daughter, at Cairo, and on the same day the wife of Noureddin Ali, at Balsora, brought into the world a boy, who was named Bedreddin Hassan. The grand vizier of Balsora testified his joy by vast gifts to the poor and by instituting public rejoicings on the birth of his grandson. To prove his affection for Noureddin Ali, he afterwards went to the palace to entreat the sultan to grant him leave to transfer his office, that he might have the satisfaction, before he died, of seeing his son-in-law in his place.

"The sultan, who had seen Noureddin Ali immediately after his marriage, and had since that time heard him spoken of favourably, readily granted to his vizier the wished-for favour, and he ordered Noureddin Ali to be clothed in his presence in the dress of a grand vizier.

"The happiness of the father-in-law was complete when he saw Noureddin Ali presiding at the council in his place, and performing all the functions of his exalted office. Noureddin Ali acquitted himself of his new duties so well that he appeared to have exercised his office all his life. He presided at the council whenever the infirmities of age would not allow his father-in-law to be present. The good old man died four years after this marriage, with the satisfaction of seeing a descendant firmly established, who promised to sustain the honour and credit of his family.

"Noureddin Ali performed the last duties to his dead father-in-law with the greatest tenderness and gratitude; and as soon as Bedreddin Hassan, his son, had reached the age of seven years, he placed him under the care of an excellent master, who began the boy's education in a way suitable to his birth. He found in his pupil a quick and penetrating lad, capable of profiting by the instruction, he received.

"By the time Bedreddin Hassan had been two years with his tutor, he had learned to read, and could write the Koran by heart. Noureddin Ali, his father, then procured him other masters, and he made such a rapid progress in his studies that at the age of twelve years he was no longer in need of their assistance. By that time the features of his countenance had become so beautiful that he was the admiration of all who saw him.

"Till then Noureddin Ali had only sought to make his son study, and had not brought him out into the world. He now took him to the palace, and had the honour of introducing him to the sultan, who received him very favourably. The people in the streets who saw Bedreddin Hassan as he went along were so struck with his beauty that they cried out in amazement, and showered blessings upon his head.

"As his father wished to make him capable of one day filling the situation he himself held, he spared nothing to qualify him for it; and by making him enter into affairs of the most difficult nature he prepared him early for the career he intended him to follow. In short, he neglected nothing that could tend to the advancement of his dearly beloved son; and he had begun to enjoy the fruits of his care, when he was suddenly attacked by a disease so violent that he felt his end was approaching. He therefore did not deceive himself with hopes of recovery, but prepared to die like a good Mussulman. In these precious moments he did not forget his beloved son Bedreddin Hassan; he caused him to be called to his bedside, and thus addressed him: 'My son, you see that this world is perishable; that world only to which I am shortly going is eternal. You must from this moment begin to prepare to take this journey without regret; your conscience acquitting you of having neglected any of the duties of a Mussulman, or of an honest man. With regard to your religion, you have been sufficiently instructed in that by the masters you have had, as well as by what you have read. As to your duty as an honest man, I will now give you some advice, by which I hope you will endeavour to profit. As it is right you should know who you are, and you cannot possibly have that knowledge without knowing who I am, I will now inform you.

"'I was born in Egypt; my father was prime minister to the sultan of that country. I, too, had the honour of being one of the viziers of the same sultan, jointly with my brother, your uncle, who I believe is still alive, and is called Schemseddin Mohammed. I was compelled to separate from him, and I came into this country, where I attained the rank which I have till now enjoyed. But you will learn all these things more fully from a packet which I shall give you.'

"Noureddin Ali then took out a scroll, which he had written with his own hand, and which he always carried about him, and gave it to Bedreddin Hassan. 'Take it,' he said; 'read it at your leisure; you will find in it, among other things, the date of my marriage, and that of your birth. These are particulars which may be useful to you in the end, and you must, therefore, carefully preserve the record.' Bedreddin Hassan, truly grieved at seeing his father in such a state, and, touched by his discourse, received the packet with tears in his eyes, promising never to let it go out of his possession.

"Noureddin Ali was seized with a fainting fit, which, it was feared, would terminate his existence; but he recovered, and spoke the following words to his son:—

"'The first maxim I wish to impress on your mind is, not to impart your confidence with all kinds of persons. The way to live in safety is to be reserved, and not too communicative.

"'The second maxim is, to commit violence on no one; for were you to do so all the world would revolt against you, and you must regard the world as a creditor to whom you owe moderation, compassion, and toleration.

"'Thirdly, never reply when you are spoken to in anger. "He is out of danger," says the proverb, "who remains silent." On such occasions, in particular, you should attend to this. You know also what one of our poets has written on this subject: "Silence is the ornament and safeguard of life; nor should we in speaking resemble the stormy rain, which spoils everything." We never repent having been silent, but often regret having spoken.

"'The fourth maxim is, to abstain from drinking wine, for it is the source of all vice.

"'The fifth, to manage your fortune with economy; if you do not spend it extravagantly, you will have what you require to help you in case of need. Beware, however, of too much parsimony, lest you become a miser. If you have only a little, and yet spend that with propriety, you will gain many friends; but if, on the contrary, you possess great riches, and do not make a good use of them, every one will despise and abandon you.'

"Noureddin Ali continued to give similar counsels to his son till the last moments of his life; and after his death he was interred with all the honours due to his rank and dignity. Bedreddin Hassan, of Balsora, as he was called, from being born in that town, was inconsolable at the death of his father. Instead of mourning for one month, as is the custom, he passed two in retreat, overwhelmed by his sorrow; during which time he would not see any one, nor did he even go out to pay his respects to the sultan, who, displeased with this neglect, which he considered as a mark of contempt towards him and his court, suffered his anger to rise to a great height. He summoned the new grand vizier whom he had elected in the place of Noureddin Ali, and ordered him to go to the house of the deceased minister, and to confiscate it, together with all Noureddin Ali's other houses, grounds, and effects; nor was anything to be left for Bedreddin Hassan, whose person also he ordered the officer to seize.

"The grand vizier, accompanied by a number of the officers of the palace, immediately

BEDREDDIN HASSAN AND THE JEW ISAAC.

set out to execute his commission. One of the slaves of Bedreddin Hassan, who had by chance joined the crowd at the council, no sooner learnt the intention of the grand vizier than he hastened to warn his master of the danger. He found him seated in the vestibule of his house, as full of affliction as if his father were but just dead. The slave threw himself at his master's feet quite out of breath, and kissing the hem of Bedreddin Hassan's robe, exclaimed, 'Fly, my lord, fly quickly!' 'What is the matter?' inquired Bedreddin Hassan, raising his head, 'what news hast thou?' 'My lord,' replied the slave, 'you have not a moment to lose. The sultan is enraged against you, and they are now coming by his order to confiscate all your possessions, and even to seize your person.'

"This news brought by the faithful and affectionate slave occasioned Bedreddin Hassan some perplexity. 'But,' said he, 'cannot I return and take even some money and jewels?' 'My dear lord,' replied the slave, 'the grand vizier will be here in a moment. Depart instantly and make your escape.' Bedreddin Hassan immediately got up from the sofa on which he was sitting, and put on his slippers; then covering his head with one corner of his robe to conceal his face, he fled, without knowing whither to turn his steps to avoid the danger which threatened him. The first thought that occurred to him was to make for the nearest gate of the city. He ran without stopping till he came to the public cemetery, and as evening was approaching, determined to pass the night near his father's tomb. This tomb was a large edifice of magnificent appearance, built in the shape of a dome, which Noureddin Ali had erected during his lifetime; but Bedreddin Hassan in his way met with a very rich Jew, a banker and merchant by profession. This man was returning to the city from a place where he had been on business.

"This Jew, who was called Isaac, knew Bedreddin Hassan, and he stopped and saluted him very respectfully: after kissing his hand, he said, 'My lord, may I take the liberty of asking you where you are going to at this hour alone, and seemingly so agitated? Is there anything that disturbs you?' 'Yes,' replied Bedreddin Hassan, "I fell asleep just now, and my father appeared to me in a dream. His countenance was threatening, as if he had been very angry with me. I awoke much terrified, and I set off immediately to come and pray at his tomb.' 'My lord,' replied the Jew, who did not know the real cause of Bedreddin Hassan's quitting the city, 'as the late grand vizier your father, of happy memory, had several vessels laden with merchandise, which are still at sea and now belong to you, I entreat you to grant me the preference over any other merchant. I am in a position to purchase for ready-money the cargoes of all your vessels; and as a proof of what I say, if it please you, I will give you a thousand sequins for the first which arrives in port; I have the money here in a purse, and am ready to pay it.' Saying this, he drew out from under his robe a large purse, sealed with his seal, which he showed to Bedreddin Hassan.

"Forced from his home, and robbed of everything he possessed, Bedreddin Hassan looked upon this proposition of the Jew as a favour from Heaven, and accepted the offer with great joy. 'O my master,' said the Jew, 'you grant me then the cargo of the first of your vessels that arrives for one thousand sequins?' 'I do,' replied Bedreddin Hassan, 'the bargain is made.' The Jew then put the purse of sequins into his hands, at the same time offering to count them, but Bedreddin Hassan saved him the trouble by saying he trusted in his honour. 'Then, my lord,' resumed the Jew, 'will you have the goodness to write an acknowledgment of the bargain we have made?' He then pulled from his girdle an ink-horn, and taking a cane prepared for writing, he presented it to the young man, with a leaf of paper which he found in his pocket-book, and while he held the ink, Bedreddin Hassan wrote these words:—

"'*This writing is to witness, that Bedreddin Hassan, of Balsora, has sold the cargo of the first of his ships which shall arrive at this port to the Jew Isaac, for the sum of one thousand sequins, received.* 'BEDREDDIN HASSAN, OF BALSORA.'

"This writing he gave to the Jew, who put it in his girdle, and they separated; Isaac pursuing his way to the city, while Bedreddin Hassan proceeded to the tomb of his father, Noureddin Ali. When he had reached it, he prostrated himself with his face towards the earth, and with many tears began to lament his miserable fate. 'Alas!' said he, 'unfortunate Bedreddin, what will become of thee? Where wilt thou find refuge from the unjust prince who persecutes thee? Was it not affliction enough to lose so dear a father? Why would fortune add another grief to those thou hast already suffered?' He remained a considerable time in this state; but at length he arose, and, leaning his head on his father's sepulchre, he renewed his lamentations, and continued to weep and sigh until, overtaken by sleep, he laid himself down on the pavement, where he fell into a gentle slumber.

"He had scarcely begun to taste the sweets of repose, when a genie, who had chosen this cemetery as his retreat during the day, and who was about to set forth on his nightly excursions, perceived this young man in the tomb of Noureddin Ali. He entered, and, as Bedreddin Hassan lay with his face upwards, the genie was struck with admiration at his beauty; and, after gazing at him for some time, he said to himself, 'To judge of this creature by his countenance, it can only be an angel sent by Allah from the terrestrial paradise to enchant the world with its beauty.' After he had contemplated the sleeper again, he rose into the air, where by chance he met a fairy. They saluted each other, and the genie said, 'I entreat you to descend with me to the cemetery where I live, and I will show you a prodigy of beauty, who will awaken your admiration as he has excited mine.' The fairy consented, and they both instantly descended. When they came to the tomb, the genie, showing Bedreddin Hassan to her, exclaimed, 'Tell me, did you ever see so handomse a youth as this?'

"The fairy examined Bedreddin Hassan attentively, and then replied, turning towards the genie, 'I confess that he is very handsome, but I have just seen at Cairo an object still more wonderful; and will tell you something concerning it if you will attend to me.' 'That I will, with pleasure,' replied the genie. 'You must know, then,' resumed the fairy, 'that the Sultan of Egypt has a vizier, named Schemseddin Mohammed, and this Schemseddin Mohammed has a daughter about twenty years of age. She is the most beautiful and perfect creature ever seen. A few days since, the sultan, hearing from every one of the extraordinary beauty of this young lady, sent for the vizier her father, and said to him, 'I understand you have a daughter who is marriageable, and I wish to make her my wife; will not you give her to me?' The vizier, who did not at all expect such a proposal, was rather disconcerted, but he was not dazzled by the prospect of such a marriage for his daughter; and, instead of accepting the offer with joy, as many in his place would have done, he replied to the sultan, 'O sultan, I am not worthy of the honour your majesty would confer on me; and I humbly entreat you not to be displeased that I should decline your offer. You know that I had a brother called Noureddin Ali, who, like myself, had the honour of being one of your viziers. We had a quarrel, in consequence of which he suddenly disappeared, and I have never heard of him since that time till within these four days, when I learnt that he had lately died at Balsora, where he enjoyed the dignity of grand vizier to the sultan. He has left one son; and, as we formerly agreed that our children, if ever we had any, should marry each other, I am certain that when he died he had not abandoned his design. For this reason I wish, on my part, to perform my promise; and I supplicate your majesty to permit me to do so. There are many nobles in this court who have daughters as fair as mine, and who will be deeply grateful for the honour of your alliance.'

"'The Sultan of Egypt was extremely irritated by this answer of Schemseddin Mohammed, and said to him, in a sudden transport of anger, 'Is it thus you return the condescension with which I proposed my alliance to your family? You dare to show preference to another over me? I swear to you that your daughter shall have for her husband the meanest and ugliest of my slaves.' With these words he dismissed the vizier, who returned home full of confusion and much mortified.

"'To-day the sultan ordered to be brought to him one of his grooms, who is very much deformed, and so ugly it is impossible to look at him without terror; and, after commanding Schemseddin Mohammed to give his consent to the marriage of his daughter with this horrible slave, he had the contract drawn up, and signed by witnesses in his presence. The preparations for these strange nuptials are now completed, and at this moment all the slaves of the nobles of the Egyptian court are at the door of a bath, each with a torch in his hand; they are waiting for the humpbacked groom, who is in the bath, to come out, that they may lead him to his bride, who is already dressed to receive him. At the time I left Cairo the ladies were assembled to conduct her, in her nuptial ornaments, to the hall, where she is to receive her deformed bridegroom, and where she is now expecting him. I saw her, and assure you that it is impossible to behold her without admiration.'

"When the fairy had ceased speaking, the genie replied that he could not believe it possible for the beauty of this damsel to surpass that of the youth who lay sleeping before them. 'I will not dispute with you,' said the fairy; 'I will only say that he deserves to marry the charming lady who is destined for the groom; and I think we should perform a good action were we to frustrate the injustice of the sultan, and to substitute this young man for the slave.' 'You speak wisely,' resumed the genie, 'and you cannot conceive how much I admire you for this idea. Let us disappoint the vengeance of the sultan, console an afflicted father, and make his daughter as happy as she now believes herself to be miserable. I will omit nothing to make this project succeed; and I am persuaded that on your part you will not spare in your exertions. I take upon me to carry this youth to Cairo without waking him; and I leave to you the task of disposing of him after we have executed our enterprise.'

"After the genie and the fairy had decided together what they should do, the genie gently raised Bedreddin Hassan, transported him through the air with inconceivable swiftness, and placed him at the door of a public apartment adjoining the bath from whence the groom was to come, accompanied by the slaves who were waiting for him.

"Awaking at this instant, Bedreddin Hassan was much astonished to find himself in a city quite unknown to him, and was going to inquire where he was, when the genie gave him a gentle tap on the shoulder, and warned him not to speak a word; then putting a torch in his hand, he said to him, 'Go and join the people whom you see at the door of yonder bath, and walk with them till you come to a hall where a wedding is going to be celebrated. You will easily distinguish the bridegroom by his being deformed. Place yourself on his right hand when you enter; and from time to time open the purse of sequins which you have in your bosom, and distribute the money among the musicians and dancers as you go along. When you have reached the hall, do not fail to give some also to the female slaves whom you will see about the bride when they approach you. But remember, whenever you put your hand in your purse, to draw it out full of sequins, and see that you do not spare your gold. Do exactly as I have told you. Be bold, and be not surprised at anything; fear no one, and trust for the consequence in the power of one who will dispose of everything as he thinks best for you.'

"The young Bedreddin Hassan, thus instructed in what he was to do, advanced towards the door of the bath. The first thing he did was to light his torch by that of a slave; then mixing with the rest as if he had been sent by a nobleman of Cairo, he walked with them, and accompanied the groom, who came out of the bath and mounted one of the horses from the sultan's stable.

"Finding himself near the musicians and dancers who preceded the humpbacked groom, Bedreddin Hassan frequently drew from his purse handfuls of sequins, which he distributed amongst them. As he conferred these bounties with admirable grace and with a very liberal air, all those who received them cast their eyes on him, and no sooner had they seen him than they were fascinated by him, so great was his beauty and the symmetry of his figure.

"At length the procession arrived at the palace of Schemseddin Mohammed, who little thought his nephew was so near him. To prevent confusion, some of the officers stopped all the slaves who carried torches, and would not suffer them to enter. They also wanted to exclude Bedreddin Hassan; but the musicians and dancers, for whom the doors were opened, declared they would not proceed if he were not allowed to accompany them. 'He is not one of the slaves,' said they, 'you have only to look at him to be fully convinced of that. He must be some young stranger who wishes from curiosity to see the ceremonies observed at weddings in this city.' Saying this, they placed him in their midst, and made him go in, in spite of the officers. They took from him his torch, and when they had brought him into the hall they placed him on the right hand of the groom, who was seated on a magnificent throne, next to the daughter of the vizier.

"The bride was dressed in her richest ornaments, but her countenance displayed a melancholy, or rather a desponding sorrow, the cause of which was easily divined by any one who saw by her side the humpbacked bridegroom who seemed so little deserving her

BEDREDDIN HASSAN GIVING AWAY SEQUINS.

love. The throne of this ill-matched pair was erected in the middle of a large divan; the wives of the emirs, viziers, and officers of the sultan's chamber, together with many other ladies of the court and of the city, were seated a little below on each side, according to their rank; and all were so brilliantly and richly dressed, that the whole scene formed a beautiful spectacle. Each person held a lighted flambeau.

"When they saw Bedreddin Hassan enter, they all fixed their eyes on him, and could not cease looking at him, so much were they struck with the beauty of his figure and countenance. The difference between Bedreddin Hassan and the crooked groom, whose person excited disgust and horror, gave rise to some murmurs in the assembly. 'This handsome youth,' exclaimed the ladies, 'ought to be married to our bride, and not this deformed wretch.' They went further than this, and even ventured to utter imprecations against the sultan, who was abusing his absolute power by uniting deformity to beauty. They also vented execrations on the groom, and put him quite out of countenance, much to the diversion of the spectators, who by their hootings for some time interrupted the music which was playing. At length the musicians again began their concert, and the women who had dressed the bride approached her.

"Each time the bride changed her dress, which according to custom she was obliged to do seven different times, she arose, and, followed by her women, passed before the groom, without deigning to look at him, and went to present herself to Bedreddin Hassan, to show herself to him in her new ornaments. Remembering the instructions he had received from the genie, Bedreddin Hassan on each of these occasions put his hand into the purse and drew it out full of sequins, which he distributed to the women who attended the bride. He did not forget the musicians and dancers, but gave them some money also. They testified their gratitude, and told him by signs that they wished him to marry the bride instead of the humpbacked groom. The women who were about her said the same thing to her, not caring whether the humpback heard them; for they played him all kinds of tricks, to the great amusement of the spectators.

"When the ceremony of changing the dresses was completed, the musicians ceased playing and retired, making signs to Bedreddin Hassan to remain. The ladies also motioned him to stay, and took their leave, together with all those who did not belong to the house. The bride went into a closet, where her women followed to undress her, and there remained no one in the hall except the humpbacked groom, Bedreddin Hassan, and some servants. The humpback, who was furiously enraged with Bedreddin Hassan, gave him a scowling look out of the corners of his eyes, and cried out, 'What art thou waiting for? Get thee gone! Why dost thou not depart with the rest?' As Bedreddin Hassan had no pretext for remaining, he retired somewhat out of countenance; but he had scarcely left the vestibule when the genie and the fairy appeared before him, and stopped him. 'Whither art thou going?' said the genie. 'Return, for the hunchback has left the hall; you have nothing to do but to go in and proceed at once to the chamber of the bride. When you are alone with her tell her confidently that you are her husband, that the sultan only intended to put off a jest upon the hunchback, and that to appease this pretended husband you have ordered him a large dish of cream in his stable. Use all the arguments you can think of to persuade her of the truth of this. A handsome man like yourself will not find much difficulty in doing this, and she will be delighted with so agreeable an exchange. We will take proper precautions so that the hunchback shall not return to prevent you from visiting your bride, for she is yours, not his.'

"While the genie was thus encouraging Bedreddin Hassan, and instructing him in the part he was to play, the hunchback had really quitted the hall. The genie went and sought him out, and assuming the figure of a large black cat, began to mew in a terrific manner. The hunchback clapped his hands and made a noise to frighten the creature away; but the cat, instead of retreating, set up its back and fixed its fiery eyes fiercely on him, mewing louder than before. It then began to swell, increasing in size until it was larger than an ass. The hunchback at this sight was going to call for assistance, but he was so terrified that he could not utter a sound, and remained with his mouth open unable to speak. To increase his terror, the genie suddenly changed himself into a large buffalo, and under this shape cried with a loud voice, 'O miserable hunchback!' At these words the frightened groom fell on the floor; and covering his head with his robe to avoid seeing this horrible beast, he replied, trembling, 'Sovereign prince of the buffaloes, what dost thou require of me?' 'Ill befall thee!' replied the genie; 'thou hast the temerity to dare to marry my mistress?' 'O my lord!' cried the hunchback, 'I entreat you to pardon me; if I have erred it is through ignorance alone. I did not know that the lady had a buffalo for her lover. Command me in whatever you please, I swear I am ready to obey.' 'I swear to thee,' resumed the genie, 'that if thou quittest this spot or breakest silence before the sun rises, nay, if thou utterest but a syllable, I will crush thy head to atoms. At sunrise I permit thee to leave this house; but I command thee to fly quickly, and not to look behind thee; and if thou hast ever the audacity to return, it shall cost thee thy life.' Thus saying the genie transformed himself into a man, and took the hunchback by the heels; then, holding him against the wall with his head downwards, he added, 'If thou darest to stir before the sun rises I repeat to thee that I will take thee by the feet and dash thy head into a thousand pieces against this wall.'

"Meanwhile Bedreddin Hassan, encouraged by the genie and by the fairy, who was present, had re-entered the hall, and proceeded privately into the nuptial chamber, where he seated himself, waiting with anxious expectation the issue of his adventure. After some time the bride arrived, conducted by an old woman, who stopped at the door without looking in to see if the hunchback or another were in the room; she then shut the door and retired.

"The young bride was extremely surprised when, instead of the hunchback, she beheld Bedreddin Hassan, who presented himself to her with the utmost grace. 'O my friend!' exclaimed she, 'how came you here at this hour? I suppose you are one of my husband's comrades?' 'No, madam,' replied Bedreddin Hassan, 'I have nothing to do with that disgusting hunchback. Be undeceived: such beauty as yours will not be sacrificed to the most despicable of men. I am the happy mortal to whom you are married. The sultan chose to amuse himself by playing off this little jest on the vizier your father, and has selected me for your real husband. You must have observed that the ladies, the musicians, the dancers, your women, in short, all who belonged to your household, were diverted with this comedy. We have dismissed the hunchback to his stable, where he is now regaling himself with a dish of cream; and you may be assured that he will never more appear before your beautiful eyes.'

"At this discourse the daughter of the vizier, who had entered the nuptial chamber more dead than alive, changed countenance, and regained an air of cheerfulness, which added so much to her beauty that Bedreddin Hassan was quite charmed with her. 'I did not expect so agreeable a surprise,' said she, 'I considered myself condemned to pass the rest of my days in misery, but my happiness is so much the greater in being united to a man so worthy of my affection.' Bedreddin Hassan was delighted to find himself in possession of so beautiful a spouse. He quickly undressed, putting his clothes on a chair, together with the purse which the Jew had given him, and which was still full, notwithstanding all the gold he had taken from it. He took off his turban to put on a cap suitable for wearing at night, which had been prepared for the hunchback, and lay down.

"When the two lovers were asleep, the genie, who had sought out the fairy, told her it was now time to complete the task they had so well begun and so happily conducted thus far. 'Let us not,' said he, 'be surprised by daylight, which will now soon appear; go and take away the young man without waking him.'

"The fairy repaired to the chamber of the lovers, who were both sleeping profoundly, and stole away Bedreddin Hassan, dressed as he was in his shirt and drawers. Accompanied by the genie, she flew with wonderful swiftness to the gates of Damascus, in Syria. They arrived precisely at the time when the muezzin was calling the people to prayers at break of day. The fairy gently placed Bedreddin Hassan on the ground, near the gate, and then flew away, the genie vanishing with her.

"Presently the gates were opened; and the people, who had assembled in great numbers to go out, were extremely surprised at seeing Bedreddin Hassan lying on the ground in only his shirt and drawers. One said, 'This man was obliged to decamp from some haunt in such haste that he had not time to dress himself.' 'See,' said another, 'to what accidents a man may be exposed: he has passed the night drinking with his friends, and, being inebriated, went out, and has wandered here, not knowing what he did, and has been overtaken by sleep.' Others formed different opinions, but no one could guess by what chance Bedreddin Hassan came there. A slight breeze which was beginning to rise blew aside the cap which shaded his face. They were all surprised at the whiteness of the skin, and they exclaimed so loudly in their admiration that they awakened the young man. His astonishment was not less than theirs on finding himself at the gate of a city where he had never been, and on seeing a crowd of people, who were examining him attentively. He cried out, 'Friends, I entreat you to inform me where I am, and what you want of me.' One of the spectators replied, 'Young man, the gates of this city are but just opened, and when we came out we found you lying here, just as you now are; and we stopped to look at you. Have you passed the night here, and do you know that you are at one of the gates of Damascus?' 'At one of the gates of Damascus!' exclaimed Bedreddin Hassan, 'you do but jest with me; when I went to bed last night I was at Cairo.' At these words some of the people, moved with compassion, said it was a pity that so handsome a youth should have lost his senses; and so they passed on.

"A venerable old man next addressed him. 'My son,' he said, 'you must be mistaken; for how could you be last night at Cairo, and this morning at Damascus? That cannot be.' 'It is very true, notwithstanding,' replied Bedreddin Hassan; 'and I assure you, moreover, that I passed the whole of yesterday at Balsora.' He had scarcely uttered these words when they all burst into a laugh, and cried, 'He is mad, he is mad!' Some, however, pitied him on account of his extreme youth; and a man who was looking on said, 'My son, you have lost your reason: you know not what you say. How is it possible that a man should be in one day at Balsora, in the same night at Cairo, and the next morning at Damascus? You surely cannot be fully awake: try to collect your thoughts.' 'What I tell you,' persisted Bedreddin Hassan, 'is as true as that I was last night married in the city of Cairo.' All those who had laughed before burst into fresh shouts at hearing this. 'Take care,' resumed the person who had addressed him before, 'you must have dreamt all this, and the illusion still remains impressed on your mind.' 'I know what I am saying,' replied the youth, 'I have not dreamt I was at Cairo, for I am persuaded I was there in reality. My bride was conducted seven times before me, each time in a different dress; and I saw a hideous hunchback, to whom they were going to marry her. But can you tell me what is become of my robe, my turban, and the purse of sequins I had at Cairo?'

"Although he assured them that all this was true, yet the people who listened to him only laughed at what he said, and their shouts and jeering so confused him that he did not know himself what to think of all that had happened. At length he rose, and walked into the city; but the crowd followed him, crying out, 'A madman! a madman!' On hearing this, some of the inhabitants ran to the windows, others came out at their doors, and some joined the throng who had surrounded Bedreddin Hassan, and joined in the cry, 'A madman!' without knowing why they shouted. Tormented by his pursuers, he came to the house of a pastrycook who was opening his shop, and entered the house to escape from the hooting of the mob who followed him.

"This pastrycook had formerly been the chief of a troop of wandering Arabs who attacked caravans; and although he was now established at Damascus, where no one had any reason to complain of his conduct, yet he was feared by all who knew anything of his former life. His appearance soon dispersed the mob that followed Bedreddin Hassan. The pastrycook began to question the young man, inquiring who he was, and what had led him to Damascus. Bedreddin Hassan related the story of his birth, and told of the death of the grand vizier his father. He then proceeded to relate how he had left Balsora; how, after falling asleep on the tomb of his father, he had awaked to find himself at Cairo, where he had married a lady. Lastly, he expressed his surpise at seeing himself in Damascus without being able to understand any of these miracles.

"'Your history is very astonishing,' said the pastrycook; 'but if you will follow my advice, you will not disclose to any one the facts you have related to me; wait patiently until Heaven shall put a period to the misfortunes with which it is pleased to afflict you. You may remain with me till your fortunes change; and, as I have no

BEDREDDIN HASSAN AND THE PASTRYCOOK.

children, I will adopt you as my son, if you consent. You may then go freely about the city, and will no longer be exposed to the insults of the populace.'

"Although this proposal conferred no great honour on the son of a grand vizier, Bedreddin Hassan nevertheless accepted the pastrycook's offer, judging, very properly, that it was the only step he could take in his present situation. The pastrycook procured him clothes; and, taking witnesses with him, went before a cadi to declare that he adopted the young man as his son. Bedreddin Hassan resided with him, and, only calling himself by the simple name of Hassan, soon learned the art of making pastry.

"Whilst this was passing at Damascus, the daughter of Schemseddin Mohammed awoke; and, not finding Bedreddin Hassan by her side, concluded that he had risen softly, not to interrupt her slumbers, and that he would soon return. She was still expecting him, when her father, the vizier Schemseddin Mohammed, came to the door of her apartment. He was much affected by the affront he conceived had been put upon him by the Sultan of Egypt, and came to bewail with her on the unhappy destiny to which she had been abandoned. He called her by her name; and she no sooner heard his voice than she rose up to open the door to him. She kissed his hand, and received him with an air of so much satisfaction that the vizier, who expected to find her bathed in tears, and in grief equal to his own, was extremely surprised. 'Miserable one!' cried he, in an angry tone, 'is it thus you appear before me? Bearing the horrid fate to which you have been sacrificed, can you present yourself to me with a countenance which bespeaks content?' When the bride perceived her father's displeasure at the joy which brightened her features, she replied, 'My lord, I entreat you not to reproach me so unjustly. I have not been married to that monster the hunchback, who is more detestable in my eyes than death itself; all the company treated him with such derision and contempt that he was obliged to go away and hide himself, and make room for a charming young man, who is my real husband.' 'What story is this?' cried the grand vizier; 'was not the hunchback married to you last night?' 'No, my lord,' returned she, 'my husband is the young man I was speaking of, who has large eyes and fine black eyebrows.' At these words Schemseddin Mohammed lost all patience, and put himself in a violent rage with his daughter. 'Ah, foolish girl!' said he, 'will you make me lose my senses by the lies you tell?' 'It is you, father,' replied she, 'who almost drive me out of my senses by your incredulity.' 'Is it not true,' persisted the vizier, 'that the hunchback——' 'Let us talk no more of the hunchback,' interrupted she; 'evil befall the hunchback! Must I for ever hear nothing but the hunchback's name repeated in my ears? I again tell you,' she continued, 'that he has not passed the night in my chamber, but my dear husband, whom I have mentioned to you; and indeed he cannot be now at any great distance from hence.'

"Schemseddin Mohammed went out immediately to look for this husband; but, instead of finding him, he was in the greatest astonishment at seeing the humpbacked fellow standing on his head with his feet in the air, and in the very position in which the genie had left him. 'What is the meaning of all this?' he asked him. 'Who placed you in that situation?' The hunchback, who instantly recognised the vizier, answered, 'You are the man who wishes to give me in marriage to the mistress of a buffalo; to one who is in love with a villainous genie? But I won't be your dupe, I promise you; so do not think to deceive me in that manner.'

"Schemseddin Mohammed thought the hunchback was out of his senses when he heard him talk in this manner. 'Get up,' he cried, 'and stand upon your legs.' 'I will beware how I do that,' answered he, 'unless, indeed, the sun be risen. You must know, that as I was coming here yesterday evening, a large black cat suddenly appeared to me; and it kept increasing in size till it was as large as a buffalo. I shall never forget what it said to me; therefore mind your own concerns, and leave me here.' Instead of complying, the vizier took hold of the hunchback by the legs and obliged him to get up. As soon as he was on his legs he ran away as fast as he could, without stopping once to look behind him. He went directly to the palace, and presented himself before the Sultan of Egypt, who was highly amused at the account he gave of the manner in which the genie had treated him.

"Schemseddin Mohammed then went back to his daughter's apartment, still more astonished than before, and quite uncertain how to think or act. 'Unhappy girl,' he said to his daughter, 'can you give me no farther account of this adventure, which confuses and distracts me?' 'My father,' she replied, 'I cannot tell you anything more than I have already had the honour to relate to you. But see,' she added, 'here is some part of my husband's dress, which he has left on this chair, and perhaps this may throw some light on what you wish to discover.' So saying, she presented the turban of Bedreddin Hassan to the vizier, who examined it attentively. He then said, 'I should conjecture this to be a turban that belonged to a vizier if it were not made in the fashion of those of Moussoul.' As he was thus turning it over in his hands, he felt something sewn up in the inside of the turban between the folds. He asked, therefore, for scissors, and on unripping the turban, he discovered a paper folded up. This was the packet which Noureddin Ali on his death-bed had given to his son Bedreddin Hassan, who had concealed it in his turban as the best method of preserving it. On opening the packet, Schemseddin Mohammed instantly knew the handwriting of his brother Noureddin Ali, and read the following direction:—'*For my son, Bedreddin Hassan.*' Before he had time to reflect on these circumstances, his daughter put into her father's hands the purse which she had found in Bedreddin Hassan's pocket. He immediately opened it, and saw it filled with sequins; for, through the care of the genie and fairy, it had remained full in spite of all the gold that Bedreddin Hassan had bestowed on those around him. Upon a sort of ticket attached to the purse the vizier read these words:—'*A thousand sequins belonging to the Jew Isaac.*' And under them was the following inscription, which the Jew had written before he had left Bedreddin Hassan:—'*Delivered to Bedreddin Hassan, in payment for the cargo of the first vessel that arrives in port belonging to him, and which belonged to Noureddin Ali, his father, of happy memory.*' The vizier had scarcely finished reading these words, when he uttered a loud cry and fainted away.

"When the vizier Schemseddin Mohammed was recovered from his fainting-fit, by the assistance of his daughter and the women she had called, he exclaimed, 'My daughter, be not surprised at the accident which has just happened to me; so wonderful is the adventure which has caused it, that you will hardly give credit to it. The husband who has passed the night with you is no other than your cousin, the son of Noureddin Ali. The thousand sequins in this purse remind me of the quarrel I had with my dear brother. Doubt not, this is the wedding-present he makes you. Allah be praised for all these things, and particularly for this wonderful adventure, which so manifestly proves His power!' He then looked at the writing in his brother's hand, and kissed it many times, bathing it with his tears. 'Why cannot I see Noureddin Ali himself here,' he exclaimed, 'and be reconciled to him, as well as I see his handwriting, which causes me so much joy?'

"He read the packet through and found the dates of his brother's arrival at Balsora, of his marriage, and of the birth of Bedreddin Hassan; then, comparing these dates with those of his own marriage, and of his daughter's birth at Cairo, he could not help wondering at the coincidence; and remembering that his nephew was his son-in-law, he gave himself up entirely to the emotions of pleasure to which all these circumstances gave rise. He took the packet and the ticket off the purse, and showed them to the sultan, who forgave him the past, and who was so pleased with the history that he ordered it to be written down that it might descend to posterity.

"Nevertheless Schemseddin Mohammed could not understand why his nephew had disappeared: he expected him to arrive every moment, and awaited his coming with the greatest impatience. When seven days had passed, and no Bedreddin Hassan appeared, he ordered him to be sought for in every part of Cairo; but he could hear no tidings of him, and this caused him much uneasiness. 'This is, indeed,' said he, 'a singular adventure; surely such a strange fate never befell mortal before.'

"Uncertain what might happen in the course of time, he thought proper himself to write the account of what had taken place, detailing the manner in which the nuptials were celebrated, and how the hall and the chamber of his daughter were furnished. He also carefully preserved the turban, the purse, and the rest of the dress of Bedreddin Hassan.

"After some time the daughter of Schemseddin Mohammed gave birth to a son. A nurse was provided for the child, with other women and slaves to attend upon him, and his grandfather named him Agib.

"When the young Agib had attained the age of seven years, the vizier Schemseddin Mohammed, instead of having him taught to read at home, sent him to school to a master who had a great reputation for his learning; and two slaves had the care of conducting him to school and bringing him back every day. Agib used to play with his comrades; and as they were all of much inferior condition to himself they treated him with great deference, and in this the schoolmaster set the example by excusing many faults in Agib which he did not pass over in other scholars. The blind submission with which Agib was treated completely spoiled him. He became proud and insolent; he expected his companions to bear everything from him, but would not in return comply with any of their wishes. He domineered everywhere, and if anyone dared to thwart or contradict him, he vented his anger in abusive language, and often even in blows. At last he made himself so obnoxious to all the scholars that they complained of him to the master of the school. The master at first exhorted them to have patience; but perceiving that by so doing he only increased the insolence of Agib, and being tired himself of the trouble that headstrong boy gave, he said to them, 'My boys, I see that Agib is an insolent fellow. I will tell you how to mortify him in a way that will prevent his tormenting you any longer; indeed, it may perhaps prevent his returning any more to school. To-morrow when he comes, and you are going to play together, place yourselves round him and let one of you say aloud, 'We are going to play, but every one who wishes to join in the game must tell his name, and that of his father and mother. Those who refuse to do so we shall consider as bastards, and they shall not play with us.'' The master then explained to them how mortified Agib would be, and they all went home with the greatest satisfaction.

"The following day, when they were assembled, they did not fail to do as their master had instructed them. They surrounded Agib, and one of them said, 'Let us play at some game, but on condition that he who cannot tell his name, and that of his father and mother, shall not play with us.' Agib and all the rest agreed to these conditions. Then the boy who had spoken first interrogated them all, and each answered satisfactorily till Agib's turn came. The boy said, 'I am called Agib, my mother is named the Queen of Beauty, and my father is Schemseddin Mohammed, the vizier of the sultan.'

"At these words all the children cried, 'Agib, this is not true; that is not the name of your father, but of your grandfather.' 'Woe to you!' replied he, angrily, 'do you dare to say that the vizier Schemseddin Mohammed is not my father?' The scholars then all laughed at him, and cried out, 'No, no! he is only your grandfather, and you shall not play with us; we will take care not to come near you.' Then they left him and continued to laugh among themselves. Agib was so mortified at their jeering that he began to cry.

"The master, who had been listening and heard all that passed, now made his appearance, and said to Agib, 'Do not you yet know, Agib, that the vizier Schemsheddin Mohammed is not your father? He is your grandfather, and the father of your mother, the Queen of Beauty. Like yourself, we are ignorant of the name of your father; we only know that the sultan wished to marry your mother to one of his grooms who was deformed, but that a genie took the groom's place. This is unpleasant for you, but it ought to teach you to treat your companions with less haughtiness than you have hitherto shown.'

"Vexed at the jokes of his schoolfellows, little Agib immediately left the school, and returned home in tears. He went first to the apartment of his mother, who, alarmed at seeing him in such grief, anxiously inquired the cause. He could only answer by broken words, interrupted by sobs, so great was his grief; but at length he managed to explain the reason of his sorrow. When he had told her his adventure, he cried out, 'In the name of God, mother, tell me who is my father?' 'My son,' replied she, 'your father is the vizier Schemseddin Mohammed, who embraces you every day.' 'You do not tell me the truth,' said Agib, 'he is not my father, but yours. But whose son am I?' At this question the Queen of Beauty, recalling to her mind the night of her marriage, which had been followed by so long a widowhood, began to weep bitterly, mourning the loss of a husband so amiable as Bedreddin Hassan.

"The Queen of Beauty and her son Agib were still weeping when the vizier Schemseddin Mohammed entered, and desired to know the cause of their grief. His daughter related the mortification her son had met with at school. This account very much affected the vizier, who joined his tears with theirs. Being very much disturbed by this cruel reflection, he went to the palace of the sultan, prostrated himself at his master's feet, and humbly entreated permission to take a journey into the provinces of the Levant, and more particularly to Balsora, to seek his nephew Bedreddin Hassan, for he could not bear that the whole city should suppose his daughter had been married to a genie. The sultan felt for the grief of the vizier, approved his intention, and gave him leave to

AGIB AND HIS SCHOOLFELLOWS.

execute it; he even wrote a letter of recommendation in the most gracious manner to the princes and nobles in whose dominions Bedreddin Hassan might be, requesting them to authorise the young man's departure with the grand vizier.

"Schemseddin Mohammed could not find words to express his gratitude to the sultan for all his goodness towards him. He could only prostrate himself a second time before the throne; but the tears which flowed from his eyes sufficiently proved his feelings. He took leave of the sultan, after wishing him every kind of prosperity. On reaching his house, he immediately began to prepare for his departure, and took his measures with so much diligence that at the end of four days he set off, accompanied by his daughter and by Agib his grandson.

"They took the road to Damascus, and travelled for nineteen days without stopping; but on the twentieth they halted in a beautiful meadow, at a little distance from the gates of that city, and had their tents pitched on the banks of a river which runs through the city, and renders the surrounding country very agreeable.

"The vizier Schemseddin Mohammed declared his intention of remaining two days in this beautiful spot, proposing to continue his journey on the third. He allowed the persons in his suite to visit Damascus. They almost all availed themselves of this permission; some from curiosity to see a city they had heard so favourably spoken of; others to dispose of Egyptian merchandise which they had brought with them, or to buy the silks and rarities with which the place abounded.

"The Queen of Beauty, who wished that her son Agib should also have the gratification of walking about this celebrated city, ordered the black eunuch who held the office of governor to the child to take Agib into the town, admonishing him to be very careful that the boy did not meet with any accident.

"Agib, who was magnificently dressed, set out with the eunuch, who carried a large cane in his hand. Directly they entered the city, Agib, who was as beautiful as the morning, attracted the admiration of every one. Some ran out from their doors to see him nearer; others came to the windows; and people who were walking in the streets, not satisfied with stopping to look at him, ran by his side to have the pleasure of contemplating his beauty for a longer time. In short, every one admired him, and showered blessings on the father and mother who had brought into the world so sweet a boy. The eunuch and Agib came by chance to the shop where Bedreddin Hassan was; and, pressed by the throng that surrounded them, they were obliged to stop at his door.

"The pastrycook who had adopted Bedreddin Hassan as his son had been dead some years, and to this adopted son had left his shop and all his property. Bedreddin Hassan, therefore, was now master of the shop, and exercised the trade of a pastrycook so successfully that he had acquired a great reputation in Damascus. Observing many people assembled round his door to look at Agib and the black eunuch, Bedreddin Hassan also began to examine them attentively.

"Directly he cast his eyes on Agib he felt himself agitated, without knowing why. He was not struck, like the crowd, with the extreme beauty of the boy; his emotion arose from another cause, which he could not understand. It was the force of nature which moved this tender father, and caused him to leave his occupation, approach Agib, and say to him, with an engaging air, 'My little lord, you have won my heart; I beg you will do me the favour to walk into my shop, and eat some of my pastry, that I may have the pleasure of admiring you at my leisure.' He pronounced these words with so much tenderness that the tears came into his eyes. Little Agib was affected by his manner, and, turning towards the eunuch, said, 'This good man has a countenance that pleases me, and he speaks to me in so affectionate a manner that I cannot avoid doing what he requests; let us go in and eat some of his pastry.' 'Not so,' replied the eunuch; 'it would be a pretty tale to tell that the son of a vizier had gone into a pastrycook's shop to eat; do not think that I shall allow it.' 'Alas! my young master,' cried Bedreddin Hassan, 'those are very cruel who trust you with a man who treats you so harshly.' Then addressing the eunuch, he continued, 'My good friend, do not prevent this young gentleman from doing me the favour I ask; do not mortify me so. Rather do me the favour of coming in with him, and thus you will evince that, although you are without as brown as the chesnut, you are as white as that nut within. Do you know,' continued he, 'that I have a secret which will change your colour from black to white?' The eunuch began to laugh on hearing this, and asked Bedreddin Hassan what this secret was. 'I will tell you,' replied the pastrycook; and immediately he recited some verses in praise of black eunuchs, calling them guardians of sultans, of princes, and of all great men. The eunuch was delighted with these verses, and no longer resisted the entreaties of Bedreddin Hassan. He suffered Agib to go into the pastrycook's shop, whither he also accompanied him.

"Bedreddin Hassan was extremely pleased at having obtained his request; and, returning to his work, which he had left, he said, 'I was making some cheesecakes; you must if you please, eat some, for I feel sure you will find them excellent. My mother, who makes them admirably, taught me how to make them also, and men come from all quarters of the town to buy them of me.' Saying this, he drew a cheesecake out of the oven, and, having strewed on it some grains of pomegranate and sugar, he served it to Agib, who found it delicious. The eunuch, to whom Bedreddin Hassan presented one likewise, was of the same opinion.

"Whilst they were both eating, Bedreddin Hassan examined Agib with the greatest attention; and, reflecting that perhaps the charming wife from whom he had been so soon and cruelly separated might have brought him such a son, he could not supresss some tears. He was preparing to question the little Agib on the reason of his journey to Damascus, but had not time to satisfy his curiosity; for the eunuch, who was anxious that he should return to the tents of his grandfather, took him away as soon as he had done eating. Bedreddin Hassan was not satisfied with following him with his eyes only; but, immediately shutting up his shop, he went out after them, and overtook them by the time they had reached the gate of the city.

"The eunuch, perceiving that he followed them, was very much surprised, and said to him, angrily, 'Importunate man! what do you want?' 'My good friend,' replied Bedreddin Hassan, "do not be displeased; I have a little business just beyond the city, which I have thought of; and I must go and give orders concerning it.' This answer did not satisfy the eunuch, who turned to Agib, and said, 'See what you have brought on me; I foresaw that I should repent of my complacence. You would go into this man's shop, but indeed I was a fool to suffer it.' 'Perhaps,' said Agib, 'he may really have business beyond the city, and the road is free to all.' They then continued walking, without looking behind them, till they had reached the tents of the grand vizier; they then looked back, and saw that Bedreddin Hassan still followed them closely. Agib, perceiving that the pastrycook was within a few paces of him, became red and pale by turns with mingled anger and fear. He feared that the vizier his grandfather would learn that he had been in a pastrycook's shop to eat. Urged by this fear, he took up a large stone that lay at his feet, and threw it at Bedreddin Hassan. It struck him in the middle of his forehead, and covered him with blood. Agib then ran away as fast as he could into the tent of the eunuch, who called back to Bedreddin Hassan that he must not complain of a misfortune which he deserved and had brought upon himself.

"Bedreddin Hassan returned to the city, staunching the blood from his wound with his apron, which he had not taken off. 'I was wrong,' said he to himself, 'to leave my house and occasion so much trouble to the child; for he only treated me thus because he no doubt supposed that I had some bad design against him.' When he reached home he had his wound dressed, and consoled himself with the reflection that there were many people in this world more unfortunate than himself.

"Bedreddin Hassan continued to exercise the business of a pastrycook at Damascus, and his uncle Schemseddin Mohammed left the city three days after his arrival. The vizier took the road to Emaus, and went from thence to Hamah, and thence to Aleppo, where he rested two days. From Aleppo he crossed the Euphrates, entered Mesopotamia, and after traversing Mardin, Moussoul, Sengira, Diarbekir, and several other towns, he arrived at last at Balsora, where he directly requested an audience of the sultan. That prince, who had been informed of the rank of Schemseddin Mohammed, immediately granted his request. He received him very favourably, and asked him the cause of his journey to Balsora. 'O King!' replied the vizier Schemseddin Mohammed, 'I am come to learn tidings of the son of Noureddin Ali, my brother, who had the honour of serving your majesty.' 'It is a long time since Noureddin Ali died,' said the sultan; 'and as for his son, all that I can tell you is that, about two months after the death of his father, he suddenly disappeared, and no one has seen him since, notwithstanding the pains I have taken to discover him. But his mother, who was the daughter of one of my viziers, is still living.' Schemseddin Mohammed requested permission to see this lady, and to conduct her into Egypt. The sultan consented, and Schemseddin Mohammed, unwilling to defer till the morrow so great a gratification, inquired for the abode of this lady, and went to her immediately, accompanied by his daughter and her son.

"The widow of Noureddin Ali lived in the same house which had been occupied by her deceased husband. It was a handsome mansion, built in a costly style, and ornamented with columns of marble; but Schemseddin Mohammed did not stop to admire it. On entering it he kissed the door and a marble tablet, on which the name of his brother was written in letters of gold. He desired to speak to his sister-in-law, whose servants informed him that she was in a small edifice, built in the shape of a dome, which they showed him in the middle of a spacious court. This affectionate mother was accustomed to pass the greater part of the day and night in this building, which she had erected to represent the tomb of Bedreddin Hassan, whom she supposed to be dead, after she had long and vainly expected his return. She was then weeping for the loss of this dear son, and Schemseddin Mohammed found her plunged in the deepest affliction.

"He saluted her on entering, and having entreated her to suspend her tears and lamentations, he informed her that he had the honour of being her brother-in-law; and also told her the reason which had caused him to leave Cairo and travel to Balsora. After he had made his sister-in-law acquainted with all that had happened at Cairo on the night of his daughter's nuptials, and the surprise which the discovery of the packet that was found sewn up in Bedreddin Hassan's turban had occasioned, he presented Agib and the Queen of Beauty to her.

"When the widow of Noureddin Ali, who had hitherto remained seated, like one who took no interest in the affairs of this world, understood by the conversation of Schemseddin Mohammed that the dear son she so much regretted might still be alive, she rose up and tenderly embraced the Queen of Beauty and little Agib, in whom she recognised the features of Bedreddin Hassan. The tears that now fell from her eyes were different from those she had long been in the habit of shedding. She kissed the child again and again, and he received her embraces with every demonstration of joy. 'It is time, madam,' said Schemseddin Mohammed, 'to forget your sorrows and to dry your tears; for you must now arrange your affairs, and go with us into Egypt. The Sultan of Balsora has given me permission to take you with me, and I trust you will not refuse to come. I hope we shall have the good fortune to meet with my nephew your son; and if we should be so fortunate, your history and mine, and that of my son and daughter, will be worthy of being written down and transmitted to after ages.'

"The widow of Noureddin Ali listened to this proposal with great pleasure, and instantly began to make preparations for departure. Schemseddin Mohammed requested another audience of the sultan, to take leave of that monarch, who sent him back laden with honours. Entrusted with a considerable present for the Sultan of Egypt, he left Balsora, and again took the road to Damascus.

"As soon as they arrived in the vicinity of that city, Schemseddin Mohammed ordered his servants to pitch the tents just without the gate by which they were to enter. He told his people he should remain there three days, that he might rest himself, and also to purchase whatever things were most curious and worthy of being presented to the Sultan of Egypt. While he himself was occupied in selecting the most beautiful stuffs, which the principal merchants brought to him, Agib entreated the black eunuch, his governor, to go and walk with him in the city, declaring that he was desirous of seeing whatever he had not had time to visit when he was there before, and that he was also very anxious to get some news of the pastrycook whom he had wounded with the stone. The eunuch agreed to the proposal, and walked into the city with him, having first obtained leave of Agib's mother, the Queen of Beauty.

"They entered Damascus by the gate which led to the palace, and which was the one nearest to the tents of the vizier Schemseddin Mohammed. They walked through the great squares, saw the public buildings, and the covered market where the richest merchandise was sold. They then came to the ancient mosque of the Ommiades, about the time when the people were assembling for prayers between noon and sunset. They then passed by the shop of Bedreddin Hassan, whom they found still engaged in making cheesecakes. 'Hail to you!' said Agib to him. 'Look at me; do you not remember to have seen me before?' At these words Bedreddin Hassan cast his eyes upon the boy, and

AGIB AND THE EUNUCH WITH BEDREDDIN HASSAN.

instantly recognised him. At the very same moment—Oh, surprising effect of paternal love!—he felt the same emotion he had experienced at his first meeting with Agib. He was greatly troubled; and, instead of answering him, he stood for some time unable to speak a single word. At length, recollecting himself, he said, 'Do me the favour, my young lord, once more to come into my shop with your governor, and eat a cheesecake.

I beg you will pardon me for the displeasure I caused you by following you out of the city. I was beside myself, and knew not what I did. It was a sort of charm which drew me after you, and which I could neither resist nor explain to myself.'

"Surprised at this speech of Bedreddin Hassan's, Agib replied, 'The friendship you profess towards me is carried to excess, and I will not come into your house unless you promise faithfully not to follow me when I go away. If you pledge your word and keep it, I will come again to-morrow while the vizier my grandfather is making purchases for a present to the Sultan of Egypt.' 'My little master,' answered Bedreddin Hassan, 'I will do anything you desire me.' Agib and the eunuch then entered his shop.

"Bedreddin Hassan immediately set before them some cheesecakes, which were as delicate and good as those they had tasted at their first visit. 'Come,' said Agib, 'sit down by me and eat with us.' When Bedreddin Hassan was seated he was going to embrace Agib, to express to him the joy he experienced at being near him; but Agib pushed him back, saying, 'Be quiet; your friendship is too tender. Be content with looking at and conversing with me.' Bedreddin Hassan obeyed, and began to sing a song which he composed at the moment in praise of Agib. He did not eat, but was attentive to serve his guests. When they had finished eating he gave them water to wash their hands, and a very white and delicate napkin to wipe them. He then took a vase of sherbet, and prepared a large china bowlful, in which he put some snow, and presenting the bowl to little Agib, 'Take it,' cried he; 'it is rose sherbet, the most delicious that this city can produce; you never tasted any so good.' Agib drank some with great pleasure; Bedreddin Hassan then took the bowl and offered it to the eunuch, who drained it to the last drop.

"When Agib and his governor were satisfied they thanked the pastrycook for the good entertainment they had received, and returned as quickly as they could, as it was late. They arrived at the encampment of Schemseddin Mohammed, and went first to the tent which the ladies occupied. The grandmother of Agib was rejoiced to see him again; and as she had always her son Bedreddin Hassan in her mind, she could not refrain from tears on embracing the boy. 'Ah, my child,' cried she, 'my happiness would be complete if I could have the pleasure of embracing your father Bedreddin Hassan as I embrace you.' She was just going to supper. She made him sit next her, and asked him many questions about his walk; then saying that he must be hungry, she helped him to a piece of cheesecake of her own making; and it was excellent, for, as we have already said, she could make these cakes better than any pastrycook. She gave some to the eunuch also; but they had both eaten so much that they could hardly touch it.

"Agib had scarcely begun to eat the cheesecake before him when, pretending that it did not suit his palate, he put it back on his plate; and Schaban, for this was the name of the eunuch, did the same. Vexed at seeing her grandson so indifferent about her cheesecake, the widow of Noureddin Ali said, 'What, my son! do you scorn the work of my hands in this way? Let me tell you that no one in the world can make such good cheesecakes excepting your father Bedreddin Hassan, to whom I myself taught the curious art of making them.' 'Ah, my good grandmother,' cried Agib, 'if you cannot make them better than this, there is a pastrycook in this city who surpasses you in skill; we have just been eating one in his shop, which is a great deal better than this.'

"At these words the grandmother cast an angry look at the eunuch. 'How! Schaban,' said she, 'is my grandson entrusted to your care that you should take him to eat at a pastrycook's like a beggar's child?' 'O lady,' replied the eunuch, 'it is true that we have been talking to a pastrycook, but we did not eat at his house.' 'Indeed,' interrupted Agib, 'we went into his shop and ate a cheesecake.' The lady, more angry than ever at the eunuch's deceit, left the table abruptly, and ran to the tent of Schemseddin Mohammed, whom she informed of this misdemeanour of the eunuch in terms likely to exasperate the vizier against the delinquent.

"Schemseddin Mohammed, who was naturally of a warm temper, flew into a violent passion. He immediately repaired to the tent of his sister-in-law, and said to the eunuch: 'Wretch! hast thou the temerity to abuse the confidence I have placed in thee?' Schaban, although sufficiently convicted by the testimony of Agib, thought proper still to deny the fact. But the child maintained the contrary. 'Grandfather,' said he to Schemseddin Mohammed, 'I assure you we have eaten so much that we do not want any supper. The pastrycook also regaled us with a large bowl of sherbet.' 'Now, thou wicked slave,' cried the vizier, turning to the eunuch, 'after this wilt thou deny that you both went into a pastry-shop and ate there?' Schaban had the effrontery to swear that it was not true. 'Thou art a liar!' said the vizier, 'I believe my grandson rather than thee. Nevertheless, if thou canst eat the whole of the cheesecake which is on this table I shall be persuaded that thou speakest the truth.'

"Though he was full to the very throat, Schaban submitted to this trial and took a bit of the cheesecake; but he was obliged to take it out of his mouth again, for his stomach turned against it. He, however, persisted in his falsehood, declaring that he had eaten so much the preceding day that his appetite was not yet returned. Irritated by the repeated falsities of the eunuch, and fully convinced that he was guilty, the vizier had him laid on the ground and ordered him to receive the bastinado. The unhappy wretch uttered loud cries on suffering this punishment, and confessed his fault. 'It is true,' cried he, 'that we did eat a cheesecake at a pastry-shop; and it was an hundred times better than that which is on this table.'

"The widow of Noureddin Ali thought it was through spite to her and to mortify her that Schaban praised the pastrycook's cheesecake; therefore, addressing herself to him, she said, 'I cannot believe that the cheesecakes of this pastrycook are more excellent than mine. I will be satisfied on this point: thou knowest where the man lives; go to him and bring me back a cheesecake directly.' She then ordered some money to be given to the eunuch that he might buy the cheesecake; and he set off. When he came to Bedreddin Hassan's shop he said, "Here, my good pastrycook, is some money for you; give me one of your cheesecakes; one of our ladies wishes to taste them.' There happened to be some hot cakes on the table, just out of the oven; Bedreddin Hassan chose the best, and giving it to the eunuch, said, 'Take this, I warrant it to be excellent; and I can assure you that no one in the world can make such cheesecakes excepting my mother, who perhaps is still living.'

"Schaban returned quickly to the tent with his cheesecake. He placed it before the widow of Noureddin Ali, who was impatiently expecting it. She broke off a piece to taste it; but it had scarcely touched her lips when she uttered a loud cry and fainted away. Schemseddin Mohammed, who was present, was very much surprised at this accident. He threw some water on his sister-in-law's face, and did all in his power to restore her. As soon as she was recovered from her fainting, she exclaimed, 'By Allah! it must have been my son, my dear son Bedreddin Hassan, who made this cake.'

"When the vizier Schemseddin Mohammed heard his sister-in-law say that it was Bedreddin Hassan who had made the cheesecake brought by the eunuch, he felt inexpressible joy; but then reflecting that this joy was altogether premature, and that according to all appearance the conjecture of the widow of Noureddin Ali was unfounded, he said to her, 'But, madam, what makes you think this? Cannot there be a pastrycook in the world who is able to make cheesecakes as well as your son?' 'I allow,' replied she, 'that there may be pastrycooks capable of making them as good, but as I make them in a very peculiar manner, and as no one except my son possesses this secret, it must certainly have been he who made this. Let us rejoice, my dear brother,' added she, in a transport of joy; 'we have at length found him whom we have been so long and so anxiously seeking.' 'Madam,' said the vizier, 'I entreat you to moderate your impatience; we shall soon know what to think of this adventure. We have only to desire the pastrycook to come here; if he be Bedreddin Hassan, you and my daughter will recollect him. But you must conceal yourselves, and see him without his seeing you, for I do not wish the discovery to take place at Damascus.'

"He then left the ladies in their tent and retired to his own. Then he summoned fifty of his people before him, and said to them, 'Take each of you a stick, and follow Schaban, who will conduct you to a pastrycook's in the city. When you get there break everything you find in his shop; if he inquires why you commit such an outrage, only ask if it was not he who made the cheesecake that was bought of him by a eunuch; if he acknowledges the fact, seize him; bind him securely, and bring him to me, but take care that you do not strike or hurt him. Go, and lose no time.'

"The vizier was quickly obeyed; his people, armed with sticks and led by the black eunuch, repaired to the house of Bedreddin Hassan, where they broke in pieces the plates, the boilers, the saucepans, the tables, and all the other furniture and utensils they could discover, so that Bedreddin Hassan's shop was deluged with sherbet, cream, and confectionery. At this sight Bedreddin Hassan was much astonished, and said to them in a pitiful tone: 'My good people, why do you treat me thus? What is the matter? What have I done?' 'Was it you,' asked they in return, 'who made the cheesecake which you sold the eunuch who is with us?' 'Yes,' said Bedreddin Hassan, 'I made it myself. What fault have you to find with it? I defy anyone to make a better!' Instead of answering him they continued to break everything in the shop, and the oven itself was not spared.

"The neighbours were by this time attracted by the noise, and much surprised to see fifty armed men committing such depredations. They inquired the cause of this violent usage. Bedreddin Hassan once more said to those who were engaged in the work of destruction: "I entreat you to inform me what crime I have committed that you should thus break and destroy everything in my house?' 'Is it not you,' replied they, 'who made the cheesecake that you sold to this eunuch?' 'Yes, yes! I am the person,' he exclaimed; 'and I will maintain that it is excellent, and that I do not deserve this unjust treatment.' Hereupon they seized his person, and having torn off the linen of his turban, they made use of it to tie his hands behind him; then they dragged him by force out of his shop.

"The populace, who had gathered round, were touched with compassion for Bedreddin Hassan. They took his part, and were inclined to oppose the designs of the people of Schemseddin Mohammed; but at this moment some officers of the governor of the city arrived, and dispersing the mob, favoured the carrying off of Bedreddin Hassan; for Schemseddin Mohammed had been to the governor of Damascus to acquaint him with the order he had given, and to request his assistance and guard; and this governor, who ruled over Syria in the name of the Sultan of Egypt, did not dare to refuse anything to the vizier of his master. Bedreddin Hassan was therefore dragged away.

"On his arrival, the vizier inquired for the pastrycook. When he was brought before him, poor Bedreddin Hassan said, with tears in his eyes, 'Oh, my lord, my lord, do me the favour to tell me in what I have offended you?' 'How, wretch!' exclaimed the vizier, 'was it not thou who madest the cheesecake thou sentest me?' 'I confess that it was,' replied Bedreddin Hassan, 'but what crime have I committed by doing so?' 'I will punish thee as thou deservest,' resumed Schemseddin Mohammed, 'and thou shalt pay with thy life for having made so bad a cake.' 'Woe is me!' cried Bedreddin Hassan; 'what do I hear? Is it a crime worthy of death to have made a bad cheesecake?' 'Yes,' replied the vizier, 'and expect not from me any other treatment.'

"As Schemseddin Mohammed had resolved to set off that same night, he ordered the tents to be struck and all preparations to be made for the commencement of the journey. As for Bedreddin Hassan, the vizier gave instructions that he might be put in a well-fastened case and carried on a camel. As soon as everything was in readiness for their departure, the vizier and the people in his suite began their march. They travelled the whole of that night and the following day without resting; at the approach of night they stopped. They then took Bedreddin Hassan out of his case to give him some food; but they were careful to keep him at a distance from his mother and his wife; and during the twenty days they occupied by their journey they treated him in the same manner.

"On reaching Cairo they encamped without the city walls, by order of the vizier Schemseddin Mohammed, who desired his servants to bring Bedreddin Hassan before him. When the prisoner was come, Schemseddin Mohammed said to a carpenter, whom he had sent for on purpose, 'Go, and get some wood, and cut me a large stake immediately.' 'Oh, my lord,' cried Bedreddin Hassan, 'what are you going to do with this stake?' 'To fasten you to it,' replied the vizier, 'and then have you carried through all the quarters of the city, that everyone may behold in thee a vile pastrycook, who makes cheesecakes without putting pepper in them.' At these words Bedreddin Hassan exclaimed in so comic a manner that Schemseddin Mohammed had difficulty to refrain from laughter: 'Oh, Allah! is it then for not having put pepper in a cheesecake that I am condemned to suffer a cruel and ignominious death? What!' said Bedreddin Hassan, 'was everything in my house to be broken and destroyed, myself imprisoned in a box, and at last a stake prepared for my execution! was all this done only because I did not put pepper in a cheesecake? Powers of Heaven! who ever heard of such a thing? Are these actions worthy of Mussulmen, of persons who profess to practise justice, probity, and all kinds of good works?' Saying this, he burst into tears, and recommenced his lamentations. 'No,' continued he, 'no one was ever treated so unjustly and so rigorously! Is it possible that they should deprive a man of life for not having put pepper into a cheese-

AGIB REFUSES TO EAT HIS GRANDMOTHER'S CHEESECAKES.

cake? Cursed be all cheesecakes, and the hour in which I was born! would I had died at that instant!'

"As the night was now far advanced, the vizier Schemseddin Mohammed ordered Bedreddin Hassan to be put back into his case, and said to him, 'Remain there till to-morrow; the day shall not pass before I order thee to be put to death.' The case was taken away and placed on the camel that had brought it from Damascus; all the other camels were reladen, and the vizier mounting his horse, ordered that the camel which carried his nephew should go before him: thus he entered the city, followed by all his equipage. After passing through several streets, where no one appeared, as the inhabitants had retired to rest, he arrived at his house, where the case was deposited with strict charge not to open it till he should think proper.

"Whilst they were unloading the other camels, Schemseddin Mohammed took aside the mother of Bedreddin Hassan and his daughter, and addressing the latter, said, 'God be praised, my dear daughter, that we have so happily met with your cousin and husband. I dare say you recollect the state in which your chamber was on the night of your nuptials? Go and have everything placed as it was then. If by chance you do not remember it, I can supply the defect in your memory by the description I wrote at the time. On my part, I will go and give orders for the rest.'

"The Queen of Beauty went joyfully to execute the commands of her father, who began to place all the things in the hall in the same position as when Bedreddin Hassan was there with the humpbacked groom of the Sultan of Egypt. As he read the writing, his servants put each piece of furniture in its place. The throne was not forgotten, nor the lighted torches. When everything was prepared in the hall, the vizier entered the chamber of his daughter, where he placed the clothes of Bedreddin Hassan, together with the purse of sequins. Then he said to the Queen of Beauty: 'Undress yourself, my daughter, and go to bed; and when Bedreddin Hassan comes into this chamber, begin to complain of his long absence, and tell him that you were much surprised when you awoke not to find him by your side. Press him to return to bed; and to-morrow morning you will entertain your mother-in-law and me with the account of what he says.' At these words, he went out of his daughter's chamber, and left her.

"Schemseddin Mohammed commanded all the servants, excepting only two or three, to go out of the hall, and to these he gave directions to take Bedreddin Hassan out of the case, to put him on a shirt and drawers, and thereupon to bring him into the hall, where they were to leave him alone, and shut the door. In spite of his unhappy condition, Bedreddin Hassan had fallen so soundly asleep, that the servants of the vizier took him out of the case, and put on his shirt and drawers, without waking him; and then they carried him so quickly into the hall that they did not give him time to recollect himself. When he found himself alone in the hall, he looked round; and the things he saw reminding him of his marriage, he perceived with astonishment, on a closer inspection, that this was the same hall in which he had seen the humpbacked groom. His surprise increased when, drawing near to the door of a chamber which he found open, he saw his clothes in the same spot where he remembered to have placed them on the night of his nuptials. 'Good heavens!' said he, rubbing his eyes, 'am I asleep or awake?'

"The Queen of Beauty, who watched him, was much amused at his astonishment. She drew aside the curtains of the bed, and advancing her head, said in a tender voice, 'My lord, what are you doing at the door? Come and lie down again. You have been absent a long time: I was much surprised, when I awoke, not to find you by my side.' Bedreddin Hassan's countenance changed when he perceived that the lady who spoke to him was the same charming person to whom he had been married years ago. He went into the chamber; but instead of going to bed, as his mind was full of the thoughts of what had passed during the last ten years, and he could not persuade himself that so many events had taken place in only one night, he approached the chair where his clothes and purse of sequins were. These he examined with great attention, and then exclaimed, 'By the great living God! these are things which I cannot understand.' The lady, who was diverted at his embarrassment, said to him, 'Once more, my dear lord, let me beg you to come to bed; what troubles you thus?' At these words, he advanced towards the Queen of Beauty, and said, 'I entreat you, madam, to acquaint me if it is long since I left you.' 'The question surprises me,' replied she; 'did you not just now rise from the bed? Your mind must be strangely disturbed.' 'Madam,' resumed Bedreddin Hassan, 'my spirits certainly are not very composed. I remember to have been with you, it is true; but I also remember to have lived ten years at Damascus. If I have really slept with you this night, I cannot have been absent so long.' 'Yes, my lord,' replied the Queen of Beauty, 'you have no doubt dreamt that you were at Damascus.' 'What a ridiculous thing is this!' cried Bedreddin Hassan, bursting into a laugh; 'I assure you, madam, that this dream will appear to you very laughable. I found myself at the gates of Damascus in my shirt and drawers, just as I am at this moment; I entered the city amidst the shouts and hisses of the populace, who followed to insult me; I took refuge with a pastrycook, who adopted me, taught me his business, and left me all his property when he died; after his death I kept his shop. In short, madam, a great number of adventures befell me, which would be too tedious to relate; all I can say is, that I did well to awake, for they were going to nail me to a stake.' 'And why,' said the Queen of Beauty, pretending surprise, 'why were you to suffer so cruelly? You must have committed some heinous crime.' 'No, indeed,' replied Bedreddin Hassan, 'it was for the most comical and ridiculous thing you can conceive. My only crime was that I had sold a cheesecake in which I had not put any pepper.' 'I must confess,' said the lady, laughing heartily, 'that you were treated very unjustly.' 'O madam,' resumed he, 'this was not all; on account of this cursed cheesecake, in which I was accused of not having put any pepper, they broke and destroyed everything in my shop; they bound me with cords, and shut me up in a case, where I was so closely confined that I feel as if I were still in it. At last they sent for a carpenter, and ordered him to prepare a stake to crucify me. But God be praised that all this is only a dream.'

"Bedreddin Hassan did not pass the night very quietly; he awoke from time to time, and asked himself whether he was dreaming or awake. He doubted his good fortune; and, wishing to ascertain the truth, he undrew the curtains, and cast his eyes round the room. 'I am not deceived,' said he; 'this is the same chamber into which I came instead of the hunchback, and where I saw the beautiful lady who was destined for him.' Daylight, which now began to appear, had not removed his uneasiness when the vizier Schemseddin Mohammed, his uncle, knocked at the door, and entered to wish him good day. Bedreddin Hassan was extremely surprised to see a man with whom he was so well acquainted appear immediately after; but the visitor no longer bore the appearance of the terrible judge who had pronounced the decree of his death. 'Ah!' cried he, 'it is you who have treated me so cruelly, and condemned me to a death, the thoughts of which still fill me with horror, for having made a cheesecake without putting pepper in it!' The vizier laughed; and, to dispel Bedreddin Hassan's fears, related how, by the interference of a genie (for the account he had received from the hunchback made him suspect the truth) the young man had been conveyed to his house, and had married his daughter instead of the groom belonging to the sultan. He then acquainted him that it was by means of the packet written by Noureddin Ali that he had discovered him to be his nephew; and at last told him how, in consequence of this discovery, he had left Cairo, and had gone to Balsora in search of him. 'My dear nephew,' added he, embracing Bedreddin Hassan with the greatest tenderness, 'I beg your pardon for all I have made you suffer since I have discovered you. I wished to bring you here before I acquainted you with your good fortune, which you must find so much the more pleasant, as it has cost you so much pain. Console yourself for all your afflictions with the joy you must experience at being again with those who are most dear to you. Whilst you dress yourself, I will go and summon the lady your mother, who is all impatience to embrace you; and I will bring you your son, whom you saw at Damascus, and towards whom you felt so much affection without knowing him.'

"No words can give any idea of the joy of Bedreddin Hassan when he saw his mother and his son Agib. These three persons embraced each other with all the transports which nature and the tenderest affection can inspire. The mother said the most affecting things to Bedreddin Hassan. She described to him the sorrow which his long absence had caused, and the tears she had shed on his account. Little Agib, instead of avoiding the embraces of his father, as he had done at Damascus, flew to receive them; and Bedreddin Hassan, divided between two objects so worthy of his love, thought he could never lavish on them sufficient proofs of his affection.

"Whilst these things were passing in the house of Schemseddin Mohammed, the vizier himself had gone to the palace, to give the sultan an account of the happy success of his journey. The sultan was so delighted at the account of this wonderful history, that he ordered it to be written and carefully preserved among the archives of his kingdom. When Schemseddin Mohammed returned home, as a noble banquet had been prepared, he sat down to table with all his family; and his whole household passed the day in great festivity and rejoicings."

"The vizier Giafar, having concluded the history of Bedreddin Hassan, said to the Caliph Haroun Alraschid, 'Commander of the Faithful, this is what I had to relate to your majesty.' The caliph thought this history so surprising that he did not hesitate to grant a pardon to the slave Rihan; and to console the young man for the loss of a wife he tenderly loved, the caliph married him to one of his slaves.

BEDREDDIN HASSAN'S SURPRISE.

"But, my lord," added Scheherazade, "however entertaining the history I have related may have been, I know another which is far more wonderful: if your majesty will but hear it to-morrow night, I am sure you will think so too." Shahriar arose without making any reply, for he was doubtful what he should do. "This good sultana," said he to himself, "relates very long stories; and when she has once begun one, there is no possibility of refusing to hear the whole of it. I do not know whether I ought not to order her death to-day; yet no, I will not do anything precipitately. The story she promises me is, perhaps, the most amusing of any I have yet heard, and I must not deprive myself of the pleasure of hearing it. After she has finished it I will give orders for her execution."

Dinarzade did not fail on the following morning to wake the sultana before daybreak, according to her usual custom. And Scheherazade, having requested permission of Shahriar to relate the history she had promised him, began as follows:—

THE HUNCHBACK SINGS TO THE TAILOR'S WIFE.

## THE HISTORY OF THE LITTLE HUNCHBACK.

"In the city of Casgar, which is situated near the confines of Great Tartary, there formerly lived a tailor, who had the good fortune to possess a very beautiful wife, between whom and himself there existed the strongest mutual affection. One day, while this tailor was at work in his shop, a little hunchbacked fellow came and sat down at the door, and began playing on a timbrel, and singing to the sound of this instrument. The tailor was much pleased with his performance, and resolved to take him home, and introduce him to his wife, that the hunchback might amuse them both in the evening with his pleasant and humorous songs. He therefore immediately proposed this to the little hunchback, who readily accepted the invitation; and the tailor directly shut up his shop, and took his guest home with him.

"So soon as they reached the tailor's house, his wife, who had already set out the table, as it was near supper-time, put before them a very nice dish of fish which she had been dressing. Then all three sat down; but in eating his portion the little hunchback had the misfortune to swallow a large fish-bone, which stuck fast in his throat, and almost instantly killed him, before the tailor or his wife could do anything to assist him. They were both greatly alarmed at this accident; for, as the mishap had happened in their house, they had great reason to fear it might come to the knowledge of some of the officers of justice, who would punish them as murderers. The husband, therefore, devised an expedient to get rid of the dead body.

"He recollected that a Jewish physician lived in his neighbourhood; and he formed a plan, which he directly began to put in execution. He and his wife took up the body, one holding it by the head and the other by the feet; and thus they carried it to the physician's house. They knocked at the door, at the bottom of a steep and narrow flight of stairs leading to the physician's apartment. A maid-servant immediately came down without even staying for a light; and, opening the door, she asked them what they wanted. 'Have the kindness to tell your master,' said the tailor, 'that we have brought him a patient who is very ill, and for whom we request his advice.' Then he held out a piece of money in his hand, saying, 'Give him this in advance, that he may be assured we do not intend he should give his labour for nothing.' While the servant went back to inform her master, the Jewish physician, of this good news, the tailor and his wife quickly carried the body of the little hunchback upstairs, placed him close to the door, and returned home as fast as possible.

"In the meantime the servant went and told the physician that a man and a woman were waiting for him at the door, and that they had brought a sick person with them, whom they requested him to see. She then gave him the money she had received from the tailor. Pleased at the thought of being paid beforehand, the physician concluded this must be a most excellent patient, and one who ought not to be neglected. 'Bring a light directly,' cried he to the girl, 'and follow me.' So saying, he ran towards the staircase in a hurry, without even waiting for the light; and, stumbling against the little hunchback, he gave him such a blow with his foot as sent him from the top of the stairs to the bottom; indeed he had some difficulty to prevent himself from following him. He called out to the servant, bidding her come quickly with the light. She at last appeared, and they went downstairs. When the physician found that it was a dead man who had rolled downstairs, he was so alarmed at the sight that he invoked Moses, Aaron, Joshua, Esdras, and all the other prophets of the law, to his assistance. 'Wretch that I am!' exclaimed he, 'why did I not wait for the light? Why did I go down in the dark? I have completely killed the sick man whom they brought to me. I am the cause of his death! I am a lost man! Alas, alas! they will come and drag me hence as a murderer!'

"Notwithstanding the perplexity he was in, he took the precaution to shut his door, lest any one passing along the street might perchance discover the unfortunate accident of which he believed himself to be the cause. He immediately took up the body, and carried it into the apartment of his wife, who almost fainted when she saw him come in with his fatal load. 'Alas!' she cried, 'we are quite ruined if we cannot find some means of getting rid of this dead man before to-morrow morning. We shall certainly be slain if we keep him till day breaks. What a misfortune! How came you to kill this man?' 'Never mind, in this dilemma, how it happened,' said the Jew; 'our only business at present is to remedy this dreadful calamity.'

"The physician and his wife then consulted together to devise means to rid themselves of the body during the night. The husband pondered a long time. He could think of no stratagem likely to answer their purpose; but his wife was more fertile in invention, and said, 'A thought occurs to me. Let us take the corpse up to the terrace of our house, and lower it down the chimney into the warehouse of our neighbour the Mussulman.'

"This Mussulman was one of the sultan's purveyors; and it was his office to furnish oil, butter, and other articles of a similar kind for the sultan's household. His warehouse for these things was in his dwelling-house, where the rats and mice used to make great havoc and destruction.

"The Jewish physician approved of his wife's plan. They took the little hunchback and carried him to the roof of the house; and, after fastening a cord under his arms, they let him gently down the chimney into the purveyor's apartment. They managed this so cleverly, that he remained standing on his feet against the wall, exactly as if he were alive. As soon as they found they had landed the hunchback, they drew up the cords, and left him standing in the chimney-corner. They then went down from the terrace, and retired to their chamber. Presently the sultan's purveyor came home. He had just returned from a wedding-feast, and he had a lantern in his hand. He was very much surprised when he saw by the light of his lantern a man standing up in the chimney; but, as he was naturally brave and courageous, and thought the intruder was a thief, he seized a large stick, with which he directly ran at the little hunchback. 'Oh, oh!' he cried, 'I thought it was the rats and mice who ate my butter and tallow; and I find you come down the chimney and rob me. I do not think you will ever wish to visit me again.' Then he attacked the hunchback, and gave him many hard blows. The body at last fell down, with its face on the ground. The purveyor redoubled his blows; but, at length remarking that the person he struck was quite motionless, he stooped to examine his enemy more closely. When he perceived that the man was dead his rage gave place to fear. 'What have I done, unhappy man that I am!' he exclaimed. 'Alas, I have carried my vengeance too far! May Allah have pity upon me, or my life is gone! I wish all the butter and oil were destroyed a thousand times over before they had caused me to commit so great a crime.' Thus he stood, pale and confounded. He imagined he already saw the officers of justice coming to conduct him to his punishment; and he knew not what to do.

"While the Sultan of Casgar's purveyor was beating the little hunchback he did not perceive his hump; the instant he noticed it, he poured out a hundred imprecations on it. 'Oh, you rascal of a hunchback! you dog of deformity! would to Heaven you had robbed me of all my fat and grease before I had found you here! O ye stars which shine in the heavens,' he cried, 'shed your light to lead me out of the imminent danger in which I am!' Hereupon he took the body of the hunchback upon his shoulders, went out of his chamber, and walked into the street, where he set it upright against a shop; and then he made the best of his way back to his house, without once looking behind him.

"A little before daybreak, a Christian merchant, who was very rich, and who furnished the palace of the sultan with most things which were wanted there, after passing the night in revelry and pleasure, had just come from home on his way to a bath. Although he was much intoxicated, he had still sufficient consciousness to know that the night was far advanced, and that the people would very soon be called to early prayers. Therefore he was making all the haste he could to get to the bath, for fear any Mussulman, on his way to the mosque, should meet him, and order him to prison as a drunkard. He happened to stop at the corner of the street, close to the shop against which the sultan's purveyor had placed the little hunchback's body. He pushed against the corpse, which at the very first touch fell directly against the merchant's back. The latter fancied himself attacked by a robber, and therefore knocked the hunchback down with a blow of his fist on the head. He repeated his blows, and began calling out, 'Thief! thief!'

"A guard, stationed in that quarter of the city, came directly on hearing his cries; and seeing a Christian beating a Mussulman (for the little hunchback was of our religion), asked him how he dared ill-treat a Mussulman in that manner. 'He wanted to rob me,' answered the merchant; 'and he came up behind me to seize me by my throat.' 'You have revenged yourself,' replied the guard, taking hold of the merchant's arm and pulling him away, 'therefore let him go.' As he said this, he held out his hand to the hunchback to assist him in getting up; but, observing that he was dead, he cried, 'Is it thus that a Christian has the impudence to assassinate a Mussulman?' Hereupon he laid hold of the Christian merchant, and carried him before the magistrate of the police, who sent him to prison till the judge had risen and was ready to examine the accused. In the meantime the merchant became completely sober, and the more he reflected upon this adventure the less could he understand how a single blow with the fist could have taken away the life of a man.

"Upon the report of the guard, and after examining the body which they had brought with them, the judge interrogated the Christian merchant, who could not deny the crime imputed to him, although he in fact was not guilty of it. As the little hunchback belonged to the sultan (for he was one of the royal jesters), the judge determined not to put the Christian to death till he had learnt the will of the prince. He went, therefore, to the palace, to give the sultan an account of what had passed. On hearing the whole story, the monarch cried, 'I have no mercy to show towards a Christian who kills a Mussulman. Go and do your duty.' The judge of the police accordingly went back and ordered a gibbet to be erected; and then sent criers through the city to make known that a Christian was going to be hanged for having killed a Mussulman.

"At last they took the merchant out of prison, and brought him on foot to the gallows. The executioner had fastened the cord round the merchant's neck, and was just going to draw him up into the air, when the sultan's purveyor forced his way through the crowd, and, rushing straight towards the executioner, called out, 'Stop, stop! It is not he who has committed the murder, but I.' The judge of the police, who superintended the execution, immediately interrogated the purveyor, who gave him a long and minute account of the manner in which he had killed the little hunchback; and he concluded by saying that he had carried the body to the place where the Christian merchant had found it. 'You are going,' added he, 'to slay an innocent person, for he cannot have killed a man who was not alive. It is enough for me that I have slain a Mussulman; I will not further burden my conscience with the murder of a Christian, an innocent man.'

"When the purveyor of the Sultan of Casgar thus publicly accused himself of having killed the hunchback, the judge could not do otherwise than immediately release the merchant. 'Let the Christian merchant go,' said he to the executioner, 'and hang in his stead this man, by whose own confession it is evident that he is the guilty person.' The executioner immediately unbound the merchant, and put the rope round the neck of the purveyor; but at the very instant when he was going to put this new victim to death, he heard the voice of the Jewish physician, who exclaimed that the execution must be stopped, that he himself might come and take his place at the foot of the gallows.

"'Sir,' said he, directly he appeared before the judge, 'this Mussulman whom you are about to deprive of life does not deserve to die; I alone am the unhappy culprit. About the middle of last night, a man and a woman, who are total strangers to me, came and knocked at my door. They brought with them a sick person: my servant went instantly to the door without waiting for a light, and, having first received a piece of money from one of the visitors, she came to me and said that they wished I would come down and look at the sick person. While she was bringing me this message they brought the patient to the top of the stairs, and went their way. I went out directly, without waiting till my servant had lighted a candle; and falling over the sick man in the dark, I gave him an unintentional kick, and he fell from the top of the staircase to the bottom. I then discovered that he was dead. He was a Mussulman, the very same little hunchback whose murderer you now wish to punish. My wife and myself took the body, and carried it to the roof of our house, whence we let it down into the warehouse of our neighbour the purveyor, whose life you are now going to take away most unjustly, as we were the persons who placed the body in his house by lowering it down the chimney. When the purveyor discovered the hunchback, he took him for a thief, and treated him as such. He knocked him down, and believed he had killed him; but this is not the fact, as you will have understood by my confession. I alone am the perpetrator of the murder; and, although it was unintentional, I am resolved to expiate my crime, rather than burden my conscience with the death of two Mussulmen, by suffering you to take away the life of the sultan's purveyor. Therefore dismiss him, and let me take his place; for I alone have been the cause of the hunchback's death.'

THE HUNCHBACK FOUND BY THE JEWISH PHYSICIAN.

"Convinced that the Jewish physician was the true murderer, the judge now ordered the executioner to seize him, and set the purveyor at liberty. The cord was placed round the neck of the physician, and in another moment he would have been a dead man, when the voice of the tailor was heard entreating the executioner to stop; and presently the tailor pushed his way to the judge of the police, to whom he said, 'You have very nearly caused the death of three innocent persons; but if you will have the patience to listen to me, you shall hear who was the real murderer of the hunchback. If his death is to expiated by that of another person, I am the person who ought to die.

"'As I was at work in my shop yesterday evening, a little before dark, feeling in a merry humour, this little hunchback came to my door half tipsy, and sat down. He immediately began to sing, and had been doing so for some time, when I proposed to him to come and pass the evening at my house. He agreed to my proposal; and I took him home with me. We sat down to table almost directly, and I gave him a little piece of fish. While he was eating it a bone stuck fast in his throat, and, in spite of everything that my wife and I could do to relieve him, he died in a very short time. We were grieved and alarmed at his death; and for fear of being called to account for it, we carried the body to the door of the Jewish physician. I knocked, and told the servant who let me in to go back to her master as soon as possible, and request him to come down to see a patient whom we had brought to him; and that he might not refuse I charged her to put into his own hand a piece of money which I gave her. Directly she had gone I carried the little hunchback to the top of the stairs, and laid him on the first step, and leaving him there my wife and myself made the best of our way home. When the physician came out of his room to go downstairs he stumbled against the hunchback, and rolled him down from the top to the bottom; this made him suppose that he was the cause of the little man's death. But seeing how the case stands, let the physician go, and take my life instead of his.'

"The judge of the police and all the spectators were filled with astonishment at the various strange events to which the death of the little hunchback had given rise. 'Let the physician then depart,' said the judge, 'and hang the tailor, since he confesses the crime. I most candidly own that this adventure is very extraordinary, and worthy of being written in letters of gold.' When the executioner had set the physician at liberty, he put the cord round the tailor's neck.

"While all this was going on, and the executioner was preparing to hang the tailor, the Sultan of Casgar, who never allowed any length of time to pass without seeing the little hunchback his jester, ordered that he should he summoned into his presence. One of the attendants replied, 'The little hunchback whom your majesty is so desirous to see yesterday became tipsy, and escaped from the palace, contrary to his usual custom, to wander about the city; and this morning he was found dead. A man has been brought before the judge of the police, accused of his murder, and the judge immediately ordered a gibbet to be erected. At the very moment they were going to hang the culprit another man came up to the gallows, and then a third. Each of these accused himself, and declared that the rest were innocent of the murder. All this took up some time, and the judge is at this moment in the very act of examining the third of these men, who says he is the real murderer.'

"On hearing this report the Sultan of Casgar sent one of his attendants to the place of execution. 'Go,' he cried, 'with all possible speed, and command the judge to bring all the accused persons instantly before me, and order them also to bring the body of the poor little hunchback, whom I wish to see once more.' The officer instantly went, and arrived at the very moment when the executioner was beginning to draw the cord, in order to hang the tailor. The messenger called out to them as loud as he could to suspend the execution. As the hangman knew the officer, he dared not proceed, so he desisted from hanging the tailor. The officer now came up to the judge and declared the will of the sultan. The judge obeyed, and proceeded to the palace with the tailor, the Jew, the purveyor, and the Christian merchant; and ordered four of his people to carry the body of the hunchback.

"As soon as they came into the presence of the sultan, the judge prostrated himself at the monarch's feet; and when he rose he gave a faithful and accurate detail of everything that related to the adventure of the little hunchback. The sultan thought it so very singular that he commanded his own historian to write it down, with all its particulars; then, addressing himself to those who were present, he said, 'Has any one of you ever heard a more wonderful adventure than this which has happened to the hunchback my jester?' The Christian merchant prostrated himself so low at the sultan's feet that his head touched the ground; then he spoke as follows: 'Powerful monarch, I think I know a history still more surprising than that which you have just heard, and if your majesty will grant me permission I will relate it. The circumstances are so wonderful that no person can hear them without being affected at the narrative.'

The sultan gave the merchant permission to speak; and the latter began his story in these words:—

### The Story told by the Christian Merchant.

O GREAT KING, I was not born in any spot within the limits of your empire. I am a stranger; a native of Cairo in Egypt, of Coptic parents, and by religion a Christian. My father was a corn dealer by trade, and had amassed a large fortune, which he left to me when he died, and I continued to carry on his business. One day, when I was in the public corn-market at Cairo, which is frequented by those who deal in all sorts of grain, a young and handsome merchant, richly dressed, and mounted upon an ass, accosted me. He saluted me, and opening a handkerchief in which he had a sample of sesamè, he showed it to me, and inquired how much a large measure of grain of a similar quality was worth. I examined the sample which the young merchant had put into my hands, and told him that, according to the present price, a large measure was worth a hundred drachms of silver. Then he said, 'Find me a merchant who will buy it at that price, and come to the gate called Victory, where you will see a khan standing apart from every other house, and I will wait for you there.' Thereupon he went away, and left me the sample of sesamè, which I showed to different merchants on the spot. They all said they would take as much as I would sell them at one hundred and ten drachms of silver a measure; and at this rate I should gain ten drachms for each measure sold.

"Elated at so large a profit, I went directly to the gate called Victory, where the merchant was waiting for me. He took me into his warehouse, which was full of sesamè. I had the heap measured, and there were about fifty large measures. I then loaded the corn upon asses, and went and sold it for five thousand drachms of silver. Then the young man said to me, 'You have a right, according to our agreement, to five hundred drachms of this money, at the rate of ten drachms a measure; the rest belongs to me, but as I have no immediate use for it, go and put it by for me till I shall come and demand it of you.' I told him it should be ready at any time when he came for it or sent any one to demand it. I kissed his hand, and he left me; and I went home very well satisfied with his generosity.

"A whole month passed without my seeing him; at the end of that time he appeared. Then he said: 'Where are the four thousand five hundred drachms of silver which you owe me?' 'They are all ready,' I replied, 'and I will immediately count them out to you.' As he was mounted upon an ass, I requested him to alight and do me the honour to eat with me before he received his money. 'No,' he answered, 'I have not time. I have some urgent business which requires my presence, and therefore I cannot stay; but on my way back I will call for my money.' So saying he went away. I waited for him a long time, but it was to no purpose, for he did not return till a month afterwards. 'This young merchant,' thought I to myself, 'places a deal of confidence in me, to leave the sum of four thousand five hundred drachms of silver in my hands without knowing anything of me. Any one but he would certainly fear I should make away with the money.' At the end of the third month I saw him come back mounted upon the same ass, but much more magnificently dressed than he had been before.

"As soon as I perceived the young man, I went out to meet him. I entreated him to alight; and asked whether he wished me to count out the money which I had in trust for him. 'Never mind that,' he replied, in a lively and contented manner; 'I am in no hurry. I know it is in good hands; and I will come and take it when I have spent all I now have, and there is nothing left. Farewell,' he added; 'expect me again at the end of the week.' At these words he gave his ass a stroke with his whip, and was out of sight in a moment. 'This is excellent,' said I to myself; 'he has told me to expect him in a week, and yet, if I may judge from his conversation, I may not see him for a long time. Why should not I, in the meantime, make some use of his money? It will be of considerable advantage to me.'

"I was not mistaken in my conjecture; for a whole year passed before I heard anything of the young man. At the end of that time he again appeared, as richly dressed as when he last came; but it seemed to me that there was something which affected his spirits. I entreated him to honour me by entering my house. 'I agree to do so for this once,' he replied; 'but it is only on condition that you put yourself to no additional trouble or expense on my account.' 'I will do exactly as you please,' I said, 'if you will favour me by coming in.' He immediately alighted, and came in with me. I then gave orders for refreshments; and while my servants were making ready, we entered into conversation; and, when the repast was served, we sat down to table. Directly he began to eat, I observed he fed himself with his left hand, and I was much astonished to observe that he never made use of his right. I knew not what to think of it, and said to myself, 'From the very first moment I have known this merchant, I have always seen him behave with the greatest politeness; it is impossible that he can act thus out of contempt for me. What can be the reason that he makes no use of his right hand?' This matter continued to puzzle me extremely.

"When the repast was over, and my servants had cleared everything away and left the room, we went and sat down on a sofa. I then offered my guest a very excellent kind of lozenge. He took it; but still with his left hand. 'I entreat you, sir,' I cried at last, 'to pardon the liberty I take in asking you how it happens that you always make use of your left hand, and never of the right: some accident surely has happened to you?' At this speech of mine he gave a deep sigh, and instead of answering me, he drew out his right arm from his robe, under which he had till now quite concealed it, when I saw to my utter astonishment that his hand had been cut off! 'You were much shocked,' he said, 'at seeing me eat with my left hand; but you now see I could not do otherwise.' 'May I inquire,' I asked, 'how you had the misfortune to lose your right hand?' At this request he began to shed tears: after some time, however, he told the following history:—

"'I must in the first place inform you,' said the young man, 'that I am a native of Bagdad. My father was extremely rich, and one of the most eminent men, both as to rank and possessions, in that city. I had hardly begun to take part in the business of the world, when I was struck with the accounts which many people who had travelled in Egypt gave of the wonderful and extraordinary sights to be seen in that country, and particularly in Grand Cairo. Their conversation made a deep impression on my mind; and I became very anxious to journey thither. But my father would not give me permission. He at length died; and, as his death left me master of my own actions, I resolved to go to Cairo. I directly invested a large sum of money in the purchase of different sorts of the fine stuffs and manufactures of Bagdad and Moussoul, and began my travels.

"'When I arrived at Cairo I stopped at a khan, which they call the khan of Mesrour. I took up my abode there, and also hired a warehouse, in which I placed the bales of merchandise I had brought with me on camels. When I had arranged this business I retired to my chamber, to rest myself and recover from the fatigue of my journey. In the meantime my servants, to whom I had given some money, went and bought some provisions, and began to dress them. After I had satisfied my hunger, I went to see the castle, the mosques, the public places, and everything else that was worthy of notice.

"'The next morning I dressed myself very carefully; and took from my bales some very beautiful and rich stuffs, which I purposed carrying to a bazaar, to know what buyers would offer me for them. I gave these pieces of stuff to some of my slaves, and we went to the bazaar of the Circassians. I was instantly surrounded by a multitude of brokers and criers, who had been informed of my arrival. I gave specimens of my different stuffs to several criers, who went and showed them all over the place; but

THE YOUNG MAN RELATING HIS STORY TO THE MERCHANT.

no merchant offered me even so much as the original cost of the merchandise and the expenses of the carriage. This vexed me very much, and the criers were witness to my anger and disappointment. 'If you will depend upon us,' they said, 'we will show you how you may lose nothing by your stuffs.' I asked them what method I should adopt to sell my goods to advantage. They replied thus:—'Distribute them among different merchants, who will sell them in small quantities, and you may come twice every week, and receive the money for which the goods have been sold. By this method you will make some profit, instead of losing anything, and the merchants also will have an advantage in the business. In the meantime you will have opportunity and leisure to walk about and view the town, and to embark upon the Nile.'

" 'I followed their advice, and took them with me to my warehouse, from whence I brought out all my goods; and, returning to the market-place, I distributed the stuffs among those of the merchants whom the criers pointed out to me as the most trusty and creditable. The merchants gave me a receipt in due form, properly signed and witnessed, and stipulated that I should make no demand upon them for the first month.

" 'Having thus arranged all my business, I gave myself up entirely to pleasure and gaiety. I made acquaintance with several young men about my own age, who contributed very much to make my time pass agreeably. When the first month had elapsed, I began to call upon my merchants regularly twice every week, taking with me a proper public officer to examine their books, and a money-changer to ascertain the goodness and different values of the various sorts of money they paid me. In this manner I constantly brought away a considerable sum of money, which I took with me to the khan of Mesrour, where I lodged. This business did not prevent me from going, on the intervening days of the week, to pass the morning sometimes with one merchant, and sometimes with another; and I was much pleased with their conversation, and amused at the various scenes in the bazaar.

" 'One Monday, while I was sitting in the shop of one of these merchants, whose name was Bedreddin, a lady, richly attired and of a distinguished air, and accompanied by a female slave neatly attired, entered the shop, and sat down close to me. Her appearance, and a certain natural grace which accompanied her every movement, interested me very much in her favour, and excited a great desire in me to know more of her. I know not whether she perceived that I took a pleasure in beholding her, or whether my attention pleased her or not, but she lifted up the thick crape veil that hung over the muslin which concealed the lower part of her face, and thus gave me an opportunity of seeing her black eyes, by which I was quite charmed. She completed her conquest, and made me quite in love with her, by the pleasant tone of her voice, and by the obliging and modest manner with which she addressed the merchant, and inquired after his health.

" 'After she had conversed some time upon various subjects, she told him that she was in search of a particular sort of stuff, with a gold ground. She said that she came to his shop because it contained a better assortment of goods than any in the bazaar; and that, if he had such a thing, he would much oblige her by letting her see it. Bedreddin having spread out a great many different pieces, she at length selected one, and asked the price of it. He said he could afford to sell it her for eleven hundred drachms of silver. 'I will agree to give you that sum,' she replied, 'though I have not the money about me; but I hope you will give me credit for it till to-morrow, and suffer me to carry the stuff home; and I will not fail to send you the eleven hundred drachms in the course of to-morrow.' 'Lady,' answered the merchant, 'I would gladly give you credit, and you should have full permission to take the stuff home with you, if it belonged to me; but it is the property of this young man, whom you see here, and this is one of the days upon which I must give an account of the money for which his goods are sold.' 'How comes it,' cried the lady, 'that you treat me in this manner? Am I not in the habit of coming to your shop? And every time I have bought any stuffs you have desired me to carry them home without first paying for them. Have I ever failed to send you the money on the following day?' The merchant agreed that she was right. 'It is all very true, lady,' he answered, 'but to-day I require the money.' Thereupon she threw down the stuff in anger, and said: 'Take your stuff; and may Allah confound you, and all your fellow-merchants, for you are all alike, and have no regard for any one but yourselves!' So she rose up in a passion, and went away greatly enraged against Bedreddin.

"'When I saw that the lady was gone, I began to feel very much interested about her; and before she was out of hearing I called her back, and said: 'Lady, I beg you to come back, and perhaps I shall find a way to accommodate and satisfy both you and the merchant.' She came back, but made me understand that she did this entirely on my account. Then I said to the merchant, 'How much do you wish to receive for this stuff which belongs to me?' 'Eleven hundred drachms of silver,' he replied; 'nor can I possibly let it go for less.' 'Then give it to the lady,' said I, 'and permit her to carry it home. I will give you one hundred drachms for your profit, and you shall have an order to take this sum out of the payments for the other merchandise which you have of mine.' I immediately wrote the order, signed it, and put it into the hands of Bedreddin. Then presenting the stuff to the lady, I said, 'O lady, you have now full power to take it away with you; and with respect to the money, you may send it to-morrow, or on the next day; or if you will do me the honour to accept of the stuff, it is quite at your service.' 'That,' replied the lady, 'is very far from my intention. You have behaved with so much kindness, that I should be unworthy of appearing in the presence of men if I did not prove my gratitude to you. May Heaven increase your fortune, and suffer you to live a long time after I am gone; may the gates of heaven be opened at your death; and may all the city publish the report of your generosity!'

"'This speech gave me courage, and I said to her, 'Lady, permit me as a favour to see your face.' At these words she turned towards me, and lifting up the muslin which covered her face, she displayed a countenance of amazing beauty. I was so much struck that I could think of nothing to express the delight I felt. I was unable to take my eyes off her face; but she quickly dropped her veil, for fear any one should perceive her; and, taking up the piece of stuff, she went out of the shop. My mind continued greatly troubled for some length of time. Before I left the merchant, I asked if he knew who the lady was; and he told me she was the daughter of a deceased emir, who had left her an immense fortune.

"'So soon as I had returned to the khan of Mesrour my people brought up supper; but I was unable to eat a morsel. I could not close my eyes during the whole night, which appeared to me of interminable length. As soon as it was day I got up, in hopes that I should again behold the object who had thus disturbed my repose; and with the wish that I might be so fortunate as to please her, I dressed myself still more carefully than I had done the day before. I then returned to the shop of Bedreddin.

"'I had not been there long before I saw the lady approach, followed by her slave. She was much more magnificently dressed than on the preceding day. Paying no attention to the merchant, she addressed herself only to me. 'You see,' she said, 'I have kept my word with you very exactly. I promised to pay the money to-day, and have now come on purpose to bring you the sum for which you had the goodness to trust me, without knowing anything of me. This is an act of generosity I shall never forget.' I replied, 'Lady, there was not the least necessity for hurry. I was quite satisfied with respect to my money, and am sorry for the trouble you have given yourself.' She said, 'It would not have been just in me to misuse your good-nature.' And with these words she put the money into my hands, and sat down near me.

"'Taking advantage of this opportunity of conversing with her, I declared to her the love I felt, but she got up and left me so hastily that I believed she was offended at my confession. I followed her with my eyes as long as I could see her, and when she was quite out of sight I took my leave of the merchant, and left the bazaar without knowing whither I went. I was meditating upon this adventure, when I felt some person touch me. I instantly turned round to see who it was, and recognised the young slave belonging to the lady by whom my whole mind was absorbed. I was delighted to behold her. She said: 'My mistress, the young lady who conversed with you in the shop of the merchant, wishes to speak a few words to you, if you will have the goodness to follow me.' I instantly went with her, and found her mistress waiting for me in the shop of a money-changer.

"'The lady directly invited me to sit down near her, and said, "Be not surprised that I quitted you just now so abruptly: I did not think it prudent before that merchant to give anything like a favourable answer to the acknowledgment you made of your affection for me. Yet I was not offended at your words: I own to you, it afforded me great pleasure to hear you say that I was not indifferent to you; and I esteem myself happy in having gained the esteem of a man of your worth and merit. I know not what impression the sight of me may have made upon you, but from the very first moment I saw you, I felt a very great inclination towards you. Ever since yesterday morning I have thought of nothing but what you said, and my haste and anxiety to discover you this morning ought to be sufficient to convince you that you are not indifferent to me.' 'Madam,' I exclaimed, transported with love and filled with delight, 'nothing I could possibly hear would give me half so much pleasure as what you have now had the goodness to say to me. It is impossible for any one to feel a stronger regard than I have felt for you, from that happy moment when my eyes first beheld you. They were quite dazzled with your many charms, and my heart yielded without the least resistance.' 'Then,' she said, interrupting me, 'let us not lose any time in useless protestations: I do not doubt your sincerity, and you shall immediately be convinced of mine. Will you do me the honour of visiting my house? Or, if you prefer it, I will accompany you.' 'Madam,' replied I, 'I am quite a stranger in this city, and have only lodgings at a khan, which is by no means a proper place in which to receive a lady of your rank and quality. It will surely be much better that you should have the goodness to acquaint me with your residence, where I shall be delighted to have the honour of waiting upon you.' The lady consented to this plan. 'On the day after to-morrow,' she said, 'come directly after mid-day prayers into the street called Devotion-street. You have only to inquire for the house of Abon Schamma, surnamed Bercour, formerly chief of the emirs: at that place you will find me.' Hereupon we separated; and I passed the whole of the next day in a state of the greatest impatience.

"'When Thursday came, I rose very early, and dressed myself in the handsomest robe I had. I put a purse containing fifty pieces of gold into my pocket, and I set out mounted upon an ass, which I had ordered the day before, and accompanied by the man of whom I had hired it. When we had reached Devotion-street, I desired the owner of the ass to inquire the whereabouts of the house which I was seeking: a bystander immediately pointed it out. I alighted at the door, rewarded the man very liberally, and dismissed him; desiring him at the same time to observe well the house at which he left me, and not to fail to return for me the next morning, to take me back to the khan of Mesrour.

"'I knocked at the door. Two little slaves, as white as snow, very neatly dressed, immediately appeared and opened it. 'Enter, my lord,' they said; 'our mistress has been waiting very impatiently for you. For two whole days she has never ceased talking of you.' I went into a court, and came to a pavilion, raised about seven steps from the ground, and surrounded with trellis-work, which divided it from a very beautiful garden. Some majestic trees embellished the spot, and sheltered it from the rays of the sun; and a great number of others were loaded with all kinds of fruit. I was charmed with the warbling of a great many birds, whose notes mingled with the murmurs of a fountain that threw its water to a vast height, in the midst of a parterre enamelled with flowers. The fountain also was gorgeous to behold. Four large gilt dragons seemed to guard the four corners of the reservoir, which was exactly square; and these dragons threw up the water in great abundance, in jets clearer and more brilliant than rock crystal. The two little slaves desired me to go into a saloon magnificently furnished; and while one of them went to inform her mistress of my arrival, the other remained with me, and pointed out all the beauties of the saloon.

"'I had not been long in this place before the lady with whom I was so much in love made her appearance, adorned with the finest diamonds and pearls; but the lustre of her eyes was more brilliant than the sheen of her jewels. Her form, now no longer concealed by her walking dress, as when I met her in the city, seemed to me to be the finest and most striking in the world. I can never express to you the delight we felt at again beholding each other; indeed, the most eloquent description would fail to do justice to our feelings. After the first compliments were over, we both sat down on a sofa, where we conversed with the greatest satisfaction. They then served up a repast, consisting of the most delicate and exquisite dishes. We sat down to table, and recommenced our conversation, which lasted till the evening set in. The attendants then brought us some most excellent wine, and some dried fruits well adapted to excite a desire for drinking; and we drank to the sound of instruments, on which slaves played, accompanying the music with their voices. The lady of the house also sang, and thus completely confirmed her conquest. Her song rendered me the most passionate of lovers

"'The next morning I rose and bade the lady farewell, after secretly putting the purse with fifty pieces of gold in it, which I had brought with me, under her pillow. Before I went, she asked me when I would return again. 'I promise you, madam,' I

THE YOUNG MAN AND THE LADY.

replied, 'to come back this evening.' She seemed delighted with my answer, accompanied me herself to the door, and at parting conjured me not to forget my promise.

"'The man who had brought me the day before was now waiting for me with his ass. I immediately mounted, and returned to the khan of Mesrour. On dismissing the man I told him I would not pay him, but that he might come again with his ass after dinner, at an appointed hour.

"'As soon as I returned to my khan, I sallied forth again and purchased a lamb and several sorts of cakes, which I sent by a porter as a present to the lady. I then transacted my more important affairs, till the owner of the ass arrived, when I went with him to the lady's house. She received me with as much joy as she had shown on the day before, and regaled me in quite as magnificent a style. When I left her the next morning

I again put a purse containing fifty pieces of gold under the pillow, and returned to the khan of Mesrour.

"'I continued thus to visit the lady every day, and each time I left with her a purse with fifty pieces of gold. I pursued this plan till the merchants to whom I had given my merchandise to sell, and whom I visited regularly twice a week, had nothing more of mine in their hands; I then found myself without money, and without the least chance of obtaining any.

"'I was ready to give myself up to despair. I went out of my khan, without knowing what I was about, and walked towards the castle, where a great multitude of people had assembled to behold a spectacle given by the Sultan of Egypt. When I came to the post where the crowd was collected, I plunged into the thickest part of it; and by chance I found myself near a gentleman who was well mounted, and very handsomely dressed. To the pommel of his saddle there was fastened a little half-open bag, from which hung a green string. I touched the outside of the bag, and it seemed to me that the green string which hung down belonged to a purse. At the very moment when this thought crossed my mind, a porter carrying a large bundle of wood passed so close to the horseman on the other side of his horse, that he was obliged to turn away, to prevent the wood from touching him and tearing his dress. The devil at this moment tempted me; and laying hold of the string with one hand, while with the other I enlarged the opening of the bag, I drew out the purse unperceived by any. It was very heavy, and I made sure that it was filled either with gold or silver.

"'So soon as the porter had gone past, the person on horseback, who seemed to have had some suspicion of my intention, instantly put his hand into the bag and missed the purse. He gave me such a blow that I fell to the ground. The spectators who saw this violent attack directly began to take my part. Some seized the bridle of the man's horse, to stop him, and asked him what he meant by thus knocking me down, and how he durst ill-treat a Mussulman. 'What have you to do with it?' he answered, in an angry tone. 'I know what I am about: he is a thief.' At these words I got up. On seeing me, every one took my part, and said he lied; for it seemed very improbable that a young man of my appearance and manners could be guilty of the infamous crime laid to my charge. In short, the bystanders insisted that I was innocent; but while they were holding my accuser's horse to favour my escape, unfortunately for me one of the officers of the police came by, accompanied by some of his men. He came up to us and inquired what had happened. Every one immediately accused the man on horseback of having used me ill, under the pretence that I had robbed him.

"'The officer of the police was by no means satisfied with this account. He asked the horseman if he suspected any one besides me of having robbed him. The latter replied in the negative, and informed the officer of the reasons which he had for his suspicions. After he had attentively listened to him, the officer ordered his attendants to seize and search me. They instantly obeyed; and one of them, discovering the purse, held it up to public view. This disgrace was too much for me to bear; I fainted away. The officer of the police then desired that the purse should be brought to him.

"'As soon as the officer had taken the purse, he asked the man on horseback if it belonged to him, and how much money there was in it. The latter immediately knew it to be the purse which had been taken from him, and assured the officer that it contained twenty sequins. The judge instantly opened it, and, finding exactly that sum in the purse, gave it back to the horseman. After this he ordered me before him. 'Young man,' said he, 'confess the truth; acknowledge that you stole the purse; and do not wait till I order you to the torture to make you tell the truth.' Holding down my head, I reflected within myself that, as the purse was found upon me, they could only consider it as a falsehood and an evasion if I denied the fact. To avoid, therefore, being doubly punished as a liar and a thief, I raised my head and acknowledged that I had taken it. Directly I had made this confession, the officer wrote down the evidence, and ordered my right hand to be cut off. This sentence was executed upon the spot, and excited the compassion of all the spectators; and I observed the accuser himself was moved to pity. The judge, indeed, wished to punish me still farther by cutting off my right foot; but I begged the person from whom I had taken the purse to intercede for me that the judge might remit that part of the sentence. The horseman pleaded for me, and obtained his request.

"'Directly the officer had gone away, the person whom I had attempted to rob came up to me, and offered me the purse, saying: 'I am convinced that necessity alone compelled you to commit so disgraceful an action, and one so unworthy a young man of your appearance. Here is this fatal purse; take it—and I am truly sorry for the misfortune it has occasioned you.' With this speech he left me; and as I was very weak and faint from the quantity of blood I had lost, some people who lived in that neighbourhood had compassion on me, and took me home with them, and gave me wine to drink. They also dressed my arm, and put my hand, which had been cut off, in a piece of linen cloth; and I fastened it to my girdle.

"'When I had returned to the khan of Mesrour, I did not find that assistance of which I stood in need. It seemed to me that I should run a great risk by presenting myself to the young lady. I said to myself, 'She will not wish to see me any more when she hears of the infamous action I have done.' I nevertheless determined to see her again; and as soon as the crowd who had followed me was dispersed, I went by the most unfrequented streets to her house. When I arrived, I found myself so weak and worn out from pain and fatigue, that I instantly threw myself on a sofa, taking care to keep my right arm under my robe, as I was anxious to hide my misfortune from my friend.

"'In the meantime, the lady being informed of my arrival, and having been told that I seemed very ill, came to me in the greatest haste. She exclaimed, on seeing me pale and faint, 'My dear lord! what is the matter with you?' I concealed the real cause of my illness, and told her that I had a most violent headache which very much tormented me. At this she appeared much distressed. 'Sit down,' she said, for I had risen to receive her, 'and tell me how this has happened to you. You were very well the last time I had the happiness to see you here. There is surely something else which you conceal from me. Tell me, I pray you, what it is.' As I remained silent the tears fell from my eyes. 'I cannot comprehend,' she added, 'what can possibly cause you so much grief. Have I unintentionally given you any offence? Do you come to tell me you no longer love me?' 'It is not that, madam,' I replied; 'and even a suspicion of the sort augments my misery.'

"'I could not make up my mind to discover the true cause of my illness to her. When evening approached supper was served up. My entertainer entreated me to eat; but as I could only make use of my left hand, I requested her to excuse me, saying I had no appetite. 'Your appetite will come back,' said she, 'if you will unfold to me what you so obstinately conceal. Your distaste doubtless arises from the pain you suffer by remaining silent.' 'Alas madam,' I replied, 'it is very necessary that I should make that determination and adhere to it.' I had no sooner said this than she poured me some wine, and presenting it to me, 'Drink this,' she replied, 'it will give you strength and courage.' I held out my left hand, and took the glass.

"'When I had received the glass, my tears flowed afresh and my sighs increased. 'Why do you lament and sigh so bitterly?' said the lady to me. 'And why do you take the glass in your left hand rather than your right?' 'Alas! lady,' I replied, 'be not angry with me, I entreat you; for I have a swelling on my right hand.' 'Show me this swelling,' said she, 'and I will open it for you.' I excused myself by saying it was not yet ripe; I then drank all the contents of the glass, which was a very large one. The strength of the wine, added to my fatigue and the low state in which I was, soon made me very drowsy, and I then fell into a profound sleep that lasted till the next morning.

"'While I slept, the lady wishing to know what accident had happened to my right hand, lifted up my robe, and saw with the greatest astonishment that it was cut off, and that I had it with me wrapped up in a linen cloth. She had now no difficulty in understanding why I so strongly resisted all her entreaties. All night she was thinking of the disgrace that had happened to me, not doubting but that my love for her had been the cause of it.

"'When I awoke the next morning, I perceived in her countenance the grief that oppressed her; but she did not utter a word to me on the subject, lest she should give me pain. She obliged me both to eat and drink, in order, as she said, to recruit the strength of which I had so much need. I then wished to take my leave of her, but she took hold of my robe and detained me. 'I will not suffer you,' she said, 'to go from hence; for although you will not confess it, I am certain that I am the cause of the misfortune which has happened to you. The grief which I feel will quickly kill me; but before I die I must execute a design which I meditate in your favour.' Thereupon she ordered some of her people to bring an officer of justice and some witnesses, and on their arrival she made a will, bequeathing all her fortune to me. These people she dismissed, after paying them handsomely for their trouble, and opened a large chest, where all the purses that I had ever brought her since the commencement of our acquaintance had been placed. 'There they all are,' said she to me, 'just as you left them; I have not touched one of them. Here is the key: take it, for they belong to you.' I thanked her for her kindness and generosity; but she added, 'I do not reckon this as anything in comparison with what I intend to do for you. Nor shall I be happy until by my death I prove to you how much I love you.' I conjured her by our mutual love not to contemplate so terrible a design, but I was unable to divert her thoughts from it. The sorrow and chagrin she felt at seeing me maimed brought on a serious illness, which terminated in her death at the end of five or six weeks.

"'After mourning for her loss as much as became me, I took possession of all her fortune, and the sesamè which you sold for me was part of her property.'

"When the young man of Bagdad had finished his story, he added: 'What you have now heard ought to be a sufficient excuse for my having eaten in your company with my left hand. I thank you for the trouble you have taken on my account. I cannot sufficiently laud your fidelity and probity; and as I have, praised be Allah! a very plentiful fortune, although I have expended a great deal, I must beg that you will accept as a present the small sum for which you sold the sesamè. I have moreover another proposal to make to you. Unable to remain at Cairo with any comfort or satisfaction to myself, after the melancholy accident that has befallen me, I am resolved to leave it, and never to return. If you choose to accompany me, we will trade as brothers, and we will divide the profits we make.'

"When the young man of Bagdad had concluded his history," said the Christian merchant, "I said to him, 'Many thanks to you, my master, for the present you have done me the favour to make me. With respect to the proposal of travelling with you, I accept it with all my heart; and assure you that your interest will be always as dear to me as my own.'

"We fixed a day for our departure; and when it came we began our journey. We passed through Syria and Mesopotamia. We travelled over Persia; and, after visiting many cities, we at length came, O sultan, to your capital. After some little time the young man informed me that he had taken the resolution of going back into Persia, and of settling there. We then made up our accounts and separated, perfectly satisfied with each other. He departed, and I remained in this city, where I have the honour of being employed in the service of your majesty. This is the history which I had to relate to you. Does it not seem to your majesty much more surprising than that of the little hunchback?"

"The Sultan of Casgar was very angry with the Christian merchant. 'Thou art very bold and insolent,' said he to the merchant, 'to dare to make a comparison between a history so trifling and unworthy my attention and that of my hunchback. Dost thou flatter thyself that thou canst make me believe the foolish adventures of a young debauchee are more wonderful than those of my jester? I will, in truth, hang all four of you to revenge his death.'

THE GENTLEMAN OFFERS THE PURSE.

"At these words the terrified purveyor threw himself at the sultan's feet. 'O my lord!' he cried, 'I entreat your majesty to suspend your just wrath, and to listen to me; and if the narrative I shall relate shall seem to you more interesting than that of the little hunchback, perchance you will do us the favour to extend your pardon to us all.' 'Speak,' said the sultan; 'I grant thy request.' The purveyor then began as follows:—

## THE STORY TOLD BY THE PURVEYOR OF THE SULTAN OF CASGAR.

WAS yesterday, great monarch, invited by a man of great position and fortune to the wedding of one of his daughters. I did not fail to be at his house by the appointed hour; and found a large company of the best inhabitants of the city. When the ceremony was over, the feast, which was very magnificent, was served up. We sat down to table, and each person ate what was most agreeable to his taste. There was one dish dressed with garlic, which was so very excellent that every one wished to try it. We remarked, however, that one of the guests avoided eating any, although the dish stood directly before him. We invited him to help himself to some, as we did; but he requested us not to press him to touch it. 'I shall be very careful,' said he, 'how I touch a ragout dressed with garlic. I have not yet forgotten the consequences to me the last time I tasted one.' We inquired the cause of the aversion he seemed to have to garlic; but the master of the house called out, without giving him time to answer our inquiries, 'Is it thus you honour my table? This ragout is delicious. Do not, therefore, refuse to eat of it; you must do me that favour, like the rest of the company.' 'My master,' replied his guest, who was a merchant of Bagdad, 'I certainly will obey your commands if you insist; but it must only be on condition that, after eating the ragout of garlic, you will permit me to wash my hands forty times with alkali, forty times with the ashes of the plant from which that substance is procured, and as many times with soap. I hope you will not be offended at this design of mine, for it is in consequence of an oath I have taken, and which I must not break, never to eat a ragout with garlic without observing these ceremonies!'

"As the master of the house would not excuse the merchant from eating some of the ragout, he ordered his servants to get ready some basins, containing a solution of alkali, ashes of the same plant, and soap, that the merchant might wash as often as he pleased. After giving these orders, he said to the merchant, 'Come, now, do as we do, and eat; neither the alkali, the ashes of the plant, nor the soap shall be wanting.'

"Although the merchant was angry at the sort of compulsion to which he was subjected, he put out his hand, and took a small quantity of the ragout, which he put to his mouth with fear and trembling, and ate with a repugnance that very much astonished us all. But we remarked with still greater surprise that he had only four fingers, and no thumb. No one had noticed this circumstance until now, although he had eaten of several other dishes. The master of the house then said, 'You seem to have lost your thumb; how did such an accident happen? There must have been some singular circumstances connected with it; and you will afford this company great pleasure if you will relate them.'

"'It is not only on my right hand that I have no thumb,' replied the guest; 'my left is also in the same state.' He held out his left hand as he spoke, that we might be convinced he told the truth. 'Nor is this all,' he added; 'I have lost the great toe from each of my feet. I have been maimed in this manner through a most extraordinary adventure, which I have no objection to relate if you will have the patience to listen to it; and I think it will not excite your compassion equally with your astonishment. First of all, however, permit me to wash my hands.' So saying, he rose from table; and after washing his hands one hundred and twenty times, he sat down again, and related the following story:—

"'You must know, my masters, that my father lived at Bagdad, where I also was born, during the reign of the Caliph Haroun Alraschid, and he was reckoned one of the richest merchants in that city. But as he was a man much addicted to pleasure and dissipation, he very much neglected his affairs; instead, therefore, of inheriting a large fortune at his death, I found myself greatly embarrassed, and was obliged to use the greatest economy to pay the debts he left behind him. By dint of great attention and care, however, I at last discharged them all, and my small fortune then began to assume a favourable appearance.

"'One morning, as I was opening my shop, a lady, mounted upon a mule, accompanied by an eunuch, and followed by two slaves, came riding towards my warehouse, and stopped in front of my door. The eunuch directly assisted her to alight; he then said to her, 'I am afraid, lady, you have arrived too soon; you see, there is no one yet come to the bazaar. If you had believed what I said, you would not have had the trouble of waiting.' She looked round on every side, and finding that there was, in fact, no other shop open but mine, she came up, and saluting me, requested permission to sit down till the other merchants arrived. I replied civilly that my shop was at her service.

"'The lady entered my shop and sat down; and as she observed there was no one to be seen in the bazaar except the eunuch and myself, she took off her veil in order to enjoy the air. I had never seen any one so beautiful, and to gaze upon her and to be passionately in love were with me one and the same thing. I kept my eyes constantly fixed upon her, and I thought she looked as if my admiration was not unpleasing to her; for she gave me full opportunity of beholding her during the whole time of her stay, nor did she put down her veil till the fear of the approach of strangers obliged her to do so. After she had adjusted her veil, she informed me that she had come with the intention of looking at some of the finest and richest kinds of stuff, which she described to me, and inquired whether I had any such wares. 'Alas! lady,' I said, 'I am but a young merchant, and have not long begun business; I am not yet rich enough to trade so largely; and it is a great mortification to me that I have none of the things for which you came into the bazaar; but to save you the trouble of going from shop to shop, let me, as soon as the merchants come, go and get from them whatever you wish to see. They will tell me exactly the lowest price, and you will thus be enabled, without having the trouble of seeking farther, to procure all you require.' To this she consented, and I began a conversation with her which lasted a long time, as I made her believe that those merchants who had the stuffs she wanted were not yet come.

"'I was not less delighted with her wit and understanding than I had been with her personal charms. I was, however, at last compelled to deprive myself of the pleasure of her conversation, and I went to seek the stuffs she wanted. When she had decided upon those she wished to have, I informed her that they came to five thousand drachms of silver. I then made them up into a parcel, and gave them to the eunuch, who put them under his arm. The lady immediately rose, took leave of me, and went away. I followed her with my eyes until she had reached the gate of the bazaar, nor did I cease to gaze at her till she had mounted her mule.

"'When the lady was out of sight, I recollected that my love had caused me to be guilty of a great fault. My beautiful visitor had so wholly engrossed my attention that I had not only omitted taking the money for the goods, but even neglected to inquire who she was, and where she lived. This led me immediately to reflect that I was accountable for a very large sum of money to several merchants, who would not, perhaps, have the patience to wait. I then went and excused myself to them in the best way I could, telling them I knew the lady very well. I returned home as much in love as ever, although very much depressed at the idea of the heavy debt I had incurred.

"'I requested my creditors to wait a week for their money, which they agreed to do. On the eighth morning they did not fail to come and demand payment; but I again begged the favour of a little further delay, and they kindly granted my request; but on the very next morning I saw the lady coming along on the same mule, with the same persons attending her, and exactly at the same hour as at her first visit.

"'She came directly to my shop. She said, 'I have made you wait a little for your money in payment for the stuffs which I had the other day, but I have at last brought it you. Go with it to a money-changer, and see that it is all good, and that the sum is right.' The eunuch who had the money went with me to a money-changer. The sum was exactly correct, and all good silver. After this I had the happiness of a long conversation with the lady, who stayed till all the shops in the bazaar were open. Although we conversed only upon common topics, she gave a certain grace and novelty to the whole discourse, and confirmed me in my first impression, that she possessed much wit and good sense.

"'As soon as the merchants were come and had opened their shops, I took the sum I owed to each of those from whom I had purchased the stuffs on credit; and I had now no difficulty in getting from them other pieces which the lady had desired to see. I carried back with me brocades worth a thousand pieces of gold, all of which she took away with her; and not only did she omit to pay for them, but never mentioned the subject, or even informed me who she was or where she lived. What puzzled me the most was that she ran no risk and hazarded nothing, while I remained without the least security, and without any chance of being indemnified in case I should not see her again. I said to myself, 'She has certainly paid me a very large sum of money, but she has left me responsible for a debt of much greater amount. Is it possible she can intend to cheat me, and thus, by paying me for the first quantity, has only enticed me to more certain ruin? The merchants themselves do not know her, and depend only upon me for payment.'

"'My love was not powerful enough to prevent me from making these distressing reflections for one entire month. My fears kept increasing from day to day, and time passed on without my having any intelligence whatever of the lady. The merchants at last began to grow very impatient, and in order to satisfy them I was going to sell off everything I had; when, one morning, I saw the lady coming with exactly the same attendants as before. 'Take your weights,' she said to me, 'and weigh the gold I have brought you.' These few words put an end to all my fears, and my regard for her was greater than ever.

"'Before she began to count out the gold, she asked me several questions; and among the rest inquired if I was married. I told her I was not, nor had I ever been. Thereupon she gave the gold to the eunuch, and said to him: 'Come, let us have your assistance to settle our affairs.' The eunuch could not help smiling; and taking me aside he made me weigh the gold.

"'While I was thus employed, the eunuch whispered the following words in my ear:—'I have only to look at you to see that you are desperately in love with my mistress; and I am surprised that you have not the courage to declare your passion to her. She loves you, if possible, more than you love her. Don't suppose that she wants any of your stuffs; she only comes here out of affection for you; and this was the reason why she asked you whether you were married. You have only to declare yourself, and if you wish it, she will not hesitate even to marry you.' 'It is true,' I replied, 'that I felt emotions of love arise in my breast the very first moment I beheld your lady; but I never thought of aspiring to the hope of having pleased her. I am wholly her own, and shall not fail to remember the good service you have done me.'

"'When I had finished weighing the gold, and while I was putting it back into the bag, the eunuch went to the lady, and said that I was very well satisfied. This was the expression they had agreed upon between themselves. The lady, who was seated, immediately rose and went away, telling me first that she would send back the eunuch, and that I must do exactly as he directed.

"'I then went to all the merchants to whom I was indebted, and paid them. After this I waited with the greatest impatience for the arrival of the eunuch; but it was some days before he made his appearance. At length he appeared.

"'I received him in the most kind and friendly manner, and made many inquiries after the health of his mistress. He replied: 'You are certainly the happiest lover in all the world: she is absolutely dying for love of you. It is impossible you can be more anxious to see her than she is for your company; and if she were able to follow her own inclinations, she would instantly come to you, and gladly pass every moment of her future life with you.' 'From her noble air and manner,' I replied, 'I have concluded she is a lady of great rank and consequence.' 'Your opinion is quite correct,' said the eunuch; 'she is the favourite of Zobeidè, the sultana, who is strongly attached to her, and has brought her up from her earliest infancy; and Zobeidè's confidence in her is so great that she employs her in every commission she wishes to have executed. Inspired with affection for you, she has told her mistress Zobeidè that she has cast her eyes upon you, and has asked the sultaness to consent to the match. Zobeidè has listened favourably, but has requested in the first instance to see you, that she may judge whether her favourite has made a good choice; and in case she approves of you, she will herself bear the expenses of the wedding. Know, therefore, that your happiness is certain. As you have pleased the favourite you will please her mistress, whose sole wish is to be kind to her attendant, and who has not the least desire of putting any restraint upon the lady's inclination. The only thing, therefore, you have to do is to go to the palace; and this was the reason of my coming here. You must now tell me what you determine to do.' 'My resolution is already taken,' I replied; 'and I am ready to follow you when and where you choose to conduct me.' 'That is well,' said the eunuch; 'but you must recollect that no man is permitted to enter the apartments belonging to the ladies in the palace, and that you can be introduced there only by such means as will keep your presence a profound secret. The favourite has thought of a scheme by which she may effect this; and you must on your

THE FAVOURITE VISITING THE MERCHANT OF BAGDAD.

part do everything to facilitate it. But above all things you must be discreet, or your life may be the forfeit.'

"'I assured him that I would obey his directions exactly. 'You must then,' he said, 'go this evening to the mosque which the lady Zobeidè has caused to be built on the banks of the Tigris; and you must wait there till we come to you.' I agreed to do everything he wished, and waited with the greatest impatience till the day was gone. When the evening fell, I set out and went to prayers, which began an hour and a half before sunset, at the appointed mosque, and remained there till every one else had left.

"'Almost immediately after prayers I saw a boat come to shore, rowed by eunuchs. They landed and brought a great number of chests into the mosque. Hereupon they all went away except one, whom I soon recognised as the man who had accompanied the lady, and who had spoken with me that very morning. Presently I saw the lady herself come in. I went up to her, and was explaining to her that I was ready to obey all her orders, when she said, 'We have no time to lose in conversation.' She opened one of the chests and ordered me to get in, adding, 'It is absolutely necessary both for your safety and mine. Fear nothing, and leave me to manage this affair.' I had gone too far to recede; therefore I did as she desired, and she immediately shut down the top of the chest, and locked it. The eunuch who was in her confidence then called the other eunuchs who had brought the chests, and ordered them to carry the boxes back on board the boat. The lady and the eunuch then embarked, and they began to row toward the apartments of Zobeidè.

"'As I lay in the chest I had leisure to make the most serious reflections; and I repented most heartily of having exposed myself to the danger I was in. I gave vent to alternate prayers and regrets; but both were now useless and out of season.

"'The boat came ashore exactly before the gate of the caliph's palace. The chests were all landed and carried to the apartment of the officer of the eunuchs, who keeps the key of the ladies' dwelling, and who never permits anything to be carried in without first examining it. The officer had gone to bed; it was therefore necessary to wake him and make him get up. He was greatly out of humour at having his rest thus disturbed. He quarrelled with the favourite because she returned so late. 'You shall not finish your business so soon as you think,' said he to her, 'for not one of these chests shall pass till I have opened and examined them narrowly.' Accordingly he commanded the eunuchs to bring them to him one after the other, that he might open them. They began by taking the very chest in which I was shut up, and set it down before him. At this I was more terrified than I can express, and thought the last moment of my life was approaching.

"'The favourite, who had the key, declared she would not give it him, nor suffer that chest to be opened. 'You know very well,' she said, 'that I do not bring anything in here but what is ordered by our mistress Zobeidè. This chest is filled with very valuable articles that have been entrusted to me by some merchants who have just arrived. There are also a great many bottles of water from the fountains of Zemzem at Mecca; and if one of these comes to be broken all the other things will be spoiled, and you will be answerable for them. The wife of the Commander of the Faithful will know how to punish your insolence.' She said this in so peremptory a tone, that the officer had not courage to persist in his resolution of opening the chest in which I was, or any of the others. 'Begone, then!' he angrily cried: 'go!' The door of the ladies' apartment was immediately opened, and the chests were all carried in.

"'Scarcely had they been placed on the ground, when I suddenly heard the cry of 'The caliph! the caliph is coming!' These words increased my fears to such a degree that I was almost ready to die on the spot. Presently the caliph came in. 'What have you there in those chests?' said he to the favourite. 'Commander of the Faithful,' she replied, 'they are some stuffs lately arrived, which Zobeidè my mistress wished to inspect.' 'Open them,' said he, 'and let me see them also.' She endeavoured to excuse herself by saying they were only fit for females, and that Zobeidè would not like to be deprived of the pleasure of seeing them before any one else. 'Open them, I tell you,' he answered; 'I command you!' She still remonstrated, alleging that the sultaness would be very angry if she did as his majesty ordered. 'No, no,' replied the caliph, 'I will promise you that she shall not be angry. Only open them, and do not detain me longer.'

"'It was then absolutely necessary that the favourite should obey. My fears were again excited; and I tremble, even now, every time I think of that dreadful moment. The caliph seated himself, and the favourite ordering all the chests to be brought, opened them one after the other, and displayed the stuffs before him. To prolong the business as much as possible, she pointed out to him the peculiar beauties of each individual stuff, in the hope that she might tire out his patience; but she did not succeed. At last all the chests had been inspected except the one in which I lay. 'Come,' said the caliph, 'let us make haste and finish this business; we have now only to see what is in yonder chest.' On hearing these words, I knew not whether I was alive or dead; for I now lost all hope of escaping the terrible danger I was in.

"'When the favourite saw that the caliph was determined she should open the chest in which I was concealed, she said, 'Your majesty must be content. There are some things in that chest which I cannot show, except in the presence of the sultana my mistress.' 'Be it so,' replied the caliph, 'I am content: let them carry the chests in.' The eunuchs immediately took them up, and placed them in Zobeidè's chamber, where I again began to breathe freely.

"'As soon as the eunuchs who brought in the chests retired, the favourite quickly opened that in which I was a prisoner. 'Come out,' she cried; and, showing me a staircase which led to a chamber above, she added, 'Go up, and wait for me there.' She had hardly shut the door after me when the caliph came in, and sat down upon the very chest in which I had been locked up. The motive of this visit was a fit of curiosity, which did not in the least relate to me. The caliph only wished to ask the favourite some questions as to what she had seen and heard in the city. They conversed a long time together: at last he left her, and went back to his own apartment.

"'So soon as she was at liberty she came into the apartment in which I waited, and made a thousand excuses for the alarm I had suffered. 'My anxiety and fear,' she said, 'quite equalled your own. This you ought not to doubt, since I suffered both for you, from my great regard for you, and for myself, on account of the great danger I ran. I think few persons in my position would have had the address and courage to extricate themselves from so delicate a situation. It required equal boldness and presence of mind, or rather all the love I felt for you was required to sharpen my wits in that terrible dilemma, to get out of such an embarrassment. But compose yourself now: there is nothing more to fear.' After we had gratified ourselves some time with mutual avowals of our affection, she said, 'You want repose; you are to sleep here, and I will not fail to present you to my mistress Zobeidè some time to-morrow. This is a very easy matter, as the caliph will be absent.' Encouraged by this account, I slept with the greatest tranquillity. If my rest was at all interrupted, it was by the pleasant ideas that arose in my mind from the thought that I should soon marry a lady of remarkable understanding and beauty.

"'The next morning, before the favourite of Zobeidè introduced me to her mistress, she instructed me how I should behave in her presence. She informed me almost word for word what Zobeidè would ask me, and dictated appropriate answers. She then led me into a hall, where everything was very magnificent, very rich, and very well chosen. I had not been long there when twenty female slaves, all dressed in rich and uniform habits, came out from the cabinet of Zobeidè, and immediately ranged themselves before the throne in two even rows with the greatest modesty and propriety. They were followed by twenty other female slaves, very young, and dressed exactly like the first, with this difference only, that their dresses were much more splendid. Zobeidè, a lady of very majestic aspect, appeared in the midst of the young slaves. She was so loaded with precious stones and jewels that she could scarcely walk. She went immediately and seated herself upon the throne. I must not forget to mention that her favourite lady accompanied her, and remained standing close on her right hand, while the female slaves were grouped altogether at a little distance on both sides of the throne.

"'As soon as the caliph's consort was seated, the slaves who came in first made a sign for me to approach. I advanced between two ranks, which they formed for that purpose, and prostrated myself till my head touched the carpet which was under the feet of the princess. She ordered me to rise, and honoured me so far as to ask my name, and to inquire concerning my family and the state of my fortune. In my answers to all these questions I gave her perfect satisfaction. I was confident of this, not only from her manner, but from a thousand kind things she had the condescension to say to me. 'I have great satisfaction,' said she, 'in finding that my daughter (for as such I shall ever regard her, after the care I have taken of her education) has made such a choice. I entirely approve of it, and agree to your marriage. I will myself give orders for the necessary preparations. But for the next ten days before the ceremony can take place I shall require my daughter's services; and during this time I will take an opportunity of speaking to the caliph, and obtaining his consent; meanwhile you shall remain here, and shall be well taken care of.'

"'I spent these ten days in the ladies' apartments; and during the whole time I was deprived of the pleasure of seeing the favourite, even for one moment; but, by her direction, I was so well treated that I had great reason to be satisfied in every other respect.

"'Zobeidè in the meantime informed the caliph of the determination she had taken to give her favourite in marriage; and the caliph not only left her at liberty to act as she pleased in this matter, but even gave a large sum of money to the favourite as his contribution towards setting up her establishment. The appointed time at length came, and Zobeidè had a proper contract of marriage prepared, with all the necessary forms. Preparations for the nuptials were made; musicians and dancers of both sexes were ordered to hold themselves in readiness; and for nine days the greatest joy and festivity reigned through the palace; the tenth was the day appointed for the concluding ceremony of the marriage. The favourite was led to a bath on one side, and I proceeded to one situate on the other. In the evening I sat down to table, and the attendants served me with all sorts of dishes and ragouts. Among other things, there was a ragout made with garlic, similar to the dish of which you have now forced me to eat. I found it so excellent that I hardly touched any other food. But, unfortunately for me, when I rose from table I only wiped my hands, instead of well washing them. This was a piece of negligence of which I believe I had never before been guilty.

"'As it was now night, a grand illumination was made in all the ladies' apartments. The sweet tones of instruments of music resounded through the building. The guests danced, they joined in a thousand sports, and the palace re-echoed with exclamations of joy and pleasure. My bride and I were led into a large hall, and seated upon two thrones. The maidens who attended on the bride changed her dress several times, according to the general practice on these occasions. Every time they thus changed her dress they presented her to me.

"'When all these ceremonies were finished, I approached my bride to embrace her. But she forcibly repulsed me, and called out in the most lamentable and violent manner; so much so, that the women all rushed towards her, desirous of learning the reason of her screams. As for myself, my astonishment was so great that I stood quite motionless, without having even power to ask the cause of this strange behaviour. 'What can possibly have happened to you?' the women said to my bride: 'inform us, that we may help you.' Then she cried: 'Take away, instantly take from my sight, that infamous man!' 'Alas! madam,' I exclaimed, 'how can I possibly have incurred your anger?' 'You are a villain,' said she, in the greatest rage. 'You have eaten garlic, and have not washed your hands. Do you think I will suffer a man who can be guilty of so dirty and so filthy a negligence to approach me? Lay him on the ground,' she added, speaking to the women, 'and bring me a whip.' They immediately threw me down; and while some held me by the arms, and others by the feet, my wife, who had been very quickly obeyed, beat me without the least mercy as long as she had any strength. She then said to the females, 'Take him before an officer of the police, and let him have that hand cut off with which he fed himself with the garlic ragout.'

"'At these words I exclaimed, 'Merciful Allah! I have been abused and whipped, and to complete my misfortune I am to be still further punished by having my hand cut

THE FAVOURITE LOCKS THE MERCHANT IN THE BOX.

off! And all for what? Because, forsooth, I have eaten of a ragout made with garlic, and have forgotten to wash my hands! What a trifling cause for such anger and revenge! Curses on the garlic ragout! I wish that the cook who made it, and the slave who served it up, were at the bottom of the sea!'

"'But now every one of the women present, who had seen me already so severely punished, pitied me very much when they heard the favourite talk of having my hand cut off. 'My dear sister and my good lady,' said they to her, 'do not carry your resentment so far. It is true that he is a man who does not appear to know how to conduct himself, and who seems not to understand your rank, and the respect that is due to you. We entreat you, however, not to take further notice of the fault he has committed, but to pardon him.' 'I am not yet satisfied,' she cried; 'I wish to teach him how to behave, and require that he should bear such lasting marks of his ill breeding, that he will never forget, so long as he lives, having eaten garlic without remembering to wash his hands after it.' They were not discouraged by this refusal. They threw themselves at her feet, and kissing her hand, cried, 'My good lady, in the name of Allah, moderate your anger, and grant us the favour we ask of you.' She did not answer them a single word; but got up, and, after abusing me again, went out of the apartment. All the women followed her, and left me quite alone in the greatest possible affliction.

"'I remained here ten days, seeing no one except an old slave who brought me some food. I asked her for some information concerning my bride. 'She is very ill,' she said, 'from grief at your usage of her. Why did you not take care to wash your hands after eating of that diabolical ragout?' 'Is it possible, then,' I answered, 'that these ladies are so dainty? and that they can be so vindictive for so slight a fault?' But I still loved my wife, in spite of her cruelty, and could not help pitying her.

"'One day the old slave said to me, 'Your bride is cured: she is gone to the bath; and she told me that she intended to come and visit you to-morrow. Therefore have a little patience, and endeavour to accommodate yourself to her humour. She is very just and very reasonable; and is moreover very much beloved by all the women in the service of Zobeidè our royal mistress.'

"'My wife really came to see me the next day; and she immediately said to me: 'You must think me very good to come and see you again, after the offence you have given me; but I cannot bring myself to be reconciled to you till I have punished you as you deserve for not washing your hands after having eaten the ragout with garlic.' When she had said this she called to the women, who instantly entered, and laid me down upon the ground according to her orders; and after they had bound me, she took a razor, and had the barbarity with her own hands to cut off my two thumbs and two great toes. One of the women immediately applied a certain root to stop the bleeding; but this did not prevent me from fainting, partly from loss of blood, and partly from the great pain I suffered.

"'When I had recovered from my fainting fit, they gave me some wine, to recruit my strength and spirits. 'Ah! lady,' I then said to my wife, 'if it should ever fall to my lot again to partake of a ragout with garlic, I swear to you that instead of washing my hands once, I will wash them one hundred and twenty times; with alkali, with the ashes of the plant from which alkali is made, and with soap.' 'Then,' replied my wife, 'on this condition I will forget what has passed, and live with you as your wife.'

"'This is the reason,' continued the merchant of Bagdad, addressing himself to all the company, 'why I refused to eat of the garlic ragout which was served up just now.

"'The women not only applied the root to my wounds, as I have told you, to stop the blood, but they also put some balsam of Mecca to them, which was certainly unadulterated, since it came from the caliph's own store. By the virtue of this excellent balsam I was perfectly cured in a very few days. After this, my wife and I lived together as happily as if I had never tasted the garlic ragout. Still, as I had always been in the habit of enjoying my liberty, I began to grow very weary of being constantly shut up in the palace of the caliph; but I did not give my wife any reason to suspect that this was the case, for fear of displeasing her. At last, however, she perceived it; and, indeed, she wished as anxiously as I did to leave the palace. Gratitude alone attached her to Zobeidè. But she possessed both courage and ingenuity; and she so well represented to her mistress the constraint I felt myself under, in not being able to live in the city and associate with men of my own position, as I had always been accustomed to do, that the excellent princess preferred to deprive herself of the pleasure of having her favourite near her rather than refuse her request.

"'Thus it happened, that about a month after our marriage I one day perceived my wife come in, followed by many eunuchs, each of whom carried a bag of money. When they had withdrawn, my wife said to me, 'You have not complained to me of the uneasiness and languor which your long residence in the palace has caused you; but I have nevertheless perceived it, and I have fortunately found out a method to put you at your ease. My mistress Zobeidè has permitted us to leave the palace; and here are fifty thousand sequins, which she has given us, that we may live comfortably and commodiously in the city. Take ten thousand, and go and purchase a house.'

THE FAVOURITE CUTS OFF HER HUSBAND'S THUMBS.

"'I very soon bought one for that sum; and, after furnishing it most magnificently, we went to live there. We took with us a great number of slaves of both sexes, and we dressed them in the handsomest manner possible. In short, we began to live the most pleasant kind of life; but, alas! it was not of long duration. At the end of a year my wife fell sick; and in a few days she died.

"'I should certainly have married again, and continued to live in the most honourable manner at Bagdad; but the desire I felt to see the world put other thoughts in my head. I sold my house; and, after purchasing different sorts of merchandise, I attached myself to a caravan, and travelled into Persia. From thence I took the road to Samarcand, and at last came and established myself in this city.'

"'This, O king!' said the purveyor to the Sultan of Casgar, 'is the history which the merchant of Bagdad related to the company at the house where I was yesterday.'

'Truly, it comprises some very extraordinary details,' replied the sultan; 'but yet it is not to be compared to the story of my little hunchback.' The Jewish physician then advanced, and prostrated himself before the throne of the sultan; and, on rising, said to him, 'If your majesty will have the goodness to listen to me, I flatter myself that you will be very well satisfied with the history I shall have the honour to relate.' 'Speak,' said the sultan; 'but if thy story be not more wonderful than that of the hunchback, do not hope I shall suffer thee to live.' "

THE STORY TOLD BY THE JEWISH PHYSICIAN.

HILE I was studying medicine at Damascus, and when I had even begun to practise that admirable science with considerable success, a slave one day came to inquire for me; and desired me to go to the house of the governor of the city, to visit a person who was ill. I accordingly went, and was introduced into a chamber, where I perceived a very handsome young man; but he seemed very much depressed, apparently from some pain he suffered. I saluted him, and went and sat down by his side. He returned no answer to my salutation, but showed me by a look that he understood me, and was grateful for my kindness. 'Will you do me the favour, my friend,' I said to him, 'to put out your hand, that I may feel your pulse?' Hereupon, instead of giving me his right hand as is the usual custom, he held out his left. This astonished me very much. 'Surely,' said I to myself, 'it is a mark of great ignorance of the world not to know that it is the constant custom to present the right hand to a physician.' I nevertheless felt his pulse, wrote a prescription, and then took my leave.

" I continued to visit him regularly for nine days; and every time that I wished to feel his pulse he still held out his left hand to me. On the tenth day he appeared to be so much recovered, that I told him he no longer required me, or indeed any medical help but the bath. The governor of Damascus was present; and, in order to prove how well he was satisfied with my abilities and conduct, he at once had me dressed in a very rich robe, and appointed me physician to the hospital of the city, and physician in ordinary to himself. He told me, moreover, that I should be always welcome to his house, where there was constantly a place provided at the table for me.

" The young man whom I had cured also gave me many proofs of his friendship, and requested me to accompany him to the bath. I complied; and when we had gone in and his slaves had undressed him, I perceived that he had lost his right hand. I even remarked that it had been lately cut off. This had been the real cause of his disease, which he had concealed from me; and, while the strongest applications had been secretly used to cure his arm as quickly as possible, his friends had only called me in to prevent any bad consequences arising from a fever which had come on. I was astonished and distressed to see him thus maimed. My countenance showed the sympathy I felt for him. The young man remarked it, and said to me: 'Do not be surprised at seeing me without my right hand. I will one day inform you how I lost it; and you will hear a most wonderful and strange adventure.'

" On our return from the bath, we sat down to table and began to converse. He asked me if he might safely take a walk out of the city to the garden of the governor. I replied that it would be very beneficial to him to go into the air. 'Then,' said he, 'if you choose to accompany me, I will there relate my history.' I told him I was at his service for the rest of the day. He immediately ordered his people to prepare a slight repast, and we set out for the garden of the governor. We walked two or three times round the enclosure, and then seated ourselves on a carpet, which his people spread under a tree that formed a delightful shade around. Then the young man began to tell his history in these words :—

THE TRAVELLERS RESTING BEFORE DAMASCUS.

"'I was born at Moussoul, and am a member of one of the chief families in that city. My father was the eldest of ten children, who were all living and all married when my grandfather died. But among this number of brothers my father was the only one who had any children, and I was his only son. He took great care of my education, and had me taught everything which a boy in my station in life ought to be acquainted with.

" 'I was grown up, and had begun to associate with the world, when one Friday I went to the noonday prayers in the great mosque of Moussoul with my father and my uncles. After the prayers were over every one retired, except my father and my uncles, who seated themselves on the carpet which covered the whole floor of the mosque. I sat down with them; and, as we discoursed on various topics, the conversation happened to turn on travel. The beauties and peculiarities of various kingdoms, and of their principal towns, were discussed and praised. But one of my uncles said, that if the account of a great number of travellers might be believed, there was not in the world a more beautiful country than Egypt on the banks of the Nile, which all agreed in praising. What he related of this land gave me such an opinion of its beauties, that from that moment I formed the wish to travel thither. All that my other uncles could say in favour of Bagdad and the Tigris, when they vaunted Bagdad as the true abode of the Mussulman religion and the metropolis of all the cities in the world, did not make half so much impression on me. My father maintained the opinion of that brother who had spoken in favour of Egypt; and I was very glad of this. 'Let people say what they will,' cried he; 'the man who has not seen Egypt has not seen the greatest wonder in the world! The earth in that country is all gold! I mean to say it is so fertile that it enriches the inhabitants like a golden soil. All the women enchant the beholder by their beauty or their agreeable manners. What river can be more delightful than the Nile? What stream rolls with water so pure and delicious? The residue that remains after its overflowings enriches the ground, and makes it produce without any trouble a thousand times more than other countries yield with all the labour that can be bestowed on their cultivation. Hear what a poet, who was obliged to quit Egypt, wrote to the natives of that country: "Your Nile heaps riches on you every day; it is for you alone that it travels so far. Alas! now that I must leave you, my tears will flow as abundantly as its waters! You will continue to enjoy its pleasures, whilst I, longing to partake of them, am condemned to exile!"

" 'If you cast your eyes on the island which is formed by the two largest branches of the Nile,' continued my father, 'what a variety of verdure will you behold! What a beautiful enamel of all kinds of flowers! What a prodigious number of cities, towns, canals, and a thousand other pleasing objects! If you turn on the other side, looking towards Ethiopia, how many different causes for admiration! I can only compare the verdure of all those meadows, watered by the various canals in the island, to the lustre of emeralds set in silver! Is not Cairo the largest, the richest, the most populous city in the universe? How magnificent the edifices, private and public! If you go to the pyramids you are lost in astonishment! You are struck speechless at the sight of those enormous masses of stone, whose lofty summits are lost in the clouds! You are forced to confess that the Pharaohs, who employed so many men and such immense riches in the construction of these gigantic monuments, surpassed in magnificence and invention all the monarchs who have succeeded them, not only in Egypt, but in the whole world! These monuments, which are so ancient that the learned are at a loss to fix the period of their erection, still brave the ravages of time, and will remain for ages. I say nothing of the maritime towns of the kingdom of Egypt, such as Damietta, Rosetta, and Alexandria, where so many nations traffic for various kinds of grain and stuffs, and a thousand other things for the comfort and pleasure of mankind. I speak of the country from my own knowledge: I spent some years of my youth there, which I shall ever esteem the happiest of my life.'

" 'In reply to my father, my uncles could but agree to all he had said about the Nile, Cairo, and the whole of the kingdom of Egypt. As for me, my imagination was so filled with it that I could not sleep all night. A short time afterwards my uncles also showed how much they had been struck with my father's discourse. They all proposed to him a journey into Egypt. He acceded to the plan; and, as they were rich merchants, they resolved to take with them such goods as they might dispose of with profit. I heard of their preparations for the journey: I went to my father, with tears in my eyes, and entreated his permission to accompany them, with a stock of merchandise to sell on my own account. 'You are too young,' said he, 'to undertake such a journey. The fatigue would be too much for you; moreover, I feel sure you would be a loser by your bargains.' This rebuff did not diminish my desire to travel. I persuaded my uncles to intercede for me with my father; and they at length obtained his permission that I should go as far as Damascus, where they would leave me, whilst they continued their journey into Egypt. 'The city of Damascus,' said my father, 'has its beauties; and he must be satisfied that I give him leave to go thus far.' Much as I wished to see Egypt after the accounts I had heard, I was obliged to relinquish the thought; for my father had a right to my obedience, and I submitted to his will.

"'I set off from Moussoul with my father and my uncles. We traversed Mesopotamia, crossed the Euphrates, and arrived at Aleppo, where we remained a few days. From thence we proceeded to Damascus, the first appearance of which agreeably surprised me. We all lodged in the same khan. I found the city large and well fortified, populous, and inhabited by civilized people. We passed some days in visiting the delightful gardens which beautify the suburbs, and we agreed that the report we had heard of Damascus was true—that it was in the midst of Paradise. After staying here some time, my uncles began to think of proceeding on their journey, having first taken care to dispose so advantageously of my merchandise, that I gained a large profit. This produced a considerable sum for me, with the possession of which I was quite delighted.

"'My father and my uncle left me at Damascus, and continued their journey. After their departure I was very careful not to spend my money in extravagance. Still, I hired a magnificent house. It was built entirely of marble, and ornamented with paintings; and there was a garden attached to it, in which were some very fine fountains. I furnished the house, not indeed so expensively as the magnificence of the place required, but at least sufficiently for a young man of my condition. It had formerly belonged to one of the principal grandees of the city, named Modoun Abdalraham, and it was now the property of a rich jeweller, to whom I paid only two scherifs* a month for the use of it. I had a numerous retinue of servants, and lived in good style. I sometimes invited my acquaintances to dine with me, and frequented entertainments at their houses. Thus I passed my time at Damascus during the absence of my father. No grief or anxiety disturbed my repose, and to enjoy the society of agreeable people was my chief pleasure.

"'One day, when I was sitting at the door of my house, a lady, handsomely dressed and of a good figure, came towards me, and asked me if I did not sell stuffs; and she immediately entered my house. Thereupon I rose and shut the door, and ushered her into a room, where I entreated her to be seated. 'Lady,' said I, 'I have had some stuffs which were worthy of your notice, but it grieves me to say I have not any now.' She took off the veil which concealed her face, and discovered to my eyes a countenance of remarkable beauty. 'I do not want any stuffs,' said she; 'I come to see you, and to pass the evening in your company, if you approve of me.'

"'Delighted with my good forture, I immediately gave my people orders to bring us several kinds of fruits and some bottles of wine. We sat down to table, and ate and drank and regaled ourselves till midnight; in short, I had never passed an evening so agreeably before. Before she left me, the lady put ten scherifs into my hand, saying, 'I insist on your accepting this present from me; if you refuse I will never see you more.' I dared not decline a gift thus pressed upon me; and the lady continued: 'Expect me in three days, after sunset.' She then took her leave, and I felt that she carried away my heart with her.

"'At the expiration of three days, she returned at the appointed hour. I had expected her with impatience, and received her with joy. We passed the evening as agreeably as at our former meeting, and when she left me, again promising to return in three days, she obliged me, as before, to accept ten scherifs from her.

"'On her third visit, when both of us were merry with wine, she said to me, 'My dear friend, what do you think of me? Am I not handsome and pleasing?' 'O lady,' replied I, 'these questions are very useless; all the proofs of affection I give you ought to

* Eastern money.

convince you I love you. You are my queen, my sultana; you form the sole happiness of my life.' 'Indeed,' she resumed, 'I am sure you would change your tone, if you were to see a friend of mine who is younger and handsomer than I am. She has such lively spirits, that she would make the most melancholy of men laugh. I must bring her to you. I have mentioned you to her, and have given her such an account that she is dying with impatience to see you. She begged me to procure her this pleasure, but I did not dare to comply with her request till I had mentioned it to you.' 'O lady,' said I, 'you must do according to your will; but in spite of all you say about your friend, I defy all her charms to captivate my heart, which is so devotedly yours that nothing can ever alter my attachment.' 'Beware of protestations,' replied she. 'I warn you that I am going to put your heart to a great trial.'

"'We said no more at the time; but this time the lady gave me fifteen scherifs instead of ten at her departure. 'Remember,' said she, 'that in two days a new guest will visit you. Prepare to give her a good reception. We shall come at the usual hour after sunset.'

"'I had the room decorated, and prepared a sumptuous collation on the day when they were to come. I waited for them with great impatience. At length, when the evening was closing in, they came. They both unveiled; and if I had been surprised with the beauty of the first lady, I had much more reason to be astonished at the charms of her friend. Her features were regular and perfectly formed. She had a glowing complexion, and eyes of such brilliancy that I could scarcely bear their lustre. I thanked her for the honour she conferred on me, and entreated her to excuse me if I did not receive her in the style she deserved. 'I ought to thank you,' she replied, 'for having allowed me to accompany my friend hither; but as you are so good as to allow me to remain, let us put aside all ceremony.'

"'I had given orders for the collation to be served as soon as the ladies arrived; accordingly we sat down to table. I was opposite to my new guest, who did not cease to look smilingly at me. I could not resist her winning glances; and she quickly made herself mistress of my heart. But while she inspired me with love, she felt the flame herself; and far from practising any restraint, she said a number of tender things to me.

"'The other lady, who observed us, at first only laughed. 'I told you,' said she, addressing herself to me, 'that you would be charmed with my friend, and I perceive you have already become inconstant towards me.' 'Lady,' replied I, laughing, 'you would have reason to complain, if I were wanting in politeness towards a lady whom you love, and have done me the honour to bring here; both of you would reproach me if I failed in the duties of hospitality.'

"'We continued feasting; but in proportion as we became heated with wine, the new lady and I exchanged compliments with so little precaution, that her friend conceived a violent jealousy, of which she soon gave us a fatal proof. She rose and went out, saying that she should soon return; but a few minutes afterwards, the lady who had remained with me changed countenance; she fell into strong convulsions, and expired in my arms, whilst I was calling my servants to my assistance. I went out immediately, and inquired for the other lady; my people told me that she had opened the street door, and had gone away. I then began to suspect, and indeed I had good reason to do so, that she had occasioned the death of her friend. In fact, she had had the cunning and the wickedness to put a strong poison into a cup of wine which she herself had presented to her.

"'I was horror-struck at this terrible event. 'What shall I do?' said I to myself. 'What will become of me?' As I felt sure that I had no time to lose, I ordered my people to raise up by the light of the moon, and as quietly as possible, one of the largest slabs of the marble with which the court of my house was paved. They obeyed me, and dug a grave in which they interred the body of the young lady. After the marble was replaced, I put on a travelling dress; and, taking all the money I possessed, I locked up everything, even the door of my house, on which I put my own seal. I went to the jeweller who was the proprietor, paid him what I owed, and a year's rent in advance besides. I gave him the key, and begged him to keep it for me. 'A very important affair,' said I, 'obliges me to be absent for some time; I must go to visit my uncles at Cairo.' I then took my leave of him, instantly mounted my horse, and set off with my people, who were waiting for me.

"'My journey was prosperous, and I arrived at Cairo without any mishap. I found my uncles astonished to see me. I accounted for my coming by saying that I was tired of waiting for them; and that, receiving no intelligence of them, my uneasiness had induced me to undertake the journey. They received me very kindly, and promised to intercede with my father, that he might not be displeased at my quitting Damascus without his permission. I lodged in the same khan with them, and saw everything that was worth seeing in Cairo.

"'As they had sold all their merchandise, they talked of returning to Moussoul, and were already beginning to make preparations for their departure; but as I had not seen

THE YOUNG MAN AND THE GOVERNOR OF DAMASCUS.

all that I wished to see in Egypt, I left my uncles. I went to lodge in a quarter very distant from their khan, and did not make my appearance till they had set off. They sought me in the city for a considerable time; but failing to find me, they supposed that, displeased with myself at coming to Egypt against the will of my father, I had returned privately to Damascus; and they left Cairo in the hope of meeting me at Damascus, where I could join them and return home.

"'I thus remained at Cairo after their departure, and lived there three years gratifying my curiosity and beholding all the wonders of Egypt. During that time I took care to send my rent to the jeweller; always desiring him to keep my house for me, as it was my intention to return to Damascus, and reside there for some years. I did not meet with any remarkable adventure at Cairo; but you will, no doubt, be very much surprised to hear what befel me on my return to Damascus.

"'When I came to this city, I dismounted at the jeweller's, who received me with joy, and insisted on accompanying me to my house, to show me that no one had been in it during my absence. The seal was still entire on the lock. I entered, and found everything as I had left it.

"'In cleaning and sweeping the room in which I had feasted the two ladies, one of my servants found a golden necklace in the form of a chain, in which were set, at intervals, ten very large and perfect pearls. He brought it me, and I knew it to be the necklace which I had seen on the neck of the young lady who was poisoned. I supposed that the clasp had given way, and it had fallen without my perceiving it. I could not look at it without shedding tears; for it brought to my recollection the charming creature whom I had seen expire in such a cruel manner. I wrapped it up and put it carefully in my bosom.

"'In a few days I had recovered from the fatigue of my journey. I began to visit the friends with whom I had been formerly acquainted. I gave myself up to all kinds of pleasure, and gradually spent all my money. Embarrassed for the want of funds, instead of selling my goods I resolved to dispose of the necklace; but my ignorance of the value of pearls brought me into trouble, as you will hear.

"'I went to the bazaar, where I called aside one of the criers. Showing him the necklace, I told him I wished to sell it, and begged him to exhibit it to the principal jewellers. The crier was surprised at the splendour of the ornament. 'Ah, what a beautiful thing!' cried he, when he had admired it for some time. 'Our merchants have never seen anything so rich and costly. They will be glad to buy it; and you need not doubt their setting a high price on it, and bidding against each other.' He led me into a shop, which I found belonged to the owner of my house. 'Wait for me here,' said the crier; 'I shall soon return and bring you an answer.'

"'Whilst he went about with great secresy to the different merchants to show the necklace, I seated myself by the jeweller, who was very glad to see me; and we entered into conversation on various subjects. The crier returned; and taking me aside, instead of telling me, as I expected he would, that the necklace was valued at two thousand scherifs at the least, he assured me, that no one would give me more than fifty. 'They say,' added he, 'that the pearls are false: determine whether you will let it go at that price.' As I believed what he said, and was in want of money, I replied: 'I will trust your word and the opinion of men who are better acquainted with these matters than I am; deliver up the necklace, and bring me the money directly.'

"'The crier had, in fact, been sent to offer me fifty scherifs by one of the richest jewellers in the bazaar, who had only mentioned this price to sound me, and ascertain if I knew the worth of the article I wanted to sell. So soon as he received my answer, he took the crier with him to an officer of the police, to whom he showed the necklace, saying: 'Sir, this is a necklace that has been stolen from me; and the thief, who is disguised as a merchant, has had the effrontery to offer it for sale, and is now actually in the bazaar. He is content to receive fifty scherifs for jewels that are worth two thousand: nothing can be a stronger proof that he has stolen the necklace.'

"'The officer of the police sent immediately to arrest me; and when I appeared before him, he asked me if the necklace he had in his hand was the one which I had offered for sale in the bazaar. I acknowledged the fact. 'And is it true,' continued he, 'that you would dispose of it for fifty scherifs?' I confessed this also. 'Then,' said he, in a sneering tone, to his followers, 'let him have the bastinado. He will soon tell us, in spite of his fine merchant's dress, that he is nothing better than a thief; let him be beaten till he confesses.' The anguish of the blows made me tell a lie: I confessed, contrary to truth, that I had stolen the necklace; and immediately the officer of police ordered that my hand should be cut off.

"'This occasioned a great noise in the bazaar, and I had scarcely returned to my house when the owner of it came to me. 'My son,' said he, 'you seem to be a prudent and well educated young man; how is it possible that you have committed so base an action as a theft? You told me the amount of your property, and I doubt not that you spoke the truth. Why did not you ask me for money? I would willingly have lent you some. But after what has passed I cannot allow you to remain any longer in my house. Determine what you will do; for you must seek another home.' I was extremely mortified at these words, and entreated the jeweller, with tears in my eyes, to suffer me to stay in his house three days longer; and he granted my request.

"'Alas!' cried I, 'what a misfortune is this! What shame have I endured! How can I venture to return to Moussoul? All that I can say to my father will never persuade him that I am innocent.' Three days after this calamity had befallen me, a number of the attendants of the police officer came into my house, to my great astonishment, accompanied by my landlord and the merchant who had falsely accused me of having stolen the necklace from him. I asked them what they wanted; but instead of replying they bound me with cords, and loaded me with execrations, telling me that the necklace belonged to the governor of Damascus, who had lost it about three years before; and that at the same time one of his daughters had disappeared. Judge of my consternation at this intelligence! But I quickly determined how to act. 'I will tell the truth,' thought I; 'the governor shall decide whether he will pardon me or put me to death.'

"'When I appeared before the governor, I observed that he looked on me with an eye of compassion; and I considered this to be a favourable omen. He ordered me to be unbound. Then, addressing the merchant who was my accuser, and the landlord of my house, 'Is this,' he said, 'the young man who offered the pearl necklace for sale?' They immediately answered, 'Yes.' 'Then,' the governor continued, 'I am convinced that he did not steal the necklace; and I am astonished at the unjust sentence that has been executed upon him.' Encouraged by this speech, I cried, 'My lord, I swear to you that I am innocent. I am certain, also, that the necklace never belonged to my accuser, whom I never saw before, and to whose horrible duplicity I owe the calamity that has befallen me. It is true that I confessed the theft; but I made the avowal against my conscience, compelled by the torments I was made to suffer, and for a reason which I am ready to relate, if you will have the goodness to listen to me.' 'I know enough already,' replied the governor, 'to be able to render you part of the justice which is your due. Let the false accuser be taken hence,' continued he, 'and let him undergo the same punishment which he caused to be inflicted on this young man, of whose innocence I am convinced.'

"'The sentence of the governor was instantly executed. The merchant was led out and punished as he deserved. Then the governor desired all who were present to withdraw, and thus addressed me: 'My son, relate to me, without fear, in what manner this necklace fell into your hands, and disguise nothing from me.' I disclosed to him all that had happened; and owned that I preferred passing for a thief to revealing this tragical adventure. 'O Allah!' exclaimed the governor, as soon as I had done speaking, 'thy judgments are incomprehensible, and we must submit without murmuring: I receive with entire submission the blow which thou hast been pleased to strike.' Then he addressed himself to me in these words: 'My son, I have heard the account of your misfortune, for which I am extremely sorry. I will now relate mine. Know that I am the father of the two ladies you have entertained.

"'The first lady, who had the effrontery to seek you even in your own house, was the eldest of all my daughters. I married her at Cairo to her cousin, the son of my brother. Her husband died, and she returned here, corrupted by a thousand vices which she had learnt in Egypt. Before her arrival, the youngest, who died in so deplorable a manner in your arms, had been very obedient, and had never given me any reason to complain of her conduct. Her eldest sister formed a very close friendship with her, and by insensible degrees led her away into the path of wickedness.

"'The day following that on which the youngest died, I missed her when I sat down to table, and inquired for her of her sister, who had returned home; but instead of making any reply, my eldest daughter began to weep so bitterly, that I foreboded some misfortune. I pressed her to answer my question.

"'My father,' replied she, sobbing, 'I can tell you nothing more than that my sister yesterday put on her best dress, and her beautiful pearl necklace, and went out, and she has never returned.' I caused search to be made for my daughter through the city, but could learn no tidings of her fate. In the meantime my eldest daughter, who, no doubt, began to repent of her fit of jealousy, continued to weep and to bewail the death of her sister: she even deprived herself of all kinds of food, and at length starved herself to death.

"'Such, alas!' continued the governor, 'is the condition of man. Such are the evils to which he is exposed. But, my son, as we are both equally unfortunate, let us unite our sorrows, and never abandon each other. I will bestow my third daughter on you in marriage: she is younger than her sisters, and her conduct has been irreproachable. She is even more beautiful than her sisters were. My house shall be your home, and after my death you and she will be my only heirs.' 'My lord,' said I, 'I am overwhelmed by your kindness, and shall never be able to testify my gratitude.' 'It is enough,' interrupted he; 'let us not waste time in useless words.' Hereupon he caused witnesses to be summoned, and I married his daughter without further delay.

"'The merchant, who had falsely accused me, was further punished by having all his property, which was very considerable, confiscated to my use. As you come from the governor, you may have observed in what high estimation he holds me. I must also tell you that a man, who was sent expressly by my uncles to seek me in Egypt, discovered, on passing through this city, that I resided here, and yesterday brought me letters from them. They inform me of the death of my father, and invite me to go to Moussoul to take possession of my inheritance; but as my alliance and friendship with the governor attach me to him, and I cannot think of quitting him, I have sent back the messenger with authority to my uncles legally to transfer all that belongs to me. And now I trust you will pardon me the incivility I have been guilty of, during my illness, in presenting you my left hand instead of my right.'

"'This," said the Jewish physician to the Sultan of Casgar, 'is the story which the young man of Moussoul related to me. I remained at Damascus as long as the governor lived; after his death, as I was still in the prime of my life, I felt an inclination to travel. I traversed all Persia, and went into India; at last I came to establish myself in your capital, where I exercise, with some credit to myself, the profession of a physician."

"The Sultan of Casgar thought this story entertaining. 'I confess,' said he to the Jew, 'that thou hast related wonderful things; but to speak frankly, the story of the hunchback is still more extraordinary and much more entertaining, so do not flatter thyself with the hope of being reprieved any more than the others; I shall have you all four hanged.' 'Vouchsafe me a hearing,' cried the tailor, advancing, and prostrating himself at the feet of the sultan; 'since your majesty likes pleasant stories, I have one to tell which will not, I think, displease you.' 'I will listen to thee also,' replied the sultan; 'but do not entertain any hopes that I shall suffer thee to live if thy story be not more diverting than that of the hunchback.' Then the tailor, with the air of a man who knew what he did, boldly began his tale in the following words:—

### The Story told by the Tailor.

TWO days since, a tradesman of this city did me the honour of inviting me to an entertainment which he purposed giving to his friends. I repaired to his house yesterday at an early hour, and found about twenty people assembled.

"We were waiting for the master of the house, who had gone out on some sudden business, when we saw him come, accompanied by a young stranger. This young man was handsomely dressed, and of a good figure; but he was lame. We all rose, and, to do honour to the master of the house, we begged the young man to sit with us on the sofa. He was just going to sit down, when, perceiving a certain barber among the company, he abruptly stepped back, and turned as if to go. Surprised at this, the master of the house stopped him. 'Where are you going?' said he; 'I have brought you here that you may give me the honour of your company at an entertainment I am going to give my friends, and you scarcely enter before you want to depart!' 'In the name of Allah, sir,' replied the stranger, 'I entreat you not to detain me, but suffer me to go. I cannot without horror behold that abominable barber who is sitting yonder. Although he was born in a country where the complexion of the people is white, he looks like an Ethiopian; but his mind is of a dye deeper and more horrible than his visage.'

"We were all very much surprised at this speech, and began to form a very bad opinion of the barber, though we knew not what reason the young stranger had for speaking of him in such terms. We even went so far as to declare that we would not

THE YOUNG MAN DESIRING TO DEPART.

admit at our table a man of whom we had heard so terrible a character. The master of the house begged the stranger to let us know the cause of his hatred to the barber. 'My master,' said the young man, 'you must know, that I am lame through this barber's fault, and he has moreover brought upon me the most cruel affair which is possible to be conceived. For this reason I have made a vow to quit any place where he may be. I will not even reside in any town where he lives: for this reason I left Bagdad, where he was, and undertook a long journey to come and settle in this city, where, in the centre of Great Tartary, I flattered myself I should be secure of never beholding him again. However, contrary to my hopes and expectations, I find him here: this obliges me, my masters, to deny myself the honour of partaking of your feast. I will this day leave your city, and go to hide myself, if I can, in some place where yonder barber can never again offend my sight.' With this speech he was going to leave us; but the master of the house still detained him, and entreated him to relate to us the cause of the aversion he had against the barber, who all this time had kept his eyes fixed on the ground, without speaking a word. We joined our entreaties to those of the master of the house; and at last the young man, yielding to our importunities, seated himself on the sofa and, turning his back towards the barber, lest he should see him, began his history in these words:—

"'My father, who lived in Bagdad, was entitled by his rank to aspire to the highest offices of state; but he preferred leading a quiet and tranquil life to all the chances of gaining honour. I was his only child; and when he died I had completed my education, and was old enough to manage the large possessions he had bequeathed me. I did not waste them in folly, but employed them in a way that procured me the esteem of every one.

"'I had not yet felt the tender emotions of love, and I will confess, perhaps to my shame, that I carefully avoided the society of women. One day, as I was walking in a street, I saw a great number of ladies coming towards me. To avoid them, I turned into a little street that lay before me, and sat down on a bench near a door. Opposite me, in a window, stood a number of very fine flowers, and my eyes were fixed on them, when the window opened, and a lady appeared whose beauty dazzled me. She cast her eyes on me; and as she watered the flowers with a hand whiter than alabaster, she looked at me with a smile, which inspired me with as much love for her as I had hitherto felt aversion towards the rest of her sex. After she had tended her flowers and bestowed on me another look, which completed the conquest of my heart, she shut the window, and left me in a state of pain and perturbation which I cannot describe.

"'I should have remained a considerable time in thought had not a noise I heard in the street brought me to my senses. I turned my head as I got up, and saw one of the first cadis of the city approaching, mounted on a mule, and accompanied by five or six of his people. He alighted at the door of the house where the young lady had opened the window; and from this I concluded he was her father.

"'I returned home, agitated by a passion all the more violent from its being the first attack. I was seized with a raging fever, which caused great affliction in my household. My relations, who loved me, alarmed by my sudden illness, came quickly to see me, and importuned me to tell them the cause; but I was very careful to keep my secret. My silence increased their alarm, nor could the physicians dissipate their fears for my safety, for they knew nothing of my disease, which was only increased by the medicines they administered.

"'My friends began to despair of my life, when an old lady who had been informed of my illness arrived. She looked at me with a great deal of attention, and at length discovered, I know not how, the cause of my disorder. She took my relations aside, and begged them to order my people to retire, and to leave her alone with me.

"'When the room was cleared she seated herself near my pillow. 'My son,' said she, 'you have hitherto persisted in concealing the cause of your illness; nor do I require you to confess it now; I have sufficient experience to penetrate into this secret, and I am sure you will not deny what I am going to declare. You are love-sick. I can probably accomplish your cure, provided you will tell me the name of the happy lady who has been able to wound a heart so insensible as yours; for you have the reputation of a woman-hater; however, what I foresaw has at last come to pass, and I shall be delighted if I can succeed in relieving you from your pain.'

"'The old lady waited to hear my answer; but although this speech had made a strong impression on me I did not dare open my heart to her. I turned towards her and uttered a deep sigh, but said not a word. Then she said, 'Is it shame that prevents you from speaking, or is it want of confidence in my power to assist you? Can you doubt my promise? I could mention to you an infinite number of young people of your acquaintance who have endured the same pain that you now feel, and for whom I have obtained consolation.'

"'In short, the good lady said so much to me that at length I described to her the street where I had seen the lady, and related all the circumstances of my adventure. 'If you succeed,' continued I, 'and procure me the happiness of seeing this enchanting beauty, and of expressing to her the love with which I burn, you may rely on my gratitude.' 'My son,' replied the old lady, 'I know the person you mention. You were quite right in supposing her to be the daughter of the principal cadi in this city. I am not surprised that you should love her. She is the most beautiful as well as the most amiable lady in Bagdad; but I am grieved to inform you that she is very haughty and difficult of access. Many of our officers of justice are very exact in making women observe the laws which subject them to irksome restraint. They are especially strict in their own families, and the cadi is more rigid on this point than all the others. The daughters are as circumspect as their fathers. I do not say that this is absolutely the case with the daughter of the principal cadi; yet I am much afraid I shall have as much difficulty with her as with her father. Would to Heaven you loved any other lady! I should not have so many difficulties to surmount as I foresee here. I will nevertheless employ all my art, but I shall require time for my advances. Nevertheless, take courage, and place confidence in me.'

"'The old lady left me; and as I reflected with anxiety on all the obstacles she had represented to me, the fear that she would not succeed took hold on me, and increased my disease. My old friend came to visit me the following day, and I soon read in her countenance that she had no favourable intelligence to announce. She said: 'My son, I was not mistaken; I have a greater difficulty to surmount than merely to baffle the vigilance of a father. You love one who delights in letting those burn with unrequited passion who suffer themselves to be charmed with her beauty. She listened to me with pleasure whilst I talked to her only of the pain she made you suffer; but as soon as I opened my mouth to persuade her to allow you an interview, she cast an angry look at me, and said, 'You are very insolent to attempt to make such a proposition; and I desire you will never see me more, if you intend to hold such language as this!'

"'But let not that afflict you,' continued the old lady: 'I am not easily discouraged; and provided you do not lose your patience, I hope at last to accomplish my design.'

"'Not to protract my narration,' continued the young man, 'I will only say that this good messenger made several fruitless attempts in my favour with the haughty enemy of my peace. The vexation I endured increased my disorder to such a degree that the physicians gave me over. I was considered as a man at the point of death, when the old lady came to give me new life.

"'That no one might hear her, she whispered in my ear: 'Determine what present you will make me for the good news I bring you.' These words produced a wonderful effect upon me. I raised myself in my bed, and replied with transport, 'The gift shall be worthy of you; what have you to tell me?' 'My good friend' resumed she, 'you will not die this time; and I shall soon have the pleasure of seeing you in perfect health, and well satisfied with me. Yesterday I went to the lady with whom you are in love, and found her in very good humour. I at first put on a mournful countenance, uttered a number of sighs, and shed some tears. 'My good mother,' said the lady; 'what is the matter? Why are you in such affliction?' 'Alas! my dear and honourable lady,' replied I, 'I have just come from the young gentleman of whom I spoke to you the other day. He is at the point of death, and all for love of you. Alas! this is a sad misfortune, and you are very cruel.' 'I do not know,' said she, 'why you should accuse me of being the cause of his death: how can I be blamed for his illness?' 'How!' replied I, 'did I not tell you that he seated himself before your window, just as you opened it to water your flowers? He beheld this prodigy of beauty, these charms, which your mirror reflects every day. He has languished for you, and his disease has taken such a hold on him that he is now reduced to the pitiable state I have described to you. You may remember, lady,' continued I, 'how harshly you reproved me lately, when I was going to tell you of his illness, and propose to you a method of relieving him in his dangerous condition. I returned to him after I left you, and when he perceived from my countenance that I did not bring a favourable report than his malady at once increased. From that time he has been in the most imminent danger of death; and I do not know whether you could now save his life, even if you were inclined to take pity on him.'

"'This was what I told her,' said the old lady.

"'The fear of your death startled her, and I saw her face change colour. 'Is what you say to me quite true?' said she, 'and does his illness proceed only from his love for me?' 'Ah, lady,' replied I, 'it is but too true; would to Heaven it were false!' 'And do you really think, resumed she, 'that the hope of seeing and speaking to me would diminish the peril in which he lies?' 'Very probably,' said I; 'and if you desire me, I will try this remedy.' 'Then,' replied she, sighing, 'let him hope he may see me; but he must not expect my acceptance if he aspires to marry me, unless my father gives his consent.' 'O lady,' said I, 'you are very good: I will go directly to this young man, and announce to him that he will have the delight of seeing and conversing with you.' 'I do not know,' said she, 'that I can fix a more convenient time for our interview than Friday next, during the midday prayer. Let him observe when my father goes out to the mosque; and then let him come immediately to this house, if he is well enough to leave his home. I shall see him from my window, and will come down to let him in. We will converse together during the hour of prayer, and he will retire before my father returns.'

"'Whilst the good lady was talking, I felt my disorder diminish, and by the time she had concluded her discourse I found myself quite recovered. 'Take this,' said I, giving her my purse full of gold; 'to you alone I owe my cure; I think this money better employed than all I have given to the physicians, who have done nothing but torment me during my illness.'

"'The lady left me; and presently I found myself sufficiently strong to get up. My relations were delighted to see me so much better, congratulated me on my recovery, and took their leave.

"'On the appointed morning the old lady came, whilst I was dressing, making choice of the handsomest garments my wardrobe contained. 'I do not ask you,' said she, 'how you feel; the business you are engaged in tells me what I am to think; but will not you bathe before you go to the principal cadi's?' 'That would consume too much time,' replied I. 'I shall content myself with sending for a barber to shave my head and beard.' I then ordered one of my slaves to seek a barber who was expert and expeditious in his business.

"'The slave brought me this unlucky barber who is here present. After saluting me, he said, 'My master, to judge by your looks, I should say you are unwell.' I replied that I was recovering from a very severe illness. 'May Allah preserve you from all kinds of evils,' continued he, 'and may His favour accompany you everywhere.' 'I hope He will grant this wish,' said I, 'and I am much obliged to you.' 'As you are now recovering from illness,' resumed the barber, 'I pray Allah that he will preserve you in health. Now tell me what is your pleasure: I have brought my razors and my lancets; do you wish me to shave or to bleed you?' 'Did I not tell you,' returned I, 'that I am recovering from an illness? You may suppose, then, that I did not send for you to bleed me. Be quick and shave me, and do not lose time in talking, for I am in a hurry, and have an appointment precisely at noon.'

"'The barber was very slow in spreading out his apparatus and preparing his razors. Instead of putting water into his basin, he drew out of his case a very neat astrolabe, went out of my room, and walked with a sedate step into the middle of the court, to take the height of the sun. He returned as deliberately as he had gone out, and said, on entering the chamber, 'You will, no doubt, be glad to learn, sir, that this is the eighteenth day of the moon of Safar, in the year six hundred and fifty-three from the Hægira of our great Prophet from Mecca to Medina, and in the year seven thousand three hundred and twenty of the epoch of the great Iskander with the two horns; and that the conjunction of Mars and Mercury signifies that you cannot choose a better time to be shaved than the present day and the present hour. But on the other side, this conjunc-

THE YOUNG MAN AND THE BARBER.

tion carries with it a bad omen for you. It demonstrates to me that you will this day encounter a great danger; not, indeed, a risk of losing your life, but the peril of an inconvenience which will remain with you all your days. You ought to thank me for warning you to be careful of this misfortune; I should be sorry if it befel you.'

"'I was sincerely vexed at having fallen into the hands of this chattering and ridiculous barber. How mortifying was this delay to a lover who was preparing for a tender meeting with his mistress! I was quite exasperated. 'I care very little,' said I, angrily, 'for your advice or your predictions: I did not send for you to consult you on astrology. You came here to shave me; therefore either perform your office or begone, that I may send for another barber.'

"'My master,' replied he, in so unconcerned a tone that I could scarcely contain myself, 'what reason have you to be angry? Do not you know that all barbers are not like me, and that you would not find another like myself, even if you had him made expressly for you? You only asked for a barber, and in my person you see united the best barber of Bagdad, an experienced physician, a profound chemist, a never-failing astrologer, a finished grammarian, a perfect rhetorician, a subtle logician; a mathematician, thoroughly accomplished in geometry, arithmetic, astronomy, and in all the refinements of algebra; an historian, thoroughly versed in the history of all the kingdoms in the universe. Besides these sciences, I am well instructed in all the points of philosophy, and have my memory well stored with all our laws and all our traditions. I am moreover a poet, and an architect; but what am I not? There is nothing in nature concealed from me. Your late honoured father, to whom I pay a tribute of tears every time I think of him, was fully convinced of my merit. He loved me, caressed me, and never failed to quote me on all occasions as the first man in the whole world. My gratitude and friendship for him attach me to you, and urge me to take you under my protection, and secure you from all misfortunes with which the planets may threaten you.'

"'Notwithstanding my anger, I could not help laughing at this speech. 'When do you mean to have done, impertinent chatterer?' cried I, 'and when do you intend to begin shaving me?'

"'Indeed,' replied the barber, 'you do me an injury by calling me a chatterer: for you must know that I everywhere enjoy the honourable appellation of 'Silent.' I had six brothers, whom you might with some reason have termed chatterers; and that you may be acquainted with them, I will tell you that the eldest was named Bacbouc, the second Bakbarah, the third Bakbac, the fourth Alcouz, the fifth Alnaschar, and the sixth Schacabac. These men were indeed most tiresome talkers; but I, who am the youngest of the family, am very grave and sparing of my words.'

"'Think what a situation was mine! What could I do with so cruel a tormentor? 'Give him three pieces of gold,' said I to the slave who managed the expenses of my house, 'and send him away, that I may be rid of him; I will not be shaved to-day.' 'My master,' cried the barber at hearing this, 'what am I to understand by these words? It was not I who came to seek you; it was you who ordered me to come; and that being the case, I swear by the faith of a Mussulman I will not quit your house till I have shaved you. If you do not know my value, it is no fault of mine: your late honoured father was more just to my merits. Each time when he sent for me to bleed him, he used to make me sit down by his side, and then it was delightful to hear the clever things with which I entertained him. I kept him in continual admiration; I enchanted him; and when I had finished speaking he would cry, "Ah, you are an inexhaustible fund of science; no one can approach the profundity of your knowledge." "My dear master," I used to reply, "you do me more honour than I deserve. If I say a good thing, I am indebted to you for the favourable hearing: it is your liberality that inspires me with those sublime ideas which have the good fortune to meet your approbation." One day, when he was quite charmed with an admirable discourse I had just delivered, he exclaimed: "Give him an hundred pieces of gold, and dress him in one of my richest robes!" I received this present immediately; and at the same time I drew out his horoscope, which I found to be one of the most fortunate in the world. I carried the proofs of my gratitude still further, for I cupped him instead of merely bleeding him with a lancet.'

"'He did not stop; he began another speech which lasted a full half-hour. Tired out with hearing him, and vexed at finding the time pass while I made no progress, I knew not what more to say. At length I exclaimed, 'Indeed it is not possible that there can be in the whole world a man who takes a greater delight in making others mad.'

"'I then thought I might succeed better by gentle means. 'In the name of Allah,' I said to him, 'leave off your fine speeches, and despatch me quickly: I have an affair of the greatest importance, which obliges me to go out, as I have already told you.' At these words he began to laugh. 'It would be very praiseworthy,' said he, 'if our minds were always calm and equable; however, I am willing to believe that when you put yourself in a passion with me, it was your late illness which ruffled your temper; on this account, therefore, you are in need of some instructions, and you cannot do better than follow the example of your father and your grandfather. They used to come and consult me in all their affairs; and I may safely say, without vanity, that they were always the better for my advice. Let me tell you, that a man scarcely ever succeeds in any enterprise if he has not recourse to the opinions of enlightened persons. No man becomes clever, says the proverb, unless he consults a clever man. I am entirely at your service, and you have only to command me.'

"'Cannot I persuade you,' interrupted I, 'to desist from these long speeches, which only drive me mad, and prevent me from keeping my appointment? Shave me directly, or leave my house.' So saying I arose, and angrily struck my foot against the ground.

"'When he saw that I was really exasperated with him, he said, 'O master, do not be angry; I will begin directly.' In fact, he washed my head and began to shave me; but he had not touched me four times with his razor, when he stopped to say, 'My master, you are hasty; you should abstain from these gusts of passion, which only come from the devil. Moreover, I deserve that you should have some respect for me on account of my age, my knowledge, and my striking virtues.'

"'Go on shaving me,' said I, interrupting him again, 'and speak no more.' 'You mean to tell me,' replied he, 'that you have some pressing affair on your hands. I'll lay a wager that I am not mistaken.' 'I told you this two hours ago,' returned I; 'you ought to have shaved me long since.' 'Moderate your impatience,' replied he: 'perhaps you have not considered well what you are going to do; what a man does precipitately is almost always a source of repentance. I wish you would tell me what this affair is about which you are in such haste, and I will give you my opinion on it. You have plenty of time, for you are not expected till noon, and it will not be noon these three hours.' 'That is nothing to me,' said I; 'men who keep their word are always before the time appointed. But in reasoning thus with you, I am imitating the faults of chattering barbers. Finish shaving me at once.'

"'The more anxious I was for despatch, the less willing was he to obey me. He put down his razor to take up his astrolabe; and when he put down his astrolabe, he took up his razor.

"'He seized his astrolabe a second time, and left me, half shaved, to go and see precisely what o'clock it was. When he returned, 'My master,' said he, 'I was certain I was not mistaken; it wants three hours to noon, I am well assured, or all the rules of astronomy are false.' 'Mercy of Allah!' cried I, 'my patience is exhausted, I can hold out no longer. Cursed barber! ill-omened barber! I can hardly refrain from falling upon thee and strangling thee.' 'Be calm, my master,' said he, coolly, and without showing any emotion or anger; 'you seem to have no fear of bringing on your illness again: do not be so passionate, and you shall be shaved in a moment.' Saying this, he put the astrolabe in its case, took his razor, which he sharpened on a strap that was fastened to his girdle, and began to shave me; but whilst he was shaving he could not help talking. 'If,' said he, 'you would inform me what this affair is that will engage you at noon, I would give you some advice, which you might find serviceable.' To satisfy him, I told him that some friends expected me at noon to give me a feast and rejoice with me on my recovery.

"'Directly the barber heard me mention a feast, he exclaimed, 'May Allah bless you on this day as well as on every other! You bring to my mind that yesterday I invited four or five friends to come and regale with me to-day; I had forgotten it, and have not made any preparations for them.' 'Let not that embarrass you,' said I: 'although I am going out, my table is always well supplied, and I make you a present of all that has been prepared for it to-day; I will also give you as much wine as you want, for I have some of excellent quality in my cellar. Only be quick and finish shaving me; and remember that, instead of making you presents to hear you talk, as my father did, I give them to you for being silent.'

"'He was not content to rely on my word. 'May Allah recompense you,' cried he, 'for the favour you do me. But show me these provisions directly, that I may judge if there will be enough to regale my friends handsomely; for I wish them to be satisfied with the good cheer I give them.' 'I have,' said I, 'a lamb, six capons, a dozen fowls, and sufficient meat for four courses.' I gave orders to a slave to produce the whole supply, together with four large jugs of wine. 'This is well,' replied the barber; 'but we shall want some fruit, and some herbs for sauce to the meat.' I desired my slaves to give him what he wanted. He left off shaving me to examine each thing separately; and as this examination took up nearly half an hour, I stamped and cried out with impatience: but I might excite myself as I pleased, the rascal did not hurry the more. At length, however, he again took up the razor, and for a few minutes went on shaving me; then stopping suddenly, he cried, 'I should never have supposed that you had been of so liberal a turn; I begin to discover that your late father, of honoured memory, lives a second time in you. Certainly I did not deserve the favours you heap on me; and I assure you that I shall retain an eternal sense of my obligation; for I may as well tell you, for your future information, that I have nothing but what I get from generous people like yourself. In this I resemble Zantout, who rubs people at the bath, and Sali, who sells little burnt peas about the streets, and Salouz, who sells beans, and Akerscha, who sells herbs, and Abou Mekares, who waters the streets to lay the dust, and Cassem, who belongs to the caliph's guard. All these people rigidly avoid melancholy. They are neither sorrowful nor quarrelsome. Better satisfied with their fortune than the caliph himself in the midst of his court, they are always gay, and ready to dance and sing; and each of them has his peculiar dance and song with which he entertains the whole city of Bagdad. But what I esteem most highly in them is, that they are not great talkers, any more than your slave who has the honour of speaking to you. Now, my master, I will give you the song and the dance of Zantout, who rubs the people at the bath: look at me, and you will see an exact imitation.'

"'The barber sang the song and danced the dance of Zantout; and, notwithstanding all I could say to make him cease his buffoonery, he would not stop till he had given a similar imitation of each of the men he had mentioned. After that he said, 'Sir, I am going to invite all these good people to my house; and, if you will take my advice, you will be of our party, and leave your friends, who are perhaps great talkers, and will only disturb you by their tiresome conversation, and will worry you into an illness still worse than that from which you have just recovered; whereas at my house you will enjoy only pleasure.'

"'Notwithstanding my anger, I could not avoid laughing at his folly. 'I wish,' said I, 'that I had no other engagement; then I would gladly accept your proposal. I would with all my heart make one among your merry friends; but I must entreat you to excuse me: I am too much engaged to-day. I shall be more at liberty another day, and we will have this party. Finish shaving me, and hasten away; for perhaps your friends are already waiting for you.' 'O my master,' replied he, 'do not refuse me the favour I ask of you. Come and amuse yourself with the good company I shall have. If you could only behold them, you would be so pleased with them that you would give up your friends readily.' 'Say no more about it,' said I; 'I cannot be present at your feast.'

"'I gained nothing by gentleness. 'Since you will not come with me,' replied the barber, 'you must allow me to accompany you. I will carry home the provisions you have given me; my friends shall eat of them if they like, and I will return immediately. I cannot be guilty of such an incivility as to suffer you to go alone: you deserve any

THE ALARM.

exercise of friendship on my part.' 'Good heaven!' exclaimed I, on hearing this, 'am I then condemned to bear the tormenting of this creature for this whole day? In the name of Allah,' said I to him, 'make an end of your tiresome speeches; go to your friends, eat and drink, and enjoy yourselves, and leave me at liberty to go to mine. I will go alone, and do not want any one to accompany me; and, indeed, if you must know the truth, the place where I am going is not one in which you can be received; I only can be admitted.' 'You jest, my master,' replied he. 'If your friends have invited you to an entertainment, what reason can prevent me from accompanying you? You will very much oblige them, I am sure, by taking with you a man like me, who has the art of entertaining a company and making them merry. Say what you will, I am resolved to go in spite of you.'

"'These words threw me into the greatest embarrassment. 'How can I possibly contrive to get rid of this horrible barber?' thought I to myself. 'If I continue obstinately to contradict him, our contest will be never-ending. The first call to noon prayers has already sounded.' It was, indeed, now almost the moment to set out. I determined, therefore, not to answer a single word, but to appear as if I agreed to everything my tormentor said. He finished shaving me, and, directly this was done, I said to him, 'Take some of my people with you to carry these provisions to your home; then return hither. I will wait, and not go without you.'

"'He accordingly went out, and I finished dressing myself as quickly as possible. I only waited till I heard the last summons to prayers, and then set forth on my errand. But this malicious barber, who seemed aware of my intention, took care only to accompany my people to within sight of his own house. So soon as he had seen them go in, he concealed himself at the corner of the street to observe and follow me. Accordingly, when I got to the door of the cadi, I turned round and perceived him at the end of the street. I was greatly enraged at this sight.

"'The cadi's door was half-open, and when I went in I found the old lady waiting for me. As soon as she had shut the door, she conducted me to the apartment of the young lady with whom I was in love. But I had hardly commenced a conversation with her, when we heard a great noise in the street. The young lady ran to the window, and, looking through the blinds, perceived that the cadi her father was already returning from prayers. I looked out at the same time, and saw the barber seated exactly opposite the house, on the same bench from whence I had beheld the lady for the first time.

"'I had now two subjects for alarm—the arrival of the cadi, and the presence of the barber. The young lady quieted my fears on the one subject, by telling me that her father very rarely came up into her apartment. Moreover, as she had foreseen that such an occurrence might take place, she had prepared the means of my escape in case of necessity; but the presence of that unlucky barber caused me great uneasiness: and you will soon perceive that my anxiety was not without cause.

"'As soon as the cadi had returned home, he began beating a slave who had deserved punishment. The slave uttered loud cries, which could be plainly heard in the street. The barber thought I was the person who was being ill-treated, and that these were my cries. Fully persuaded of this, he began to call out as loud as he could. He tore his clothes, threw dust upon his head, and shouted for help to all the neighbours, who soon ran out of their houses. They inquired what was the matter, and why he called for help. 'Alas!' exclaimed he, 'they are murdering my master, my dear lord.' And, without waiting for further details, he ran to my house, crying out all the way, and returned followed by all my servants armed with sticks. They knocked furiously at the door of the cadi, who sent a slave to know what the noise meant. But the slave returned quite frightened to his master. 'My lord,' said he, 'more than ten thousand men are determined to come into your house by force, and are already beginning to break open the door.'

"'The cadi himself ran to the door, and inquired what the people wanted. His venerable appearance did not inspire my people with any respect, and they shouted insolently, 'Cursed cadi! dog of a cadi! why are you going to murder our master? What has he done to you?' 'My good friends,' replied the cadi, 'why should I murder your master, whom I do not know, and who has never offended me? My door is open; you may come in and search my house.' 'You have been beating him,' said the barber: 'I heard his cries not a minute ago.' 'But how,' persisted the cadi, 'can your master have offended me, that I should ill-treat him thus? Is he in my house? And if he is here, how could he get in, or who could have admitted him?' 'You will not make me believe you, for all your great beard, you wicked cadi!' cried the barber. 'I know what I mean. Your daughter loves our master, and arranged to meet him in your house during the mid-day prayers. You must have found this out, and returned quickly; you surprised him here, and ordered your slaves to give him the bastinado. But your cruelty shall not remain unpunished: the caliph shall be informed of it, and will execute severe and speedy justice on you. Set him free, and let him come out directly, or we will go in and take him from you to your shame.' 'There is no occasion to talk so much,' said the cadi, 'nor to make such a riot. If what you say is true, you have only to go in and search for your master; I give you full permission.' Directly the cadi had spoken these words, the barber and my servants burst into the house like madmen, and began to ransack every corner in search of me.

"'As I heard every word the barber said to the cadi, I endeavoured to find some place in which I might conceal myself. The only hiding-place I could discover was a large empty chest, into which I immediately crept, and shut the lid down upon myself. After the barber had searched every other place, he at last came into the apartment where I lay. He ran directly to the chest, and opened it; and, finding me crouching there, he took it up and carried it away upon his head. He rushed down the staircase, which was very high, into a court, through which he quickly passed, and at last reached the street.

"'As he was carrying me along, the lid of the chest unfortunately opened. I had not resolution enough to bear the shame and disgrace of my exposure to the populace who followed us, and jumped down so hastily into the street that I hurt myself seriously, and have been lame ever since. I did not at first feel the full extent of the injury I had suffered; I therefore made haste to get up, and ran away from the people who were laughing at me. I scattered among them a handful or two of gold and silver, with which I had filled my purse, and while they were stopping to pick up the prize, I made my escape by hurrying through several quiet streets. But the wretched barber, taking advantage of the stratagem I had made use of to get rid of the crowd, followed me closely, and never once lost sight of me; and as he followed me, he continued calling aloud, 'Stop, my master! why do you run so fast? You know not how much I pity you for the ill-usage you have received from the cadi; and well I may, for you have been very generous to me and my friends, and we are under great obligations to you. Did I not tell you truly, that you would endanger your life through your obstinacy in not allowing me to accompany you? All this happened to you through your own fault; and I know not what would have become of you, if I had not obstinately determined to follow you, and notice which way you went. Whither would you run, my master? I pray you, wait for me.'

"Thus the unlucky barber kept calling out to me all through the street. Not satisfied with having humiliated me completely in the quarter where the cadi resided, he seemed to wish that the whole city should know of my disgrace. This put me into such a rage that I could have stopped and strangled him; but that would only have increased my difficulties. I therefore went another way to work. As I perceived that his calling out attracted the eyes of every one towards me, for some persons looked out of their windows, and others stopped in the street to stare at me, I went into a khan, the master of which was known to me. I found him at the door, whither he had been attracted by the noise and uproar. 'In the name of Allah,' I cried, 'prevent that mad fellow from following me in here.' He promised me to do so, and he kept his word, although not without great difficulty; for the obstinate barber attempted to force an entrance in spite of him. But the wretch would not retire without uttering a thousand abusive words; and all the way home he continued to tell every one he met the very great service he pretended to have done me.

"'Thus I got rid of this tiresome man. The master of the khan asked me to give him an account of my adventure. I did so, and begged him in return to let me have an apartment in his house till I was quite cured. He replied: 'You will be much better accommodated in your own house.' 'I do not wish to return there,' I answered, 'for that detestable barber will be sure to find me out, and I shall be pestered with him every day; and to have him constantly before my eyes would absolutely kill me with vexation. Besides, after what has happened to me this day, I am determined not to remain any longer in this city. I will wander wherever my unhappy destiny may lead me.' Accordingly, as soon as I was cured, I took as much money as I thought would be sufficient for my journey, and gave the remainder of my fortune to my relations.

"'I set out from Bagdad, and arrived here. I had every reason at least to hope that I should be free from this mischievous barber in a country so distant from my own; and I now discover him in your company! Be not therefore surprised at my anxiety and eagerness to retire. You may judge of the pain I feel at the sight of this man, by whose means I became lame, and was reduced to the dreadful necessity of giving up my family, my friends, and my country.'

"After speaking thus, the lame young man rose and went out. The master of the house accompanied him to the door, assuring his guest that it gave him great pain to have been the innocent cause of his great mortification.

"When the young man was gone, we sat in great astonishment thinking of his history. We cast our eyes towards the barber, and told him that he had done wrong, if what we had just heard was true. 'My master,' answered he, raising his head, which he had till now kept bent towards the ground, 'the silence which I have imposed upon myself, while this young man was telling you his story, ought to prove to you that he has asserted nothing but the truth; but notwithstanding all he has told you, I still maintain that I was right in acting as I did: and I shall leave you to judge. Was he not thrown into a position of great danger, and would he have escaped from it but for my assistance? He may think himself very fortunate to have endured nothing worse than lameness. Did I not expose myself to a much greater danger to rescue him from a house where I thought he was being ill-treated? How then can he complain of me, and attack me with injurious reproaches? This is the reward of the man who serves the ungrateful. He accuses me of being a chatterer: that is mere calumny. Of the seven brothers who comprise our family, I am the one who speaks least, and yet who possesses the most wit. To convince you of this, my masters, I have only to relate to you my history and that of my brothers. I entreat you to favour me with your attention.'

## The History of the Barber.

URING the reign of the Caliph Mostanser Billah, a prince famous for his great liberality towards the poor, there were ten robbers who infested the roads in the neighbourhood of Bagdad, and for a long time made themselves famous by their great depredations and horrible cruelties. At last their crimes came to the ears of the caliph; and that prince summoned the chief of the police into his presence some days before the feast of Bairam, and commanded him under pain of death to bring all the ten robbers to his throne. The chief of the police made great exertions; and sent out so many of his men into the country, that the ten robbers were taken on the very day of the feast. I happened to be walking on the banks of the Tigris, when I saw ten very handsomely dressed men embark on board a boat. I might have known they were robbers if I had noticed the guard who accompanied them; but I observed only the men themselves; and thinking that they were a company going to enjoy themselves and pass the day in festivity, I embarked in the boat with them, without saying a word, in the hope that they would suffer me to accompany them. We rowed down the Tigris, and the guards made us land at the caliph's palace. By this time I had found an opportunity of noticing the men more closely, and perceived that I had formed a wrong opinion of my companions. When we quitted the boat, we were surrounded by a fresh party of the guards belonging to the chief of the police. We were bound and carried before the caliph. I suffered myself to be pinioned like the rest without saying a word; for what would it have profited me had I remonstrated or made any resistance? I should only have been ill-treated by the guards, who would have paid no attention to my expostulations; for these men are brutes who will not hear reason. I had been in company with the robbers, and that was quite enough to make the guards believe that I was myself a thief.

"As soon as we had come before the caliph, he ordered the immediate execution of the ten rascals. 'Strike off the heads of these ten robbers,' said he. The executioner immediately ranged us in a line, within reach of his arm; and fortunately I stood last in the row. Then, beginning with the first, he struck off the heads of the ten robbers; but when he came to me he stopped. The caliph, observing that the executioner did not cut off my head, called out in anger, 'Have I not ordered thee to cut off the heads of the ten robbers? Why then hast thou executed only nine?' 'Commander of the Faithful,' replied the executioner, 'Allah forbid that I should neglect your majesty's orders. Here are ten bodies on the ground, and ten heads which I have cut off;' and he counted the corpses at his feet. When the caliph himself saw that the executioner was right, he looked at me with astonishment; and finding that I had not the appearance of a robber, he said, 'Good old man, by what accident were you found among these wretches, who deserved a thousand deaths?' 'Commander of the Faithful,' I replied, 'I will tell you the entire truth. This morning I saw these ten persons, whose punishment is a proof of your majesty's justice, get into a boat; considering they were people who were going to enjoy themselves together, to celebrate this day, the great festival of our religion, I embarked with them.'

"The caliph could not help laughing at my adventure; and (very different from the lame young man, who treated me as a babbler) he admired my discretion and power of keeping silence. 'Commander of the Faithful,' said I, 'let not your majesty be astonished that I have held my tongue in circumstances under which most persons would have been most anxious to speak. I make it my particular study to practise silence, and by the possession of this virtue I have acquired the glorious surname of The Silent. My friends call me thus, to distinguish me from six brothers of mine. Silence is an art which my philosophy has taught me; in short, this virtue is the cause of all my glory and my happiness.' 'I heartily rejoice,' answered the caliph, 'that you have earned a title to which you show so excellent a claim. But inform me what sort of men your brothers were: did they at all resemble you?' 'Not in the least,' I answered 'they were all of them chatterers; and in person not one of us resembled another. The first of my brothers was humpbacked; the second was toothless; the third had but one eye; the fourth was quite blind; the fifth had lost his ears; the sixth was hare-lipped. The various adventures which happened to them would enable your majesty to judge of their characters, if I might have the honour to relate their story.' As I thought the caliph evidently wished to hear the history of my brothers, I went on without waiting for his answer."

### The History of the Barber's First Brother.

MY eldest brother, O caliph! was called Bacbouc the Humpback, and was a tailor by trade. As soon as he had passed through his apprenticeship, he hired a shop, which happened to be opposite a mill; and as he had not at first a great deal of business, he found some difficulty in getting a livelihood. The miller, on the contrary, was very wealthy, and had also a very beautiful wife. As my brother was one morning working in his shop, he happened to look up, and perceived the window of the mill open, and the miller's wife looking into the street. She seemed to him so very handsome that he was quite enchanted with her; but she paid not the least attention to him, but shut the window, and did not make her appearance any more that day.

"In the meantime the poor tailor continued looking towards the mill all the time he was at work. The consequence was, that he pricked his fingers very often, and his work was not that day so neat and regular as usual. When the evening came, and he was forced to shut up his shop, he had hardly resolution to depart, because he still hoped he should again see the miller's wife. At last, however, he had no choice but to shut up his store, and retire to his small house, where he passed a very restless night. The next morning he rose very early, and ran to his shop, so impatient was he to behold the mistress of his heart. But he was not more fortunate than the day before; for the miller's wife looked out of window only for one instant. That moment, however, was quite sufficient to render him like a man bewitched. On the third day he had indeed more reason to be satisfied, for the miller's wife accidentally cast her eyes upon him, and actually caught him gazing fervently at her; and she readily divined the secret thoughts of his breast.

"On making this discovery, instead of being angry or vexed, she resolved to amuse herself with my brother. She looked at him with a smiling air, and he returned her glances in so comical a manner that she was obliged to shut the window as quick as possible, for fear her bursts of laughter should make him find out she was turning him into ridicule. Bacbouc was so innocent that he interpreted this conduct of hers in his own favour, and flattered himself, that she had looked upon him with favour.

"The miller's wife then resolved to play off a jest at my brother's expense. She happened to have in her possession a piece of handsome stuff, which she had for a long time intended to make up into a garment. She wrapped it up, therefore, in a beautiful handkerchief embroidered with silk, and sent it to the tailor by a young female slave. This slave, instructed for the purpose, came to my brother's shop, and said, 'My mistress salutes you, and desires you to make a robe out of this piece of stuff that I have brought, according to the pattern she sends with it. She very often renews her dress, and her custom will be valuable to you.' My brother did not for a moment doubt but that the miller's wife was in love with him. He thought that she had given him this employment so soon after what had passed between them only to show that she understood the state of his heart; and he felt quite sure of the progress he had made in her affections. Impressed with this good opinion of himself, he desired the slave to tell her mistress that he would put aside all other work for hers, and that the dress should be ready by the next morning. He really worked with so much diligence and assiduity that the dress was finished the same day.

"The next morning the young slave came to see how the dress was progressing. Bacbouc immediately gave it her, neatly folded up, and said, 'I am sincerely desirous of obliging your mistress, and I wish by my diligence to persuade her to employ no one else but myself.' The slave then took a few steps, as if she meant to go; but suddenly turning back, she said in a low voice to my brother, 'I had nearly forgotten part of my errand: my mistress charged me to salute you, and to ask you how you had passed the night; for she, poor lady, is so much in love with you, that she has not slept a moment.' 'Tell her,' answered my poor simpleton of a brother, in a transport, 'that my passion for her is so violent, I have not closed my eyes these four nights.' This kind message from the miller's wife raised his hopes to the most inordinate height.

"The slave had not left my brother above a quarter of an hour before he saw her return with a piece of satin. 'My mistress,' said she, 'is quite satisfied with her dress, which fits her perfectly; but as it is very handsome, she is desirous of having a new under-garment also to wear with it; and she entreats you to make her one, as soon as possible, out of this piece of satin.' 'It is sufficient,' answered Bacbouc: 'it shall be done before I leave my shop to-day; and you have only to come and fetch it in the evening.' The miller's wife showed herself very often to my brother at the window, and used all her fascinations in order to encourage him to work. It was wonderful to see how he stitched away. The clothes were soon made, and the slave came to take them away; but she brought the tailor no money for what he had laid out in the trimmings for both the garments he had made, or to pay him for his own work. Moreover, this unfortunate lover, who thus unconsciously made sport for his tormentors, had eaten nothing the whole of that day, and was obliged to borrow some money to purchase a supper.

"The day following, as soon as my brother had entered his shop, the young slave came to him, and told him the miller wished to speak to him. 'My mistress,' added she, 'has shown him your work, and has said so much in your favour, that he also wants you to work for him. She has acted thus, because she wishes to make use of every chance that may assist her in making your acquaintance.' My brother was easily persuaded to believe this, and went with the slave to the mill. The miller received him kindly, and showed him a piece of cloth. 'I require some shirts,' said he, 'and wish you to make me twenty out of this piece of cloth: if any of the material is left, you can return it to me.'

THE MILLER OBLIGES BACBOUC TO TURN THE MILL.

"My brother had five or six days of hard work before he finished the twenty shirts for the miller; who, immediately after, gave him another piece of cloth to make him twenty pairs of trousers. When they were finished, Bacbouc carried them to the miller, who asked him what he demanded for his trouble. My brother upon this said that he should be satisfied with twenty drachms of silver. The miller immediately called the young slave, and ordered her to bring the scales, that he might weigh the money he was going to pay. The slave, who knew what was expected of her, looked at my brother angrily, to make him understand that he would spoil everything if he received the money. He understood her very well; and therefore refused to take any part of the sum, although he was so much in want of money that he had been obliged to borrow to purchase the thread with which he had made the shirts and trousers. On leaving the miller he came directly to me, and entreated me to lend him a trifle to buy some food, telling me that his customers did not pay him. I gave him some copper money which I had in my purse; and upon this he lived some days. It is true he ate nothing but broth, and had not even enough of that.

"My brother one day went to the miller's. This man was busy about his mill; and thinking my brother might have come to ask for his money, he offered it to him: but the young slave, who was present, again prevented his accepting his due, and made him tell the miller, in answer, that he did not come for payment, but only to inquire after his health. The miller thanked him for his kindness, and gave him a cloak to make. Bacbouc brought it home the next day, and the miller took out his purse. But the young slave came in at that moment, and looked at my brother, who then said to the miller: 'There is no hurry, neighbour; we will settle the business another time.' Thus the poor dupe returned to his shop, burdened by three great evils: he was in love, he was hungry, and he was pennyless.

"The miller's wife was both avaricious and wicked. She was not satisfied with preventing my brother from receiving his pay, but she excited her husband to revenge himself for the profession of love which the tailor had made; and to accomplish this they took the following means. The miller invited Bacbouc one evening to supper; and after having treated him with but indifferent fare, he thus addressed him: 'It is too late, brother, for you to return home; you will do better, therefore, to sleep here.' Thereupon he showed him a place where there was a bed; and leaving his guest there, he returned, and went with his wife to the room where they usually slept. In the middle of the night the miller came back to my brother, and called out to him, 'Are you asleep, neighbour? My mule is taken suddenly ill, and I have a great deal of corn to grind; you will therefore do me a very great favour if you will turn the mill for my mule.' To prove his readiness to oblige his host, my brother undertook the strange duty required of him, asking only to be informed how he should set about it. The miller then harnessed him by the middle of his body, like a mule, to make him turn the mill; and immediately giving him a good cut upon his loins with the whip, cried out, 'Get on, neighbour.' 'Why do you strike me?' inquired my brother. 'It is only to encourage you,' replied the miller, 'for without the whip my mule will not stir a step.' Bacbouc was astonished at this treatment, but he dared not complain. When he had gone five or six rounds, he wished to rest himself; but the miller immediately gave him a dozen sharp cuts with the whip, calling out, 'Courage, neighbour! don't stop, I beg of you: you must go on without taking breath, or you will spoil my flour!'

"The miller thus obliged my brother to turn the mill during the rest of the night; and as soon as daylight appeared, he went away without unfastening him, and returned to his wife's chamber. Bacbouc remained for some time harnessed in the mill. At last the young slave came, and untied him. 'Alas! how my good mistress and myself have pitied you,' cried the cunning slave. 'We are not at all to blame for what you have suffered; we have had no share in the wicked trick which her husband has played you.' The unfortunate Bacbouc answered not a word, for he was thoroughly exhausted, and moreover bruised with the beating. He got back to his own house, and firmly resolved to think no more of the miller's wife.

"The recital of this history," continued the barber, "made the caliph laugh. 'Go,' said he to me, 'return home; 'you shall receive something, by my order, to console you for the loss of the festivities in which you expected to share.' 'Commander of the Faithful,' replied I, 'I entreat your majesty not to think of giving me anything till I have related the histories of my other brothers.' The caliph showed by his silence that he was disposed to listen to me; and I continued in the following words:—

### The History of the Barber's Second Brother.

"My second brother, Bakbarah, called the Toothless, was walking one day through the city, when he met an old woman in a retired street. She accosted him in the following terms: 'I have a word to say to you, if you will stay a moment.' He immediately stopped, and asked her what she wished. 'If you have time to go with me,' she replied, 'I will take you to a magnificent palace, where you shall see a lady more beautiful than the day. She will receive you with a great deal of pleasure; and will feast you royally and give you excellent wine. I do not think I need say more.' 'But is this true that you tell me?' asked my brother. 'I am not given to lying,' replied the old woman. 'I am telling you the plain truth; but you must remember what I require you to do. You must be prudent, speak little, and comply with every request that is made.' Bakbarah agreed to the conditions. The old woman walked on, and he followed her. They arrived at the gate of a large palace, where were a great number of officers and servants. Some of these men wished to stop my brother, but the old woman spoke to them, and they let him pass. She then turned to my brother and said, 'Remember, that the young lady to whose house I have brought you likes to see

BAKBARAH AND THE OLD WOMAN.

mildness and modesty, and cannot bear to be contradicted. If you satisfy her in this, there is no doubt but you will obtain from her whatever you wish.' Bakbarah thanked her for this advice, and promised to profit by it.

"She then led him into a very splendid apartment, which formed part of a square building. It corresponded with the magnificence of the palace. There was a gallery all round it, and in the midst was a very beautiful garden. The old woman made him sit down on a gorgeously decorated sofa, and desired him to wait there a moment, while she went to inform the young lady of his arrival.

"As my brother had never before been in so supurb a place, he immediately began to examine all the beautiful things he beheld; and judging of his good fortune by the magnificence around him, he could hardly contain his joy. He almost immediately heard a great noise, which came from a long array of slaves, who were in a state of much merriment, and who came towards him, bursting at intervals into violent fits of laughter. In the midst of the slaves he perceived a young lady of most extraordinary beauty, whom he easily knew to be their mistress by the deference they paid her. Bakbarah, who expected to have had a private conversation with the lady, was very much surprised at the arrival of so large a company. The slaves put on a serious air as they approached him; and when the young lady was near the sofa, my brother, who had risen, made a most profound reverence. She took her seat, and then, motioning him to be seated also, said to him in a smiling manner: 'I am delighted to see you, and wish that your every desire may be fulfilled.' 'Lady,' replied Bakbarah, 'I cannot wish for a greater honour than that of appearing before you.' 'Your wit is equal to your good humour,' she replied, 'and I doubt not we shall pass our time very agreeably together.'

"She immediately ordered the slaves to bring a collation, and they covered the table with baskets of various fruits and sweetmeats. The lady sat down at the table, with my brother and the slaves around her. As he happened to sit directly opposite to her, she observed, as soon as he opened his mouth to eat, that he had no teeth. She remarked this circumstance to her slaves, and they all laughed immoderately. Bakbarah, who from time to time raised his head to look at the lady, and saw that she was laughing, imagined that her mirth arose from the pleasure she felt at being in his company; and flattered himself she would soon order the slaves to retire, and that he should enjoy her conversation in private. The lady guessed his thoughts, and took a pleasure in continuing a delusion which seemed so agreeable to him. She said a thousand soft and tender things to him, and she presented him with some of the choicest dishes with her own hand.

"When the collation was finished, she rose from table. Ten slaves instantly took some musical instruments, and began to play and sing, while the rest danced. In order to make himself agreeable, my brother also began dancing, and the young lady herself joined in the amusement. After they had danced for some time, they all sat down to take breath. The lady called for a glass of wine, and then cast a smile at my brother, to intimate that she was going to drink his health. He instantly rose up, and stood while she drank. When she had emptied the glass, instead of returning it, she had it filled again, and presented it to my brother, that he might pledge her.

"Bakbarah took the glass, and, as he received it from the young lady, he kissed her hand. Then he drank to her, standing the whole time, to show his gratitude for the favour she had done him. After this the young lady made him sit down by her side, and began to caress him. She put her arm round his neck, and patted him several times gently with her hand. Delighted with these favours, he thought himself the happiest man in the world. He felt tempted to return the caresses the charming lady lavished upon him, but he dared not take this liberty before the slaves, who had their eyes upon him, and who continued to laugh at this trifling. The young lady had at first tapped him gently; but at last she began to give him such forcible slaps that he grew angry. He reddened, and got up, intending to sit further away from so rude a playfellow. At this moment the old woman who had brought my brother there gave him a look which made him understand that he was wrong, and had forgotten the advice she had before given him. He acknowledged his fault; and, to repair it, he again approached the young lady, pretending that he had not moved away from any angry feeling. She then took hold of him by the arm, and drew him towards her, making him again sit down close by her, and continuing to bestow on him a thousand pretended caresses. Her slaves, whose only aim was to divert her, began to take a part in the sport. One of them gave poor Bakbarah a fillip on the nose with all her strength; another pulled his ears almost off, while the rest kept slapping him in a way that went beyond jesting.

"My brother bore all this ill-usage with the most exemplary patience. He even affected to be amused by it, and looked at the old woman with a forced smile. 'You were right,' said he, 'when you said that I should find a very agreeable and charming young lady. How much am I obliged to you!' 'Oh, this is nothing yet,' replied the old woman: 'let her alone, and you will see something very different by and bye.' The young lady then said to my brother: 'You are a brave man, and I am delighted at finding in you so much kindness and forbearance for all my little whims. I see you possess a disposition conformable to mine.' 'O lady,' replied Bakbarah, who was delighted with this speech, 'I am no longer myself, but am entirely at your disposal; you have full power to do with me as you please.' 'You give me the greatest happiness,' said the lady, 'by showing so much submission to my will. I am perfectly satisfied with you; and I wish you to be satisfied with me.' Then she called to the attendants to bring perfumes and rose-water. At these words two slaves went out, and instantly returned. One carried a silver vase, containing exquisite aloe-wood, with which she perfumed my brother; the other bore a flagon of rose-water, which she sprinkled over his face and hands. My brother could not contain himself for joy at seeing himself so handsomely and honourably treated.

"When this ceremony was finished, the young lady commanded the slaves who had before sung and played to recommence their concert. They obeyed; and while the music was going on, the lady called another slave, and ordered her to take my brother with her. 'You know what you have to do,' she said, 'and when you have done it, bring him back to me.' Bakbarah, who heard this order given, immediately got up; and going towards the old woman, who had also risen to accompany the slave, requested her to tell him what they wished him to do. 'Our mistress,' replied she, in a whisper, 'is very eccentric. She wishes to see how you would look disguised as a female. This slave, therefore, has orders to take you with her, to paint your eyebrows, shave off your moustache, and dress you like a woman.' 'You may paint my eyebrows,' said my brother, 'as much as you please: to that I readily agree, because I can wash the paint off again; but as to being shaved, that I will by no means allow. How can I appear in the streets without my moustache?' 'Beware,' answered the woman, 'how you refuse anything that is required of you. You will quite spoil your fortune, which is now prospering greatly. She loves you, and wishes to make you happy. Will you, for the sake of a paltry moustache, forego the greatest happiness any man can possibly enjoy?'

"Bakbarah at length yielded to the old woman's arguments; and without further opposition he suffered the slave to lead him to an apartment, where they painted his eyebrows red. They shaved off his moustache, and were absolutely going to remove his beard. But the easiness of my brother's temper did not carry him quite so far as to make him suffer that. 'Not a single stroke,' he exclaimed, 'shall you make at my beard.' The slave represented to him that it was in vain he had parted with his moustache, if he would not also agree to lose his beard: that a hairy countenance did not at all coincide with the dress of a woman; and she declared herself astonished that a man who was about to gain the hand of the most beautiful woman in Bagdad should care for his beard. The old woman sided with the slave, and adduced fresh reasons, threatening my brother with her mistress's displeasure. She said so much, that Bakbarah at last permitted them to do what they wished.

"As soon as they had dressed him like a woman, they brought him back to the young lady, who burst into so violent a fit of laughter at his appearance that she fell back on the sofa on which she was sitting. The slaves all began to clap their hands, and my brother was put quite out of countenance. The young lady then rose, still laughing, and said, 'After the good-nature you have shown to me, I should be wrong if I did not bestow my whole heart upon you; but you must do one thing more for love of me: it is only to dance before me in your present costume.' Bakbarah obeyed; and the young lady and the slaves danced with him, laughing all the while as if they were crazy. After they had danced for some time, they all surrounded the poor dupe, and gave him so many blows and kicks that he fell down almost fainting. The old woman came to his assistance, and without giving him time to express his indignation at such ill-treatment, whispered in his ear: 'Be comforted, for you have now reached the end of your sufferings, and are about to receive your reward. You have only one thing more to do,' added she, 'and that is a mere trifle. You must know that my mistress is accustomed, whenever she is in a merry mood, like to-day, not to suffer any of her favourites to come near her, unless they have run a race with her. You must be stripped to your shirt, and then she will start a few paces before you, and run through the gallery, and from room to room, till you have caught her. This is one of her fancies. Now, whatever start she may take, you, who who are so light and active, can easily catch her. Therefore undress yourself quickly, and do not make any difficulty about it.'

"My brother had already carried his compliance too far to stop. The young lady now took off her robe, in order to run with greater ease. When they were both ready to begin the race, the lady took a start of about twenty paces, and then began running with wonderful swiftness. My brother followed her as fast he could, amid shouts of laughter from the slaves, who kept clapping their hands as he ran. Instead of losing any of the advantage she had first taken, the young lady kept continually gaining upon my brother. She ran round the gallery two or three times, then turned off down a long dark passage, and escaped through a side door unperceived by my brother. Bakbarah, who kept constantly following her, had lost sight of her in this passage; moreover, he was obliged to slacken his pace on account of the darkness. At last he perceived a light, towards which he made with all possible haste: he passed through a door, which was instantly shut upon him.

"You may imagine what was his astonishment when he found himself in the middle of a street inhabited by curriers. They were equally surprised at seeing a man among them in his shirt, his eyebrows painted red, and without either beard or moustache. They began to clap their hands, to hoot at him, aud some even ran after him and beat him with strips of leather. They then seized him, and set him on an ass which they accidentally found, and led him through the city, exposed to the laughter and shouts of the mob.

"To complete his misfortunes, they led him through the street where the judge of the police lived; and this magistrate immediately sent to inquire the cause of the uproar. The curriers informed him that they had seen my brother come out, exactly in the state in which he then was, from the gate leading to the apartments of the women belonging to the grand vizier, which opened into their street. The judge immediately commanded that the unfortunate Bakbarah should receive a hundred strokes upon the soles of his feet, and that he should be thrust out of the city, and forbidden ever to enter it again.

"'This, O Commander of the Faithful,' said I to the Caliph Mostanser Billah, 'is the history of my second brother, which I wished to relate to your majesty. He knew not, poor man, that the ladies of our great and powerful nobles amuse themselves by playing off jests of this kind upon any young man who is silly enough to trust himself in their hands.'

"The barber then proceeded at once to tell the history of his third brother."

## The History of the Barber's Third Brother.

OMMANDER of the Faithful," the barber said to the caliph, "my third brother, who was called Bakbac, was quite blind; and his condition was so wretched that he was reduced to beg, and passed his life in going from door to door asking charity. He had been so long accustomed to walk through the streets alone that he required no one to lead him. He used to knock at the different doors, and never to speak till somebody came and opened them to him.

"He happened one day to knock at the door of a house when the master was sitting alone. 'Who is there?' he called out. My brother made no answer, but knocked a second time. Again the master of the house inquired who was at the door, but Bakbac did not answer. He then came down, opened the door, and asked my brother what he wanted. 'Bestow

THE THREE BLIND MEN WATCHED BY THE THIEF.

something upon me, for the love of God,' answered Bakbac. 'You seem to me to be blind,' said the master of the house. 'Alas! it is true,' replied my brother. 'Hold out your hand,' cried the other. My brother, who made sure of receiving something, immediately put his hand out; but the master of the house only took hold of it to assist him in going upstairs to his apartment. Bakbac imagined that the master of the house would give him some food; for he often received provisions at other houses. When they had reached the upper chamber, the master of the house let go my brother's hand, and sat down in his place; he then again asked him what he wanted. 'I have already told you,' replied Bakbac, 'that I beg you to give me something for the love of God.' 'My good blind man,' answered the master, 'all I can do for you is to wish that Allah may restore your sight to you.' 'You might have told me that at the door,' said my brother, 'and spared me the labour of coming upstairs.' 'And why, good foolish man that you are,' replied the master of the house, 'did you not answer me, after you had knocked the first time, when I asked you what you wanted? Why do you give people the trouble of coming down to open the door when they speak to you?' 'What do you mean to do for me?' asked Bakbac. 'I tell you again,' replied the master, 'that I have nothing to give you.' 'Help me at least to get back to the door, as you brought me up,' said my brother. 'The staircase is before you,' the master of the house answered, 'and if you wish it, you may go down alone.' My brother then began to descend; but missing his footing about half-way down, he fell to the bottom of the stairs, and bruised his head and strained his back cruelly. He got up with difficulty, and went away muttering curses at the master of the house, who did nothing but laugh at his fall.

"As he turned away from the house, two of his companions, who were also blind, happened to pass by, and knew his voice. They stopped to ask him what success he had met with. He told them what had just befallen him; and added, that he had received nothing during the whole day. 'I conjure you,' continued he, 'to accompany me home, that I may in your presence take some of the money which we have in store, to buy something for my supper.' The two blind men agreed to his proposal, and he conducted them home.

"It is necessary here to observe, that the master of the house in which my brother had been so ill-treated was a thief, and a man of cunning and malicious disposition. He had overheard, from his window, what Bakbac had said to his comrades: he therefore came downstairs and followed them; and passed with them unobserved into an old woman's house, where my brother lodged. As soon as they were seated, Bakbac said to the other two: 'We must shut the door, brothers, and take care that there is no stranger among us.' At these words the robber was very much embarrassed; but perceiving a rope that hung from a beam in the middle of the room, he took hold of it, and swung in the air, while the blind men shut the door, and felt all round the room with their sticks. When this was concluded, and they were again seated, he let go the rope, and sat down by the side of my brother, in perfect silence. The latter, thinking there was no one in the room but his blind companions, thus addressed them: 'O my comrades, as you have made me the keeper of all the money we three have collected for a long time past, I wish to prove to you that I am not unworthy of the trust. The last time we reckoned, you remember, we had ten thousand drachms, and we put them into ten bags: I will now show you that I have not touched one of them.' Having said this, he groped about among some old rags and clothes, and drew out the ten bags, one after another; and giving them to his companions, he continued: 'Here are all the bags, and you may judge by the weight that they are quite full; or you may count the money if you like.' They answered that they were perfectly satisfied with his honesty. He then opened one of the bags, and took out ten drachms, and the other two blind men did the same.

"My brother replaced the bags in the spot from which he had taken them. One of the blind men then said there was no occasion to spend anything for supper that night, as he had received from the charity of some good people sufficient provisions for all three; and he took out of his wallet some bread, cheese, and fruit, which he placed upon a table. They then began to eat; and the robber, who sat on the right hand of my brother, chose the best pieces, and ate of their provisions with them. But in spite of all the care he took to avoid making the least noise, Bakbac heard him chew, and instantly exclaimed: 'We are betrayed! there is a stranger among us!' As he said this he stretched out his hand, and seized the robber by the arm. He then fell upon him, calling out, 'Thief!' and giving him many blows with his fist. The other blind men joined in the cry, and beat the robber, who on his part defended himself as well as he could. As he was both strong and active, and had the advantage of seeing where he planted his blows, he laid about him furiously, first on one and then on the other, whenever he was able, and called out, 'Thieves! robbers!' louder than his enemies.

"The neighbours assembled at the noise, broke open the door, and with much difficulty separated the combatants. Having at last put an end to the fray, they inquired the cause of their disagreement. 'O my masters,' cried my brother, who had not yet let the robber go, 'this man, whom I have got hold of, is a thief; he came in here with us for the purpose of robbing us of the little money we possess.' Directly he saw the people enter, the robber had shut his eyes, and pretended to be blind. He now exclaimed, 'He is a liar, my masters. I swear by the name of Allah, and by the life of the caliph, that I am one of their companions and associates, and that they refuse to give me the share of our money which belongs to me. They all three have joined against me, and I demand justice.' The neighbours, who did not wish to interfere with the disputes of these blind men, carried them all four before the judge of the police.

"When they were come before this magistrate, the robber, who still pretended to be blind, began to speak, without waiting to be questioned. 'Since you, my lord, have been appointed to administer justice in behalf of the caliph,' he said, 'whose power may Allah prosper, I will declare to you that we are all equally guilty. But as we have pledged ourselves by an oath not to reveal anything except we receive the bastinado, you must order us to be beaten if you wish to be informed of our crime; and you may begin with me.' My brother now wished to speak, but the officers compelled him to hold his tongue. They then began to bastinado the robber.

"He had the resolution to bear twenty or thirty strokes; and then, pretending to be overcome with pain, he opened first one eye, and then the other; calling out at the same time for mercy, and begging the judge of the police to order a remission of his punishment. When he saw the robber with both his eyes open, the judge was very much astonished. 'Scoundrel!' he cried, 'what does this mean?' 'O my lord,' replied the robber, 'I will discover a most important secret, if you will have the goodness to pardon me; and as a pledge that you will keep your word, give me the ring you have on your finger, and which you often use as a seal. Then I will reveal the whole mystery to you.'

"The judge ordered his people to stop beating the robber, and promised to pardon him. 'Trusting to your promise,' replied the robber, 'I now declare to you, my lord, that my companions and I can see perfectly well. We all four feign blindness, in order that we may enter houses without molestation, and even penetrate into the apartments of the women, whose charity we sometimes take advantage of. I moreover confess to you, that we have collected among us at least ten thousand drachms by this cunning trick. This morning I demanded of my companions two thousand five hundred drachms, which came to my share; but because I declared I would break off all connection with them, and from fear that I should discover their artifice, they refused to give me my money. When I continued to insist on having it they all fell upon me, and ill-treated me in a shameful manner, as the people who have brought us before you can bear witness. I wait here for you to do me justice, my lord, and expect that you will make them deliver up the two thousand five hundred drachms which are my due. If you wish that my comrades should acknowledge the truth of what I advance, order them to receive three times as many blows as you have given me, and you will see them open their eyes as I did.'

"My brother and the other two blind men began to exclaim loudly against this infamous imposture; but the judge would not hear a word. 'Rascals!' he cried, 'is it thus that you counterfeit blindness, and go about deceiving people; and, under pretence of deserving their charity, are guilty of such wicked actions?' 'He is an impostor!' exclaimed my brother: 'what he says is false! We are not able to see at all; and we are ready to swear by Allah that we are blind.'

"But all my brother's protestations were useless. He and his companions each received two hundred strokes of the bastinado. The judge every moment expected them to open their eyes, and attributed to their great obstinacy the non-performance of what it was impossible for them to do. During the whole of this time the robber kept saying to the blind men: 'My good friends, open your eyes, and do not wait till you almost die under the punishment.' Then he added, addressing himself to the judge of the police, 'I see very well, my lord, that they will be obstinate to the end, and that they will never open their eyes; doubtless they are anxious to avoid the shame of reading their own condemnation in the countenances of those who surround them. Would it not be better to pardon them now, and send some one with me to take the ten thousand drachms they have concealed?'

"The judge did not intend to neglect securing the money. He therefore commanded one of his people to accompany the robber, and they brought the ten bags back with them. He then ordered two thousand five hundred drachms to be counted out and given to the robber, and kept the remainder for himself. With respect to my brother and his companions, he commanded them to quit the city, and thought he had dealt very leniently with them. So soon as I heard what had happened to Bakbac I sought him out. He related his misfortunes to me, and I brought him privately back into the city. I might, perhaps, have been able to prove the innocence of my brother before the judge of the police, and the robber would have been punished as he deserved; but I dared not attempt this, for fear of bringing some misfortune upon my own head.

"This is the conclusion of the melancholy adventure of my third brother, who was blind.

"The caliph laughed as much at this story as he had done at those he had before heard. He again ordered that something should be given to me; but without waiting to receive it, I began the history of my fourth brother."

## The History of the Barber's Fourth Brother.

HE name of my fourth brother was Alcouz. How he lost his eye I shall have the honour to relate to your majesty. He was a butcher by trade; and, as he had a particular talent in bringing up rams, and teaching them to fight, he had become introduced to the acquaintance and friendship of some of the principal people, who were much amused with combats of this kind, and who even kept fighting-rams at their own houses. He had moreover a very good business; and there was always in his shop the finest and freshest meat that was to be found in the market; for he was very rich, and did not spare expense in buying the best.

"As he was one day in his shop, an old man, who had a very long and white beard, came in to purchase six pounds of meat. He paid for his purchase, and went away. My brother observed that the money the old man paid was very beautiful, new, and well-coined. He resolved, therefore, to lay it by in a separate part of his closet. During five months the same old man came regularly every day for the same quantity of meat, and paid for it with the same sort of money, which my brother as regularly continued to lay by.

"At the end of five months Alcouz, who wished to purchase a certain quantity of sheep, resolved to pay for them out of this particular money. He therefore went to his box, and opened it; but great was his astonishment when he discovered, instead of his money, only a parcel of leaves of a round shape. He immediately began to beat his breast, and made so great a noise that he brought all his neighbours about him. Their surprise was as great as his own when he informed them of what had happened. 'Would to Allah,' cried my brother, with tears in his eyes, 'that this treacherous old man came here now with his hypocritical face!' He had hardly spoken these words, when he saw the old man at a distance coming towards him. My brother ran in the greatest hurry to meet him, and having seized hold of him, vociferated with all his force, 'Mussulmen, assist me! Hear me tell the shameful trick that this infamous man has played me!' He then related to a large crowd of people, who had gathered round him, the story he had before just told to his neighbours. When he had finished his tale, the old man, without the least emotion, quietly answered: 'You will do best to let me go, and thus make amends for the affront you have offered me before so many people. Unless you do this I may revenge myself in a more serious manner, which I should be sorry to do.' 'And what have you to say against me?' replied my brother. 'I am an honest man in my business, and I fear you not.' 'You wish that I should make it public?' returned the old man in the same tone of voice. 'Listen,' added he, addressing himself to the

ALCOUZ AND THE OLD MAN.

people, 'and hear me tell you that, instead of selling the flesh of sheep, as he ought to do, this man sells human flesh!' 'You are an impostor!' cried my brother. 'No, no!' answered the other: 'at this very moment in which I am speaking, there is a man with his throat cut hanging up on the outside of your shop like a sheep! Let these people go there, and we shall soon know whether I have spoken the truth.'

"That very morning, before my brother had opened the box in which the leaves were, he had killed a sheep, and had dressed and exposed it outside his shop as usual. He therefore declared that what the old man had said was false; but, in spite of all his protestations, the credulous mob, enraged at the idea that a man could be guilty of so shocking a crime, wished to ascertain the fact on the spot. They therefore obliged my brother to let the old man go; and, seizing Alcouz himself, ran precipitately to his shop. There, indeed, they saw a man with his throat cut, hanging up exactly as the accused had stated; for this old man was a magician, and had blinded the eyes of all the people, as he had formerly done those of my brother, when he made him take the leaves that were offered him for real good money.

"At sight of this, one of the men who held Alcouz gave him a great blow with his fist, and at the same time cried, 'You wretch! would you make us eat human flesh?' The old man also, who had followed them, immediately gave him another blow that knocked out one of his eyes. Every one who could get near my brother joined in beating him. Nor were they satisfied with ill-treating him in this manner. They dragged him before the judge of the police, carrying with them the corpse, which they had taken down as a proof of the criminal's guilt. 'O my lord,' said the old magician to the judge, 'you see before you a man who is so barbarous as to kill men, and sell their flesh for that of sheep. The people expect that you will punish him in an exemplary manner.' The judge of the police listened with great patience to what my brother had to say; but the story of the money that had been changed into leaves appeared so utterly incredible, that he treated my brother as an imposter; and, choosing rather to believe his own eyes, he ordered that Alcouz should receive five hundred blows. After this he obliged him to reveal where his money was, confiscated the whole of it, and condemned him to perpetual banishment, after having exposed him for three successive days, mounted on a camel, to all the city.

"At the time that this dreadful adventure happened to Alcouz, my fourth brother, I was absent from Bagdad. He retired to a very obscure part of the city, where he remained concealed till the wounds his punishment had produced were healed. It was on the back that he had been most cruelly beaten. As soon as he was able to walk he travelled, during the night and through unfrequented roads, to a city where no one knew him: there he took a lodging, from whence he hardly ever stirred. But tired at last of his exclusive life, he one day went to walk in the suburbs of the town. Suddenly he heard a great noise of horsemen coming along behind him. He happened just at this instant to be near the door of a large house; and as he was afraid of everybody, after what had happened to him, he fancied that these horsemen were in pursuit of him in order to arrest him. He therefore opened the door for the purpose of concealing himself. After shutting it again, he went into a large court; but directly he entered, two servants came up to him and seized him by the collar, saying, 'Allah be praised that you have come of your own free will to deliver yourself into our hands. You have disturbed us so much for these last three nights, we have been unable to sleep; and you have spared our lives only because we have frustrated your wicked intention of taking them.'

"You may easily imagine that my brother was not a little surprised at this welcome. 'My good friends,' said he to the men, 'I know not what you would have with me; doubtless you mistake me for another person.' 'No, no,' replied they; 'we know well enough that you and your comrades are thieves. You were not satisfied with having robbed our master of all he possessed, and reducing him to beggary—you wished to take his life. Let us see if you have not the knife about you which you had in your hand when we pursued you last night.' Hereupon they began to search him, and found that he had a knife. 'So, so,' cried they, as they snatched it from him; 'and have you the assurance still to deny that you are a robber?' 'How!' answered my brother, 'cannot a man carry a knife in his pocket without being a thief? Listen to my story,' he added, 'and instead of having a bad opinion of me, you will pity me for my misfortunes.' But instead of listening to him, they immediately fell upon him, trampled him under their feet, pulled off his clothes, tore his shirt; and then, observing the scars upon his back, they redoubled their blows. 'You scoundrel! do you wish to make us believe you are an honest man, when your back is so covered with scars?' 'Alas!' cried my brother, 'my sins must be very great, since, after having been once most unjustly treated, I am served so a second time, without having committed the least fault.'

"The two servants paid no attention to my brother's complaints. They carried him before the judge of the police. 'How dare you,' said the judge, 'break into people's houses, and pursue them with a knife in your hand?' 'O my lord,' answered poor Alcouz,

'I am one of the most innocent men in the world. I shall be undone, if you will not do me the favour patiently to listen to me. No man is more worthy of compassion than I am.' 'O judge,' cried one of the servants, 'will you listen for a moment to a robber, who breaks into people's houses, pillages them, and murders the inhabitants? If you refuse to believe, look at his back, and that will prove the truth of our words.' When he had said this, they uncovered my brother's back, and showed it to the judge, who, without inquiring any further into the matter, ordered that he should at once receive a hundred strokes with a leathern strap on his shoulders. He then commanded him to be led through the city upon a camel, while a crier going before him called out, 'THUS SHALL MEN BE PUNISHED WHO FORCIBLY BREAK INTO HOUSES.'

"When this punishment was over, they set Alcouz down outside the town, and forbade him ever to enter it again. Some people who accidentally met him after this second disgrace informed me where he was. I set out directly to find him, and then brought him secretly to Bagdad, where I did everything in my power to assist him.

"The Caliph Mostanser Billah did not laugh so much at this history as at the others, for he was kind enough to commiserate the unfortunate Alcouz. He then wished to give me something and send me away; but without giving his servants time to obey his orders, I said, 'You may now have observed, most sovereign lord and master, that I speak very little. Since your majesty has had the goodness to listen to me thus far, and as you express a wish to hear the adventures of my two other brothers, I hope and trust they will not afford you less amusement than the histories you have already heard. They will then form a complete chronicle, which will not be unworthy of being placed amongst your archives.'"

### THE HISTORY OF THE BARBER'S FIFTH BROTHER.

HAVE the honour to inform you that the name of my fifth brother was Alnaschar. While he lived with my father he was excessively idle. Instead of working for his bread, he was not ashamed to beg sufficient for his support every evening, and to live upon it the next day. Our father at last died at a very advanced age, and all he left us consisted of seven hundred drachms of silver. We divided it equally among us, and each took one hundred for his share. Alnaschar, who had never before possessed so much money at one time, found himself very much embarrassed how to dispose of it. He debated this subject a long time in his own mind, and at last determined to lay out his hundred drachms in the purchase of glasses, bottles, and other glass articles, which he procured at a large wholesale merchant's. He put his whole stock into an open basket, and chose a very small shop, where he sat down with his basket before him; and, leaning his back against the wall, waited till customers should come to buy his merchandise.

"As he sat thus, with his eyes fixed upon his basket, he began to meditate; and, in the midst of his reverie, he pronounced the following speech, so loud that a tailor who was his neighbour could hear him. 'This basket,' said he, 'cost me one hundred drachms, and that is all I had in the world. Selling its contents by retail, I shall manage to make two hundred drachms; these two hundred I shall employ again in purchasing glassware, so that I shall make four hundred drachms. By continuing this trade, I shall, in time, amass the sum of four thousand drachms. With these four thousand I shall easily make eight, and as soon as I have gained ten thousand I will leave off selling glassware, and turn jeweller. I will then deal in diamonds, pearls, and all sorts of precious stones. When I have got together as much wealth as I wish to have, I will purchase a beautiful house, large estates, eunuchs, slaves, and horses: I will entertain my friends handsomely and largely, and shall make some noise in the world. I will make all the musicians and dancers, male and female, who live in the city, come to my house.

But I will not leave off trading till I have realised, if it shall please Allah, one hundred thousand drachms. And when I thus become rich, I shall think myself equal to a prince; and I will send and demand the daughter of the grand vizier in marriage. I shall represent to him that I have heard most astonishing reports of the beauty, wisdom, wit, and every other good quality of his daughter; and, in short, that I will bestow upon her, the very night of our nuptials, a thousand pieces of gold. If the vizier should be so ill-bred as to refuse me his daughter—though I know that will not be the case—I will go and take her away before his face, and bring her home in spite of him.

"'As soon as I have married the grand vizier's daughter, I shall purchase ten very young and handsome black eunuchs for her. I will dress myself like a prince, and ride in procession through the town, mounted on a fine horse, the saddle of which shall be of pure gold, and the caparisons of cloth of gold, enriched with diamonds and pearls. I will be accompanied by slaves, some marching before and some behind me; and thus we shall proceed to the palace of the vizier, with the eyes of all fixed upon me, both nobles and common people, who will pay me the most profound reverence as I go along. When I have dismounted at the grand vizier's, and come to the foot of the staircase, I will ascend the stairs, while my servants stand ranged in two rows to the right and left; and the grand vizier, rising to receive me as his son-in-law, will give me his place, and seat himself before me to show me the greater respect. Two of my men shall have each a purse containing one thousand pieces of gold, which I had ordered them to bring. I will take one of these purses, and present it to the grand vizier with these words: 'Behold the thousand pieces of gold which I have promised you on the first night of my marriage.' Then offering him the other purse, I will add, 'To show you that I am a man of my word, and to prove that I give more than I promise, receive this other purse of equal value.' After such an act, my generosity will be talked of by all the world.

"'I will then return home with the same pomp with which I set out. My wife must send an officer to compliment me on my visit to her father. I shall bestow a beautiful robe of honour on the officer, and send him back with a rich present. If she shall wish to make me a present in return, I will refuse it, and dismiss the person who brings it. I will not, moreover, permit her to leave her apartments upon any account whatever without first obtaining my permission; and whenever I visit her, it shall always be in a way that shall impress her with the greatest respect for me. In short, no house shall be so well regulated as mine. I will always appear magnificently dressed; and whenever I wish to pass the evening with my wife, I will sit in the most honourable seat, where I will assume a grave and solemn air, not turning my head to the right or to the left. I will speak but little; and when my wife, beautiful as the full moon, presents herself before me in all her splendour, I will pretend not to see her. Her women, who will be standing round her, must say: 'O our dear lord and master, behold before you your spouse, the humblest of your slaves. She waits for you to caress her, and is much mortified that you do not deign to take the least notice of her. She is greatly fatigued at standing so long before you; permit her, therefore, to sit down.' I will not answer a word to this speech, and my continued silence will greatly augment their surprise and grief. They will then throw themselves at my feet, and after they have remained prostrate before me a considerable time, entreating and begging me to notice them, I will at last lift up my head, and casting upon my wife a careless glance, will resume my former attitude. Thinking, perhaps, that my wife may not be dressed or adorned to my taste, they will lead her back to her room to change her habit; and in the meantime I will return to my apartment, and put on a more magnificent dress than I wore before. They will then return a second time, and renew their entreaties; and I shall again have the pleasure of disregarding my wife, till they have prayed and besought me as long and earnestly as before. And I will thus begin, on the very first day of my marriage, to teach her how she may expect to be treated during the remainder of her life.

"'After the various ceremonies of our nuptials are over,' continued Alnaschar, 'I will take from the hands of one of the attendants a purse containing five hundred pieces of gold, which I will give to the female attendants, and then they will leave me alone with my

ALNASCHAR AND HIS BASKET OF GLASS.

spouse. After they have retired, I will treat my wife with such utter indifference that she will not fail to complain to her mother, the lady of the grand vizier, of my pride and neglect; and this will very much delight me. Her mother will then come to visit me. She will kiss my hands respectfully, and say to me, 'My master,' (for she will not dare to call me son-in-law, for fear that her familiarity should displease me), 'I entreat you not to despise my child in such a manner, nor keep her at a distance. I assure you she will always endeavour to please you, and I know her whole heart is devoted to you.' Although my mother-in-law addresses me so respectfully and kindly, I will not answer her a word, but remain as grave and solemn as ever. She will then throw herself at my feet, and kissing them repeatedly, will say, 'My lord, you surely have no fault to find with my daughter? I assure you I have never suffered her to go out of my sight; and you are the first man who has ever seen her face. Forbear to inflict so great a mortification upon her, and do her the favour to look at and speak to her, and thus strengthen her good intention of endeavouring to satisfy and please you in everything.'

"'All this shall have no effect upon me; and my mother-in-law, observing my indifference, will take a glass of wine, and putting it into my wife's hand, will say, 'Go and offer him this glass of wine yourself; he will not have the cruelty to refuse it from so beautiful a hand.' My wife will then take the glass and stand before me trembling. When she observes that I do not relent towards her, and that I persist in my sullen behaviour, she will address me thus, with her eyes bathed in tears: 'My heart, my dear soul, my amiable lord, I conjure you, by the favours which Heaven has so plentifully bestowed on you, to have the goodness to take this glass of wine from the hand of the humblest of your slaves.' I shall, however, neither look at her nor speak. 'My charming husband,' she will continue to say, with renewed tears, and coming closer to me with the glass of wine, 'I will not cease to entreat you until you do me the favour of drinking it.' At last, tired and annoyed with her solicitations and prayers, I will throw a terrible glance at her, and give her a blow on her cheek, and push her so violently from me with my foot, that she will fall down beside the sofa.'

"My brother was so entirely absorbed in these chimerical visions, that he thrust out his foot as if the whole scene were a reality; and he unfortunately struck his basket of glassware so violently that it fell from his shopboard into the street, where it was all broken to pieces.

"His neighbour the tailor, who had heard the whole of Alnaschar's extravagant speech, burst into a fit of laughter when he saw the basket overturned. 'O cruel wretch!' said he to my brother, 'ought you not to die with shame for thus ill-treating a young wife, when she has given you no reason for complaint? You must be hard-hearted indeed to pay no attention to the tears of so amiable a lady, and to be insensible to her charms. If I were your father-in-law, the grand vizier, I would order you a hundred blows with a leathern strap, and send you round the city, with a man to proclaim your crime, as you deserve.'

"This most unfortunate accident brought my brother to his senses; and knowing that it had been caused by his own insufferable pride, he beat his breast, tore his garments, and shrieked so violently and so loud that all the neighbours came running up; and the people who were going by to mid-day prayers stopped to inquire what was the matter; and as this happened to be Friday, there were more people than usual. Some pitied Alnaschar; others laughed at his folly. But the vanity which he had before shown was now entirely subdued by the loss of his property; and he continued bewailing his hard and cruel fate, when a lady of considerable rank passed by, mounted on a mule richly caparisoned. The sight of my brother's distress excited her compassion. She asked who he was, and the reason of his violent grief. The people replied that he was a poor man, who had laid out the little money he possessed in a basket of glassware, and that the basket had fallen down, and all his glass was broken. The lady immediately turned to a eunuch who accompanied her, and ordered him to give my brother what money he had with him. The eunuch obeyed, and put a purse containing five hundred pieces of gold into my brother's hand. Alnaschar was ready to expire with joy at sight of this wealth. He bestowed a thousand blessings on the lady; and after shutting up his shop, where there was now nothing to keep him, he went home.

"He made many serious reflections on the good fortune which had so unexpectedly come to him; and while he was thus employed, he heard some person knock at his door. He asked who was there; and perceiving that his visitor was a female, he admitted her.

'My son,' said she, addressing my brother, 'I have a favour to request of you. It is now the time for prayers, and I wish to wash myself, that I may be fit to perform my devotions. Suffer me, I entreat you, to come into your house, and bestow on me a basin of water.' My brother looked at her, and saw she was somewhat advanced in years; and although he did not know her, he nevertheless acceded to her request. He gave her a vessel of water, and then resumed his seat. He again fell to thinking of his adventure: he took his gold and put it into a sort of long and narrow purse, which he could easily carry at his girdle. The old woman in the meantime said her prayers; and when she had done, she approached my brother, and prostrated herself twice at his feet till her forehead touched the ground; then rising, she wished Alnaschar all manner of prosperity, and thanked him for his kindness.

"As she was very meanly dressed, and humbled herself so much before him, my brother thought that she meant to ask charity; he therefore offered her two pieces of gold. The old woman drew back with as great an appearance of surprise as if my brother had done her an injury. 'O Allah!' cried she, 'what do you mean by this? Is it possible, my master, that you can take me for one of those poor wretches who make a practice of impudently going into men's houses and begging? Put back your money, for I have no need of it, Allah be praised! I belong to a young lady in this city, whose beauty is incomparable, and she is so rich that she does not let me want for anything.'

"My brother was not wise enough to see through the cunning of the old woman, who refused the two pieces of gold only to dupe him the more. He asked her if she could not procure him the honour of seeing this lady. 'Certainly,' answered she; 'and you may even succeed in marrying her; and, in becoming her husband, you will get possession of all her fortune: take your money, and follow me.' Delighted that his singular good fortune in receiving such a large sum of money should be followed by the acquisition of a beautiful and rich wife, Alnaschar forgot every thought of prudence. He took his five hundred pieces of gold, and suffered the old woman to lead him away.

"She went on before, and he followed her till they came to the door of a large house, at which she knocked. He came up just as a young female Greek slave opened the door. The old woman made Alnaschar enter first. He passed through a well-paved court, and she then brought him into a hall, whose handsome furniture confirmed him in the high opinion he had conceived of the mistress of the house. While the old woman went to inform the young lady of his arrival, he sat down; and, as the day was warm, he took off his turban, and laid it by his side. The lady of the house presently made her appearance; and he was much more struck with her beauty than with the magnificence and richness of her dress. He rose up the moment he saw her. The lady requested him with a pleasing air to resume his seat, and placed herself by his side. She expressed great pleasure at seeing him; and, after some kind speeches, she said to him, 'We are not here sufficiently at our ease; come, give me your hand.' So she led him to a distant apartment, where they remained some time in conversation; she then left him, with a promise to return in a few moments. He had waited some time, when, instead of the lady, a large black slave entered with a scimitar in his hand; and he cried, casting a terrible look at my brother, 'What do you here?' Alnaschar was seized with so violent a fright, he could not make any answer. The black immediately stripped him, took away his gold, and gave him several wounds with his scimitar. Poor Alnaschar fell down on the ground, where he remained motionless, though he did not lose his senses. The black slave, thinking he had killed my brother, called for some salt, and the Greek slave brought him a large dishful. They rubbed the salt over my brother's wounds; and although the pain he felt was almost intolerable, he had the presence of mind to show no signs of life. The black slave and the young Greek now went away; and the old woman who had caught my brother in this snare came in. She took him by the legs, and drew him towards a trap-door, which she opened. She then threw him in; and he found himself in a subterraneous vault, surrounded by the bodies of different people who had been murdered. It was some time, however, before he knew this, as the violence of the fall had stunned him and taken away his senses. The salt with which his wounds had been rubbed had preserved his life. He soon felt himself sufficiently strong to sit up. At the end of two days he opened the trap-door in the night; and observing a place in a court-yard in which he could conceal himself, he remained there till daybreak. He then saw the wicked old woman come out: she opened the street-door, and went away in search of more prey. As soon as she was out of sight, he escaped out of this den of murderers, and fled to my house. He then informed me of the numerous adventures he had encountered in the last few days.

"At the end of a month, he was quite cured of his wounds, by means of the sovereign remedies I made him apply. He then resolved to avenge himself on the old woman who had so cruelly deceived him. For this purpose he took a purse large enough to hold five hundred pieces of money, but instead of putting gold in it, he filled it with pieces of glass.

"My brother then tied the purse to his girdle, and disguised himself as an old woman, taking with him a scimitar concealed under his dress. He went out early one morning, and soon met the old hag, who was already prowling about the city, seeking to entrap some unwary passenger. Alnaschar accosted her, and, in a feigned woman's voice, he said, 'Can you do me the favour to lend me some scales for weighing money? I am a Persian, and have just arrived in this city. I have brought five hundred pieces of gold from my own country, and I wish to see if they are the proper weight.' 'My good woman,' replied the old hag, 'you could not have addressed yourself to a more proper person than myself. You need only follow me, and I will take you to the house of my son, who is a money-changer, and he will be glad to weigh the gold for you himself, and save you the trouble. Let us lose no time, lest he should be gone to his shop.' My brother followed her to the same house whither she had led him the first time, and the door was opened by the Greek slave.

"The old woman conducted my brother into the hall, where she bade him wait a moment, while she went to find her son. The pretended son then appeared in the form of the villainous black slave. 'Come, my old woman,' he called out, 'get up, and follow me.' Having spoken this, he walked on before to the place where he committed his murders. Alnaschar rose and followed the black slave; but as he went, he drew his scimitar from under his robe, and struck the slave such a blow on the hinder part of the neck that he cut his head completely off. He then took the head up in one hand, and with the other he drew the body after him to the entrance of the subterraneous vault, into which he cast both head and body. The Greek slave, who was used to this business, quickly appeared with a basin of salt; but when she saw Alnaschar with the scimitar in his hand, and without the veil that had concealed his face, she let the basin fall, and ran away; but my brother, who was very active, soon overtook her, and struck her head from her shoulders. Hearing the noise they made, the wicked old woman ran to see what was the matter; but Alnaschar seized her before she had time to make her escape. 'Wretch!' he exclaimed, 'dost thou not know me?' 'Alas! my master, she tremblingly answered, 'I do not remember to have ever seen you before; who are you?' 'I am the man into whose house you came the other day to request leave to wash yourself, and say your hypocritical prayers. Do you not recollect it?' She instantly fell down on her knees, and begged for mercy; but he cut her into four pieces.

"Now the lady alone remained; and she knew nothing at all of what was passing. My brother went to look for her, and discovered her in a chamber. When she saw him enter she nearly fainted. She begged him to spare her life, and he had the generosity to grant her prayer. Then he said, 'How can you, lady, live with such wretches as those on whom I have even now so justly revenged myself?' She answered: 'I was the wife of a very worthy merchant; and that wicked old woman, whose treacherous character I did not know, sometimes came to see me. She said to me one day, 'O lady, we are going to have a merry and splendid wedding at our house, and you will be well entertained there if you will honour us with your company.' I suffered myself to be prevailed upon to go; and I dressed myself in my richest habit, and took a hundred pieces of gold with me. I followed her till she came to this house, where I saw this black, who detained me here by force; and it is now three years that I have been kept here as a prisoner.' My brother replied: 'To judge by the time he has continued his proceedings, this black must have amassed great wealth.' 'So much,' she answered, 'that if you could carry it away you would never be poor again. Follow me, and I will show it you.' She conducted Alnaschar into a room, where he really saw so many coffers filled with gold that he could not conceal his astonishment. The lady said to him, 'Go and bring here a sufficient number of persons to carry all this away.'

THE LADY SHOWS ALNASCHAR THE HIDDEN TREASURE.

"My brother needed no second bidding. He went away, and had quickly collected ten men together. He brought them back with him, and was much astonished to find the door of the house open; but his astonishment was still greater when, on going into the room where he had left the coffers, he could not find a single one. The lady had been more cunning and more diligent than he, and she and the coffers had vanished during my brother's absence. That he might not return with empty hands, he ordered the men to take whatever moveables they could find in the chambers and different apartments, whence he carried off much more than sufficient to repay him the value of the five hundred pieces of gold of which he had robbed. But when he left the house, my brother forgot to shut the door; and the neighbours, who knew Alnaschar, and had seen the porters come and go, went and gave information to the judge of what appeared to them to be a very suspicious business.

"Alnaschar passed the night quite comfortably; but early the next morning, as he was going out, he encountered twenty men belonging to the police, who immediately seized him. 'You must come with us,' they cried: 'our master wants to speak with you.' My brother begged them to have patience, and offered them a sum of money if they would permit him to escape; but instead of paying any attention to what he said, they bound him, and compelled him to go with them. In the street they met an old friend of my brother's, who stopped them to know the reason why they led him away in this manner. He also offered to give them a considerable sum if they would allow Alnaschar to escape, and report to the judge that they were unable to find him. But he could not prevail with them, and they carried Alnaschar before the judge of the police.

"As soon as he came into the judge's presence, that officer said to him, 'I desire you to inform me from what place you got all that furniture you caused to be brought home yesterday.' 'O judge,' replied Anaschar, 'I am ready to tell you the whole truth; but permit me in the first place to implore your favour, and to beg that you will pledge me your word that nothing shall happen to me.' 'I promise it,' said the judge. My brother then related, without disguise, every circumstance that had happened to him from the time when the old woman first came to his house to request leave to say her prayers, till his return to the chamber in which he had left the young lady, after having killed the black, the Greek slave, and the old woman. With regard to what he had carried home, he entreated the judge to suffer him to keep at least a part of it, as amends for the five hundred pieces of gold of which he had been robbed.

"The judge immediately sent some of his people to my brother's house to bring away everything, without promising to let Alnaschar keep any part of the spoil; and as soon as the things were deposited in his own warehouse, he ordered my brother instantly to leave the city, and forbade him to return again on pain of death; because he was fearful that if my brother remained in the city he would go and complain to the caliph of the judge's injustice. Alnaschar obeyed the order without a murmur. He departed from the city, and fled for refuge to another town. But on the road he fell among robbers, who took from him everything he had, and stripped him naked. So soon as I heard of this new misfortune I took some clothes with me, and went to find him out. I consoled him as well as I could, and brought him back with me, and made him enter the city quite privately; and I took as much care of him as of my other brothers."

## The History of the Barber's Sixth Brother.

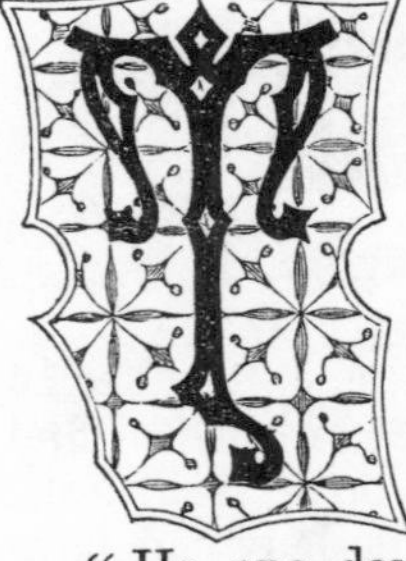

HE history of my sixth brother is the only one that now remains to be told. He was called Schacabac, the Hare-lipped. He was at first sufficiently industrious to employ the hundred drachms of silver which came to his share in a very advantageous manner; but at length he was reduced, by reverse of fortune, to the necessity of begging his bread. In this occupation he acquitted himself with great address; and his chief aim was to procure admission into the houses of the great, by bribing the officers and domestics; and when he had once managed to get admitted to them, he failed not to excite their compassion.

"He one day passed by a very magnificent building, through the door of which he could see a spacious court, wherein were a vast number of servants. He went up to one of them, and inquired of them to whom the house belonged. 'My good man,' answered the servant, 'where can you come from, that you ask such a question? Any one you met would tell you it belonged to a Barmecide.' My brother, who well knew the liberal and generous disposition of the Barmecides, addressed himself to the porters, for there were more than one, and requested them to bestow some charity upon him. 'Come in,' answered they, 'no one prevents you, and speak to our master —he will send you back well satisfied.'

"My brother did not expect so much kindness; and after returning many thanks to the porters, he with their permission entered the palace, which was so large that he spent some time in seeking out the apartment belonging to the Barmecide. He at length came to a large square building very handsome to behold, into which he entered by a vestibule that led to a fine garden, the walks of which were formed of stones of different colours, with a very pleasing effect to the eye. The apartments which surrounded this building on the ground floor were almost all open, and shaded only by some large curtains which kept off the sun, and which could be drawn aside to admit the fresh air when the heat began to subside.

"My brother would have been highly delighted with this pleasant spot had his mind been sufficiently at ease to enjoy its beauties. He advanced still farther, and entered a hall, which was very richly furnished, and ornamented with foliage painted in azure and gold. He perceived a venerable old man, whose beard was long and white, sitting on a sofa in the most distinguished place. He judged that this was the master of the house. In fact, it was the Barmecide himself, who told him in an obliging manner that he was welcome, and asked him what he wished. 'My lord,' answered my brother, in a lamentable tone, 'I am a poor man, who stands very much in need of the assistance of such powerful and generous persons as yourself.' He could not have done better than address himself to the person to whom he spoke, for this man possessed a thousand amiable qualities.

"The Barmecide was much astonished at my brother's answer; and putting both his hands to his breast, as if to tear his clothes, as a mark of commiseration, he exclaimed: 'Is it possible that in Bagdad such a man as you should be so much distressed as you say you are? I cannot suffer this to be.' At this exclamation my brother, thinking the Barmecide was going to give him a singular proof of his liberality, wished him every blessing. 'It shall never be said,' replied the Barmecide, 'that I leave you unsuccoured. I intend that you shall not leave me.' 'O my master,' cried my brother, 'I swear to you that I have not even eaten anything this day.' 'How!' cried the Barmecide, 'is it true that at this late hour you have not yet broken your fast? Alas! poor man, you will die of hunger! Here, boy,' added he, raising his voice, 'bring us instantly a basin of water, that we may wash our hands.'

"Although no boy appeared, and my brother could see neither basin nor water, the Barmecide began to rub his hands, as if some one held the water for him; and as he did so, he said to my brother, 'Come hither, and wash with me.' Schacabac by this supposed that the Barmecide loved his jest; and as he himself was of the same humour, and knew the submission the rich expected from the poor, he imitated all the movements of his host.

"'Come,' said the Barmecide, 'now bring us something to eat, and do not keep us waiting.' When he had said this, although nothing had been brought to eat, he pretended to help himself from a dish, and to carry food to his mouth and chew it, while he called out to my brother, 'Eat, I entreat you, my guest. You are heartily welcome. Eat, I beg of you: you seem, for a hungry man, to have but a poor appetite.' 'Pardon me, my lord,' replied Schacabac, who was imitating the motions of his host very accurately, 'you see I lose no time, and understand my business very well.' 'What think you of this bread?' said the Barmecide; 'don't you find it excellent?' 'In truth, my lord, answered my brother, who in fact saw neither bread nor meat, 'I never tasted anything more white or delicate.' 'Eat your fill then,' rejoined the Barmecide; 'I assure you, the slave who made this excellent bread cost me five hundred pieces of gold.' He continued to praise the female slave who was his baker, and to boast of his bread, which my brother only devoured in imagination. Presently he said, 'Boy, bring us another dish. Come my friend,' he continued, to my brother, though no boy appeared, 'taste this fresh dish, and tell me if you have ever eaten boiled mutton and barley better dressed than this.' 'Oh, it is admirable,' answered my brother, 'and you see that I help myself very plentifully.' 'I am rejoiced to see you,' said the Barmecide; 'and I entreat you not to suffer any of these dishes to be taken away, since you find them so much to your taste.' He presently called for a goose with sweet sauce, and dressed with vinegar, honey, dried raisins, grey peas, and dried figs. This was brought in the same imaginary manner as the mutton. 'This goose is nice and fat,' said the Barmecide; 'here, take only a wing and a thigh, for you must save your appetite, as there are many more courses yet to come.' In short, he called for many other dishes of different kinds, of which my brother, who felt completely famished, continued to pretend to eat. But the dish the Barmecide praised most highly of all was a lamb stuffed with pistachio nuts, and which was served in the same manner as the other dishes. 'Now this,' said he, 'is a dish you never met with anywhere but at my table, and I wish you to eat heartily of it.' As he said this he pretended to take a piece in his hand, and put it to my brother's mouth. 'Eat this,' he said, 'and you will not think I said too much when I boasted of this dish.' My brother held his head forward, opened his mouth, and pretended to take the piece of lamb, and to chew and swallow it with the greatest pleasure. 'I was quite sure,' said the Barmecide, 'you would think it excellent.' 'Nothing can be more delicious,' replied Schacabac. 'Indeed, I have never seen a table so well furnished as yours.' 'Now bring me the ragout,' said the Barmecide; 'and I think you will like it as much as the lamb.—What do you think of it?' 'It is wonderful,' answered my brother: 'in this ragout we have at once the flavour of amber, cloves, nutmegs, ginger, pepper, and sweet herbs; and yet they are all so well balanced that the presence of one does not destroy the flavour of the rest. How delicious it is!' 'Do justice to it then,' cried the Barmecide, 'and I pray you eat heartily. Ho! boy,' cried he, raising his voice, 'bring us a fresh ragout.' 'Not so, my master,' said Schacabac, 'for in truth I cannot indeed eat any more.'

"'Then let the dessert be served,' said the Barmecide: 'Bring in the fruit.' He then waited a few moments, to give the servants time to change the dishes; then resuming his speech, he said, 'Taste these almonds: they are just gathered, and very good.' They then both pretended to peel the almonds, and eat them. The Barmecide after this invited my brother to partake of many other things. 'You see here,' he said, 'all sorts of fruits, cakes, dried comfits, and preserves; take what you like.' Then stretching out his hand, as if he was going to give my brother something, he said, 'Take this lozenge: it is excellent to assist digestion.' Schacabac pretended to take the lozenge and eat it. 'There is no want of musk in this, my lord,' he said. 'I have these lozenges made at home,' replied the Barmecide, 'and in their preparation, as well as everything else in my house, no expense is spared.' He still continued to persuade my brother to eat, and said, 'For a man who was almost starving when he came here, you have really eaten hardly anything.' 'O my master,' replied Schacabac, whose jaws were weary of moving with nothing to chew, 'I assure you I am so full that I cannot eat a morsel more.'

"'Then,' cried the Barmecide, 'after a man has eaten so heartily, he should drink a little. You have no objection to good wine?' 'My master,' replied my brother, 'I pray you to forgive me—I never drink wine, because it is forbidden me.' 'You are too scrupulous,' said the Barmecide; 'come, come, do as I do.' 'To oblige you I will,' replied Schacabac, 'for I observe you wish that our banquet should be complete. But as I am not in the habit of drinking wine, I fear I may be guilty of some fault against good breeding, and even fail in the respect that is due to you. For this reason, I still entreat you to excuse my drinking wine; I shall be well satisfied with water.' 'No, no,' said the Barmecide, 'you must drink wine.' And he ordered some to be brought. But the wine, like the dinner and dessert, was imaginary. The Barmecide then pretended to pour some out, and drank the first glass. Then he poured out another glass for my brother, and presenting it to him, he cried, 'Come, drink my health, and tell me if you think the wine good.'

"My brother pretended to take the glass. He held it up, and looked to see if the

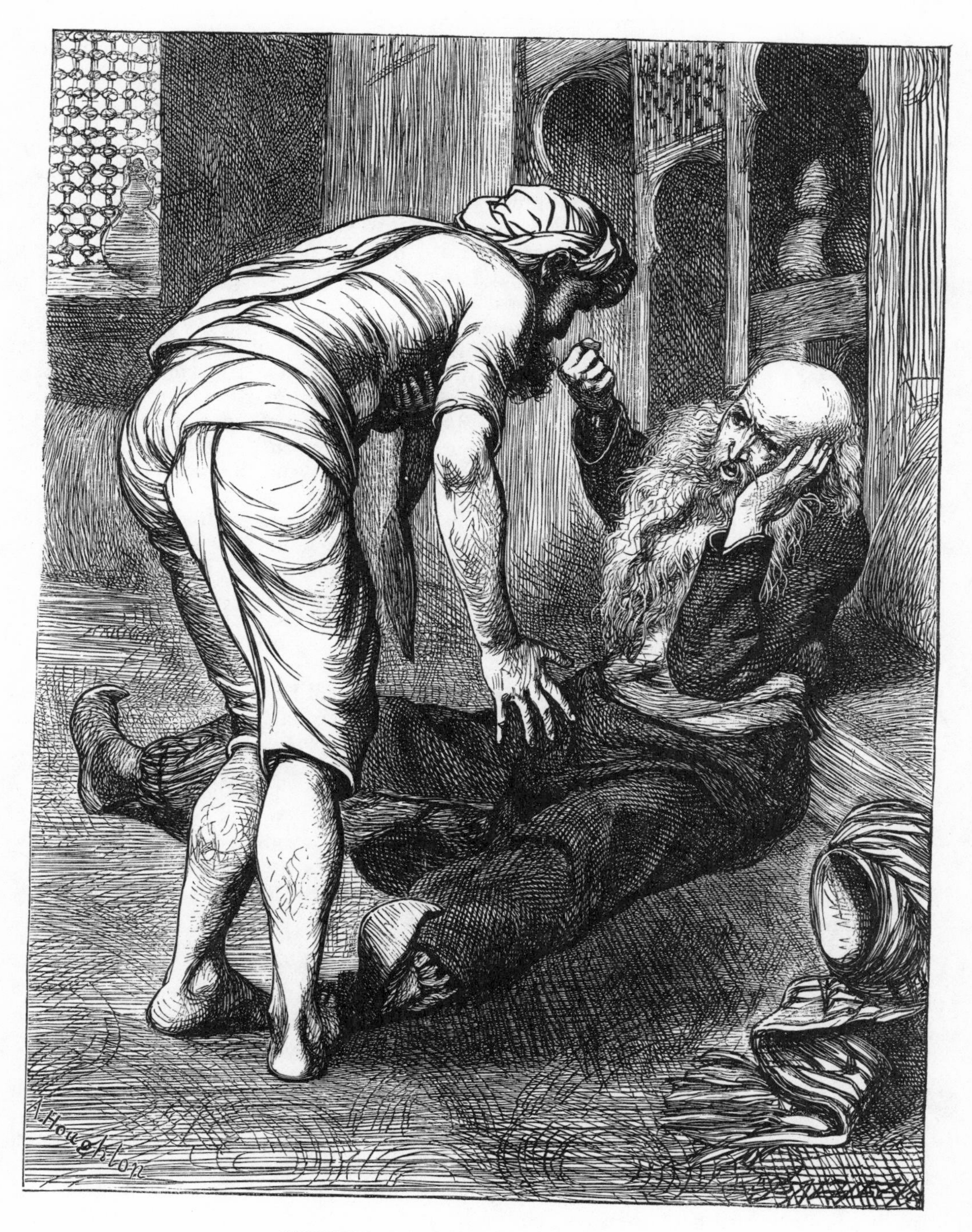


SCHACABAC KNOCKS DOWN THE BARMECIDE.

wine were of a good bright colour; he put it to his nose to test its perfume; then, making a most profound reverence to the Barmecide, to show that he took the liberty to drink his health, he drank it off; pretending that the draught gave him the most exquisite pleasure. 'My master,' he said, 'I find this wine excellent; but it does not seem to me quite strong enough.' 'You have only to command,' replied the other, 'if you wish for a stronger kind. I have various sorts in my cellar. We will see if this will suit you better.' He then pretended to pour out wine of another kind for himself and for my brother. He repeated this action so frequently that Schacabac pretended that the wine had got into his head, and feigned intoxication. He raised his hand, and gave the Barmecide such a violent blow that he knocked him down. He was going to strike him a second time, but the Barmecide, holding out his hand to ward off the blow, called out, 'Are you mad?' My brother then pretended to recollect himself, and said, 'O my master, you had the goodness to receive your slave into your house, and to make a great feast for him: you should have been satisfied with making him eat; but you compelled him to drink wine. I told you at first that I should be guilty of some disrespect; I am very sorry for it, and humbly ask your pardon.

"When Schacabac had finished this speech, the Barmecide, instead of putting himself in a great passion and being very angry, burst into a violent fit of laughter. 'For a long time,' said he, 'I have sought a person of your disposition. I not only pardon the blow you have given me, but from this moment I look upon you as one of my friends, and desire that you make my house your home. You have had the good sense to accommodate yourself to my humour, and the patience to carry on the jest to the end; but we will now eat in reality.' So saying he clapped his hands, and this time several slaves appeared, whom he ordered to set out the table and serve the dinner. His commands were quickly obeyed, and my brother was now in reality regaled with all the dishes he had before partaken of in imagination. As soon as the table was cleared, wine was brought; and a number of beautiful and richly attired female slaves appeared, and began to sing some pleasant airs to the sound of instruments. Schacabac had in the end every reason to be satisfied with the kindness and hospitality of the Barmecide, who took a great fancy to him, and treated him as a familiar friend, giving him moreover a handsome dress from his own wardrobe.

"The Barmecide found my brother possessed of so much knowledge of various sorts, that in the course of a few days he entrusted to him the care of all his house and affairs; and my brother acquitted himself of his charge, during a period of twenty years, to the complete satisfaction of his employer. At the end of that time the generous Barmecide, worn out with old age, paid the common debt of nature; and as he did not leave any heirs, all his fortune fell to the state; my brother was even deprived of all his savings. Finding himself thus reduced to his former state of beggary, he joined a caravan of pilgrims going to Mecca, intending to perform the pilgrimage as a medicant. During the journey the caravan was unfortunately attacked and plundered by a party of Bedouin Arabs, who were more numerous than the pilgrims.

"My brother thus became the slave of a Bedouin, who for many days in succession gave him the bastinado in order to induce him to get himself ransomed. Schacabac protested that it was useless to ill-treat him in this manner. 'I am your slave,' said he, 'and you may dispose of me as you like; but I declare to you that I am in the most extreme poverty, and that it is not in my power to ransom myself.' My brother tried every expedient to convince the Bedouin of his wretched condition. He endeavoured to soften him by his tears and lamentations. But the Bedouin was inexorable; and through revenge at finding himself disappointed of a considerable sum of money, which he had fully expected to receive, he took his knife and slit my brother's lips. By this inhuman act he endeavoured to revenge himself for the loss he considered he had suffered.

"This Bedouin had a wife who was rather handsome; and her husband soon after left my brother with her, when he went on his excursions. At such times his wife left no means untried to console Schacabac for the rigour of his situation. She even gave him to understand she was in love with him; but he took every precaution to avoid being alone with her, whenever she seemed to wish it. At length she became so much accustomed to joke and amuse herself with the hard-hearted Schacabac whenever she met him, that she one day forgot herself, and jested with him in the presence of her husband. As ill luck would have it, my poor brother, without in the least thinking he was observed, returned her pleasantries. The Bedouin immediately imagined his slave and his wife loved each other. This suspicion put him into the greatest rage. He sprang upon my brother, and after mutilating him in a barbarous manner, he carried him on a camel to the top of a high rugged mountain, where he left him. This mountain happened to be on the road to Bagdad, and some travellers, who accidently found my brother there, informed me of his situation. I made all the haste I could to the place; and I found the unfortunate Schacabac in the most deplorable condition possible. I afforded him every assistance and aid, and brought him back with me into the city.

"This was what I related to the caliph Montanser Billah," said the barber in conclusion. "The caliph very much applauded my conduct, and expressed his approval by reiterated fits of laughter. He said to me, 'They have given you with justice the name of The Silent, and no one can say you do not deserve it. Nevertheless, I have some private reasons for wishing you to leave the city; I therefore order you immediately to depart. Go, and never let me hear of thee again.' I yielded to necessity, and travelled for many years in distant lands. At length I was informed that the caliph was dead; I therefore returned to Bagdad, where I did not find one of my brothers alive. It was on my return to this city that I rendered to this lame young man the important service of which you have heard. You are also witnesses of his great ingratitude, and of the injurious manner in which he has treated me. Instead of acknowledging his great obligations to me, he has chosen rather to quit his own country in order to avoid me. As soon as I discovered that he had left Bagdad, although no person could give me any information concerning the road he had taken, or tell me into what country he had travelled, I did not hesitate a moment, but instantly set out to seek him. I passed on from province to province; and I accidently met him to-day when I least expected it. And least of all did I expect to find him so irritated against me."

"Having in this manner related to the Sultan of Casgar the history of the lame young man, and of the barber of Bagdad, the tailor went on as follows:—

"'When the barber had finished his story, we plainly perceived the young man was not wrong when he called him a great chatterer. We nevertheless wished that he should remain with us and partake of the feast which the master of the house had prepared for us. We sat down to table, and continued to enjoy ourselves till the time of the sunset prayers. All the company then separated; and I returned to my shop, where I remained till it was time to shut it up, and go to my house.

"'It was then that the little hunchback, who was half drunk, came to my shop, in front of which he sat down, and sang to the sound of his timbrel. I thought that by taking him home with me I should afford some entertainment to my wife; and it was for this reason only that I invited him. My wife gave us a dish of fish for supper. I gave some to the little hunchback, who began to eat without taking sufficient care to avoid the bones; and presently he fell down senseless before us. We tried every means in our power to relieve him, but without effect; and then, in order to free ourselves from the embarrassment into which this melancholy accident had thrown us, and, in the great terror of the moment, we did not hesitate to carry the body out of our house, and induce the Jewish physician to receive it in the manner your majesty has heard told. The Jewish physician let it down into the apartment of the purveyor, and the purveyor carried it into the street, where the merchant thought he had killed the poor man. This, O sultan,' added the tailor, 'is what I have to say to your majesty in my justification. It is for you to determine whether we are worthy of your clemency or anger; whether we deserve to live or die.'

"The Sultan of Casgar's countenance expressed so much satisfaction and favour that it gave new courage to the tailor and his companions. 'I cannot deny,' said the monarch, 'that I am more astonished at the history of the lame young man and of the barber, and the adventures of his brothers, than at anything in the history of my buffoon. But before I send you all four back to your own houses, and order the little hunchback to be buried, I wish to see this barber, who has been the cause of your pardon. And since he is now in my capital, it will not be difficult to produce him.' He immediately ordered one of his attendants to go and find the barber out, and to take with him the tailor, who knew where the *silent* man was.

"The officer and the tailor soon returned, and brought back with them the barber, whom they presented to the sultan. He appeared a man of about ninety years of age. His beard and eyebrows were as white as snow; his ears hung down to a considerable length, and his nose was very long. The sultan could scarcely refrain from laughter at the sight of him. 'Man of silence,' said he to the barber, 'I understand that you are acquainted with many wonderful histories. I desire that you will relate one of them to me.' 'O sultan!' replied the barber, 'for the present, if it please your majesty, we will not speak of the histories which I can tell; but I most humbly entreat permission to ask one question, and to be informed for what reason this Christian, this Jew, this Mussulman, and this hunchback, whom I see extended on the ground, are in your majesty's presence.' The sultan smiled at the freedom of the barber, and said, 'What can that matter to thee?' 'O sultan!' returned the barber, 'it is of importance that I should make this inquiry, in order that your majesty may know that I am not a great talker, but, on the contrary, a man who has very justly acquired the title of The Silent."

"The Sultan of Casgar graciously satisfied the barber's curiosity. He desired that the adventures of the little hunchback should be related to him, since the old man seemed so very anxious to hear it. When the barber had heard the whole story, he shook his head, as if there were something in the tale which he could not well comprehend. 'In truth,' he exclaimed, 'this is a very wonderful history: but I should vastly like to examine this hunchback a little more attentively.' He then drew near to him, and sat down on the ground. He took the hunchback's head between his knees, and after examining him very closely he suddenly burst out into a violent fit of mirth, and laughed so immoderately that he fell backwards, without at all considering that he was in the presence of the Sultan of Casgar. He got up from the ground, still laughing heartily. 'You may very well say,' he at length cried, 'that no man dies without a cause. If ever a history deserved to be written in letters of gold, it is this of the hunchback.'

"At this speech every one looked upon the barber as a buffoon, or an old madman, and the sultan said:

"'Man of silence, answer me: what is the reason of your clamorous laughter?' 'O sultan!' replied the barber, 'I swear by your majesty's good-nature that this hunchback fellow is not dead: there is still life in him; and you may consider me a fool and a madman if I do not instantly prove it to you.' Hereupon he produced a box in which there were various medicines, and which he always carried about with him, to use on any emergency. He opened it, and taking out a phial containing a sort of balsam, he rubbed it thoroughly and for a long time into the neck of the hunchback. He then drew out of a case an iron instrument of peculiar shape, with which he opened the hunchback's jaws; and thus he was enabled to put a small pair of pincers into the patient's throat, and drew out the fish-bone, which he held up and showed to all the spectators. Almost immediately the hunchback sneezed, stretched out his hands and feet, opened his eyes, and gave many other proofs that he was alive.

"The Sultan of Casgar, and all who witnessed this excellent operation, were less surprised at seeing the hunchback brought to life, although he had passed a night and almost a whole day without the least apparent sign of animation, than delighted with the merit and skill of the barber, whom they now began to regard as a very great personage in spite of all his faults. The sultan was so filled with joy and admiration that he ordered the history of the hunchback, and that of the barber, to be instantly committed to writing, that the knowledge of a story which so well deserved to be preserved might never be forgotten. Nor was this all. In order that the tailor, the Jewish physician, the purveyor, and the Christian merchant might ever remember with pleasure the adventures which the hunchback's accident had caused them, he gave to each of them a very rich robe, which he made them put on in his presence before he dismissed them. And he bestowed upon the barber a large pension, and kept him ever afterwards near his own person."

THE BARBER EXTRACTS THE BONE FROM THE HUNCHBACK'S THROAT.

Thus the Sultana Scheherazade finished the story of the long series of adventures to which the supposed death of the hunchback had given rise. Her sister Dinarzade, observing that Scheherazade had done speaking, said to her: "My dear princess, my sultana, I am much the more delighted with the story you have just finished, from the unexpected incident by which it was brought to a conclusion. I really thought the little hunchback was quite dead." "This surprise has also afforded me pleasure," said Shahriar: "I have also been entertained by the adventures of the barber's brothers." "The history of the lame young man of Bagdad has also very much diverted me," rejoined Dinarzarde. "I am highly satisfied, my dear sister," replied Scheherazade, "that I have been able thus to entertain you and the sultan our lord and master; and since I have had the good fortune not to weary his majesty, I shall have the honour, if he will have the goodness to prolong my life still further, to relate to him the history of the loves of Aboulhassan Ali Ebn Becar, and of Schemselnihar, the favourite of the Caliph Haroun Alraschid—a story not less worthy than the history of the hunchback to attract his attention and yours." The Sultan of India, who had been much entertained by everything Scheherazade had hitherto related, was determined not to forego the pleasure of hearing this new history which she promised. He therefore arose and went to prayers, and then sat in council; and the next morning Dinarzade did not fail to remind her sister of her promise, and Scheherazade began her new story in the following words:—

## THE HISTORY OF ABOULHASSAN ALI EBN BECAR, AND OF SCHEMSELNIHAR, THE FAVOURITE OF THE CALIPH HAROUN ALRASCHID.

URING the reign of the Caliph Haroun Alraschid, there lived at Bagdad a druggist whose name was Aboulhassan Ebn Thaher. He was a man of considerable wealth, and was also very handsome, and reckoned an agreeable companion. He possessed more understanding and more politeness than can be generally found among people of his profession. His ideas of rectitude, his sincerity, and the liveliness of his disposition made him beloved and sought after by every one. The caliph, who was well acquainted with his merit, placed the most implicit confidence in him. He esteemed him so highly that he even entrusted to him the sole care of procuring for his favourite ladies everything they required. It was the druggist who chose their dresses, the furniture of their apartments, and their jewellery, and in all his purchases he gave proofs of a most excellent taste.

"His various good qualities and the favour of the caliph caused the sons of the emirs and other officers of the highest rank to frequent this man's house, which, in this manner, became the rendezvous of all the nobles of the court. Among other young nobles who made almost a daily practice of going there, was one whom Ebn Thaher esteemed above all the rest, and with whom he contracted a most intimate friendship. This young nobleman's name was Aboulhassan Ali Ebn Becar, and he derived his origin from an ancient royal family of Persia. This family still continued to live at Bagdad from the time when the Mussulman arms made a conquest of that kingdom. Nature seemed to have taken pleasure in combining in this young prince every mental endowment and personal accomplishment. He possessed a countenance of the most finished beauty. His figure was fine, his air elegant and easy, and the expression of his face so engaging that no one could see him without instantly loving him. Whenever he spoke he used the most appropriate words, and his every speech had a certain turn of expression equally novel and agreeable. There was something even in the tone of his voice that charmed all who heard him. To complete the description of him, as his understanding and judgment were of the first rank, so all his thoughts and expressions were most admirable and just. He was moreover so reserved and modest, that he never made an assertion till he had taken every possible precaution to avoid all suspicion of preferring his own opinions or sentiments to those of others. It is not to be wondered at that Ebn Thaher distinguished this excellent young prince in a particular manner from the other young noblemen of the court, whose vices, for the most part, served only to make his virtues appear the more brilliant by contrast.

"The prince was one day at the house of Ebn Thaher when a lady came to the door, mounted upon a black and white mule, and surrounded by ten female slaves, who accompanied her on foot. These slaves were all very handsome, as far as could be judged from their air and through the veils that covered their faces. The lady herself wore a rose-coloured girdle at least four fingers in width, upon which were fastened diamonds and pearls of the largest size; and it was no difficult matter to conjecture that her beauty surpassed the charms of her attendants as much as the moon at its full exceeds the crescent of two days old. She came for the purpose of executing some commission; and as she desired to speak to Ebn Thaher, she went into his shop, which was very large and commodious. He received her with every mark of respect, begged her to be seated, and, taking her by the hand, conducted her to the most honourable place.

"The Prince of Persia in the meantime did not choose to neglect such an excellent opportunity of showing his politeness and his gallantry. He placed a cushion, covered with cloth of gold for the lady to rest upon, and then immediately retired, that she might sit down. After this he made his obeisance by kissing the carpet at her feet, then rose and stood before her at the end of the sofa. As the lady felt herself quite at home in Ebn Thaher's house, she took off her veil, and displayed to the eyes of the Prince of Persia a beauty so extraordinary that it pierced him to the bottom of his heart. Nor could the lady on her part help looking at the prince, whose appearance made an equal impression on her. She said to him in an obliging manner, 'I beg you, my lord, to be seated.' The Prince of Persia obeyed, and sat down on the edge of the sofa. He kept his eyes constantly fixed upon the beautiful lady, and swallowed large draughts of the delicious poison of love. She soon perceived what passed in his mind, and this discovery aroused a kindred feeling in her own breast. She rose and went to Ebn Thaher, and after she had imparted to him, in a whisper, the motive of her visit, she inquired of him the name and country of the Prince of Persia. 'O lady,' replied Ebn Thaher, 'this young prince, of whom you are speaking, is called Aboulhassan Ali Ebn Becar, and is of the blood royal of Persia.'

"The lady was delighted to find that the man whose appearance had won her esteem was of such a high rank. She replied: 'I understand from what you say that he is descended from the kings of Persia.' 'In truth, lady,' returned Ebn Thaher, 'the kings of Persia are his ancestors; and since the conquest of that kingdom, the princes of his family have always been held in esteem at the court of our caliphs.' 'You will do me a great favour,' said the lady, 'if you will make me acquainted with this young prince.' She added: 'I shall shortly send this attendant,' pointing to one of her slaves, 'to request you to come and see me, and I beg you will bring him with you; I very much wish him to see the splendour and magnificence of my palace, that he may publish to the world that avarice does not hold her court among people of rank at Bagdad. Understand and give heed to my words. Fail not to remember my request. If you do I shall be very angry with you, and will never come and see you again so long as I live.'

"Ebn Thaher possessed too much penetration not to understand by this speech what were the sentiments of the lady. 'Allah forbid, my princess,' replied he, 'that I should give you any cause to be offended with me. To execute your orders will ever be my delight.' Having received this answer, the lady took leave of Ebn Thaher by an inclination of her head; and after casting a most obliging look at the Prince of Persia, she mounted her mule and departed.

"The prince was violently moved with admiration for this lady. He continued looking at her as long as she was in sight; and even after she had disappeared it was a long time before he turned away his eyes from the direction in which she had gone. Ebn Thaher then remarked to him that he was observed by some people, who were inclined to make merry at his expense. 'Alas!' said the prince, 'you and all the world would have compassion upon me if you knew that this beautiful lady, who has just left your house, had carried away by far the better part of me; and that what remains cannot live separate from her. Tell me, I conjure you,' added he, 'who this tyrannical lady is that thus compels people to love her without giving them time to combat their feelings?' 'My lord,' replied Ebn Thaher, 'that lady is the famous Schemselnihar, the first favourite of our sovereign master the caliph.' The prince rejoined: 'She is indeed with great justice and propriety named Schemselnihar, since she is more beautiful than the cloudless meridian sun.' 'It is true,' cried Ebn Thaher; 'and the Commander of the Faithful loves her, or I may rather say, adores her. He has expressly commanded me to furnish her with everything she wishes, and even to anticipate her thoughts, if it were possible, in anything she may desire.'

"Ebn Thaher told all these particulars to the prince to prevent the young man from giving way to a passion which could only end unfortunately; but the druggist's words only served to inflame him the more. 'I cannot hope,' cried he, 'charming Schemselnihar, that I shall be suffered to raise my thoughts to you. I nevertheless feel, although I am destitute of all hope of being beloved by you, that it will not be in my power to cease from adoring you. Therefore I will continue to love you, and will bless the fate that has made me the slave of the most beautiful object that the sun shines on.'

"While the Prince of Persia was thus consecrating his heart to the beautiful Schemselnihar, that lady, as she went home, continued to think upon the means she should pursue in order to see and converse with freedom with this prince. So soon as she reached the palace she sent back to Ebn Thaher the female slave whom she had pointed out to him, and in whom she placed the most implicit confidence. The slave brought to the druggist a request that he would see her mistress without delay, and bring the Prince of Persia with him. The slave arrived at the shop of Ebn Thaher while he was still conversing with the prince, and while he was using the strongest arguments in his endeavour to persuade him to think no more of the favourite of the caliph. When the slave thus saw them talking together she said, 'My most honourable mistress Schemselnihar, the first favourite of the Commander of the Faithful, entreats you both to come to the palace, where she awaits you.' In order to show how ready he was to obey the summons, Ebn Thaher instantly got up, without answering the slave one word, and followed her, though with much inward reluctance. As for the prince, he followed her without at all reflecting on the perils which might arise to him from this visit. The presence of Ebn Thaher, who had free admission to the favourite, made him feel perfectly at his ease. The two men followed the slave, who walked a little in advance of them. They went into the palace of the caliph, and joined her at the door of the smaller palace appropriated to Schemselnihar, which was already open. The slave introduced them into a large hall, and motioned them to be seated.

"The Prince of Persia thought himself in one of those delightful abodes which are promised to us in a future world. He had hitherto seen nothing that at all approached the magnificence of the place where he now was. The carpets, cushions, and coverings of the sofas, together with the furniture, ornaments, and decorations, were most exceeding rich and beautiful. The visitors had not long remained in this apartment, before a black slave, handsomely dressed, brought in a table covered with the most delicate dishes, the delicious fragrance of which gave token of the richness of the repast prepared for them. While they were eating, the slave who had conducted them to the palace did not leave them: she was very diligent in pressing them to eat of those ragouts and dishes she knew to be best. In the meantime other slaves poured them out some excellent wine, with which they regaled themselves. When the feast was over, the attendants presented to the Prince of Persia and to Ebn Thaher each a separate basin, and a beautiful golden vase, full of water, to wash their hands. They afterwards brought them some perfume of aloes in a beautiful vessel, which was also of gold, and with this perfume the guests scented their beards and dress. Nor was the perfumed water forgotten. It was brought in a golden vase made expressly for this purpose, enriched with diamonds and rubies, and it was poured into both their hands, with which they rubbed their beards and their faces, according to the usual custom. They then sat down again in their places; but in a very few moments the slave requested them to rise up and follow her. She opened a door which led from the hall where they had feasted; and they entered a very large saloon wonderfully constructed. The ceiling was a dome of elegant form, supported by a hundred columns of marble as white as alabaster. The pedestals and capitals of these columns were all ornamented with quadrupeds and birds of various species, worked in gold. The carpet of this splendid saloon was composed of a single piece of cloth of gold, upon which were worked bunches of roses in red and

THE CONCERT AT THE PALACE OF SCHEMSELNIHAR.

white silk; the dome itself was painted in arabesque, and exhibited to the spectator a multitude of charming objects. There was a small sofa in every interval between the columns, ornamented in the same manner, together with large vases of porcelain, of crystal, jasper, jet, porphyry, agate, and other valuable materials, all enriched with gold and inlaid with precious stones. The spaces between the columns contained also large windows, with balconies of a proper height, and furnished in the same style of elegance as the sofas, with a view into the most delicious garden in the world. The walks in this garden were formed of small stones of various colours, which represented the carpet of the saloon under the dome; and in this manner, when the spectator turned his eyes towards the ground, either in the saloon or garden, it seemed as if the dome and the garden, with all their beauties, formed one splendid whole. The view from every point was terminated at the end of the walks by two pieces of water, as transparent as rock crystal, in which the circular figure of the dome was reproduced. One of these was raised above the other, and from the higher the water fell in a large sheet into the lower one. On their banks, at certain distances, were placed beautiful bronze and gilt vases, all decorated with shrubs and flowers. These walks also separated from each other large lawns, which were planted with lofty and thick trees, in whose branches a thousand birds warbled the most melodious sounds, and diversified the scene by their various flights, and by the battles they fought in the air, sometimes in sport, and at others in a more serious and cruel manner.

"The Prince of Persia and Ebn Thaher stopped a long time to examine the great magnificence of this place. They expressed strong marks of surprise and admiration at everything that struck them. The Prince of Persia especially had never before seen anything at all comparable to this dwelling. Ebn Thaher, too, although he had been before in this enchanting spot, could not refrain from admiring its beauties, which always appeared to possess an air of novelty. In short, the guests had not ceased from their admiration of the singular spectacle around them, and were still agreeably engaged in examining its various beauties, when they suddenly perceived a company of ladies very richly dressed. They were all sitting in the garden, at some distance from the dome, each on a seat made of Indian plantain wood, enriched with silver inlaid in compartments. Each had a musical instrument in her hands, and seemed waiting for the appointed signal to begin to play on it.

"Ebn Thaher and the Prince of Persia went and placed themselves in one of the balconies, from whence they had a direct view of these ladies; and on looking towards the right hand, they saw before them a large court, with an entrance into the garden up a flight of steps. The whole of this court was surrounded with very elegant apartments. The slaves had left them, and as they were alone, they conversed together for some time. 'I do not doubt,' said the Prince of Persia to Ebn Thaher, 'that you, who are a sedate and wise man, look with very little satisfaction upon all this exhibition of magnificence and power. In my eyes nothing in the whole world can be more surprising; and when I add to this reflection the thought that it is the splendid abode of the too beautiful Schemselnihar, and that the foremost monarch of the world makes it the place of his retreat, I confess to you that I think myself the most unfortunate of men. It seems to me that there cannot be a more cruel fate than mine, for I love a being who is completely in the power of my rival; and being in the very spot where my rival is so powerful, I am at this very instant not even secure of my life.'

"To this speech of the Prince of Persia Ebn Thaher thus replied: 'Would to Allah, O prince, that I could give you as perfect an assurance of the happy issue of your attachment as I can of the safety of your person. Although this superb palace belongs to the caliph, it was erected expressly for Schemselnihar, and is called the Palace of Continual Pleasures; and although it forms a part, as it were, of the sultan's palace, yet be assured this lady here enjoys the most perfect liberty. She is not surrounded by eunuchs placed to watch her minutest actions. These buildings are appropriated to her sole use, and she has absolute power to dispose of the whole as she thinks proper. She goes out and walks about the city wherever she pleases, without asking leave of any one; she returns at her own time; and the caliph never comes to visit her without first sending Mesrour, the chief of the eunuchs, to give her notice of his intention, that she may have time to prepare for his reception. Your mind, therefore, need not be disturbed, but you may consider yourself in perfect safety to listen to the concert with which I perceive Schemselnihar is going to entertain us.'

"At the very instant when Ebn Thaher had done speaking, the Prince of Persia and he both observed the slave who was the confidante of the favourite, come and order the women seated in front of them to sing, and play on their several instruments. They all immediately began a sort of prelude, and after playing thus for some time, one of them sang alone, and accompanied herself on a lute most admirably. As she had been informed of the subject upon which she was to sing, the words of her song were in such perfect unison with the feelings of the Prince of Persia, that he could not help applauding her at the conclusion of the strain. 'Is it possible,' he cried, 'that you can have the faculty of penetrating the inmost thoughts of others, and that the knowledge you have of what passes in my heart has enabled you to give my feelings utterance in the sound of your delightful voice? I could not myself have expressed in more appropriate terms the passion of my heart.' To this speech the minstrel answered not a word. She resumed, and sang several other stanzas, which so much affected the Prince of Persia, that he repeated some of them with tears in his eyes; and that he applied the song to Schemselnihar and himself was sufficiently evident. When the lady had finished all the couplets, she and her companions stood up and sang all together some words to the following effect: *The full moon is going to arise in all its splendour, and will soon approach the sun.* The meaning of which was, that Schemselnihar was about to appear, and that the Prince of Persia would immediately have the pleasure of seeing her.

"Indeed, looking towards one side of the court, Ebn Thaher and the prince observed the confidential slave approach, followed by ten black females, who with difficulty carried a large throne of massive silver most elegantly wrought, which the slave made them place at a certain distance from the prince and Ebn Thaher. After they had deposited their burden, the black slaves retired behind some trees at the end of a walk. Then twenty very beautiful females, richly and uniformly dressed, advanced in two rows, singing and playing on different instruments; and they ranged themselves on each side of the throne.

"The Prince of Persia and Ebn Thaher beheld all these preparations with the greatest possible attention, eager and curious to know in what the scene would end. At last they saw, issuing from the same door whence the ten black slaves who had brought the throne and the twenty other slaves had emerged, ten other women, as beautiful and as handsomely adorned as the first group. They stopped at the door for some moments waiting for the favourite, who then issued forth, and placed herself in the midst of them. It was very easy to distinguish her from the rest, alike by her beauteous person and majestic air, and by a sort of mantle, of very light materials enriched with azure and gold, which she wore fastened to her shoulders over the rest of her dress, which was the most appropriate, the most elegant, and the most magnificent that could be. The diamonds, pearls, and rubies which ornamented her garb were not scattered in a confused manner: they were few in number, properly arranged, and of inestimable value. She advanced with a degree of majesty which might well be likened to that of the sun in his course, in the midst of clouds which receive its rays without diminishing its splendour. She then proceeded, and seated herself upon the silver throne that had been brought for that purpose.

"As soon as the Prince of Persia perceived Schemselnihar, he had eyes only for her. 'We cease our inquiries after the object of our search,' said he to Ebn Thaher, 'when it appears before us; and we are no longer in a state of doubt when the truth is evident. Look at this divine beauty: she is the cause of all my sufferings; sufferings, indeed, which I bless, however severe they have been, and however lasting they may prove. When I behold this charming creature, I am no longer myself: my restless soul revolts against its master, and I feel that it strives to fly from me. Go, then, my soul; I permit thee to stray; but let thy flight be for the advantage and preservation of this weak frame. It is you, too cruel Ebn Thaher, who are the cause of my woes. You thought to give me pleasure by bringing me here; and I find that I am come only to court my destruction.—Pardon me,' he added, recovering himself a little; 'I deceive myself, for I was determined to come, and can accuse only my own folly.' At these words he wept violently. 'I am rejoiced to find,' said Ebn Thaher, 'that you at least do me justice. When I told you that Schemselnihar was the first favourite of the caliph, I did so for the express purpose of nipping this direful and fatal passion, which you seem to take a pleasure in nourishing in your heart. Everything you see here ought to make you endeavour to disengage yourself, and should excite in you only sentiments of gratitude and respect for the honour Schemselnihar has been willing to do you, when she ordered me to introduce you here. Therefore be a man; recall your wandering reason, and be ready to appear before her in a way her kindness and condescension deserve. See, she approaches. If these things were to happen again, I would in truth act very differently; but the thing is done, and I trust in Allah that we shall not have to repent it. I have nothing more to say,' added he, 'but that love is a traitor who, if you give him sway, will plunge you in an abyss from which you can never again extricate yourself.'

"Ebn Thaher had no time to say more, as Schemselnihar now came up. She seated herself on the throne, and saluted both her visitors with an inclination of her head. Her eyes, however, were fixed only upon the prince. He was not slow to answer her in the same way, and they both spoke a silent language intermingled with sighs, by which, in a short time, they uttered more than they would have said in an age in actual conversation. The more Schemselnihar looked at the prince, the more did his looks tend to confirm her opinion that she was not indifferent to him; and, thus convinced of his passion, Schemselnihar thought herself the happiest being in the whole world. At length she ceased gazing at him, and ordered the women who had sung to approach. They rose up, and as they came forward the black slaves came from the walk where they had remained, and brought their seats, and placed them near the balcony, in the window of which the Prince of Persia and Ebn Thaher were. They were arranged in such a way that, together with the favourite's throne, and the women who were on each side of her, they formed a semicircle before the two guests.

"When those who had before been seated had again taken their places, by the permission of Schemselnihar, who gave them a sign for that purpose, the charming favourite desired one of her women to sing. After employing a little time in tuning her lute, the woman sang a song, the words of which had the following meaning:—When two lovers, who are sincerely fond of each other, are attached by a boundless passion; when their hearts, although in two bodies, form but one; when an obstacle opposes their union, they may well say mournfully, with tears in their eyes, 'If we love each other, because each finds the other amiable, ought we to be censured? Fate alone is to blame: we are innocent.'

"Schemselnihar evidently showed, both by her looks and manner, that she thought these words applicable to herself and the prince; and he was no longer master of himself. He rose, and advancing towards the balustrade, he leaned his arm upon it, and contrived to catch the attention of one of the women who sang. As she was not far from him, he said to her, 'Listen to me, and do me the favour to accompany with your lute the song I am now going to sing.' He than sang an air, the tender and impassioned words of which perfectly expressed the violence of his love. As soon as it was finished, Schemselnihar, following his example, said to one of her women, 'Attend to me also, and accompany my voice.' She then sang in a manner that increased and heightened the flame that burnt in the heart of the Prince of Persia, who only answered her by another air still more tender and impassioned than the one he had sung before.

"These two lovers having thus declared their mutual affection by their songs, Schemselnihar at length completely yielded to the strength of her feelings. She rose from her throne, almost forgetting what she did, and proceeded towards the door of the saloon. The prince, who was aware of her intention, instantly rose also, and hurried to meet her. They encountered each other at the very door, where they seized each other's hands, and embraced with so much transport that they both fainted on the spot. They would have fallen to the ground, if the female attendants who followed Schemselnihar had not supported them. They bore them in their arms to a sofa; and by throwing perfumed water over them, and applying various stimulants, they restored the prince and Schemselnihar to their senses.

"The first thing Schemselnihar did, as soon as she had recovered, was to look round on all sides; and not seeing Ebn Thaher, she eagerly inquired where he was. Ebn Thaher had retired out of respect to her, while the slaves were employed in attending their mistress; for he greatly feared, and not without reason, that some unfortunate consequence would arise from this adventure. As soon as he heard that Schemselnihar had asked for him, he came forward and presented himself before her.

"She seemed highly satisfied at the appearance of Ebn Thaher, and expressed her joy in these flattering words: 'I know not, Ebn Thaher, by what means I can ever repay the obligations I am under to you; but for you I should never have become acquainted with the Prince of Persia, nor have gained the affections of the most amiable being in the world. Be assured, however, that I shall not be ungrateful, and that my gratitude shall, if possible, equal the benefit I have received through your means.' Ebn Thaher could only answer this obliging speech by an inclination of his head, and by wishing the favourite the attainment of every blessing she could desire.

"Schemselnihar then turned towards the Prince of Persia, who was seated by her side; and looking at him, not without confusion at the thought of what had passed between them, she said to him: 'My friend, I cannot but be perfectly assured that you love me; and however strong your passion for me may be, you cannot, I think, doubt that it is thoroughly reciprocated. But do not let us delusively flatter ourselves; whatever unison there may be between your sentiments and mine, I can look forward only to pain, disappointment, and misery for us both. And no consolation, alas! remains to befriend us in our misfortunes, but perfect constancy in love, entire submission to the will of Heaven, and patient expectation of whatever it may please to decree as our destiny.'

"'O lady,' replied the Prince of Persia, 'you would do me the greatest injustice in the world, if you could for a moment doubt the constancy and fidelity of my heart. My affection has so completely taken possession of my soul, that it forms in fact a part of my very existence; nay, I shall even preserve it beyond the grave. Neither misery, torments, nor obstacles of any kind can ever succeed in lessening my love for you.' At the conclusion of this speech his tears flowed in abundance; nor could Schemselnihar restrain her own grief.

"Ebn Thaher took this opportunity to speak to the favourite. 'O my mistress,' said he, 'permit me to say that, instead of thus despairing, you and the prince ought rather to feel the greatest joy in finding yourselves so fortunately in each other's society. I do not understand the motive for your grief. If it overwhelms you already, what must you feel when necessity shall compel you to separate? But why do I say 'shall compel' you? we have already tarried too long here, and, lady, you must know that it is now necessary we should take our departure.' 'Alas!' replied Schemselnihar, 'how cruel you are! Have not you, who well know the cause of my tears, any pity for the unfortunate situation in which you see me? Oh, miserable destiny! why am I compelled to submit to the hardship of being for ever unable to be united to him who absorbs my whole affection?'

"As, however, she was well persuaded that Ebn Thaher had said nothing but what was dictated by friendship, she was by no means angry at his speech. She even profited by it; for she directly made a sign to the slave her confidante, who immediately went out, and soon returned with a small collation of various fruits upon a silver table, which she placed between the favourite and the Prince of Persia. Schemselnihar chose the fruit she thought the most delicate, and presented it to the prince, entreating him to eat it for her sake. He took it, and instantly carried it to his mouth, taking care that the very part which had felt the pressure of her fingers should first touch his lips. The prince in his turn then presented some fruit to Schemselnihar, who directly took and ate it in the same manner. Nor did she forget to invite Ebn Thaher to partake of the collation with them: but as he knew he was now staying in the palace longer than was perfectly safe, he would rather have returned home, and he therefore joined them only through complaisance. As soon as the table had been removed, the slaves brought some water in a vase of gold, and a silver basin, in which the two friends washed their hands at the same time. After this they returned to their seats, and then three of the ten black women brought each, upon a golden tray, a cup formed of beautiful rock crystal, and filled with the most exquisite wine, which thev placed before Schemselnihar, the Prince of Persia, and Ebn Thaher.

"In order to be more at her ease, Schemselnihar retained near her only the ten black slaves and the other ten women who were skilled in music and singing. After she had dismissed all the remaining attendants, she took one of the cups, and holding it in her hand, she sang some tender words, while one of the females accompanied her voice with a lute. When this was finished she drank the wine. She then took one of the other cups, and, presenting it to the prince, requested him to drink it for love of her in the same manner as she had drunk hers. He received it in a transport of love and joy. But before he drank the wine he sang in his turn an air, accompanied by the instrument of another woman; and while he sang the tears fell in abundance from his eyes: the words also which he sang expressed the idea that he knew not whether it was the wine that he was drinking, or his own tears. Schemselnihar then presented the third cup to Ebn Thaher, who thanked her for the honour and attention she had shown him.

"When this was over, the favourite took a lute from one of the slaves, and accompanied her own voice in so impassioned a manner that she was absolutely carried beyond herself; and the Prince of Persia, with his eyes intently fixed upon her, remained perfectly motionless, like one enchanted. In the midst of this scene the trusty slave of the favourite entered in great alarm, and told her mistress that Mesrour and two other officers, accompanied by a number of eunuchs, were at the door, and desired to speak ot her, bringing a message from the caliph. When the Prince of Persia and Ebn Thaher heard what the slave said, they changed colour and trembled, as if they had been betrayed. Schemselnihar, however, who perceived this, soon dispelled their fears.

"After she had endeavoured to quiet their alarm, she charged her confidential slave to go and keep Mesrour and the two officers of the caliph in conversation while she prepared herself to receive them; and said she would then send to have them introduced. She directly ordered all the windows of the saloon to be shut, and the paintings on silk, which were in the garden, to be taken down; and after having again assured the prince and Ebn Thaher that they might remain where they were in perfect safety, she opened the door that led to the garden, went out, and shut it after her. In spite, however, of all her assurances that they were quite secure from discovery, they could not avoid feeling very much alarmed all the time they were alone.

"As soon as Schemselnihar came into the garden with the women who attended her, she made them take away all the seats on which the women who had sung and played had sat, near the window from whence the prince and Ebn Thaher had heard them. When she saw that everything was arranged as she wished, she sat down on the silver throne, and then sent to inform her confidential slave that she might introduce the chief of the eunuchs and the two officers who accompanied him.

"They appeared, followed by twenty black eunuchs, all handsomely dressed. Each of them had a scimitar by his side, and a large golden belt round his body four fingers in breadth. As soon as they saw the favourite, although they were still at a considerable distance from her, they made a most profound reverence, which she returned them from her throne. When they approached nearer she rose up, and went towards Mesrour, who walked first. She asked him what was his errand; to which he replied, 'O lady, the Commander of the Faithful, by whose orders I am come, has charged me to say to you that he cannot live any longer without the pleasure of beholding you. He purposes, therefore, to pay you a visit this evening; and I am come in order to inform you of this, that you may prepare for his reception. He hopes, my mistress, that you will feel as much joy in receiving him as he feels impatience to behold you.'

"When the favourite observed that Mesrour had finished his speech, she prostrated herself on the ground, to show the submission with which she received the commands of the caliph. When she rose she said to him, 'I beg you will inform the Commander of the Faithful that it will ever be my glory to fulfil the commands of his majesty, and that his slave will endeavour to receive him with all the respect that is due to him.' At the same time she gave orders to her confidential slave to make all the necessary preparations in the palace for the caliph's reception, by the hands of the black slaves who were kept for this purpose. Then, in dismissing the chief of the eunuchs, she said to him, 'You must see that the necessary preparations will occupy some time; go, therefore, I pray you, and arrange matters so that the caliph may not be very impatient, and that he may not arrive so soon as to find us quite in confusion.'

"The chief of the eunuchs then retired with his attendants; and Schemselnihar returned to the saloon very much grieved at the necessity she was under of sending the Prince of Persia away sooner than she had intended. She went to him with tears in her eyes; and her apparent confusion very much increased the alarm of Ebn Thaher, who seemed to conjecture from it some unfortunate event. 'I see, O lady,' said the prince to her, 'that you come for the purpose of announcing to me that we must separate. If, however, this is the only misfortune I have to dread, I trust that Heaven will grant me patience, which I greatly need, to enable me to support your absence.' 'Alas! my love, my dear life,' cried the tender Schemselnihar, interrupting him, 'how happy do I find your lot when I compare it with my more wretched fate! You doubtless suffer greatly from my absence, but that is your only grief; you can derive consolation from the hopes of seeing me again; but I—just Heaven! to what a painful task am I condemned! I am not only deprived of the enjoyment of the only being I love, but am obliged to bear the sight of one whom you have rendered hateful to me. Will not the caliph's arrival constantly bring to my recollection the necessity of your departure? And absorbed as I shall be continually with your dear image, how shall I be able to express to that prince any sign of joy at his presence?—I who have hitherto always received him, as he often remarks, with pleasure sparkling in my eyes! When I address him my thoughts will be distracted; and when I must speak to him in the language of affection, my words will be a dagger in my very soul! Can I possibly derive the least pleasure from his kind words and caresses? How dreadful is the idea! Judge, then, my prince, to what torments I shall be exposed when you have left me.' The tears, which ran in streams from her eyes, and the convulsive throbs of her bosom, prevented her further utterance. The Prince of Persia wished to make a reply, but he had not sufficient strength of mind. His own grief, added to what he saw Schemselnihar suffer, took from him all power of speech.

"Ebn Thaher, whose only object was to get out of the palace, was obliged to console them, and beg them to have a little patience. At this moment the confidential slave broke in upon them. 'O lady,' she cried, 'you have no time to lose; the eunuchs are beginning to assemble, and you know from this that the caliph will very soon be here.' 'Oh, Heavens!' exclaimed the favourite, 'how cruel is the separation! Hasten,' she cried to the slave, 'and conduct them to the gallery which on one side looks towards the garden, and on the other towards the Tigris; and when night shall have hidden the face of the earth in darkness, let them out of the gate that is at the back of the palace, that they may retire in perfect safety.' At these words she embraced the Prince of Persia, without having the power of saying another word; and then went to meet the caliph, with her mind in a disordered state, as may easily be imagined.

"In the meantime the confidential slave conducted the prince and Ebn Thaher to the gallery whither Schemselnihar had ordered her to repair. As soon as she had introduced them into it she left them there, and went out, shutting the doors after her, after she had first assured them that they had nothing to fear, and that she would come at the proper time and let them out.

"The slave, however, was no sooner gone, than both the prince and Ebn Thaher forgot the assurances she had given them that they had no cause for alarm. They examined the gallery all round; and were extremely frightened when they failed to discover a single outlet by which they could escape, in case the caliph or any of his officers should by any chance happen to come there.

"A sudden light, which they saw through the blinds, in the direction of the garden, induced them to go and examine from whence it came. It was caused by the flames of a hundred flambeaux of white wax, which a hundred young eunuchs carried in their hands. These eunuchs were followed by more than their own number of others who were older. All of them formed part of the guard continually on duty at the apartments of the ladies of the caliph's household. They were dressed and armed with scimitars, in the same way as those I have before mentioned. The caliph himself walked after these, with Mesrour, the chief of the eunuchs, on his right hand, and Vassif, the second in command, on his left.

"Schemselnihar waited for the caliph at the entrance of one of the walks. She was accompanied by twenty very beautiful young women, who wore necklaces and ear-rings made of large diamonds, and whose heads were also profusely ornamented with gems of the same description. They all sang to the sound of their instruments, and gave a most delightful concert. When the favourite saw the caliph appear, she advanced towards him, and prostrated herself at his feet. But at the very instant she thus did homage to her master, she said to herself, 'If your mournful eyes, O Prince of Persia, were witness to what I am now compelled to do, you would be able to judge of the hardness of my lot. It is before you alone that I would wish thus to humble myself; my heart would not then feel the least repugnance.'

"The caliph was delighted to see Schemselnihar. 'Rise, beautiful lady,' he cried, as he approached her, 'and come near to me. I have felt myself but ill at ease while I have been deprived for so long a time of the pleasure of beholding you.' So saying, he took her by the hand, and continuing to address the most kindly and obliging words to her, he seated himself on the throne of silver which she had ordered to be brought. Thereupon she took her seat before him; and the other twenty women formed an entire circle round them, sitting down on cushions; while the hundred young eunuchs who carried the flambeaux, dispersed themselves at certain distances from each other all over the garden; and the caliph in the meantime at his ease enjoyed the freshness of the evening air.

"When the caliph had taken his seat, he looked round him, and observed with great satisfaction that the garden was illuminated with a multitude of other lights besides those which the eunuchs carried. He noticed, however, that the saloon was shut up: at this he seemed surprised, and asked the reason of this strange appearance. It had been done, in fact, on purpose to astonish him; for he had no sooner spoken than all the windows at once suddenly opened, and he saw the hall lighted up both within side and without with more complete and magnificent illuminations than he had ever yet beheld. 'Charming Schemselnihar," he cried at this sight, 'I understand your meaning: you wish me to acknowledge that the night may be made as beautiful as the day. And after what I now see I cannot deny it.'

"Let us now return to the Prince of Persia and Ebn Thaher, whom we left shut up in the gallery. Although he felt himself in a very disagreeable situation, the latter could not help admiring everything that passed, and wondered at the splendour of which he was a spectator. 'I am not a young man,' he cried, 'and have in the course of my life beheld many beautiful sights; but I really think I never saw any spectacle so surprising or grand as this. Nothing that has been related, even of enchanted palaces, at all equals the glories we have now before our eyes. What a profusion of magnificence and riches!'

"But none of these brilliant sights seemed to have any effect upon the Prince of Persia, who derived no pleasure from them like Ebn Thaher did. His eyes were only intent upon watching Schemselnihar, and the presence of the sultan plunged him into the greatest affliction. 'Dear Ebn Thaher,' he cried, 'would to Heaven I had a mind sufficiently at ease to be interested, like yourself, in everything that is splendid and admirable around us. But, alas! I am in a very different state of mind; and all things serve but to increase my torment. How can I possibly see the caliph alone with her I adore, and not die in despair? Ought an affection, so tender and indelible as mine, to be disturbed by so powerful a rival? Heavens! how extraordinary and cruel is my destiny!

Not an instant ago I thought myself the happiest and most fortunate lover in the world; and at this moment I feel a pang at my heart that will cause my death. No, dear Ebn Thaher, I cannot resist it. My patience is worn out; my misfortune completely overwhelms me, and my courage sinks under it.' As he spoke these last words he observed something going on the garden which obliged him to be silent and give his attention.

"The caliph had commanded one of the women who stood around Schemselnihar that was near to take her lute and sing. The words she sang were very tender and impassioned. The caliph felt assured that she sang them by order of Schemselnihar, who had often given him similar proofs of her affection, and he accordingly interpreted them in favour of himself. But at that moment any compliment to the caliph was very far from the intention of Schemselnihar. She in her heart applied the words to her dear Ali Ebn

THE PRINCE OF PERSIA AND EBN THAHER ESCAPE FROM THE PALACE.

Becar, the Prince of Persia; and the misery she felt at having, in his stead, a master whose presence she could not endure, had such an effect upon her that she fainted. She fell back in her chair, and would have sunk on the ground if some of her women had not quickly run to her assistance. They carried her away, and bore her into the saloon.

"Astonished at this incident, Ebn Thaher, who was in the gallery, turned his head towards the Prince of Persia, and was yet more surprised when, instead of seeing him leaning against the blind, and looking out into the darkness as he himself had been doing, he found the prince stretched motionless at his feet. By this display of emotion, he judged of the strength of the Prince of Persia's love for Schemselnihar, and could not help wondering at this strange effect of sympathy, which distressed him the more on account of the place they were then in. He did all he could to recover the prince, but without success. Ebn Thaher was in this embarrassing situation when the confidante of

Schemselnihar opened the door of the gallery, and ran in quite out of breath, and like one who did not know what course to take. 'Come instantly,' cried she, 'that I may let you out. Everything here is in such confusion that I believe our very lives are in jeopardy.' 'Alas!' replied Ebn Thaher, in a tone which bespoke his grief, 'how can we depart? Come hither, and see what a state the Prince of Persia is in.' When the slave saw that he had fainted, she ran immediately to get some water, without losing time in conversation, and returned in a few moments.

"After they had sprinkled water on his face, the Prince of Persia at length began to recover. When Ebn Thaher saw symptoms of returning animation, he said to him, 'Prince, we both run a great risk of losing our lives by remaining here any longer, therefore make an effort, and let us fly as quickly as possible.' The prince was so weak that he could not rise without assistance. Ebn Thaher and the confidante gave him their hands, and, supporting him on each side, they came to a little iron gate, which led towards the Tigris. They went out by this gate, and proceeded to the edge of a small canal communicating with the river. The confidential slave clapped her hands, and instantly there appeared a little boat rowed by one man, and it came towards them. Ali Ebn Becar and his companion embarked in it, and the slave remained on the bank of the canal. As soon as the prince was seated in the boat, he stretched out one hand towards the palace, and placing the other on his heart, cried in a feeble voice, 'Dear object of my soul, receive from this hand the pledge of my faith, while with my other I assure you that my heart will ever cherish the flame with which it now burns.'

"The boatman rowed with all his strength, and the slave walked on the bank of the canal to accompany the Prince of Persia and Ebn Thaher till the boat was floating in the current of the Tigris. Then, as she could not go any farther, she took her leave of them, and returned.

"The Prince of Persia continued extremely weak. Ebn Thaher said all he could do console him, and exhorted him to take courage. 'Remember,' said he, 'that when we disembark we shall still have a long way to go before we arrive at my house; for, considering the state in which you now are, to conduct you to yours, which is so much farther, at this hour, would, I think, be very imprudent. We might also run a risk of meeting the watch.' They at length got out of the boat, but the prince was so feeble that he could not walk; and this very much increased Ebn Thaher's embarrassment. He recollected that he had a friend in the neighbourhood, and, with great difficulty, led the prince to that friend's house. Ebn Thaher's friend received his visitors very cordially, and when he had made them sit down, he asked them from whence they came at that late hour. Ebn Thaher replied, 'I heard this evening that a man who owes me a considerable sum of money intended to set out on a very long journey; I therefore immediately went in search of him, and on my way I met this young lord whom you see, and to whom I am under many and great obligations; as he knows my debtor, he did me the favour to accompany me. We had some difficulty in gaining our point, and inducing my debtor to behave with justice towards me. However, at last we succeeded, and this is the reason why we are wandering so late in the city. As we were returning this young lord, for whom I have the utmost regard, felt himself suddenly seized with illness at a few paces from your house; and this induced me to take the liberty of knocking at your door. I flattered myself that you would have the goodness to give us a lodging for this night.'

"The friend of Ebn Thaher was easily imposed on by this fable. He told them they were welcome, and offered the Prince of Persia, whom he did not know, every assistance in his power. But Ebn Thaher, taking upon himself to answer for the prince, said that his friend's illness was of a nature that required no remedy but repose. The druggist's friend also understood by this speech that both his guests wanted rest. He therefore conducted them to an apartment, where he left them alone.

"The Prince of Persia soon fell asleep. But his repose was disturbed by the most distressing dreams, representing Schemselnihar fainting at the feet of the caliph, and thus his affliction did not at all subside. Ebn Thaher, who was excessively impatient to get to his own house, for he doubted not that his family were in the utmost distress, because he made it a rule never to sleep from home, got up and departed very early, after taking leave of his friend, who had risen by daybreak to go to early prayers. They at length arrived at Ebn Thaher's house. The Prince of Persia, who had exerted himself very much to walk so far, threw himself upon a sofa, feeling as much fatigued as if he had accomplished a long journey. As he was not in a fit state to go home, Ebn Thaher ordered an apartment to be prepared for him; and that none of the prince's people might be uneasy about their master, he sent to inform them where he was. In the meantime he begged the prince to endeavour to make his mind easy, and order everything about him as he pleased. The Prince of Persia replied: 'I accept with pleasure the obliging offers you make; but that I may not be any embarrassment to you, I entreat you to attend to your own affairs as if I were not with you. I cannot think of staying here a moment if my presence is to be any restraint upon you.'

"As soon as Ebn Thaher had time to collect his thoughts, he informed his family of everything that had occurred in the palace of Schemselnihar, and finished his recital by returning thanks to God for having delivered him from the danger he had escaped. The principal servants of the Prince of Persia came to receive their orders from him at Ebn Thaher's; and soon afterwards several of his friends arrived who had been informed of his indisposition. His friends passed the greater part of the day with him; and although their conversation could not entirely banish the sorrowful reflections which occasioned his illness, at least it was thus far of advantage, that it gave him some relaxation.

"Towards the close of the day the prince wished to take his leave of Ebn Thaher; but this faithful friend found him still so weak that he induced him to remain till the following morning. In the meantime, to dissipate his gloom, he gave him in the evening a concert of vocal and instrumental music; but this only served to recall to the prince's memory the beautiful strains he had enjoyed the preceding night, and increased his grief instead of assuaging it; so that the next day his indisposition seemed to be augmented. Finding this to be the case, Ebn Thaher no longer opposed the prince's wish to return to his own house. He undertook the care of having him conveyed thither, and also accompanied him; and when he found himself alone with the prince in his apartment, he represented to him in strong terms the necessity of making one great effort to overcome a passion which could not terminate happily either for him or the favourite. 'Alas! dear Ebn Thaher,' cried the prince, 'it is easy for you to give this advice; but how difficult a task for me to follow it! I see and confess the importance of your words, without being able to profit by them. I have already said it: the love I have for Schemselnihar will accompany me to the grave.' When Ebn Thaher perceived that he could make no impression on the mind of the prince, he took his leave with the intention of retiring, but the prince would not let him depart. 'Kind Ebn Thaher,' said he to the druggist, 'though I have declared to you that it is not in my power to follow your prudent counsel, I entreat you not to be angry with me, nor to desist on that account from giving me proofs of your friendship. You could not do me a greater service than by informing me of the fate of my beloved Schemselnihar, if you should hear any tidings of her. The uncertainty I am under respecting her situation, and the dreadful apprehensions I feel on account of her fainting, cause the continuance of the languor and illness for which you reproved me so bitterly.' 'My lord,' replied Ebn Thaher, 'you may surely hope that her fainting has not produced any bad consequences, and that her confidential slave will shortly come to acquaint me how the affair terminated. As soon as I know the particulars, I will not fail to come and communicate them to you.'

"Ebn Thaher left the prince with this hope, and returned home; where he waited all the rest of the day in expectation of the arrival of Schemselnihar's favourite slave; but he waited vainly. She did not make her appearance even on the morrow. The anxiety he felt to learn the state of the prince's health did not allow him to remain any longer without seeing his friend; and he went to him with the design of exhorting him to have patience. He found him stretched upon the bed, and quite as ill as before. Around his couch stood his friends, and several physicians, who were exerting all their professional skill to endeavour to discover the cause of his disease. As soon as he perceived Ebn Thaher, he cast a smiling look on him, which denoted two things: one, that he was rejoiced to see him; the other, that his physicians were deceived in their conjectures on his disease, the cause of which they could not guess.

"The physicians and the friends retired, one after the other, so that Ebn Thaher remained alone with the sick prince. He approached his bed, to inquire how he had felt since he last saw him. 'I must own to you,' replied the Prince of Persia, 'that my love, which every day acquires increased strength, and the uncertainty of the destiny of the lovely Schemselnihar, heighten my disease every moment, and reduce me to a state which causes much grief to my relations and friends, and baffles the skill of the physicians, who cannot understand it. You little imagine,' added he, 'how much I suffer at seeing so many people, who constantly importune me, and whom I cannot dismiss without seeming ungrateful. You are the only one whose company affords me any comfort; but do not disguise anything from me, I conjure you. What news do you bring of Schemselnihar? Have you seen her favourite slave?' Ebn Thaber answered that he had not seen the slave of whom his friend spoke: and he had no sooner communicated this sorrowful intelligence to the prince, than the tears came in the young man's eyes: he could make no reply, for his heart was full. 'Prince,' resumed Ebn Thaher, 'allow me to say that you are too ingenious in tormenting yourself. In the name of Allah, dry your tears; some of your servants might come in at this moment, and you are well aware how cautious you ought to be to conceal your sentiments, which might be discovered from the emotion you are exhibiting.' But all the remonstrances of this judicious counsellor were ineffectual to stop the prince's tears, which he could not restrain. 'Wise Ebn Thaher,' cried he, when he had regained the power of speech, 'I can prevent my tongue from revealing the secret of my heart, but I have no power over my tears, while my heart is distracted with anxiety for Schemselnihar. If this adorable and only delight of my soul were no longer in this world, I should not survive her one moment.' 'Do not harbour so afflicting a thought,' replied Ebn Thaher; 'Schemselnihar still lives; you must not doubt it. If she has not sent you any account of herself, it is probably because she has not been able to find an opportunity, and I hope this day will not pass without your receiving some intelligence of her.' He added many other consoling speeches, and then took his leave.

"Ebn Thaher had scarcely returned to his house, when the favourite slave of Schemselnihar arrived. She had a sorrowful air, which prepared him to hear news of which he conceived an unfavourable presage. He inquired after her mistress. 'First,' said she, 'give me some intelligence of yourselves, for I was in great anxiety on your account, seeing the state in which the Prince of Persia appeared to be when you departed together.' Ebn Thaher related to her all she wished to know; and when he had concluded his narrative, the slave spoke in the following words: 'If the Prince of Persia suffers on my mistress's account, she does not endure less pain for him. After I had quitted you,' continued she, 'I returned to the saloon, where I found Schemselnihar, who had not yet recovered from her fainting fit, notwithstanding all the remedies that had been applied. The caliph was seated by her side, showing every symptom of real grief. He inquired of all the women, and of me in particular, if we had any knowledge of the cause of her indisposition; but we all kept the secret, and told him quite the contrary to what we knew to be the fact. We were all in tears at the sight of her sufferings, and tried every means that we thought might relieve her. It was quite midnight when she came to herself. The caliph, who had waited patiently until now, showed great joy, and asked Schemselnihar what had caused this illness. As soon as she heard the caliph's voice she made an effort to sit up, and kissed his feet before he had time to prevent her. 'O my lord,' she said, 'I ought to complain of Heaven for not having suffered me to die at your majesty's feet, that I might thus convince you how sincerely I am penetrated by the sense of all your goodness to me.'

"'I am convinced that you love me,' replied the caliph, 'but I command you to take care of yourself for my sake. You have probably made some exertion to-day, which has been the cause of this illness; you must be more careful, and I beg you to avoid a repe-

SCHEMSELNIHAR'S DISTRESS.

tition of anything that may be injurious. I am happy to see that you are partly recovered, and I advise you to pass the night here, instead of returning to your apartment, for moving might be hurtful to you.' He then ordered some wine to be brought, of which he made her take a small quantity to give her strength, and he then took his leave of her, and retired to his chamber.

"'So soon as the caliph was gone, my mistress made signs to me to approach her. She anxiously inquired after you. I assured her that you had long since quitted the palace, and set her mind at ease on that subject. I took care not to mention the fainting of the Prince of Persia, for fear she should relapse into the state from which we had with so much difficulty recovered her. But my precaution was useless, as you will shortly hear. 'O prince,' cried Schemselnihar, 'from this time I renounce all pleasures so long as my eyes shall be deprived of the gratification of beholding you: if I understand your heart, I am but following your example. You will not cease your tears until you are restored to me; and it is but just that I should weep and lament until you are given back to my prayers.' With these words, which she pronounced in a manner that denoted the violence of her love, she fainted a second time in my arms.

"'It was long before my companions and I could recall her to her senses. At length her consciousness returned. I then said to her, 'Are you resolved, lady, to suffer yourself to die, and to make us die with you? I conjure you in the name of the Prince of Persia, in whom you are so interested, to endeavour to preserve your life. I entreat you to hear me, and to make those efforts which you owe to yourself, to your love for the prince, and to our attachment to you.' 'I thank you sincerely,' returned she, 'for your care, your attention, and your advice. But, alas! how can they be serviceable to me? We are not permitted to flatter ourselves with any hope; and it is only in the bosom of the grave that we may expect a respite from our torments.'

"'One of my companions wished to divert our lady's melancholy ideas by singing a little air to her lute; but Schemselnihar desired her to be silent, and ordered her, with the rest, to quit the room. She kept only me to spend the night with her. Heavens! what a night it was! She passed it in tears and lamentations, calling continually on the name of the Prince of Persia. She bewailed the cruelty of her fate, which had thus destined her for the caliph, whom she could not love, and had deprived her of all hope of being united to the Prince of Persia, of whom she was so passionately enamoured.

"'The next day, as it was not convenient for her to remain in the saloon, I assisted to remove her into her own apartment. So soon as she was installed there all the physicians of the palace came to see her, by order of the caliph; and it was not long before he himself made his appearance. The remedies prescribed by the physicians for Schemselnihar had no effect; for these men were ignorant of the cause of her illness; and the restraint she felt in the presence of the caliph increased her sufferings. She has, however, enjoyed a little rest last night, and as soon as she awoke, she charged me to come to your house to obtain some intelligence of the Prince of Persia.' 'I have already informed you of the state he is in,' replied Ebn Thaher; 'therefore return to your mistress, and assure her that the Prince of Persia expected to hear from her with as much impatience as she could feel to hear news of him. Exhort her especially to moderate and conquer her feelings, lest some word escape her lips in the presence of the caliph, which may prove the destruction of us all.' 'As for me,' returned the slave, 'I am in constant apprehension, for she has very little command over herself. I took the liberty of telling her what I thought on that subject, and I am certain she will not take it amiss if I give her your message also.'

"Ebn Thaher, who had but just left the Prince of Persia, did not judge it proper to return again so soon. He had, moreover, to transact some important business which would keep him at home; thus he did not see his friend again till the close of day. The prince was alone, and was no better than he had been in the morning. 'Ebn Thaher,' said he, when he saw the druggist enter the room, 'you have, no doubt, many friends; but those friends do not know your worth as I know it; for I have witnessed the zeal, the care, and the pains you take when an opportunity offers to do your friend a service. I am quite confused at the thought of all you do for me. You show so much friendship and affection, that I shall never be able to repay you for your goodness.'

"'Prince,' replied Ebn Thaher, 'let us not speak on that subject. I am ready not only to lose one of my eyes to preserve one of yours, but even to sacrifice my life for you. But this is not the business I am come upon: I came to tell you that Schemselnihar sent her confidential slave to me, to inquire after your health, and at the same time to give you some information respecting herself. You may imagine that the message I sent must confirm her belief of the excess of your love for her mistress, and of the constancy with which you adore her.' Ebn Thaher then gave the prince an exact detail of everything the slave had told him. The prince heard the account with all the different emotions of fear, jealousy, tenderness, and compassion, which such a relation was likely to inspire; and during the progress of the narrative, he made on each circumstance of an afflicting or consoling nature such reflections as so passionate a lover could be capable of.

"The conversation had lasted so long that the night was now far advanced. Accordingly the Prince of Persia made Ebn Thaher remain at his house. The next morning, as this faithful friend was returning home, he saw a woman coming towards him, whom he soon recognised to be the confidential slave of Schemselnihar. She came up to him and said, 'My mistress salutes you, and I come from her to beg you to deliver this letter to the Prince of Persia.' The friendly Ebn Thaher took the letter, and returned to the prince, accompanied by Schemselnihar's attendant.

"When they came to the prince's house, Ebn Thaher begged her to remain a few minutes in the antechamber and wait for him. As soon as the prince saw his friend, he anxiously inquired what news he had to tell. 'The best you can possibly wish,' replied Ebn Thaher: 'you are beloved as tenderly as you love. Schemselnihar's confidential slave is in your antechamber; she brings you a letter from your mistress, and only waits your orders to appear before you.' 'Let her come in!' cried the prince in a transport of joy. And saying this he raised himself in his bed to receive her.

"As the attendants of the prince had left the room when Ebn Thaher entered it, that he might be alone with their master, Ebn Thaher went to open the door himself, and desired the confidante to come in. The prince recollected her, and received her with great distinction. 'My lord,' said she, 'I know all the pains you have suffered since I had the honour of conducting you to the boat which waited to take you home; but I hope that the letter I bring you will contribute to your recovery.' She then presented to him the letter. He took it and after having kissed it several times, he opened it, and read the following words:—

"'Schemselnihar to Ali Ebn Becar, Prince of Persia.

"'The person who will deliver this letter to you will give you an account of me better than I myself can give; for all outward things are nothing to me, since I ceased beholding you. Deprived of your presence, I seek to continue the illusion, and converse with you by means of these ill-formed lines; and this occupation affords me some pleasure, while I am debarred from the happiness of speaking to you

"'I have been told that patience is the remedy for all evils; yet the ills I suffer are increased rather than relieved by it. Although your image is indelibly engraven on my heart, my eyes wish again to behold you in person; and their sight will forsake them if they remain longer deprived of that gratification. Dare I flatter myself that yours experience the same impatience to see me? Yes, I may; they have sufficiently proved it to me by their tender glances. Happy would Schemselnihar be, happy would you be, O prince, if my wishes, which are the counterpart of yours, were not opposed by insurmountable obstacles! These obstacles occasion me a grief that is the sharper for being the cause of sorrow to you.

"'These sentiments which my fingers trace, and in the expression of which I feel such inconceivable consolation that I cannot repeat them too often, proceed from the bottom of my heart—from that incurable wound you have made in it; a wound which I bless a thousand times, notwithstanding the cruel sufferings I endure in your absence. I should care little for all the obstacles that oppose our love, were I only permitted to see you occasionally without restraint. I should then enjoy your society; and what more could I desire?

"'Do not imagine that my words convey more than I feel. Alas! whatever expressions I may use, I shall still leave unsaid much more than I can ever say. My eyes, which never cease looking for you, and incessantly weep till they shall behold you again; my afflicted heart, which seeks but you; my sighs, which pour from my lips whenever I think of you, and I am thinking of you continually; my memory, which never reflects any object but my beloved prince; the complaints I utter to Heaven of the rigour of my fate; my melancholy, my uneasiness, my sufferings, from which I have had no respite since you were torn from my gaze, are all sufficient pledges of the truth of what I write.

"'Am I not truly unfortunate to be born to love—to love, without indulging the hope that the object of my affections will ever be mine? This dreadful reflection overpowers me to such a degree that I should die were I not convinced that you love me. But this sweet consolation counteracts my despair, and attaches me to life. Tell me that you love me still. I will preserve your letter as a treasure of price: I will read it a thousand times a day; and I shall then bear my sorrows with less impatience. I pray that Heaven may no longer be angry with us, but may grant us an opportunity of revealing to each other, without restraint, the tender affection we feel, and of mutually declaring that we will never cease to love. Farewell.

"'I salute Ebn Thaher, to whom we are both under so many obligations.'

"The Prince of Persia was not satisfied with reading this letter only once. He thought he had not bestowed sufficient attention on it; he read it again more deliberately, and while thus engaged he frequently uttered deep sighs, and as frequently wept. He then would burst into transports of joy and tenderness, according to the different emotions he experienced from the contents of the letter. In short, he could not withdraw his eyes from the characters traced by that beloved hand, and he was going to read the writing a third time, when Ebn Thaher represented to him that the slave had no time to lose, and that he must prepare an answer. 'Alas!' cried the prince, 'how can I reply to so obliging and kind a letter? In what terms shall I describe the anguish of my soul? My mind is agitated by a thousand distressing thoughts, and my sentiments are obliterated before I have time to express them by others, which in their turn are erased as soon as formed. While my bodily frame shares the agitation of my mind, how shall I be able to hold the paper and guide the reed to form the letters?'

"Saying this, he drew from a little writing case, which was near him, some paper, a cut reed, and an ink-horn; but before he began to write he gave the letter of Schemselnihar to Ebn Thaher, and begged him to hold it open before him, that, by occasionally casting his eyes over it as he wrote, he might be better enabled to answer it. He took up the writing-cane to begin; but the tears, which flowed from his eyes on the paper, frequently obliged him to stop to allow them a free course. He at length finished his letter, and gave it to Ebn Thaher, with these words: 'Do me the favour to read it, and see if the agitation of my spirits has allowed me to write a proper answer.' Ebn Thaher took the paper, and read as follows:—

"'The Prince of Persia to Schemselnihar.

"'I was sunk in the deepest affliction when your letter was delivered into my hands. At the sight of the words traced by your pen, I was transported with a joy I cannot express; but on reading the lines which your beautiful hand had sent to comfort me, my eyes were sensible of greater pleasure than that which they lost when yours so suddenly closed on the evening when you fell senseless at my rival's feet. The words contained in your beloved letter, are so many luminous rays, that enliven the obscurity in which my soul was wrapped. They convince me how much you suffer for me, and also prove that you sympathise with the anguish I endure for you, and thus console me in my pain. At one moment they cause my tears to flow in abundant streams; at another they inflame my heart with an inextinguishable fire, which supports it, and prevents my expiring with grief. I have not tasted one instant's repose since our too cruel separation. Your letter alone afforded me some relief from my misery. I preserved an uninterrupted silence till it was placed in my hands; but that has restored to me the power of speech. I was wrapped in the most profound melancholy; but that has inspired me with joy, which instantly proclaimed itself in my eyes and countenance. My surprise at receiving a favour so unmerited was so great, that I knew not how to express myself, or in what words to testify my gratitude. I have kissed it a thousand times, as the precious pledge of your goodness; I read it again and again, till I was quite lost in the excess of my happiness. You tell me to say that I love you still; alas! had my love for you been less passionate, less tender than is the passion that fills my whole soul, could I have done otherwise than adore you, after all the proofs you give me of the strength and endurance of your affection? Yes, I love you, my dearest life; and to the end of my existence shall glory in the pure flame which you have kindled in my heart. I will never complain of the vivid fire which consumes my being; and however rigorous may be the pains which your absence occasions, I will support them with constancy and firmness, encouraged by the hope of beholding you again. Would to Heaven I could see you to-day,

THE PRINCE SENDS HIS LETTER TO SCHEMSELNIHAR.

and that, instead of sending you this letter, I might be permitted to present myself before you, that I might die for love of you. My tears prevent me from continuing to write. Farewell.'

"Ebn Thaher could not read the last lines without himself shedding tears. He returned the letter to the prince, assuring him it needed no correction. The prince folded it up, and when he had sealed it, he said to the confidential slave, who had retired to the end of the apartment: 'I beg you to approach. This is the answer I have written to the letter of your dear mistress. I entreat you to take it to her, and to salute her from me.' The slave took the letter, and retired with Ebn Thaher, who, after he had walked some distance with her, left her and returned to his house, where he began to make serious reflections on the unhappy affair in which he found himself so unfortunately and deeply engaged. He considered that the Prince of Persia and Schemselnihar, notwithstanding the strong interest they had in concealing their sentiments, behaved with so little discretion that their love could not long remain a secret. He drew from this reflection all the unfavourable conclusions which must naturally suggest themselves to a man of good sense. 'If Schemselnihar,' thought he, 'were not a lady of such high rank, I would exert myself to the utmost of my ability to make her and her lover happy; but she is the favourite of the caliph, and no man can aspire to become the possessor of one who has gained the affections of our master with impunity. The caliph's anger will first fall on Schemselnihar; the prince will assuredly lose his life; and I shall be involved in his misfortune. But I have my honour, my peace of mind, my family, and my property to take care of; I must, then, while it is in my power. endeavour to extricate myself from the perils in which I find myself involved.'

"Ebn Thaher's mind was occupied with thoughts of this nature for the whole of that day. The following morning he went to the Prince of Persia with the intention of making one last effort to induce him to conquer his unfortunate passion. In vain he repeatedly urged upon the prince all the arguments he had already employed, declaring that the prince would do much better to exert all his courage to overcome this attachment to Schemselnihar; that he should not suffer himself to be led away to destruction by its means; and that his love for her was dangerous to himself, as his rival was so powerful. 'In short, my lord,' added he, 'if you will take my advice, you will endeavour to overcome your affection; otherwise you run the risk of causing the destruction of Schemselnihar, whose life ought to be dearer to you than your own. I give you this counsel as a friend, and some day you will thank me for it.'

"The prince listened to Ebn Thaher with evident impatience, though he allowed him to finish what he wished to say; but when the druggist had concluded he said: 'Ebn Thaher, do you suppose that I can cease to love Schemselnihar, who returns my affection with so much tenderness? She does not hesitate to expose her life for me, and can you imagine that the care of preserving mine should occupy me a single moment? No; whatever misfortunes may be the consequence, I will love Schemselnihar to the last moment of my life.'

"Offended at the obstinacy of the prince, Ebn Thaher left him abruptly, and returned home, where, recollecting his reflections on the preceding day, he began to consider very seriously what course he should pursue.

"While he was thus lost in thought, a jeweller, an intimate friend of his, came to see him. This jeweller had observed that the confidential slave of Schemselnihar had been with Ebn Thaher more frequently than usual, and that Ebn Thaher himself had been almost incessantly with the Prince of Persia, whose indisposition was known to every one, although the cause was a secret. All this had created some suspicions in the jeweller's mind. As Ebn Thaher appeared to be absorbed in thought, he supposed that some important affair occasioned this preoccupation; and thinking he had hit on the cause, he asked him what business the slave of Schemselnihar had with him. Ebn Thaher was somewhat confused at this question; but not choosing to confess the truth, he replied, that it was only on a trifling errand that she came to him so often. 'You do not speak sincerely,' resumed the jeweller; 'and by your dissimulation you will make me suspect that this trifle is of a more important nature than I had at first supposed.'

"Finding that his friend pressed him so closely, Ebn Thaher said, 'In very truth, this affair is of the utmost importance. I had determined to keep it secret; but as I know you take a lively interest in everything that concerns me, I will reveal it to you, rather than suffer you to make conclusions for which there is no foundation. I do not enjoin you to secresy, for you understand from what I am going to relate how impossible it would be to keep such a promise.' After this preface, he related to him the story of the attachment between Schemselnihar and the Prince of Persia. 'You are aware,' added he, at the conclusion of his tale, 'in what estimation I am held by the nobles and ladies of the highest rank both in the court and city. What a disgrace will it be for me, if this story becomes known! And, indeed, not only a disgrace—it would be absolute destruction to my whole family as well as to myself. This consideration embarrasses me more than all the rest; but I have resolved how to act. I owe it to my safety, and I must be firm. I intend in the speediest manner possible to collect what sums are owing to me, and satisfy those who are my creditors; and after I have secured all my property, I will retire to Balsora, where I may remain, till the storm, which I see gathering over my head, is passed. The friendship which I feel for Schemselnihar and for the Prince of Persia makes me very anxious on their account: I pray that Allah may make them sensible of the danger to which they expose themselves, and may Heaven be their shield. But if their luckless destiny condemns their attachment to be known to the caliph, I at least shall be sheltered from his resentment; for I do not suspect them of sufficient malice to entangle me in their misfortune. Their ingratitude would be black indeed if they acted thus: they would then repay with baseness the services I have done them, and the good advice I have given, particularly to the Prince of Persia, who might still draw back from the precipice if he were willing, and save his mistress as well as himself. It would be as easy for him to leave Bagdad as for me; and absence would insensibly eradicate a passion which will only increase while he remains in this city.'

"The jeweller heard the words of Ebn Thaher with very great astonishment. 'What you have now told me,' said he, 'is of such vast importance that I cannot comprehend how Schemselnihar and the Prince of Persia could be so imprudent as to give way to their violent passion. Whatever inclination they might feel for each other, they ought, instead of yielding to its influence, to have resisted it with firmness, and made a better use of their reason. Could they be blind to the dreadful consequences of their proceedings? How sadly are they mistaken, if they suppose their love can remain secret! Like yourself, I foresee the fatal termination of this affair. But you are prudent and wise, and I entirely approve the resolution you have formed; it is only by putting it in execution that you can escape the direful events you so justly fear.' After this conversation the jeweller rose, and took his leave of Ebn Thaher; but before he left him, the latter conjured him, by the friendship which united them, not to reveal their conversation to any one. 'Give yourself no uneasiness,' replied the jeweller; 'I will keep the secret at the peril of my life.'

"Two days after, the jeweller happened to pass by the shop of Ebn Thaher; and, observing that it was shut up, he concluded his friend had put his contemplated design into execution. To be quite sure, however, he inquired of a neighbour if he knew why Ebn Thaher's shop was not open. The neighbour replied that he knew no more than that Ebn Thaher had set off on a journey. This was all the jeweller wanted to hear; and now his thoughts immediately flew to the Prince of Persia. 'Unhappy prince,' thought he, 'how grieved you will be to learn this intelligence! What means can you now devise to hold intercourse with Schemselnihar? I fear despair will put a period to your existence. I feel compassion for you, and must endeavour to replace the loss of the timid friend you has deserted you.'

"The business which led him out was not of immediate consequence; he therefore neglected that, and, although he only knew the prince from having sold him some jewellery, went to his house. He requested one of the servants who stood at the door to tell his master that he wanted to speak to him on an affair of the greatest importance. The servant soon returned to the jeweller, and introduced him into the apartment of the prince, who was reclining on a sofa, with his head on the cushion. The prince, recollecting that he had seen him before, rose to receive him and give him welcome; and after having begged him to sit down, he asked the jeweller if he could render him any service, or if his visitor came on business which related to him. 'Prince,' replied the jeweller, 'although I have not the honour to be intimately known to you, yet the zealous desire I have of serving you has made me take the liberty of coming to acquaint you with a circumstance which concerns you nearly. I hope you will pardon my freedom, as it proceeds from a good intention.'

"After this introduction, the jeweller began his story, and proceeded thus: 'Prince, will you allow me the honour of telling you, that congeniality of thought between myself and Ebn Thaher, together with some affairs we had to transact with each other, has given rise to a firm friendship which knits us closely together. I know his acquaintance with you, and that he has, till now, exerted himself to serve you to the utmost of his ability. This I learned from his own lips, for we have no concealments from each other. I just now passed by his shop, and was surprised to find it shut up. I inquired the reason of one of his neighbours, who told me that Ebn Thaher had taken leave of him, and of his other acquaintances, two days since, at the same time offering them his services at Balsora, whither he said he was going on an affair of considerable importance. I was not thoroughly satisfied with this answer; and the interest I feel in whatever concerns him, induced me to come to ask you if you could tell me the particulars of this sudden departure.'

"At this speech, to which the jeweller had given the turn he thought most likely to forward his design, the Prince of Persia changed colour, and looked at the jeweller with an air which evidently proved how much he was grieved at the intelligence. He replied: 'What you tell me astonishes me: you could not have brought me intelligence more mortifying. Yes!' cried he, the tears flowing from his eyes, 'I have no hope left, if what you tell me is true! Does Ebn Thaher forsake me, who was my only consolation and support? I can live no longer after so cruel a blow!'

"The jeweller had heard enough to be fully convinced of the violence of the prince's love, of which Ebn Thaher had already told him. Simple friendship, he thought, does not express itself in such strong language; love alone has the power to inspire such violent emotion.

"The prince remained for some minutes absorbed in the most distressing reflections. At length he raised his head, and, addressing one of the attendants, said: 'Go to Ebn Thaher's house; speak to some of his servants, and inquire if it be true that their master has set out for Balsora. Run there instantly, and return as quickly as possible, that I may learn what you have heard.' While the servant was gone, the jeweller endeavoured to converse with the prince on different subjects; but his host seemed totally inattentive, and sat lost in thought. Sometimes he could not persuade himself that Ebn Thaher was really gone; then again he felt convinced of it, when he recollected the conversation he had held with his friend the last time he had seen him, and the abrupt manner in which the druggist had left him.

"At length the servant of the prince returned, and said that he had spoken with one of the people belonging to Ebn Thaher, who assured him that his master was no longer in Bagdad, but that he had set off two days before for Balsora; and he added these words: 'As I was coming out of the house of Ebn Thaher, a well-dressed female slave accosted me; and after asking me if I had not the honour of being one of your attendants, she said that she wanted to speak to you, and therefore begged me to allow her to come with me. She is in the antechamber, and, I believe, has a letter to deliver from some person of consequence.' The prince immediately desired that she might be admitted, not doubting that it was the confidential slave of Schemselnihar; and he was not mistaken in his conjecture

"The jeweller knew this woman from having met her sometimes at Ebn Thaher's, who had told him who she was. She could not have arrived at a more seasonable time to prevent the prince from giving way to despair. She saluted him, and he returned her greeting. The jeweller had risen as soon as she entered, and had withdrawn to a little distance, to leave them at liberty to converse together. After an interview of some length with the prince, the slave took her leave, and went away. She left him quite altered from what he had been before: his eyes appeared to sparkle, and his countenance was more cheerful. These appearances led the jeweller to suppose that the confidential slave had been saying something favourable to his hopes.

"The jeweller resumed his place near the prince, and said to him with a smile, 'I see, prince, you have some important affairs at the palace of the caliph.' Surprised and alarmed at this speech, the prince replied, 'What induces you to think that I have any affairs at the palace of the caliph?' 'I conclude so,' resumed the jeweller, 'from your speaking to the slave who has just left you.' 'And to whom do you suppose this slave belongs?' resumed the prince. 'To Schemselnihar, the favourite of the caliph,' replied the jeweller. 'I know this slave,' he continued, 'and her mistress also, who has sometimes done me the honour of coming to my shop to buy jewellery. I know, moreover, that this slave is admitted into all the secrets of Schemselnihar. I have seen her for some days past continually walking about the streets with a pensive air, and from this I imagine she is now concerned in something of consequence which relates to her mistress.'

"These words of the jeweller confused the Prince of Persia. 'This man would not talk to me thus,' thought he, 'if he did not suspect, or rather if he did not know, my secret.' He remained silent for a few minutes, not knowing how to act. At length he roused himself, and said to the jeweller, 'You tell me some things which lead me to think you know still more than you have revealed. It is very necessary to my peace of

THE JEWELLER AND THE LETTER.

mind that I should know everything; I entreat you, therefore, to conceal nothing from me.'

"The jeweller, who desired no better opportunity, then gave the prince an exact detail of the conversation he had had with Ebn Thaher, and thus let him know that he was well aware of the intercourse that subsisted between him and Schemselnihar. He did not omit telling his hearer that Ebn Thaher, alarmed at the danger in which he was placed by his position as the prince's friend, had imparted to him the design he had formed of quitting Bagdad for Balsora, where he intended to remain until the storm which he dreaded had passed away. 'This design he has put in execution,' continued the jeweller, 'and I am surprised that he could prevail on himself to abandon you in the state in which he described you to be. As for me, prince, I confess to you that I was moved with compassion for your sufferings, and I have come to offer you my services; if you will do me the honour to accept them, I promise to observe the same fidelity towards you that Ebn Thaher has observed; and engage, moreover, to continue more firm and constant than he has been. I am ready to sacrifice my life and honour in your service; and, that you may have no doubts of my sincerity, I swear by everything most sacred in our holy religion to preserve your secret inviolably. Be assured, then, prince, that in me you will find a friend equal to him you have lost.'

"This speech afforded the Prince of Persia great consolation, and reconciled him to the desertion of Ebn Thaher. He replied: 'I am very fortunate to find in you so good a substitute for the loss I have suffered. I cannot sufficiently express the gratitude I feel to you; and I trust that God will amply recompense your generosity. I accept, therefore, with great pleasure, the kind offer you have made me.' A moment afterwards he resumed: 'Should you suppose that Schemselnihar's confidential slave has been talking to me of you? She told me that it was you who advised Ebn Thaher to leave Bagdad. These were the very last words she said as she left me, and she seemed thoroughly persuaded of their truth. But she did you great injustice; and everything you have now told me convinces me that she was completely deceived.' 'Prince,' replied the jeweller, 'I have had the honour to give you both a literal and a faithful narrative of the conversation that took place between Ebn Thaher and myself. It is true that, when he told me of his intention of retiring to Balsora, I did not dissuade him from his design. I even told him I thought him both prudent and wise; but this ought not to prevent you from putting your whole confidence in me. I am ready to give you my time and faithful services, and to exert myself most warmly and indefatigably in your cause. If you doubt me and decline my offer, I will nevertheless keep the solemn oath I have made, and religiously preserve your secret.' To this the prince replied: 'I have already told you that I place not the least confidence in anything the slave has said. It is her zeal only that has raised these suspicions in her mind, and I am convinced they have not the least foundation. You ought, therefore, to excuse her on that account, as I do.'

"They continued their conversation for some time longer, and consulted together upon the best and most suitable means of keeping up a correspondence between the prince and Schemselnihar. The first point upon which they agreed was the necessity of undeceiving the confidante, who was so unjustly prejudiced against the jeweller. The prince took upon himself the task of explaining this matter the first time he should see her; and also to desire her, whenever she brought any more letters, or had any message from her mistress, to apply directly to the jeweller. They thought it imprudent that she should make her appearance at the prince's house so often; for her continual presence there might cause disclosures of circumstances it was so much the interest of all parties to conceal. The jeweller then rose, and, after again assuring the prince he might place entire confidence in him, took his leave.

"As the jeweller turned away from the Prince of Persia's house, he observed a letter in the street which some one seemed to have dropped. As it was not sealed he unfolded it, and found it contained the following words:—

"'Schemselnihar to the Prince of Persia.

"'I am now about to inform you, by means of my slave, of a circumstance which causes me as much affliction as it will occasion you. In losing Ebn Thaher we truly suffer a great loss; but do not let this, beloved prince, prevent you from taking care of yourself. If the friend in whom we trusted has abandoned us through a dread of the consequences, let us consider it as an evil we could not avoid, and let us console ourselves under the misfortune. I own to you that Ebn Thaher has forsaken us at a time when his presence and aid were most necessary; but let us fortify ourselves with patience under this most unexpected event; nor let our affection fail us even for an instant. Strengthen your mind against this disastrous event. Remember that we seldom attain our wishes without difficulty. Do not, then, let this misfortune damp our courage; let us hope that Heaven will be favourable; and that after all our numerous sufferings we shall at last arrive at the full and happy completion of our wishes. Farewell.'

"While the jeweller had been engaged in conversation with the Prince of Persia, the confidante had had time to return to the palace, and give her mistress the disastrous intelligence of Ebn Thaher's departure. Schemselnihar had in consequence immediately written the foregoing letter, and sent her slave back to carry it to the prince without delay; and the slave had accidentally dropped it as she went along.

"The jeweller was much pleased at finding it; for this letter afforded him an excellent method of justifying himself in the mind of Schemselnihar's slave, and bringing the matter to the point at which he wished to see it. As he finished reading the letter, he perceived the slave herself, who was looking for the lost writing in great distress and anxiety. He directly folded it up and put it in his bosom; but the woman, who observed this action, ran up to him. 'My master,' she said, 'I have dropped the letter which you had just now in your hand; I beg you to have the goodness to return it me.' The jeweller pretended not to hear her, and continued to walk on till he came to his own house, without answering a word: he did not shut the door after him, that the confidante, who still followed him, might come in if she pleased. This she immediately did; and when she had reached his apartments, she said to him: 'My master, you can make no use of the letter you have found, and you would not hesitate for a moment to give it back to me if you knew from whom it comes, and to whom it is addressed. Give me leave to tell you, also, that you do not act justly in detaining it.'

"Before he returned any answer to the slave, the jeweller made her sit down. He then said to her: 'Is it not true that the letter of which you speak is from Schemselnihar, and that it is addressed to the Prince of Persia?" The slave, who did not expect this question, turned pale. 'This question seems to embarrass you,' continued the jeweller; 'but understand that indiscreet curiosity is not my motive for asking it. I could have given you the letter in the street, but I wished to induce you to follow me here, because I am desirous of explaining my motives to you. Tell me, is it just to impute a disastrous event to a man who has not in the most distant manner contributed to it? This, however, is exactly what you did when you told the Prince of Persia that I advised Ebn Thaher for his own security to leave Bagdad. I will not lose time in justifying myself to you; it is enough that the Prince of Persia is fully convinced of my innocence on this point. I will only say that, instead of having aided Ebn Thaher in his departure, I am extremely mortified at it; not so much on account of my friendship for him, as from my sincere compassion for the situation in which he has left the prince, of whose intercourse with Schemselnihar he made me aware. As soon as I was certain that Ebn Thaher was no longer in Bagdad, I ran and presented myself to the prince, with whom you found me. I informed him of this news, and at the same time offered him the same offices which Ebn Thaher had performed till his departure. I have succeeded in my design; and provided you place as much confidence in me as you did in Ebn Thaher, it will be your own fault if I am not as useful as he has ever been. Go and report to your mistress what I have now said to you, and assure her that, though I may lose my life by my participation in the dangerous enterprise, I shall never repent having sacrificed myself for two lovers so worthy of each other.'

"The confidential slave listened with great satisfaction to the words of the jeweller. She requested him to pardon her for the bad opinion she had entertained of him, a misconception which had arisen merely from the zeal she felt for Schemselnihar's interests. She continued: 'I rejoice greatly that the favourite and the Prince of Persia have been fortunate enough to find in you a proper person to supply the place of Ebn Thaher; and I will not fail to give my mistress a favourable account of the strong inclination you have to serve her.'

"After Schemselnihar's slave had thus expressed the pleasure it afforded her to find the jeweller so disposed to be useful to Schemselnihar and the Prince of Persia, the jeweller took the letter out of his bosom, and gave it her. 'Take it,' he cried, 'and carry it immediately to the prince; and then come back this way, that I may see what answer he sends. And remember also to give him an account of our conversation.'

The slave took the letter, and carried it to the Prince of Persia, who answered it without delay. She then returned to the jeweller's to show him the reply, which contained these words :—

"'The Prince of Persia to Schemselnihar.

"'Your dear letter has produced a great effect upon me ; but yet not such an effect as I could wish. You endeavour to console me for the loss of Ebn Thaher. Alas ! however sensible I may be of this misfortune, it is only the least of the evils I endure. You know what those evils are ; and you know that your presence alone can cure them. Oh ! when will the period arrive in which I can enjoy that dear presence without the dread of being again deprived of it ? How distant does it appear to me ! Perhaps, indeed, we ought not to flatter ourselves that we shall ever meet again. You tell me to be careful of my health : I will obey you, since I have made every inclination of my heart subservient to you. Farewell.'

"When he had read this letter, the jeweller returned it to the slave, who said to him, as she was departing, 'I am going to induce my mistress to place the same confidence in you which she placed in Ebn Thaher. To-morrow you shall have some intelligence from me.' Accordingly she came the very next day, with great satisfaction expressed in her countenance. 'Your very appearance,' said he, 'proves to me that you found Schemselnihar in the disposition of mind you wished.' 'It is true,' she answered ; 'and you shall hear the manner in which I brought it about. I found her yesterday waiting for me with the greatest impatience. I put the letter of the prince into her hand, and while she read it her eyes filled with tears. As I perceived she was going to give herself up to her accustomed grief, I said, 'O dear lady, it is doubtless the departure of Ebn Thaher which so much grieves you ; but permit me to conjure you, in the name of Allah, not to alarm yourself any more on that subject. We have found another friend like him, who has offered to engage in your service with equal zeal, and, what is of more consequence, with greater courage.' I then mentioned you to her, and told her the motives which induced you to visit the Prince of Persia. In short, I assured her that you would ever preserve inviolable the secret of her attachment to the prince, and that you were determined to aid their cause with all your power. She appeared greatly consoled at this speech, and exclaimed, 'How greatly bound ought we to feel ourselves to the excellent man of whom you speak ! I wish to know him, to see him, to hear from his own lips what you have now told me, and to thank him for his almost unheard-of generosity towards persons who have not the slightest reason to expect him to interest himself so zealously in their behalf. His presence will afford me pleasure, and I will omit nothing that I think may confirm him in his good opinion and intentions. Do not fail to go to him to-morrow morning, and bring him here.' Therefore, my master, I beg you to take the trouble to go with me to her palace.

"These words of the slave of Schemselnihar very much embarrassed the jeweller. He replied : 'Your mistress must permit me to say, that she has not thought sufficiently of what she has required of me. The free access which Ebn Thaher had to the caliph gave him admission everywhere ; and the officers and attendants, who knew him, suffered him to go backwards and forwards unnoticed and unquestioned in the palace of Schemselnihar. But how dare I enter that dwelling ? You must yourself see that this is impossible. I entreat you, therefore, to explain to Schemselnihar the reasons which prevent me from giving her this satisfaction, and represent to her all the unpleasant consequences that might happen from my acquiescence. And if she will quietly reconsider the matter, she will easily see that she exposes me to a very great danger without gaining the least advantage.'

"The confidential slave endeavoured to encourage the jeweller. She said, 'Do you suppose that Schemselnihar is so regardless of your safety as to expose you, from whom she expects a continuance of the most important services, to the least danger, in ordering you to come to her ? Reflect for a moment, and you will find there is not even the appearance of danger. Both my mistress and myself are too much interested in this affair to engage you in it without due consideration. You may therefore very safely trust me

SCHEMSELNIHAR AND THE JEWELLER.

to conduct you; and you will readily acknowledge, when the interview is over, that your alarms are without foundation.'

"The jeweller yielded to the arguments of the confidential slave, and rose up to follow her. But in spite of all the courage he piqued himself upon possessing, his fears so far got the better of him that he trembled from head to foot. Thereupon the slave said: 'Judging by the state in which you appear to be, I am sure you had better remain at home, and let Schemselnihar devise some other mode of seeing you; and I have no doubt that her great anxiety to behold you will induce her to come and seek you herself. Therefore I request you will not go out; for I am convinced it will not be long before you see her arrive.' The woman was not wrong in her conjectures; for when she informed Schemselnihar of the jeweller's alarm, the favourite instantly made preparations to go to his house.

"He received her with every mark of the most profound respect. As soon as she had seated herself, for she was somewhat fatigued with her walk, she took off her veil, and revealed so much beauty to the eyes of the jeweller, that he instantly confessed in his own mind how natural it was that the Prince of Persia should have devoted his heart to the favourite of the caliph. She accosted the jeweller in the kindest manner, and said to him: 'I could not possibly become acquainted with the great interest you take in the welfare of the Prince of Persia and myself, without at once determining to thank you in person; and I am truly grateful to Heaven for having so soon and so completely supplied the great loss we suffered in the departure of Ebn Thaher.'

"Schemselnihar said much more that was complimentary and kind to the jeweller, and then returned to her palace. The jeweller himself instantly went and gave an account of this visit to the Prince of Persia, who called out, when he saw him arrive, 'I have been waiting for you with the greatest impatience. The confidential slave has brought me a letter from her mistress; but this letter has afforded me no comfort. Although the amiable Schemselnihar may endeavour to give me every encouragement, yet I dare not indulge any hope, and my patience is quite exhausted. I know not what plan to pursue. The departure of Ebn Thaher has thrown me into despair. He was my great support; and in losing him I have lost everything; for in the free access he had to Schemselnihar I flattered myself with some hopes of success.'

"To these words, which the prince uttered in a very expressive manner, and so rapidly that the jeweller had no opportunity of putting in a word, the jeweller replied: 'O prince, no one can take a greater interest in your misfortunes than I, and if you will have the patience to listen to me you will find that I can afford you some comfort.' On hearing these words the prince held his tongue, and listened eagerly while the jeweller continued: 'I very clearly see that the only means of satisfying you is to enable you to see and to converse with Schemselnihar without any restraint. This is a satisfaction I wish to procure you; and I will set about the task to-morrow. I trust it will not be necessary to expose you to the risk of going to the palace of Schemselnihar. You know from experience how dangerous a plan that is. I am acquainted with a much safer place for this interview—a place where you will both be in safety.' When the jeweller had spoken thus, the prince embraced him with the greatest transport.

"'By this delightful promise,' he exclaimed, 'you give new life to an unfortunate lover, who felt himself already condemned to death. From what I have already heard, I am sure the loss of Ebn Thaher has been fully supplied to me. Whatever you undertake will, I know, be done well; and I give myself up entirely to your direction.'

"The prince again thanked the jeweller for the zeal he had shown in his service, and the latter then returned home. The confidential slave of Schemselnihar came the next morning to seek him. He informed her that he had given the Prince of Persia some hopes of speedily seeing Schemselnihar. She replied: 'I am come expressly to concert some measures with you for that purpose. It appears to me that this very house is well adapted for their meeting.' 'I should not have the least objection to their coming here,' said the jeweller, 'but I think they will be much more at liberty in another house which belongs to me, and which is entirely uninhabited. I will immediately have it handsomely furnished and prepared for their reception.' 'In that case,' rejoined the slave, 'nothing remains to be done but to procure the consent of the favourite. I will go and speak to her on the subject, and will return in a very short time, and bring you her answer.'

"It was not long before the slave came back; and she told the jeweller that Schemselnihar would not fail to be at the appointed place towards the close of the day.

At the same time she put a purse into his hands, and told him to provide an excellent collation. The jeweller directly brought the slave to the house where the lovers were to meet, that she might know where to find it, and be able to conduct her mistress thither; and after he had dismissed her he went to borrow some gold and silver plate, and certain very rich carpets and cushions, and other furniture, with which he furnished the house in the most magnificent manner. When everything was in readiness, he went to the Prince of Persia.

"Great was the joy of the prince when the jeweller informed him that he had come for the purpose of conducting him to a house which had been prepared for the reception of Schemselnihar and her lover. This intelligence made the prince forget all his vexations, all his disappointments, and all his sufferings. He put on a most magnificent dress, and went out, without even one attendant, with the jeweller, who led him to the house through many unfrequented streets, in order that no one might observe them, and introduced him into his new abode, and there they remained in conversation till the arrival of Schemselnihar.

"They had not long to wait for the coming of the beautiful favourite. She arrived directly after sunset prayers, accompanied by her confidential attendant and two other slaves. It would be useless to attempt to express the excess of joy these two lovers evinced at the sight of each other. They sat down upon a sofa, and at first looked at each other without being able to utter a single word, so much were their minds absorbed in the contemplation of their happiness. But when after a time they recovered the use of their speech, they made ample amends for their former silence. They expressed themselves in so tender and affecting a manner that the jeweller, the confidante, and the two slaves, could not refrain from shedding tears. The jeweller was the first to recover himself; he went out, and returning, set the collation before them with his own hands. The lovers ate and drank very sparingly; after which they returned to the sofa, and Schemselnihar asked the jeweller if he could procure her a lute, or any other instrument. The jeweller, who had taken care to provide everything which might afford them pleasure, immediately brought a lute. After a few moments occupied in tuning it, the favourite began to sing.

"While Schemselnihar was thus delighting the Prince of Persia, by expressing her love for him in words which she improvised as she sang, they suddenly heard a great noise; and a slave, whom the jeweller had brought with him, presently rushed in, breathless with alarm, and said that some people were forcing the door. He had demanded to know what they wanted, but instead of returning any answer, they redoubled their blows. The jeweller, greatly alarmed, left Schemselnihar and the Prince of Persia, to go and ascertain the meaning of this interruption. He had advanced as far as the court, when, through the obscurity of the place, he observed a troop of men, armed with scimitars, who had already forced the door, and were coming directly towards him. The jeweller pressed close to the wall as quickly as possible, and he saw them pass by, to the number of ten, without being himself observed.

"As he thought he could be of no assistance to the Prince of Persia and Schemselnihar, he contented himself with lamenting their sad situation, and fled as fast as possible. He ran out of his own house, and took refuge in the abode of a neighbour, who was not yet retired for the night; not doubting that this unforeseen and violent attack was made by order of the caliph, who had by some means been informed of the place where the favourite and the Prince of Persia had appointed to meet. The house to which he fled for safety was so near that he distinctly heard the noise the invaders made at his own; and this noise continued till midnight. Then, as everything appeared to be silent, the jeweller requested his neighbour to lend him a sabre, armed with which he sallied forth. He went to the door of his own house; and entering the court, to his great alarm, encountered a man, who demanded who he was. He instantly recognised the voice of his own slave. 'How have you been able,' cried the jeweller, 'to escape being taken by the guard?' 'O master,' replied the slave, 'I concealed myself in the corner of the court, and I came out as soon as the noise had ceased. It was not the guard that broke into your house, but a band of robbers, who for some days past have invested this quarter of the city, and plundered a great many dwellings. They have doubtless remarked the quantity of rich furniture that has been brought here; and it was to steal this that they came.'

"The jeweller thought the conjecture of his slave very probable. He examined the house, and found that the robbers had really carried off the beautiful furniture of the apartment in which he had received Schemselnihar and her lover, and stolen all the gold and silver plate, not leaving a single piece behind them. At this sight he was quite in despair. 'Oh, Heavens!' he exclaimed, 'I am undone without the chance of redress or recovery! What will my friends say? And what excuse can I make to them, when I have to tell them the thieves have broken open my house, and robbed me of everything they had so generously lent me? How can I ever compensate them for the loss they have suffered through me? And what can have become of Schemselnihar and the Prince of Persia? This affair will make a great noise, and it must certainly reach the ears of the caliph. He will hear of this meeting, and I shall be the victim of his rage.' The slave, who was very much attached to his master, tried to console him. He said, 'O master, with regard to Schemselnihar, there is no doubt but that the robbers would be content with despoiling her of her valuables. You may be assured she will return to her palace with her slaves; and the Prince of Persia has probably fared no worse. You have every reason, therefore, to hope that the caliph will remain in total ignorance of this adventure. As for the loss which your friends have suffered, it is a misfortune you cannot help, nor can you be said to have caused it. They know very well that the robbers are here in great numbers, and that they have had the boldness to pillage not only the houses I have mentioned to you, but many others belonging to the principal noblemen of the court. It is also well known that, in spite of the orders which have been issued to seize these miscreants, not one of them has hitherto been taken, notwithstanding all the exertions and diligence that have been used. Even after you have made every recompense to your friends, by paying them the full value of the things you have been robbed of, thanks be to Allah you will still have a tolerable fortune remaining.'

"While they were waiting for daylight the jeweller made the slave mend the door of the house that had been forced, as well as he could. He then went back with his slave to the abode he commonly lived in, and during his walk he made the most melancholy reflections. He said to himself: 'Alas! Ebn Thaher has been wiser than I; he has foreseen this misfortune, into which I have blindly run headlong. Would to Heaven I had never meddled in this unfortunate business, which may perhaps cost me my life.'

"With the returning daylight the report that his house had been broken open and pillaged spread through the city, and in consequence a great number of the jeweller's friends and neighbours assembled. The greater number came under the pretext of expressing their sorrow for this accident, but really only to hear the particulars of the affair. He did not forget to thank them for the kindness of their inquiries; and he had at least the consolation of finding that no one mentioned either the Prince of Persia or Schemselnihar, and this led him to hope that they had either returned home or had retired to some place of safety.

"When the jeweller was again alone his people served up a repast; but he could not eat anything. It was about mid-day, when one of his slaves came and informed him there was a man at the door, a stranger, who said he wanted to speak with him. As the jeweller did not wish to admit an unknown man into his house, he rose up and went to speak to him at the door. His visitor said: 'Although you do not know me, I am not unacquainted with you, and I am come to you upon a most important affair.' On hearing these words the jeweller requested him to come into the house. 'By no means,' replied the stranger; 'I must request you to take the trouble to go with me to your other house.' 'How came you to know,' asked the jeweller, 'that I have any house besides this?' The stranger replied, 'I am very well aware of that, and therefore you have only to follow me, and fear nothing: I have something to communicate to you that will give you pleasure.' The jeweller then went with him; but informed him by the way in what manner his house had been robbed the day before, and that it was not in a state for the reception of visitors.

"When they had arrived opposite to the house, and the stranger perceived that the door was broken, he said to the jeweller, 'I see, indeed, that you have spoken the truth; I will conduct you to a place where we shall be better accommodated.' When he had said this, they continued walking on, nor did they stop during the remainder of the day. Fatigued with the distance they had come, vexed at seeing night so near at hand, and wondering at the stranger's obstinate silence respecting the place they were going to, the jeweller began to lose all his patience; but at length they arrived at an open place, which led down to the Tigris. When they had come to the banks of that river they embarked in a small boat, and passed over to the other side. The stranger then conducted the jeweller down

THE JEWELLER AND HIS STRANGE VISITOR.

a long street, where he had never before been; and after passing through a great number of unfrequented lanes, he stopped at a door, which he opened. He desired the jeweller to go in, and following, shut the door after him, and fastened it with a large iron bar. He then conducted his guest into an apartment where there were ten other men, as completely unknown to the jeweller as the one who had brought him there.

"These ten men received the jeweller without much ceremony. They desired him to sit down, and he complied. He had, indeed, great occasion for repose, for he was not only fatigued and out of breath from his long walk, but the alarm which had seized him when he found himself with strangers under such novel circumstances was so great that he was hardly able to stand. As they only waited for the chief before they went to supper, the meal was served up when he made his appearance. The men first washed their hands, and compelled the jeweller to do the same; they then made him sit down at table with them. After supper was over they asked him if he was aware with whom he was conversing. The jeweller answered that he knew them not, nor did he even know either the quarter of the city or the place he was in. They said: 'Relate to us, then, your adventure of last night, and do not conceal anything from us.' The jeweller was much astonished at this demand, and answered, 'O my masters, I doubt not you are already acquainted with it.' 'True,' replied they, 'the young man and young lady who were with you yesterday evening have related it to us; but we wish nevertheless to know it from your own lips.'

"This was quite enough to make the jeweller understand that he was now speaking to the very robbers who had broken open and pillaged his house. 'Masters,' said he, 'I am in great distress about that young man and that young lady. Can you give me any information concerning them?' They answered: 'Do not fear on their account; they are in a place of safety, and are quite well.' Thereupon they pointed out two small apartments to the jeweller, and they assured him the persons in question were there. 'They informed us,' added the strangers, 'that you were the only person who is acquainted with their affairs, and interested about them. As soon as we knew that we took all possible care of them on your account. So far from having made use of the least violence towards them, we have, on the contrary, done them every service in our power, and not one of us has attempted to treat them ill; we assure you also of the same fair usage, and you may place the fullest confidence in us.'

"Encouraged by this speech, and delighted to find that Schemselnihar and the Prince of Persia were in safety, at least with respect to their lives and persons, the jeweller endeavoured to engage the robbers still further in their service. He praised and flattered them, and returned them a thousand thanks. He said to them: "I confess, my friends, that I have not the honour of knowing you; but it is a very great happiness to me to find that you are not unacquainted with me, and I cannot sufficiently thank you for the gratification you have afforded me by making yourselves known. Not to speak of the great humanity and kindness of this action, I see very clearly that it is only among men like you that a secret can be faithfully kept, where there is any danger of a discovery to be dreaded; and if there be any enterprise of a nature more than usually difficult, you well know how to carry it through, by your alacrity, your courage, and your intrepidity. Relying upon these qualifications, which appear so brilliantly in you, I shall make no difficulty in relating my history, and also that of the two persons whom you found at my house, with all the distinctness and truth you can require.'

"After the jeweller had taken all these precautions to interest the robbers in everything he was going to reveal to them, he gave them a complete detail, without omitting a single circumstance, of the attachment and adventures of the Prince of Persia and Schemselnihar, from the very beginning till the time of the meeting he had procured them at his house.

"The robbers were in the greatest astonishment at what they heard. 'What!' they cried, when the jeweller had concluded his narration, 'is it possible that this young man is the illustrious Ali Ebn Becar, Prince of Persia, and this lady the beautiful and celebrated Schemselnihar?' The jeweller swore that he had told them nothing but the strict and literal truth, and added, that they ought not to think it strange that persons of such exalted rank as Schemselnihar and Ali Ebn Becar should be unwilling to make themselves known.

"Upon this assurance the robbers all went, one after the other, and threw themselves at the feet of Schemselnihar and the Prince of Persia, entreating their pardon, and protesting that nothing of what had happened should have taken place if they had known the rank of the guests before they broke open the jeweller's house. They added: 'We will now endeavour to make some reparation for the fault we have committed.' They then returned to the jeweller, and said: 'We are very sorry that we are unable to restore everything we have taken from you, as some part of it is no longer at our disposal; we beg that you will, therefore, be satisfied with the plate and silver articles, which shall be immediately given up to you.'

"The jeweller thought himself very fortunate to regain what the robbers promised to give. They accordingly restored to him the articles in question, and then they requested the Prince of Persia and Schemselnihar to come, and informed them and the jeweller that they were ready to conduct them back to a certain place, from whence each might return to his own house; but before they did this they wished to bind each of their prisoners by an oath not to betray them. The Prince of Persia, Schemselnihar, and the jeweller, all said they were ready to pledge their word; and added, that if the robbers particularly wished it, they would swear solemnly to preserve the whole transaction a most profound secret. Upon this, perfectly satisfied with their oath, the robbers went out with them.

"As they were going along, the jeweller, who felt much disturbed at not seeing either the confidante or the other two slaves, went up to Schemselnihar, and requested her to inform him if she knew what was become of them. She replied: 'I know nothing about them; all that I can tell you is, that they carried us with them from your house, that we were taken across the river, and at last brought to the house where you found us.'

"This was all the conversation which the jeweller had with Schemselnihar. They then suffered themselves, together with the prince, to be escorted by the robbers, and they soon came to the side of the river. The robbers immediately took a boat, embarked with them, and landed them on the opposite bank.

"At the instant when the Prince of Persia, Schemselnihar, and the jeweller were stepping ashore, they heard a great noise. It was caused by the horse patrol, who came towards them, and arrived the moment after they had landed, and while the robbers were rowing back to the other side with all their strength.

"The officer of the guard demanded of the prince, Schemselnihar, and the jeweller, where they were coming from at that late hour, and who they were. As they were all in a state of considerable alarm, and therefore fearful of saying anything that might lead them into difficulties, they remained silent. It was, however, absolutely necessary to make some answer; and the jeweller took upon himself to reply, as he was not quite so disturbed as his companions. 'My lord,' he replied, 'let me assure you, in the first place, that we are people of character, who live in the city. The men who are in the boat from which we have just landed are robbers, who last night broke open the house where we were. They despoiled it of everything, and carried us away with them. Ever since our capture we made use of every means in our power, by persuasions and entreaties, to procure our liberty, and have at last succeeded, and in consequence of this they brought us to this spot. Nay, they even did more—they restored to us a part of the plunder they had taken, and we now have it with us.' He then showed the officer the parcel of plate the robbers had returned to him.

"The commander of the patrol was by no means satisfied with this answer of the jeweller's. He went up to him and to the Prince of Persia, and said to them, looking in their faces, 'Tell me the strict truth; who is this lady? How came you acquainted with her, and in what quarter of the city do you live?'

"These questions very much embarrassed them, and they knew not what answer to make. Schemselnihar, however, came to their assistance. She took the officer aside, and had no sooner spoken to him, than he got off his horse, and showed her every mark of great respect and honour. He directly ordered some of his attendants to bring two boats.

"When these were brought, the officer requested Schemselnihar to embark in one, while the prince and the jeweller went into the other. Two of the officer's attendants were also placed in each, with orders to conduct the passengers wherever they wished to go. The two boats then began to steer each a different course: and we will now only follow that in which the Prince of Persia and the jeweller had embarked.

"In order to save the persons whom the officer had ordered to conduct them home some trouble, the prince told them he would take the jeweller home with him, and told them of the part of the city in which he lived. Upon this information the attendants rowed the boat towards the shore close to the caliph's palace. The Prince of Persia and the jeweller were in the greatest possible alarm, although they durst not betray their fears. Notwithstanding that they had heard the order which the officer had given, they nevertheless were fully convinced that they were going to be taken to the guard-house for the night, and that they should be brought before the caliph in the morning.

"This was, however, by no means the intention of their conductors; for as soon as they had landed, as they themselves were obliged to return to their party, they transferred their passengers to an officer belonging to the caliph's guard, who sent two soldiers with them to attend them by land to the Prince of Persia's house, which was at a considerable distance from the river. They at length arrived there, so worn out with toil and fatigue that they could scarcely move.

"In addition to this great weariness, the Prince of Persia felt so much grieved at the unfortunate and disastrous interruption he and Schemselnihar had experienced, and which seemed for ever to shut out all hope of another interview, that when he threw himself down on the sofa he absolutely fainted. While most of his people were employed in assisting to recover him, the rest surrounded the jeweller, and requested him to inform them what had happened to the prince, whose absence had occasioned them the greatest anxiety.

"The jeweller, who took good care to reveal to them nothing they ought not to know, told them that the adventure was a very extraordinary one; but that he had not then sufficient leisure to give them the particulars, but advised them to turn their attention to assisting their master. The prince fortunately at this moment recovered his senses, and those persons, therefore, who had so recently asked the questions, retired to a distance, and showed the greatest respect; and at the same time evinced much joy that his fainting fit had lasted but a short time.

"Although the Prince of Persia had recovered his consciousness, he remained in such a weak state that he could not open his lips to speak a word. He answered only by signs, even when his relations spoke to him. He continued in the same condition till the next morning, when the jeweller took his leave of him. The prince answered his farewell only by a glance of his eye; at the same moment he took the jeweller by the hand; and as he observed that he was encumbered with the bundle of plate which the robbers had returned to him, he made a sign to one of his attendants to accompany the jeweller, and carry it home for him.

"The jeweller's return had been expected by his family with the greatest impatience during the whole of the day on which he had gone out with the man who had called to inquire for him. Who this man could be they did not know; and when the time by which the jeweller ought to have returned had elapsed, they were convinced some accident even worse than the robbery had happened to him. His wife, his children, and servants were all in the greatest alarm, and were in tears when he arrived. Their joy at seeing him was great for the moment, but it was soon succeeded by pain and regret at finding him so much altered during his short absence. The excessive fatigue of the preceding day, succeeded by a long night passed in sleeplessness and in the midst of alarms, were the causes of this change; and many of his people, for a moment, hardly knew him again. As he felt himself very much weakened, he remained two whole days at home without once stirring out. During that time he saw only his most intimate friends, whom he had ordered to be admitted.

"On the third day, the jeweller, who felt his strength partly re-established, thought that a walk in the open air would contribute to his recovery. He went, therefore, to the shop of a rich merchant, with whom he had been upon a friendly footing for some length of time. As he rose to take his leave and go away, he perceived a female, who made him a sign; and he instantly recognised her as the confidential slave of Schemselnihar. Her appearance confounded him with such a mixture of joy and alarm, that he went out of the shop without returning her greeting. She, however, followed him, as he was convinced she would do, for the place they were then in was not proper for conversation. As he walked rather quickly, the confidential slave could not overtake him, and therefore from time to time called out to him to stop. He heard her distinctly, but, after what

LANDING FROM THE BOAT.

had happened to him, he did not choose to speak to her in public, through the dread of giving rise to suspicion that he had any acquaintance with Schemselnihar. For it was very well known throughout Bagdad that this slave belonged to the favourite, who employed her upon every occasion. The jeweller continued to walk rapidly on, till he came to a mosque, which was but little frequented, and where he knew there would not be any one at that time of the day. The slave followed him into the mosque, and they had there an opportunity for a long conversation without any danger of interruption.

"The jeweller and the confidante of Schemselnihar felt great pleasure in seeing each other again after the singular adventure with the robbers, and after the fear each had felt for the other, not to mention the alarm they had endured on their own account. The jeweller wished the confidential slave to inform him, in the first instance, by what means she and her two companions had been able to make their escape, and if she had gained any intelligence of Schemselnihar since he had seen her. The confidante herself, however, was so very eager to learn what had happened to him since their unexpected separation, that he was obliged to satisfy her curiosity. 'This,' said he, when he had finished his story, 'is all that you wish to know from me; now, therefore, I beg of you, tell me in your turn what I desire to know.'

"The slave of Schemselnihar replied: 'As soon as I saw the robbers make their appearance, I took them for some soldiers belonging to the caliph's guard, imagining that the caliph had been informed of Schemselnihar's expedition, and that he had sent them with orders to kill her, the Prince of Persia, and all of us. I therefore instantly ran up to the terrace on the top of your house, while the robbers went into the apartment where the prince and Schemselnihar were sitting; the other two slaves also made haste to follow my example. We hastened away, stepping from the terrace of one house to that of another, till we came to a habitation belonging to some people of good character, who received us with great kindness, and under whose protection we passed the night.

"'The next morning, after thanking the master of the house for the favour he had done us, we returned to Schemselnihar's palace. When we arrived we were in the greatest anxiety and alarm; and felt the more distressed, as we were entirely ignorant of the destiny of these two unfortunate lovers. The other female attendants of Schemselnihar were much surprised at seeing us return without their mistress. We told them, as we had previously agreed between ourselves to do, that we had left her at the house of a lady who was one of her friends, and that she would send for us again to accompany her home when she intended to return. With this excuse they were quite satisfied.

"'You may imagine that I passed the day in the greatest uneasiness. When night came on, I opened the small private gate, and saw a boat upon the canal that branched off from the river and terminated at the gate. I called out to the boatman, and begged him to row up and down by the banks of the river, and look if he could not see a lady; and, if he met with one, to bring her over.

"'The two slaves were with me, and as much distressed as myself. We waited till midnight in expectation of his return. Then the same boat came back with two other men in it, and a woman, who was lying down in the stern. When the boat reached the shore, the two men assisted the lady to rise, and she landed. I immediately discovered her to be Schemselnihar; and my joy at seeing and finding her again was greater than I can possibly express to you. I instantly gave her my hand to assist her in getting out of the boat. Indeed, she had no little need of my assistance; for she was so agitated she could scarcely stand. As soon as she was on shore, she whispered in my ear, and in a tone which bore witness to her sufferings, desired me to go and get a purse containing a thousand pieces of gold, and give it to the two soldiers who accompanied her. I then entrusted her to the two slaves to help her along, and charging the soldiers to wait a moment, I ran for the purse, and returned with it almost instantly. I gave it to them, paid the boatman, and then shut the gate.

"'I soon overtook Schemselnihar, who had not yet reached her apartment. We lost no time in undressing and putting her to bed, where she continued all night in such a state that we thought her soul was on the eve of quitting its habitation.

"'The next day her other attendants expressed a great desire to see her; but I told them she had returned home very much fatigued, and had great need of repose to recruit her strength. In the meantime the other two slaves and myself afforded her all the assistance and comfort we could impart, and which she could possibly expect from our zeal. At first she seemed determined not to eat anything; and we should have despaired of her life, if we had not perceived that the wine which we gave her, from time to time, very much supported and strengthened her. At length, by means of our repeated entreaties, and even prayers, we prevailed on her to eat something.

"'As soon as I saw that she was able to speak without injury to herself (for she had hitherto done nothing but shed tears, intermingled with dismal groans), I requested her to do me the favour of informing me by what fortunate accident she had escaped from the power of the robbers. 'Why do you ask me,' she replied, with a profound sigh, 'to recall to my recollection a subject that causes me so much affliction? Would to Heaven the robbers had taken my life, instead of preserving me. My woes would then have been at an end; but now my sufferings will, I know, long continue to torment me.'

"'O lady,' I answered, 'I beg of you not to refuse my request. You cannot be ignorant that the unhappy sometimes derive a degree of consolation when they open their hearts by relating even their worst misfortunes. My request, then, will be of service to you, if you will have the goodness to comply.'

"'Listen, then,' she replied, 'to a narrative of the most distressing circumstances that could possibly happen to any one so much in love as I am, and one who had almost dared to hope for happiness in her love. When I saw the robbers enter each with a sabre in one hand and a poniard in the other, I concluded the very last moment of my existence was at hand, and that the Prince of Persia was in equal danger. I did not indeed lament my own death. I felt a kind of satisfaction in the reflection that we should die together. But instead of instantly falling upon us, and plunging their weapons in our hearts, as I fully expected they would have done, two of the robbers stood by us to guard us, while the others were engaged in packing up whatever they could find in the room where we were, and in the other apartments. When they had finished their preparations, and had taken all the plunder upon their shoulders, they went out, and made us go with them.

"'While we were on the way, one of those who accompanied us demanded our names. I told him that I was a dancing woman. He asked the same question of the prince, who replied that he was a citizen.

"'When we arrived at the robbers' dwelling we experienced new alarms. They collected round me, and, after examining my dress and the valuable jewels with which I was adorned, they seemed very much to doubt the truth of my assertion. 'A dancing girl,' they said, 'is not likely to be dressed as you are. Tell us truly what is your name and rank.'

"'As they found I was not inclined to give them any answer, they put the same question to the Prince of Persia. 'Inform us,' they cried, 'who you are. We can easily see that you are not a common citizen, as you wish us to believe by your former answer.' But the prince gave them no greater satisfaction than I had done. He only told them that, in order to amuse himself, he had come on a visit to a certain jeweller, whose name he mentioned, and that the house, where they found us, belonged to him.

"'One of the robbers, who seemed to have some authority among them, cried out, 'I know that jeweller, and I am under some obligations to him, although he is not perhaps aware of it: I know also that he has another house. To-morrow I will make it my business to bring him hither, and we will not release you till we know from him who you are. In the meantime be assured that no harm shall happen to you.'

"'The jeweller was brought here the next day, and as he thought to oblige us (and in fact he did so), he informed the robbers precisely who we were. They immediately came and begged my pardon, and I believe they likewise asked pardon of the prince, who was in another apartment. They protested to me, at the same time, that if they had known that the house where they discovered us belonged to the jeweller, they would not have broken it open. They then took us all three, and conducted us to the banks of the Tigris; they put us on board a boat, in which we crossed the water; but at the very instant when we landed, a party of the guard came up to us on horseback.

"'I took the commander aside, told him my name, and informed him that on the evening before, as I was visiting one of my friends, some robbers met and stopped me, and then carried me with them; and that only on my informing them who I was would they release me. I also added that on my account they set at liberty the two persons the officer then saw with me, because I assured them I knew who they were. The officer of the guard immediately alighted, as a mark of respect to me, and after expressing his joy at being able to oblige me in anything, he ordered two boats to come to the shore. Into one of these he put me and two of his people, whom you saw, and who escorted me hither. The Prince of Persia and the jeweller embarked in the other, with two more of his soldiers, who were charged to conduct them safely home.

"'I hope,' added Schemselnihar, with her eyes swimming in tears, as she finished this account, 'that no fresh misfortune has happened to them since our separation; and I firmly believe that the grief and distress of the prince is equal to mine. The jeweller who has served us with so much zeal and affection deserves at least to be reimbursed for the loss he has sustained through his friendship for us; do not, therefore, fail to take to him to-morrow morning, on my behalf, two purses with a thousand pieces of gold in each; and at the same time ask some intelligence from him concerning the Prince of Persia.'

"'When my good mistress had concluded her story, I endeavoured, when she thus ordered me to obtain some information of the Prince of Persia, to persuade her to make use of every method to conquer her feelings; urging the greatness of the danger she had just encountered, and from which she had escaped only as it were by a miracle. But she replied: 'Answer me not, but do as I command you.'

"'I was therefore obliged to hold my tongue, and immediately set out to obey her orders. I first proceeded to your house, where I did not find you; and feeling quite uncertain whether I should meet with you at the place where they told me you were gone, I was on the point of going to the Prince of Persia's house, but was afraid to make the attempt. I left the two purses, as I came hither, with a person of my acquaintance. If you will wait here a little while for me, I will go and bring them.'

"The confidential slave then departed, but returned almost directly to the mosque where she had left the jeweller. She gave him the two purses, and said: 'Take these, and make compensation to your friends for their losses.' 'There is much more in those purses,' replied the jeweller, 'than is necessary to reimburse my friends; but I dare not refuse the present which so kind and generous a lady wishes to make to the humblest of her slaves. I beg you to assure her that I shall for ever preserve the recollection of her kindness.' He then made an agreement with the confidential slave, that she should come and inquire for him at the house where she at first met him whenever she had anything to communicate from Schemselnihar, or wished to gain any intelligence of the Prince of Persia. And thus they separated.

"The jeweller returned home very well satisfied with the ample sum of money he had received for the purpose of making up the loss his friends had suffered, and greatly relieved in his mind; for he was sure no person in Bagdad knew that the Prince of Persia and Schemselnihar had been discovered in his other house, which had been robbed. He had certainly acquainted the robbers themselves with that fact; but he was tolerably secure that they would keep the secret for their own sakes. Besides, he thought they did not mix sufficiently with the world to cause him any danger, even if they did divulge it. The next morning he saw the friends to whom he was under obligations for the loan of the furniture, and he had no difficulty in giving them perfect satisfaction; and, after paying all expenses, he had enough money remaining to furnish his other house again very handsomely. He did this, and sent some of his domestics to inhabit it. Thus employed, he quite forgot the danger which he had so lately escaped; and in the evening he went to visit the Prince of Persia.

"The officers and attendants of the prince who received him told him he came very opportunely; for that since he left him the prince had fallen into a state which alarmed them for his life, and that they had not been able to get him to speak a single word. They introduced him into the young man's chamber without making the least noise; and he found the prince lying in his bed with his eyes shut, and in a state which very much excited his compassion. He saluted the sufferer, took him by the hand, and exhorted him to keep up his spirits.

"The Prince of Persia perceived that it was the jeweller who spoke to him. He opened his eyes, and gave him a look which plainly evinced how much he was afflicted, and how much more he now suffered than when he first saw Schemselnihar. He took the jeweller's hand, and pressed it, as a mark of his friendship; and at the same time said, in a very feeble tone of voice, how much he felt himself obliged to this friendly visitor for the trouble he took in coming to see so unfortunate and wretched a being as himself.

"The jeweller replied: 'I beseech you, prince, do not speak of the obligations you are under to me. I wish most earnestly that the good offices which I endeavour to do

THE PRINCE AND THE JEWELLER.

you were more effectual. Let us think only of your health. From the state in which I find you, I fear you suffer yourself to be too much depressed, and that you do not take so much nourishment as is absolutely necessary.'

"The attendants who were in waiting seized this opportunity to inform the jeweller that they had tried every method in their power to induce their master to eat something, but all their efforts had been in vain; and that the prince had taken nothing for a very long time. This compelled the jeweller to request that the Prince of Persia would suffer his servants to bring him something to eat; and, after much entreaty, he at length obtained his consent.

"When, through the persuasions of the jeweller, the Prince of Persia had eaten much more heartily than he had hitherto done, he ordered his people to retire, that he might be alone with his visitor. And after the attendants were gone out, he addressed these words to the jeweller: 'In addition to the misfortune which overwhelms me, I feel very great pain for the loss that you have suffered from your regard to me; and it is but just that I should think of some means to recompense you. But in the first place, after requesting you most earnestly to pardon me, I entreat you to inform me if you have heard how Schemselnihar fared after I was compelled to separate from her.'

"As the jeweller had before received the whole account from Schemselnihar's confidential slave, he now related what he knew of her arrival at her own palace, and described the state she had been in from that moment; and added that she now felt herself so much better as to be able to send her confidante to get some intelligence of him.

"To this speech of the jeweller's the prince answered only by his sighs and tears. He then made an effort to get up: he called his people, and went himself to the room where he kept his valuables, and ordered it to be opened. He then caused his servants to bring forth many pieces of rich furniture and plate, and ordered that these should be carried to the jeweller's.

"The jeweller wished to decline accepting the present of the Prince of Persia; but, although he represented to him that Schemselnihar had already sent him much more than sufficient to replace everything that his friends had lost, the prince nevertheless would be obeyed. Therefore the only thing the jeweller could do was to express how much he felt confused at the prince's great liberality, and to assure him he could not be sufficiently thankful for all this kindness. He then wished to take his leave, but the prince desired him to remain; and they passed the greater part of the night in conversation.

"Before he went away the next morning the jeweller saw the prince again, and the latter made him sit down near him. He said: 'You know very well that there must be an end to everything. All the aspirations and wishes of a lover are centred in her he loves: if he once loses sight of this hope, it is certain that he can no longer wish to live. You must be well convinced that I am in a very miserable situation. Twice, when I have flattered myself that a happier time was beginning to dawn upon me, have I been torn from the object of my affections in the most cruel manner. I have now, therefore, only to think of death. I would myself put an end to my very unhappy existence, but that my religion prevents my becoming a self-murderer. I feel, however, that I have no occasion to hasten the approach of death, for I am well convinced I shall not have long to await its arrival.' After these words the prince was silent, and then gave full vent to his tears; nor did he endeavour to suppress his sighs and lamentations.

"The jeweller, who knew of no better method to pursue to lead the prince away from this hopeless and despairing train of thought than by recalling Schemselnihar to his recollection and holding out some slight ray of hope, told him that he was afraid the confidential slave was already come, and he declared that it would not therefore be right if he delayed his departure. To this the prince replied: 'I permit you to go; but, if you see the slave, I entreat you to urge her to assure Schemselnihar that if I die, as I really expect very soon to be the case, I shall adore her with my last breath, nor will my affection cease even in the tomb.'

"The jeweller then returned home, and remained there in hopes that the slave would soon make her appearance. She arrived a few hours afterwards; but she came bathed in tears and in the greatest disorder. Alarmed at seeing her in this condition, the jeweller eagerly inquired what was the matter.

"The slave replied, 'We are all undone! Schemselnihar, the Prince of Persia, you, myself—every one of us! Listen to the terrible news I heard yesterday, when I left you and returned to the palace.

"'For some fault or other, Schemselnihar had ordered one of the two slaves who were with us at your house to be punished. Enraged at this ill-treatment, and finding a door of the palace open, the slave ran out, and we doubt not that she went and told everything to one of the eunuchs of our guard, with whom she has stayed ever since.

"'Nor is this all: the other slave, her companion, has also fled, and has taken refuge in the palace of the caliph, to whom we have every reason to believe she has revealed all she knew; and what confirms this opinion is, that the caliph this morning sent twenty eunuchs to bring Schemselnihar to his palace. I found an opportunity to steal away, and to come and give you information of all this. I know not what has happened, but, I conjecture, nothing good. Whatever it may be, I entreat you to keep our secret.'

"The slave then added, that she thought it would be proper that the jeweller should go, without losing a moment, to the Prince of Persia, and inform him of the whole affair, that he might hold himself in readiness for any turn events might take; and also to admonish him that he might be true and faithful to the common cause. She said not another word, but suddenly went away, without even waiting for an answer.

"And what, indeed, could the jeweller have answered in the confusion of mind this speech produced? He stood motionless, like a person stunned by a blow. He was nevertheless aware that the business required decisive and prompt measures. Therefore he made all the haste he could to the Prince of Persia's house, and as soon as he saw him he accosted him with an air that instantly showed he was the messenger of bad news. 'Prince,' he cried, 'arm yourself with patience, constancy, and courage; prepare for the most dreadful shock you have ever encountered.'

"The prince replied: 'Tell me briefly what has happened, and do not thus keep me in suspense. I am ready to die, if it must be so.'

"The jeweller then related to him everything he had heard from the confidential slave, and said, moreover, 'You see that your destruction is inevitable. Arise up, then, and endeavour to escape without a moment's delay. Time is precious. You ought not to expose yourself to the anger of the caliph, still less to confess anything, although you should be in the midst of torments.'

"Very little more would at this moment have actually killed the prince, so much was he already broken down by affliction, sorrow, and terror. He at length recollected himself, and inquired of the jeweller what plan he advised him to pursue in these critical circumstances, when prompt decision was so absolutely necessary. 'There is nothing that you can do,' replied the jeweller, 'but to get on horseback as soon as possible, take the road to Anbar, and endeavour to reach that place before daylight to-morrow. Let as many of your people as you think necessary accompany you, and some good horses, and suffer me to escape with you.'

"The Prince of Persia, who knew of no better method to pursue, gave orders to have such preparations made as were quite necessary for the journey. He carried some money and jewels with him, and after taking leave of his mother, set out, and made all speed to get at a distance from Bagdad, in company with the jeweller and the attendants he had chosen.

"They travelled for the rest of the day, and most of the following night, without making any stay on the road, till about two or three hours before day, when the fatigue of the long journey, and the absolute exhaustion of their horses, compelled them to alight, and take some little repose.

"They had hardly had time to breathe before they were attacked by a considerable troop of robbers. They defended themselves for some time with the greatest courage, till all the attendants of the prince were killed; the prince and the jeweller then laid down their arms, and yielded at discretion. The robbers spared their lives; but, after taking their horses and baggage, they rifled and even stripped the persons of their victims, and then retreating with their plunder, left them where they were.

"Directly the robbers were at some distance, the prince said to the jeweller, who was in the utmost distress, 'What think you of our late adventure, and of the state in which we are now left? Do you not rather wish that I had remained at Bagdad, and had there awaited my death, in what manner soever it might have come upon me?' The jeweller replied: 'O prince, we must submit to the decrees of Allah. It is His will that we should suffer affliction upon affliction. It is not for us to murmur, but we must receive everything, whether good or evil, from His hands with absolute submission. However, we must not stay here; let us push on, and endeavour to find out some place where we shall be able to obtain relief in our misfortune.'

"But the Prince of Persia cried, 'Leave me here, and suffer me to end my days in this place; for of what consequence is it where I breathe my last? Perhaps at this very instant, while we are speaking, Schemselnihar is suffering death, and it is not my wish, nor is it even in my power, to outlive her.' At length, with much entreaty, the jeweller persuaded him to move. They walked on for a long time, and at last came to a mosque, which they found open. They went in, and passed the rest of the night there.

"At daybreak only one person came into the mosque. He said his prayers, and when he had finished them was retiring, when he perceived the Prince of Persia and the jeweller, who were seated in a corner. He went up to them, saluted them with great civility, and thus accosted them: 'O my masters, if I may judge from your appearance, you seem to me to be strangers.' The jeweller, who took upon himself to be spokesman, answered: 'You are not wrong in your supposition. Last night, in coming along the road from Bagdad, we were robbed, as you may conjecture, if you notice the state we are in; and we have great need of assistance, but know not to whom to apply.' The stranger replied: 'If you will take the trouble to come to my house, I will very readily give you all the help and assistance in my power.'

"On hearing this obliging offer, the jeweller turned towards the Prince of Persia, and whispered in his ear that he thought this man did not know either of them, and that if they waited until other people came, they might be recognised. He continued: 'We ought not, therefore, to refuse the favour which this good man offers us.' The prince replied: 'It is for you to decide; I agree to everything you wish.'

"As the stranger saw the prince and the jeweller consulting together, he thought that they were reluctant to accept the proposal he had made them. He asked, therefore, on what they had determined. 'We are ready to follow you,' replied the jeweller; 'but what causes us the greatest distress is that we are almost naked, and we feel ashamed to appear in this condition.' Fortunately the man had sufficient clothes about him to be able to bestow enough on them to cover them while they followed him to his house. So soon as they arrived at his dwelling, their host ordered a dress to be brought for each of them; and, as he naturally imagined that they were greatly in want of food, and would be much more at ease if they ate by themselves, he sent a female slave with a variety of dishes. But they could scarcely touch anything, particularly the prince, who was reduced to such a languid state, and was so worn out, that the jeweller felt considerable alarm for his life.

"Their host visited them several times during the day, and he left them early in the evening, as he knew they stood in great need of repose. But the jeweller was obliged to call him again almost immediately, to help him in attending on the Prince of Persia, who, he thought, was very near death. The jeweller perceived that the prince's respiration was difficult and rapid, and from this he judged he had only a few moments to live. He went up to him, and then the prince said: 'As you must perceive, the moment is at hand when I must die, and I am well satisfied that you should be present to witness the last sigh I shall ever breathe. I resign my life with much satisfaction, nor need I inform you why I do so: you know the reason. All the regret I feel is because I do not breathe my last in the arms of my dearest mother, who has always shown the tenderest affection for me, and to whom, I trust, I have always shown due love and respect. She will grieve much that she had not the melancholy consolation of closing my eyes, or even of burying me with her own hands. I beg of you to tell her that I have also grieved for this; and request her, on my behalf, to have my body conveyed to Bagdad, that she may water my grave with her tears, and may afford me the benefit of her prayers.' He did not forget the master of the house where he lay. He thanked him for the generous reception he had afforded to two strangers; and after requesting that his body might be allowed to remain in the house till his own attendants came to bury it, he expired.

"The day after the death of the Prince of Persia, the jeweller took advantage of a large caravan which happened at that time to be going to Bagdad; travelling with these, he arrived there in safety. He immediately went to his own house, and, after changing his dress, he proceeded to the abode of the deceased Prince of Persia, where the inmates were all much alarmed at not seeing the prince himself come back with him. He desired the attendants to inform the prince's mother that he wished to speak to her; and it was not long before they introduced him into a hall, where she sat surrounded by many of her women. 'O my princess,' said the jeweller on entering, but in a tone and manner that evidently proved he was the messenger of ill news, 'may Allah preserve you, and heap abundance of His favours upon you. But I need not remind you that the Almighty disposes of mortals according to His will.'

"The lady gave the jeweller no time to say more. She at once exclaimed, 'You come to announce the death of my son!' and immediately began to utter the most melancholy cries, and her women joined in their lamentations; and this pitiful sight renewed the grief of the jeweller, and made his tears flow afresh. She continued to suffer these torments,

THE JEWELLER RETURNING HOME.

and remained a long time overcome by affliction before she would permit the jeweller to go on with what he had to say. At length she suppressed for a time her lamentations and tears, and begged him to continue his account, and not to conceal any circumstance of this melancholy history. He complied with her desire; and when he had concluded, she asked him if the prince her son had not charged him with any particular message to give to her while he was lying at the point of death. He assured her that Ali Ebn Becar only expressed the greatest regret at breathing his last at a distance from his affectionate mother, and that the only thing he wished was that she would take care and have his body brought to Bagdad. Accordingly, early the next morning the princess set out, accompanied by all her women and a great number of slaves.

"When the jeweller, who had been detained by the mother of the Prince of Persia, had seen her take her departure, he returned home, his eyes cast down, and in the most melancholy state of mind; for he himself deeply regretted the death of so accomplished and amiable a prince, who had thus perished in the very flower of his age.

"As he was walking along meditating thus within himself, a woman came up, and stopped directly before him. He raised his eyes, and perceived the confidential slave of Schemselnihar. She was dressed in mourning, and her eyes were bathed in tears. This sight renewed the jeweller's grief to a great degree; and without even opening his lips to speak to her, he continued walking on till he came to his own house. The confidential slave followed him, and entered the house at the same time with him.

"They sat down, and the jeweller began the conversation by asking her, with a deep sigh, if she had already been informed of the death of the Prince of Persia, and if it was for him that she wept. 'Alas, no!' she answered: 'is that amiable prince dead? Truly he has not long survived his adorable Schemselnihar. O happy spirits!' added she, alluding to the departed lovers, 'in whatever place you may be, you are now much to be envied; for in future you may love each other without any obstacle. Your life here was an invincible hindrance to your wishes, and Heaven has freed you from them that your souls may be united.'

"The jeweller, who had not heard until now of the death of Schemselnihar, and who had not noticed the circumstance of the confidential slave's being in mourning, felt an additional pang when he learnt this intelligence. 'Schemselnihar dead too!' he exclaimed. 'Is she no more?' 'Alas! it is too true,' replied the slave, with a fresh burst of tears. 'It is for her that I wear this mourning garb. The circumstances attending her death are singular; and it is proper that you should be made acquainted with them. But before I relate these events to you, I beg of you to inform me of everything relative to the death of the Prince of Persia, whose loss I shall continue all my life to lament, as I now mourn the death of my dear and amiable mistress Schemselnihar.'

"The jeweller related to the confidante all the circumstances she wished to know, and as soon as he had finished his account of what had passed, from the time when he last saw her, to the moment when the prince's mother began her journey for the purpose of bringing her son's body to Bagdad, she went on as follows: 'I have already told you how the caliph sent for Schemselnihar to his own palace. It was true, as we had reason to believe, that the caliph had been informed of the attachment and meeting between Schemselnihar and the Prince of Persia. The two slaves, whom he had separately questioned, had betrayed the secret. You may perhaps imagine that he was in great anger against the favourite, and that he showed strong feelings of jealousy and revenge against the Prince of Persia. But this was not the case. He thought not for an instant about his rival. He only pitied Schemselnihar. Nay, it is thought he attributed what had happened only to himself, and to the permission which he had given her to go freely about the city unaccompanied by any eunuchs. At least we cannot form any other conjecture from the extraordinary manner in which he conducted himself towards her from first to last. You shall hear what he did.

"'The caliph received Schemselnihar with an open countenance. He perceived the traces of the grief with which she was overwhelmed, but which nevertheless did not in the least diminish her beauty, for she appeared before him without any symptoms either of surprise or fear. He addressed her thus, with his usual air of kindness: 'Schemselnihar, I cannot bear that you should appear before me with a countenance so strongly impressed by sorrow. You know with what ardour I have always loved you: you must be convinced of my sincerity by all the proofs I have given you of it. I am not changed, for I still love you more than ever. You have some enemies, and these enemies have spread evil reports of the manner in which you conduct yourself; but everything that they can say of you makes not the least impression upon my mind. Therefore drive away this melancholy, and dispose yourself to receive me this evening with as amusing and diverting an entertainment as you used to provide.' He continued to say many other obliging things to her, and then conducted her into a magnificent apartment near his own, where her requested her to await his return.

"'The wretched Schemselnihar was sensibly affected at these kindly proofs of the caliph's concern for her person; but the more she felt herself under obligations to him, the more was her bosom penetrated with grief at being separated, perhaps for ever, from the Prince of Persia, without whom she was convinced she could not exist.'

"The confidential slave continued her narrative thus: 'This interview between the caliph and Schemselnihar took place while I was coming to speak to you; and I learnt the particulars of it from my companions who were present. But as soon as I left you I hastened back to Schemselnihar, and was witness to what passed in the evening. I found my mistress in the apartment I have mentioned; and as she was very sure I came from your house, she desired me to approach her; and, without being overheard by any one, she said to me: 'I am much obliged to you for the service you have just now rendered me. I feel that it will be the last I shall require at your hands.' This was all she said; and it was not a place where I could say anything that might afford her consolation.

"'The caliph in the evening entered Schemselnihar's palace to the sound of instruments, which were touched by the females belonging to the favourite; and a banquet was served on his arrival. The caliph took Schemselnihar by the hand, and made her sit near him upon a sofa. The effort she made in complying with this invitation had such a violent effect upon her feelings, that in a few moments after we saw her expire. She was in fact hardly seated before she fell back dead. The caliph thought that she had only fainted, nor had we at first any other idea. We rendered her every assistance in our power; but she never breathed again. This, then, was the manner in which this great misfortune came upon us.

"'The caliph honoured her with tears, which he was unable to restrain; and before he retired to his apartment, he gave orders that all the musical instruments should be instantly destroyed, and his command was at once obeyed. I remained near the body the whole night, and washed and prepared it for burial with my own hands, almost bathing it with my tears. It was the next day interred, by the command of the caliph, in a magnificent tomb, which he had once ordered to be built in a spot that Schemselnihar had herself chosen. And since you have told me the body of the Prince of Persia is to be brought to Bagdad, I am determined that it shall be placed in the same tomb with that of the favourite.'

"The jeweller was very much astonished at the resolution thus announced by Schemselnihar's attendant. 'You do not surely recollect,' said he, 'that the caliph will never allow it.' 'You may believe the thing impossible,' she replied, 'but I assure you it is not. And you will agree with me, when I have informed you that the caliph has given freedom to all the slaves that belonged to Schemselnihar, with a pension to each of them sufficient to support herself; and that he has moreover appointed me to take care of and watch the favourite's tomb, with a considerable salary both for its repair and my subsistence. Besides, the caliph, who, as I have told you, is not ignorant of the attachment of Schemselnihar and the Prince of Persia, and who is not now offended or hurt at it, will never have any objection to this proceeding.' In answer to this the jeweller had nothing to say; he only requested the confidante to conduct him to the tomb, that he might offer up his prayers there. When he arrived he was greatly surprised at seeing a crowd of people of both sexes, who had collected from all parts of Bagdad. He could not even get near the tomb, and could only pray at some distance. When he had finished his prayers, he said to the confidante in a satisfied tone of voice, 'I do not now think it impossible to accomplish what you so affectionately planned. We need only make known the various facts we know concerning the favourite and the Prince of Persia, and particularly the death of the latter, which took place almost at the instant when Schemselnihar died.' Before his body arrived all Bagdad agreed in demanding that the two thus strangely associated should not be separated in the grave. The scheme succeeded, and on the day in which it was known the body would arrive, a multitude of people went out as far as twenty miles to meet it.

"The confidential slave waited at the gate of the city, where she presented herself before the mother of the Prince of Persia, and requested her, in the name of all the inhabitants, who so ardently desired it, to allow the bodies of the two lovers, whose hearts had formed but one from the commencement of their attachment to the last moment of their lives, to be united in the tomb. The lady agreed to the proposal; and the body was carried to the tomb of Schemselnihar, followed by an immense number of people of all ranks; and it was placed by her side. From that time all the inhabitants of Bagdad, and even strangers from all parts of the world where Mussulmen are known, have never ceased to feel a great veneration for that tomb, and many go to offer up their prayers before it.

"This, O great king," said Scheherazade, "is what I had to relate to your majesty concerning the history of the beautiful Schemselnihar, the favourite of the Caliph Haroun Alraschid, and the amiable Aboulhassan Ali Ebn Becar, Prince of Persia."

When Dinarzade perceived that the sultana her sister had concluded her story, she thanked her most heartily for the pleasure she had afforded her by the recital of that interesting history. Scheherazade replied, "If the sultan would suffer me to live till to-morrow, I would relate to him the history of Prince Camaralzaman, which he would find still more agreeable than that of Schemselnihar." She was then silent; and Shahriar, who could not yet determine to give orders for her death, deferred passing the sentence, that he might listen to the new story which the sultana began to relate on the following night.

## THE HISTORY OF CAMARALZAMAN, PRINCE OF THE ISLE OF THE CHILDREN OF KHALEDAN, AND OF BADOURA, PRINCESS OF CHINA.

KING, about twenty days' sail from the coast of Persia, there is in the open sea an island, which is called the Isle of the Children of Khaledan. This island is divided into several large provinces, containing many large, flourishing, and well-peopled towns, and it forms altogether a very powerful kingdom. It was formerly governed by a king named Schahzaman, who, as was the custom, had four wives, all daughters of kings, and sixty concubines.

"Schahzaman esteemed himself the happiest sovereign on the whole face of the earth, for his reign had been a scene of prosperity and peace. One thing only diminished his happiness; he was already far advanced in years, and he had no children, notwithstanding the great number of his wives. He could not account in any way for this circumstance; and in the moments of his affliction he considered it the greatest misfortune that could befall him, to die without leaving one of his descendants as successor to the throne. For a considerable time he concealed the tormenting anxiety that preyed upon him, and he suffered the more from endeavouring to assume an air of cheerfulness. At length he broke silence; and one day, having complained of his misfortune in the bitterest terms of sorrow, in a private conversation he had with his grand vizier, he asked the minister if he knew of any means to remedy so great an evil.

"The wise vizier replied: 'If what your majesty requires depended on the common application of human wisdom, you might soon have the gratification you so ardently desire; but I confess my experience and knowledge are not equal to solve the question you ask. To Allah alone you must apply in such cases: in the midst of our prosperity, which often makes us forget what we owe Him, He sometimes mortifies us by refusing one of our wishes, that we may turn our thoughts to Him, acknowledge His universal power, and ask of Him that which we cannot obtain but at His hand. You have amongst your subjects some men who devote themselves to the particular profession of knowing and serving Him, and who lead a life of penance and hardship for the love of Him: my advice is that your majesty should bestow alms on them, and request them to join their prayers

BIRTH OF CAMARALZAMAN.

to yours; perhaps, among the great number of these men, one may be sufficiently pure and acceptable to the Almighty to obtain from Him the completion of your wishes.'

"The king approved this advice, and thanked his grand vizier for it. He ordered alms to a considerable amount to be presented to each of these communities of people consecrated to prayer; he then desired the rulers of their houses to come to him; and after regaling them with a repast suited to their frugal manner of living, he declared his intention, and begged them to impart what he told them to the communities who were under their authority.

"Schahzaman obtained from heaven what he so much desired. One of his wives gave him hopes of an heir, and, at the expiration of nine months, presented him with a son. To testify his gratitude he sent fresh presents to the communities of devout Mussulmen, presents which were worthy of his dignity and greatness; and the birth of the prince was celebrated by public rejoicings for a whole week, not only in his capital, but throughout his extensive dominions. The young prince was brought to his father immediately on his birth, and Schahzaman thought him so very beautiful that he gave him the name of Camaralzaman, which means the Moon of the Age.

"Prince Camaralzaman was educated with all possible care, and when he reached a proper age, the sultan awarded him a prudent governor and able preceptors. These persons, who were distinguished by their superior understandings, found in the prince a boy of a docile and intelligent disposition, capable of receiving all the instruction they wished to give him for the forming of his morals and the cultivation of his mind in such acquirements as a prince in his situation ought to possess. As he advanced in years he learned various exercises with a great degree of facility, and acquitted himself with so much grace and address, that he charmed every beholder, but more particularly the sultan his father.

"When the prince had attained the age of fifteen years, Schahzaman, who loved him with the greatest tenderness, and gave him every day new and stronger proofs of his affection, conceived the design of bestowing on him the most striking mark of his regard, by descending from the throne himself, and raising his son to that distinguished position. He communicated his intention to his grand vizier, and added these words: 'I fear that in the idleness of youth my son will lose not only those advantages which nature has bestowed on him, but also those he has successfully acquired by the good education I have given him. As I have now reached an age which makes me think of retiring from the world, I have almost resolved to give up the government to him, and to pass the rest of my days in retirement, satisfied to see him reign. I have laboured a long time, and I now want repose.'

"The grand vizier would not at that time represent to the sultan all the reasons that might dissuade him from putting this design into execution; on the contrary, he appeared to concur in his master's wish. He replied: 'O my lord, the prince is still too young, I think, to be entrusted at so early a period with a duty so heavy as that of governing a powerful state. Your majesty is fearful that he may be corrupted, if he be suffered to lead a life of inactivity and indolence. Your fears are reasonable; but to remedy that evil, would it not in your opinion be more proper to marry him first? Marriage is likely to render his affections steady, and to prevent him from plunging into dissipation; besides this, your majesty might give him admission to your councils, so that he might learn by degrees to sustain with dignity the brilliancy and weight of your crown; and when he is found sufficiently qualified, and you by experience consider him equal to the undertaking, you might still resign the crown in his favour.'

"Schahzaman thought this advice from his prime minister very reasonable and prudent; he therefore summoned his son, Prince Camaralzaman, to attend him as soon as the grand vizier had taken his leave.

"The prince, who hitherto had only seen the sultan at certain stated hours, without requiring a summons, was rather surprised at this order. Therefore, instead of presenting himself before him in his usual frank manner, he saluted his father with great respect, and stopped as soon as he was in his presence, fixing his eyes on the ground, and assuming an appearance of deep humility.

"The sultan perceived the reserve of the prince, and said to him, in a tone intended to inspire him with confidence, 'My son, do you know on what account I sent for you?' 'My lord,' replied the prince, modestly, 'Allah alone can penetrate into the recesses of the heart: I shall rejoice greatly to learn the reason from your majesty's lips. 'The sultan resumed: 'I sent for you to let you know that I wish you to marry. What do you think of my proposal?'

"Prince Camaralzaman heard these words with great concern. He was quite disconcerted; a burning flush arose on his face; and he knew not how to reply. After some moments passed in silence, he said, 'O my lord, I entreat you to pardon me if I appear confused at the declaration your majesty has just made; I did not expect such a proposal at my very youthful age. I do not even know whether I shall ever be able to submit myself to the bonds of marriage, for I am well aware of the embarrassment and trouble occasioned by women; moreover, I have frequently read in our authors of their arts, their cunning, and their perfidy. Perhaps I may not always retain this opinion; at any rate, I feel that I should require a considerable length of time to induce me to agree to the design your majesty proposes to carry out.'

"This answer of the prince's greatly afflicted the sultan his father. The monarch felt real grief at finding his son entertained so great a repugnance to matrimony. He did not, however, think proper to treat his answer as disobedience, or to employ the authority of a parent. He contented himself with saying: 'I will not use any undue influence over you on this subject. I give you time to think of it, and to consider that a prince, destined as you are to govern a large kingdom, ought in the first place to turn his thoughts to provide a successor in his own family. In giving yourself this satisfaction you will afford me very great joy; for I desire to see myself live again in you and in the children who are to prolong my race.'

"Schahzaman said no more to Prince Camaralzaman. He allowed him free entrance to the councils of state, and in every other respect gave him reason to be satisfied with the affection and confidence he showed towards him. At the expiration of a year he took the prince aside, and said: 'Well, my son, have you remembered to reflect on the design I formed last year of finding a wife for you? Will you still refuse me the joy I should experience from your compliance with my wishes, and do you intend that I should die without experiencing this satisfaction?'

"The prince appeared less disconcerted than on the former occasion, and did not long hesitate to reply with firmness in these words: 'I have not, my lord, omitted to reflect upon the subject; I gave it all the attention which it deserves; but, after having maturely considered it, I am confirmed in my resolution to live without binding myself in the chains of marriage. The numberless evils which women have from time immemorial been the occasion of in the world, and of which I have been well informed by our histories, and the daily accounts I hear of their cunning and malice, are the reasons which determine me never to have any connection with them. Therefore your majesty will pardon me, if I venture to assure you that any arguments you may use to endeavour to persuade me to marry will be fruitless.' He ceased speaking, and left the presence of the sultan in an abrupt manner, without even waiting for his father's answer.

"Any monarch but Schahzaman would with difficulty have restrained himself if his son had made him a reply so rude and stubborn as this answer of Camaralzaman's, and would have ordered him some punishment; but the king tenderly loved his son, and wished to employ every gentle means of persuasion before he had recourse to more rigid means. He communicated the new cause of sorrow, which Camaralzaman had given to him, to his prime minister. He said: 'I have followed your advice, but my son is still more averse to matrimony than he was the first time I spoke to him on the subject; and he explained himself in such a determined manner that I needed all my reason and moderation to restrain my anger. Men who pray as ardently as I did that they may have children are madmen and fools, who seek to deprive themselves of that repose and quiet which they might otherwise tranquilly enjoy. Tell me, I entreat you, by what means I can reclaim a mind so rebellious to my desires.'

"The grand vizier answered: 'O my lord, a great many things are accomplished by the help of patience. Perhaps this may not be a difficulty that can be conquered by such means; but your majesty will not have to reproach yourself with being too precipitate, if you consent to allow the prince another year to alter his determination. If during this interval he does not return to his duty, you will have a much greater satisfaction in the consciousness of having employed no method but that of paternal kindness, to obtain his obedience. If, on the contrary, he persists in his obstinacy, then, when the year is expired, I think your majesty will be fully justified in declaring to him, before the whole council, that the good of the state requires his marriage. It is not possible that he should be wanting in respect towards you before an assembly of enlightened and celebrated men whose deliberations you honour with your presence.'

"The sultan, who so passionately and ardently wished to see his son married that a year's delay appeared ages to him, was very reluctant to consent to wait so much longer. But he was persuaded by the arguments of the grand vizier, which he could neither contradict nor disapprove.

"When the prime minister had retired, the Sultan Schahzaman went to the apartment of the mother of Prince Camaralzaman, to whom he had long since imparted the ardent desire he had of marrying his son. When he had related to her the painful disappointment he had just met with in this second refusal, and also the indulgence he still intended to grant the prince by the advice of his grand vizier, 'O lady,' he added, 'I know that he has more confidence in you than in me, that you converse with him, and that he listens to you with great respect; I entreat you, therefore, to take an opportunity to speak to him seriously on this subject; and to make him sensible that, if he persists in his obstinacy, he will oblige me at last to have recourse to extremities, which I should be sorry to adopt, and which would make him repent of his disobedience.'

"Fatima (for this was the name of the prince's mother) informed Camaralzaman, the next time she had a conversation with him, that she had made been acquainted with his fresh refusal to marry, which he had testified to the sultan, and expressed herself much chagrined that the prince had given his father so great a cause for anger. 'O lady,' Camaralzaman replied, 'do not, I entreat you, renew my grief on this affair; I fear that, in my present state of mind, I might be guilty of saying something disrespectful to you.' Fatima knew by this answer that it would be worse than useless to continue the subject; she therefore let it rest for the time.

"Some time after this Fatima thought she had met with an opportunity of renewing the conversation, and with more prospect of success in obtaining a hearing. She said: 'My son, if it be not painful to you, pray tell me what are the reasons that have given you so great an aversion to marriage. If you have none stronger than the art and wickedness of women, believe me, you could not have chosen a plea more weak or unreasonable. I will not undertake the defence of artful or cunning women, for that there are numbers of that description I am well persuaded; but it is the most flagrant injustice to accuse the whole sex of this vice. Surely, my son, you do not form your opinion from the few examples which your books mention, of women who have, I confess, occasioned great disorder and confusion in the world! I will not attempt to justify such characters; but why, on the other hand, do you not remark also the many monarchs, sultans, and lesser princes, whose tyranny, barbarity, and cruelty excite the deepest horror, and are related in those histories, which I have read as well as yourself. For one woman who has been guilty of the crimes which frighten you, you will find a thousand men who have been barbarians and tyrants. And do you think the poor women who have the misfortune to be married to these wretches, and who are perhaps good and prudent wives, can be very happy?'

"'O lady!' replied Camaralzaman, 'I do not doubt that there are in the world a great number of prudent, good, and virtuous women, of gentle dispositions and good morals. Would to Allah all women resembled you! But what deters me is the doubtful choice a man is obliged to make when he marries; or rather the fact, that he is often deprived of the liberty of making that choice himself.'

"He continued in these words: 'Let us suppose that I had consented to contract a marriage, as the sultan my father so impatiently wishes me to do; whom would he give me for my wife? A princess, in all probability, whom he would demand of some neighbouring prince, and who would, no doubt, think us greatly honoured. Handsome or ugly, she must be received; but even supposing she excels every other princess in beauty, who can ensure that her mind will be equal to her appearance? that she will be gentle, obliging, affable, and engaging? that her conversation will not be frivolous? that she will not always be discoursing of dress, of ornaments, of good looks, and a thousand other trifles which must create contempt in a man of good sense? In a word, that she is not proud, haughty, irascible, disdainful—one who will ruin a whole kingdom by her frivolous expenses in dresses, jewels, trinkets, or in tasteless and empty magnificence?

THE SULTAN ENTREATS FATIMA TO INDUCE CAMARALZAMAN TO MARRY.

"'Now you see, madam, if we consider only this one point, how many things there are to give rise to my antipathy to matrimony. But even if this princess be so perfect and so accomplished that she is irreproachable on all these points, I have a great number of reasons still stronger than any I have expressed to make me continue in the same opinion, and adhere to my resolution.'

"Fatima hereupon exclaimed: 'How, my son, can you add more objections to those you have already stated? I was going to answer you, and refute your arguments with one word.' The prince answered: 'Lady, I beg you to speak: I shall probably have some reply to make to your answers.'

"'I was going to say, my son,' resumed Fatima, 'that it is easy for a prince who should have the misfortune to marry a princess of the character you describe, to leave her, and also to adopt such measures as might prevent her from ruining the state.'

"'Then, madam,' said Prince Camaralzaman, 'do you not consider what a cruel mortification it must be to a prince to be under the necessity of having recourse to such extremities? Is it not much better both for his peace of mind and for his reputation that he should not expose himself to it?'

"But Fatima still persisted, and said, 'My son, from the way in which you treat this matter, I conclude that you intend to be the last king of the race from which you are descended, and which has so gloriously filled the throne of the Island of the Children of Khaledan.'

"The prince retorted: 'Madam, I have no wish to survive the king my father. Even should I die before him, he ought not to be surprised, since there are many examples of children dying before their parents. But it is always glorious for a race of kings to end with a prince so worthy of being a sovereign as I should endeavour to make myself, by imitating my predecessors, and him with whom the line began.'

"After this, Fatima frequently had conversations on the same subject with the prince her son; and she left no means untried which might in any way eradicate his aversion to the married state. But he confuted all the reasons she could produce by others equally strong, to which she knew not what to reply; and he remained unshaken in his determination.

"The year passed, and to the great regret of the Sultan Schahzaman, Prince Camaralzaman did not show the least appearance of having altered his sentiments. At length one day when the grand council met, and the first vizier, the lesser viziers, the principal officers of the crown, and the generals of the army were assembled, the sultan thus addressed the prince: 'It is now a long time, my son, since I expressed to you the anxious desire I have of seeing you married; and I expected that you would accede to the wishes of a father who required of you nothing but what was reasonable. The long resistance you have made has entirely exhausted my patience; and I now repeat to you, in the presence of my council, the request I once made in private. By persisting in your refusal you not only disoblige your father, but the welfare of my dominions requires your compliance; and all these nobles join with me in requesting it. Declare your sentiments in their presence, that from the answer you make me I may know what measures to adopt.'

"Prince Camaralzaman answered with so little respect, or rather with so much warmth, that the sultan, justly irritated by this behaviour of his son before the full council, exclaimed, 'How, undutiful son! have you the insolence to speak thus to your father and your sultan?' He immediately ordered some of the officers who were present to take the prince into their custody, and to carry him to an ancient tower which had long stood empty and neglected. Here the prince was confined, with only a bed and very little furniture, a few books, and one slave to attend him.

"Satisfied with the permission which was granted him to amuse himself with his books, Prince Camaralzaman bore his imprisonment with sufficient patience. Towards evening he washed himself, said his prayers, and, after reading some chapters in the Koran as tranquilly as if he had been in his own apartment in the palace of the sultan, he lay down without extinguishing his lamp, which he left by his bedside, and fell asleep.

"In this tower there was a well, which during the day formed a retreat of a fairy called Maimounè, the daughter of Damriat, the king or chief of a legion of genii. It was about midnight when Maimounè lightly darted to the top of the well, to prepare for her nightly excursion, as was her usual custom, and to wander about the world, wherever curiosity might lead her. She was much surprised to see a light in the chamber of Camaralzaman. She entered it; and without being stopped by the slave who was stationed at the door, she approached the bed, the magnificence of which attracted her attention. But her surprise was much increased at observing that somebody was lying asleep in the bed.

"Camaralzaman's face was half concealed by the covering as he lay. Maimounè raised the covering a little, and beheld the handsomest youth she had ever seen in any part of the world, through the whole of which she had passed in her travels. She said to herself, 'What brilliancy, or rather what a world of beauty must those eyes display, when no longer concealed, as they now are, by their well-formed eyelids! What cause can he have given to be treated in a manner so unworthy of his rank?' For she had already heard of the prince's disgrace, and did not doubt that this was he.

"Maimounè could not cease admiring the beauty of Prince Camaralzaman; at length, however, she kissed him gently on the cheek, and on the middle of his forehead, without waking him; then she replaced the covering as it was before, and flew away through the air. When she had risen very high towards the middle region of the clouds, she suddenly heard the sound of wings; and curiosity induced her to fly to the quarter from whence it came. On approaching she found that the noise had been occasioned by a genie—one of those rebellious spirits who rose up against the Almighty. Maimounè was, on the contrary, one of those angels whom the great Solomon had compelled to acknowledge his power.

"This genie, who was named Danhasch, and who was the son of Schamhourasch, recognised Maimounè, and was greatly terrified at meeting with her. He knew that she possessed considerable superiority over him, in consequence of her submission to Allah. He would fain, therefore, have avoided this encounter, but he found he was so close to her that he must either risk a battle or submit.

"Danhasch was the first to speak. He said, in a supplicating tone: 'Good Maimounè, swear to me, by the great name of Allah, that you will not hurt me, and I promise you, on my part, not to annoy you.'

"'Cursed genie,' cried Maimounè, 'what harm canst thou do me? I fear thee not. But I will grant thee this favour, and I take the oath thou requirest. Now tell me whence thou comest, what thou hast seen, and what thou hast done this night?' 'Beautiful lady,' replied Danhasch, 'we meet opportunely, for I can tell you wonderful news. Since you wish it, I will inform you that I come from the extremity of China, where its coast overlooks the farthest islands of this hemisphere. But, charming Maimounè,' cried Danhasch, interrupting himself, for he trembled with fear in the presence of this fairy, and had some difficulty in speaking before her, 'you promise at least to forgive me, and to permit me to depart, when I shall have satisfied your curiosity?'

"'Proceed with thy story, thou wretch,' replied Maimounè, 'and fear nothing. Dost thou think I am as perfidious as thyself, and that I can break the terrible oath I have taken? But take heed to thyself that thou relatest nothing but what is true; otherwise I will cut thy wings and treat thee as thou deservest.'

"Danhasch felt a little relief by these words of Maimounè's. He continued: 'O beauteous lady, I will tell you nothing but what is very true; have but the goodness to listen to me. The country of China, from whence I come, is one of the largest and most powerful kingdoms in the world, and attached to it are the most extreme isles of this hemisphere, of which I spoke just now. The present king is named Gaiour. He has an only daughter, the most beautiful creature that ever was beheld on earth since this world has been a world. Neither you, nor I, nor the genii to whom you or those to whom I belong, nor all mankind together, can find words sufficiently expressive, or eloquence fiery enough, to convey the most distant idea of what she is in reality. Her hair is of a fine brown, and of such length that it reaches below her feet. It grows in such abundance that when she wears it in curls on her head it resembles a fine bunch of grapes, with berries of extraordinary size. Under her hair appears her well-formed forehead, as smooth as the finest polished mirror; her eyes are of a brilliant black, and full of fire; her nose is neither too long nor too short; her mouth small and tinted with vermillion; her teeth are like two rows of pearls, but surpass the finest of those gems in whiteness;

and when she opens her mouth to speak, she utters a sweet and agreeable voice, and expresses herself in words which prove the liveliness of her wit. The most beautiful alabaster is not whiter than her neck. In short, from this feeble sketch, you may easily suppose that there is not a more perfect beauty in the world.

"'A stranger who should behold the conduct towards her of the king her father would imagine, from the various proofs of affection he is continually giving her, that he is in love with her. The most tender lover was never known to do so much for the most beloved mistress as he has done for his daughter. The most violent jealousy never took such precautions as his love has caused him to take to render her inaccessible to every one, except the fortunate person who is destined to marry her; and that she might not feel the retreat irksome to which he has confined her, he has had seven palaces built for her, which surpass everything that was ever heard of in magnificence.

"'The first palace is built of rock crystal, the second of bronze, the third of the finest steel, the fourth of another kind of bronze, more precious than the first description or the steel, the fifth of loadstone, the sixth of silver, and the seventh of massive gold. The king has furnished these palaces in the most sumptuous style, each in a manner appropriate to the materials of which it is built. Nor has he forgotten to embellish the gardens which surround the castles with everything that can delight the senses—smooth lawns, or pastures enamelled with flowers; fountains, canals, cascades; groves thickly planted with trees, through whose deep shades the rays of the sun never penetrate; and each garden has its own peculiar arrangement. King Gaiour's paternal love alone has induced him to incur the enormous expense all this has occasioned.

"'The fame of this princess's incomparable beauty induced the most powerful of the neighbouring kings to send the most solemn embassies to demand her hand in marriage. The King of China received all their proposals with the same degree of ceremony; but as he had determined not to marry the princess except with her own entire consent, and as she did not approve of any of the offers made her, the ambassadors returned to their own countries with their mission unfulfilled; yet they were all highly gratified by the civilities and attentions they had received.

"'The princess spoke to the King of China in the following terms: 'O my lord, you wish to marry me, and you think by so doing to make me happy. I know your motive, and feel thankful to you for your kindness. But where should I find such gorgeous palaces and such delicious gardens as these that are mine in the territories of your majesty? Moreover, thanks to your goodness, I am under no restraint, and I receive the same honours that are paid to your own person. These are advantages which I should not enjoy in any other part of the world, to whatever prince I might be united. Husbands ever will be masters, and it is not in my nature to brook command.'

"'After several embassies had been sent away, one at last arrived from a king who was richer and more powerful than any who had before applied for the hand of Giaour's daughter. The King of China proposed this royal suitor to his daughter, and enlarged on all the advantages which would result from such an alliance. The princess entreated him to excuse her from obeying, urging the same reasons she had employed on former occasions.

"'Her father pressed her to accede; but instead of obeying, she forgot the respect due to the king, and angrily cried, 'O king, speak to me no more of this marriage, nor of any other; if you persist in your importunities I will plunge a dagger into my heart, and thus free myself from them.'

"'The King of China was extremely irritated against the princess, and he replied in these words: 'My daughter, you are mad, and I must treat you accordingly.' In fact, he had her confined in an apartment of one of his palaces, and allowed her only ten old women as associates and attendants, the principal of whom was her nurse. Then, that the neighbouring kings, who had sent embassies to request her hand, might not cherish any further hopes of obtaining her, he despatched envoys to announce to them all her absolute repugnance to marriage. And as he supposed that his daughter had really lost her senses, he commanded the same envoys to make known in each court that, if there were any physician sufficiently skilful to restore her, he should receive the hand of the princess in marriage as a recompense.'

"The genie Danhasch proceeded in these words: 'Beautiful Maimounè, matters are at present in this state, and I do not fail to go regularly every day to contemplate this wonderful beauty, whom I should be loth to injure in the slighest degree, notwithstanding my natural malicious inclinations. I entreat you to come and see her: you will be well repaid for your pains. When you are convinced by your own eyes that I do not tell an untruth, I am sure you will thank me for having shown you a princess who has no equal in beauty. I am ready to conduct you to her, and you have only to command.'

"Instead of replying to Danhasch, Maimounè burst into a loud fit of laughter, which

HOW THE SLAVE PRESENTED HIMSELF BEFORE KING SCHAHZAMAN.

continued for some time, and which very much astonished the genie, who did not know to what cause to attribute it. At last, however, she composed herself, and said, 'Of a truth thou thinkest to impose on me. I thought thou wouldst have related to me something very surprising and extraordinary, and thou talkest to me only of a blear-eyed wench. Shame on thee! What wouldst thou say, thou wretch, if thou hadst seen the beautiful prince whom I have just been watching, and whom I esteem as he deserves? He indeed is a model of beauty. Thou wouldst run crazy for admiration of him.

"To this speech Danhasch replied: 'Amiable Maimounè, may I inquire who this prince can be of whom you speak?' 'Know,' said the fairy, 'that nearly the same thing has happened to him as to the princess of whom thou hast been talking. The king his father insisted that he should take a wife; and after long and repeated importunities, the prince has frankly declared that he would not agree to the proposal. For this reason he is at this moment imprisoned in an ancient tower, where I take up my abode, and where I have had an opportunity of admiring him.'

"'I will not absolutely contradict you,' resumed Danhasch, 'but, O my mistress, until I have seen your prince, you will give me leave to think that no mortal, either man or woman, can equal or even approach the beauty of my princess.' 'Peace, wretch!' replied Maimounè; 'I tell thee again that thou art wrong.' Danhasch hereupon said very humbly, 'I will not obstinately oppose you; the only means by which you can decide whether I speak truth or not, is that you accept the proposal I have made you to come and see my princess, and afterwards to show me your prince.' 'There is no occasion that I should take so much trouble,' said Maimoune, 'there is another method, by which we can both be satisfied; that is, to bring thy princess and place her beside my prince on his bed. We can then easily compare them with each other, and thus settle our dispute.'

"Danhasch consented to do as the fairy desired, and was going instantly to set off for China, but Maimounè stopped him, saying: 'Stay; come with me first, that I may show thee the tower whither thou art to bring thy princess.' They flew together to the tower; and when Maimounè had shown it to Danhasch, she said, 'Now go and bring thy princess; be quick, and thou wilt find me here. But listen: I intend thou shalt pay me a forfeit if my prince proves to be handsomer than thy princess. I also will pay thee one, if thy princess is the most beautiful.'

"Danhasch quitted the fairy, flew to China, and returned with inconceivable swiftness, bearing in his arms the beautiful princess fast asleep. Maimounè took her from his hands, and carried her into the chamber of Prince Camaralzaman, where she placed her on the bed by the prince's side.

"When the prince and princess were thus close to each other, a grand contest arose on the subject of their beauty between the genie and the fairy. They stood for some time admiring and comparing them in silence. Danhasch was the first to speak, and he addressed Maimounè in these words: 'Now I trust you are convinced; I told you that my princess was more beautiful than your prince. Have you still any doubt?'

"'How! any doubt?' cried Maimounè, 'yes, truly, I have great doubt. Thou must be blind not to see that my prince is infinitely superior to thy princess. She is beautiful, I confess; but be not over-hasty—compare them well one with the other, without prejudice, and then thou wilt see that I am right.'

"'Were I to compare them for ever,' Danhasch replied, 'I should not think otherwise than I think now. I saw at the first glance what I now see, and time would show me no more than what is now visible to my eyes. This, however, will not prevent me from believing your judgment rather than mine, charming Maimounè, if you wish it.' 'It shall not be so,' exclaimed the fairy; 'I will never suffer a cursed genie, such as thou art, to show me favour. I will submit the contest to an arbitrator, and if thou dost not consent, I shall win the cause by thy refusal.'

"Danhasch, who was ready to show any degree of complaisance to Maimounè, at once consented, and the fairy struck the ground with her foot. The earth opened, and instantly a hideous genie appeared. He was hunchbacked, lame, and blind with one eye; he had six horns on his head, and long crooked claws on his hands and feet. As soon as he had risen to the surface, and the ground had closed under him, he perceived Maimounè, and threw himself at her feet; and, kneeling on one knee, he asked in what his very humble services could be useful to her.

"'Rise, Caschcasch,' said Maimounè (for this was the name of the genie); 'I sent for you, that you might be judge in a dispute which has arisen between me and this cursed Danhasch. Cast your eye on that bed, and tell us, without favour, which appears to you the more beautiful, the young man or the young lady?'

"Caschcasch looked very attentively at the prince and princess, and showed every token of great surprise and admiration. After he had contemplated them very accurately for a long time, without being able to make up his mind, he said to Maimounè: 'O my mistress, I confess to you that I should deceive you and dishonour myself, if I were to tell you that I thought one of these persons more handsome than the other. The more I examine them, the more each seems to me to have separately that sovereign perfection of beauty which they jointly possess; and neither has the least defect from which we can assert the other to be free, and consequently superior. If, indeed, any difference can be found between them, there seems to be only one method of discovering that difference. And this method is, to wake them separately, and to agree that the person who feels for the other the most violent love, and proves it by the strongest and most ardent expressions, shall be considered in some point or other to be the less beautiful.'

"The proposal of Caschcasch was approved both by Maimounè and by Danhasch. Maimounè then transformed herself into a flea, and jumped upon the neck of Camaralzaman. She gave him so sharp a bite that he awoke, and put his hand to the place; but he caught nothing, for Maimounè, prepared for this movement, had jumped away, and, taking her original form, became invisible, while with the other two genii she stood by the bedside in order to watch what would happen.

"As he drew back his hand, the prince let it fall upon that of the Princess of China. He opened his eyes, and his looks expressed great surprise at finding a lady by his side, and one, too, who possessed such marvellous beauty. He lifted his head up and supported it on his elbow, in order the better to observe her. The youth of the princess, and her incomparable beauty, kindled in an instant a flame in his heart to which he had hitherto been a stranger, and excited a feeling which he had till now never experienced.

"A passion of the most animated kind now took possession of his soul; and he could not help exclaiming: 'What beauty! what charms! O my heart, my soul!' and thus saying, he kissed her forehead, her cheeks, and her lips, with so little precaution, that he must have broken her slumbers if she had not, through the enchantment of Danhasch, slept more soundly than usual.

"'How! my beautiful lady,' said the prince, 'will not these marks of the love of Camaralzaman disturb your repose? Whoever you may be, here is one not unworthy of your affection.' He was then going to wake her in good earnest; but he suddenly paused, exclaiming, 'There cannot be a doubt but that this is the princess to whom the sultan my father wished to marry me. He has been much to blame not to let me see her sooner. I should not then have offended him by my disobedience and my rude behaviour towards him in the council; and he would thus have spared himself the sorrow which I have caused him.' Prince Camaralzaman repented most heartily of the fault of which he had been guilty, and was again upon the point of waking the Princess of China, saying, 'Perhaps, indeed, the sultan my father wished to surprise me; and he has therefore sent this lady to ascertain whether I really have so great an aversion to marriage as I have always shown. Who knows if he may not have brought her here himself—and perhaps he is concealed somewhere in the room, in order to see how I conduct myself, and make me ashamed of my former delusion. This second fault would be much worse than my first; but I will at least claim this ring in remembrance of her.'

"The Princess of China had a very beautiful ring on her finger; and as the prince concluded his speech, he drew it quietly off, and put one of his own in its place. He then turned from the fair lady, and it was not long before, through the enchantment of the genie, he fell into as deep a sleep as that which had first held him.

"As soon as Prince Camaralzaman's eyes were completely closed, Danhasch, in his turn, transformed himself into a flea, and bit the princess directly under her lip. She awoke suddenly, and starting up, opened her eyes. Great was her astonishment at finding the prince sleeping beside her. From surprise she passed to admiration, and from admiration to joy, which became apparent as soon as she saw that her companion was a young, handsome, and agreeable man.

"She exclaimed: 'Are you the prince whom the king my father has destined for my husband? How unfortunate am I in not having known this before! I should then never have thought with aversion of a husband whom I now feel that I shall love with my whole soul. Awake, and arouse yourself; it ill becomes a husband to sleep thus soundly on the very first night of his nuptials.'

"So saying, the princess shook Prince Camaralzaman by the arm in so violent a manner, that he must have started up, if Maimounè had not at that instant made deeper his sleep by means of enchantment. The princess shook him in this manner several times; then, as she found she could not prevent him from sleeping, she called out, 'What can possibly have happened to you? What rival, jealous of our mutual happiness, has had recourse to magic, and thus thrown you into this marvellous fit of stupefaction, from which it seems almost impossible to rouse you?' She then took hold of his hand, and, tenderly kissing it, she perceived the ring which he had on his finger. It appeared so like her own that she felt convinced it was the same; and at the same moment she observed that she herself had on a ring which was strange to her. She could not comprehend how this exchange of rings had been effected; but she did not for an instant doubt that it was a sure proof of her marriage. Fatigued with the useless efforts she had made to wake the prince, and satisfied, as she thought, that he could not leave her, she cried, 'Since I am unable to awaken you from your sleep, I will continue no longer to attempt to interrupt it. We shall see each other again.' And kissing his cheek as she pronounced these words, she lay down, and in a short time fell asleep

"When Maimounè perceived that she might speak without danger of being heard by the Princess of China, she said to Danhasch: 'Well, wretch, hast thou observed, and art thou convinced that thy princess is less beautiful than my prince? Begone, I forgive thee the wager thou hast lost; but another time believe me when I assert anything.' Then turning towards Caschcasch, she added, 'As for you, I thank you. Do you and Danhasch take the princess, and carry her back to the palace whence he brought her.' Danhasch and Caschcasch executed the orders of Maimounè, while the latter retired to her well.

"When Prince Camaralzaman awoke the next morning, he looked on every side to see if the lady whom he had found by him in the night was still there; but when he perceived she was gone, he said to himself, 'It is as I suspected; the king my father wished to surprise me: I am, however, happy that I was aware of his intention.' He then called the slave, who was still asleep, and desired him to make haste and dress himself, but he did not say a word to him in explanation of the reason why he was in such a hurry. The slave brought a basin and water; the prince then washed himself, and, after saying his prayers, took a book and read for some time.

"After he had concluded his usual occupations, Prince Camaralzaman called the slave towards him, and said: 'Come here, and be sure you do not tell me a falsehood. Inform me how the lady who slept with me last night came here, and who brought her.'

"'O prince,' the slave replied, in the greatest astonishment, 'of what lady are you speaking?' 'Of her, I tell you,' answered the prince, 'who either came or was brought here, and who passed the night with me.' The slave returned: 'O prince, I swear to you that I know nothing about the matter. How could any lady possibly get in while I slept at the door?' 'Thou art a lying rascal!' cried the prince, 'and art in league with some one to vex and distress me.' So saying, he gave the slave a blow and knocked him down; then, after having trampled on him, he tied the rope of the well round his body, and let him down into it, and plunged him several times in the water, exclaiming, 'I will drown thee if thou dost not immediately acquaint me who the lady is, and who brought her hither.'

"The poor slave, who was in a sorry plight, half in and half out of the water, thought the prince had certainly lost his senses through grief, and that his only chance of safety lay in telling an untruth. So he cried, in a supplicating tone, 'O prince, grant me my life, I conjure you, and I promise to tell you exactly how the matter stands.'

"The prince drew the slave up to the surface, and commanded him to speak. When he was out of the well, 'O prince,' the slave said, trembling, 'you must be sensible that I cannot satisfy you in the state I am now in; allow me time to change my dress.' 'I grant it thee,' replied the prince · 'but make haste, and look that thou dost not disguise the truth from me.'

THE PRINCE PRESENTS THE RING TO KING SCHAHZAMAN.

"The slave went out, and, after fastening the door on the prince, he ran to the palace wet as he was. The king was engaged in conversation with his grand vizier, and was complaining of the restless night he had passed in consequence of his grief at the disobedience and ill-judged rashness of the prince his son in thus opposing his will.

"The minister endeavoured to console his master, and convince him that the prince, by his disrespectful behaviour, had justly merited the punishment he endured. 'O my lord,' said he, 'your majesty ought not to repent of having imprisoned him. If you will have the patience to suffer him to remain in confinement, you may be assured that he will lose this youthful impetuosity, and that he will at length be glad to perform whatever you may require of him.'

"The grand vizier had just uttered these words when the slave presented himself before King Schahzaman, and spoke the following words: 'O king, I am sorry to be obliged to announce to your majesty a piece of intelligence that will no doubt occasion you great sorrow. The prince insists on speaking of a lady who slept with him last night; and this, together with the manner in which he has treated me, as your majesty may perceive, too plainly proves that he is not in his senses.' He then gave an account of everything that Prince Camaralzaman had said, and of the violence he had been guilty of towards himself; and the scared manner in which he related this confirmed the truth of the account.

"The king, who was not prepared for this new affliction, exclaimed to the grand vizier, 'This is indeed a very distressing event, and one which does not justify the hopes you flattered me with just now. Go, lose not a moment, and examine yourself into the truth of this affair, and then come and inform me of what you discover.' The grand vizier immediately obeyed. When he entered the chamber of the prince, he found Camaralzaman seated with a book in his hand, which he was reading with apparent composure. He saluted the prince, and seating himself by his side, said: 'I am very angry with the slave who attends you, for having alarmed your father by the intelligence he has just now brought him.' 'What is this intelligence,' inquired the prince, 'that has occasioned my father so much alarm? I have also great reason to complain of my slave.'

"The vizier replied: 'O prince, Heaven forbid that what he has just said of you be true! The tranquil state in which I find you, and in which I pray that Allah may preserve you, convinces me there is no truth in his report.' 'Perhaps,' said the prince, 'he has not explained himself properly; but as you are here, I am glad to have an opportunity of asking you, who must know something about the matter, where the lady is who slept with me last night?'

"The grand vizier was quite astonished at this inquiry. He exclaimed: 'Prince, do not be surprised at the astonishment this question causes me. How can it be possible that any man whatever, much less any lady, could have penetrated in the night into this place, to which there is no other entrance but by the door? and even then, how could any one enter without trampling on your slave, who was guarding it? I entreat you to collect your thoughts, and I am convinced you will find that some dream has left a strong impression on your mind.'

"'I shall pay no attention to your arguments,' resumed the prince, in a loud and angry voice: 'I insist upon knowing what has become of this lady; I am in a position to make you obey me.' This firmness of speech and manner embarrassed the grand vizier inexpressibly, and he now only thought of the best means to extricate himself from the difficulty. He tried the prince with soft words, and asked him, in the most humble and conciliating manner, if he had himself seen the lady.

"Camaralzaman answered: 'Yes, indeed, I saw her, and soon perceived that you had placed her here with instructions to rouse my curiosity. She played the part you assigned her excellently well: she would not say a word, but pretended to sleep, and conveyed herself away as soon as I fell asleep again. You know all this, I doubt not: she has certainly given you an account of the whole transaction.' 'O prince,' cried the grand vizier, 'I swear to you that all you have been saying is a mystery to me, and that neither the king your father nor I sent you the lady you mention; we never had such an idea. Allow me once more to say, that this lady could only have appeared to you in a dream.'

"Then the prince cried out angrily, 'Hast thou, too, come hither to mock me, and to tell me that what I have seen was only a dream?' He then seized his visitor by the beard, and beat him most unmercifully, till his strength quite failed him. The poor grand vizier bore all this treatment from Prince Camaralzaman in a very resigned manner, merely saying to himself, 'Here am I, precisely in the same situation as the slave; happy shall I be, if, like him, I can escape from this great danger.' While the prince was still employed in beating him, he cried, 'I entreat you, prince, to listen to me for one moment.' The prince, tired of his own violence, suffered him to speak.

"The grand vizier said, as soon as he had liberty to speak: 'I own to you, prince, that your suspicions are not unfounded; but you know that a minister is compelled to execute the orders of the king his master. If you will have the goodness to suffer me to go, I am ready to take to the king your father any message with which you will entrust me.' The prince answered: 'I give you leave to go. Tell my father that I will marry the lady whom he sent or brought me, and who slept with me last night. Be speedy, and bring me the answer.' The grand vizier made a profound reverence on quitting the prince; but he hardly considered himself safe till he was out of the tower, and had fastened the door. He presented himself before King Schahzaman with an air of sorrow, which alarmed that monarch, who at once asked in what condition he had found his son. 'O my lord,' replied the vizier, 'what the slave related to your majesty is but too true.' He then gave the king an account of the conversation he had had with Camaralzaman, of the angry violence of the prince when he attempted to convince him that the lady he spoke of could not possibly have slept with him, of the cruel treatment inflicted upon himself, and of the excuse by which he had escaped from the prince's fury.

"Schahzaman, who was the more grieved at this report, inasmuch as he had always loved the prince with the greatest tenderness, wished to investigate the truth of it himself: he went at once to the tower, and took the grand vizier with him. Prince Camaralzaman received his father with the greatest respect. The king sat down, and after requesting the prince to sit next him, he asked his son many questions, to which the young man replied with perfect good sense; so that from time to time he looked at the vizier, as if to say that the prince his son was not deranged in his intellects, as the minister had asserted, and that the prince's conduct must have been misrepresented.

"At length the king mentioned the lady. He said: 'My son, I beg you to tell me who this lady is, who, as I hear, slept with you last night.' 'My father,' replied Camaralzaman, 'I entreat your majesty not to add to the vexation I have already had to endure on this subject; rather do me the favour to bestow her on me in marriage. Whatever aversion I may hitherto have evinced against women, this young and beautiful lady has so charmed me, that I feel no difficulty in confessing I have been wrong. I am ready to receive her from your hands, and to prove my gratitude in every possible way.'

"King Schahzaman was thunderstruck on receiving from the prince an answer which appeared to him so inconsistent with the good sense his son had shown in his former replies. He said: 'O my son, you speak to me in a way that astonishes me beyond measure. I swear to you by the crown which is to adorn your brow when I shall be no more, that I know nothing of the lady of whom you speak. If any one has been with you I know nothing of her visit; but how is it possible that a lady should have penetrated into this tower without my consent? As to what my grand vizier said to you, he only invented a story to appease your anger. This supposed visit must have been a dream: recollect yourself I conjure you, and take some pains to ascertain the truth.'

"'My lord,' resumed the prince, 'I should be for ever unworthy of your majesty's goodness, if I refused to give credence to the solemn assurance you have given me; but I request you to have the patience to listen to me, and then judge if what I shall have the honour of relating to you can be a dream.'

"Prince Camaralzaman then told the king his father how he had suddenly awoke in the night. He gave him a glowing description of the beauty and charms of the lady he had found by his side, confessed the love which had instantaneously been kindled in his breast, and related all his fruitless endeavours to awaken the lady. He did not even conceal what had made him wake; and added that he fell asleep again after he had exchanged his ring for that of the lady. When he concluded, he took the ring from his finger, and presented it to the king, saying, 'O my lord, you know the appearance of my ring, for you have seen it several times. After this, I hope you will be convinced that I have not lost my senses, as others would fain persuade you.'

"The king was so fully convinced of the truth of what the prince had related to him, that he had nothing to reply. His astonishment, moreover, was so excessive that he remained a considerable time incapable of answering a single word.

"The prince took advantage of these moments of silent amazement to say to the king: 'O my father, the passion I feel for this charming lady, whose precious image is so deeply engraven on my heart, has already risen to so violent a pitch that I am sure I have not strength to endure it. I humbly supplicate you to feel compassion for the state I am in, and to procure me unspeakable happiness by bestowing her on me, and allowing me to call her mine.'

"To this Schahzaman answered: 'After what I have now heard, my son, and after the evidence of this ring, I can no longer doubt the reality of your love, or question that you did absolutely see the lady whose appearance you have described. Would to Allah I knew her! Your wish should be gratified this very day, and I should be the happiest of fathers. But where am I to seek her? How and by what means could she enter here without my consent or knowledge? Why did she come only to sleep with you, to show you her beauty, to inspire you with love while she slept, and disappear as soon as you fell asleep again? I cannot comprehend this strange adventure; and, unless Heaven assists us, it will perhaps bring both you and me to the grave.' The good king then took the prince by the hand, and added, in a mournful voice, 'Come, my son, let us go and mingle our lamentations together; you, for loving without hope; I, for seeing your affliction without possessing the means of relieving it.'

"Schahzaman took the prince out of his prison, and led him to the palace, where the prince, quite in despair at feeling so violent a passion for an unknown lady, at once fell into a grievous sickness. The king shut himself up from all society for several days, and sat weeping with his son, desisting entirely from attending to the usual concerns of his kingdom.

"His prime minister, who was the only man to whom he did not refuse admission to his presence, came one day to represent to him that his whole court, as well as the people generally, began to murmur at not seeing their monarch administering justice, as it had been his daily custom to do; and the vizier added that no one could calculate the discontents and disorders that might arise in consequence of his seclusion. He continued: 'I entreat your majesty to pay some attention to these complaints. I am convinced that your presence only serves to nourish the affliction of the prince, as the sight of his grief increases yours; but you must not suffer everything to go to decay. Allow me to propose to you, that you should remove with the prince to the castle on the little island situated at a short distance from the port, and that you should hold a council and audience twice a week only. This duty will oblige you to quit the prince occasionally, while the beauty of the spot, the delicious air, and the charming prospects of the surrounding country, will enable him to support these short absences with patience.'

"The king approved of this advice; and as soon as the castle, which had not been inhabited for some time, was furnished and prepared for his reception, he removed thither with the prince, whom he never left except to hold the two stipulated audiences. He passed the rest of the time by his son's pillow sometimes endeavouring to console him, and sometimes giving vent to his own grief.

"While these things were happening in the capital of King Schahzaman, the two genii, Danhasch and Caschcasch, had carried back the Princess of China to the palace where the king her father had confined her, and placed her in her bed.

"The next morning, when she awoke, the Princess of China looked about on each side of her; and when she found that Prince Camaralzaman was no longer near her, she called her women in so brisk a voice that they all came running quickly to her, and

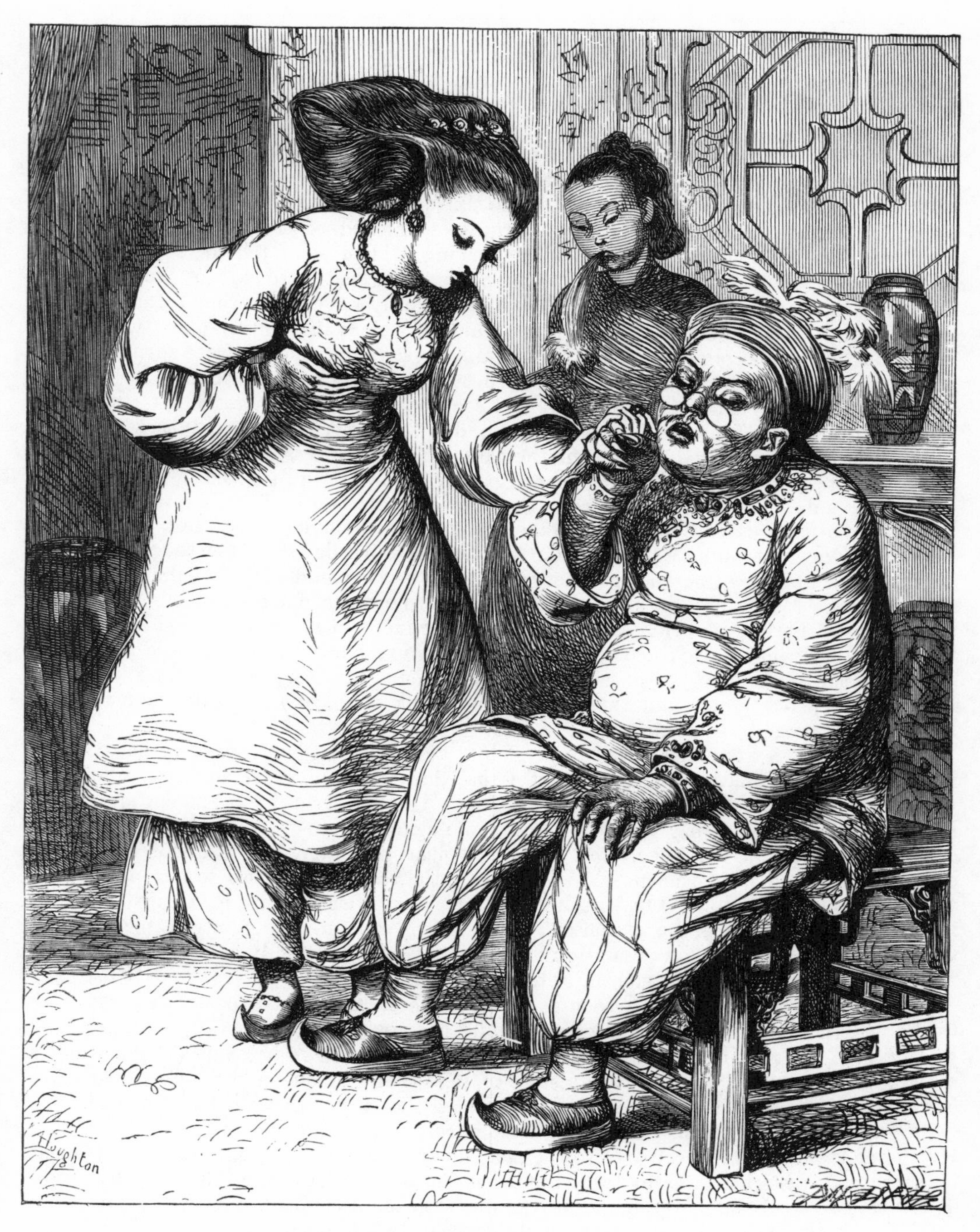

THE PRINCESS SHOWS THE RING TO THE KING OF CHINA.

surrounded her. Her nurse approached her pillow, and asked her what she wished, and if anything had happened to her.

"The princess replied, 'Tell me what is become of the young man who slept with me last night; for I love him dearly.' 'My princess,' said the nurse, 'we cannot understand your meaning unless you explain yourself more clearly.' The princess hereupon cried:

'I tell you that a young man of the most beautiful and elegant appearance that can be imagined slept by my side last night: I spoke to him for a considerable time, and did all I could to wake him, but in vain. I ask you where he is?'

"The nurse said: 'O my princess, this is some merry jest of yours: will you please to rise now?' 'I speak seriously,' said the princess, 'and I desire to know where he is.' But the nurse protested: 'My dear princess, you were alone when we put you to bed last night, and no one has entered this place since, at least to our knowledge.'

"The Princess of China's patience was quite exhausted. She seized her nurse by the head, and gave her several cuffs and blows, crying, 'Thou shalt tell me the truth, thou old witch, or I will murder thee.' The nurse struggled hard to get free from the princess's hands: she at length succeeded, and instantly ran to seek the Queen of China, the mother of the princess. She presented herself before the queen, with tears in her eyes, and her face swollen and disfigured. Her appearance excited great surprise in the queen, who inquired what was the cause of her being in such a condition.

"The nurse replied: 'O my queen, you see the effects of the treatment I have just received from the princess: she would have killed me entirely if I had not escaped as I did.' She then related to the queen the cause of the princess's anger and subsequent violent behaviour, at which the queen was greatly surprised and grieved. In conclusion the nurse said: 'You see, my mistress, that the princess is out of her senses: you may judge of the fact yourself if you will take the trouble of coming to see her.'

"The Queen of China was too tenderly attached to her daughter not to feel extremely anxious, after the news she had just heard from the nurse; and she immediately went to the princess. When she reached the apartment where her daughter was confined, she seated herself beside the princess; first inquired tenderly if she was in good health, and then asked her what cause of complaint she had against her nurse that could have made her treat the old woman so cruelly as she had done. 'Indeed, my daughter,' said the queen, 'you acted wrong, and a princess of your rank ought never to suffer herself to be led away by passion to commit such excesses.'

"The princess answered: 'O lady, I plainly perceive that your majesty has come to mock me; but I solemnly declare that I shall have neither peace nor rest till I have married the amiable and charming youth whom I saw last night. You certainly must know who he is; and I beg you to let him come again.'

"To this speech the queen replied: 'My dear daughter, you astonish me, and I cannot understand what you mean.' Forgetting the respect she owed to her mother, the princess answered hotly: 'O my mother, the king my father and you have persecuted me for some time, to compel me to marry when I had no wish to change my state; but now the wish has at length taken possession of my breast, and I am fully determined either to marry the young man I told you of, or to kill myself.'

"The queen now attempted to prevail by gentle means, and expostulated thus with the princess: 'You know well, my dear child, that you are alone in your chamber, and that no man can possibly enter it.' But, instead of listening to her mother, the princess interrupted her, and fell into such a state of rage that the queen was obliged to leave her to calm herself, while she went and acquainted the king with what had happened.

"The King of China wished to convince himself in person of the truth of this report. He therefore immediately repaired to the apartment of the princess, and asked her if what he had heard was true. 'O my lord,' replied the princess, 'let us not talk thus idly; only do me the favour to suffer the husband who was with me last night to return to me.'

"The king exclaimed, in amazement: 'What do I hear? Did any one visit you last night?' 'How can you ask me such a question, my lord?' interrupted the princess, 'your majesty cannot be ignorant of the fact. He is the handsomest young man who was ever beheld under heaven. I entreat you to send him to me again; do not refuse my request, I conjure you. That your majesty may not entertain any doubts that I have seen this youth,' she added, 'that I have been with him, spoken to him, and used every effort to awaken him without success, look, I pray you, upon this ring.' She held out her hand, and the King of China knew not what to think, when he perceived that she wore a man's ring on her finger. But as he could not comprehend in the least what she said, and had shut her up originally because he considered she was mad, he now thought her still worse than before. So without speaking again to her, lest he should provoke her to commit violence on her own person, or on any one who might approach her, he had her chained and more closely confined than before; and ordered that no one, except her nurse, should approach her, and that a strong guard should be placed at her door.

"Quite inconsolable for the misfortune that had befallen the princess his daughter, in what he supposed to be a fit of madness, the King of China set himself to consider what methods should be taken to effect her recovery. He assembled his council, and after having announced the state in which she was, he made the following proclamation: 'If any one who is here present is sufficiently skilful to undertake her cure, and to succeed in effecting it, I will bestow her on him in marriage, and will make him the heir of my crown and dominions.'

"The desire of winning so beautiful a princess, together with the hope of governing at some future period the large and powerful empire of China, made a strong impression on the mind of an emir who was present. Although he was already far advanced in years, being well skilled in magic he flattered himself he should succeed in curing the princess. He therefore offered his services to the king. The monarch replied: 'I consent to let you make the attempt, but I must first inform you that it is on condition that you lose your head if you do not succeed. It would not be fair that you should have the prospect of gaining so great and desirable a reward without a corresponding risk. What I propose to you will, in the same way, be proposed to all who present themselves after you, in case you do not agree to the conditions, or in case you fail.'

"The emir accepted the conditions, and the king himself conducted him to the apartment of his daughter. The princess covered her face as soon as she perceived the emir, and said to her father: 'My lord, your majesty surprises me, by bringing into my presence a man who is unknown to me, and to whom, as you well know, our holy religion forbids me to show my face.' 'O my daughter,' the king replied, 'do not suffer your delicacy to be wounded by his presence; he is one of my emirs, who requests your hand in marriage.' The princess said: 'This is not the husband you have already bestowed on me, whose faith is pledged to me by the ring I wear; be not angry if I refuse to accept any other.'

"The emir expected to find the princess behaving violently, and saying extravagant things. He was much surprised to find her collected and tranquil, and to hear the sensible words she spoke. He therefore was soon convinced that her supposed madness was nothing but a strong attachment to some object that had engaged her love. He did not, however, dare to explain his real sentiments to the king, who could not have endured the idea that his daughter had bestowed her heart on any other than the man whom he should present to her. So the emir prostrated himself at the feet of the king, and said: 'O king, after what I have just heard from the lips of the princess, it would be in vain that I should undertake to cure her. I have no remedies that can be of any service to her in her present state; my life, therefore, is in your majesty's hands.' The king, irritated at the emir's confession of his incompetency, and angry at the trouble he had occasioned him, ordered his head to be struck off.

"That he might not have to reproach himself with neglect of anything that could conduce to the recovery of the princess, this monarch ordered it to be proclaimed in his capital, a few days afterwards, that if there were any physician, astrologer, or magician inhabiting it, who was sufficiently experienced in his profession to restore the princess to her senses, he might appear before the council under the before-mentioned condition of losing his head if he failed in the attempt. He sent an order to have the same proclamation published in all the principal towns in his dominions, and also in the courts of the neighbouring princes.

"The first man who presented himself was an astrologer and magician, whom the king ordered to be conducted by an eunuch to the prison of the princess. The astrologer took from a little bag, which he had brought under his arm, a parchment covered with mystical signs, a small globe, a chafing-dish, various kinds of drugs proper for fumigation, a copper vessel, and several other things; and he requested that fire should be brought.

"The Princess of China asked the meaning of all this apparatus. The eunuch replied: 'O princess, it is to conjure the evil spirit that possesses you, that he may be shut up in this copper vessel, and thrown into the sea.'

"'Wretched astrologer!' cried the princess, 'know that I want none of thy preparations: I am in my right mind, and it is thou who art mad. If thy power extend so far, bring me but the prince I love, and then thou wilt indeed do me a service.' 'If this is true,' replied the astrologer, 'I can be of no use, O princess; the king your father can alone relieve your woes.' He then replaced in his bag all the things he had taken from it, and went out, truly mortified at having so inconsiderately undertaken to cure an imaginary disease.

"When the eunuch had brought the astrologer back to the King of China, the magician did not wait till the eunuch should speak to the king, but spoke to him at once in a firm tone, saying, 'O king, your majesty published to the world, and repeated to me, that the princess your daughter was mad; and I doubted not my power to restore her to her senses by means of my secret knowledge. But so soon as I saw her I was convinced that her only malady is violent love; and my art does not extend to the cure of pangs like these. Your majesty can best prescribe the remedy, if you will please to give her the husband for whom she pines.' The king, angry at what he considered insolence in the astrologer, immediately commanded his head to be struck off.

"Not to weary your majesty with many repetitions, I will only say that, including astrologers, physicians, and magicians, one hundred and fifty men successively presented themselves, and shared the same fate; and their heads were ranged over the various gates of the city.

"The nurse of the Princess of China had a son, named Marzavan, the foster-brother of the princess, who had been nursed and brought up with her. During their childhood their friendship had been so intimate, that they treated each other as brother and sister so long as they lived together; and even when their more advanced age obliged them to be separated, their regard for each other continued.

"Among the various sciences which Marzavan had cultivated from his earliest youth, his inclination had led him more particularly to the study of judicial astrology, geomancy, and other secret sciences, in all of which he had attained considerable proficiency. Not satisfied with the information he could obtain from the masters under whose tuition he had studied, he began to travel as soon as he felt himself sufficiently strong to bear the fatigue. Every man who was celebrated for learning in any science or art did Marzavan seek out, even in the most distant countries; and he continued to associate with them until he had gained from them all the information and knowledge they had to bestow.

"After an absence of several years, Marzavan at length returned to the capital of China. The sight of the heads, which he observed ranged over the gate by which he entered the city, surprised him very much. As soon as he had arrived at his house he inquired the reason why they were placed there; but, above all, his chief inquiries were concerning the health of the princess his foster-sister, whom he had not forgotten. As the answer to his first question included a reply to his second, he heard news which soon occasioned him much pain; but he waited till his mother, the princess's nurse, could give him full information of the whole affair. Although she was closely occupied by her attendance on the princess, yet so soon as she heard of the arrival of her beloved son, she contrived to steal away, to embrace him and pass a few moments in his company. After she had informed him, with tears in her eyes, of the pitiable state to which the princess was reduced, and the reason why the King of China had ordered her to be so harshly treated, Marzavan asked her if she could not procure him an interview with the princess without the knowledge of the king. The nurse meditated for some minutes; she then said: 'I cannot give any reply to such a proposition at present; but I will meet you to-morrow at this hour, and I will then give you an answer.'

"No one, except the nurse, had access to the apartment of the princess without the permission of the eunuch who commanded the guard at the door. The nurse, knowing that he had been only lately appointed to his office, and was ignorant of what had previously taken place at court, addressed herself to him thus: 'You know that I have nursed and brought up the princess from her earliest infancy; but perhaps you do not also know that at the same time I nursed a daughter of my own, who was of the same age. She is lately married; and the princess, who still does her the honour of feeling attached to her, desires to see her; but she wishes that the interview should be so contrived that no one may see my daughter come in or go out.'

"The nurse was going to add more, but the eunuch stopped her. 'It is well,' said he; 'I will always, with the greatest pleasure, do everything in my power to oblige the princess. You may either tell your daughter to come, or go yourself to bring her hither

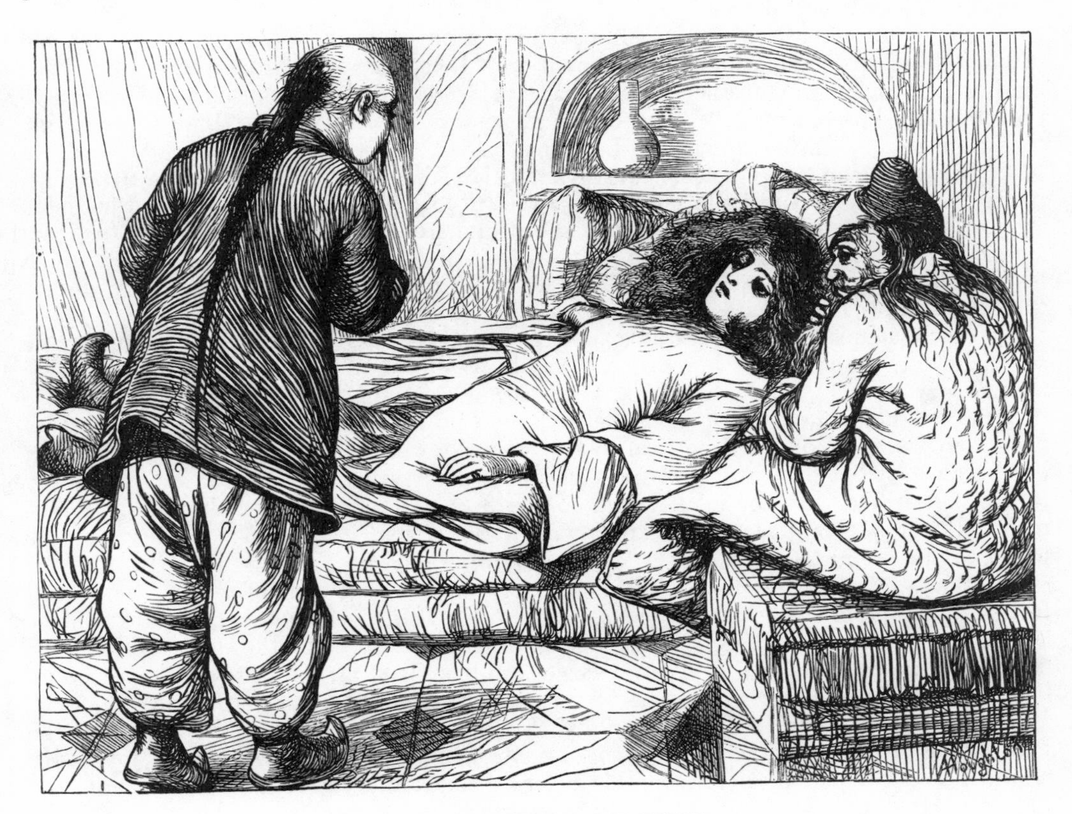

MARZAVAN DISCOVERS THE PRINCE.

at night, after the king has retired; the door shall be open to you.' As soon as night came on the nurse went to her son Marzavan. She disguised him in woman's clothes, so that no one could have suspected he was not a woman, and took him with her. The eunuch, who doubted not that he was admitting the nurse's daughter, opened the door, and let them both go in.

"Before she presented Marzavan, the nurse went to the Princess Badoura, and said: 'O lady, this is not a woman whom you see: it is my son Marzavan, who has just arrived from his travels, and whom I have found means to introduce into your chamber, disguised in this dress. I hope you will permit him to have the honour of paying his respects to you.'

"When she heard the name of Marzavan, the princess expressed great joy. She immediately cried out: 'Come hither, O my brother, and take off that veil: it is not forbidden to a brother and sister to see each other's faces.' Marzavan saluted her with great respect, but the princess would not allow him time to speak. She continued: 'I am delighted to see you again in good health after an absence of so many years, during which time no one, nay, not even your good mother, ever received any intelligence from you.'

"'I am infinitely obliged to you for your kindness, O gracious princess,' replied Marzavan. 'I expected and hoped on my arrival to receive better accounts of you than those I have heard, and I am much grieved to find you in this condition. I feel very happy, however, to think that after the failure of so many men, I have arrived in time to administer the remedy you need for your disorder. If I have derived no other advantage from my studies and travels than that of being instrumental to your recovery, I shall deem it sufficient recompense.'

"As he uttered these words, Marzavan drew out a book and other things he had furnished himself with, which he supposed would be necessary, from the accounts his mother had given him of the illness of the princess. So soon as she perceived these preparations, she exclaimed: 'What, brother! are you too deluded like those who imagine that I am mad? Listen to me, and be undeceived!'

"The princess then related to Marzavan all her history. She did not omit the most trifling circumstance; and she showed him the ring which had been exchanged for hers. In conclusion she said: 'I have disguised nothing from you. In what I have told you I acknowledge that there is something mysterious which I cannot comprehend, and which leads them all to suppose that I am not in my right senses; but they pay no attention to the circumstances of my story, which are exactly as I have related.'

"When the princess had ceased speaking, Marzavan, who was filled with unutterable astonishment, remained for some time with his eyes fixed on the ground, unable to pronounce a syllable. At length, raising his head, he said: 'If, O princess, what you have told me is true, as indeed I am persuaded it is, I do not despair of procuring you relief from your woes. I only entreat you to arm yourself with patience for some time longer, until I have visited those countries in which I have not yet been. When you hear of my return, be assured that the man for whom you now sigh with so much love and tenderness will not be very far distant from you.' So saying, Marzavan took leave of the princess, and set forth on his travels on the following day.

"Marzavan wandered from city to city, from province to province, and from island to island. Wherever he went, rumour spoke of the Princess Badoura (for that was the name of his foster-sister), and of her extraordinary history. At the expiration of four months, Marzavan arrived at Torf, a large and populous maritime town, where he no longer heard of the Princess Badoura; for here every one was talking of Prince Camaralzaman, who was said to be ill; and the history they told was nearly similar to that of the Princess of China. Marzavan was seized with an indescribable transport of joy. He inquired in what part of the world this prince resided, and received the information he sought. He found there were two ways of reaching that country—one by land, and the other by sea. The latter was the shorter; therefore Marzavan chose it, and embarked in a merchant vessel, which had a good voyage till it came within sight of the capital of the kingdom of Schahzaman. But unfortunately, through the unskilfulness of the pilot, as the vessel was entering the harbour it struck on a rock, went to pieces, and sank just in sight of the castle in which Prince Camaralzaman passed his life, and where his father King Schahzaman was at that moment conversing with his grand vizier.

"Marzavan was an expert swimmer. He therefore did not hesitate to throw himself into the sea, and made his way to the castle of King Schahzaman, where he was taken, and every assistance was given him, according to the orders of the grand vizier, who had received the king's commands on this subject. Marzavan was provided with dry garments, and was treated with the greatest kindness. When he had recovered from his fatigue he was brought before the grand vizier, who had desired to see him.

"As Marzavan was a youth of a good appearance and engaging air, the vizier treated him with the utmost civility, and, from the sensible and proper answers he received to all the questions he asked his guest, soon conceived a great respect and esteem for the shipwrecked stranger. He discovered almost insensibly that Marzavan was a very learned man. At length he could not refrain from saying to him, 'I plainly perceive from conversing with you that you are a man of no common ability. Would to Heaven that in the course of your travels you had learned some secret that could cure a young man, whose illness has for some time past plunged this court into the deepest affliction.'

"Marzavan replied, that if he were made acquainted with the disease under which the person in question laboured, he might be able to find a remedy for it. The grand vizier then explained to Marzavan the state of Prince Camaralzaman, relating the whole history from the very beginning. He concealed nothing from him. He spoke of the joy of the king at his birth, of his education, of the desire of King Schahzaman to see him married at an early age, and the extraordinary aversion the prince had shown to the idea of matrimony. He then went on to speak of the prince's behaviour before the council, his subsequent imprisonment, and the extravagant actions he committed in prison, which had suddenly changed into a violent love for an unknown lady—a love for which there was no other foundation than a ring, which the prince persisted had belonged to this lady, who perhaps was not in existence. In short, the vizier related every circumstance of the prince's case with the most faithful exactness.

"This account gave Marzavan great joy: he felt sure that in consequence of his shipwreck he had fortunately met with the object of his search and inquiry. He felt convinced, beyond all doubt, that Prince Camaralzaman was the person with whom the Princess of China was so deeply in love, and that the princess was equally the object of the prince's ardent attachment. He did not mention his thoughts to the grand vizier; he only said to him, that an interview with the prince would better enable him to judge what remedies it might be necessary to administer. 'Follow me,' said the vizier; 'you will find the king with him, and the king has already expressed a wish of seeing you.'

"The first thing that struck the eyes of Marzavan, when he entered the chamber, was the figure of the prince, who reclined on his bed with a languid air, and his eyes closed. Regardless of the situation in which he found King Schahzaman, who was seated by the side of the bed, and of the prince himself, whom such an exclamation might have alarmed and agitated, Marzavan exclaimed, 'O Heavens! who ever saw so strong a likeness!' He alluded to the prince's resemblance to the Princess of China, for, indeed, there was a great similiarity in their features.

"These words of Marzavan's excited the curiosity of Prince Camaralzaman, who opened his eyes and looked at him. Marzavan, who had great quickness of invention, took advantage of this circumstance, and instantly repeated some complimentary verses, taking care to use such mysterious terms that the king and grand vizier did not comprehend the meaning of his words. He so well explained what had happened to him with the Princess of China, that the prince at once understood that his visitor knew her, and would be able to give him some information respecting her; and at the hope of hearing of her he felt a degree of joy that soon displayed itself in his eyes and countenance. When Marzavan had finished his compliment, the prince took the liberty of making a sign of entreaty to his father, begging that Schahzaman would rise from his seat, and permit Marzavan to take his place.

"Delighted to see in his son a change which gave a hope of his recovery, the king rose, and taking Marzavan by the hand, obliged him to sit down in the place he had just quitted. He asked him who he was, and whence he came; and after Marzavan had replied, that he was a subject of the King of China, and that he came from that monarch's dominions, the king said to him, 'May Heaven grant that you may restore my son to health, and divert his mind from the profound melancholy in which it is sunk; my obligations to you will be without bounds, and the proofs of my gratitude shall be of such a nature that the whole world shall say, "Never was service so largely recompensed."' As he spoke these words he left the prince at liberty to converse with Marzavan, and went away with his grand vizier, rejoicing at this fortunate occurrence.

"Marzavan approached very close to Prince Camaralzaman, and said to him in a low voice: 'O prince, the time is come when you may cease to pine thus piteously. The lady for whom you suffer is well known to me: she is the Princess Badoura, daughter of the King of China, whose name is Gaiour. From what she has herself related to me of her adventure, and from what I have already learned of yours, I am certain that I am speaking the truth. The princess is suffering as much from love of you as you endure from your affection towards her.' He then related all that he knew of the history of the princess, since the fatal night of her very remarkable meeting with Camaralzaman. He did not omit also to inform him of the punishment that had been inflicted, by order of the King of China, on all those who undertook to cure the Princess Badoura of her supposed madness, and who had failed in the attempt. He concluded his speech with these words: 'You are the only one who can accomplish her perfect recovery, and you may, therefore, present yourself for that purpose, without fear of incurring the dreadful penalty that attaches to failure. But before you can undertake so long a journey, you must yourself be in good health; we will then take the necessary measures for our departure. Endeavour, therefore, to regain your strength as quickly as possible.'

"This discourse of Marzavan produced a wonderful effect upon the hearer: Prince Camaralzaman was so comforted by the hope which had just been poured into his bosom, that he felt sufficiently strong to rise, and, with an air and countenance which gave the king his father inexpressible joy, he entreated King Schahzaman, who had again entered the apartment, to allow him to dress himself.

"Without inquiring the means by which so surprising a change had been instantaneously effected, the king embraced Marzavan, to express his thanks, and immediately went out of the room with the grand vizier, to proclaim this agreeable intelligence. He ordered public rejoicings for several days; he distributed presents to his officers and the populace; gave alms to the poor; and had all prisoners set at liberty. Joy and gladness reigned in the capital, and this happy change very soon spread its influence throughout the dominions of King Schahzaman.

"Prince Camaralzaman, who had been extremely weakened by continued want of sleep, and by his long abstinence from almost all kinds of food, soon recovered his usual health. So soon as he found himself sufficiently strengthened to be able to support the fatigue of a long journey, he took Marzavan aside, and said to him: 'O beloved Marzavan, it is now time to fulfil the promise you have made me. The impatience I feel to see this charming princess, and to put an end to the dreadful torments she endures for my sake, will soon throw me back into the state in which you first saw me, unless we set out immediately. One circumstance alone grieves me, and makes me fear an obstacle to my departure; that is, the tender affection of my father, who will never be able to grant me permission to leave him. His refusal will drive me to despair, if you cannot devise some scheme to obviate it. I feel assured that he will never suffer me to quit his sight.' The prince could not refrain from tears as he uttered these last words.

"Marzavan replied: 'O prince, I have before now foreseen the great obstacle you mention; it remains with me so to act that your father will not prevent our departure. The first intention of my journey was to procure for the Princess of China a cure for her grief and sufferings. This I owed to the mutual friendship that has united us almost from our birth, and to the zeal and affection with which it is my duty to serve her. I should fail in that duty were I to neglect any means of obtaining consolation for her, and for you at the same time—if I failed to employ all the art I possess for that purpose. Listen, therefore, to the scheme I have devised to remove the difficulty of obtaining the king's permission to accomplish what we both so earnestly desire. You have not left this apartment since I arrived here: express to your father a wish to take some exercise, and ask his leave to go on a short hunting excursion with me for two or three days. There is no reason to suppose he will refuse you this indulgence. When he has granted your request, you will give orders to have two good horses ready for each of us: one on which to set out, and the other for change; and leave the rest to me.'

"The next day Prince Camaralzaman watched his opportunity, and told the king his father how much he wished to go forth into the woods, and begged leave of absence to hunt for a day or two with Marzavan. The king replied: 'I do not object to your departure; but you must promise me not to remain away longer than one night. Too much exercise at first might be injurious, and a longer absence would be painful to me.' The king gave orders for the best horses to be chosen for the prince and Marzavan, and took care himself that all things necessary should be provided for the expedition. When everything was ready he embraced him, and having earnestly recommended him to the care of Marzavan, he let him depart.

"Prince Camaralzaman and Marzavan reached the open country; and, to deceive the two attendants who led the spare horses, they pretended to hunt, and got as far distant from the city as possible. At night they stopped at a caravanserai, where they slept till about midnight. Marzavan, who was the first to wake, called Prince Camaralzaman, without waking the attendants. He begged him to give him his dress, and to put on another, which one of the attendants had brought for him. They then mounted the fresh horses, and set out at a quick pace Marzavan leading one of the groom's horses by the bridle.

"At daybreak the travellers found themselves in a forest, at a place where four roads met. At this spot Marzavan begged the prince to wait for him a moment, and rode into the thickest of the forest. He there killed the groom's horse, tore the dress which the prince had worn on the preceding day, and dipped it in the horse's blood. When he returned to the prince he threw the blood-stained garments into the middle of the path where the road divided.

"The prince asked Marzavan why he did this. Marzavan answered: 'When the king your father perceives that you do not return to-night, as you promised, and when he hears from the servants that we set out without them while they were asleep, he will undoubtedly send people out in different directions to search for us. Those who come this way and find this blood-stained cloak will conclude that some beast of prey has devoured you, and that I have made my escape, to avoid the king's anger and vengeance. Your father, thinking from their account that you are no longer alive, will desist from his search after us, and thus afford us the opportunity of continuing our journey without interruption, and we need not fear pursuit. The stratagem is certainly a violent one, and will occasion a tender parent the afflicting alarm of having lost a son whom he fondly loves; but the joy of your father will be beyond all bounds when he shall again discover that you are alive and happy.' 'O wise Marzavan,' cried the prince, 'I cannot but approve your ingenious invention, and feel additional obligations to you for your forethought.'

"The prince and Marzavan, who were well supplied with valuable jewels to defray their expenses, continued their travels by land and by sea, and found no obstacle but the length of the journey to prevent them from fulfilling their enterprise.

"They at length arrived at the capital of China. Instead of conducting the prince to his own house, Marzavan made him alight at a public khan for the reception of travellers. In this place they remained three days, to recover from the fatigue of the journey; and during this interval Marzavan had an astrologer's dress made as a disguise for the prince. When the three days had expired, the friends went together to the bath, where Marzavan made the prince put on the astrologer's dress; and when they left the bath, he conducted him within sight of the palace of the King of China, and there left Camaralzaman, while he himself went and acquainted his mother, the nurse of Princess Badoura, of his arrival, that she might prepare the princess for the interview.

"The prince, instructed by Marzavan as to his future proceedings, and furnished with everything necessary to support his assumed dress and character, approached the gate of the palace; and stopping before it, cried out with a loud voice, in the hearing of the guard and porters: 'I am an astrologer, and I come to effect the cure of the illustrious Princess Badoura, daughter of the great and puissant monarch, Gaiour King of China, according to the conditions proposed by his majesty:—to marry her if I succeed, or to lose my life if I fail.'

"The novelty of this proclamation quickly drew together round Prince Camaralzaman a multitude of people, besides the guard and porters belonging to the palace. Indeed, it was a long time since either physician, astrologer, or magician had presented himself, such terror had been caused by the many tragical examples of people who had failed in their enterprise. It was supposed the race of astrologers was extinct, or at least that there remained none of the tribe so foolish as to expose themselves to almost certain death.

"On noticing the elegant figure of the prince, his noble air, and the extreme youth which was discernible in his countenance, every one present felt compassion for him. 'What are you thinking of, O my master?' said those who were nearest to him; 'what can be your motive for thus sacrificing to certain death a life which seems to presage such flattering hopes? Have not the heads, which you have seen ranged at the top of the gates of the city, filled you with horror? In the name of Heaven, abandon this useless and fatal design, and withdraw.'

"The prince remained firm, notwithstanding all these remonstrances, and instead of listening to the entreaties of these people, as he saw that no one appeared to introduce him into the palace, he repated his proclamation with an oath, which made every one shudder; and all the bystanders exclaimed, 'He is resolved to die: may Allah have pity on his youth and on his soul!' But the prince cried aloud, repeating his proclamation a third time, and then the grand vizier came forth himself, by order of the King of China.

"The minister conducted him into the presence of the king. So soon as the prince perceived the monarch seated on the throne, he prostrated himself, and kissed the earth before him. Among all the adventurers whose immeasurable presumption had lost them their heads, the king had not yet seen one so worthy of his attention as this youth; and he felt unfeigned compassion for Camaralzaman, when he considered the danger to which he exposed himself. He even showed him great honour; desiring him to approach and seat himself by his side. He said: 'O fair young man, I can scarcely believe that at your youthful age you can have acquired sufficient experience to undertake the cure of my daughter. I wish you may be able to succeed; I would bestow her on you in marriage, not only without reluctance, but with the greatest possible pleasure and joy, whereas I should have felt truly unhappy if any of those men who have applied before you had obtained her. But I must declare to you, although it gives me pain to inform you of this condition, that if you fail, neither your youth, nor your noble and engaging appearance, can mitigate the penalty you will incur, and you must lose your head.'

"'O mighty king,' replied Prince Camaralzaman, 'I am greatly obliged to your majesty for the honour you confer on me, and for the kindness you show to one who is an entire stranger to you. The country I come from is not so distant from your dominions that its name should be unknown there, and that I might, therefore, abandon my project with impunity. What would be said of my want of firmness were I to relinquish so great and praiseworthy a design, after having undergone so much danger and fatigue as I have already encountered? Would not your majesty lose that esteem which you already entertain for me? If I am to lose my life in the attempt, O king, I shall at least die with the satisfaction of not forfeiting that esteem after having obtained it. I entreat you, then, not to let me remain any longer in my present state of suspense, but let me prove the infallibility of my art by the means I am now ready to employ.'

"The King of China commanded the eunuch who guarded the Princess Badoura, and who was then present, to conduct Prince Camaralzaman to the apartment of his daughter. But before the prince departed, the king told him he was still at liberty to relinquish his enterprise. But the prince would not listen to him; he followed the eunuch with a resolution, or rather with an ardour, which astonished all beholders.

"Thus Prince Camaralzaman went with the eunuch; and when they reached a long gallery at the end of which the princess's apartment was situated, the prince, delighted to find himself so near the dear object for whom he had shed so many tears and heaved so many fruitless sighs, hastened his pace and got before the eunuch. The eunuch mended his pace, but he had some difficulty to overtake the prince. 'Where are you going so fast?' said he, taking hold of his arm. 'You cannot enter those apartments without me. You must be very desirous to get rid of life, that you run so eagerly into the arms of death.

Not one of the astrologers I have seen and conducted to the place where you will arrive but too soon ever showed so much anxiety.'

"'Friend,' replied Prince Camaralzaman, looking at the eunuch, and slackening his pace, 'the reason is, that all the astrologers you speak of were not so sure of their science as I am of mine: they were certain of losing their lives if they did not succeed, and they were not sure of success; they had therefore some reason to tremble as they approached the place whither I am going, and where I am convinced I shall meet with happiness and joy.' As he pronounced these words they reached the door. The eunuch opened it, and brought the prince into a large room, which led to the chamber of the princess, and was divided from it only by a slight door. Before he entered the prince stopped; and speaking in a much lower tone of voice than he had yet employed, lest he should be heard in her apartment, he said to the eunuch: 'To convince you that neither presumption, caprice, nor the fire of youthful ardour has stimulated me to this enterprise, I submit two alternatives to your choice: which do you prefer—that I should cure the princess while in her presence, or here, without going any farther, and without even seeing her?'

"The eunuch was extremely astonished at the confidence with which the prince spoke. He ceased to taunt him, and said seriously: 'It matters not which course you pursue. In whatever manner you accomplish the business, you will acquire immortal glory, not only in this kingdom, but over all the habitable world.' The prince answered: 'Then it is better that I cure her without seeing her, that you may be a witness of my skill. However great may be my impatience to see the princess of exalted rank who is to be my wife, I will nevertheless, to gratify you, deprive myself for some moments of that happiness.' As he was furnished with everything appropriate to his assumed character of an astrologer, he drew out his writing materials and some paper, and wrote the following letter to the Princess of China:—

"'PRINCE CAMARALZAMAN TO THE PRINCESS OF CHINA.

"'Adorable princess! The love-stricken Prince Camaralzaman does not tell you of the inexpressible woes he has endured since the fatal night when your charms deprived him of that liberty which he had resolved to maintain to the end of his life. He only assures you that he gave you his heart during your sweet sleep; a sleep that prevented him from viewing the animated brilliancy of your eyes, notwithstanding all his efforts to induce you to open them. He even had the presumption to place his ring upon your finger, as a token of his love, and in exchange to take yours, which he sends you enclosed in this letter. If you will condescend to return it to him as a reciprocal pledge of your affection, he will esteem himself the happiest and most fortunate of lovers. But should you not comply with his prayer, your refusal will cause him to submit to the stroke of death with the greater resignation, as he will have sacrificed his life to the love he bears you. He awaits your answer in your antechamber.'

"When Prince Camaralzaman had finished this letter, he wrapped it up in a small packet with the princess's ring, which he enclosed without letting the eunuch see what the parcel contained which he placed in the hands of that officer, saying: 'Take this, friend, and carry it to your mistress. If she is not cured the moment she has read this note and seen its contents, I allow you to proclaim to the world that I am the most worthless and impudent astrologer who has ever existed in the past, or can ever exist in the future.'

"The eunuch went into the princess's chamber, and carried to her the packet from Prince Camaralzaman, saying: 'O princess, an astrologer has just arrived, who, if I am not mistaken, has more assurance than any who have yet appeared. He declares that you will be cured as soon as you read this note, and see what it encloses. I wish he may prove neither a liar nor an impostor.' The Princess Badoura took the packet and opened it with the utmost indifference; but when she recognised the ring, she scarcely allowed herself time to read it. She got up precipitately, and with an extraordinary effort broke the chain which confined her, and then ran to the door and opened it. The princess

THE MEETING OF THE PRINÇE AND BADOURA.

instantly recollected the prince, who at once recognised her. They ran into each other's arms, and were locked in the tenderest embrace, without being able to utter a word from excess of joy. They gazed at each other for a considerable time with emotions not to be described, mingled with surprise at the singularity of their interview, after their former meeting, which neither of them could comprehend. The nurse, who had run out with the princess, made them go into the chamber, where the princess returned her ring to the prince, saying, 'Take it; I could not keep it without returning yours, which I am resolved not to part with till my dying day. Neither of our rings can be in better hands.'

"The eunuch in the meantime had gone to report this strange occurrence to the King of China. 'O great king,' said he, 'all the physicians, astrologers, and magicians, who have hitherto presented themselves to undertake the recovery of the princess, were but ignorant fools. This last has not made use either of magic books, or of conjurations of

CAMARALZAMAN FOLLOWS THE BIRD.

wicked spirits, or of perfumes, or of any of the apparatus they employed; he has cured her without even seeing her.' He related the manner in which the prince had proceeded, and the king went immediately, in a very agreeable surprise, to the apartment of the princess, whom he tenderly embraced. He embraced the prince also, took hold of his hand, and placing it in that of the princess, he exclaimed: 'Happy stranger, whoever you may be, I keep my promise, and give you my daughter in marriage. But I feel assured within myself that you are not what you appear to be, and that you have only assumed a disguise.'

"Prince Camaralzaman thanked the king in the most submissive terms, the better to express his gratitude. 'O king,' he said, 'as for my station, it is true that I do not practise astrology as my profession, as your majesty very rightly judged; I only put on the habit of one of that craft to ensure the success of my endeavour to obtain an honourable alliance with the most powerful monarch in the universe. I am a prince by birth, the son of a king and queen: my name is Camaralzaman, and my father is King Schahzaman, who reigns over the well-known Island of the Children of Khaledan.' He then related his adventures, and the marvellous events which had originated his love for the princess: he declared furthermore that her affection for him was conceived at the same time, and that both these assertions were fully proved by the exchange of the two rings.

"The king exclaimed: 'So extraordinary a history deserves to be handed down to posterity. I will have it written and deposited amongst the archives of my kingdom; then I will make it public, that from my dominions the knowledge of it may pass to the neighbouring nations.' The ceremony of the nuptials was performed on that very day; and the most solemn festivities and rejoicings were held throughout the extensive dominions of China. Marzavan was not forgotten. The king granted him admission to the court, and bestowed on him an honourable office, with the promise that in time he should be promoted to others yet more considerable.

"Prince Camaralzaman and the Princess Badoura, who had thus reached the summit of their wishes, enjoyed the blessings of married love, and for several months the King of China did not cease to testify his happiness by continual feasts and entertainments.

"In the midst of these pleasures, Prince Camaralzaman one night had a dream, in which King Schahzaman, his father, appeared before him, lying at the point of death; and he seemed to say: 'This son, whom I have begotten, whom I have tenderly cherished, has forsaken me, and he is the cause of my death.' He awoke with so deep a sigh that it roused the princess also, and made her inquire the cause of his unhappiness.

"'Alas!' cried the prince, 'perhaps, at this very moment while I am speaking, the king my father is breathing his last.' He then told the princess his reason for giving way to these melancholy thoughts. The princess, who had no wish but to give him pleasure, and who knew that his earnest desire to see his father once more might diminish the satisfaction he felt at living with her in a country so distant from his native home, said nothing more at the time; but on that very day she availed herself of an opportunity of speaking to the King of China in private. 'O my father,' said she, respectfully kissing his hand, 'I have a favour to request of your majesty; and I entreat you not to refuse it me. But lest you should imagine that the prince my husband has any part in the prayer I am about to make, I must first assure you that he is not acquainted with my intention. My petition is, that you would permit me to accompany him on a visit to my father-in-law, King Schahzaman.'

"'Whatever sorrow such a separation may occasion me,' the king answered, 'I cannot disapprove of your resolution: it is worthy of you thus to despise the fatigue you must experience from so long a journey. Go—I give my consent; but it is only on condition that you remain no longer than one year at the court of King Schahzaman. He will not, I hope, object to this proposal, and that we should have you to reside with us alternately, that he may welcome his son and daughter-in-law, and I my daughter and son-in-law.' The princess announced her father's consent to Camaralzaman, who was much rejoiced at it, and thanked her for this new proof of her affection towards him.

"The King of China gave orders that the necessary preparations should be made for the journey; and when everything was ready, he set out with the young pair, and accompanied them for several days. At length they took leave of each other, not without many tears on either side. The king embraced his children tenderly, and after having begged the prince to continue to love his daughter with the same affection he had manifested until then, he left them to continue their journey, and returned to his capital, following the chase as he went.

"When the prince and princess had dried their tears, they began pleasurably to anticipate the joy that King Schahzaman would experience in seeing and embracing them, and their own delight when they should behold him.

"After they had been travelling about a month they came to a plain of vast extent, planted here and there with trees, which formed a very agreeable shade. As the heat on that day was great, Prince Camaralzaman thought it expedient to encamp here. He asked the Princess Badoura if she had any objection to this plan. The princess declared that she was at that moment going to propose that very measure to him. They immediately alighted in this beautiful spot; and as soon as their tents were pitched, the princess, who had been resting in the shade, retired to her pavilion, while Prince Camaralzaman went to give orders to the rest of the party. That she might be more at her ease, she took off her girdle, which her women placed by her side; she then fell asleep from fatigue, and her attendants left her alone.

"When Prince Camaralzaman had given all necessary orders, and made the requisite arrangements in the camp, he returned to the tent, and as he perceived that the princess had fallen asleep, he came in and sat down as silently as possible. As he reclined thus, himself half overcome by sleep, the girdle of the princess caught his eye. He examined one by one the different diamonds and rubies with which it was enriched, and he perceived a small silk purse sewn neatly to the girdle, and tied with a silken thread. On touching this purse, he felt that it contained something hard; curious to know what it was, he opened the purse and took out a cornelian, on which were engraven different figures and characters, all of them unintelligible to him. 'This cornelian,' said he to himself, 'must certainly be of very great value, or my princess would not carry it about with her, and take such great care not to lose it.' This cornelian was in truth a talisman, which the Queen of China had given to her daughter to ensure her happiness, assuring her that she would always be prosperous so long as she wore this about her.

"The better to examine this talisman, and as the tent was rather dark, Prince Camaralzaman went to the entrance; but as he held the jewel in his hand, a bird made a sudden dart from the air upon it, and carried it away.

"Nothing could exceed the astonishment and grief of the prince when he found the talisman thus unexpectedly snatched from him by the bird. This accident, the most tormenting that could have befallen him, and occasioned too by his own ill-timed curiosity, deprived the princess of a precious gift. This reflection rendered him for some minutes speechless with vexation.

"The bird flew away with his prize, but alighted on the ground at a little distance with the talisman still in his beak. Prince Camaralzaman ran towards him, in the hope the bird might drop it; but as soon as he approached, the bird flew a little way, and then stopped again. The prince continued to pursue him; the bird then swallowed the talisman, and took a longer flight. The prince again followed him, thinking to kill him with a stone. The farther the bird got from him, the more was Camaralzaman determined not to lose sight of him till he had recovered the talisman.

"Over hills and valleys the bird drew the prince after him for the whole day, always getting farther from the spot where he had left the Princess Badoura; and at the close of the day, instead of perching in a bush, in which Camaralzaman might have surprised him during the night, he flew to the top of a high tree, where he was in safety.

"The prince was extremely mortified at having taken so much useless trouble, and he began to deliberate whether he should return to his camp. 'But,' thought he, 'how shall I return? Shall I climb the hills and traverse the valleys over which I came? Shall I not lose my way in the dusk of evening? and will my strength hold out? And even if I could find my way back, should I venture to present myself before the princess without her talisman?' Absorbed in these disconsolate reflections, and overcome with fatigue, with hunger, thirst, and want of sleep, he lay down, and passed the night at the foot of the tree.

"The next morning Camaralzaman was awake before the bird had quitted the tree; and as soon as he saw the winged robber take flight, he got up to pursue him, and followed him the whole of that day with as little success as he had met with on the preceding one. He satisfied his hunger with the herbs and fruits he found in his way.

He continued the pursuit till the tenth day, always keeping his eyes on the bird, and sleeping at night at the foot of the tree, while the bird perched on its highest branches.

"The bird constantly flew on, and Camaralzaman as constantly pursued it, till on the eleventh day they arrived at a great city. When the bird was near the walls he soared very high above them, and winged his course far away, so that the prince entirely lost sight of him, and with him lost the least hope of ever recovering the talisman of the Princess Badoura.

"Bowed down with many griefs, and hopeless of procuring relief to his sorrows, he entered the city, which was built on the sea shore and had a very fine harbour. He walked for a considerable time through the streets, not knowing where he was or whither he should go; at length he came to the harbour. Still more uncertain what to do, he walked along the shore till he came to the gate of a garden, which was open, and there he paused. The gardener, a good old man, who was at work among his flowers, happened to raise his head as Camaralzaman stood there. Directly he perceived the prince, and knew him to be a stranger and a Mussulman, he invited him to come in quickly and shut the gate. Camaralzaman accordingly entered, and, going up to the gardener, asked him why he had made him take this precaution of closing the gate. The gardener replied: 'I did this because I see that you are a stranger newly arrived, and a Mussulman; and this city is inhabited for the most part by idolaters, who have a mortal hatred to Mussulmen, and ill-treat the few who dwell here, and who profess the religion of our prophet. I suppose you are ignorant of this circumstance; and I look on it as a miracle that you should have proceeded thus far without meeting with any disagreeable adventure. In fact, these idolaters are above all things watchful to observe the arrival of Mussulmen strangers, and they never fail to lay snares for those who are not aware of their wickedness. I praise Allah that he has led you into a place of safety.'

"Camaralzaman thanked this good man very gratefully for the retreat he so generously offered to shelter the stranger from insult. He was going to say more, but the gardener interrupted him, saying: 'Let us have no more compliments: you are fatigued, and you must want food; come and rest yourself.' He took his guest into his little house, and, after the prince had refreshed himself with the food and drink the gardener set before him with a cordiality that quite won the prince's heart, he begged of him to have the goodness to relate the reason of his coming.

"Camaralzaman satisfied his host's curiosity; and when he had finished his story, in which he disguised nothing, he asked, in his turn, by what means he might get back to the dominions of the king his father; 'For,' said he, 'were I to attempt to go back to the princess, how should I find her, after I have been separated from her for eleven days by my luckless adventure? How do I know even that she is still alive?' At this sorrowful reflection he could not avoid bursting into tears.

"In answer to the prince's questions, the gardener told him that the city to which he had wandered was a whole year's journey distant from those countries were Mussulmen lived, and which were governed by princes of their religion; but that by sea he might reach the Isle of Ebony in a much shorter time; and that from the latter country it would be more easy to pass to the Island of the Children of Khaledan. He added, that every year a merchant ship sailed to the Isle of Ebony, and that the prince might avail himself of that opportunity to return to the Island of the Children of Khaledan. 'If you had arrived some days sooner,' continued he, 'you might have embarked in the vessel which sailed this year. But if you will wait till the sailing of next year's ship, and like to live with me in the meantime, I offer you freely the hospitality of my house, such as it is.'

"Prince Camaralzaman esteemed himself very fortunate in having thus met with an asylum in a place where he knew no one, and had no interest to procure him acquaintances. He accepted the offer, and remained with the gardener; and while he waited the departure of a merchant vessel for the Isle of Ebony, he employed himself every day in working in the garden; but he passed the nights, when nothing prevented his thoughts from dwelling on his dear Princess Badoura, in sighs, tears, and lamentations.

We will quit him to return to the Princess Badoura, whom we left sleeping in her tent.

THE OLD GARDENER AND CAMARALZAMAN.

"The princess slept for some time; and when she woke was surprised that Prince Camaralzaman was not with her. She called her women, and asked them if they knew where he was. Whilst they were assuring her that they had seen him go into the tent, but had not noticed how or when he left it, she happened to take up her girdle, and at once perceived that the little bag was open, and that the talisman was no longer in it.

She did not doubt that the prince had taken the jewel out to examine it, and that he would bring it back. She expected him till night with the greatest impatience, and could not imagine what could oblige him to be absent from her so long. When she perceived that night came on, and that it was already quite dark, and yet he did not return, she gave herself up to the deepest grief. She cursed the talisman a thousand times, and cursed the maker of it; and if respect had not restrained her tongue, she would have cursed the queen her mother, who had bestowed on her that fatal gift. Although she was distracted at her misfortune, which was the more afflicting inasmuch as she could not imagine why the talisman should be the cause of the prince's departure, she did not lose her presence of mind, but, on the contrary, formed a design which showed a courage not usually given to her sex.

"None but the princess and her women knew of Camaralzaman's disappearance; for when he went away his people had all retired, and were sleeping in their tents. As she feared they might betray her if his absence came to their knowledge, she endeavoured to control her grief, and commanded her women not to say or do anything that might create the slightest suspicion. She then changed her dress for one of Camaralzaman's; and, thus attired, she resembled the prince so strongly that his attendants mistook her for him when she made her appearance on the following morning, and commanded them to pack up the baggage and prepare to continue their journey. When all was ready, she made one of her women take her place in the litter, while she herself mounted Camaralzaman's horse, and they set off.

"After a journey of several months, by land and by sea, the princess, who had retained her disguise as a means of reaching the Island of the Children of Khaledan, arrived at the capital of the Isle of Ebony. The reigning king of this island was named Armanos. Those of the servants of the princess who disembarked first to seek a lodging for her, published in the town that the vessel which had just arrived carried Prince Camaralzaman returning from a long voyage, and obliged by bad weather to make for this port; and the intelligence soon reached the palace of the king.

"King Armanos, accompanied by the greater part of his court, immediately set out to receive the princess, and met her just as she quitted the vessel to proceed to the lodging that had been prepared for her. He gave her a welcome befitting the son of a king who was his friend and ally, and with whom he had always lived on terms of amity; and conducted her to his palace, where he lodged her and her whole suite, notwithstanding her earnest entreaties that he would allow her to have a lodging to herself. He conferred upon her many and great honours, besides entertaining her for three days with extraordinary magnificence.

"When the three days had expired, and King Armanos found that the princess, whom he still supposed to be Prince Camaralzaman, talked of re-embarking and continuing her voyage, he spoke privately to her (for he was quite charmed with the appearance and manners, as well as with the wit and knowledge, of the supposed prince). Therefore he spoke these words: 'O prince, at the advanced age to which you see I have attained, and with little hope of living much longer, I endure the mortification of having no son to whom I can bequeath my kingdom. Heaven has bestowed on me an only daughter, who is possessed of beauty that might worthily be bestowed upon a prince of your high birth and honour, and of such mental and personal accomplishments as distinguish you. Instead, therefore, of preparing to return to your own country, remain with us, and receive her at my hands, together with my crown, which from this moment I resign in your favour. It is now time for me to repose, after having borne the weight of empire for so many years: I cannot retire with more satisfaction to myself than at a period when I am likely to see my state governed by so worthy a successor.'

"This generous offer of the King of the Island of Ebony, to give his only daughter in marriage to the Princess Badoura, who, being a woman, could not accept her, and of giving up to her all his dominions, occasioned his visitor a degree of embarrassment which she little expected. As she had told the king that she was Camaralzaman, and had supported the character with complete success, she thought it would be unworthy of a princess of her rank to undeceive him, and to declare that, instead of being the man she had represented herself, she was only his wife. But if she refused his offer, she had just reason to fear, from the extreme desire he had evinced for the arrangement of the marriage, that the king might change his friendship and good-will towards her into enmity and hatred, and might even attempt her life. Moreover, she could not be certain that she would find Camaralzaman at the court of King Schahzaman his father.

"These considerations, together with the prospect of acquiring a new kingdom for the prince her husband, when the time came that she should ever see him again, made Badoura resolve to accept the proposals of King Armanos. After a few minutes' consideration, therefore, she replied, with her face overspread with blushes, which the king attributed to modesty: 'O great king, I am under infinite obligations to your majesty for the good opinion you have conceived of me, and for the honour you propose to confer upon me, by offering me so great a favour, which I by no means deserve, yet dare not refuse. But, my lord, I cannot accept so great an alliance, except on condition that your majesty will assist me with your counsel; and that I undertake no measures of which you shall not previously have expressed your approval.'

"The marriage being thus agreed on and concluded, the ceremony of the nuptials was fixed for the following day; and the Princess Badoura took that opportunity of acquainting her officers, who still supposed her to be Prince Camaralzaman, of this new turn of affairs, that they might not be astonished at it; and she assured them that the Princess Badoura had given her consent. She spoke of the coming event to her women also, charging them to continue faithfully to keep her secret.

"The King of the Island of Ebony, overjoyed at having gained a son-in-law in whose favour he was entirely prepossessed, assembled his council on the morrow, and declared that he bestowed the princess his daughter in marriage on Prince Camaralzaman, whom he brought with him, and seated beside him near his throne; he told the nobles, moreover, that he resigned his crown to the prince, and enjoined them to accept him as their king, and to pay him homage. When he had concluded, he descended from the throne, and made the Princess Badoura ascend and take his place, where she received the oaths of fidelity and allegiance from the principal nobles who were present.

"When the council broke up, the new king was solemnly proclaimed throughout the city. Festivities were ordered for several days, and couriers were despatched to all parts of the kingdom, that the same ceremonies and the same demonstrations of joy might be everywhere observed.

"In the evening the whole palace was illuminated, and the Princess Haiatalnefous (for this was the name of the daughter of the King of the Island of Ebony) was presented, magnificently dressed, to the Princess Badoura, whom every one supposed to be a man. After the marriage ceremonies were concluded, the newly married pair were left alone, and retired to rest.

"The next morning, while the Princess Badoura received the compliments of a large assembly of courtiers on her marriage and her accession to the throne, King Armanos and his queen repaired to the apartment of the new queen their daughter. Instead of making any reply to their congratulations, she cast her eyes on the ground, and, by the expression of sorrow which overspread her countenance, plainly showed that she was dissatisfied with her marriage.

"In order to console Queen Haiatalnefous, the king said to her: 'My dear daughter, be not disquieted: when Prince Camaralzaman landed here he only sought to return, as soon as possible, to King Schahzaman his father. Although we have prevented him from putting his design in execution by an arrangement with which he must be well satisfied, we must nevertheless expect that he feels much disappointment at being so suddenly deprived of the hope of ever again seeing his father, or any one belonging to his family. But you may be certain that when these emotions of filial tenderness are a little subsided, he will be as attentive to you as a good husband can.'

"In the character of Camaralzaman, and as the King of the Island of Ebony, the Princess Badoura passed the whole of that day in receiving the compliments of her court.

and in reviewing the regular troops belonging to the household. She also performed several other royal duties, with a dignity and ability which earned her the approbation of the whole court.

"The night was advanced when she entered the apartment of Queen Haiatalnefous, and she soon perceived, by the coldness with which the bride received her, that she was not satisfied with her husband. The Princess Badoura endeavoured to dissipate the sadness of Queen Haiatalnefous by a long conversation, in which she employed all her eloquence, of which she had no inconsiderable share, to persuade the bride that she loved her exceedingly. She at last gave her time to go to bed, and during this interval she began to say a prayer; but she remained so long thus employed that Queen Haiatalnefous fell asleep. Then the Princess Badoura ceased from praying, and lay down by her side without waking her. For her own part, she could not sleep, so much afflicted was she by the hard necessity of acting a character which did not become her, and by the loss of her beloved Prince Camaralzaman, whom she unceasingly lamented. She rose the next morning at break of day, before Queen Haiatalnefous awoke. and went to the council, attired in her magnificent royal robes.

"King Armanos did not fail to visit the queen his daughter again on this second day, and he again found her in tears. He at once surmised that her husband's neglect was the cause of her affliction. Quite indignant at the affront which he thought had been put upon her, and of which he could not comprehend the cause, he said: 'Daughter, have patience for one night more. I have raised your husband to my throne, but I have the power to cast him down, and to banish him hence with shame and ignominy, if he does not treat you properly. So indignant am I at seeing you treated with such neglect, that I do not know whether I shall be satisfied with merely driving him hence. It is not to you only, but to my person, that this unpardonable affront is offered.'

"The Princess Badoura returned to the chamber of Queen Haiatalnefous as late on that evening as on the preceding night. She conversed with her as she had done before, and was then going to say her prayers while the bride went to bed; but Queen Haiatalnefous prevented her, and obliged her to sit down again. 'I see,' said she, 'you intend to treat me this night as you did last night and the night before. Tell me, I entreat you, in what way I have displeased you—I, who not only love, but adore you, and esteem myself the happiest of all princesses in the possession of so amiable a prince as you are for my husband? Any other princess who had been affronted as you have affronted me would have revenged herself by abandoning you to your luckless fate; but, even did I not love you as I do, the compassion I feel for the misfortunes even of those who are totally indifferent to me would cause me to warn you that the king my father is extremely displeased with your conduct, and that he only waits till to-morrow to make you feel the full effect of his anger, if you continue this usage of me. I conjure you not to drive to despair a princess who cannot help loving you.'

"This speech occasioned the Princess Badoura inexpressible embarrassment. She could not doubt the sincerity of Queen Haiatalnefous; the coolness which King Armanos had shown towards herself on that day fully indicated his displeasure. The only method that occurred to her of justifying her conduct, was to confess her sex to Queen Haiatalnefous. But although she had foreseen that she should be obliged to make this declaration, yet the uncertainty whether the princess would take it in good part made her tremble. But at last—when she reflected that if Prince Camaralzaman was still alive, he must necessarily stop at the Isle of Ebony on his way to the dominions of King Schahzaman, that she ought to be careful of herself for his sake, and that she could maintain her position only by discovering herself to Queen Haiatalnefous—she hazarded the confession.

"As the Princess Badoura stood silent and confused, Queen Haiatalnefous, becoming impatient, was going to speak again, when the Princess Badoura interrupted her with these words: 'Too amiable and charming princess, I confess I am in fault, and I blame myself greatly; but I hope you will pardon me, and that you will keep inviolate the secret I am going to impart to you for my justification.' So saying, the Princess Badoura uncovered her bosom, and continued: 'See, if a woman and a princess, like yourself, does

CAMARALZAMAN FINDS THE TALISMAN OF THE PRINCESS BADOURA.

not deserve your pardon. I feel certain you will grant it freely when I have related my history to you, and when you are made acquainted with the misfortune which has obliged me to act a deceitful part.

"When the Princess Badoura had concluded her narration, and made herself known to the Princess of the Isle of Ebony, she entreated Queen Haiatalnefous a second time not to betray her secret, but, on the contrary, to help her to maintain the delusion, and pretend that Badoura was really her husband, until the arrival of Prince Camaralzaman, whom she hoped shortly to see again.

"Haiatalnefous replied: 'O princess, it would indeed be a singular destiny if so happy a marriage as yours has been should have really come to an end after a mutual affection, conceived and preserved through so many marvellous trials and adventures. I sincerely wish with you that Heaven may soon re-unite you to your husband. Be assured in the meantime that I will most religiously preserve the secret you have imparted to me. I shall feel the greatest pleasure at being the only person in the great kingdom of the Isle of Ebony who really knows you, while you govern the land with the wisdom you have displayed at the commencement of your reign. I asked you to love me, but now I declare to you that I shall be fully satisfied if you do not refuse me your friendship.' After this conversation the two princesses tenderly embraced, and, with many reciprocal promises of respect and esteem, they lay down to rest.

"The princesses lived together in great amity, as though they had really been husband and wife. Not only were the female attendants of the Princess Haiatalnefous deceived, but King Armanos, the queen his consort, and his whole court had no suspicion of the truth. And from this time the Princess Badoura continued to govern the kingdom in great tranquillity, to the complete satisfaction of the king and all his subjects.

"While these events were occurring in the Isle of Ebony, in which the Princesses Badoura and Haiatalnefous, King Armanos, the queen, the court, and indeed the whole kingdom were so closely interested, Prince Camaralzaman was still in the city of idolaters, dwelling with the gardener who had offered him a retreat.

"One morning very early, while the prince was preparing to work in the garden, according to his usual custom, the good old gardener came to him, and spoke these words: 'The idolaters have a grand festival to-day, and as they abstain from all kinds of labour, and pass the time in public assemblies and rejoicings, they will not suffer Mussulmen to work; and to preserve peace and amity with the natives, the Mussulmen enter into their amusements, and are present at the various spectacles, which are well worthy of notice: so you may allow yourself a holiday to-day. I shall leave you here; and as the time approaches when the merchant vessel which I mentioned to you will sail for the Island of Ebony, I shall go to see some friends, and will inquire of them what day it is to set sail; and at the same time I will arrange matters for your embarkation.' The gardener then put on his best dress, and went out.

"When Prince Camaralzaman found himself alone, instead of taking part in the public rejoicings which enlivened the whole city, he sat down alone, and the leisure he enjoyed brought to his mind in stronger colours than ever the sad recollection of his ever-beloved princess. Lost in melancholy reflection, he sighed and lamented as he walked through the garden, when suddenly the noise made by two birds, who had perched on a tree near him, attracted his attention, and induced him to lift up his head and watch them.

"Camaralzaman observed that these birds were fighting desperately, pecking each other with their beaks; and in a few minutes he saw one of them fall dead at the foot of a tree. The bird who remained conqueror flew away, and soon disappeared.

"At the same moment two other birds of a larger size, who had seen the combat from a distance, came flying down from a different quarter, and alighted, one at the head, the other at the feet of the dead bird. They gazed at it for a considerable time, shaking their heads, with gestures expressive of grief, and then dug a grave for the bird with their claws, and buried it.

"As soon as the birds had filled the grave with the earth they had thrown out, they flew away, and a short time afterwards returned, dragging between them the murderer, one holding him by the wing, and the other by the leg. The criminal uttered dreadful screams, and made violent efforts to escape. They brought him to the grave of the bird he had destroyed in his rage, and there inflicted upon him the just punishment he merited for the cruel murder he had committed; for they deprived him of life by pecking him with their beaks. They then tore open his body, and, leaving the corpse on the ground, flew away.

"Camaralzaman had remained all this time in silent admiration at this surprising spectacle. He now approached the tree where the scene had taken place, and casting his eyes on the body of the criminal, which lay extended on the ground, he perceived something red protruding from the stomach of the bird that had been torn to pieces. He took up the mangled remains, and taking out the red substance which had attracted his notice, he found it to be the talisman of the Princess Badoura, his dear and tenderly-beloved princess, the loss of which had cost him so much anxiety, pain, and regret. 'Cruel bird!' cried he, as he gazed at the talisman, 'thou didst delight in evil actions, and I have great cause to complain of the grief thou hast caused me. But in proportion to what I have suffered through thee, do I wish well to those who have avenged my injuries, while they revenged the death of their companion.'

"It is impossible to express the joy of Prince Camaralzaman at this adventure. 'Dearest princess,' he exclaimed again, 'this fortunate moment, in which I thus recover what is so valuable to you, is no doubt a happy omen that announces my meeting with you in the same unexpected manner, perhaps even sooner than I dare to hope! Blessed be the day in which I taste this happiness, and which, at the same time, opens to me the delightful prospect of the greatest joy that can be mine.'

"As he spoke these words Camaralzaman kissed the talisman; and, wrapping it up carefully, tied it round his arm. Since his separation from the princess he had passed almost every night without closing his eyes, and racked by tormenting reflections. He slept very tranquilly the whole of the night which succeeded this happy event; and the next morning, at break of day, he put on his working dress, and went to the gardener to receive directions for his labour. The gardener begged him to cut and root up a particular tree which he pointed out to him, for it was old, and no longer bore fruit.

"Camaralzaman took an axe, and set to work. As he was cutting a part of the root he struck something which resisted the axe, and made a loud noise. He removed the earth, and discovered a large plate of brass, under which he found a staircase with ten steps. He immediately descended, and when he had reached the bottom, he found himself in a sort of cave or vault, about fifteen feet square, in which he counted fifty large bronze jars, ranged round the walls, each with a lid. He uncovered these vases, one after the other, and found them filled with gold dust. He then left the vault, quite overjoyed at having discovered this rich treasure. He replaced the plate over the staircase, and continued to root up the tree, while he waited for the gardener's return.

"The gardener had been informed on the preceding day, that the vessel which sailed annually to the Isle of Ebony was to depart very soon; but those who had given him this intelligence could not acquaint him with the precise day on which it would sail; they promised, however, to tell him this on the morrow. He had been to gain the information he wanted, and returned with a countenance which displayed the joy he felt at being the bearer of good news for Camaralzaman. 'My son,' said he to him, for by his great age he claimed the privilege of addressing the prince by this endearing title, 'rejoice, and hold yourself in readiness to embark in three days; the vessel will certainly sail in that time, and I have agreed with the captain about your passage and departure.'

"'O my friend,' Camaralzaman replied, 'you could not at the present moment come to me with more joyful news. But, in return, I also have intelligence to communicate to you, which will give you great pleasure. Have the goodness to follow me, and you will see the good fortune that Heaven has sent you.' Camaralzaman conducted the gardener to the spot where he had rooted up the tree, and made him go down into the vault; then, showing him the number of jars it contained, all filled with gold dust, he expressed his joy that Heaven, his kind protector, had given the good man a reward for all the toil and pain he had undergone for so many years.

"The gardener answered: 'O my son, what is this you say? Do you suppose that I will possess myself of this treasure? No; it is all your own: I have no claim to any part of it. During the eighty years that I have worked in this garden since my father's death, I have never chanced to discover it. This is a sign that it was destined for you alone, since Heaven led you to find it. This wealth is more suited to a prince like you than to me, who am on the brink of the grave, and want nothing more. Allah sends it to you very opportunely at the time when you are about to return to the kingdom which is to belong to you, and where you will make a good use of it.'

"Prince Camaralzaman would not be behindhand with the gardener in generosity, and they had a great contest on this point. He at length solemnly protested that he would not touch any of the gold unless the gardener retained half for his own share. At length the gardener consented to this proposal, and they divided the jars, each taking twenty-five.

"After the division had been made, the gardener said, 'My son, this is not all; we must now devise some plan for embarking this wealth on the vessel, and taking them with you so secretly as not to give any suspicion of its presence, otherwise you might run a risk of losing your gold. There are no olives in the Isle of Ebony, and those which come from here are in great request. As you know, I have a good stock of olives, gathered from my own garden. You must, therefore, take the fifty jars, and fill the lower half of each with the gold dust, and the other half with olives up to the top; and we will have them taken to the ship when you yourself embark.'

"Camaralzaman adopted this advice, and employed himself for the rest of the day in filling and arranging the fifty jars; and as he feared that he might lose the talisman of the Princess Badoura if he wore it constantly on his arm, he took the precaution to put it in one of these jars, on which he set a mark to know it again. By the time he had completed his work, and the jars were ready for removal, night was approaching. Therefore he went home with the gardener, and entering into conversation with him, related the battle of the two birds, and the circumstances by which he had recovered the talisman of the Princess Badoura. The gardener was surprised, and rejoiced at this account for the sake of his guest.

"Whether it was from his great age, or because he had taken too much exercise on that day, the gardener passed a bad night; his illness increased on the following day, and the third morning he found himself still worse. As soon as it was day, the captain of the vessel, with some of his seamen, came and knocked at the garden-gate. Camaralzaman opened it, and they inquired for the passenger who was to embark on board their vessel. The prince replied: 'I am he. The gardener who took my passage is ill, and cannot speak to you; however, pray come in, and take away these jars of olives, together with my baggage; and I will follow you as soon as I have taken my leave of my old friend.'

"The seamen carried away his jars and baggage, and, on leaving Camaralzaman, desired him to follow them immediately; For: the captain said, 'the wind is fair, and I only wait for you to set sail.'

"As soon as the captain and seamen were gone, Camaralzaman returned to the gardener, to bid him farewell and thank him for all his kindness towards a desolate stranger; but he found the old man at the point of death; and had scarcely obtained from him the profession of his faith, which all good Mussulmen repeat on their death-bed, when the gardener fell backward, and expired.

"The prince, who was under the necessity of embarking immediately, used the utmost diligence in performing the last duties to the deceased. He washed the body, wrapped it in grave-clothes, and dug a grave in the garden; for, as Mahometans were barely tolerated in the city of idolaters, they had no public cemetery. The burial of his friend occupied him till the close of the day. He then set out to embark; and that he might lose no time, he took the key of the garden with him, intending to deliver it to the proprietor, or, if he could not find him, to give it to some trusty person, in the presence of witnesses, that it might be sent to the owner. But when he arrived at the harbour, he was informed that the ship had weighed anchor some time before, and it was already out of sight. His informant added that it waited for him three full hours before it had set sail.

"As may be supposed, Camaralzaman was vexed and distressed to the utmost degree when he found himself obliged to remain in a country where he had no motive for wishing to form any acquaintance, and where he must wait another year before the opportunity he had just lost would again present itself. He was still more mortified to think that he had parted with the talisman of the Princess Badoura, which he now gave up for lost. Nothing was left for him but to return to the garden he had left, to rent it of the landlord to whom it belonged, and to continue to cultivate the ground, while he deplored his misfortune. As the labour of cultivating the garden was more than he could endure alone, he hired a boy to assist him; and that he might not lose the second half of the treasure, which came to him by the death of the gardener, who had died without heirs, he put the gold dust into fifty other jars, and covered them with olives, as he had done in

DEATH OF THE OLD GARDENER.

the first instance, intending to take them with him when the time came for him to embark.

"While Prince Camaralzaman was thus entering upon another year of toil, sorrow, and impatience, the vessel continued its voyage with a favourable wind, and arrived without mishap at the capital of the Isle of Ebony.

"As the palace was on the sea shore, the new king, or rather the Princess Badoura, who happened to notice the vessel sailing into port with all its flags flying, inquired what ship it was, and was told that it came every year, at that season, from the city of idolaters, and that it was in general laden with very rich merchandise.

"The princess, who, in the midst of all the state and splendour that surrounded her, had her mind constantly occupied with the idea of Camaralzaman, imagined that he might have embarked on board that vessel, and it occurred to her that she might go to meet him when he landed—not with the intention to make herself known to him, for she was convinced he would not recognise her; but to observe him, and take the measures she thought most proper for their meeting. Under pretence, therefore, of inspecting the merchandise, and even of being the first to see and to choose the most valuable for herself, she ordered a horse to be brought to her. She went to the harbour, accompanied by several officers who happened to be present at the time, and arrived at the moment when the captain came on shore. She desired him to come to her, and inquired of him from whence he had sailed, how long he had been at sea, what good or evil fortune he had met with during his voyage, and if he had among his passengers any stranger of distinction. Above all, she required to know of what his cargo consisted.

"The captain gave satisfactory answers to all these questions. As regarded passengers, he assured her he had none except the merchants who were accustomed to trade to the Island of Ebony, and that they brought very rich stuffs from different countries, linens of the finest texture, white and dyed, precious stones, musk ambergris, camphor, civet, spices, medicinal drugs, olives, and many other articles.

"The Princess Badoura happened to be exceedingly fond of olives. Directly she heard them mentioned, she said to the captain, 'I will buy all you have on board. Let them be unladen immediately, that I may purchase them of you. As for the other merchandise, you will request the owners to bring me the most beautiful and valuable of their goods before they show them to any one.'

"'O king,' replied the captain, 'there are fifty large jars of olives on board, but they belong to a merchant who was left behind. I had informed him of my intended departure, and even waited for him for some time. But as I found he did not come, and that his delay would prevent my profiting by a favourable wind, I lost all patience, and set sail without him.' 'Let them be carried ashore nevertheless,' said the princess; 'this shall not prevent my purchasing them.'

"The captain sent his boat to the ship, and it soon returned, bringing the jars of olives. The princess inquired what the value of the fifty jars might be in the Isle of Ebony. The captain replied: 'O king, the merchant is very poor; your majesty will confer a great obligation on him by giving him a thousand pieces of silver.' 'That he may be perfectly satisfied,' said the princess, 'and in consideration of his great poverty, you shall have a thousand pieces of gold counted out to you, which you will take care to deliver to him.' She gave orders for the payment of this sum, and, after she had desired that the jars might be taken away, she returned to the palace.

"When evening came the Princess Badoura retired to the interior of the palace, and went to the apartment of the Princess Haiatalnefous, where she had the fifty jars of olives brought to her. She opened one of the jars to taste the contents, and poured some into a dish, when, to her great astonishment, she found the olives mixed with gold dust. 'What a wonderful circumstance!' she exclaimed. She immediately ordered the other jars to be opened and emptied in her presence by the women of Haiatalnefous, and her surprise increased when she perceived that the olives in each jar were mixed with gold dust. But when that jar was emptied in which Camaralzaman had deposited the talisman, her emotions on beholding it were so powerful that she was quite overcome, and fainted away.

"The Princess Haiatalnefous and her women ran to her assistance, and, by throwing water on her face, at length brought her to herself. When she had recovered her senses, she took up the talisman, and kissed it several times; but as she did not choose to reveal her secret before the princess's women, who were ignorant of her disguise, and as it was moreover time to retire to rest, she dismissed them. But she said to Haiatalnefous, as soon as they were alone, 'O princess, after what I have related to you of my adventures, you no doubt guessed that it was the sight of this talisman which caused my fainting. It is mine, and has been the fatal cause of the separation that has taken place between my beloved husband, Prince Camaralzaman, and myself. But as it was the occasion of an event so painful to both of us, I feel certain it will be the means of our speedy reunion.'

"The next morning, as soon as day appeared, the Princess Badoura sent for the captain of the vessel. When he came into her presence, she said to him, 'I beg you to give me some additional particulars concerning the merchant to whom the olives belonged that I bought yesterday. I think you told me that you left him in the city of idolaters: can you inform me what was his occupation there?'

"The captain answered: 'O great king, I can answer your majesty with certainty, for I know how the merchant employed himself. The bargain for his passage was made with a gardener, who was extremely old, and who told me that I should find my passenger in his garden, the situation of which he pointed out to me, and where he told me this merchant laboured: this made me tell your majesty that he was poor. I went to this very garden to seek him, and to tell him that I was going to embark, and spoke to him there myself.'

"Then the princess said: 'If what you tell me is true, you must set sail again to-day, and return to the city of idolaters to search for this young gardener, and bring him hither, for he is my debtor. If you refuse, I declare that I will confiscate not only all the goods which belong to you and those of the merchants you have on board, but will also make your life and the life of every one on board your ship to answer for my debtor. By my command the magazines where your cargo is deposited shall be sealed up, and the seals shall not be taken off until you have delivered into my hands the young man I require. This is what I have to say to you. Go and obey my orders.'

"The captain dared not demur at this command, for he saw that to disobey would involve him and all his friends in one common ruin. He reported the supposed king's words to them, and they were no less anxious than himself for the immediate departure of the vessel. He laid in a store of water and provisions for the voyage, and made his preparations with so much expedition that he set sail on that very day.

"The ship had a very good voyage, and the captain made such haste that he arrived by night at the city of idolaters. When he was as near land as he thought necessary, he did not cast anchor, but while the vessel lay to he got into his boat, and disembarked at a spot not far from the harbour. From thence he went to the garden of Camaralzaman, accompanied by six of his most resolute seamen.

"The prince was not asleep. His separation from the beautiful Princess of China still overwhelmed him with affliction, and he mourned and cursed the moment when he had suffered himself to be tempted by curiosity first to touch and then to examine her girdle. In this manner he was passing the hours which should have been dedicated to repose, when he heard a knocking at the gate of the garden. He went, half dressed, to open it, and directly he appeared the captain and sailors, without speaking a word, seized him and dragged him by main force to the boat. They then put him on board the ship, which set sail again as soon as they had re-embarked.

"Camaralzaman, who, as well as the captain, and seamen, had till then preserved a profound silence, now asked the captain, whose features he recollected, what reason he had for thus violently dragging him away. 'Are you not a debtor to the King of the Island of Ebony?' inquired the captain in his turn. 'How can I be a debtor to the King of the Island of Ebony?' exclaimed Camaralzaman, with amazement: 'I do not know him; I never had any dealings with him, nor did I ever set my foot in his dominions.' 'You must know more about that matter than I can tell you,' replied the captain; 'but you shall speak to him yourself; however, remain here quietly, and be patient.'

"The vessel had as successful a voyage in carrying Camaralzaman to the Isle of Ebony as it had experienced in going for him to the city of idolaters. Although night had closed in when they arrived in port, the captain at once went ashore to take Prince Camaralzaman to the palace, where he requested to be admitted to the king's presence.

"The Princess Badoura had already retired to the inner palace; but as soon as she was informed of his return, and of the arrival of Camaralzaman, she went out to speak to him. When she had cast her eyes on her beloved prince, for whom she had shed so many tears since their separation, she instantly recognised him, even in his labourer's dress. As for the prince, who trembled in the presence of a king to whom he was to answer for an imaginary debt, he had not the least idea that he stood in the presence of her whom he desired so ardently to meet. Had the princess yielded to her inclinations, she would have run to him, and made herself known by her tender embraces; but she restrained her emotions, as she thought it for the interest of both that she should continue to sustain the character of king for some time longer, before she revealed her secret to the prince. She contented herself with recommending Camaralzaman particularly to the care of an officer who was present, charging him to pay his prisoner every attention, and treat him well until the following day.

"When the Princess Badoura had arranged everything that related to Prince Camaralzaman, she turned towards the captain, to recompense him for the important service he had rendered her. She immediately despatched an officer to take off the seal which had been placed on his merchandise, as well as that of the merchants, and dismissed him with a present of a rich and precious diamond, which fully repaid him the expense of the second voyage. She told him also that he might keep for himself the thousand pieces of gold which had been paid for the jars of olives, and that she would settle the matter with the merchant he had brought back with him.

"She at length returned to the apartment of the Princess of the Isle of Ebony, to whom she told how successful her project had been. She begged Queen Haiatalnefous not to disclose the secret, and to entrust her with the measures she thought it necessary to adopt, before she discovered herself to Prince Camaralzaman and acknowledge who he himself was. 'There is,' she said, 'so great a distance between the rank of a great Prince and that of a gardener, that there might be some danger in his passing from one of the lowest classes of the people to the very highest station, however just his claim to the higher rank might be.' Far from being faithless to her promise, the Princess of the Isle of Ebony concurred with Badoura in the design she had formed. She even assured her that she would contribute all in her power to forward it, on receiving instructions as to her mode of proceeding.

"The next day, after taking care to have Prince Camaralzaman conducted to the bath very early in the morning, and afterwards dressed in the robe of an emir, or governor of a province, the Princess of China, under the name, habit, and authority of King of the Isle of Ebony, introduced him into the council, where he attracted the attention of all the nobles present by his stately and majestic air, and his handsome appearance.

"The Princess Badoura herself was charmed once more to see a husband who had always appeared amiable in her eyes, and she felt additional interest in extolling him to the council. After he had taken his place in the rank of emirs, according to her directions, she said, addressing the other emirs: 'My lords, Camaralzaman, whom I this day present to you as your colleague, is not unworthy of the position he occupies amongst you. I have in my travels had sufficient experience of his worth to be able to answer for him; and I can assure you that he will make himself celebrated and admired by all for his valour, and for a thousand other good and amiable qualities, characteristic of the greatness of his mind.'

"Camaralzaman was extremely surprised when he heard his own name mentioned by the King of the Isle of Ebony, whom he little suspected to be a woman, much less his adored princess; and when he heard the king assure the assembly that he knew the stranger, when he was himself convinced that he had never met the king in his life, he was still more astonished at the unexpected praise the monarch bestowed on him.

"This praise, however, although pronounced by royal lips, did not disconcert him; he received it with a modesty that proved he deserved it, but that it did not excite his vanity. He prostrated himself before the throne of the king, and when he rose he said: 'O great king, I cannot find words to express my thanks to your majesty for the great honour you have conferred on me, and for all your kindness. I will exert myself to the utmost to deserve the favour you have vouchsafed to me.'

"When he left the council, the prince was conducted by an officer to a large mansion, which the Princess Badoura had already caused to be furnished and prepared for his reception. In this handsome dwelling he found officers and servants ready to receive his commands, and a stable filled with very fine horses. The whole establishment was suited to the dignity which had just been conferred on him; and when he went into his closet, his steward brought him a coffer full of gold for his expenses. Totally unable as he was to guess from what quarter this good fortune came, his surprise and admiration were intense; but he never entertained the least suspicion that it was his own princess who was thus showering benefits upon him.

"At the end of two or three days, the Princess Badoura, who wished to afford

CAMARALZAMAN AND BADOURA.

Camaralzaman more frequent access to her presence, so that she might raise him gradually to higher distinction, bestowed on him the office of grand treasurer, which had become vacant. He performed the duties of this new office with so much integrity, and was so considerate to all around him, that he not only acquired the friendship of all the nobles about the court, but also won the hearts of the common people by his rectitude and generosity.

"Camaralzaman would have been the happiest of men, on finding himself in such high favour with a king who, as he supposed, was an entire stranger to him, and thus obtaining the daily increasing esteem of every one, had he possessed his princess also. But in the midst of all his splendour he never ceased lamenting her loss, and deploring that he could gain no information respecting her in a country where he concluded she must have sojourned, since the time when he had been separated from her by the unfortunate accident of the lost talisman. He might have suspected the truth if the Princess Badoura had retained the name of Camaralzaman, which she had assumed with his dress. But when she ascended the throne, she changed her adopted name for that of Armanos, in compliment to the former king, her father-in-law; so that she was now known only by the name of King Armanos the Younger; and there were only a few courtiers who remembered the name of Camaralzaman, which she had borne on her first arrival at the Island of Ebony. Camaralzaman had not yet had sufficient communication with these courtiers to learn this circumstance; but he might in the end have been informed of it.

"As the Princess Badoura feared that the secret might be thus betrayed, and as she wished Camaralzaman to be indebted to her only for the discovery, she resolved at length to put an end to her own suspense and to the grief with which she saw the prince was oppressed. She had remarked that when she conversed with him on the affairs relating to his office, he frequently heaved deep sighs, and was evidently possessed by some mournful remembrance. She herself lived in a state of constant restraint, which she was determined to end without further delay. Moreover, the friendship of the nobles which Camaralzaman had gained by his judicious conduct, added to the zeal and affection of the people, contributed to persuade her that the crown of the Island of Ebony might be placed on his head without any risk.

"When once the Princess Badoura had formed this resolution, in concert with the Princess Haiatalnefous, she spoke to Prince Camaralzaman in private, on the same day, in the following words: 'I wish to converse with you on an affair which will require some discussion, and on which I want your advice. Come to me this evening; tell your people not to wait for you, for you will remain here for the night.'

"Camaralzaman did not fail to repair to the palace at the hour appointed by the princess. She took him with her into the inner palace, and telling the chief of the eunuchs, who was preparing to follow her, that she did not require his attendance, but desiring him to keep the door fastened, she conducted the prince into a different apartment from that of the Princess Haiatalnefous, in which she was accustomed to sleep.

"When the prince and princess were thus left alone together, the princess fastened the door. Thereupon she took the talisman out of a little box, and showed it to Camaralzaman, saying: 'It is not long since an astrologer gave me this talisman, and as I know you are well versed in every science, you perhaps can tell me its peculiar properties.' Camaralzaman took the talisman, and approached a light to examine it. He at once recognised it, and exclaimed, with a cry of surprise which delighted the princess, 'O king, do you ask me the properties of this talisman? Alas! its power is such that it will make me die with grief and sadness, if I do not shortly find the most charming and amiable princess ever beheld under heaven! To her this talisman belonged, and it was the cause of my losing her. The adventure was of so singular a nature, that the recital of it would excite your majesty's compassion for me, the unfortunate husband and lover, if you would have the patience to listen to it.'

"To this the princess replied: 'You shall relate it to me some other time; but I am very happy to tell you that I know something concerning the talisman. Wait for me here; I will return in a moment.'

"Thereupon the princess went into a closet, where she took off the royal turban, and in a few minutes put on a woman's dress, together with the girdle she had worn on the day of their separation. Then she returned to the chamber where she had left the prince.

"Camaralzaman instantly knew his dear princess. He ran to her, and embraced her with the utmost tenderness, exclaiming, 'Ah! how much I am obliged to the king for having surprised me so agreeably!' 'Do not expect to see the king again,' replied the princess, embracing him in her turn, with tears in her eyes. 'Look upon me, and you behold the king. Sit down, that I may explain this enigma to you.'

"They seated themselves, and the princess related to Camaralzaman the resolution she had formed in the plain where they had encamped together for the last time, when she discovered that she waited for him in vain. She told him how she had kept this resolution until her arrival at the Isle of Ebony, where she had been obliged to marry the Princess Haiatalnefous, and to accept the crown which King Armanos had offered her in consequence of the marriage. She related to Camaralzaman how generously the princess, whose merits she spoke of in the warmest terms, had received the declaration she had made of the sex of her supposed husband; and finally acquainted him with the adventure of the talisman, found in one of the jars of olives and gold dust which she had purchased, which had induced her to send for him to the city of idolaters.

"When the Princess Badoura had concluded her narrative, she begged the prince to inform her by what accident the talisman had occasioned his departure. He related his adventure, and when he had concluded it, he complained to her in an affectionate manner of her cruelty in making him languish so long without the hope of seeing her again. She gave him the reasons that had induced her to postpone the discovery; and now at length the loving pair were reunited.

"The next morning, as soon as it was day, the princess arose. She now no longer wore the royal robe, but resumed her own dress, and when she was ready, she despatched the chief of the eunuchs to request that King Armanos, her father-in-law, would honour her by coming to her apartment.

"When King Armanos arrived, he was very much surprised to see a lady whom he did not remember ever to have seen, and to find in her presence the grand treasurer, who was not allowed to enter the inner palace, any more than the other nobles belonging to the court. When he had taken his seat, he inquired for the king.

"The princess replied: 'O King Armanos, yesterday I was a king; to-day I am only the Princess of China, the wife of the true Prince Camaralzaman, who is the son of King Schahzaman. If your majesty will have the patience to listen to our separate histories, I flatter myself you will not condemn me for the innocent deceit I have conceived and practised.' King Armanos granted her an audience, and listened to her adventures with the utmost astonishment from beginning to end.

"When the Princess Badoura had concluded the history of her life, she added: 'O great king, although the ordinance by which our religion permits men to have several wives is not very agreeable to our sex, yet if your majesty will consent to give the Princess Haiatalnefous, your daughter, in marriage to Prince Camaralzaman, I will cheerfully resign the dignity and title of queen, which properly belongs to her, and will myself be content with the second rank. Even if this preference were not her due, I should have insisted on her accepting it, after the obligation she has conferred upon me by so generously keeping the secret with which I entrusted her. If your majesty's determination depends upon her consent, I have already obtained her acquiescence in this arrangement, and am certain she will be happy.'

"King Armanos listened with every mark of admiration to this discourse of the Princess Badoura; and when she had finished speaking, he turned to Prince Camaralzaman, and spoke in the following words: 'My son, since the Princess Badoura your wife, whom a deception of which I cannot now complain caused me to consider as my son-in-law, has offered that you should marry my daughter, I have nothing to do but to inquire if you also are willing to marry her, and to accept the crown, which the Princess Badoura would well deserve to wear for the rest of her life, if her love for you did not induce her to resign it.' Camaralzaman replied: 'O king, however strong may be my desire of seeing my father, the obligations I owe to your majesty and to the Princess Haiatalnefous are so great and powerful, that I am ready to do all you wish.'

"Camaralzaman was therefore proclaimed king, and espoused the Princess Haiatalnefous the same day with the greatest magnificence; and he was thoroughly satisfied with the beauty, wit, and affection of his new wife.

"The two queens continued to live together in the same friendship and union which they had hitherto shown, and were well contented with the equality which King Camaralzaman observed in his conduct towards them.

"They each presented him with a son in the same year, and nearly at the same time, and the births of the two princes were celebrated by great public rejoicings. To the first-born son, the child of the Queen Badoura, Camaralzaman gave the name of Amgiad, or 'The Most Glorious,' while the babe whom the Queen Haiatalnefous had brought into the world was called Assad, or 'The Most Happy.'"

## THE HISTORY OF PRINCE AMGIAD, AND OF PRINCE ASSAD.

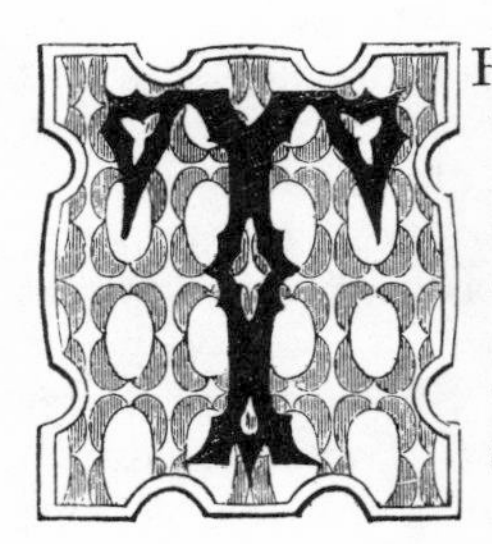

HESE two princes were brought up with great care. When they were of a proper age, they had each the same governor, and the same masters in all those sciences and branches of learning in which King Camaralzaman wished them to be skilled. One person also taught both of them the necessary lessons of physical strength and endurance. The great regard they showed for each other, even from their infancy, produced a certain uniformity in all their thoughts and actions, which in itself tended to augment their friendship.

"When they had attained the age at which each of them might expect to have a separate house and establishment, they were so strongly attached to each other that they requested their father to suffer them still to live together. They obtained their wish: and thus the same officers were appointed for both of them. They were served by the same attendants, rode in the same cavalcade, slept in the same apartment, and dined at the same table. Camaralzaman gradually learned to place such implicit confidence both in their ability and their rectitude, that when they were about nineteen years old he did not hesitate to appoint them alternately to preside at the council, whenever he was absent for a few days on a hunting expedition.

"These two princes were of equal beauty, both in face and figure, and had always been esteemed very handsome from their infancy, and the two queens felt an almost incredible attachment to them. Now it also happened, in accordance with destiny, that two ladies in the palace, on whom King Camaralzaman had set his affections, conceived a great regard for the Princes Amgiad and Assad; and as the princes advanced in age, this regard, which had commenced in friendship, changed to a more tender feeling, and at length became the most violent love. The princes, indeed, appeared in the eyes of the two ladies possessed of so many accomplishments, that they were absolutely blinded and led away by the fascinations of the young men. They made the greatest efforts to resist their passion; but the frequency of their meetings—for they saw the princes every day—and the habit they had acquired of admiring and praising them from their earliest infancy—a habit which it was scarcely in their power to break themselves of—so unfortunately increased their infatuation that they could get no rest. To heighten their misfortune and that of the princes, Amgiad and Assad became so accustomed to these demonstrations of affection, that they had not the slightest suspicion of the real state of the case.

"As the two ladies had not entrusted to each other the secret of their passion, and as neither of them had the audacity openly to make a declaration of it in person to the prince whom she loved, they separately determined to explain it by letter. In order to execute this fatal design, they took advantage of the absence of King Camaralzaman, who had gone on a hunting party for a few days.

"The day after the king's departure Prince Amgiad presided at the council, and was employed for two or three hours in the afternoon in hearing complaints and administering justice. As he came out from the council chamber, and was returning to the palace, an eunuch took him aside, and gave him a letter from his enamoured. Amgiad immediately

CAMARALZAMAN COMMANDS GIONDAR TO PUT THE PRINCES TO DEATH.

opened it, and was struck with horror when he read its contents. 'What!' cried he to the eunuch, drawing his sabre the moment he had perused the letter, 'is this the fidelity thou owest to thy king and master?' and with these words he struck off the eunuch's head.

"Directly he had done this, Amgiad went in the greatest possible indignation to his mother, Queen Badoura; and with a look that plainly showed his anger, he held out the letter to her, and informed her of the contents, telling her also from whom it came. But instead of listening to him, the queen herself flew into a violent rage. 'I am convinced, my son,' she replied, 'that what you tell me is nothing but a calumnious falsehood. The lady is both prudent and wise; and indeed I consider it a great act of boldness in you to speak against her with so much insolence.' To this speech of the queen's the prince retorted, 'You are one as bad as the other, and were it not for the respect I owe to the king my father, this day should be the last of her life.'

"From the manner in which Prince Amgiad had received the declaration of his enamoured, the lady who loved Prince Assad might have judged what to expect, the prince being as noble-minded as his brother, and who would not therefore receive a similar declaration more favourably. This, however, did not prevent her from pursuing her detestable plan. The next day, therefore, she wrote a letter to Assad, which she entrusted to an old woman, who had free admission to the palace.

"This old woman chose the moment when Prince Assad left the council, where he went to preside in his turn, as a proper opportunity to execute her commission. The prince took the letter, but he did not even finish the perusal of it. When he had read enough to understand its nature, he was so transported with rage that he drew his sabre, and punished the old woman with the death she deserved. He then ran to the apartment of Queen Haiatalnefous his mother, with the letter in his hand, intending to show it her. But she did not give him time to do so, or even to open his lips. 'I know why you have come hither,' she cried: 'you are as insolent as your brother Amgiad. Go! begone—never again dare to appear in my presence!'

"Assad was overwhelmed with astonishment at these words, for which he was totally unprepared. So transported was he with anger that he was upon the point of showing the most direful marks of his wrath; he, however, had the resolution to restrain himself, and retired without making any reply, lest a word should escape him unworthy of his greatness of soul. As Prince Amgiad had not mentioned to him the letter he had received the day before, Assad went to his brother to chide him for his silence, and that they might mingle their griefs together, and console each other in their sorrows.

"The two ladies were driven almost to desperation at finding that the princes regarded them and their proceedings with horror. The consciousness of the detestation they inspired, instead of bringing them back to a sense of their duty, made them renounce every natural feeling, and conceive for the princes a most intense hatred. They consulted together how they might destroy them. They made their women believe that the princes, and not they, were the criminals in this matter; and attempted to pass off this deception for a reality by shedding abundance of tears, and by exhausting themselves in lamentations and invectives. They went and slept in the same bed, as if to condole with each other in their deep distress.

"When King Camaralzaman returned the next day from the chase, he was greatly astonished at finding the two ladies in bed together, bathed in tears, and in a condition of pretended grief and horror that greatly excited his compassion. He eagerly inquired of them what had happened.

"To this question they cunningly answered by redoubled sighs and groans. At length, in reply to his tender and repeated inquiries, one of them broke silence, and said, 'O my gracious lord, the deep and matchless grief with which we are afflicted should make us hide our faces even from the light of the sun. The princes Amgiad and Assad have insulted our honour beyond all endurance. With a craft and subtlety altogether unworthy of their illustrious birth, they have had the boldness and insolence during your absence to attempt irrevocably to defame us. We entreat your majesty not to make any further inquiries. Our grief must explain to you the nature of the insult they have offered us.' The king then ordered the two princes to be called, and would absolutely have killed them with his own hand, if old King Armanos, his father-in-law, who happened to be present, had not prevented him. The old king exclaimed: 'O my son, what are you about to do? Do you wish to embrue your hands in the blood of your own offspring, here in your very palace? There are means of punishing the princes if they are really guilty of the crime you lay to their charge.' In this manner he endeavoured to appease King Camaralzaman, and entreated him thoroughly to examine whether it was quite certain the princes had meditated the crime imputed to them.

"King Camaralzaman so far got the better of his rage as to refrain from being the executioner of his own children. However, he ordered them to be arrested, and desired an emir, called Giondar, to come in the evening to him; and he then commanded that officer to conduct the princes beyond the city, and at a proper distance from the capital to put them to death. As a proof that he had executed the orders he thus received, Giondar was not to return without the blood-stained garments of the two brothers.

"Giondar continued travelling with the princes the whole night; and the next morning, dismounting from his horse, he informed the princes, with tears in his eyes, of the orders he had received. 'O beloved princes,' said he to them, 'this is indeed a cruel command, and great is my grief that I have been chosen for the executioner. Would to heaven it were otherwise.' 'Do your duty,' replied Amgiad and Assad; 'we know well enough that you are not the cause of our death, and sincerely do we pardon you.' With these words they embraced, and took an eternal farewell of each other with so much tenderness and affection, that it was a long time before they could separate. Prince Assad was the first who prepared himself to receive his death at the hands of Giondar. 'Kill me first,' said he, 'that I may not have the grief of seeing my dear brother Amgiad die.' Amgiad opposed this plan, and Giondar was unable to restrain his bitter tears at the sight of an amiable contest, which so evidently proved the sincerity and strength of their mutual affection.

"This interesting dispute was at last terminated by their entreating Giondar to bind them both together, in such a way that they might both, as nearly as possible, receive their death at the same moment. They said to him, 'Do not refuse to afford two unfortunate brothers the consolation of dying together; two brothers who, even to their innocence in this affair, have from their earliest infancy possessed everything in common.' Giondar granted the prayer of the two princes. He bound them, and having placed them, as he thought, in the most convenient position for striking off both their heads at one blow, he asked them if they had any request to make to him before their death. 'There is only one thing,' answered the princes, 'which we wish you to do. Assure the king our father, upon your return, that we die innocent: but that we nevertheless do not impute to him the crime of shedding our blood. We know, indeed, that he is deceived concerning the infamous offence of which we are accused.' Giondar promised that he would not fail to do what they desired. Then he drew his scimitar to execute his terrible duty; but his horse, which was fastened to a tree, alarmed at this action, and also at the glittering of the blade, broke its bridle, and began to gallop away over the country at full speed.

"This horse was very valuable, and also very richly caparisoned, and Giondar was vexed at the thought of losing him. Therefore, instead of cutting off the heads of the princes, he threw down his scimitar and ran after his horse, endeavouring to catch it. The horse, a vigorous and playful animal, gallopped about for some time just before Giondar, who was led in the pursuit close to a wood, into which the horse ran. The emir followed the beast, when the neighing of the horse disturbed a lion, which lay sleeping in the wood. The lion instantly roused itself, but instead of pursuing the horse, it ran directly at Giondar, as soon as it perceived him.

"Giondar then thought no more of his horse, but was in the greatest distress how to save his own life. He endeavoured to escape the attack of the lion, who never lost sight of him, but kept pursuing him among the trees. In this extremity he said to himself, 'Allah would not have inflicted this punishment upon me, if the princes, whom I have been ordered to kill, were not innocent. Unfortunately, too, I have not my scimitar to defend myself with.'

"During the absence of Giondar, the two princes experienced a burning thirst, brought on by the fear of death, which they felt, notwithstanding their manly and generous resolution to summit to the cruel order of their father. Prince Amgiad then observed to his brother that they were not far from a spring of water, and proposed to him that they should unbind themselves, and quench their thirst. 'It is not worth the trouble, my brother,' said Assad, 'for the few moments we have to live: we shall have to bear this thirst only for a short time longer.' Amgiad, however, paid no attention to this speech, but unbound both himself and his brother, against the inclination of Assad. They went to the spring; and when they had refreshed themselves, they heard the roaring of the lion, accompanied by lamentable and most piercing cries, which issued from the wood into which Giondar had run after his horse. Amgiad instantly caught up the scimitar which Giondar had thrown down. 'Brother,' he cried, 'let us hasten to the assistance of the unfortunate Giondar; perhaps we may arrive in time to deliver him from danger, and save his life.'

"The two princes rushed into the wood, and entered it at the very instant when the lion had pulled Giondar down to the ground. No sooner did the animal observe Prince Amgiad approaching, scimitar in hand, than he let his prey go, and ran at this new assailant with the greatest fury. The prince waited with intrepidity and coolness to receive the furious creature, and gave him a blow with so much strength and skill, that the lion fell instantly dead at his feet.

"When Giondar perceived that he was indebted for his life to the two princes, he threw himself at their feet, and thanked them most fervently for the favour and assistance they had shown him. 'O beloved princes,' said he to them when he rose, while his tears fell upon their hands, 'Allah forbid that I should ever attempt to take your lives, after the noble manner in which you have saved mine. It shall never be said that the Emir Giondar was capable of such black ingratitude.'

"To this speech Prince Amgiad replied: 'The service we have done you ought by no means to prevent you from executing your orders. Go and take your horse, and let us return to the spot where you left us.' They had now no difficulty in catching the horse; its spirit had been quelled by the appearance of the lion, and it now stood trembling and submissive. But though the princes urged upon Giondar, as they returned to the spring, that it was his duty to fulfil his master's commands, they could not persuade him to be the instrument of their death. On the contrary, he said: 'The only thing that I take the liberty to ask of you, and which I beg you not to refuse, is that you will clothe yourselves in my garments, as well as you can, and let me have yours; and that you will escape to such a distance that the king your father may never again hear tidings of you.'

"The princes at length promised to comply with all his wishes; and after giving him some of their garments, they put on as much as he could spare of his clothes. Giondar then obliged them to take all the money he had about him, and departed.

"After the emir had left the princes, he went again into the wood, where he dipped their clothes in the blood of the lion, and then journeyed back to the capital of the Isle of Ebony. On his arrival, King Camaralzaman asked him if he had faithfully executed the orders he had received. Giondar held up the blood-stained garments of the two princes, and said: 'O king, behold the proofs of my fidelity.' 'Inform me,' said Camaralzaman, 'in what manner they behaved on suffering the punishment I ordered to be inflicted on them.' 'They received it, O my lord,' answered Giondar, 'with the most exemplary fortitude, and with a perfect resignation to the decrees of Allah, who has fully proved the sincerity of their belief in their religion. Above all, they spoke of your majesty with the greatest respect, and showed most entire submission to your order for their deaths. Their words were, "We are innocent, but we do not murmur at our fate. We receive our death from the hands of Allah, and we heartily forgive the king our father. We well know that he has been deceived in this matter!"' King Camaralzaman was sensibly affected at the account given by Giondar. It occurred to him that he would examine the garments of his sons, and he began by feeling in the pockets of Amgiad. He found there a letter, which he opened and read. When he discovered, not only by the handwriting, but by a small lock of hair which was within the letter, where it came from, he groaned aloud in anguish. Then with trembling hands he searched the pockets of Prince Assad, and found the letter he had received. This new discovery had such a violent and sudden effect upon him, that he fell fainting to the ground.

"Never was king so overwhelmed with grief as was Camaralzaman, when he at length recovered his senses. 'What hast thou done, O barbarous father?' he exclaimed. 'Thou hast destroyed thine own offspring. O my innocent sons! could not your sense, your modesty, your obedience, your entire submission to his wishes, nor even your virtues, defend you from his rage? O blind misguided parent, dost thou think that the

THE GRIEF OF CAMARALZAMAN.

earth ought to bear thee after so execrable a crime? I have brought this calamity on myself; and Allah has inflicted this punishment upon me. I will not, ye detestable women, wash away your crime with your blood; no, you are not even worthy of my anger: but may Heaven itself hurl destruction on my head, if ever I see you again!'

"The king kept his oath most religiously. He ordered on the very same day that the two ladies should be conveyed each to a separate apartment, where they should always remain well guarded; and to the last day of his life he never once went near them.

"While Camaralzaman was thus inconsolable for the loss of the princes his sons, a misfortune of which he had himself been the cause by his precipitate conduct, the two princes wandered about in desert places, endeavouring to avoid every trace of human habitation, and afraid of meeting with any living being. They satisfied their hunger with herbs and wild fruits, and drank only the stagnant rain-water which they found in the crevices and holes of rocks. And when night approached, they watched by turns, in order to guard against wild beasts.

"At the end of about a month, they came to the foot of a very steep mountain, composed entirely of a sort of black stone, and which appeared to them quite inaccessible. At length, however, they perceived a path; but they found this path so narrow and difficult that they durst not attempt to climb it. Hoping that they might discover another road less rugged and steep, they kept wandering round the foot of the mountain for about five days. All the trouble they took was to no purpose; and they were compelled to return to the path they had at first neglected. It appeared to them so absolutely impracticable that they took a long time to consult whether they should attempt to ascend it or not. At last, however, they encouraged each other, and began to mount.

"The farther they advanced, the higher and steeper the mountain seemed to be, and they were more than once tempted to abandon their enterprise. As soon as one of them perceived that the other was tired, he stopped, and they both took breath together. Sometimes they were both so fatigued that their strength failed them; and they gave up all thoughts of proceeding, and expected to die through weariness and exhaustion. But after a little time, as their strength returned, they took fresh courage, animated each other, and resumed their efforts.

"In spite, however, of all their diligence, their perseverance, and their exertions, they were unable to reach the summit before the evening. Night overtook them, and Prince Assad found himself so wearied and worn out that he suddenly stopped. He said to Amgiad, 'My dear brother, I can go no farther; I must lie down in this spot and die.' 'Let us rest ourselves here,' replied Amgiad, stopping at the same time, 'as long as you please, and get fresh courage and strength. You may observe, that we have not much farther to ascend, and the moon will favour our progress.'

"After they had rested for above half an hour, Assad made a fresh effort; and at length they reached the summit of the mountain, where they again sat down for some time. Amgiad was the first to rise; and going forward a little distance, he descried a tree not far off. He went up, and found it to be a pomegranate tree, the branches of which were almost borne down with the weight of the fruit. A fountain, or small stream, also washed the foot of the tree. He instantly ran to inform Assad of this good news, and led him to the margin of the fountain under the tree. They ate a pomegranate, which refreshed them greatly, and then they fell asleep.

"The next morning when the princes awoke, Amgiad said to Assad: 'Let us proceed, brother, on our way: I see this mountain is much less rugged and steep on this side than we found it on the other, and we have now only to descend.' Prince Assad, however, was so exhausted with the labours of the preceding day, that he required at least three days to recover his strength. They passed this time in conversation, as they had already passed many weary hours. All their discourse turned upon the horrible calumny through which they had been brought to their present deplorable state. 'But,' said they, 'inasmuch as Allah has declared in our favour in so evident a manner, we ought to bear our misfortunes with patience, and to console ourselves with the hope that happier days may be in store for us.'

"The three days passed away, and the brothers pursued their journey. As the mountain on this side did not form one regular descent, but was varied by a considerable surface of even ground several times before they could arrive at its base, it took them five days to reach the plain. They at length discovered a large city, the sight of which greatly delighted them. 'Do you not think, my brother,' said Amgiad to Assad, 'that it will be better for you to remain in some place without the town, where on my return I shall be able to find you, while I go and learn in what country we are, what this place is called, and what language is spoken here? When I come back I will bring some fresh provisions with me. I think, moreover, it will be much the best that we do not go together, in case there should be any danger.' 'I highly approve of your opinion,' replied Assad; 'it is both prudent and wise. But, my dear brother, if one of us must separate from the other for this purpose, I will never suffer you to be the person who incurs the probable danger: you must permit me to undertake this enterprise. What agony should I not endure were any accident to happen to you!' 'But, my brother,' answered Amgiad, 'ought not I to fear the very same thing on your account which you do for me? I entreat you, therefore, suffer me to go; and do you wait patiently for me in this place.' 'I will never permit it,' said Assad; 'and if anything should happen to me, I shall at least have the consolation of knowing that you are in safety.' Amgiad was at length obliged to yield to Assad's entreaties, and he sat down under some trees at the foot of the mountain.

"Prince Assad took some money out of the purse which Amgiad kept, and continued his journey to the town. He had not walked far in the first street he came to before he met with a venerable-looking old man of decent appearance, leaning upon a staff. As he believed the old man to be a person of some consequence, and one therefore not likely to deceive him, Assad accosted him, begging the venerable man to inform him which was the way to the market-place.

"The old man looked at the prince with a smiling countenance, and said to him: 'My son, you seem to be a stranger; otherwise surely you would not put such a question to me.' Assad replied: 'I am indeed a stranger here.' 'You are welcome,' resumed the old man, 'and our country ought to esteem itself highly honoured that a handsome young man like yourself takes the trouble to come and visit it. Pray inform me what business carries you to the public market-place?' 'O my friend,' replied Assad, 'it is nearly two months since my brother and I set out from a very distant country. We have been all this time on our journey, and arrived here only yesterday. My brother was so much fatigued by the length of the way that he is waiting for me at the foot of the mountain, while I am come to purchase some provisions for us both.'

"You could not possibly have arrived more opportunely, my son,' replied the old man; 'and I heartily rejoice at your coming, out of respect for you and your brother. I have this very day given a great entertainment to many of my friends, and there is a great quantity of provisions left at my house untouched. Come home, therefore, with me, and I will give you abundance to eat; and when you have satisfied your hunger, I will give you as much as will be sufficient for yourself and your brother for many days. You have no need, therefore, to take the trouble of going and spending your money in the market: travellers, you know, are seldom too well provided. Besides, while you are refreshing yourself, I will inform you of all the peculiarities and customs of our city, concerning which I can better enlighten you than most people. A person like myself, who has filled all the most honourable offices with distinction and credit to himself, ought not to be ignorant of our customs. You may indeed think yourself particularly fortunate in having addressed yourself to me rather than to any other person; for I am truly sorry to say that all our townspeople are not like myself; some of them, I assure you, are very wicked. Come with me, and I will show you the difference between an honest man, like myself, and those who boast of their character without possessing any qualification to entitle them to praise.' To this harangue Prince Assad answered: 'I am infinitely obliged to you for the kindness and good intentions you express. I put myself entirely under your protection, and am ready to go wherever you please.'

"The old man walked on with the prince by his side. He was laughing in his sleeve all the time; and for fear Assad should perceive this, he conversed with him on many subjects, that the stranger might continue to have the same good opinion of him he at first had formed. Among other things he kept repeating, 'I declare that it is a fortunate circumstance that you addressed me in preference to any other person. I thank Allah that I have met you; you will know why I say this so earnestly when you come to my house.'

"The old man at length arrived at his own home, and introduced Assad into a large room, where he saw forty old men sitting in a circle, round a lighted fire, which they were worshipping. Prince Assad felt a sensation of horror at thus seeing human beings so far deprived of their reason as to offer that reverence to the creature which they owed to the Creator. He was also considerably alarmed at seeing himself so deceived, and in such an abominable and wicked place.

"While the prince stood quite motionless with astonishment and horror, the artful old man who had brought him saluted the forty inmates. 'Fervent and devout adorers of fire,' said he to them, 'this is a most happy day for us. Where is Gazban?' he added; 'let him come in.' As these words were spoken in a loud voice, a negro, who had heard them outside the room, immediately made his appearance. This black, who was the Gazban of whom the old man spoke, no sooner perceived the disconsolate Assad, than he understood for what purpose he was called. He ran towards the prince, and with a blow that he gave him knocked him down; he then bound his arms with surprising quickness. When this had been done, the old man called out: 'Carry him below, and do not fail to tell my daughters, Bostana and Cavama, to be careful that he has enough of the bastinado every day, with only one piece of bread night and morning for his subsistence. That quantity will be quite enough to keep him alive till the departure of the vessel for the blue sea and the mountain of fire: we will offer him as a most acceptable sacrifice to our divinity.'

"When the old man had given these cruel orders, Gazban seized Assad in a rough and brutal manner, and dragged him to a place under the room. After passing through several doors, they came to a dungeon, into which they descended by twenty steps; and here the black fastened Assad by his legs to a large and very heavy chain. As soon as he had done this, Gazban went to inform the old man's daughters of the prisoner's arrival; their father had, however, already spoken to them himself. 'My daughters,' he said to them, 'go down into the dungeon, and bestow the bastinado on the prisoner, in the manner you know that every Mussulman whom I make captive ought to receive it; and see you do not spare him. Thus you may best evince that you are true worshippers of fire.'

"Bostana and Cavama, who had been brought up with the greatest detestation of all Mussulmen, accepted this office with joy. They immediately went down to the dungeon, and beat Assad so inhumanly that he was covered with blood, and at last fainted. After this inhuman proceeding, they placed a piece of bread and a jar of water by his side, and left him. It was a long time before the prince regained his senses. He shed torrents of tears, and deplored his miserable fate; consoling himself, however, with the idea that this misfortune had happened to himself, and not to his brother Amgiad.

"In the meantime, Prince Amgiad waited for his brother at the foot of the mountain till sunset with the greatest impatience. When he found that one, two, three, and even four hours of the night were gone, and that Assad did not make his appearance, he began to feel the utmost anxiety and alarm. He passed the night in a very distressed and anxious state, and as soon as day appeared he set out towards the town. The almost entire absence of Mussulmen in the streets greatly astonished him. He stopped the first of that religion whom he met, and asked him the name of the place. The Mussulman replied that it was called the City of the Magi, because the Magi, who were worshippers of fire, lived there in great numbers, and that there were very few Mussulmen. Amgiad inquired also how far they reckoned it to the Isle of Ebony; when he was told for answer, that by sea it was about four months' voyage, and a year's journey by land. The man to whom the prince had addressed himself abruptly left him, after having satisfied him in these particulars, and continued his road, as he was in haste.

"Amgiad, who had not been more than six weeks in coming from the Isle of Ebony with his brother Assad, could not comprehend how they had travelled so far in so short a time, unless it were by enchantment, or that the road over the mountain which they had traversed was much shorter than the usual route, though not at all frequented, on account of its difficulty and danger. In his walk through the town, he stopped at the shop of a tailor, whom he knew to be a Mussulman by his dress, as he had also known the former person whom he had accosted. Entering the shop, he saluted the tailor, and then sat down and informed him of his own great distress, and of its cause.

"When Prince Amgiad had finished his story, the tailor said to him: 'If your brother

PRINCE ASSAD AND THE WORSHIPPERS OF FIRE.

has fallen into the hands of any one of the Magi, you may make up your mind never to see him again. He is lost past recovery; and I advise you to be consoled, and only to endeavour to preserve yourself from the same disastrous fate. To assist you in this, I will allow you, if you please, to remain with me, and I will inform you of all the cunning and artful tricks of the Magi, in order that you may be upon your guard against them when you go out.' Amgiad was greatly grieved at the loss of his brother. He accepted the tailor's offer, thanking the kind Mussulman a thousand times for the goodness he showed him.

"For a whole month Amgiad did not go out of the house, except in company with the tailor. At the end of that time he ventured to go alone to the bath. As he returned, he passed through a street where he did not see a single person, except a lady, whom he met, and who came up to him.

"Observing him to be a handsome and agreeable young man, fresh from the bath, the lady lifted up her veil, and asked him with a smiling countenance whither he was going, and as she spoke she cast on him a glance of admiration. Amgiad was unable to resist the appearance of this lady, who was indeed very charming, and in reply said, 'I am going to my own house, or to yours, whichever you like best.' 'O my friend,' answered the lady, with an engaging smile, 'ladies of my rank and disposition never carry men to their houses, they only accompany them.'

"Amgiad was in the greatest embarrassment at this answer, which was quite unexpected. He was afraid to bring this lady to the house of his host, who might be much scandalized at her appearance, and he should thus run the risk also of losing his host's protection, which was very necessary in a town where so many precautions were to be taken. The little experience also he had in the ways of the town made him ignorant of any place to which he might carry her; but he could not resist the temptation of improving her acquaintance. In this uncertainty he determined to leave everything to chance; and without answering the lady a word, he walked on, and she followed him.

"Prince Amgiad wandered for a long time from street to street and from square to square. He and his companion were at last greatly fatigued with their long ramble, when they came down a street, at the end of which was a large door belonging to a house of handsome appearance, with a bench, or seat, on each side of it. Amgiad sat down on one of these seats, to take breath, and the lady, even more tired than he, sat down on the other.

"'Is this your house?' said she to Prince Amgiad, as soon as he was seated. 'You see it is, O lady,' replied the prince. 'Why do you not then open the door?' asked the fair one; 'what do you wait for?' 'My charming friend,' answered Amgiad, 'I have not the key. I left it with my slave, to whom I gave some commissions to execute, and he has not yet returned; and as I ordered him, after fulfilling his errand, to go and purchase some provisions for a good dinner, I am afraid that we shall have to wait a considerable time.'

"The difficulty in which the prince found himself began to damp his ardour, and make him regret the adventure in which he found himself involved. He had therefore invented the excuse he made in hopes that the lady would take offence, and in her anger would leave him, to go and seek some more suitable admirer: but he was mistaken. 'What an impertinent slave is yours,' said she, 'to make you wait thus! I will chastise him myself as he deserves, if you do not punish him well, when he comes back. It is very humiliating that I should have to remain here alone at the door with a man.' So saying, she rose and took a large stone to break the lock, which, according to the custom of that country, was made of wood, and not very strong.

"Amgiad knew not what to do, nor how to prevent her from fulfilling her intention. 'O lady,' he cried, 'what are you going to do? Do me the favour to have a little more patience.' 'What are you afraid of?' said she; 'is not the house your own? There is no great harm in breaking a wooden lock; and it will be very easy to get another.' She then broke the lock; and as soon as the door was open she entered the house, and walked on before Amgiad. When the prince saw the house broken open he gave himself up for lost. He hesitated whether he should go in, or endeavour to make his escape from a danger which seemed to him to increase every moment; and he was on the point of determining upon the latter plan, when the lady came back, and found he was not going in. 'How is this,' she said, 'that you do not come into your own house?' 'I am looking, O lady,' he answered, 'to see if my slave is returning, because I am afraid we shall find nothing prepared for us.' 'Come, come,' cried she; 'we can wait much better in the house than standing here waiting for him in the street.'

"Much against his will, the prince went into a very large and handsome paved court. From this they ascended by a few steps to a grand vestibule, where he and the lady, his companion, perceived a large open room handsomely furnished. One table was set out with numerous excellent dishes, another was covered with a variety of fine fruits, and on a sideboard there appeared a goodly supply of wine. When Amgiad saw these preparations, he no longer doubted that his destruction was near at hand. 'You are a lost man, poor Amgiad,' said he to himself: 'you will not long survive your dear brother Assad.' The lady, on the contrary, was delighted at this agreeable sight. 'Ah! my friend,' she cried, 'you were fearful that nothing was ready; and you may now perceive that your slave has even exceeded his orders, and done more than you expected. But, if I do not deceive myself, these preparations are for some other lady, and are not intended for me. No matter: let her come; I promise you I shall not be jealous of her. The only favour that I ask of you is, that you will suffer me to attend upon you both.'

"Notwithstanding the melancholy and painful apprehensions he felt, Amgiad could not help laughing at the pleasantry of the lady. 'O lady,' said he, totally absorbed in the afflicting reflections that preyed upon his mind, 'I assure you that you are much mistaken in your conjectures: these are only the preparations made daily for me.' As he could not resolve to sit down at a table that had not been prepared for him, he was going to a sofa, but the lady prevented him. 'What are you doing?' she cried; 'after having gone into the bath, you ought to be almost famished with hunger. Come, let us sit down at the table, and eat and enjoy ourselves.'

"The prince was obliged to do as the lady wished. They therefore sat down, and began to eat. After she had eaten a mouthful or two, she took a bottle and glass, and poured out some wine. She drank the first glass to the health of Amgiad. Thereupon she filled the same glass again, and presented it to the prince, who pledged her in return.

"The more he reflected upon his adventure, the more astonished was he at finding not only that the master of the house did not make his appearance, but that not a single domestic was to be seen in a house so handsome and so richly furnished. 'My happiness and good fortune will be extraordinary indeed,' said he to himself, 'if the master should not make his appearance at all, and I should safely get out of this dilemma.' While these thoughts, as well as others of a more distressing nature, continued to occupy his mind, the lady was employed in eating and drinking, from time to time obliging him also to do the same. They were already eating their dessert when the master of the house came home.

"The proprietor was the master of the horse to the King of the Magi, and his name was Bahadar. This house belonged to him, but he had another, in which he commonly lived. He only made use of this for the occasional reception of three or four chosen friends, and for this purpose everything was brought from his usual dwelling; and this was exactly what had been done on that day by some of his people, who had left the house only a few moments before Amgiad and the lady entered it.

"Bahadar himself arrived without any attendants, and in disguise, as was his usual custom; and he came rather before the time on which he had appointed to meet his friends. He was greatly surprised at finding the door of his house forced open. He went in, therefore, as silently as possible; and as he heard people talking and enjoying themselves in the saloon, he crept round by the wall, and put his head half into the room, to see who they might be. When he observed only a young man and a female, who were eating at the table which had been prepared for himself and his friends, and noticed that the mischief they had done was confined to the eating of his provisions, he resolved to divert himself with them.

"The lady, who had her back towards the door, did not perceive Bahadar; but Amgiad saw him at once, while he was in the act of drinking. At sight of the stranger he instantly turned pale, and fixed his eyes upon Bahadar, who made him a sign not to say a word, but to come out and speak to him. Amgiad drank off his glass of wine, and got up. 'Where are you going?' inquired the lady. 'Remain here a moment, I beg of you, my friend,' replied he; 'I will be back instantly: a matter of business obliges me to go out.' The prince found Bahadar waiting for him in the vestibule; and they both went down into the court, that the lady might not hear their conversation.

"When they had come into the court, Bahadar asked the prince how he came to be in his house with the lady, and why he had forced the door? 'O my lord,' replied Amgiad, 'I must in your eyes appear very much to blame; but if you will have the patience to hear my story, I hope you will be convinced of my innocence.' He then, in a few words, related to Bahadar his adventure just as it had occurred, without disguising a single circumstance; and, to prove to him that he was unable to commit so disgraceful an action as that of breaking open a house, he did not even conceal from him that he was a prince, or why he had come to the city of the Magi.

"Bahadar, who was exceedingly fond of foreigners, was highly delighted at having an opportunity of obliging a stranger of the high rank and illustrious quality of Amgiad. In fact, the prince's air, his manner, his well-chosen and correct conversation, left no doubt of the perfect truth of his account. 'O prince,' said Bahadar, 'I am exceedingly happy at thus finding an opportunity of obliging you, and am delighted at so accidental, singular, and pleasant a meeting as the present. So far from disturbing your festivity, I shall take great pleasure in contributing all in my power to your satisfaction. Before I speak to you any further on this subject, I must tell you that I am master of the horse to the king, and that my name is Bahadar. I have another house in which I commonly live, and this is the place where I sometimes come to enjoy myself with my friends without any ceremony. You have made your lady believe that you have a slave, though in fact you have none. I will be that slave; and that I may not distress you by this proposal, and that you may not wish to excuse yourself from having it so, I repeat again to you that I particularly wish it, and you shall hereafter know my motives for this conduct. Go, therefore, and take your place again, and continue to divert yourself; and when, after some time, I shall return, and present myself before you dressed like a slave, rate me soundly, and do not be afraid even of striking me. I will attend upon you all the time you are at table, and even till night. You shall both remain here, and you shall send the lady back in the most honourable manner. After this, I will endeavour to render you a service of greater consequence. Go, therefore, and lose no time.' Amgiad wished to make some reply, but Bahadar would not suffer him to speak. He compelled him to go back directly to the lady.

"Amgiad had scarcely returned to the room where he had left the lady, when the friends arrived whom Bahadar had invited. He requested them as a favour to excuse him from entertaining them on that day; giving them to understand that they would approve of his conduct when they knew the cause, of which they should be informed on the first opportunity. So soon as the guests were gone, he went out and procured a slave's habit, in which he dressed himself.

"The prince went back to the lady, highly delighted at having thus fortunately chanced to enter a house belonging to a person of so much consequence, and one who treated him so kindly in his embarrassing dilemma. 'O lady,' said he, as he again sat down to the table, 'I beg you a thousand pardons for my incivility, and for the ill-humour I exhibited on account of my slave's absence. The rascal shall pay dearly for it. I will let him see that he shall not neglect my commands with impunity.' 'Do not let this disturb you,' replied the lady; 'it shall only be so much the worse for him. If he commits any fault he shall suffer for it. Trouble yourself no more about him, but let us only think of enjoying ourselves.'

"They continued feasting at table with much more pleasure and delight than before, because Amgiad was no longer uneasy at the consequences that might have arisen from the indiscretion of the lady, who ought not to have forced the door, even though the house had belonged to Amgiad. He did not now feel himself in a worse humour than the lady herself; and while they continued to drink more than they ate, they amused themselves with conversation, saying a thousand pleasant and humorous things, till Bahadar arrived in his disguise.

"He came in, looking like a slave who was much mortified at finding his master had come with company before he returned. He immediately threw himself at Amgiad's feet, and kissing the ground, begged his pardon for being so late. And when he got up he stood still, with his hands crossed and his eyes cast down, waiting to receive his master's commands. 'Impudent fellow!' cried Amgiad, in a tone and manner that well counterfeited extreme anger, 'tell me if there is in the whole world a worse slave than yourself? Where have you been? What have you been about, that you have stayed

PRINCE AMGIAD AND THE WICKED LADY.

away so long?' 'O my lord,' replied Bahadar, 'I entreat your pardon; I have just returned from executing the orders you gave me, and I did not think you would return so early.' 'You are a rascal!' said the prince, 'and I will give you a good beating, to teach you not to neglect your duty, and afterwards to tell falsehoods.' He then got up, took a stick, and gave the pretended slave three or four very slight blows, after which he returned to the table.

"The lady, however, was not satisfied with the trifling punishment inflicted by Amgiad. She rose in her turn, and, taking the stick, she beat Bahadar so unmercifully that the tears came into his eyes. Amgiad was excessively annoyed at the liberty which she took in a strange house, and at the manner in which she treated one of the first officers of the king. He begged her to desist, crying that she had beaten the slave quite enough; but she nevertheless went on striking him. 'Let me alone,' she cried; 'I wish to satisfy myself, and teach him not to be absent so long another time.' She continued to beat Bahadar with so much violence, that Amgiad was forced to get up, and take the stick out of her hands, and he had some difficulty in getting it from her. When she found she could no longer beat the slave, she sat down in her place, and continued to abuse him roundly.

"Bahadar dried his tears, and remained standing behind Amgiad and the lady to pour out their wine. As soon as he saw that they had finished eating and drinking, he took away all the things and set the room in order, putting everything in its proper place; and when night came on he lighted up the candles. Every time that he went out or came in the lady began again to scold, threaten, and abuse him, to the great annoyance of Amgiad, who would willingly have prevented her, but was afraid to remonstrate. After attending to all the comforts of the intruders, Bahadar went to another apartment, where in a very short time he fell asleep, through the great fatigue he had undergone.

"Amgiad and the lady continued in conversation for at least half an hour longer; and before they retired to rest, the lady, having occasion to pass through the vestibule, heard Bahadar, who was already fast asleep, breathing heavily. As she had observed that there was a scimitar hanging up in the room where they had feasted, she went back, and said to Amgiad: 'I beg of you to do one thing for love of me.' 'What can I do to please you?' asked the prince. 'Oblige me by taking this scimitar,' replied she, 'and go and cut off the head of your slave.'

"This proposal excited the greatest astonishment in the prince; and he had no doubt that it was prompted by the effect of the wine the lady had taken. 'O my friend,' he replied, 'let us not regard my slave; he is not worthy of your notice: I have punished him, and so have you; let this be sufficient. Besides, I am very well satisfied with him upon the whole, as he is not in general accustomed to commit these faults.' 'That is of no consequence to me,' replied the angry woman; 'I wish the rascal dead, and if he is not to be killed by your hands, he shall perish by mine.' With these words she snatched up the scimitar, drew it from the scabbard, and ran out, to put her diabolical design in execution.

"Amgiad followed her, and overtook her in the vestibule. 'I must do your bidding,' he cried, 'since you insist upon it. I am, however, determined that no one but myself shall kill my slave.' As soon as she had given him the scimitar he said, 'Follow me, and do not make any noise, for fear of waking him.' They went into the chamber where Bahadar lay; but instead of striking Bahadar with the scimitar, Amgiad aimed a blow at the lady, whose head fell upon Bahadar. If the noise made by the action of cutting off the lady's head would not have disturbed his sleep, the blow that the head itself gave him as it fell upon him was sufficient to rouse the sleeping man. Astonished at seeing Amgiad standing by him with the bloody scimitar in his hand, and the headless body of the female upon the ground, Bahadar eagerly inquired the meaning of all this. The prince related everything to him exactly as it had occurred, and in conclusion added: 'To prevent this furious creature from taking your life, I could discover no other method than that of destroying hers.'

"'O my lord,' replied Bahadar, impressed with the greatest gratitude, persons of your rank and generous character are not capable of aiding such wicked actions as this woman purposed to commit. You are my preserver, and I cannot sufficiently thank you.' So great was his sense of the obligation, that he instantly embraced Amgiad. 'Before the day breaks,' said he, 'this body must be concealed. I will undertake to do this.' Amgiad, however, opposed the project, and said that he would take that danger upon himself, as he had been the cause of the lady's death. 'A stranger in this place, like yourself, will not be so well able to manage it,' replied Bahadar. 'Leave it to me, and do you retire to rest. If I do not return before daybreak, you may be assured that the watch has captured me. For fear this should happen, I will now make over to you, in writing, this house and all it contains, and you may live here at your ease.'

"As soon as Bahadar had written a sufficient transfer of the house to Amgiad, and had put this deed of gift into his hands, he took the lady's body and head, and placed them in a sack. He then threw it across his shoulders, and walked along, from street to street, towards the sea. He had not, however, proceeded very far, before he encountered the officer of the police, who was going his rounds in person. The attendants stopped Bahadar, and, opening the sack, discovered the body and head of the murdered lady. The officer, who knew the master of the horse notwithstanding his disguise, took him away as a prisoner, as he durst not put a person of Bahadar's high rank and dignity to death without referring the matter to the king. The next morning, therefore, he took Bahadar into the royal presence. When the king had heard from the report of the officer of the cruel act which Bahadar appeared, from all the circumstances, to have perpetrated, he loaded him with abuse. 'Is it thus,' he exclaimed, 'that you murder my subjects, in order to plunder them, and then throw their bodies into the sea, to prevent the discovery of your wickedness? Let the city be freed from such a monster! Hang him up instantly!'

"Notwithstanding that Bahadar knew himself to be quite innocent, he received the sentence of death with perfect resignation, and said not a word in his own justification. The judge led him back to prison, and while the gibbet was preparing, criers were sent to publish in all the quarters of the city, the sentence which was going to be executed at noon, on the grand master of the horse, for the crime of murder.

"Prince Amgiad, who had waited in vain for Bahadar, was seized with inexpressible consternation when he heard the crier proclaiming this sentence, from the house where he lay concealed. 'If any one is to die to expiate the death of so wicked a woman,' said he to himself, 'it is not Bahadar who should be executed, but myself; and I cannot bear that the innocent should be punished for the guilty.' Without delay he went at once to the spot where the execution was to take place, and mingled with the crowd, which was collecting from all parts.

"As soon as Amgiad saw the judge appear, leading Bahadar to the gibbet, he went and presented himself before him. 'My lord,' said he, 'I come to declare to you most solemnly, that the master of the horse, whom you are going to lead to execution, is quite innocent of the death of the lady whom he is supposed to have murdered. It was I who committed this crime—if indeed it can be called a crime to deprive a detestable woman of life, who was on the point of murdering the master of the horse.' And the prince proceeded to tell the whole story.

"When Prince Amgiad had informed the judge how the lady had accosted him on his coming out of the bath, and how she had been the cause of his entering the house of Bahadar, and of all that had happened, until he found himself obliged to cut off her head to save the life of Bahadar, the judge suspended the execution, and took them both before the king.

"The monarch desired to be informed of the whole affair by Amgiad himself; and in order to exculpate himself, as well as the master of the horse, the better, the prince took advantage of the opportunity to relate the whole of his history, together with that of Prince Assad his brother, from their banishment until that very day.

"When the prince had concluded his narrative, the king said to him: 'I am much pleased, O prince, that this affair has afforded me the opportunity of becoming acquainted with you. I not only grant you your life, and that of the master of the horse, whose good conduct towards you I commend and admire, and whom I re-establish in his office, but I also confer on you the dignity of grand vizier, to console you for the unjust, although excusable, treatment you have experienced from the king your father. As for Prince Assad, I give you free permission to exercise all the authority with which you are invested to discover where he is.'

"Amgiad thanked the King of the City of the Magi for his favour, and entered at once upon the duties of his office of grand vizier. He made use of every method he could devise to find the prince his brother. He proclaimed by means of the public criers, in all quarters of the city, that a considerable reward would be given to any one who should produce Assad to him, or even give information where he might be found. He employed people to make inquiries in every quarter; but, notwithstanding all his researches, he could obtain no intelligence of his brother.

"Assad, in the meantime, was languishing in chains in the dungeon where he had been confined through the artifice of the old man; and Bostana and Cavama, his daughters, continued to treat him in a cruel and inhuman manner. The solemn festival of the fire worshippers drew near. The vessel which usually sailed to the mountain of fire was equipped and ready to start, and a captain, named Behram, a zealous follower of the religion of the Magi, undertook to lade it with merchandise. When the ship was ready to put to sea, Behram contrived that Assad should be placed in a case half filled with merchandise, in which sufficient space had been left between the planks to admit air for him to breathe; and then the case was let down into the hold of the ship.

"Before the vessel set sail, the grand vizier Amgiad, who had been informed that the worshippers of fire made it an annual custom to sacrifice a Mussulman on the fiery mountain, and who suspected that Assad, who had probably fallen into their hands, might be the destined victim of this bloody ceremony, determined to search the vessel. He went in person, and ordered all the seamen and passengers to come on deck while his people made their search; but Assad was too well concealed to be discovered.

"The search being concluded, the ship left the harbour; and when it had reached the open sea, Behram took Assad out of the case, but kept him chained; fearing that, as the prisoner well knew the fate for which he was destined, he might, in despair, throw himself headlong into the sea.

"After they had sailed for some days, the wind, which had at first been favourable, suddenly veered round, and increased to such a degree that it at length rose to a furious tempest. The vessel was not only thrown out of its course, but Behram and the pilot did not know where they were, and feared every moment they should be dashed on a rock, and go to pieces. The storm was at its height when they discovered land. Behram found that he had gained the harbour and capital of Queen Margiana, a circumstance which occasioned him great vexation and sorrow.

"This Queen Margiana, who was a Mussulman, cherished a mortal enmity to the worshippers of fire. She not only refused to tolerate one of those idolaters in her dominions, but she would not even suffer any of their vessels to come into her ports.

"It was, however, totally out of the power of Behram to avoid making for the harbour of this city, without exposing himself to the certainty of being cast away on the dangerous rocks which lined the shore. In this extremity, he held a council with his pilot and seamen, and said: 'My good friends, you see the necessity we are reduced to. Of two things we must choose one; we must either be swallowed up by the waves, or take refuge in Queen Margiana's capital; but you well know her implacable hatred to our religion, and to all who profess it. She will not fail to seize our ship, and put us all to death without mercy. I see but one stratagem which may perhaps succeed. I propose that we take off the chains from the Mussulman, whom we have on board, and dress him as a slave. When Queen Margiana sends for me to appear before her, and asks me concerning my trade, I will tell her that I am a merchant who sells slaves, that I have sold all I had, with the exception of one, whom I have reserved for myself as a sort of secretary, because he can read and write. She will desire to see him; and as he is handsome, and moreover professes her religion, she will be moved with compassion for him, and will, no doubt, propose to purchase him of me. But I will only sell him on condition that we remain in her harbour until the weather is fair. If you can propose a better plan, speak, and I will hear you.' The pilot and seamen applauded the captain's device very much, and they all resolved to put it in practice.

"Behram ordered his men to take off Prince Assad's chains, and had him neatly dressed, that he might appear as a slave who filled the office of writer, or secretary, to his ship, in which character he wished him to appear before the queen. Assad was scarcely

QUEEN MARGIANA ASKS PRINCE ASSAD TO WRITE.

dressed and prepared for his part, when the vessel entered the harbour, and cast anchor. Queen Margiana's palace was situated near the sea, with a garden extending along the shore. So soon as she perceived the ship at anchor in the port, she sent to the captain to come to her; in her anxiety to learn what this ship might be, she went to meet him in the garden.

"Behram, who expected this summons, went on shore with Prince Assad, after exacting a promise from the prisoner that he would confirm what Behram should say of his being a slave and secretary to the ship. They were conducted to the queen; and Behram, throwing himself at her feet, described to her the necessity he had been under of taking refuge in her harbour. He then told her that he was a merchant dealing in slaves, and that Assad, whom he had brought with him, was the only one remaining; but that he kept this slave for himself in the capacity of secretary.

"Margiana had felt a predilection for Assad from the first moment she cast her eyes on him; and she was delighted to hear that he was a slave. Determined, therefore, to purchase him at any price, she asked Assad his name. The prince replied, with tears in his eyes, 'O mighty queen, does your majesty wish to know the name I formerly bore, or that by which I am now called?'

"'Have you two names?' inquired the queen. 'Alas!' replied the prince, 'it is indeed so. I was formerly called Assad, or The Most Happy, but my name now is Motar, or Destined for Sacrifice.'

"Margiana, who could not understand the true meaning of this reply, supposed that Assad applied it to his present state of slavery; at the same time she saw he had a ready wit. 'As you are a secretary,' said she, 'I conclude you can write very well; let me see some of your writing.' Assad had been provided with an ink-horn, which was fastened to his girdle, and some paper; for Behram had not forgotten anything that might confirm the queen in the belief that he was in reality secretary to the ship. He withdrew to a little distance, and wrote the following sentences, which had their application to his miserable condition.

"'The blind man avoids the ditch into which the clear-sighted stumbles. The ignorant man raises himself to the highest dignities by speeches which signify nothing; while the wise man remains neglected as the dust, though he possesses the greatest eloquence. The Mussulman languishes in the deepest misery; but the infidel triumphs in the midst of prosperity. We must not hope that things will change; the Almighty decrees that they should remain as they are.'

"Assad presented the paper to Queen Margiana, who was charmed alike with the morality of the sentences, and with the beauty of the writing. These sentences sufficed to win her affection, and make her feel unfeigned compassion for the unfortunate youth. When she had finished reading the paper she spoke to Behram as follows: 'Choose which you will do; either sell me this slave, or give him to me; perhaps you may find the latter course most to your advantage.' Behram replied in a very insolent manner, that he had no choice to make, for that he required the services of his slave, and should therefore keep him.

"Irritated by this behaviour, Margiana said no more to Behram, but, taking Assad by the arm, made him walk before her till they came to the palace. Then she sent to acquaint Behram that she should confiscate all his property and set fire to his vessel in the harbour itself if he dared to remain there through the night. Thus the captain was obliged to return to his vessel greatly dejected in his mind, and to prepare with the utmost diligence for sailing, although the tempest had not entirely subsided.

"On her return to the palace, the queen ordered that supper should be instantly served. She herself conducted Prince Assad to her apartment, where she made him sit next her. Assad wished to remonstrate, saying that such an honour was too great to be conferred on a slave. But the queen replied: 'A moment since you were a slave, but you are now a captive no longer. Sit down by me, and let me hear your history; for I am certain, by what you wrote just now, as well as by the insolence of that merchant, that your adventures must be very extraordinary.'

"Prince Assad obeyed; and when he was seated he began thus: 'Most powerful queen, your majesty is not mistaken; my history is indeed extraordinary—more marvellous, perhaps, than you can imagine. The grief, the almost inconceivable torments I have undergone, and the cruel kind of death to which I was destined, and from which you have delivered me with a generosity truly royal, bear witness to the magnitude of your kindness, which will be indelibly impressed on my memory. But before I relate a circumstance which can only excite horror, you must permit me to begin from the earliest date of my misfortunes.'

"After this preface, which very much increased the curiosity of Margiana, Assad began his tale by acquainting his protectress with his royal birth, together with that of his brother, Prince Amgiad. Then he spoke of their reciprocal friendship, of the passicn conceived for them by two ladies, which had so suddenly changed into an implacable hatred, and thus became the cause of their singular misfortunes. He then told her of the anger of the king his father, of the almost miraculous manner in which his own life and that of his brother had been preserved, and lastly of the great grief he had suffered from the loss of Amgiad, and the long and cruel imprisonment from which he had just been relieved, and which was to have ended in his immolation on the fiery mountain.

"When Assad had finished his story, Margiana, more than ever irritated against the worshippers of fire, said to him: 'Prince, notwithstanding the aversion I have always felt against the worshippers of fire, I have nevertheless always treated them with great humanity; but the barbarous treatment you have experienced from them, and their execrable design of sacrificing you as a victim to their idol, cause me to declare implacable war against them.' She would have given utterance to further invectives on this subject had not supper been announced; and she sat down to table with Prince Assad, charmed with his bearing, and delighted to listen to him. Already she felt conscious of a rising regard and affection, which she purposed to take an early opportunity of disclosing to him. 'Prince,' she said, 'we must now make amends for all the fastings and privations which the pitiless fire-worshippers obliged you to endure. You want nourishment after so many sufferings.' With these words, and others of the same nature, she pressed him repeatedly both to eat and drink; the repast lasted a considerable time, and Assad drank more than he could well bear.

"When the table had been cleared, Assad wished to breathe the fresh air, and took the opportunity of going out unperceived by the queen. He went down into the court; and seeing the gate of the garden open, he entered it. Attracted by the various beauties of the spot, he wandered about for some time. At length he went towards the fountain, which formed one of the principal ornaments of the garden, and washed his hands and face in it to refresh himself; then, sitting down to rest on the lawn which surrounded the fountain, he fell asleep.

"Night was approaching gradually, and Behram, who did not wish to give Margiana an opportuuity of fulfilling her threats, had already weighed anchor, not a little vexed at the loss of Assad, and by which his intention of sacrificing a victim was frustrated. He endeavoured, however, to console himself with the reflection that the storm had ceased, and that a land breeze favoured his departure. As soon as he was clear of the harbour, having towed out his ship with the assistance of his boat, he said to the sailors who were in it, before he drew it up into the ship, 'Stay a little, my friends, and don't come up yet: I am going to give you the casks that you may bring fresh water, and I will wait for you just off the shore.' The sailors, who did not know where they could procure a supply, wished to excuse themselves; but Behram had remarked the fountain while he was speaking with the queen in the garden: accordingly he said, 'Go ashore at the garden of the palace, get over the wall, which is not very high, and you will find plenty of water in the basin in the middle of the garden.

"The sailors went on shore to the place described to them by Behram, and each taking a cask on his shoulders, they easily got over the wall. As they approached the basin, they perceived a man lying asleep on the bank; and when they drew nearer they recognised Assad. Thereupon they divided into two parties; and whilst one was filling the casks as quietly and quickly as possible, the other surrounded Assad, and kept watch to secure him in case he should wake. But he continued to sleep soundly; and when the casks were filled, and lifted on to the shoulders of the men who were to carry them, the others seized Assad, and took him away before he had time to recollect himself. They dragged him over the wall, put him in the boat with their casks, and rowed with all their strength to the ship. When they approached their vessel, they cried out with shouts of joy, 'O captain, sound your hautboys and your drums: we bring you back your slave.'

"Behram, who could not conceive how his seamen had been able to find and capture Assad, and who could not discern him in the boat, owing to the darkness of the night, waited with impatience for their coming on board to inquire what they meant; but when he saw the prince before him, he could not contain himself for joy; and without staying to hear how his men had managed to effect so valuable a capture, he put Assad once more in chains, and ordering the boat to be hauled up as quickly as possible, he bent his course with full sails towards the mountain of fire.

"Margiana, in the meantime, was in the greatest alarm. She did not feel uneasy at first, when she perceived the absence of Prince Assad, for she did not doubt he would soon return. She waited patiently for him; but finding after a considerable time had elapsed that he did not make his appearance, she began to be very uneasy. She commanded her women to search for him. They sought him accordingly, but to no purpose, and they could bring her no intelligence of him. Night came on, and she caused the search to be continued with lights; but all her endeavours were ineffectual.

"In a state of the greatest impatience and alarm, Margiana went herself to look for the prince by the light of the flambeaux; and as she observed that the garden gate was open, she went in with her women, supposing he might be there. Passing near the fountain, she noticed on the bank a slipper, which, when examined, she, as well as her women, recognised as one of those worn by the prince. This circumstance, and the quantity of water spilt on the edge of the basin, led her to the conclusion that Behram must have taken the prince away by force. She immediately sent to inquire if the fire-worshipper's ship was still in the harbour; and she was informed that he had sailed just before night came on, that he had lain to for some time off the shore, and that his boat had been to fetch water from her garden. She immediately despatched a messenger to the commander of ten ships of war, which were always kept in port fully equipped and ready to sail on the shortest notice, to acquaint him that she intended to embark the following day, about an hour after sunrise.

"The commander was diligent in obeying the queen's orders. Meanwhile Margiana assembled the captains and other officers, the sailors and soldiers, and by the appointed hour everything was ready. She embarked, and when her squadron got out to sea, and was in full sail, she thus declared her intention to the commander: 'You must use all expedition, and pursue the merchant vessel which sailed from the harbour yesterday evening. I give it up to you as a prize, if you take it; but if you fail, your life shall be the forfeit.'

"The ten ships chased Behram's vessel for two whole days, without being able to get within sight of it. On the third they discovered it, at break of day; and by noon they had come so near that it could not escape. So soon as the cruel Behram perceived the ten vessels, he concluded they must be the squadron of Queen Margiana, and he immediately inflicted the bastinado on Prince Assad. Indeed, he had continued that practice daily, from the time he had left the city of the Magi; and he now inflicted the chastisement with more violence than usual. He was extremely embarrassed, when he found himself on the point of being surrounded on all sides. If he kept Assad, his guilt would be manifest. If he put his prisoner to death, he was fearful that some mark might remain as a token of the murder. He therefore had him unchained, and the prince was then made to come up from the hold of the ship, where he was confined, and appear before the captain, who shouted furiously to him: 'It is thou who art the cause of our being pursued!' and on saying this he threw the unfortunate prince into the sea.

"Prince Assad was a strong swimmer, and made use of his hands and feet with so much success, that, assisted by the waves, which bore him towards the shore, he had sufficient strength to hold out till he reached land. When he found himself in safety, the first thing he did was to return thanks to Heaven for having delivered him from so great a peril, and again favoured his escape from the hands of the worshippers of fire.

PRINCE ASSAD AFTER SWIMMING ASHORE.

He then undressed himself and wrung the water from his clothes, which he then spread on the rock to dry. This he soon effected, being assisted by the heat of the sun, and that of the rock, which had received considerable warmth from its rays.

"Assad lay down for some time, and began to deplore his miserable fate, for he was a stranger in the country on whose shore he had been cast, and uncertain which way to go. He then took up his clothes, put them on, and began to proceed along the shore; he continued walking till he came to a road. He pursued this path or road for ten days, through a country that seemed to be without inhabitants. He found nothing along the banks of the rivulets but wild fruits and a few plants, on which he lived. He at last arrived at a town, which he immediately knew to be the city of the Magi, where he had been so ill-used, and where his brother Amgiad was grand vizier. He was much rejoiced to find himself again in an inhabited place; but was determined to address himself to no one whom he knew to be a fire worshipper, but only to speak to Mussulmen; for he remembered to have remarked a few men of that religion as he came into the city the first time. As it was late, and he knew very well that all the shops were shut up, and that few people were abroad at that hour, he resolved to go into a cemetery which was close to the town, and pass the night there, as there were many tombs in it built in the form of mausoleums. Looking around he discovered one, the door of which was open. He went in, and determined to remain there till morning.

"Behram, the captain in whose ship Assad had been a prisoner, tried in vain to escape from his pursuers. Very soon after he had thrown Assad into the sea, his vessel was surrounded on all sides by the fleet of Margiana. He was first boarded by the ship in which the queen herself was; and unable to make any resistance, Behram at her approach hauled down his sails as a sign that he surrendered.

"Margiana immediately went on board the vessel, and asked Behram where the secretary was whom he had had the audacity either to take away, or to cause others to carry away from her palace. 'O queen,' replied Behram, 'I swear to your majesty that he is not on board my vessel; if you will order it to be searched you will then know my innocence.'

"Margiana commanded that the vessel should be searched with the greatest possible strictness; but he whom she was so desirous of finding, as much for the love she had for him as from her natural goodness of disposition, could not be found. She at first felt inclined to kill Behram with her own hand; but she restrained herself, and was content with confiscating the vessel and its cargo, and turning the captain and all the sailors adrift in their open boat, to reach the shore as they best could. Behram and his crew landed, and made their way back to the city of the Magi, where they arrived on the very same night on which Assad had taken refuge in the burial-ground. As the gate of the city was shut, Behram and his crew were also obliged to have recourse to the cemetery, and to find some tomb to wait in till day should appear, and the gate be again opened.

"Unfortunately for Assad, Behram came to the very tomb in which he was. On entering, the captain at once saw a man asleep, with his head wrapped in his turban. The prince awoke at the noise of Behram's entrance, and lifting up his head, demanded who was there. Behram immediately recognised him, and exclaimed: 'Ah, dog! is it you, who are the cause of my being ruined for the rest of my life? You have for the present escaped being sacrificed, but you shall not evade your fate next year.' So saying, he threw himself upon Assad, put his handkerchief into the prince's mouth, to prevent his calling out, and then made the sailors bind him.

"The next morning, as soon as the gate of the city was open, Behram found it no difficult matter to carry Assad back to the house of the old man, who had so completely deceived him by his cunning tricks, by taking him through unfrequented streets; he was sure of not being discovered, for the majority of the inhabitants had not yet risen. As soon as he came to the old man's house, he thrust Assad into the same dungeon from whence he had been brought, and then went and informed the old man of the unfortunate cause of his return, and of the failure of his voyage. That wicked wretch did not forget to impress upon his two daughters very strongly the necessity of treating the unfortunate prince, if possible, still worse than before.

"Assad was extremely surprised at finding himself again in the place where he had already suffered so much, and was broken-hearted at having to anticipate a renewal of the tortures from which he had thought himself delivered for ever. He wept, and was lamenting the hardness of his destiny, when he saw Bostana enter the dungeon, carrying a stick, a piece of bread, and a pitcher of water. He trembled at sight of this merciless creature, and groaned aloud when he reflected upon the daily torments he was again to endure for another whole year, before he should be led forth to suffer a cruel death.

"Bostana, however, did not treat the unfortunate Assad in so cruel a manner as she had done when he was in the prison the first time. The lamentations, the complaints, and the continual tearful entreaties of the prince to spare him, were at length so powerful, that Bostana could not avoid being softened by them; and she even mingled her tears with his. 'O stranger,' she said to Assad, as she again covered his shoulders, 'I ask you a thousand pardons for the cruelty with which I have till now treated you. Hitherto I have been afraid of disobeying my father, who is unjustly angry with you, and who is determined upon your destruction. But I now detest and abhor his barbarity. Console yourself, therefore, for your sufferings are at an end; and I am going by better treatment to make amends for all my crimes, the enormity of which I am well aware of. You have hitherto looked upon me as an infidel; you must for the future regard me as a Mussulman. I have already received much instruction from a female slave who attends me; I hope that you will complete the good work she has begun. To prove to you my good intentions, I ask pardon of Heaven for all my offences against, and all my cruelty towards you; and I have full confidence that Providence will discover to me the means of restoring you to your full liberty.'

"This speech afforded Prince Assad great consolation. He offered up his grateful thanks for the happy change that had taken place in the heart of Bostana, and for her conversion to the true religion. After first thanking her for the good intentions she had expressed towards him, he neglected nothing that he thought would confirm her in her new opinions. Not only did he endeavour to instruct her still further in the various doctrines of the Mussulman religion, but he gave her a long and faithful account of himself, of all his misfortunes, and his illustrious descent. So soon as he was convinced of her firmness in the good resolutions she had taken, he asked her how she would be able to prevent her sister Cavama from becoming acquainted with this change, and also from ill-using him when it should be her turn to guard him. Bostana replied: 'Let not that trouble you; I know very well how to adjust matters so that she shall give herself no further trouble about you.'

"Indeed, Bostana found some means of intercepting Cavama every time the latter expressed a wish to go into the dungeon. She herself, however, saw the prince very often; and instead of carrying only bread and water to him, as she was ordered to do, she brought him wine, and a variety of excellent provisions prepared by twelve Mussulman slaves who attended on her. She also frequently partook of his repasts with him, and did everything in her power to console him.

"Some days after Prince Assad's return to the city of the Magi, Bostana happened to be at the door of her house when she heard the public crier making an announcement. As she could not understand what the crier said, because he was far off, and as she observed him coming towards the house, she went in, but left the door ajar, and listened. She saw the crier walking on before the grand vizier, Amgiad, Prince Assad's brother, who was surrounded by several officers of state, and a great multitude of people were following.

"The crier had not gone many steps from the door before he made the following proclamation in a loud voice: 'The most excellent and illustrious grand vizier, who is now present, comes in person to inquire after, and seek for, his dear brother, who has been separated from him for more than a year. The description of his person is thus and thus. If any person have given the vizier's brother shelter in his house, or know where he is, his excellency commands him to bring him forth, or to give some information concerning him; and he promises to reward them handsomely. But for those persons who shall conceal and detain him, if he be afterwards discovered, his excellency declares that such persons shall be punished with death, together with their wives, their children, and all their family; and their houses shall be razed to the ground.'

"When Bostana heard these words she instantly shut the door, went to the dungeon where Assad was, and cried to him in a joyful tone, 'Prince, your misfortunes are at length terminated: follow me as quickly as possible.' Assad, whom she had released from his chains on the very day he had been brought back to the dungeon, followed her into the street, and on her arrival there she instantly cried out: 'Behold him! behold him!' The grand vizier, who had not proceeded far, turned round. Assad instantly recognised his brother, ran towards him, and fell into his arms. Amgiad, too, knew and embraced him with transport. He then made him mount the horse of one of his officers, and conducted him in triumph to the palace, where he presested him to the king, who appointed Assad one of his viziers.

"After this event Bostana did not wish to return to her father's, whose house was razed to the ground the very same day. She followed Prince Assad till he arrived at the palace, and she was sent to an apartment belonging to the queen. The old man her father, and Behram, with both their families, were brought the next day before the king, who commanded that they should all lose their heads. On this, they threw themselves at his feet, and implored his mercy. The king replied: 'You shall have no mercy shown you unless you renounce the worship of fire, and embrace the Mussulman religion.' By adopting this course they saved their lives; and so also did Cavama, the sister of Bostana, and the whole family.

"In consideration of Behram's being converted to the Mussulman faith, and in order to give him some recompense for the loss he had suffered in the confiscation of his ship, Amgiad made him one of his principal officers, and lodged him at his own house. A few days after, when Behram was made acquainted with the adventures of his benefactor Amgiad, and of the vizier's brother Assad, he proposed to fit out a vessel, and carry them back to their father Camaralzaman. He said: 'There is no doubt that the king is by this time convinced of your innocence, and is impatient to see you again. If, however, he should still be angry, it is very easy to be informed of that before you land, and then, if he is found to be implacable, you will find no difficulty in returning.'

"The two brothers accepted Behram's offer. They mentioned their design to the king, who not only approved of the project, but gave orders for the immediate equipment of a vessel. Behram hastened the preparations as much as possible; and when he was ready to set sail, the princes went and took leave of the king on the morning before they embarked. While they were making their acknowledgments, and thanking the monarch for all his kindness to them, they heard a great bustle and tumult in the city; and at the same moment an officer came, and announced that a very large army was approaching, and that no one could tell to whom it belonged.

"Observing the alarm that this bad news gave the king, Amgiad said to him: 'O mighty king, although I am now come for the purpose of resigning the office of grand vizier with which you have honoured me, I am, notwithstanding, ready to take upon myself the duty of rendering you any service in my power; and I entreat you to suffer me to go and see who this enemy is that thus comes to attack you in your very capital without having first declared war.' The king gave Amgiad the required permission, and he instantly set out with very few attendants.

"It was not long before Prince Amgiad came in sight of the army, which appeared very formidable, and continued to approach. The advanced guard, who had received their orders, gave him a favourable reception, and brought him into the presence of a princess, who stopped, with her whole army, to hold a conference with him. Prince Amgiad made her a most profound reverence. He asked her if she came as a friend or an enemy; and if she came as an enemy, he requested to be informed what cause of complaint she had against the king his master. The princess replied: 'I come as a friend, and have no cause whatever for complaint against the King of the Magi. His dominions and mine are so situated with regard to each other, that it is almost impossible we can ever have any dispute together. I come only to require the surrender of a slave, whose name is Assad, and who has been taken away from me by a captain belonging to this city, who is called Behram, and is the most insolent of men. And I trust your king will do me justice, when he learns that my name is Margiana.'

"'O powerful queen,' replied Amgiad, 'I am the brother of that slave whom you seem to seek with so much interest and concern. I had lost him, and have now recovered him. Come with me, and I will give him up to you, and I shall likewise have the honour to inform you of every particular of his escape. The king my master will be delighted to see you.'

"Queen Margiana then ordered her army to encamp in the spot where they then were, while she herself accompanied Prince Amgiad through the city to the palace, where he presented her to the king. When the monarch had received her with all possible honour, Prince Assad, who was present, and who knew her the moment she appeared, came and paid his respects to her. She expressed great joy at seeing him again; but at that very instant an officer entered, and announced to the king that another army, much

PRINCE AMGIAD CONDUCTS PRINCE ASSAD TO THE PALACE.

more powerful than the first, had made its appearance on the other side of the city. The King of the Magi seemed more alarmed now than he had been when the army belonging to Margiana came in sight; for this new host appeared much the more numerous, if he might judge from the clouds of dust raised by its approach, and which seemed to darken the whole air. 'What will become of us, O Amgiad?' he cried; 'here is a fresh army approaching to overwhelm us.' The prince knew what the king wished him to do. He therefore mounted his horse, and rode as fast as possible to meet this second army. He demanded of the first troops whom he encountered to speak to their commander, and they conducted him before one who was a king, as he instantly conjectured, from a crown which the commander had upon his head. As soon as he caught sight of this king, Amgiad alighted, and as he approached, he prostrated himself on the ground, and asked what the stranger monarch wished of the king, Amgiad's master.

"'My name is Gaiour,' replied the monarch, 'and I am King of China. The desire to gain some intelligence of a daughter, named Badoura, whom many years since I gave in marriage to Prince Camaralzaman, son of Schahzaman, King of the Island of the Children of Khaledan, is the cause why I have left my dominions. I gave that prince permission to visit his father on condition that he should come and spend every second year with me, and bring my daughter with him. But for a great length of time I have been unable to hear anything of them. Your king, therefore, will greatly oblige an afflicted father if he can give him the least information on the subject.'

"Prince Amgiad, who instantly knew by this speech that the stranger was his grandfather, kissed his hand with great tenderness, and said to him: 'Your majesty will pardon this liberty, when you hear that I kiss your royal hand as a mark of respect to you as my grandfather. I am the son of Camaralzaman, who is at this time king of the Island of Ebony, and of Queen Badoura, on whose account you are so much distressed; and I do not doubt that they are at this time in their dominions, in perfect health.' The King of China embraced Amgiad in the most affectionate manner; and greatly was he delighted at thus seeing his grandson. This very unexpected and happy meeting drew tears from the eyes of both. On King Gaiour's asking what was the reason he thus found Amgiad in a foreign country, the prince related his history, and that of his brother Assad. When it was finished, the King of China replied: 'My son, it is not just that two princes so innocent as you and your brother should experience any further effects of injustice and wrong. Console yourself; I will carry both you and your brother to King Camaralzaman, and will make your peace. Go, and make my arrival known to your brother.'

"While the King of China ordered his army to encamp in the place where Prince Amgiad had encountered him, the latter went back to give an account of the interview to the King of the Magi, who was waiting for him with the greatest impatience. The King of the Magi was extremely surprised to hear that so powerful a monarch as the King of China had undertaken such a long and painful journey through the desire of gaining some intelligence of his daughter. He immediately gave orders that King Giaour should be honourably entertained, and made preparations to go and receive him in person.

"But now considerable clouds of dust were again seen. They seemed to rise from a third side of the city; and the news soon came that a third army was approaching. This circumstance obliged the king to stop, and request Amgiad again to go and see what was the cause of this new visit. The prince departed, and this time he took his brother Assad with him. This proved to be the army of Camaralzaman their father, who was coming in search of them. He had reproached himself so bitterly for his hastiness in ordering their execution, that the emir Giondar at last informed him in what manner he had preserved their lives. This made the king resolve to go and discover his sons, in whatever country they might be.

"This afflicted father embraced the two princes with tears of joy. They were the first tears he had for a long time shed which had not arisen from the deepest affliction. When the princes informed him of the arrival of his father-in-law, the King of China, he went with them, accompanied by a very few attendants, to see King Giaour in his camp. They had not proceeded far on their road before they perceived a fourth army, which seemed to advance in perfect order, and to come from the direction of Persia. Camaralzaman desired his sons to go and see to whom that army belonged, and said that he would wait for their return. They departed immediately; and when they met the army on its approach, they presented themselves to the king who commanded it. After saluting him with the greatest respect, they asked him his motive for thus coming to the capital of the King of the Magi.

"The grand vizier, who was present, took upon himself to reply in the following words: 'The monarch to whom you have addressed yourself is called Schahzaman, King of the Island of the Children of Khaledan. He has been travelling for a long time, with all the attendants you see, in search of his son, Prince Camaralzaman, who left his dominions many years ago without acquainting his father with his intention. If you should happen to know anything concerning Prince Camaralzaman, you will afford the king the greatest possible pleasure by giving him the information.' To this speech the princes made reply that they would come back in a little time with an answer. They then set off at full speed to Camaralzaman, to announce to him the cause of the arrival of the last army, and that it belonged to King Schahzaman, who commanded it in person.

"Astonishment and joy, not unmingled with remorse at having left the king his father without taking leave of him, had so powerful an effect upon Camaralzaman, that he absolutely fainted when he heard that his father was so near him. At length the assistance of Amgiad and Assad, who did all they could to comfort him, restored him to his senses; and when he thought he had acquired sufficient strength, he went out and threw himself at his father's feet. Never was witnessed a more tender or affecting interview between a parent and son. Schahzaman affectionately chid Camaralzaman for his unkindness in leaving him in so unfeeling and cruel a manner; and the latter showed the deepest regret and compunction at the fault which love alone had caused him to commit.

"The three kings and Queen Margiana continued three days at the court of the King of the Magi, who entertained them in the most magnificent and splendid manner. These three days also witnessed the celebration of the marriage of Prince Assad with Queen Margiana, and that of Bostana with Prince Amgiad, who married the idolater's daughter in consideration of the essential service she had afforded Prince Assad. At length the three kings and Queen Margiana, with her husband, retired to their separate dominions. But the King of the Magi, who had attained a very advanced age, felt so strong an attachment to his vizier, Prince Amgiad, that he placed the crown upon his head. King Amgiad then used all his endeavours to abolish the idolatrous worship of fire, and instead of it to establish the Mussulman religion throughout the kingdom.

## THE HISTORY OF NOUREDDIN AND THE BEAUTIFUL PERSIAN.

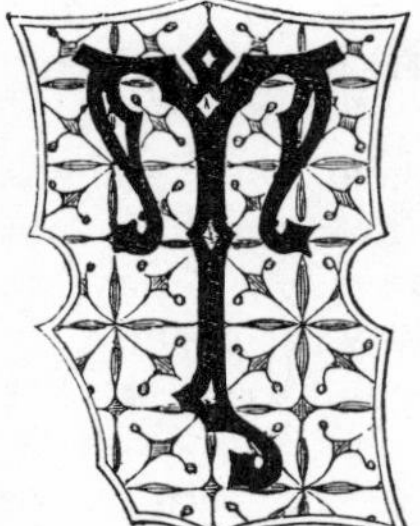

HE city of Balsora was for a long time the capital of a kingdom tributary to the caliphs. During the life of the Caliph Haroun Alraschid it was governed by a king named Zinebi. The great caliph and the king were the offspring of two brothers, and were, therefore, closely related. Zinebi, who was unwilling to trust the administration of his government to one vizier only, chose two to preside in his council. They were named Khacan and Saouy.

"The character of the vizier Khacan was distinguished by mildness, liberality, and kindness. His greatest pleasure consisted in obliging all who came in contact with him. He granted every favour that he could accord consistently with that justice he held himself bound to administer. The whole court of Balsora, the city, and every part of the kingdom held him in the highest esteem, and the whole region echoed with his well-earned praise.

"Saouy, on the other hand, was a very different man. His mind was a constant prey to fretfulness and chagrin. Without distinction of rank or quality, he repulsed every applicant who approached him. His avarice was so great that, instead of doing good and earning blessings by the use of the immense wealth he possessed, he even denied himself the common necessaries of life. No one could love such a man; nor was a word ever uttered in his praise. And what increased the general aversion in which the people held him was his great hatred of Khacan, whose benevolent and generous actions he always endeavoured to represent in a bad point of view, that they might tell to the disadvantage of that excellent minister. He was also continually on the watch to undermine Khacan's credit with the king.

"One day, after holding a council, the king indulged in familiar conversation with these two ministers, and some other members of the court. The subject happened to turn upon those female slaves whom it is the custom to purchase, and who are considered by their possessors nearly in the light of lawful wives. Some of the nobles present were of opinion that beauty and elegance of form in a slave were a full equivalent for the qualifications possessed by those ladies of high birth, with whom, either for the sake of a splendid connection, or from motives of interest, alliances of marriage were frequently formed.

"Others, among whom was the vizier Khacan, maintained that mere beauty and charms of person by no means comprehended all that was requisite in a wife; that these qualities should be accompanied by wit, intelligence, modesty, and pleasing manners; and heightened, if possible, by a variety of acquirements and accomplishments. To persons who have important concerns to transact, and who have passed a tedious day in close application to their affairs, nothing, they contended, can be so grateful, when they retire from bustle and fatigue, as the company of a well instructed wife, whose conversation will equally improve and delight. On the other hand, they contended, a slave whose sole recommendation is her beauty, could never compare in attractions with such a companion.

"The king was of the latter party, and proved himself so by ordering Khacan to purchase for him a slave, who, perfect in all exterior charms of beauty, should, above everything, possess a well cultivated mind.

"Saouy, who had been of a contrary opinion to Khacan, was jealous of the honour shown to his colleague by the king, and said to Zinebi: 'O my lord, it will be extremely difficult to find so accomplished a slave as your majesty requires; and if such a woman be found, which I can scarcely believe possible, she will be cheaply bought at the expense of ten thousand pieces of gold.' 'Saouy,' replied the king, 'you seem to think this too large a sum. It would be so, perhaps, for you; but is not excessive for me.' At the same time he ordered his grand treasurer, who was present, to pay ten thousand pieces of gold to Khacan.

"As soon as Khacan returned home, he sent to summon a number of men, who traded in slaves, and charged them, when they should find such a female slave as he described, to give him immediate notice of it. Equally anxious to oblige the vizier Khacan, and to promote their own interest, the slave merchants promised to use every means in their power to procure such a slave as he wished to purchase; and, indeed, a day seldom passed, in which they did not bring some woman to him, but he found some fault with each one.

"Early one morning, while Khacan was on his way to the royal palace, a merchant presented himself with great eagerness, and seizing the vizier's stirrup, informed him that a Persian merchant, who had arrived very late on the preceding evening, had a slave to sell, whose beauty far surpassed anything he had ever beheld; and, with respect to intelligence and knowledge, the merchant assured him, that she surpassed everything the world had ever known.

"Delighted with the news, which would, he hoped, afford him a good opportunity of making his court, Khacan desired that the slave might be brought to him on his return from the palace, and thereupon he continued his way.

"The merchant did not fail to wait upon the vizier at the hour appointed; and Khacan found that the slave possessed charms so far above his expectation, that he immediately gave her the name of the Beautiful Persian. Being a man of great knowledge and penetration, he soon discovered, by the conversation he held with her, that he might seek in vain for any slave, who could excel her in all the qualities required by the king. He enquired, therefore, of the merchant, what was the sum demanded for her by the Persian trader who had brought her.

"'O my lord,' replied the merchant, 'the trader, who is a man of few words, protests that he cannot consent to make the smallest abatement of ten thousand pieces of gold. He has assured me in the most solemn manner, that without taking into account his own care, pains, and time, he has expended very nearly that sum in engaging various masters for the improvement of her mental accomplishments; and then there is the unavoidable expense of dress and maintenance. From the very moment when he purchased her, in her early infancy, he considered her worthy of royal regard. He spared nothing in her

PURCHASE OF THE BEAUTIFUL PERSIAN.

education, that might enable her to attain so high an honour. She plays on every instrument, sings and dances to admiration, writes better than the most skilful masters, and makes exquisite verses. There are no books she has not read; nor am I exceeding the truth when I assert, that there never existed, till now, so accomplished a slave.'

"The vizier Khacan, who understood the merits of the Beautiful Persian much better than the merchant, who merely repeated what the trader had told him, was unwilling to defer the purchase to a future day. Accordingly he sent one of his people to the place where the merchant informed him the trader might be found, to desire the immediate attendance of the Persian.

"As soon as he arrived, Khacan said: 'It is not for myself that I am desirous to purchase your slave, but for the king. You must, however, propose a more moderate price than the sum which the merchant has mentioned to me.'

"'O vizier,' replied the Persian, 'it would be to me an infinite honour were I allowed to present my slave to his majesty; but I am aware that such a proceeding would not become a stranger like myself. All that I desire is to be reimbursed for the money which I have actually expended in her education. I may, I think, assert with confidence that his majesty will be perfectly content with his purchase.'

"The vizier Khacan was not inclined to dispute the matter. He ordered the required sum to be paid to the merchant, who, before he withdrew, addressed Khacan as follows: —'O vizier, since the slave you have purchased is intended for the king, allow me the honour to inform you, that she is exceedingly fatigued with the long journey she has so lately made; and, though her present beauty may well seem incomparable, yet she will appear to far greater advantage if you keep her in your own house about a fortnight, allowing her, in the meantime, such attentions as she may require. When you present her to the king at the end of that time, she will ensure you honour and reward, and entitle me, I hope, to your thanks. You may perceive that the sun has rather injured her complexion; but when she has used the bath a few times, and has been adorned in the manner your taste will direct, you may be sure, my lord, she will be so changed, that you will find her beauty infinitely beyond what you can at present imagine.'

"Khacan thought the advice of the merchant very good, and determined to follow it. He allotted to the Beautiful Persian an apartment near that of his wife, whom he requested to allow the slave a place at her own table, and to treat her with all the respect due to a lady belonging to the king. He farther desired that his wife would cause the most magnificent dresses to be made, and to choose apparel peculiarly becoming to the beautiful stranger, whom he thus addressed: 'The good fortune I have just procured to you could not possibly be greater. I have purchased you for the king, whose joy in possessing you will, I trust, be even greater than the satisfaction I feel in having acquitted myself of the commission with which I have been charged. But it is right that I should inform you that I have a son, who, though he does not want intelligence, has all the inconsiderate rashness of youth. As you cannot avoid sometimes meeting him, I mention this to put you on your guard.' The Beautiful Persian thanked the vizier for his information and advice, and assured him she would profit by it. Thereupon the vizier withdrew.

"Noureddin, the son of whom the vizier had spoken, was accustomed, without restraint, to enter the apartment of his mother, with whom he usually took his meals. He was very handsome to look upon—young, agreeable, and intrepid. He had, moreover, a great deal of wit; and, accustomed to express himself with extraordinary facility, he had the enviable gift of being able to carry by persuasion every point he wished to gain. From the moment when Noureddin first saw the Beautiful Persian, although he knew from the solemn assurance of his father that she had been purchased for the king, he put no constraint upon himself, nor did he strive against the feeling of love that began to possess him, but permitted himself to be allured by the charms of the fair stranger, with which he had been struck from the first. His passion increased with the delight he experienced in conversing with her, and he determined to employ every means in his power to procure her for himself.

"The Beautiful Persian was also mucn struck by the graces of Noureddin. 'The vizier does me great honour,' said she to herself, 'in purchasing me for the king of Balsora. I should, however, have esteemed myself very happy, if he had designed me for his own son.'

"Noureddin never failed to profit by the opportunities he had of beholding the Beautiful

Persian; and his delight was to converse, to laugh, to jest with her. Never did he quit her till he was driven away by his mother, who would often say: 'It is not, my son, becoming in a young man, like you, to waste so much time in a woman's apartment. Go, and labour to render yourself worthy of one day succeeding to the office and dignity of your father.'

"In consequence of the long journey which the Beautiful Persian had lately taken, much time had elapsed since she had enjoyed the luxury of the bath. Accordingly, about five or six days after she had been purchased, the wife of the vizier gave orders to have the bath in their house prepared for her use. She sent thither the Beautiful Persian, accompanied with a train of female slaves, who were commanded to render her every possible service and attention. The fair slave quitted the bath, arrayed in a most magnificent dress, which had been provided for her. The vizier's lady had given herself the more trouble on this occasion, from a desire to please her husband; for she wished to show him how much she interested herself in whatever concerned his happiness.

"A thousand times handsomer than when Khacan purchased her, the Beautiful Persian appeared before the wife of the vizier, who scarcely knew her again.

"Having gracefully kissed the hand of Khacan's wife, the fair slave thus addressed her: 'I know not, O lady, how I may appear to you in the dress you have had the goodness to order for me. Your women assure me it so well becomes me, they hardly know me again—but I fear they are flatterers. It is to yourself that I wish to appeal. If, however, they should speak the truth, it is to you, O my mistress, that I am indebted for all the advantage this apparel gives me.'

"'O my daughter,' replied the vizier's lady, with a look of great delight, 'what my women have told you is no flattery. I am better able to judge than they; and without taking into account your dress, which, however, becomes you wonderfully, be assured you bring with you from the bath a beauty so infinitely above what you possessed before, that I cannot sufficiently marvel at it. If I imagined the bath were still sufficiently warm, I would use it myself.' 'O, my mistress,' replied the Beautiful Persian, 'I have no words to express my sense of the kindness you have shown me, who have done nothing to merit your favour. With respect to the bath, it is admirable; but if you intend to use it, there is no time to be lost, as I have no doubt your women will inform you.'

"The wife of the vizier reflecting that many days had elapsed since she bathed, was desirous of profiting by the opportunity. She made known her intention to her women, and they soon prepared all the requisites for the occasion. But before the vizier's lady went to the bath she commanded two little female slaves to remain with the Beautiful Persian, who had retired to her apartment, giving them a strict order not to admit Noureddin if he made his appearance during her absence.

"While the lady was in the bath Noureddin came; and, not finding his mother in her apartment, he went towards that of the Beautiful Persian. In the ante chamber, he found the two slaves. He enquired of them for his mother, and they informed him she was in the bath. Then he asked, 'Where is the Beautiful Persian?' They replied, 'She is just returned from thence, and is now in her chamber. But we cannot allow you to enter, having been strictly forbidden to do so by our lady, your mother.'

"The chamber of the Beautiful Persian was only shut off by a tapestry curtain. Noureddin was determined to enter. The two slaves tried to prevent him from doing so, but he took each of them by the arm and turned them out of the ante chamber. They ran to the bath, making loud and bitter complaints; and in tears informed their lady that Noureddin had driven them from their post, and in contempt of their remonstrance had entered the chamber of the Beautiful Persian.

"The excessive boldness of her son angered the good lady extremely. She instantly quitted the bath, and dressed herself with all possible haste. But before she could get to the chamber of the Beautiful Persian, Noureddin had left it, and had gone away.

"The Beautiful Persian was extremely astonished, when she saw the wife of the vizier enter, bathed in tears, and looking like a distracted person. 'O, my mistress,' said she, 'may I presume to ask what it is that thus grieves you? Has any accident befallen you at the bath, that you have been compelled to quit it so soon?'

"'How!' cried the vizier's lady, 'can you ask with so tranquil an air why I am thus disordered, when my son, Noureddin, has been in your chamber alone with you? Could a greater misfortune possibly happen either to him or to me?'

"'I beseech you, O lady,' returned the Beautiful Persian, 'to inform me what evil can happen to yourself, or your son, in consequence of his having been in my chamber?'

"'Has not my husband informed you,' cried the vizier's lady, 'that you were purchased for the king; and has he not already cautioned you not to allow Noureddin to approach you?'

"To this speech the Beautiful Persian replied, 'I have not forgotten his injunction, madam; 'but Noureddin came to inform me that the vizier, his father, had altered his plans concerning me; and that, instead of reserving me for the king as he had purposed, I was destined to be the wife of Noureddin. I believed what he told me, and felt no regret at the change in my destiny; for I have conceived a great affection for your son, notwithstanding the few opportunities we have had of seeing each other. I resign, without regret, the hope of belonging to the king, and shall esteem myself perfectly happy if I am allowed to pass my whole life with Noureddin.'

"'Would to Heaven,' cried the vizier's lady, 'that what you tell me were true. It would give me very great delight. But believe me, Noureddin is an impostor; he has deceived you. It is impossible that his father should have made the change he talks of. O unhappy young man! and unhappy parents! and thrice unhappy father, who must suffer the dreadful consequences of the king's wrath! Neither my tears nor my prayers will be able to soften Khacan, or to obtain pardon for his son, whom he will sacrifice to his just resentment, when he shall be informed of the boldness of which Noureddin has been guilty.' Having spoken these words, she wept bitterly, and her slaves, who were all anxious for the safety of Noureddin, mingled their tears with hers.

"The vizier Khacan, who came home soon after, was greatly astonished to find his wife and slaves bathed in tears, and the Beautiful Persian extremely melancholy. He inquired the cause of their grief; upon which, instead of replying, they redoubled their moans and tears. This conduct so increased his surprise, that addressing himself to his wife, he said, 'I insist upon being informed of the cause of this sorrow.'

"The unhappy lady was thus obliged to speak. But first she said to her husband, 'Promise me that you will not impute blame to me in what I am going to tell you. I assure you the calamity has not happened from any fault of mine.' Then without waiting for his reply, she continued; "While I was in the bath, attended by my women, your son came home, and availed himself of this fatal opportunity to persuade the Beautiful Persian that you had relinquished your intention of giving her to the king, and that you intended her for his wife. I leave you to imagine what I felt at hearing he had told so terrible a falsehood. This is the cause of my grief, on your account, and on account of our son also, for whom I have not the courage to entreat your clemency.'

"It is impossible to describe the mortification of the vizier Khacan, when he was informed of the insolence of Noureddin. 'Ah!' cried he, beating his breast, wringing his hands, and tearing his beard, 'is it thus, wretched youth—unworthy to live—is it thus that you precipitate your father into a pit of destruction from the highest degree of happiness? You have ruined him, and with him destroy yourself. In his anger at this offence, committed against his very person, the king will not be satisfied with your blood or mine.'

"His wife endeavoured to comfort him, and said, 'Do not thus despair, I can easily, by disposing of a part of my jewels, procure ten thousand pieces of gold, with which you may purchase a slave more beautiful than this, and one more worthy of the king.' 'What! do you believe,' returned the vizier, 'that the loss of ten thousand pieces of gold thus troubles me? It is not this that afflicts me; what I lament is the loss of honour which to me is the most precious of all earthly things.' 'Nevertheless,' observed the lady, 'it appears to me, my lord, that a loss that can be repaired by money is not of such very great importance.'

"But the vizier resumed: 'Surely, you are not ignorant that Saouy is my most inveterate enemy. Can you not see, that as soon as he shall become acquainted with the affair, he will go immediately to the king to triumph at my expense? "Your majesty," he will say, "is accustomed to speak of the affection and zeal which Khacan shows for your service. He has, however, lately proved how little he is worthy of your generous confidence. He has received ten thousand pieces of gold to purchase you a slave. He has duly acquitted himself of his honourable commission, and the slave he has bought is the handsomest ever beheld; but, instead of bringing her to your majesty, he has thought proper to make a present of her to his son. He has said, as it were, my son, take this

THE VIZIER'S VEXATION.

slave; you are more worthy of her than the king." Then will my enemy add, with his usual malice, "His son is now the possessor of this slave, and every day rejoices in her charms. That the affair is precisely as I have had the honour to state your majesty may be assured by examining into it yourself." Do you not perceive,' added the vizier, 'that should it occur to Saouy to calumnate me thus, I am every moment liable to have the guards of the king entering my house, and carrying off the beautiful slave. It is easy to imagine all the terrible evils which will ensue.'

"To this discourse of the vizier, her husband, the lady answered: 'Sir, the malice of Saouy is certainly great, and should this affair come to his knowledge, he will be certain to represent it unfavourably to the king. But how can he, or any person, be informed of what happens in the interior of this house? And even if it should be suspected, and the king should interrogate you on the subject, you may easily say that on a nearer acquaintance with the slave you did not find her so worthy of his majesty's regard as she at first appeared; that the merchant had deceived you; that she indeed possessed incomparable beauty; but was beyond measure deficient in those qualities of the mind which she had been supposed to possess. The king will rely on your word, and Saouy will once more have the mortification of failing in his plans to ruin you, which he has already so often attempted in vain. Take courage, then; and if you allow me to advise, send for the brokers, inform the slave merchants that you are by no means satisfied with the Beautiful Persian, and direct them to look out for another slave.'

"This counsel appeared to the vizier Khacan very judicious. His mind accordingly became more tranquil, and he determined to follow his wife's advice. He did not, however, in the least abate his anger towards his son.

"Noureddin did not appear for the rest of the day. Fearing to take refuge with any of those young friends whose houses he was in the habit of frequenting, lest his father would have him searched for there, he went to some distance from the city, and concealed himself in a garden, where he had never before been, and was wholly unknown. He did not return home till very late at night, and long after the time when he well knew his father was accustomed to go to rest. He prevailed upon his mother's women to let him in, and they admitted him with great caution and silence. He went out the next morning before his father had risen, and was obliged to take the same precautions for a whole month, to his great chagrin and mortification. The women, however, did not in the least flatter him. They told him frankly, that the vizier, his father, was exceedingly angry with him, and had, moreover, determined to kill him at the first opportunity, whenever he should come in his way.

"The vizier's lady knew from her women that Noureddin returned home every night; but she had not the courage to solicit her husband to pardon him. At length she summoned resolution to mention the subject. 'O my husband,' said she, 'I have not ventured hitherto to speak to you concerning your son. I entreat you now to allow me to ask what you intend to do with him. No son can behave worse towards a parent than Noureddin has behaved towards you. He has deprived you of great honour, and of the satisfaction of presenting to the king a slave so highly accomplished as the Beautiful Persian. All this I acknowledge. But, after all what do you purpose doing? Do you wish to destroy him utterly? Are you aware that by doing so you may bring upon yourself a very heavy calamity, in addition to the comparatively light misfortune which you have already sustained? Do you not fear that malicious or malignant persons, in their endeavours to discover the reason why your son is driven from you, may ascertain the real cause, which you are so anxious to conceal? Should this happen, you will have fallen into the very misfortune which you have strenuously endeavoured to avoid.'

"The vizier replied, 'What you say is perfectly just and reasonable; but I cannot resolve to pardon Noureddin till I have chastised him in some degree as he deserves.' 'He will be sufficiently punished,' urged his wife, if you put in execution the plan that has this moment occurred to me. Your son returns home every night, and departs in the morning, before you rise. Wait this evening for his arrival, and let him suppose that you intend to kill him. I will come to his assistance; and by appearing to grant his life to my prayers, you may oblige him to take the Beautiful Persian on any terms you wish. I know he loves her, and the beautiful slave does not dislike him.'

"Khacan was well pleased with this advice. Accordingly, before Noureddin, who arrived at his accustomed hour, was allowed to enter the house, the vizier placed himself behind the door, and so soon as it was opened rushed out upon his son, and threw him to the ground. Noureddin, looking up, beheld his father standing over him with a poniard in his hand, ready to stab him.

"The mother of Noureddin arrived at this moment, and seizing the vizier by the arm, exclaimed: 'What are you doing, my lord?' 'Let me alone,' replied he, 'that I may kill this unworthy son.' 'Ah, my lord, exclaimed the mother, 'you shall first kill me; never will I permit you to imbrue your hands in your own blood.' Noureddin took advantage of this moment's respite. 'My father.' cried he, his eyes suffused with tears,

'I entreat your pity and forbearance. Grant me the pardon I presume to ask, in the name of that Being from whom you will yourself hope forgiveness on the day when we shall all appear before him.'

"Khacan suffered the poniard to be wrested from him, and released Noureddin, who instantly threw himself at his father's feet, which he passionately kissed, to express how sincerely he repented having given him offence. 'Noureddin,' said the vizier, 'thank your mother, for it is out of respect to her that I pardon you. I will even give you the Beautiful Persian, on condition that you engage, on oath, not to consider her as a slave, but as your lawful wife, whom you will never, on any account, sell or repudiate. As she has infinitely more understanding and good sense than you, she may be able to moderate those fits of youthful indiscretion by which you seem likely to be ruined.'

"Noureddin, who had not dared to expect so much indulgence, thanked his father with the warmest expressions of gratitude, and readily took the oath required of him. The Beautiful Persian and he were perfectly satisfied with each other, and the vizier was very well pleased at their union.

"Under these circumstances Khacan did not think it prudent to wait till the king spoke to him of the commission he had received. He took every opportunity of himself introducing the subject, and of pointing out the difficulties he experienced in acquitting himself in this affair to his majesty's satisfaction. He played his part with so much address, that in a short time the king thought no more of the matter. Saouy had indeed heard some rumours of what had happened; but Khacan continued so much in favour that he did not venture to speak of his suspicions

"More than a year elapsed; and this delicate business had gone on much more prosperously than the vizier Khacan could have any reason to expect. But one day, when he had indulged himself with a bath, some very urgent affair obliged him to hasten to the palace, heated as he was. The cold air struck him so forcibly that it brought on a sudden and grievous fever, which confined him to his bed. His illness continuing to increase, he soon became sensible that his last moments were approaching. He therefore addressed Noureddin, who never quitted his side, in these terms: 'My son, I know not whether I have made a good use of the great riches which the goodness of Allah has bestowed upon me. You see that my possessions are of no avail to protect me from the hand of death. But the one thing that I am anxious to impress upon your mind, at this awful moment, is the duty of remembering the promise you have made me with respect to the Beautiful Persian. In full confidence of your integrity I die happy.'

"These were the last words, which the vizier uttered. He expired immediately afterwards, to the inexpressible grief of his family, the city, and the court. The king lamented the loss of a wise, zealous, and faithful minister; the city wept for its friend and benefactor. Never was there seen at Balsora so magnificent a funeral. The viziers, emirs, and indeed all the nobles of the court, were eager to support the bier, which they bore, in succession, on their shoulders to the place of burial, while all the citizens, rich and poor, accompanied the procession with weeping and lamentations.

"Noureddin showed every token of profound grief for the loss he had sustained. For a long time he suffered no person to have access to him. At length, however, he one day gave permission that one of his intimate friends should be admitted. This friend endeavoured to comfort him, and finding him inclined to listen to advice, represented to Noureddin, that since every token of respect which duty and affection could claim had been paid to the memory of his father, it was time for him to re-appear in the world, to associate with his friends, and to assert that rank and character to which, by virtue of his birth and merits, he could lay claim. 'We offend against the laws of nature and civilised life,' said this judicious counseller, 'if we do not render to our deceased parents every respect which tenderness dictates; and the world will very justly censure, as a proof of savage insensibility, any omission in these rites of tenderness and duty; but when we have acquitted ourselves in such a manner as to be above the possibility of reproach, it becomes us then to resume our former habits, and to live in the world like persons who have a character to sustain. Therefore dry your tears. and strive to recover that air of gaiety which was wont to diffuse such universal joy amongst all who had the pleasure of your acquaintance.'

"The advice of this friend was reasonable enough, and Noureddin would have been spared many misfortunes which afterwards befell him if he had followed it in moderation. But impetuous in all he did, he yielded even too implicitly to the persuasions of his friend, whom he immediately entertained with great good will; and when the friend was retiring, Noureddin begged that he would visit him again the next day, and bring with him three or four of their common friends. By degrees, he formed a society of ten persons, all nearly of his own age, with whom he spent his time in continual feasts and scenes of pleasure; and not a day passed on which he did not dismiss every one of them withsome present.

"Sometimes, to make his house even more agreeable to his friends, Noureddin would request the Beautiful Persian to be present at their feast. Though she had the good nature to comply cheerfully with his commands, she greatly disapproved his excessive expenditure; on which subject she freely gave him her opinion: 'I have no doubt,' she said, 'that the vizier, your father, has left you great riches; but be not angry if I, a slave, remind you that however great your wealth may be, you will assuredly come to the end of it, if you continue your present style of living. It is reasonable sometimes to regale, and entertain friends; but to run every day into the same unbounded expense is to pursue the sure road to want and wretchedness. It were far better, for your reputation and honour, that you followed the steps of your deceased father, and put yourself in the way of obtaining those offices, in which he gained so much glory.'

"Noureddin listened to the Beautiful Persian with a smile, and when she had finished, he replied, 'My love, I beg you will cease this solemn discourse, and let us talk only of pleasure. My late father held me constantly in such great restraint that I am now very glad to enjoy the liberty for which I so often sighed in former days. There will be always time enough to adopt the regular plan you recommend; a man of my years ought to indulge in the delights of youth.'

"What contributed, perhaps, more than any thing else to the embarrassment of Noureddin's affairs, was his extreme aversion to reckon with his steward. Whenever the steward and his book appeared, they were instantly dismissed. Noureddin would say, 'Get you gone, I can trust your honesty. Only take care that my table be always handsomely furnished.' Then would the steward reply, 'O Noureddin, you are my master. Allow me, nevertheless, very humbly to remind you of the proverb, which says, "he who spends much, and reckons little, will be a beggar before he is a wise man." It is not only the enormous expense of your table, but your profusion in other respects is utterly without bounds. Were your treasures as huge as mountains, they would not be sufficient to maintain your expenses.' 'Begone, I tell you,' repeated Noureddin, 'I want none of your lectures; continue to provide for my table, and leave the rest to me.'

"In the meantime, the friends of Noureddin were very constant guests at his table, and lost no opportunity of profiting by his easy temper. They were ever praising and flattering him, and pretending to discover some extraordinary virtue, or grace, in his most trifling action. But, especially, they never neglected to extol to the skies every thing that belonged to him; and indeed, they found it very profitable to do so. One of them would say, 'O my friend, I passed the other day by the estate which you have in such and such a place; nothing can be more magnificent, or better furnished than the house; and the garden belonging to it is an absolute paradise of delights.' 'I am quite delighted that you are pleased with it,' answered Noureddin. 'Ho, there! bring us pen, ink, and paper; the place is yours; I beg to hear no words on the subject; I give it you with all my heart.' Others had only to commend one of his houses, baths, or the public inns erected for the accommodation of strangers—a property very valuable from the considerable revenue it brought in—and these were instantly given away. The Beautiful Persian represented to Noureddin the injury he did himself; but, instead of regarding her admonitions, he continued in the same course of extravagance till he had parted with every thing he possessed.

"In short, Noureddin, for the space of a year, attended to nothing but feasting and

THE BEAUTIFUL PERSIAN REMONSTRATES WITH NOUREDDIN AGAINST HIS EXTRAVAGANCE.

merriment; and thus he lavished away the vast property which his ancestors, and the good vizier, his father, had acquired, and managed with so much care and attention. The year had hardly gone by, when, while he was at table one day, he heard a rapping at the door of his hall. He had dismissed his slaves and shut himself up with his friends, that they might enjoy themselves free from interruption.

"One of his companions offered to rise and open the door, but Noureddin prevented him, and went to the door himself. He found the visitor was his steward; and withdrew a little way out of the hall, to hear what was wanted, leaving the door partly open.

"The friend, who had risen, had perceived the steward; and curious to hear what he might have to say to Noureddin he placed himself between the hangings and the door, and heard him thus address his master: 'O my lord, I beg you will pardon me for interrupting you in the midst of your pleasures; but what I have to communicate appears to me to be of such great importance, that I could not, consistently with my duty, avoid intruding upon you. I have just been making up my accounts, and I find that what I have long foreseen, and of which I have often warned you, has now arrived; that not a single coin is left of all the sums I have received from you to defray your expenses. Whatever other funds you have paid over to me are also exhausted; and your farmers and various tenants have made it appear to me so very evident, that you have made over to others the estates they rented of you, that I can demand nothing from them. Here are my accounts, my lord, examine them; if you wish that I should continue to serve you, provide me with fresh funds; or permit me to retire.' Noureddin was so astonished at this intelligence that he could not answer a word.

"The friend, who had been listening, and who had heard all that passed, returned immediately to the rest of the party, and communicated the news. 'You will do as you please,' said he, 'in the use you make of this information; with regard to myself, I declare to you, that this is the last time you will ever see me in Noureddin's house.' The others replied, 'If things are really as you have represented, we have no more business here than yourself, and our foolish young friend will scarcely see us again.'

"Noureddin returned at this moment, and, though he endeavoured to put a good face upon the matter, and to diffuse the accustomed hilarity among his friends, he could not so dissemble but that they readily conjectured the truth of what they had just heard. Accordingly, he had hardly returned to his seat, when one of the company rose and thus addressed him: 'O my friend, I am very sorry that I cannot enjoy the pleasure of your society any longer, therefore I hope you will excuse my departure.' 'What obliges you to leave us so soon?' said Noureddin. 'My lord,' replied the guest, 'my wife is brought to bed to-day, and you are well aware that in such cases the presence of a husband is peculiarly necessary.' He then made a very low bow, and departed. Immediately afterwards another guest withdrew upon some pretence, and the whole party, one after another, followed the example, till there remained not one of all the friends who till this day had been the constant companions of Noureddin.

"Noureddin had not the least suspicion of the resolution his friends had taken not to see him again. He went to the apartment of the Beautiful Persian, to consult with her in private on the information he had received from his steward; and he openly expressed his sincere regret at having reduced his affairs to such great disorder.

"'My lord,' said the Beautiful Persian, 'permit me to remind you, that, on this subject you never would listen to my counsel; you now see the result. I was not in the least deceived when I foretold the melancholy consequences you might expect, and great has been my concern that I could not make you at all conscious of the evil times that awaited you. Whenever I was anxious to speak to you on the subject you always replied: "Let us enjoy ourselves, and rejoice in the happy moments when fortune is favourable. The sky will probably not always be so bright." Still I was not wrong when I reminded you, that we are ourselves able to build up our own fortune by the wisdom of our conduct. You would never listen to me; and I was compelled, in spite of my forebodings, to leave you to yourself.'

"'I must acknowledge,' replied Noureddin, 'that I have been very wrong in neglecting the prudent advice you have given me, and in disregarding the dictates of your admirable wisdom; but, if I have expended all my estate, consider that it has been with a few select friends, whom I have long known; men of worth and honour, and who, full of kindness and gratitude, will not assuredly now abandon me.' 'My lord,' said the Beautiful Persian, 'if you have no other resource than the gratitude of your friends, believe me your hopes are ill-founded, as you will doubtless discover in a very short time.'

"'O charming Persian,' cried Noureddin, 'I have a better opinion than you seem to have of my friends' disposition to serve me. I will go round to all of them to-morrow morning, before their ordinary hour of coming hither, and you shall see me return with a large sum of money, which they will unite in subscribing for my wants. I have fully resolved that I will then change my manner of life, and use the money I obtain in some way of merchandise.'

"On the next day Noureddin accordingly visited his ten friends, who all lived in the same street. He knocked at the door of the first, who happened to be one of the richest of them. A female slave appeared, and, before she opened the door, enquired who was there. 'Tell your master,' said Noureddin, 'that it is Noureddin, son of the late vizier Khacan.' The slave admitted him, and introduced him into a hall; then she went to the chamber, where her master was, to inform him that Noureddin was waiting to see him. 'Noureddin!' repeated the friend, in a tone of contempt, and so loudly that Noureddin heard him: 'Go, tell him I am not at home—and whenever he comes again, give him the same answer.' The slave returned, and informed Noureddin, that she had thought her master was at home, but that she had been mistaken.

"Noureddin went away confused and astonished. 'Oh! the perfidious, pitiful wretch,' cried he, 'it was only yesterday that he protested to me I had no sincerer friend than himself, and now he treats me thus unworthily!' He proceeded to the door of another who sent out the same reply. He then waited on a third, and went to all the rest in succession, receiving everywhere the same answer, though at the time they were every one at home.

"These repulses naturally aroused the most serious reflections in the mind of Noureddin, and he clearly saw the fault he had committed in relying so fondly on these false friends, who had so assiduously surrounded his person. He now saw the vanity of protestations of regard, uttered amidst the enjoyment of splendid entertainments, and awakened only by an entertainer's boundless liberality. 'It is true,' said he to himself, as tears flowed from his eyes, 'it is only too true, that a man, situated as I have been, resembles a tree full of fruit; so long as any fruit remains on the tree it is surrounded by those who come to partake of its gifts, but when there is nothing more to be had, it is regarded no longer, but stands alone, stripped, and abandoned.' So long as he was in the streets he endeavoured to put some restraint upon his feelings; but when he re-entered his house, he went to the apartment of the Beautiful Persian, and gave full vent to his grief.

"So soon as the Beautiful Persian saw Noureddin return downcast and melancholy she understood that he had not derived from his friends the assistance he had expected. Therefore she said to him, 'O my lord, are you now convinced of the truth of what I foretold?' 'Ah, my love,' he replied, 'what you foresaw is but too true. Not one of those men would receive me—see me—speak to me. Never could I have believed it possible that persons, who owe me so many obligations, and for whom I have deprived myself of all I possessed, could have treated me so cruelly. I am no longer master of my reason, and I much fear that, in the deplorable and wretched condition in which I now am, I may do something desperate, unless assisted by your kind and prudent counsels.' 'My lord,' said the Beautiful Persian, 'I know no other remedy for your misfortune than that of selling your slaves and furniture; you can thus raise a sum of money on which you may subsist till Heaven shall point out some other way of extricating you from your difficulties.'

"The remedy appeared to Noureddin extremely severe, but his present wants were very urgent. Therefore he first sold his slaves, who had become a useless burden, and for whose maintenance he could no longer provide. He lived for some time upon the money thus obtained, and, when this supply began to fail, he caused his furniture to be conveyed to the public mart, where it was sold greatly below its real value, as some of it was extremely rich, and had cost immense sums. Thus he was enabled to live for a considerable time. But at length this resource failed also; and now, as there remained nothing more to dispose of, he came again, and poured his griefs into the bosom of the Beautiful Persian.

"Noureddin did not in the least expect the proposal this prudent and generous woman now made him: 'My lord,' said she, 'I am your slave, and you know the late vizier, your father, purchased me for ten thousand pieces of gold. I am well aware that I am not so valuable as I was at that time; but I flatter myself I may still produce a sum not much short of it. Therefore I counsel you to send me to the market and sell me immediately. With the money you thus obtain, which will be a very considerable sum, you may commence business as a merchant in some place where you are not known, and thus procure the means of living, if not in opulence, at least in a way that may render you happy and contented.'

"'O charming, beautiful Persian!' cried Noureddin, 'is it possible that you can entertain such a thought? Have I given you so few proofs of my affection that you believe me capable of such meanness? And even if I could be so unworthy, should I not add the foulest perjury to my baseness, after the oath I made to my late father, which I would sooner die than break. No, never can I separate myself from one whom I love more than life itself; though your making to me so unaccountable a proposal proves only too clearly how far your affection to me falls short of that which I feel for you.'

"'My lord,' replied the Beautiful Persian, 'I am convinced your love for me is as great as you describe it; and Heaven is my judge that my affection for you is not the less; and Heaven knows with what extreme repugnance I prevailed on myself to make the proposal which has so much displeased you; but, to meet the objection you offer, I have only to remind you that necessity has no law. Believe me, my love for you cannot possibly be exceeded by yours for me, nor can it ever change, or cease, to whatever master I may belong. Never can I know any joy so great as that of being re-united to you, if, as I hope may be the case, your affairs should ever be so prosperous as to enable you to re-purchase me. The necessity to which we are now driven is extremely severe; but, alas! what other means are left to extricate us from the poverty which now surrounds us!'

"Noureddin, who knew too well the truth of what the Beautiful Persian had been saying to him, and who had no other resource against the most ignominious poverty, was compelled to adopt the measure she proposed. Therefore, though with the most inexpressible regret, he conveyed her to the market-place, where female slaves were sold; and, addressing himself to a broker, said, 'Hagi Hassan, I have a slave here whom I wish to sell; I beg of you to learn what price the purchasers will give for her.'

"Hagi Hassan desired Noureddin and the Beautiful Persian to enter a chamber, where the latter removed the veil that concealed her face; Hagi Hassan was struck with astonishment and said, 'Can I be deceived? Is not this the slave whom the late vizier, your father, purchased for ten thousand pieces of gold?' Noureddin assured him this was the Beautiful Persian herself; and Hagi Hassan, giving him reason to expect a large sum, promised to exert all his ability to obtain for her the best price possible.

"Hagi Hassan and Noureddin left the chamber where the Beautiful Persian remained. They went in search of the merchants who were occupied in purchasing various slaves, Greeks, Franks, Africans, Tartars, and others. Thus Hagi Hassan was obliged to wait till they had completed their business. When they were ready, and again assembled together, he said, with much pleasantry in his look and manner, 'My good fellow-countrymen, every round thing is not a nut; every long thing is not a fig; every red thing is not flesh; and every egg is not fresh. I will readily agree that in the course of your lives you have seen and purchased many slaves; but never have you beheld a single one who can in the least compare with her I am about to show you. She is, in truth, a perfect slave. Come with me and look at her. I wish you yourselves to fix the price at which I ought to offer her.'

"The merchants followed Hagi Hassan, who opened the door of the apartment where the Beautiful Persian was. They beheld her with astonishment, and immediately agreed that, to begin with, they could not possibly set a smaller price upon her than four thousand pieces of gold. They then left the room, and Hagi Hassan, after fastening the door, followed them out a little way, crying, with a loud voice, '*The Persian slave for four thousand pieces of gold.*'

"Not one of the merchants had yet spoken; and they were consulting together about the sum they should bid for her, when the vizier Saouy made his appearance. He had perceived Noureddin in the market, and said to himself, 'It appears that Noureddin is still raising money from the sale of his effects'—for he knew that the young man had been selling some of his furniture—'and is come hither to purchase a slave.' As he was advancing, Hagi Hassan cried out a second time, '*The Persian slave for four thousand pieces of gold.*'

"Saouy imagined, from hearing this high price, that the slave must possess very

SALE OF THE BEAUTIFUL PERSIAN.

extraordinary beauty. He immediately felt a strong desire to see her, and urged his horse forward towards Hagi Hassan, who was surrounded by the merchants. 'Open the door,' said he, 'and let me see this slave.' It was contrary to custom to permit a slave to be seen by any indifferent person after the merchants had seen her, and while they were bargaining for her; but they had not the courage to urge their right against the authority of the vizier, nor could Hagi Hassan avoid opening the door. He therefore made a sign to the Beautiful Persian to approach, so that Saouy might see her without alighting from his horse.

"When Saouy beheld the extraordinary beauty of this slave, he was beyond measure surprised; and knowing the name of the agent employed to sell her, who was a person with whom he had occasionally had business, he said, 'Hagi Hassan, four thousand pieces of gold is, I think, the price at which you value her.' 'Yes, my lord,' replied Hassan.

'The merchants whom you see here, have just now agreed that I should put her up at that price. I now expect them to advance upon the price, and expect much more by the time they have done bidding.' 'I will give the money myself,' said Saouy, 'if no one offers more.' He immediately gave the merchants a glance, which sufficiently expressed that he must not be outbidden. He was, indeed, so much feared by them all, that they took especial care not to open their lips, even to complain of the manner in which he had violated their rights.

"When the vizier had waited some time, and found that none of the merchants would bid against him: 'Well, what do you wait for?' he said to Hagi Hassan. 'Go, find the seller, and conclude the bargain with him for four thousand pieces of gold, or learn what he intends farther.' He did not at the time know that the slave belonged to Noureddin.

"Hagi Hassan locked the chamber door, and went to talk over the affair with Noureddin. 'My lord,' said he, 'I am very sorry to be obliged to communicate very unpleasant intelligence: your slave is about to be sold for a miserable price.' 'How is this?' enquired Noureddin. 'My lord,' said Hagi Hassan, 'the business at first looked promising enough. The moment they had seen her, the merchants, without any doubt or hesitation, desired me to put her up at four thousand pieces of gold. Just as I had cried her at that price the vizier Saouy arrived. His presence immediately shut the mouths of all the merchants, who were evidently disposed to raise her to at least the price which she cost the late vizier, your father. Saouy will only give four thousand pieces of gold, and I assure you it is with great reluctance that I am come to report to you his inadequate offer. The slave is yours; and I cannot advise you to part with her at that price. You and all the world know the character of the vizier. Not only is the slave worth infinitely more than the sum he has offered, but he is so unprincipled a man that he will very likely invent some pretence for not paying you even the money he now offers.'

"'Hagi Hassan,' replied Noureddin, 'I am much obliged to you for your advice. Do not imagine that I shall ever permit my slave to be sold to the enemy of my house. I am certainly in great need of money, but I would sooner die in the most abject poverty than part with her to Saouy. I have, therefore, one favour to request of you—that, as you are acquainted with all the customs and artifices of this kind of business, you will tell me what I must do to prevent Saouy from obtaining her?'

"Hagi Hassan replied, 'That is easily done. Pretend, that having been in great wrath with your slave, you swore you would expose her in the public market, and that you have accordingly done so. But say that you had no intention of selling her, but merely wished to redeem your oath. This will satisfy every one, and Saouy will have nothing to say against it. Be ready, then; and in the moment when I shall present her to Saouy, come up and say that though her bad conduct made you threaten to sell her, you never intended to part with her in earnest.' Thereupon he led forth the Beautiful Persian to Saouy, who was already before the door, 'My lord,' said he, leading her to him, 'there is the slave, take her, she is yours.'

"Hagi Hassan had hardly finished these words, when Noureddin seized hold of the Beautiful Persian, and, drawing her towards him, gave her a box on the ear. 'Come here, thou stubborn one,' said he, in a tone sufficiently loud to be heard by every one, 'and get thee gone. Your abominable temper compelled me to take an oath to expose you in the public market; but I shall not sell you at present. It will be time enough to do that when every other means fail.'

"The vizier was very angry at this action of Noureddin's. 'Wortbless spendthrift,' he exclaimed, 'would you have me believe that you have anything left to dispose of except this slave?' As he spoke he rode his horse at Noureddin, and endeavoured to seize the Beautiful Persian. Stung to the quick by the affront which the vizier had put upon him, Noureddin let the Beautiful Persian go, and desiring her to wait, threw himself immediately upon the horse's bridle, and compelled him to fall back three or four paces. 'You despicable old wretch,' said he, to the vizier, 'I would tear you to pieces this instant, if I were not restrained by regard for those about me.'

"As the vizier Saouy was not loved by any one, but, on the contrary, was hated by all, those present were delighted at the mortification he had received, and made known their satisfaction to Noureddin by various signs; giving him to understand that if he revenged himself in any way he chose he would experience no opposition from them.

"Saouy made every effort to oblige Noureddin to let go his horse's bridle; but the latter being a young man of great strength, encouraged by the good wishes of those present, pulled the vizier from his horse into the middle of the street, and after giving him a great many blows, dashed his head forcibly against the pavement, till it was covered with blood. Half a score of slaves who were in waiting on the vizier would have drawn their sabres, and fallen upon Noureddin, but were prevented by the merchants. 'What are you about to do?' said these, 'if one is a vizier, do you not know that the other is a vizier's son? Let them decide their own quarrel; perhaps one day they may become friends, but in any case, should you kill Noureddin, your master, powerful as he is, will not be able to screen you from justice.' Noureddin, fatigued with beating the vizier, left him in the middle of the street, and again taking charge of the Beautiful Persian, returned home, amidst the acclamations of all the people, who much commended him for what he had done.

"Exceedingly bruised by the blows he had received, Saouy, assisted by his servants, with the greatest difficulty got up, and was extremely mortified to find himself besmeared all over with blood and mire. Supporting himself upon the shoulders of two of his slaves, he went, in that forlorn condition, immediately to the palace; and it increased his confusion to see that, though all gazed at him with surprise, he was pitied by none. When he arrived near the apartment of the king, he began to weep and to cry out for justice, in a most pathetic manner. The king ordered him to be admitted; and as soon as he appeared, desired to know how it happened that he had been so ill-treated, and who had put him into so lamentable a state. 'O great king,' exclaimed Saouy, 'it is because I am honoured with your majesty's favour, and am allowed a share in your important counsels, that I have been treated in the shocking manner you now behold.' 'Let me have no useless words,' said the king; 'tell me at once what is the meaning of the affair, and who is the offender. If any one has done you a wrong, I shall know how to bring him to repentance.'

"'O my king,' said Saouy, who took care to give everything a turn in his own favour, 'I was going to the market of female slaves, in order to purchase a cook, whom I required. On my arrival there, I heard them crying a slave for four thousand pieces of gold. I desired to see this slave, and I found her the most beautiful creature that eyes ever beheld. After looking upon her with the most extreme satisfaction, I asked to whom she belonged, and I was informed that Noureddin, the son of the late vizier Khacan, wished to sell her.'

"'Your majesty may remember that about two or three years since you ordered to be paid to that minister ten thousand pieces of gold, with which he was charged to purchase a slave. He employed it in purchasing the one in question; but instead of bringing her to your majesty, whom it would appear he thought unworthy of her, he presented her to his son. Since his father's death this son has, by the most unbounded extravagance of every sort, dissipated his whole fortune, so that nothing remained to him but this slave, whom he at length determined to sell, and who was in fact this day brought to market. I sent to speak with him; and without alluding in any way to the prevarication, or rather perfidy, of which his father had been guilty towards your majesty, I said to him, in the civillest manner possible, "Noureddin, the merchants, as I understand, have put up your slave at four thousand pieces of gold; and I doubt not that the competition which seems likely to take place, will raise the price very considerably; but trust to me, and sell her for the four thousand pieces of gold; I wish to purchase her for the king, our lord and master. This transaction will give me a good opportunity of recommending you to his majesty's favour, which you will find of infinitely more value than any sum of money the merchants can give you."

"'Instead of answering me with the courtesy and civility I had a right to expect,

Noureddin cast upon me a look of the most insolent contempt. "Thou detestable old wretch," said he, "sooner than sell my slave to thee, I would give her to a Jew for nothing." "But, Noureddin," cried I, without allowing myself to be carried away by passion, however great the provocation I had received, "when you thus speak, you do not consider the insult you are offering to the king, to whose kindness your father, like myself, owed all that he enjoyed."

"'This remonstrance, which ought to have softened him, only irritated him the more. He rushed upon me like a madman, and without any regard for my age or dignity, pulled me off my horse, beat me till he was weary, and at last left me in the condition in which your majesty now sees me. I beseech you to consider that it is through my zeal for your interests that I have suffered this shocking insult.' Having finished his speech, he hung down his head, and turning away, gave free course to his tears, which flowed in abundance.

"The king, imposed upon by this artful tale, and highly incensed against Noureddin, showed by his countenance how violent was his anger; and turning round to the captain of the guard who was near him, said, 'Take forty of your men; go and sack Noureddin's house, and after ordering it to be razed to the ground, return hither with him and his slave.'

"The captain of the guard did not quit the apartment so expeditiously, but that a groom of the chamber, who had heard the order given, got the start of him. The name of this officer was Sangiar. He had been formerly a slave belonging to the vizier Khacan, and had been introduced by him into the king's household, where by degrees he had raised himself to the rank he held.

"Full of gratitude to his dead master, and of affection for Noureddin, whom he had known from the hour of his birth, and fully aware of the hate which Saouy had long entertained against the house of Khacan, Sangiar trembled with apprehension when he heard the order. He said to himself, 'The conduct of Noureddin cannot be so bad as Saouy represents it. The malicious vizier has prejudiced the king, who will condemn Noureddin to death without giving him the least opportunity of justifying himself.' Sangiar therefore ran with such speed, that he arrived just in time to inform Noureddin of what had happened at the palace, and to give him an opportunity of escaping with the Beautiful Persian. He knocked at the door in so violent a manner that Noureddin, who for a long time had been without a servant, came and opened it himself, without a moment's delay. 'O my dear lord,' said Sangiar to him, 'there is no safety for you at Balsora; depart, and escape from the city without losing an instant.'

"'How is this?' replied Noureddin. 'What has happened that I should depart so soon?' 'Go, I entreat you,' resumed Sangiar, 'and take your slave with you. Saouy has just related to the king, in such a manner as best suited his purpose, the encounter he had with you to-day, and the captain of the guard will be here in an instant with forty soldiers to sieze you and your slave. Take these forty pieces of gold to assist you in gaining some place of safety; I would give you more, but this is all I have about me. Excuse me if I depart at once—I leave you with great reluctance—but it is for the benefit of us both, as I am very anxious that the captain of the guard should not see me.' Sangiar received the thanks of Noureddin, and immediately withdrew.

"Noureddin went to acquaint the Beautiful Persian of the necessity they were both under of making their escape that very instant. She only stayed to put on her veil; and then they quitted the house together, and had the good fortune not only to get out of the city without being discovered, but even to reach the mouth of the Euphrates, which was not far distant, and to embark on board a vessel then ready to weigh anchor.

"Indeed, at the very moment when they appeared, the captain was upon the deck in the midst of his passengers. 'My friends,' said he, 'are you all here? Have any of you any business in the city, or have you forgotten any thing?' To this the passengers replied they were all ready, and he might sail whenever he pleased. Directly Noureddin came on board, he enquired to what place the vessel was bound, and was delighted to

SAOUY COMPLAINS TO THE KING.

find it was going to Bagdad. The captain then gave orders to weigh anchor and set sail; and favoured by the wind, the ship had soon left Balsora far behind.

"Let us now relate what happened at Balsora, while Noureddin, accompanied by the Beautiful Persian, was escaping from the anger of the king.

"The captain of the guard hastened to the house of Noureddin, and knocked at the door.

As no one answered, he caused it to be broken open; and immediately the soldiers rushed in, and searched every part of the house, but could find neither Noureddin nor his slave. The captain then ordered enquiries to be made, and himself examined some of the neighbours, as to whether they had seen any thing of them. But this was fruitless, for even if these people could have given any account of the fugitives, they were so cordially attached to Noureddin, that not one of them would have said any thing to his injury. While the men were plundering and destroying the house, the captain went to inform the king of his failure. 'Let every place, where it is possible they can be concealed, be searched,' said the king; 'I must have them found.'

"The captain of the guard accordingly went back to make fresh enquiries, and the king, unwilling any longer to detain the vizier, dismissed him with honour. 'Go home,' said he, 'and give yourself no further concern about the punishment of Noureddin. I will take care that his insolence is chastised.'

"That no means might be left untried, the king ordered it to be proclaimed through the city, that a thousand pieces of gold should be paid to any one who should apprehend Noureddin and his slave; and that whoever concealed them should be severely punished; but, notwithstanding all his care and diligence, he could obtain no information of them; so that the vizier Saouy had no consolation but that of having the king on his side.

"In the meantime Noureddin and the Beautiful Persian were pursuing their journey with all the good fortune possible; and in due time they arrived at the city of Bagdad. As soon as the captain perceived the place, glad to be so near the completion of his voyage, he exclaimed, addressing himself to the passengers, 'rejoice, my friends, there is the great and wonderful city, to which people from every part of the world are constantly flocking. You will there find inhabitants without number; and, instead of the chilling blasts of winter, or the oppressive heats of summer, you will perpetually feel the mildness and beauty of spring, and enjoy the delicious fruits of autumn.'

"When they had cast anchor a little below the city, the passengers quitted the ship and went to their respective habitations. Noureddin gave five pieces of gold for the passage, and landed with the Beautiful Persian. As he had never before been at Bagdad he was wholly ignorant where to seek shelter. They walked, for a considerable time, by the side of the gardens which bordered the Tigris, one of which was bounded by a long and handsome wall. When they came to the end of this, they turned into a long well-paved street, in which they perceived the garden gate, near a very delightful fountain.

"The gate, which was extremely magnificent, was locked. Before it was an open vestibule, with a sofa on each side. 'Here is a most convenient place,' said Noureddin to the Beautiful Persian. 'Night is coming on; and as we refreshed ourselves with food before we left the ship, I recommend that we remain here. To-morrow morning we shall have ample time to look for a lodging. What say you?' 'You know, my lord,' replied the Beautiful Persian, 'that I have no wish but to please you; if you desire to remain here I shall be happy to stay. Then each of them took a draught from the fountain, and seating themselves on one of the sofas conversed for some time, till, lulled by the agreeable murmur of the waters, they fell into a profound sleep.

"This garden, which belonged to the caliph, had in the middle of it a grand pavilion, called the painted pavilion; because it was ornamented with pictures in the Persian style, painted by masters whom the caliph had sent for from Persia. The grand and superb saloon which this pavilion contained was lighted by eighty windows, with a large chandelier in each; but, by the express command of the caliph, these were never lighted up except when he was there; but when lighted they made a most beautiful illumination, which could be seen at some distance in the country, and over a great part of the city.

"This garden was inhabited only by the person who kept it in order; a very aged officer, named Scheich Ibrahim, to whom the caliph had given this post as a reward for former services. He had received very particular injunctions not to admit into it all persons indiscriminately; and particularly, to prevent the visitors from sitting or resting upon the sofas placed without the gate, which were to be constantly kept with the greatest care; and, therefore, all whom he found offending were to be punished.

"This officer, who had been called out on some business, had not yet returned; but coming home before the day closed he perceived two persons sleeping on one of the sofas, their heads covered with a linen turban to protect them from the gnats. 'So, so!' said Scheich Ibrahim to himself, 'it is thus that you disobey the commands of the caliph? But I shall teach you to respect them.' He then, without any noise, let himself out through the gate, and soon after returned with a large cane in his hand and his sleeve tucked up. Just as he was going to strike with all his force, he paused: 'Scheich Ibrahim,' said he to himself, 'you are going to beat these people without considering that, perhaps, they are strangers, who know not where to lodge, and are ignorant of the caliph's prohibition. It will be better, first, to know who they are.' He then gently raised up the linen which covered their heads, and was much surprised when he saw a young man of an extremely good, pleasing countenance, and a young woman of extraordinary beauty. He then roused Noureddin, by pulling him softly by the feet.

"Noureddin immediately lifted up his head; and, as soon as he saw an old man with a long white beard at his feet, he rose up on the sofa in a kneeling position, and seizing the visitor by the hand, which he kissed, he said, 'good father, may Heaven preserve you; what do you wish of me?' 'My son,' said Scheich Ibrahim, 'who are you? whence come you?' 'We are strangers, who have just arrived,' returned Noureddin, 'and we wish to stay here till to-morrow morning.' 'You will be very badly lodged here,' replied Scheich Ibrahim; 'you will do better to go in with me. I will furnish you with a much more suitable place to sleep in; and the view of the garden, which is very beautiful, will delight you during the short portion of day that remains.' 'And is this garden yours?' said Noureddin. 'Certainly it is,' said Scheich Ibrahim, smiling, 'it is an inheritance I received from my father. Come in, I entreat you; you will not repent seeing it.'

"Noureddin rose and expressed to Scheich Ibrahim how much he was obliged by his politeness. Thereupon he went with the Beautiful Persian into the garden. Scheich Ibrahim locked the gate; and, walking before his guests, conducted them to a place whence they might see at one view the arrangement, grandeur, and beauty of the whole.

"Noureddin had seen many very beautiful gardens at Balsora, but never one that could be compared to this. When he had well observed everything, and had been amusing himself for some time by walking along the paths, he turned round to the old man who accompanied him, and asked his name. As soon as he had learned it, he said: 'Scheich Ibrahim, I must confess that your garden is wonderful: may Heaven spare you many years to enjoy it. We cannot sufficiently thank you for the favour you have done us in showing us a place so extremely worth seeing: it is only right that we should in some way express our gratitude. Take, therefore, I pray you, these two pieces of gold, and endeavour to procure us something to eat, that we may all make merry together.'

"At the sight of the two pieces of gold, Scheich Ibrahim, who had a great admiration for that metal, could not help laughing in his sleeve. He took the money; and, as he had no assistant, left Noureddin and the Beautiful Persian by themselves, while he went to execute the commission. 'These are good people,' said he to himself, gleefully. 'I should have done myself no small injury if I had ill-treated or driven them away. With the tenth part of this money I can entertain them like princes, and the remainder I may keep for my trouble.'

"While Scheich Ibrahim was gone to purchase some supper, of which he remembered that he was himself to partake, Noureddin and the Beautiful Persian walked about the garden till they came to the painted pavilion, situated in the middle of it. They stopped for some time to examine its wonderful structure, size, and loftiness; after they had gone round it, surveying it on all sides, they ascended by a grand flight of steps, formed of white marble, to the door of the saloon, which they found locked.

"They had just descended the steps when Scheich Ibrahim returned, laden with provisions. 'Scheich Ibrahim,' said Noureddin, in great surprise, 'did you not say that this garden belonged to you?' 'I did say so, and I say it again,' returned Scheich Ibrahim; 'but why do you ask the question?' 'And is this superb pavilion yours also?' asked Noureddin. Scheich Ibrahim had not expected this question, and felt somewhat embarrassed. 'If I should say it is not mine,' thought he, 'they will ask me immediately how it is possible that I can be master of the garden and not of the pavilion?' Therefore, having pretended that the garden was his, he found it necessary to assert the same of the pavilion. 'My son,' he replied, 'the pavilion is not detached from the garden; both of them belong to me.' 'Since it is yours,' replied Noureddin, 'and you allow us to be your guests to-night, I entreat you to grant us the favour of letting us see the interior; for to judge from its external appearance, it must be beyond measure magnificent.'

"Scheich Ibrahim felt that it would not be civil in him to refuse Noureddin's request after the handsome way in which the young stranger had treated him. He considered, too, that the caliph, who had not sent him the notice that always preceded a royal visit, would not be there that night; and that, therefore, his guests and himself might safely take their repast in the pavilion. Having, therefore, placed the provisions he had brought upon the first step of the staircase, he went to his apartment to find the key, and, returning with a light, opened the door.

"Noureddin and the Beautiful Persian entered the saloon, which they found so very splendid that they were for a long time wholly engrossed in admiring its riches and beauty. The sofas and ornaments, as well as the pictures, were in the highest degree magnificent; and, besides the lustres which hung at every window, there were between the frames silver branches, each containing a wax taper. Noureddin could not behold these objects without calling to mind the splendour in which he himself had lived, and heaving a sigh of regret.

"In the meantime Scheich Ibrahim brought the provisions, and prepared a table upon one of the sofas; and, now that everything was ready, he sat down to supper with Noureddin and the Beautiful Persian. When they had finished, and had washed their hands, Noureddin opened one of the windows, and calling the Beautiful Persian, said, 'Come hither and admire with me the charming view, and the beauty of the garden in the light of the moon. Nothing can be more delightful.' She obeyed, and they together enjoyed the sight, while Scheich Ibrahim was removing the cloth from the table.

"When he had done this, and had returned to his guests, Noureddin asked him if he had nothing in the way of liquor with which he could regale them. 'Would you like some sherbet?' said Scheich Ibrahim; 'I have some that is exquisite; but you know, my son, sherbet is never taken after supper.' 'That's very true,' replied Noureddin; 'but it is not sherbet we want. There is, you know, another kind of beverage; I am surprised you don't understand what I mean.' 'You must surely mean wine,' said Scheich Ibrahim. 'You have guessed it exactly,' replied Noureddin. If you have any, you will oblige us much by bringing a bottle; for you know it will pass away the time very agreeably from supper till bed time.'

"'Allah forbid that I should ever touch wine!' exclaimed the old man, 'or that I should approach the place where it is kept! A man who, like me, has made the pilgrimage to Mecca four times, has renounced wine for the rest of his days.'

"'Still you would do us a great kindness to procure us some,' returned Noureddin, 'and, if it will not be disagreeable to you, I will teach you a method of doing so without entering a tavern, or even touching the vessel that contains it.' 'I will agree on these conditions,' returned Scheich Ibrahim; 'only tell me what I am to do.'

"Noureddin resumed: 'As we came here we saw an ass tied up at the entrance of your garden. I conclude it to be yours; and, therefore, you ought to make use of it in cases of necessity. Here, take these two pieces of gold; lead your ass with his panniers and proceed towards the first tavern; but do not approach it nearer than you like; give something to the first person who passes by, and beg him to go to the tavern with the ass and procure two pitchers of wine, one for each pannier; then let him lead the ass back to you, after he has paid for the wine with the money which you will give him. You have then nothing to do but to drive the ass before you hither, and we ourselves will take the pitchers out of the panniers. Thus, you see, you will do nothing that can give your conscience the least offence.'

"The two new pieces of gold which Scheich Ibrahim had now received, produced a wonderful effect upon his mind. When Noureddin had finished speaking, he exclaimed, 'O my son, well do you understand things; without your assistance I could never have imagined any possible means by which I could have procured you wine, without feeling some compunction.' He left them to set about his commission, which he executed in a very short time. As soon as he returned Noureddin, descended the steps, drew the pitchers from the panniers, and carried them up into the saloon.

SCHEICH IBRAHIM AND HIS VISITORS.

"'Scheich Ibrahim now led back the ass to the place from whence he had taken it. When he returned, Noureddin said to him, 'O worthy Scheich Ibrahim, we cannot sufficiently thank you for the trouble you have taken; but still there is one thing wanting.' 'What is there I can yet do to serve you?' asked Scheich Ibrahim in reply. 'We have no cups to drink out of,' said Noureddin; 'and a little fruit of some sort, if you have any, would be very acceptable.' 'You have only to command,' said Scheich Ibrahim, 'and you shall want for nothing you can desire.'

"He then went down, and in a short time had provided them a table with all sorts of fruit in dishes of the most beautiful porcelain, and with a variety of cups of gold and silver; and when he had asked them if they required anything more he withdrew, though they earnestly solicited his company.

"Noureddin and the Beautiful Persian again sat down to the table, and each of them took a cup of the wine, which they found excellent. 'Tell me, my love,' said Noureddin to the Beautiful Persian, 'are we not the most fortunate people in the world to have thus come by accident into so delightful a place? Let us enjoy our good fortune, and endeavour to make amends for the bad fare of our voyage. Can happiness be more complete than mine, now that I have you on one side of me and good wine on the other.' They filled their cups frequently, and conversed together in the most agreeable manner, occasionally amusing themselves with a song.

"As they had most excellent voices, and the Beautiful Persian especially sang in a ravishing manner, their singing presently attracted Scheich Ibrahim, who listened to them a long time with the greatest pleasure, standing near the top of the stairs where he could not be seen. At length, unable to contain himself any longer, he pushed his head in at the door, and said to Noureddin, whom he believed to be already intoxicated, 'Bravely sang, O my friend; I am delighted to see you so happy.'

"'Ah! Scheich Ibrahim,' cried Noureddin, turning towards him, 'you are a worthy man, and we are much obliged to you. We dare not ask you to drink with us; but come in nevertheless. At least give us the honour of your company.' 'Go on, go on,' replied Scheich Ibrahim; 'I am sufficiently pleased with hearing your charming songs.' Having said this he disappeared

"The Beautiful Persian perceiving that Scheich Ibrahim only retreated as far as the top of the stairs, mentioned that fact to Noureddin. 'My lord,' said she, 'you see what an aversion he expresses for wine. Yet I do not despair of making him drink some, if you will do what I propose.' 'What is that?' exclaimed Noureddin. 'You have only to speak, and I will do whatever you wish.' 'Then persuade him merely to come in and give us his company. When he has been here some time, pour out a cup of wine and offer it to him; if he refuse drink it yourself. Then feign to be asleep, and leave the rest to me.'

"Noureddin was not slow to enter into the Beautiful Persian's design. He called to Scheich Ibrahim, who re-appeared at the door. 'Scheich Ibrahim,' said Noureddin, 'we are your guests, and you have entertained us in the most noble manner possible. Will you not grant us the request we make, that you will honour us with your company? We will not ask you to drink; we only solicit the pleasure of having you with us.'

"Scheich Ibrahim allowed himself to be persuaded. He came in and placed himself at the edge of the sofa which was nearest the door. 'You are badly seated there,' said Noureddin, 'and, besides, we have not the honour of seeing you. Come forward, I entreat you, and take a seat near the lady; it will gratify her much.' 'I will do whatever you desire,' returned Scheich Ibrahim. He accordingly approached with a smiling countenance, pleased at the idea of being near so charming a woman, and seated himself at some little distance from the Beautiful Persian. Noureddin requested her to sing, in acknowledgment of the honour which Scheich Ibrahim had done them. She complied, and acquitted herself in a manner that moved him to ecstacy.

"When the Beautiful Persian had finished her song, Noureddin poured out a cup of wine, and offered it to Scheich Ibrahim. 'Scheich Ibrahim,' said he, 'let me entreat you to drink this to our healths.' 'My lord,' replied Scheich Ibrahim, starting back, as if the very sight of wine inspired him with horror, 'I beg of you to excuse me; I have already told you that I have renounced wine long ago.' 'Then since you positively will not drink our healths,' said Noureddin, 'you must allow me to drink yours.'

"While Noureddin was drinking, the Beautiful Persian cut half an apple which she presented to Scheich Ibrahim. 'You have refused to drink with us,' said she; but I flatter myself you will not have the same aversion to taste this apple; it is a most excellent one.' Scheich Ibrahim could not refuse the fruit from so fair a hand; he took it, with a slight inclination of his head, and began to eat it. The Beautiful Persian was saying many civil things to him, when Noureddin fell back on the sofa, and pretended to go to sleep. The Beautiful Persian immediately advanced towards Scheich Ibrahim and said to him, in a low voice: 'Look at my lord, this is always his way whenever we begin to enjoy ourselves together; he has no sooner drunk a cup or two of wine than he falls asleep, and leaves me alone; but you, I hope, will have the goodness to give me your company while he is sleeping there.'

"The Beautiful Persian then took a cup, filled it with wine, and presented it to Scheich Ibrahim. 'Take this,' said she, 'and drink my health; I will pledge you.' Scheich Ibrahim made a great many difficulties, and was very anxious that she would desist from her request; but she pressed him in so lively a manner, that, overcome by her charms and entreaties, he took the cup and drank it off.

"The good old man loved wine heartily; but was ashamed of indulging before people with whom he was not acquainted. Like many others, he was in the habit of going to the tavern in private; and had not thought it necessary to take the precautions which Noureddin had recommended when he went to obtain the wine they were then drinking. Under cover of the night he had gone to purchase it himself of an innkeeper whom he knew, and had thus saved the money which, according to Noureddin's instructions, he was to give the person whom he might employ.

"After he had taken his cup Scheich Ibrahim was eating the remainder of his apple, when the Beautiful Persian filled him another goblet, which he took with much less difficulty than he had made in drinking the first. To the third he made no objection whatever. He was going on to drink a fourth, when Noureddin, ceasing to feign sleep, rose up on his seat, and looking hard at the old man, burst out into a violent fit of laughter. 'Ha, ha,' said he, 'Scheich Ibrahim; I have caught you. You told me you had renounced wine, and that you could not bear even the sight of it.'

"Scheich Ibrahim was somewhat disconcerted by this unexpected address, which caused the colour to mount rapidly into his cheeks; he did not, however, desist from draining his cup. When he had finished it he replied, smiling: 'My friend, if what I have done is a sin, it ought not to be laid to my charge, but to that of this fair lady; how is it possible to resist so many charms?'

"The Beautiful Persian, who perfectly understood Noureddin, pretended to take the part of Scheich Ibrahim. 'Scheich Ibrahim,' she said, 'let him talk on; do not suffer him to interrupt us; continue to drink and enjoy yourself.' Some little time after Noureddin poured out some wine for himself, and afterwards offered some to the Beautiful Persian. When Scheich Ibrahim saw that Noureddin gave him none, he took a cup and held it out to him, saying, 'Come now, why am I not to drink as well as you?'

"At this speech of Scheich Ibrahim's Noureddin and the Beautiful Persian laughed very heartily. Noureddin filled his host's cup, and they continued to enjoy themselves, laughing and drinking till midnight. About this time the Beautiful Persian noticed that there was only one light on the table. Accordingly she said to the good old officer: 'O Scheich Ibrahim, you have allowed us only one taper, while there are so many handsome ones about the room. Do us the favour, I beseech you, to light them, that we may see a little more clearly.' Scheich Ibrahim, full of the generosity which wine inspires when the head becomes a little heated, and unwilling, moreover, to break off a conversation he was then holding with Noureddin, called out to the beautiful lady, 'Light them yourself. It is an office much more fitted for your age than mine; but take care not to light more than five or six: that will be sufficient.' The Beautiful Persian rose, and taking a wax taper in her hand, proceeded to light up the whole eighty, without at all regarding the injunction of Scheich Ibrahim.

"Some time after, while Scheich Ibrahim was conversing with the Beautiful Persian upon some other subject, Noureddin, in his turn, requested him to light up some of the lustres. Without observing that all the tapers were burning, 'You must,' the old man answered, be extremely indolent, or have weaker limbs than mine, if you cannot light them yourself. Go, then, and light them; but remember, not more than three.' Instead of confining himself to this number, Noureddin lighted up the whole number, and afterwards opened the fourscore windows, unobserved by Scheich Ibrahim, who was earnestly engaged in conversation with the Beautiful Persian.

"The Caliph Haroun Alraschid had not yet retired to his chamber. He was in a hall of his palace, which fronted the Tigris, and on one side commanded a view of the garden and the painted pavilion. By accident he opened a window on that side and was exceedingly surprised to see the pavilion brilliantly illuminated; the more, as from the great splendour of the light he at first imagined there was a fire in some part of the city. The grand vizier Giafar was still with him, waiting for the moment when the caliph should retire, to return to his own home. The caliph called out to him in a great rage: 'Come here, thou careless vizier, come this way: look at the painted pavilion, and tell me why it is lighted up when I am not there.'

"The grand vizier trembled exceedingly from the mere fear that what the caliph said might be true; but he trembled much more when he looked and saw that it really was so. He was compelled, however, to find some pretence to appease his master. 'Commander of the Faithful,' said he, 'I can give your majesty no other information on the subject, except that, about four or five days since Scheich Ibrahim came and informed me that he had an intention of holding an assembly of the ministers belonging to his mosque, in order to observe some ceremony which he was anxious to perform, under your majesty's most happy reign. I asked him in what way he expected me to serve him in the affair; upon which he entreated me to obtain permission of your majesty that he might hold the meeting and perform the ceremony in the pavilion. I dismissed him, and said that he might do what he wished, and that I would not fail to speak to your majesty on the subject; and I entreat your pardon for having, through forgetfulness, neglected to do so. It would appear that Scheich Ibrahim has chosen this day for the ceremony; and has doubtless, in the course of entertaining the ministers, lighted up the pavilion for their pleasure.'

"'Giafar,' replied the caliph, in a tone that showed he was somewhat appeased, 'it appears from your own account that you have committed three most unpardonable faults. First, you erred in giving permission to Scheich Ibrahim to perform this ceremony in the pavilion, for the mere keeper of a garden is not an officer of sufficient consideration to be allowed so great an honour; secondly, you were wrong in neglecting to speak to me on the subject; and thirdly, in not having revealed the real object of this good old man. I am convinced that he had no other view in his application to you than to try if he could obtain some gratuity to assist him in his undertaking. You had not the penetration to find this out, and I think he has done right to avenge himself for your omission by putting us to the greater expense of this illumination.'

"The grand vizier, delighted to see the caliph treat the affair in this pleasant way, readily acknowledged himself guilty of the faults with which he was reproached, and freely confessed that he had been very wrong in not having presented Scheich Ibrahim with a few pieces of gold. 'Since that is the case,' added the caliph, smiling, 'it is proper you should be punished for your faults; your punishment, however, will not be very severe; it shall be to accompany me, and pass the remainder of this night with these good people, whom I should much like to see. Therefore while I go and put on the dress of a citizen, you and Mesrour must disguise yourselves in the same manner, and then accompany me.' The grand vizier humbly represented to the caliph that it was very late, and the company would probably have gone before his majesty could arrive; but the caliph persisted in his intention. As there was not a shadow of truth in what the vizier had been saying, Giafar felt extremely embarrassed at this resolution of his master's, but he was compelled to obey, and not reply.

"The caliph then sallied out from his palace in the disguise of a citizen, accompanied by the grand vizier Giafar, and Mesrour, the chief of the eunuchs. He proceeded through the streets of Bagdad until he arrived at the garden, the gate of which he found open. This was owing to the negligence of Scheich Ibrahim, who had forgotten to lock it when he returned from purchasing the wine. The caliph was very angry at this circumstance. 'Giafar,' said he to the grand vizier, 'what do you say to the gate's being open at this hour? Is it possible that Scheich Ibrahim should make it a custom thus to leave it open all night? I would rather hope that the neglect has been occasioned by the hurry and confusion arising from the entertainment that Scheich Ibrahim is giving.' The caliph

THE CALIPH PEEPING INTO THE PAVILION.

then entered the garden. When he had reached the pavilion, he felt unwilling to go up into the saloon before he knew what was going forward there. He, therefore, consulted with the grand vizier about climbing one of the nearest trees, in order to make his observations. But in looking towards the door of the saloon, the grand vizier perceived that it was not entirely closed, and called the caliph's attention to the fact. Scheich Ibrahim had left the door half open when he had been persuaded to enter the room, and join the party of Noureddin and the Beautiful Persian.

"The caliph upon this gave up his first design, and ascended cautiously, without noise, to the door of the saloon, which he found so far open that he was able to see the people in the room without being himself observed. His surprise was great indeed when he saw a lady of incomparable beauty, and an extremely handsome young man, sitting at table with Scheich Ibrahim, who was holding a cup in his hand, and thus addressing the Beautiful Persian: 'My charming lady, a good companion will never continue drinking all the evening without mixing music with his wine. Therefore do me the honour to listen to me, and I will sing you a very pleasant song.'

"He then began to sing, at which the caliph was exceedingly astonished, as he had never imagined till this moment that Scheich Ibrahim would indulge in wine, and had always believed him the grave sober man he appeared to be. He now withdrew from the door as cautiously as he had approached it, and returning to the grand vizier, who stood upon the staircase a few steps below. 'Come up,' said he to Giafar, 'and see if the persons who are here are ministers of the mosque, as you wished me to believe.'

"The tone with which the caliph pronounced these words showed the grand vizier but too plainly that affairs were going on very badly for him. He went up, and looking through the opening of the door, trembled with alarm when he saw three persons carousing to their hearts' content. He returned to the caliph utterly confused, and wholly at a loss what to say. 'What insolence is this?' exclaimed Haroun. 'Who are these people who presume to come and divert themselves in my garden and pavilion; and how can Scheich Ibrahim allow it, and even join in their festivities? Still I do not believe that a handsomer young man, and a lovelier young woman, or a better matched pair could be easily found. Before, therefore, I give way to my indignation, I wish to know more about them, and to learn who they are, and for what purpose they have come here.' So saying the caliph returned to the door to observe them again, and the vizier, who followed, remained behind his master, while Haroun looked at the group. They both heard Scheich Ibrahim say to the Beautiful Persian: 'My lovely lady, is there anything you can desire to render our pleasure this evening more complete?' 'It appears to me,' replied the Beautiful Persian, 'that our entertainment would be perfect if there were an instrument on which I could play. If you have one do me the favour to bring it for me.' 'O fairest lady,' replied Scheich Ibrahim, 'can you play on the lute?' 'Bring me one,' said the Beautiful Persian, 'and you shall hear.'

"Without going far from where he sat, Scheich Ibrahim took a lute out of a closet, and offered it to the Beautiful Persian, who began to put it in tune. The caliph in the meantime turned round to the grand vizier and said: 'Giafar, the young lady is going to play upon the lute. If she plays well I will pardon her, and also the young man for her sake: but as to you, you shall certainly be hanged.' 'Commander of the Faithful,' replied the grand vizier, 'I pray to Heaven she may play ill.' 'Why so?' asked the caliph. 'The more of us there are to suffer,' replied the grand vizier, 'the better we shall console ourselves, that we die in good and pleasant company.' The caliph, who was fond of a jest, laughed at this speech, and turning round towards the door he applied his ear to hear the Beautiful Persian play.

"The Beautiful Persian was already preluding in such a way that the caliph at once perceived by her manner of touching the strings, that she was perfectly mistress of the instrument. She afterwards sang an air, accompanying her excellent voice on the lute, and performed with so much skill and in so exquisite a style, that the caliph was quite charmed.

"As soon as the Beautiful Persian had finished her song, the caliph descended the stairs, followed by the vizier Giafar. When he reached the foot of the steps he said to the vizier, 'On my life I have never heard so good a voice, nor a better player on the lute. Isaac, whom I believed the best lute-player in the world, is much inferior to her. I am so well satisfied that I wish to go in and hear her play before me; but the difficulty is to find out how I can obtain admittance.'

"'Commander of the Faithful,' replied the vizier, 'if you were to enter, and Scheich Ibrahim were to recognise you, he would infallibly die with terror.' 'This is my embarassment,' returned the caliph. 'I should be sorry to be the cause of the old man's death, after he has served me so many years. A plan comes into my mind which may answer. Stay you here with Mesrour, and wait in the nearest walk till I come back.'

"The vicinity of the Tigris had enabled the caliph, by means of a channel he had made under ground, to form a very handsome piece of water in his garden, to which resorted many of the finest fish of the river. With this fact the fishermen were well acquainted, and had often wished to have the liberty of fishing there; but the caliph had expressly forbidden Scheich Ibrahim to give any one that privilege. Nevertheless, that very night a fisherman, who was passing the garden gate which the caliph had left open as he found it, took advantage of the opportunity, and stealing into the garden had proceeded as far as the piece of water.

"He had thrown in his nets, and was just going to take them up, when the caliph, who suspected what might happen from the negligence of Scheich Ibrahim, and resolved to avail himself of the circumstance, came to the place. Notwithstanding his disguise, the fisherman knew Haroun immediately, and, throwing himself at his feet entreated his pardon, pleading the excuse of poverty for his fault. 'Rise, and fear nothing,' said the caliph; 'only take up your nets, and let me see what fish you have got.'

"The fisherman, taking courage, readily performed what the caliph desired, and drew up five or six very fine fish. The caliph took the two largest and fastened them together, by means of a twig passed through their gills. He then said to the fisherman, 'Give me your clothes and take mine.' The exchange was made in a few moments, and the caliph found himself completely disguised as a fisherman from head to foot. He then sent the man away, saying, 'Take up your nets and go about your business.'

"When the fisherman was gone, very much pleased with his good fortune, the caliph took the two fish in his hand, and went to look for the grand vizier Giafar and Mesrour. He stopped when he approached the grand vizier, who, not knowing him, angrily cried out, 'What do you want, fellow? Go your ways.' The caliph laughed heartily at this speech, and the grand vizier recognised him, and exclaimed: 'O, Commander of the Faithful, is it possible it can be you? I did not know you in that disguise, and I beg a thousand pardons for my rudeness. You may immediately enter the saloon, without the smallest fear that Scheich Ibrahim will know you.' 'Do you, then, and Mesrour stay here,' said the caliph, 'while I go and play my part.'

"The caliph ascended the stairs of the saloon, and knocked at the door. Noureddin, who first heard him, spoke to Scheich Ibrahim, who inquired who was there? The caliph opened the door and advanced one step into the saloon, in order that he might be seen. Then he said: 'Scheich Ibrahim, I am Kerim, the fisherman: I was told you were entertaining your friends; and, as I have this moment caught two very fine fish, I come to ask you if you would like to have them.'

"Noureddin and the Beautiful Persian were delighted to hear of the arrival of these fish. The Beautiful Persian said to him immediately, 'Scheich Ibrahim, pray do us the favour to make him come in, that we may see his fish.' Scheich Ibrahim, who was no longer sufficiently sober to think of asking this pretended fisherman how he came there or whence he came, could refuse no request of the Beautiful Persian; therefore, turning his head towards the door, with great difficulty from the quantity of wine he had drank, he, with a stammering voice addressed the caliph, whom he took for a fisherman. 'Come hither,' said he, 'my fine thief of the night; come hither, and let me see thee.'

"The caliph advanced, counterfeiting perfectly the manners of a fisherman, and showed his two fish. 'These are really very fine,' said the Beautiful Persian, 'and I should like to taste them if they were dressed and served up.' 'The lady is right,' cried Scheich Ibrahim. 'What can we do with your fish in this state? Go and prepare them yourself, and bring them to us; you will find everything you want in my kitchen.'

"The caliph went back to the grand vizier Giafar, and said: 'I have been extremely well received, but they want me to dress these fish.' 'I will go and prepare them,' replied the grand vizier; it shall be done in an instant.' But the caliph said: 'I am so very desirous to accomplish my whole purpose myself, that I will even take the trouble of cooking these fish. Since I have acted the fisherman so well, I can surely personate the cook. In my youth I often went into the kitchen, and have not badly acquitted myself there.' He then went towards Scheich Ibrahim's apartment, followed by the grand vizier and Mesrour.

"They all three set to work; and though the kitchen of Scheich Ibrahim was not very spacious, yet, as it contained everything necessary, the fish were soon prepared. The caliph carried up the dish, and served it with a lemon to each guest. They ate with much appetite, particularly Noureddin and the Beautiful Persian; and the caliph remained standing before them.

"When they had finished Noureddin looked up at the caliph, and said: 'O fisherman, it is impossible to eat better fish; you have done us the greatest favour in the world.' At the same time he put his hand into his bosom and drew out his purse, in which there still remained thirty pieces of gold out of the forty, which Sangiar, the officer of the king of Balsora had given him before his departure. 'Here,' he said, 'take this; if I had more, I would give it you. Had I known you before I spent my fortune, I would have placed you beyond the reach of poverty. But you must accept this with as good a grace as if the present were more considerable.'

"The caliph took the purse, and thanked Noureddin. Perceiving that it contained gold, he cried, 'O my lord, I cannot sufficiently acknowledge your generosity. I am particularly fortunate to have dealings with such noble gentlemen as you; but before I go away I have one request to make, which I entreat you to grant. I see a lute yonder, from which I conclude the lady plays. If you could prevail on her to favour me with a single tune I should return home the most contented creature in the world—for it is an instrument of which I am passionately fond.'

"'Beautiful Persian,' said Noureddin, addressing himself to her, 'permit me to request of you this favour, which I hope you will not refuse.' She took the lute, and having tuned it, she sang and played an air that charmed the caliph. When this was finished, she continued to play without singing, and performed with so much taste and expression that he was delighted to ecstacy. When the Beautiful Persian had done playing, the caliph cried, 'Ye Heavens! what a voice! what a hand! what skill! was there ever such a singer!—such a player? No one ever saw or heard her equal!'

"Noureddin who was accustomed to give away whatever belonged to him to those who praised it, cried out: 'O fisherman, I see clearly that you understand the matter; since she pleases you so much, she is yours—I make you a present of her.' So saying he rose and taking his robe, which he had put off, was about to depart, and leave the caliph, whom he knew only as a fisherman, in possession of the Beautiful Persian.

"Exceedingly astonished at the liberality of Noureddin, the Beautiful Persian stopped him. 'O my lord,' said she, looking at him tenderly, 'where do you mean to go? Resume your place, I beseech you, and listen to what I am going to sing and play.' He did as she requested. Then touching the lute, and continuing to look upon him with her eyes bathed in tears, she sang some improvised verses, in which she keenly upbraided him with his heartlessness, which had made him so readily, and even so cruelly, abandon her to Kerim. She wished to express her sentiments by these means to Noureddin, without explaining herself further to a fisherman, such as Kerim appeared to be; for she had no more idea than had Noureddin himself that this was the caliph. When she had concluded she laid down her lute by her side, and put a handkerchief to her face to conceal the tears she was unable to restrain.

"Noureddin answered not a word to her reproaches, and seemed to express by his silence that he did not repent the donation he had made. But the caliph, surprised at what he had heard, said to him: 'From what I see, sir, this beautiful, rare, and accomplished lady, whom you have just presented to me with so much generosity, is a slave—and you are her master.' 'You have spoken truth, Kerim,' replied Noureddin; 'and you would be more astonished than you appear at present, if I were to relate to you all the misfortunes I have sustained on her account.' 'I pray you, my lord,' returned the caliph, carefully preserving his assumed character, 'be so kind as to make me acquainted with your history.'

"Noureddin who had just been conferring on him favours of much greater importance, was unwilling to refuse the pretended fisherman this further instance of his good will. He recounted to him his whole history, from the time of the purchase of the Beautiful Persian, by the vizier, his father, for the King of Balsora; and omitted nothing of what he had done, or suffered, from that day to his arrival at Bagdad, and even to the very moment when he was speaking.

"When Noureddin had finished his story the caliph said to him: 'Where do you

A PRESENT FOR THE FISHERMAN.

intend to go now?' 'Where am I going?' repeated he, 'why! where Heaven shall direct me.' 'If you will trust to me,' replied the caliph, 'you will go no further; indeed it is important that you should return to Balsora. I will write you a short note which you shall give the king from me. You will find after he has read it he will receive you very graciously, and that no one will say anything against you.'

"'Kerim,' replied Noureddin, 'what you say to me is very extraordinary. Who ever heard that a fisherman like you could correspond with a king?' 'This ought not to surprise you,' resumed the caliph, 'we pursued our studies together under the same masters, and have always been the best friends in the world. It is true fortune has not equally favoured us. He has become a king, and I a fisherman: but this inequality has not lessened our friendship. He has often wished to raise me up from my present condition, and has offered me his protection with all the kindness imaginable. I am satisfied, however, in the belief that he will refuse nothing I may ask for the benefit of my friends. Leave the affair to me, and you shall see it will prosper.'

"Noureddin consented to do what the caliph desired: and as there was in the saloon everything necessary for writing, the caliph wrote the following letter to the King of Balsora, adding at the top, near the edge of the paper in very small characters, *In the name of Allah the most merciful;* an established form to express that he required the most implicit obedience.

"'The Caliph Haroun Alraschid to the King of Balsora.

"'Haroun Alraschid, son of Mahdi, sends this letter to Mahomed Zinebi, his cousin. As soon as Noureddin, son of the late vizier Khacan, and the bearer of this letter, shall have delivered it, and you have read its contents, strip yourself instantly of the royal mantle, put it upon his shoulders, and resign to him your crown. Herein fail not. Farewell.'

"The caliph folded up the letter and sealed it, without informing Noureddin of its contents. 'Take it,' said he, 'go and embark without delay; the vessel will weigh anchor very soon, as it departs every day about this hour; you may sleep after you are on board.' Noureddin took the letter, and set off with only the little money he had in his pocket at the time when Sangiar gave him his purse; and the Beautiful Persian, inconsolable at his departure, withdrew to a sofa, where she gave full vent to her tears.

"Scarcely had Noureddin left the saloon when Scheich Ibrahim, who had sat in silent astonishment during the whole transaction, looked hard at the caliph, whom he still believed to be the fisherman Kerim, and said, 'Hark ye Kerim, you came here to bring two fish, which at most were not worth more than twenty pieces of copper, and for them you have received a purse and a slave. Do you imagine that you are going to keep all this to yourself? I declare that I will have half the value of the slave: and with respec- to the purse show me what it contains: if it be silver, you shall take one piece of it for yourself; if gold, I will take the whole, and give you some pieces of copper I have about me.'

"To make what follows intelligible, it is necessary to remark that the caliph, before he carried the fish into the saloon, had ordered the grand vizier to repair with all diligence to the palace, and bring back with him a royal garment, and four of those servants who attended on his person; and to wait on the other side of the pavilion till he should strike one of the windows with his hand. The grand vizier had acquitted himself of his commission, and he, Mesrour, and the four servants, were waiting at the place appointed till the signal should be given.

"The caliph, still in the character of a fisherman, boldly replied: 'Scheich Ibrahim, what there may be in the purse, be it silver or gold I know not, I will share it with you with all my heart: but with respect to the slave, I will keep her to myself. If you are unwilling to agree to these conditions you shall have nothing at all.'

"Furious with rage at this insolence, as he deemed it, of a fisherman, Scheich Ibrahim snatched up one of the porcelain dishes that stood upon the table and threw it at the caliph's head. The caliph very easily avoided a dish thrown by a drunken man; it struck the wall and broke into a thousand pieces. More angry than ever at having missed his aim, Scheich Ibrahim took the candle from the table, rose staggering from his seat, and went down the back stairs to find a cane.

"The caliph took this opportunity to give the signal at one of the windows, by striking it with his hand; and the grand vizier, Mesrour, and the four servants were with him in an instant. The servants very soon divested the caliph of the fisherman's dress, and put on him that which they had brought. They were still employed about the caliph, who was seated on the throne which stood in the saloon, when Scheich Ibrahim, flushed with wine and anger, re-entered the room, flourishing a large cane with the full intention of giving the pretended fisherman a good beating. Instead of finding the object of his wrath he could perceive only the fisherman's clothes lying in the middle of the saloon, while he beheld the caliph seated on the throne, with the grand vizier and Mesrour at his side. He started at the sight, scarcely knowing whether he was awake or asleep. The caliph laughed at his surprise, and exclaimed, 'Scheich Ibrahim, what do you want?—whom seek you?'

"Scheich Ibrahim, who was now convinced that it was the caliph who had personated Kerim, threw himself immediately at his master's feet, his face and long beard touching the ground. 'O Commander of the Faithful,' he cried, 'your vile slave hath offended you. He implores your mercy; he entreats your forgiveness!' As the attendants had now finished dressing him, the caliph descended from his throne, saying, 'Rise, I pardon thee.'

"The caliph hereupon addressed himself to the Beautiful Persian, who had checked her tears as soon as she heard that the garden and pavilion belonged to the caliph, and not to Scheich Ibrahim, as the latter had pretended, and that it was Haroun Alraschid himself who had been dressed as a fisherman. 'O, Beautiful Persian,' said he, 'rise and follow me. After what you have seen I need not inform you who I am, and that I am of too exalted a rank to take advantage of the power which, with a generosity never equalled, Noureddin has bequeathed to me in making me your master. I have sent him to ascend the throne of Balsora, and you shall follow him and share his honours as soon as I have forwarded the despatches necessary for the full establishment of his authority as king. In the meantime I will order you an apartment in my palace, where you shall be treated with all the respect you deserve.'

"These noble words of the caliph's reanimated the hopes of the Beautiful Persian, by enabling her to look for consolation in the hope of Noureddin's elevation and success. She was now fully repaid for her affliction by the joy she felt on hearing that Noureddin, whom she passionately loved, was about to be raised to the summit of grandeur. The caliph did not fail to keep his word with her. He even recommended her to the care of his wife Zobeidè, to whom he imparted the high proof of his esteem which he had been conferring on Noureddin.

"Noureddin's journey to Balsora was prosperous, though he arrived there sooner by some days than was quite desirable for his own sake. On his arrival he saw neither relation nor friend, but went immediately to the palace of the king, who was then holding a public court. He made his way through the crowd, holding the letter up in his hand. Every one made way, and he presented the missive to the king, who took it and read it, showing his emotion by the frequent changes in his countenance. He kissed the paper thrice, and was going to obey the directions it gave, when it occurred to him to show the letter to the vizier Saouy, the mortal enemy of Noureddin.

"Saouy, who had seen Noureddin's arrival, and was anxiously conjecturing in his own mind what all this could possibly mean, was as much surprised by the contents of the letter as the king himself. Feeling that his own fortunes were at stake, he in a moment bethought himself of a way to elude them. Pretending not to have read the letter perfectly he turned aside, as if to hold it up to the light that he might peruse it a second time. Then, unperceived by all present, and with such dexterity that his proceedings could only be discovered on a very near examination, he tore off the top of the letter containing the words which expressed the caliph's injunction of immediate and implicit obedience. This he conveyed to his mouth, and swallowed it.

"After this perfidious action, Saouy turned round to the king, and giving him the letter, said in a very low voice, 'O king, what is your majesty's intention?' 'To do as the caliph commands me,' answered the king. 'Be on your guard, my lord,' returned the wicked vizier; 'the writing is indeed the caliph's, but the important superscription is wanting.' The king had, indeed, read the superscription; but, in the perturbation he was in, he imagined he might have been deceived, since it was not now to be seen.

"'O mighty king,' continued the vizier, 'it cannot be doubted that the caliph has given Noureddin this letter merely to get rid of his importunity, in consequence of the complaints he has been urging against your majesty and me; for it is not to be imagined that you are to execute the command it contains. It is, moreover, to be considered that no messenger has been sent with the firman appointing Noureddin in your place, without which the letter is useless. A king, like your majesty, is not to be deposed without some formality. Another claimant may arrive, even with a forged letter. Such irregular proceedings never have been, nor never can be allowed. Your majesty may be sure that I speak the truth; and I will take upon myself the whole responsibility, and bear all the consequences of your refusal.'

"The king allowed himself to be persuaded, and gave Noureddin entirely into the hands of the vizier Saouy, who, with the aid of a considerable escort, had him conducted to his own house. As soon as Noureddin arrived there he received the bastinado till he was to all appearance dead; and in this condition he was conveyed to a prison, where he was confined in the darkest and deepest cell, the keeper receiving strict orders to give him nothing but bread and water.

"When Noureddin, who had been half killed by the blows he had received, began to recover his senses and saw the dismal place he was in, he gave way to the most bitter lamentations, and deplored his unhappy fate. 'O cruel fisherman,' cried he, 'how you have deceived me, and how credulous was I to believe you. But how could I expect so cruel a return for the benefits I had bestowed on you? Heaven bless you, nevertheless: I can never believe that your intention was wicked, and I will even fortify myself with patience for the end of my woes.'

"The unhappy Noureddin remained six days in this forlorn state. Not that he was forgotten by the vizier: that revengeful minister had resolved to take his enemy's life in the most public and disgraceful manner; but he durst not perpetrate that deed on his own authority. In order to succeed in his base designs he loaded a number of his own slaves with rich presents, and, placing himself at their head, went to the king. 'O my lord,' said he, with the deepest malice, 'see the present which the new king entreats your majesty to accept on his accession to the crown.'

"The king fully comprehended what Saouy wished him to understand. 'What!' said he, 'is that wretch still living? I thought you had taken care to punish him as he deserved.' 'O, great king,' replied Saouy, 'it is not in my province to order the execution of any man; that power belongs to your majesty.' 'Go then,' cried the king, 'order that his head be cut off immediately! I give you full permission.' 'My lord,' said Saouy, 'I am infinitely obliged to your majesty for this act of justice; but, as Noureddin affronted me, as your majesty knows, in so very public a manner, I request the favour that you will permit the sentence to be executed before the palace, and that the criers may go and proclaim it in all parts of the city. As all the inhabitants were witnesses of the indignity that I endured, I wish that all may witness the reparation.' The king granted the vizier's request. The criers performed their duty, and occasioned a general sadness through the whole city. The recollection of the father's virtues, still fresh in the minds of all, made them learn with indignation that the son was going to be ignominiously sacrificed at the solicitation and through the revengeful malice of the vizier Saouy.

"That wicked minister went to the prison in person, accompanied with twenty of his slaves, ministers of his cruelty. They led away Noureddin, and obliged him to mount an old broken-down horse, without a saddle. When Noureddin thus saw himself delivered into the hands of his enemy, he cried, 'You are now triumphant, and glory in the abuse of your power: but I have confidence in the words written in one of our wise books: "*You judge unjustly, and in a short time you shall yourself be judged.*" The vizier Saouy was indeed exulting in his heart, and he replied angrily: 'What! insolent wretch, dare you still insult me? However, I pardon you; I care not what happens if I have the pleasure of seeing your head taken off in the sight of all Balsora. Let me remind you of what another of our books says: "*Who regards dying the day after the death of his enemy?*"'

"This implacable minister, surrounded by a number of armed slaves, ordered that Noureddin should be conducted before him by the rest, and they set off towards the palace. The people were ready to tear Saouy in pieces, and would certainly have stoned him, if any one had began the attack. When he had led Noureddin to the open space before the palace, opposite to the king's apartment, Saouy left him in the hands of the executioner, and went immediately to the king, who was already in his cabinet, eager to feast his eyes with the bloody scene about to be enacted.

"The king's guard and the slaves of the vizier Saouy formed a large circle about Noureddin. But they had great difficulty to restrain the populace, who made all possible efforts, though without success, to force their way to the prisoner and bear him away.

THE CALIPH REMINDED OF NOUREDDIN.

The executioner now approached him: 'O my master,' said he, 'I entreat you to pardon me the part I take in your death. I am only a slave, and am compelled to do my duty. If you have nothing further to say, be pleased to prepare for death; the king is going to command me to strike.'

"At this dreadful moment the disconsolate Noureddin turned to those about him and said: 'Will no one, for charity, bring me a drop of water to quench my thirst?' They instantly brought some in a cup for him, and handed it to him. The vizier Saouy, perceiving the delay from the window of the king's cabinet, cried out to the executioner,

'Strike, what do you wait for?' These barbarous and inhuman words excited such universal indignation that the whole place resounded with loud and deep imprecations against the minister; while the king, naturally jealous of his authority, by no means approved the boldness of Saouy in his presence, and his displeasure appeared in his immediately crying out to desire the executioner to stop. He had, indeed, another reason for doing this: at this very moment, turning his eyes towards a wide street before him which led to the place of execution, he perceived a troop of horsemen, who were approaching at full speed. 'O vizier,' said he immediately to Saouy, 'look yonder, what is that?' Saouy, who suspected what it might be, urged the king to give the signal to the executioner. 'No,' replied the king, 'I wish to know first who these horsemen are.' They were the grand vizier Giafar and his suite, who had come from Bagdad by the order of the caliph.

"To account for this minister's arrival at Balsora, it is necessary to observe that after the departure of Noureddin with the caliph's letter, Haroun Alraschid had forgotten, not only on the next day, but for some days after, to send an express with the firman of which he had spoken to the Beautiful Persian. But soon after, passing one of the apartments in the inner palace, which belonged to his women, his attention was attracted by the sounds of a beautiful voice. He stopped, and hearing some words which expressed grief at absence, demanded of an officer of eunuchs, who attended him, what lady lived in that apartment. The officer told him it was the slave belonging to the young lord whom he had sent to Balsora to be king, in the room of Mohammed Zinebi.

"'Alas, poor Noureddin, son of Khacan!' cried the caliph, 'I had indeed forgotten thee! Despatch,' he added, 'and order Giafar to come to me immediately.' The minister came accordingly. 'O Giafar,' said the caliph, 'I have forgotten to send the firman which was necessary to confirm Noureddin as king of Balsora. There is no time now to prepare one. Therefore, use the utmost speed and repair to Balsora, with some of your servants, with all possible diligence. If Noureddin has been executed, and they have been the cause of his death, cause the vizier Saouy to be hanged. If Noureddin is still alive bring him hither, with the king and the vizier.'

"The grand vizier Giafar made no delay; but mounting his horse immediately, departed with a considerable number of the officers of his house. He arrived at Balsora at the time and in the manner already mentioned. As soon as he appeared at the place of execution all the people gave way to make room for him, crying out, 'A pardon for Noureddin!' He proceeded, with his whole train, to enter the palace, not alighting from his horse till he arrived at the foot of the stairs.

"The king of Balsora knew the prime minister of the caliph; and going out to meet him received him at the entrance of his apartment. The grand vizier desired to know if Noureddin were yet alive, and demanded, if he still lived, that he might be immediately sent for. The king answered that Noureddin lived, and ordered him to be brought before them. He soon made his appearance, bound, and a prisoner, but, at the command of the grand vizier, he was at once set at liberty; and Giafar further commanded that the cords taken from Noureddin should be put on Saouy.

"The grand vizier made a very short stay at Balsora. He quitted the city the next day, and, according to the orders he had received, took with him Saouy, the King of Balsora, and Noureddin, whom on his arrival at Bagdad he presented to the caliph. When he had given an account of his journey, and particularly mentioned the state in which he found Noureddin, and the manner in which the caliph's envoy had been treated, through the counsel and animosity of Saouy, Haroun Alraschid, extremely incensed at this conduct, proposed that Noureddin should himself cut off the vizier's head. 'O Commander of the Faithful,' replied Noureddin, 'whatever injury this wicked man may have done me, or may have attempted to do my late father, I should esteem myself the most infamous of men were I to stain my hands with his blood.' The caliph, well pleased with Noureddin's generosity, ordered the common executioner to perform his office.

"The caliph wished to send Noureddin back to Balsora to reign there, but the latter humbly solicited leave to decline the honour. 'O Commander of the Faithful,' said he, 'the city of Balsora is, and will ever be, after what has happened to me there, so distasteful to me that I venture to entreat your majesty to allow me to keep an oath I have taken—never to return thither as long as I live. I wish to place my whole glory in the performances of such services as I may perform near your majesty's person, if you will grant me so great an honour as to allow me to remain here.' The caliph hereupon placed him among those courtiers with whom he was most intimate; restored to him the Beautiful Persian, and bestowed on him so ample a fortune, that he and his wife lived together during the rest of their lives, in the enjoyment of all the happiness they could desire.

"With regard to the king of Balsora, the caliph, after duly pointing out to him how much it was his duty and interest to be very circumspect in the choice of his viziers, sent him back to his kingdom.

## THE HISTORY OF BEDER, PRINCE OF PERSIA, AND OF GIAUHARE, PRINCESS OF THE KINGDOM OF SAMANDAL.

ERSIA is a country of such vast extent, that its ancient monarchs did not without reason assume the lofty title of king of kings. Not to speak of the various kingdoms that had been added by conquest, each separate province was governed by its own sovereign, who not only paid a large tribute to the supreme prince, but was subject to his authority, in the same manner as the governors of other kingdoms are placed under the authority of their respective monarchs.

"One of these mighty princes, who had begun his reign by very fortunate and extensive conquests, continued to govern for many years with a success and tranquility which rendered him the most contented of sovereigns. There was only one thing in which he esteemed himself unfortunate. He was far advanced in years, and not one of all his wives had given him a prince, who might succeed to the throne after his death. He had, however, more than a hundred wives, who all dwelt in the most magnificent apartments, with female slaves to wait upon, and eunuchs to guard them. But, notwithstanding all his solicitude to render them happy, and even to anticipate their wishes, not one of them fulfilled his anxious expectation. Many good actions did he perform to propitiate the favour of Heaven. He gave away considerable sums in alms to the poor, and made very large donations to the holy men of his religion. Moreover, he instituted new foundations for their benefit, with a magnificence truly royal, in order to obtain, by their prayers, the accomplishment of his wishes in the birth of an heir.

"According to the constant usage of the kings, his predecessors, during their residence in the capital, he was accustomed every day to hold an assembly of his courtiers, to which were invited the ambassadors and foreigners of distinction who attended his court. The conversation at these times was not usually confined to business of state, but turned upon the sciences, history, literature, poetry, and, indeed, every topic which could agreeably interest the mind. On one of these assembly days, an eunuch came to inform him that a merchant, just arrived from a very remote country with a slave whom he had bought, requested permission to present this slave to his majesty. 'Desire him to enter and wait,' said the king; 'I will speak to him as soon as the assembly is over.' The merchant was accordingly introduced, and placed in such a position that he was able not only to see the king perfectly, but to hear him converse with those immediately about his person

"It was the custom of the king thus to treat all strangers who had occasion to speak to him. It was done with the benevolent intention that they might become accustomed to his presence; and witnessing the familiarity and kindness that characterised his intercourse with those about him, they might obtain confidence to address him, and not suffer themselves to be awed by the state and grandeur by which he was surrounded. For, indeed, this pomp and glory was sufficient to repress all freedom of speech in persons unused to such magnificence. He observed a similar conduct towards ambassadors from foreign princes. He first partook of their repasts, made enquiries after their health, the incidents of their journey, and the peculiarities of their country; and when, by these means, he had given them sufficient confidence to sustain an official interview, he appointed a day of audience.

"When the council broke up, and all had retired, the merchant was introduced. He prostrated himself before the throne, his face to the earth, praying for the accomplishment of all the king's desires. As soon as the merchant had raised himself from this attitude of reverence, the king asked if he were the man who had brought with him the slave of whom he had been informed, and if she was as handsome as report described her.

"'O mighty monarch,' replied the merchant, 'your majesty has, I doubt not, many beautiful slaves, as you have them sought for with so much care in every part of the world; but I can assure you, without the least apprehension of setting too high a value upon the fair maiden I bring, that you have never seen one that can compare with her, either in point of beauty, form, captivating manners, or all the various accomplishments which heighten personal charms.' 'Where is she?' enquired the king. 'Let her be brought to me.' 'My lord,' answered the merchant, 'I left her in charge of an officer belonging to your eunuchs. Your majesty may, if you please, command her appearance instantly.'

"The slave was brought in. Immediately on seeing her the king became charmed with her fine figure and graceful manner. He then entered his cabinet, whither the merchant and some of the attendant eunuchs followed him. The slave had on a veil of red satin worked with gold, which concealed her face. When the merchant removed it, the King of Persia beheld a lady who surpassed in beauty all he then possessed or had ever seen. He instantly fell passionately in love with her, and enquired of the merchant the price he fixed upon her.

"'O king,' replied the merchant, 'I gave to the person of whom I purchased her a thousand pieces of gold; and I have expended as great a sum in the three years during which I have been travelling to your court. It does not become me to mention a price to so great a prince; I entreat, if it be agreeable to your majesty, that you will accept her as a present.' 'I thank you for your offer,' returned the king, 'but it is not my custom to receive presents from merchants, who come from so great a distance with the intention of serving me. I shall give orders to my treasurer to pay you ten thousand pieces of gold. Will that satisfy you?'

"'O great king,' replied the merchant, 'I should have been extremely happy if your majesty had deigned to accept her without paying a price; but I presume not to refuse your liberal recompense; nor shall I fail to proclaim your generosity in my own country, and in every place through which I pass,' The sum was paid to the merchant, and before he withdrew from the king's presence he was arrayed, by his majesty's order, in a robe of gold brocade.

"By desire of the king the beautiful slave was installed in the most magnificent apartment of the palace, that alone excepted which was appropriated to the royal use. The king appointed a great many matrons and other female slaves to wait upon her. He ordered them to conduct her to the bath, and to dress her in the most magnificent habit they could possibly obtain. They were instructed also to procure the most beautiful pearl necklaces, and diamonds of the greatest brilliancy, and other precious stones of the highest value, that she herself might choose those she thought proper for her adornment.

"The matrons, her attendants, who had no other wish but to please the king, were themselves struck with admiration, when they beheld this maiden's extraordinary beauty. Being perfectly skilled in their business, their leader said to the king: 'O mighty monarch, if your majesty will have patience to grant us only three days, we engage in the course of that time so much to improve the lady's appearance, that you shall scarcely know her

THE BEAUTIFUL SLAVE.

again. Though very unwilling to be so long deprived of the pleasure of her society, the king granted their request. 'I agree,' said he, 'on condition that you punctually keep your promise.'

"The capital of the King of Persia was situated in an island, and his palace, which was extremely grand, was built on its shore. The apartment of the king, and also that of the beautiful slave, situated near the king's, commanded a view of the sea, which rolled its majestic waves to the foot of the walls.

"At the end of three days the king was informed that the beautiful slave was ready to receive him. When he entered she was sitting, most magnificently adorned, upon a sofa alone in her chamber, resting her arm on one of the windows, which opened towards the sea. Her attention being drawn by a footstep heavier than that of her female attendants, she immediately turned her head to see who it was that approached her. On perceiving the king she testified not the least surprise, nor did she rise from her seat to receive him with any marks of courtesy, but she continued in the same posture, as though he had been a person of no importance.

"The King of Persia was exceedingly astonished that a slave of so much beauty and of such graceful deportment should know so little of the customs of the world. He attributed this defect to the bad education she had received, and to the neglect of those with whom she had lived to instruct her in the rules of good manners. He advanced towards her as far as the window, and found that, notwithstanding the cold and careless manner in which she had just received him, she did not prevent him from admiring and caressing her as much as he wished.

"After his first rapture of surprise was over the monarch paused a moment to look at her. 'O thou charming and enchanting creature,' exclaimed he, with enthusiasm, 'tell me, I entreat thee, from whence thou comest? Who and where are the happy parents who have given to the world so beautiful and enchanting a being? You have captivated my heart! Never have I felt for any woman what I feel for you! Although I have seen, and continue every day to see, great numbers of your sex, I have never beheld such a blaze of charms; and I feel that I am entirely, devotedly yours. My dearest love,' he added, 'will you not answer me? Will you not deign to afford some sign that you appreciate the many proofs I give of my great love? You do not even turn your eyes that mine may meet them, and convince you that it is impossible to feel more affection than I feel for you. Why do you persevere in a silence that chills my soul? Why do you appear with such a serious, or rather such a melancholy mein? You fill me with sorrow. Do you lament the loss of country, of parents, or of friends? Cannot a King of Persia, who loves, who adores you, give you consolation, and supply the place of every thing the world could offer?'

"All the protestations of love the King of Persia made, and all he could say to induce the fair slave to speak, was powerless to alter her cold and lifeless demeanour; with her eyes always fixed on the ground, she never deigned to cast a single look on the king, and her mouth remained closed in obstinate silence.

"The King of Persia, delighted with the dazzling beauty of his slave, did not press her further. He hoped that kind treatment and attention would produce a change in her behaviour. He clapped his hands, and immediately several females entered, whom he ordered to bring in a collation. As soon as it was prepared, 'O my charmer,' he said to the slave, 'come hither, and let us eat together.' She rose from the place where she was sitting, and when she had placed herself opposite the king, he served her before he began to eat anything himself, observing the same ceremony with every dish that was brought on the table. The slave partook with him of the entertainment; but her eyes were still cast down, nor did she reply with a single syllable to his frequent enquiries whether the dishes were to her taste.

"In order to change the conversation, the king asked the beautiful slave her name. He enquired if she was pleased with her dress and jewels—what she thought of her apartment—whether she approved the furniture—and if the view of the sea afforded her any amusement? But to all these questions she made no reply. The king, not knowing what to think of such invincible silence, at length imagined that the slave must be really dumb. 'But,' said he to himself, 'is it possible that Allah should have formed so beautiful, so perfect, so accomplished a creature, and have left her with so great a defect? It would, indeed, be a sad misfortune; but be this as it may, I cannot cease to love her.'

"When the king rose from table, he retired to one side of the room to wash his hands, while the slave was washing hers at the other. He availed himself of this opportunity to enquire of the women, who presented the basin and napkin, if she had spoken to them. 'O king,' said one of them, replying for the rest, 'we have not any more than your majesty heard her utter a single syllable. We have attended her at the bath, we have waited on her in her chamber, have dressed her hair, and assisted in putting on her apparel; but she has never opened her lips to say that she was satisfied with our attention. We asked her if she wanted anything? If there was anything she wished us to do? We declared that we were ready to obey her commands. Whether it be sullenness, sorrow, stupidity, or that she is absolutely dumb, we cannot tell; we can only assure your majesty that we have never been able to induce her to say a single word.'

"The King of Persia was more than ever surprised at what he now heard. As he believed the slave was depressed by some severe affliction he used every means in his power to soothe her; amongst other amusements he gave a grand entertainment to the ladies of his palace. Many of these ladies entertained the company by their musical performances on various instruments; the rest either sung or danced, and sometimes they all amused themselves together; afterwards they played at such games as were known to be agreeable to the king. The beautiful slave alone took no part in their diversions; she remained in one place, her eyes constantly fixed on the ground, and preserved an aspect of passive indifference, which was not less astonishing to the ladies than to the king himself. At length the guests retired to their apartments, and left the king alone with the beautiful slave.

"For a long time the affection of the king for his new wife, far from abating, continued steadily to increase. He did not fail to make known his affection to his courtiers; in short, he resolved to attach himself altogether to this lady; and he kept his resolution. After a time he dismissed all his other ladies, presenting them with the rich dresses, jewels, and other articles of value, in which they were accustomed to appear, and giving to each of them a large sum of money, and permission to marry whenever they pleased. He retained only the matrons and other aged females, whose attendance was required on the beautiful slave. A whole year passed away, during which he had not the pleasure of hearing her utter a single word. He did not, however, in the least waver in his love for her; but, with all the complaisance imaginable, continued to give her the most signal proofs of his ardent attachment.

"A year had passed away, when the king was one day sitting by the side of his beloved fair one. He warmly protested to her that his love, instead of diminishing, more and more increased. 'O my queen,' said he, 'I cannot guess what are your sentiments on this subject; but I now solemnly swear that I have not known what it is to form a wish since I have had the happiness of possessing you. My kingdom, great and powerful as it is, is of no value, in my estimation, compared to the pleasure of seeing you, and of telling you a thousand times a day how much I love you. Nor have I proved my love by words only. Surely you cannot doubt my sincerity, when I have sacrificed to your society all the numerous wives who were residing in my palace. You may remember that a year has passed away since I dismissed them all; and at this moment I as little regret what I have done as I did at the instant when I sent them away; nor shall I ever repent it. Nothing would be wanting to my satisfaction, my happiness, or my delight, if, but by a single word, you inform me that you are sensible of my attachment. But how can you gratify me in this if you are really dumb! Alas! I am too much afraid that this is the case; and how can I avoid entertaining such fears, when, after the lapse of a whole year, during every day of which I have entreated you a thousand times to speak to me, you still preserve your distressing silence. If it is impossible that I can attain this happiness, may Heaven at least grant that you may give me a son to succeed me on the throne. I feel that I am growing older every day, and even at the present time I require some one to assist me in sustaining the fatigues of government. Again do I impress upon you the ardent desire I have to hear you speak. Something whispers to me you are not absolutely dumb. For heaven's sake, lady, I conjure you, cease to treat me with such reserve. Speak to me a single word, and I shall die happy.'

"At this discourse the beautiful slave, who had listened to the king, as usual, with downcast eyes, and whose cold, passionless manner had given him reason to suspect not only that she was dumb, but that she had never laughed in her life, suffered her countenance to be illumined with a smile. The King of Persia perceived this with surprise, and the change occasioned him to burst out into an exclamation of delight; and, as he doubted not that she was going to speak, he awaited the moment with the most lively attention and with inexpressible impatience.

"The beautiful slave at length broke the long silence she had maintained. 'O my lord,' said she, 'I have so many things to tell your majesty, now that I have begun to speak, that I know not where to begin. I believe, however, that it is my first duty to thank you for all the favours and honours you have heaped on me, and to pray that Heaven will make you prosperous, and put to confusion all the plots of your enemies; and, instead of dying, may your life be happy and prolonged for many years. I think, moreover, you will be pleased to hear that I hope to present you with an heir to your throne, and that I hope, with you, it may be a son. What I have more to say, O king,' added she, 'is this. I entreat your majesty to pardon my sincerity when I avow that were it not for the hope of which I have just informed you, I had resolved never to love you, and to maintain a perpetual silence; and that at present I love you as much as it is my duty to do.'

"The King of Persia, enchanted alike to hear her speak, and to hear that there was a prospect of the fulfilment of his most ardent hopes, very tenderly embraced her. 'Dearest light of my eyes,' said he, 'I cannot realise so great a happiness as you bestow upon me. You have spoken, and you have declared I may hope for an heir. I scarcely know what or where I am, after two such unexpected causes of delight.'

"The King of Persia said nothing more at that time to the beautiful slave. He left her; but made it very apparent by his manner that he meant soon to return. He desired that the cause of his happiness might be made public, and accordingly announced it to his officers; and having summoned his grand vizier, he gave him orders to distribute a hundred thousand pieces of gold amongst the priests, among the men who had made a vow of poverty, the hospitals, the poor, and to be employed in acts of charity. This commission was punctually performed by the minister.

"Hereupon the King of Persia returned to the beautiful slave. 'O, lady,' said he, 'pardon me for leaving you so abruptly. You yourself were the cause of my departure. But permit me to defer my explanation till another time, as I am very anxious to learn from you some things of the greatest importance to me. Tell me, I entreat you, what motive can possibly have operated with you so strongly, that, while you lived with me as my wife for a twelvemonth, you could preserve unshaken a resolution, not merely of keeping an unbroken silence, but even of refraining from letting me know whether you understood a single word I addressed to you. This astonishes me; as I cannot conceive how you could possibly put so great a restraint upon yourself. The cause must be something very extraordinary.'

"To satisfy the king's curiosity, this beautiful woman replied, 'O my lord, to be a slave—to be far removed from my country—to have lost all hope of ever returning thither—to have a heart pierced with grief, at seeing myself separated for ever from my mother, my brother, my relations, and my friends—these are surely motives sufficient to produce that silence which has appeared to your majesty so strange. The love of country is not less natural than the love of children to their parents; and the loss of liberty is insupportable to every one who has sufficient good sense to know the value of freedom. The body may, indeed, be subjected to the authority of a master who has force and power in his hands; but the mind can never be subdued; that remains ever free. Your majesty has seen an instance of this in me. It is some merit that I have not followed the example of many of those wretched persons of both sexes, whom the love of liberty has reduced to the melancholy resolution of seeking death in a thousand ways, by the exercise of that freedom which none can take away.'

"'O lady,' replied the King of Persia, 'I am fully convinced of what you say; but still it appears to me that a person, beautiful and accomplished, of excellent sense and refined understanding, with all those other qualities such as you possess, and who has been reduced by ill fortune to a state of slavery, might think herself happy in finding a king for her master.'

"'Great king,' said the lady, 'though fortune may destine me to be a slave, yet, as I have just now told your majesty, the will is not to be subdued, even by royal authority. But you were speaking of a slave happy enough to please a monarch, and to make herself beloved by him. A slave born in an inferior condition, and raised to a great

THE BROTHER AND SISTER.

height by royal notice may, I will readily admit, think herself happy in the midst of her calamity. But, after all, what is her happiness? She cannot but consider herself as a slave, torn from the arms of her parents, and, perhaps, from the embraces of a lover, whom, for the rest of her life she can never cease to lament. But if we are to suppose the case of a slave not inferior in rank to the king who has obtained her, your majesty can easily conceive the rigour of her destiny; and you will be able to judge how severe must be her misery—how extreme her affliction, and what resolutions she may be able to maintain.'

"The King of Persia was astonished at what he heard. 'Is it possible, fair lady,' he cried, 'as your conversation leads me to think, that you yourself are of royal descent? For heaven's sake explain this matter, and do not augment my impatience. Tell me who are the happy parents who were blessed with so beautiful a child? Who are your brothers, your sisters, your relations, and, above all things, tell me what is your name?'

"'O king,' replied the beautiful slave, 'my name is Gulnarè of the Ocean. My father, who is dead, was one of the most powerful kings of the sea. At his death, he left his kingdom to my brother Saleh, and to the queen my mother. My mother was a princess, the daughter of another very powerful king of the sea. We were living in our kingdom in great harmony, and in most profound peace, when an enemy, envious of our happiness, invaded our states with an immense army, and penetrated even to our capital, of which he soon made himself master. We had, indeed, scarcely time to escape, by withdrawing to a place very difficult of access, and almost impenetrably hidden, whither we were attended by some faithful officers who would not abandon us.'

"'My brother did not remain idle in this retreat. He endeavoured to discover, if possible, some means by which he might expel the unjust usurper from his kingdom. He one day took me aside, and said in the most serious manner, "O my sister, the result of the most trivial enterprises is ever uncertain. I may possibly fail in the execution of a scheme I have long meditated for the recovery of my kingdom. But I feel less concerned on my own account than at the thought of the misfortunes which may befal you. To guard against disasters, and to put you in a position of security, I am anxious to see you married before I make my attempt; but in the forlorn state in which our affairs now are, it does not seem possible that you should be united to any prince of the sea. I wish you could be prevailed on to adopt my opinion, which is, that you should marry some prince of the earth. I am ready to give you every assistance in my power. With the beauty you possess, I am confident there is many a king who would be delighted to share his throne with you."'

"'This proposal of my brother's excited my extreme indignaiton. "O brother," I replied, "like yourself I trace my descent, both on my father's and mother's side, from kings and queens of the sea, who have never condescended to any alliance with the kings of the earth. I have no desire, any more than they, to make a disgraceful connection; and I took a firm resolution not to do so from the moment I attained sufficient knowledge to understand the grandeur and antiquity of our house. The state to which we are now reduced will not induce me to change my purpose; and if you should unhappily die in the execution of your project, I am ready to perish with you, rather than to follow a counsel which I little expected you could give."'

"'My brother, who was strongly prepossessed in favour of his scheme, however unpleasant it might appear to me, went on to represent that there were many kings of the earth not at all inferior to the monarchs of the sea. This angered me exceedingly, and urged me to passionate remonstrances that drew some severe speeches from him, which pierced me to the soul. He departed as little satisfied with me as I was with him. In my paroxysm of anger I darted from the bottom of the sea, and made my way to the island air.'

"'Notwithstanding the piercing sorrow which had induced me to throw myself upon this island, I lived tolerably content, taking care to keep myself in the most retired situations. My precautions, however, did not avail. A man of some distinction, accompanied by his servants, surprised me while I was sleeping, and brought me away with him. He expressed a great deal of love, and neglected nothing to persuade me to marry him. When he found that he gained nothing by gentle means, he imagined that he should succeed better by force; but I soon made him repent of his insolence. Then he resolved to dispose of me, and in consequence sold me to the merchant who brought me to your majesty. This merchant was a prudent, gentle, humane man; and in the very long journey which he made me take, gave me no occasion to speak of him but in terms of sincere commendation.'

"'As regards your majesty,' continued the Princess Gulnarè, if you had not shown me all those obliging attentions you so unceasingly lavished upon me—if you had not given me so many marks of affection, with a sincerity which left no room for doubt—if, without hesitation, you had not dismissed all your women—I will not affect to conceal that I had fully intended not to remain with you. I should have thrown myself into the sea through that window where I stood when you addressed me when you first visited me in my apartment, and should have gone to seek my brother, my mother, and my friends. I continued to cherish this intention for a considerable time, and would certainly have executed it, if, after a certain period, I had not gained the hope of becoming a mother. In the state I am now in I have wholly relinquished the idea, as nothing I could say to my mother and my brother would induce them to believe that I had been the companion of a king like your majesty. They would for ever upbraid me with having made a voluntary sacrifice of my honour. This being the case, whether it be a prince or princess whom I bring into the world, the child will be a constant pledge to your majesty of my never leaving you. I only hope that you will cease to consider me as a slave, and regard me as a princess not unworthy of your alliance.'

"Thus it was that the Princess Gulnarè made herself and her history known to the King of Persia. 'My charming, my adorable princess,' exclaimed the monarch, 'what wonders are these, that I hear! What ample matter to excite curiosity! How I long to overwhelm you with questions in regard to things so wholly new! But first let me thank you for your goodness, and for the patience you have shown in waiting for the proofs of my sincere and unalterable love. I do not believe it possible to love any one more than I have loved you; yet, since I have been informed that you are so great a princess, my respect for you is increased a thousand times. Why do I call you princess? You are not so now; you are my queen; as much the queen of Persia as I am the king; and this title shall soon resound through my whole dominions. To-morrow it shall be proclaimed in my capital, with such rejoicings as have never been seen; your splendid descent shall be made known, and it shall be published that you are my wife. All this would have been done long since, if you had relieved me sooner from my error; as, from the very moment I first saw you, I have entertained the same resolution I hold at present, to love you always and to love none but you.'

"'In the meantime, that I myself may be fully satisfied, and may, moreover, be instructed how to render you all due respect, let me beseech you to give me some particulars concerning the states and people of the sea, on which subject I am wholly ignorant. I have, indeed, heard of persons living in the sea, but I have always considered such stories as mere fables. But after what you have told me I cannot but believe it to be true; I have, indeed, a convincing proof in the presence of yourself, a sea princess, and are now my wife; an honour which has never fallen to the lot of any other inhabitant of the earth. There is still one thing that seems unaccountable, and respecting which I beg you to give me information. I cannot comprehend how you are able to live, breathe, and move in the water, without being drowned. Among us there are but few persons who have the art of remaining under water; and they perish there, if they do not rise to the surface in a certain time, when their power of endurance is exhausted.'

"'O king,' replied the Princess Gulnarè, 'I will satisfy your majesty on this point with the greatest pleasure. We are accustomed to walk at the bottom of the sea in the same manner in which you walk upon the earth, and are enabled to breathe in the water as others do in the air. Instead, therefore, of our being suffocated, as would be the case with you, the water nourishes our existence. What may seem also very remarkable is that it does not wet our clothes; and when, therefore, we visit the earth we have no necessity of drying our garments. Our ordinary language is the same as that in which the inscription on the seal of the great prophet Solomon the son of David is written.'

"'I should not omit to tell you that the water does not in the least prevent us from seeing, for we can open our eyes in it without sustaining the least inconvenience; and as our sight is for the most part extremely good, we can, notwithstanding the depth of the sea, perceive objects in the water as clearly as others do upon earth. It is the same with us at night. We have the moon to give us light, and the planets and stars are not hidden from our gaze. With respect also to our kingdoms, as the sea is much more spacious than the earth, it includes a greater number of empires, and some of them of greater extent than any terrestrial realm. They are divided into provinces; and in every province there are a great many well-peopled towns. In short, there exist among us an infinity of nations, showing different manners and customs, in the same way as in the kingdoms upon the earth.'

"'The palaces of our kings and princes are extremely gorgeous and magnificent. They are formed of marble of different colours, of rock crystal, with which the sea abounds, of mother of pearl, coral, and other most valuable materials. Gold, silver, and every sort of precious stones are found here in greater abundance than upon the earth. I do not mention pearls; the very largest that are seen on land would be held in no estimation among us, and they are worn only by the common people.'

"'As we have the power of transporting ourselves wherever we wish with incredible velocity, we have no occasion for carriages. Yet all our kings possess great stables and studs of marine horses, but these are for the most part only made use of for amusement, or when we have feasts or public rejoicings. Some kings take great pains in training them for riding, and afterwards mount them to show their ability in the race; others harness them to cars made of mother of pearl, ornamented with a thousand different sorts of shells, all of the most brilliant colours. These cars are made open, with a throne in the middle, in which our kings are accustomed to sit when they show themselves to their people. They are themselves extremely skilful in the management of these chariots, and, therefore, have no need of drivers. I must pass over a great number of other curious particulars in regard to these marine countries, a recital of which would give your majesty very great pleasure; but you must allow me to resume the conversation when we have more time to pursue it. At present I wish to speak to you of something of the greatest importance. It is necessary that I should inform you, my lord, that the women of the sea are attended in illness in a different manner from the women of the earth; and I have reason to fear that the assistance which this country affords would not in my case be perfectly safe if I were to fall sick. As your majesty is greatly interested in the state of my health, I think it proper, if it meets your wishes, to summon hither the queen my mother, and several of my female cousins; at the same time I should like to see the king my brother, with whom I much wish to be reconciled. My relations will be delighted to see me again, especially when I inform them of my history, and they learn that I am the wife of the most powerful King of Persia. I entreat your majesty to comply with my wishes. My family will be extremely glad to pay you their respects, and I can promise you that you will be very well pleased to see them.'

"'O queen,' replied the King of Persia, 'you are here sole mistress. Do whatever you please; it shall be my endeavour to receive your friends with all the honours to which their rank entitles them. But I request to know how you propose to convey to them your wish to see them, and also when they will arrive, that I may order everything necessary for their reception, and may myself be ready to introduce them to my court.' 'My lord,' replied Queen Gulnarè, 'there is no necessity for these ceremonies; they will be here in an instant, and your majesty shall see in what manner they will arrive. Only take the trouble to go into this little closet, and look through the lattice.'

"When the King of Persia had entered the closet, the queen ordered a brazier and some fire to be brought her by one of her women, whom she then dismissed, charging her to fasten the door after her. On being left alone she took a small piece of wood of aloes from a box, and put it in the brazier. As soon as she saw the smoke rise, she pronounced some words in a language wholly unknown to the King of Persia, who observed with great attention all that was going forward. She had scarcely finished speaking when the sea began to be agitated. The closet, to which the king had retired, was so situated that he had a view of the sea through the lattice.

"At length at some distance the sea opened, and immediately there arose from it a young man, extremely handsome, and of a very commanding figure, with mustachios of a sea-green colour. A lady, somewhat advanced in years, but of a most majestic air, rose at the same time, a little behind him; and around her were five young ladies, whose beauty equalled that of the queen herself.

GULNARE SUMMONING HER RELATIVES.

"Queen Gulnarè, who presented herself at one of the windows, immediately recognised the king her brother, the queen her mother, and her other relations, who as instantly knew her. The party advanced as if borne on the surface of the sea, and when they had all reached the shore, they bounded lightly, one after another, through the window at which Queen Gulnarè had appeared, and from whence she had retired to give them room. As soon as they entered, King Saleh, the queen his mother, and all her relations embraced Queen Gulnarè with the greatest tenderness, their eyes suffused with tears.

"When Queen Gulnarè had received them with all possible honour, and made them sit down on a sofa, the queen her mother addressed her in these words: 'I have very great pleasure, my daughter, in seeing you again after so long an absence; and I am sure that your brother and your other relations do not feel less than myself. Your departure, which you took without having said a word to any one, occasioned us all inexpressible affliction, and we cannot now tell you how many tears we have shed. We could conceive no cause which could induce you to take so unexpected a step, unless it were a conversation with your brother, of which he informed us. The advice he gave you appeared to him advantageous, considering the position in which you and all of us then were. There was no cause for such great alarm, though it were disagreeable to you; and you must allow me now to tell you that you considered the matter in a very false and exaggerated light. But let us not renew a subject which will only bring to our recollection causes of complaint and sorrow, which we will now endeavour to forget. Do you, rather, inform us of what has happened to you in the long time we have been separated, and how you are now situated; but, above everything, inform us if you are happy.'

"Queen Gulnarè immediately threw herself at the feet of the queen her mother, and humbly kissed her hand. Then rising, she said: 'O my mother, I have I confess been guilty of a great fault, and I can ascribe to nothing but your goodness the pardon you have been so kind as to grant me. What I have to relate, in obedience to your commands, will make you clearly perceive how absurd it is to feel a strong repugnance to measures of which we know nothing. I have experienced in myself that the very step to which my will was most opposite, is precisely that to which my destiny has led me.' She then related to her mother all that had happend since her indignation had induced her to quit the bottom of the sea. When she had proceeded in her history till she came to the time when she was sold to the King of Persia, with whom she now dwelt, the king her brother exclaimed: 'O my sister, you have been much in the wrong to suffer so many indignities, and have had no one to blame but yourself. You have always had the power of setting yourself free, and I am astônished at your patience in continuing so long in slavery. Come at once, and return with us to my kingdom, which I have re-conquered from my fierce enemy, who, as you know, had made himself master of it.'

"The King of Persia, who heard these words from the closet, where he was concealed, was in the greatest alarm and consternation. 'Alas! woe is me,' said he to himself, 'if my queen, my Gulnarè, should listen to this cruel advice. I can no longer live without her, and they wish to take her from me.' Queen Gulnarè, however, did not leave him long in this state of painful apprehension.

"'My dear brother,' said she, smiling, 'the proposition you now make convinces me more fully than ever of the sincerity of your regard for me. Formerly I could not endure the advice you gave me to marry a prince of the earth. To-day I am almost angry with you for recommending me to quit my present abode, where I dwell with the most powerful and most renowned of all princes. But I do not dwell here as a slave with her master. It would be easy to restore the ten thousand pieces of gold I have cost the king. My position here is that of a wife with a husband; of a wife who has never had occasion for complaint in a single instance. The monarch to whom I am united is religious, wise, moderate, and has given me the most unequivocal marks of his affection. He could not possibly have done me a more distinguished one than in dismissing, from the very commencement of his acquaintance with me, the great number of ladies who belonged to him, and whom he sent away in order to attach himself solely to me. I am his wife; and he has just declared me Queen of Persia, and a partner in his rule. I have also to inform you that I hope to give him an heir, and if heaven so much favours me as to give me a son, it will unite me to him still more inseparably.'

"'Thus, my dear brother,' continued the queen, 'far from being able to follow your advice, all these considerations, as you will readily perceive, oblige me not only to love the King of Persia as much as he loves me, but to remain and pass my life with him, as well from a feeling of gratitude as from duty. I hope that neither you, my mother, nor my good cousins, will disapprove either my resolution to remain here, or the alliance I have accidentally made, which does honour equally to the monarchs of the sea and the earth. Pardon my boldness in having given you the trouble of coming here from the depths of the ocean to make you acquainted with these facts, and that I might enjoy the happiness of seeing you after so long a separation.'

"'My dear sister,' replied King Saleh, 'the proposal I made to you, after hearing your adventures, to which I have listened with the greatest astonishment, was suggested altogether by my sincere affection for you. I hope I need not say how much I honour you, and you will readily believe that there is nothing in the world which touches me so nearly as any question that concerns your happiness. For these reasons I cannot, for my own part, refrain from giving my high approval to the very laudable and queenly resolution you have taken, after what you have told us of the King of Persia, and of the great obligations you are under to him. With respect to the queen, our mother, I feel assured that she will entertain the same opinion.'

"The Queen of the Sea confirmed what her son had said. 'My daughter,' observed she, addressing herself to Queen Gulnarè, 'I am quite delighted you are so happy; and I have nothing to add to what the king your brother has been saying, but to express my entire concurrence in his sentiments. I should be the first to condemn you, if you did not feel all suitable gratitude to a monarch who loves you with so much ardour as the King of Persia has shown, and who has given you such generous proofs of his affection.'

"The King of Persia was still in the closet, where he had concealed himself at the commencement of this interview. In proportion to his grief and alarm at the fear of losing his beloved queen, was the delight he felt when he heard her resolve never to abandon him. As he could no longer doubt her affection, after so clear a declaration, he loved her even more than ever, and cordially resolved within himself to show his gratitude by every means in his power.

"While the King of Persia was joyfully forming these resolutions within himself Queen Gulnarè clapped her hands, and commanded some slaves, who entered immediately, to serve up some refreshments. As soon as these were brought she invited her mother, her brother, and her other relations, to partake of them. But they were all of opinion that as they were then without permission in the palace of a most potent monarch, whom they had never seen and to whom they were wholly unknown, it would be a mark of the greatest incivility to sit down to his table without some previous introduction. The colour immediately mounted into their cheeks, and so great was their emotion that flames shot from their nostrils and their mouths, and their eyes seemed to flash fire.

"The King of Persia was inexpressibly alarmed at a phenomenon so entirely unexpected, and of which he so little knew the cause. Queen Gulnarè, who imagined what his feelings might be, and perfectly comprehended the intention of her friends, rose from her seat, saying that she should soon return. She went immediately to the king, who was much comforted by her presence; 'O my lord,' said she, 'I doubt not that your majesty is fully satisfied with the proof I have just given of my regard, and of the grateful sense I feel of the vast obligations I owe you. I might, without hindrance, have acceeded to the wishes of my friends, and have returned with them to our country; but I am incapable of such ingratitude, and, indeed, should be the first to condemn it in others.' 'Ah! my queen,' cried the King of Persia, 'do not talk of obligations; you are under none to me. But I owe you a debt that I can never pay. I could not have believed that you love me as it appears you do. You have assured me of your affection in the most satisfactory way.' 'O great king,' returned Queen Gulnarè could I possibly do less than I have done? It seems but a small return for all the honours I have received, for the many favours you have heaped upon me, the many instances of love, to which I could not be insensible.'

"'But, my lord,' added she, 'allow me to break off this discourse, and assure you of the sincere friendship of the queen my mother, and the king my brother. They are very anxious to see you, and to assure you of their gratitude and reverence. I had intended to sit down with them at the table I have had furnished with refreshments before I solicited an introduction; but I now entreat your majesty to have the goodness to enter, and to honour them with your presence.'

"'My beloved princess,' replied the King of Persia, 'I shall have great pleasure in being introduced to any persons who are so nearly connected with you; but the flames which I have observed to proceed from their mouths and nostrils somewhat alarm me.' 'Great king,' said the queen, smiling, 'do not allow these flames to give you the least uneasiness. They merely express my friends' unwillingness to partake of the collation prepared, till your majesty will honour them with your presence.'

"Encouraged by this declaration, the King of Persia rose from his place and entered the chamber with Queen Gulnarè, who presented him to the queen her mother, to the king her brother, and to her cousins, who immediately prostrated themselves with their faces to the earth. The King of Persia ran to them immediately, raised them up, and embraced each of them in turn. When they were all seated King Saleh spoke the following words to the King of Persia: 'O great king, we cannot sufficiently express to your majesty the joy we feel at the good fortuue of Queen Gulnarè my sister, who has been taken from a position of disgrace, and placed under your mighty protection. Permit us to assure you that she is not unworthy the high rank to which she has been thus fortunately raised. We have ever felt so great an affection and tenderness for her, that we could not prevail on ourselves to part with her to one of the most powerful princes of the sea, who had solicited her in marriage, even before she was of age. Heaven reserved her for you, O king, and we cannot better return thanks for the favour it has done both her and us, than in offering the supplication for your majesty, that you may long experience with your queen every sort of prosperity and happiness.'

"'It is evident,' replied the King of Persia, 'that the bounty of Heaven reserved her for me, as you have observed. The affection I feel for her makes me fully sensible that till I saw her I never really loved. I cannot sufficiently express the gratitude I feel to the queen, the mother of my Gulnarè, and to you prince, and the rest of your family, for the generous manner in which you have received me into an alliance that confers on me so much glory.' Having said this he invited them to take a seat at the table, at which he placed himself by the side of his queen. When they had partaken of a repast the King of Persia continued in conversation with them till the night was far advanced; at length, when it became necessary to retire, he conducted them himself to the several apartments that had been prepared for them.

"The King of Persia made continual feasts for the entertainment of his illustrious guests, displaying in his whole conduct the greatest grandeur and magnificence, and thus insensibly led them on to continue at his court till the time of the queen's delivery. When this event approached he gave orders that everything should be prepared which could possibly be necessary at so important a juncture. The queen at length presented the king with a son, to the infinite joy of the queen her mother, who was present on the occasion; as soon as the child was arrayed in the magnificent robes prepared for him, his grandmother brought him to his royal father.

"The King of Persia received the present with an excess of delight, more easy to conceive than to express. The countenance of the young prince was open in its expression and of transcendent beauty. It seemed, therefore, to his father that he could not give the child a more characteristic name than that of Beder. To express his thanks to Heaven, he ordered considerable alms to be given to the poor, released the prisoners throughout his empire from their confinement, gave liberty to all his slaves of both sexes, and distributed large sums of money amongst the ministers and holy men of his religion. He also made great presents to his court and his people; and public festivals were held by his order for many days in every part of the city.

"After Queen Gulnarè had recovered from her confinement, the King of Persia, the queen her mother, King Saleh her brother, and the princesses her relations, were one day conversing together in the chamber of the queen when the nurse entered with Prince Beder in her arms. King Saleh rose immediately from his place, ran to the little prince, and taking him from the nurse's arms began to caress him with every appearance of tenderness. He played for some time with the babe, making several turns about the chamber, and holding him up between his hands; then on a sudden, in a transport of joy, he darted through the window which was open and plunged with the infant prince into the sea.

"The King of Persia was wholly unprepared for this event. He gave a dreadful shriek, in the belief that he should never again see his beloved son, or, at least, that he should never again behold him alive. His affliction had nearly deprived him of his

THE KING'S GRIEF.

senses; but a flood of tears came to his relief. 'Oh my lord,' said Queen Gulnarè, with perfect composure of countenance and manner, 'may it please your majesty to dismiss your fears. The young prince is my son as well as yours, and my love for him is not less than yours; you see, however, that I am not in the least alarmed; indeed I have no occasion to be so. I assure you he runs no risk whatever, and you will soon see the king his uncle, re-appear and restore him to us in perfect safety. Although he is descended from you, yet as he belongs to me also, he has no doubt inherited the advantage we enjoy of being equally able to live either in the sea or on the earth.' The queen, the mother of Gulnarè, and the princesses her relations, gave the king the same assurances; but their assertions had little effect in removing his fears, which kept possession of him so long as Prince Beder was absent from his sight.

"The sea at length became agitated, and soon after King Saleh re-appeared, rising from the waves, with the little prince in his arms. He flew rapidly through the air, and returned by the same window through which he had gone out. The King of Persia was delighted; but expressed much surprise to see Prince Beder looking as tranquil as when he left the room. 'Was not your majesty alarmed,' asked King Saleh, 'when you saw me plunge into the sea with the prince, my nephew?' 'Ah! my friend,' replied the King of Persia, 'I cannot express to you how much I was terrified. From the moment when my son disappeared, I believed him irrecoverably lost: in bringing him back to me you have given me new life.' 'Great king,' replied King Saleh, 'I was apprehensive you would be distressed, but there was not the least occasion for your alarm. Before I threw myself into the sea I pronounced over my nephew some mysterious words, which were graven on the seal of the great king Solomon, the son of David. We observe the same ceremony with regard to all the children who are born amongst us in the depths of the sea, and in virtue of these words they obtain the privilege of that we possess over all the inhabitants of the earth. From what your majesty has just witnessed, you may easily judge of the great advantages Prince Beder derives in being descended from Queen Gulnarè, my sister. While he lives he may, whenever it pleases him, plunge freely into the sea and visit the vast empires which are contained within its hidden depths.'

"When King Saleh had said this, he restored the little Prince Beder to the arms of its nurse. He then opened a box, which he had brought from his palace during the short time of his absence. It contained three hundred diamonds, each as large as a pigeon's egg, three hundred rubies of very extraordinary size, a number of emerald wands, each six inches long, and thirty pearl necklaces, every necklace consisting of ten rows. This box he brought to the King of Persia, and offered it to him in the following terms: 'O king, when we were summoned hither by the queen my sister, we knew not in what part of the world she dwelt, and that she had the honour of being married to a great monarch. It was for this reason that we came with empty hands. As it was not then in our power to give your majesty any immediate mark of our gratitude, we humbly entreat that you will now deign to accept this slight acknowledgment of the very extraordinary favours you have had the goodness to confer on my sister; favours for which we are all equally grateful.'

"It is impossible to paint the king's surprise when he saw such abundance of riches contained in so small a space. 'What! my prince,' he exclaimed, 'do you call it a slight mark of your gratitude to bestow upon me, to whom you owe nothing, so inestimable a present? I declare to you again, that neither the queen your mother, nor yourself are under any obligation whatever to me. I feel happy in having obtained your consent to the alliance I have contracted with your family. My princess,' said he, turning round to Queen Gulnarè, 'the king your brother overwhelms me with confusion, and I would fain entreat him to allow me to decline his present, did I not fear that I should offend him. Do you, therefore, request him to excuse me from accepting it.'

"King Saleh replied: 'I am not surprised that your majesty should think this present somewhat extraordinary; I am aware that upon the earth it is not usual to see jewels of this quality, and in this abundance. But if you knew, as I do, where the mines are from whence they are drawn; and if you were aware that it is in my power to collect from thence a greater treasure than is possessed by all the kings of the earth, your majesty would be justly astonished that I have presumed to make you so trivial an acknowledgment of your kindness. We beg, therefore, that you will not consider our present in respect to its intrinsic value, but as a pledge of that sincere friendship which has induced us to offer it. Inflict not on us the severe mortification of a refusal to receive it, but accept it rather in the same spirit of amity with which it is bestowed.' This generous behaviour compelled the King of Persia to accede to King Saleh's wish. He expressed his deep sense of the obligation he was under to the illustrious donor and his royal mother.

Not long after this King Saleh found it necessary to speak to the King of Persia on the subject of his departure. He declared that the queen his mother, the princesses his relations, and himself would with great pleasure pass their whole life at the King of Persia's court; but as they had now been long absent from their kingdom, and as their presence there was become necessary, he begged the king not to be displeased if they took their leave of him and of Queen Gulnarè. The King of Persia assured his guests that he was extremely sorry not to have it in his power to repay their civility by returning the visit. 'But as I am convinced,' added he, 'that you will not forget Queen Gulnarè, but will be anxious to visit her from time to time, I hope to have the honour of seeing you frequently.'

"When the moment of separation arrived many tears were shed on both sides. King Saleh was the first who withdrew; the queen his mother and the princesses were obliged, in order to follow him, to tear themselves from the embraces of Queen Gulnarè, who could not summon courage to allow them to depart. As soon as this royal party had disappeared the King of Persia could not refrain from saying to Queen Gulnarè: 'Princess, if any one had told me, as truths, the marvellous things I have seen with my own eyes since your illustrious family first honoured my palace with their presence, I should have looked upon him as a person who wished to practise on my credulity. But I cannot distrust my own eyes; never shall I forget what I have seen, or cease to thank Heaven for having selected me from among the princes to receive its most valuable gift.'

"Prince Beder was brought up in the palace, under the immediate inspection of his royal parents, who saw him increase in stature and beauty with the most lively satisfaction. Their happiness was daily augmented as he advanced in age, by the continued good humour he displayed, by his agreeable manner in everything he did, and by the correct judgment and quickness of understanding which showed themselves in all he said. Still more complete did their happiness become by being frequently shared with King Saleh, the young prince's uncle, the queen his grandmother, and the princesses his cousins, who often came to visit him. No difficulty was found in teaching the young prince the necessary branches of education; nor did he fail to learn with equal facility all the sciences with which a prince of his elevated rank should be familiar.

"When the Prince of Persia had reached the age of fifteen years, he acquitted himself in all his exercises with infinitely more skill and address than his masters could show. He was, moreover, endowed with extraordinary wisdom and prudence. The King of Persia had observed in him, almost from the hour of his birth, the seeds of all the virtues necessary to a sovereign, and had seen them augment with his years. Moreover he found that the infirmities of age daily increased upon himself; and thus he became desirous that the prince's succession to the throne should not depend on his own life; he wished immediately to resign to him the kingdom. He had no difficulty in inducing his council to accede to his wishes; and the people heard of his resolution with much satisfaction, being fully satisfied that the prince was in every respect worthy to rule over them. Prince Beder had, indeed, for a very considerable time been accustomed to appear in public, and his subjects had had opportunities of remarking that he did not carry himself in that haughty and forbidding manner which many princes assume, who look upon everything beneath them with an intolerable air of loftiness and disdain. They had observed, on the contrary, that he behaved towards all with a benignity of manner that invited their approach; that he listened attentively to those who had occasion to speak to him; and that he answered them with a kindness and courtesy peculiar to himself, refusing no man's request, provided it was just and reasonable.

"The day for the ceremony came. Surrounded by his council, which was on this occasion more than usually numerous, the King of Persia descended from the throne on which he was sitting. He then took the crown from his own head, and placed it upon that of the prince; then, having assisted him to ascend the throne he had quitted, he kissed the new king's hand as a mark that he had given up to him all his power and sovereignty; after which he took a seat amongst the viziers and emirs.

"The nobles of the court and all the principal officers immediately came forward to prostrate themselves at the feet of the new king, and each took the oaths of fidelity and allegiance according to his rank. This ceremony concluded, the grand vizier made a report to King Beder of some important affairs of government; and on every subject the new king delivered himself with so much wisdom that he became the admiration of the council. He afterwards deposed many governors who had been convicted of malversation, and set up others in their places, showing in his choice an amount of equity and discernment that drew praise from every one—commendations which were more honourable as they were free from flattery. He at length quitted the council and, accompanied by his father, went to the apartment of Queen Gulnarè. The queen no sooner saw him with the crown upon his head than she ran and embraced him with the greatest tenderness, expressing her ardent wishes that his reign might be long and happy.

"During the first year of his reign King Beder acquitted himself of all the royal duties with the greatest assiduity. Above everything, he took care to make himself acquainted with the real state of affairs, and with every matter which could contribute to the happiness of his subjects. The following year, after making every arrangement for the administration of affairs with his council, and acting with the approbation of the old king his father, he left his capital under the pretext of taking the diversion of hunting: but his real intention was to visit all the provinces of his kingdom, in order to correct abuses, to establish everywhere good order and discipline, and, by showing himself upon the frontiers, to take away from the princes his neighbours, who were nourishing projects of hostility, the hope of effecting anything against the peace and security of his states.

"For the fulfilment of this useful design at least a year was required. Not long after his return, the king his father became so dangerously ill as to be convinced from the first that his end was approaching. He looked forward to death with the most perfect tranquillity, having no other anxiety but to recommend to the ministers and lords of the court to persevere in the fidelity they had sworn to his son. They all renewed their oaths with the same readiness they had before shown in taking them. The old king soon afterwards died, to the great affliction of King Beder and Queen Gulnarè, who had the body deposited in a superb mausoleum with all the pomp befitting the exalted rank of the departed king.

"After the funeral was over, King Beder fulfilled his own wish in complying with the custom of Persia of bewailing the dead for one entire month, during which time no visitor was to be received. He would have mourned the loss of his father his whole life long had he followed merely the dictates of his heart, and had it been consistent with the duties of so great a king to abandon himself wholly to grief. In the meantime, the queen, the mother of Queen Gulnarè, and King Saleh, with the princesses their relations, came and shared in the affliction of the queen and her son before they ventured to speak to them of consolation.

"When the month was past the king could no longer avoid giving admittance to the grand vizier and all the lords of his court, who entreated him to lay aside his mourning, to appear before his subjects, and to resume the direction of public affairs. He at first expressed great unwillingness to accede to this request. The grand vizier was obliged to take up the subject and thus address him: 'O great king, I have no need to represent to your majesty that to continue in perpetual mourning gives an appearance of female obstinacy. We cannot doubt that you are fully sensible of this, and that it is by no means your intention to present such a spectacle. Neither our tears nor yours can restore to life the king your father, though we continued to weep for the remainder of our days. He has submitted to the common fate of all men, and paid the inevitable debt of our nature. We cannot, however, say absolutely that he is dead since we behold him again in your sacred person. He himself felt convinced, even in dying, that he should live again in you: it behoves, therefore, your majesty to prove that he was not deceived.'

"King Beder was unable to resist these pressing entreaties. He put off his mourning garments from that moment, and having re-assumed the habiliments and ensigns of royalty, he began to provide for the necessities of his kingdom, and of his individual subjects with the attention he had always shown before his father's death. He acquitted himself in every particular in such a way as to gain universal approbation, and, as he was very exact in following the ordinances of his predecessors, the people were hardly sensible of any change of authority.

KING BEDER IN LOVE

" King Saleh, who had returned to his kingdom of the sea with the queen his mother and the princesses, as soon as King Beder had re-assumed the reins of government, at the end of the year revisited King Beder and Queen Gulnarè, who were delighted to see him.

" One evening, when the table had been removed and they were left by themselves, the conversation turned on a variety of subjects. King Saleh after a time began praising the king his nephew, and remarked to his sister how fully he was satisfied with the wisdom with which King Beder governed, and which had gained the new king a great reputation, not only among the kings his neighbours, but even in far distant kingdoms. King Beder who felt much embarrassed at hearing himself so highly commended, and was yet too complaisant to request the king his uncle to be silent, rested on his elbow and pretended to sleep, while he rested his head upon a cushion that was placed behind him.

"After having noticed the extraordinary prudence of King Beder, as shown in his conduct, and his quick understanding as displayed in his enterprises, King Saleh went on to observe on the king's personal perfections, and spoke of him as a prodigy never equalled on earth, nor in any of the countries beneath the waters of the sea. 'O sister,' he suddenly exclaimed, 'so perfect as he is, and such as he must appear to you, I am astonished that you have not yet thought of seeing him united with some princess in marriage. If I am not mistaken he is now in his twentieth year, an age at which so distinguished a prince should not remain without a consort. Since you seem to pay no attention to this, I feel inclined myself to undertake the task of finding, in some princess of our kingdoms, a queen worthy of him.'

"'O my brother,' replied Queen Gulnarè, 'you bring to my notice a duty which, I must confess to you, has never till the present moment in the least occupied my thoughts. As my son has never expressed any desire to be married, the idea had never occurred to me, and I am extremely glad that you have put it into my mind. As I entirely approve your design of uniting my son to one of our princesses, I must depend on your goodness to procure him one, who will, I hope, be so handsome and accomplished that my son will feel perfectly happy with her.'

"'I know a princess worthy of him,' observed King Saleh, in a low tone of voice; 'but before I tell you who she is, I must beg you to see whether the king my nephew is really asleep. I will give you my reason why I think it right to take this precaution.' The queen turned and looked at her son, and as she saw King Beder in his former position she had no suspicion but that he was in a profound sleep. King Beder, however, far from being unconscious of what was going on, redoubled his attention, that he might not lose the least word of what his uncle was going to impart with so much secrecy. 'You need not fear,' said the queen to her brother; 'you may speak as freely as you please, without the smallest fear of being overheard.'

"'It is not desirable,' returned King Saleh, 'that the king my nephew should at once hear what I am going to say. Love, you know, sometimes gains admission by the ear; and it may not be convenient that he should love on report the lady I am about to mention, as I foresee great difficulties to be surmounted; not, I am inclined to believe, on the part of the princess, but on that of the king her father. I am sure you remember the Princess Giauharè and the King of Samandal.'

"'What is this you say, brother?' cried Queen Gulnarè. 'Is not the Princess Giauharè yet married? I remember to have seen her a little while before I left you. She was then about eighteen months old, and even then her beauty was really astonishing. She must now be quite a wonder of the world, if her beauty has gone on increasing from that time. She is but little older than my son, and that need not to deter us from our endeavours to procure for him so advantageous a match. The first thing necessary is to learn what the difficulties are you will have to encounter; the second, to find the means of surmounting them.'

"'My dear sister,' replied King Saleh, 'I apprehend much opposition from the King of Samandal. His vanity is so excessive, that he looks upon himself as superior to all other kings; and it seems hardly probable that he will consent to treat on the subject of this alliance. But I will myself wait upon him, to request for my nephew the hand of the princess his daughter, and if he refuses, we will address ourselves where we may expect a more favourable reply. For this reason, you perceive, it is very desirable that my nephew should know nothing of our purpose till we are certain of the King of Samandal's consent. An affection for the Princess Giauharè might take strong possession of him, and we may be at last unable to succeed in obtaining her father's consent.' They continued to converse for some time upon this subject, and before they separated it was agreed that King Saleh should return immediately to his kingdom, and should demand of the King of Samandal the hand of the Princess Giauharè for the King of Persia.

"Queen Gulnarè and King Saleh, who had no doubt that King Beder was asleep, roused him as they were about to retire, and the king succeeded perfectly in making them believe he was really awakening from a deep sleep. But the real truth was, that he had not lost a single word of their conversation; and the picture they had drawn of the Princess Giauharè had excited a passion altogether new in his breast. He formed to himself so exalted an idea of her beauty, that the hope of winning her made him pass the whole night in great agitation, nor was he able to close his eyes for a moment.

"King Saleh proposed to take his departure the next day. Accordingly he bade farewell to Queen Gulnarè and to the king his nephew. The young King of Persia, who was well aware that his uncle's intention in leaving them so soon was to avoid any loss of time in the execution of the scheme he had formed for his happiness, could not hear of his departure without showing evident marks of interest by frequent changes of countenance. His passion was already so strong that he could not endure the idea of being precluded from beholding the object that had awakened it, during the long time that would be necessary to arrange a formal treaty of marriage. He, accordingly, resolved to request his uncle to take him with him; but as he was desirous that his mother should know nothing of the matter, in order that he might have an opportunity of speaking to King Saleh in private, he induced him to defer his journey for a day or two, and to set forth on a hunting party with him, resolving to profit by this opportunity to make his wishes known.

"The hunting expedition set out, and King Beder several times found himself alone with his uncle; but he could never summon courage to utter a single word of what he had before determined to say. In the heat of the chase, when King Saleh had separated from him, and no one of his officers or attendants remained near him, he alighted from his horse, near a brook; and having fastened the animal to a tree, which, with many others, made a beautiful shade beside the water, he reclined upon the grass and gave free vent to his tears which flowed in abundance, accompanied by frequent sighs. He remained a long time in this state wholly absorbed in reflection, without uttering a single word.

"In the meantime King Saleh, who presently missed his nephew, was extremely anxious to know what was become of him, but could find no one who could give the least information. He then separated himself from the huntsmen to go in search of King Beder, and soon perceived him at some distance. He had observed the day before, and more evidently on the present day, that his nephew was perturbed in mind; that, contrary to custom, he was pensive and reserved, and by no means ready to give an answer to any question that was proposed to him. But King Saleh had not the least suspicion of the cause of this change. Now, however, when he found King Beder sitting alone and disconsolate he had not a doubt in his mind but that the king had overheard the conversation between himself and the queen his mother, and that he was thoroughly in love. He dismounted from his horse at some distance, and having tied it to a tree, approached by a circuitous path, and without making the least noise till he came sufficiently near to hear the young king pronounce these words:

"'Amiable princess of the kingdom of Samandal,' 'it is only a feeble sketch that has been given me of your beauty, which I doubt not excels that of all the princesses in the world as much as the splendour of the sun outshines that of the moon or of the stars. I would go this moment to make you an offer of my heart, did I but know where to find you. It is yours, and never shall any princess but yourself possess it.'

"King Saleh did not wish to hear more; he advanced so that King Beder could see him, and spoke thus: 'From what I see, nephew, you have overheard what the queen your mother and myself were yesterday saying about the Princess Giauharè. We should have been more on our guard, but that we believed you were asleep.' 'My dear uncle,' returned King Beder, 'I did not lose a single word of your conversation, and I have fully experienced the effect you foresaw, and which you were so anxious to prevent. I induced you to defer your departure for the express purpose of informing you of the state of my heart; but the confusion I felt when I wished to have made known my weakness, if indeed it be a weakness to love a princess so worthy of my affections, absolutely closed my lips. I entreat you, therefore, by all the friendship you entertain for a prince who has the honour of being so nearly allied to you, that you will extend your pity to me, and not delay to procure me a sight of the divine Princess Giauharè till you have obtained the consent of the King her father to our marriage; unless, indeed, you wish me to die for love of her before I see her.'

"The King of Persia's speech extremely embarrassed King Saleh, who represented to him the great difficulty there would be in obtaining for him the boon he craved; that he could not do it without taking King Beder with him, while the King of Persia's presence in his own kingdom was so necessary, that much inconvenience might be apprehended from his absence. He entreated him to moderate his passion till things could be put in a proper train, assuring him that he would employ every means in his power to secure the success they both wished, and that he would at all events see his nephew again in a very few days to give an account of his mission. The King of Persia was deaf to all these arguments. 'O unkind uncle,' he exclaimed, 'it is too apparent that you do not love me so much as I believed, and that you would rather see me pine and die, than grant me the first favour that I ever asked of you in my life.'

"'I am ready to convince your majesty,' replied king Saleh, 'that there is nothing I will not do to oblige you; but I cannot possibly agree to your departing with me till you have mentioned the subject to the queen your mother. What would she say of us both? I am willing to take you with me if she consents, and I will even add my entreaties to your own.' 'You must be aware,' replied the King of Persia, 'that my mother will never consent to my leaving her; this excuse, therefore, makes me perceive more clearly how averse you are to oblige me. If you loved me as much as you would sometimes make me believe you do, you would undoubtedly return to your kingdom this very moment, and take me with you.'

"Compelled to yield to the King of Persia's solicitation, King Saleh drew off a ring which he had on his finger, and on which were the same mysterious names of the Deity as were engraven upon the seal of Solomon, and which by their virtue had produced such miraculous effects. He gave the ring to his nephew with these words: 'Take this ring, put it upon your finger, and fear neither the waters nor the depth of the sea.' The King of Persia took the ring and put it on his finger. Thereupon King Saleh said to him, 'Do as I do.' At the same time they rose together lightly into the air, and proceeding towards the sea, which was not very distant, they immediately plunged into it.

"It was not long before the King of the Sea arrived at the palace, accompanied by the King of Persia his nephew, whom he immediately conducted to the apartment of the queen, and presented to her. The King of Persia kissed the hand of the queen his grandmother, who in her turn embraced him with the greatest demonstrations of joy. 'I need not enquire concerning your health,' said she; 'I perceive that you are perfectly well, and it delights me to find you so; but I am very anxious to hear some news of my daughter, Queen Gulnarè.' The King of Persia took especial care not to divulge the fact that he left his palace without taking leave of his mother; on the contrary, he assured his grandmother that Queen Gulnarè was in perfect health, and that he was charged to present her most dutiful and affectionate greeting. The queen presented him afterwards to the princesses, and while they were engaged in conversation together she withdrew into her closet with King Saleh, who informed her of the love which the King of Persia had conceived for the Princess Giauharè, on the mere description of that lady's beauty—though he had taken every precaution in the matter; he added that, unable to resist the solicitations of the king, he had brought King Beder with him, and was now going to adopt such measures as seemed most likely to obtain the hand of the princess for his nephew.

"Although in strict truth King Saleh was innocent of the King of Persia's passion, the queen was nevertheless much dissatisfied with his conduct, in having spoken in his nephew's presence with so little precaution of the Princess Giauharè. 'Your imprudence,' said she 'is unpardonable; can you hope that the King of Samandal, whose character you so well know, will have more respect for you than for the numerous sovereigns whose suit he has rejected with open marks of contempt? Do you wish to be sent away with similar disgrace?'

"'O lady,' replied King Saleh, 'I have already observed to you that my being overheard by the king my nephew, in the description I gave to my sister concerning the

THE RAGE OF THE KING OF SAMANDAL.

beauty of the Princess Giauharè was wholly contrary to my wish or intention. But the mischief is done; and we must now remember that King Beder is passionately in love, and that he will die with grief if we do not by some means obtain her for him. It becomes me, too, to reflect that, however innocently I have acted, it is I who have done the evil, and that it is, therefore, my duty, as it is my inclination, to contribute everything in my power towards providing a remedy. I hope you will approve the resolution I have taken, to visit myself the King of Samandal, to offer him a rich present of jewels, and to demand the hand of the princess his daughter for the King of Persia your grandson. I cherish some hope that he will not refuse me, and that he will consent to an alliance with one of the most powerful monarchs of the earth.'

"'It would be well,' replied the queen, 'if we had not been reduced to the necessity of making this request, where we are so likely to plead in vain; but as it is the object of our present consideration to give repose and happiness to the king my grandson, I shall not withhold my consent to your scheme. Above all things, since you so well know the humour of the King of Samandal, take care I entreat you to address him with all the respect which is due to him, and make your request in such agreeable terms that he cannot possibly take offence.'

"The queen herself prepared the present which King Saleh was to take with him. It consisted of diamonds, rubies, emeralds, and rows of pearls; these were deposited in an extremely rich and beautiful casket. Next day King Saleh took leave of the queen his mother, and of the King of Persia, and departed with a small and select retinue of officers and servants. He soon reached the capital and entered the palace of the King of Samandal, who, as soon as he heard of the strange king's arrival, gave him audience. He rose from his throne at the appearance of King Saleh who was willing for a few moments to forget his own rank and prostrate himself at the feet of the monarch of Samandal, wishing him the accomplishment of all he could desire. The king of Samandal stooped immediately to raise his visitor, whom he seated near himself, assuring him of the satisfaction he had in seeing him. Then he requested to know if there were anything he could do to serve his visitor.

"'O mighty king,' replied King Saleh, 'if in the journey I have taken I had no other motive than to pay my respects to one of the most powerful princes the world has known, and to behold a prince equally distinguished by his wisdom and his valour, I should but freely express to your majesty how much I esteem and honour you. If you could penetrate the thoughts of my heart you would perceive the great veneration I entertain for your majesty, and the ardent desire I have to give you some proofs of my attachment.' Having thus spoken, he took the casket from the hands of one of his attendants, and presenting it to the King of Samandal, entreated that he would have the goodness to accept this gift.

"'O prince,' replied the King of Samandal, 'you would not offer a present of this value if you had not some proportionate favour to ask. If it be anything that stands within my power I shall have the greatest pleasure in acceding to your wish. Speak and tell me freely in what way I can serve you.'

"'It is true, great king,' replied King Saleh, 'that I have a favour to ask of your majesty. You may be assured that I should be careful not to request what it is not in your power to grant; the thing, indeed, depends so entirely upon yourself that it would be altogether useless to apply to any other person. I venture, therefore, to urge my petition with all possible earnestness, and to beg that you will not refuse my prayer.' 'In that case,' replied the King of Samandal, 'you have only to inform me of your wishes, and you shall see how ready I am to oblige you in anything within the limits of my authority.'

"'O king,' said King Saleh, 'your majesty having encouraged me to place so great a confidence in your good will, I will no longer withhold from you that I am come hither to entreat you to honour my family with your alliance, through the marriage of the Princess Giauharè, your illustrious daughter; and thus to confirm that amity and good understanding which have been for a long time maintained between our two kingdoms.'

"At this proposal the King of Samandal burst into a violent fit of laughter, throwing himself back in his seat, and leaning against the cushion behind him in a manner that was highly insulting to King Saleh; 'O King Saleh,' said he, with an air of contempt, 'I had always looked upon you as a wise and prudent prince, a monarch who could boast of much good sense, and I am sorry to find, from what I have just heard from you, how entirely I have been deceived. Tell me, I beg, where could your understanding possibly be wandering when you first entertained so extravagant a chimera as that of which you have been speaking? Could you really seriously think of aspiring to the hand of a princess descended from so great and powerful a monarch as myself. You ought well to have considered the immense distance there is between you and me ere you came hither to sacrifice by a moment's folly the good opinion I have for years entertained of you.'

"King Saleh was exceedingly offended at this insolent answer, and had great difficulty in subduing his just resentment: he replied, however, with all possible moderation. 'May Heaven reward your majesty as you deserve; allow me the honour to tell you that I do not solicit the princess your daughter in marriage for myself; though had this been the case, far from its being a cause of just offence either to your majesty or to the princess herself, I cannot but flatter myself that the alliance would have done equal honour to all concerned. Your majesty cannot but know that I am, like yourself, one of the kings of the sea; that the kings, my predecessors, are second to no monarchs in the antiquity and splendour of their race; and that the kingdom which I inherit from them is not less flourishing or powerful than it has ever been. But, putting this aside, had I not been interrupted you would have been informed that the favour I asked was not for myself, but for the young King of Persia, my nephew, with whose power, grandeur, and personal qualities you cannot be unacquainted. It is universally known that the Princess Giauharè is the most beautiful lady beneath the sky; but it is not less true that the young King of Persia is the handsomest and most accomplished young man who lives on the earth, or in any of the kingdoms of the sea; these are facts admitted on all sides. As, therefore, the favour I request will reflect much honour both on yourself and the Princess Giauharè you can have no reason to apprehend that your consent to so proper and equal an alliance will not meet with universal approbation. The princess is undoubtedly worthy of the King of Persia; but the king is no less worthy of her. No monarch or prince in the world would question the justice of his claims.'

"The King of Samandal would not have given King Saleh an opportunity of making so long a speech had not rage deprived him of all power of utterance. As it was, King Saleh had ceased speaking some time before the King of Samandal could find words to reply. He at length broke out in terms of the grossest abuse, and in words altogether unworthy of a great king. 'O dog,' he exclaimed, 'dare you to hold this insolent language, and even to utter the name of my daughter? Do you imagine that the son of your sister Gulnarè can enter into comparison with my daughter? Who are you? Who was your father? Who is your sister? Who is your nephew? Was not his father a reptile, and the son of a reptile like yourself? Ho, seize this insolent wretch this moment and cut off his head.'

"Some officers who were about the person of the King of Samandal prepared immediately to obey his orders; but as King Saleh was in the full vigour of life, and extremely light and active, he escaped before they had drawn their sabres, and gained the palace gate where he met a thousand of his relations and friends, who had just arrived well armed and equipped. The queen his mother, considering how few attendants he had taken with him, and entertaining some apprehension of the kind of reception the King of Samandal might give him, had sent off this party, entreating them to follow their master with the greatest possible diligence. King Saleh's relations, who marched at the head of the troop, were much gratified at having arrived so very opportunely, when they saw him approaching in haste and his people following in great disorder, with the King of Samandal's officers pursuing them. 'Oh, king,' cried they, the moment he came up to them, 'what means this? We are ready to avenge you; you have only to command us.'

"King Saleh, in a very few words, informed them of the insult that had been offered him. He then put himself at the head of a considerable party, and returned towards the palace, leaving the rest in possession of the gate which they had seized. The few officers and guards who had pursued him having been dispersed, he re-entered the hall of the King of Samandal, who being abandoned by those about him, was instantly seized. King Saleh having left a sufficient number of his party about the king to guard against his escape, went from room to room in search of the Princess Giauharè; but at the very beginning of the confusion this lady, accompanied by the females her attendants. had darted to the surface of the sea, and escaped to a desert island.

"Whilst these events were passing at the palace of the King of Samandal, some of King Saleh's people, who had taken flight on the first menaces they had heard against their royal master, returned home, and put the queen his mother into very great alarm by informing her of the danger in which they had left him. The young King Beder, who was present when they came, was the more shocked, as he considered himself the first and chief cause of all the mischief which might ensue. He did not feel sufficiently strong to support the presence of the queen his grandmother, and her expected reproaches concerning the forlorn situation in which he believed King Saleh to be placed entirely on his account. While, therefore, she was occupied in giving such orders as were necessary in the present posture of affairs, he darted to the surface of the sea, and ignorant of the road to Persia, ascended to the same island to which the Princess Giauharè had already made her escape.

"This prince seated himself, in a very dejected state of mind, at the foot of a great tree which was surrounded by many others. While he sat there endeavouring to recover his calmness, he heard the sound of a voice. He immediately began to listen attentively; but being too distant from the voice to understand a syllable of what he heard, he rose from his seat, and advancing without the least noise to the place whence the sound came, he perceived through the foliage a lady of such exquisite beauty that her presence wholly dazzled him. 'Doubtless,' said he to himself, while he stopped and surveyed her with an eye of astonishment, 'doubtless this is the Princess Giauharè, who has been compelled by terror to quit the palace of the king her father, but whosoever she be, she seems quite worthy that I should love her with my whole heart.' He did not pause any longer, but immediately approached the princess, with profound reverence. 'O beautiful lady,' said he, 'I cannot sufficiently thank Heaven for the favour it has done me, in presenting to my view so much loveliness; no greater happiness can possibly befall me than the privilege of offering you my most humble services. I entreat you to accept them; a lady like you cannot be in such a solitude as this without having need of assistance.'

"The Princess Giauharè replied, with an air of great melancholy: 'It is, indeed, a very unusual thing for a lady of my rank to find herself in the forlorn state I am now in. I am a princess, daughter of the King of Samandal, and am called Giauharè. I was sitting very quietly in my father's palace, when I heard suddenly a most dreadful noise. Some of my people came immediately to inform me that King Saleh, for I know not what reason, had stormed the palace, and seized on the king my father, after having overpowered those of his guard who had made resistance. I had barely time to escape, and to seek an asylum from his rage in this place.'

"On hearing this account from the princess, King Beder, in much confusion, silently reproached himself for having so abruptly quitted the queen his grandmother, without having waited for the arrival of more accurate information, than the report of a few terrified fugitives. Nevertheless he was delighted that the king his uncle had made himself master of the King of Samandal's person; for he felt sure that the latter, for the sake of regaining his liberty, would readily give his consent to the marriage of the princess. 'O adorable princess,' he replied, 'your concern is just; but it is easy to put an end to your anxiety, and to the captivity of the king your father. You will surely agree with me when you hear that my name is Beder, that I am King of Persia, and that King Saleh is my uncle. I can confidently assure you that he has no intention of seizing on the dominions of the king your father; nor has he any other object in view than to prevail with the monarch of Samandal to allow me the honour and happiness of being his son-in-law, by receiving you from his royal hand. I have already given you my heart on the mere report of your charms. Far from repenting of the gift, I now entreat you to receive it, and to be assured that my heart will never beat but for you. I presume to hope that you will not refuse me, and that you will even be of opinion that a king who has quitted his throne solely to make you an offer of his love, has some claims on your gratitude. Permit me, then, beautiful princess, to have the honour of presenting you to my uncle. When once the king your father has given his consent to our marriage, he will immediately be left master of his kingdom as before.'

"This declaration of King Beder did not produce the effect which he had expected from it. At the first view of him, the princess, struck with his fine figure, gallant air, and the finished address with which he had accosted her, could not behold him without rising sentiments of partiality; but when she learned from his own mouth that he had been the

KING BEDER TRANSFORMED INTO A BIRD.

cause of the bad treatment which the king her father had experienced, of the grief which she herself had endured, and of the terrors she had felt for her own safety; when she found it was through him that she had been obliged to take refuge on this desert island; when all these things presented themselves to her mind, she regarded him as an enemy, with whom she was bound to have no dealings. Whatever disposition she herself might have had to consent to the marriage, yet as she believed one of the strongest objections on the part of her father arose from the fact that King Beder was descended from a sovereign of the earth, she was resolved, in a matter so important to the dignity of their house, to submit entirely to the paternal will. She, nevertheless, concealed her resentment from King Beder, being anxious to escape out of his hands. Therefore she affected to regard him with kindness, and replied with all possible courtesy: 'O prince, you are the son of Queen Gulnarè, so celebrated for her extraordinary beauty. It gives me much pleasure to hear this, and I am delighted to see in you a prince so worthy of your beautiful mother. The king my father was very wrong to oppose himself so violently to our union; but let him once see you, and he will readily consent to render us both happy.' Having thus addressed him, she offered him her hand in token of friendship.

"King Beder now imagined himself at the very summit of human happiness. He extended his hand, and taking that of the princess, bent forward in order to kiss it respectfully. The princess did not allow him time. 'Thou wretch,' said she, motioning him away, and spitting in his face, 'quit the human form, and take the shape of a white bird with red beak and feet.' As she pronounced these words King Beder, to his infinite mortification and astonishment, was changed into a bird of the kind she had named. 'Take this bird,' said she to one of her women, 'and convey it to the barren island.' This island was nothing but a frightful rock, which offered not a single drop of water.

"The woman took the bird; but, as she turned away to fulfil the order of the Princess Giauharè, she could not but compassionate the hard fate of King Beder. 'It would be a great pity,' said she to herself, 'that a prince so worthy to live should die of hunger and thirst. The princess, who is of a kind and gentle disposition, will probably herself repent having given this cruel order, so soon as she shall be a little recovered from her present anger. It will be much better that I carry him to some place where he may die a natural death.' She accordingly conveyed the transformed prince to an inhabited island, and left him in a very pleasant country, planted with all kinds of fruit trees, and, watered by abundance of streams

"Let us now return to King Saleh. After he and his people had sought the Princess Giauharè in vain through every part of the palace, he ordered the King of Samandal to be secured in his own hall under a strong guard, and then, giving the necessary orders for the government of the kingdom during his absence, he returned to the queen, his mother, to report to her what had happened. On his arrival he immediately enquired after the king, his nephew, and learned, with the greatest surprise and alarm, that King Beder had disappeared. 'They came to inform us,' said the queen his mother, 'of the great danger you were in from the King of Samandal; and, while I was giving orders to send you fresh succour, either to defend you or to avenge your wrongs, your nephew disappeared. He must have been terrified to hear of the danger you were in, and perhaps, was even alarmed for his own safety while he remained with us.'

"This news filled King Saleh with deep grief. He now repented his own easiness of disposition in submitting to the wishes of King Beder, without having previously communicated with Queen Gulnarè concerning the affair. He sent every way in search of his nephew; but, notwithstanding all the diligence he could use, no one brought the least information concerning King Beder, and the pleasure he had experienced in having so far promoted a marriage which he considered as his own work, was changed into the most mortifying chagrin at a disappearance so disastrous and unexpected. In the meanwhile, till he should obtain some information, good or bad, he left his kingdom under the administration of the queen his mother, and went to preside in the capital of the King of Samandal, whom he continued to guard with much vigilance, though he showed him all the respect due to so illustrious a personage.

"The same day on which King Saleh had departed to return to the kingdom of Samandal, Queen Gulnarè arrived at the court of the queen her mother. Queen Gulnarè had suffered little concern on the first day of her son's absence; she readily imagined that, as sometimes happened, the ardour of the chase had carried him on further than he expected. But when she found that he returned not on the next day, nor on the third, she began to feel all the serious alarm which the feeling of maternal tenderness could not fail to inspire. This alarm was greatly increased when she learned from the officers who had accompanied King Beder, and who had been obliged to return after a long and fruitless search, that something disastrous must have happened to him and King Saleh; or that they were still in some retreat which the officers could not possibly discover. They had, they acknowledged, soon found the horses of the two kings, but with respect to the riders, notwithstanding all the diligence they could use, they could not gain the least information. The queen, upon hearing the whole of this report, judged it prudent to dissemble, and for the present to conceal her affliction; she ordered the officers once more to pursue their former route, and to make the strictest inquiry possible. In the meanwhile she had determined on the plan she herself would adopt; therefore, without speaking to any one, and telling her women that she wished to be alone, she threw herself into the sea in order to test the truth of a suspicion she had formed, that King Saleh had drawn away the King of Persia with him.

"This great queen would have been received by her mother with every expression of delight if the elder lady had not, from the first moment she saw her, suspected the cause of Queen Gulnarè's visit. 'My daughter,' said she, 'I am convinced that I am not the cause of your coming. You are come to obtain news concerning the king your son; and unhappily I have none to give you, but what will augment your grief as well as mine. I felt the greatest possible satisfaction when I saw the King of Persia arrive with his uncle; but I no sooner understood that he had departed without your knowledge than I sympathised very sincerely in the pain you would necessarily suffer.' She then gave her daughter an account of the zealous manner in which King Saleh had undertaken in person to solicit the hand of Princess Giauharè, and of what had happened in consequence, concluding with King Beder's departure. 'I have sent to seek him,' added she, 'and the king my son, who has just set off to take upon himself the government of the kingdom of Samandal, has also used all diligence on his part. Hitherto all has been without success; but let us hope that we shall see King Beder again when we least expect it.'

"The disconsolate Queen Gulnarè could not at first comfort herself with so feeble a hope; she looked upon the king, her dear son, as for ever lost, and wept most bitterly, imputing the whole blame to the king her brother. The queen her mother was very urgent to convince her that it behoved her in some measure to conceal her affliction. 'It is true,' said she, 'that the king your brother ought not to have spoken to you of this marriage with so little precaution, or even to have consented to bring away the king my grandson without your previous assent; but as it is not absolutely certain that the King of Persia has perished, you ought to put all means in practice to preserve his kingdom for him. Do not then waste your time here, but return immediately to your capital, where your presence is necessary. You will find it easy to keep matters in their present tranquil state, provided you proclaim that the King of Persia has left his dominions only for the purpose of honouring us with a visit.'

"These arguments were sufficiently weighty to convince Queen Gulnarè. She immediately prepared to follow the advice of her royal mother, of whom she took an affectionate leave. She came back to the palace of the capital of Persia before her absence had even been perceived. She immediately despatched some of her people to bring back the officers whom she had sent in search of the king her son, informing them that she knew where he was, and that he would return soon. She also caused this report to be spread through the whole city, while, aided by the first minister and the council, she carried on the business of government with the same tranquillity and order as if King Beder had been present.

"Let us now return to King Beder, whom the servant of the Princess Giauharè had carried and left in an island. This monarch was exceedingly astonished when he found himself alone, in the form of a bird. He felt so much the more unhappy at his transformation as he knew not where he was, nor in what part of the world the kingdom of Persia was situated. But even if he had known this, and had been sufficiently assured of the strength of his wings to hazard a journey across the seas that separated him from

Persia, and had been able eventually to regain his kingdom, what would he have derived from his success, but the misery of finding himself oppressed by the same evils he now experienced? No one would have known him to be the King of Persia, or even supposed him to have ever belonged to the human species! He must have remained an inhabitant of the fields as he was now, supporting life upon the same food as other birds of his kind, and passing his nights upon a tree.

"The king had remained for some days in this disconsolate state, when a peasant, who was very skilful in catching birds, came with his nets to the place where King Beder was, and was much delighted when he perceived a beautiful bird, of a species quite unknown to him, although he had for many years followed the sport in which he was now engaged. He employed all the address he could command, and took his measures so well, that they were at length crowned with success. Delighted to find the bird in his possession, which on account of its beauty and rarity, he esteemed of infinitely more value than the birds he usually caught, he secured it in a cage, and carried it to the city. As he carried it across the market a citizen stopped him, and asked what price he asked for the bird.

"Instead of replying to this question, the peasant, in his turn, desired to know of the citizen what he intended to do with the bird in case he bought it? 'My good man,' replied the citizen, 'what can you imagine I should do with it, but roast and eat it?' 'In that case,' said the peasant, 'you would think you had bought it dear were you to give me only the smallest piece of silver. I value it so highly that I would not part with it were you even to give me a piece of gold. I am now an old man, but never, since I can remember, have I seen a bird of this kind. I will go and make a present of it to the king; he will know its value better.'

"Instead of remaining in the market, the peasant made his way to the palace, and on his arrival there stopped in front of the royal apartment. The king was near a window, from whence he could see everything that took place in the court. As soon as he perceived the beautiful bird, he sent one of the officers of his eunuchs with an order to purchase it. The officer came to the peasant, and inquired what he wanted for the bird. 'If it is for his majesty,' replied the peasant, 'I entreat that he will allow me to present it to him.' The bird was brought to the king, who found it so singularly beautiful that he desired the officer to take ten pieces of gold back to the peasant, who retired perfectly content; whereupon the bird was put into a magnificent cage, and supplied with grain and water in the most costly vessels.

"The king, who was then ready to mount his horse for the purpose of going out hunting, and who had not had sufficient time thoroughly to examine the bird, desired on his return to have it again set before him. An officer brought the cage, which the king opened; and in order to view the bird more fully he took it in his hand. Surveying it with much admiration, he enquired of the officer if he had ever seen it eat. 'O my lord,' replied the officer, 'your majesty may perceive that the vessel containing its food is still full. I have not observed that it has even touched a seed.' The king then ordered them to give it various kinds of food, that it might choose what it most liked.

"The table was already spread, and they were serving up the dinner, when the king gave this order. The bird, as soon as they had brought the dishes, escaped from the king's hand, and clapping his wings flew upon the table, where he began to peck at the bread and the various meats, hopping from dish to dish. The king was so much surprised that he sent the officer of the eunuchs to beg that the queen would come and witness this astonishing sight. The officer conveyed the message to her majesty in as few words as possible, and the queen came immediately. But, as soon as she saw the bird, she covered her face with her veil, and wished to retire. The king, astonished at this action, the more so as there were only eunuchs and some of the queen's women who had followed her, present in the chamber, requested to know the reason of this unusual proceeding.

"'O my lord,' replied the queen, 'your majesty will not be astonished when you learn that this bird is not the creature you suppose, but a transformed man.' 'Lady,' replied the king, still more surprised than before, 'you are assuredly jesting with me. But

THE BIRDCATCHER SNARES KING BEDER.

you shall not persuade me that a bird is a man.' 'Heaven forbid, my lord, that I should mock or deceive your majesty; what I have the honour to tell you is perfectly true; and I assure you, further, that in yonder bird you behold Beder, King of Persia, son of the celebrated Queen Gulnarè, princess of one of the renowned kingdoms of the sea. He is nephew of King Saleh, the reigning monarch, and grandson of Queen Farasche, the mother of Queen Gulnarè and of King Saleh; and, moreover, it is the Princess Giauharè, daughter of the King of Samandal, who has thus metamorphosed him.' In order entirely to remove the king's doubts, she related to him how the Princess Giauharè had thus taken revenge for the injury which King Saleh had inflicted on the King of Samandal her father.

"The king was easily made to believe all the particulars the queen related to him of this extraordinary history, as he knew her to be more skilled in magic than almost any one the world had ever seen. To her wonderful knowledge of events he had frequently been indebted for early and important information, that had enabled him to counteract the hostile designs of neighbouring monarchs. Touched with compassion for the King of Persia, he entreated the queen with much importunity to dissolve the enchantment, by the force of which the unfortunate prince was imprisoned in so unworthy a form.

"The queen most readily consented. She said to the king: 'Will it please your majesty to take the trouble of retiring to your cabinet with the bird, and I will in a few moments make him appear before you in his own royal form; and I will engage that you shall find him highly worthy of your consideration.' The bird, who had ceased eating in order to attend to the conversation of the king and queen, did not give his majesty the trouble of taking him up, but walked at once into the cabinet, where the queen arrived soon after, with a vessel full of water in her hand. She pronounced over this vessel some words, which the king could not understand. Presently the water began to boil; she then immediately took some in her hand, and throwing it upon the bird, cried: 'By the virtue of the holy and mysterious words I have just pronounced, and in the name of the Creator of heaven and earth, who revives the dead, and supports the universe, quit your present form of a bird, and resume that which was given you by the great author of your existence.'

"The queen had scarcely finished these words when, instead of a bird, the king saw before him a young prince, of a very handsome and manly figure, and with a commanding air and noble countenance, which quite charmed him. King Beder immediately prostrated himself before him, returning thanks to Heaven, for the great kindness he had just received. Afterwards, in rising, he seized the hand of the monarch, and kissed it, in order to evince his gratitude. The king embraced him with every expression of delight, and assured him of the very high satisfaction he felt in seeing him. King Beder was desirous of thanking the queen also, but she had already retired to her apartment. The king then desired King Beder's company at table. When they had finished their repast, he further requested to know for what possible reason the Princess Giauharè could have been so cruel as to transform into a bird so amiable a prince. Upon this subject the King of Persia gave him full information. When he had finished his story the king, quite indignant at the conduct of the princess, began to speak of her in terms of severe censure. 'It was commendable,' said he, 'in the Princess of Samandal to feel indignant at the treatment which the king her father had received; but that she should carry her revenge to such an extreme against a prince who was in no respect to blame, betrays a malignity of temper which nothing can justify or excuse. But let us quit this unpleasant subject, and tell me if there is anything in which I can further serve you.'

"O gracious king,' replied King Beder, 'the obligation I am under to your majesty is so great that I ought to remain with you for the rest of my life to give you a proof of the gratitude I feel; but since your generosity is so great, may I presume to request that you will grant me a vessel to take me back to Persia, where I fear my absence, which has been already too long, may be the occasion of some disturbance. Indeed, the queen my mother, from whom I concealed my departure, may fall a victim to anxiety and grief in the painful uncertainty she must now be under with regard to my fate.'

"The king granted King Beder's request with all possible readiness. He gave orders for the immediate equipment of one of the best built and swiftest ships in his whole navy. The vessel was very soon completely rigged, and provided with sailors, soldiers, and all necessary stores. As soon as the wind became favourable King Beder embarked, having first taken leave of the king, and thanked him for his numerous favours.

"The ship set sail with a very favourable wind, and as the breeze continued propitious without any change for the space of ten days, they proceeded far on their voyage. But on the eleventh day from their departure the wind blew hard from an adverse quarter, and rapidly increased to a furious storm. The bark was, in consequence, not only driven out of its course, but was so violently tossed about by the fury of the tempest that all the masts at length gave way. The ship was now wholly at the mercy of the elements; it struck upon a rock, and was there dashed to pieces.

"The greater part of the crew instantly sank to the bottom; of the remainder, some confiding in the strength of their arms endeavoured to save themselves by swimming, while others trusted to a plank or a piece of the wreck. King Beder was amongst the latter class, and was carried about by waves and currents long doubtful as to his fate, till he at length perceived that he was near land, and not far from a city of magnificent appearance. He put forth all his remaining strength in the endeavour to reach the shore, and at length came so near it that he was able to touch the bottom with his feet. He immediately cast away the piece of wood which had rendered him such important service, and was making his way forward, in order to gain the dry land, when he was astonished to see running towards him from all quarters a number of horses, camels, mules, asses, oxen, cows, bulls, and other animals, which ranged themselves along the shore, and seemed determined to prevent his landing. He had the greatest possible difficulty to get the better of their opposition, and to open himself a passage. When he had at length succeeded in passing them, he chose for himself a position amongst the rocks where he was secured from further molestation, till he could in some measure recover his breath, and dry his clothes in the sun.

"When the prince attempted to advance towards the city he had again to encounter the same opposition from the animals. They seemed anxious to turn him from his purpose, and to make him understand that danger awaited him.

"King Beder, however, at length made his way into the city, where he saw a great number of handsome and spacious streets; but was much astonished at not meeting a single inhabitant. This marvellous solitude made him suspect that he had been opposed not without reason by the numerous animals who had done all in their power to induce him to fly the place. He ventured, however, to proceed; and observing that a number of shops stood open, was led to conclude that the city was not so utterly uninhabited as he had at first imagined. He approached one of these shops where a variety of fruits, displayed to much advantage, were exposed for sale, and accosted an old man, who was sitting there as if waiting for customers.

"The old man, who happened at that moment to be occupied, immediately raised his head. Seeing before him a youth of commanding aspect, he enquired, with an air which marked great surprise, from whence the stranger came, and what chance had brought him thither? King Beder informed him of his shipwreck in a very few words. Then the old man went on to enquire whether the young man had met no one in his way? The king replied: 'You are the first person I have seen, and I cannot in the least comprehend how or why so beautiful and magnificent a city as this should be deserted in the manner it appears to be.' 'Come in; do not stay an instant longer at the door,' replied the old man, 'lest some evil befall you. When I have time I will satisfy your curiosity, and tell you why it is necessary that you should take this precaution.'

"King Beder did not require to be invited twice; he entered, and took a seat near the old man, who, conceiving from what he had heard of the prince's misfortunes that his guest must be in great need of refreshment, offered him immediately such food as he thought would best restore his strength; and although King Beder had entreated him to explain for what reason he had urged him so earnestly to come in from the street, the old man would not say a word till the repast was finished; for he feared that what he had to communicate might prevent the king from eating with the appetite and relish he showed. At length, when he saw that King Beder would eat no more, he said: 'You ought to return thanks to Allah that you have arrived so far as my house without any unpleasant accident.' 'Why? For what reason?' returned King Beder, much alarmed.

"'I have to inform you,' replied the old man, 'that this city is called the City of

Enchantment, and that it is governed, not by a king, but by a queen. This queen is the most beautiful woman in the world, and is, moreover, an enchantress of such remarkable and dangerous powers that her equal has never been known. You will be convinced of this when I inform you that all the horses, mules, and other animals which you saw on your landing have once been men like you and me, but by her infernal art she has thus transformed them. All the handsome young men who, like yourself, approach the city, are intercepted by some of her vile emissaries. These men, with or without their consent, conduct them before the queen. She receives them in the most obliging manner possible; caresses them, regales them with every dainty, lodges them in most magnificent apartments, and endeavours to persuade them, by the attentions she lavishes on them, that she is really in love. She rarely fails to make them believe her; but she permits her unhappy dupes only for a short time to enjoy their imaginary good fortune; for at the end of forty days she changes every one of them into some beast or bird, as it pleases her fancy. You have mentioned to me the animals you encountered on the shore who endeavoured to prevent your landing and your approach hither. This was the only way in which they could try to make you comprehend the danger to which you were exposing yourself, and they did all that was in their power to persuade you to depart.'

"This narrative of the old man excited the most serious alarm in the mind of the king. 'Alas!' he cried, 'to what a condition am I reduced by my evil destiny! Scarcely delivered from one enchantment, which I look back upon with horror, I see myself exposed to another still more terrible.' The recollection of his former transformation gave him occasion to relate to the old man his history at length, to inform him of his birth and rank, of his love for the Princess of Samandal, and of the cruelty she had shown in transforming him into a bird at the moment of their first interview, and immediately after he had made a declaration of his passion.

"When the prince proceeded in his narrative to mention his good fortune in having found a queen who had dissolved his enchantment, and at the same time gave evident tokens of the apprehension he entertained of experiencing a similar or a worse evil, the old man became anxious to appease his guest's fears. 'Although,' he said, 'what I have told you of the sorceress queen, and of her cruel proceedings, is perfectly true, yet you need not in consequence give way to the great disquietude which seems at present to possess you. I am beloved throughout this whole city, and am not unknown to the queen herself. I may venture to add she has a great regard for me. You may therefore esteem it a piece of singular good fortune that you have addressed yourself to me rather than to any one else. You are in perfect safety in my house, where, if it be agreeable, I would recommend you to remain. I can give you the most positive assurance that while you are under my roof nothing will happen which can afford you the least occasion to question my good faith; nor need you here be under any restraint whatever.'

"King Beder thanked the old man for the hospitality he offered, and for the protection he so readily extended to him. He sat down at the entrance of the shop. So soon as he appeared there, his youth and his handsome appearance drew upon him the eyes of all that passed; many stopped to compliment the old man upon having obtained so well-looking a slave, for such they imagined King Beder to be. They appeared at the same time much surprised, as they could not imagine how so handsome a young man had escaped the vigilance of the queen. 'Do not imagine,' replied the old man, 'that the person you see is a slave; you know I am not sufficiently rich, or in a condition of life to keep a slave for myself. The young man is my nephew, the son of a deceased brother; and, as I have no children, I have invited him to come and live with me.' The bystanders heartily congratulated him on the satisfaction he must feel at his nephew's arrival; but at the same time could not refrain from expressing their fears that the queen would take the youth away. 'You know her,' said they, 'as well as we do, and cannot, after all the examples you have seen, be ignorant of the danger to which you expose yourself. How extreme will be your grief if she should treat him in the same manner as she has done so many others, whose melancholy fate we know too well.'

"'I am extremely obliged to you,' returned the old man, 'for the kind concern you have expressed, and for the interest you take in a matter so near my heart; and I return you my best thanks. I am, however, far from thinking that the queen will show the least unkindness to me, on whom she so frequently bestows the most signal marks of her favour. Should she hear of the young man's arrival, and be inclined to speak to me on the subject, I cannot but hope and believe that when she learns he is my nephew, she will think fit to leave him unmolested.'

"The old man was delighted to hear the praises which were bestowed on the King of Persia, for whom he was disposed to feel as much affection as if King Beder had really been his son. His friendship and good opinion seemed to increase every moment of the king's sojourn with him, as it gave fresh opportunity for the display of the young guest's many virtues. They had thus lived together about a month. King Beder was sitting one

KING BEDER WASHED ASHORE.

day, according to his custom, at the entrance of the shop, when he saw the retinue of Queen Labè, for thus was the royal enchantress called, approaching the house of the old man with great pomp. So soon as King Beder perceived the guards who were advancing before the queen, he rose and re-entered the shop, to enquire of the old man, his host, the meaning of this great procession. 'The queen is going past,' the old man replied, 'but remain where you are, and fear nothing.'

"The guards of Queen Labè, dressed in a very rich uniform of a purple colour, and very nobly mounted and equipped, marched four deep with their sabres drawn. They were about a thousand in number, and there was not amongst them a single officer who did not salute the old man in passing before his shop. These guards were followed by a thousand eunuchs dressed in brocaded silk, and better mounted than the guards; the officers of the eunuchs also bowed as they passed by the old man. After these came as many young ladies, all of exquisite and nearly equal beauty, richly dressed and decked with jewels. These marched on foot with a solemn step. Each of them had a short pike in her hand, and in their midst appeared Queen Labè, seated on a horse covered with the most brilliant diamonds, and with a saddle entirely of gold, and housings of most inestimable value. The young ladies also, in passing, saluted the old man; and the queen, struck by the handsome appearance of King Beder, stopped before the shop. 'O Abdallah,' said she, calling to the old man by his name, 'Tell me, I beg, does this comely and charming slave belong to you? Has he been long in your possession?'

"Before he replied to the queen, Abdallah prostrated himself to the earth, and when he arose from this posture of submission and respect, he said, 'O mighty queen, he is my nephew, the son of a brother who died not long since. As I have no children of my own I have adopted this nephew as my son, and have brought him hither to be my companion while I live, and to receive the little property I may leave at my death.'

"Queen Labè, who had never yet seen any man worthy to be compared with King Beder, and who at first sight conceived a violent affection for him, was thinking, after what she had heard, in what manner to address the old man, so as to prevail upon him to give up his nephew to her. 'My good father,' said she, 'will you not do me a favour by giving this young man to me? Do not refuse me I entreat you; I swear by the fire and by the light, I will make him so great and powerful, that he shall enjoy a more exalted fortune than has ever fallen to the lot of any mortal being. Even if I wished to inflict evil on the whole of the human race, he at least would be one whom I should anxiously preserve from ill. I have the fullest confidence that you will comply with my request, relying more on the friendship which I know you have for me, than on the esteem which I entertain and always have entertained for yourself.'

"'O Lady,' replied the good Abdallah, 'I am greatly indebted to your majesty for all your goodness to me, and for the honour you wish to confer on my nephew. He is not worthy to approach so great a queen as yourself: may it please your majesty, therefore, to abandon your kind intentions in his favour.'

"'Abdallah,' replied the queen, 'I had flattered myself that you loved me more than it appears you do. I could never believe you would have given me so evident a proof of the slight regard in which you hold me; but I again swear by the fire, and by the light, and by everything I hold most sacred in my religion, that I will not go my way till I have subdued your opposition. I fully understand what it is that you fear on his behalf, but I give you my solemn promise that you shall not have the least cause to repent having obliged me in an affair which I feel is important to my happiness.'

"Old Abdallah was inexpressibly embarrassed, both on his own account and on that of King Beder, but he felt himself compelled to yield to the solicitation of the queen. 'Gracious mistress,' he replied, 'I should be very sorry to give your majesty the least occasion to imagine that I am wanting in the respect I owe you, or that I lack inclination or zeal to do everything in my power that may contribute to your pleasure. I put entire reliance on your word; and you will, I doubt not, keep it faithfully. I only entreat that you will not confer on my nephew the high good fortune you intend for him till you pass this way again.' 'That then will be to-morrow,' replied the queen, and as she said these words she bowed to Abdallah to express the obligation she was under. She then continued her way towards her palace.

"When Queen Labè with all her pompous retinue had passed by, the good Abdallah said to King Beder, 'O my son,'—for thus he was accustomed to address the king, that he might not be led inadvertently, when speaking of him in public, to betray the prince's rank—'O my son, I was not able, as you yourself must acknowledge, to refuse the queen what she solicited with so much earnestness without incurring the risk of her displeasure, and being exposed in consequence to some open or secret violence, which, by the aid of magic, she would find means of effecting. Probably, to gratify her spirit of revenge against me as well as you, she would bring upon you some evil more dreadful than any she has yet inflicted on those unhappy sufferers of whom I have informed you. I have some reason to believe, from the especial regard she has for me, that she will not fail in her promise to use you well. You must have yourself remarked from the conduct of her whole court, who were all forward to pay me honour, that I have some amount of influence with her. She would, indeed, be the most infamous of beings if she deceived me. She shall not cheat me with impunity. If she plays me false, I shall find a way of being revenged.'

"These assurances appeared too vague to have much effect in tranquillising the mind of King Beder. 'After all that you have told me of the wicked actions of this queen,' he replied, 'I cannot conceal from you with what fear and repugnance I approach her. I might perhaps disregard all that you have said to me, and suffer myself to be dazzled by the splendour and magnificence with which she is surrounded, did I not already know by experience what it is to be at the mercy of a magician. The condition to which I was reduced through enchantment by the Princess Giauharè, and from which I seem to have been delivered only to be brought again almost instantly into a similar state, makes me look forward to my fate with horror.' Tears now choked his utterance, and expressed by their abundance his extreme grief at the fatal necessity he was under of placing himself in the power of Queen Labè.

"'My son,' said old Abdallah, 'do not be thus cast down; I will confess to you that it would be folly to put any great faith in the promises or even the oath of so wicked a queen as Labè. I wish you, however, to know, that she is not able to exert the least authority over me. She is well aware of this power, and it is for this reason, more than for any real affection, that she confers on me so many marks of favour. I shall find means to prevent her from doing you the least injury, should she be so perfidious as to harbour the intention; you may trust to me, and provided you follow exactly the advice I shall give you before I resign you to her, you may rest fully satisfied that she will have no more power over you than she has over me.'

"The sorceress queen appeared punctually the next day in front of the shop of Abdallah, with the same pomp she had displayed on the preceding morning. The old man attended her with the greatest respect. She said to him when she stopped, 'O my good father, you may judge of the impatience I feel to have the pleasure of your nephew's company by my punctuality in appearing before you to claim the performance of your promise. I know that you are a man of your word, and I cannot believe that you have changed your intention.'

"Abdallah, who had prostrated himself to the earth as soon as he saw the queen approaching, rose when she ceased speaking; and, as he was anxious that no one should hear what he had to say to her, advanced respectfully near to her horse's head, and addressed to her these words in a low tone of voice: 'Most potent queen, I am convinced that your majesty will not take amiss the reluctance I yesterday expressed at parting with my nephew; you will readily understand the motive which influenced me. To-day I am all submission to your pleasure, and resign him to your majesty with perfect good will; but I entreat you to have the goodness to lay aside all the power of the magic art which you possess in such perfection. I look upon my nephew as if he were my son; and your majesty would plunge me in the deepest despair if you were to treat him unworthily, or in any way to swerve from the gracious promises you have given me.'

"'I most willingly repeat those promises,' replied the queen, 'and I again assure you by the same oath I took yesterday, that both you and he will have abundant reason to be satisfied with me. I see very well,' added she, 'that you do not sufficiently know me; you have seen me at present only in an unfavourable light; but, if I find your nephew worthy of my friendship, I shall be happy to convince you that I am not unworthy of his.' Having finished this speech she permitted King Beder, who had approached with old Abdallah, to survey her incomparable beauty, with which, however, he was but little affected. For he said to himself, 'Beauty alone is not sufficient. The conduct should be as pure as the features are beautiful.'

"While King Beder was making these reflections with his eyes fixed upon the queen, the venerable Abdallah turned towards him, and having taken him by the hand, presented him to her majesty: 'Mighty queen,' said he, 'I presume to entreat once more that you will not forget this young man is my nephew; and that you will allow him sometimes to come and see me.' The queen promised compliance; and to assure Abdallah of her gratitude, made him a present of a purse which she had ordered to be brought with her, containing a thousand pieces of gold. He at first declined to receive it, but she insisted so earnestly that he should accept it, that he could no longer refuse. She had ordered a horse as richly caparisoned as her own to be brought for the King of Persia. It was brought to him, and while he was putting his foot in the stirrup, the queen said to Abdallah, 'I forgot to enquire of you your nephew's name.' As soon as he had answered that he was called Beder, 'This is a strange mistake,' she said, 'he certainly ought to have been named Schems.' By this she meant: instead of the 'Full Moon,' he should have been called 'The Sun.'

"As soon as King Beder had mounted the horse provided for him, he was going to take his place behind the queen, but she obliged him to ride on her left hand, and desired that he would keep by her side. She then again turned to Abdallah, and taking leave of him with a courteous inclination of her head, proceeded on her way.

"Instead of remarking in the countenance of the people a certain satisfaction accompanied with respect, at the sight of their sovereign, King Beder perceived on the contrary that they beheld her with scorn, and that many of them even uttered secret imprecations against her. 'The sorceress,' said one, 'has found a new subject on which to exercise her malice; will Heaven never deliver the world from her tyranny?' 'Unhappy stranger,' muttered another, 'you are completely deceived if you imagine that your good fortune will be of long continuance; you are raised so high only that your fall may be the deeper.' These words were sufficient to convince the king that Abdallah had painted the character of the queen in true colours; but as he could no longer depend upon his venerable friend to extricate him from his danger, he resigned himself to Providence, trusting wholly to the powers above to decide his fate.

"The sorceress queen arrived at her palace. She alighted from her horse, and obliged King Beder to give her his hand. Thus, accompanied by her women and the officers of her eunuchs, she entered her splendid abode. She herself showed King Beder all the apartments, which were decorated with massive gold and precious stones, and contained furniture of wonderful magnificence. When she had conducted him into her cabinet she proceeded with him to a balcony, from whence she pointed out to him a garden of enchanting beauty. King Beder praised everything he saw with much intelligent discrimination, but at the same time he was careful to raise no doubt in the queen's mind as to his being really the nephew of old Abdallah. They conversed on a variety of indifferent subjects, till an attendant came to announce to her majesty that dinner was ready.

"The queen and King Beder immediately rose, and proceeded to the dining-room, where the table and all the dishes were of solid gold. They began to eat, but drank nothing till just before the dessert was served, when the queen ordered her cup to be filled with some excellent wine, which she drank off to the health of King Beder. Then, holding the cup in her hand, she desired it might be again filled, and presented it to the king, who received it with every mark of respect, and, by a very low inclination of his head, humbly expressed that he would drink her health in return.

"Ten women belonging to the queen now entered with musical instruments, with which they accompanied their voices, thus forming a most agreeable concert; the united charms of wine and music passed the time during a great part of the night. At length, in consequence of their repeated libations, they began both of them to be considerably elated, so much so, that King Beder forgot insensibly that the queen was a magician, and looked upon her only as the most beautiful woman in the world. As soon as the queen perceived that she had wrought him up to the desired point, she made a sign to her eunuchs and women to retire. She then remained for a considerable time alone with her guest in converse.

"The next day the queen and King Beder went to the bath; upon the king's quitting it, the women who were to wait upon him, presented him with linen of a snowy

QUEEN LABE UNVEILS BEFORE KING BEDER.

whiteness and with a dress of unequalled magnificence. The queen also attired herself much more splendidly than on the preceding day, and having summoned the king, they went together to her apartment, where they partook of an excellent repast; after which they passed the day most agreeably, sometimes sauntering in the garden, at other times occupying themselves in some interesting amusement.

"In this manner Queen Labè amused and regaled King Beder for the space of forty days, according to her usual mode of treating her admirers. On the night of the fortieth, while they were on a sofa together, and when she believed King Beder was asleep, she rose without making any noise. The king, who was only dozing, roused himself, and imagining that something extraordinary was going forward, feigned himself asleep, while he paid strict attention to her proceedings. As soon as she had risen she opened a casket, from whence she drew a box full of a yellow powder. She took some of this powder, and with it laid a train across the chamber. Thereupon the powder was transformed into a stream of transparent water, to the great astonishment of King Beder. He trembled with fear, and became more anxious than ever to keep up the appearance of deep slumber, that the queen might not discover that he was awake.

"Queen Labè took some of the water of this stream in a vessel and poured it into a basin, in which there was some flour; of this flour she made a paste, which she continued to knead for a long time. She afterwards added to it certain drugs, taken from different boxes, and thus she made a cake, which she put into a covered baking pan. As she had been very careful to provide a good fire, she drew from it some of the burning coals, on which she placed the baking pan; and, while the cake was preparing, she returned the vessels and boxes that had been used to their places. The stream, which was still flowing in the middle of the chamber, disappeared in a moment at certain words she pronounced. When the cake was ready she removed it from the coals and conveyed it to a closet; and then returned to the sofa, where King Beder had so well dissembled that she had not the least suspicion of his being acquainted with anything that had passed.

"Absorbed in luxury and pleasure, the young king had forgotten the good old Abdallah, his host, from the time he quitted him: he now called him to remembrance, and began to think, after what he had seen of Queen Labè's conduct during the night, that he had need of the old man's counsel. As soon as he rose he expressed to the queen a desire to visit Abdallah, and entreated her to give him permission to go. 'What! my dear Beder,' replied the queen, 'are you already tired not only of dwelling in this superb palace, where I should imagine your time passed in continual delight, but also of the company of a queen who loves you passionately, and who has given you abundant proofs of her love?'

"'O great queen,' replied King Beder, 'how can I be tired of the many and great favours which your majesty has had the goodness to heap upon me! Far from it, gracious lady; I ask leave to pay this visit only to give an account to my uncle of the infinite obligations I owe your majesty, and to convince him that he is not forgotten. I will not deny that the latter motive has the greater weight with me; for I know that Abdallah loves me with the greatest tenderness; and as forty days have elapsed since he has seen me, I do not wish, by deferring any longer to visit him, to give him occasion to think that I am insensible to his kindness.' 'Go, then,' replied the queen, 'I wish you to visit him; but do not delay your return, for you must remember that I am not able to live without you.' She then ordered a horse to be richly caparisoned, and King Beder mounted it and rode away.

"The good Abdallah was delighted to behold King Beder again. Without thinking of the rank of his guest he tenderly embraced him. The king embraced him in return, so that no one could possibly suspect that he was not the old man's nephew. When they were seated Abdallah said to the king: 'Tell me how goes it with you, and how have you fared with that faithless woman, that sorceress?'

"King Beder replied: 'I have the satisfaction to tell you that hitherto she has shown for me all imaginable regard, and has endeavoured by every means and with all possible earnestness to persuade me that she is entirely devoted to me. I have, however, this last night observed a circumstance which leads me to suspect that the whole of her conduct has been dictated by profound dissimulation. She believed that I was sound asleep, though it happened that I was awake; then I saw her steal from my side with the greatest precaution. This conduct of hers excited my suspicion; instead, therefore, of giving way again to sleep, I merely feigned slumber and began to observe her very carefully.' He proceeded with his story, and related to Abdallah how, and with what mystic ceremonies he had seen the queen prepare the cake, and added in conclusion, 'Till this time I will confess I had nearly forgotten you, and all the cautions you gave me on the subject of Queen Labè's malice; but this strange action made me fear that she would violate the promises she had given you, and the oaths she so solemnly made. I immediately thought of you, and esteem myself happy that I have been permitted to see you, with far less opposition on her part than I had ventured to expect.'

"'You have judged rightly,' replied old Abdallah, with a smile, which sufficiently expressed that he himself had never imagined that the queen would pursue a different conduct. 'Nothing will ever produce amendment in this perfidious woman. But fear nothing; I know a way to make the evil recoil on herself which she intends to inflict upon you. The suspicion you have conceived was extremely fortunate and happy, and you could not possibly have done better than to communicate your observations to me. She does not retain her lovers more than forty days, and, instead of dismissing them in a handsome manner, changes them into animals, with which she furnishes her forests, parks, and the country in general; but I yesterday took some necessary measures to prevent her from serving you in the same manner. The earth has too long endured this monster; it is high time that she should meet the fate she deserves.'

"As he said these words Abdallah put into the hands of King Beder two cakes, which he desired him to keep carefully, and to use in the way he was going to point out. 'You have told me,' continued he, 'that the sorceress has this very night prepared a cake. You may be certain she intends it for you; but take especial care not to taste it. You must, however, take a piece when she offers it; but instead of putting it in your mouth, substitute, without her perceiving it, one of those which I have given you, and eat it instead of Queen Labè's. When she believes that you have swallowed some of her cake she will endeavour to transform you into some animal; and, failing in her design, will attempt to turn the whole affair into a jest, as if she had only done it in sport, in order to frighten you, while she will in her heart be exceedingly chagrined, and will impute her failure to some defect in the composition of her cake. With respect to the second cake which I have given you, you must make her a present of it, and press her to eat it; this she will do to remove, by a seeming reliance on you, any suspicions you may have formed of her conduct. When she has eaten some of this cake of yours, take a little water in the hollow of your hand, and throwing it in her face, address her in these words: *Quit this present form, and take that of*—adding the name of any animal you please. When you have proceeded thus far come to me with the transformed queen, and I will instruct you concerning your further proceedings.'

"King Beder signified to the old man, in the warmest terms, how much he felt obliged to him for the interest this good protector took in his behalf, and for the kind endeavours he used to protect him from the snares of the wicked and cruel sorceress. They continued in conversation for a short time, and then King Beder bade farewell to Abdallah, and returned to the palace. On his arrival he was informed that Queen Labè was waiting for him in the garden with the greatest impatience. He went to seek her. As soon as she saw him she approached with extreme eagerness. 'My dear Beder,' said she, 'that is a true saying which tells us that the absence of a beloved object best enables us to know the extent and force of our passion. I have had no enjoyment while you were away from me. It appears to me as if years had rolled tediously by since I saw you last; if you had deferred your return any longer I should have prepared to come and seek you myself.'

"'O lady,' replied King Beder, 'I can assure your majesty that my impatience to return has been great indeed; but I could not refuse to converse for a few minutes with an uncle who loves me, and who had not seen me for a long time. He wished me to stay, but I have torn myself from his embraces, to come where love invites; and have been content with a single cake, which I have brought away from a collation he had prepared on my account.' King Beder had wrapped up one of the two cakes in a rich handkerchief, and when he had unfolded it he presented the cake to the queen, and added, 'This is the cake, lady; I entreat that you will partake of it.'

"'I accept it,' said the queen, 'with all my heart, and shall eat of it with pleasure, both for your sake and for that of my good friend your uncle; but I wish, first, that you will oblige me by eating a piece of this, which I have made in your absence.' 'O beautiful queen,' said King Beder, receiving it with every mark of respect, 'from hands such as your majesty's nothing can come but what is excellent; I am unable to express the gratitude I feel for the favour you show me.'

"King Beder very cleverly substituted for the cake the queen had produced the second cake he had received from Abdallah, of which he broke off a piece, which he conveyed to his mouth. 'Ah, queen,' he exclaimed as he ate it, 'I have never tasted anything so exquisite.' As they were at the time near a fountain that threw up a sparkling jet of water, the sorceress, who perceived that he had swallowed the piece of cake and was proceeding to eat more, took some water in the hollow of her hand, and throwing it in his face, cried: 'Wretch, quit thy present form of a man, and take that of a despicable, lean, halting, one-eyed horse.'

"These words produced no effect, to the great astonishment of the sorceress, who saw before her King Beder still retaining the form of a man, but giving signs of extreme fear. The colour flew into her cheeks from disappointment; when, however, she perceived that she had failed in her purpose, she quickly said: 'My dear Beder, be calm; I have no intention of doing you harm; what I have just done, which seems to have alarmed you, was only to see how you would behave. Should I not be the most abandoned and execrable of women if I could be guilty of so base an action? if I could break the oaths I have taken, and nullify the proofs of love I have given you?'

"'Most potent queen,' replied King Beder, 'however convinced I may be that your majesty has no intention but to divert yourself, I cannot suppress a feeling of surprise. For who could hear without emotion words that seem capable of effecting so strange and terrible a result? But, lady, let us pursue this subject no farther; and since I have eaten of your cake, do me the favour now to taste of mine.'

"Queen Labè, who had no better way of justifying herself than by giving this mark of her confidence in the King of Persia, broke off a small piece of the cake, and ate it. The instant she had swallowed it she appeared exceedingly troubled, and stood rigid and motionless. King Beder lost not a moment; he took some water from the fountain and throwing it in her face he exclaimed: 'Abominable enchantress, quit thy present form, and be changed into that of a mare.'

"At the same instant Queen Labè became transformed into a very handsome mare: and so great was her confusion and sorrow at seeing herself thus enchanted, that she shed abundance of tears. She bent down her head to the feet of King Beder, as if to move him with compassion; but even if he had been disposed to relent, it was not in his power to alter the change he had made. He led the mare to the stable of the palace, where he put her into the hands of a groom to saddle and bridle her; but of all the bridles which the groom tried not one was found that would suit her. He then ordered two horses to be got ready, one for himself and one for the groom, whom he commanded to follow him to the house of Abdallah, leading the mare by a halter.

"Abdallah perceived King Beder and the mare approaching from a distance, and doubted not but that the King of Persia had done as he had recommended him. 'O cursed sorceress,' said he to himself, in a transport of delight, 'Heaven at length has chastised you as you deserve.' King Beder alighted immediately, and entered into the shop of Abdallah, whom he cordially embraced, thanking him for the many important services the good old man had rendered him. He gave an account of the events that had just taken place, and observed to his old friend that he could find no bridle proper for the mare. Abdallah, who had them for horses of every sort, bridled the mare himself: and as soon as King Beder had sent away the groom with the two horses, he said: 'O king, you have no occasion to stop any longer in this place; mount your mare and return to your kingdom. The only thing

I have to recommend to your attention is that, in case you are disposed to part with your mare, you take especial care to give her up with the bridle on her.' King Beder promised that he would not forget this injunction, and after they had bidden each other adieu, he departed.

"Directly he was out of the city the young King of Persia, full of joy at having escaped so great a danger, and at seeing the sorceress in his power, became negligent, not reflecting that he had still great need of circumspection. Three days after his departure

ABDULLAH GIVES KING BEDER THE CAKE.

he arrived at a large city. As he passed through the suburbs he was met by an old man of respectable appearance, who was going on foot to his retreat in the country. 'O friend,' says the old man, addressing him, 'may I ask from whence you come?' The king stopped to reply; and while the old man went on to ask more questions, an elderly woman approached, who likewise, when she came up to them, stopped, and looking upon the mare, began to weep bitterly.

"King Beder and the old man suspended their conversation to observe the woman, and King Beder asked her what was the occasion of her grief. 'O my master,' said she, 'your mare so perfectly resembles one lately belonging to my son, and which, for his sake, I yet regret, that I should believe her to be the very same were his mare still alive. Sell her to me,' I entreat you. I will pay you whatever you ask, and think myself under great obligation to you.'

"'My good mother,' replied King Beder, 'I am very sorry it is not in my power to grant your request—my mare is not to be sold.' 'Ah! good sir,' exclaimed the old woman, 'I beseech you in the name of Heaven not to refuse me; both I and my son will die with grief if you deny us this favour.' 'My good mother,' remonstrated King Beder, 'I should grant your request very willingly if I had any intention of parting with so good a mare; but even if this were the case, I do not believe that you would choose to give a thousand pieces of gold for her, and I certainly should not value her at less.' 'Why should I not give it?' said the old woman; 'if you will only sell the mare I am ready at this moment to pay the money.'

"Observing that the old woman was dressed very meanly, King Beder did not imagine that she could be in circumstances to raise a thousand pieces of gold. To try, therefore, if she would keep to the bargain, he said, 'Give me the money, and the mare is yours.' Immediately the old woman untied a purse, which was fastened round her waist, and presenting it to him, said: 'Take the trouble to dismount, and we will see whether this purse contains the sum required. If it does not I shall soon be able to provide the rest; my house is not far off.'

"The astonishment of King Beder when he saw the purse was very great: 'My good mother,' said he, 'do not you see that what I have been saying was merely meant as a joke; I repeat to you that my mare is not to be sold.'

"The old man, who had listened to the whole conversation, now put in his word: 'My son,' said he to King Beder, 'it is right that you should be made acquainted with a matter of which I perceive you are ignorant. No man is permitted in this city to tell any kind of falsehood whatever under pain of death. It is absolutely necessary, therefore, that you should take this good woman's money, and give up your mare, since the price you asked has been offered to you. You will do better to yield the point quietly than to expose yourself to the evil which may rise from your refusal.'

"Angry with himself for having thus inconsiderately betrayed his own interests, King Beder dismounted from his mare with deep regret. The old woman was ready in an instant to seize the bridle and strip it off; she was, if possible, still more brisk in possessing herself of some water from a stream that flowed in the middle of the street; and taking some drops in her hand she threw it on the mare, pronouncing these words: 'My daughter, quit this form, which does not belong to you, and re-assume your own.' The change was made in an instant; and King Beder, who fainted away as soon as Queen Labè again appeared before him, would have fallen to the ground if the old man had not supported him.

"The old woman, who was the mother of Queen Labè, and who had instructed her in all the secrets of magic, at the queen's recovery embraced her daughter in the fulness of her joy. Thereupon she whistled; and there appeared a genie of hideous shape, and of truly gigantic size. The genie took King Beder immediately upon one arm, while he embraced the old woman and the sorceress queen with the other, and in a few moments transported them to the palace of Queen Labè, in the City of Enchantments.

"When they were once again in the palace Queen Labè began to reproach King Beder with the air of a fury, 'Ungrateful wretch,' said she, 'is it thus that your unworthy uncle and you have given proofs of you gratitude after all that I have done for you? I will reward you both as you deserve.' She paused no longer, but taking some water in her hand, and throwing it upon his face, she cried: 'Quit thy present form, and take that of a filthy owl.' The change instantly took place when she commanded one of her women 'to confine the hateful creature in a cage, and to give it nothing to eat or drink.'

"The woman took the cage; but in opposition to the commands of the queen, placed in it both food and water; being, moreover, a friend of old Abdallah, she sent secretly to inform him of the queen's conduct in regard to his nephew, and of her intention to destroy both uncle and nephew. She gave him this warning that he might use the necessary precautions and provide for his own safety.

"Abdallah saw immediately that the time was past for keeping any terms with Queen Labè. He therefore whistled in a particular manner, and immediately an enormous genie with four wings appeared before him, and desired to know for what purpose he was called. 'O Lightning!' said Abdallah, for thus was the genie named, 'It is our present business to preserve the life of King Beder, the son of Queen Gulnarè. Go to the palace of the sorceress and transport from thence instantly to the capital of Persia that compassionate woman to whom she has given charge of the cage, in order that Queen Gulnarè may be informed of the danger to which her son is exposed, and of the necessity of sending him prompt assistance. Take care not to alarm Queen Gulnarè when you present yourself before her, and tell her from me what I wish her to do.'

"Lightning disappeared, and in an instant arrived at the palace of the sorceress. He gave the necessary instructions to the woman, and conveying her aloft through the air, transported her to the capital of Persia, where he placed her upon a terraced roof which communicated with the apartment of Queen Gulnarè. The woman descended the staircase, which led to this apartment, where she found Queen Gulnarè and Queen Farachè her mother, conversing upon the subject of their mutual affliction. She saluted the two queens with most profound reverence, and then gave such an account of King Beder as made them instantly perceive the necessity of sending him immediate succour.

"Queen Gulnarè was so transported with joy at the news she heard that she rose from the place where she sat and cordially embraced the worthy messenger, to express how much she was obliged by the service she had received. Immediately after this she left her apartment, and commanded the trumpets, drums, and other instruments of the palace to be sounded, to announce to the whole city that the King of Persia would soon return. She then sought out King Saleh her brother, whom Queen Farachè had already brought there by means of an incantation she frequently practised. 'O brother,' said she, to him, 'the king your nephew, my dear son, is in the City of Enchantments, under the power of Queen Labè. It is your business and mine to go and deliver him: there is no time to be lost.'

"From his marine dominions King Saleh assembled a powerful army, which soon arose from the sea. He called also to his assistance the genie, his allies, who appeared with another army more numerous than his own. When these two forces had joined, he put himself at their head, with Queen Farachè, Queen Gulnarè, and the princesses, who were desirous to take part in the action. They mounted into the air, and very soon descended on the palace in the City of Enchantments, where the sorceress queen, her mother, and all the worshippers of fire were destroyed in the twinkling of an eye.

"Queen Gulnarè had ordered that the woman of Queen Labè, who had arrived with the information of King Beder's calamitous change and imprisonment, should accompany her; and she gave her a strict charge that in the midst of the battle and confusion she should have no object whatever in view but to secure the cage, and bring it to Queen Gulnarè. This order was faithfully executed. The queen opened the cage herself, and drew thence the owl, on whom she threw some water which she had caused to be brought: 'Oh, my dear son,' said she, 'quit this strange form, and re-assume thy natural figure of a man.'

"In the same moment the owl disappeared, and the queen saw before her King Beder her son, whom she embraced immediately in a transport of delight. What she was unable to say in words from the emotion which overcame her was expressed by abundance of tears. She could not prevail on herself to let her son go, and Queen Farachè was obliged to tear him from her arms to embrace him in her turn. When these ladies could bear to part with him, he was warmly welcomed by the king his uncle, and by the princesses his relations.

"The first care of Queen Gulnarè was to make inquiry after old Abdallah, to whom she was indebted for the King of Persia's restoration. As soon as the old man was conducted to her, she said: 'The obligation I am under to you is so great, that there is nothing I am not ready to do to express my gratitude; tell me how I can serve you most to your satisfaction, and be assured I shall not refuse your request.' 'O great queen,' he replied, 'if the lady whom I sent to your majesty will freely and willingly consent to accept in marriage the man who now offers himself to her, and if the King of Persia will permit me to remain at his court, I do now with my whole heart devote the remainder of my life to his service.' Queen Gulnarè immediately turned towards the lady, whose modest blushes and embarrassed demeanour fully expressed that she felt willing to accede to the proposal; Queen Gulnarè, therefore, joined their hands together, while she and the King of Persia assured them both of future protection and favour.

"This marriage gave the King of Persia an opportunity to enlarge on the subject; addressing himself, therefore, to the queen his mother, he said, smiling, 'O queen, I am delighted with the marriage you have just made; but there is another match which demands your attention.' Queen Gulnarè did not immediately understand of what marriage he was speaking, but a moment's reflection showed her the full meaning of his speech. She replied, 'You allude to your own marriage; I consent to it most willingly.' She immediately addressed herself to the marine subjects of the king her brother, and to the genii who were present. 'Go,' said she, 'and examine all the palaces of the sea and of the earth, and bring us information of the most beautiful princess, and the one most worthy of the king, my son, that you can anywhere find.'

"'O honoured lady,' replied King Beder, 'It will be useless to take this trouble. Doubtless you know already that I have given my heart to the Princess of Samandal, upon the simple statement of her beauty; I have seen her and do not repent of the choice I have made. Indeed, neither upon the earth nor under the sea can there possibly exist a princess who deserves to be put in comparison with her. Upon the declaration I made of myself and my passion, she certainly behaved to me in a way that would have extinguished the flame of a love less ardent than mine. She was, however, not to be blamed; she could not without failing in her filial duty, and disregarding the honour of her family, treat me with less rigour after she had discovered that I, however innocently, was the cause of the imprisonment of the king her father. It may be that by this time the King of Samandal has altered his sentiments, and that the princess will no longer refuse me her heart and hand when she has obtained the sanction of her royal parent.'

"'O my son,' replied Queen Gulnarè, 'if there be in the world no one but the Princess Giauharè who can make you happy, it is not my intention to oppose your union if it is possible for you to obtain her. The king your uncle has only to bring the King of Samandal hither, and we shall soon learn if he is not more amenable to reason than formerly.'

"Although the King of Samandal had been strictly guarded during his captivity by King Saleh's orders, he had all the time been treated with so much attention that his haughty spirit was much subdued, and he condescended to live on easy terms with the officers who surrounded him. King Saleh ordered a chafing-dish full of coals to be brought him, upon which he threw a certain composition, at the same time pronouncing some mysterious words. As soon as the smoke began to ascend the whole palace trembled, when immediately the King of Samandal appeared with the officers of King Saleh who attended him. The King of Persia threw himself instantly at the King of Samandal's feet, and remained with his knee upon the ground: 'O mighty monarch,' said he, 'it is no longer King Saleh who solicits of your majesty to honour the King of Persia with your alliance, it is the King of Persia himself who now entreats you to grant that great favour, and who cannot believe that you wish to be the death of a king who can live no longer if he be denied the possession of the amiable Princess Giauharè.'

"The King of Samandal no longer allowed the King of Persia to remain kneeling at his feet. He embraced him and besought him to rise. 'O king,' said he, 'I should be extremely sorry to contribute in the least to the death of so worthy a monarch. If it be true that a life so precious can only be preserved by an union with my daughter, rise, she is yours. She has always been perfectly obedient to my will, and I do not apprehend that she will now oppose me.' He then charged one of his own officers, who by King Saleh's desire had remained about his person, to go in search of the Princess Giauharè, and to bring her to them instantly.

"The Princess Giauharè had all this time remained on the island where the King of Persia had met her. The officer found her there, and was soon seen returning accompanied by her and her women. The King of Samandal embraced the princess, and said, 'O my daughter, I have given you a husband. The King of Persia, whom you see before you, is the most accomplished monarch in the whole universe; the preference he gives you above all other princesses obliges both you and me to give him every token of our gratitude.'

"'O my father,' returned the Princess Giauharè, 'your majesty knows that I have never failed in the obedience I owe to all your commands. I am ready to comply in the present instance; and only hope that the King of Persia will forget the bad treatment he has received from me. He is, I believe, sufficiently generous to impute it to its real cause, the necessity of showing my duty to you.'

"The nuptials were celebrated in the palace of the City of Enchantments with the greater pomp, as all the victims of the sorceress queen, who had regained their original form from the moment of her death, and who came to return their thanks to the King of Persia, Queen Gulnarè and King Saleh, attended on the occasion. They were all sons of kings, or persons of very high rank.

"After this time King Saleh conducted the King of Samandal back to his own dominions, and reinstated him in the full possession of his kingdom. The King of Persia had attained the summit of his wishes. He returned to the capital of Persia, accompanied by Queen Gulnarè, Queen Farachè, and the princesses; the latter, with Queen Farachè, remained there until King Saleh came back to them and took them home to his dominions under the sea.

## THE HISTORY OF GANEM, SON OF ABOU AIBOU, THE SLAVE OF LOVE.

MIGHTY king, said Scheherazadè to the Sultan of the Indies, there lived formerly at Damascus a merchant, who by his industry and attention to business, had amassed a large fortune, on which he lived in a very respectable way. His name was Abou Aibou, and he had a son and a daughter. The son was originally called Ganem, but afterwards acquired the name of the Slave of Love. He was very handsome, and his understanding, which was naturally good, had been cultivated by the best masters, whom his father had been careful to provide for his education. The daughter was called Alcolomb, that is, "subduer of hearts," because she was so very beautiful, that all who saw her became enamoured of her charms.

"Abou Aibou died, and left immense riches. A hundred bales of brocade and other rich silks, which were found in his warehouse, formed but a small part of his wealth. These bales were all ready packed, and upon each of them was written in large characters, *For Bagdad.*

"At that time Mohammed, surnamed Zinebi, the son of Soliman, reigned at Damascus, the capital of Syria. His relation, Haroun Alraschid, who resided at Bagdad, had bestowed upon him this tributary kingdom.

"A short time after the death of Abou Aibou, Ganem was conversing with his mother on family affairs, and mention was made of the goods which were in the warehouse; Ganem asked his mother what was the meaning of the writing which he observed on every bale. 'O my son,' replied his mother, 'your father being accustomed to travel into various provinces, used, before his departure. to write upon each bale the name of the place to which he proposed consigning it. He had arranged everything for his journey to Bagdad, and was ready to set off when death—' She was unable to proceed; the lively remembrance of the loss she had sustained choked her utterance, and she shed a torrent of tears.

"Ganem could not see his mother thus affected without feeling very acutely himself. The two remained silent for some minutes; but at length Ganem recovering himself, addressed his mother in the following words, as soon as he saw her able to attend to him: 'Since my father destined this merchandise for Bagdad, and has not been permitted to execute his design, I will prepare to take the journey myself. I think, indeed, I ought to hasten my departure as much as possible lest the goods should take harm in the state in which they are now, or we should lose the opportunity of disposing of them to advantage.'

"The widow of Abou Aibou, who tenderly loved her son, was much alarmed at hearing this resolution; 'My son,' answered she, 'I quite approve that you should wish to imitate your father; but think how young you are, how inexperienced, and how entirely unaccustomed to the fatigue of long journeys. And then, would you abandon me, and add a new affliction to that with which I am already overwhelmed? Is it not better to dispose of these goods to the merchants of Damascus, and content ourselves with a moderate profit, than that you should expose yourself to so many dangers?'

"But it was in vain she opposed Ganem's design; he was too eager in the prosecution of his scheme to yield to her arguments. The desire of travelling, and of improving his mind by a more extensive survey of the world, urged him to depart, and prevailed over the remonstrances, prayers, and even tears of his mother. He went to the market where slaves were sold, and bought such as he thought suited to his purpose. He hired a hundred camels, and having provided himself with everything necessary, set off with five or six merchants of Damascus, who were going to trade at Bagdad.

"These merchants, who were attended by their slaves and accompanied by several other travellers, made up so large a caravan that they had nothing to fear from the Bedouins, or wandering Arabs, whose custom it is to scour the country, attacking and pillaging all the caravans that are not strong enough to resist their assaults. They had nothing to encounter but the fatigues incident to a long journey, which were soon forgotten when they came in sight of the city of Bagdad, where they arrived in perfect safety.

"They alighted at the finest and best frequented khan of the city; but Ganem, who wished to be lodged more privately and commodiously, did not make any long stay there. He took care to leave his merchandise in a place of safety, and then hired in the neighbourhood an excellent house, richly furnished, and with the most delightful garden that can be imagined, abounding in beautiful groves and fountains.

"The young merchant had been for some days established in his house, and had recovered from the fatigue of his journey, when he dressed himself very handsomely in order to proceed to the public place where the merchants assembled to buy and sell their goods. He was followed by a slave who carried a parcel containing several pieces of fine stuffs and linens.

"The merchants received Ganem with much civility; and their chief, or syndic, to whom he first addressed himself, bought the stranger's whole parcel at the several prices marked on the tickets which were fastened respectively to each piece. Ganem continued disposing of his wares with so much success, that he sold every day whatever merchandise he brought out.

"At last one bale only remained, which he had ordered to be taken out of the warehouse and brought to his own home before he went down to the market; but when he arrived there he found all the shops shut. This appeared to him very extraordinary. He enquired the cause, and was told that one of the principal merchants, a man with whom he had been acquainted, was dead, and that, according to custom, all the fraternity were gone to attend the dead man's funeral.

"Ganem took pains to learn the whereabouts of the mosque where prayers were to be offered, and whence the corpse was to be carried to the place of interment. Thereupon he sent away his slave with the merchandise, and proceeded towards the mosque. He arrived there while prayers were still being recited, in a room hung with black satin. The corpse was soon afterwards taken up, and was followed by all the relations, by the merchants, and Ganem to a burying-place at a considerable distance from the city. The tomb was a stone edifice, in the form of a dome, destined to receive the bodies of the family of the deceased; and as it was small tents, had been erected round it that the company might be sheltered when interments took place. The tomb was opened, and after the corpse had been placed in it the doors were closed. Then the Iman and the other ministers of the mosque, sitting in a circle upon carpets in the principal tent, recited the rest of the prayers. They also read the chapters of the Koran appointed for the burial of the dead, while the relations and merchants, following the example of the ministers, sat in a circle around.

THE LADY REVIVING.

"It was almost night before all the ceremonies were finished. Ganem, who had not expected they would last so long, began to be uneasy; and his disquietude increased when he saw preparations made for serving a repast in honour of the deceased, according to the custom of Bagdad. He was told that the tents had been pitched not only to guard against the heat of the sun, but as a protection also from the dampness of the night, and that the company were not to return to the city till the next morning. This news alarmed him. 'I am a stranger,' said he to himself, 'and am accounted rich. Thieves may take advantage of my absence and rob my house. My slaves even may be tempted by so rare an opportunity. They may abscond with the money I have received for my merchandise, and then how shall I be able to pursue them?' Greatly disturbed by these thoughts, he hastily ate a few morsels, and stole away from the company.

"He set out to return home with the utmost diligence; but, as it often happens, that those who make the most haste, through some adverse accident, have the worst speed, so he, mistaking one road for another, got so bewildered in the dark, that it was nearly midnight when he arrived at the gate of the city. To complete his misfortune he found the gate shut. This circumstance brought with it a new difficulty. He was now obliged to look out for some place where he might pass the remainder of the night, and wait till the gate should be opened. He entered a burying-ground of vast extent, reaching from the city to the place he had just quitted. He proceeded till he came to some high walls, which surrounded a private place of burial belonging to a particular family; and in this enclosure he observed a large palm tree. There were a great many other private burial-places, the doors of which had not been carefully secured. Finding that one open in which he had seen the palm tree, Ganem entered, and shut the door after him: he then lay down upon the grass in the hope of obtaining some repose; but the uneasiness he felt at his situation did not allow him to sleep. He rose, and after walking several times backwards and forwards before the door, opened it, without well knowing why he did so; immediately he perceived at a distance a light, which seemed to approach. He was seized with fear at the sight, and quickly closed the door, which shut only with a latch. Then he hastily climbed to the top of the palm tree, which in his alarm he considered to be the most secure situation he could find

"When he had established himself in the tree he saw, by means of the light which had alarmed him, three men enter the burying-ground. He knew by their dress that these men were slaves. One walked in front with a lantern, and the two others followed, carrying a chest about five or six feet long, which they bore upon their shoulders. They set it down, after which one of the three slaves said to his comrades: 'Comrades, if you will take my advice, let us leave the chest here and return to the city.' 'No, no,' replied another, 'we must not neglect the orders of our mistress in this manner. We shall certainly repent it if we disobey them: let us bury the chest, since she has commanded us so to do.' The other slaves consented, and they began to turn up the earth with some instruments they had brought for the purpose. When they had dug a deep hole they put in the chest, and threw back the earth they had removed. They then left the burying-ground, and went away.

"Ganem, who from the top of the palm tree had heard what the slaves had been saying, knew not what to think of this adventure. He imagined that this chest must contain something very precious, and that the person to whom it belonged had some particular reason for having it hidden in this burying-ground. He immediately resolved to satisfy himself on the subject, and accordingly came down from the palm tree. The departure of the slaves had relieved him from his fears. He went to work to scratch up the earth, and so well employed his hands and feet upon the spot, that he soon came down to the chest, but he found it fastened by a large padlock. He was much mortified at finding a new obstacle to prevent him from satisfying his curiosity. Still he would not give the matter up, and the light now beginning to dawn, showed him several large flints which were lying about in the burying-ground. He took up one of these, and with it he forced open the padlock without much difficulty. Then, full of impatience, he opened the chest. Instead of finding money in it, as he had expected, Ganem was inexpressibly surprised when he beheld a young lady of extraordinary beauty. Her fresh colour, and the beautiful bloom on her cheeks, and still more her soft and regular breathing, satisfied him that she was alive; but, supposing her to have been only asleep, he could not understand the reason of her not waking at the noise he had made in forcing the padlock. She was magnificently dressed; her bracelets and ear-rings were of diamonds, and her necklace of the largest and finest pearls. Therefore he could not for a moment doubt but that she was one of the first ladies of the court. At the sight of this charming lady Ganem not only felt all that compassion and desire of relieving distress which is natural to man, but a stronger feeling came upon him, which he did not then well understand, and which led him to do everything in his power to assist this beautiful young creature.

"His first care was to shut the door of the burying-ground, which the slaves had left open. He then returned to the lady, took her in his arms, and lifting her out of the chest, laid her upon the earth he had just removed. Released from her confined situation and exposed to the open air, the lady began to sneeze, and a slight effort she made in turning her head caused a liquid to flow from her mouth, which seemed to have been given to stupify her; then half opening her eyes and rubbing them, she exclaimed, without seeing Ganem, in a voice which delighted him by its clear sweetness: 'Zohorob Bostan, Schagrom Marglan, Cassabos Souccar, Nouronnihar, Nagmatos Sohi, Nouzhetos Zaman, speak, where are you?' She was pronouncing the names of the female slaves who usually attended her. She continued to call them, and was much astonished that no one answered. At last she opened her eyes; and finding herself in a burying-ground she was much alarmed. 'What,' cried she, in a louder tone of voice, 'are the dead come to life? Is the day of judgment come? What strange transformation do I behold since last night!'

"Ganem was unwilling to leave the lady any longer in a state of suspense. He immediately presented himself before her, with all possible respect and politeness. 'O lady,' said he, 'I can but faintly express the happiness I feel at the accident which, by bringing me here, has enabled me to do you a service; permit me to offer you that further assistance which in your present condition you must still need.'

"To inspire the lady with confidence, Ganem immediately told her who he was and by what accident he had come into the burying-ground. He afterwards gave her an account of the coming of the three slaves, and of the manner in which they had buried the chest. The lady, who had covered her face with a veil as soon as Ganem appeared before her, was very deeply affected when she learned the extent of her obligation to him. 'I thank Heaven,' said she, 'for having sent a worthy person like yourself to deliver me from death. But since you have begun this charitable work, I conjure you not to leave it unfinished. Go, I beseech you, to the town and find a muleteer who will convey me in this chest on a mule to your house; for were I to go with you on foot, my dress, which is different from that usually worn in the city, would attract attention, and might occasion my being followed, and it is very important that this should be avoided. When we are safe in your house you shall hear my whole history: in the meantime be assured you have not conferred your favours on an ungrateful person.'

"Before he quitted the lady the young merchant drew the chest from the hole in which it had been left and filled up the cavity with the earth; he then replaced the lady in the chest, which he shut in such a manner as to make it appear as if the padlock had not been forced. But for the safety of the occupant he avoided shutting the chest so close as to prevent all admission of air. Then he left the burying-ground, closing the door after him, and finding the city gates open he had soon an opportunity of obtaining the services of a muleteer. He returned to the burying-ground with all despatch, and helped the muleteer to place the chest across his mule; and to remove any suspicion the man might entertain, told him that he had arrived late in the night with another muleteer, who being in haste to return, had left the chest in the burying-ground.

"Ganem, who since his arrival at Bagdad had been entirely engrossed by his business, had never yet known the force of love. He now felt its power for the first time. It was impossible to see the young lady without admiring her, and the agitation he experienced whilst he followed the muleteer at a distance, and his fear lest some accident should deprive him of his prize, led him to suspect the real cause of the strange sensations he felt. Great was his joy on reaching home to see the chest safely deposited there. He sent away the muleteer, and having ordered one of his slaves to fasten the door that led to the street, opened the chest and helped the lady out of it. Then he offered her his hand to conduct her to his apartment, lamenting the sufferings she must have endured in her close imprisonment. 'I am well recompensed,' said she to him, 'for all I have suffered by the kindness you have shown me, and by the pleasure I feel at finding myself now in safety.'

"The apartment of Ganem, although richly furnished, attracted the attention of the lady less than did the fine figure and handsome countenance of her deliverer, whose politeness and engaging manners inspired her with the most lively gratitude. She sat down on a sofa; and to give the merchant some proof that she was not insensible to, or ungrateful for, the important service he had rendered her, took off her veil. Ganem on his part was fully impressed with the favour conferred on him by so charming a woman in appearing with her face uncovered; and his admiration for her grew into a violent passion. Whatever service he had rendered her, he thought himself amply rewarded by so great an indulgence.

"The lady guessed Ganem's sentiments, and was not alarmed by them, for his behaviour was perfectly respectful. Supposing that she must wish to eat, and not choosing to rely on any one to provide for so lovely a guest, he went out himself, followed by a slave, to order a sumptuous repast from a neighbouring tavern. From thence he went to a fruiterer's shop where he selected the finest and choicest fruits. He provided also some excellent wine, and some of the kind of bread which is eaten in the palace of the caliph.

"As soon as he returned home, he with his own hands arranged the fruit he had bought in a pyramidal form, and presented it himself to the lady in a dish of beautiful porcelain: 'O beautiful lady,' said he, 'whilst you are waiting for a more complete and more suitable repast, let me entreat you to take some of this fruit.' He wished to show his respect, and therefore remained standing; but the lady assured him she would not touch a morsel unless he would sit down and partake with her. He obeyed. Whilst they were eating the fruit, Ganem, remarking that the lady's veil which she had placed near her on the sofa, was embroidered at the edge with letters of gold, asked to look at it. The lady took up the veil immediately, and holding it towards him, asked if he could read. 'Fair lady,' replied he, with an air of modesty, 'a merchant would ill transact his commercial affairs if he did not at least know how to read and write.' 'Then,' said the lady, 'read the words which are written upon this veil: they will give me an opportunity to relate my story to you.'

"Ganem took the veil and read the following words: 'I AM THINE AND THOU ART MINE, O DESCENDANT OF THE UNCLE OF THE PROPHET!' This descendant of the uncle of the prophet was the caliph Haroun Alraschid, the reigning monarch at that time, who was descended from Abbas, the uncle of Mahomet.

"As soon as Ganem understood the meaning of the words which had attracted his notice, he exclaimed in a melancholy tone, 'Alas, beautiful lady, I have been the means of preserving your life, and this writing will deprive me of mine! I do not quite understand this mystery; I see, however, but too well, that I am the most unhappy of men: pardon the liberty I take in saying so. It was impossible for me to see you without surrendering you my heart. You must have seen distinctly that it was beyond my power to resist your charms; and this alone can afford any excuse for my presumption. I had hoped to touch your heart by my respect, my attentions, my care, my assiduity, my submission, or at least by my constancy; and scarcely have I conceived the flattering design, when I find all my hopes dashed to the ground. I can hardly flatter myself that I shall be long able to endure so great a misfortune; but, whatever may be the issue, I shall have the consolation of living or dying wholly yours. Proceed, O lady, I conjure you, and let me know the whole extent of my misery!'

"He could not utter these words without shedding tears. The lady was affected by his sorrow; and, far from being displeased at the declaration she had just heard, she felt a secret satisfaction on hearing it, as her heart also began to be touched. Still she concealed her feelings, and replied as if she had not given the slightest attention to what Ganem said, 'I should have taken great care not to let you see my veil, had I imagined the sight could have caused you so much uneasiness; nor am I at all aware that what I have to relate ought to render your fate so deplorable as you apprehend.'

"'In order that you may understand my history,' she continued, 'I must first tell you that I am called Fetnab, or "the Tormentor of Hearts," a name which was given me at my birth, it being foreseen that the sight of me would one day cause much misery. You can scarcely be unacquainted with this name, since there is no one in Bagdad who

GANEM PRESENTING THE TWO SLAVES TO FETNAB.

does not know that the caliph Haroun Alraschid, my sovereign master and yours, has a favourite so called.'

"'I was brought to Haroun's palace in my infancy, and have been educated with all the care and attention which is usually bestowed on young persons of my sex, who are destined to a position in the royal harem. I was quick at learning such accomplishments as it was thought necessary to teach me; and these acquirements, joined to a little beauty, gained me the friendship of the caliph, who gave me a private apartment near his own. The prince lavished upon me other marks of favour. He appointed twenty women, and as many eunuchs, to attend me; and from time to time has made me such considerable presents that I am become richer than any queen in the world. You will readily imagine that Zobeidè, the wife and relative of the caliph, could not behold my good fortune without jealousy. The truth is, that although Haroun Alraschid pays her all imaginable attention, she has sought every possible opportunity to effect my destruction.'

"'I had many times successfully evaded her snares. But this last effort of her jealousy conquered me, and but for you I should have been at this moment the prey of an inevitable death. I have no doubt that she suborned one of my slaves to give me in my lemonade last night a certain drug, which produced complete insensibility; and this made it easy for my captors to dispose of me. This insensibility is indeed sometimes so deep that for seven or eight hours nothing can dispel it. I have the greater reason to entertain this opinion, as my sleep is naturally very light, and I wake at the slightest noise.'

"'In order to execute her wicked design, Zobeidè has taken advantage of the absence of the caliph, who set out a few days since to put himself at the head of his troops, in order to punish the audacity of some neighbouring kings, who are in league together to make war upon him. But for this circumstance my rival, exasperated as she is, would not have ventured to attempt my life. By what arts she intends to keep the affair concealed from the caliph I cannot discover; but you see that it is of the utmost importance that you should not betray the place of my abode, as my life depends upon your secrecy. If my residence here were known, I should not be in safety a moment whilst the caliph is absent from Bagdad. Indeed you are yourself interested in concealing my adventure; for if Zobeidè were to know the obligation I am under to you, she would certainly punish you for having preserved me.'

"'At the return of the caliph I shall have less occasion to be cautious. I shall manage to inform him of all that has occurred, and I am convinced he will be still more earnest than myself to reward a service which restores me to his love.'

"When the beautiful favourite of Haroun Alraschid had ceased to speak, Ganem replied in the following words: 'Beautiful lady, I return you a thousand thanks for having given me the information I was bold enough to request; and I beg you will believe that you are here in perfect safety. The sentiments with which you have inspired me will insure my discretion. As for my slaves I confess their secrecy is not to be trusted. They might fail in the fidelity they owe me if they knew by what accident, and in what place, I had the happiness of meeting with you. But it is impossible for them to guess the truth, and I will even venture to assure you that they will not have the smallest curiosity to learn the particulars of the affair. It is so usual for young men to search for beautiful slaves that they will not be at all surprised to see you here, as they will naturally conjecture that you are one whom I have just bought. They will think, too, that I may have my reasons for bringing you here in a secret and hidden manner. Therefore, set your mind at ease on this subject, and be assured that you shall be treated with all the respect due to the favourite of so great a monarch as Haroun Alraschid. But whatever greatness may surround you, permit me to declare to you, adorable lady, that nothing will ever make me revoke the offering I have made you of my heart. I also know, nor shall I ever forget, that *what belongs to the master is forbidden to the slave;* but I loved you before I knew that your faith was pledged to the caliph. It is entirely beyond my power to conquer a passion, which, though still in its infancy, has all the strength of love fortified by long continuance. I wish that your august, too happy lover, may frustrate the malignity of Zobeidè, by recalling you to his presence: and when you are restored to his society may you sometimes think of the unfortunate Ganem, who is your admirer equally with the caliph. Powerful as this prince is, if you are sensible to tenderness alone, not even he, I think, will be able wholly to efface me from your memory. He cannot love you with an ardour greater than mine, and never shall I cease to adore you, to whatever part of the world I may go to bewail my loss, and die.'

"Fetnab could not avoid perceiving that Ganem was agitated by the most violent grief, nor could she avoid feeling pity for his distress; but, aware of the embarrassment that the continuance of such a conversation must produce, and which might lead her insensibly to betray the inclination she felt towards him, she hastily rejoined, 'I see that this conversation gives you pain; let us not continue it; and allow me to express

ZOBEIDE AND THE OLD LADY.

the infinite obligations I feel towards you. I have, indeed, no words to paint my gratitude, when I reflect that without your succour I should probably at this moment have been among the dead.'

"Fortunately for both of them some one now knocked at the door. Ganem rose to see who it might be, and found one of his slaves, who came to announce the arrival of the master of the tavern to him. For greater security Ganem had prevented his slaves from entering the apartment where Fetnab was. He now went out to bring in what he had previously ordered at the tavern, and served it himself to his beautiful guest, who, in her own mind, was delighted with the attention the ardent young man paid her.

"After the repast was finished, Ganem took all the things away in the same careful manner; and having given them to his slaves, who remained at the door, he said to Fetnab, 'O lady, you will now, perhaps, be glad to take some repose. I will leave you; and when you have rested yourself, you will find me ready to receive your commands.' As soon as he had said this, he went out and bought two female slaves. He also purchased some very fine linen, and everything necessary for a toilet worthy of the favourite of the caliph. He brought the slaves home with him, and presented them to Fetnab, saying, 'A person like you, lady, must have occasion for at least two slaves to wait upon her: permit me to offer you these.'

"Fetnab was charmed with Ganem's attention, and replied: 'O my lord, I see you are not a man to do things imperfectly. You increase my obligations to you by your manner of conferring them;—but I hope I shall not die without giving you proofs of my gratitude; and I pray that Heaven may soon place me in a situation to acknowledge all your generosity towards me.'

"When the slaves had retired to an adjoining apartment, into which the young merchant sent them, Ganem sat down upon the same sofa with Fetnab, but at some distance from her, to show his respect. He again turned the conversation upon his passion; and said some very affecting things upon the invincible obstacles which deprived him of all hope. 'I dare not even flatter myself,' said he, 'that my tenderness may excite any favourable emotion in a heart like yours, which belongs to the most powerful prince in the world. Alas! it would be some consolation in my wretchedness, if I could flatter myself that you did not look with indifference upon the madness of my love.' 'My lord!' replied Fetnab. 'Alas, lady,' interrupted Ganem, 'it is the second time you have treated me with a degree of ceremony to which I have no title. The presence of the female slaves prevented me from saying what I wished on the former occasion; but now, I conjure you, do not treat me with a respect to which I have no claim. Command me, as your slave, I beseech you: I am your slave, and never shall be anything more.'

"'No, no,' interrupted Fetnab, in her turn, 'I can never think of treating a man who has saved my life otherwise than with respect. I should be very ungrateful if I said or did anything that would imply forgetfulness of your claims. Let me follow the dictates of my gratitude, and do not require, as the price of your services, that I should treat you with incivility; for I can never consent to do so. I am too much impressed with your respectful conduct to abuse the liberty you give me; and I will confess to you, that I cannot look with an eye of indifference on the attentions you have shown me. It is impossible for me to say more: you know the reasons which condemn me to silence.'

"Ganem was delighted with this declaration. He even wept for joy; and, unable to find terms sufficiently strong to express his thanks to Fetnab, merely observed, that if she knew what was due from her to the caliph, he on his part was not ignorant that *what belongs to the master is forbidden to the slave.*

"When he perceived that night was coming on, he left the room to procure a light, which he brought himself, with something by way of supper, a customary meal in Bagdad, where, after the principal meal at noon, people pass the evenings in eating fruit and drinking wine, agreeably enlivening each other with conversation.

"They placed themselves at table, and each, with much politeness, pressed the other to eat of the fruits which were before them. The excellence of the wine insensibly led them to drink; and when they had taken two or three cups, they determined to drink no more without singing. Ganem sang some verses he composed at the moment, expressive of the violence of his passion; and Fetnab, animated by his example, improvised and sang a variety of airs which had relation to her late adventure, and in which there was always some passage that Ganem might interpret in his favour. This was the only instance in her whole conduct in which she at all deviated from her fidelity to the caliph. The repast was of long duration, and the night far advanced before they thought of separating. Ganem, however, at length retired to another apartment, and left Fetnab in the room she already occupied, where the female slaves he had purchased soon came to wait upon her.

"In this manner Ganem and Fetnab lived together for several days. The young merchant never left his house but when he was called away by business of the greatest importance; and then he chose those times when the lady took her repose, for he could not bear to lose a single moment that he was permitted to pass in her company. He thought of nothing but his dear Fetnab; and she, prompted by inclination as well as gratitude, could not help at length confessing that her affection for him was not less than what he professed for her. At the same time, much as they were enamoured of each other, their respect for the caliph was sufficiently strong to keep them within due bounds; though this restraint certainly served to increase their passion.

"Whilst Fetnab, snatched as it were from the jaws of death, passed her time so agreeably with Ganem, Zobeidè was by no means free from disquietude in the palace of Haroun Alraschid.

"Soon after the three slaves, the ministers of her vengeance, had taken away the chest, ignorant of what it contained, and, like people accustomed to execute blindly the command of a superior, not even desirous of learning, she became a prey to the most distressing anxiety. A thousand importunate reflections disturbed her repose. She could not for a moment enjoy the sweets of sleep: her nights were passed in the endeavour to devise means of concealing her crime. 'My lord the caliph,' said she, 'loves Fetnab more than he has ever loved any of his favourites. What shall I say when, at his return, he asks for her?' Several stratagems occurred to her mind, but she was satisfied with none of them: some difficulty always presented itself, and she knew not on what to determine. She had about her an old attendant who had brought her up from her earliest infancy, whom she ordered to come to her at daybreak; and after confiding her secret to her she said: 'My good mother, you have always assisted me with your excellent advice: if ever I required it I do so now, when my troubled mind seeks for something to calm its agitation, and when some explanation must be devised to satisfy the caliph.'

"'My dear mistress,' replied the old lady, 'it would have been much better if you had not brought yourself into this difficulty; but, as the mischief is now done, we must say no more about it, and only think of some stratagem to deceive the Commander of the Faithful. I am of opinion, that you should immediately get a piece of wood carved to appear like a corpse: we will wrap it up in old linen, enclose it in a coffin, and cause it to be buried in some place belonging to the palace: then, without loss of time, you must cause a marble mausoleum, in the form of a dome, to be built over the place of burial, and an effigy to be erected which shall be covered with black cloth, surrounded with chandeliers and large wax-lights. There is another thing,' added the old lady, 'which must not be omitted: you should go into mourning, and order your own women to do the same: Fetnab's attendants also, as well as your eunuchs, and all the officers of the palace must be commanded to appear in the same garb. When the caliph returns, and sees the whole palace in mourning, and yourself also, he will immediately ask the reason of it. You will then have an opportunity of recommending yourself to his affections by saying, that out of respect to him you were anxious to render the last offices to Fetnab, who had been carried off by sudden death. You must inform him that you have caused a mausoleum to be built, in order that every honour might be conferred on the memory of his favourite, and all rites as religiously observed as if he himself had been present. As his affection for her was great, he will no doubt shed tears over her grave. Perhaps, too,' said the old lady, 'he will not believe that she is really dead; but may suspect that you have driven her from the palace through jealousy. If so, he will look upon this mourning merely as an artifice to deceive him, and to prevent him from making any search. It is not unlikely that he may have the coffin taken up and opened. But he will certainly be convinced of her death when he sees what appears to be a corpse. He will then feel very grateful to you for what you have done, and will warmly express his gratitude. As to the piece of wood, I will take care to have it carved by an artificer in the city, who will not know for what purpose it is required. Do you, O my mistress, order the woman who gave Fetnab her lemonade last night to tell her companions that she has just found her mistress dead in her bed; and, in order that they may lament Fetnab without wishing to go into her chamber, let her add that she has informed you of the calamity, and that you have already given orders to Mesrour for the favourite's interment.'

"As soon as the old lady ceased speaking, Zobeidè took a fine diamond ring from her casket, and, putting it upon her nurse's finger, embraced her in a transport of joy, saying, 'Ah, my good mother, how much I am indebted to you! I should never have thought of so ingenious an expedient. It cannot fail of success, and I feel my tranquillity already returning. I rely upon you for providing the wooden image; and I will go and give orders about the rest.'

"The image was prepared with all the diligence Zobeidè could desire, and carried by the old lady herself into the apartment of Fetnab, where it was attired like a corpse and placed in the coffin; then Mesrour, who was himself deceived, ordered the coffin and the figure representing Fetnab to be carried away, and buried with the customary ceremonies in the place which Zobeidè had appointed. The procession started amidst the tears and lamentations of the favourite's women, who were strongly incited to a great display of grief by the example of the slave who had given Fetnab the lemonade.

"On the same day Zobeidè sent for the architect of the palace and various mansions belonging to the caliph; and, in pursuance of the orders she gave him, the mausoleum was very soon finished. A princess so powerful as the wife of a monarch whose rule extends from the setting to the rising sun, is obeyed with unusual alacrity, and her orders are executed rapidly. Zobeidè also, with her whole court, were soon clad in mourning, a circumstance which immediately caused the report of Fetnab's death to be spread abroad, so that the news was quickly known throughout the whole city.

"Ganem was one of the last to hear of it; for he scarcely ever went from home. At last, however, the report reached even him. 'O lady,' said he to the beautiful favourite of the caliph, 'your death is generally believed in Bagdad; and I do not doubt but Zobeidè is perfectly sure that the belief is well-founded. I thank Heaven, however, for being the cause and happy witness of your existence. Would to Heaven that, taking advantage of this false report, you could be persuaded to unite your fate with mine; and, flying with me far from hence, to reign the sole possessor of my heart! But whither does my transport hurry me? I forget that you are born to be the delight of the most powerful prince on earth, and that Haroun Alraschid alone is worthy of you. Thus, even if you would consent to resign him for me—if you would even join your fate to mine—ought I to consent to it? No! it would still be my duty to keep constantly in remembrance that *what belongs to the master is forbidden to the slave.*'

"The amiable Fetnab, though far from indifferent to the tender emotions which he manifested, had sufficient command over herself to conceal what she felt in return. 'O my lord,' said she, 'we cannot hinder the present success of Zobeidè. I am not surprised at the artifice she has made use of to conceal her crime; but let her do what she will, I flatter myself her triumph will be but short, and disgrace will quickly follow. The caliph will ere long return, and we shall find means privately to inform him of all that has passed. In the meantime let us take greater precautions than ever to prevent her from suspecting that I am still alive. I have already told you what would be the consequences if she discovered my retreat.'

"At the end of three months the caliph returned to Bagdad, covered with glory and victorious over all his enemies. He entered his palace, impatient to return to Fetnab, and lay his laurels at her feet. How great was his astonishment at seeing all his officers clothed in black! He shuddered involuntarily at the sight, and his heart misgave him when he reached the apartment of Zobeidè, and perceived that the princess and her whole train of women were in deep mourning. He instantly and anxiously asked the reason of these signs of mourning. 'Commander of the Faithful,' answered Zobeidè, 'I wear this mourning for your slave Fetnab, who died so suddenly as to render it

GANEM'S ESCAPE.

impossible to apply any remedy to her disease.' She would have proceeded, but the caliph did not allow her time. He was so overcome by the intelligence that he uttered a shriek and fell senseless into the arms of his vizier Giafar, who accompanied him. But he soon recovered, and in a voice which betrayed his deep affliction, requested to know where his dear Fetnab had been buried. 'My lord,' said Zobeidè, 'I have myself taken care to have her obsequies performed with suitable magnificence. I have caused a marble mausoleum to be erected at the place where she lies buried. I will conduct you thither if you wish to see it.'

"The caliph did not choose to give Zobeidè the trouble, and was satisfied with the attendance of Mesrour. He proceeded to the place immediately without changing his dress. When he saw the effigy covered with black cloth, the tapers burning round it, and the magnificence of the monument, he was astonished that Zobeidè should have performed the obsequies of her rival with so much pomp; and as he was naturally suspicious began to doubt the reality of this apparent generosity, and to think it possible that his favourite might not be really dead; but that Zobeidè, taking advantage of his long absence, might have driven her from the palace, and have caused her to be conveyed to so great a distance that she should never be heard of more. He suspected nothing worse; for he did not believe Zobeidè wicked enough to attempt the life of his favourite.

"In order to assure himself of the truth, the caliph ordered the effigy to be taken down, the grave to be opened, and the coffin uncovered in his presence; but when he saw the linen which enveloped the piece of wood he did not dare to proceed further. The pious caliph feared to offend against the laws of religion if he permitted the body of the deceased to be touched; and this devout scruple prevailed over both curiosity and love. He no longer doubted the death of Fetnab. He ordered that the coffin should be again closed, the grave filled up, and the effigy replaced in its former position.

"Thinking it necessary to pay some tribute of respect at the tomb of his favourite, the caliph sent for the ministers of religion, those of the palace, and the readers of the Koran; and during the time which elapsed while they were assembling, he remained in the mausoleum, bedewing with his tears the earth which covered the image of his mistress. When the ministers arrived he placed himself at the head of the effigy, and they ranging themselves around it recited long prayers, after which several chapters of the Koran were read.

"The same ceremony was performed every day for a month, both morning and evening, and always in the presence of the caliph, of the grand vizier Giafar, and of the principal officers of the court, who were all in mourning like the caliph himself. During the whole time he never ceased to honour with his tears the memory of Fetnab; nor could he be prevailed upon to transact any business whatever.

"On the last day of the month the prayers and reading of the Koran continued from morning till daybreak on the following day; the whole series of ceremonies being now finished every one returned to his own house. Haroun Alraschid, fatigued by his long vigils, went to rest himself in his apartment, and fell asleep upon a sofa between two of the ladies of his palace, one of whom sat at his feet and the other at his head. These ladies were employed in working embroidery and kept the most profound silence during his sleep.

"The attendant who sat at his head, and who was called Nouronnihar, perceiving the caliph to be asleep, said in a low voice to the other lady, 'Nagmatos Sohi,' for that was the name of the second, 'there is great news. The Commander of the Faithful, our dear lord and master, will be delighted when he wakes, to learn what I have to communicate. Fetnab is not dead, she is in perfect health.' 'O Heavens,' cried Nagmatos Sohi, 'is it possible that the beautiful, the charming, the incomparable Fetnab can be still alive?'

"Nagmatos Sohi spoke these words with so much vivacity, and in so loud a voice that the caliph awoke. He enquired why his sleep had been interrupted. 'Ah, my lord,' replied Nagmatos Sohi, 'pardon my indiscretion; I could not hear without emotion that Fetnab still lives. The wonderful news inspired me with a transport I could not restrain.' 'What then is become of her,' said the caliph, 'if it be true that she is not dead?' 'Commander of the Faithful,' replied Nouronnihar, 'I received this evening from a person unknown a note without any signature, but evidently in the handwriting of Fetnab, who relates her misfortune and desires me to inform you of it. I delayed executing my commission till you had taken some moments of repose, knowing how necessary it must be to you after so much fatigue; and' —— 'Give me, give me the note,' interrupted the caliph, with great eagerness, 'your delay was very ill-judged.'

"Nouronnihar immediately presented the note to Haroun Alraschid who opened it with extreme impatience. Fetnab had detailed at length all that had happened to her, but had dwelt a little too much on the attentions she had received from Ganem. The caliph, naturally of a jealous disposition, instead of being softened by a consideration of the hardships his favourite had experienced from the cruelty of Zobeidè, was only sensible to the infidelity of which he imagined her to have been guilty. 'What!' said he, when he had perused the note, 'perfidious wretch! after having lived four months with a young merchant, has she the effrontery to boast of his attentions to her? It is thirty days since I returned to Bagdad, and she has never troubled herself to let me hear of her till now! Ungrateful creature! whilst I was consuming whole days in lamenting her, she passed them in betraying me. I will instantly revenge myself on the faithless wretch, and on the presumptuous youth who has dared to injure me.' The prince rose as he spoke these words, and proceeded towards a large hall where he was accustomed to show himself, and to give audience to the great men of court. The door of the hall was open, and the courtiers who were waiting for his appearance entered. The grand vizier Giafar approached, and prostrated himself before the throne on which the caliph was seated. He then rose and stood before his master, who said in a tone which demanded prompt obedience, 'Giafar, your diligence is required in the execution of an important commission with which I am going to entrust you. Take with you four hundred of my guards. Enquire out the residence of a merchant of Damascus called Ganem, the son of Abou Aibou; when you have discovered his abode raze the house to the ground;—but first seize Ganem, and bring him hither with Fetnab my slave, who has been living with him these four months. I wish not only to chastise her, but to make a public example of the bold wretch who has with so much insolence been unmindful of the respect he owes to his sovereign.'

"The grand vizier, upon receiving this express command, made a profound obeisance to the caliph, putting his hand to his head to show that he would rather lose his head than be wanting in obedience: after this he at once withdrew to carry out the caliph's directions. The first step he took was to send to the syndic of the merchants who dealt in foreign silks, or fine cloths, in order to ascertain the house and street in which Ganem lived. The officer to whom this order was given soon brought back word that for some months Ganem had scarcely ever made his appearance, and that the reason why he remained so much at home was unknown; and it was even doubtful whether he had not quitted Bagdad. The same officer also informed Giafar of the situation of Ganem's house, and told him the widow's name of whom Ganem had hired it.

"On obtaining this intelligence, upon which he could rely, the minister immediately set off without loss of time, at the head of the soldiers whom the caliph had ordered him to take with him. He went to the officer of police, whom he desired to accompany him; then, followed by a great number of masons and carpenters, and furnished with the necessary implements, he proceeded to Ganem's house. As it stood alone, he made the soldiers surround it in order to prevent the young merchant from making his escape.

"Fetnab and Ganem were just at dinner. The lady was seated near a window, which opened towards the street. Hearing a noise, she looked through the lattice, and seeing the grand vizier approaching with his train, conjectured there was some design afoot against Ganem and herself. She saw that her note had been received, but she had little expected such an answer; she had hoped the caliph would have taken her communication in a very different manner. She knew not that the prince had been so long at Bagdad, and therefore, though aware of his tendency to jealousy, had felt no apprehension on that account. Still the sight of the grand vizier and his soldiers made her tremble, not, indeed, for herself, but for Ganem. She felt quite sure that she should be able to justify herself provided the caliph would consent to hear her. With regard to Ganem, whom she loved less through gratitude than from inclination, she foresaw that his irritated rival would probably demand to see him, and then condemn him to death, in anger at his youth and handsome person. Full of this idea, she turned towards the young merchant, and said: 'Ah, Ganem, we are ruined! They are come in search of us.' Ganem immediately looked through the lattice, and was extremely alarmed when he perceived the caliph's guards with drawn swords, and the grand vizier with the police officer at their head. He was so terrified at the sight that he stood motionless, unable to utter a single word. 'O Ganem,' said the favourite, 'there is no time to be lost. If you love me you will at once put on the dress of one of your slaves, and rub your face and arms with soot from the chimney. Then place one of these dishes upon your head, and they will take you for the servant from the tavern, and will let you pass. If you are asked where the master of the house is, say without hesitation that he is at home.' 'Alas, beautiful lady,' said Ganem, less alarmed for himself than for Fetnab, 'you are thinking only of me; what is to become of you?' 'Do not distress yourself about me,' replied the lady, 'I shall take care of myself. With regard to your property in this house, I will provide for its safety, and it will all, I hope, be faithfully restored to you when the caliph's anger shall have subsided; but let me entreat you to escape from its first violence. The orders which Haroun Alraschid gives in the first moments of his rage are always fatal.' The young merchant was so much afflicted that he knew not on what to determine. He would have suffered himself to be taken by the caliph's soldiers, had not Fetnab eagerly pressed him to disguise himself. He gave way to her entreaties, put on a slave's dress, and besmeared himself with soot. He was barely in time; for a knocking was presently heard at the door. All that the two friends could do was to take one tender embrace before they parted, for they were too deeply moved to utter a syllable. Thus they took leave of each other. Ganem went out with the dishes upon his head, and being really taken for the servant of the tavern, was allowed to pass without molestation. The grand vizier, who met him first, made way for him, not having the most distant idea that this was the very person whom he was seeking. The guards who were behind the grand vizier drew back in the same manner, and thus favoured Ganem's escape. He reached one of the gates of the town with all possible despatch, and passed through it without a moment's delay.

"Whilst by this stratagem Ganem was flying from the pursuit of the grand vizier, that minister entered the apartment of Fetnab, whom he found seated on a sofa. The room was filled with a great number of chests containing goods belonging to Ganem, and money which he had made by the sale of his merchandise.

"As soon as Fetnab saw the grand vizier enter, she prostrated herself with her face to the ground, and remained in that posture like one who was prepared to receive the stroke of death. 'My lord,' she said, "I am ready to submit to the sentence that the Commander of the Faithful has pronounced against me; you have only to declare it.' 'O lady,' replied Giafar, also prostrating himself till she had risen, 'Allah forbid that any one should dare to touch you with unauthorised hands. I have no design to give you the least cause of displeasure. My orders are simply to request that you will come with me to the palace, and I am to conduct you thither, with the merchant who inhabits this house.' 'My lord,' replied the favourite, rising, 'let us depart; I am ready to attend you. With regard to the young merchant to whom I owe my life he is not here. He departed nearly a month ago for Damascus, whither his affairs called him; and has left me the care of the chests you see till his return. I beseech you to permit them to be carried to the palace, and to give orders that they may be put in a place of safety, as I am very desirous to keep the promise I made him, and to take all possible care of them.

"'You shall be obeyed, lady,' replied Giafar; and he immediately sent for some porters who took up the chests, and carried them to Mesrour.

"As soon as the porters were gone Giafar whispered something to the officer of police, whom he commissioned to see the house completely razed to the ground: but not till a thorough search had first been made after Ganem, whom he suspected to be still concealed in it, notwithstanding what Fetnab had said. He then went away, carrying with him the young lady, followed by the two female slaves who had attended her. As to Ganem's

FETNAB SENT TO THE DARK TOWER.

slaves, no attention was paid to them. They mingled indiscriminately with the crowd, and no one knew what became of them.

"So soon as Giafar had quitted the house the masons and carpenters began their work of destruction; and they did their duty so well that in less than an hour not a vestige of the building remained. But the officer of the police was not able to find Ganem, though he made the most diligent scrutiny. He therefore sent to inform the grand vizier of his ill success, before that minister reached the palace. 'Tell me,' said Haroun Alraschid, when he saw the vizier enter his cabinet, 'have you executed my orders?' 'Yes, O Commander of the Faithful,' replied Giafar; 'the house which Ganem inhabited is totally demolished, and I bring with me your favourite Fetnab: she is at the door of your apartment, and will enter when you command her to appear. The young merchant could nowhere be found, though the most diligent search was made for him. Fetnab asserts that he has been gone to Damascus nearly a month.'

"Never did rage equal the anger of the caliph when he heard that Ganem had made his escape. With regard to his favourite, persuaded as he was that she had been unfaithful to him, he would neither see nor communicate with her. 'Mesrour,' said he, to the chief of the eunuchs, who was present, 'take the ungrateful, perfidious Fetnab, and shut her up in the dark tower.' This tower was within the walls of the palace, and was generally used as a prison for those favourites who had offended the caliph.

"Mesrour was accustomed to execute the orders of his master, however violent they might be, without question or reply; but he obeyed this command with regret. He expressed his sorrow to Fetnab, who was the more disconcerted at this turn of affairs, as she had persuaded herself that the caliph would not refuse to speak with her. But there was now no way of escape from her melancholy fate. She followed Mesrour, who shut her up in the dark tower, and there left her.

"In the meantime the enraged caliph dismissed his grand vizier; and, blinded by his own fury, wrote with his own hand the following letter to the King of Syria, who was his cousin, and tributary to him:—

"'THE CALIPH HAROUN ALRASCHID TO MOHAMMED ZINEBI, KING OF SYRIA.

"'O Cousin, this letter is to inform you that a merchant of Damascus, called Ganem, the son of Abou Aibou, has seduced Fetnab, the most beautiful of my slaves, and has since fled. It is my desire that upon the receipt of this you cause strict search to be made for the above Ganem, and that you have him put into safe custody. As soon as he is in your power I desire that he may be loaded with irons, and for three successive days let him receive fifty lashes. Then cause him to be led through all the quarters of the city, preceded by a crier, who shall proclaim these words: "Behold the very lightest punishment which the Commander of the Faithful inflicts on the man who insults his sovereign, and seduces one of his monarch's slaves." After that you shall send him to me, under a strong guard. But this is not all; I desire that you give up Ganem's house to be razed to the ground, and as soon as it is destroyed, let the materials be carried without the town, and scattered in the open fields. Moreover, if he has a father, mother, sisters, wives, daughters, or any other relations, let them be completely stripped, and in this state exposed in the town for three days, with the penalty of death to any who shall give them shelter. And let there be no delay in the execution of my commands.

"'HAROUN ALRASCHID.'

"As soon as he had written this letter, the caliph delivered it to a courier, whom he ordered to use all possible dispatch, and to take some pigeons with him, that the caliph might receive, in the quickest manner possible, the information he wished to obtain from Mohammed Zinebi.

"There are pigeons in Bagdad which have the peculiar property of returning to that city, more particularly when they have young ones, however distant the place may be from which they are let loose. The way in which they are made use of is by tying a letter under the wing of the bird; and in this manner intelligence is very soon conveyed from the place whence the bird is set free.

"The caliph's messenger travelled night and day, to gratify the impatience of his master. When he arrived at Damascus, he proceeded immediately to the palace of King Zinebi, who, seated on his throne, received the letter of the caliph. The courier presented it to the king, who instantly took it, and immediately recognising the hand, rose from his seat as a proof of his respect, kissing the letter, and putting it to his head, to show that he was ready to execute, with all submission, whatever orders it might contain. He thereupon opened and read it; after which he descended from his throne, and mounted his horse without delay, ordering the principal officers of his household to attend him. He also sent for the chief officer of the police; and, followed by his whole guard, proceeded to Ganem's house.

"During the whole time that the young merchant had been absent from Damascus his mother had not received any letter from him, though the merchants whom he accompanied to Bagdad had returned in safety. They all told her that they had left him in perfect health; but as he did not come home, and neglected to send her any direct information, the affectionate mother was induced to believe that her son was dead. She was so thoroughly convinced of this, that she wore mourning for him, and lamented him as sincerely as if she had seen him die, and had herself closed his eyes. No mother ever showed more heartfelt grief; and, far from seeking consolation, she took a melancholy pleasure in indulging her affliction. She caused a dome to be erected in the court belonging to her house. Under this dome she placed a statue of her son, and with her own hands covered it with black cloth. In this building she passed whole days and nights, lamenting her son in the same manner as if his body had been buried there; the beautiful Alcolomb, her daughter, the companion of her grief, mingling her tears with those of the afflicted mother.

"They had already passed some time in this melancholy state, pitied by the whole neighbourhood, who heard their lamentable cries and exclamations of sorrow, when King Mohammed Zinebi came, and knocked at the door. A female slave opened it, whereupon he hastily entered, asking for Ganem, the son of Abou Aibou.

"As the slave had never seen the king, she concluded from his numerous suite that he was one of the principal officers of Damascus. 'O my lord,' said she, 'Ganem, whom you inquire for, is dead. My mistress, his mother, is now at his tomb, which you see before you, lamenting his loss.' Without paying attention to the words of the slave, the king ordered his guards to make strict search for Ganem throughout the house. He afterwards himself proceeded towards the tomb, where he beheld the mother and daughter bathed in tears, seated upon a common mat near the figure which represented Ganem. As soon as they perceived a man at the door of the building, the mourning women covered themselves with their veils. But the mother, who recognised the king, immediately rose, and ran to throw herself at his feet. 'Worthy lady,' said the prince to her, 'I seek your son Ganem; is he here?' 'Alas, great king,' cried she, 'he has been long dead. Would to Heaven I had been permitted to perform the last offices for him with my own hands—that I had been allowed the consolation of depositing his bones within this tomb! Oh, my son, my beloved son!' She would have said more, but her grief was so violent that it choked her utterance.

"King Zinebi was affected at her distress; for he was a prince of a mild disposition, and very compassionate towards the suffering and unhappy. 'If Ganem alone is guilty,' said he to himself, 'why punish his mother and sister, who are innocent? Cruel Haroun Alraschid, how much you distress me by making me the minister of your vengeance, and obliging me to injure those who have never offended you!'

"The guards, whom the king had sent to seek for Ganem, now came to inform their master that their search had been fruitless. He quite expected this report; for the tears of the two women would not permit him to entertain a doubt of the truth of their report. He was miserable at finding himself reduced to the necessity of executing the caliph's orders; but whatever compassion he might feel, he did not dare to deceive the great caliph by screening them from his resentment. 'My good lady,' said he to Ganem's mother, 'leave this tomb; you and your daughter are not here in safety.' When they came out, to preserve them from insult, he took off his robe, which was very large, and covered them both with it, recommending them to keep near him. Having thus secured their personal safety, he ordered the populace to be admitted, and the pillaging of the house commenced with eagerness, and with shouts which terrified the mother and sister of Ganem the more, as they were perfectly ignorant of the cause of these proceedings. The most valuable furniture was seized, with chests full of money, Persian and Indian carpets, cushions covered with gold and silver stuffs, the finest porcelain—in short, everything was carried off, and nothing left but the bare walls of the house. It was a melancholy sight for these unhappy women to see all they possessed given up to plunder, without at all knowing why they were so cruelly treated.

"When the house had been thoroughly plundered, Mohammed ordered the police officer to have it utterly razed, and the tomb likewise. Whilst the men were employed at this work, he conducted Alcolomb and her mother to his palace. It was then that he doubled their grief by declaring to them the will of the caliph. 'Haroun Alraschid orders,' said he, 'that you shall be stripped and exposed naked before all the people during three days. It is with extreme repugnance that I execute this cruel and ignominious sentence.' The king uttered these words in a tone which proved how sincerely he felt the sorrow and compassion he expressed. Although the fear of being dethroned prevented him from giving way to the suggestions of pity, he nevertheless softened in some degree the rigour of Haroun Alraschid's commands, by ordering for Alcolomb and her mother a coarse garment made of horsehair, and without sleeves.

"The next day these unfortunate victims of the caliph's resentment were stripped of their clothes, and dressed in the rough garments provided for them. Their head-dresses were also taken off, and their dishevelled hair left to hang loose over their shoulders. Alcolomb's was of a light colour, the most beautiful hue imaginable, and reached down to the ground. In this state they were exposed to the gaze of the people. The police officer, followed by his attendants, accompanied them, and led them through the city. They were preceded by a crier, who from time to time proclaimed in a loud voice: 'This is the punishment of those who draw upon themselves the indignation of the Commander of the Faithful.' Whilst they were thus paraded about Damascus, their arms and feet naked, in so strange a dress, and endeavouring to conceal their confusion by covering their faces with their hair, the people were melted even to tears at the affecting sight.

"The women especially, looking through the lattices at these innocent sufferers, as they justly esteemed them, and feeling especial pity for the youth and beauty of Alcolomb, made the air resound with their piteous cries, as these unresisting victims passed under their windows. The children, too, terrified by the lamentations, and by the sight which occasioned them, added their cries to the general uproar, and increased the horror of the scene. In short, had the enemies of the state taken possession of Damascus, put the people to the sword, and set fire to the place, there could not have appeared greater marks of consternation.

"It was almost night before this dreadful spectacle came to a conclusion. The mother and daughter were then brought back to the palace of the king, where they no sooner arrived than they fainted away, from the anguish they endured and the fatigue they had undergone in walking barefoot. It was a long time before they could be brought to themselves. The Queen of Damascus, struck with deep pity for their misfortunes, sent some of her women to comfort them with all kinds of refreshments, and wine to restore their strength, notwithstanding the prohibition of the caliph.

"The queen's women found them still insensible, and far too much exhausted to be benefited by the relief which they brought them. However, by means of proper applications they were at last recovered. The mother of Ganem immediately expressed her sense of their kindness. 'Worthy lady,' said one of the queen's women, 'your misfortunes move us very sensibly. We were greatly rejoiced when our mistress the Queen of Syria commissioned us to afford you all the assistance in our power. We can assure you that her majesty and the king her husband take great interest in your unhappy situation.' Ganem's mother begged that the queen's women would return their most grateful acknowledgments to that princess for her kindness to her and Alcolomb. Then, addressing the lady who had spoken, she added: 'Kind lady, the king has never told me why the Commander of the Faithful has sentenced us to suffer such cruel outrages: let me beseech you to inform me what crimes we have committed.' 'My good lady,' replied the queen's attendant, 'your misfortunes originate with your son Ganem: he is not dead as you imagine. He is accused of having carried off the most beloved of the caliph's favourites; and, as he has escaped the effects of the prince's resentment by a hasty flight, the punishment has fallen upon you. Every one condemns the violence of the caliph, but at the same time every one fears him; and King Zinebi himself, as you

GANEM'S MOTHER AND SISTER PERSECUTED.

perceive, dares not disobey his orders, through fear of his displeasure. Thus all we can do is to testify our compassion, and exhort you to patience.'

"'I know my son's disposition,' said the mother of Ganem; 'I have taken great pains with his education, and have always brought him up with a strong sense of respect for the Commander of the Faithful. He has not committed the crime of which he is accused: I will be answerable for his innocence. But I shall no longer murmur or complain, since it is for him I suffer, and since I know that he is not dead. O Ganem,' she exclaimed, transported by mingled emotions of joy and tenderness, 'Oh, my dear son, is it possible you are still alive? I no longer regret the destruction of my property; and, to whatever excess the caliph may carry his resentment, I can pardon all, since Heaven has preserved my son. It is for my daughter only that I grieve; her woes alone distress me. I believe her, however, to be so good a sister, that she will easily follow my example.'

"At these words, Alcolomb, who had till then appeared unmoved, turned towards her mother and cried fervently, throwing her arms round her neck: 'Yes, my dear mother, I will always follow your example, whatever extremities your affection for my brother may lead you to endure!'

"Thus, mingling their tears and sighs, mother and daughter remained for a considerable time tenderly locked in each other's arms. In the meantime, the queen's women, who were much affected at the scene, used every persuasion to induce the mother of Ganem to take some refreshment. She ate a morsel only, merely to satisfy them, and Alcolomb did the same.

"It was the caliph's order that the relatives of Ganem should be exposed three days successively to the people in the degraded position which has been described. Therefore Alcolomb and her mother appeared as a public spectacle for the second time during the whole of the next day. But things were now conducted in a very different manner. On this and the following day, the streets, which before had been crowded with people, were deserted. The merchants, indignant at the treatment which the widow and daughter of Abou Aibou had received, shut up their shops, and scrupulously avoided coming out of their houses. The women, instead of looking through their lattices, retired to the back of their houses. Not a creature was to be seen in all the squares and streets through which the poor persecuted women were obliged to pass; it seemed as if the town had been abandoned by its inhabitants.

"On the fourth day Mohammed Zinebi, who wished faithfully to execute the caliph's orders, although he did not approve them, sent criers into all quarters of the city to publish to every citizen of Damascus, and also to all foreigners of whatsoever condition, that they should not presume to give shelter to the mother and sister of Ganem, or furnish them with a morsel of bread or a drop of water, under pain of death and of being afterwards thrown as food to the dogs; in a word, the whole city was prohibited from affording them the smallest assistance, or from having any communication with them.

"After the criers had executed the king's commands, Zinebi further ordered that the mother and her daughter should be sent out of the palace, and be permitted to go whichever way they chose. They no sooner appeared in the street than every one fled to avoid them, so strong was the impression made on the minds of the people by the proclamation they had heard. These unhappy women soon discovered that they were shunned by all; and being ignorant of the cause of this seeming hatred, they were much surprised at it. Their astonishment was painfully increased when, on entering one of the streets, they perceived among many others several of their particular friends, who, as soon as they appeared, fled with as much precipitation as the rest. 'What!' said the mother of Ganem, 'do we carry the plague with us? Has the unjust and barbarous treatment we have received made us hateful to our fellow-citizens? Come, my child,' continued she, 'let us leave Damascus—let us not stay another moment in a place where we create horror even in our best friends.'

"Full of these melancholy thoughts these two unfortunate ladies reached one of the extremities of the town, and betook themselves to a miserable ruin, where they hoped to find shelter for the night. Some Mussulmen, actuated by motives of charity and compassion, came as soon as it was dark to bring them some provision; but they dared not stop a moment to console them for fear of being discovered, and punished for disobeying the orders of the caliph.

"In the meantime King Zinebi had sent forth a pigeon, in order that Haroun Alraschid might be informed of the punctual fulfilment of his orders. He informed the caliph at the same time of all that had passed, and begged to be instructed in what way he was to proceed in regard to the mother and sister of Ganem. By the same mode of conveyance he very soon received the caliph's answer. Haroun Alraschid desired that they might be for ever banished from Damascus. The King of Syria immediately sent people to the ruin where the mother and sister of Ganem had taken refuge, with orders to conduct them three days' journey from Damascus, and there to leave them, with strict injunctions never to return to that city.

"King Zinebi's people performed their task; but, less exact than their master had been in executing the orders of Haroun Alraschid, they compassionately bestowed on Alcolomb and her mother some small pieces of money to procure them food. They also gave each of them a bag, which they put round their necks, to hold their provisions.

"In this deplorable state the two ladies arrived at the first village from Damascus. The female peasants gathered round them; and as they could not help observing through the strangers' disguise that they were people of condition, they asked them what had obliged them to travel in a dress to which they were evidently unaccustomed. Instead of answering these questions they began to weep. This tended to increase the curiosity of the peasants, and at the same time to inspire them with compassion. The mother of Ganem related all that she and her daughter had suffered. The good villagers were moved at the recital, and endeavoured to console the sufferers, nor did they fail to entertain them in the best way their poverty would allow. They obliged them to take off their coarse garments of horsehair, which much incommoded them, and to put on other clothes which they gave them. They likewise provided them with shoes. and with something to cover their heads in order to protect their hair.

"After heartily thanking the charitable peasants of this village, Alcolomb and her mother proceeded towards Aleppo by short journeys. They were accustomed to retire to the neighbourhood of the mosques or into one of those buildings towards dusk, and there they passed the night upon the mats, if there were any, which covered the pavement; otherwise they lay down on the pavement itself, or lodged in one of those public places which are built to serve as an asylum for travellers. They were sufficiently supplied with food, as they often came to places where bread, boiled rice, and other provisions were distributed to any traveller who asked for it.

"They at last arrived at Aleppo; but they did not choose to stay there, and continuing their way towards the Euphrates, they crossed that river and entered into Mesopotamia, which they penetrated as far as Moussoul. From thence, undeterred by their sufferings, they proceeded to Bagdad. That was the place whither all their desires tended, for they hoped to meet with Ganem, although they ought not to have flattered themselves that he could be in the same town in which the caliph resided; but they cherished the hope because they had the wish. Instead of diminishing, their affection for him increased, notwithstanding all their sufferings. He was generally the subject of their conversation; they even made inquiry concerning him of all whom they met.

But we must here leave Alcolomb and her mother, and return to Fetnab.

"That lady had been strictly confined in the dark tower from the day which proved so disastrous to her and Ganem. However disagreeable her prison might be to her, she was less distressed at her own sufferings than at Ganem's. The uncertainty she felt respecting his fate caused her the most poignant anguish. There was scarcely a moment in which she did not lament his sad destiny.

"One night when the caliph was walking alone round his palace, as was his frequent custom—for this prince possessed a very large share of curiosity, and sometimes became aware, in his noctural excursions, of things which happened in his palace, and which would never otherwise have come to his knowledge—one night his road led him near the dark tower. Thinking he heard some one speaking within, he stopped; approaching the door to listen, he distinctly heard these words, which Fetnab, still a prey to grief at the remembrance of Ganem, uttered in a voice of piercing grief: 'O Ganem, unhappy Ganem! What has become of you? Whither has your unfortunate destiny led you? Alas! I have been the unhappy cause of your misfortunes! Why did you not rather leave me to perish miserably, than afford me your generous assistance? What a sad reward have you received for all your care and respect! The Commander of the

Faithful, who ought to reward you, becomes your persecutor: for having alway respected me as consecrated to him you lose all your property, and are obliged to seek safety in flight. Ah, caliph! barbarous caliph! what can you say for yourself, when you shall appear with Ganem before the awful tribunal of the Supreme Judge, and when the angels shall in your presence bear testimony to the truth? All your present power, before which half the earth trembles, will not in that day save you from the condemnation and punishment due to your unjust violence.' Here Fetnab ceased to speak, for sighs and tears choked her utterance.

"What he now heard was sufficient to make the caliph reflect upon his past conduct. He clearly perceived that if what Fetnab said was true, she must of necessity be innocent, and that he had been too precipitate in the orders he had issued against Ganem and his family. In order to investigate thoroughly an affair in which his character for equity, which had hitherto stood high, seemed to be involved, he instantly returned towards his apartment, and, as soon as he entered it, ordered Mesrour to go to the dark tower, and bring Fetnab before him.

"The chief of the eunuchs inferred from this order, and still more from the caliph's manner, that Haroun Alraschid intended to pardon and recall his favourite. He was delighted to entertain this hope, as he loved Fetnab, and was much grieved at her disgrace. He instantly hastened to the tower, and said to Fetnab, in a tone expressive of the satisfaction he felt, 'O lady, have the goodness to follow me. I hope you will never again return to this gloomy, dismal place. The Commander of the Faithful wishes to speak with you, and I augur well from this circumstance.'

"Fetnab followed Mesrour, who introduced her into the caliph's cabinet. She immediately fell prostrate before her master, and remained in that posture with her face bathed in tears. 'O Fetnab,' said the caliph, without desiring her to rise, 'it appears that you accuse me of violence and injustice. Tell me who is this man of whom you say, "In spite of the respect and attention he has preserved towards me, he is reduced to so dreadful a situation?" Speak you know that I am naturally of a forgiving disposition, and inclined to do justice.'

"The favourite understood by what the caliph said that he had overheard her lamentations; and, taking advantage of so excellent an opportunity of justifying her beloved Ganem, she replied: 'Commander of the Faithful, if any expression has escaped me which displeases your majesty, I humbly entreat your pardon. Ganem, the unfortunate son of Abou Aibou, a merchant of Damascus, is the man concerning whose innocence and sufferings you have deigned to question me. He it was who saved my life, and gave me an asylum in his house. I will confess that when he first saw me he may perhaps have entertained the idea of devoting himself to me, in the hope that I would repay his attention; this, at least, I inferred from the zeal he showed in my behalf, and from the eagerness he showed to render me every assistance in the mournful position in which I stood. But as soon as he was aware that I had the honour to belong to you, he exclaimed: "O lady, *what belongs to the master is forbidden to the slave.*" I must do him the justice to say that his conduct from that moment never belied his words. At the same time you know, O Commander of the Faithful, with what rigour you have treated him; and for this rigour you will have to answer before the tribunal of Allah.'

"The caliph was not displeased with Fetnab for the freedom she used in expressing her sentiments. He replied: 'But can I rely on the assurances you give me of Ganem's honour?' 'Yes,' said she, 'you may. I would not on any account disguise the truth from you; and to prove that I am sincere, I will make a confession, which will perhaps displease you; but I solicit beforehand your majesty's forgiveness.' 'Speak, daughter,' replied Haroun Alraschid; 'I freely pardon you, provided you conceal nothing from me.' 'Know, then, O Commander of the Faithful,' replied Fetnab, 'that the respectful attentions of Ganem, added to the essential services he rendered me, led me to esteem him very highly—I even went further. You yourself have experienced the tyranny of love. I felt that he inspired me with the tenderest sentiments: he perceived it; but, far from profiting by my weakness, and notwithstanding the ardour of his passion, he

FETNAB AND THE CALIPH.

continued firm in his duty. All that his regard for me ever drew from him was the saying I have already repeated to your majesty: "*What belongs to the master is forbidden to the slave.*"'

"This ingenuous confession would perhaps have irritated many monarchs, but it completely softened Haroun Alraschid. He commanded her to rise, and, seating her near himself, desired her to relate her history from beginning to end. She obeyed his command, acquitting herself with much spirit and address. She passed slightly over the circumstances which regarded Zobeidè. She enlarged upon her obligations to Ganem, upon the expense he had been at on her account; and she particularly dwelt on his discretion, wishing by that means to make the caliph understand that her concealment in Ganem's house had been necessary in order to deceive Zobeidè. She concluded with the flight of the young merchant, a measure which she frankly told the caliph she had advised Ganem to take, in order to avoid the effects of his displeasure.

"When she had concluded the caliph said to her: 'I believe all you have told me; but why did you so long delay to give me some intelligence of yourself? Was it necessary to wait a whole month after my return before you informed me where you were?'

"'Commander of the Faithful,' replied Fetnab, 'Ganem so seldom went out of his house, that you can scarcely be surprised when I tell you that for a long time we were not aware of your return. Besides, it was a long time before he could find a favourable opportunity to deliver into the hands of Nouronnihar the note I had written, and of which he took charge.'

"'It is enough, Fetnab,' said the caliph; 'I acknowledge my error, and am willing to repair it by heaping all kinds of honour upon this young merchant. Thou shalt see how much I will do: ask for him what thou wilt, I will grant it.' At these words the favourite threw herself at the caliph's feet, bowing her face to the ground; then raising herself, she said: 'Commander of the Faithful, after first returning your majesty my sincere thanks for Ganem, I humbly beseech you to order it to be proclaimed throughout your dominions that you pardon the son of Abou Aibou, and that you command him to appear before you.' 'I will do more than that,' replied the caliph; 'in order to reward him for having preserved your life, and for the respect he has shown towards me, and also to make him amends for the loss of his property, and repair the injury his family has sustained, I bestow you upon him as his wife.' Fetnab was powerless to find words wherein she could sufficiently express her gratitude to the caliph for his generosity. She now retired into the apartment she had occupied before her unfortunate adventure. The same furniture remained in it: nothing had been touched. But she was best pleased of all to find the chests and packages belonging to Ganem, which Mesrour had taken care to have conveyed there.

"The next day Haroun Alraschid gave orders to the grand vizier to have it proclaimed in every town of his dominions that he pardoned Ganem, the son of Abou Aibou; but this proclamation seemed to produce no effect, for a considerable time passed and nothing was heard of the young merchant. Fetnab thought that he had certainly been unable to survive the misery of having lost her, and the sharpest anxiety took possession of her mind; but hope is the last thing that abandons lovers. She begged the caliph's permission to go herself in search of Ganem. Haroun Alraschid consented; and taking out of her casket a purse containing a thousand pieces of gold, Fetnab left the palace one morning, mounted upon a mule very richly caparisoned, with which she had been provided from the stables of the caliph. Two black eunuchs attended her, one walking on each side with his hand on the mule's bridle.

"Fetnab proceeded from mosque to mosque, distributing alms to devout men of the Mussulman religion, imploring their prayers for the accomplishment of an important affair, on which, she told them, the happiness of two persons depended. She employed the whole day and spent her thousand pieces of gold in acts of charity at the mosques, and in the evening returned to the palace.

"The following day she took another purse containing a thousand sequins, and with the same attendants repaired to the place where the jewellers were accustomed to assemble. She stopped at the entrance, and without dismounting, ordered one of the eunuchs to desire the syndic to come and speak with her. The syndic, who was a very charitable man, and who expended more than two-thirds of his income in relieving poor strangers afflicted with sickness, or any way distressed in their affairs, immediately attended on Fetnab, whom he knew by her dress to be a lady belonging to the palace.

'I apply to you,' said she, putting her purse into his hands, 'as to a man whose piety is much commended through the whole city. I beg you to distribute these pieces of gold among the poor people you are accustomed to assist, for I am well aware that it is your laudable practice to succour the distresses of all strangers who apply to you for charity. I know, too, that you are even anxious to anticipate their wants, and that nothing is more pleasing to you than to find opportunities of relieving distress.' 'O worthy lady,' replied the syndic, 'I shall execute your commands with pleasure; but if you are desirous of dispensing your charity with your own hands, and will take the trouble to come to my house, you will there see two women worthy of all your compassion. I met them yesterday as they entered the city. They were in a most miserable state, and I was the more moved by their distress as they appeared to be people of condition. Through the wretched rags which covered them, and in spite of all the injury their faces had received from the heat of the sun, I was struck by an air of superiority which I have rarely met with in those poor objects to whom I have extended my aid. I conducted them both to my house, and placed them under the care of my wife, who formed the same judgment concerning them that I had made. She ordered her slaves to prepare good beds, while she employed herself in assisting the strangers to wash their faces, and in providing a change of linen. We do not yet know who they are, because we wished them to take some repose before we importuned them with questions.'

"Fetnab felt a curiosity to see them which she could not well account for. The syndic thought it his duty to attend her to his house; but she would not suffer him to take that trouble, and was conducted to his abode by one of his slaves. When she came to the door she alighted from her mule, and followed the syndic's slave, who entered first to announce her to his mistress, whom he found in the apartment occupied by Alcolomb and the mother of Ganem; for these were the women of whom the syndic had been speaking to Fetnab.

"The syndic's wife, informed by her slave that one of the ladies of the palace was in the house, was coming out of the chamber to receive her; but Fetnab followed the slave so closely that she did not give her time, and entered the apartment at once. The syndic's wife prostrated herself before her visitor, as a mark of her respect towards every one who belonged to the caliph. Fetnab raised her and said: 'My good lady, I entreat your permission to speak to the two strangers who arrived at Bagdad last night.' 'O my mistress,' replied the wife of the syndic, 'they are now lying in the two little beds which you see standing together.' The favourite immediately approached the couch in which the mother reclined, and looking at her attentively, said: 'My good woman, I am come to offer you some assistance. I am not without influence in this city, and I may, perhaps, be useful to you and your companions.' 'I see, beautiful lady,' replied the mother of Ganem, 'by your kind offer of assistance, that Heaven has not yet forsaken us. We have had reason to fear that we were cast off, after all we have suffered.' When she had spoken these words she began to weep so bitterly that Fetnab and the wife of the syndic could not refrain from tears.

"Then the caliph's favourite presently dried her eyes, and said to the mother of Ganem: 'I beseech you to relate to us the history of your life and misfortunes. You cannot speak to people more disposed to use every effort in their power to console and assist you.' 'O lady,' replied the unfortunate widow of Abou Aibou, 'the cause of all our sufferings is a favourite of the Commander of the Faithful, a lady called Fetnab.' The favourite was thunderstruck at this declaration; but suppressing her confusion and agitation, she did not interrupt the mother of Ganem, who proceeded as follows: 'I am the widow of Abou Aibou, a merchant of Damascus. I had a son called Ganem, who, being drawn by his business to Bagdad, was accused there of carrying off this Fetnab. The caliph caused him to be sought for, in order to put him to death; and not being able to find him, wrote to the King of Damascus, ordering him to have our house plundered and destroyed; to have my daughter and myself exposed to the gaze of the people for three successive days; and then commanded that we should both be banished for ever from Syria. But with whatever indignity we have been treated, I could still be happy if I knew that my son lived, and I could again meet with him. What delight would it be to me and to his sister to behold him once more! When we embraced him we should forget the loss of our property, and all we have suffered on his account. Alas! I am convinced that if he is the cause, he is the innocent cause of our misfortunes, and that he is as free from wrong towards the caliph as towards his sister and myself.' 'No, undoubtedly,' interrupted Fetnab, 'he is no more criminal than you are. I can testify to his innocence, because I am that very Fetnab of whom you have so much reason to complain. It is my unhappy fate to have caused all your distresses. To me you must impute the loss of your son, if he really is no more; but if I have been the cause of your sufferings I have also the power to alleviate them. I have already justified Ganem in the sight of the caliph. That monarch has proclaimed throughout his dominions a pardon to the son of Abou Aibou; and be assured he will now serve you as effectually as he has before injured you. You are no longer his enemies. He only waits for the arrival of Ganem to reward him, by uniting our fates for ever, for the important service he has rendered me. He intends to give me to Ganem as his wife. Look upon me, then, as your daughter, and permit me to assure you of my eternal friendship.' As she said this she leaned affectionately over the mother of Ganem, whose astonishment rendered her unable to answer. Fetnab folded her a long time in her arms, and left her only to fly to the other bed, to embrace Alcolomb, who sat up extending her arms to receive her.

"After having lavished upon the mother and daughter every mark of tenderness and affection which they might expect from the wife of Ganem, the charming favourite of the caliph said: 'Do not grieve; for the valuable bales which Ganem had in this city are not lost: they are safe in my apartment in the caliph's palace. I am well aware that all the treasures in the world could not console you for the loss of Ganem; at least, I judge by my own feelings of the hearts of his mother and sister. The feeling of relationship is not less powerful than love in exalted minds. Do not let us despair of seeing him again: we shall find him. The happiness I experience in having thus met with you gives me the greater encouragement to entertain hope. Perhaps this very day may be the last of your misfortunes, and the commencement of happiness even still greater than you enjoyed at Damascus before Ganem quitted you.'

"Fetnab was still speaking when the syndic of the jewellers arrived. 'O lady,' said he, 'I have just witnessed a very affecting spectacle. A young man has been brought by a camel-driver to the hospital at Bagdad. He was fastened with cords upon the camel, for he had not sufficient strength to support himself. They had just unbound him and were about to carry him to the hospital when I passed. I approached the young man, and looked at him attentively, and it struck me that I had already seen his face. I asked some questions relative to his family, but I could not draw from him any answer but sighs and tears. I took pity on him; and knowing, from the custom I have of seeing sick persons, that there was urgent necessity for him to be immediately taken care of, I would not allow him to be left at the hospital. Well knowing the manner in which the sick are neglected in those places, and the incapacity of the physicians, I ordered him to be brought hither by my slaves, who have placed him in a separate apartment, and, by my desire, given him some of my own linen to wear; and they wait upon him in the same manner as I should be waited upon myself.'

"Fetnab started on hearing this account, and felt an emotion she could not explain. She said to the syndic: 'Let me go into the sick man's chamber: I must see him.' The syndic immediately conducted her there; and whilst she was absent, Ganem's mother said to Alcolomb: 'Ah, daughter! however miserable the situation of this sick stranger may be, it is possible that your unhappy brother, if he be still alive, is in as lamentable a condition.'

"As soon as the favourite of the caliph entered the sick man's apartment, she approached the bed where the syndic's slaves had placed the sufferer. She saw a young man, with his eyes closed, his face pale and disfigured and bathed in tears. She looked at him attentively, and her heart beat violently, for she thought she recognised the countenance of Ganem; but she could scarcely believe her eyes. If in some respects she found a resemblance to him in the person before her, in others he appeared so different, that she durst not flatter herself this could be Ganem whom she beheld. Unable to resist her desire of obtaining certainty on this subject, 'Ganem,' said she, with a trembling voice, 'is it you?' At these words she paused, in order to give him time to answer; but perceiving that he remained apparently insensible, she exclaimed: 'O Ganem, then it is not you to whom I speak! My imagination, too strongly impressed with your image, has painted the deceitful resemblance on this stranger. No illness could render the son of Abou Aibou deaf to the voice of Fetnab.' At the name of Fetnab, Ganem (for it was indeed he) raised his eyes, and turned his head towards the person who addressed him; and recognising the favourite of the caliph, he murmured: 'Ah, beautiful lady, can it be you? By what miracle ——' He could not go on; his

MEETING AGAIN.

emotions of joy overpowered him, and he fainted. Fetnab and the syndic eagerly flew to his assistance; but, as soon as he showed signs of recovery, the syndic begged the lady to retire, fearing lest the sight of her should increase Ganem's disorder.

"When the young man had recovered his senses, he looked round, and not perceiving her he sought, he cried: 'Beautiful Fetnab, where are you? Did you not appear to my eyes, or was it only an illusion?' 'No, my friend,' said the syndic, 'it is no illusion: I begged the lady to retire, but you shall see her as soon as you are strong enough to bear an interview. You now stand in need of repose, and nothing must prevent you from taking it. Your affairs wear a much better aspect; for I imagine you must be that Ganem for whom the Commander of the Faithful has caused a pardon for past offences to be proclaimed in Bagdad. Rest satisfied for the present with this intelligence. The lady who has just been with you will, in due time, give you more ample information. Think of nothing at present, but how best to regain your health; it shall be my endeavour to do everything in my power to contribute towards your recovery.' When he had said this, he left Ganem to his repose, and went to order whatever was necessary to restore the strength of the sick man, exhausted as he was by want and fatigue.

"During this time, Fetnab was in the apartment of Alcolomb and her mother, where a similar scene took place; for when Ganem's mother heard that the sick stranger whom the syndic had brought to his house was Ganem himself, she was so overjoyed that she also fainted away. When the care and attention of Fetnab and the syndic's wife had brought her to herself, she instantly wished to rise and go to her son; but the syndic, who arrived at this juncture, prevented her, by representing that Ganem was so weak and emaciated, that his life would be endangered if such violent emotions were excited in him as the unexpected sight of a beloved mother and sister must occasion. The syndic did not find it necessary to use any stronger arguments to persuade the mother of Ganem to desist from her purpose. The idea of the injury she might do her son was a consideration sufficiently powerful to make her instantly give up the pleasure she expected in seeing him. Fetnab now exclaimed: 'Blessed be Heaven for again bringing us together! I shall now return to the palace, and inform the caliph of these events; and to-morrow morning I will be with you again.' She then embraced the mother and daughter, and went away.

"As soon as she arrived at the palace, she requested a private audience of the caliph, which she instantly obtained. She was introduced into the monarch's cabinet, where he sat alone. She immediately threw herself at his feet, bowing her head to the ground, according to the usual custom. He desired her to rise and be seated, and then asked her if she had heard anything of Ganem. 'Commander of the Faithful,' said she, 'I have succeeded so well that I have found him, and his mother and sister also.' The caliph was curious to know how she could have discovered them in so short a time. She satisfied his curiosity, and spoke so handsomely of the mother of Ganem and of Alcolomb, that he had a great desire to see them, and also the young merchant.

"If Haroun Alraschid was at times violent, and allowed himself to be hurried by the heat of passion to the commission of acts of cruelty, yet he was in his nature the most equitable and generous of princes when once his anger was appeased, and he became sensible of his injustice. Being now convinced that he had unjustly persecuted Ganem and his family, and that he had publicly injured them, he resolved upon giving them public satisfaction. 'I am delighted,' said he to Fetnab, 'that you have been so fortunate as to make this discovery; I rejoice at it less on your account than on my own. I will punctually keep the promise I have given you. You shall marry Ganem; and I declare that from this moment you are no longer my slave—you are now free! Return to the young merchant; and, as soon as he has recovered his health, bring him to me, with his mother and sister.'

"Very early the next morning, Fetnab did not fail to repair to the syndic of the jewellers, impatient to learn the state of Ganem's health, and to communicate to the mother and daughter the news of the good fortune which awaited them. The first person she met was the syndic, who told her that Ganem had passed a very good night; and that as his disorder arose entirely from melancholy, and the cause was now removed, he would very soon recover.

"The son of Abou Aibou was in reality much stronger. Repose, the excellent remedies he had taken, and, more than all, the effect produced on his mind by the happy change in his situation, were so efficacious, that the syndic was of opinion he might with safety see his mother, sister, and mistress, provided he was prepared for the interview; for it was much to be feared that, wholly ignorant as he was of the arrival of his mother and sister at Bagdad, his surprise and joy at the sight of them might be attended with bad consequences. It was determined, therefore, that Fetnab should first enter Ganem's apartment alone, and should make a sign to the two other ladies to enter, when she judged they might safely appear.

"Affairs being thus arranged, Fetnab was introduced by the syndic to the sick man, who was so overjoyed at the sight of her that he almost fainted once more. 'Behold, Ganem!' said she, approaching his bed, 'you see your Fetnab again, whom you imagined lost to you for ever.' 'O beautiful lady,' interrupted he, eagerly, 'by what miracle do you again bless my sight? I thought you had been in the palace of the caliph. Doubtless he has listened to you: you have dispelled his suspicions, and are restored to his affection.' 'Yes, my dear Ganem,' replied Fetnab, 'I am justified in the opinion of the Commander of the Faithful, who, in order to repair the evils he has made you sustain, promises to bestow me on you in marriage.' These last words gave Ganem such extreme delight, that he was quite incapable at first of manifesting his joy otherwise than by the expressive and tender silence so well known to lovers. But he at last broke out into exclamations of rapture. 'Ah, beautiful Fetnab!' he cried, 'may I credit what you tell me? Can I believe that the caliph really gives you up to the son of Abou Aibou?' 'It is perfectly true,' replied the lady: 'the same monarch who was lately so desirous to take away your life, and who, in his anger, has made your mother and sister suffer a thousand indignities, now wishes to see you, in order to reward you for the respect you have shown towards him; and there is no doubt that he will give ample proofs of his favour to your whole family.'

"Ganem desired to know in what manner the caliph had ill-treated his mother and sister; whereupon Fetnab told him the mournful story of their sufferings. He could not hear the sad tale without tears, notwithstanding the happy state of his mind from the recent promise of his approaching marriage with his beloved mistress. But when Fetnab told him that his mother and sister were actually at Bagdad, and, moreover, in the same house with him, he showed such extreme impatience to see them that Fetnab could no longer delay the boon he so anxiously craved. She immediately called them: they were at the door, awaiting the glad summons. They entered, ran towards Ganem, and embracing him by turns, kissed him again and again; and many were the happy tears shed in the midst of these embraces. Ganem's countenance was bedewed with them; his mother and sister, and Fetnab also, wept abundantly. Even the syndic and his wife were unable to refrain from tears at so affecting a spectacle; nor could they sufficiently admire the secret ways of Providence, which had thus restored to each other four persons whom fortune had so cruelly separated.

"After they had all wiped away their tears, Ganem again awakened their compassion by the account he gave of all he had suffered, from the day when he left Fetnab to the moment when the syndic had brought him to his house. He told them that, having taken refuge in a small village, he had there fallen ill; that some charitable peasants had taken care of him; but as he exhibited no signs of recovery, he was given in charge to a camel-driver to be conveyed to the hospital at Bagdad. Fetnab also recounted the hardships she had sustained in her prison, and the accident of the caliph's overhearing her in the tower, and of his sending for her into his cabinet; nor did she omit to make mention of the conversation which restored her to his good opinion. At last, when they had all informed each other of what had befallen them respectively, 'Let us thank Heaven,' Fetnab said, 'for having thus united us, and think only of the happiness that now awaits us. As soon as Ganem's health is re-established, it will be necessary that he shall appear before the caliph, with his mother and sister; but as they are not at present in a condition to make a suitable appearance, I must undertake to remove this obstacle, and therefore beg you will excuse me for a moment.'

"So saying, she left the room, and went immediately to the palace, whence she soon returned to the syndic's house with another purse containing a thousand pieces of gold. She gave it the syndic, begging him to purchase proper dresses for Alcolomb and her mother. The syndic, who was a man of great taste, chose very elegant materials, and had them made up with all possible expedition. The dresses were ready in three days; and Ganem, finding himself sufficiently recovered, prepared for the important visit. But on the day which he had fixed upon for his visit to the caliph, just as he and his mother and sister were making the necessary preparations, the grand vizier Giafar arrived at the house of the syndic.

The minister was on horseback, and a long train of officers followed him. 'My lord,' said he to Ganem as he entered, 'I come from the Commander of the Faithful, your master and mine; the commission with which I am now entrusted is very different from my former task, which I do not wish to call to your remembrance. I am ordered to bring you with me, and present you to the caliph, who much wishes to see you.' To these civilities of the grand vizier Ganem replied only by a profound inclination of his head; he then mounted a horse which had been brought for him from the stables of the caliph, and showed very great dexterity and grace in its management. The mother and sister of Ganem were mounted on mules brought from the palace; and whilst Fetnab, mounted also on a mule, proceeded with them to the residence of the caliph by a private way, Giafar conducted Ganem by a public road, and introduced him into the hall of audience. The caliph was seated on his throne, surrounded by his emirs, viziers, the principal officers of the palace, and numerous other courtiers from his different dominions. There were Arabs, Persians, Egyptians, Africans, and Syrians, not to mention strangers who lived in countries not dependent upon the caliph.

"When the grand vizier had brought Ganem to the foot of the throne, the young merchant made his obeisance by prostrating himself with his face to the ground; then rising, he addressed an elegant compliment in verse to the caliph. The verses, though composed at the moment, obtained the applause of the whole court. When Ganem had finished his speech the caliph desired him to approach, and said, 'I am very glad to see you, and wish to learn from your own lips where you found my favourite, and what you have done to serve her.' Ganem accordingly told his story, and appeared so entirely frank and open, that the caliph was convinced of his sincerity. Haroun Alraschid ordered a very rich robe to be presented to him, according to the custom always observed towards those to whom audience was given. He then said: 'Ganem, I wish that you should remain at my court.' 'Commander of the Faithful,' replied the young merchant, 'the slave has no other will than that of his master, who is the arbiter of his life and fortune.' The caliph was well satisfied with Ganem's answer, and gave him a large pension. Hereupon, Haroun Alraschid descended from his throne, and ordering Ganem and the grand vizier only to follow him, he retired to his own apartment.

"As he did not doubt that Fetnab was at the palace with the mother and daughter of Abou Aibou, he ordered them to be summoned. They prostrated themselves before him. He desired them to rise, and was so struck with the beauty of Alcolomb that, after contemplating her with great attention, he said, 'I am so much concerned at having treated your charms so unworthily, that I think a reparation due to them which may exceed the offence I have committed. I take you, Alcolomb, for my wife, and by that means I shall punish Zobeidè, who will thus become the remote cause of your happiness, as she has been of your misfortunes. I will do yet more,' added he, turning towards the mother of Ganem. 'You, lady, are still young, and will not disdain an alliance with my grand vizier. I give you to Giafar; and you, Fetnab, shall be the wife of Ganem. Let a cadi and witnesses be brought hither, and let the three contracts be immediately drawn up and signed.' Ganem represented to the caliph that his sister would be too much honoured in being ranked among the number of the royal favourites; but the prince was determined to marry her.

"He thought this history of Ganem so extraordinary, that he ordered a famous historian to commit it to writing. It was afterwards deposited in the caliph's treasury, whence several copies from the original have been taken, and thus the story became public."

When Scheherazade had finished the history of Ganem, the son of Abou Aibou, the Sultan of the Indies expressed how much pleasure he had received from the relation. 'O mighty monarch,' said the sultana, 'since this history has amused you, I humbly entreat that your majesty will listen to the tale of Prince Zeyn Alasnam and the King of the Genii: you will be as much satisfied with it as with this.' Schahriar consented; but as the day began to dawn, the telling of the story was deferred to the following night. The Sultana then began the history as follows:—

THE KING REWARDS THE ASTROLOGERS.

## THE HISTORY OF PRINCE ZEYN ALASNAM, AND OF THE KING OF THE GENII.

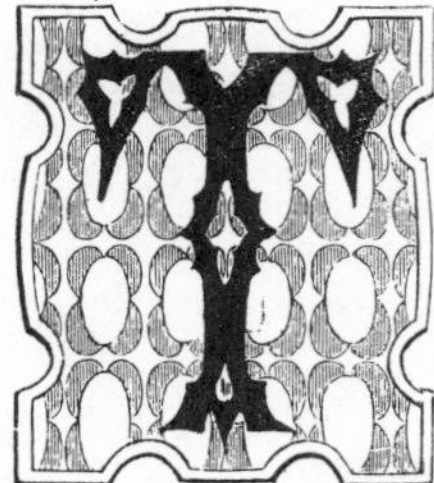

HERE was once a King of Balsora who possessed immense riches, and was much beloved by his subjects; but he had no children, and this grieved him greatly. All the holy men of his kingdom were engaged by very considerable donations to petition Heaven to grant the king a son. At length their prayers were answered. The queen became the mother of a prince, who was named Zeyn Alasnam, which means the Beauty of Statues.

"The king called an assembly of all the astrologers in his kingdom, and ordered them to calculate the nativity of his son. They discovered by their observations that the prince's life would be long; that he would be of a firm and courageous temper; and that he would need all his courage to sustain and support him through the evils that would threaten him. The king was not disconcerted at this prediction. He replied: 'My son will have no reason to complain, since he will possess courage. It is good for princes to experience misfortune: adversity purifies virtue, and makes rulers better acquainted with the duties of government.'

"The king rewarded the astrologers and dismissed them. The young prince was brought up with all possible care. Masters in every department of knowledge were provided, as soon as he was old enough to profit by their instructions. His father was in fact determined to give the prince a very complete education; but the good king was very suddenly attacked by a disease which his physicians were unable to cure. Finding that he was on his death-bed, he called his son, whom he recommended, among other things, to make himself beloved rather than feared by his people; never to lend an ear to flatterers; and to be equally slow in rewarding and in punishing, since it frequently happened that kings, misled by false appearances, heaped benefits on the bad, and oppressed the good.

"So soon as the king was dead, Prince Zeyn clothed himself in mourning, which he continued to wear for seven days. On the eighth he ascended the throne, removed his father's seal from the royal treasure, which he sealed with his own signet. And now he began to taste all the sweets of empire. The pleasure of seeing his courtiers bend before him, of beholding them engaged in no other study than how to prove their obedience and zeal; these, and the other charms of sovereign power, took firm possession of his mind. He thought only of the duties which his subjects owed to him, without reflecting on the important return which they had a right to claim from him. He took little interest in the affairs of government, but plunged into all sorts of debauchery, with a set of voluptuous young men, on whom he conferred all the first offices of the state. As he was naturally prodigal, and put no restraint whatever upon his bounties, it soon came to pass that his numerous favourites had insensibly exhausted his treasures.

"The queen, his mother, was still living. She was a princess of great wisdom and prudence, and had many times unsuccessfully attempted to check the extravagant courses of the king her son, by representing to him that unless he soon changed his conduct he would not only dissipate his riches, but completely lose the affection of his people, and bring on a rebellion which would in all probability cost him both his crown and his life. What his mother predicted nearly took place. The people began to exclaim against the government; and their murmurs would infallibly have produced a general revolt, if the queen had not had the address to prevent the outbreak. This princess, informed of the unhappy state of affairs, admonished the king of his danger in very serious terms; and Zeyn Alasnam at last allowed himself to be convinced. He deprived his vicious companions of all share in the government, and supplied their places by sage old men, who knew better how to keep his subjects within their duty.

"Finding all his riches dissipated so quickly, King Zeyn began to repent that he had made no better use of them. He had fallen into a profound melancholy which nothing could divert, when one night an old man appeared to him in a dream, and, advancing towards him with a smiling countenance, addressed him in these words: 'Know, O King Zeyn, that there is no sorrow which may not be succeeded by joy, no misfortune which may not draw happiness in its train. If you wish to see your sorrow turned into joy, arise, depart into Egypt, and visit Cairo, where good fortune awaits you.'

"The prince was much struck with this dream. He spoke of it very seriously to the queen his mother, who was disposed to treat it with disdain. 'You would not, surely, my son,' said she, 'travel into Egypt on the faith of this curious dream?' 'And why not, lady?' retorted King Zeyn; 'do you imagine that all dreams are mere chimeras, or casual impressions of the brain? No, no; be assured some of them are of mysterious and weighty import. My preceptors have related to me a thousand histories which have firmly convinced me of this. Besides, if I were not even fully convinced, I could not avoid attaching importance to my own dream. The old man who appeared to me had something supernatural in his glance. He was not one of those whom age alone renders respectable; there was an air of divinity diffused over his whole person. He looked just as our great Prophet is represented; and if you wish that I should give you my opinion, I believe that he was the Prophet himself, who, touched by my misfortunes, wishes to alleviate them. I am disposed to put full reliance in the hopes he has inspired me with; I confide in his promises, and am resolved to obey his voice.' The queen attempted to dissuade her son from his purpose, but her arguments were unavailing. The king entrusted to her the care of his kingdom, and quitted the palace one night very secretly, taking the road to Cairo unaccompanied by any one.

"After enduring much hardship and fatigue, he arrived at that famous city, with which few can compare either in extent or beauty. He alighted at the door of a mosque; and, finding himself overcome with weariness, he lay down to rest. Scarcely had he fallen asleep, when he saw in a dream the same old man, who said to him: 'O my son, I am fully satisfied with you; you have relied on my words. You have come hither without suffering the length or difficulties of the way to abate your resolution; but learn that I have made you undertake this long journey merely to prove you. I see that you have courage and firmness. You deserve to be rendered the most rich and happy prince in the whole world. Return to Balsora: you will find in your palace immense riches, such as no king ever possessed.'

"The prince was by no means satisfied with this dream. 'Alas!' said he to himself when he awoke, 'how great has been my error! This old man, whom I believed to be our venerable Prophet, is nothing but a creation of my own troubled mind. With my fancy so thoroughly imbued with him, it is not wonderful that I should see him a second time. I will return to Balsora; for why should I tarry here? I am glad, however, that I did not communicate the object of my journey to any one but my mother. Were it known why I came I should become the mockery of my people.'

"He then retraced his steps to Balsora. As soon as he arrived there, the queen asked him if he returned contented. He related to her everything that had happened, and appeared so much mortified at having shown himself so credulous, that his mother, instead of increasing his chagrin by raillery or reproaches, endeavoured to console him. 'Cease to afflict yourself, my son,' she said to him; 'if Allah destines you to be rich, you will acquire wealth without effort: all that I have to recommend to you is to be virtuous. Renounce the vain delights of dancing, of music, and of purple wine. Fly those destructive pleasures; they have already nearly ruined you. Strive rather to render your subjects happy: in securing their good you will obtain your own.'

"King Zeyn declared that in future he would follow the counsels of his mother and of those sage viziers whom he had made choice of to sustain the weight of government. But on the first night after his return to his palace he again, for the third time, saw the old man in a dream. And the vision said to him: 'Valiant Zeyn, the time of your prosperity is at length arrived. To-morrow morning, as soon as you rise, take a pickaxe and dig with it in the cabinet of the deceased king: you will there discover a great treasure.'

"So soon as the king awoke he rose from his bed, and running to the queen's apartment, related to her with much earnestness the dream he had just had. 'In truth, my son,' said the queen, smiling, 'this is a most obstinate old man; he is not content with having deceived you twice. Do you feel inclined to trust him again?' 'No, my mother,' replied Zeyn, 'I believe nothing of what he has said to me; but still, from curiosity, I feel anxious to pay a visit to my father's cabinet.' 'Oh! I have no doubt of it,' exclaimed the queen, with a burst of laughter. 'Go, my son, satisfy yourself: it is a great comfort to me that your present purpose is not altogether so fatiguing as a journey to Egypt.'

"'Indeed, honoured lady,' replied the king, 'I must confess to you that this third dream has revived my confidence, it is so evidently connected with the two former visions. Let us examine all the words of the old man. He first commanded me to go to Egypt; he there told me that he had ordered me to take the journey merely that I might give proof of my courage and resolution. "Return," said he then, "to Balsora, and there you will discover treasures." He has this night pointed out to me the precise spot where these treasures are. In these three dreams there is, it appears to me, a manifest unity of design: they have nothing equivocal about them; not a single circumstance to create disbelief. They may indeed be wholly a delusion; but I would rather make a useless search than be obliged to reproach myself all my life for having failed to obtain great riches, because I very unadvisedly chose to indulge in the pride of disbelief.'

"So saying he left the queen's apartment. He then provided himself with a proper instrument, and entered alone into the cabinet of the deceased king. He immediately began his work, and raised more than half the squares of the pavement, without perceiving the least appearance of treasure. He discontinued his labour for a moment to rest himself, saying in his heart: 'I very much fear that my mother will have reason to laugh at me.' However, he took fresh courage and resumed his task. He had no cause to repent his perseverance. Suddenly he discovered a white stone. He eagerly raised it, and found beneath it a door, secured by a steel padlock. He broke this in with the instrument in his hand, and opened the door, under which he found a staircase of white marble. King Zeyn now lighted a wax taper, with which he descended by this staircase into a chamber inlaid with porcelain; the ceiling and floor were of crystal. But his attention was chiefly attracted by four shelves, upon each of which stood ten urns of porphyry. The king supposed these to be full of wine. 'Good,' said he to himself; 'this wine must be very old, and I doubt not it is excellent.' He went up to one of the urns and took off the lid; then, with equal surprise and joy, he discovered that the vessel was full of gold. He examined all the urns on the four shelves, one after another, and found them full of sequins. He took a handful of the coin, which he carried to the queen.

"As may be imagined, the queen was greatly astonished when she heard the king's account of what he had seen. 'O my son,' she exclaimed, 'take care not to dissipate these riches in the inconsiderate manner in which you have already wasted the royal treasure; let not your enemies have so fair an occasion for exultation.' 'No, my mother,' replied King Zeyn, 'I shall hereafter live in a manner that will not displease you.'

"The queen requested that the king her son would conduct her into this astonishing vault, which her departed husband had caused to be made so very secretly that she had never heard of it, or had any suspicion of its existence. King Zeyn accompanied her to the cabinet, assisted her to descend the marble staircase, and led her to the apartment which contained the urns. She gazed at everything with an eye of extreme curiosity, and presently remarked in a corner of the room a small urn of the same materials as the rest, which the prince had not seen. He took it in his hand, and on opening it, found it contained a small golden key. 'My son,' said the queen to him, 'this is, without doubt, the key of some new treasure. Let us search diligently, and, if possible, discover the lock which it is intended to open.'

"They examined the room with the greatest attention, and at length discovered, in the middle of one of the panels of the wainscot, a lock, which they immediately supposed was that to which the key belonged. The king at once made trial of it. The door opened in an instant, and another apartment was exposed to their view, in the middle of which were nine pedestals of massive gold. Eight of these supported each a statue made of a single diamond, the lustre of which was so great as completely to illuminate the room.

"'O Heavens!' cried King Zeyn, in the greatest astonishment, 'where could my father possibly find anything so rare and beautiful as these statues?' When he came to the ninth pedestal his astonishment was increased; for above it was placed a piece of white satin, on which were written these words: 'My dear son, to acquire these eight statues has been a work of great labour; but, beautiful as they may appear, know that there is in the world a ninth statue which greatly excels them. This ninth statue is in itself of a thousand times greater value than all you behold. If you wish to become the possessor of it, repair to the city of Cairo, in Egypt, where resides one of my old slaves called Mobarec. You will have no trouble in finding him: the first person you meet will inform you where he dwells. Go to him, and tell him what you have discovered. He will know that you are my son, and will lead you to the place where this marvellous statue is to be found, and instruct you how you may certainly obtain it.'

"When King Zeyn had read these words he said to the queen: 'I have a great desire to obtain this ninth statue. It must be a piece of unheard-of excellence, since all these together do not equal it in value. I am resolved to set off for Grand Cairo; and I am sure, my mother, that you will not wish to dissuade me from my purpose.' 'No, my son,' replied the queen, 'I have no objection to make: you are evidently under the direction of our great Prophet, who will not permit you to perish on the journey. Depart when you please. I and your viziers will, in your absence, manage the kingdom.' The king ordered his travelling train to be prepared, and set off with only a few slaves, not choosing to be attended by a numerous retinue.

KING ZEYN CONDUCTS THE QUEEN MOTHER TO THE VAULT.

"He accomplished his journey without any disagreeable accident, and in due time arrived at Cairo, where he inquired after Mobarec. He learned that the man whom he sought was one of the richest people of the place; that he lived in the style of a great nobleman, and that his house was constantly open, particularly to strangers. King Zeyn requested a citizen whom he met to conduct him thither. He knocked at the door, which was opened by a slave, who desired to know his name and business. 'I am a stranger,' replied the king, 'and as I have heard much of the generosity of your master Mobarec, I am come to take up my abode with him.' The slave requested King Zeyn to wait a moment, while he went to speak to his master, who immediately ordered that the stranger should be admitted. The slave returned to the door to assure the stranger that he was welcome.

"King Zeyn then entered the house, and having crossed a large court, passed into a hall magnificently ornamented, where Mobarec, who was waiting for him, received him with great civility, and thanked him for the honour he did him in taking up his abode at his house. The king made a suitable reply to this compliment, and then addressed him as follows: 'In me you behold the son of the late King of Balsora: my name is Alasnam.' 'The King of Balsora,' said Mobarec, 'was formerly my master; but, my lord, I never knew that he had a son. How old are you?' 'I am twenty years of age,' replied King Zeyn: "how long is it since you quitted my father's court?' 'Nearly two-and-twenty years,' said Mobarec; 'but how can you convince me that you are his son?' 'My father,' returned King Zeyn, 'had a vault under his cabinet, in which I have found forty urns of porphyry all filled with gold.' 'And what did you see there besides?' replied Mobarec. 'There are,' said the king, 'nine pedestals of massive gold, upon each of which are diamond statues; and above the ninth is suspended a piece of white satin, upon which my father has written what it is necessary for me to do that I may obtain another statue more valuable than all the rest. I doubt not that you know where this statue is, since it is written upon the satin that you are to conduct me to it.'

"He had scarcely spoken these words, when Mobarec threw himself on his knees, and kissing one of King Zeyn's hands a great many times, exclaimed: 'I return thanks to Heaven for conducting you hither. I am now satisfied that you are the King of Balsora's son. If you wish to visit the place where the marvellous statue is to be found, I will lead you to it; but it is necessary that you should first remain here some short time, to recover from your fatigue. This day I give an entertainment to the principal people of Cairo. We were at table when the news of your arrival came. Will you condescend, my lord, to come and join our party?' 'By all means,' replied King Zeyn; 'I shall be delighted to partake of your feast.' Mobarec immediately conducted him to a hall under a lofty dome, where the company was assembled. He caused King Zeyn to take his seat at the table, and began to serve him on his knees. The grandees of Cairo expressed much surprise at this spectacle, saying to each other in a low tone, 'Who can this stranger be whom Mobarec waits upon with so much respect?'

"When they had finished eating, Mobarec thus addressed the company: 'Be not astonished, gentlemen, at the profound respect you have seen me pay to this young stranger. Know that he is the son of the King of Balsora, my former master. His father purchased me with money from his own treasure, and died without having granted me my liberty. I am, therefore, still a slave! Consequently, I myself and all my property of right belong to this young king, the sole heir of my dead master.' King Zeyn here interrupted him: 'O Mobarec,' said he, 'I declare before all these worthy guests that you are free from this moment, and that I renounce every claim I may have on yourself or to anything belonging to you. I only wish to know what I can further do to serve you.' At these words Mobarec kissed the earth, and expressed in appropriate terms the infinite obligation he was under to the young king. Wine was afterwards brought in, and they continued to drink during the remainder of the day; and in the evening presents were distributed to the guests before they retired.

"The next day King Zeyn said to Mobarec: 'I have had sufficient rest; and since my journey to Cairo has not been undertaken with any view to pleasure, but merely with the intention of procuring the ninth statue, I think it is time that we should set off in search of it.' 'O my lord,' replied Mobarec, 'I am ready to fulfil your wish; but you know not all the dangers you must encounter if you are determined to obtain this precious statue.' 'Be the danger what it may,' replied the king, 'I am resolved to face it, and will perish rather than yield. Every event that can befall is under the direction of an all-ruling Providence. Therefore I beg you to accompany me, and let your fortitude equal mine.'

"Mobarec, seeing his young master determined to depart, summoned his domestics, and ordered them to provide what was necessary. King Zeyn and Mobarec afterwards performed the ceremony of ablution, and the usual religious rite, after which they set out on their journey. They remarked upon the road a great number of very rare and surprising objects; and, continuing their route during many days, at length reached a very delicious retreat, where they alighted from their horses. Mobarec then said to the servants who attended them: 'Remain in this place, and keep good guard till we return.' Then, addressing himself to King Zeyn, he said: 'Come, my lord, let us now advance by ourselves; we are near the dreadful place where the ninth statue is concealed. You will have need of all your courage.'

"They soon came to the margin of a lake. Mobarec seated himself upon the bank, and thus addressed the king: 'It is requisite that we should pass this water.' 'How is that possible,' replied King Zeyn, 'when we have no boat?' 'You will see one appear in a moment,' returned Mobarec: 'an enchanted bark, belonging to the King of the Genii, will come to receive you; but be careful to remember what I now tell you. You must preserve a strict silence, and on no account address one syllable to the boatman. However singular his appearance may seem, whatever you may see to excite your astonishment, speak not a word; for I tell you beforehand, that if you once open your lips after we have embarked, the vessel will sink in an instant.' 'I will take especial care to be silent,' said King Zeyn; 'you have only to tell me what I have to do, and I will follow your instructions very exactly.'

"While he was saying this, he suddenly perceived, traversing the lake, a bark of red sandal-wood, having a mast of fine amber, with a streamer of blue satin. There was only one being to guide it—a creature whose head resembled that of an elephant, and whose body was shaped like that of a tiger. When the vessel had come to where the prince and Mobarec stood, the boatman took them up, one after another, with his trunk, and lifted them into the boat. He then passed to the other side of the lake in an instant, and, taking them up as before, set them down on the opposite shore. Thereupon he and his bark disappeared.

"'We may now speak freely,' said Mobarec. 'The island on which we now are belongs to the King of the Genii, and no spot on earth deserves to be compared with it. Examine it closely, and tell me, prince, if it is not a most charming retreat. It appears to me a just image of that delightful abode which is prepared by Allah above for the faithful observers of our law. See how the fields are enamelled with flowers and with every sort of odoriferous herb. Admire these beautiful trees, bending to the earth with their burden of delicious fruit. Listen to the exquisite harmony which fills the air on every side from the songs of innumerable birds of species unknown in every other country.' King Zeyn, forgetting all his fatigue, could not desist for a moment from surveying the beauties that surrounded him. As he advanced into the island, a variety of new charms were constantly presenting themselves to his view.

"At length they came in front of a palace, built of the finest emeralds, and surrounded by a large moat, on the borders of which at due distances were planted trees, which had grown to so vast a height as to cover the whole palace with their shade. Opposite the gate, which was of massive gold, was a bridge made of the single shell of a fish, but measuring at the least twelve yards in length and six in breadth. At the head of the bridge appeared a troop of genii of gigantic height, who guarded the entrance of the castle with immense clubs of Chinese steel.

"'Let us advance no farther,' said Mobarec; 'if we attempt it these genii will destroy us; and if we wish to prevent their coming hither, we shall have to perform a certain magic ceremony.' So saying, he drew from a purse, which he had under his robe, four bands of yellow taffeta, one of which he passed round his waist, and another along his back; the remaining two he gave to the king, who made a similar use of them. After this, Mobarec spread upon the earth two large cloths or carpets, upon the borders of which he strewed a variety of precious stones, with a quantity of musk and amber. They then sat down each on a carpet, and Mobarec addressed the prince in these terms: 'My lord, I am about to summon the King of the Genii, who inhabits this palace. He will not, I hope, arrive in an angry mood; but I must confess to you I am not without anxiety on the subject. If our arrival in this island be disagreeable to him, he will appear under the form of a most hideous monster; but if he approves our purpose, he will assume the appearance of a handsome man. As soon as he appears, you must rise and salute him, but without quitting your carpet, for if you leave it you will infallibly perish. You must say to him, "Sovereign lord of the genii, my father your servant hath been summoned away by the angel of death; may it please your majesty to extend to me the same gracious protection you bestowed on my deceased parent." If the King of the Genii,' added Mobarec, 'desires to know what is the favour you request of him, answer as follows: "My sovereign lord, I humbly entreat to be put in possession of the ninth statue."'

"Having in this way imparted to the king the instructions he thought necessary, Mobarec began his magic arts. The eyes of the two men were immediately struck by a vivid flash of lightning, which was followed by a loud clap of thunder. The whole island was involved in thick darkness; a furious storm arose; horrid cries were heard; and the earth, trembling to its base, was disturbed by a commotion like that which Asrafyel will produce at the dreadful day of final retribution.

"King Zeyn felt considerable alarm, and began to forebode all kinds of evil from the noise and confusion around him; but Mobarec, who better knew what to think of the matter, began to smile, and said: 'O king, take confidence; everything goes well.' Presently the King of the Genii made his appearance under the form of a handsome man, retaining, however, a certain fierceness of aspect.

"As soon as he perceived the King of the Genii, King Zeyn delivered the compliment which Mobarec had dictated. The King of the Genii received him with a smile, and replied: 'O my son, I loved your father, and whenever he came to pay me his respects I presented him with a statue to take back with him. My affection for you is not less than the love I bestowed on him. Some days before your father's death, I obliged him to write upon the piece of white satin the inscription you read; I promised him to take you under my protection, and to give you the ninth statue, which surpasses in beauty all those in your possession. I have already begun to keep my word. It was I who appeared to you in a dream under the form of an old man. It was I who revealed to you the secret apartments where the urns and statues stand. In everything that has happened to you I have played a part, or rather I have been the mover of the whole. I know the purpose for which you are here: you shall obtain your wish. If I had not given my promise to your father, I would most willingly have granted your request on your own account. But it is first necessary that you should swear by the most sacred of oaths that you will return to this island, and bring back with you a girl in the fifteenth year of her age—a virgin of surpassing loveliness and virtue. It is further necessary, that though she possesses the most perfect beauty, you should be so completely master of yourself, that, in conducting her hither, you should form no desire to appear in any other character than that of her protector.'

"King Zeyn took the rash oath which the King of the Genii required. 'But, great king,' said he afterwards, 'suppose I should be fortunate enough to meet with the extraordinary person you have described, how shall I be able to know when I have found her whether she is virtuous?' 'I confess,' replied the King of the Genii, smiling, 'that in these cases appearances may deceive. Certain knowledge is not to be attained by the sons of Adam; nor have I any intention of relying altogether on your sagacity in so delicate an affair. I will give you a mirror, to which you may more safely trust than to your conjectures. As soon as you see a perfectly beautiful girl of the age required, you will have only to look in your mirror, where you will behold her image. If the glass remains perfectly pure and unsullied, you may be assured that the damsel is virtuous; but if, on the contrary, it shows the least dimness, this will be a certain proof that she has not been always upon

THE KING OF THE GENII GIVES THE MIRROR TO KING ZEYN.

her guard, or that there have been moments when she might have done what is wrong. Do not forget the oath you have taken, or I shall be obliged to deprive you of life, notwithstanding the regard I feel for you.' King Zeyn Alasnam declared again that he would keep his word most exactly.

"The King of the Genii then put a mirror into King Zeyn's hands, saying at the same time, 'My son, you may return whenever you please; and, with the aid of this mirror, may you accomplish your purpose.' King Zeyn and Mobarec took leave of the King of the Genii, and proceeded towards the lake. The boatman with the elephant's head came to them with his bark, and put them across in the same manner as he had brought them. They found their retinue waiting for them, and returned to Cairo.

"Prince Alasnam remained some days with Mobarec to recover from his fatigue. At length he said to him: 'Let us depart for Bagdad, and seek out a damsel for the King of the Genii.' 'What!' replied Mobarec, 'are we not in Grand Cairo? Do you suppose we cannot in this place find plenty of handsome women?' 'You are right,' replied the king; 'but how shall we discover the places where they are to be found?' 'Give yourself no concern on that account, my lord,' replied Mobarec; 'I know a very expert old woman, whom I will employ in this matter. I have no doubt she will acquit herself very skilfully.'

"The old woman had, in truth, all the requisite address. She soon found means to give the king a sight of a great number of very beautiful girls of the age of fifteen; but when he came to consult his mirror, the glass, the fatal touchstone of their virtue, was constantly clouded. All the women of the court and of the city who were in their fifteenth year underwent in succession the severe scrutiny, and in no instance did the glass preserve itself pure and unsullied.

"When they found that they could meet with no damsels of sufficient purity at Cairo, they repaired to Bagdad. They here rented a magnificent palace in one of the best parts of the city, and began to show very liberal hospitality. Their table was free to all comers; and, when the numerous guests in the palace were satisfied, what remained was conveyed to the dervises, who thence derived a very comfortable subsistence.

"In the part of the city where they lived was an Iman named Boubekir Muezin, a vain, proud, and envious man. He hated the rich because he himself was poor, and allowed his own poverty to exasperate him against the prosperity of his neighbour. He frequently heard of King Zeyn Alasnam, and of the abundance which reigned in his house, and this was enough to inspire him with an extreme aversion to the prince. He even carried his hatred so far, that one day in the mosque, after evening prayers, he said to the people: 'I have heard, my brethren, that a stranger, who has lately taken up his abode in our quarter of the town, daily expends very large sums. I can find no one who knows anything of him. He is probably some villain who, having been a thief in his own country, has come to this large and populous city to enjoy his ill-gotten riches. Be upon your guard, my friends; for should the caliph learn that a person of this character is living among us, we have great reason to fear that he will punish us severely for not having informed him of the fact. With respect to myself, I shall stand acquitted whatever may happen. No omission of duty can ever be imputed to me.' The people, who usually allow themselves to be very easily persuaded, cried out with one voice to Boubekir: 'It is your own affair; do you, therefore, give information to the council.' The Iman hereupon returned home perfectly satisfied, and employed himself in composing a memorial upon the subject, with the intention of presenting it to the caliph the next day.

"But Mobarec, who had attended prayers, and with the rest had heard the Iman's harangue, put five hundred sequins of gold in a handkerchief, and prepared a parcel of several pieces of silk; thereupon he made the best of his way to Boubekir's house. The Iman, in a very rough tone of voice, desired to know what he wanted. 'I am your neighbour and servant,' replied Mobarec, with an air of great mildness, as he put the gold and the pieces of silk in the hands of the astonished Boubekir. 'I come in behalf of King Zeyn, who lives in this part of the town. He has heard much of your merit, and has commanded me to come and tell you how much he wishes for the pleasure of your acquaintance; in the meantime, he begs you to accept this small present.' Boubekir, transported with joy, replied to Mobarec: 'Have the goodness, my master, to make my most humble excuses to the prince. Assure him that I am much concerned and ashamed at my negligence in not having yet visited him; that I will take an early opportunity to repair my fault; and that to-morrow he may expect that I shall pay my respects.'

"On the following day, after morning prayers, Boubekir thus addressed the people: 'Be assured, my brethren, there is no one living who is without enemies. Envy attacks all, but chiefly those who have large possessions. The stranger of whom I spoke to you yesterday is not a villainous character, as some ill-intentioned persons represented him to be, but a young prince possessed of a thousand virtues. Let us not, then, by any injurious report, give the caliph a false impression of so worthy a man.'

"Having by this discourse effaced from the people's mind the opinion he had given of King Zeyn the preceding day, Boubekir returned to his house. He then clothed himself in his dress of ceremony, and set off to wait upon the young king, who received him very graciously. After many compliments on both sides, Boubekir said to the king: 'Do you propose, my lord, to remain long at Bagdad?' 'I shall continue here,' replied King Zeyn, 'till I have found a woman who is in her fifteenth year, possessed of perfect beauty, and who at the same time shall be of such unsullied virtue that she must never have harboured an evil thought.' 'You seek what is not easily found,' replied the Iman, 'and I should greatly fear that your labour would be useless, if I did not myself know a young lady of the character you describe. Her father, who was formerly vizier, has long since quitted the court. He has for many years been living in a very retired position, and has wholly devoted himself to the education of his daughter. I will, if you approve, wait upon this man on your behalf; he, I have no doubt, will be delighted to have a son-in-law of your birth and elevated rank.' 'Not so fast,' replied King Zeyn; 'I shall certainly not marry this young lady till I am assured that she is the sort of person I seek. With respect to her beauty, I can readily rely upon what you say; but with regard to her virtue, what proofs can you give me on this subject?' 'Proofs!' said Boubekir, 'what proofs would you wish to have?' 'It is necessary,' said King Zeyn, 'that I should see her face: that will be enough to satisfy me.' 'You are, then, exceeding expert in the science of physiognomy,' replied the Iman, smiling. 'However, come with me to the old vizier, and I will beg his permission that you may see her for a single moment in his presence.'

"So saying, he conducted the prince to the vizier's house. When the old man was informed of the birth and intentions of King Zeyn, he gave orders that his daughter should appear; and when she entered, he commanded her to remove her veil. Never had the young King of Balsora beheld so perfect and captivating a beauty. He surveyed her for some time in silent astonishment. When at length he sufficiently recovered himself to make the important trial whether she was as virtuous as fair, he drew forth his mirror, and the polished surface remained pure and unsullied!

"Having at last discovered the damsel he sought, he begged of the vizier to give her up to him. A cadi was immediately summoned, a marriage contract was prepared, and the ceremony of prayer performed; after which King Zeyn attended the vizier to his house, where he entertained him very magnificently, and made him large presents. He afterwards sent a large number of jewels to the lady by Mobarec, whom he charged to conduct her to his palace, where the nuptials were celebrated with all the pomp suitable to the high rank of King Zeyn. When all the company had retired, Mobarec said to his master: 'Let us depart, my lord; we have no further business at Bagdad. It is necessary that we now return to Cairo: remember the promise you made to the King of the Genii.' 'Let us depart at once,' replied the king; 'I am determined most faithfully to fulfil my engagement. I will, however, confess to you, my dear Mobarec, that in obeying the King of the Genii I do small violence to my inclination. The person whom I have just married is very amiable, and I feel strongly inclined to convey her immediately to Balsora, and place her on my throne.'

"'Ah, my lord!' cried Mobarec, 'resist with all possible fortitude so dangerous a wish. Learn to subdue your inclinations; and, whatever it may cost you—how great soever the conflict you sustain—keep your promise to the King of the Genii.' 'Then, Mobarec,' said the prince, 'be careful to conceal from me this charming girl; let not my eyes ever behold her more; I fear, indeed, that I have already seen her but too often.'

"Mobarec caused all things to be prepared for their departure. They returned to Cairo, and from thence betook themselves to the island of the King of the Genii. When they arrived there, the lady, who had travelled all the way in a litter, and had never seen the prince from the day of their marriage, inquired of Mobarec where they then were. 'Shall we not,' said she, 'soon reach the dominions of the king my husband?' 'Beautiful lady,' replied Mobarec, 'it is time to undeceive you. King Zeyn has had no other view in marrying you than to draw you from the protection of your father. Not to make you sovereign of Balsora has he pledged his faith to you: his intention is to deliver you to the King of the Genii, who has required from him a damsel of perfect beauty and perfect virtue.' At these words the lady began to weep bitterly, and to show an amount of distress which very much affected both the prince and Mobarec. 'Have pity on me, I beseech you!' she exclaimed; 'I am here a helpless stranger. You will have to answer to Heaven for the treachery you have practised towards me!'

"All her tears and complaints were vain. She was delivered up to the King of the Genii, who, after looking fixedly upon her for some time, said to King Zeyn: 'O king, I am fully satisfied with your conduct. The damsel you have brought me is as virtuous as she is beautiful; and your meritorious perseverance in keeping your word faithfully is highly pleasing to me. Return to your dominions; and when you revisit the subterranean apartment where the eight statues stand, you will find the ninth I promised you; I shall take care to have it transported thither by the aid of my genii.' King Zeyn returned his best thanks to the king. He then took his leave, and with Morabec again set out on the road to Cairo. At that city he made a very short stay, his impatience to possess the ninth statue urging him to proceed as fast as possible. But for all his haste he did not cease to think frequently of the damsel he had espoused; and bitterly remorseful for the deceit he had used, he regarded himself as the sole cause of her misfortune. 'Alas!' said he to himself, 'I have stolen her from an affectionate father to sacrifice her to a genie. O charming, incomparable beauty! how much better a fate did you deserve!"

"Full of these reflections, King Zeyn pursued his journey till he arrived at Balsora, where his subjects, delighted at his return, made very great rejoicings. He first waited upon the queen his mother, to give her an account of his journey. The queen learned with the greatest satisfaction that he was so certain to obtain the ninth statue. 'Come, my son,' said she 'let us go and view it instantly; for we may be certain it is in the subterraneous apartment, where the King of the Genii has instructed you to seek it.' The young king and his mother, burning with impatience to see this marvellous statue, descended into the vault and entered the hall of statues together. But how great was their surprise when, instead of a diamond statue, they perceived on the ninth pedestal a young damsel of perfect beauty, whom the prince immediately recognised as the lady he had carried to the island of the genii. 'You are much surprised, O king,' said the young lady, 'to see me here: you expected to find something much more precious, and, I doubt not, at this very moment you heartily repent of the trouble you have taken. You expected to receive some worthier recompense.' 'No, beautiful lady,' replied King Zeyn, 'Heaven is my witness how much I wished to preserve you to myself, and how frequently I wished to break my promise to the King of the Genii. Whatever may be the value of a diamond statue, can it possibly be equal to the pleasure of possessing you? Be assured I love you better than all the diamonds and all the riches of the world.'

"Just as he was concluding this speech, a clap of thunder was heard which shook the whole subterranean hall. The mother of King Zeyn was much alarmed; but the King of the Genii, who instantly appeared, dissipated her terrors. 'Worthy queen' said he, 'I protect and love your son. I was desirous to know whether at his age he would be able to obey the dictates of reason. I am well aware that the charms of this beauteous lady have touched his heart, and that he did not exactly keep the promise he had made, not even to wish to be more than her protector; but I am at the same time too well acquainted with the weakness of human nature to be much offended at this; and I am delighted with the virtue and moderation he has shown. Behold here the ninth statue, bestowed upon him as the reward of his merit. It is infinitely more rare and more precious than all the others. Live, O King Zeyn,' added he, addressing himself to the prince, 'live happy with this young lady; she is your wife; and, if you wish that she should preserve for you a pure and constant faith, love her always, and love none but her. Take care to give her no rival, and I will be answerable for her fidelity.' With these words the King of the Genii disappeared, and King Zeyn, delighted with his good fortune, had his beauteous wife proclaimed Queen of Balsora the same day. This virtuous pair, always faithful and always affectionate, lived together for a great number of years in perfect happiness."

When the Sultana of the Indies had thus finished the story of Prince Zeyn Alasnam, she begged permission to begin another. Schahriar granted the required permission for the next night, as daylight was now beginning to appear. Therefore on the following evening the princess began her new narrative in these words:—

## THE HISTORY OF PRINCE CODADAD AND HIS BROTHERS, AND OF THE PRINCESS OF DERYABAR.

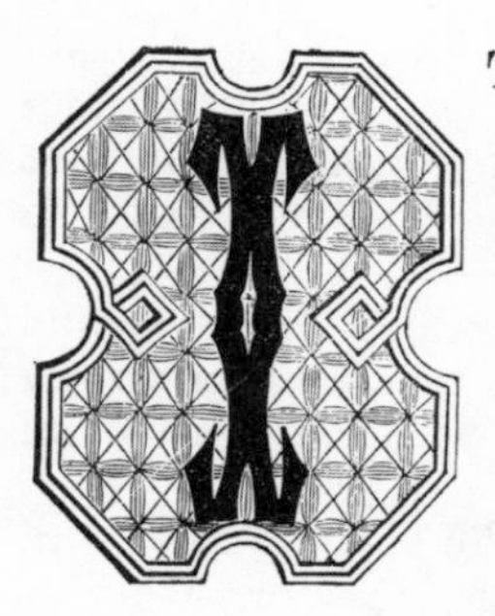

T is related by the historians of the kingdom of Diarbekir, that in the city of Harran there once reigned a most magnificent and powerful monarch, whose regard for his subjects was equalled by their affection for him. He was a pattern of every virtue, and wanted nothing to make him perfectly happy but the blessing of an heir. Although he had among his wives the most beautiful women in the world, he still had no children. He incessantly offered up his prayers to Heaven that this blessing might be vouchsafed to him. One night, while he was enjoying the sweets of sleep, a man of venerable appearance, indeed a prophet, stood before him, and said: 'Thy prayers are heard, thou shalt obtain what thou so earnestly desirest. Rise as soon as thou art awake, and instantly begin praying; then go into the gardens belonging to the palace, call the gardener, and desire him to bring thee a pomegranate; eat some of the seeds, as many as thou mayest desire, and thy wishes shall be fulfilled.'

"The king, as soon as he awoke, recollected his dream, and returned thanks to Heaven. He rose, addressed himself to prayer, and performed the requisite ceremonies; he then went into his garden, took fifty pomegranate seeds, which he counted one by one, and ate them. He had fifty wives, and some time after this each seemed likely to make him a father, with the exception of one lady, named Pirouzè; consequently he took a dislike to this lady, and was desirous to put her to death. 'Her barrenness,' said he, 'is a sure proof that Heaven deems her unworthy to be the mother of a prince. It is my duty to rid the world of a creature on whom Heaven looks with displeasure.' He formed this cruel resolution; but his vizier dissuaded him from it, by representing to him that all women were not of the same temperament and constitution, and that it was not impossible Pirouzè might yet have a son, though there seemed as yet no cause to expect such an event. 'Then,' replied the king, 'let her live; but she must not remain in my court, for her presence is hateful to me.' 'Will your majesty be pleased,' suggested the vizier, 'to send her to Prince Samer, your cousin?' The king approved the advice: he sent Pirouzè to Prince Samer with a letter, in which he desired his cousin to treat her with proper attention, and, if she became a mother, to give him information of it as soon as the child was born.

"Soon after Pirouzè arrived in Prince Samer's dominions it was discovered that she was likely to have a child. In due time she became the mother of a prince, beautiful as the day. Prince Samer wrote immediately to the King of Harran, to make him acquainted with the birth of this son, and to congratulate him on the happy event. This information gave his majesty very great pleasure, and, in reply, he wrote to Prince Samer in these terms: 'Dear cousin, each of my other wives has been delivered of a prince, so at present we have a great number of children here. I beg, therefore, that you will take charge of Pirouzè's infant, and give him the name of Codadad. I will send to you when I wish to have him home.'

"Prince Samer spared no pains in the education of his nephew. Prince Codadad was taught to ride, to shoot with the bow, and all other exercises suitable to the son of a king, and showed such aptitude that at the age of eighteen years he was esteemed a perfect prodigy. This young prince, perceiving in himself a courage worthy of his birth, said one day to his mother: 'I begin, madam, to be tired of this country. I feel within myself an ardent love of glory; permit me, then, to go and seek it amidst the dangers of war. The King of Harran my father has many enemies; some neighbouring princes are at this time preparing to disturb his peace. Why does he not demand my aid? Why am I left here to pass my time in fruitless tutelage? I ought even now to be at his court. While all my brothers have the privilege of sharing the dangers of war by his side, must I alone pass my life in torpid indolence?' 'My dear son,' replied Pirouzè, 'I am quite as impatient as you can be to see you in the way of obtaining fame and honour; I much wish that you had already distinguished yourself against the enemies of the king your father; but we are obliged to wait till he requires your assistance.' 'No, my mother,' replied Prince Codadad, 'I have waited already but too long. I burn with desire to see the king my father, and I feel myself strongly inclined to go and offer him my services as a young warrior who is unknown to him. He will certainly not refuse my help, and I intend not to discover myself till I have performed a thousand glorious exploits. I earnestly wish to merit my father's esteem before he shall know me to be his son.'

"Pirouzè much approved this generous resolution; and lest Prince Samer should oppose it, Prince Codadad, without imparting to him his intention, took an opportunity one day of leaving the country, under pretence of diverting himself with the pleasures of the chase.

"He was mounted upon a white horse, which had a golden bridle and was shod with gold. The saddle and housings were of blue satin and thickly embroidered with pearls. He wore at his side a sabre, the hilt of which was formed of a single diamond, and the scabbard was made of sandal-wood, ornamented with emeralds and rubies. His bow and quiver hung across his shoulders. Thus equipped in a manner which set off his handsome person to the greatest advantage, he arrived at the city of Harran. He soon found an opportunity of being presented to the king, who, charmed with his beauty and noble bearing, or perhaps drawn by the secret ties of blood, gave him a very favourable reception, and inquired his name and rank. 'O mighty king,' replied Prince Codadad, 'I am the son of an emir of Cairo. My desire to travel has induced me to quit my country; and as I learned, in passing through your dominions, that you are at war with some of your neighbours, I betook myself to your court, with the intention of offering the assistance of my sword to your majesty.' The king listened to him very graciously, and immediately gave him a distinguished position in his army.

"Prince Codadad soon found occasion to prove his valour. He acquired the esteem of the officers and excited the admiration of the soldiers; and, as his intellect was equal to his courage, he so effectually secured himself in the good graces of the king, that he soon became the prime favourite at court. A day never passed on which the ministers and other courtiers did not attend to pay their respects to Prince Codadad, seeking his friendship with much eagerness, while they wholly disregarded the other sons of the king.

"These young princes could not observe this neglect without feeling themselves much offended; and imputing their humiliation entirely to the esteem in which the stranger was held, they all conceived the greatest hatred to him. At the same time the king, becoming every day more attached to Prince Codadad, was continually giving him marks of his affection. He wished him to be constantly about his person. He was charmed

PRINCE CODADAD AND HIS MOTHER.

with the young stranger's conversation, which he found replete with wit and knowledge; and, to give indisputable proof of the high opinion he entertained of his wisdom and prudence, he gave him authority over the other princes, although the young warrior was not older than they; and thus Prince Codadad became the governor of his brothers.

"This, as may be supposed, only increased their hatred. 'What!' said they, 'is not the king content with bestowing on this stranger the affection which he owes to us, but must he also make him our governor, so that we are to do nothing without his permission? This is more than we can or ought to endure. We must rid ourselves of this encroacher on our rights.' Then one of them suggested: 'Let us go all of us together in search of him, and fall on him with our sabres.' 'No, no,' said another; 'we must not wreak vengeance upon him ourselves. His death would render us hateful to the king, who would, perhaps, in consequence, declare us all unworthy to reign. Let us manage this affair with more dexterity. I propose that we ask leave to go out hunting, and when we are at a considerable distance from the palace, let us take the road to some other city, where we will go and remain for some time. Our absence will alarm the king, who, not seeing us return, will lose all patience, and most likely condemn the stranger to death. Most certainly he will be dismissed from court, for having allowed us to leave the palace.'

"All the princes applauded this artifice. They went immediately in search of Prince Codadad, and entreated him to give them permission to take their pleasure in hunting, promising to return the same day. The son of Pirouzè fell into the snare, and granted the request which his brothers made. They departed, but failed to return. They had already been absent three days, when the king said to Prince Codadad: 'Where are the princes? It is a long time since I saw them.' 'O great king,' he replied, with an air of the deepest respect, 'they have been out on a hunting party for the last three days: they promised me that they would return much sooner.' The king became anxious about his sons, and his uneasiness increased when on the following day he found that the princes did not make their appearance. He was no longer able to restrain his anger, but said in a tone of reproach to Prince Codadad: 'Imprudent stranger! how dared you permit my sons to go away without accompanying them? Is it thus that you acquit yourself of the important charge committed to you? Go and seek them out instantly, and bring them to me, or be assured that your life shall be sacrificed.'

"At these words of the king the unhappy son of Pirouzè was seized with fear. He immediately provided himself with his usual arms, mounted his horse, and left the city to go in search of his brothers, scouring the country like a shepherd who has lost his flock. He inquired in every village if they had been seen to pass through it: but, obtaining no information whatever, he at length abandoned himself to despair. 'Alas! my brothers,' he exclaimed, 'where are you gone? Oh, me! perhaps you have fallen into the hands of enemies, and are at this moment enduring every hardship their malice can inflict. Would to Heaven I had never come to the court of Harran! I alone am to blame for this terrible misfortune. How can I repair the evil I have done?' In these and similar expressions he poured forth his lamentations at the disastrous event which had taken place, and of which he considered himself the sole author.

"After spending some days in a fruitless search he came to a plain of vast extent, in the middle of which was a palace built of black marble. On approaching it he saw at the window a lady of exceeding beauty. But her charms, great as they were, owed nothing to the aid of ornament; her hair was dishevelled, her garments were torn, and her countenance was expressive of the utmost grief. As soon as she perceived Prince Codadad, and he was near enough to hear what she said, she addressed him in these words: 'O young man, fly from this fatal place, or you will soon find yourself in the power of the monster who inhabits it. A negro, who gorges himself with human blood, has his abode here: he seizes every one who is compelled by hard fortune to pass through this plain, and shuts them up in dark dungeons, whence they are never released but to be devoured.'

"'Beautiful lady,' replied Prince Codadad, 'inform me who you are, and have no fear for my safety.' 'I am a person of rank, and come from Cairo,' replied the lady: 'I was passing near this castle on my way to Bagdad, when I met the negro, who killed all my servants, and brought me hither. I wish I had nothing worse to fear than death; but, to increase my misery, this wretch has the audacity to pretend an affection for me, and if I do not to-morrow consent to be his, I am threatened with unheard-of tortures. Once more,' added she, 'let me entreat you to seek safety in flight. The negro will soon return:

THE LADY WATCHES THE CONFLICT.

he is gone in pursuit of some travellers whom he observed at a distance on the plain. You have no time to lose; and I know not whether even the most rapid flight will now enable you to escape.'

"She had scarcely finished these words when the negro appeared. He was a monster of gigantic size and terrific appearance. He was mounted on a very powerful Tartar horse, and carried at his side a scimitar so large and heavy that none but himself could wield it. Prince Codadad, on seeing him, was astonished at the immense stature of this wretch. He offered up his prayers to Heaven to entreat its favour and protection; then drawing his sabre, he waited in a firm posture of defence till the negro should attack him. The giant, scorning so feeble a foe, summoned him to surrender without conflict; but Prince Codadad soon made him sensible, by his undaunted countenance, that he intended to defend his life; for he approached and dealt his adversary a violent blow on the knee. The negro, perceiving himself wounded, uttered a most dreadful cry, which resounded through the whole plain. He became furious, and at last foamed with rage; and rising in his stirrups, prepared in his turn to strike Prince Codadad with his tremendous scimitar. The blow was aimed with so much force that the young prince would have been inevitably killed, if he had not rapidly avoided the stroke by the most skilful management of his horse. The scimitar descended through the air with a loud hissing sound; but before the negro had time to aim a second blow Prince Codadad struck him with his sword with so much force that he cut off his right arm. The dreadful scimitar fell powerless with the hand that held it, and the negro, overcome by the violence of the blow, lost his stirrups and his seat, and fell headlong to the ground, which shook with the force of his fall. The prince immediately sprang from his horse, threw himself upon his enemy, and cut off his head. At this moment the lady, who had been all the time a witness of the combat, and who was still offering her ardent vows to Heaven for the young hero, at whom she gazed with admiration, uttered a shout of joy; she then cried enthusiastically to Prince Codadad: 'O Prince—for the victory you have just gained, as well as your noble air, fully persuade me that you can be of no common condition—finish your work. The negro has the keys of the castle; take them, and come and release me from prison.' The prince followed the lady's directions; and searching the dress of the wretched negro, who lay extended in the dust, found a number of keys in his pockets.

"He opened the first gate of the castle, and entered a large court, where he saw the lady approaching to meet him. She wanted to throw herself at his feet, to express her gratitude; but he would not permit her. She commended his valour, and exalted him above all the heroes of the world. To all her compliments he replied in proper terms; and, as she appeared to him more lovely than ever, now he saw her near than when he beheld her at a distance, it is difficult to say which of them felt more delighted—she at being released from her perilous situation, or he at having rendered an important service to so charming a woman.

"Their conversation was now interrupted by cries and groans. 'What do I hear?' exclaimed Prince Codadad, 'whence come these lamentable sounds which assail my ears?' 'O my friend,' said the lady, pointing towards a low door which was in the court, 'they come from yonder place, where are confined a number of unhappy prisoners, whose unpropitious stars threw them into the negro's hands. They are all in chains; and every day this monster dragged forth one of them for his horrid repast.'

"'I am rejoiced to find,' said the prince, 'that my victory saves the lives of so many unfortunate persons. Come, beautiful lady, come and partake with me the pleasure of restoring them their liberty; you can judge by your own feelings of the happiness we are going to confer.' They accordingly advanced towards the door of the dungeon: in proportion as they approached it, they heard more distinctly the cries of the prisoners. Prince Codadad felt the most anxious sympathy for these unhappy sufferers; and, impatient to put an end to their misery, he applied, without delay, one of the keys to the lock. He did not at first find the right one; he therefore tried another. The noise alarmed the wretched captives. They were fully convinced that it was the negro, who, according to custom, was bringing them their daily food, and coming to seize on one of their number. They redoubled their groans and lamentations; and it seemed as if the dismal sounds proceeded from the centre of the earth.

"But the prince quickly opened the door, and discovered a very steep staircase, by means of which he descended into a vast and profound cave, rendered more horrible by the feeble light which it received from a single small aperture. Within were more than a hundred persons fastened to stakes, with their hands bound. 'Unfortunate travellers,' said Prince Codadad, 'miserable victims, who had nothing to expect but a cruel death, return thanks to Heaven, which has this day delivered you by the assistance of my arm. I have killed the horrible negro in whose power you were, and am now come to loosen your chains.' The prisoners had no sooner heard these words, than they altogether set up a cry of surprise and joy. Prince Codadad and the lady began to unbind them, and those who were released from their chains assisted in giving freedom to the rest; so that in a very short time the whole company was at liberty.

"They fell upon their knees, and thanked Prince Codadad for saving them from destruction: thereupon they quitted the cave. When they ascended into the court, how great was the astonishment of the prince to see amongst the prisoners the very brothers of whom he was in search, and whom he had despaired of ever beholding more. 'O princes!' he exclaimed on seeing them, 'do not my eyes deceive me? May I still hope to restore you to the arms of the king your father, who is now inconsolable for your absence? Are you all safe? Has no one of you fallen a prey to the horrible monster? Alas! the death of only one amongst you would be sufficient to poison all the joy I feel at having saved the rest.'

"The forty-nine princes all presented themselves before Prince Codadad, who embraced them one after another, and told them of the great grief and anxiety which their absence had occasioned the king. They bestowed on their deliverer all the praises he merited. In this they were joined by the rest of the prisoners, who were yet unable to find terms sufficiently strong to express the gratitude they felt at their release. Hereupon Prince Codadad, accompanied by all those whom he had rescued from the dungeon, explored the whole castle, in which they found goods of immense value, consisting of fine cloths, gold brocades, Persian carpets, Chinese satins, and an infinity of other merchandise, which the negro had taken from the caravans he had pillaged. A great part of this plunder belonged to the prisoners whom Prince Codadad had just released, and each of whom knew and claimed his own property. The prince ordered that every one should take the bales that belonged to him; and he afterwards divided equally amongst them the rest of the merchandise. He then said to them, 'But how will you remove these goods? We are here in a desert, where there seems not the least probability of our being able to procure horses.' 'My lord,' replied one of the prisoners, 'the negro took our camels when he robbed us of our other property. Perhaps they are still in the stables belonging to this castle.' 'It is not impossible,' returned Prince Codadad; 'let us go and see.' They went accordingly to the stables, where they found not only the camels of the merchants, but even the horses belonging to the sons of the King of Harran. At this they all rejoiced greatly. There were in the stables a number of black slaves, who, seeing the prisoners freed, and concluding from this fact that the negro was killed, took the alarm, and immediately made their escape by a variety of circuitous paths with which they were acquainted. No one had the least desire to follow them. The merchants, delighted that with their liberty they had recovered their camels and goods, prepared to depart; but before they went they again made their most grateful acknowledgments to their deliverer.

"When they were gone, Prince Codadad addressed himself in the following words to the lady: 'May I inquire, fair one, where you wish to go? To what country were you wending your way when you were captured by the negro? It is my wish and intention to conduct you to whatever place you may have fixed on for your retreat; and I have no doubt that these princes have formed the same resolution.' The sons of the King of Harran protested to the lady that they would not leave her till they had restored her to her friends.

"'Dear princes,' said she to them, 'I belong to a country far distant from this place; and, besides that, it would be an abuse of your generosity to take you so much out of your way; I must confess to you, that I have left my home for ever. I told you a little while since that I was a lady of Cairo; but after the kindness you have shown me, and the great obligation I owe to you, my deliverer,' added she, addressing her speech to Prince Codadad, 'I can have no reason to conceal from you the real truth. Know, then, that I am the daughter of a kind. An usurper took away my father's life, and seized upon his throne. Fearing to meet with the same untimely end, I had recourse to flight as the only means to save my life.' In consequence of this avowal, Prince Codadad and his brothers entreated the princess to relate her history; assuring her that they took all possible interest in her misfortunes, and that there was nothing they were not ready to do to promote her happiness. She thanked them warmly for their new offers of service; and, believing that she could not, with any civility refuse to gratify their curiosity, she began the following recital of her adventures:—

"'There is in a certain island a large city called Deryabar. This city was for a long time governed by a great, powerful, and virtuous monarch, who would have wanted nothing to render him completely happy had he been blessed with children. He was perpetually offering prayers to Heaven for a son; but the queen his wife after long and earnest expectation, gave to the world only a daughter.

"'I am this unhappy daughter. My father felt disappointment rather than pleasure at my birth; but he submitted to the will of Heaven. He had me educated with all imaginable care, being resolved, since he had no son, that I should be instructed in the art of government, and succeed to the throne at his decease.

"'One day, while he was pursuing the diversion of hunting, he perceived a wild ass, which he immediately chased, separating himself from the rest of his party. His ardour carried him so far that, without thinking how far he strayed, he continued the pursuit till night. He then alighted from his horse, and seated himself at the entrance of the wood, into which he had observed that the ass entered. Scarcely had the day closed when he perceived a light amongst the trees, which led him to suppose that he was not far distant from some village; and he rejoiced at the thought of being able to pass the night there, and also of finding some one whom he might send to the people of his suite, to inform them where he was. He rose, and proceeded toward the light, which served as a guide to his footsteps.

"'He very soon discovered that he had been deceived; and that this light proceeded from a fire in a hut not far distant. He approached it, and was much astonished to behold a tall black man, or rather a horrible giant, who was sitting upon a sofa. This monster had before him a large pitcher of wine, and was roasting upon some coals an ox which he had just flayed. He was busily engaged, employing himself alternately in drinking out of the pitcher and cutting pieces out of the ox, which he greedily devoured. But the attention of the king my father was chiefly attracted by a beautiful woman whom he saw in the hut. She appeared to be sunk in profound melancholy; her hands were tied; at her feet was a little child, between two and three years of age, who, as if he were already sensible to the misfortunes of his mother, wept unceasingly, making the air resound with his cries.

"'My father was so much moved by what he saw, that he felt at first a strong inclination to enter the hut and attack the giant; but, reflecting that this combat would be too unequal, he restrained himself, and resolved to achieve by surprise what he despaired of being able to effect by force. In the meantime, the giant, after emptying the pitcher and eating more than half the ox, turned towards the lady, and said, 'Charming princess, why will you, by your obstinacy, compel me to treat you with so much rigour? You may be perfectly happy if you like. Only take the resolution to love and be faithful to me, and you may be certain of the most kind and gentle treatment.' 'Thou hateful monster!' replied the lady, 'never hope that time will diminish the horror I feel in beholding thee; thou wilt ever be odious in my eyes.' These words were followed by so many injurious expressions that the giant became irritated. 'This is too much!' he exclaimed in a furious tone. 'Love thus scorned turns to rage; your hatred has at length excited mine; it now takes such entire possession o me, that I have never so ardently wished to gain your love as I now wish your destruction.' Having spoken these words, he seized the unhappy woman by her hair, and with one hand holding her suspended in the air, while he drew his scimitar with the other, he was preparing to cut off her head, when the king my father discharged an arrow which pierced his breast: the giant staggered, and in an instant fell down lifeless.

"'My father entered the hut. He untied the lady's hands, and then requested to know who she was, and by what accident she had been brought to such a place. 'O stranger,' she replied, 'there are living upon the sea-shore a certain number of Saracenic families, whose chief was a prince to whom I am married. This giant, whom you have just killed, was one of his principal officers. The wretch conceived a violent passion for me, which he took great pains to conceal, till he should find a favourable opportunity of executing a scheme he had formed of carrying me away by force. It would appear that fortune more frequently favours the enterprises of the wicked than the resolutions of the good. The giant surprised me one day, with my child, in a retired place, and carried us

THE MONSTER AND THE WIFE OF THE PRINCE OF THE SARACENS.

both off; and to render useless all the inquiries which he naturally supposed my husband would make as to my whereabout, he travelled to a great distance from the country inhabited by the Saracens, and brought us to this wood, where he has kept me for some days.

"'But however deplorable my destiny may be, I do not fail to derive much secret consolation, when I reflect that this giant, rude and cruel as he was, never had recourse to violence with me. It is true he was threatening me perpetually that he would proceed to the most horrible extremities unless I consented to marry him; and I confess to you, that frequently, when I have by the bitterness of my language excited his anger, I have been fearful of the worst that could befall me.

"'This, noble stranger,' continued the wife of the Prince of the Saracens, 'is my history; and you will, I doubt not, think me so far worthy of your pity as not to repent the generous assistance you have given me.' 'Indeed lady,' replied my father, 'your misfortunes interest me much; I feel myself very strongly affected by them, nor shall it be my fault if your future destiny is not very different from the sufferings you have lately experienced. To-morrow, as soon as the morning rays have dispersed the shades of night, we will leave this wood, and seek the road to the great city of Deryabar, of which I am sovereign; and, if it be agreeable to you, you shall remain in my palace till the prince your husband comes to demand you.'

"'The lady accepted the proposal; and the next day departed with the king my father. Immediately on quitting the wood he descried the officers of his suite, who had passed the night in searching for him, and were in great anxiety on his account. Their delight at seeing him again was not greater than their astonishment on beholding him accompanied by a lady of such exquisite beauty. He related to them in what manner he had met with her, and the danger he had run in approaching the hut, where he would, without doubt, have lost his life if the giant had seen him. One of the officers took the lady on his horse, and another took charge of the child.

"'They arrived in this manner at the palace of the king my father, who immediately ordered that an apartment should be prepared for the fair Saracen, and had her son educated with the greatest attention. The lady was extremely sensible of the king's goodness; she felt towards him all the gratitude he could wish. She at first seemed rather uneasy and impatient at hearing nothing from the prince her husband; but her disquietude gradually diminished. The constant respect that was paid her by my father charmed away her regrets: so much so, indeed, that she would at last, I believe, have considered herself more unfortunate in being restored to her relations, than in having been at first separated from them.

"'In due time the son of this lady attained manhood. He was extremely handsome, and, as he by no means lacked understanding, he readily found the way of pleasing the king my father, who conceived a great regard for him. This was quickly perceived by the people about the court, who imagined in consequence that this young man would be my husband. Acting on this opinion, and looking upon him as heir to the crown, they attached themselves to him with much assiduity, and every one of them very strenuously endeavoured to gain his confidence. The young man had sufficient penetration to discover the motive of their attachment. The idea was so grateful to him that, forgetting the difference of our position, he cherished the hope that my father had conceived so great an affection for him as to prefer his alliance to that of all the princes of the world. He went even further. The king being, in his opinion, too tardy in offering him my hand, he presumed to demand it.

"'However great might be the punishment due to such audacity, my father contented himself with telling the bold suitor, without testifying any particular marks of displeasure, that he had other views for me. The haughty youth was extremely irritated at the refusal, and felt as much offended at the refusal of his addresses as if he had demanded in marriage a common person, or as if his birth had equalled mine. His resentment was not inactive. He resolved to revenge himself on the king; and with an excessive ingratitude of which there are, I trust, few examples, he conspired against his benefactor, struck a poniard to the king's heart, and caused himself to be proclaimed King of Deryabar by a great number of discontented persons, whose disaffection he well knew how to turn to account. His first care, after he had slain my father, was to come himself to my apartment, at the head of a party of the conspirators. His design was either to take my life or to compel me to marry him. But I had time to escape. While he was employed in murdering my father, the grand vizier, who had always been faithful to his master, came, and hurrying me from the palace, conveyed me to a place of safety in the house of one of his friends. He kept me concealed in this retreat till a vessel, secretly prepared by his order, was ready to sail. I then quitted the island, accompanied only by a female attendant and by this generous minister, who preferred following the daughter of his late master, and sharing her misfortunes, to giving his allegiance to a tyrant.

"'It was the intention of the grand vizier to proceed with me to the courts of some neighbouring monarchs, in order to implore their assistance, and excite them to avenge the death of my father; but Heaven did not favour a resolution which to us appeared just and reasonable. After some days' sailing there arose so violent a tempest that, in spite of all the skill of the sailors, our vessel, carried away by the violence of the winds and waves, split upon a rock. There is no need that I should give you a description of our shipwreck. I should fail were I to attempt a description of the manner in which the grand vizier and all those who accompanied me were swallowed up in the dreadful abyss of waters; the fear which took possession of me did not allow me to see all the horrors of our fate. I soon lost my senses; nor can I tell whether I was carried on shore upon some pieces of wreck, or if Heaven, in order to reserve me for further calamity, wrought a miracle for my preservation. I only know that when I recovered my senses I found myself on shore.

"'Misfortune often renders us unjust towards others. Instead of thanking Allah for the signal favour bestowed on me, I impiously lifted up my eyes to reproach Heaven for the protection it had granted. Far from lamenting the vizier and my attendant, I envied their fate; and my reason giving way by degrees under the frightful images which had taken possession of my mind, I formed the desperate resolution of throwing myself into the sea. But just as I was going to rush forward I heard behind me a great noise of men and horses. I naturally turned my head to see what the noise meant, when I beheld a number of armed horsemen, among whom was one mounted upon an Arabian horse. He was attired in a robe embroidered with silver, and wore a girdle of precious stones, and a crown of gold upon his head. If his dress had not sufficiently indicated him as the chief of the party, I should have discovered it from the air of grandeur which was diffused over his whole person. He was a young man of extremely noble appearance, and beautiful as the morning. Surprised to see a lady by herself in so retired a place, he sent forward some of his officers to inquire who I was. I could make no reply but by a flood of tears. As the shore was covered with wreck from our vessel, they concluded that a ship had lately been cast away on the coast, and that I was one of the passengers who had escaped. This conjecture, and the very lively grief I expressed, excited the curiosity of the officers, who began to ask me a thousand questions, assuring me that their king was a generous prince, and that I should find at his court everything that could comfort and console me.

"'The king himself, impatient to learn who I was, became weary of waiting for the return of his officers. He approached me himself, and gazed upon me with great attention; and as I still continued to weep and moan, without being able to reply to my questioners, he forbade them to trouble me any longer with their importunities, and addressed me in the following terms: 'O lady, I entreat you to moderate your grief. If Heaven, in its anger, has made you feel its rigour, are you on that account to abandon yourself to despair? I entreat you to summon up your fortitude. The pains as well as the pleasures of this life endure but for a time. Your fate may soon change. I venture to assure you that if your distresses can be alleviated, my dominions shall offer you every consolation. I proffer to you the asylum of my palace. You will be near the queen my mother, who will endeavour by every kind attention to mitigate your grief. Though I know not at present who you are, I feel myself much interested in your behalf.'

"'I thanked the young king for his goodness, and accepted the obliging offers he made me; and to prove to him that I was not beneath his regard, I discovered to him my name and rank. I told him of the audacity of the young Saracen, and had only occasion to give a very simple narrative of my sufferings to excite his compassion and that of all his officers. After I had done speaking the prince once again assured me that he took a great interest in my misfortunes. He afterwards conducted me to the palace, where he presented me to the queen his mother. I was here obliged again to relate the history of my adventures, the remembrance of which made my tears flow afresh. The queen showed herself extremely kind to me in my affliction, and conceived for me the tenderest regard. The king her son became passionately in love with me, and soon offered me his hand and his crown. My mind had been hitherto so much engrossed by the various disasters I had suffered, that the prince, amiable as he was, had not made that impression on me which under different circumstances he probably would have made. Penetrated, however, with gratitude, I did not refuse to promote his happiness. I gave my consent, and our marriage was solemnised with all the pomp imaginable.

"'While all the citizens were occupied in celebrating the nuptials of their sovereign, a hostile prince of a neighbouring state came one night with a considerable army, and made a descent upon the island. This formidable foe was the King of Zanguebar. He came upon us entirely by surprise, and cut in pieces all the subjects of the king my husband who resisted him. He was on the point of taking both the king and myself as his prisoners; for he was already in the palace with some of his people before we found means of saving ourselves, and of gaining the sea shore, where we threw ourselves into a fisherman's bark, which we had the good fortune to find. For two days we were driven at the mercy of the winds, without knowing what would be our fate; on the third we perceived a ship, which approached us in full sail. We were at first delighted at the sight, supposing that this was some merchant vessel coming to our relief; but how great was our surprise and fear, when, on the nearer approach of the vessel, we saw on the deck ten or twelve armed corsairs. They immediately proceeded to board us. Five or six threw themselves into the bark, seized upon us both, bound the prince my husband, and made us enter their own vessel. Here they immediately removed my veil. My youthful appearance struck them: they were all of them indeed so anxious to have me as a prize, that instead of drawing lots for me, every one insisted on his own right, and resolved that I should become his property. The dispute grew warm, and from words they soon proceeded to blows, fighting like madmen. Soon the deck was covered with dead bodies, and the conflict continued to rage till all the pirates were slain, with the exception of one man, who, finding himself my undoubted possessor, thus addressed me: 'You now belong to me. It is my intention to carry you to Cairo; I shall there make a present of you to a friend of mine, to whom I have promised a handsome slave. But,' added he, observing the king my husband, 'who is that man? What brought him into your company? Are you allied by blood, or is it love that has brought you together?' 'My master,' I replied to him, 'he is my husband.' 'If that be so,' cried the corsair, 'I must get rid of him out of pity. He must not have the grief of seeing you transferred to my friend.' At these words he took the unhappy prince, who lay bound and helpless, and threw him into the sea, notwithstanding all the efforts I could make to prevent it.

"'This cruel action drew from me the most dreadful shrieks; and I should certainly have plunged into the waves if the pirate had not prevented me. Perceiving that I was determined, if possible, to put an end to my existence, he bound me with cords to the mainmast, and then setting sail, proceeded with a favourable wind towards the shore, where we soon landed. I was now released from my bonds, and my new master led me towards a small town, where he purchased camels, tents, and slaves, and then took the road towards Cairo, with the intention, as he frequently said, of fulfilling his promise to his friend.

"'We had been some time on our way, when yesterday, as we passed through this plain, we encountered the negro who inhabited this castle. When we first saw him at a distance we supposed him to be a tower, and afterwards, when he approached us, we had great difficulty in believing that he was a man. He drew his enormous scimitar, and summoned the pirate to surrender himself prisoner, with all his slaves and the lady who accompanied him. The corsair was a brave man, and, seconded by his slaves, who all promised to be faithful to him, he attacked the negro. The combat was long and hot; but the pirate at length fell under the blows of his enemy, with the slaves, who were determined to die rather than abandon their master. Thereupon the negro conveyed me to the castle, bearing with him the body of the pirate, which he devoured for supper. Towards the end of this horrible repast he said to me, observing that I did nothing but weep: 'Fair lady, instead of thus giving way to grief, prepare to take me for your husband. Let me recommend you to yield with a good grace to what you cannot avoid. I will allow

THE PRINCESS OF DERYABAR A PRISONER ON BOARD THE PIRATES' VESSEL.

you till to-morrow to reflect upon the affair, in the hope that I shall then see you consoled for your misfortunes in the delight you must feel at being destined for my wife.' When he had finished this speech he conducted me to a chamber, and then retired to his own, first securing all the doors of the castle; these he opened again this morning, taking care to fasten them after him when he went forth in pursuit of some travellers whom he observed at a distance, but who probably made their escape, since he was returning alone, and without plunder, when you attacked him.'

"When the princess had thus concluded the history of her adventures, Prince Codadad assured her that he sympathised most sincerely in her misfortunes: 'But, fair lady,' he added, 'it lies entirely in your own power to render your future life more tranquil than the past has been. The sons of the King of Harran offer you an asylum in their father's court. Let me entreat you to accept it. You will find a kind protector in the king, and will be respected by every one; and, if you do not disdain to be the wife of him who has had the good fortune to be your deliverer, allow me to offer you my hand. Only consent to be mine, and let the princes be witnesses of our engagement.' The princess yielded to his entreaty, and the marriage was solemnised in the castle on the same day. Every sort of provision was found ready for the occasion, the kitchens being full of meats and various dishes, which the negro was accustomed to devour after he had satisfied himself with human flesh. They found also a variety of fruits, all excellent of their kind; and to complete their good fortune they came upon a great store of liquors and exquisite wines.

"They all sat down to table. When they had eaten and drunk as much as they wished they packed up the rest of the provisions and left the castle, with the intention of returning to the King of Harran's court. They continued their journey many days, encamping in the most agreeable spots they could find. When they had arrived at their last resting-place, within a day's journey of Harran, they drank the remainder of their wine, with that spirit of festivity which people feel who have no longer any occasion to save; thereupon Prince Codadad addressed the party as follows: 'O princes,' said he, 'I can no longer conceal from you my real name and rank; you behold in me your brother Codadad. Like yourselves, I am a son of the King of Harran. I was educated by the Prince of Samer, and the Princess Pirouzè is my mother. Charming lady,' added he, addressing himself to the Princess of Deryabar, 'pardon me if I have made a mystery of my birth to you. I might, perhaps, by revealing it sooner, have spared you some unpleasant reflections, which you can scarcely have failed to make on a marriage that must have appeared to you so very unequal.' 'No, my lord,' replied the princess, 'the sentiments of regard with which you at first inspired me have been strengthened every moment: nor was it at all necessary to my happiness that you should be of the high station to which you can lay claim.'

"The princes congratulated Prince Codadad on the revelation he had made, and were profuse in expressing every outward mark of joy, though at the bottom of their hearts they were ill at ease; for their hatred to their amiable brother increased every moment. In the middle of the night they assembled in a retired place, and held a council together, while Prince Codadad and the princess were enjoying the sweets of repose in their tent. These ungrateful and envious wretches, disregarding what they owed to the courageous son of Pirouzè, and never remembering that without his aid they would all have been devoured by the negro, took the horrid resolution of assassinating him. 'It is the only thing we can do,' said one of these treacherous men. 'As soon as the king learns that this stranger, whom he loves so much, is his son, and that this youth has sufficient prowess alone to overpower a giant whom our united strength was unable to resist, he will load him with new favours, will be eloquent in his praise, and declare him his heir, to the prejudice of all his other sons, who will be obliged to prostrate themselves before this new-found brother, and yield him obedience.' To these arguments he added many others, which made so strong an impression on the jealous minds of his hearers that they sallied forth instantly, in the hope of finding Prince Codadad asleep. They really found him slumbering, and as he lay in this helpless state they fell upon him with a thousand strokes of their poniards, and leaving him apparently dead in the arms of the princess, they departed, directing their course to the city of Harran, where they arrived the next day.

"The king their father was much delighted at their return; the more so as he had despaired of ever seeing them again. He inquired the cause of their delay, which they took especial care to conceal: they mentioned not a word either of the negro or Prince Codadad, but merely stated that, unable to resist the curiosity they felt to inspect the country, they had made a short stay in several of the neighbouring cities.

"In the meantime Prince Codadad lay stretched in his tent weltering in his blood, and showing hardly any symptoms of life, attended by the princess his wife, who seemed in a condition as miserable as his own. She filled the air with her cries, tore her hair, and bathing the body of her husband with her tears, exclaimed incessantly: 'Ah, Prince Codadad! my dear Codadad! Is it thus I now behold you, on the brink of the grave? What cruel hands must those have been that have reduced you to this state? Can I believe your own brothers have thus dreadfully mangled you? brothers who owe their life to your valour? No! they must be demons, who have taken the form of your relations, and have come hither to wreak their malice upon you. Oh, wicked and barbarous men! Could you thus repay with the vilest ingratitude the service he has done you? But why, unhappy Codadad, should I lay the blame on your brothers? It is to me alone you owe your death. You desired to link your fate with mine, and therefore all the ill-fortune which has pursued me since I left the palace of my father has fallen on you. O Heaven! by whose hard decree I am condemned to lead a wandering wretched life, if thou dost forbid me to have a husband, why am I allowed to meet with any one who wishes to marry me? This is the second husband I have lost, just as I began to feel an affection for him.'

"In such passionate expressions as these, and in other exclamations even more affecting, the unhappy Princess of Deryabar gave utterance to her grief, while she saw the unfortunate Prince Codadad lying senseless before her. He was not, however, entirely dead. He still continued to breathe; and the princess his wife, noticing these signs of life, ran instantly towards a large town which appeared in the plain, in order to procure a surgeon. She found one, who returned with her immediately; but when they came to the tent, Prince Codadad was nowhere to be found. They searched everywhere for him in vain; at length they concluded that some wild beast had seized and devoured him. The princess again gave vent to her grief in the most bitter cries and lamentations. The surgeon was much affected at the sight of her despair; and, unwilling to abandon the unhappy lady in her affliction, he proposed to her to return to the town, and made her an offer of his house and services.

"She suffered herself to be persuaded. The surgeon, therefore, conducted her to his house; and, without knowing at all who she was, treated her with all imaginable attention and respect. He endeavoured in his conversation to bring forward every topic of consolation; but all his efforts failed, for he only increased the sorrows he wished to assuage. 'Beautiful lady,' said he to her one day, 'I entreat you to communicate to me the cause of your distress. Tell me what is your country, and what your rank: I may, perhaps, be able to give you good advice, when I have been informed of all the circumstances of your misfortunes. You now do nothing but mourn, without reflecting that it is often possible to discover remedies even for the most desperate evils.'

"The surgeon spoke with so much good sense, that he at length persuaded the princess to relate to him all her adventures. When she had finished her story, the surgeon addressed her in his turn: 'Lady,' said he, 'allow me to represent to you, that, under the circumstances you have related, you ought not to abandon yourself thus to grief. Endeavour rather to arm yourself with sufficient fortitude to perform what your situation demands: your character and duty as a wife call upon you to avenge your husband. I am ready, if you wish, to serve as your attendant. Let us go to the King of Harran's court. He is a good and just prince: you will have only to represent in true colours the treatment which Prince Codadad has received from his brothers, and I am sure the king will do you justice.' 'I submit to your reasoning,' replied the princess. 'Yes, I feel that the disastrous fate of my dear husband calls upon me for vengeance; and as you are so kind and generous as to offer to accompany me, I am ready to depart.' When she had formed this resolution the surgeon undertook to provide two camels; and on these they set out upon their journey, and soon arrived at the city of Harran.

"They alighted at the first caravanserai they found, and inquired of the master what was the news at court. 'The court,' said he, 'is thrown into mourning. The king had a son, who lived with him here for a long time without revealing his true birth, and no one knows what is become of him. A wife of the king, named Pirouzè, the mother of the prince, has caused innumerable inquiries to be made, but they have all hitherto proved fruitless. Every one is sorry for the young prince, as he possessed great merit. The king has forty-nine other sons, all by different mothers; but there is not one amongst them who can console the king for the death of Prince Codadad: I say the death, for it is scarcely possible he can be still living; since, notwithstanding all the search that has been made, he has not yet been heard of.'

"On hearing this account from the master of the caravanserai, the surgeon was of opinion that the most proper plan the Princess of Deryabar could pursue, was to go to Pirouzè; but this step could hardly be taken without danger, and required many precautions. There was great risk that, if the sons of the King of Harran heard of the arrival and intention of their sister-in-law, they would find means to dispose of her before she had an opportunity of speaking to the mother of Prince Codadad. Having made all these reflections, and sensible of the danger to which he himself might be exposed, the surgeon was anxious to conduct the affair with all possible prudence. He therefore begged the princess to continue at the caravanserai, while he went to the palace, in order to discover in what manner he might, with the least risk, introduce her to the mother of Prince Codadad.

"He then betook himself to the city, and continued his way towards the palace as a man might do who was drawn thither by no other motive than a desire to see the court. Suddenly he perceived a lady mounted upon a richly-caparisoned mule: she was followed by a troop of females, who were also mounted upon mules, and by a great number of guards and black slaves. As she approached, the people ranged themselves in two rows to see her pass, and saluted her with their faces bowed towards the earth. The surgeon greeted her in the same manner, and then inquired of a calender who was near him whether this lady was not one of the king's wives. 'Yes, brother,' replied the calender, 'she is, and the wife whom the people most love and honour, because she is the mother of the brave and wise Prince Codadad, whose renown must have reached your ears.'

"The surgeon did not wait to hear more. He followed Pirouzè to a mosque, which she entered to distribute alms, and to attend the public prayers which the king had ordered for the return of Prince Codadad. The people, who were greatly interested in the fate of the young prince, ran in crowds to join their prayers to those of the priests; so many came that the mosque was soon completely filled. The surgeon made his way through the multitude, and advanced towards the guards of Pirouzè. When the princess was about to depart, he accosted one of her slaves, and said to him in a whisper, 'Brother, I have a very important secret to reveal to the Princess Pirouzè. Can I not, with your good help, be introduced into her apartment?' 'If this secret,' answered the slave, 'concerns Prince Codadad, I can venture to promise that you shall, on this very day, be admitted to the audience you wish to have; but if it concerns anything else, it will be useless for you to make any attempt to be presented to the princess; for at the present time she is incapable of attending to anything unconnected with her son, nor does she choose to speak on any subject that does not concern him.' 'It is on this subject alone that I wish to address her,' replied the surgeon. 'If that be the case,' said the slave, 'you will do well to follow us to the palace; and you shall soon have the opportunity you desire.'

"Accordingly, as soon as Pirouzè had returned to her apartment, the slave came to inform her that an unknown person had something of great importance to communicate to her, and that it concerned Prince Codadad. On receiving this communication, Pirouzè showed the most lively impatience to obtain an interview with the stranger. The slave introduced him immediately into the cabinet of the princess, who sent out all her women, with the exception of two whom she honoured with her confidence. As soon as she saw the surgeon, she asked of him with the greatest eagerness what it was that he had to communicate concerning her son. 'O lady,' answered the surgeon, after prostrating himself with his face to the earth, 'I have to tell you a long story, in which are many events that will doubtless surprise you.' He then gave her a full account of everything that had happened between Prince Codadad and his brothers. She listened to his recital with the most eager attention; but when he came to speak of the assassination, this tender mother, as if she had been herself struck by the blows inflicted on her son, fell senseless upon a sofa. Her two women flew eagerly to her assistance, and used every means to restore her; and when she was able to attend, the surgeon proceeded with his narrative. When he had concluded, the princess said to him: 'Return to the Princess of Deryabar, and inform her from me that the king will soon acknowledge

THE PRINCESS OF DERYABAR AND THE SURGEON ON THEIR JOURNEY TO THE CITY OF HARRAN.

her as his daughter-in-law; and with respect to yourself, be assured that your services shall be well rewarded.'

"After the surgeon was gone, Pirouzè remained on the sofa in a violent paroxysm of grief, the remembrance of her dear Prince Codadad exciting every tender emotion in her breast. 'O my son!' said she, 'shall I then never more behold you? Are you, alas! gone for ever? When I permitted you to depart to visit this court, when I received your last tender farewell, little did I imagine that far away from me a cruel death awaited you. O unhappy Prince Codadad! wherefore did you leave me? You could not, certainly, have acquired so much glory had you stayed with me; but you would have been still alive, and your mother would have been spared this bitter affliction.' As she said these words she wept bitterly; and her confidential women, sympathising with her grief, mingled their tears with hers.

"While they were thus mourning in company (each seeming to vie with the rest in expressions of sorrow), the king entered the apartment; and, observing the state they were in, inquired of Pirouzè whether she had heard bad news of Prince Codadad. 'Alas! my lord,' said she, 'all is lost! My dear son is no more; and, to increase my woe, I am precluded from paying him funeral honours; for, according to all appearances, his beloved remains have become a prey to ravenous beasts.' Thereupon she related to the king everything the surgeon had told her, and did not fail to enlarge on the cruel manner in which Prince Codadad had been murdered by his brothers.

"The king scarcely gave her time to finish her narrative. Transported with rage, and giving way to his passion, he said to the princess: 'O lady, these perfidious wretches, whose cold and cruel treachery has occasioned you these bitter tears, and given to me, their father, the most bitter grief, shall soon experience the punishment they deserve.' Thereupon, with fury sparkling in his eyes, the king repaired to the hall of audience, where his courtiers, and those among the people who had any petitions to prefer, were waiting for him. They were astonished when they beheld his enraged countenance. Imagining that he had conceived some cause of anger against his subjects, their hearts were struck cold with terror. He ascended his throne, and desired his grand vizier to approach. Then he said publicly: 'O Hassan, I have an order to give you. Go immediately and take a thousand soldiers of my guard, and seize all the princes my sons. Shut them up in the tower where assassins are imprisoned; and take care that my orders are performed with the utmost dispatch.' All who were present trembled at this surprising order; while the grand vizier, without answering a word, put his hand upon his head, to express that he was ready to obey, and left the hall, that he might at once execute the king's command, at which he was as much surprised as the rest. The king meanwhile dismissed the persons who were come to solicit audience; and publicly declared, that for the ensuing month he would not be spoken with on any matter of business whatever. He was still in the hall when the vizier returned. 'How now, vizier!' said he; 'are all my sons in the tower?' 'Yes, great king,' replied the minister, 'your commands are obeyed.' 'It is not sufficient,' replied the king; 'I have another order to give you.' With these words he left the hall of audience, and returned to the apartment of Pirouzè with the vizier, who followed him. He desired to know of the princess where the widow of Prince Codadad was lodged. Pirouzè's women gave him the information he required; for the surgeon had not omitted to mention it. The king then, turning towards his minister, said, 'Go to that caravanserai, and conduct hither a young princess who lodges there: and be careful to treat her with all the respect due to her rank.'

"The vizier was not long in obeying this order. He mounted on horseback with all the emirs and other great personages of the court, and repaired to the caravanserai where the Princess of Deryabar resided, to whom he showed his order; and at the same time presented to her, in the name of the king, a beautiful white mule, with a bridle and saddle of gold, splendidly ornamented with rubies and emeralds. She immediately mounted it; and, surrounded by all the considerable persons of the court, betook herself to the palace. The surgeon accompanied her, mounted also upon a handsome Tartar horse, which had been given to him by the vizier's order. All the people ran to their windows, or into the streets, to see the magnificent cavalcade; and, as it was soon reported that the princess who was being thus conducted to court with so much state was the wife of Prince Codadad, nothing was heard but shouts of applause. The air resounded with incessant cries of joy, which would, however, have been converted into groans had the people known the melancholy story of the young prince, so much and so universally was he beloved.

"The Princess of Deryabar found the king waiting at the palace gate to receive her. He took her by the hand and led her to the apartment of Pirouzè, where a most affecting scene took place. The wife of Prince Codadad found all her grief renewed at the sight of the father and mother of her husband; nor were the latter able to behold so near and dear a relation of their son without showing the most painful emotion. She threw herself at the king's feet, and bathed them with her tears. Presently she was seized with a violent paroxysm of grief, which deprived her of utterance. Pirouzè was not in a less deplorable state, for she was penetrated to the soul by the affliction she saw and experienced. The king was so wholly subdued by the sight of this deep grief that he appeared for a time as if his senses and reason had left him. The three bereaved persons, mingling their sighs and tears, continued for a long time to maintain a tender and mournful silence. The Princess of Deryabar, having at length in some measure recovered her composure, related the adventures of the castle, and the cruel fate of Prince Codadad; and then demanded justice on the princes. 'Yes, lady,' said the king to her, 'these ungrateful wretches shall surely perish; but it will be first necessary to make known the death of Prince Codadad, in order that the punishment of his brothers may not amaze the minds of my subjects. Besides, although we do not possess the body of my son, it is not the less necessary that we pay him the last honours.' He then addressed himself to his vizier, and ordered him to have a dome of white marble erected in the beautiful plain in the midst of which the city of Harran stands. He moreover provided in his palace a most splendid apartment for the Princess of Deryabar, whom he acknowledged as his daughter-in-law.

"Hassan set about his work with so much diligence, and employed so many workmen, that the dome was finished in a few days. A tomb was erected under it, upon which a figure representing Prince Codadad was placed. As soon as the work was finished the king ordered prayers to be performed, and appointed a day for the funeral rites of his son.

"When the solemn day came all the inhabitants of the city were scattered over the plain to see the ceremony, which was conducted in the following manner:—

"The king, attended by his vizier and the principal lords of the court, proceeded towards the dome; when he had reached it he, with his attendants, entered the structure, and they seated themselves on carpets of black satin flowered with gold; after this a large troop of guards on horseback, with their heads bowed down and their eyes nearly closed, approached the dome. They rode round it twice, observing the most profound silence; but the third time they stopped before the entrance, and said one after another in a loud voice: 'O prince, son of the king, were it possible, by the keen stroke of our scimitars and the display of our valour, to lessen the severity of thy fate, we should soon restore thee to the light; but the King of kings has commanded, and the Angel of Death has obeyed.' Having uttered these words they retired to give room to a hundred old men, who were all mounted upon black mules, and who wore long and snowy beards.

"These were persons of austere life, who, from their youth upwards, had lived concealed in caves, never appearing to human view except when they came forward to attend the obsequies of the kings of Harran, or of any of his royal house. Each of these venerable personages carried on his head a large book, which he held with one hand. They all then made the circuit of the dome three times without speaking; stopping afterwards at the entrance, one of them pronounced these words: 'O prince, what is there that we can do for thee? If either prayers or knowledge could restore thee to life, we would wipe thy feet with our white beards—we would address thee in words of wisdom; but the King of the universe has taken thee away for ever!'

"This part of the ceremony being concluded, the old men retired to a distance from the dome, and immediately fifty young maidens of exquisite beauty approached. They were all mounted on small white horses, wore no veils, and carried in their hands golden baskets, filled with every kind of precious stone. They also went round the dome three times, and stopping at the place where the rest had paused, the youngest of the party delivered the following speech: 'O prince, formerly so beautiful, what succour canst thou hope from us? If it were possible that our charms could reanimate thee, we would readily become thy slaves; but thou art no longer sensible to beauty, nor hast thou occasion for aught that we can give!'

"When the young maidens had withdrawn the king and his courtiers arose, and walked in procession three times round the figure within the tomb. The king then broke silence in these terms: 'O my dear son, light of my eyes; have I then lost thee for ever?' He accompanied these words with heavy sighs, and moistened the tomb with his tears, his courtiers following his example. After this ceremony the door of the tomb was shut, and every one returned to the city. On the next day public prayers were repeated at all the mosques, and these prayers were continued for eight days. It was the king's determination that on the ninth the princes his sons should be beheaded. All the people, indignant at the usage Prince Codadad had experienced, seemed to await with impatience the punishment of the criminals. The scaffolds were already being prepared; but the people were obliged to put off the work for the present, because it was suddenly discovered that the neighbouring princes, who had already made war on the King of Harran, were advancing with a more numerous army than before, and that they were already at no great distance from the city. It had been long known that they were preparing for war; but the preparations had occasioned little alarm. This news, however, caused a general consternation, and furnished fresh matter of regret for the fate of Prince Codadad, who had greatly signalised himself in the preceding war against the same enemies. 'Ah!' said the people, 'if the intrepid Prince Codadad were still alive, we should feel very little alarm about the princes who are coming against us.' But the king, instead of giving way to any faint-heartedness or fear, made a hasty levy of his people. He brought together a considerable army, and being of too courageous a disposition to wait quietly within the walls till his enemies should come to seek him there, he sallied out, and marched forward to meet them. The enemy, on their side, having learned by their spies that the King of Harran was advancing to attack them, waited in the plain, and disposed their army in order of battle.

"As soon as the king perceived them he also arranged and disposed his troops for combat. He commanded them to sound the charge, and made his attack with great vigour. The enemy resisted in the same manner. Much blood was shed on both sides, and for a long time victory seemed doubtful. It was at last about to declare itself for the enemies of the King of Harran, who, having the advantage in numbers, were on the point of surrounding the king, when on a sudden there appeared in the plain a large body of horsemen, who approached the combatants in good order. The view of these fresh soldiers equally astonished both parties, who knew not what to think of their appearance; but this state of uncertainty did not long continue. This troop advanced, attacked the enemies of the King of Harran in flank, and charged with so much fury that they instantly threw them in disorder, and very soon put them to rout. They did not remain long in this state. Their enemies pursued them briskly, and cut almost the whole of their army in pieces.

"The King of Harran, who had observed all that had passed with much attention, had greatly admired the intrepidity of the horsemen by whose unexpected aid the victory had been determined in his favour. He had been particularly delighted with their chief, whom he had observed fighting with extraordinary valour, and was anxious to know the name of this generous hero. Impatient to see and to thank him, he went to meet him, while the conqueror himself was advancing towards the king. When the two princes approached one another the King of Harran recognised in this brave warrior, who thus brought him such important succour and had so completely subdued his foes, his beloved son Prince Codadad! The king remained motionless with excess of surprise and delight. 'Great king,' said Prince Codadad to him, 'you have, without doubt, much reason to be astonished at thus seeing on a sudden before you a man whom you have probably supposed to be dead. I should have perished if Heaven had not preserved me, in order that I might still serve you against your enemies.' 'Ah, my son!' replied the king, 'is it possible that you can be restored to me? Alas! I had wholly despaired of ever seeing you more.' So saying he held out his arms to the young prince, who willingly resigned himself to his father's affectionate embraces.

"'I know perfectly, my son,' said the king, after he had for a long time encircled him in his arms, 'I know perfectly in what way your brothers have repaid you the service you rendered them in delivering them from the hands of the negro; but to-morrow you shall be revenged on their treachery. In the meantime repair to the palace; your mother, who has shed so many tears on your account, is waiting to rejoice with me at the defeat of our enemies; what delight will be hers when she learns that I owe my victory to you!' 'O king,' said Prince Codadad, 'allow me to ask you how you became acquainted with the adventures of the castle? Has any one of my brothers, wounded by the stings of conscience, made a confession to you?' 'No,' replied the king, 'it is the Princess of Deryabar who has informed us of everything. She arrived a short time since at my palace, whither she came for the avowed purpose of demanding justice of your guilty brothers.' Prince Codadad was transported with joy at learning that the princess his wife was at the court. 'Come, my father,' he exclaimed with transport, 'let us wait on my mother, who expects us; I burn with impatience to dry her tears, as well as those of the Princess of Deryabar.'

PRINCE CODADAD AND THE PEASANT.

"The king immediately returned towards the city, at the head of his army, which he soon dismissed; he re-entered his palace amidst general congratulations. The air resounded with the acclamations of the people, who thronged around him, and earnestly petitioned Allah to prolong his days, while the name of Prince Codadad was raised to the skies. These two princes found Pirouzè and her daughter-in-law waiting to congratulate the king; but it is impossible to express their transports of delight when they saw the young prince attending his father. Their embraces were mingled with tears; but these tears were of a very different nature from those they had before shed on his account. When the first fervour of their joy had in some degree abated, the king and the ladies were anxious to know from Prince Codadad by what miracle it happened that he was yet alive.

"He informed them that a peasant, mounted upon a mule, had by accident entered the tent, where he lay senseless. This person, seeing him alone and pierced with so many wounds, had taken him upon his mule and carried him to his house, where he applied a variety of bruised herbs, which had cured Prince Codadad in a very short time. 'When I found myself perfectly recovered,' added he, 'I thanked the peasant, and presented him with all the diamonds I possessed. I then set forward towards the city of Harran; but, having learned on the road that some neighbouring princes had collected an army, and were approaching to attack the subjects of the king, I made myself known in all the villages, and excited the zeal of the people to rise in their own defence. I armed a great number of young men, and, putting myself at their head, arrived at the very time when the two armies were fighting.'

"When Prince Codadad had done speaking, the king said: 'Let us return thanks to Heaven for having preserved Prince Codadad; but it is only just that the traitors who intended his death should all of them perish this day.' 'O merciful king,' replied the generous son of Pirouzè, 'ungrateful and wicked as they undoubtedly are, remember that they are of your own blood. They are my brothers; I pardon them their crime, and presume to request of you the same favour for them.' These noble sentiments drew tears from the king. He caused the people to be assembled, and declared Prince Codadad his heir. He afterwards caused the princes to be led forth. They came forward loaded with irons. The son of Pirouzè loosed their chains and embraced them, one after another, with as much cordiality as he had shown in the court of the negro's castle. The people were charmed with the generous disposition displayed by Prince Codadad, and bestowed on him a thousand blessings. The surgeon was likewise loaded with benefits, as a reward for the important services he had rendered to the Princess of Deryabar."

"The Sultana Scheherazade had related the history of Ganem in so agreeable a manner, that the Sultan of the Indies, her husband, could not help declaring to her that he had heard it with very great pleasure. "Mighty king," replied the sultana, "I have no doubt but your majesty had much satisfaction in seeing the caliph Haroun Alraschid change his opinion in favour of Ganem, Ganem's mother, and his sister Alcolomb; and I have no doubt you were moved at the misfortunes of the one and the ill-treatment shown to the others; but I am convinced that if your majesty would listen to the story of the 'Sleeper Awakened,' instead of all those emotions of indignation and compassion which the history of Ganem must have excited in your heart, and which still remain, this story would occasion you only mirth and laughter."

When he had heard the title of the story which the sultana had mentioned, Schahriar, who expected from it very entertaining and quite novel adventures, would fain have heard the narrative that very morning. But it was time to rise; he therefore deferred it till the following morning; and this new story served for many days and nights to prolong the sultana's life. Dinarzade having called her at the appointed time, she began the narrative as follows:—

## THE SLEEPER AWAKENED.

DURING the reign of the caliph Haroun Alraschid, there lived at Bagdad a very rich merchant, whose wife was far advanced in years. They had an only son, called Abou Hassan, who had been in every respect brought up with great strictness.

"The merchant died when this son was thirty years old; and Abou Hassan, who was his sole heir, took possession of the vast wealth which his father had amassed, by great parsimony and a constant industry in business. The son, whose views and inclinations were very different from those of his father, very soon began to dissipate his fortune. As his father had not allowed him in his youth more than was barely sufficient for his maintenance, and as Abou Hassan had always envied young men of his own age who had been more liberally supplied, and who never denied themselves any of those pleasures in which young men too readily indulge, he determined in his turn to distinguish himself by making an appearance consistent with the great wealth with which fortune had favoured him. Accordingly, he divided his fortune into two parts. With the one he purchased estates in the country and houses in the city, and, although these would produce a revenue sufficient to enable him to live at his ease, he resolved to let the sums arising from them accumulate; the other half, which consisted of a considerable sum of ready money, was to be spent in enjoyment, to compensate him for the time he thought he had lost under the severe restraint in which he had been kept during his father's lifetime: but he laid it down as a primary rule, which he determined inviolably to keep, not to expend more than this sum in the jovial life he proposed to lead.

"Abou Hassan soon brought together a company of young men, nearly of his own age and rank in life; and he thought only how he should make their time pass agreeably. To accomplish this he was not content with entertaining them day and night, and giving the most splendid feasts, at which the most delicious viands, and wines of the most exquisite flavour were served in abundance; he added music to all this, engaging the best singers of both sexes. His young friends, on their part, while they indulged in the pleasures of the table, often joined their voices to those of the musicians, and, accompanied by soft instruments, formed a concert of delightful harmony. These feasts were generally followed by balls, to which the best dancers in the city of Bagdad were invited. All these amusements, which were daily varied by new pleasures, were so extremely expensive to Abou Hassan, that he could not continue his profuse style of living beyond one year. The large sum of money which he had devoted to this prodigality ended with the year. So soon as he ceased giving these entertainments his friends disappeared; he never even met them in any place he frequented. In short, they shunned him whenever they saw him; and if by accident he encountered any one of them, and wished to detain him in conversation, the false friend excused himself under various pretences.

"Abou Hassan was more distressed at the strange conduct of his friends, who abandoned him with so much faithlessness and ingratitude after all the vows and protestations of friendship they had made him, than at the loss of all the money he had so foolishly expended on them. Melancholy and thoughtful, with his head sunk upon his breast, and a countenance full of bitter emotion, he entered his mother's apartment and seated himself at the end of a sofa at some distance from her.

"'What is the matter, my son?' asked his mother, when she saw him in this desponding state. 'Why are you so moody, so cast down, and so different from your former self? Had you lost everything you possessed in the world you could not appear more miserable. I know at what an enormous outlay you have lived; and ever since you engaged in that course of dissipation I thought you would soon have very little money left. Your fortune was at your own disposal, and I did not endeavour to oppose your irregular proceedings, because I knew the prudent precaution you had taken of leaving half of your means untouched; while this half remains I do not see why you should be plunged into this deep melancholy.' Abou Hassan burst into tears at these words, and in the midst of his grief exclaimed, 'Oh, my dear mother, I know from woeful experience how insupportable poverty is. Yes, I feel very sensibly that as the setting of the sun deprives us of the splendour of that luminary, so poverty deprives us of every sort of enjoyment. Poverty buries in oblivion all the praises that have been bestowed on us, and all the good that has been said of us, before we fell into its grasp. It reduces us at every step to take measures to avoid observation, and to pass whole nights in shedding the bitterest tears. He who is poor is regarded but as a stranger, even by his relations and his friends. You know, my mother,' continued Abou Hassan, 'how liberally I have conducted myself towards my friends for a year past. I have exhausted my means in entertaining them in the most sumptuous manner; and now that I cannot continue to do so, I find myself abandoned by them all. When I say that I have it no longer in my power to entertain them as I have done, I mean that the money I had set apart to be employed for that purpose is entirely exhausted. I thank Heaven for having inspired me with the idea of reserving what I call my income, under the rule and oath I made not to touch it for any foolish dissipation. I will strictly observe this oath, and I have resolved to make a good use of what happily remains; but first I wish to see to what extremity my friends, if indeed I can still call them so, will carry their ingratitude. I will see them all, one after another; and when I represent to them the lengths to which I have gone from my regard to them, I will solicit them to raise amongst themselves a sufficient sum of money in some measure to relieve me in the unhappy situation to which I am reduced by contributing to their amusement. But I mean to take this step, as I have already said, only to see whether I shall find in these friends the least sentiment of gratitude.'

"'My son,' replied the mother of Abou Hassan, 'I will not take upon myself to dissuade you from executing your plan; but I can tell you beforehand that your hope is unfounded. Believe me, it is useless to attempt this trial; you will receive no assistance but from the property you have yourself reserved. I plainly see you do not yet know those men who, among people of your description, are commonly styled friends; but you will soon know them: and I pray Heaven it may be in the way I wish—that is, for your good.' 'My dear mother,' cried Abou Hassan, 'I am convinced of the truth of what you tell me: but it will be a more convincing proof to me of those men's baseness and want of feeling if I learn it by my own experience.'

"Abou Hassan set out immediately; and he timed his visits so well that he found all his friends at home. He represented to them the great distress he was in, and besought them to lend him such a sum of money as would be of effectual assistance to him; he even promised to enter into a bond to every one individually to return the sums each should lend him, so soon as his affairs were re-established; but he still avoided letting them know that his distresses were in a great measure arising from them; for he wished to give them every opportunity of displaying their generosity. And he did not forget to hold out to them the hope that he might one day be again in a position to entertain them as he had done.

"Not one of his convivial companions was the least affected by Abou Hassan's distresses and afflictions, though he represented his embarrassments in the most lively colours, hoping he should persuade his friends to relieve him. He had even the mortification to find that many of them pretended not to know him, and did not even remember ever to have seen him. He returned home, his heart filled with grief and indignation. 'Alas! my mother,' cried he, as he entered her apartment, 'you have told me the truth; instead of friends I have found only perfidious, ungrateful men, unworthy of my friendship. I renounce them for ever, and I promise you I will never see them again.

"Abou Hassan kept firmly to the resolution he had made, and took every prudent precaution to avoid being tempted to break it. He bound himself by an oath never to ask any man who was an inhabitant of Bagdad to eat with him. He then took the strong box which contained the money arising from his rents from the spot where he had laid it by, and put it in the place of the coffers he had just emptied. He resolved to take from it for the expenses of each day a regular sum that should be sufficient to enable him to invite one person to sup with him; and he took a second oath, declaring that the person he entertained should not be an inhabitant of Bagdad, but a stranger who had only tarried in the city one day; and determined that he would send him away the next morning, after giving him only one night's lodging.

"In carrying out his design Abou Hassan took care every morning to make the necessary provision for this limited hospitality; and towards the close of each day he went and sat at the end of the bridge of Bagdad, and as soon as he saw a stranger, whatever the appearance of the wayfarer, he accosted him with great civility, and invited him to sup and lodge at his house on that, the night of his arrival. He at once informed his guest of the rule he had laid down, and the bounds he had set to his hospitality; and thereupon conducted him to his house.

"The repast which Abou Hassan set before his guest was not sumptuous; but it was such as might well satisfy a man, especially as there was no want of good wine. They

ABOU HASSAN AND THE STRANGER.

remained at table till almost midnight; and instead of discoursing to his guest, as is customary, on affairs of state, family matters, or business, he used, on the contrary, to talk gaily and agreeably of indifferent things: he was naturally pleasant, good-humoured, and amusing, and whatever the subject was he knew how to give such a turn to his conversation as would enliven the most melancholy of his visitors.

"When he took leave next morning of his guest, Abou Hassan always said: 'To whatever place you go, may Allah preserve you from every sort of calamity. When I invited you to sup with me yesterday, I informed you of the rule I had laid down for myself: for which reason you must not take it ill if I tell you that we shall never drink together again, nor shall we ever meet each other any more at my house, or any other place. I have my reasons for this course of conduct, which I need not explain to you. May Allah guard you!'

"Abou Hassan observed this rule with great exactness; he never again noticed or addressed the strangers whom he had once received in his house: when he met them in the streets, the squares, or public assemblies, he appeared not to see them, and even turned from them if they accosted him. In short, he avoided the slightest intercourse with them. And for a long time he continued this course of life. But one day, a little before sun-set, as he was seated in his usual manner at the end of the bridge, the caliph Haroun Alraschid appeared; but so completely disguised that none of his subjects could know him.

"Although this monarch had ministers and officers of justice, who performed their duty with great exactness, he wished, nevertheless, to look into the working of everything himself. With this design, as we have already seen, he often went in different disguises through the city of Bagdad. He was even accustomed to visit the high environs; and on this account he made it a custom to go on the first day of every month into the high roads which lead to the city, sometimes choosing one road, and sometimes another. That day, the first of the month, he appeared disguised as a merchant from Moussoul, just landed on the other side of the bridge, and was followed by a strong and sturdy slave.

"As the caliph looked in his disguise like a grave and respectable man, Abou Hassan, who believed him to be a merchant from Moussoul, rose from the place on which he was seated. He saluted the stranger with a bland and courteous air, and addressed him thus: 'O my master, I congratulate you on your happy arrival; I entreat you will do me the honour to sup with me, and pass the night at my house, that you may rest yourself after the fatigue of your journey.' And to induce the supposed merchant to comply with his request, he told him, in a few words, the rule he had laid down to himself—of every day receiving, for one night only, the first stranger who presented himself.

"The caliph found something so singular in the whimsical taste of Abou Hassan, that he felt an inclination to know something further of him. Therefore, preserving the character of a merchant, he assured Abou Hassan he could not better reply to so great and unexpected a civility, on his arrival at Bagdad, than by accepting the obliging invitation; and accordingly begged his entertainer to lead the way, declaring himself ready to follow him.

"Abou Hassan, who was ignorant of the high rank of the guest whom chance had just presented to him, treated the caliph as if he had been his equal. He took him to his house, showed him into an apartment very neatly furnished, where he seated him on a sofa in the most honourable place. Supper was ready, and the cloth was spread. Abou Hassan's mother, who was an adept in the culinary art, sent in three dishes. One was a fine capon, garnished with four fat pullets; the other two dishes were a fat goose and a ragout of pigeons. This was the whole provision; but the dishes were well chosen, and excellent of their kind.

"Abou Hassan placed himself at table opposite his guest; and the caliph and he began eating with a good appetite, helping themselves to what they liked best, without speaking and without drinking, according to the custom of their country. When they had done, the slave of the caliph brought them water to wash their hands, while the mother of Abou Hassan took away the dishes, and brought the dessert, which consisted of a variety of the fruits then in season, such as grapes, peaches, apples, pears, and several kinds of cakes made of dried almonds. As the evening closed in they lighted the candles; and then Abou Hassan brought out bottles and glasses, and took care that his mother provided supper for the caliph's slave.

"When the pretended merchant of Moussoul and Abou Hassan were again seated at table, the latter, before he touched the fruit, took a cup, and filling it for himself, held it out in his hand, 'O my master,' said he to the caliph, whom he took to be only a merchant, 'you know as well as I do that the cock never drinks till he has called his hens about him to come and drink with him; therefore I invite you to follow my example. I know not what your sentiments may be; but, for my own part, it seems to me that a man who hates wine, and would fain be thought wise, is certainly foolish. Let such men deem themselves wise with their stupid and melancholy disposition, but let us enjoy ourselves; I see pleasure sparkling in the cup, and it will assuredly yield much pleasure to those who empty it.'

"While Abou Hassan was drinking, the caliph took hold of the cup that was intended for him, and replied: 'I agree with you. You are what may be called a jolly fellow. I love you for your humour, and I expect you will fill my cup to the brim as you have filled yours.'

"When Abou Hassan had drunk, he accordingly filled the cup which the caliph held out; 'Taste it, my friend,' said he, 'you will find it excellent.' 'I have no doubt of that,' returned the caliph, laughing; 'no doubt a man of discernment like you knows how to procure the best of everything.'

"While the caliph was drinking, Abou Hassan observed, 'any man who looks at you may observe at first sight that you are one of those who have seen the world, and know how to enjoy it. If my house,' added he, quoting some lines of Arabian poetry, 'were capable of any feeling, and could be alive to the pleasure of receiving you within its walls, it would loudly express its joy, and throwing itself at your feet, would cry out, "Ah! what delight, what happiness is it, to see myself honoured with the presence of a person so respectable, and at the same time so condescending, as the man who now deigns to come under my roof!" In short, my master, my joy is complete, and I count the day fortunate on which I have met with a man of your merit.'

"These sallies of Abou Hassan very much diverted the caliph, who was naturally of a merry disposition, and took pleasure in inducing him to drink, that by means of the gaiety which wine would excite, he might become better acquainted with him. To engage him in conversation he asked him his name, and what was his employment, and how he passed his time. 'O stranger,' replied his host, 'my name is Abou Hassan; I have lost my father, who was a merchant, not indeed a very rich man, but one of those who, at Bagdad, manage to live very much at their ease. At his death he left me an inheritance sufficient to support me creditably in the rank I held. As he had kept me very strictly during his lifetime, and at the time of his death I had passed the best part of my youth under great restraint, I wished to try to make up for all the time I considered I had lost.

"'Nevertheless,' continued Abou Hassan, 'I regulated my proceedings with more prudence than is practised by young people in general. They usually give themselves up to intemperance in a very thoughtless way; they indulge in every dissipation till, reduced to their last sequin, they exercise a forced abstinence during the remainder of their life. In order to avoid future distress, I divided my property into two parts; the one consisted of rents, the other of ready money. I devoted the ready money to the enjoyments I purposed indulging in; and made a firm resolution not to touch my rents. I brought together a company of people I knew, men nearly of my own age; and, with the ready money which I freely lavished, I every day gave the most splendid entertainments, living with my friends in luxury which pleased us all well. But this did not last long; at the end of a year I found my purse empty, and at once all my convivial friends disappeared. I made it my business to call upon each of them in turn; I represented to each the wretched state to which I was reduced, but not one of them would give me any assistance. I therefore renounced their friendship; and, reducing my expenses within the limits of my income, I determined that in future I would entertain no one at all, except every day one stranger whom I should meet on his arrival at Bagdad; and I made it a condition that I entertained him for that day only. I have told you the rest, and I thank my good fortune which to day has thrown in my way a stranger of so much merit.'

"Very well, satisfied with this explanation, the caliph said to Abou Hassan, 'I cannot sufficiently commend the step you took, and the caution with which you acted, when you entered upon your free course of life. You conducted yourself very differently from young men in general; and I respect you still more for keeping your resolution with so much steadiness as you have shown. You walked in a very slippery path; and I cannot sufficiently wonder, after you had spent all your ready money, that you had the moderation to confine yourself within the income arising from your rents; and that you do not mortgage your estate. To tell you what I think of the matter, I firmly believe you are the only man of pleasure that ever did, or ever will, conduct himself in such a manner. In short, I declare that I envy your good fortune. You are the happiest man on earth, thus to have every day the company of a respectable person, with whom you can converse agreeably, and to whom you give an opportunity of telling the world the good reception you have afforded him. But we forget ourselves. Neither you nor I perceive how long we have been talking without drinking; come, drink, and I will pledge you.' The caliph and Abou Hassan continued drinking a long time, and conversing most agreeably together.

"The night was now far advanced; and the caliph, pretending to be much fatigued with his day's journey, said to Abou Hassan that he was much inclined to go to rest. 'I should be loth,' added he, 'that, on my account, you should lose any of your sleep. Before we part—for perhaps I shall be gone to-morrow from your house before you are awake—let me have the satisfaction of saying how sensible I am of the civility, the good cheer, and the hospitality with which you have treated me in so obliging a manner. I am only anxious to know in what way I can best prove my gratitude. I entreat you to inform me, and you shall find that I am not an ungrateful man. It is hardly possible that a person like you should not have some business that might be done, some want that should be supplied, some wish that is yet ungratified. Open your heart to me, and speak freely. Though I am but a merchant as you see, I am in a position, either alone, or with the help of my friends, to serve my friends.'

"At these offers of the caliph, whom Abou Hassan all along supposed to be a merchant, he replied, 'My good friend, I am thoroughly convinced that is not out of mere compliment you address me in this generous manner. But, upon the word of a man of honour, I can assure you that I have no distress, no business, no want; that I have nothing to ask of any one. I have not the smallest degree of ambition, as I have already told you, and am perfectly contented with my lot; so that I have only to thank you, as well for your kind offers as for the kindness you have shown in conferring upon me the honour of taking a poor refreshment at my house.

"'I will say, nevertheless,' continued Abou Hassan, 'that one thing gives me some concern, though it does not very materially disturb my repose. You know the city of Bagdad has several divisions, and that in every division there is a mosque. Each mosque has an Iman, who assembles all the people of the division at the accustomed hours to join with him in prayer. The Iman of this division is a very old man, of an austere countenance; he is a complete hypocrite, if ever there was one in the world. He assembles in council four other dotards, my neighbours, very much of the same character with himself, and they meet regularly every day at his house. When they get together there is no sort of slander, calumny, and mischief which they do not raise and propagate against me, and against the whole quarter; they disturb our quiet, and stir up dissensions among us. They make themselves formidable to some, and threaten others. They wish, in short, to be our masters, and desire that each of us should behave himself according to their caprice, while, at the same time, they cannot govern themselves. To say the truth, I cannot bear to see them busying themselves with everything except the Koran, and it angers me that they cannot let their neighbours live in peace.'

"'So then,' replied the caliph, 'you seem desirous of finding means to check this abuse?' 'I am, indeed,' returned Abou Hassan; 'and the only thing I would beg of Heaven for this purpose is, that I might for one day be caliph in the room of the Commander of the Faithful, our sovereign lord and master, Haroun Alraschid.' 'What would you do,' demanded the caliph, 'if that should happen?' 'One very important thing would I do,' replied Abou Hassan, 'which would give satisfaction to all good people. I would order that one hundred strokes on the soles of the feet be given to each of the four old men, and four hundred to the Iman himself, to teach them that it is not their business to disturb and vex their neighbours.'

"The caliph was much amused by the conceit of Abou Hassan; and, as he had naturally a turn for adventures, it suggested to him a desire to divert himself at his host's expense in a very extraordinary manner. 'Your wish pleases me the more,' said

ABOU HASSAN FALLS ASLEEP.

the caliph, 'because I see it springs from an upright heart, and is the sentiment of a person who cannot bear that the malice of wicked men should go unpunished. I should have great pleasure in procuring its fulfilment, and perhaps it is not impossible that what you have imagined may come to pass. I feel certain that the caliph would readily trust his power in your hands for twenty-four hours if he only knew of your good intention, and the excellent use you would make of the opportunity. Although I am but a merchant, and a stranger, I am nevertheless not without a degree of interest which may possibly forward this business.'

"'I see plainly,' replied Abou Hassan, 'that you are diverting yourself with my foolish fancy—and the caliph would laugh at it also if he came to hear of such a ridiculous whim. Still, it might have the effect of inducing him to inquire into the conduct of the Iman and his counsellors, and order them to be punished.'

"'I am by no means laughing at you,' replied the caliph; 'Heaven forbid that I should cherish so unbecoming a thought towards a person like you, who have entertained me so handsomely, though I was quite a stranger to you; and I can assure you the caliph himself would not laugh at you. But let us make an end of this conversation; it is near midnight, and time to go to bed.'

"'Then,' said Abou Hassan, 'we will cut short our discourse, and I will not prevent you from taking your repose: but, as there is a little wine still left in the bottle, I pray you let us finish that, and then we will retire. The only thing I have to recommend is, when you leave the house to-morrow morning, if I should not have risen, that you would not leave the door open, but that you would trouble yourself to shut it after you.' This the caliph faithfully promised to do.

"While Abou Hassan was speaking, the caliph laid hands on the bottle and the two cups. He helped himself first, and made Abou Hassan understand that he drank to him a cup of thanks. When he had done so, he slily threw into Abou Hassan's cup a little powder, which he had with him, and poured upon it the remainder of the wine from the bottle. Presenting it to Abou Hassan, he said, 'you have had the trouble of helping me throughout the evening; the least I can do, in return, is to spare you that trouble now at our parting cup: I beg you will take this from my hand, and drink this time for my sake.'

"Abou Hassan took the cup; and the better to prove to his guest with how much pleasure he accepted the honour done him, he swallowed the whole contents at a draught. But scarcely had he set down the cup on the table, when the powder began to take effect. He instantly fell so soundly asleep, and his head dropped almost upon his knees so suddenly, that the caliph could not help laughing. The slave who attended the caliph had returned as soon as he had supped, and had been for some time on the spot, ready to obey his master's orders. 'Take this man upon your shoulders,' said the caliph to him, 'but be careful to notice the spot where this house stands, that you may bring him back hither when I shall bid you.'

"The caliph, followed by his slave, who bore Abou Hassan on his shoulders, went out of the house; but he did not close the door as Abou Hassan had requested him to do. Indeed, he left it open on purpose. When he arrived at the palace he entered by a private door, and ordered the slave to carry Abou Hassan to his own apartment, where all the officers of the bed-chamber were in waiting. 'Undress this man,' said he to them, 'and lay him in my bed; I will afterwards tell you my intention.'

"The officers undressed Abou Hassan, clothed him in the caliph's night dress, and put him to bed, as they were ordered. No one in the palace had yet retired to rest. The caliph ordered that all the ladies, and all the other officers of the court should be summoned; and when they were all in his presence, he said, 'I desire that all those who usually come to me when I rise shall not fail in their attendance here to-morrow morning upon this man, whom you see asleep in my bed; and that upon his waking each shall perform the same services for him which are usually performed for me. I desire also that the same respect be observed towards him that is shown to my own person; and that he be obeyed in all that he shall command. He shall be refused nothing he may demand. All his orders are to be fulfilled, nor is he to be contradicted in any desire he shall express. On every occasion, where it shall be proper to speak to him or to answer him, let him be always treated as the Commander of the Faithful. In one word, I require that no more attention be paid to me by any one all the time you are about him than if he were really what I am, caliph and Commander of the Faithful. Above all, let the utmost care be taken that the deception is carried through, even to the most trifling circumstance.'

"The officers and ladies, who soon perceived the caliph had some jest in hand, answered only by a low obeisance; and from that moment all of them prepared to contribute everything in their power, each in his or her peculiar function, to support the deception with exactness.

"On his return to the palace the caliph had sent the first officer in waiting to summon the grand vizier Giafar, and the vizier had just arrived. The caliph said to him: 'Giafar, I sent to you to warn you not to seem astonished when, at the audience to-morrow morning, you shall see the man who is now asleep on my bed seated upon my throne, and dressed in my robes of state. Address him in the same form you employ towards me, and pay him the same respect you are in the habit of paying to me; treat him exactly as if he were the Commander of the Faithful. Wait upon him, and execute punctually all his orders, just as if they were mine. He will most probably make large presents, and you will be entrusted with the distribution of them: fulfil all his commands in this matter, even to the hazard of exhausting my treasury. Remember also to warn my emirs, my ushers, and all the officers not within the palace, that to-morrow at the public audience they shall pay him the same honours they accord to my person, and bid them act their parts so well that he shall be thoroughly deceived, and that the amusement I propose to give myself may not in the smallest particular be broken. You may now retire; I have nothing further to order; but be careful to give me in this matter all the satisfaction which I demand.'

"After the grand vizier had retired, the caliph passed on to another apartment; and as he went to bed he imparted to Mesrour, chief of the eunuchs, the orders which were to be executed, so that everything might succeed in the manner intended; for the caliph wished both to fulfil the wish of Abou Hassan, and to see the use he would make of the royal power and authority during the short time he would possess them. Above all, he enjoined Mesrour not to fail in coming to call him at the usual hour, and before Abou Hassan should be awake, because he wished to be present at all that might take place.

"Mesrour awakened the caliph punctually at the time he was ordered. As soon as Haroun Alraschid had entered the room where Abou Hassan slept, he placed himself in an adjoining closet, whence he could see through a lattice all that took place, without being himself seen. All the officers and all the ladies who were to be present when Abou Hassan rose came in at the same time, and were posted in their accustomed places, according to their rank, and in profound silence, just as if the caliph himself had been about to rise, and they were waiting ready to perform the duties of their various offices.

"As the day already began to break, and it was time to get up for early prayer before sunrise, the officer who was nearest Abou Hassan's pillow applied to the sleeper's nose a small piece of sponge dipped in vinegar.

"Abou Hassan sneezed and turned his head, without opening his eyes. Thereupon his head sank back on the pillow. Presently he opened his eyes; and, as far as the dim light permitted him, he saw himself in a large and magnificent chamber, superbly furnished, the ceiling painted with various figures, and elegant borders, and ornamented throughout with vases of massive gold, and with tapestry and carpets of the richest kind. He found himself surrounded by young ladies of enchanting beauty, many of whom had different musical instruments, which they were preparing to play upon; and by black eunuchs richly dressed, and standing ranged in attitudes of deep humility and respect. As he cast his eyes upon the coverlid of the bed, he saw it was of crimson and gold brocade, ornamented with pearls and diamonds; by the bed side lay a dress of the same materials, ornamented in similar style; and near it, on a cushion, a caliph's cap.

"At the sight of all this splendour Abou Hassan was inexpressibly astonished and bewildered. He looked upon the whole as a dream—but a dream of so charming a nature that he hoped it might prove a reality. 'Truly,' said he to himself, 'it seems I am caliph; but,' added he, after a pause, on recovering himself, 'I must not deceive myself, this is a dream, merely an effect of the wish I formed in conversation with my guest—' so he shut his eyes again as if he intended to go to sleep.

"But at that moment an eunuch drew near. 'O Commander of the Faithful,' said he, respectfully, 'your majesty will be pleased not to sleep again. It is time to rise for early prayer. The day begins to break.' Abou Hassan, very much astonished at this address, said again to himself, 'Am I awake, or do I sleep? No, I am certainly asleep—' continued he, keeping his eyes still closed—'I must not doubt it.'

"O Commander of the Faithful,' resumed the eunuch, who observed that Abou

Hassan gave no answer, and showed no signs of intending to rouse himself, 'your majesty will allow me to repeat that it is time to rise, unless your majesty means to disregard the hour of morning prayer, which you are accustomed to attend; and the sun is even now appearing.'

"'I was deceiving myself,' said Abou Hassan, 'I am not asleep, I am awake. Those who sleep never hear anything; and I certainly hear that I am spoken to.' Then he opened his eyes again. It was now daylight, and he saw distinctly what he had before only imperfectly beheld. He sat up in his bed with a cheerful countenance, like a man much rejoicing at finding himself in a situation very far above his rank; and the caliph, who watched him without being himself seen, penetrated his thoughts with great satisfaction.

"Then the beautiful ladies of the palace bowed down before Abou Hassan, with their faces towards the ground; and those among them who had instruments of music saluted him on his awaking with a concert of soft-toned flutes, hautbois, lutes, and various other instruments. This so enchanted him, and raised him to such an excess of delight, that he knew not where he was, and almost lost consciousness. He recurred, nevertheless, to his first thought, and again doubted whether what he saw and heard was a dream or reality. He covered his eyes with his hands, and bending his head repeated to himself, 'What does all this mean? Where am I? What has happened to me? What is this palace? Whence come these eunuchs, these gallant handsome officers, these beauteous damsels, and these enchanting musicians? Is it possible that I should not be able to distinguish whether I am dreaming, or whether I have all my senses about me!' At last he took his hands from his face; and opening his eyes to look up, he saw the sun darting its first rays through the window of the chamber in which he lay.

"At this moment Mesrour, the chief of the eunuchs, came in. He bowed down, with his face to the ground, before Abou Hassan, and as he rose said, 'Commander of the Faithful, your majesty will permit me to represent that you have not been accustomed to rise so late, nor have you ever suffered the hour of morning prayer to pass unregarded. Unless your majesty has had a bad night, or is otherwise indisposed, you will now be pleased to mount your throne, to hold your council, and to give audience as usual. The generals of your armies, the governors of your provinces, and the other great officers of your court, await the moment when the door of the council chamber shall be opened.

"At this address of Mesrour, Abou Hassan was, as it were, convinced against his own judgment that he was not asleep, and that the splendours which he saw around him were not a dream. He was much perplexed; he felt bewildered at the position he was in, and uncertain what part he should take. At length he fixed his eyes upon Mesrour, and, in a serious tone, demanded of him, 'Whom are you addressing? Who is it that you call Commander of the Faithful? I know you not; you must certainly take me for some other person.'

"Any man but Mesrour would have been disconcerted at Abou Hassan's questions; but, instructed by the caliph, he played his part wonderfully well. 'O my most honoured lord and master,' cried he, 'your majesty surely talks thus to me to-day in order to try me! Is not your majesty the Commander of the Faithful, the monarch of the world from the east to the west? and upon earth vicar of the prophet sent from Allah, who is master of all, both in Heaven and in earth? Your poor slave Mesrour has not forgotten all this, after the many years during which he has had the honour and happiness of paying his duty and services to your majesty! He would think himself the most miserable of men if he were to lose your good opinion. He most humbly entreats your majesty to have the goodness to restore him to your favour, and humbly ventures to think some disagreeable dream has disturbed your majesty's repose.'

"Abou Hassan burst into such a violent fit of laughter at this speech of Mesrour's that he fell back on his pillow, to the great amusement of the real caliph, who would have laughed as loudly as did the pretended one, but for the fear of putting an end to the pleasant scene which he had determined to have exhibited before him.

"After he had laughed till he was out of breath, Abou Hassan sat up again in his

ABOU HASSAN AS CALIPH.

bed, and speaking to a little eunuch as black as Mesrour, cried, 'Hark ye, tell me who I am.' 'O mighty sovereign,' said the little eunuch, in a very humble manner, 'your majesty is the Commander of the Faithful, and vicar upon earth of the Lord of both worlds.' 'Thou art a little liar, thou sooty-face!' replied Abou Hassan.

"He then called one of the ladies who was nearer to him than the rest. 'Come hither,' said he, as he held out his hand towards her, 'take the end of my finger and bite it, O thou fair one, that I may feel whether I am asleep or awake.'

"The damsel, who knew the caliph from his hiding place saw all that was going on, was delighted with an opportunity of showing how well she could play her part where the business was to afford her master amusement. She came towards Abou Hassan with the most serious air imaginable, and closing her teeth upon the end of his finger, which he had held out to her, she bit it pretty sharply.

"Abou Hassan drew back his hand in a hurry. 'I am not asleep,' he cried, I am most assuredly not asleep. By what miracle have I become caliph in one night? This is the most surprising, the most marvellous thing in the world.' Speaking again to the same damsel he resumed, 'Now, in the name of Allah, in whom you put your trust, as I also do, I beseech you tell me exactly the truth. Am I really and truly the Commander of the Faithful?' 'Your majesty,' replied she, 'is in truth and actually the Commander of the Faithful; and we, who are your slaves, are all amazed to think what can make your majesty doubt the fact.' 'You lie.' replied Abou Hassan, 'I know very well who I am.'

"As the chief of the eunuchs perceived that Abou Hassan meant to rise, he offered his hand to assist him in getting out of bed. As soon as the pretended caliph stood up, the whole chamber resounded with the salutation which all the officers and ladies pronounced with acclamation in these words: 'O Commander of the Faithful, in the name of Allah, we wish your majesty good morning.'

"'Oh, Heavens!' cried Abou Hassan, 'what miracle is this! Last night was I Abou Hassan, and this morning I am the Commander of the Faithful! I cannot at all understand this very sudden and surprising change.' The officers whose business it was to dress the caliph speedily performed their office. When this was accomplished, as the other officers, the eunuchs, and the ladies, had ranged themselves in two lines, extending to the door through which he was to go into the council chamber, Mesrour led the way, and Abou Hassan followed. The arras was drawn back, and the door opened by an usher. Mesrour entered the council chamber, and went on before Abou Hassan quite to the foot of the throne, where he stopped to assist him in ascending it. He supported the caliph by placing his hand under his shoulder on one side, while another officer, who followed, assisted him in the same way on the other.

"Thus Abou Hassan sat on the royal throne amidst the acclamations of the attendants, who wished him all kinds of happiness and prosperity; and looking to the right and left he saw the officers of the guards ranged in two rows in exact military order.

"Directly Abou Hassan entered the council chamber, the caliph quitted the closet in which he had been concealed, and passed to another closet from whence he could see and hear all that took place in the council when the grand vizier presided there instead of him, if at any time it was inconvenient for him to be there in person. He was not a little diverted to see Abou Hassan representing him upon the throne, and presiding with as much gravity as he could himself have shown.

"When Abou Hassan had taken his seat, the grand vizier, who was present, prostrated himself at the foot of the throne, and, as he rose, said in a solemn voice: 'O Commander of the Faithful, may Allah pour upon your majesty all the blessings of this life, and receive you into paradise in the next, and cast your enemies into the flames of hell!'

"After all that had happened to him since he awoke, and what he had just heard from the mouth of the grand vizier, Abou Hassan no longer doubted that his wish had been fulfilled, and that he was really the caliph. So without examining how, or by what means this unexpected transformation had been brought about, he immediately began to exercise his power. Looking at the grand vizier with profound gravity, he asked him whether he had anything to report.

"O Commander of the Faithful, replied the grand vizier, 'the emirs, the viziers, and the other officers who belong to your majesty's council, are at the door, anxiously waiting till you shall give them permission that they may enter, and pay their accustomed respects.' Abou Hassan immediately gave the word to open the door, and the grand vizier, turning round, said to the chief usher who stood expectant, 'O chief usher, the Commander of the Faithful enjoins you to do your duty.'

"The door was opened; and at once the viziers, the emirs, and the principal officers of the court, all in their magnificent habits of ceremony, entered in exact order. They came forward to the foot of the throne, and paid their respects to Abou Hassan, each according to his rank, bending the knee, and prostrating themselves with their faces to the ground, just as they would have done in presence of the caliph himself. They saluted him by the name of Commander of the Faithful, according to the instructions given by the grand vizier. They then took their places in turn when each had gone through this ceremony. When this was ended, and they had all returned to their places, there was a profound silence.

"Then the grand vizier, standing before the throne, began to make his report of various matters from a number of papers which he held in his hand. This report was a matter of routine, and of little consequence. Nevertheless the caliph was in constant admiration of Abou Hassan's conduct; for the new caliph never was at a loss, nor appeared at all embarrassed. He gave just decisions upon the questions which came before him; for his good sense suggested whether he was to grant or refuse the demands that were made.

"Before the vizier had finished his report, Abou Hassan caught sight of the chief officer of the police, whom he had often seen sitting in his place. 'Stay a moment,' said he, interrupting the grand vizier, 'I have an order of importance to give immediately to the officer of the police.'

"This officer, who had his eyes fixed upon Abou Hassan, and who perceived that he looked at him in particular, hearing his name mentioned, rose immediately from his place, and gravely approached the throne, at the foot of which he prostrated himself with his face towards the ground. 'O officer,' said Abou Hassan to him, when he had raised himself, 'go immediately, without loss of time, to such a street in such a quarter of the town,' and he mentioned the name of his own street. 'In this street is a mosque, where you will find the Iman and four old grey-beards. Seize their persons, and let the four old men have each a hundred strokes on the feet, and let the Iman have four hundred. Thereupon you shall cause all the five to be clothed in rags and mounted each on a camel, with their faces turned towards the tail. Thus equipped, you shall have them led through the different quarters of the town preceded by a crier, who shall proclaim with a loud voice, "This is the punishment for those who meddle with affairs which do not concern them, and who make it their business to sow dissension among neighbouring families, and to cause strife and mischief." I command you, moreover, that you enjoin them to leave the part of the town in which they now live, and forbid them ever to set foot again in the place whence they are driven. While your deputy is leading them in the procession I have just ordered, you must return to report to me the execution of my commands.'

"The officer of police placed his hand upon his head, to signify that he was ready to execute the order he had received, and should expect to lose his head if he failed in any point. He prostrated himself a second time before the throne, then rose and went away.

"The order thus judiciously given gave the caliph great satisfaction; for he was now convinced that Abou Hassan had been in earnest in wishing to punish the Iman and his four old counsellors, when he declared that was the original motive for his wishing that he might have the caliph's power for a single day.

"The grand vizier went on with his report, which he had very nearly ended, when the officer of the police presented himself to give an account of what he had done. He approached the throne, and, after the usual ceremony of prostration, said to Abou Hassan: 'O Commander of the Faithful, I found the Iman and the four old men in the mosque of which your majesty spoke, and to prove that I have duly executed the orders I received from your majesty, I bring a written account of the proceeding, signed by many principal people of that part of the town who were witnesses.' So saying, he took from his bosom a paper, and gave it to the pretended caliph.

"Abou Hassan took the paper and read it from beginning to end, even to the names of the witnesses, all of whom were people whom he knew; and when he had finished, he said with a smile to the officer of the police: 'You have done well; I am satisfied and pleased; resume your place.' And he added to himself, with an air of satisfaction, 'Hypocrites who undertake to comment upon my actions, and think it wrong that I should receive and entertain respectable people at my house, richly deserve this disgrace and punishment.' The caliph, who watched him, saw into his mind and highly approved of the proceedings of his substitute.

"After that Abou Hassan addressed the grand vizier: 'Let the grand treasurer,' said he, 'make up a purse of a thousand pieces of gold, and go with it into the quarter of the city whither I sent the officer of the police, and give it to the mother of one Abou Hassan, called the Reveller. The man is well known throughout that quarter by that name; any man will show you his house. Go, and return quickly.'

"The grand vizier Giafar put his hand to his head to mark his readiness to obey; and after prostrating himself before the throne, departed, and went to the grand treasurer, who gave him the purse. He ordered one of the slaves who attended him to take it, and proceed to convey it to Abou Hassan's mother. On coming to her house, he said the caliph had sent her this present, and departed without explaining himself farther. Abou Hassan's mother was much surprised at receiving the purse, as she could not conceive what should induce the caliph to make her so handsome a present; for she knew not what was passing at the palace.

"During the absence of the grand vizier, the officer of the police made a report of many matters in his department; and this lasted until the vizier returned. As soon as Giafar reached the council-chamber, and had assured Abou Hassan that he had executed his commission, Mesrour, the chief of the eunuchs, who, after he had conducted Abou Hassan to the throne had passed into the inner apartments of the palace, came back and made a sign to the viziers, emirs, and all the officers, that the council was ended, and that every one might retire. They accordingly withdrew, after taking their leave by making a profound reverence at the foot of the throne, in the same order as they observed upon their entrance. There then remained with Abou Hassan only the officers of the caliph's guard and the grand vizier.

"Abou Hassan did not continue long on the throne of the caliph. He descended from it as he had mounted it, with the assistance of Mesrour and of another officer of the eunuchs. Each of his companions took him by an arm and attended him to the apartment in which he was at first. Then Mesrour, walking before him to show him the way, led him into an inner room, where a table was set out. The door of the apartment was open, and a great many eunuchs ran to tell the female musicians that the pretended caliph was coming. They immediately began a very harmonious concert of vocal and instrumental music, which delighted Abou Hassan to such a degree that he was transported with satisfaction and joy, and was quite at a loss what to think of all he saw and heard. 'If this is a dream,' said he to himself, 'it is a dream of a long continuance. But it cannot be a dream,' continued he, 'I am perfectly sensible, I make use of my understanding—I see—I walk—I hear. Be it what it may, I am in the hands of Heaven, and must be content. Still, I cannot possibly believe that I am not the Commander of the Faithful; for none but the Commander of the Faithful could be surrounded with the magnificence I find here. The honours and respect which have been, and are still paid to me, and the rapid execution of my orders, are clear proofs of it.'

"Abou Hassan was at last convinced that he was the caliph and the Commander of the Faithful; and this conviction was confirmed in him when he found himself in a very large and richly furnished saloon. Gold shone on all sides, intermixed with the most vivid colours. Seven bands of female musicians, all women of the most exquisite beauty, were posted around this saloon. Seven golden lustres, with the same number of branches, hung from different parts of the ceiling, which was painted in a beautiful pattern—a skilful mixture of gold and azure. In the midst was a table on which gleamed seven large dishes of massive gold, which perfumed the room with the odour of the richest spices used in seasoning the several delicacies. Seven young and very beautiful damsels, dressed in habits of the richest stuffs and most brilliant colours, stood round the table. Each held a fan in her hand, which was for the purpose of refreshing their lord the caliph while he sat at table.

"If ever mortal was delighted, that mortal was Abou Hassan when he entered this magnificent saloon. At every step he paused to look about him, and contemplate at his leisure all the wonderful things which were presented to his view. Each moment he turned from side to side in sheer amazement, to the high delight of the caliph, who watched him with the utmost attention. At length he walked forward towards the middle of the room and took his place at the table. Immediately the seven beautiful damsels began agitating the air with their fans to refresh the new caliph. He looked at them all in succession; and after admiring the graceful ease with which they performed their office,

ABOU HASSAN AND THE SEVEN DAMSELS.

he said to them, with a gracious smile, that he supposed one of them at a time would be able to give him all the air he wanted; and he desired that the other six should place themselves at the table with him, three on his right and three on his left, and give him their company. The table was round; and Abou Hassan placed these fair companions in such a manner at it that whichever way he looked his eyes rested on objects of beauty and delight.

"At his behest the six damsels placed themselves round the table. But Abou Hassan perceived that out of respect to him they forbore to eat. This induced him to help them himself, inviting and pressing them to eat in the most obliging manner. He desired to know their names, and each in turn replied to his questions.

"Their names were Neck-of-Alabaster, Lip-of-Coral, Fair-as-Moonlight, Bright-as-Sunshine, Eye's-desire, Heart's-delight. He put the same question to the seventh, who held the fan, and she answered that her name was Sugar-Cane. The agreeable things he said to each of them on the subject of their names showed that he had abundance of wit; and this display of his powers greatly heightened the esteem which the caliph had already entertained for him.

"When the damsels saw that Abou Hassan had ceased eating, one of them said to the eunuchs who were in waiting: 'The Commander of the Faithful desires to walk into the saloon where the dessert is prepared; let water be brought.' They all rose from the table at the same time; and one took from the hands of the eunuchs a golden basin, another a pitcher of the same metal, the third a napkin, and these they presented on their knees to Abou Hassan, who was still sitting, that he might have an opportunity of washing his hands. Thereupon he rose; and at the same moment an eunuch drew back the arras, and opened the door of another saloon into which he was to go.

"Mesrour, who had not quitted Abou Hassan, walked before him, and conducted him into a saloon as large as that he had left, but adorned with a variety of splendid pictures, and ornamented in quite a different manner, with vases of gold and silver. The carpets and other furniture were of the most costly kind. In this saloon there were also seven other bands of female musicians, different from the former, and these seven choirs of music began a new concert the moment Abou Hassan appeared. This saloon was furnished with seven other large lustres; and on the table in the middle stood seven large golden basins, in which every sort of fruit in season, the finest, best chosen, and most exquisite was piled up in pyramids; and round the table stood seven other young women more beautiful than the first, each with a fan in her hand.

"These new splendours raised in Abou Hassan's mind a still greater admiration than he had felt before; and he paused for a moment manifesting the deepest surprise and astonishment. At length he reached the table, and when he was seated at it and had surveyed the seven damsels very leisurely one after another, with a sort of embarrassment which showed he could not tell to whom among them to give the preference, he ordered them all to lay aside their fans and to sit down and eat with him, saying, 'that the heat was not so troublesome to him as to make him require their services.'

"When the damsels had taken their places on either side of Abou Hassan, he at once proceeded to inquire their names; and he found that they had different names from those of the seven in the former saloon, but that their names also marked some excellence of mind or body by which they were distinguished from each other. This amused him extremely; and he showed his wit in the lively and appropriate speeches he used when he offered to each, in turn, some fruit of the different sorts before him. To her who was called Heart's-chain he gave a fig, saying: 'Eat this for my sake, and make the chains lighter which I have worn from the moment I first saw you.' And giving some grapes to Soul's-grief, he said, 'Take these grapes upon condition that you ease the grief I endure from the love with which you have inspired me;' and he addressed a similar compliment to each of the other damsels. By his behaviour on this occasion Abou Hassan made the caliph, who was much pleased with all he did and all he said, more and more delighted; for Haroun Alraschid rejoiced greatly at having found in Abou Hassan a man who could so agreeably amuse him, and at the same time furnish him with the means of knowing his character more thoroughly.

"When Abou Hassan had eaten of those sorts of fruit on the table which he liked best, he rose; and immediately Mesrour, who never quitted him, again walked before him, and led him into a third saloon, furnished, decorated, and enriched in the same magnificent manner as the two former.

"There Abou Hassan found seven other bands of music, and seven other damsels, waiting round a table, set out with seven golden basins containing liquid sweetmeats of various sorts and colours. After stopping to look at the multitude of new objects for admiration he encountered on all sides, he walked up to the table amidst the loud harmony of the seven bands of music, which ceased when he had taken his seat. At his command these seven damsels also took their places at the table with him. And as he could not dispense these liquids with the same grace, and with the same polite attention he had shown in distributing the fruits, he begged that the ladies would themselves make choice of such as they liked best. He asked their names too; and he was not less pleased with these than with those of the former damsels; for the variety of their appellations furnished him with new matter for conversing with the ladies, and addressing them with tender expressions, which gave them as much pleasure as this new proof of Abou Hassan's wit gave the caliph, who did not lose a word that he said.

"The day was drawing towards a close when Abou Hassan was conducted into a fourth saloon. This apartment was decorated like the rest with the most costly and most magnificent furniture. Here, too, were seven grand lustres of gold with lighted tapers; and the whole room was illuminated by a vast number of other lights, which had a novel and wonderful effect. Abou Hassan found in this last saloon, as he had found in all the others, seven bands of female musicians. These began to play a strain of a gayer cast than had been performed in the other saloons, and one which seemed intended to inspire cheerfulness and mirth. Here, too, he saw seven other damsels, who stood in waiting round a table. On this table glittered seven basins of gold, filled with cakes and pastry, with all sorts of dry sweetmeats, and with a number of other compounds, provocative of drinking. But Abou Hassan observed here what he had not seen in the other saloons; this was a side-board, upon which were seven large flagons of silver filled with the most exquisite wines; and seven glasses of the finest rock crystal, of excellent workmanship, stood near each of these flagons.

"In the three first saloons Abou Hassan had drunk only water, in compliance with the custom observed at Bagdad, equally by the common people, by the upper ranks, and by the court of the caliph, namely, to drink wine only at night. All those who drink it before evening are looked upon as dissipated persons; and they dare not appear in the day time. This custom is the more to be commended, as during the day a man requires a clear head to transact business; and, again, as wine is not taken till night at Bagdad, drunken people are never seen making disturbances in open day in the streets of that city.

"Abou Hassan entered this fourth saloon and walked up to the table. When he was seated he remained a long time in a kind of ecstasy of admiration at the seven damsels who stood about him, and whom he thought still more lovely than those he had seen in the other saloons. He had great desire to know the name of each of them, but as the loud sound of the music, and especially of the cymbals, which were used in all the bands, did not allow his voice to be heard, he clapped his hands to put an end to the performance; and instantly there was a profound silence.

"Thereupon he took the hand of the damsel who was nearest him on the right. He made her sit down, and after presenting her with a rich cake, he asked her name. 'Commander of the Faithful,' answered the damsel, 'I am called Cluster-of-Pearls.' 'You could not have a better name,' cried Abou Hassan, 'or one more expressive of your charms. Without prejudice to those who gave you this name, I must think your beautiful teeth, certainly surpass the finest-coloured pearls in the world. Cluster-of-Pearls,' added he, 'since that is your name, do me the favour take a glass, fill it, and let me drink it from your fair hand.'

"The damsel went instantly to the side-board, and came back with a glass of wine, which she presented to Abou Hassan with all imaginable grace. He took it with pleasure, and looking at her tenderly said, in a voice of admiration, 'Cluster-of-Pearls, I drink your health; I desire you would fill the glass for yourself and pledge me in return.' She quickly ran to the side-board and returned with a glass in her hand; but before she drank Cluster-of-Pearls sung a song, which delighted her hearer not less from its novelty than by the charm of her voice, which was still more fascinating.

"When Abou Hassan had drunk he took from the basins a supply of what he liked best, and presented it to another damsel, whom he desired to come and sit near him. He enquired her name also. She answered, that her name was Morning-Star. 'Your fine eyes,' resumed he, 'are brighter and more brilliant than the star whose name you bear. Go, and do me the favour to bring me a glass of wine;' she complied in a moment, with the best grace possible. He paid a similar compliment to the third damsel who was called Light-of-Day, as well as to all the rest, who each presented him wine which he drank, to the high delight of the caliph.

"When Abou Hassan had emptied as many glasses as there were damsels, Cluster-of-Pearls, to whom he had first spoken, went to the side-board and took a glass which she filled with wine, after having thrown into it a little of the powder which the caliph had made use of the day before. Presently she came and presented it to him with these words: 'Commander of the Faithful,' I entreat your majesty, by my anxiety for the preservation of your health, to take this glass of wine, and before you drink it to hear a song which I dare flatter myself will not be disagreeable to you. I composed it only this morning, and no one has yet heard me sing it.' 'I grant your request with pleasure,' said Abou Hassan, as he took the glass which she presented to him; 'and as Commander of the Faithful I lay my injunctions upon you to sing, as I feel assured that so charming a person as you can say nothing but what is most agreeable and very lively.'

"The damsel took her lute and sang a song, accompanying herself on this instrument with so much accuracy, grace, and expression, that she kept Abou Hassan entranced from beginning to end. He thought her song so charming that he called for it a second time, and was no less pleased with it than he had been before.

"When she had finished singing, Abou Hassan, who was desirous of praising her as she deserved, drank off at a draught the glass of wine she had filled for him. Then turning his head towards the damsel to speak to her, he was suddenly overcome by the effect of the powder which he had taken, and could only open his mouth without uttering a single word distinctly. Presently his eyes closed; and letting his head fall upon the table, like a man thoroughly overcome with sleep, he became as completely forgetful of all outward things as he had been the day before, about the same time when the caliph had administered the powder to him, and one of the damsels near him caught the glass which he let fall from his hand. The caliph, who had derived an amount of amusement beyond his expectation from the events of the day, and who saw what happened now as well as whatever Abou Hassan had done before, came out of his closet and appeared in the saloon, quite delighted at having succeeded so well in his design. He first ordered that the caliph's habit in which Abou Hassan had been dressed in the morning, should be taken from him; and that he should be clothed again in the garments which he had worn twenty-four hours before, at the time the slave, who accompanied the caliph, had brought him to the palace. He ordered the same slave to be called; and upon his appearing he said, 'Take charge once more of this man,' and carry him back to his own bed as silently as you can; and when you come away be careful to leave the door open.'

"The slave took up Abou Hassan, carried him off by the secret door of the palace, and placed him in his own house as the caliph had ordered him. Then he returned in haste to give an account of what he had done. Then the caliph said: 'Abou Hassan wished to be in my place for one day only that he might punish the Iman of the mosque in his neighbourhood, and the four scheiks, or old men, whose conduct had displeased him; I have procured him the means of doing what he wished. Therefore he ought to be satisfied.'

"Abou Hassan, who had been deposited on his sofa by the slave, slept till very late the next day. He did not awake until the effect of the powder which had been put into the last glass he drank had passed away. Then, upon opening his eyes, he was very much surprised to find himself at his own house. 'Cluster-of-Pearls! Morning-Star! Break-of-day! Coral-lips! Moonshine!' cried he, calling the damsels of the palace who had been sitting with him each by their name as he could recollect them, 'Where are you? Come to me!'

"Abou Hassan called as loudly as he could. His mother, who heard him from her apartment, came running up at the noise he made; 'What's the matter with you, my

ABOU HASSAN AND HIS MOTHER.

son?' she asked. 'What has befallen you?' At these words Abou Hassan raised his head, and looking at his mother with an air of haughtiness and disdain, replied, 'Good woman, who is the person you call your son?' 'You are he,' answered the mother, with much tenderness, 'are not you my son, Abou Hassan? It would be the most extraordinary thing in the world if, in so short a time, you should have forgotten it.' 'I your son, you execrable old woman!' cried Abou Hassan, 'you know not what you are saying. You are a liar. I am not the Abou Hassan you speak of: I am the Commander of the Faithful.'

"'Be silent, my son,' rejoined the mother, 'you do not consider what you say: to hear you talk men would take you for a madman.' 'You are yourself a mad old woman,' replied Abou Hassan, 'I am not out of my senses, as you suppose; I tell you again I am Commander of the Faithful, and vicar upon earth of the Lord of both worlds.' 'Ah, my son!' cried the mother, 'how comes it that I now hear you utter words which clearly prove that you are not in your right mind? What evil genius possesses you that you hold such language. The blessing of Allah be upon you, and may he deliver you from the malice of Satan! You are my son, Abou Hassan, and I am your mother.'

"After having given him all the proofs she could think of to convince him of his error in order to bring him to himself, she continued to expostulate in these words: 'Do you not see that the chamber you are now in is your own, and not the chamber of a palace fit for the Commander of the Faithful; and that living constantly with me you have dwelt in this house ever since you were born! Reflect upon all I have been saying to you, and do not let your mind be troubled with thoughts which are not, and cannot be true; once more, my son, consider the matter seriously.'

"Abou Hassan heard these remonstrances of his mother with composure. He sat with his eyes cast down, and resting his head upon his hand, like a man who was recollecting himself and trying to discover the truth of what he saw and heard: 'I believe you are right,' said he, to his mother, a few moments afterwards, looking up as if he had been awakened from a deep sleep, but without altering his posture. 'It seems,' said he, 'that I am Abou Hassan, that you are my mother, and that I am in my own chamber. Once more,' added he, throwing his eyes around the chamber, and attentively contemplating the furniture it contained, 'I am Abou Hassan; I cannot doubt it, nor can I conceive how I could take this fancy into my head.'

"His mother thought in good earnest that her son was cured of the malady which disturbed his mind, and which she attributed to a dream. She was preparing to laugh with him, and question him about his dream, when on a sudden he sat up, and looking at her with an angry glance, cried: 'Thou old witch, thou old sorceress, thou knowest not what thou art saying; I am not thy son, nor art thou my mother. Thou deceivest thyself, and thou dost endeavour to impose upon me. I tell thee I am Commander of the Faithful, and thou shalt not make me believe otherwise.' 'For Heaven's sake, my son, put your trust in Allah, and refrain from holding this kind of language, lest some mischief befall you. Let us rather talk of something else. Allow me to tell you what happened yesterday to the Iman of our mosque, and to the four scheiks of our neighbourhood. The officer of the police caused them to be apprehended, and after having given them each in turn I know not how many strokes on the feet, he ordered it to be proclaimed by the crier, that this was the punishment of men who meddled with affairs that did not concern them, and who made it their business to sow dissension among the families of their neighbours. Then he caused them to be led through all parts of the town, while the same proclamation was repeated before them, and he forbade them ever to set foot again in our neighbourhood.'

"Abou Hassan's mother, who could not imagine her son had any concern in the event she was relating, had purposely turned the conversation, and supposed that the narration of this affair would be a likely mode of effacing the whimsical delusion under which he laboured of being the Commander of the Faithful.

"But the effect proved quite otherwise, and the recital of this story, far from effacing the notion which he now entertained, that he was the Commander of the Faithful, served only to recall it to his mind, and to impress still more deeply on his imagination the firm conviction that it was not a delusion, but a real fact. Thus, the moment his mother had finished her story, Abou Hassan exclaimed, 'I am no longer your son, nor Abou Hassan, I am assuredly the Commander of the Faithful, and it is not possible for me to have any furthur doubt after what you yourself have just told me. Know then, that it was by my orders that the Iman and the four scheiks were punished in the manner you have related; I tell you, in good truth, I am the Commander of the Faithful; say therefore no longer that it is a dream. I am not now asleep, nor was I dreaming at the time I am telling you of. You have greatly pleased me by confirming what the officer of the police, to whom I gave the orders for the punishment you described, had already reported to me; that is to say, that my commands were punctually executed; and I am the more pleased at this because this Iman and these four scheiks were consummate hypocrites. I should be glad to know who it was that brought me here. Allah be praised for everything. The truth is this, that I am most assuredly the Commander of the Faithful, and all your reasoning will never persuade me to the contrary.'

"His mother, who could not guess or even imagine why her son maintained with so much obstinacy and so much confidence that he was the Commander of the Faithful, felt quite assured that he had lost his senses when she heard him assert things which in her mind were so entirely beyond all belief, though in that of Abou Hassan they had a good foundation. Under this persuasion she said, 'My son, I pray Heaven to pity and have mercy upon you. Cease, my son, from talking a language so utterly devoid of common sense. Look up to Allah, and entreat him to pardon you, and give you grace to converse like a man in his senses. What would be said of you if you should be heard talking in this manner. Do you not know that walls have ears?'

"These remonstrances, far from softening Abou Hassan's anger, served only to irritate him still more. He inveighed against his mother with greater violence than ever. 'O old woman,' said he, 'I have already cautioned thee to be quiet. If thou continuest to talk any longer I will rise and chastise thee in a manner thou wilt remember all the rest of thy life. I am the caliph, the Commander of the Faithful, and thou art bound to believe me when I tell thee so.' Then the poor mother, seeing that Abou Hassan was wandering still farther and farther from his right mind, instead of returning to the subject gave way to tears and lamentations. She bent her face and bosom; she uttered exclamations, which testified her astonishment and deep sorrow at seeing her son in such a dreadful position—lunatic and deprived of understanding.

"Abou Hassan, instead of being calm, and suffering himself to be affected by his mother's tears, on the contrary, forgot himself so far as to lose all sort of natural respect for her. He rose and suddenly seizing a stick he came towards her with his uplifted hand, raging like a madman. 'Thou cursed old woman,' said he, in his fury, and in a tone of voice sufficient to terrify any other than an affectionate mother, 'tell me this moment who I am!' 'My son,' answered his mother, looking most kindly at him, and far from being afraid, 'I do not believe you so far abandoned by Allah as not to know the woman who brought you into the world, or to know who you yourself are. I am perfectly sincere in telling you that you are my son Abou Hassan, and that you are quite wrong in claiming for yourself a title, which belongs only to the caliph Haroun Alraschid, your sovereign lord and mine; and this is the more culpable, at a time when our monarch has been heaping benefits upon both you and me, by the present he sent me yesterday. In fact, I have to tell you that the grand vizier Giafar took the trouble yesterday to come hither to me, and putting into my hands a purse of a thousand pieces of gold, he bade me pray to Allah to bless the Commander of the Faithful, who made me this present; and does not this liberality concern you more than me, seeing I have but a few days to live?'

"At these last words Abou Hassan lost all command over himself. The circumstances of the caliph's liberality, which his mother had just related, assured him he did not deceive himself, and convinced him more firmly than ever that he himself was the caliph, because the vizier had carried the purse by his own order. 'What! thou old sorceress!' cried he, 'wilt thou not be convinced when I tell thee that I am the person who sent these thousand pieces of gold by my grand vizier Giafar, who merely executed the order which I gave him as Commander of the Faithful? Nevertheless, instead of believing me thou art seeking to make me lose my senses by thy contradictions, maintaining, with wicked obstinacy, that I am thy son. But I will not suffer thy insolence to be long unpunished.' Upon this, in the height of his frenzy, he was so unnatural as to beat her most unmercifully with the stick he held in his hand.

"When his poor mother, who had not supposed her son would so quickly put his threats in execution, found herself beaten, she began to cry out for help as loudly as she could; and as the neighbours came crowding round, Abou Hassan never ceased striking her, calling out at every stroke, 'Am I the Commander of the Faithful?' And each time the mother affectionately returned, 'You are my son.'

"Abou Hassan's rage began to abate a little when the neighbours came into his chamber. The first who appeared at once threw himself between his mother and him; and snatching the stick from his hand cried out, 'What are you doing, Abou Hassan? have you lost all sense of duty, or are you mad? Never did a son of your condition in life dare to lift his hand against his mother! And are not you ashamed thus to ill-treat her who so tenderly loves you?'

"Abou Hassan, still raging with fury, looked at the person who spoke without giving him any answer. Then casting his wild eyes on each of the others who had come in, he demanded, 'Who is this Abou Hassan you are speaking of? Is it me you call by that name?' This question somewhat disconcerted the neighbours. 'How!' replied the man who had just spoken, 'do not you acknowledge this woman for the person who brought you up, and with whom we have always seen you living? in one word, do not you acknowledge her for your mother?' 'You are very impertinent,' replied Abou Hassan; 'I know neither her nor you; and I do not wish to know her. I am not Abou Hassan, I am the Commander of the Faithful; and if you do not know it yet, I will make you know it to your cost.'

"At this speech the neighbours were all convinced that he had lost his senses. And to prevent his repeating towards others the outrageous conduct he had been guilty of towards his mother, they seized him, and, in spite of his resistance, bound him hand and foot, and deprived him of the power of doing any mischief. But though he was thus bound, and apparently unable to hurt anybody, they did not think it right to leave him alone with his mother. Two of the company hastened immediately to the hospital for lunatics, to inform the keeper of what had happened. That officer came directly, with some of the neighbours, followed by a considerable number of his people, who brought with them chains, handcuffs, and a whip made of thongs of leather for the purpose of restraining the supposed lunatic.

"On their arrival, Abou Hassan, who did not in the least expect such vigorous proceedings, made great efforts to free himself; but the keeper, who was prepared to use his whip, soon quieted him by two or three strokes well applied to his shoulders. This treatment had such an effect upon Abou Hassan that he soon lay motionless, and the keeper and his assistants did with him what they pleased. They chained him, and put handcuffs and fetters on him; and when they had thus secured him they carried him out of his house, and took him to the hospital for lunatics.

"Abou Hassan was no sooner in the street than he found himself surrounded by a great crowd of people. One gave him a blow with the fist, another struck him in the face; and others reproached him in the most abusive language, treating him as a fool and a madman.

"While he was suffering all this bad treatment he said to himself: 'There is no greatness and strength but in Allah, the lofty and omnipotent. It is determined that I am a madman, although I am certainly in my senses: I bear these injuries and suffer all this indignity, resigned to the will of Heaven.

"Thus Abou Hassan was conveyed to the hospital appropriated to madmen. There he was bound and shut up in an iron cage. But before he was left to himself the keeper, who had become hardened in the exercise of his office, belaboured his back and shoulders most unmercifully with fifty strokes of his whip; and for more than three weeks he continued to give him every day the same number of blows, always repeating these words: 'Recover your senses, and tell me whether you are still Commander of the Faithful.' 'I have no need of your correction,' answered Abou Hassan, 'I am no madman; but if

I were likely to go mad, nothing would so quickly bring that misfortune upon me as the blows you give me.'

"Abou Hassan's mother came constantly to see her son; and she could not refrain from tears when she saw him daily losing his flesh and strength, and heard his sighs and lamentations at the sufferings he endured. In fact, his shoulders, his back, and sides were black and bruised; nor could he procure any rest, try how he would. His skin came off more than once during his abode in that dreadful mansion. His mother was desirous of conversing with him, endeavouring to console him, and to find out whether he continued uniformly in the same state of mind on the subject of his pretended dignity of caliph and Commander of the Faithful. But every time she opened her mouth to touch upon this point, he contradicted what she said with so much rage and fury, that she

ABOU HASSAN TRYING TO AVOID THE MERCHANT.

was forced to yield and quit the subject, inconsolable at seeing him so obstinate in his opinion.

"The strong and lively recollections which were impressed upon the mind of Abou Hassan, of having been dressed in the caliph's robes, of having actually discharged the office of the caliph, of having exerted his authority, of having been obeyed and treated in all respects as the caliph—all these facts which had persuaded him, upon his awaking from sleep, that he actually was Commander of the Faithful, and had made him persevere so long in his error, began now insensibly to wear out. 'If I were caliph and Commander of the Faithful,' said he sometimes to himself, 'why should I have found myself after my sleep at my own house, and dressed in my own clothes? Why should I not have seen myself surrounded by the chief eunuch and his fellows, and by the very large assembly of damsels? Why should the grand vizier Giafar, whom I have seen at my feet, and all those emirs, governors of provinces, and other officers by whom I have seen myself surrounded—why should they all have deserted me? They would certainly long since have delivered me from the wretched situation in which I am now if I still retained any authority over them. All this has been only a dream, and I ought to acknowledge it as such. I certainly ordered an officer of the police to punish the Iman and the four old men his counsellors; and I ordered the grand vizier Giafar to carry a thousand pieces of gold to my mother, and my orders were obeyed. This makes me hesitate, and I cannot understand these things. But how many things more are there which I cannot comprehend, and never shall be able to understand? I refer all to Allah, who knows and who can guide everything.'

"Abou Hassan was one day absorbed in these thoughts and reflections when his mother came in. She saw him so emaciated and so weak that her tears fell more abundantly than ever. In the midst of her sobs she addressed him in the usual way, and Abou Hassan returned her salutation with a humility he had never shown since his arrival at the hospital. She thought this a good omen. 'Well, my son,' said she, wiping away her tears, 'how do I find you to-day? In what state of mind are you? Have you given up all those fancies and that language which the evil spirit suggested to you' 'O my dear mother,' answered Abou Hassan, with a settled and composed voice, and in a tone that marked the concern he felt for the violence of which he had been guilty towards her; 'I acknowledge my error, and I entreat you to forgive the horrid treatment to which I have subjected you, and of which I sincerely repent. I also crave pardon of our neighbours for the offence which I have given them. I have been deceived by a dream; but this dream was so extraordinary and so like reality, that I would engage that any other person who happened to dream it would be as much deluded by it as I was, and would fall into greater extravagances, perhaps, than you have seen me commit. I am still so much disturbed while I am speaking to you, that I can scarcely persuade myself that what I have experienced is a dream; so much did it resemble a real event, and so fully awake did I appear to be.'

"'Be this, however, as it may, I must acknowledge my error, and cannot but continue to think it a dream, or an illusion. I am even convinced that I am not that phantom of a caliph and Commander of the Faithful, but your son Abou Hassan. O my mother, whom I have always honoured till that fatal day, the recollection of which covers me with confusion; I honour you now, and ever will honour you in a manner worthy of myself as long as I live.'

"At these coherent and sensible words, the tears of grief, of compassion, and distress, which Abou Hassan's mother had been shedding during a long time, were changed into tears of joy, of comfort, and of tender affection for her dear son, whom she thus recovered. 'O my son,' cried she, in a transport of delight, 'I am as joyful and happy to hear you talk so rationally as if I had just now brought you into the world a second time. I must tell you my opinion of your adventure, and call your attention to a circumstance which, perhaps, you have overlooked. The stranger whom you brought home to supper with you one night, went away without, as you desired him, shutting your chamber door; and that, I believe, gave an opportunity to the evil spirit to come in and throw you into that dreadful illusion under which you have laboured. Therefore, my son, you are bound to thank Heaven for having given you this deliverance, and to pray that you may be preserved from again falling into the snares of this demon.'

"'You have discovered the source of my misfortune,' answered Abou Hassan; 'and it was on that very night that I had the dream which has so turned my head. I had, however, expressly cautioned the merchant to shut the door after him; and I am now certain that he did not do so. Therefore I think with you, that the devil found the door open, entered, and put all these imaginations into my head. At Moussoul, surely, from whence this merchant came, they cannot be aware of what we know only too well at Bagdad, that the devil comes in to occasion all those sad dreams which disturb our night's rest when the chambers in which we sleep are left open. In the name of Allah, my mother, since through His mercy I am perfectly restored to my senses, I entreat you, as earnestly as it is possible for a son to entreat so good a mother as you are, to deliver me as soon as may be out of this place of torment, and rescue me from the hand of the barbarous keeper who will infallibly shorten my days if I remain here any longer.'

"Perfectly comforted and much affected at seeing her son entirely recovered from the mad fancy of being caliph, Abou Hassan's mother went immediately to seek the keeper who had brought him to the madhouse, and who had till then the management of him; and when she had assured him that her son was perfectly restored to his reason, he came and examined him; and, finding she spoke the truth, released him then and there.

"Abou Hassan returned to his house, and remained there many days to recover his health, and recruit his strength with better food than he had received in the hospital for madmen. But as soon as he had a little recovered his spirits, and no longer felt the bad effects of the hard usage he had experienced during his confinement, he began to think it tiresome to pass his evenings without company. For this reason he soon returned to his usual way of life; and presently began again to provide a banquet every day to entertain a new guest at night.

"The day on which he renewed his custom of going towards sunset to the foot of the bridge of Bagdad in order to stop the first stranger who should approach, and invite him to do him the honour of coming to sup at his house, was the first of the month; and it has been already mentioned that this was the day on which the caliph amused himself with passing through one of the gates of the city in disguise that he might himself see whether anything was done contrary to the established laws. This he did in pursuance of a determination made in the beginning of his reign.

"Abou Hassan had not long taken his seat on a bench placed against the parapet when, casting his eyes towards the other end of the bridge, he saw the caliph coming towards him in his old disguise of a merchant of Moussoul, and attended by the same slave who had once accompanied him to Abou Hassan's house. Convinced that all the misery he had suffered arose only from the circumstance that the caliph, whom he thought to be only a merchant from Moussoul, had left the door open when he went out of his chamber on the former occasion, Abou Hassan trembled at the sight of him. 'Allah preserve me!' said he to himself, 'if I am not mistaken this is the very sorcerer who laid his spell upon me.' He immediately turned his head and looked stedfastly into the stream, leaning over the parapet that the supposed merchant might not see him as he passed by.

"The caliph, who wished for a renewal of the amusement he had derived from Abou Hassan, had taken great care to be informed of all that he had said and done the day after he awoke and was carried back to his house, and had been told of everything that had happened to the unfortunate man. He felt fresh pleasure at each new particular that was told him, and was amused even at the ill treatment which Abou Hassan had undergone at the hospital for madmen. But as this monarch was very just and generous, and as he discovered in Abou Hassan a turn of mind likely to afford him still further amusement, and as he also doubted whether, after having given up his assumed dignity of caliph, Abou Hassan would return to his usual way of life, he thought fit to bring the young man again near his person; and to effect this purpose he considered it best to disguise himself on the first day of the month like a merchant of Moussoul, as he had done before. He perceived Abou Hassan almost as soon as he was himself seen by the latter; and from Abou Hassan's turning away, he found immediately how dissatisfied his former host was with him, and that he meant to avoid him. This induced him to walk on that side of the bridge where Abou Hassan was, and to approach him as closely as possible. When he came up to him he stooped down and looked in his face. 'It is you, brother Abou Hassan?' said he. 'I salute you; suffer me, I beseech you, to embrace you.'

'"For my part,' answered Abou Hassan, bluntly, without looking at the pretended merchant of Moussoul, 'I am not desirous of saluting you. I want neither your salutation nor your embraces; go your way.' 'What,' resumed the caliph, 'do not you know me? Do not you recollect the evening we passed together a month ago this day at your house, when you did me the honour to entertain me so hospitably?' 'No,' replied Abou Hassan, in his former rough tone of voice, 'I know you not, nor can I guess what you are talking of. Therefore, I say again, go about your business.'

"The caliph did not resent Abou Hassan's rough answer. He knew that one of the rules Abou Hassan had laid down for himself was to have no farther acquaintance with a person whom he had once entertained. Abou Hassan had told him this, but he chose to pretend ignorance of it. 'I cannot believe that you do not recollect me,' he said. 'It is not a great while since we have seen each other; and it is scarcely possible that you should have so easily forgotten me. Surely some misfortune must have befallen you, that you should speak to me thus strangely. You must remember, nevertheless, that I showed my gratitude by my good wishes; and that upon one point, which you held near your heart, I made an offer of my services, which are not to be slighted.' 'I know not,' replied Abou Hassan, 'what may be your influence, nor am I desirous of putting it to the proof. This I know, that your wishes had only the effect of driving me mad. Therefore, I say once again, go your way, and plague me no more.'

"'Ah, brother Abou Hassan,' replied the caliph, embracing him, 'I do not mean to part from you in this manner. Since I have been so fortunate as to meet with you a second time, you must again extend to me the same hospitality you showed me a month ago, and I must have the honour of drinking with you again.' For that very reason Abou Hassan protested he would be upon his guard. 'I have sufficient power over myself,' he cried, 'to prevent myself from again associating with a man who carries mischief about him as you do. You know the proverb, which says, "Take up your drum and march;" apply it to yourself. Why should I repeat what I have so many times said? May Heaven direct you! You have done me much harm, and I would not willingly expose myself to more at your hands.'

"'My good friend Abou Hassan,' returned the caliph, embracing him once more, 'you treat me with a harshness I did not expect. I beseech you not to hold so unpleasant a language towards me, but, on the contrary, to be convinced of my friendship. Do me the favour to relate to me what has befallen you; confide in me who have ever wished you well, who still wish you well, and who would be glad of an opportunity to do you any service in order to make amends for any misfortune you may have suffered through me, if, indeed, you have suffered through my fault.' Abou Hassan gave way to the entreaty of the caliph; and, after having made him take a seat near him, he said, 'Your earnestness, and your importunity towards me, have overcome my resistance; but you shall judge from what I am about to tell you whether I complain of you without reason.'

"The caliph seated himself close to Abou Hassan, who gave him an account of all the adventures that had befallen him from the time of his waking at the palace to the moment of his second waking at his own chamber; and he told everything as if it were really a dream, not omitting a multitude of circumstances which the caliph knew as well as he did himself, and the recital of which gave his hearer fresh pleasure. He then dwelt fervently on the impression which this dream had left upon his mind of his being caliph and Commander of the Faithful. 'This delusion,' added he, 'led me into the wildest extravagances; until at last my neighbours were obliged to bind me like a madman, and have me conveyed to the hospital for lunatics, where I was treated in a manner which all must allow to have been cruel, barbarous, and inhuman; but what will surprise you, and what, without doubt, you do not expect to be told is, that all these misfortunes have come upon me entirely through your fault. You must remember how earnestly I requested you to shut the door of my chamber when you left me after supper. This request you utterly disregarded, for you left the door open, and the devil entered and filled my head with this dream which, agreeable as it then appeared to me, has nevertheless occasioned all the evils of which I have so much reason to complain. You, therefore, by your negligence are the cause of all, which makes you responsible for the crime, the dreadful and horrid crime which I have committed, not only of lifting my hand against my mother, but of almost killing her and committing matricide! And all

THE CALIPH LOOKING THROUGH THE LATTICE.

this for a reason, which makes me blush for shame whenever I think of it—because she called me her son, as in truth I am, and would not acknowledge me to be the Commander of the Faithful, as I maintained, and actually believed myself to be. You, too, are the cause of that offence I gave my neighbours, when running to our house at the cries of my poor mother, they found me so exasperated against her that I beat her violently, which would not have happened if you had been careful to shut my chamber door when you left me, as I had entreated you to do. The neighbours could not have come into my house without my permission, and they would not have been witnesses of my extravagances, for it is this exposure which mortifies me most of all. I should not have thought it necessary to strike them in defending myself, and they would not have ill-treated me and bound me hand and foot, and caused me to be conveyed to the lunatics' hospital and shut up there, where I can assure you every day during my imprisonment in that infernal place I had to submit to be beaten most severely with a whip of thongs.'

"Abou Hassan related to the caliph all these grievances with much warmth and vehemence. The caliph knew better than he all that had occurred, and was delighted within himself at having succeeded so well, and having contrived to bring Abou Hassan into that state of illusion in which he still saw him; but he could not hear this narrative detailed in so artless a manner without bursting into a fit of laughter.

"Abou Hassan, who thought his story would excite compassion, and that all the world must sympathise with him, was highly offended at this violent laughter of the pretended merchant of Moussoul. 'Are you making a jest of me,' said he, 'by thus laughing in my face, or do you think I am bantering you when I am talking to you very seriously? Do you wish for actual proof of what I advance? Here, look and see yourself, and tell me if this is a jest.' As he said this he bent forward, and baring his breast and shoulders he let the caliph see the scars and bruises occasioned by the beatings he had received.

"The caliph was shocked at the sight. He felt compassion for poor Abou Hassan, and was extremely sorry the jest had been carried so far. He ceased laughing, and cordially embracing Abou Hassan he said, with a very serious air, 'Rise, my dear brother, I beseech you let us go to your house, I wish to have again the pleasure of being your guest this evening; to-morrow, if it please Heaven, all will be found to have turned out for the best.'

"Notwithstanding his resolution, and in opposition to the oath he had taken not to entertain a stranger a second time at his house, Abou Hassan could not withstand the flattering importunities of the caliph, whom he all along supposed to be a merchant from Moussoul. 'I consent,' said he, to the pretended merchant, 'but only upon a condition which you shall bind yourself by an oath to observe. It is this: that you do me the favour to shut my chamber door when you leave my house that the devil may not come to turn my brain as he did before.' The pretended merchant gave his promise. Thereupon the two men rose and walked towards the town. The better to engage Abou Hassan, the caliph said to him, 'Put confidence in me, and I promise you, as a man of honour, that I will not fail of my word. After this you will not hesitate to rely upon a person like me, who wishes you all kinds of prosperity and happiness.'

"'I do not require this,' rejoined Abou Hassan, suddenly stopping short—'I give way with all my heart to your importunity, but I can dispense with your good wishes, and I beg for Heaven's sake that you will not invoke any blessings upon me. All the ills that have befallen me to the present time have no other source than those wishes of yours.' 'Good,' replied the caliph, smiling within himself at the still disordered imagination of Abou Hassan, 'since you will have it so, you shall be obliged. I promise to express no more good wishes for you.' 'I am heartily rejoiced to hear you say so,' said Abou Hassan, 'and I have nothing else to ask. And if you keep your word in this, I will lay no further conditions upon you.'

"Abou Hassan and the caliph, followed by the caliph's slave, walked on conversing in this manner: the day began to close when they reached Abou Hassan's house. He immediately called his mother, and ordered a light to be brought. He requested the caliph to take a seat on the sofa, and he seated himself near his guest. In a short time supper was served on a table that was placed before them. They fell to without ceremony. When they had finished Abou Hassan's mother came to clear the table, and placed the fruit upon it, near her son, with the wine and glasses; she then retired and appeared no more.

"Abou Hassan first poured out wine for himself, and then for the caliph. They drank six or seven glasses each, conversing on indifferent matters. When the caliph saw Abou Hassan beginning to grow merry, he led him to a more interesting subject, and asked him if he had ever been in love.

"'Brother,' replied Abou Hassan, in a very familiar manner, for he thought he was talking with a guest of his own rank, 'I have never considered either love or marriage but as a slavery to which I have always felt a reluctance to submit; and to this moment I will confess to you I have never loved anything but the pleasures of the table, and especially good wine; my idea of enjoyment, in a word, is to amuse myself and converse agreeably with my friends. I will not go so far as to say that I should be indifferent to marriage, or incapable of attachment if I could meet with a woman as beautiful and as agreeable in disposition as one of the many whom I saw in my dream on that fatal night when I received you here the first time, and when, to my misfortune, you left my chamber door open; one who would pass the evenings feasting with me, who could sing and play on the lute and converse agreeably with me, and who had no other wish but to please and amuse me. On the contrary, I believe all my indifference would be changed into the warmest attachment to such a person, and I could live very happily with her. But where shall a man meet with such a woman as I have described, except in the palace of the Commander of the Faithful; at the house of the grand vizier; or of those very powerful lords of the court with whom there is no want of silver and gold. I would rather, therefore, confine myself to my bottle, which is a pleasure I have at little expense, and which I can enjoy as well as they.' As he said this, he took a glass and filled it with wine. 'Do you take a glass also, which I will fill for you,' said he to the caliph, 'and let us prolong the enjoyment of this delightful evening.'

"When the caliph and Abou Hassan had emptied their glasses, the former resumed: ''Tis a great pity that so gallant a man as you are, and one who is not indifferent to love, should lead such a retired and solitary life.' 'I infinitely prefer,' said Abou Hassan, 'the composed kind of life you see me leading, to the company of a woman who perhaps, in respect of beauty, might not hit my taste, and who besides might plague me in a thousand ways by her faults and her ill temper.

"They continued their conversation on this subject to a great length; and the caliph, who saw Abou Hassan had quite reached the point he wished, then said; 'Leave the matter to me, and since you have a good taste and are an honest fellow, I will find a lady to your mind without causing you either expense or trouble. So saying, he took the bottle and Abou Hassan's glass, into which he dexterously put a small quantity of the powder he had made use of before, filled a bumper for his host, and, presenting the glass to him, merrily observed: 'Take this, and drink beforehand to the health of the beauty who is to make your life happy; depend upon it you shall be pleased with her.'

"Abou Hassan took the glass with a smile, and shook his head. 'Happy be the event,' said he, 'since you will have it so; I cannot bear to be guilty of an incivility toward you, nor will I disoblige so agreeable a guest as you are for a thing of so little importance; I will then drink to the health of this beauty you promise me, although I am content with my present situation, and do not greatly reckon upon gaining any new happiness.'

"So soon as Abou Hassan had swallowed the drugged wine a deep sleep overpowered his senses, as it had done twice before, and the caliph was again enabled to deal with him as he pleased. He immediately ordered the slave who attended him to take Abou Hassan and carry him to the palace. The slave accordingly carried him off; and the caliph, who had no design of sending Abou Hassan back, shut the chamber door when he quitted it.

"The slave followed with his burden; and when the caliph reached the palace he ordered Abou Hassan to be laid on a sofa in the fourth saloon, whence he had been carried back to his own house, fast asleep, on the former occasion. Before Abou Hassan was left alone to finish his sleep, the caliph ordered the same dress to be put upon him in which he had been clad on the day when he supported the character of the caliph; and the royal garments were put upon Abou Hassan in the caliph's presence. Then the latter bade all in the palace go to bed; and also ordered the officers of the eunuchs, the officers of the bed-chamber, the female musicians, and the same damsels who had been in this saloon when Abou Hassan drank the last glass of wine which brought on his sleep to be ready without fail the next day at sunrise when Abou Hassan should awake; and charged all of them to play their parts exactly.

"The caliph went to bed, after having told Mesrour to come and rouse him early, that he might go into the closet where he had before been concealed.

"Mesrour did not fail to wake the caliph exactly at the appointed hour. The caliph immediately dressed, and went out towards the chamber where Abou Hassan was still asleep. He found the officers of the eunuchs, those of the bed-chamber, the damsels, and the female musicians, at the door waiting his arrival. He told them in a few words what his intention was; then he went in and proceeded to place himself in the closet, whose lattices concealed him. Mesrour, all the other officers, the damsels, and the female musicians, came in after him, and stood round the sofa on which Abou Hassan was sleeping, ranging themselves in such a way as not to prevent the caliph from seeing and observing whatever the sleeper might do.

"When everything was thus arranged, and Abou Hassan had slept off the effects of the caliph's powder, he awoke, but without opening his eyes. Directly he stirred in the bed the seven choirs of female singers raised their delightful voices, mingled with the sound of hautbois, soft flutes, and other instruments, so as to make a most agreeable concert.

"Abou Hassan was very much astonished when he heard such sweet harmony. He opened his eyes, and his astonishment increased beyond measure when he perceived the damsels and the officers who stood round him, and who he thought he recollected. The saloon where he now lay seemed the same as that which he had seen in his first dream; for he recognised the lights, the furniture, and the ornaments.

"The concert presently ceased, for the performers wished to give the caliph an opportunity of observing the countenance of his new guest, and hearing all that Abou Hassan should say in his astonishment. The damsels, Mesrour, and all the officers of the bed-chamber remained in their places, standing in profound silence, with every mark of respect. 'Alas!' cried Abou Hassan, biting his fingers, and speaking in a loud voice, to the delight of the caliph, 'here am I again fallen into the same dream and the same illusion which I experienced a month ago; and what have I to expect but the same scourging, the hospital for madmen, and the iron cage? O Allah the merciful! I resign myself into the hands of Thy divine providence. He whom I received yesterday evening at my house is a most wicked rascal to bring upon me this delusion, and all the misery I shall suffer in consequence of it. Perfidious traitor! He had promised with an oath that he would shut my chamber door after him when he left my house; but he has not done so, and the evil spirit has entered, and is now again turning my brain with this cursed dream about the Commander of the Faithful, and all the other fancies by which he fascinates my eyes. May Allah confound thee, Satan, and heap a mountain of stones upon thy head!'

"When he had spoken these words Abou Hassan shut his eyes, and remained sunk in deep thought, with a mind thoroughly confused. A moment afterwards he opened them, and looking by turns on all the objects around him he cried again, but with rather less astonishment, and with a smile, 'I resign myself into the hands of Thy providence; O Allah, preserve me from the temptation of Satan!' Then closing his eyes again, he continued, 'I know what I will do—I will sleep till Satan leaves me, and goes back to the place whence he came; I will sleep though I should stay here till noon.'

"But the bystanders would not give him time to sleep again, as he proposed. Heart's-Delight, one of the damsels whom he had seen at his first visit to the palace, came up to him and seated herself at the end of the sofa. 'Commander of the Faithful,' said she, in a very respectful manner, 'I beseech your majesty to pardon me, if I take the liberty of advising you not to sleep again, but to endeavour to rouse yourself and get up; the day is beginning to appear.' 'Get thee from me, Satan,' said Abou Hassan, when he heard this voice; then looking up at Heart's-Delight he asked, 'Do you call me Commander of the Faithful? You certainly take me for another person.'

"But Heart's-Delight resumed: 'I am addressing your majesty by the title which belongs to you as sovereign of all the mussulman world; I address you, whose most humble slave I am, and to whom I have now the honour to speak. Your majesty is doubtless pleased to jest,' added she, 'in thus affecting not to know who you are; or perhaps you have been troubled by some unpleasant dream; but if your majesty will be pleased to open your eyes, the cloud, which perhaps hangs over your imagination, will be dissipated, and you will see that you are in your palace, surrounded by your officers, and by us, the humblest of your slaves, ready to render you our accustomed services. Nor ought your majesty to be surprised at finding yourself in this saloon, and not in your

THE CALIPH'S LAUGHTER.

bed; you yesterday fell asleep so suddenly that we were unwilling to wake you, even to conduct you to your bed-chamber, and we were accordingly content with placing you that you might sleep conveniently on this sofa.'

"Heart's-Delight said so many other things to Abou Hassan which appeared quite probable to him, that at length he rose and sat up. He opened his eyes and recognised her, and likewise Cluster-of-Pearls, and the other damsels whom he had seen before. Then they all approached him at once, and Heart's-Delight resuming her discourse: 'Commander of the Faithful, and vicar of the prophet upon earth,' said she, 'your majesty will allow us to remind you again that it is time to rise; you see it is day-light.'

"'You are very troublesome and impertinent,' retorted Abou Hassan, rubbing his eyes; 'I am not Commander of the Faithful, I am Abou Hassan, as I very well know; and you shall not persuade me to the contrary.' 'We know nothing of Abou Hassan, of whom your majesty speaks,' replied Heart's-Delight; 'we have no desire to know him; we know your majesty to be Commander of the Faithful, and you will never persuade us that you are any other person.'

"Abou Hassan cast his eyes around him, and felt as if he were bewitched, when he saw himself in the saloon in which he knew he had been before; but he attributed this appearance to a dream, like that he had already experienced, and he dreaded the consequences that were to come. 'Heaven have mercy upon me,' cried he, lifting up his hands and eyes, 'into its hands I resign myself. From what I now see I cannot doubt but that the devil who entered my chamber besets and disturbs my imagination with all these visions.' The caliph, who was observing him, and had just heard all his exclamations, felt so strong a disposition to laugh that he had some difficulty to avoid betraying himself.

"Abou Hassan was by this time once more lying down, and had shut his eyes again. 'Commander of the Faithful,' immediately said Heart's-Delight, 'since your majesty does not rise after being told it is day-light, a fact we are bound to announce to you, and that it is necessary your majesty should pay attention to the business of the empire which is entrusted to your government, we shall make use of the permission you have given us for such occasions.' As she said this she took Abou Hassan by one arm, and called the other damsels to assist her in making him rise from the place where he lay; and they carried him, almost by force, into the midst of the saloon, where they placed him on a seat. Then they took each other by the hand and danced and skipped about him to the sound of the cymbals and all the other instruments, which they rattled about his head as loud as possible.

"Abou Hassan found himself perplexed beyond expression: 'Can I be really caliph and Commander of the Faithful?' said he to himself. At last, uncertain what to think, he tried to call out, but the loud sounds of the instruments prevented his being heard. He beckoned to Cluster-of-Pearls and Morning-Star, who were dancing about him, holding each other by the hand, and signified that he wished to speak. Morning-Star immediately put a stop to the dance, and silenced the noise of the instruments, and came near him. 'Now speak out honestly,' said he, with great simplicity, 'and tell me truly who I am.'

"'Commander of the Faithful,' answered Morning-Star, 'your majesty is pleased to astonish us by putting this question, as if you did not yourself know that you are the Commander of the Faithful, and the vicar upon earth of the Prophet of Allah, who is Lord both of this world and the other; of the world in which we now are, and of that which is to come after death. If this is not the case, some extraordinary dream must have made your majesty forget who you are. Something of this sort may well have happened when we consider that your majesty has slept to-night a much longer time than usual. Nevertheless, if your majesty gives permission, I will bring to your recollection everything you did yesterday through the whole day.' She then reminded him of his coming into the council, of the punishment of the Iman and the four old men by the officer of the police. She told him of the present of a purse of gold sent by his vizier to the mother of a person called Abou Hassan. She related what was done in the interior of the palace, and what passed at the three refreshment tables which were served in the three saloons. And when she came to speak of the last she said: 'Your majesty, after having made us sit near you at the table, did us the honour of listening to our songs, and taking wine from our hands, till the moment when your majesty fell fast asleep in the manner just related by Heart's-Delight. Since then your majesty, contrary to your usual habit, has remained sunk in a deep sleep till the beginning of this day. Cluster-of-Pearls, all the rest of the slaves, and all the officers present will prove the same thing—and will it please your majesty to prepare to go to prayers, for it is now time.'

"'Well, well,' returned Abou Hassan, shaking his head, 'you would fain impose upon me if I would hearken to you. For my part,' he went on, 'I say you are all mad, and have all lost your senses. 'Tis a great pity, however, since you are all so handsome. But let me tell you, that since I saw you I have been at my own house, have treated my mother very ill, and have been thrown into the lunatics' hospital, where I remained much against my will more than three weeks, during which time the keeper never failed to treat me every day with fifty lashes—and would you have all this to be nothing but a dream? Surely you are jesting.' 'Commander of the Faithful,' replied Morning-Star, 'we are all ready, all that are here present, to swear by whatever your majesty holds most dear, that what you tell us is only a dream. You have not left this room since yesterday, and you have slept through the whole night till this moment.'

"The confidence with which this damsel assured Abou Hassan that all she said was true, and that he had not left the saloon since he first entered it, plunged him into the greatest bewilderment. He knew not and could not tell what to believe—who he was, or what he saw. He remained some time quite lost in thought. 'O Heaven!' said he to himself, 'am I Abou Hassan? Am I Commander of the Faithful? May Allah enlighten my understanding, and cause me to distinguish the truth that I may know what to believe.' He then uncovered his shoulders, still black with the strokes he had received, and showing them to the damsels he cried out, 'look for yourselves and judge whether such scars could come from a dream when a man is sleeping. I can assure you I think them real; and the pain I still feel from them is so sure a proof of their reality that I can have no doubt. If all this has befallen me in my sleep, it is the most extraordinary and the most astonishing thing in the world; I must confess it passes my comprehension.'

"In his bewilderment of mind Abou Hassan called one of the officers who stood near him: 'Come hither,' said he, 'and bite the tip of my ear that I may determine whether I am asleep or awake.' The officer stepped up to Abou Hassan, took the top of his ear between his teeth, and bit so hard that Abou Hassan set up a yell of pain.

"When he thus cried out all the instruments began to play at the same time, and the damsels and the officers began to dance, to sing, and skip about Abou Hassan with so much noise, that he fell into a sort of frenzy, which made him commit a thousand extravagances. He began to sing with the rest. He stripped off the fine dress of the caliph which they had put upon him. He threw upon the floor the cap he had on his head; and with only his shirt and trowsers on, he sprang off his couch and threw himself between the two damsels, whom he took by the hand, and began to skip and dance with them so actively, so violently, and with so many droll and ridiculous twistings of his body, that the caliph in his hiding place could no longer restrain himself. This sudden outburst of Abou Hassan made him laugh so violently that he fell backwards, and his laughter was heard above all the noise of the musical instruments and cymbals. For a long time he was quite unable to master his merriment. At length he rose up and opened the lattice. Then putting out his hand he cried, still laughing: 'Abou Hassan, Abou Hassan, are you determined to make me die with laughter?'

"When the caliph spoke every one was silent, and the loud music ceased. Abou Hassan paused with the rest, and turned his head towards the place whence the voice came. He knew the caliph, and discovered that it was he who had personated the merchant of Moussoul. He was not disconcerted at this; he knew in a moment that he was quite awake, and that everything which had befallen him was perfectly real and no dream. He fell in with the humour and design of the caliph: 'Ah, ha!' cried he, looking at him with an air of confidence, 'you are there, you merchant of Moussoul! How can you complain that I make you die with laughing; you who are the cause of my bad behaviour towards my mother, and of all I myself suffered during my long confinement in the hospital for lunatics—you who have so ill-treated the Iman of the mosque in our part of the town, and our four scheiks, my neighbours—for I had nothing to do with it, I wash my hands of it—you who have occasioned so much distress and so many cross accidents. I ask you, are not you the aggressor, and am not I the sufferer?' 'You are in the right, Abou Hassan,' replied the caliph, who was still laughing, 'but for your comfort and to make amends for all your sufferings, I am ready—and I call Heaven to witness it—to recompense you in any way you wish, and to grant all you shall think proper to demand.'

"As soon as he had said this, the caliph came down from his closet and entered the saloon. He caused one of his best habits to be brought, and bade the damsels and the officers of the chamber employ themselves, according to their duty, in dressing Abou Hassan in it. When they had done so the caliph embraced him, and said, 'You are my brother, ask of me whatever will best please you and I will grant it.' 'Commander of the Faithful,' replied Abou Hassan, 'I beseech your majesty to have the goodness to inform me what you did to turn my brain, and what was your design; at present this is of more importance to me than anything else, to bring my mind back again to its former state.'

"The caliph was ready to give Abou Hassan this satisfaction. 'You must in the first place understand then,' said he, 'that I very often disguise myself, and especially by night, that I may find out whether proper order is preserved in all respects in the city of Bagdad; and as I am also glad to learn what happens in the neighbourhood, I set apart a certain day, the first of every month, to make a circuit beyond the walls, sometimes on one side, sometimes on the other; and I always return by the bridge. I was returning from my round on the evening when you invited me to sup with you. In the course of our conversation, you observed that your greatest wish was to be caliph and Commander of the Faithful only for twenty-four hours, that you might punish the Iman of the mosque in your neighbourhood, and the four scheiks, his counsellors. From this wish of yours I thought I might derive great amusement; and with that view I at once devised means to procure you the satisfaction you desired. I had about me a powder which brings on a deep sleep the moment it is taken, and keeps the person who has taken it asleep during a certain time. Without your perceiving it, I put a dose of that powder into the last glass which I presented to you, and you swallowed it. You were immediately overcome by sleep, and I ordered you to be taken away and carried to my palace by the slave who waited upon me: and when I went away I left your chamber door open. I need not tell you what happened to you at my palace after your waking, and during the whole of that day you spent here; at night, after you had been well entertained by my order, one of my female slaves who waited upon you put another dose of the same powder into the last glass which she presented to you, and which you drank. A sound sleep immediately seized you, and I caused you to be carried back to your own house by the same slave who had brought you, with an order to leave again the chamber door open when he came out of it. You had yourself told me all that befell you on the next day and immediately after. I did not imagine you would have to undergo so much as you suffered on this occasion; but I have given you my word I will do everything to console you, and will, if possible, make you forget all your sufferings. Consider, therefore, what I can do for your satisfaction, and freely ask me to give you whatever you wish.'

"'O Commander of the Faithful,' returned Abou Hassan, 'great as have been the ills I have suffered, they are effaced from my memory now that I know they were occasioned by my sovereign lord and master. With regard to the generosity with which your majesty offers to shower benefits upon me, I can have no doubt, after your irrevocable word has passed, that it will be fulfilled; but as self-interest had never much power over me, since your majesty gives me this liberty, the favour I shall presume to ask is that you allow me free access to your person, that I may have the happiness of admiring your greatness all my life long.'

"This last proof of Abou Hassan's disinterestedness completely gained the caliph's esteem. 'I most readily comply with your request,' said he; 'I grant you free access to me in my palace at all hours, and in whatever part of it I may be:'—and he immediately assigned to Abou Hassan an apartment in the palace. He chose rather that his new retainer should be about his person, than that Abou Hassan have any particular office in his treasury, and upon the spot ordered a thousand pieces of gold to be paid him from the privy purse. Abou Hassan made the humblest acknowledgements to the caliph, who then left him in order to hold his usual council.

"Abou Hassan took this opportunity of going immediately to his mother to inform

ABOU HASSAN PAYING THE COOK.

her of all that had occurred, and to acquaint her with his good fortune. He made her understand that all which had befallen him was by no means a dream; that he had really been caliph; that he had actually discharged all the royal functions, and received all the honours paid to the caliph during the space of twenty-four hours; and assured her that she need not doubt the truth of what he was telling her, since he had it confirmed to him by the caliph's own mouth.

"The news of Abou Hassan's adventure soon spread throughout the city of Bagdad; it passed even into the neighbouring provinces, and thence into the most distant regions, and was repeated with all the singular and amusing circumstances which accompanied it.

"This newly acquired distinction of Abou Hassan brought him constantly about the caliph's person. As he was naturally of a good temper, and diffused much cheerfulness wherever he came by his wit and pleasantry, the caliph scarcely knew how to do without him, and never engaged in any scheme of amusement but he made Abou Hassan one of the party. He sometimes brought him even to his wife Zobeidè, to whom he had related his history, which entertained her much. Princess Zobeidè was very well pleased with Abou Hassan; but she observed that whenever he attended the caliph in his visits to her, he had always his eye upon Nouzhatoul Aouadat, one of her slaves. This circumstance she determined, therefore, to communicate to the caliph; and said to him one day, 'Commander of the Faithful, you do not observe, perhaps, as I do, that every time Abou Hassan comes hither with you he constantly fixes his eyes upon Nouzhatoul Aouadat, and that she never fails to blush and cast down her eyes. You will hardly doubt that this is a sure sign she does not dislike him. If, therefore, you will take my advice, we will arrange a marriage between them.' 'Lady,' returned the caliph, 'you bring to my recollection a thing I ought not to have forgotten. Abou Hassan has told me his opinion on the subject of marriage, and I have always promised to give him a wife, with whom he shall have every reason to be satisfied. I am glad you have spoken to me about it, and I cannot conceive how the thing could have escaped my memory. But it is better that Abou Hassan should follow his own inclination in the choice he is to make for himself. Besides, since Nouzhatoul Aouadat does not seem averse to the match, we should not hesitate about this marriage. Here they are both; they have nothing to do but to declare their consent.'

"Abou Hassan threw himself at the feet of the caliph and of Princess Zobeidè, to testify his gratitude at their kindness towards him. 'I cannot,' said he, as he rose, 'receive a bride from better hands; but I dare not hope that Nouzhatoul Aouadat will give me her hand as cordially as I am ready to give her mine.' As he said this he looked at the slave of the princess, who, on her part, by a respectful silence and by the colour which rose into her cheeks, plainly showed that she was entirely disposed to follow the advice of the caliph and of the Princess Zobeidè her mistress.

"The marriage presently took place. The nuptials were celebrated in the palace with great demonstrations of joy, which lasted many days. Princess Zobeidè considered it a point of honour to make her slave rich presents to please the caliph; and the caliph, on his part, out of regard for the Princess Zobeidè, was equally generous towards Abou Hassan.

"The bride was conducted to the apartments which the caliph had assigned to Abou Hassan her husband, who awaited her coming with impatience. He received her with the sound of all sorts of musical instruments, mingled with the voices of singers of both sexes belonging to the palace, raised together in a loud and harmonious concert.

"Many days passed in the festivities and rejoicings usual upon such occasions. At length the newly married pair were left to each other's society. Abou Hassan and his new wife were charmed with each other. They were so perfectly united in affection that, except the time employed in attendance, one on the caliph, the other on the Princess Zobeidè, they lived entirely together. Nouzhatoul Aouadat had all the qualities that would inspire love and attachment in a man like Abou Hassan; for she corresponded to those wishes he had expressed so plainly to the caliph, and was especially fitted to be his companion at table. With such dispositions they could not fail to pass their time together most agreeably. Their table was constantly covered at every meal with the most delicious and the rarest dishes that cooks, with the utmost care, could prepare and furnish. Their sideboard was always provided with the most exquisite wine, which was so disposed as to be conveniently within the reach of either as they sat at table. There they enjoyed themselves to their heart's content in private, and entertained each other with a thousand pleasantries, which made them laugh more or less, according to the degree of the wit and humour which they contained. Their evening repast was more peculiarly devoted to pleasure. At that time were served only the best sorts of fruits, almond cakes, and the most exquisite confectionery. At every glass they drank, their spirits were raised by new songs, often composed at the moment, and suggested by the subject of their conversation. These songs were sometimes accompanied by a lute, or some other instrument, on which both of them were able to perform.

"Abou Hassan and Nouzhatoul Aouadat passed a long time in the enjoyment of mirth and jollity. They took no thought about the expense of their way of living. The cook whom they had chosen had hitherto furnished everything without demanding payment. It was but right that he should receive some money. He therefore presented his account to them. The amount was found to be very considerable. There was, moreover, a demand made for marriage garments of the richest stuffs for the use of both, and for jewels of high value for the bride; and so very large was the sum that they perceived, but too late, that of all the money they had received from the liberality of the caliph and the Princess Zobeidè when they were married, there remained no more than was sufficient to discharge the debt. This made them reflect seriously on their past conduct; but their reflections brought no remedy for the present evil. Abou Hassan was inclined to pay the cook, and his wife had no objection. They sent for the cook accordingly, and paid him his demand, without showing the least sign of the embarrassment they knew must immediately follow upon the payment of this money.

"The cook went away quite rejoiced at being paid in such new and very excellent coin; for none of an inferior sort was ever seen at the caliph's palace. Abou Hassan and Nouzhatoul Aouadat had thought their purse would never be empty. They sat in profound silence, with downcast eyes, and much confounded at finding themselves reduced to a penniless condition the very first year after their marriage.

"Abou Hassan remembered that the caliph on receiving him at his palace promised that he should never want for anything. But when he reflected that he had squandered in a little time the bounty he had so liberally received from the hand of Haroun Alraschid, he felt no disposition to make a request; nor could he bear to expose himself to the shame of avowing to the caliph the use he had made of his bounty, and the necessity he was under of receiving a fresh supply of money. He had given up all his own property to his mother, as the caliph had retained him near his person; and he was very unwilling to have recourse to her for assistance; for she would know from such a step that he had again fallen into the state of distress he had been in soon after the death of his father.

"In the same way Nouzhatoul Aouadat, who regarded the generosity of the Princess Zobeidè, and the liberty she had given her of marrying, as more than a sufficient recompense for her services and attachment, did not think she had any claim to request farther favours.

"At last Abou Hassan broke silence; and looking at Nouzhatoul Aouadat with an open countenance, he said: 'I plainly see that you are in the same embarrassment I myself feel, and that you are considering what we are to do in our deplorable situation, when our money fails us all at once before we had made provision for such a failure. I know not what you may think of the matter; for my part, whatever may be the consequence, I am determined not to retrench in the smallest degree from my usual expenses, and I believe you are not disposed to give up yours. The point is, to find means to provide for our wants without our having the meanness to apply either to the caliph or to the Princess Zobeidè; and I think I have discovered a way to get over this difficulty. But in this matter we must resolve to assist each other.'

"This speech of Abou Hassan's gave Nouzhatoul Aouadat much satisfaction and some degree of hope. 'I was thinking upon this very matter,' said she; 'and if I did not speak out it was because I could see no remedy. I must confess that the declaration you have just made gives me the greatest satisfaction possible. But since you say you have discovered the means of relief for us both; and since my assistance is necessary to our success, you have only to tell me what I am to do, and you shall see that I will exert myself to the utmost.' 'I entirely expected,' replied Abou Hassan, 'that you would not fail me in a matter which concerns you equally with myself. I have devised a scheme to procure money in our necessity, at least for some time to come. It consists in a little piece of deceit which we must practise towards the caliph and the Princess Zobeidè, and which I am assured will cause them amusement, and not be unprofitable to us. The deceit which I propose is that we should both of us die.'

"'That we should both of us die!' repeated Nouzhatoul Aouadat in astonishment. 'You may die, if you please; but, for my part, I am not yet tired of life, and without wishing to give you offence, I must say I have no intention of dying quite so soon. If you have no better scheme to propose you may execute that one yourself; for I can assure you I will have nothing to do with it.' 'You are a woman,' replied Abou Hassan —'I mean you are surprisingly ready and quick with your reply. You give me no time to explain myself. Hear me for a moment patiently, and you shall find that you will have no objection to dying in the way I mean to die. You must understand that I do not mean to talk of a real, but a feigned death.'

"'Ah! good!' said Nouzhatoul Aouadat briskly: 'since you speak of nothing more than a feigned death, I am at your service: you may depend upon my assistance. You shall see with what zeal I will second you in this sort of death; but, to tell you the truth, I have a most unconquerable aversion to the thoughts of dying so soon in the way I first understood you to mean.' 'Very well,' said Abou Hassan, 'you may be satisfied. This is what I mean: in order to carry out my scheme I am going to play the dead man. You shall immediately take a sheet, and you must put me in a coffin as if I were actually dead. You shall lay me out in the middle of the chamber in the usual way, with a turban on my face, and my feet turned towards Mecca, and with every preparation made for carrying me to the grave. When all this has been done, you are to begin weeping and lamenting, as is usual upon such occasions, rending your garments and tearing your hair; and in this state of grief, and with dishevelled locks, you shall go and present yourself to the Princess Zobeidè. Your mistress will wish to know the reason of your tears; and when you have informed her of my death, in broken words mingled with sobs, she will not fail to pity you, and to make you a present of a sum of money to assist you in defraying the expenses of my funeral, and to purchase a piece of brocade to serve for a pall and to give a splendour to my obsequies, as well as to purchase a new dress for yourself, as a substitute for that which she will see you have torn. As soon as you have returned with this money and this piece of brocade, I will rise from the ground where I have been lying, and you shall take my place. You shall pretend to be dead; and, after you have been put into a coffin, I will go in my turn to the caliph, and tell him the same tale you tell to the Princess Zobeidè; and I dare promise myself that the caliph will not be less liberal to me than the Princess Zobeidè will have been to you.'

"When Abou Hassan had sufficiently explained himself concerning his intended project, Nouzhatoul Aouadat replied: 'I believe the trick will be very amusing, and am mistaken if the caliph and the Princess Zobeidè will not think themselves much obliged to us for it. But we must take care to manage it properly. So far as my part is concerned, you may be sure it shall be well performed—at least, as well as I suppose you will perform yours; and we shall both act with zeal and attention in proportion as we expect to derive benefit from the scheme. Let us lose no time. Whilst I am getting a sheet, do you take off your upper garments. I know how to manage funerals as well as anybody; for whilst I was in the service of the Princess Zobeidè, if any slave died among my companions I was always appointed to superintend the burial.'

"Abou Hassan was not long in carrying out the recommendations of Nouzhatoul Aouadat. He lay down on his back on the sheet which had been spread upon the carpet in the middle of the chamber, crossed his arms, and suffered himself to be wrapped up in a manner which made him look as if he were only waiting to be placed on the bier and to be carried out for burial. His wife turned his feet towards Mecca, covered his face with the finest muslin, and then placed his turban over it in such a manner as not to interfere with his breathing. She then pulled off her head-dress, and with tears in her eyes, and her hair hanging loose and dishevelled, while she pretended to pull it with great outcries, she struck her cheeks, beat her breast violently, and showed every other sign of the most passionate grief. In this manner she went out and crossed a spacious court, intending to go to the apartment of the Princess Zobeidè.

"Nouzhatoul Aouadat shrieked and lamented so loudly that the Princess Zobeidè heard her from her apartment. Princess Zobeidè ordered her female slaves who were then in waiting to inquire whence the cries and lamentations which she heard proceeded. They instantly ran to the lattice, and came back to tell the Princess Zobeidè that Nouzhatoul Aouadat was coming that way apparently in very great distress. Thereupon

THE TRICK SUCCESSFUL.

the princess, impatient to know what had befallen her favourite, rose, and went to meet her as far as the door of her antechamber.

"Nouzhatoul Aouadat played her part to perfection. The moment she perceived the Princess Zobeidè, who herself held back the tapestry and kept the door of the antechamber half open, waiting for her, she redoubled her lamentations, and as she advanced tore off her hair by handfuls, struck her cheeks and breast more violently, and threw herself at her mistress's feet, bathing them with her tears. Princess Zobeidè, astonished to see her slave in such terrible grief, asked her what was the matter, and what misfortune had befallen her.

"Instead of answering her, Nouzhatoul Aouadat continued sobbing for some time, apparently taking the utmost pains to suppress her grief. 'Alas! my ever-honoured lady and mistress,' she cried at last, her voice much broken with sobs, 'what greater, what more fatal evil could befall me, than the dreadful calamity which obliges me to come and throw myself at the feet of your majesty in the extreme distress to which I am reduced! May Heaven grant you long life and the most perfect health, my most honoured mistress, and bestow upon you many and happy years! Abou Hassan—the poor Abou Hassan, whom you have honoured with your bounty, and whom you and the Commander of the Faithful gave me for a husband—is dead!'

"So saying, Nouzhatoul Aouadat redoubled her tears and sobs, and threw herself again at the feet of her mistress. Princess Zobeidè was extremely surprised at this news. 'Is Abou Hassan dead?' crid she: 'a man who appeared in such good health, who was so agreeable and amusing; I did not expect to hear so soon of the death of such a man, who promised to live to a great age, and so well deserved to do so.' She could not help expressing her concern by her tears. The female slaves who were in waiting, and who had often enjoyed the pleasantries of Abou Hassan when he was admitted to familiar conversation with the Princess Zobeidè and the caliph, testified by their weeping the regret they felt at her loss and their sympathy in her distress.

"Princess Zobeidè, her female slaves, and Nouzhatoul Aouadat remained a long time with their handkerchiefs at their eyes, weeping and sobbing at this fancied calamity. At length the princess broke silence: 'Wretch!' cried she, speaking to the supposed widow, 'perhaps thou hast caused his death. Thou hast plagued him so much by thy sad temper, that thou hast at last brought him to the grave.'

"Nouzhatoul Aouadat appeared greatly mortified at this reproach of the Princess Zobeidè. 'Ah, honoured lady,' cried she, 'I did not believe I had ever, during the whole time I had the honour of being your slave, given your majesty the smallest reason for entertaining so disadvantageous an opinion of my behaviour towards a husband so dear to me. I should think myself the most unhappy of women if you were really convinced of its truth. I have paid every fond attention to Abou Hassan which a wife can pay to a husband whom she dotes upon; and I can say without vanity that I have felt for him all the tenderness which he deserved for his ready compliance with my moderate wishes, and which indeed showed that his affection was sincerely given to me. I am convinced he would fully justify me on that subject in your majesty's opinion if he were still living. But madam,' added she, her tears flowing afresh, 'his hour was come: that alone was the cause of his death.'

"In truth, Princess Zobeidè had always observed in her slave a kind and even temper, much unaffected sweetness, a great degree of docility, and a zeal in everything she undertook in her service, which arose more from inclination than duty. She therefore did not hesitate to believe her on her word, and ordered the superintendent of her treasury to bring a purse of a hundred pieces of gold, and a piece of brocade. The superintendent returned immediately with the purse and the piece of brocade, which, at the Princess Zobeide's order, she delivered to Nouzhatoul Aouadat.

"Upon receiving this handsome present the pretended widow threw herself at the Princess Zobeidè's feet, and made her the most humble acknowledgments, with great secret satisfaction that she had succeeded so well. 'Go,' said the Princess Zobeidè, 'let the piece of brocade be used to spread over your husband on his bier, and spend the money in defraying the expense of a funeral that shall do him the honour he is worthy of. And, as soon as you can control yourself, moderate the excess of your affliction: I will take care of you.'

"As soon as Nouzhatoul Aouadat was safely out of the presence of the Princess Zobeidè, she joyfully dried up her tears, and returned as soon as possible to give Abou Hassan an account of the success she had met with in playing her part. As she entered, Nouzhatoul Aouadat burst into a violent fit of laughing at finding Abon Hassan lying in the same position in which she had left him in the middle of the room, and ready prepared for his funeral. 'Get up,' said she, still laughing, 'and behold the fruits of my visit to the Princess Zobeidè. We shall not die of hunger to-day.' Abou Hassan quickly got up, and rejoiced with his wife when he saw the purse and the piece of brocade.

"Nouzhatoul Aouadat was so pleased at the happy success of the artifice she had just practised upon her mistress, that she could not contain her joy. 'This is not enough,' said she to her husband, laughing; 'I must pretend to die in my turn; and you shall see whether you will be clever enough to get as much from the caliph as I have from the Princess Zobeidè.' 'This is exactly the humour of women,' replied Abou Hassan; 'it is very justly said they have always the vanity to think they are superior to men, although they seldom do anything well but by the men's advice. It is hardly likely that I should not succeed with the caliph as well as you have done, considering it was I who contrived the scheme. But let us lose no time in idle chat; do you now pretend to be dead, and you shall soon see whether I do not manage as well as you have done.'

"Abou Hassan laid out his wife in the same place and in the same manner as he himself had been laid, turned her feet towards Mecca, and went out of his chamber in great disorder, with his turban awry, like a man in great affliction. Thus he went to the caliph, who was then holding a particular council with the grand vizier Giafar and the other viziers in whom he placed the most confidence. Abou Hassan presented himself at the door, and the usher, who knew that he always had free access, opened it to him. He entered, with one hand holding a handkerchief before his eyes to conceal the tears which he feigned to be shedding in abundance, and with the other violently beating his breast, while he uttered exclamations expressive of the greatest grief.

"The caliph, who was accustomed to see Abou Hassan with a cheerful countenance, and considered him as a man who always inspired others with joy, was surprised at seeing him appear in so melancholy a condition. He broke off the business they were then transacting in the council, in order to ask him the occasion of his grief.

"O Commander of the Faithful,' answered Abou Hassan, with repeated sighs and sobs, 'a greater misfortune could not possibly happen to me than that for which you now see me immersed in grief. May Allah grant a long life to your majesty, and preserve you on that throne which you fill with so much glory. Nouzhatoul Aouadat, whom in your goodness you were pleased to bestow upon me, that I might pass the remainder of my life with her, is, alas——!' After this exclamation Abou Hassan pretended that his heart was so oppressed that he could not utter another word, but he shed tears abundantly.

"The caliph, who now understood that Abou Hassan came to inform him of the death of his wife, appeared extremely affected at it. 'Heaven have mercy upon her!' said he, with an air that showed how much he regretted her. 'She was a good slave, and the Princess Zobeidè and I gave her to you with the design of making you happy: she was worthy of a longer life.' The tears trickled from his eyes, and he was forced to take his handkerchief to wipe them away.

"The grief of Abou Hassan and the tears of the caliph drew tears from the grand vizier Giafar and the other viziers. They all lamented the death of Nouzhatoul Aouadat, who, in the meantime, was becoming extremely impatient to know how Abou Hassan had succeeded.

"The caliph for a moment entertained the same opinion of the husband that the Princess Zobeidè had held of the wife, and imagined he had been the cause of her death. He said, in an angry tone of voice, 'Wretch! hast thou not destroyed thy wife by thy ill-treatment of her? Alas! I have no doubt of it. Thou shouldst at least have had some regard for the Princess Zobeidè my wife, who loved her more than any of her slaves, and who only parted with her in order to give her to thee. Is it thus thou hast shown thy gratitude?'

"'Commander of the Faithful,' answered Abou Hassan, pretending to weep more bitterly than ever, 'can your majesty for a moment entertain the thought that Abou Hassan, whom you have loaded with your bounty and favours, and on whom you have conferred honours to which he presumed not to aspire, could be capable of so much ingratitude? I loved Nouzhatoul Aouadat my wife as much on account of the generosity that had given her to me, as because she possessed so many excellent qualities that I could not withhold from her all the attachment, all the tenderness, and all the love she deserved. But, alas! your majesty, she was to die, and Heaven has chosen to take away from me the happiness which I held from the bounty of your majesty and that of the Princess Zobeidè your beloved wife.'

"In short, Abou Hassan found means to counterfeit grief so perfectly, with all the outward marks of a true affliction, that the caliph, who indeed had never heard that he had behaved ill to his wife, gave credit to all he said, and never doubted his sincerity. The treasurer of the palace was present, and the caliph ordered him to go to the treasury and give Abou Hassan a purse of a hundred pieces of gold, together with a fine piece of brocade. Abou Hassan immediately threw himself at the feet of the caliph, in token of his gratitude. 'Follow the treasurer,' said the caliph; 'the piece of brocade will serve you to lay over your dead wife, and the money to provide a funeral worthy of her: I have no doubt you will give her this last proof of your love.'

"Abou Hassan made no answer to these kind words of the caliph's, but bowed profoundly as he retired. He went with the treasurer, and when the purse and the piece of brocade had been delivered to him, he returned to his house perfectly satisfied, and thoroughly happy in himself at having so readily and so easily found means to supply his present necessities, which had occasioned him much anxiety.

"Nouzhatoul Aouadat, tired at the length of time she was kept in imprisonment, did not wait till Abou Hassan should bid her quit her uncomfortable position. As soon as she heard the door open she ran towards him. 'Tell me,' said she, 'has the caliph been as easily imposed upon as the Princess Zobeidè was?' 'You see,' replied Abou Hassan, laughing, and showing her the purse and the piece of brocade, 'that I know how to counterfeit affliction for the death of a wife who is alive and hearty, as well as you do to mourn for a husband who is not yet dead.'

"Abou Hassan was very sure that this twofold artifice must have its consequences, therefore he cautioned his wife as well as he could upon all that was likely to happen, in order that they might act in concert; and he added, 'The better we succeed in placing the caliph and Princess Zobeidè in some sort of embarrassment, the more pleased they will at last be, and perhaps they will testify their satisfaction by some fresh marks of their kindness.' This last consideration induced them to carry on their artifice to the greatest possible length.

"Although there were affairs of importance to settle in the council which was then sitting, the caliph, impatient to go to the Princess Zobeidè to condole with her on the death of her slave, rose very soon after Abou Hassan's departure, and adjourned the council to another day. The grand vizier and the other viziers took their leave and retired.

"As soon as they were gone, the caliph said to Mesrour, chief of the eunuchs of the palace, who was almost always near his person, and who besides was acquainted with all his designs, 'Come with me, and sympathise in the grief of the princess for the death of her slave Nouzhatoul Aouadat.'

"They went together to Princess Zobeidè's apartment. When the caliph was at the door he put back the tapestry a little way, and perceived his wife sitting upon her sofa in great affliction, with her eyes still bathed in tears.

"The caliph entered, and walked up towards Princess Zobeidè. 'Lady,' said he, 'it is unnecessary to tell you how completely I share your affliction, since you are well aware I sympathise in all that gives you pain and in all that gives you pleasure; but we are all mortal, and we must give back to Allah that life which He hath given us whenever He requires it. Nouzhatoul Aouadat your slave had in truth qualities which deservedly gained your esteem, and I think it quite right that you give proofs of it even after her death. Consider, however, that your sorrow will never bring her back again to life. Therefore, if you will follow my advice, you will take comfort upon this loss, and be more careful of your own life, which you know to be very precious to me, and which constitutes the whole happiness of mine.'

"If Princess Zobeidè was, on the one hand, charmed with the tender sentiments which accompanied the caliph's compliment, she was, on the other, much surprised to

MESROUR'S VISIT TO THE HOUSE OF ABOU HASSAN.

hear of the death of Nouzhatoul Aouadat, which she did not expect. This intelligence threw her into such a state of astonishment that she remained for some time unable to reply. Her surprise was so much increased to hear an account so entirely different from what she had just been told, that it deprived her of speech; at length, upon recovering herself and regaining her voice, she said, with an air and tone still expressive of her astonishment, 'Commander of the Faithful, I am very grateful for all the tender sentiments which you express towards me; but allow me to say that I do not at all understand the intelligence you give me of the death of my slave. She is in perfect health. Heaven preserve us both, my lord; but you see me afflicted at the death of Abou Hassan her husband, your favourite, whom I esteem as much for the regard I know that you have for him, as because you have had the goodness to introduce him to my acquaintance, and he has sometimes very agreeably entertained me. But, my lord, the indifference which I see you manifest at his death, and the forgetfulness you show in so very little time after the proofs you have given me of the pleasure you derived from having him near you, fill me with surprise and astonishment. And this insensibility appears to me the more strange from the confusion you seem disposed to make by telling me of the death of my slave, instead of speaking of his death.'

"The caliph, who supposed he was perfectly well informed of the death of the slave, and who had reason to feel certain from what he had seen and heard, began to laugh when he heard Princess Zobeidè talk in this manner. 'Mesrour,' said he, turning towards the chief of the eunuchs, 'what say you to this speech? Is it not true that ladies have sometimes strange wanderings of the understanding that one can scarcely believe? For you have both heard and seen the particulars of this affair as well as myself.' And turning again to Princess Zobeidè he resumed: 'Lady, shed no more tears for Abou Hassan, for he is perfectly well. Weep rather for the death of your dear slave. It is scarcely a moment since her husband came into my council hall in tears, and so much afflicted as to give me pain, to announce to me the death of his wife. I ordered a purse of a hundred pieces of gold and a piece of brocade to be given him towards defraying the funeral expenses of his dead wife. Mesrour here was witness of all that happened, and can tell you the same thing.'

"Princess Zobeidè could not believe the caliph was serious when he spoke thus. She thought he only meant to impose upon her. 'Commander of the Faithful,' replied she, 'although it be your custom to jest, I must say that this is not a proper time to do so. What I have been telling you is quite a serious matter. It is not my slave who is dead, but her husband, Abou Hassan, whose fate I lament, and which you ought to lament with me.'

"'And I,' replied the caliph, becoming now much more serious, 'tell you without jesting that you are mistaken. It is Nouzhatoul Aouadat who is dead, and it is Abou Hassan who is alive and in perfect health.'

"Princess Zobeidè was piqued at the caliph's direct contradiction. 'Commander of the Faithful,' she resumed in an earnest tone, 'may Heaven keep you from remaining long under this mistake. You would make me suppose that you are not in your right mind. Allow me to repeat once more that it is Abou Hassan who is dead, and that Nouzhatoul Aouadat my slave, widow of the deceased, is certainly alive. It is not an hour since she left me. She came hither quite in despair, and in a state of affliction the very sight of which would have drawn tears from me, even though she had not, amidst continual sobs, told me the real cause of her grief. All my women have been weeping with me, and they can give you the most convincing proofs of the truth of what I say. They will tell you also that I made Nouzhatoul Aouadat a present of a purse of a hundred pieces of gold and a piece of brocade; and the grief you observed in my countenance when you entered was as much caused by the death of her husband as by the distress in which I had just seen her. I was even going to send you the expression of my sympathy at the time you made your appearance.'

"'My good lady,' cried the caliph, with a loud laugh at these words of Princess Zobeidè, 'this is a very strange obstinacy of yours; and for my part I must tell you,' he continued, resuming his serious tone, 'that it is Nouzhatoul Aouadat who is dead.' 'No, I tell you!' replied Princess Zobeidè, instantly and earnestly, 'it is Abou Hassan who is dead, you shall never make me believe otherwise.'

"The caliph's eyes sparkled with anger. He sat down on the sofa, but at a great distance from Princess Zobeidè, and, speaking to Mesrour, said, 'Go this moment and see which of the two is dead, and instantly bring me word. Although I am quite certain that Nouzhatoul Aouadat is dead, I would rather take this step than be any longer obstinate in a matter of which I am nevertheless perfectly convinced.'

"The caliph had hardly finished speaking before Mesrour was gone. 'You will see in a moment,' continued he, speaking to Princess Zobeidè, 'who is right, you or I.' 'For my part,' replied Princess Zobeidè, 'I very well know that I am right, and you will yourself see that it is Abou Hassan who is dead, as I told you.' 'And I,' retorted the caliph, 'am so assured that it is Nouzhatoul Aouadat that I will bet you any wager you please that she is dead, and that Abou Hassan is very well.' 'Do not think to carry your point so,' replied Princess Zobeidè: 'I accept your wager. I am so convinced of the death of Abou Hassan that I am ready to stake whatever I hold most precious against what you please, be it of never so little value. You very well know my tastes and likings, and, therefore, what I love best; you have only to choose and propose. I will abide by your word, be the consequence what it may.' 'Since this is the case,' said the caliph, 'I stake my garden of delights against your palace of pictures. One is as good as the other.' Princess Zobeidè replied, 'Whether your garden is better than my palace is not at present the question between us. The business is for you to select whatever you please of mine to set against what you may bet on your part. I will consent to it, and the wager is settled. I shall not be the first to retract, I declare to Heaven.' The caliph, on his part, replied just as positively, and they waited in expectation of Mesrour's return.

"While the caliph and Princess Zobeidè were contending so earnestly and with so much warmth whether it was Abou Hassan or Nouzhatoul Aouadat who was dead, Abou Hassan, who had foreseen that altercation would ensue upon this point, was on the alert to be prepared for whatever might happen. When he saw Mesrour at a distance through the lattice near which he sat conversing with his wife, and observed that the chief of the eunuchs was coming straight to their apartments, he immediately understood for what purpose he had been sent. He told his wife to pretend to be dead once more, as they had before agreed, and to make her preparations quickly.

"In fact there was no time to lose, and it was as much as he could do before Mesrour arrived to place his wife upon the ground again, and to spread over her the piece of brocade which the caliph had ordered to be given to him. He then opened the door of his apartment, and with a melancholy and dejected countenance, holding his handkerchief before his eyes, seated himself at the head of the pretended corpse.

"Scarcely was he ready when Mesrour entered the chamber. The funereal preparations which met the eyes of the chief of the eunuchs gave him secret pleasure as far as it regarded the commission with which he was entrusted by the caliph. As soon as Abou Hassan saw him he rose to meet him, and respectfully kissing his hand said, sighing and lamenting, 'O my friend, you see me in the greatest affliction possible for the death of my dear wife Nouzhatoul Aouadat, whom you honoured with your kindness.'

"Mesrour was much affected at this address, and could not refuse the tribute of a few tears to the memory of the dead lady. He lifted up the cloth which covered the body that he might look at her face; and letting it fall again, after he had glanced at her countenance, he said, with a deep sigh: 'There is no other God but Allah: we must all submit to His will, and every creature must return to Him. Nouzhatoul Aouadat, my good sister!' added he, sighing again, 'your destiny has been very quickly fulfilled. May Heaven have mercy upon you!' He then turned towards Abou Hassan, who was bathed in tears, and observed: 'The saying is true which tells us that women sometimes know not what they say, which cannot be excused. Princess Zobeidè, my most excellent mistress, is now in this predicament. She persisted in maintaining to the caliph that it was you who were dead, and not your wife. And, let the caliph say what he will to the contrary, to convince her by the strongest and most serious assurances, he cannot succeed in altering her conviction. He even called me as a witness to vouch for the truth of his assertion, since you well know I was present when you came to tell him this afflicting news; but all was to no purpose. They were so earnest and obstinate in their altercation, that it would never have ended if the caliph, in order to convince the

Princess Zobeidè, had not determined to send me hither to ascertain the truth. But I am afraid it will be in vain; for try your very utmost with women to make them understand a matter, and you will find them unconquerably obstinate when once they have taken a thing into their heads.'

"'Heaven preserve the Commander of the Faithful in the possession and good use of his excellent understanding,' replied Abou Hassan, the tears still in his eyes, and his words interrupted by sobs. 'You see the state of the case, and that I have not imposed upon his majesty; and would to Heaven,' cried the deceiver, the better to carry on the cheat, 'that I had never had occasion to go to him with such melancholy, such heart-rending information. Alas! I cannot find words to express the irreparable loss I have this day sustained.' 'You speak truth,' replied Mesrour; 'and I can assure you I sympathise very sincerely in your affliction. However, you must be comforted, and not thus entirely give way to your grief. I must now reluctantly leave you to return to the caliph; but I beg as a favour,' continued he, 'that you will not let the body be carried away until I return; for I am desirous of being present at my poor friend's interment, and wish to follow her with my prayers.'

"Mesrour was going away to give the caliph an account of his commission, when Abou Hassan, who accompanied him to the door, observed that he had no claim to the honour the chief of the eunuchs intended him. Lest Mesrour should turn back immediately to say something else, he followed him with his eyes for some time; and when he saw him at a considerable distance, he came back to his chamber and freed Nouzhatoul Aouadat from the covering under which she lay. 'This is a new scene in our play,' said he; 'but I suppose it will not be the last. The Princess Zobeidè will certainly not pay any regard to Mesrour's report, but, on the contrary, will laugh at him: she has every reason to disbelieve him; so that we must expect some new event.' While Abou Hassan was saying this, Nouzhatoul Aouadat had time to put on her dress again. Then they resumed their seats near the lattice, and waited to see what would happen next.

"In the meantime Mesrour reached the Princess Zobeidè's apartment. He entered her cabinet, laughing and clapping his hands as a man would do who had something agreeable to communicate. The caliph was naturally of an impatient temper. He wished to have the matter instantly cleared up; besides, he was urged on to it by his wife's challenge. As soon, therefore, as he saw Mesrour, he cried out: 'Thou wicked slave, this is no time for laughing. What hast thou to say? Speak out boldly: who is dead—the husband or the wife?'

"'Commander of the Faithful,' immediately answered Mesrour, putting on a serious countenance, 'it is Nouzhatoul Aouadat who is dead; and Abou Hassan is still as much overwhelmed with grief as when he lately appeared before your majesty.'

"Without giving Mesrour time to say more, the caliph broke out into a loud fit of laughter. 'Good news!' cried he; 'only a moment since, the Princess Zobeidè, your mistress, was the owner of the palace of pictures; it is now mine. It was betted against my garden of delights since you left us; so that you could not have given me greater pleasure than by the news you bring. I will take care to reward you. But no more of this: tell me every particular of what you have seen.'

"'Commander of the Faithful,' Mesrour went on, 'when I reached Abou Hassan's apartments I went into his chamber, which was open. I found him still weeping, and in deep grief at the death of his wife Nouzhatoul Aouadat. He was seated near the head of the dead lady, who was lying in the middle of the room, with her feet turned towards Mecca. The corpse was covered with the piece of brocade which your majesty lately presented to Abou Hassan. After expressing my sympathy with his grief, I drew near; and, lifting the covering from the face of the deceased, I knew Nouzhatoul Aouadat, whose face was already swollen and much changed. I very earnestly exhorted Abou Hassan to be comforted; and, when I came away, I expressed my wish to be present at the interment of his wife, and requested that he would not suffer the corpse to be carried to the grave till I should come. This is all I have to tell your majesty with regard to the fulfilment of the order which you gave me.'

"When Mesrour had finished his report, the caliph laughed very heartily, and said, 'I will ask you no more questions; I am perfectly satisfied with your exactness.' And, addressing the Princess Zobeidè, he continued: 'Now, lady, have you anything still to say in opposition to such evidence as this? Do you continue to think that Nouzhatoul Aouadat is still living, and that Abou Hassan is dead? and do you not confess that you have lost your wager?'

"Princess Zobeidè was by no means satisfied that Mesrour had made a true report. 'How, my lord, can you think that I shall believe this slave?' she retorted; 'he is an impertinent fellow, who knows not what he says. I am neither blind nor deprived of my reason. I have seen with my own eyes Nouzhatoul Aouadat in the greatest affliction. I have myself spoken to her, and I heard perfectly what she told me concerning the death of her husband.'

ALTERCATION BETWEEN THE NURSE AND MESROUR.

"'Lady,' returned Mesrour, 'I swear by your life, and by the life of the Commander of the Faithful (the most precious things in the world to me), that Nouzhatoul is dead, and that Abou Hassan is alive.' 'Thou liest, vile and contemptible slave!' cried the Princess Zobeidè, in a violent passion; 'and I will confound thee in a moment.' She immediately called her women by clapping her hands. They instantly entered at her summons. 'Come hither,' said the princess to them; 'tell me the truth: who was it that came to me a short time before the Commander of the Faithful made his visit here?' The women all answered that it was the poor wretched Nouzhatoul Aouadat. And, speaking to her treasuress, the Princess Zobeidè demanded: 'What was it I ordered you to give her when she went away?' 'O lady,' replied the treasuress, 'I gave to Nouzhatoul Aouadat, by your majesty's order, a purse with a hundred pieces of gold, and a piece of brocade, which she took away with her.' 'Well, then, thou wretch! thou unworthy slave!' said the Princess Zobeidè to Mesrour, in great indignation, 'what canst thou say to all thou hast now heard? Whom thinkest thou I am now to believe; thee, or my treasuress, my women, and my own eyes?'

"Mesrour might easily have answered his mistress to some purpose; but, as he was afraid of irritating her still more, he chose to play a prudent part, and remain silent, thoroughly convinced all the while by the proofs he had seen that Nouzhatoul Aouadat was dead, and not Abou Hassan.

"During this altercation between the Princess Zobeidè and Mesrour, the caliph, who had heard the proofs brought on both sides, and which each party thought convincing, and who felt assured, as well by what had passed in his own conversation with Abou Hassan as by what Mesrour had just reported, that the Princess Zobeidè was wrong, laughed heartily at seeing the Princess Zobeidè in such a rage with Mesrour. 'Lady, let me observe once more,' said he to her, 'that I know not who it was that said women are sometimes beside themselves; allow me to say that you make the truth of that saying very apparent. Mesrour is but just returned from Abou Hassan's apartments: he tells you he has seen with his own eyes Nouzhatoul Aouadat lying dead in the middle of her chamber, and Abou Hassan sitting near the corpse; and notwithstanding this testimony, which cannot reasonably be doubted, you persist in your former opinion. It is a matter I cannot understand.'

"Princess Zobeidè seemed not to attend to this remonstrance of the caliph. 'Commander of the Faithful,' returned she, 'pardon me if I have a little suspicion of you. I see plainly that you are leagued with Mesrour in a design to thwart me, and to try my patience to the utmost. And as I perceive that the report which Mesrour has made was arranged between you, I beg you will allow me to send a person on my part to Abou Hassan's apartments, that I may know whether I am really in error.'

"The caliph gave his consent, and his wife sent her nurse upon this important errand. This nurse was a woman far advanced in life. She had always remained with the Princess Zobeidè from her infancy, and was now present with the other women. 'Nurse,' said the lady, 'attend to what I say. Go to Abou Hassan's house, or rather to that of Nouzhatoul Aouadat, since Abou Hassan is dead. You hear the discussion I have had with the Commander of the Faithful and with Mesrour. I need not say any more to you. Clear up the whole matter to me; and if you bring me back a good account a valuable present shall be made to you. Go quickly, and return without delay.'

"The nurse departed, to the great joy of the caliph, who was delighted to see the Princess Zobeidè in this embarrassment; but Mesrour, extremely mortified at seeing his mistress so angry with him, was pondering by what means he should appease her, and contrive that the caliph and the Princess Zobeidè should both be satisfied with him. For this reason he was delighted when he saw the Princess Zobeidè determined to send her nurse to Abou Hassan's, because he felt convinced that the report the nurse would make would correspond entirely with his own, and would serve to justify him and restore him again to her favour.

"Meanwhile Abou Hassan, who had been keeping watch at the lattice, perceived the nurse at some distance. He immediately conjectured what must be the errand on which the Princess Zobeidè had sent her. He called his wife, and without a moment's hesitation as to what was to be done, said: 'Here comes your lady's nurse to inquire into the truth. I must again play the dead man in my turn.'

"Everything was soon ready. Nouzhatoul Aouadat placed Abou Hassan upon the ground, threw over him the piece of brocade which the Princess Zobeidè had given her, and placed the turban on his face. The nurse, in her eagerness to execute her commission, was meanwhile approaching as quickly as she could. Entering the chamber, she perceived Nouzhatoul Aouadat, all in tears, with her hair dishevelled, beating her breast and cheeks, and uttering loud lamentations.

"She drew near this pretended widow, and said in a very melancholy tone of voice:

'O my dear Nouzhatoul Aouadat, I am not come to disturb your grief, nor to prevent your shedding tears for a husband who loved you so tenderly.' 'Ah, my good mother,' instantly replied the disconsolate widow, in a tone that seemed to speak the deepest grief, 'you see to what a wretched situation I am reduced, overwhelmed as I am with distress at the loss of my dear Abou Hassan, whom the Princess Zobeidè, my dear mistress and yours, and the Commander of the Faithful had given me for a husband. Abou Hassan, my beloved husband,' cried she again, 'what have I done that you should so soon abandon me? Have I not always followed your inclination rather than my own? Alas! what will become of the poor Nouzhatoul Aouadat?'

"The nurse was in utter astonishment at seeing a state of things entirely opposite to what the chief of the eunuchs had reported to the caliph. 'The curse of Allah be upon this black-faced Mesrour!' exclaimed she earnestly, raising her hands on high, 'for having been the occasion of so great a quarrel between my good mistress and the Commander of the Faithful by the notorious lies he has told them!' Then addressing herself to Nouzhatoul Aouadat, she continued: 'My dear child, I must tell you the wickedness and falsehood of this wretch Mesrour, who has maintained with inconceivable impudence to our good mistress that you were dead, and that Abou Hassan was living.' 'Alas! my good mother,' cried Nouzhatoul Aouadat, 'would to Heaven he had spoken the truth! I should not be overwhelmed with affliction as you see me now, nor be lamenting a husband who was so dear to me.' At these last words she melted into tears, and bewailed her forlorn state with renewed cries and lamentations.

"The nurse was much affected by the tears of Nouzhatoul Aouadat. She seated herself near the supposed widow, and shed many tears. Then she silently approached the head of Abou Hassan, raised his turban a little, and uncovered his face, to see whether she would know him. 'Ah, poor Abou Hassan,' said she, covering him again almost directly, 'I pray Heaven to have mercy upon you! Farewell, my child,' she continued, turning to the mourner; 'if I could stay with you a longer time I should be glad to do so. But I must not stop a moment; my duty urges me to go instantly, and deliver my good mistress from the distressful state of anxiety into which that black villain has thrown her by his impudent falsehood, in assuring her with an oath that you were dead.'

"Princess Zobeidè's nurse had scarcely closed the door upon leaving them when Nouzhatoul Aouadat, who was well satisfied the visitor would not come back, as she was in such haste to return to the princess, wiped her eyes and took off the things in which Abou Hassan was wrapped. Then they returned together to their places on the sofa, patiently waiting for the event of their artifice, and prepared to get out of the difficulty whatever turn the matter should take.

"Princess Zobeidè's nurse in the meantime, notwithstanding her great age, returned even more quickly than she had gone. The pleasure of bringing the princess a good account, and still more the hope of a reward for herself, winged her steps. She entered the cabinet of the princess almost out of breath, and gave an account of her commission, relating in an artless manner all she had seen.

"Princess Zobeidè heard the nurse's report with a satisfaction she could not conceal. The moment her messenger had ceased speaking, she said to the nurse, in a tone of triumph at having gained her point: 'Repeat what you have told me to the Commander of the Faithful, who looks upon us as deprived of our senses, and who besides would have it thought that we have no sentiment of religion—that we have no fear of Allah! And speak to this wicked black slave, who has the insolence to maintain to my face what is not true in a matter which I understand better than he does.'

"Mesrour, who expected that the nurse's expedition and the report she was to make would prove favourable, was excessively mortified to find that all had turned out quite differently. Besides, he was very much chagrined at the great displeasure which the Princess Zobeidè showed towards him about a matter which appeared to him the simplest thing in the world. For this reason he was much pleased at having an opportunity of explaining himself freely to the nurse rather than to the princess, whom he did not presume to answer, for fear of being thought guilty of disrespect. 'Thou toothless old woman,' said he to the nurse, 'I tell thee plainly thou art a liar: there is not a word of truth in what thou sayest. I saw with my own eyes Nouzhatoul Aouadat lying dead in the middle of her chamber.' 'Thou art a liar, a notorious liar, thyself!' replied the nurse, with a furious air, 'to dare to maintain such a falsehood to me, who am just returned from Abou Hassan's house. I saw him lying dead; and I left his wife in great grief, but perfectly alive.'

"'I am not an impostor,' replied Mesrour; 'it is thou who art trying to mislead us.' 'What a gross piece of impudence,' retorted the nurse, 'to presume thus to charge me with a falsehood in the presence of their majesties, when I am just returned from seeing with my own eyes the truth of what I have the honour of reporting!' 'Nurse,' rejoined Mesrour, 'thou hadst better say no more; thou art doting.'

"Princess Zobeidè could no longer bear this want of respect in Mesrour, who was treating her nurse so contemptuously in her presence. Without, therefore, giving her nurse time to make answer to this atrocious reproach, she cried out to the caliph: 'O Commander of the Faithful, I appeal to your justice respecting this insolent behaviour, which concerns you as much as myself.' She could say no more. Her vexation overcame her, and she burst into tears.

"The caliph, who had heard all this altercation, was very much embarrassed. It was to no purpose that he silently gave all possible attention to the matter. He knew not what to think of so much contradiction. The princess, for her part, as well as Mesrour, the nurse, and the female slaves who were present, knew not what to think of it, and were all silent. The caliph at last spoke. 'Lady,' said he, addressing himself to the Princess Zobeidè, 'I see clearly we are all liars; I first, you next, then Mesrour, and then the nurse; at least it appears that no one of us is more worthy of credit than the rest. So let us rise and go ourselves, that we may see with our own eyes on which side the truth lies. I see no other way of clearing up our doubts and quieting our minds.'

"Saying this, the caliph rose. The Princess Zobeidè followed him, and Mesrour walked before to open the door. 'Commander of the Faithful,' said he, 'I am much rejoiced your majesty has taken this step; and I shall be still more glad when I have convinced the nurse, not that she is doting, because that expression has had the misfortune to offend my good mistress, but that the report she made is not true.' The nurse replied angrily: 'Hold thy tongue, blackface! there is no dotard here but thyself.'

"Princess Zobeidè, who was unusually angry with Mesrour, could not bear that he should again attack her nurse. She took her follower's part. 'Thou vile slave!' said she, 'whatever thou mayest say, I still maintain that my nurse has spoken the truth; thee I can only regard as a liar.' 'O my gracious mistress,' answered Mesrour, 'if the nurse is so truly assured that Nouzhatoul Aouadat is alive, and that Abou Hassan is dead, let her lay some wager with me: she would not dare.' The nurse was ready with an answer. 'I will readily dare,' said she, 'and take thee at thy word. Let us see whether thou wilt stand to it.' Mesrour kept his word. The nurse and he made a wager, in the presence of the caliph and the Princess Zobeidè, of a piece of gold brocade with silver flowers, the pattern to be chosen by the winner.

"The apartment which the caliph and the Princess Zobeidè left, although at some distance from those in which Abou Hassan and Nouzhatoul Aouadat lived, was directly opposite to them. Abou Hassan, who saw them coming, preceded by Mesrour and followed by the nurse with a great number of the Princess Zobeidè's women, immediately apprised his wife of this circumstance, telling her that he was greatly mistaken if they were not to be soon honoured by a royal visit. Nouzhatoul Aouadat looked through the lattice, and saw the procession coming. Although her husband had told her beforehand what was likely to happen, she was nevertheless surprised. 'What shall we do?' cried she; 'we are ruined!' 'Not at all; don't be afraid,' returned Abou Hassan, very coolly; 'have you already forgotten what we have said upon this subject? Let us both pretend to be dead, as we have each of us pretended before, and as we have agreed we would do,

ABOU HASSAN WINNING THE THOUSAND PIECES OF GOLD.

and you shall see that all will turn out well. At the rate at which they are coming we shall be ready before they reach the door.'

"In fact, Abou Hassan and his wife determined to cover themselves as well as they could; and, after they had placed themselves one beside the other in the middle of the chamber, each under a piece of brocade, they waited quietly for the arrival of the company who were coming to visit them.

"The illustrious visitors presently appeared. Mesrour opened the door, and the caliph and the Princess Zobeidè entered the chamber, followed by all their attendants. They were much surprised, and stood silent for a time, looking at the dismal spectacle which presented itself to their view. No one knew what to think of the matter. Princess Zobeidè at last broke silence. 'Alas!' said she to the caliph, 'both are dead! This is your doing,' she went on, looking at the caliph and Mesrour. 'Why did you obstinately endeavour to impose upon me that my dear slave was dead? Indeed she is dead now, doubtless for grief at having lost her husband.' 'Say rather,' replied the caliph, with a contrary prejudice, 'that Nouzhatoul Aouadat died first, and that the poor Abou Hassan expired under the affliction of seeing his wife, your dear slave, die. So you must allow that you have lost your wager, and that the palace of pictures is now fairly mine.' 'And I,' replied the Princess Zobeidè, with a spirit excited by the contradiction of the caliph, 'maintain that you have lost, and that your favourite garden belongs to me. Abou Hassan died first; did not my nurse tell you, as well as I, that she saw his wife alive, and lamenting her husband's death?'

"This altercation of the caliph with Princess Zobeidè brought on another debate. Mesrour and the nurse were as unconvinced as their superiors. They too had betted, and each claimed to be the winner. The dispute was extremely warm between the chief eunuch and the nurse, who were proceeding to abuse each other roundly.

"At last the caliph, reflecting upon all that had happened, agreed that the Princess Zobeidè had as much reason as himself to maintain that she was the winner. Mortified at not being able to come at the truth in this matter, he drew near the two dead bodies, and seated himself near their heads, endeavouring to think of some method which should determine the wager in his own favour and against the Princess Zobeidè. 'Yes,' cried he, a moment after, 'I swear by the holy name of Allah that I will give a thousand pieces of my own money to the person who shall ascertain for me which of the two died first.'

"The caliph had scarcely said these last words when he heard a voice from under the brocade which covered Abou Hassan cry out, 'Commander of the Faithful, it was I who died first: give me the thousand pieces of gold.' And at the same time Abou Hassan freed himself from the brocade which covered him, and threw himself at the caliph's feet. His wife rose up in the same manner, and ran to throw herself at the feet of Zobeidè; but out of decency she wrapped herself in the brocade. Princess Zobeidè set up a loud cry, which increased the terror of all those who were present. The princess at last recovered from her fright, and was overjoyed at seeing her dear slave living again, for she had felt inconsolable at having seen her dead. 'Ah, you wicked one!' cried she, 'you have made me suffer much for your sake in more ways than one! I pardon you, however, from the bottom of my heart, since I find that you are not really dead.'

"The caliph on his part had not taken the thing so much to heart. Far from being afraid when he heard Abou Hassan's voice, he was nearly bursting with laughter when he saw the pair of corpses freeing themselves from their coverings, and heard Abou Hassan very seriously demanding the thousand pieces of gold which he had promised to the person who should ascertain which died first. 'So, then, Abou Hassan,' said the caliph, laughing very heartily, 'have you determined to make me die with laughter? How came it into your head thus to surprise both the Princess Zobeidè and I, in a way against which we could not possibly guard?'

"'Commander of the Faithful,' replied Abou Hassan, 'I will tell you the whole truth without disguise. Your majesty very well knows that I always had a love for good living. The wife you gave me has not taught me economy in this point; on the contrary, I have found in her an inclination to encourage this propensity. With such dispositions, your majesty will easily believe that had our purse been as deep as the sea, and had we possessed all the wealth of your majesty, we should soon have found the means of squandering it. Ever since we have been together we have saved nothing, but have lived merely upon your majesty's bounty. This morning, after settling accounts with our cook, we found upon satisfying his demand and paying some other debts that there remained nothing of all the money you had given us. Then reflections on the past and resolutions to do better in future crowded on our minds: we proposed a thousand schemes, each of which we had to abandon. At last, the shame of seeing ourselves reduced to so wretched a situation, and our reluctance to inform your majesty of it, set us upon inventing this plan to supply our wants, by amusing you with a little artifice, which we entreat your majesty will have the goodness to forgive.'

"The caliph and Princess Zobeidè were very well satisfied with the sincerity of Abou Hassan. They did not seem at all angry at what had occurred; on the contrary, the Princess Zobeidè, who had hitherto taken the matter in too serious a light, could not help laughing, in her turn, at the thought of all that Abou Hassan had devised to bring about his design. The caliph, who had scarcely once ceased laughing, so singular did the scheme appear to him, said to Abou Hassan and his wife, as he rose, 'Follow me, both of you: I will give you the thousand pieces of gold that I promised you, for the joy I feel that you are neither of you dead.'

"'Commander of the Faithful,' resumed Princess Zobeidè, 'content yourself, I beseech you, with causing the thousand pieces of gold to be given to Abou Hassan; you owe them only to him: leave me to content his wife.' So saying, she ordered her treasuress, who had come with her, to give a thousand pieces of gold to Nouzhatoul Aouadat also, as a token of the joy she felt to see that her favourite was still alive.

"Abou Hassan and Nouzhatoul Aouadat for a long time preserved the favour of the Caliph Haroun Alraschid and of Princess Zobeidè, and gained enough from their bounty abundantly to supply all their wants for the remainder of their lives."

The Sultana Scheherazade, when she had finished the history of Abou Hassan, promised Schahriar to relate to him on the morrow another story which should amuse him just as much as the adventure of the Sleeper Awakened. Dinarzade did not fail to remind her of her promise before it was daylight, and the sultan having expressed a wish that she should begin, Scheherazade immediately related the following history:—

## THE HISTORY OF ALADDIN, OR THE WONDERFUL LAMP.

IN the capital of one of the richest and most extensive provinces of the great empire of China there lived a tailor whose name was Mustapha. This tailor was very poor. The profits of his trade barely sufficed for the subsistence of himself, his wife, and the one son whom Heaven had sent him.

"This son, whose name was Aladdin, had been brought up in a very negligent and careless manner, and had been so much left to himself that he had contracted many very bad habits. He was obstinate, disobedient, and mischievous, and regarded nothing his father or mother said to him. As a lad he was continually absenting himself from home. He generally went out early in the morning, and spent the whole day in the public streets, playing with other boys of his own age who were as idle as himself.

"When he was old enough to learn a trade, his father, who was too poor to have him taught any other business than his own, took him to his shop, and began to show him how to use his needle. But neither kindness nor the fear of punishment could restrain Aladdin's volatile and restless disposition, nor could his father succeed in making him attend to his work. No sooner was Mustapha's back turned than Aladdin was off, and returned no more during the whole day. His father frequently chastised him, but Aladdin remained incorrigible; and with great sorrow Mustapha was obliged at last to abandon him to his idle vagabond course. This conduct of his son's gave him great pain; and the vexation of not being able to induce young Aladdin to pursue a proper and reputable course of life, brought on a virulent and fatal disease that at the end of a few months put a period to poor Mustapha's existence.

"As Aladdin's mother saw that her son would never follow the trade of his father, she shut up Mustapha's shop, and sold off all his stock and implements of trade. Upon the sum thus realised, added to what she could earn by spinning cotton, she and her son subsisted.

"Aladdin was now no longer restrained by the dread of his father's anger; and so regardless was he of his mother's advice, that he even threatened her whenever she attempted to remonstrate with him. He gave himself completely up to idleness and vagabondism. He continued to associate with boys of his own age, and became fonder than ever of taking part in all their tricks and fun. He pursued this course of life till he was fifteen years old, without showing the least token of good feeling of any sort, and without making the slightest reflection upon what was to be his future lot. Affairs were in this state when, as he was one day playing with his companions, according to his custom, in one of the public places, a stranger who was going by stopped and looked attentively at him.

"This stranger was a magician, so learned and famous for his skill that by way of distinction he was called the *African* Magician. He was, in fact, a native of Africa, and had arrived from that part of the world only two days before.

"Whether this African Magician, who was well skilled in physiognomy, thought he saw in the countenance of Aladdin signs of a disposition well suited to the purpose for which he had undertaken a long journey, or whether he had any other project in view, is uncertain; but he very cleverly obtained information concerning Aladdin's family, discovered who he was, and ascertained the sort of character and disposition he possessed. When he had made himself master of these particulars he went up to the youngster, and, taking him aside from his companions, asked him if his father was not called Mustapha, and whether he was not a tailor by trade. 'Yes, sir,' replied Aladdin; 'but he has been dead a long time.'

"On hearing this, the African Magician threw his arms round Aladdin's neck, and embraced and kissed him repeatedly, while the tears ran from his eyes, and his bosom heaved with sighs. Aladdin, who observed his emotion, asked him what reason he had to weep. 'Alas! my child,' replied the magician, 'how can I refrain? I am your uncle: your father was my most excellent brother. I have been travelling hither for several years; and at the very instant of my arrival in this place, when I was congratulating myself upon the prospect of seeing him and rejoicing his heart by my return, you inform me of his death. How can I be so unfeeling as not to give way to the most violent grief when I thus find myself deprived of all my expected pleasure? However, my affliction is in some degree lessened by the fact that, as far as my recollection carries me, I discover many traces of your father in your countenance; and, on seeing you, I at once suspected who you were.' He then asked Aladdin where his mother lived; and, when Aladdin had informed him, the African Magician put his hand into his purse and gave him a handful of small money, saying to him: 'My son, go to your mother, make my respects to her, and tell her that I will come and see her to-morrow if I have an opportunity, that I may have the consolation of seeing the spot where my good brother lived so many years, and where his career closed at last.'

"As soon as the African Magician, his pretended uncle, had quitted him, Aladdin ran to his mother, highly delighted with the money that had been given him. 'Pray tell me, mother,' he cried as he entered the house, 'whether I have an uncle.' 'No, my child,' replied she, 'you have no uncle, either on your poor father's side or on mine.' 'For all that,' answered the boy, 'I have just seen a man who told me he was my father's brother and my uncle. He even wept and embraced me when I told him of my father's death. And to prove to you that he spoke the truth,' added he, showing her the money which he had received, 'see what he has given me! He bade me also be sure and give his kindest greeting to you, and to say that if he had time he would come and see you himself to-morrow, as he was very desirous of beholding the house where my father lived

THE AFRICAN MAGICIAN EMBRACING ALADDIN.

and died.' 'It is true, indeed, my son,' replied Aladdin's mother, 'that your father had a brother once; but he has been dead a long time, and I never heard your father mention any other.' After this conversation they said no more on the subject.

"The next day the African Magician again accosted Aladdin while he was playing in another part of the city with three other boys. He embraced him as before, and putting two pieces of gold in his hand, said to him: 'Take this, my boy, and carry it to your mother. Tell her that I intend to come and sup with her this evening, and that I send this money that she may purchase what is necessary for our entertainment; but first inform me in what quarter of the city I shall find your house.' Aladdin gave him the necessary information, and the magician took his departure.

"Aladdin carried home the two pieces of gold to his mother; and, when he had told her of his supposed uncle's intention, she went out and purchased a large supply of good provisions. And as she did not possess a sufficient quantity of china or earthenware to hold all her purchases, she went and borrowed what she wanted of her neighbours. She was busily employed during the whole day in preparing supper; and in the evening, when everything was ready, she desired Aladdin to go out into the street, and if he saw his uncle, to show him the way, as the stranger might not be able to find their house.

"Although Aladdin had pointed out to the magician the exact situation of his mother's house, he was nevertheless very ready to go; but, just as he reached the door, he heard some one knock. Aladdin instantly opened the door, and saw the African Magician, who had several bottles of wine and different sorts of fruit in his hands, that they might all regale themselves.

"When the visitor had given to Aladdin all the things he had brought, he paid his respects to the boy's mother, and requested her to show him the place where his brother Mustapha had beeen accustomed to sit upon the sofa. She pointed it out, and he immediately prostrated himself before it and kissed the sofa several times, while the tears seemed to run in abundance from his eyes. 'Alas, my poor brother!' he exclaimed, 'how unfortunate am I not to have arrived in time to embrace you once more before you died!' The mother of Aladdin begged this pretended brother to sit in the place her husband used to occupy; but he would by no means consent to do so. 'No,' he cried, 'I will do no such thing. Give me leave, however, to seat myself opposite, that if I am deprived of the pleasure of seeing him here in person, sitting like the father of his dear family, I may at least look at the spot and try to imagine him present.' Aladdin's mother pressed him no further, but permitted him to take whatever seat he chose.

"When the African Magician had seated himself, he began to enter into conversation with Aladdin's mother. 'Do not be surprised, my good sister,' he said, 'that you have never seen me during the whole time you have been married to my late brother Mustapha, of happy memory. It is full forty years since I left this country, of which, like my brother, I am a native. In the course of this long period I have travelled through India, Persia, Arabia, Syria, and Egypt; and, after passing a considerable time in all the finest and most remarkable cities in those countries, I went into Africa, where I resided for many years. At last, as it is the most natural disposition of man, however distant he may be from the place of his birth, never to forget his native country, nor lose the recollection of his family, his friends, and the companions of his youth, the desire of seeing mine, and of once more embracing my dear brother, took so powerful a hold on my mind, that I felt sufficiently bold and strong once more to undergo the fatigue of this long journey. I therefore set about making the necessary preparations, and began my travels. It is useless to say how long I was thus employed, or to enumerate the various obstacles I had to encounter and all the fatigue I suffered before I came to the end of my labours. But nothing so much mortified me or gave me so much pain in all my travels as the intelligence of the death of my poor brother, whom I tenderly loved, and whose memory I must ever regard with a truly fraternal respect. I have recognised almost every feature of his countenance in the face of my nephew; and it was his likeness to my brother that enabled me to distinguish him from the other boys in whose company he was. He can inform you with what grief I received the melancholy news of my brother's death. We must, however, praise Heaven for all things; and I console myself in finding him alive in his son, who certainly has inherited his most remarkable features.'

"The African Magician, who perceived that Aladdin's mother was very much affected at this conversation about her husband, and that the recollection of him renewed her grief, now changed the subject, and, turning towards Aladdin, asked him his name. 'I am called Aladdin,' he answered. 'And pray, Aladdin,' said the magician, 'what is your occupation? Have you learned any trade?'

"At this speech Aladdin hung his head, and was much disconcerted; but his mother seeing this, answered for him. 'Aladdin,' she said, 'is a very idle boy. His father did all he could to make him learn his business, but could not get him to work; and since my husband's death, in spite of everything I can say, Aladdin will learn nothing, but leads the idle life of a vagabond, though I remonstrate with him on the subject every day of my life. He spends all his time at play with other boys, without considering that he is no longer a child; and if you cannot make him ashamed of himself, and induce him to listen to your advice, I shall utterly despair that he will ever be good for anything. He knows very well that his father left us nothing to live upon; he can see that though I pass the whole day in spinning cotton, I can hardly get bread for us to eat. In short, I am resolved soon to turn him out of doors, and make him seek a livelihood where he can find it.'

"As she spoke these words, the good woman burst into tears. 'This is not right, Aladdin,' said the African Magician. 'Dear nephew, you must think of supporting yourself, and working for your bread. There are many trades you might learn: consider if there be not any one you have an inclination for in preference to the rest. Perhaps the business which your father followed displeases you, and you would rather be brought up to some other calling. Come, come, don't conceal your opinion; give it freely, and I may perhaps assist you.' As he found that Aladdin made him no answer, he went on thus: 'If you have any objection to learning a trade, and yet wish to grow up as a respectable and honest man, I will procure you a shop, and furnish it with rich stuffs and fine linens. You shall sell the goods, and with the profits that you make you shall buy other merchandise; and in this manner you will pass your life very respectably. Consult your own inclinations, and tell me candidly what you think of the plan. You will always find me ready to perform my promise.'

"This offer greatly flattered the vanity of Aladdin; and he was the more averse to any manual industry, because he knew well enough that the shops which contained goods of this sort were much frequented, and the merchants themselves well dressed and highly esteemed. He therefore hinted to the African Magician, whom he considered as his uncle, that he thought very favourably of this plan, and that he should all his life remember the obligation laid upon him. 'Since this employment is agreeable to you,' replied the magician, 'I will take you with me to-morrow, and have you properly and handsomely dressed, as becomes one of the richest merchants of this city; and then we will procure a shop of the description I have named.'

"Aladdin's mother, who till now had not been convinced that the magician was really the brother of her husband, no longer doubted the truth of his statement when she heard all the good he promised to do her son. She thanked him most sincerely for his kind intentions; and charging Aladdin to behave himself so as to prove worthy of the good fortune his uncle had led him to expect, she served up the supper. During the meal the conversation turned on the same subject, and continued till the magician, perceiving that the night was far advanced, took leave of Aladdin and his mother, and retired.

"The African Magician did not fail to return the next morning according to promise to the widow of Mustapha the tailor. He took Aladdin away with him, and brought the lad to a merchant's where ready-made clothes were sold, suited to every description of people, and made of the finest stuffs. He made Aladdin try on such as seemed to fit him, and after choosing those he liked best, and rejecting others that he thought improper for him, he said, 'Dear nephew, choose such as please you best out of this number.' Delighted with the liberality of his new uncle, Aladdin made choice of a garment. The magician bought it, together with everything that was necessary to complete the dress, and paid for the whole without asking the merchant to make any abatement.

"When Aladdin saw himself thus handsomely dressed from head to foot, he overwhelmed his uncle with thanks; the magician on his part again promised never to forsake him, but to continue to aid and protect him. He then conducted Aladdin to the most frequented parts of the city, particularly to the quarter where the shops of the most opulent merchants were situated; and when he had come to the street where fine stuffs and linens were sold in the shops, he said to Aladdin, 'You will soon become a merchant like those who keep these shops. It is proper that you should frequent this place, and become acquainted with them.' After this he took him to the largest and most noted mosques, to the khans where the foreign merchants lived, and through every part of the sultan's palace where he had leave to enter. When they had thus visited all the chief parts of the city, they came to the khan where the magician had hired an apartment. They found several merchants with whom he had made some slight acquaintance since his arrival, and whom he had now invited to partake of a repast, that he might introduce his pretented nephew to them.

"The entertainment was not over till the evening. Aladdin then wished to take leave of his uncle, and go home. The African Magician, however, would not suffer him to go alone. He went himself, and conducted Aladdin back to his mother's. When she saw her son so handsomely dressed, the good woman was transported with joy. She invoked a thousand blessings on the magician, who had been at so great an expense on her dear child's account. 'O generous relation,' she exclaimed, 'I know not how to thank you for your great liberality. My son, I know, is not worthy of such generosity, and he will be wicked indeed if he ever proves ungrateful to you, or fails to behave in such a way as to deserve and be an ornament to the excellent position you are about to place him in. I can only say,' added she, 'I thank you with my whole soul. May you live many happy years, and enjoy the gratitude of my son, who cannot prove his good intentions better than by following your advice.'

"Aladdin,' replied the magician, 'is a good boy. He seems to pay attention to what I say. I have no doubt that we shall make him what we wish. I am sorry for one thing, and that is that I shall not be able to perform all my promises to-morrow. It is Friday, and on that day all the shops are shut. It will be impossible to-morrow either to take a shop or furnish it with goods, because all the merchants are absent and engaged in their several amusements. We will, however, settle all this business the day after to-morrow, and I will come here to-morrow to take Aladdin away with me, and show him the public gardens, in which people of reputation constantly walk and amuse themselves. He has probably hitherto known nothing of the way in which men pass their hours of recreation. He has associated only with boys, but he must now learn to live with men.' The magician then took his leave and departed. Aladdin, who was delighted at seeing himself so well dressed, was still more pleased at the idea of going to the gardens in the suburbs of the city. He had never been beyond the gates, nor had he seen the neighbouring country, which was really very beautiful and attractive.

"The next morning Aladdin got up very early and dressed himself, in order to be ready to set out the very moment his uncle called for him. After waiting some time, which he thought an age, he became so impatient that he opened the door and stood outside to watch for his uncle's arrival. The moment he saw the magician coming, he went to inform his mother of the fact; then he took leave of her, shut the door, and ran to meet his uncle.

"The magician received Aladdin in the most affectionate manner. 'Come, my good boy,' said he, with a smile, 'I will to-day show you some very fine things.' He led the boy out at a gate that led to some large nnd handsome houses, or rather palaces, to each of which there was a beautiful garden, wherein they had the liberty of walking. At each palace they came to he asked Aladdin if it was not very beautiful; but the latter often anticipated this question by exclaiming when a new building came in view, 'O uncle, here is one much more beautiful than any we have yet seen.' In the meantime they were advancing into the country, and the cunning magician, who wanted to go still farther, for the purpose of putting into execution a design which he had in his head, went into one of these gardens, and sat down by the side of a large basin of pure water, which received its supply through the jaws of a bronze lion. He then pretended to be very tired, in order to give Aladdin an opportunity of resting. 'My dear nephew,' he said, 'like myself, you must be fatigued. Let us rest ourselves here a little while, and get fresh strength to pursue our walk.'

"When they had seated themselves, the magician took out from a piece of linen cloth which hung from his girdle various sorts of fruits and some cakes with which he had provided himself. He spread them all out on the bank. He divided a cake between himself and Aladdin, and gave the youth leave to eat whatever fruit he liked best. While they were refreshing themselves he gave his pretended nephew much good advice, desiring him to leave off playing with boys, and to associate with intelligent and prudent

ALADDIN'S MOTHER SURPRISED AT SEEING HER SON SO HANDSOMELY DRESSED.

men, to pay every attention to them, and to profit by their conversation. 'You will very soon be a man yourself,' he said, 'and you cannot too early accustom yourself to the ways and actions of men.' When they had finished their slight repast they rose, and pursued their way by the side of the gardens, which were separated from each other by small ditches, that served to mark the limits of each without preventing communication among them. The honesty and good understanding of the inhabitants of this city made it unnecessary that they should take any other means of guarding against injury from their neighbours. The African Magician insensibly led Aladdin far beyond the last of these gardens; and they walked on through the country till they came into the region of the mountains.

"Aladdin, who had never in his whole life before taken so long a walk, felt very much tired. 'Where are we going, my dear uncle?' said he; 'we have got much farther than the gardens, and I can see nothing but hills and mountains before us. And if we go on any farther I know not whether I shall have strength enough to walk back to the city.' 'Take courage, nephew,' replied his pretended uncle; 'I wish to show you another garden that far surpasses in magnificence all you have hitherto seen. It is not much farther on, and when you get there you will readily own how sorry you would have been to have come thus near it without going on to see it.' Aladdin was persuaded to proceed, and the magician led him on a considerable distance, amusing him all the time with entertaining stories, to beguile the way and make the distance seem less.

"At length they came to a narrow valley, situate between two mountains of nearly the same height. This was the very spot to which the magician wished to bring Aladdin, in order to put in execution the grand project that was the sole cause of his journey to China from the extremity of Africa. Presently he said to Aladdin: 'We need go no farther. I shall here unfold to your view some extraordinary things, hitherto unknown to mortals; when you shall have seen them you will thank me a thousand times for having made you an eye-witness of such marvels. They are indeed such wonders as no one but yourself will ever have seen. I am now going to strike a light; and do you in the meantime collect all the dry sticks and leaves that you can find, in order to make a fire.'

"So many pieces of dried sticks lay scattered about this place that Alladin had collected more than sufficient for his purpose by the time the magician had lighted his match. He then set them on fire; and as soon as they blazed up the African threw upon them a certain perfume, which he had ready in his hand. A thick and dense smoke immediately arose, which seemed to unfold itself at some mysterious words pronounced by the magician, and which Aladdin did not in the least comprehend. A moment afterwards the ground shook slightly, and opening near the spot where they stood, discovered a square stone of about a foot and a half across, placed horizontally, with a brass ring fixed in the centre, by which it could be lifted up.

"Aladdin was dreadfully alarmed at these doings, and was about to run away, when the magician, to whom his presence was absolutely necessary in this mysterious affair, stopped him in an angry manner, at the same moment giving him a violent blow that felled him to the ground and very nearly knocked some of his teeth out, as appeared from the blood that ran from his mouth. Poor Aladdin, with tears in his eyes and trembling in every limb, got up and exclaimed, 'What have I done to deserve so severe a blow?' 'I have my reasons for it,' replied the magician. 'I am your uncle, and consider myself as your father, therefore you should not question my proceedings. Do not, however, my boy,' added he, in a milder tone of voice, 'be at all afraid: I desire nothing of you but that you obey me most implicitly; and this you must do if you wish to render yourself worthy of the great advantages I mean to afford you.' These fine speeches in some measure calmed the frightened Aladdin; and when the magician saw him less alarmed, he said: 'You have observed what I have done by virtue of my perfumes and the words that I pronounced. I must now inform you that under the stone which you see here there is concealed a treasure, which is destined for you, and which will one day render you richer than the most powerful potentates of the earth. It is moreover true that no one in the whole world but you can be permitted to touch or lift up this stone, and go into the region that lies beneath it. Even I myself am not able to approach it and take possession of the treasure which is below it. And, in order to insure your success, you must observe and execute in every respect, even to the minutest point, the instructions I am going to give you. This is a matter of the greatest consequence both to you and myself.'

"Overwhelmed with astonishment at everything he had seen and heard, and full of the idea of this treasure which the magician said was to make him for ever happy, Aladdin forgot everything that had happened. 'Well, my dear uncle,' he exclaimed, as he got up, 'what must I do? Tell me, and I am ready to obey you in everything.' 'I heartily rejoice, my dear boy,' replied the magician, embracing Aladdin, 'that you have made so good a resolution. Come to me, take hold of this ring, and lift up the stone.'

'I am not strong enough, uncle,' said Aladdin; 'you must help me.' 'No, no,' answered the African Magician, 'you have no occasion for my assistance. Neither of us will do any good if I attempt to help you; you must lift up the stone entirely by yourself. Only pronounce the name of your father and your grandfather, take hold of the ring, and lift it; it will come up without any difficulty.' Aladdin did exactly as the magician told him; he raised the stone without any trouble, and laid it aside.

"When the stone was taken away a small excavation was visible, between three and four feet deep, at the bottom of which there appeared a small door, with steps to go down still lower. 'You must now, my good boy,' then said the African Magician to Aladdin, 'observe exactly every direction I am going to give you. Go down into this cavern; and when you have come to the bottom of the steps which you see before you, you will perceive an open door, which leads into a large vaulted space divided into three successive halls. In each of these you will see on both sides of you four bronze vases, as large as tubs, full of gold and silver; but you must take particular care not to touch any of this treasure. When you get into the first hall, take up your robe and bind it closely round you. Then be sure you go on to the second without stopping, and from thence in the same manner to the third. Above everything, be very careful not to go near the walls, or even to touch them with your robe; for if any part of your dress comes in contact with them, your instant death will be the inevitable consequence. This is the reason why I have desired you to fasten your robe firmly round you. At the end of the third hall there is a door which leads to a garden, planted with beautiful trees, all of which are laden with fruit. Go straight forward, and pursue a path which you will perceive, and which will bring you to the foot of a flight of fifty steps, at the top of which there is a terrace. When you have ascended to the terrace, you will observe a niche before you, in which there is a lighted lamp. Take the lamp and extinquish it. Then throw out the wick and the liquid that is in it, and put the lamp in your bosom. When you have done this, bring it to me. Do not be afraid of staining your dress, as the liquid within the lamp is not oil; and when you have thrown it out, the lamp will dry directly. If you should feel desirous of gathering any of the fruit in the garden you may do so; there is nothing to prevent your taking as much as you please.'

"When the magician had given these directions to Aladdin, he took off a ring which he had on one of his fingers, and put it on the hand of his pretended nephew; telling him at the same time that it was a preservative against every evil that might otherwise happen to him. Again he bade him to be mindful of everything he had said to him. 'Go, my child,' added he, 'descend boldly. We shall now both of us become immensely rich for the rest of our lives.'

"Aladdin gave a spring, jumped into the opening with a willing mind, and then went on down the steps. He found the three halls, which exactly answered the description the magician had given of them. He passed through them with the greatest precaution possible, as he was fearful he might perish if he did not most strictly observe all the directions he had received. He went on to the garden, and without stopping ascended to the terrace. He took the lamp which stood lighted in the niche, threw out it contents, and observing that it was, as the magician had said, quite dry, he put it into his bosom. He then came back down the terrace, and stopped in the garden to look at the fruit, which he had only seen for an instant as he passed along. The trees of this garden were all laden with the most extraordinary fruit. Each tree bore large balls, and the fruit of each tree had a separate colour. Some were white, others sparkling and transparent like crystal; some were red and of different shades; others green, blue, or violet; and some of a yellowish hue; in short, there were fruits of almost every colour. The white globes were pearls; the sparkling and transparent fruits were diamonds; the deep red were rubies; the paler a particular sort of ruby called balass; the green emeralds; the blue turquoises; the violet amethysts; those tinged with yellow sapphires; and all the other coloured fruits, varieties of precious stones; and they were all of the largest size, and the most perfect ever seen in the whole world. Aladdin, who knew neither their beauty nor their value, was not at all struck with their appearance, which did not suit his taste, as the figs, grapes, and other excellent fruits common in China would have done. As he was not yet of an age to be acquainted with the value of these stones, he thought they were only pieces of coloured glass, and did not therefore attach any importance to them. Yet the variety and contrast of so many beautiful colours, as well as the brilliancy and extraordinary size of these fruits, tempted him to gather some of each kind; and he took so many of every colour, that he filled both his pockets, as well as the two new purses that the magician had bought for him at the time he made him a present of his new dress, that everything he wore might be equally new; and as his pockets, which were already full, could not hold his two purses, he fastened them one on each side of his girdle or sash. He also wrapped some stones in its folds, as it was of silk and made very full. In this manner he carried them so that they could not fall out. He did not even neglect to fill his bosom quite full, putting many of the largest and handsomest between his robe and shirt.

"Laden in this manner with the most immense treasure, but ignorant of its value, Aladdin made his way hastily through the three halls, that he might not make the African Magician wait too long. Having traversed them with the same caution he had used before, he began to ascend the steps he had come down, and presented himself at the entrance of the cave, where the magician was impatiently waiting for him. As soon as Aladdin perceived him he called out, 'Give me your hand, uncle, to help me up.' 'My dear boy,' replied the magician, 'you will do better first to give me the lamp, as that will only embarrass you.' 'It is not at all in my way,' said Aladdin, 'and I will give it you when I am out of the cave.' The magician still persisted in demanding the lamp before he helped Aladdin out of the cave; but the latter had in fact so covered it with the fruit of the trees, that he could not readily get at it, and absolutely refused to give it up till he had got out of the cave. The African Magician was then in such despair at the obstinate refusal of the boy, that at length he fell into the most violent rage. He threw a little perfume on the fire, which he had taken care to keep up; and he had hardly pronounced two magic words when the stone which served to shut up the entrance to the cavern returned of its own accord to its place, and the earth covered it exactly in the same way as when the magician and Aladdin first arrived there.

"There is no doubt that this African Magician was not the brother of Mustapha the tailor, as he had pretented to be, and consequently not the uncle of Aladdin. He was most probably a native of Africa, as that is a country where magic is more studied than in any other. He had given himself up to it from his earliest youth, and after nearly forty years spent in enchantments, experiments in geomancy, fumigations, and reading books of magic, he had at length discovered that there was in the world a certain wonderful lamp, the possession of which would make him the most powerful monarch of the universe, if he could succeed in laying hands on it. By a late experiment in geomancy he discovered that this lamp was in a subterranean cave in the middle of China, in the very spot that has just been described. Thoroughly convinced of the truth of this discovery, he had come from the farthest part of Africa, and after a long and painful journey had arrived in the city that was nearest the depository of this treasure. But though the lamp was certainly in the place which he had found out, yet he was not permitted to take it away himself, nor to go in person into the cave where it was. It was absolutely necessary that another person should go down to take it, and then put it into his hands. For this reason he had addressed himself to Aladdin, who seemed to him to be an artless youth, well adapted to perform the service he required of him; and he had resolved, as soon as he had got the lamp from the boy, to raise the last fumigation, pronounce the two magic words which produced the effect already seen, and sacrifice poor Aladdin to his avarice and wickedness, that no witness might exist who could say he was in possession of the lamp. The blow he had given Aladdin, as well as the authority he had exercised over him, were only for the purpose of accustoming the youth to fear him, and obey all his orders without hesitation, so that when Aladdin had possession of the wonderful lamp he might instantly deliver it to him. But the event disappointed his hopes and expectations, for he was in such haste to sacrifice poor Aladdin, for fear that

THE MAGICIAN COMMANDING ALADDIN TO GIVE UP THE LAMP.

while he was contesting the matter with him some person might come and make that public which he wished to be kept quite secret, that he completely defeated his own object.

"When the magician found all his hopes and expectations for ever blasted, there remained but one thing that he could do, and that was to return to Africa; and, indeed, he set out on his journey the very same day. He was careful to travel the by-paths, in order to avoid the city where he had met Aladdin. He was also afraid to meet any person who might have seen him walk out with the lad, and come back without him.

"To judge from all these circumstances, it might naturally be supposed that Aladdin was hopelessly lost; and, indeed, the magician himself, who thought he had thus destroyed the boy, had quite forgotten the ring which he had placed on his finger, and which was now to render Aladdin the most essential service, and to save his life. Aladdin knew not the wonderful qualities either of the ring or of the lamp; and it is indeed astonishing that the loss of both these prizes did not drive the magician to absolute despair; but persons of his profession are so accustomed to defeat, and so often see their wishes thwarted, that they never cease from endeavouring to conquer every misfortune by charms, visions, and enchantments.

"Aladdin, who did not expect to be thus wickedly deceived by his pretended uncle, after all the kindness and generosity which the latter had shown to him, was in the highest degree astonished at his position. When he found himself thus buried alive, he called aloud a thousand times to his uncle, telling him he was ready to give up the lamp. But all his cries were useless, and having no other means of making himself heard, he remained in perfect darkness, bemoaning his unhappy fate. His tears being at length exhausted, he went down to the bottom of the flight of stairs, intending to go towards the light in the garden where he had before been. But the walls, which had been opened by enchantment, were now shut by the same means. He groped along the walls to the right and left several times, but could not discover the smallest opening. He then renewed his cries and tears, and sat down upon the steps of his dungeon, without the least hope that he should ever again see the light of day, and with the melancholy conviction that he should only pass from the darkness he was now in to the shades of an inevitable and speedy death.

"Aladdin remained two days in this hopeless state, without either eating or drinking. On the third day, regarding his death as certain, he lifted up his hands, and joining them as in the act of prayer, he wholly resigned himself to the will of Heaven, and uttered in a loud tone of voice: 'There is no strength or power but in the high and great Allah.' In this action of joining his hands he happened, quite unconsciously, to rub the ring which the African Magician had put upon his finger, and of the virtue of which he was as yet ignorant. When the ring was thus rubbed, a genie of enormous stature and a most horrid countenance instantly rose as it were out of the earth before him. This genie was so tall that his head touched the vaulted roof, and he addressed these words to Aladdin: 'What dost thou command? I am ready to obey thee as thy slave—as the slave of him who has the ring on his finger—both I and the other slaves of the ring.'

"At any other moment, and on any other occasion, Aladdin, who was totally unaccustomed to such apparitions, would have been so frightened at the sight of this startling figure that he would have been unable to speak; but he was so entirely taken up with the danger and peril of his situation, that he answered without the least hesitation, 'Whoever you are, take me if you can out of this place.' He had scarcely pronounced these words when the earth opened, and he found himself outside the cave, at the very spot to which the magician had brought him. It will easily be understood that, after having remained in complete darkness for so long a time, Aladdin had at first some difficulty in supporting the brightness of open day. By degrees, however, his eyes became accustomed to the light; and on looking round him he was surprised to find not the smallest opening in the earth. He could not comprehend in what manner he had so suddenly emerged from it. But he could recognise the place where the fire had been made, which he recollected was close to the entrance into the cave. Looking round towards the city, he descried it in the distance, surrounded by the gardens, and thus he knew the road he had come with the magician. He returned the same way, thanking Heaven for having again suffered him to behold and revisit the face of the earth, which he had quite despaired of ever seeing more. He arrived at the city, but it was only with great difficulty that he got home. When he was within the door, the joy he experienced at again seeing his mother, added to the weak state he was in from not having eaten anything for the space of three days, made him faint, and it was some time before he came to himself. His mother, who had already mourned for him as lost or dead, seeing him in this state, used every possible effort to restore him to life. At length he recovered, and the first thing he said to his mother was, 'O my dear mother, bring me something to eat before you do anything else. I have tasted nothing these three days.' His mother instantly set what she had before him. 'My dear child,' said she as she did so, 'do not hurry yourself, for that is dangerous. Eat but little, and that slowly; and you must take great care what you do in your exhausted state. Do not even speak to me. When you have regained your strength you will have plenty of time to relate to me everything that has happened to you. I am full of joy at seeing you once more, after all the grief I have suffered since Friday, and all the trouble I have also taken to learn what was become of you, when I found that night came on and you did not return home.'

"Aladdin followed his mother's advice. He ate slowly and sparingly, and drank with equal moderation. When he had done he said: 'I have great reason, my dear mother, to complain of you for putting me in the power of a man whose object was to destroy me, and who at this very moment supposes my death so certain that he cannot doubt either that I am no longer alive, or at least that I shall not survive another day. But you took him to be my uncle, and I was also equally deceived. Indeed, how could we suspect him of any treachery, when he almost overwhelmed me with his kindness and generosity, and made me so many promises of future advantage? But I must tell you, mother, that he was a traitor, a wicked man, a cheat. He was so good and kind to me only that, after answering his own purpose, he might destroy me, as I have already told you, and neither you nor I would ever have been able to know the reason. For my part, I can assure you I have not given him the least cause for the bad treatment I have received; and you will yourself be convinced of this from the faithful and true account I am going to give you of everything that has happened from the moment when I left you till he put his wicked design in execution.'

'Aladdin then related to his mother all that had happened to him and the magician on the day when the latter came and took him away to see the palaces and gardens round the city. He told of what had befallen him on the road and at the place between the two mountains, where the magician worked such wonders; how, by throwing the perfume into the fire and pronouncing some magical words, he had caused the earth instantly to open, and discovered the entrance into a cave that contained inestimable treasures. He did not forget to mention the blow that the magician had given him, and the manner in which this man, after having first coaxed him, had persuaded him by means of the greatest promises, and by putting a ring upon his finger, to descend into the cave. He omitted no circumstance that had happened, and told all he had seen in going backwards and forwards through the three halls, in the garden, or on the terrace whence he had taken the wonderful lamp. He took the lamp itself out of his bosom and showed it to his mother, as well as the transparent and different coloured fruits that he had gathered as he returned through the garden. He gave the two purses that contained these fruits to his mother, who did not set much value upon them. The fruits were, in fact, precious stones; and the lustre which they threw around them by means of a lamp that hung in the chamber, and which almost equalled the radiance of the sun, ought to have shown her they were of the greatest value; but the mother of Aladdin knew no more of their value than her son. She had been brought up in comparative poverty, and her husband had never been rich enough to bestow any jewels upon her. Besides, she had never even seen any such treasures among her relations or neighbours; and therefore it was not at all surprising that she considerd them as things of no value—mere playthings to please the eye by the variety of their colours. Aladdin therefore put them all behind one of the cushions of the sofa on which they were sitting.

"He finished the recital of his adventures by telling his mother how, when he came back and presented himself at the mouth of the cave and refused to give the lamp to the magician, the entrance of the cave was instantly closed by means of the perfume that the magician threw on the fire and by some words that he pronounced. He could not refrain from tears when he represented the miserable state he found himself in, as it were buried alive in that fatal cave, till the moment he obtained his freedom and emerged into the upper air by means of the ring, of which he did not even now know the virtues. When he had finished his story, he said to his mother: 'I need not tell you more, for you know the rest. This is a true account of my adventures and of the dangers I have been in since I left you.'

"Wonderful and amazing as this relation was, distressing too as it must have been for a mother who tenderly loved her son in spite of his defects, the widow had the patience to hear it to the end without once interrupting him. At the most affecting parts, however, particularly those that revealed the wicked intentions of the African Magician, she could not help showing by her gestures how much she detested him, and how much he excited her indignation. But Aladdin had no sooner concluded than she began to abuse the pretended uncle in the strongest terms. She called him a traitor, a barbarian, a cheat, an assassin, a magician, the enemy and destroyer of the human race. 'Yes, my child,' she cried, 'he is a magician; and magicians are public evils! They hold communication with demons by means of their sorceries and enchantments. Blessed be Heaven that has not suffered the wickedness of this wretch to have its full effect upon you! You, too, ought to return thanks for your deliverance. Your death would have been inevitable if Heaven had not come to your assistance, and if you had not implored its aid.' She added many more words of the same sort, showing also her complete detestation of the treachery with which the magician had treated her son; but as she was exclaiming in this manner, she perceived that Aladdin, who had not slept for three days, wanted rest. She made him, therefore, retire to bed, and soon afterwards went herself.

"As Aladdin had not been able to take any repose in the subterraneous place in which he had been as it were buried with the prospect of certain destruction, it is no wonder that he passed the whole of that night in the most profound sleep, and that it was even late the next morning before he awoke. He at last rose, and the first thing he said to his mother was, that he was very hungry, and that she could not oblige him more than by giving him something for breakfast. 'Alas! my child,' replied his mother, 'I have not a morsel of bread to give you. Last night you finished all the trifling store of food there was in the house. But have a little patience, and it shall not be long before I will bring you some. I have here a little cotton I have spun; I will go and sell it, and purchase something for our dinner.' 'Keep your cotton, mother,' said Aladdin, 'for another time, and give me the lamp which I brought with me yesterday. I will go and sell that; and the money it will bring will serve us for breakfast and dinner too—nay, perhaps also for supper.'

"Aladdin's mother took the lamp from the place where she had deposited it. 'Here it is,' she said to her son; 'but it seems to me to be very dirty. If I were to clean it a little perhaps it might sell for something more.' She then took some water and a little fine sand to clean the lamp, but she had scarcely begun to rub it, when instantly, and in the presence of her son, a hideous and gigantic genie rose out of the ground before her, and cried with a voice as loud as thunder: 'What are thy commands? I am ready to obey thee as thy slave, and the slave of those who have the lamp in their hands; both I and the other slaves of the lamp!' The mother of Aladdin was too much startled to answer this address. She was unable to endure the sight of an apparition so hideous and alarming; and her fears were so great, that as soon as the genie began to speak she fell down in a fainting-fit.

"Aladdin had once before seen a similar appearance in the cavern. He did not lose either his presence of mind or his judgment; but he instantly seized the lamp, and supplied his mother's place, by answering for her in a firm tone of voice: 'I am hungry: bring me something to eat.' The genie disappeared, and returned a moment after with a large silver basin, which he carried on his head, and twelve covered dishes of the same material filled with the choicest meats properly arranged, and six loaves as white as snow upon as many plates. He carried two bottles of the most excellent wine and two silver cups in his hands. He placed all these things upon the sofa, and instantly vanished.

"All this had occurred in so short a time, that Aladdin's mother had not recovered from her fainting-fit before the genie had disappeared the second time. Aladdin, who had before thrown some water over her without any effect, was about to renew his endeavours, but at the very instant, whether her fluttered spirits returned of themselves, or that the smell of the dishes which the genie had brought had a reanimating effect, she quite recovered. 'My dear mother,' cried Aladdin, 'there is nothing the matter. Come and eat; here is something that will put you in good spirits again, and at the same time satisfy my hunger. Come, do not let us suffer these good things to get cold before we begin.'

"AH, MY SON, TAKE THE LAMP OUT OF MY SIGHT!"

"His mother was extremely astonished when she beheld the large basin, the twelve dishes, the six loaves, the two bottles of wine and two cups, and perceived the delicious odour that exhaled from them. 'O my child!' she cried, 'how came all this abundance here? And whom have we to thank for such liberality? The sultan surely cannot have been made acquainted with our poverty, and have had compassion upon us?' 'My good mother,' replied Aladdin, 'come and sit down, and begin to eat; you are as much in want of food as I am. I will tell you everything when we have broken our fast.' They then sat down, and both of them ate with the greater appetite, as neither mother nor son had ever seen a table so well supplied.

"During the repast the mother of Aladdin could not help stopping frequently to look at and admire the basin and dishes, although she was not quite sure whether they were silver or any other metal, so little was she accustomed to things of this sort. In fact, she did not regard their value, of which she was ignorant; it was only the novelty of their appearance that attracted her admiration. Nor, indeed, was her son better informed on the subject than herself. Although they both merely intended to make a simple breakfast, yet they sat so long that the dinner-hour came before they had risen. The dishes were so excellent they almost increased their appetites; and, as the viands were still hot, they thought it no bad plan to join the two meals together; and therefore they dined before they got up from breakfast. When they had made an end of their double repast, they found that enough remained, not only for supper, but even for two meals the next day as plentiful as those they had just made.

"When Aladdin's mother had taken away the things, and put aside what they had not consumed, she came and seated herself on the sofa near her son. 'I now expect, my dear son,' she said, 'that you will satisfy my impatient curiosity, and let me hear the account you have promised me.' Aladdin then related to his mother everything that had passed between him and the genie from the time when she fainted with fear till she again came to herself. At this discourse of her son, and his account of the appearance of the genie, Aladdin's mother was in the greatest astonishment. 'What is this you tell me, child, about your genie?' she exclaimed. 'Never since I was born have I heard of any person of my acquaintance who has seen one. How comes it, then, that this villanous genie should have accosted me? Why did he not rather address himself to you, to whom he had before appeared in the subterraneous cavern?'

"'Mother,' replied Aladdin, 'the genie who appeared just now to you is not the same who appeared to me. In some things, indeed, they resemble each other, being both as large as giants; but they are very different both in their countenance and dress, and they belong to different masters. If you recollect, he whom I saw called himself the slave of the ring which I had on my finger; and the genie who appeared to you was the slave of the lamp you had in your hand; but I believe you did not hear him, as you seemed to faint the instant he began to speak.' 'What!' cried his mother, 'was your lamp the reason why this cursed genie addressed himself to me rather than to you? Ah, my son, take the lamp out of my sight, and put it were you please, so that I never touch it again. Indeed, I would rather that you should throw it away or sell it than run the risk of being killed with fright by again touching it. And if you will follow my advice, you will put away the ring as well. We ought to have no commerce with genii; they are demons, and our Prophet has told us to beware of them.'

"'With your permission, however, my dear mother,' replied Aladdin, 'I shall beware of parting with this lamp, which has already been so useful to us both. I have, indeed, once been very near selling it. Do you not see what it has procured us, and that it will also continue to furnish us with enough for our support? You may easily judge, as I do, that it was not for nothing my wicked pretended uncle gave himself so much trouble and undertook so long and fatiguing a journey. He did all this merely to get possession of this wonderful lamp, which he preferred to all the gold and silver which he knew was in the three halls, and which I myself saw, as he had before told me I should. He knew too well the worth and qualities of this lamp to wish for anything else from that immense treasure. And since chance has discovered its virtues to us, let us avail ourselves of them; but we must be careful not to make any parade, lest we draw upon ourselves the envy and jealousy of our neighbours. I will take the lamp out of your sight, and put it where I shall be able to find it whenever I have occasion for it, since you are so much alarmed at the appearance of genii. Again, I cannot make up my mind to throw the ring away. But for this ring you would never have seen me again; and even if I had been alive now, I should have had but a short time to live. You must permit me, therefore, to keep and to wear it always very carefully on my finger. Who can tell if some danger may not again happen to me which neither you nor I can now foresee, and from which the ring may deliver me?' As the arguments of Aladdin appeared very just and reasonable, his mother had no further objections to make. 'Do as you like, my son,' she cried. 'As for me, I wish to have nothing at all to do with genii; and I declare to you that I entirely wash my hands of them, and will never even speak of them again.'

"At supper the next evening, the remainder of the provisions the genie had brought was consumed. The following morning, Aladdin, who did not like to wait till hunger pressed him, took one of the silver plates under his robe, and went out early in order to sell it. He addressed himself to a Jew whom he happened to meet. Aladdin took him aside, and showing him the plate, asked if he would buy it.

"The Jew, a clever and cunning man, took the plate and examined it. Directly he had satisfied himself that it was good silver, he desired to know how much the seller expected for it. Aladdin, who knew not its value, and who had never had any dealings of the sort before, merely said that he supposed the Jew knew what the plate was worth, and that he would depend upon the purchaser's honour. Uncertain whether Aladdin was acquainted with its real value or not, the Jew took out of his purse a piece of gold, which was exactly one seventy-second part of the value of the plate, and offered it to Aladdin. The latter eagerly took the money, and without staying to say anything more, went away so quickly that the Jew, not satisfied with the exorbitant profit he had made by his bargain, was very sorry he had not foreseen Aladdin's ignorance of the value of the plate, and in consequence offered him much less for it. He was almost ready to run after the young man to get something back from him out of the piece of gold he had given him. But Aladdin himself ran very fast, and was already so far away that the Jew would have found it impossible to overtake him.

"On his way home, Aladdin stopped at a baker's shop, where he bought enough bread for his mother and himself, paying for his purchase out of his piece of gold, and receiving the change. When he came home he gave the rest of the money to his mother, who went to the market and purchased as much provision as would last them for several days.

"They thus continued to live quietly and economically till Aladdin had sold all the twelve dishes, one after the other, to the same Jew, exactly as he had sold the first; and then they found they wanted more money. The Jew, who had given Aladdin a piece of gold for the first, dared not offer him less for the other dishes, for fear he might lose so good a customer; he therefore bought them all at the same rate. When the money for the last plate was expended, Aladdin had recourse to the basin, which was at least ten times as heavy as any of the plates. He wished to carry this to his merchant, but its great weight prevented him; he was obliged, therefore, to seek out the Jew, and bring him to his mother's. After ascertaining the weight of the basin, the Jew counted out ten pieces of gold, with which Aladdin was satisfied.

"While these ten pieces lasted they were devoted to the daily expenses of the house. In the meantime Aladdin, though accustomed to lead an idle life, abstained from going to play with other boys of his own age from the time of his adventure with the African Magician. He now spent his days in walking about, or conversing with men whose acquaintance he made. Sometimes he stopped in the shops belonging to wealthy merchants, where he listened to the conversation of the people of distinction and education who came there, and who made these shops a sort of meeting-place. The information he thus obtained gave him a slight knowledge of the world.

"When his ten pieces of gold were spent Aladdin had recourse to the lamp. He took it up and looked for the particular spot that his mother had rubbed. As he easily perceived the place where the sand had touched the lamp, he applied his hand to the same spot, and the genie whom he had before seen instantly appeared. But as Aladdin had rubbed the lamp more gently than his mother had done, the genie spoke to him also in a softened tone. 'What are thy commands,' said he, in the same words as before; 'I am ready to obey thee as thy slave, and the slave of those who have the lamp in their hands, both I, and the other slaves of the lamp.' 'I am hungry,' cried Aladdin: 'bring me something to eat.' The genie disappeared, and in a short time returned, loaded with a service similar to that which he had brought before. He placed it upon the sofa, and vanished in an instant.

"As Aladdin's mother was aware of the intention of her son when he took the lamp, she had gone out on some business, that she might not even be in the house when the genie should make his appearance. She soon afterwards came in, and saw the table and sideboard handsomely furnished; nor was she less surprised at the effect of the lamp this time than she had been before. Aladdin and his mother immediately took their seats at the table, and after they had finished their repast there still remained sufficient food to last them two whole days.

"When Aladdin again found that all his provisions were gone, and he had no money to purchase any, he took one of the silver dishes, and went to look for the Jew who had bought the former dishes of him, intending to deal with him again. As he walked along he happened to pass the shop of a goldsmith, a respectable old man, whose probity and general honesty were unimpeachable. The goldsmith, who perceived him, called to him to come into the shop. 'My son,' said he, 'I have often seen you pass this way, loaded as you are now, and each time you have spoken to a certain Jew; and then I have seen you come back again empty-handed. It has struck me that you went and sold him what you carried. But perhaps you do not know that this Jew is a very great cheat; nay, that he will even deceive his own brethren, and that no one who knows him will have any dealings with him? Now, I have merely a proposition to make to you, and then you can act exactly as you like in the matter. If you will show me what you are now carrying, and if you are going to sell it, I will faithfully give you what it is worth, if it be anything in my way of business; if not, I will introduce you to other merchants who will deal honestly with you.'

"The hope of getting a better price for his silver plate induced Aladdin to take it out from under his robe, and show it to the goldsmith. The old man, who knew at first sight that the plate was of the finest silver, asked him if he had sold any like this to the Jew, and if so, how much he had received for them. Aladdin plainly told him that he had sold twelve, and that the Jew had given him a piece of gold for each. 'Out upon the thief!' cried the merchant. 'However, my son, what is done cannot be undone, and let us think of it no more; but I will let you see what your dish, which is made of the finest silver we ever use in our shops, is really worth, and then you will understand to what extent the Jew has cheated you.'

"The goldsmith took his scales, weighed the dish, and after explaining to Aladdin how much a mark of silver was, what it was worth, and how it was divided, he made him observe that, valued according to weight, the plate was worth seventy-two pieces of gold, which he immediately counted out to him. 'This,' said he, 'is the exact value of your plate; if you doubt what I say, you may go to any of our goldsmiths, and if you find that he will give you more for it, I promise to forfeit double the sum. We make our profit by the fashion or workmanship of the goods we buy in this manner; and with this even the most equitable Jews are not content.' Aladdin thanked the goldsmith for the good and profitable advice he had given him; and for the future he carried his dishes to no one else. He took the basin also to this goldsmith's shop, and received the value according to its weight.

"Although Aladdin and his mother had an inexhaustible source of money in their lamp, and could procure what they wished whenever they wanted anything, they continued to live with the same frugality they had always shown, except that Aladdin devoted a small sum to innocent amusements, and to procuring some things that were necessary in the house. His mother provided her own dress, paying for it with the price of the cotton she spun. As they lived thus quietly, it is easy to conjecture how long the money arising from the sale of the twelve dishes and the basin must have lasted them. Thus mother and son lived very happily together for many years, with the profitable assistance which Aladdin occasionally procured from the lamp.

"During this interval Aladdin resorted frequently to those places where persons of distinction were to be met with. He visited the shops of the most considerable merchants in gold and silver stuffs, in silks, fine linens, and jewellery; and, by sometimes taking part in their conversation, he insensibly acquired the style and manners of good company.

ALADDIN SEES THE PRINCESS BADROULBOUDOUR ON HER WAY TO THE BATH.

By frequenting the jewellers' shops he learned how erroneous was the idea he had formed that the transparent fruits he had gathered in the garden whence he took the lamp were only coloured glass: he now knew their value, for he was convinced that they were jewels of inestimable price. He had acquired this knowledge by observing all kinds of precious stones that were bought and sold in the shops; and as he did not see any stones that could be compared with those he possessed, either in brilliancy or in size, he concluded that, instead of being the possessor of some bits of common glass which he had considered as trifles of little worth, he had really procured a most invaluable treasure. He had, however, the prudence not to mention this discovery to any one, not even to his mother; and doubtless it was in consequence of his silence that he afterwards rose to the great good fortune to which we shall in the end see him elevated.

"One day as he was walking abroad in the city, Aladdin heard the criers reading a proclamation of the sultan, ordering all persons to shut up their shops, and retire into their houses, until the Princess Badroulboudour,* the daughter of the sultan, had passed by on her way to the bath, and had returned to the palace.

"The casual hearing of this order created in Aladdin a curiosity to see the princess unveiled; but this he could only accomplish by going to some house whose inmates he knew, and by looking through the lattices. This plan, however, by no means satisfied him, because the princess usually wore a veil as she went to the bath. He thought at last of a scheme, which, on being tried, proved completely successful. He went and hid himself behind the door of the bath, which was so constructed that he could not fail to see the face of every one who passed through it.

"Aladdin had not waited long in his place of concealment before the princess made her appearance; and he saw her perfectly well through a crevice, without being himself seen. The princess was accompanied by a great crowd of women and eunuchs, who walked on either side of her, while others followed her. When she had come within three or four paces of the door of the bath, she lifted up the veil which not only concealed her face but encumbered her movements, and thus gave Aladdin an opportunity of seeing her quite at his ease as she approached the door.

"Till this moment Aladdin had never seen any woman without her veil, except his mother, who was rather old, and who, even in her youth, had not possessed any beauty. He was therefore incapable of forming any judgment respecting the attractions of women. He had indeed heard that there were some ladies who were surprisingly beautiful, but the mere description of beauty in words never makes the same impression which the sight of beauty itself affords.

"The appearance of the Princess Badroulboudour dispelled the notion Aladdin had entertained that all women resembled his mother. His opinions underwent an entire change, and his heart could not help surrendering itself to the object whose appearance had captivated him. The princess was, in fact, the most beautiful brunette ever seen. Her eyes were large, well shaped, and full of fire; yet the expression of her countenance was sweet and modest. Her nose was pretty and properly proportioned; her mouth small; her lips were like vermillion, and beautifully formed; in short, every feature of her face was perfectly lovely and regular. It is, therefore, by no means wonderful that Aladdin was dazzled and almost bereft of his senses at beholding a combination of charms to which he had hitherto been a stranger. Besides all these perfections, this princess had an elegant figure and a most majestic air, and her appearance at once enforced the respect that was due to her rank.

"Long after she had passed him and entered the bath, Aladdin stood still like a man entranced, retracing and impressing more strongly on his own mind the image by which he had been charmed, and which had penetrated to the very bottom of his heart. At last he came to himself; and recollecting that the princess was gone, and that it would be perfectly useless for him to linger in the hope of seeing her come out, as her back would then be towards him and she would also be veiled, he determined to quit his post and retire.

"When he came home Aladdin was unable to conceal his disquietude and distress from the observation of his mother. She was very much surprised to see him appear so melancholy, and to notice the embarrassment of his manner. She asked him if anything had happened to him, or if he were unwell. He gave her no answer whatever, but

* The name *Badroulboudour* signifies "The Full Moon among full moons."

continued sitting on the sofa with an air of abstraction for a long time, entirely taken up in retracing in his imagination the lovely image of the Princess Badroulboudour. His mother, who was employed in preparing supper, forbore to trouble him. As soon as the meal was ready she served it up close to him on the sofa, and sat down to table. But as she perceived that Aladdin paid no attention to what went on around him, she invited him to eat; but it was only with great difficulty she could get him to change his position. He at length began to eat, but in a much more sparing manner than usual. He sat with his eyes cast down, and kept such a profound silence that his mother could not get a single word from him in answer to all the questions she put to him in her anxiety to learn the cause of so extraordinary a change.

"After supper she wished to renew the subject, and inquire the cause of Aladdin's great melancholy; but she could not get him to give her an answer, and he determined to go to bed to escape the questions with which she plied him.

"Aladdin passed a wakeful night, occupied by thoughts of the beauty and charms of the Princess Badroulboudour; but the next morning, as he was sitting upon the sofa opposite his mother, who was spinning her cotton as usual, he addressed her in the following words: 'O my mother, I will now break the long silence I have kept since my return from the city yesterday morning, for I think, nay, indeed, I have perceived, that it has pained you. I was not ill, as you seemed to think, nor is anything the matter with me now; yet I can assure you that the pain I at this moment feel, and which I shall ever continue to feel, is much worse than any disease. I am myself ignorant of the nature of my feelings, but I have no doubt that when I have explained myself you will understand them.

"'It was not proclaimed in this quarter of the city,' continued Aladdin, 'and therefore you of course have not heard that the Princess Badroulboudour, the daughter of our sultan, went to the bath after dinner yesterday: I learnt this intelligence during my morning walk in the city. An order was consequently published that all the shops should be shut up, and every one should keep at home, that the honour and respect which is due to the princess might be paid to her, and that the streets through which she had to pass might be quite clear. As I was not far from the bath at the time, the desire I felt to see the face of the princess made me take it into my head to place myself behind the door of the bath, supposing, as indeed it happened, that she might take off her veil just before she went into the building. You recollect the situation of that door, and can therefore very well imagine that I could easily obtain a full sight of her, if what I conjectured should actually take place. She did take off her veil as she passed in, and I had the supreme happiness and satisfaction of seeing this beautiful princess. This, my dear mother, is the true cause of the state you saw me in yesterday, and the reason of the silence I have hitherto kept. I feel such a violent affection for this princess, that I know no terms strong enough to express it; and as my ardent love for her increases every instant, I am convinced it can only be satisfied by the possession of the amiable Princess Badroulboudour, whom I have resolved to ask in marriage of the sultan.'

"Aladdin's mother listened with great attention to this speech of her son's till he came to the last sentence; but when she heard that it was his intention to demand the Princess Badroulboudour in marriage, she could not help bursting out into a violent fit of laughter. Aladdin wished to speak again, but she prevented him. 'Alas! my son, she cried, 'what are you thinking of? You must surely have lost your senses to talk thus.' 'Dear mother,' replied Aladdin, 'I do assure you I have not lost my senses—I am in my right mind. I foresaw very well that you would reproach me with folly and madness, even more than you have done; but whatever you may say, nothing will prevent me from again declaring to you that my resolution to demand the Princess Badroulboudour of the sultan, her father, in marriage, is absolutely fixed and unchangeable.'

"'In truth, my son,' replied his mother, very seriously, 'I cannot help telling you that you seem entirely to have forgotten who you are; and even if you are determined to put this resolution in practice, I do not know who will have the audacity to carry your message to the sultan.' 'You yourself must do that,' answered he instantly, without the least hesitation. 'I!' cried his mother, with the strongest marks of surprise, 'I go to the sultan!—not I indeed. Nothing shall induce me to engage in such an enterprise. And pray, my son, whom do you suppose you are,' she continued, 'that you have the impudence to aspire to the daughter of the sultan? Have you forgotten that you are the son of one of the poorest tailors in this city, and that your mother's family cannot boast of any higher origin? Do you not know that sultans do not deign to bestow their daughters even upon the sons of other sultans, unless the suitors have some chance of succeeding to the throne?'

"'My dear mother,' replied Aladdin, 'I have already told you that I perfectly foresaw all the objections you have made, and am aware of everything that you can add more; but neither your reasons nor remonstrances will in the least change my resolution. I have told you that I would demand the Princess Badroulboudour in marriage, and that you must impart my wish to the sultan. It is a favour which I entreat at your hands with all the respect I owe to you, and I beg you not to refuse me, unless you would see me die, whereas by granting it you will give me life, as it were, a second time.'

"Aladdin's mother was very much embarrassed when she saw with what obstinacy her son persisted in his mad design. 'My dear son,' she said, 'I am your mother, and like a good mother who has brought you into the world, I am ready to do anything that is reasonable and suited to your situation in life and my own, and to undertake anything for your sake. If this business were merely to ask in marriage the daughter of any of our neighbours whose condition was similar to yours, I would not object, but would willingly employ all my abilities in your cause. But to hope for success, even with the daughter of one of our neighbours, you ought to possess some little fortune, or at least to be master of some business. When poor people like us wish to marry, the first thing we ought to think about is how to make a livelihood. But you, regardless of the lowness of your birth, and of your want of merit or fortune, at once aspire to the highest prize, and pretend to nothing less than to ask in marriage the daughter of your sovereign, who has but to open his lips to blast all your designs and destroy you at once.

"'I will not,' continued Aladdin's mother, 'speak of the probable consequences of this business to you: you ought to reflect upon them if you have any reason left; but I will only consider my own position. How such an extraordinary design as that of wishing me to go and propose to the sultan that he would bestow the princess his daughter upon you came into your head I cannot think. Now, suppose that I have—I will not say the courage, but—the impudence to present myself before his majesty, and make such a mad request of him, to whom should I in the first place address myself to obtain admission to his presence? Do you not see that the very first person I spoke to would treat me as a madwoman, and drive me back with all the indignity and contempt I should so justly merit? But even if I overcame this difficulty, and procured an audience of the sultan—as, indeed, I know he readily grants a hearing to all his subjects when they demand it of him for the purpose of obtaining justice; and that he even grants it with pleasure when a subject who is worthy of it would ask a favour of him—what should I do then? Are you in a position to bring forward your request? Do you think that you deserve the favour which you wish me to ask for you? Are you worthy of it? What have you done for your monarch or for your country? How have you ever distinguished yourself? If, then, you have done nothing to deserve so great a favour, and if moreover you are not worthy of it, with what face can I come forward to make the demand? How can I even open my lips to propose such a thing to the sultan? His illustrious presence and the magnificence of his whole court will instantly strike me dumb with shame. How shall I, who used to tremble before your poor father, my husband, whenever I wished to ask him any favour, even attempt such a thing? But there is another reason, my son, which you have not yet thought of; and that is, that no one ever appears before the sultan without offering him some present when a favour is sought at his hands. Presents have at least this advantage, that if, for any reason of his own, the monarch refuses your request, he will listen patiently to what you have to say.

But what present have you to offer him? And when can you ever have anything that may be at all worthy the acceptance of so mighty a monarch? What proportion can your present possibly have to the request you wish to make? Be reasonable, and reflect that you aspire to a thing it is impossible to obtain.'

"Aladdin listened with the greatest patience to all these representations by which his mother sought to dissuade him from his purpose; and after he had reflected for some time upon every part of her remonstrance, he addressed her in these words: 'I readily acknowledge to you, my dear mother, that it is a great piece of rashness in me to dare to aspire so high as I do; and that it is also very inconsiderate in me to request you with so much earnestness and warmth to go and propose this marriage to the sultan, without having first taken the proper means of procuring an audience and a favourable reception.

ALADDIN WATCHING HIS MOTHER DEPART FOR THE PALACE.

I freely ask your pardon for my folly; but you must not wonder if the violence of the passion that possesses me has prevented me from thinking of the many difficulties in the way of my enterprise. I love the Princess Badroulboudour far beyond anything you can possibly conceive; or rather, I adore her, and shall for ever persevere in my wish and intention of marrying her. This is a design on which my mind is irrevocably bent. I thank you sincerely for the hints you have given me in what you have said, and I look upon this beginning as the first step towards the complete success I hope to obtain.

"'You say that it is not customary to request an audience of the sultan without carrying a present in your hand, and tell me that I have nothing worthy of offering him. I agree with you about the present, and indeed I never once thought of it. But when you tell me I have nothing worthy of his acceptance, I must say you are wrong. Do you not suppose, mother, that the coloured fruits I brought home with me, on the day when I was saved in so wonderful a manner from an almost inevitable death, would be an acceptable present to the sultan? I mean those things I brought home in the two purses and in my sash, and which we thought were pieces of coloured glass. I know their value better now, and can inform you that they are precious stones of inestimable worth, and worthy the acceptance of a great sovereign. I became acquainted with the value of these stones by frequenting the shops of jewellers; and you may, I assure you, take my word for the truth of what I say. All the gems which I have seen at our jewellers' are not to be compared with those we have either for size or beauty, and yet they are very highly valued. In fact, we have both of us been ignorant of the worth of ours; but, as far as I can judge from the little experience I have, I feel assured the present cannot but be very agreeable to the sultan. You have a porcelain dish of a very good shape and size for holding them. Bring it to me, and let us see how the stones will look when we have arranged them according to their different colours.'

"Aladdin's mother brought the dish, and he took the precious stones out of the two purses and arranged them upon it. The effect they produced in broad daylight, by the variety of their colours, their lustre, and brilliancy, was so great that both mother and son were absolutely dazzled and astonished; for till then they had only seen them by the light of a lamp. Aladdin had certainly seen them on the trees, hanging like fruit and sparkling with great brilliancy; but as he was then little more than a child, he had looked upon these jewels only as playthings, and had never thought of their value.

"When they had for some time admired the beauty of the present, Aladdin resumed the conversation in these words: 'You cannot now excuse yourself any longer from going and presenting yourself to the sultan upon the plea that you have nothing to offer him. Here is a present which, in my opinion, will procure for you a most favourable reception.'

"Notwithstanding its great beauty and brilliancy, Aladdin's mother had no high opinion of the value of her son's present; still she supposed it would be very acceptable. She was, therefore, aware that she could make no further objection on this score. She again recurred to the nature of the request which Aladdin wished her to make to the sultan. This was a constant source of disquietude to her. 'I cannot, my son,' she said, 'possibly believe that this present will produce the effect you wish, and that the sultan will look upon you with a favourable eye. Then, if you choose me for your messenger, it becomes necessary for me to acquit myself with propriety in the business you wish me to undertake. I am convinced that I shall not have courage enough to speak. I shall be struck quite dumb, and thus not only lose all my labour, but the present also, which, according to what you say, is exceedingly rich and valuable; and after all I shall have to come back and inform you of the destruction of all your hopes and expectations. I have told you what I know will happen, and you ought to listen to me. But,' she added, 'if I should act in opposition to my own opinion, and submit to your wishes, and have sufficient courage to make the request you desire, be assured that the sultan will either ridicule me and send me away as a madwoman, or he will be in such a passion, and justly too, that both you and I will most infallibly become the victims of his wrath.'

"Aladdin's mother continued to urge upon her son many other reasons which should have made him change his mind; but the charms of the Princess Badroulboudour had made too strong an impression upon the heart of Aladdin to suffer him to alter his intentions. He persisted in requiring his mother to perform her part in his scheme; and the affection she had for him, added to her dread lest he should give himself up to some paroxysm of despair, at length conquered her repugnance, and she promised to do as he bade her.

"As it was now very late, and the time for going to the palace for an audience of the sultan was past for that day, they let the matter rest till the next morning. Aladdin and his mother talked of nothing else during the rest of the day, and the former took every opportunity of urging upon his parent all the arguments he could think of to keep her to her promise of going and presenting herself to the sultan. But notwithstanding everything he could say, his mother could not be brought to believe that she would ever succeed in this affair; and, indeed, there appeared every reason for her despondency. 'My dear son,' said she, 'even if the sultan should receive me as favourably as my regard for you would lead me to wish, and even if he should listen with the greatest patience to the proposal you wish me to make, will he not, even after giving me a gracious reception, inquire of me what property you possess, and what is your rank? for he will of course in the first instance ask about this matter rather than about your personal appearance. If, I say, he should ask me this question, what answer do you wish me to make?'

"'Do not let us distress ourselves, O my mother,' replied Aladdin, 'concerning a thing that may never happen. Let us first see how the sultan will receive you, and what answer he will give you. If he should make the inquiries you mention, I will find some answer to satisfy him. I put the greatest confidence in my lamp, by means of which we have been able for some years past to live in comfort and happiness. It will not desert me in my greatest need.'

"Aladdin's mother had not a word to say to this speech, as she might naturally suppose that the lamp which he mentioned would be able to perform much more astonishing things than simply to procure them the means of subsistence. This assurance of Aladdin's satisfied her, and at the same time smoothed away all the difficulties which seemed to oppose themselves to the business she had promised to undertake for her son respecting the sultan. Aladdin, who easily penetrated his mother's thoughts, said to her: 'Above all things, be careful to keep this matter secret; for upon that depends all the success we may either of us expect in this affair.' They then separated for the night, and retired to bed; but love, with the thought of the great schemes of aggrandisement which the son had in view, prevented him from passing the night so quietly as he wished. He rose at daybreak, and went immediately to call his mother. He was anxious that she should dress herself as soon as possible, that she might repair to the gate of the sultan's palace, and enter when the grand vizier, the other viziers, and all the officers of state went into the divan, or hall of audience, where the sultan always presided in person.

"Aladdin's mother did exactly as her son wished. She took the porcelain dish in which the present of jewels had been arranged, and folded it up in a very fine white linen cloth. She then took another which was not so fine, and tied the four corners of it together, that she might carry the dish conveniently. Thereupon she set out, to the great joy of Aladdin, and took the road towards the palace of the sultan. The grand vizier, accompanied by the other viziers and officers of the court, had already gone into the hall of audience before she arrived at the gate. The crowd, consisting of persons who had business at the divan, was very great. The doors were opened, and Aladdin's mother went into the divan with the rest. It formed a most beautiful saloon, very large and spacious, with a grand and magnificent entrance. Aladdin's mother stopped, and placed herself so that she was opposite the sultan, the grand vizier, and other officers who formed the council. The different applicants were called up one after the other, according to the order in which their petitions had been presented; and their different cases were heard, pleaded, and determined till the usual hour for breaking up the council. The sultan then rose, saluted the court, and went back to his apartment, followed by the grand vizier. The other viziers and officers who formed the council then went their various ways. All the applicants whose private business had brought them there did the same. Some went away highly delighted at having gained their causes, while others were but ill satisfied with the decisions pronounced against them; and a third set departed still anxious and in suspense, and desirous of having their affairs decided on at a future meeting.

"Aladdin's mother, who saw the sultan get up and retire, rightly imagined that he would not appear any more that day; and, as she observed that every one was going away, she determined to return home. When Aladdin saw her come back with the present in her hand, he knew not at first what to think of the success of her journey. He could hardly open his mouth to inquire what intelligence she brought him, for fear that she had something unfortunate to announce. The good woman, who had never before set her foot within the walls of a palace, and who of course knew nothing of the customs of such places, very soon relieved the mind her son from his embarrassment, by saying to him, with a satisfied air: 'I have seen the sultan, my son, and I am certain he has seen me also. I placed myself directly opposite to him, and there was no person in the way to prevent his seeing me; but he was so much engaged in speaking with those who stood around him, that I really felt compassion when I saw the patience and kindness with which he listened to them. This lasted so long, that I believe at length he was quite worn out; for he got up before any one expected it, and retired very suddenly, without staying to hear a great number of persons who were all ranged in readiness to address him in their turn. And, indeed, I was glad to see him go; for I began to lose all patience, and was extremely tired with remaining on my feet so long. But do not lose heart. I will not fail to go again to-morrow: the sultan will not then, perhaps, have so much business on his hands.'

"However violent Aladdin's passion was, he felt compelled to be satisfied with this answer, and to summon up all his patience. He had at least the satisfaction of knowing that his mother had got over a most difficult part of the business, and had penetrated into the presence of the sultan; and he therefore hoped that, like those who had pleaded their causes in her presence, she would not hesitate to acquit herself of the commission with which she was entrusted when the favourable moment for addressing the sultan should arrive.

"The next morning, quite as early as on the preceding day, Aladdin's mother set out for the sultan's palace, carrying with her the present of jewels; but again her journey was useless. She found the gate of the divan shut, and was told that the council never sat two days in succession, but only on alternate days, and that she must come again on the following morning. She went back with this intelligence to her son, who was again obliged to exercise his patience. She returned again to the palace six different times on the appointed days, always placing herself opposite the sultan. But she was each time as unsuccessful as at first; and she would have gone probably a hundred times with as little result, if the sultan, who constantly saw her standing opposite him every day the divan sat, had not taken notice of her. She might have come the more often as it was only those who had petitions to present, or causes to be heard, who approached the sultan, each in his turn pleading his cause according to his rank; and Aladdin's mother had no cause to plead.

"One day, however, when the council had broken up and the sultan had retired to his apartment, he said to his grand vizier, 'For some time past I have observed a certain woman who comes regularly every day when I hold my council, and who carries something in her hand wrapped in a linen cloth. She remains standing from the beginning of the audience till the end, and always takes care to place herself opposite to me. Do you know what she wants?'

"The grand vizier, who did not wish to appear ignorant of the matter, though in fact he knew no more about it than the sultan himself, replied: 'Your majesty must be aware that women often make complaints upon the most trivial subjects. Probably she has come to your majesty with some complaint against a person who has sold her some bad meat, or on some equally insignificant matter.' This answer, however, did not satisfy the sultan. 'The very next day the council sits,' said he to the grand vizier, 'if this woman returns, do not fail to call her, that I may hear what she has to say.' The grand vizier only answered by kissing his hand, and placing it on his head, to signify that he would rather lose it than fail in his duty.

"The mother of Aladdin had by this time become so accustomed to go to the palace on the days when the council met, that she thought it no trouble, especially as her constant attendance proved to her son that she neglected nothing that she could do, and that he had therefore no reason to complain of her. She consequently returned to the palace the next day the council met, and placed herself near the entrance of the divan, opposite the sultan, as it had been her usual practice to do.

"The grand vizier had scarcely begun to make his usual report, when the sultan perceived Aladdin's mother. Touched with compassion at the great patience she had shown, he said to the grand vizier: 'In the first place, and for fear you should forget it, do you not observe the woman whom I mentioned to you the other day? Order her to come here, and we will begin by hearing what she has to say, and giving her an answer.' The grand vizier immediately pointed out the woman in question to the chief of the ushers, who was standing near him ready to receive his orders, and desired him to go

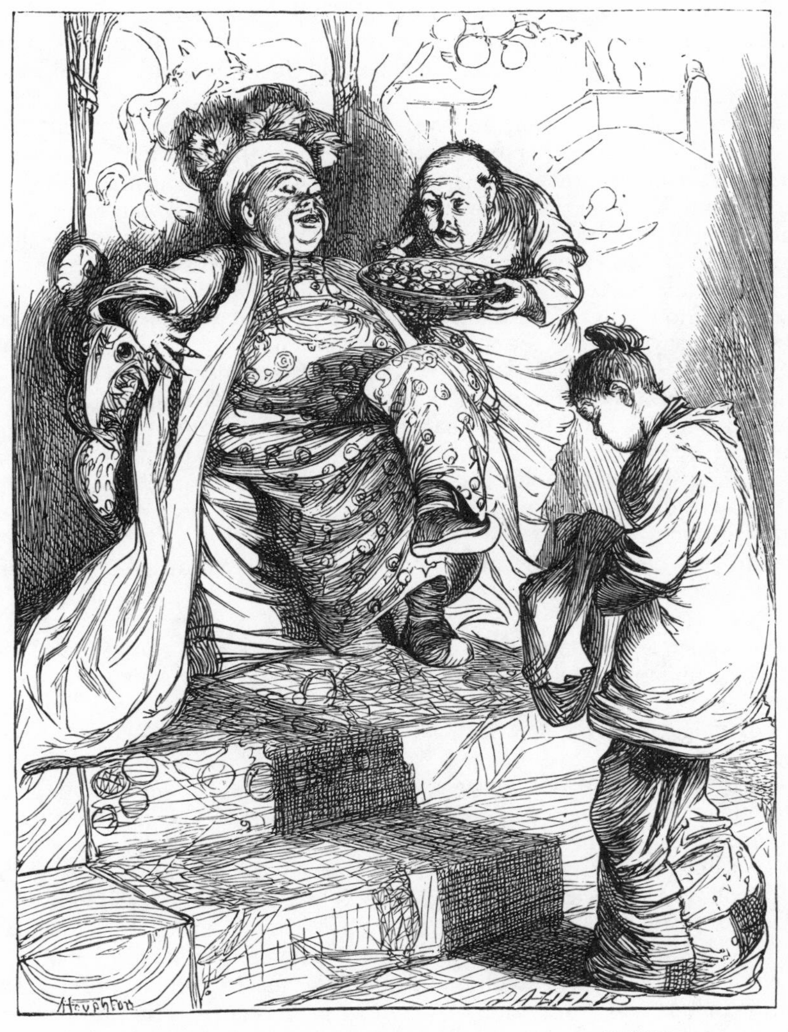

THE SULTAN'S SURPRISE AT THE BEAUTY OF THE JEWELS.

and bring her before the sultan. The officer went directly to the mother of Aladdin; and at a sign he made she followed him to the foot of the throne, where he left her, and went back to his place near the grand vizier.

"Following the example set her by many others whom she had seen approach the sultan, Aladdin's mother prostrated herself, with her face towards the carpet which covered the steps of the throne; and she remained in that position till the sultan commanded her to rise. She obeyed, and he then addressed her in these words: 'For this long time past, good woman, I have seen you regularly attend my divan, and remain near the entrance from the time the council begins to assemble till it breaks up. What is the business that brings you here?' Aladdin's mother prostrated herself a second time, and on rising answered thus: 'O gracious monarch, mightier than all the monarchs of the world! before I inform your majesty of the extraordinary and almost incredible cause that compels me to appear before your sublime throne, I entreat you to pardon the boldness, nay, I might say the impudence, of the request I am about to make. It is of so uncommon a nature that I tremble, and feel almost overcome with shame, to think that I should have to propose it to my sultan.' To give the applicant full liberty to explain herself, the sultan commanded every one to leave the divan, and remained with only his grand vizier in attendance. He then told her she might speak, and exhorted her to tell the truth without fear.

"The kindness of the sultan, however, did not perfectly satisfy Aladdin's mother, although he had thus excused her from explaining her wishes before the whole assembly. She was still anxious to screen herself from the indignation which she could not but dread the proposal she had to make would excite, and from which she could not otherwise defend herself. 'O mighty sovereign,' said she, again addressing the sultan, 'I once more entreat your majesty to assure me of your pardon beforehand, in case you should think my request at all injurious or offensive.' 'Whatever it may be,' replied the sultan, 'I pardon you in advance. Not the least harm shall happen to you from anything you may say; speak, therefore, with confidence.'

"When Aladdin's mother had thus taken every precaution, as a woman might who dreaded the anger of the sultan at the very delicate proposal she was about to make to him, she faithfully related to him by what means Aladdin had seen the Princess Badroulboudour, and with what a violent passion the sight of the princess had inspired him. She told how he had declared this attachment to her, and repeated every remonstrance she had urged to avert his thoughts from this passion. 'A passion,' added she, 'as injurious to your majesty as to the princess your daughter. But,' she went on to say, 'my son would not listen to anything I could say, nor acknowledge his temerity. He obstinately persevered, and even threatened that he would be guilty of some rash action through his despair if I refused to come and demand of your majesty the hand of the princess in marriage. I have been obliged, therefore, to comply with his wishes, although this compliance was very much against my will. And once more I entreat your majesty to pardon not only me for making such a request, but also my son Aladdin, for having conceived the rash and daring thought of aspiring to so illustrious an alliance.'

"The sultan listened to this speech with the greatest patience and good humour, and showed not the least mark of anger or indignation at the extraordinary request of Aladdin's mother, nor did he even turn it into ridicule. Before he returned any answer he asked her what she had with her tied up in a cloth. Upon this Aladdin's mother immediately took up the porcelain dish, which she had set down at the foot of the throne. She removed the linen cloth, and presented the dish to the sultan.

"It is impossible to express the utter astonishment of the monarch when he saw collected together in that dish such a quantity of the most precious, perfect, and brilliant jewels, greater in size and value than any he had ever seen. His admiration for some time was such that it struck him absolutely motionless. When he began to recollect himself, he took the present from the hand of Aladdin's mother, and exclaimed, in a transport of joy, 'Ah, how very beautiful, how glorious is this!' And then, after admiring the jewels separately, and putting each back into its place, he turned to his grand vizier, and showing him the dish, asked him if jewels so perfect and valuable had ever been seen before. The vizier was himself delighted with the jewels. 'Tell me,' added the sultan, 'what do you say to such a present? Is not the donor worthy of the princess my daughter? and must not I give her to him who comes and demands her at such a price?'

"This speech of the sultan's was very disagreeable to the grand vizier, because the monarch had some time before given that minister to understand that he had an intention of bestowing the hand of the princess upon the vizier's only son. Therefore the vizier was fearful, and not without good reason, that the sultan would be dazzled by the rich and extraordinary present, and would, in consequence, alter his mind. He therefore approached the sultan, and whispered the following words in his ear: 'O great monarch, every one must allow that this present is not unworthy of the princess; but I entreat you to grant me three months before you absolutely determine to bestow her hand. I hope that long before that time my son, for whom you have had the condescension to express to me great inclination, will be able to offer you a much more considerable present than that of Aladdin, who is an entire stranger to your majesty.' Although the sultan in his own mind was quite convinced that it was not possible for his grand vizier's son to make so valuable a present to the princess, he nevertheless paid every attention to what he said, and even granted him the delay he requested. Thereupon he turned towards Aladdin's mother, and said to her, 'Go, my good woman. Return home, and tell your son that I agree to the proposal he has made through you, but that I cannot bestow the princess my daughter in marriage until I have ordered and received certain furniture and ornaments, which will not be ready for three months. At the end of that time you may return here.'

"The mother of Aladdin went home in a very joyful mood. In the first place, she had considered that even access to the sultan, for a person in her condition, was absolutely impossible; and now she had received a favourable answer, when, on the contrary, she had expected a rebuke that would have overwhelmed her with confusion. When Aladdin saw his mother enter the house, he noticed two circumstances that led him to suppose she brought him good news. In the first place, she had returned that morning much sooner than usual; and, secondly, her countenance expressed pleasure and good humour. 'Tell me, mother,' said Aladdin, 'do you bid me hope, or am I doomed to die in despair?' When his mother had taken off her veil and had seated herself on the sofa by his side, she said: 'O my son, not to keep you any longer in suspense, I will, in the first place, tell you that so far from thinking of dying, you have every reason to be satisfied.' She then went on to explain to him in what manner she had obtained an audience before any one else was heard, which was the reason she had come back so soon. She described the precautions she had taken to make her request to the sultan in such a way that he might not be offended when he came to know that she asked nothing less than the hand of the Princess Badroulboudour in marriage for her son; and lastly, she repeated the favourable answer the sultan had given her with his own mouth. She then added that, as far as she could judge from the words and behaviour of the sultan, it was the present that had such a powerful effect upon his mind as to induce him to return so favourable an answer as that she now brought back. 'This is my belief,' added she, 'because, before the sultan returned me any answer at all, the grand vizier whispered something in his ear; and I was afraid it would lessen the good intentions he had towards you.'

"When Aladdin heard this good news he thought himself the happiest of mortals. He thanked his mother for all the pains she had taken in managing this business, and for the happy success with which her perseverance had been rewarded. Impatient as he was to possess the object of his affection, the three months that were to elapse seemed to him an age. He nevertheless endeavoured to wait with patience, as he relied upon the word of the sultan, which he considered irrevocable. Yet he could not refrain from reckoning not only the hours, the days, and the weeks, but even every moment, till this period should have passed away.

"It happened one evening, when about two months of the time had gone, that as Aladdin's mother was going to light her lamp she found that she had no oil in the house. Accordingly she went out to buy some; and on going into the city she soon perceived signs of great festivity and rejoicing. All the shops, instead of being shut up, were open, and ornamented with green branches and decorations; and every preparation was being made for an illumination, each person endeavouring to show his zeal by surpassing the rest in the splendour and magnificence of his display. The people also showed evident signs of pleasure and rejoicing. The streets were crowded with the different officers in their dresses of ceremony, mounted on horses most richly caparisoned, and surrounded by a great number of attendants and domestics on foot, who were going and coming in every direction. On seeing all this, Aladdin's mother asked the merchant of whom she bought the oil what it all meant. 'Where do you come from, my good woman,' said he, 'that you do not know that the son of the grand vizier is this evening to be married to the Princess Badroulboudour, the daughter of our sultan? The princess is just now coming from the bath, and the officers whom you see have assembled here to escort her back to the palace where the ceremony is to be performed.'

"Aladdin's mother did not wait to hear more. She returned home with all possible speed, and arrived quite out of breath. She found her son not in the least prepared for the bad news she brought him. 'All is lost, my son!' she exclaimed. 'You depended upon the fair promises of the sultan, and have been deceived.' Aladdin, who was alarmed at these words, instantly replied, 'My dear mother, why should not the sultan keep his word? How do you know anything about it?' 'This very evening,' answered Aladdin's mother, 'the son of the grand vizier is to marry the Princess Badroulboudour at the palace.' She then related to him in what way she had heard the news, and informed him of all the circumstances which had convinced her it must be true.

"Aladdin was greatly astonished at this intelligence. It came upon him like a thunder-stroke. Any person but himself would have been quite overwhelmed; but a sort of secret jealousy prevented him from remaining long inactive. He quickly bethought himself of the lamp, which had hitherto been so useful to him; and then, without indulging in vain reproaches against the sultan, or the grand vizier, or the son of that officer, he only said: 'This bridegroom, mother, shall not be so happy to-night as he expects. While I am gone for a few moments into my chamber, do you prepare supper.'

"His mother easily understood that Aladdin intended to make use of the lamp, in order, if possible, to prevent the completion of the marriage of the grand vizier's son with the Princess Badroulboudour. In this conjecture she was right; for as soon as he was in his own room he took the wonderful lamp, which he kept there that his mother might never again be alarmed as she had been when the appearance of the genie caused her to faint. He immediately rubbed it in the usual place, and the genie instantly appeared before him. 'What are thy commands?' said he to Aladdin: 'I am ready to obey thee as thy slave, and the slave of those who have the lamp in their hands, both I and the other slaves of the lamp.' 'Attend to me, then,' answered Aladdin: 'you have hitherto supplied me with food and drink when I needed it. I have now a business of more importance for you. I have demanded of the sultan the Princess Badroulboudour, his daughter, in marriage. He promised her to me, stipulating for a delay of three months; but, instead of keeping his word, he has this very evening, when the three months have not yet elapsed, given his daughter in marriage to the son of his grand vizier. I have just now been informed of the fact, and the thing is certain. What I have to order you to do is this: as soon as the bride and bridegroom have retired to rest, take them up and instantly bring them both here in their bed.' 'O master,' replied the genie, 'I will obey thee. Hast thou any further commands?' 'None at present,' said Aladdin. The genie instantly disappeared.

"Aladdin then went back to his mother, and supped with her in the same tranquil manner as usual. After supper, he entered into conversation with her for some time respecting the marriage of the princess, speaking of it as of a circumstance that did not in the least embarrass him. He afterwards returned to his chamber, and left his mother to betake herself to bed. He, of course, did not retire to rest, but waited till the genie should return and report the execution of his orders.

"In the meantime every preparation was made in the sultan's palace to celebrate the nuptials of the princess; and the whole evening was spent in ceremonies and rejoicings till the night was far advanced. When the proper time came, the son of the grand vizier retired unperceived, at a sign that the chief of the eunuchs belonging to the

THE BRIDEGROOM SHUT UP IN THE LUMBER-ROOM.

princess privately gave him; and this officer then introduced him into the apartment of the princess his wife, and conducted him to the chamber where the nuptial couch was prepared. The vizier's son retired to bed first; and in a short time the sultana, accompanied by her own women and those of her daughter, brought the bride into the room. The sultana assisted in undressing her; and, wishing her a good night, she retired with all the women, the last of whom shut the door of the chamber.

"Scarcely had this taken place, when the genie, the faithful slave of the lamp, endeavouring with the greatest exactness to execute the commands of those in whose hands it might be, took up the bed with the bride and bridegroom in it; and, to the great astonishment of them both, in an instant transported them to Aladdin's chamber, where he set them down.

"Aladdin, who was awaiting the genie's arrival with the greatest impatience, did not long suffer the son of the grand vizier to retain his place. 'Take this bridegroom,' said he to the genie, 'and shut him up in the lumber-room, and return again in the morning just at daybreak.' The genie instantly took the grand vizier's son, and transported him in his shirt to the place Aladdin had designated, where he left him, after first breathing upon him in such a way that he became paralysed in every limb, and could not stir.

"Though Aladdin felt a deep and fervent affection for the princess, he did not enter into any long conversation with her when he was with her alone. 'Fear nothing, most adorable princess,' he exclaimed, with an air of deep respect; 'you are here in safety; and however violent the love which I feel for you may be—with whatever ardour I adore your beauty and charms—be assured that I will never exceed the limits of the profound veneration I have for you. I have been forced,' he added, 'to proceed to this extremity; but what I have done has not been with the intention of offending you, but to prevent an unjust rival from calling you his, contrary to the promise which the sultan your father has made to me.'

"The princess, who knew nothing of all these particulars, paid very little attention to what Aladdin said: she was quite unable to make him any answer. The alarm and astonishment caused by this surprising and unexpected adventure had such an effect upon her that Aladdin could not get a single word from her in reply. Presently he laid himself down in the place of the grand vizier's son, with his back turned towards the princess, having first taken the precaution to place a drawn sabre between the princess and himself, as a sign that he deserved to be punished if he offended her in any way.

"Satisfied with having thus deprived his rival of the beauteous princess who had been promised to him, Aladdin slept very tranquilly. But very different was the case with the princess. Never in her whole life had she passed so unpleasant and disagreeable a night; and we need only remember in what a place and situation the genie had left the son of the grand vizier, to judge that the bridegroom spent his time in still greater discomfort.

"Aladdin had no occasion to rub his lamp the next morning to call the genie, who appeared punctually at the appointed hour, and found Aladdin dressing himself. 'I am here,' said he to Aladdin; 'what commands hast thou for me?' 'Go,' answered Aladdin, 'and bring back the son of the grand vizier from the place where you have put him. Place him again in his bed, and transport it to the palace of the sultan, whence you have brought it.' The genie instantly went to release the grand vizier's son from his imprisonment; and as soon as he appeared, Aladdin took away the sabre. He placed the bridegroom by the side of the princess; and in one moment the bed was carried back to the very same chamber of the sultan's palace whence it had been taken.

"During all these transactions the genie was invisible to the princess and the son of the grand vizier—his hideous appearance would have killed them with fright. They did not even hear a single word of the conversation that passed between Aladdin and him, and perceived only by the agitation of the bed that they were being transported from one place to another; and, indeed, it is easy to imagine that this frightened them quite enough.

"The genie had just replaced the nuptial couch in the princess's chamber, when the sultan came to visit his daughter and wish her good morning. The son of the grand vizier, who was half dead with the cold he had suffered all night, and who had not yet had time enough to warm himself, jumped out of bed as soon as he heard the door open, and went into the dressing-room where he had undressed himself the evening before.

"The sultan came up to the bedside of the princess, and kissed her between her eyes, as is the usual custom in wishing any one a good morning. He asked her, with a smile upon his face, how she had slept; but when he looked at her with greater attention, he was extremely surprised to observe that she was in the most dejected and melancholy state. She cast upon him very sorrowful looks, and showed by her whole manner that she was in a state of great alarm and grief. The sultan again spoke to her; but, as he could not get a word from her in reply, he retired. He could not, however, but suspect from her continued silence that something very extraordinary had happened. He therefore went immediately to the apartment of the sultana his wife, to whom he mentioned the state in which he had found the princess, and the reception she had given him. 'O my lord,' replied the sultana, 'I will go and see her. I shall be very much surprised if she will receive me in the same manner.'

"As soon as the sultana was dressed, she went to the apartment of the princess, who had not yet risen. She approached the bed, and, wishing her daughter a good morning, embraced her; but her surprise was great when she found that the princess was not only silent, but in the greatest distress. She therefore concluded that something which she could not yet comprehend had happened to her. Therefore she said affectionately: 'My dear daughter, what is the reason that you do not return the caresses I bestow upon you? You ought not to act thus towards your mother. But I will not suppose that you are wanting in affection towards me: something surely has occurred which I do not understand. Tell me candidly what it is, and do not suffer me to remain long in an uncertainty that distresses me beyond measure.'

"At length, with a deep sigh, the Princess Badroulboudour broke silence. 'Alas! my most honoured mother,' she cried; 'pardon me if I have failed in the respect that is due to you. My mind is so entirely absorbed by the strange and extraordinary things which happened to me last night, that I have not yet recovered from my astonishment and fears, and can scarcely summon courage to speak to you.' She then related in the greatest agitation how on the previous night the bed had been taken up and transported into an ill-furnished and dismal chamber, where she found herself quite alone, and separated from her husband without at all knowing what had become of him; and that she found in this apartment a young man, who, after addressing a few words to her which her terror prevented her from understanding, lay down in her husband's place, having first put his sabre between them; and that, when morning approached, her husband was restored to her, and the bed again brought back to her own chamber in a single instant. 'This second removal,' she added, 'was but just completed when the sultan my father came into my chamber. I was then so full of grief and distress that I could not answer him a single word, and I am afraid that he was very angry at the manner in which I received the honour he did me in visiting me. I hope, however, that he will pardon me when he is made acquainted with my melancholy adventure.'

"The sultana listened with great attention to everything the princess had to relate; but she could not give full credit to her daughter's story. 'You have done well, my child,' she said to the princess, 'not to inform the sultan your father of this matter. Take care that you mention it to no one, unless you wish to be considered a madwoman, which will certainly be the case if you talk in this way to any other person than me.' 'O my mother,' replied the princess, 'I assure you that I am in my right senses, and know what I say: you may ask my husband, and he will tell you the same thing.' 'I will take care to question him,' answered the sultana; 'but even if he gives me the same account as you have done, I shall not be convinced of its truth. In the meantime, however, I beg you will rise and drive this fantasy from your mind. It would be indeed a curious thing to see you troubled with such a delusion during the feasts that have been ordered to grace your nuptials, and which will last for many days, not only in the palace, but all over the kingdom. Do you not already hear the trumpets, cymbals, and other instruments? All this ought to inspire you with joy and pleasure, and make you forget the fanciful dreams which you have related to me.' The sultana then called her women; and after she had made her daughter get up and seen her at her toilet, she went to the sultan's apartment, and told him that some fancy seemed to have got into the head of his daughter, but that it was a mere trifle. She then ordered the son of the grand vizier to be called, in order to question him about what the princess had told her. But he felt himself so highly honoured by this alliance with the sultan, that he determined to feign ignorance. 'Tell me, my dear son-in-law,' said the sultana, 'have you the same strange ideas in your head that your wife has taken into hers?' 'Honoured madam,' he replied, 'may I be permitted to ask the meaning of this question?' 'This is sufficient,' answered the sultana; 'I do not wish to know more. I see you have more sense than she has.'

"The festivities in the palace continued throughout the day; and the sultan, who loved the princess tenderly, omitted nothing that he thought might inspire her with joy. He endeavoured to interest her in the diversions and various exhibitions that were going on; but the recollection of what had happened the preceding night made such a strong impression on her mind, that it was very clear her thoughts were unpleasantly occupied. The son of the grand vizier was equally mortified at the wretched night he had passed; but his ambitious views made him dissemble; and therefore, to judge from his appearance, any one would have thought him the happiest bridegroom in the world.

"Aladdin, who was well informed of everything that had occurred in the palace, did not doubt that the newly-married pair would again sleep together, notwithstanding the distressing adventure that had happened to them the night before. He did not, therefore, leave them to repose in quiet: a short time before night came on, he again had recourse to his lamp. The genie instantly appeared, and addressed Aladdin with the accustomed speech in which he offered his services. 'The grand vizier's son and the Princess Badroulboudour,' replied Aladdin, 'are again to sleep together this night. Go, and as soon as they have retired, bring the bed hither as you did yesterday.'

"The genie obeyed Aladdin with the same fidelity and punctuality he had shown on the previous night, and the vizier's son passed this second night in as cold and unpleasant a situation as he had passed the former; while the princess had the mortification of having Aladdin for a bedfellow, with the sabre, as before, placed between them. In the morning the genie came, according to Aladdin's orders, to carry off the bed, and took it back to the chamber of the palace whence he had taken it.

"The extraordinary reception which the Princess Badroulboudour had given to the sultan on the preceding morning had made him very anxious to learn how she had passed the second night, and whether she would again receive him in the same manner as before. He therefore went to her apartment early in the morning. The grand vizier's son, still more mortified and distressed at the misfortune that had befallen him on the second night than he had been at the first, no sooner heard the sultan than he rose as fast as possible, and ran into the dressing-room. The sultan came to her bedside, and wished the princess a good morning, after having saluted her in the same manner as on the previous day. 'Well, my daughter,' he said, 'are you as ill-humoured this morning as you were yesterday? Tell me how you slept last night.' The princess made no reply, and the sultan perceived that she was still more dejected and distressed than she had been the morning before. He could not but believe that something very extraordinary had happened to her. Irritated at the mystery she maintained with him, he drew his sabre, and exclaimed in an angry voice, 'O daughter, tell me what you thus conceal, or I will instantly strike off your head.'

"Terrified at the menaces of the sultan and at the sight of the drawn sabre, the Princess Badroulboudour at length broke silence. 'My dear father,' she exclaimed, with tears in her eyes, 'if I have offended your majesty, I most earnestly entreat your pardon. Knowing your goodness and clemency, I trust I shall change your anger into compassion, by relating to you in a full and faithful manner the occasion of the distressing and melancholy situation in which I have been placed both last night and the night before.' This appeased and softened the sultan. The princess went on to relate what had happened to her on both these horrible nights, and spoke in so affecting a manner that the sultan was penetrated with grief for the sufferings of his beloved daughter. She concluded her narrative by saying: 'If your majesty has the least doubt of the truth of any part of what I have said, you can easily inquire of the husband you have bestowed upon me: I feel very certain that he will corroborate me in everything I have related.'

"The sultan sympathised very fully with the feelings of distress this surprising adventure must have excited in his daughter's mind. 'My child,' said he, 'you were wrong not to divulge to me yesterday the strange story which you have just related, and in which I am not less interested than yourself. I have not bestowed you in marriage to render you unhappy, but, on the contrary, to increase your happiness, and to afford you

THE SULTAN DEMANDS AN EXPLANATION FROM HIS DAUGHTER.

every enjoyment you so well deserve; and therefore I bestowed you upon a husband who seemed to be very proper for you. Banish from your memory, then, the melancholy remembrance of what you have been relating to me: I will take care that you shall experience no more such nights as those which you have now suffered.'

"When the sultan got back to his apartment, he immediately sent for the grand vizier. 'Have you seen your son?' he asked him, 'and has he made any communication to you?' On the reply of the minister that he had not seen his son, the sultan reported to him everything he had heard from the Princess Badroulboudour. He then added: 'I have no doubt that my daughter has told me the truth. I wish, nevertheless, to have this matter confirmed by the testimony of your son. Go, therefore, and question him on the subject.'

"The grand vizier immediately went to his son, informed him of what the sultan had said, and commanded him not to disguise the truth, but to tell everything that had happened. 'I will conceal nothing from you, my father,' replied the son. 'Everything the princess has told the sultan is true: but she was unable to give an account of the bad treatment which I in particular have experienced. Since my marriage I have spent two of the most dreadful nights you can possibly conceive; and I cannot describe to you in adequate terms all the various evils I have gone through. I will say nothing of the fright I was in at finding myself lifted up in my bed four different times, without being able to see any one; or of being transported from one place to another, without being able to conceive in what way the movement was brought about. But you yourself can judge of the dreadful state I was in, when I tell you that I passed both nights standing upright in a sort of narrow lumber-room, with nothing upon me but my shirt, and deprived of the power of moving from the spot where I was placed, or of making the least movement, although I could not see the obstacle that rendered me thus powerless. Having told you thus much, I have no occasion to enter into further details of my sufferings. Let me add, however, that all this has by no means lessened the respect and affection which I had for the princess my wife; though I confess to you most sincerely that, in spite of all the honour and glory that I derive from having the daughter of my sovereign for my wife, I would much sooner die than continue to enjoy this high alliance, if I must continue to undergo the severe and horrible treatment I have already suffered. I am sure the princess must be of the same opinion as myself, and that our separation is as necessary for her comfort as for my own. I entreat you, therefore, my dear father, by all the affection which led you to obtain this great honour for me, to procure the consent of the sultan to have our marriage declared null and void.'

"Great as had been the ambition of the grand vizier to have his son so nearly allied to the sultan, the fixed resolution which he found the young man had formed of dissolving his union with the princess, made him think it necessary to request his son to have patience for a few days before the matter was finally settled, in order to see whether this unpleasant business might not settle itself. He then left his son, and returned to the sultan, to whom he acknowledged that everything the princess had said was true, as he had himself learnt from his son. And then, without waiting till the sultan himself spoke to him about annulling the marriage, a course to which he observed that his master was very much inclined, he requested permission for his son to leave the palace; giving as his reason that it was not just that the Princess Badroulboudour should be exposed for one instant longer to so terrible a persecution through the marriage she had contracted.

"The grand vizier had no difficulty in obtaining his request. The sultan, who had already settled the matter in his own mind, immediately gave orders that the rejoicings should be stopped, not only in his own palace, but in the city, and throughout the whole extent of his dominions, and in a short time every mark of public joy and festivity within the kingdom ceased. This sudden and unexpected change gave rise to a variety of different conjectures. Every one was inquiring why these strange orders were issued, and all affirmed that the grand vizier had been seen coming out of the palace, and going towards his own house, accompanied by his son, and that they both seemed very much dejected. Aladdin was the only person who knew the real reason of the change, and he rejoiced most sincerely at the happy success arising from the use of the lamp. And now that he knew for a certainty that his rival had left the palace, and that the marriage between the princess and the vizier's son was absolutely annulled, he had no further occasion to rub his lamp and have recourse to the genie, in order to prevent the completion of the marriage. The most singular point of all was, that neither the sultan nor the grand vizier, who had completely forgotten Aladdin and the request he had made, entertained the least idea that this forgotten suitor had any part in the enchantment which had been the occasion of the dissolution of the marriage of the princess.

"Aladdin allowed the three months, which the sultan wished to elapse before the marriage of the Princess Badroulboudour and himself, to pass without making any application. Still he kept an exact account of every day, and on the very morning after the whole period had expired he did not fail to send his mother to the palace, to put the sultan in mind of his promise. She went accordingly as her son had desired her, and stood at her usual place, near the entrance of the divan. As soon as the sultan cast his eyes that way and beheld her, he recollected her, and she instantly brought to his mind the request she had made, and the exact time to which he had deferred it. As the grand vizier approached to make some report to him, the sultan stopped him by saying, 'I perceive yonder that good woman who presented us with the beautiful collection of jewels some time since; order her to come forward, and you may make your report after I have heard what she has to say.' The grand vizier directly turned his head towards the entrance of the divan, and perceived the mother of Aladdin. He immediately called to the chief of the ushers, and pointing her out to him, desired him to conduct her forward.

"Aladdin's mother advanced to the foot of the throne, where she prostrated herself in the usual manner. After she had risen the sultan asked her what she wished. 'O mighty monarch,' she replied, 'I again present myself before the throne of your majesty, to announce to you, in the name of my son Aladdin, that the three months during which you have desired him to wait, in consequence of the request I had to make to your majesty, have expired; and to entreat that you will have the goodness to recall that circumstance to your remembrance.'

"When, on a former occasion, the sultan had desired a delay of three months before he acceded to the request of this good woman, he thought he should hear no more of a marriage which appeared to him entirely unsuited to the princess his daughter. He naturally judged of the suitor's position from the apparent poverty and low situation of Aladdin's mother, who always appeared before him in a very coarse and common dress. The application, therefore, which she now made to him to keep his word, embarrassed him greatly, and he did not think it prudent to give her an immediate and direct answer. He consulted his grand vizier, and acknowledged the repugnance he felt at concluding a marriage between the princess and an unknown man, whom fortune, he conjectured, had not raised much above the condition of a common citizen.

"The grand vizier did not hesitate to give his opinion on the subject. 'O my lord,' said he to the sultan, 'it seems to me that there is a very easy and yet very certain method to avoid this unequal marriage—a method of which this Aladdin, even if he were known to your majesty, could not complain. It is, to set so high a price upon the princess your daughter, that all his riches, however great they may be, cannot amount to the value. Then he will be obliged to desist from his bold, not to say arrogant, design, which he certainly does not seem to have considered well before he engaged in it.'

"The sultan approved of the advice of his grand vizier; and, after some little reflection, he said to Aladdin's mother: 'Good woman, it is right that a sultan should keep his word; and I am ready to adhere to mine, and to render your son happy by marrying him to the princess my daughter; but as I cannot bestow her in marriage till I have seen proofs that she will be well provided for, tell your son that I will fulfil my promise as soon as he sends me forty large basins of massive gold quite full of jewels, like those which you have already presented to me from him. These basins must be carried by forty black slaves, each of whom shall be conducted by a white slave, young, handsome, and richly dressed. These are the conditions upon which I am ready to give him the princess my daughter for his wife. Go, my good woman, and I will wait till you bring me his answer.'

"Aladdin's mother again prostrated herself at the foot of the throne, and retired. On her way home she smiled within herself at the foolish projects of her son. 'Where, indeed,' said she, 'is he to find so many golden basins, and such a great quantity of coloured glass as he will require to fill them? Will he attempt to go back into the subterraneous cavern, the entrance of which is shut up, that he may gather them off the trees? And where can he procure all the handsome slaves whom the sultan demands? He is far enough from having his wishes accomplished, and I believe he will not be very well satisfied with the result of my embassy.' Thus she entered the house, with her mind occupied by these thoughts, from which she judged Aladdin had nothing more to hope. 'My son,' said she, 'I advise you to think no more of your projected marriage with the Princess Badroulboudour. The sultan, indeed, received me with great kindness, and I believe that he was well inclined towards you. It was the grand vizier who, if I am not mistaken, made him alter his opinion, as you will yourself think when you have heard what I am going to tell you. After I had represented to his majesty that the three months had expired, and that I came on your behalf to request he would recollect his promise, I observed that he did not make me the answer I am going to repeat to you until he had spoken for some time in a low tone of voice to the grand vizier.' Aladdin's mother then gave her son a very exact account of everything the sultan had said, and of the conditions upon which he consented to the marriage of the princess his daughter with Aladdin. 'He is even now, my son,' she continued, 'waiting for your answer; but between ourselves,' she said, with a smile, 'he may wait long enough.' 'Not so long as you may think, mother,' replied Aladdin; 'and the sultan deceives himself if he supposes that by such exorbitant demands he can prevent my thinking any more of the Princess Badroulboudour. I expected to have had much greater difficulties to surmount, and thought that he would have put a much higher price upon my incomparable princess. I am very well satisfied; for what he requires of me is a trifle in comparison to what I would give him to possess such a treasure as the princess. While I am taking measures to satisfy his demands, do you go and prepare something for dinner, and leave me awhile to myself.'

"As soon as his mother was gone out to purchase provisions, Aladdin took the lamp. When he rubbed it, the genie instantly appeared, and demanded in the usual terms to know what was required of him, and stating his willingness to serve the holder of the lamp. 'The sultan agrees to give me the princess his daughter in marriage,' said Aladdin; 'but he demands of me forty large basins of massive gold, filled to the very top with the various fruits of the garden from which I took the lamp of which you are the slave. He requires also that these forty basins should be brought to him by forty black slaves, preceded by an equal number of young and handsome white slaves very richly dressed. Go and procure me this present as soon as possible, that I may send it to the sultan before the sitting of the divan is over.' The genie said that his master's commands should be instantly executed, and disappeared.

"In a very short time the genie returned with forty black slaves, each carrying upon his head a large golden basin of great weight, full of pearls, diamonds, rubies, and emeralds, which might compete for brilliancy and size with those which had already been presented to the sultan. Each basin was covered with a cloth of silver embroidered with flowers of gold. The forty black slaves with their golden basins and their white companions entirely filled the house, which was but small, as well as the court in front and a garden behind it. The genie asked Aladdin if he was satisfied, and whether he had any further commands for the slave of the lamp; and on being told that nothing further was required, he immediately disappeared.

"Aladdin's mother now returned from market; and great was her surprise on coming home to see so many persons and such vast wealth. When she had set down the provisions she had brought with her, she was going to take off her veil, but Aladdin prevented her. 'My dear mother,' he exclaimed, 'there is no time to lose. It is of consequence that you should return to the palace before the divan breaks up, that you may at once deliver to the sultan the present and dowry which he demands for the Princess Badroulboudour, that he may judge, from my diligence and exactness, of my ardent and sincere zeal to procure the honour of being received into alliance with his family.'

"Without waiting for his mother's answer, Aladdin opened the door that led into the

ALADDIN'S SLAVES CARRYING PRESENTS TO THE SULTAN.

street, and ordered all the slaves to go out one after the other. He then posted a white slave in front of each of the black ones, who carried the golden basins on their heads. When his mother, who followed the last black slave, had gone out, he shut the door and remained quietly in his chamber, fully convinced that the sultan, after receiving such a present as he had required, would now readily consent to accept him as his son-in-law.

"The first white slave who went out of Aladdin's house caused all the passers-by to stop; and before all the eighty slaves had emerged from the courtyard, the street was filled with a great crowd of people, who collected from all parts to see this grand and extraordinary sight. The dress of each slave was made of a rich stuff, and so studded with precious stones that those who thought themselves the best judges reckoned the value of each suit at many thousand gold pieces. Each dress was also very appropriate and well adapted to the wearer. The graceful manner and elegant forms of the slaves, and their great similarity to one another, together with their staid and solemn march, and the dazzling lustre that the different jewels, which were set in their girdles of massive gold, shed around—all this, added to the branches of precious stones fastened to their head-dresses, which were all of a particular make, produced in the multitude of spectators such astonishment and admiration, that they could not take their eyes from them so long as any of the slaves remained in sight. But all the streets were so thronged with people that every one was obliged to remain standing where he happened to be.

"As the procession of slaves had to pass through several streets before it could arrive at the palace, a great part of the city was traversed; and most of the inhabitants of every rank and quality were witnesses of this splendid spectacle. When the first of the eighty slaves arrived at the outer court of the palace, the porters were in the greatest haste, as soon as they perceived this astonishing prosession approaching, to open the door, as they took the first slave for a king, so richly and magnificently was he dressed. They were advancing to kiss the hem of his robe, when the slave, instructed by the genie, prevented them, and in a grave tone of voice said, 'Our master will appear at the proper time.'

"The first slave, followed by all the rest, advanced as far as the second court, which was very spacious, and contained those apartments used for the holding of the sultan's divan. The officers who were at the head of the sultan's guards were very handsomely clothed; but they were completely eclipsed by the eighty slaves who were the bearers of Aladdin's present, in which they themselves were included. Nothing throughout the sultan's whole palace appeared so beautiful and brilliant as they; and however magnificently dressed the different nobles of the court might be, they dwindled into insignificance in comparison with these splendid strangers.

"As the sultan had been informed of the march and arrival of these slaves, he had given orders to have them admitted. Accordingly, when they presented themselves at the hall of council, they found the door of the divan open. They entered in regular order, one-half going to the right and the other to the left. After they were all within the hall and had formed a large semicircle before the throne of the sultan, each of the black slaves placed upon the carpet the basin which he carried. They then all prostrated themselves so low that their foreheads touched the ground. The white slaves also performed the same ceremony. Then they all rose; and in doing so, the black slaves skilfully uncovered the basins which were before them, and then remained standing with their hands crossed upon their breasts in an attitude of profound respect.

"The mother of Aladdin, who had in the meantime advanced to the foot of the throne, prostrated herself, and thus addressed the sultan: 'O mighty ruler, my son Aladdin is well aware that this present which he has sent your majesty is very much beneath the inestimable worth of the Princess Badroulboudour. He nevertheless hopes that your majesty will graciously accept it, and that it may find favour in the eyes of the princess. He has the greater hope that his expectations will be fulfilled, inasmuch as he has tried to conform to the conditions which you were pleased to point out.'

"This complimentary address of Aladdin's mother was entirely lost upon the sultan, who paid no attention to her words. The forty golden basins, heaped up with jewels of the most brilliant lustre, the finest water, and greatest value he had ever seen, and the appearance of the eighty slaves, who seemed like so many kings, both from the magnificence of their dress and their splendid appearance, made such an impression upon him, that he could not restrain his admiration. Instead, therefore, of making any answer to the compliments of Aladdin's mother, he addressed himself to the grand vizier, who could not himself imagine whence such an immense profusion of riches could possibly have come. 'Tell me, vizier,' he exclaimed, in the hearing of all, 'what do you think of the person, whoever he may be, who has now sent me this rich and marvellous present? Do you not think that he is worthy of the princess my daughter?'

"Whatever jealousy and pain the grand vizier might feel at thus seeing an unknown person become the son-in-law of the sultan in preference to his own son, he was afraid to dissemble his real opinion on the present occasion. It was very evident that Aladdin had by his unbounded magnificence become in the eyes of the sultan very deserving of being honoured with the high alliance to which he aspired. He therefore answered the sultan in the following words: 'Far be it from me, mighty king, to suppose that he who makes your majesty so worthy a present should himself be undeserving the honour you wish to bestow upon him. I would even say that he deserved still more, if all the treasures of the universe could be put in competition with the princess your daughter.' All the nobles who were present at the divan testified by their applause that their opinion was the same as that of the grand vizier.

"The sultan hesitated no longer. He did not even think of inquiring whether Aladdin possessed the qualifications that would render him worthy of aspiring to the honour of becoming a sultan's son-in-law. The mere sight of such immense riches, and the wonderful celerity with which Aladdin had fulfilled his request without making the least difficulty about the exorbitant conditions for which he had stipulated, easily persuaded him that Aladdin must possess every necessary quality. He determined, therefore, to send back Aladdin's mother as well satisfied as she could possibly expect, and accordingly said to her: 'Go, my good woman, and tell your son that I am waiting with open arms to receive and embrace him; and that the greater diligence he uses in coming to receive from my hands the gift I am ready to bestow upon him, in the princess my daughter, the greater pleasure he will afford me.'

"When Aladdin's mother had departed, as happy as a woman could be in seeing her son exalted to a situation beyond her greatest expectations, the sultan put an end to the audience; and coming down from his throne, he ordered the eunuchs of the princess's household to be called. On their arrival, he commanded them to take up the basins and carry them to the apartment of their mistress, whither he himself went, in order to examine them with her at leisure. The chief of the eunuchs immediately saw this order executed.

"The eighty slaves were not forgotten. They were conducted into the interior of the palace; and when, soon afterwards, the sultan was speaking to the princess of their magnificent appearance, he ordered them to come opposite to her apartment, that she might see them through the lattices, and be convinced that so far from having given an exaggerated account of them, he had said much less than they deserved.

"In the meantime Aladdin's mother reached home, and instantly showed by her manner that she was the bearer of excellent news. 'You have every reason, my dear son,' she said, 'to be satisfied. Contrary to my expectations and what I have hitherto declared, I have now to announce to you that you have gained your suit. But, not to keep you any longer in suspense, I must inform you that the sultan, amid the applause of his whole court, has announced that you are worthy to possess the Princess Badroulboudour, and he is now waiting to embrace you and to conclude the marriage. It is therefore time that you should think of making some preparations for this interview, that you may endeavour to justify the high opinion he has formed of your appearance. After what I have seen of the wonders you have brought about, I feel sure you will not fail in anything. I ought not, however, to forget to tell you that the sultan waits for you with the greatest impatience, and therefore you must lose no time in making your appearance before him.'

"Aladdin was so delighted at this intelligence, and so enraptured with the thought of the enchanting object of his love, that he hardly answered his mother, but instantly retired to his chamber. He then took up the lamp that had thus far been so friendly to him by supplying all his wants and fulfilling all his wishes. He rubbed it, and immediately the genie again showed his ready obedience to its power by appearing to execute his commands. 'O genie,' said Aladdin to him, 'I have called thee to take me immediately to a bath; and when I have bathed, I command thee to have in readiness for me, if possible, a richer and more magnificent dress than was ever worn by any monarch.' So soon as Aladdin had concluded his speech, the genie rendered him invisible, took him in his arms, and transported him to a bath formed of the finest marble of the most beautiful and diversified colours. Aladdin immediately felt himself undressed by invisible hands in a large and handsome saloon. From thence he was conducted into a moderately-heated bath, and was there washed and rubbed with various sorts of perfumed waters. After having passed through the various degrees of heat in the different apartments of the bath, he emerged completely altered in appearance. His skin was white and fresh, his countenance blooming, and his whole body felt light and active. He then went back to the saloon, where, instead of the dress he had left, he found the one he had desired the genie to procure. Assisted by the genie, he dressed himself, and in doing so could not refrain from expressing the greatest admiration at each part of his costume as he put it on; and the effect of the whole was even beyond what he possibly could have conceived. As soon as this business was over, the genie transported him back into the same chamber of his own house whence he had brought him. He then inquired if Aladdin had any other commands. 'Yes,' replied Aladdin; 'I command thee to bring me as quickly as possible a horse which shall surpass in beauty and excellence the most valuable horse in the sultan's stables; the housings, saddle, bridle, and other furniture, shall be worth many thousands of gold pieces. I also order thee to get me at the same time twenty slaves, as splendidly and richly clothed as those who carried the present, to march beside and behind me, and twenty more to march in two ranks before me. Thou must also procure six females to attend upon my mother, and these slaves must be as tastefully and richly clothed as those of the Princess Badroulboudour, and each of them must carry a complete dress, fit in point of splendour and magnificence for any sultana. I also want ten thousand pieces of gold in each of ten separate purses. I have at present no further commands. Go, and be diligent.'

"When Aladdin had given his orders the genie disappeared, and a moment afterwards returned with the horse, the forty slaves, ten of whom had each a purse with ten thousand pieces of gold, and the six females slaves, each carrying a dress for Aladdin's mother wrapped up in a piece of silver tissue.

"Aladdin took only four out of the ten purses, and made a present of them to his mother, as he said that she might want them. He left the other six in the hands of the slaves who carried them, desiring them to keep the money and throw it out by handsful to the populace as they went along the streets on their way to the palace of the sultan. He ordered them also to march before him with the other slaves, three on one side and three on the other. He then presented the six female slaves to his mother, telling her that they were for her, and would in future consider her as their mistress, and that the dresses they had in their hands were for her use.

"When Aladdin had thus arranged everything for his progress to the palace, he told the genie that he would call him when he had any further occasion for his services. The genie instantly vanished. Aladdin then hastened to fulfil the wish the sultan had expressed to see him as soon as possible. He directly sent to the palace one of the forty slaves, who might have been considered the handsomest had they not all been equally well-favoured. This slave was ordered to address himself to the chief of the ushers, and inquire of him when his master might have the honour of throwing himself at the feet of the sultan. The slave had soon delivered this message, and brought word back that the sultan was waiting for his son-in-law with the greatest impatience.

"Aladdin immediately mounted his horse, and began his march in the order that has been mentioned. Although he had never been on horseback in his life, he nevertheless appeared perfectly at his ease; and those who were best skilled in horsemanship would never have taken him for a novice. The streets through which he passed were soon filled with crowds of people, who made the air resound with their acclamations and with shouts of admiration and congratulations, particularly when the six slaves who carried the purses threw handsful of gold on all sides. These expressions of joy and applause, however, did not come only from the crowd who were employed in picking up the money, but also from those of a superior rank in life, who thus publicly bestowed all the praise that such liberality as Aladdin's deserved. Those who had seen him playing about the streets like a vagabond even when he was no longer a child, did not now in the least recognise him; and those persons who had seen and known him very lately with great difficulty recognised him, so much were his features and character changed. This all arose from the power the wonderful lamp possessed, of acquiring by degrees for those who held it every quality adapted to the position they might attain by making a good

THE SIX SLAVES PRESENTED TO ALADDIN'S MOTHER.

and proper use of its virtues. The personal appearance of Aladdin thus attracted more attention than the magnificence with which he was surrounded, and which most of the spectators had before seen, when the slaves who carried and those who accompanied the present went to the palace. The horse, however, was extremely admired by all those who were judges, and were able to appreciate its beauty and excellence without being dazzled by the richness and brilliancy of the diamonds and other precious stones with which it was covered. When the report spread around that the sultan had bestowed upon Aladdin the hand of the Princess Badroulboudour—and this was soon universally known—no one ever thought about the meanness of his birth or envied him his great fortune, so entirely did he appear to deserve it.

"He at length arrived at the palace, where everything was ready for his reception. When he came to the second gate he wished to alight, according to the custom observed by the grand vizier, the generals of the army, and the governors of provinces; but the chief of the ushers, who attended him by the sultan's orders, prevented him from dismounting, and accompanied him to the hall of audience, where he assisted him from his horse, though Aladdin opposed this as much as possible, not wishing to receive such a distinction. In the meantime all the ushers formed a double row at the entrance into the hall; and their chief, placing Aladdin on his right hand, went up through the midst of them, and conducted him quite to the foot of the throne.

"When the sultan saw Aladdin coming, he was not more surprised at finding him more richly and magnificently clothed than he was himself, than he was delighted and astonished at the propriety of his manner, his graceful figure, and a certain air of grandeur, very far removed from the lowly aspect in which Aladdin's mother had appeared in his presence. His astonishment, however, did not prevent him from rising, and quickly descending two or three steps of his throne, in order to prevent Aladdin from throwing himself at his feet, and to embrace him with the most evident marks of friendship and affection. Aladdin again endeavoured to cast himself at the sultan's feet, but the sultan held his hand, and compelled him to ascend the step and sit between him and his grand vizier.

"Aladdin then addressed the sultan in these words: 'I receive the honours which your majesty has the goodness to bestow upon me, because it is your pleasure to bestow them; nevertheless I have not forgotten that I was born your slave. I am well aware of the greatness of your power, nor do I forget how much my birth places me beneath the splendour and brilliancy of that lofty rank to which you were born. If there can be the shadow of a reason,' he continued, 'to which I can in the least attribute the favourable reception which has been granted me, I candidly avow that I am indebted for it to a boldness which chance alone brought about, and in consequence of which I have raised my eyes, my thoughts, and my aspirations to the divine princess, who is the sole object of my eager hopes. I request your majesty's pardon for my rashness; but I cannot dissemble that my grief would be the death of me, if I should lose the hope of seeing my wishes accomplished.'

"'My son,' replied the sultan, again embracing him, 'you would do me injustice to doubt even for an instant the sincerity of my word. Your life is so dear to me that I shall endeavour to preserve it for ever, by presenting you with the object for which you pine. I prefer the pleasure I derive from seeing and hearing you speak to all our united treasures.'

"As he concluded this speech the sultan made a sign; and the air was immediately filled with the sound of trumpets, hautboys, and timbrels. The sultan then conducted Aladdin into a magnificent saloon, where a great feast had been prepared. The sultan and Aladdin sat down together to eat; the grand vizier and nobles of the court, each according to his dignity and rank, waited upon them during their repast. The sultan, whose eyes were always fixed upon Aladdin, so great was the pleasure he derived from seeing him, entered into conversation on a variety of different topics; and while they thus discoursed, whatever the subject happened to be, Aladdin spoke with so much information and knowledge, that he completely confirmed the sultan in the good opinion the latter had at first formed of him.

"When the repast was over, the sultan ordered the chief judge of his capital to attend, and commanded him immediately to draw up and write out a contract of marriage between the Princess Badroulboudour and Aladdin. While this was being done, the sultan conversed with Aladdin upon indifferent subjects in the presence of the grand vizier and the nobles of the court, who all equally admired the solidity of the young man's understanding and the great facility and fluency of his language.

"When the judge had drawn out the contract with all the requisite forms, the sultan asked Aladdin if he wished to remain in the palace, and conclude all the ceremonies that day. 'O mighty monarch,' he replied, 'however impatient I may be to receive the gift that your majesty's bounty destines for me, I request you to permit me to defer my happiness until I have built a palace for the princess that shall be worthy even of her merit and dignity. And for this purpose, I entreat your majesty to have the goodness to point out a suitable place near your own for its situation, that I may always be ready to pay my court to your majesty. I will neglect nothing to get it finished with all possible diligence.' 'My son,' answered the sultan, 'take whatever spot you think proper to choose. There is a large open space in front of my palace, and I have intended for some time to build upon it; but remember, that to have my happiness complete, I cannot too soon see you united to my daughter.' With these kind words he again embraced Aladdin, who now took leave of the sultan with as graceful an air as if he had been brought up and spent all his life at court.

"Aladdin then mounted his horse, and returned home in the same order in which he had come, going back through the same crowd, and receiving the same acclamations from the people, who wished him all happiness and prosperity. As soon as he had entered the court and alighted from his horse, he retired to his own chamber. He instantly rubbed the lamp, and called the genie as usual. The genie appeared directly, and offered his services. 'O genie,' said Aladdin to him, 'I have hitherto had every reason to praise the precision and promptitude with which thou hast punctually executed whatever I have required of thee, by means of the power of thy mistress, this lamp. But now, if possible, thou must show even greater zeal, and make greater dispatch than thou hast yet shown. I command thee, therefore, to build me a palace as quickly as possible, opposite to that belonging to the sultan, and at a short distance from it; and let this palace be in every way worthy to receive the Princess Badroulboudour my bride. I leave the choice of the materials to thee. Thou shalt decide whether it shall be of porphyry, of jasper, of agate, of lapis lazuli, or of the finest and rarest kinds of marble. The form of the palace also I leave to thy judgment; I only expect that at the top of the palace there shall be erected a large saloon, with a dome in the centre, and four equal sides, the walls of which shall be formed of massive gold and silver, in alternate layers, with twenty-four windows, six on each side. The lattices of each window, except one, which is to be purposely left unfinished, shall be enriched with diamonds, rubies, and emeralds, set with the greatest taste and symmetry, and in a style unequalled by anything in the whole world. I wish this palace to have a large court in the front, another at the back, and a garden. But above everything be sure that there is a room, which thou shalt point out to me, well filled with money, both in gold and silver. There must also be kitchens, offices, magazines, and receptacles for rich and valuable furniture suited to the different seasons, and all very appropriate to the magnificence of such a palace. Stables I must likewise have, filled with the most beautiful horses, also grooms and attendants; and the appliances for hunting must be there. I must have attendants for the kitchen and offices, and female slaves for the service of the princess. In short, thou canst understand what I mean. Go, and return as soon as thy task is completed.'

"The sun had already gone down when Aladdin finished giving his orders to the genie respecting the construction of the palace of which he had thus in idea formed the plan. The very next morning when the day broke, Aladdin, whose love for the princess prevented him from sleeping in tranquillity, had scarcely risen before the genie presented himself. 'O master,' said he, 'thy palace is finished. Come and see if it is built as thou didst wish.' Aladdin signified his assent, and the genie transported him to the palace in an instant. He found it exceed his utmost expectation, and could not sufficiently admire it. The genie conducted him through every part of it, and he everywhere found the greatest wealth applied with the utmost propriety. There were also the proper officers and slaves, all dressed according to their rank, and ready to engage in their different employments. Amongst other things the genie remembered to show Aladdin the treasury, the door of which was opened by the treasurer, of whose fidelity the genie confidently assured his master. Aladdin here observed large vases, filled to the very brim with purses of different sizes, each containing a sum of money, and so neatly arranged that it was quite a pleasure to behold them. The genie now led Aladdin to the stables, where he made him take notice of the most beautiful horses in the world, with servants and grooms busily employed about them. Then the genie took him into the different magazines, filled with everything that was necessary for the support of all the inmates of this vast and gorgeous building.

"When Aladdin had examined the whole palace, without omitting a single part of it, and had particularly inspected the saloon with the four-and-twenty windows, and had seen all the riches and magnificence it contained, even in greater abundance and variety than he had ordered, he exclaimed: 'O genie, no one can be more satisfied than I am, and I should be very wrong to make the least complaint. There is one thing only, which I did not mention to thee, because it escaped my recollection; it is, to have a carpet of the finest velvet laid from the gate of the sultan's palace to the door of the apartment in this which is appropriated to the princess, that she may walk upon it when she leaves the sultan's palace.' 'I will return in an instant,' replied the genie; and he had not been gone a moment, before Aladdin saw the carpet he had ordered rolled out by invisible hands. The genie again made his appearance, and carried Aladdin back to his own house, just as the gates of the sultan's palace were about to be opened.

"The sultan's porters who came to open the gates, and who were accustomed to see an open space where Aladdin's palace now stood, were much astonished at observing that space occupied by a building, and at seeing a velvet carpet, which seemed to stretch from that part directly opposite to the gate of the sultan's abode. They could not at first make out what the building was; but their astonishment increased when they distinctly beheld the superb edifice which the genii had raised for Aladdin. The news of this wonder soon spread throughout the palace; and the grand vizier, who had arrived just as the gates were opened, was no less astonished than were the rest. The first thing he did was to go to the sultan; but he tried to represent the whole business as enchantment. 'Why do you endeavour, O vizier,' replied the sultan, 'to make this appear as the effect of enchantment? You know as well as I that it is the palace of Aladdin, which I in your presence yesterday gave him permission to build for the reception of the princess my daughter. After the immense display of riches which we have seen, can you think it so very extraordinary that he should be able to build one in this short time? He wished, no doubt, to surprise us, and we every day see what miracles riches can perform. Confess that you wish through motives of jealousy to make this appear as the effect of sorcery.' The hour had now come for entering the council-hall, and this conversation was consequently broken off.

"When Aladdin had returned home and dismissed the genie, ne found that his mother was up, and had begun to put on one of the dresses which he had ordered for her the day before. About the time when the sultan usually left the council, Aladdin requested his mother to go, attended by the female slaves whom the genie had procured for her use. He desired her also, if she should see the sultan, to inform him that she came in the hope of having the honour of accompanying the Princess Badroulboudour in the evening, when the time came for the princess to go to her own palace. She accordingly set forth. But although she and her slaves were dressed as richly as sultanas, there was less crowd to see them, as they were veiled, and the rich magnificence of their habits was hidden by a sort of cloak that quite covered them. Aladdin himself mounted his horse, and left his paternal house never more to return; but he did not forget to take with him his wonderful lamp, whose assistance had been so highly advantageous to him, and had in fact been the cause of all his happiness. He went to his superb residence in the same public manner and surrounded with all the pomp with which he had presented himself to the sultan on the preceding day.

"As soon as the porters of the sultan's palace perceived the mother of Aladdin, they gave notice of her approach through the proper officer to the sultan himself. He immediately sent orders to the bands who played upon trumpets, timbrels, tabors and fifes, and hautboys, who were already placed in different parts of the terrace, and in a moment the air re-echoed with festive sounds which spread pleasure throughout the city. The merchants began to dress out their shops with rich carpets and seats adorned with foliage, and to prepare illuminations for the night. The artificers quitted their work, and all the people thronged to the great square that intervened between the palaces of the sultan

THE GRIEF OF THE PRINCESS BADROULBOUDOUR AT PARTING WITH HER FATHER.

and Aladdin. Aladdin's palace first attracted their admiration, not merely because they had been accustomed to see only that of the sultan, which could not be put in comparison with Aladdin's; but their greatest surprise arose from their not being able to comprehend by what unheard-of means so magnificent a place could have been reared in a spot where the day before there had been no materials, nor any foundation laid.

"Aladdin's mother was received with great honour, and was introduced by the chief of the eunuchs into the apartment of the Princess Badroulboudour. As soon as the princess perceived her, she ran and embraced her, and made her sit down upon her own sofa. And while the Princess Badroulboudour's women were dressing their mistress, and adorning her with the most valuable of the jewels which Aladdin had presented to her, she entertained her visitor with a most magnificent collation. The sultan, who wished to be as much as possible with the princess his daughter before she left him to go to her new home, paid great honour and respect to Aladdin's mother. She had often seen the sultan in public, but he had never yet seen her without her veil. The sultan, too, had always seen her very plainly, and indeed meanly, dressed, and he was therefore the more struck at finding her as magnificently attired as the princess his daughter. He concluded from this, that Aladdin was equally prudent and wise in all things.

"When the evening approached, the princess took leave of the sultan her father. Their parting was tender and accompanied by tears. They embraced each other several times without uttering a word; and the princess at last left her apartment, and began her progress to her new dwelling, with Aladdin's mother on her left hand, followed by a hundred female slaves, all magnificently dressed. All the bands of instruments, whose strains had been incessantly heard since the arrival of Aladdin's mother, united at once, and marched with them. These were followed by a hundred attendants and an equal number of black eunuchs in two rows, with their proper officers at their head. Four hundred young pages belonging to the sultan, marching in two troops on each side, with flambeaux in their hands, spread a great light around. The brilliancy of these flambeaux, joined to the illuminations in both palaces, rivalled the splendour of day.

"In this order did the princess proceed, walking upon the carpet which extended from Aladdin's palace to that of the sultan. And as she continued her progress, the musicians who were at the head of the procession went forward and mingled with those who were placed on the terrace of Aladdin's palace; and with their help they formed a concert which, confused and extraordinary as it was, augmented the general joy, not only amongst those in the open square, but in all the city, and even to a considerable distance around.

"The princess at length arrived at her destination, and Aladdin ran with every expression of joy to the entrance of the apartments appropriated to her, in order to welcome her. His mother had taken care to point out her son to the princess, as he stood among the officers and attendants who surrounded him; and, when she perceived him, her joy at his handsome and agreeable aspect was great. 'O adorable princess,' cried Aladdin, accosting her in the most respectful manner, 'if I should have the misfortune to have displeased you by the temerity with which I have aspired to the great honour of being allied to the daughter of my sultan, please to consider that it was to your beautiful eyes and to your charms alone that you must attribute my rashness, and not to myself.' 'O prince, for thus I must now call you,' replied the princess, 'I obey the will of the sultan my father; and now that I have seen you, I can freely own that I obey him without reluctance.'

"Aladdin was delighted at this satisfactory and charming answer. He did not suffer the princess to remain long standing after having walked so far, an exercise to which she was unaccustomed. He took her hand, which he kissed with the greatest demonstrations of joy. Then he conducted her into a large saloon, illuminated by an immense number of tapers. Here, through the attention of the genie, there was a table spread with everything rare and excellent. The dishes were of massive gold, and filled with the most delicious viands. The vases, the basins, and the goblets with which the sideboard was amply furnished, were also of gold, and of the most exquisite workmanship. The other ornaments which embellished the saloon exactly corresponded with the richness of the whole. The princess, enchanted at the sight of such a collection of riches in one place, said to Aladdin, 'O prince, I thought nothing in the whole world was more beautiful than the palace of the sultan my father; but the appearance of this saloon tells me I was deceived.'

"The Princess Badroulboudour, Aladdin, and his mother sat down to table; and instantly a band of the most harmonious instruments, played upon by women of great beauty, who accompanied the sweet strains with their voices, began a concert which lasted till the repast was finished. The princess was so delighted with the music, that she said she had never heard anything to equal it in the palace of her father. But she knew not that these musicians were fairies, chosen by the genie, the slave of the lamp.

"When supper was concluded and everything had been removed with the greatest diligence, a troop of dancers, of both sexes, took the places of the musicians. They performed dances with various figures, as was the custom of the country, and concluded by one executed by a male and female, who danced with the most surprising activity and agility, and each of whom gave the other in turn an opportunity of giving an exhibition of grace and address. It was near midnight when, according to the custon at that time observed in China, Aladdin rose and presented his hand to the Princess Badroulboudour, that they might dance together, and thus finish the ceremony of their nuptials. They both danced with such grace that they were the admiration of all present. When this ceremony was over, Aladdin did not let the hand of the princess go, but they went into the chamber together in which the nuptial bed had been prepared. In this manner did the ceremonies and rejoicings at the marriage of Aladdin and the Princess Badroulboudour conclude.

"The next morning when Aladdin arose, his chamberlains appeared to dress him. They clothed him in a new habit, but one as rich and magnificent as the dress he wore on the day of his marriage. They then brought him one of the horses appropriated to his use. He mounted it, and rode to the palace of the sultan, surrounded by a large troop of slaves. The sultan received him with the same honours he had before shown him. He embraced him, and, after placing him on the throne close by his side, ordered breakfast to be served up. 'O great king,' said Aladdin to the sultan, 'I beseech your majesty to withhold from me this honour to-day. I come for the express purpose of entreating you to come and partake of a repast in the palace of the princess, with your grand vizier, and the nobles of your court.' The sultan readily granted his son-in-law's request. He rose immediately, and, as the distance was not great, he wished to traverse it on foot. He proceeded, therefore, in this manner, with Aladdin on his right hand and the grand vizier on his left, followed by the nobles, the principal officers going before them.

"The nearer the sultan came to the palace of Aladdin, the more was he struck with its beauty; yet this impression was faint compared with the astonishment he felt on entering. His expressions of surprise and pleasure were renewed in all the apartments through which he passed. But when the company came to the hall of the twenty-four windows, to which Aladdin had requested them to ascend; when the sultan had seen its ornaments, and had above all things cast his eyes on the lattices enriched with diamonds, rubies, and emeralds, all of the finest sort and most superb size; and when Aladdin had made him observe that the outside and inside of each window was decorated with equal magnificence, the sultan was so much astonished that he stood absolutely motionless. After remaining some time in that state, he at length said to his vizier, who was near him, 'O vizier, is it possible there should be in my kingdom, and so near my own, so superb a palace, and yet that I should till this moment be ignorant of its existence?' 'Your majesty,' replied the grand vizier, 'may remember that the day before yesterday you gave permission to Aladdin, whom you then acknowledged as your son-in-law, to build a palace opposite your own. On the same day when the sun went down not the smallest part of this palace was on this spot; and yesterday I had the honour to announce to your majesty that it was built and finished.' 'I remember,' replied the sultan; 'but I never imagined that this palace would be one of the wonders of the world. Where throughout the universe will you find walls thus built with alternate layers of massive gold and silver, instead of stone or marble, and windows with lattices studded with diamonds, rubies, and emeralds? Never in the whole world has such a thing been heard of.'

"The sultan wished to examine everything more closely, and observe the beauty of the twenty-four lattices. On looking at them separately, he found only twenty-three that were equally rich, and he was therefore greatly astonished that the twenty-fourth should remain imperfect. 'Vizier,' said he to that minister, who accompanied him wherever he went, 'I am very much surprised that so magnificent a hall as this should remain unfinished in this particular.' 'O mighty monarch,' replied the grand vizier, 'Aladdin apparently was pressed for time, and therefore was unable to finish this window like the rest. But it must readily be granted that he has jewels fit for the purpose, and doubtless it will be finished at the first opportunity.'

"Aladdin, who had quitted the sultan to give some orders, came and joined them during this conversation. 'My son,' said the sultan, 'this truly is a hall worthy the admiration of all the world. There is, however, one thing at which I am astonished, and that is, to observe this lattice unfinished. Is it through forgetfulness, or neglect, or because the workmen have not had time to put the finishing-stroke to this beautiful specimen of architecture?' 'My lord,' answered Aladdin, it is not for any of these reasons that this lattice remains as your majesty now sees it. It is left unfinished on purpose; and it was by my orders that the workmen have not touched it. I wish that your majesty may have the glory of putting the finishing-stroke to this saloon and palace, and I entreat you to believe that my intention in this is that I may have a memento of the favour I have received from you.' 'If you have done it with that view,' replied the sultan, 'I take it in good part; I will give the necessary orders about it.' He accordingly ordered the jewellers, who were best furnished with precious stones, and the most skilful goldsmiths in his capital, to be sent for.

"When the sultan came down from the saloon, Aladdin conducted him into the chamber where he had entertained the Princess Badroulboudour on the evening of their nuptials. The princess herself entered a moment after, and received the sultan her father in such a manner as made it very evident that she was quite satisfied with her marriage. In this saloon two tables were set out with the most delicious viands, all served up in dishes of gold. The sultan sat down at the first table, and ate with his daughter, Aladdin, and the grand vizier. All the nobles of the court were regaled at the second, which was of great size. The repast highly pleased the sultan's taste, and he confessed that he had never partaken of so magnificent a feast. He said the same of the wine, which was in fact very delicious. But his admiration was most of all excited by four large recesses or sideboards, furnished and set out with a profusion of flagons, vases, and cups of solid gold, profusely enriched with precious stones. He was also delighted with the different bands of music, placed in various parts of the saloon; and the inspiring sounds of the trumpets, cymbals, and drums were heard at a distance, at proper intervals joining with the music within.

"When the sultan rose from the table, he was informed that the jewellers and goldsmiths whom he had caused to be summoned were come. He then went up to the hall of the twenty-four windows, and there he pointed out to the jewellers and goldsmiths who followed him that window which was imperfect. 'I have ordered you to come here,' said the sultan, 'to finish this window, and make it quite perfect like the rest. Examine these windows, and lose no time in completing the unfinished one.'

"The jewellers and goldsmiths examined all the twenty-three lattices with the closest attention; and after they had decided among themselves what each could contribute towards its completion, they presented themselves before the sultan, and the chief jeweller of the palace thus addressed him: 'We are ready, great king, to employ all our care and diligence to obey your majesty; but amongst our whole craft we have not jewels sufficient in number or in value to complete so great a work.' 'I have enough,' cried the sultan, 'and more than you want. Come to my palace; I will show you them, and you shall choose those you like best.'

"When the sultan came back to his palace, he caused all his jewels to be shown to the jewellers; and they took a great quantity of them, particularly of those which had been presented by Aladdin. They used up all these, without appearing to have made much progress in their work. They went back several times for more, and in the course of a month they had not finished more than half their task. They had used all the sultan's jewels, with as many of the grand vizier's as he could spare, and with all these they could not more than half finish the window.

"Aladdin was well aware that all the sultan's endeavours to make the lattice of this window like the others were vain, and that the jewellers would never complete their task. He therefore spoke to the workmen, and not only made them stop working, but even undo all they had yet finished, and carry back all the jewels to the sultan and the grand vizier.

"Thus all the work, which the jewellers had been four weeks in performing, was

THE JEWELLERS EXAMINING THE TWENTY-THREE LATTICES.

destroyed in a few hours. They then went away, and left Aladdin alone in the hall. He took out the lamp, which he had with him, and rubbed it. The genie instantly appeared. 'O genie,' said Aladdin to him, 'I ordered you to leave one of the twenty-four lattices of this hall imperfect, and you obeyed me. I now inform you I wish it to be completed like the rest.' The genie disappeared, and Aladdin went out of the saloon. He entered it again in a few moments, and found the lattice finished as he wished, and similar to the others.

"In the meantime the jewellers and goldsmiths arrived at the palace, and were admitted to the presence of the sultan in his own apartment. The first jeweller then produced the precious stones he had brought with him, and in the name of the rest spoke thus: 'O mighty king, your majesty knows for what length of time and how diligently we have worked, in order to finish the business on which you deigned to employ us. It was already very far advanced, when Aladdin obliged us not only to leave off, but even to destroy what we had already done, and to bring back your jewels, as well as those that belonged to the grand vizier.' The sultan then asked the jewellers whether Aladdin had given them any reason for this proceeding; and when they replied that he had said nothing on the subject, the sultan immediately ordered his horse to be brought. As soon as it came, he rode away without any other attendants than those who happened to be about his person, and who accompanied him on foot to Aladdin's palace. When he arrived there, he dismounted at the foot of the flight of stairs that led to the hall of the twenty-four windows. He immediately went up, without letting Aladdin know of his arrival; but the latter happened luckily to be in the hall, and had just time to receive the sultan at the door.

"Without giving Aladdin time to chide him for not sending word of his intention to pay him a visit, and thus causing him to appear deficient in the respect he owed him, the sultan said, 'I have come, my son, purposing to ask why you wished to leave this very rare and magnificent hall in an unfinished state?'

"Aladdin dissembled the true reason, namely, that the sultan was not sufficiently rich in jewels to go to the necessary expense. But to let the monarch see how the palace itself surpassed not only his, but also every other palace in the whole world, since he was unable to finish even a very small part of it, Aladdin replied, 'It is true, great king, that your majesty did behold this saloon unfinished; but I entreat you to look again, and tell me if at this moment there is anything wanting?'

"The sultan immediately went to the window where he had observed the unfinished lattice, but when he saw it was like the rest, he could hardly believe his eyes. He not only examined the window on each side of it, but looked at all the windows one after the other; and when he was convinced that the lattice upon which his people had so long employed themselves, and which had cost the jewellers and goldsmiths so many days, was now suddenly finished, he embraced Aladdin, and kissed him between the eyes. 'My dear son,' he cried, in astonishment, 'what a man are you, who can do such wonderful things almost instantaneously! There is not your equal in the world; and the more I know you, the more I find to admire in you.'

"Aladdin received the sultan's praises with great modesty, and made the following reply: 'O king, it is my greatest glory to deserve the kindness and approbation of your majesty, and I can assure you I shall never neglect any effort that may tend to make me more worthy of your good opinion.'

"The sultan returned to his palace in the way he had come, and would not permit Aladdin to accompany him. When he came home, he found the grand vizier waiting his arrival. Full of admiration at the wonders which he had witnessed, the sultan related everything to his minister in such terms that the vizier did not doubt for a moment the accuracy of the sultan's account. But this still more confirmed him in the belief which he already entertained, that the palace of Aladdin had been built by enchantment; and indeed he had expressed that opinion to the sultan on the very morning when the palace was first seen. He attempted to repeat his suspicions, but the sultan interrupted him with these words: 'O vizier, you have before said the same thing; but I very plainly perceive you have not forgotten the marriage of my daughter, the Princess Badroulboudour, with your son.'

"The grand vizier clearly saw that the sultan was prejudiced. He did not, therefore, attempt to enter into any dispute with him, but suffered him to retain his own opinion. Every morning, as soon as he rose, the sultan did not fail to go regularly to the apartment whence he could see the palace of Aladdin; and indeed he went often during the day to contemplate and admire it.

"Aladdin did not remain shut up in his palace, but took care to make a progress through different parts of the city at least once every week. Sometimes he went to attend prayers at various mosques; at others to visit the grand vizier, who regularly came on stated days under pretence of paying his court; and sometimes he honoured with his presence the houses of the principal nobles, whom he frequently entertained at his own palace. Whenever he went out, he ordered two of the slaves who attended him as he rode to throw handsful of gold in the streets and public places through which he passed, and where the people always collected in crowds to see him. Moreover, no poor person ever presented himself before the gate of Aladdin's palace but went away well satisfied with the liberality he experienced.

"Aladdin so arranged his different occupations, that not a week elapsed in which he did not once, at least, enjoy the diversion of the chase. Sometimes he hunted in the neighbourhood of the city, and at others he went to a greater distance; and he gave proofs of his liberality in every town and village through which he passed. His generous disposition made the people load him with blessings; and it became the common custom to swear by his head. Indeed, without giving the least cause of displeasure to the sultan, to whom he very regularly paid his court, Aladdin, in a short time, by the affability of his manners and the liberality of his conduct, won the regard and affection of all classes, and, generally speaking, he was more beloved than even the sultan himself. To all his good qualities he joined a great degree of valour and an ardent desire for the good of the state. He had an opportunity of giving the strongest proofs of his patriotism in a revolt that took place on the confines of the kingdom. So soon as he became aware that the sultan meant to levy an army to quell the insurrection, he requested to have the command of the expedition. This he had no difficulty in obtaining. He instantly put himself at the head of his troops to march against the rebels, and conducted the whole enterprise with so much judgment and activity, that the sultan had the news of the defeat, punishment, and dispersion of his enemies, quite as soon as he heard of the arrival of the army at its point of destination. This action, which made Aladdin's name celebrated throughout the whole extent of the empire, did not in the least alter his disposition. He returned victorious, but as affable and modest as ever.

"Many years passed, and Aladdin still continued by his own good conduct to advance in popularity; but during this period the African Magician, who had unintentionally procured for him the means by which he was raised to his exalted situation, frequently thought in Africa, whither he had returned, of the poor lad he had duped. Although he was well persuaded that Aladdin had met a miserable death in the subterranean cavern where he had left him, he nevertheless thought it advisable to gain certainty on the subject. As he had a complete knowledge of the science of astrology, he sat down on the sofa and placed a square instrument before him. He uncovered it, and after making the sand with which it was filled quite smooth and even, he arranged the points, drew the figures, and formed Aladdin's horoscope, with the view of discovering whether he had died in the subterranean cave. On examining it, in order to form his judgment, instead of finding Aladdin dead in the cave, he discovered that the youth had escaped out of it, that he was living in the greatest splendour, immensely rich, highly respected and honoured, and that he had married a princess.

"When the African Magician learned by his diabolical art that Aladdin was in the enjoyment of these honours, the blood rushed into his face. 'This miserable son of a tailor,' he exclaimed, in a rage, 'has discovered the secret and virtues of the lamp! I thought his death certain; but I find he enjoys all the fruits of my long and laborious exertions. I will prevent his enjoying them long, or perish in the attempt!' The magician soon made up his mind as to the method he should pursue. Early the next morning he mounted a Barbary horse which he had in his stable, and began his journey. Travelling from city to city, and from province to province, without stopping longer than was necessary to rest his horse, he at last arrived in China, and soon reached the capital where the sultan lived whose daughter Aladdin had married. He alighted at a public khan, and remained there the rest of the day and following night in order to recover from the fatigue of his journey.

"The first step the African Magician took the next morning towards fulfilling his enterprise was to inquire in what repute Aladdin stood, and to ascertain how the people spoke of him. In walking about the city, he went into the most frequented and most celebrated houses of entertainment, where people of the greatest consequence and distinction assembled to drink a warm beverage of which he had himself partaken when he was there before. He accordingly seated himself, and an attendant poured some into a cup, and presented it to him. As he took the cup, listening to what was said on every side, he heard some persons speaking of Aladdin's palace. When he had finished his cup, he approached those who were conversing on that subject, and taking his opportunity, he inquired what was the peculiar feature of this palace of which they spoke so highly. 'Surely you must be a total stranger,' said one of those to whom he addressed himself, 'and you can have arrived but lately in this city, if you have not seen, or even heard of the palace of Prince Aladdin;' for by this title Aladdin, since his union with the Princess Badroulboudour, had always been called. 'I do not say,' continued the speaker, 'that it is *one* of the wonders of the world, but I maintain it is the *greatest* wonder of the world. Nothing so rich, so grand, or so magnificent has ever been seen. You must have come from a great distance, since you seem never even to have heard of this palace; for, indeed, it has been spoken of everywhere since it has been erected. Only behold it, and you will acknowledge that I have spoken nothing but the truth.' 'Pardon my ignorance, I beseech you,' replied the African Magician; 'I arrived here only yesterday, and I have come from a great distance, even from the farthest part of Africa; the fame of this marvel had not reached that spot when I left it. And, as it was business of great importance that brought me hither, and required the utmost haste, I had no other idea during my journey than to get to the end of it as soon as possible, without stopping anywhere, or asking any news as I came along: I was, therefore, quite ignorant of what you have been telling me. I shall not, however, fail to go and see this palace. My impatience, indeed, is so great, that I would at once proceed to satisfy my curiosity if you would do me the favour to show me the way.'

"The person to whom the African Magician addressed himself was quite willing to point out to him the way he should go in order to see Aladdin's palace, and he and the magician immediately set out. When the African Magician arrived at the spot, and had accurately examined the palace on all sides, he felt fully convinced that Aladdin had availed himself of the power of the lamp in building it. He was quite aware how impossible it would be for Aladdin, the son of a tailor, to raise such a structure; but he well knew it was in the power of the genii, the slaves of the lamp, to produce such wonders—and this wonderful lamp he had once almost gained! Stung to the very soul by this evidence of the fortune and greatness of Aladdin, between whom and the sultan there seemed not the shadow of a difference, he returned to the khan where he had taken up his abode, determined at all hazards to obtain possession of the lamp which had wrought all these wonders.

"His first object was to discover the whereabouts of the lamp—whether Aladdin carried it about with him, or where he kept it; and this discovery he was able to make by a certain operation in geomancy. As soon, therefore, as he got back to his lodging, he took his square box and his sand, which he always carried with him wherever he went. His magic art informed him that the lamp was in Aladdin's palace, and his joy was so great on ascertaining this that he could hardly contain himself. 'I shall get this lamp,' he cried, 'and I defy Aladdin to prevent my having it; and I will fling him back into that native obscurity and poverty from which he has taken so high a leap.'

"It happened, most unfortunately for Aladdin, that he was absent upon a hunting expedition. This excursion was to last eight days, and only three of them had elapsed. Of this the African Magician got information in the following way. When he had finished the operation whose result had afforded him so much joy, he went to see the master of the khan, and beginning to converse with him, soon turned the talk into the desired channel. He told him that he had just returned from the palace of Aladdin; and after giving him an enthusiastic account of all the remarkable and surprising things he had seen, and describing the points that had especially attracted his attention, he continued: 'My curiosity goes still further, and I shall not be satisfied till I have seen the fortunate owner of this wonderful building.' 'That will not be at all a difficult matter,' replied the keeper of the khan, 'for hardly a day passes without affording you

"WHO WILL EXCHANGE OLD LAMPS FOR NEW ONES?"

an opportunity of seeing him when he is at home; but he has been gone these three days on a grand hunting party, which is to last for some days longer.'

"The African Magican did not want to know more: he hurriedly took leave of the master of the khan, and returned to his own apartment. 'This is the time for action,' said he to himself, 'and I must not let the opportunity escape.' He then went to the shop of a man who made and sold lamps. 'I want,' said he to the manufacturer, 'a dozen copper lamps. Can you supply me with them?' The man replied that he had not quite so many in his shop, but if his customer would wait till the next day, he would have them ready for him. The magician agreed to wait. He desired the dealer to be careful and have them very well polished; then he promised to give a good price for them, and returned to the khan.

"The next morning the African Magician received the twelve lamps, and paid the price demanded without asking for any abatement. He put them into a basket, which he had provided for the purpose, and went with this on his arm to the neighbourhood of Aladdin's palace. Here he walked to and fro, crying with a loud voice, 'Who will exchange old lamps for new ones?' As he continued thus calling, the children who were at play in the open square heard him. They ran and collected round him, hooting and shouting at him, as they took him for a fool or a madman. All who passed laughed at his apparent folly. 'That man,' said they, 'must surely have lost his senses, to offer to exchange new lamps for old ones.'

"The African Magician was not at all surprised at the shouts of the children, nor at the ridicule with which he was assailed. He seemed only intent on disposing of his merchandise, and continued to cry, 'Who will exchange old lamps for new ones?' He repeated this so often, while he walked to and fro on all sides of the palace, that at last the Princess Badroulboudour, who was in the saloon of the twenty-four windows, heard his voice; but as she could not distinguish what he said, on account of the shouting of the children who followed him, and whose numbers increased every instant, she sent one of her female slaves, who accordingly went forth from the palace to ascertain what was the reason of all the noise and bustle.

"The female slave presently returned, and entered the saloon laughing very heartily; indeed, her mirth was so violent that the princess herself, in looking at her, could not help joining in it. 'Well, thou silly one,' said the princess, 'why do you not tell me what you are laughing at?' 'O princess,' replied the slave, 'who can possibly help laughing at seeing yonder fool with a basket on his arm full of beautiful new lamps, which he will not sell, but offers to exchange for old ones. There is a crowd of children about him, and it is their mockery that makes all the noise we hear.'

"Another of the female slaves hereupon said, 'Now you speak of old lamps, I know not whether the princess has noticed one that stands on the cornice; whoever the owner may be, he will not be very much displeased at finding a new lamp instead of that old one. If the princess will give me leave, she may have the pleasure of trying whether this fellow is fool enough to give a new lamp for an old one without asking anything for the exchange.'

"This lamp of which the slave spoke was the very wonderful lamp which had been the cause of Aladdin's great success and fortune, and he had himself placed it upon the cornice, before he went to the chase, for fear of losing it. He had been in the habit of placing it there every time he hunted. But neither the female slaves, the eunuchs, nor the princess herself had paid the least attention to this circumstance till this moment. Except when he hunted, Aladdin always carried the lamp about him. His precaution, it may be said, was certainly insufficient, for he should have locked the lamp up. That is very true, but all men are liable to make such errors.

"The princess, who was ignorant of the value of the lamp and of its importance both to Aladdin and to herself, consented to make the trial, and ordered an eunuch to go and get it exchanged. The eunuch accordingly went down from the saloon, and no sooner came out of the palace gate than he perceived the African Magician. He immediately called to him, and when he came showed him the old lamp, and said, 'Give me a new lamp for this.'

"The magician at once conjectured that this was the lamp he was seeking; because he thought there would not be any other such lamp in Aladdin's palace, where everything of the kind was of gold or silver. He eagerly took the lamp from the eunuch, and after having thrust it as far as he could into his bosom, he presented his basket, and bade him take which he liked best. The eunuch chose one, and carried the new lamp to the princess. The children who saw this singular bargain made the whole square resound with their noise as they shouted in ridicule and mockery of what they thought the folly of the magician.

"The African Magician let them shout as much as they pleased. Without staying any longer near Aladdin's palace, he stole quietly to a distance, ceased his calling, and no longer invited people to exchange old lamps for new ones. He wished for no other lamp now that he had the real one. His silence, therefore, soon induced the children to leave him alone.

"As soon as he had traversed the square between the two palaces, he went through the most unfrequented streets, and as he had no further occasion either for his purchased lamps or his basket, he put his load down in the middle of a street where he thought himself unobserved. He then turned down another street, and made all the haste he could to get to one of the gates of the city. As he continued his walk through the suburb, which was very extensive, he bought some provisions; and when he was at last in the open country, he turned down a by-road where there was not a probability of meeting any person, and here he remained till he thought a good opportunity occurred to execute the design he had in view. He did not regret the horse he left at the khan where he lodged, but thought himself well recompensed by the treasure he had gained.

"The African Magician passed the remainder of the day in that retired spot, lingering there until the night was far advanced. He then drew the lamp out of his bosom, and rubbed it. The genie instantly obeyed the summons. 'What are thy commands?' cried the genie; 'I am ready to obey thee as thy slave, and the slave of those who have the lamp in their hands, both I, and the other slaves of the lamp.' 'I command you,' replied the African Magician, 'instantly to take the palace which you and the other slaves of the lamp have erected in this city; take it, exactly as it is, with everything in it, both dead and alive, and transport it, and me also, into the utmost confines of Africa.' Without making any answer, the genie, assisted by the other slaves of the lamp, took him and the whole palace, and transported both, in a very short time, to the spot he had pointed out.

"Having thus seen the African Magician, the Princess Badroulboudour, and his palace transported to Africa, let us notice what happened in the sultan's capital.

"When that monarch rose the next morning, he did not fail to go as usual to his cabinet and look out, that he might have the pleasure of contemplating and admiring Aladdin's palace. He cast his eyes in the direction where he was accustomed to see it, but saw only the open space that had been there before the palace was built. He thought he must be deceived. He rubbed his eyes, but still he could see nothing more than at first, though the air was so serene, the sky so clear, and the sun so near rising, that every object appeared distinct and plain. He looked on both sides, and out of both windows, but could not perceive what he had been accustomed to see. His astonishment was so great that he remained for some time rooted to the spot, with his eyes turned to the place where the palace had stood, but where he could no longer see it. He could by no means comprehend in what manner so large and so visible a place, which he had constantly seen every day since he had given permission to have it erected, should so suddenly and completely vanish that not the smallest vestige remained. 'I cannot be deceived,' he said to himself; 'it was in this very place that I beheld it. If it had fallen down, the materials at least would lie strewn around; and if the earth had swallowed it up, we should perceive some marks of the devastation.' In whatever way this marvellous event had come to pass, and however satisfied he was that the palace was no longer there, the sultan nevertheless waited some time to see if he were not under the influence of some delusion. He at length retired, looking once more behind him as he left the cabinet. He returned to his apartment, and ordered the grand vizier to be instantly summoned. In the meantime he sat down, his mind agitated with so many different thoughts that he knew not what steps to take.

"The grand vizier quickly obeyed the sultan's call. He came, indeed, in so much haste, that neither he nor his attendants observed, as they passed, that the palace of Aladdin was no longer where it had stood. Even the porters, when they opened the gates, did not perceive its disappearance.

"'O great king,' said the grand vizier, the moment he entered, 'the eagerness and haste with which your majesty has sent for me, leads me to suppose that something very extraordinary has happened, since your majesty is aware that this is the day on which the council meets, and that I should therefore have been here, in the discharge of my duty, in a very short time.' 'What has happened is indeed very extraordinary,' replied the sultan, 'as you will soon acknowledge. Tell me, where is Aladdin's palace?' 'I have just now passed it,' replied the vizier, with the utmost surprise, 'and it seemed to me to be where it stood before. A building so solid as that cannot be readily removed.' 'Go into my cabinet,' answered the sultan, 'and come and tell me if you can see the palace.'

"The grand vizier went as he was ordered, and was as much amazed as the sultan had been. When he was quite sure that the palace of Aladdin had really disappeared, and that not the smallest vestige of it remained, he returned to the sultan. 'Tell me,' demanded the latter, 'have you seen Aladdin's palace?' 'Your majesty may remember,' replied the grand vizier, 'that I had the honour to tell you that this palace, greatly and deservedly admired as it was for its beauty and immence riches, was the work of magic; but your majesty did not think fit to give heed to my words.'

"The sultan, who could not deny the former representations of the grand vizier, was the more angry against Aladdin, because he was also unable to answer the vizier's words. 'Where is this impostor, this wretch?' he exclaimed, 'that I may strike off his head.' 'It is some days since he came to take leave of your majesty,' answered the grand vizier; 'we must send to him, to inquire about the disappearance of his palace: he cannot be ignorant of it.' 'This would be treating him with too great indulgence!' exclaimed the monarch. 'Go, and order thirty of my horsemen to bring him before me in chains.' The grand vizier instantly gave the order, and instructed the officer how he should prevent Aladdin's escape, and make sure of taking him. The horsemen set out, and met Aladdin, who was returning from the chase, about five or six leagues from the city. The officer, when he first accosted him, declared that the sultan was so impatient to see his son-in-law that he had sent this party of horse out to meet him, and to accompany him on his return.

"Aladdin had not the least suspicion of the true cause that had brought out this detachment of the sultan's guard. He continued hunting on his way home; but when he was within half a league from the city, the soldiers surrounded him, and the officer said: 'Prince Aladdin, it is with the greatest regret that I must inform you of the orders we have received from the sultan. We are to arrest you, and bring you to the palace like a state criminal. We entreat you not to be angry with us for doing our duty, but, on the contrary, to extend your pardon to us.' This declaration astonished Aladdin beyond measure. He felt himself innocent, and asked the officer if he knew of what crime he was accused; but the officer replied that neither he nor his men could give him any information.

"As Aladdin perceived that his own attendants were much inferior in number to the detachment of soldiers, and, moreover, that they went to some distance, he dismounted, and said to the officer, 'I sumbit: execute whatever orders you have received. I must, however, declare that I am guilty of no crime either towards the person of the sultan or the state.' His captors immediately put a large and long chain about his neck, binding it tightly round his body, so that he had not the use of his arms. When the officer had put himself at the head of the troop, one of the horsemen took hold of the end of the chain, and following the officer, dragged forward Aladdin, who was obliged to follow on foot; and in this manner he was brought through the city.

"When the guards entered the suburbs, all the people they met, and who saw Aladdin led along in this way like a state criminal, felt sure that he was going to lose his head. As he was generally beloved, some seized sabres, others whatever arms they could find, and those who had no weapons whatever took up stones and tumultuously followed the guards. The soldiers who rode in the rear wheeled about, as if they wished to disperse the crowd, but the people increased so fast in number that the guards thought it better to dissemble, well satisfied if they could conduct Aladdin safe to the palace without his being rescued. In order to prevent an attempt of this kind, they took great care to occupy the whole space, sometimes extending, and at others compressing themselves, as the streets happened to be more or less wide. In this manner they arrived in

THE SULTAN'S SURPRISE AT THE DISAPPEARANCE OF ALADDIN'S PALACE.

the open square before the palace, where they all formed into one line, and faced about to keep off the armed multitude, while the officer and guard who led Aladdin entered the palace, and the porters shut the gates, to prevent any one from following.

"Aladdin was brought before the sultan, who waited for him, with the grand vizier by his side, in a balcony; and as soon as the prisoner appeared, the sultan angrily commanded the executioner, who was already present by his orders, to strike off his head, as he wished not to hear a word or any explanation whatever.

"The executioner accordingly seized Aladdin, took off the chain that was round his neck and body, and after laying down on the ground a large piece of leather stained with the blood of the many criminals he had executed, desired Aladdin to kneel down, and then tied a bandage over his eyes. Then he drew his sabre, made the three usual flourishes in the air, and waited only for the sultan's signal, to separate Aladdin's head from his body.

"At that critical instant the grand vizier perceived how the populace, who had overpowered the guards and filled the square, were in the act of scaling the walls of the palace in many places, and had even begun to pull them down in order to open a passage. Before, therefore, the sultan could give the signal for Aladdin's death, he said to him, 'I beseech your majesty to think maturely of what you are going to do. You will run the risk of having your palace torn to the ground; and if this misfortune should happen, the consequences cannot but be dreadful.' 'My palace torn down!' replied the sultan, 'who will dare attempt it?' 'If your majesty will cast your eyes towards the walls yonder,' observed the vizier, 'you will acknowledge the truth of what I say.'

"When the sultan saw the eager and violent commotion among the people, his fear was very great. He instantly ordered the executioner to sheathe his sabre, to take the bandage off Aladdin's eyes, and set him at liberty. He also commanded an officer to proclaim that he pardoned Aladdin, and that every one might retire.

"As all those who had mounted on the walls of the palace could see what occurred in the sultan's cabinet, they gave over their design and almost directly descended; and highly delighted at having thus been the means of saving the life of one whom they really loved, they instantly published this news to those that were near them, and it quickly spread among all the populace assembled in the neighbourhood of the palace. The officers also ascended the terraced roof, and proclaimed the news in the sultan's name. The justice the sultan had thus rendered Aladdin by pardoning him, disarmed the populace and quieted the tumult, so that presently every one returned home.

"When Aladdin found himself at liberty, he lifted up his head towards the balcony, and perceiving the sultan there, he raised his voice and addressed him with the most pathetic gestures. 'I entreat your majesty,' he said, 'to add a new favour to the pardon you have just granted me by informing me of my crime!' 'Thy crime, O perfidious wretch!' replied the sultan, 'dost thou not know it? Come up hither, and I will show thee.'

"Aladdin ascended to the terrace, and when he presented himself, the sultan walked on before, saying, 'Follow me,' without taking any other notice of him. He led the way to the cabinet that opened towards the place where Aladdin's palace had stood. When they came to the door, 'Enter here,' the sultan said: 'assuredly you ought to know where your own palace is. Look around, and tell me what has become of it.' Aladdin looked, but saw nothing. He perceived the space which his palace had lately occupied; but as he could not conceive how it had disappeared, this extraordinary and wonderful event so confused and astonished him, that he could not answer the sultan a single word. 'Tell me,' said the latter, impatient at his silence, 'where is your palace, and what has become of my daughter?' 'O mighty king,' replied Aladdin, at last breaking silence, 'I plainly see and must acknowledge that the palace which I built is no longer in the place where it stood. I see it has disappeared; but I can assure your majesty that I had no share whatever in removing it.'

"'I care not what has become of your palace; that gives me no concern,' replied the sultan; 'I esteem my daughter a million times beyond your palace; and unless you discover and bring her back to me, be assured that your head shall answer for it.' 'Great king,' said Aladdin, 'I entreat your majesty to grant me forty days to make the most diligent inquiries; and if I do not, within that period, succeed in my search, I give you my promise that I will lay my head at the foot of your throne, that you may dispose of me according to your pleasure.' 'I grant your request,' answered the sultan; 'but think not to abuse my favour, nor endeavour to escape my resentment. In whatever part of the world you are, I shall know how to find you.'

"Aladdin then left the sultan's presence, in the deepest humiliation, and in a state truly deserving of pity. He passed, with downcast eyes, through the courts of the palace, not even daring to look about him, so great was his confusion; and the principal officers of the court, not one of whom he had ever offended, instead of coming to console him or offer him a retreat at their houses, turned their backs upon him, alike unwilling to make it appear that they saw him, or that he should recognise them. But even if they had approached him to console him or offer him an asylum, they would not have known him: he did not even know himself. His mind seemed unhinged by his great calamity; and of this he gave evident proofs when he was out of the palace; for without thinking of what he did, he asked at every door, and of all he met, if they had seen his palace, or could give him any intelligence concerning it.

"These questions made every one think that Aladdin had lost his senses. Some even laughed at him; but the more thoughtful, and especially all those who had been on friendly terms or ever had any business with him, compassionated him most sincerely. He remained three days in the city, walking through every street, eating only what was given him in charity, and unable to come to any decision.

"At length, as Aladdin could not in his wretched condition remain any longer in a city where he had hitherto lived in splendour, he departed and bent his steps towards the country. He soon turned out of the high road, and after walking a great distance in the most dreadful state of mind, he came, towards the close of day, to the bank of a river. He now gave himself up entirely to despair. 'Whither shall I go to seek my palace?' he murmured to himself. 'In what country, in what part of the world, shall I find either my dwelling, or my dear princess, whom the sultan demands of me? Never shall I be able to succeed! It is much better, then, that I at once free myself from all my labours, which must end in nothing, and put an end at once to the woes that distract me.' He was going to throw himself into the river in pursuance of this resolution, but being a good Mussulman and faithful to his religion, he thought he ought not to quit life without first repeating his prayers. In performing this ceremony, he went close to the bank to wash his face and hands, as was the custom of his country; but as this spot was rather steep, and the ground moist from the water that had washed against it, he slipped down, and would have fallen into the river had he not been stopped by a piece of stone, or rock, that projected about two feet from the surface. Happy was it for him, too, that he still had on his finger the ring which the African Magician had given him when he made him go down into the subterranean cavern to bring away the precious lamp which had so nearly been buried with him. In grasping at the piece of rock, he rubbed the ring strongly, and the same genie instantly appeared whom he had before seen in the subterranean cavern. 'What are thy commands?' cried the genie; 'I am ready to obey thee as thy slave, and as the slave of him who has that ring on his finger, both I and the other slaves of the ring.'

"Aladdin was most agreeably surprised by the sight of this unexpected succour that came to him in his despair. He directly replied: 'Save my life, O genie, a second time, by informing me where the palace is which I have built, or by replacing it where it was.' 'What you require of me,' answered the genie, 'is beyond my power: I am only the slave of the ring; you must address yourself to the slave of the lamp.' 'If that be the case, then,' said Aladdin, 'at least transport me to the spot where my palace is, let it be in what part of the world it will; and place me under the window of the Princess Badroulboudour.' So soon as he said this, the genie took him up, and transported him to Africa, in the neighbourhood of a great city. In the midst of a large meadow in which the palace stood, he set him down directly under the windows of the apartment of the princess, and there left him. All this was the work of an instant.

"Notwithstanding the darkness of the night, Aladdin very readily recognised both his own palace and the apartment of the princess; but as the night was far advanced, and everything in the palace was still, he retired from before it, and seated himself at the foot of a tree. Full of hope, and reflecting on the good fortune which chance had procured him, he here felt more calm and collected than he had been since he was arrested by the sultan's order, placed in such imminent peril, and again delivered from the danger of losing his head. For some time he sat enjoying these agreeable thoughts; but as he had taken hardly any rest for five or six days, he could not prevent himself from being overcome by sleep, and accordingly resigned himself for a time to its influence.

"The next morning, as soon as the sun appeared above the horizon, Aladdin was most agreeably awakened by the songs of the birds, which had perched for the night upon the tree under which he lay, and also among the other thick trees in the garden of his palace. He feasted his eyes upon the beautiful building, and felt an inexpressible joy at the thought of being again master of it, and once more possessing his dear princess. He got up and approached the apartment of the Princess Badroulboudour. He walked to and fro under the window, waiting till she rose, in hopes that she might observe him. While he thus waited he tried to conjecture what could have been the cause of his misfortune; and after reflecting for some time, he felt convinced that this mishap arose from his having left his lamp about. He accused himself of negligence and carelessness in allowing the lamp to be out of his possession a single moment. He was, however, at a loss to conjecture who could be so jealous of his happiness. He would at once have understood the case if he had known that both he and his palace were in Africa; but the genie who was the slave of the ring had not informed him of this fact. The very name of Africa would have brought to his recollection his declared enemy, the magician.

"The Princess Badroulboudour rose that morning much earlier than she had risen since she had been transported into Africa by the artifice of the magician, whose hated presence she was compelled to endure once every day, as he was master of the palace; but she constantly treated him so disdainfully that he had never yet had the boldness to remain there long. When she was dressed, one of her women, looking through the lattice, perceived Aladdin, and instantly ran and told her mistress who was there. The princess, who could scarcely believe the fact, immediately went to the window and saw him herself. She opened the lattice, and at the noise she made Aladdin raised his head. He instantly recognised her, and saluted her with every demonstration of joy. 'Lose not a moment!' cried the princess: 'they are gone to open the secret door. Come to me instantly.' She then shut the lattice.

"This secret door was directly below the apartment of the princess. It was opened, and Aladdin entered his wife's apartment. It is impossible to express the joy they both felt at this meeting, after having concluded they were for ever separated. They embraced over and over again with tears of joy, and gave way to transports of the tenderest affection. At length they became calmer, and Aladdin said: 'Before you speak of anything else, my princess, tell me, in the name of Heaven, as well for your own sake and that of the sultan your ever-respected father, as for mine, what has become of that old lamp, which I placed upon the cornice of the saloon of the twenty-four windows, before I went on the hunting party?' 'Alas! my dear husband,' replied the princess, 'I greatly fear that our misfortunes are connected with that lamp; and what the more distresses me is, that it was I who meddled with it.' 'Do not, my beautiful princess,' resumed Aladdin, 'attribute any fault to yourself; I only am to blame, for I ought to have been more careful in preserving it. But let us now only think of how we may regain it; and for this purpose inform me, I beg of you, of everything that has happened, and tell me into whose hands the lamp has fallen.'

"The princess then gave Aladdin an account of all that had happened relative to the exchange of the old lamp for a new one. Then she told him how, on the following night, she had felt that the palace was flying through the air, and had found herself the next morning in the unknown country where she now was. She told him that this country was Africa, a fact she had learnt from the traitor who by his magic art had transported her thither.

"'O Princess,' replied Aladdin, interrupting her, 'in telling me that we are in Africa, you have at once unmasked the wretch who has betrayed us. He is the most infamous of men. But this is neither the time nor the place to enter into a detail of his crimes. I entreat you only to tell me what he has done with the lamp, and where he has put it.'

ALADDIN, IN DESPAIR, CONTEMPLATES SUICIDE.

'He constantly carries it carefully wrapped up in his bosom,' replied the princess: 'I am sure of this, because he once took it out in my presence, showing it as a sort of trophy.'

"'Do not be offended, my princess,' resumed Aladdin, 'at the questions I put to you; they are of the highest importance to us both. But to come at once to the point that most interests me, tell me, I conjure you, how you have been treated by this infamous wretch.' 'Since I have been in this place,' answered the princess, 'he has presented himself before me only once each day; and I am convinced that the disdain with which I have received his visits makes him repeat them less often. He has on many occasions tried to persuade me to be faithless to you, and to take him for my husband; striving to convince me that I ought never to expect to see you again; asserting that you were no longer alive, and that the sultan my father had caused your head to be cut off. He tried, moreover, to prove to me that you were an ungrateful wretch, and said that you owed all your good fortune to him; with a thousand other injurious expressions that I cannot repeat. But he never had any answer from me but complaints and tears, and was therefore obliged to retire very ill satisfied with his visit. I feel certain, nevertheless, that he means to suffer my first affliction to subside, with the hope and expectation that I shall change my mind with respect to him. What might have been the result of my continued resistance I know not; but your presence, my dear husband, at once dissipates all my fears.'

"'My princess,' interrupted Aladdin, 'I trust I am not deceived when I tell you I have discovered the means of delivering you from our enemy. For this purpose, however, I must go into the town: I will return about noon, and communicate to you the nature of my design, for you must yourself contribute towards its success. Let me, however, warn you not to be astonished if you see me return in a disguise; and be sure you give orders that I may not be kept waiting at the private door, but cause me to be admitted the instant I knock.' The princess promised that a slave should be ready to open the door on his arrival.

"When Aladdin left the palace he looked about on all sides, and at last discovered a peasant, who was going into the country. Aladdin hastened to overtake him; and when he came up with the peasant, proposed that they should exchange clothes, accompanying his offer with such a gift that the peasant readily agreed. The exchange was effected behind a small bush; and when it was completed they separated, and Aladdin took the road that led to the town. When he got there he turned down a street which led from the gate, and passing into the most frequented portions of the town, he came to that part where each avenue was occupied by a particular profession or trade. He went into a lane appropriated to druggists, and entering the shop which appeared the largest and best supplied, he asked the owner if he could sell him a certain powder, the name of which he mentioned.

"The merchant, who, from Aladdin's dress, conceived that his customer had not money enough to pay for this powder, replied that he kept it, but that it was very dear. Aladdin readily divined what was passing in the dealer's mind; he therefore took out his purse, and showing him the gold it contained, desired to have half a dram of the powder. The merchant weighed it, wrapped it up, and, giving it to Aladdin, demanded a piece of gold as the price. Aladdin immediately paid him, and without stopping any longer in the town, except to take some refreshment, returned to the palace. He had no occasion to wait at the secret door. It was instantly opened, and he went up to the apartment of the Princess Badroulboudour. 'My beloved princess,' said Aladdin to her as soon as he came in, 'the natural aversion you have expressed for this wicked magician may probably occasion you some pain in complying with the instructions I am going to give you. But permit me, in the first place, to tell you that it is absolutely necessary you should dissemble, and even offer some violence to your own feelings, if you wish to be delivered from his persecution, and if the sultan your father is to have the satisfaction of again beholding you.

"'But if you follow my advice,' continued Aladdin, 'you will this moment proceed to attire yourself in one of your most elegant dresses; and when the African Magician comes, make no difficulty in receiving him with all the affability you can assume, without appearing to act a part, or to be under any constraint. Try to speak to him with an appearance of frankness, yet still with some remains of grief, which he may easily conceive will soon be entirely dissipated. In your conversation with him give him to understand that you are making the greatest efforts to forget me; and that he may be the more convinced of your sincerity, invite him even to sup with you, and tell him that you wish to taste some of the best wine this country can produce. On hearing this, he will leave you for a time in order to procure some. In his absence, you must go to the sideboard, and put this powder into one of the cups from which you usually drink. Put the cup on one side, and tell one of your women to fill it and bring it to you at a certain signal on which you must agree, warning her not to make any mistake. On the magician's return, when you are again seated at table, after having eaten and drunk as much as you think proper, make your woman bring you the particular goblet in which the powder has been put, and then exchange cups with the magician. He will find the flavour of the wine you give him so excellent that he will not refuse it, but drink up the last drop. Scarcely shall he have emptied the cup when you will see him fall backwards. If you feel any repugnance at drinking out of his cup, you need only pretend to do so; and you can very easily manage this, for the effect of the powder will be so sudden that he will not have time to pay any attention to what you do, or to perceive whether you drink or not.'

"When Aladdin had thus proposed his plan, the princess answered: 'I must confess that I shall do great violence to my own feelings in agreeing to make these advances to the magician, although I am aware they are absolutely necessary. But what would I not resolve to undertake against such a cruel enemy? I will do as you direct, since your happiness, as well as mine, depends upon it.' When these preliminaries were all arranged with the princess, Aladdin took his leave, and passed the remainder of the day in the neighbourhood of the palace; and when the night came on, he presented himself at the secret door.

"The Princess Badroulboudour, who had been inconsolable, not only at her separation from her husband, whom, from the very first, she had loved more through inclination than duty, but also at being separated from the sultan her father, between whom and herself there existed the utmost affection, had hitherto completely neglected her personal appearance from the first moment of this distressful separation. She had not felt in spirits to dress with anything like care, particularly since the first visit of the magician, and when she had learnt from her women that he was the person who had exchanged the old lamp for a new one; for, after the infamous deception he had practised, she could not look upon him without horror. But the opportunity of taking that vengeance upon him he so justly deserved, at a time when she had given up all hope of possessing the means of accomplishing it, made her resolve to satisfy Aladdin.

"As soon, therefore, as he was gone, she went to her toilet, and made her women dress her in the most becoming manner. She put on some of her richest attire, choosing those ornaments which set off her beauty to the best advantage. Her girdle was of gold, set with diamonds of the largest size and of untold value. She put on a necklace consisting of twelve pearls, six on each side, and a central one, which was the largest and most valuable; but all these gems were so beautifully proportioned, that the proudest sultanas and the greatest queens would have thought themselves happy in possessing a necklace containing only the two smallest. Her bracelets, which were formed of diamonds and rubies mixed, admirably answered to the richness of her girdle and necklace.

"When the princess was completely dressed, she consulted her mirror, and asked the opinion of her women upon her appearance; and finding herself resplendent with all those charms that might flatter the foolish passion of the African Magician, she seated herself upon the sofa in expectation of his arrival.

"The magician did not fail to make his appearance at his usual hour. As soon as the princess saw him come into the saloon of the twenty-four windows, where she was waiting to receive him, she rose up in all the splendour of her beauty and her gorgeous array. She pointed with her hand to the most honourable seat, and remained standing while he approached it, that she might sit down at the same time with him. Altogether she treated him with a civility she had never before shown him.

"The African Magician, more dazzled by the splendid lustre of her eyes than by the brilliancy of the jewels she wore, was struck with admiration. Her majestic air, and the gracious manner she put on, so opposite to the disdain he had hitherto met with from her, absolutely confused him. He at first wished to sit at the very end of the sofa; but as he saw that the princess declined taking her seat until he had placed himself where she wished, he at last obeyed.

"When he had taken his seat, the princess, in order to free him from the embarrassment which oppressed him, looked at him with an air of kindness which made him suppose she no longer beheld him with the aversion she had till now evinced, and then said to him: 'You are doubtless astonished at seeing me appear to-day so different from what I have been; but you will no longer be surprised at it, when I tell you that my

ALADDIN AND THE DRUG MERCHANT.

natural disposition is so much averse to grief, melancholy, vexation, and distress, that I endeavour to drive them from me by every means in my power, as soon as the cause of them has departed. I have reflected upon what you said respecting the fate of Aladdin, and from the disposition of the sultan my father, which I well know, I agree with you that my late husband could not possibly escape the terrible effects of the sultan's rage. I concluded, therefore, that even if I were to weep and lament for the rest of my life, my tears would not bring Aladdin to life. Accordingly, after having paid him, even to the tomb, every respect and duty which my affection required, I thought I ought at length to admit feelings of comfort and consolation. These are the thoughts which have produced the change you see. In order, then, to drive away all sorrow, which I have now resolved to banish from my mind, and being convinced that you will assist me in these endeavours, I have ordered a supper to be prepared; but as the only wine I have is

DEATH OF THE AFRICAN MAGICIAN.

the produce of China, and as I am now in Africa, I have a great desire to taste what is made here, and I thought that, if there were any good wine to be had, you would be most likely to have the best.'

"The African Magician, who had never flattered himself that he should so soon and so easily acquire the good graces of the Princess Badroulboudour, hastened to tell her that he was unable sufficiently to express his sense of her goodness; and to put an end to a conversation which in some measure embarrassed him, he adverted to the wine of Africa which she had mentioned, and told her, that among the many advantages which that country possessed, the principal boast was that of producing excellent wine, and that this applied particularly to the part where she then was. He told her he had some wine seven years old that was not yet broached, and it was not saying too much to aver that it surpassed the produce of the whole world. 'If my princess,' added he, 'will permit me, I will go and bring two bottles of this wine, and will return immediately.' 'I should be sorry to give you that trouble,' replied the princess; 'it would be better, surely, to send some one.' 'It is necessary for me to go myself,' resumed the magician; 'no one but myself has the key of the cellar, nor does any one else know the secret of opening it.' 'The longer you are gone, the more impatient shall I be to see you again,' replied the princess: 'remember that we sit down to table on your return.'

"Full of the anticipation of his expected happiness, the African Magician hastened at his best speed to bring the wine, and was back almost instantly. The princess felt sure that he would make haste, and therefore at once threw the powder which Aladdin had given her into a goblet, and set it aside until she should call for it. They then sat down opposite to each other, the magician's back being towards the sideboard. The princess helped him with her own hands to what appeared the best on the table, and said to him, 'If you have any inclination for music, I will give you some; but as we are by ourselves, I think conversation will afford us more pleasure.' The magician regarded this speech as a fresh mark of her favour, and was almost intoxicated with delight.

"After they had feasted for some little time, the princess called for wine, and drank to the magician's health. 'You are right,' she cried, when she had drunk, 'in praising your wine; I have never tasted any so delicious.' 'O charming princess,' replied the magician, holding in his hand the goblet they had given him, 'my wine acquires a fresh flavour by the approbation you have bestowed upon it.' 'Drink to my health,' resumed the princess; 'you must confess I can appreciate good wine.' He did as she ordered him, and as he returned the goblet, observed, 'I esteem myself very happy, fair princess, to have reserved this wine for so good an occasion; and I confess I have never in my whole life emptied a cup so charmingly offered.'

"When they had continued eating some time longer, and had taken three cups each, the princess, who had most completely fascinated the African Magician by her kind and obliging manners, at length gave the signal to her woman to bring some wine, at the same time desiring her to bring her a goblet full, and also to fill the cup of the magician, which they presented to him. When they had received the goblets, 'I know not,' the princess said to the African Magician, 'what is your custom here, when two good friends drink together as we are doing now. At home in China, the gentleman presents his own goblet to the lady, who at the same time presents hers to the gentleman, and the lovers then drink to each other's health.' With these words she presented to her companion the goblet she held, and put out her other hand to receive his. The African Magician hastened to make the exchange, with which he was the more delighted as he looked upon this favour as the surest token that he had made an entire conquest of the heart of the princess; and this thought completed his happiness. 'O lovely princess,' he exclaimed, holding the goblet in his hand before he drank, 'we Africans ought to become as much refined in the art of giving a zest to pleasure by every delightful accompaniment as your nation seems to be; by instructing me, therefore, in an art of which I am ignorant, you teach me how sensible I ought to be of the favour I receive. Never shall I forget, most amiable princess, that in drinking out of your goblet, I have regained that life which your cruelty, had it continued, would most infallibly have destroyed.'

"The Princess Badroulboudour was almost worn out with the magician's absurd and tiresome compliments. 'Drink,' she cried, interrupting him, 'you may then say what you please to me.' At the same time she carried the goblet she held to her mouth, but barely suffered it to touch her lips, while the African Magician emptied his to the last drop. In draining the cup, he held his head quite back, and remained in that position till the princess, who kept the goblet to her lips, observed that his eyes were turned up, and presently he fell upon his back dead, without the least struggle.

"The princess had no occasion to order her people to go and open the secret door to admit Aladdin. Her women, who were stationed at different parts of the staircase, gave the word one to the other from the saloon; so that directly after the African Magician had fallen backwards, the door was opened.

"Aladdin went up to the saloon; and as soon as he saw the African Magician extended on the sofa, he stopped Princess Badroulboudour, who had risen to congratulate him on the joyful event. 'My princess,' he cried, 'there is at this moment no time for rejoicing. Do me the favour to retire to your apartment, and to leave me alone, while I prepare to carry you back to China as quickly as you departed thence.' So soon as the princess, her women, and the eunuchs had quitted the hall, Aladdin shut the door; and then going up to the body of the African Magician, which was lying lifeless on the sofa, he opened his vest, and took out the lamp, which was wrapped up exactly in the manner the princess had described. He took it out and rubbed it. The genie instantly presented himself, and made his usual profession of service. 'O genie,' said Aladdin, 'I have called you, to command you in the name of this lamp, your mistress, immediately to take this palace, and transport it to the same spot in China whence it was brought.' The genie testified his obedience by an inclination of his head, and forthwith vanished. The journey was made immediately, and only two slight shocks were perceptible; one, when the palace was taken up from the place where it stood in Africa, and the other when it was set down in China, opposite to the sultan's palace: and this was all the work of an instant.

"Aladdin then went down to the apartment of the Princess Babroulboudour. 'O my princess,' he exclaimed, embracing her, 'our joy will be complete by to-morrow morning.' As the princess had not finished her supper, and as Aladdin was greatly in want of refreshment, she ordered the attendants to bring the banquet from the saloon of the twenty-four windows, where the supper had been served, and whence it had not yet been removed. The princess and Aladdin drank together, and found the old wine of the magician most excellent. Then, full of the pleasure of this meeting, which could not but be delightful, they retired to their apartment.

"Since the disappearance of Aladdin's palace, and the loss of the Princess Badroulboudour, whom he did not hope to see again, the sultan had been inconsolable. He slept neither night nor day; and instead of avoiding everything that could increase his affliction, he, on the contrary, cherished every thought that was likely to remind him of it. Thus not only did he go every morning to the cabinet to indulge his grief by gazing on the spot where the vanished palace had stood, but he went several times during the day to renew his tears, and plunge in the painful sensations that arose from the thought of never again seeing what had afforded him so much delight, and from the loss of what he valued more than anything in this world. The sun had not yet risen when the sultan entered his cabinet as usual on the very morning on which Aladdin's palace had been brought back to its place. When he first came in, his mind was so much absorbed by his own feelings, and so penetrated with sorrow, that he cast his eyes towards the accustomed spot in the most melancholy manner, with the expectation of beholding nothing but a vacant space. But when he first found this void filled up, he conjectured that it was only a deluding vision. He then looked with greater attention, and at length could no longer doubt that it was the palace of Aladdin which he saw. Grief and sorrow were succeeded in his heart by the most delightful sensations of joy. He hastened back to his apartment, and instantly ordered his attendants to saddle him a horse. Directly it came he mounted it and rode away, thinking he could not arrive soon enough at Aladdin's palace.

"Aladdin, who conjectured that such a thing might happen, had risen at daybreak; and as soon as he had dressed himself in one of his most magnificent robes, he went up to the hall of the twenty-four windows. Looking through the casement, he perceived the sultan as he came along. He then descended, and was just in time to receive the monarch at the foot of the grand staircase, and assist him in dismounting. 'O Aladdin,' cried the sultan, 'I cannot speak to you till I have seen and embraced the Princess Badroulboudour, my dear daughter.'

"Aladdin accordingly conducted the sultan to the apartment of the Princess Badroulboudour, whom Aladdin had informed when he rose that she was no longer in Africa, but in China, at the capital of the sultan her father, and close to his palace. She had just finished dressing when the sultan entered. He eagerly embraced her, bathing her face with his tears, while the princess, on her part, showed the greatest delight at again beholding him. For some time the sultan could not utter a syllable, so great was his emotion at recovering his daughter after having lamented her loss as irremediable, while the princess shed tears of joy at the sight of her beloved father. 'My dear daughter,' exclaimed the sultan, at length recovering his speech, 'I am glad to perceive that the joy you feel at again seeing me makes you appear so little changed that no one would imagine what sorrows you have had. I am sure, however, that you must have suffered a great deal. No one could have been suddenly transported with a whole palace, as you have been, without feeling the greatest alarm and most dreadful anxiety. Relate to me, I beg of you, every circumstance exactly as it happened, and do not conceal anything from me.'

"The princess felt a pleasure in satisfying the affectionate curiosity of the sultan. 'O my father,' said she, 'if I appear so little altered, I beg your majesty to consider that my expectations and hopes were raised yesterday morning by the appearance of my dear husband and liberator Aladdin, whom I had till then mourned and lamented as for ever lost to me. The happiness I experienced in again embracing him restored me to my former state. Strictly speaking, my whole sorrow consisted in finding myself torn from your majesty and my husband; not only out of my affection for him, but lest he should perish from the dreadful effects of your majesty's rage, to which I did not doubt that he would be exposed, however innocent he might be; and no one could be less guilty than he in this matter. I have suffered less from the insolence of him who bore me from hence, and who has continually made proposals that gave me pain, but to which I as often put an end by the ascendency I knew how to maintain over him. I was not under more restraint than at present. Aladdin himself had not the least share in my removal, of which I was alone the cause, although the innocent one.'

"To convince the sultan that she spoke the truth, the Princess Badroulboudour gave him a detailed account how the African Magician had disguised himself like a seller of lamps, and offered to exchange new lamps for old ones. She related the jest she had intended to practise in exchanging Aladdin's lamp, the important and secret qualities of which she did not know. Then she told of the instant removal of the palace and herself in consequence of this exchange, and their being transported into Africa with the magician himself, who had been recognised by two of her women, and also by the eunuch who had made the exchange, when he had the audacity to come and present himself before her the first time after the success of his daring enterprise; and she spoke of the proposal he made to marry her. She then informed him of the persecution she continued to suffer until the arrival of Aladdin; of the measures they conjointly took to get possession of the lamp, which the magician constantly carried about him; in what manner they had succeeded, particularly by the courage of the princess in dissembling her feelings, and inviting the magician to sup with her; with everything that happened till she presented to him the goblet in which she had privately put the powder Aladdin had given her. 'With respect to the rest,' added she, 'I leave Aladdin to inform you of it.'

"Aladdin had but little to add to this account. 'When they opened the private door,' he said, 'I immediately went up to the hall of the twenty-four windows, and saw the traitor lying dead on the sofa from the effects of the powder. As it was not proper that the princess should remain there any longer, I requested her to go to her apartment with her women and eunuchs. When I was alone I took the lamp out of the magician's bosom, and made use of the same secret he had employed to remove the palace and steal away the princess. I have brought the palace back to its place, and have had the

FATIMA PAINTING THE FACE OF THE MAGICIAN.

happiness of restoring the princess to your majesty, as you commanded me. I have not deceived your majesty in this matter; and if you will take the trouble to go up to the saloon, you will see the magician has been punished as he deserved.'

"In pursuance of this invitation, the sultan rose and went up; and when he had seen the dead body of the magician, whose face had already become livid from the strength of the poison, he embraced Aladdin with the greatest tenderness. 'Do not be angry with me, my son,' cried he, 'for having used you harshly; paternal affection drove me to it, and I deserve to be pardoned for my fault, in consideration of the cause.' 'O great king,' replied Aladdin, 'I have not the least reason to complain of your majesty's conduct; you have done only what was your duty. This magician, this infamous wretch, this most detestable of men, was the sole cause of my disgrace. When your majesty has leisure to hear me, I will give you an account of another piece of treachery, not less infamous than this, which he practised towards me, from which the peculiar providence of Heaven has preserved me.' 'I will take care to find an opportunity,' said the sultan, 'and that quickly. But let us now only think of rejoicing in this happy change.'

"Aladdin ordered that the magician's body should be thrown out as a prey for the beasts and birds. In the meantime the sultan, after having commanded the drums, trumpets, cymbals, and other instruments to announce a public rejoicing, had a festival of ten days' continuance proclaimed in honour of the return of the Princess Badroulboudour and Aladdin, and of the restoration of the palace.

"It was thus that Aladdin a second time escaped an almost inevitable death. But even this was not his last peril: he was in mortal danger a third time. The circumstances of this third peril are now to be related.

"The African Magician had a younger brother, who was not inferior to him in his knowledge of magic, and who even surpassed the elder brother in wicked designs, evil intentions, and diabolical machinations. As they did not always live together, or even inhabit the same city, one sometimes being at the eastern extremity, while the other travelled in the most western part of the world, each of them did not fail once every year to ascertain, by means of their knowledge of geomancy, in what part of the world the other was, what he was doing, and whether he wanted counsel or assistance.

"Some time after the African Magician had perished in his attempt against Aladdin, his younger brother, who had not received any intelligence of him for a year, and who was not in Africa, wished to know where the elder was dwelling, whether he was well, and what he was doing. Wherever he travelled he carried with him his square geomantic box, as his brother had been accustomed to do. He took this box, and having arranged the sand, he cast the points, drew the figures, and formed his horoscope. The result was the discovery that his brother was no longer alive, but had been poisoned, and that suddenly. On searching further he found that this had happened in a capital situated in Africa, and that the man by whom his brother had been poisoned now resided in a certain part of China, was a man of low birth, but married to a princess, the daughter of the sultan.

"When the magician had thus ascertained the melancholy fate of his brother, he did not waste his time in useless regrets which could not again restore the dead man to life, but he took an immediate resolution to avenge his death. He mounted his horse and directly began his journey towards China. He traversed plains, crossed rivers, mountains, and deserts, and after a long journey, attended with incredible fatigue and difficulty, he at length reached China, and in a short time arrived at that capital which his experiment in geomancy had pointed out. Certain that he had not deceived himself, and that he had not mistaken one kingdom for another, immediately on his arrived he took up his abode there.

"The very next morning the magician walked out, not for the purpose of seeing the beauties of the place, which did not at all attract him, but with the intention of taking measures to put his pernicious design into execution. He walked abroad through the most frequented places, and was very attentive to the conversation he heard. At a house where many people were spending their time in playing a variety of games, and where, while some were playing, others were discussing the news or talking over their own affairs, he observed that they spoke much of and highly praised the virtues and piety of a woman called Fatima, who led a retired life, and of whom they asserted that she even performed miracles. As he thought that this woman might, perhaps, be in some way useful in the business he was about, he took one of the speakers aside, and begged him to give him a more particular account of this holy Fatima, and to explain what sort of miracles she performed.

"'How!' exclaimed the man: 'have you never seen or even heard of her? She is the admiration of the whole city for her strict and austere life, and for the good example she sets. Except on two days of the week, she never leaves her hermitage; but on those days she comes into the city, where she does an infinite deal of good; for there is no one afflicted with a pain in the head whom she does not cure by laying her hands upon him.'

"The magician did not want to know more on this subject, he only inquired of the same person in what quarter of the city the hermitage of this holy woman was situated. On obtaining the required information, he formed a horrible design with regard to this Fatima; and that he might be sure of its success, he observed all her conduct on the very first day she went out, and did not lose sight of her the whole day till she returned in the evening to her cell. When he had accurately remarked the spot where she dwelt, he returned to one of those places where, as has been said, a certain warm liquor is sold, and where any traveller who chooses may pass the night, particularly during the hot weather, when the inhabitants of China prefer sleeping upon a mat to resting in a bed.

"The magician, after paying the master of the house for what he had eaten and drunk, which did not amount to much, went out about midnight, and took the road to the hermitage of Fatima, or the Holy Woman, by which name she was known throughout the city. He had no difficulty in opening the door, as it was only fastened by a latch. As soon as he entered, he shut it again without making any noise. By the light of the moon he perceived Fatima lying almost in the open air, upon a couch with a ragged mat, close to the side of her cell. He approached, and after silently taking out a poniard which he had by his side, he awoke her.

"On opening her eyes, poor Fatima was very much astonished at seeing a man standing over her with a deadly weapon in his hand. Holding the point of the dagger against her breast, ready in an instant to plunge it into her heart, the magician exclaimed, 'If you cry out, or make the least noise, I will murder you. Get up, and do as I bid you.' Fatima, who always slept in her clothes, rose, trembling with fear. 'Fear nothing,' said the magician, 'I only want your cloak; give it me, and take mine.' When the magician was dressed in Fatima's clothes, he said to her, 'Paint my face to look like yours, and so that the colour will not come off.' As he saw that the Holy Woman still trembled, he added, in order to give her courage, and to induce her to obey him: 'Fear nothing, I tell you again; I swear by all that is sacred that I will spare your life.' Fatima then took him into the interior of her cell, lighted her lamp, and mixing a certain liquid in a basin, she rubbed it over his face; assuring him it would not change, and that there was now no difference in colour between her face and his. She then put upon him her own head-dress, with a veil, and she showed him how she concealed her face with this veil when she walked through the city. In conclusion, she hung round his neck a large necklace or chaplet, which came down nearly to his waist; she then put the stick she was accustomed to walk with into his hand, and gave him a mirror. 'Look at yourself,' she said, 'and you will find that you cannot resemble me more closely.' The magician found himself disguised as he wished; but he did not keep the oath he had so solemnly taken in her presence. For fear that he might be stained with her blood, which would fall if he stabbed her with his poniard, he strangled her; and when he found that she was dead, he drew the body by the feet to the cistern of the hermitage, and threw it in.

"The magician, thus disguised like the Holy Woman, passed the remainder of the night in the hermitage which he had desecrated by this horrible murder. Very early the next morning, although it was not the usual day for Fatima's appearance in the city, he sallied forth, because he conjectured that no one would ask him why he came abroad, or if they did, he could easily invent some excuse. The first thing he had done, on his arrival in the capital, had been to go and observe the palace of Aladdin; and as it was there that he intended to put the scheme he had devised into execution, he took the road towards it.

"When the people saw the Holy Woman (for every one took him for poor Fatima), the magician was surrounded by a great crowd of people. Some recommended themselves to his prayers, others kissed his hand; some kissed the hem of his robe with the greatest respect, while others, either because they had the headache, or wished to be preserved from it, bent down before him, that he might lay his hands upon them; he did so, muttering at the same time a few words that sounded like a prayer. In fact, he so well imitated the Holy Woman, that every one was deceived, and took him for her. After stopping very often to satisfy those people who fancied they received benefit from this imposition of hands, he at last arrived in the square before Aladdin's palace, where, as the crowd increased, the difficulty and press to get near him was also greater. The strongest and most zealous beat off the rest to secure a place for themselves, and hence several quarrels arose, the noise of which reached the ears of the Princess Badroulboudour, who was sitting in the hall of the twenty-four windows.

"The princess asked what was the matter, and as no person could inform her, she ordered that some one should go and see, and bring her word. One of her women, without leaving the hall, looked through the lattice, and then came and told her mistress that the noise arose from a crowd of people who were collected round the Holy Woman to be cured of pains in their heads by the laying on of her hands.

"The princess, who for some time past had heard every one speak in praise of this Holy Woman, but who had never yet beheld her, felt a desire to see and converse with her. She said as much to the chief of the eunuchs, who was present, whereupon that officer said that if she wished it, he was sure he could get Fatima to come, if his mistress would let him send for her. The princess consented to this, and he instantly dispatched four eunuchs with an order to bring back the Holy Woman with them.

"As soon as the eunuchs had gone out of the gate of Aladdin's palace, and were seen making towards the place where the Holy Woman, or rather the disguised magician, stood, the crowd began to disperse; and when the magician was thus more at liberty, and saw that they were coming towards him, he went to meet them with great glee, for he saw that his cunning scheme was likely to be successful. One of the eunuchs addressed him in these words: 'O Holy Woman, the princess wishes to see you; will it please you to follow us?' 'The princess honours me greatly,' replied the pretended Fatima: 'I am ready to obey her commands;' and he then followed the eunuchs, who immediately brought him to the palace.

"When the magician, concealing his black heart under the robe of sanctity, was introduced into the hall of the twenty-four windows, and perceived the princess, he began a prayer, which contained a long catalogue of exhortations and wishes for the happiness and prosperity of Princess Badroulboudour. He displayed all his hypocritical and deceitful rhetoric, in order to insinuate himself, under the cloak of great piety, into the good opinion of the princess. And in this he succeeded without difficulty, as the princess, who was naturally of a frank and honest disposition, fancied that all the world were at least as good as herself; particularly did she believe in all those who professed to serve Heaven by a retired life.

"When the false Fatima had finished his long harangue, the princess replied: 'My good mother, I am much obliged to you for your kind prayers; I have the greatest confidence in them, and trust Heaven will hear them. Come hither, and sit down near me.' The pretended Fatima obeyed with an appearance of the greatest modesty; and the princess, continuing her speech, said: 'My good mother, I have a request to make to you which you must not refuse me; and that is, that you come and live with me, that I may have you constantly to converse with, and may learn from your advice, and the good example you set me, to become as good and holy as you are.'

"'O princess,' replied the false Fatima, 'I entreat you not to require my compliance in a thing to which I cannot agree without giving up my life of prayer and devotion.' 'Do not let that trouble you,' resumed the princess; 'I have many apartments which are not occupied. You shall choose whichever of these you like best, and you shall have as much time for your devotions, and as much liberty, as if you were in your hermitage.'

"The magician, whose chief object was to introduce himself into Aladdin's palace, where he would have an opportunity to execute the wicked design he meditated, saw that by thus remaining under the auspices and protection of the princess, one of his chief obstacles would be removed. He therefore did not make much difficulty in acceding to the obliging offer of Princess Badroulboudour. 'O gracious princess,' he replied, 'whatever resolution a poor and miserable woman like myself may have made to renounce the world, with its pomps and vanities, I nevertheless dare not resist either the wish or the command of so pious and charitable a lady.'

"Upon this answer the princess herself arose, and said to the magician, 'Come with me, that I may show you all the apartments that are unoccupied; you may then make your choice.' The magician followed the princess through all the rooms she showed him,

THE PRETENDED FATIMA ATTEMPTS THE LIFE OF ALADDIN.

which were very pleasant and handsomely furnished. He chose the plainest and smallest of them all, saying at the same time that it was much too good for him, and that he only made choice of it to oblige the princess.

"Princess Badroulboudour wished to take the impostor back with her to the hall of the twenty-four windows, and asked him to dine with her; but as he would have been compelled to uncover his face, which he had hitherto kept concealed by the veil, and as he was afraid she might discover that he was not the holy woman Fatima, he begged her earnestly to excuse him, saying that he never ate anything but bread and dried fruits, and asked her permission to take his trifling meal in his own apartment. She readily complied with his wishes. 'My good mother,' she said, 'you are quite at liberty to follow your own wish. Do as you would in the hermitage: I will order my people to carry you in some food; but remember that I shall expect you as soon as you have finished your repast.'

"The princess then dined; and the false Fatima did not fail to return to her as soon as he had been informed by an eunuch, whom he had instructed to let him know, that his mistress had risen from the table. 'My good mother,' said the princess, 'I am delighted to enjoy the company of such a holy woman as yourself, who will, by your presence, bring down blessings upon the whole palace. And now I mention this palace, pray tell me what you think of it. But before I show you all the other apartments, tell me how you like this hall.'

"At this question the magician, who, in order to preserve his assumed aspect of humility and diffidence, had till now kept his head bent down towards the ground, without ever raising it to look on either side, at length looked up, and seemed to gaze at everything in the hall, from one end to the other. When he had thoroughly examined it, he said, 'Indeed, my princess, this saloon is truly beautiful, and worthy of admiration. But, so far as a recluse can judge who knows nothing of what is reckoned beautiful by the world in general, I think one thing is wanting.' 'What is that, my good mother?' inquired Princess Badroulboudour; 'I entreat you to tell me. For my part, I thought, and have also heard it said, that nothing was wanting; but whatever may be deficient I will have supplied.'

"'Pardon my freedom of speech, gracious lady,' replied the dissembling magician. 'My opinion, if it can be of any value, is, that if the egg of a roc were suspended from the centre of the dome, this hall would not have its equal in any of the four quarters of the globe, and your palace would be the wonder of the whole universe.'

"'My good mother,' returned the princess, 'tell me what kind of bird a roc is, and where the egg of one could be found?' 'Princess,' answered the feigned Fatima, 'the roc is a bird of prodigious size which inhabits the summit of Mount Caucasus; and the architect who designed your palace can procure you a roc's egg.'

"After thanking the pretended Fatima for her kind information and for what she thought her good advice, the Princess Badroulboudour turned the conversation upon various other subjects; but she by no means forgot the roc's egg, and determined to speak to Aladdin on the subject when he returned from hunting. He had already been absent six days; and the magician, who was aware of this circumstance, wished to take every advantage of his absence. Aladdin returned late on the same evening when the false Fatima had taken leave of the princess, and had retired to the apartment allotted to her. As soon as he entered the palace, he went to the apartment of the princess. He saluted and embraced her; but she seemed to him to receive him with less than her usual welcome. 'I do not find you, my princess, in your usual good spirits,' said Aladdin; 'has anything happened during my absence that has displeased or vexed you? Do not, in the name of Heaven, conceal it from me; for there is nothing in my power that I will not do to endeavour to dispel it.' 'I have been disturbed by a mere trifle,' replied the princess, 'and it really gives me so little anxiety that I did not suppose my discomposure would be so apparent in my face and manner that you could have perceived it. But since you have observed some alteration in me, which I by no means intended, I will not conceal the cause, inconsiderable as it is.

"'I thought, as you did yourself,' the princess continued, 'that our palace was the most superb, the most beautiful, and the most completely decorated of all the buildings in the whole world. I will tell you, however, what has come into my head on thoroughly examining the hall of the twenty-four windows. Do not you think with me that if a roc's egg were suspended from the centre of the dome, it would greatly improve the effect?' 'It is enough, my princess,' replied Aladdin, 'that you think the absence of a roc's egg a defect. You shall find, by the diligence with which I am going to repair this omission, that there is nothing I will not do for love of you.'

"Aladdin instantly left the princess, and went up to the hall of the twenty-four windows; and then taking out of his bosom the lamp, which he always carried about with him since the distress he had undergone from the neglect of that precaution, he rubbed it to summon the genie, who immediately appeared before him. 'O genie,' said Aladdin, 'a roc's egg should be suspended from the centre of this dome in order to make it perfect; I command you in the name of the lamp which I hold to get this defect rectified.'

"Aladdin had scarcely pronounced these words when the genie uttered so loud and dreadful a scream that the very room shook, and Aladdin could not refrain from trembling violently. 'How, thou wretch!' exclaimed the genie, in a voice that would have made the most courageous man shake with dread, 'is it not enough that I and my companions have done everything thou hast chosen to command? Wouldst thou repay our services by such unparalleled ingratitude, as to command me to bring thee my master, and hang him up in the midst of this vaulted dome? For this crime thou dost deserve to be instantly torn to atoms, and thy wife and palace should perish with thee. But thou art fortunate that the request did not originate with thee, and that the command is not in any way thine. Learn who is the true author of this mischief. It is done by no other than the brother of thy enemy the African Magician, whom thou hast destroyed as he deserved. That perfidious brother is in thy palace, disguised under the appearance of Fatima the holy woman, whom he has murdered; and it is he who has induced thy wife to make the horrible and destructive request thou hast made. His design is to kill thee; therefore take heed to thyself.' As the genie said this he vanished.

"Aladdin pondered well these words of the genie. He had already heard of the holy woman Fatima, and was not ignorant of the fame she had attained by her alleged cures of pains. He returned to the apartment of the princess, but did not mention what had happened to him. He sat down, and complained of a violent pain that had suddenly seized his head, and he held his hand up to his forehead with an expression of great suffering. The princess directly ordered her people to call the Holy Woman; and while they were gone she related to Aladdin the manner in which she had induced Fatima to come to the palace, where she had given her an apartment.

"The disguised magician came; and as soon as he entered, Aladdin said to him, 'I am very happy, my good mother, to see you, and it is for my advantage to have you here just now. I am tormented with a violent headache which has just attacked me. I request your assistance; and from the reliance I place on your good prayers, I hope you will not refuse me the favour which you grant to all who are thus afflicted.' When he had said this, he bent his head forward, and the magician also advanced, with his hand upon a poniard which was concealed in his girdle under his robe. Aladdin, who watched his motions, seized his hand before he could draw the weapon, and piercing him to the heart with his own dagger, stretched him dead upon the floor.

"'What have you done, my dear husband?' exclaimed the princess, in the greatest surprise; 'you have killed the Holy Woman!' 'No, no, my princess,' answered Aladdin, without the least emotion, 'I have not killed Fatima, but a villain who was going to assassinate me if I had not prevented him. This is the wretch, whom you here behold,' added he, showing the dead man's face, 'that strangled Fatima, whom you thought I had destroyed, and therefore regretted. He has disguised himself in her clothes in order to murder me; and to convince you that this is true, I have further to inform you that he is the brother of the African Magician who carried you off.' Aladdin then related to his wife in what manner he had learnt these particulars, and he then ordered the servants to remove the body.

"Thus Aladdin was delivered from the persecution of the two magicians. A few years after, the sultan died at a good old age, and as he left no male issue, the Princess Badroulboudour succeeded to the throne as his legitimate heir, and of course shared the supreme power with Aladdin. They reigned together many years, and left an illustrious and numerous posterity.

"O great king," said the Sultana Scheherazade, when she had finished the account of the adventures of Aladdin with the wonderful lamp, "your majesty has doubtless remarked in the African Magician the character of a man who has abandoned himself to the inordinate passion of acquiring wealth by the most unjustifiable methods, and one who, though he had the cleverness to gain wealth, was not suffered to enjoy it, because he was unworthy. In Aladdin, on the contrary, you see a man who from the lowest origin rose to a throne, by making use of the treasures which he had accidentally acquired as they were intended to be used, namely, as means to attain the end he had in view. In the sultan you must have observed that even a good, just, and equitable monarch runs the risk of being dethroned when, by an act of injustice, and contrary to every rule of equity, he dares with unreasonable haste to condemn an innocent man without pausing to hear his defence. Your majesty must feel horror, too, at the crimes of the two infamous magicians, one of whom sacrificed his life in the attempt to acquire treasures, and the other both his life and his religion for the sake of avenging a villain who had received the reward due to his crimes."

The Sultan of the Indies gave Scheherazade to understand that he was very much pleased with the marvellous adventures of the fortunate Aladdin, and that the other stories she had each morning told him afforded him equal satisfaction. In fact, these stories were always diverting, and each contained a good lesson. It was very evident that the sultana made them succeed each other so skilfully that the sultan was not sorry to have this excuse for delaying the fulfilment of the oath he had so solemnly taken, namely, to have a wife for but one night, and the next morning to cause her to be put to death. He now only thought whether he should not in the end absolutely exhaust the sultana's store. With this intention, after hearing the conclusion of the history of Aladdin and the Princess Badroulboudour, which was very different from any tale he had yet heard, he even got the start of Dinarzade, and himself awoke the sultana with the inquiry if she had exhausted her supply of tales.

"O my lord," replied Scheherazade, smiling at this question, "I have many yet in store: the number of my tales is so great that it would be almost impossible to give your majesty a list of them. But I fear that your majesty will grow tired of hearing me much sooner than I shall want materials to go on with." "Do not be afraid of that," replied Schahriar, "but let me hear what you have next to relate."

Encouraged by this speech, the sultana immediately began a new story in these words. "I have often, O king," said she, "entertained your majesty with some adventures of the famous Caliph Haroun Alraschid; but there are a great many others besides these of which I have not yet spoken, and I will now relate one that is not unworthy of your attention."

## THE ADVENTURES OF THE CALIPH HAROUN ALRASCHID.

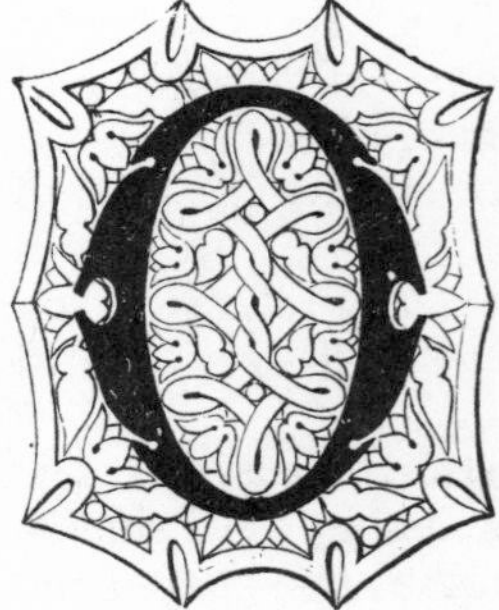

MIGHTY KING, you must be aware, and may yourself have experienced, that men sometimes give way to such extraordinary transports of joy, that they immediately communicate this passion to those around; and at others are as readily affected by the joys of their fellows. Sometimes, on the other hand, they give way so completely to melancholy, that they become a burden to themselves; and so far from being able to explain to others the cause of these extremes of feeling, they cannot even give a reason for them to themselves.

"The Caliph Haroun Alraschid was one day in this last state of mind, when Giafar, his faithful and beloved grand vizier, came into his presence. The minister found his master alone (in itself an unusual circumstance); and as he perceived upon advancing that the caliph was in a gloomy mood, and that he did not so much as lift up his eyes to look at Giafar, he stopped till Haroun Alraschid should deign to notice him. At length the caliph looked up and saw the vizier, but as quickly turned away, and resumed his former melancholy posture.

BABA ABDALLA AND THE CALIPH.

"As the grand vizier saw nothing in the caliph's countenance which indicated any displeasure towards himself, he thus addressed him: 'O Commander of the Faithful, will your majesty permit me to ask the cause of the dejection you manifest, a dejection to which I have rarely seen you subject?' 'It is true, vizier,' said the caliph, looking up, 'I seldom give way to melancholy in this manner, and but for you I should not have been aware of the disposition in which you find me, and in which I have no desire to remain. If nothing new has happened to occasion your coming to me, I must ask you to think of something that will employ and amuse me.' 'Commander of the Faithful,' replied the grand vizier, 'my duty alone has led me hither; and I take the liberty of bringing to your majesty's recollection the task you have imposed upon yourself, of witnessing in person that excellent system of regulations which you have caused to be carried out in your capital and its neighbourhood. This is the day your majesty has set apart for the performance of this business, and no occupation is more likely than this to dispel the cloud which overcasts your accustomed cheerfulness.' 'I had forgotten it,' replied the caliph, 'and you do well to remind me. Go and change your dress, and I will prepare to go out.'

"Each of them assumed the habit of a foreign merchant; and in this disguise they went unattended through a private door of the palace garden which opened into the country. They took a turn beyond the walls of the town to the banks of the river that run at some distance from the gate, without seeing anything worthy of notice. They crossed the river in the first boat they found, and when they had completed the circuit of the other part of the town opposite to that which they had first visited, they returned by way of the bridge which forms the communication.

"They passed this bridge, at the foot of which they met an old blind man who was begging. The caliph turned towards him, and dropped a piece of gold into his hand. The blind man instantly laid hold of the donor's hand, and stopped him. 'O charitable person!' said he, 'whoever you are whom Allah has inspired to give me alms, do not, I beseech you, refuse me a further favour. I request you to give me a blow on the head. I deserve this, and even a still greater punishment.' So saying, he quitted the caliph's hand, that the latter might have the power of giving him the blow, but seized his garment, for fear he should pass on without doing so.

"Surprised at this strange request and at the behaviour of the blind man, the caliph answered: 'My good friend, I cannot comply with your request; I shall certainly not care to destroy the value of my gift by the cruelty you require at my hands.' Saying this, he endeavoured to disengage himself.

"The blind man, who was prepared for this unwillingness in his benefactor, from the frequent experience he had had on similar occasions, made a still stronger effort to hold him fast. 'Sir,' said he, 'pardon my boldness and my importunity, I entreat you; give me the blow, or take back your alms. I can accept it upon no other condition without breaking a solemn oath which I have taken before Heaven; and if you knew why I had taken this oath, you would at once agree with me that the punishment I impose upon myself is very inconsiderable.'

"The caliph, who was unwilling to be any longer detained, yielded to the blind man's importunity, and gave him a slight blow. The blind man immediately let him go, with thanks and blessings. The caliph went on with the grand vizier, and after a few steps he said to him: 'Surely the reason which has induced this blind man to require a blow from all those who bestow their alms upon him must be of some importance. I should like to learn what it is; return, therefore, and tell the blind beggar who I am, and order him to come to-morrow without fail to the palace, at the time of afternoon prayers, that I may speak with him.' The grand vizier went back directly, gave a present to the blind man, and after he had also given him the required blow, told him what the caliph required; he then went back to his master.

"They re-entered the town, and passing through a square, they found themselves among a great number of people who were looking at a well-dressed young man mounted on a mare. This mare he rode at full speed round the square, whipping and spurring it most unmercifully, so that it was covered with foam and blood. The caliph, astonished at the cruelty of the young man, stopped and asked several of the spectators if they knew why he treated the animal so ill. He found that nobody could give him any information beyond the fact that the rider had for some time, every day at the same hour, engaged in this inhuman exercise.

"They continued their walk, and the caliph told the vizier to remember this square, and not fail to cause this young man to come to him the next day at the same hour at which the blind man was to receive an audience.

"Before the caliph reached the palace, in a street through which he had not passed for a long time he observed a newly-built house, which seemed to be the residence of some great man of the court. He asked the grand vizier if he could tell to whom it belonged; the latter replied he did not know, but would go and make inquiries. He then asked a neighbour, who told him that the house belonged to one Cogia Hassan, surnamed Alhabbal, from his trade of ropemaking, which he had himself seen the said Cogia Hassan carry on in a state of great poverty, and that, to the surprise of his neighbours, who knew not in what way he had been so favoured by fortune, Cogia Hassan had acquired wealth enough to erect this great building in a very splendid manner.

"The grand vizier went back to the caliph, and told him what he had learnt. 'I must see this Cogia Hassan Alhabbal,' said the caliph to him. 'Go and bid him also come to the palace, at the same hour with the other two.' The grand vizier took care punctually to execute the caliph's orders.

"The next day, when afternoon prayers were ended, the caliph returned to his apartment, and the grand vizier immediately brought in the three persons above-mentioned, and presented them to the great Haroun Alraschid. All three prostrated themselves before the throne of the sultan, and when they rose up, the caliph asked the blind man his name. He answered, 'I am called Baba Abdalla.' 'Baba Abdalla,' returned the caliph, 'your manner of asking alms yesterday appeared so extraordinary, that if I had not been influenced by certain considerations, I should have been very far from humouring you as I did; and I would instantly have put a stop to your insulting the public by making ridiculous requests. I have sent for you here to learn from yourself what motive can have urged you to take the silly oath by which you have bound yourself; and from what you tell me I shall judge whether you have done right, and whether I ought to suffer you to continue a practice which seems likely to be followed by many ill consequences. Tell me then, without disguise, whence this extravagant conceit arises; conceal nothing from me, for I require the whole truth.'

"Baba Abdalla, somewhat startled by this address, prostrated himself a second time before the throne of the caliph; and after rising, said immediately, 'Commander of the Faithful, I most humbly beg pardon of your majesty for the boldness with which I have dared to demand of you and to enforce your compliance with a condition which in truth seems very absurd. I confess my crime; but as I did not know your majesty, I implore your clemency, and hope you will mercifully consider my ignorance.

"'Your majesty has been pleased to declare that what I did was folly. I confess it seems to be so, and my behaviour must appear such in the eyes of men; but in the sight of Heaven it is but a slight penance for an enormous crime of which I have been guilty, and which I should not expiate though every man in the world should thus give me a blow: of this you will yourself judge when the history which I am about to relate in obedience to your commands shall have informed you of the heinous nature of my crime.

## The History of Baba Abdalla the Blind Man.

"I was born at Bagdad, and inherited a little property from my father and mother, who died within a few days of each other. Although I had but little experience of life, I did not, after the usual fashion of young men, waste my fortune in a short time in idle, vicious extravagance. On the contrary, I was always anxious to increase it by my industry, with all the care and trouble I could bestow. At length I became so rich that I possessed fourscore camels of my own, which I let to the caravan merchants, and which produced me large sums for every journey they made in different parts of your majesty's extended empire, and on every occasion I accompanied them.

"Thus successful, I was seized with an earnest desire to become still richer. One day

I was returning from Balsora with my camels unladen. I had driven them to that city with goods to be embarked for India. I now turned them loose to feed in a spot far distant from any habitation, and where the abundance of the pasture had induced me to halt. A dervish, who was going on foot to Balsora, came up, and sat near me to refresh himself after his fatigue. I asked him whence he came, and whither he was going; he put the same questions to me; and after we had mutually satisfied each other's curiosity, we produced our provisions, and sat down to eat and drink together.

"During our repast we conversed upon many indifferent subjects; but at length the dervish told me that in a place not far off he knew of a treasure of immense value, so large and rich, that if my fourscore camels should all be laden from thence with gold and jewels, it would seem as if nothing had been taken away from the mass.

"This good news at once surprised and delighted me. I was quite bewildered and confused with the joy I felt. I did not think the dervish would care to impose upon me. Therefore, embracing him fervently, I cried, 'My good dervish, I see plainly that you have little regard for the things of this world: of what use to you, therefore, is the knowledge of this treasure? You are alone, and could by yourself carry off but a very small part of it: show me where it is, and I will load my fourscore camels from it, and will present you with one of them in return for the profit and advantage you will have procured for me.'

"My offer was absurdly small, no doubt, but it appeared to me considerable, so entirely had avarice gained possession of my heart from the time when the dervish imparted to me this secret; and I considered the threescore and nineteen loads which would be mine as nothing in comparison with the one of which I should deprive myself by giving it to him.

"The dervish, who immediately saw my greed and covetousness, took no offence at the unreasonable offer I had just made him, but said, without the least emotion: 'O my brother, you see plainly that what you offer me is in no proportion to the favour you request. I was not obliged to say a word to you of the treasure, and might have kept my secret; but what I have so frankly told you must convince you that I had, and still have, a sincere desire to oblige you, and to give you cause to remember me for ever, by making your fortune while I make my own. I have now another proposal, more just and equitable, to make to you; it is for you to consider whether you will accept it. You said,' continued the dervish, 'that you possessed fourscore camels. I am ready to lead you to the place where the treasure lies; we will together load these camels with as much of the gold and jewels as they can carry; but upon condition that when they have all been laden you shall give up one-half of them with their burden, and shall retain the other half for yourself. Thereupon we will separate, and go where we please; you with your share, and I with mine. You see this division is perfectly equitable; for if you give up to me forty camels, you will by my means have gained enough to purchase a thousand.'

"I could not deny that the proposal of the dervish was very fair; nevertheless, instead of considering the great wealth which would accrue to me from acceding to it, I looked upon giving up the half of my camels as a great loss, particularly when I thought the dervish would be as rich as myself; so that I already repaid with ingratitude a favour of the purest generosity which I was about to receive from the dervish. But there was no room for hesitation; I must at once accept the terms, or be prepared all my life after to repent that entirely by my own fault I had lost an opportunity of making a large fortune.

"I at once collected my camels, and we proceeded together. After travelling some time, we arrived at a spacious valley, the entrance to which was very narrow. My camels could only pass one by one; but as the space by degrees grew wider, they could easily afterwards go on several together. The two mountains which bounded this valley made a sort of semicircle at its extremity, and were so high, so steep, and so inaccessible that we had no reason to fear any mortal could see us.

"When we had arrived within the pass of the mountains, the dervish said, 'Let us go no farther. Stop your camels, and make them lie down on the spot before you, that we may have no trouble in loading them; and when you have done this, I will go before you to the entrance of the place where the treasure is deposited.' I did as the dervish requested me, and went to him directly. I found him with a flint and steel in his hand, collecting a little dry wood for a fire. As soon as he had kindled a flame, he threw upon it some perfume, at the same time uttering some mystic words which I could not understand, and immediately a thick smoke rose into the air. The dervish caused this smoke to part, and in a moment, although the rock, which was between the mountains and rose perpendicularly to a considerable height, showed not the slightest trace of an opening, an entrance nevertheless appeared through the rock itself. like a passage, with folding doors admirably carved out of the solid stone.

BABA ABDALLA AND THE DERVISH IN THE TREASURE-HOUSE.

"This opening displayed to our view, in a vast cavern sunk in the rock, a magnificent palace, the work rather of genii than of man, for man would never think of undertaking any structure so bold and astonishing. But I did not think of this at the time; I was not even struck with the infinite richness of what was to be seen on all sides; but without stopping to notice the admirable order in which this great treasure had been arranged, I ran to the first heap of gold I saw, as an eagle darts upon his prey, and poured into a sack, with which I had provided myself, as much money as I thought I could carry: the sacks were large, and I would fain have filled them all, but was obliged to think of the strength of my camels. The dervish was similarly employed, but I perceived that he confined himself to the jewels. He explained to me the reason of this; I then followed his example, and we carried off a much greater proportion of precious stones than of gold. After we had filled our sacks and loaded the camels, nothing remained to be done but to close the treasure-house again and depart.

"Before we quitted the treasure, however, the dervish went to a part of the building where there were many vases of gold, in a variety of shapes and fashions, as well as some of other precious materials; and I observed that he took from one of these a small box of a certain wood, with which I was unacquainted, which he put into his bosom after he had shown me that it contained only a sort of ointment.

"The dervish went through the same ceremony on closing up the treasure that he had performed on opening it; and after he had uttered certain words the door shut upon the treasure, and the rock appeared with the same unbroken surface it had before exhibited.

"We then divided our camels, and made them all rise with their burdens. I placed myself at the head of the forty which I had reserved for myself, and the dervish began to lead away those which I had given up to him.

"We passed one by one through the same narrow path by which we had entered the valley, and then travelled on together till we came to the great road, where we were to separate; he to pursue his journey to Balsora, and I to return to Bagdad. I thanked him in the strongest terms, such as best marked my gratitude, for his great kindness in having preferred me to all others, and making me the sharer of so much wealth. We embraced each other with the highest satisfaction, and after a cordial farewell we parted.

"I had taken but a few steps towards overtaking my camels, who were accustomed to travel on in the road on which I drove them, before the demon of ingratitude and envy got possession of my heart. I lamented the loss of my forty camels, and still more the wealth they carried. 'The dervish has no occasion for all this wealth,' said I to myself. 'He is master of the whole treasure, and can help himself to as much as he chooses.' Thus I gave myself up to thoughts of the blackest ingratitude, and instantly determined to take from my benefactor his camels and their burdens.

"In order to accomplish my purpose, I made my camels halt. I then ran after the dervish, calling to him as loud as I could to make him understand that I had something more to say to him; and I made signs to him to stop his camels also, and to wait for me. He heard my voice, and stood still.

"When I had come up to him, I exclaimed: 'O my dear brother, so soon as I had quitted you, I thought of a thing which I never alluded to before, and which, perhaps, you yourself have never yet considered. You are a good dervish, used to live in great tranquillity, free from all worldly care, and with no other idea than that of serving Allah. You can have no conception, I am sure, of the trouble you have undertaken by encumbering yourself with the care of so many camels. Believe me, you had better take away only thirty; and I conjecture you will have quite difficulty enough in managing them. You may leave the rest to me—I am used to them.' 'I believe you are right,' said the dervish, who found himself in no position to dispute the matter with me; 'and I confess,' added he, 'that I never once thought of it. I was beginning to feel uneasy at the thought of what you now represent to me. Select the ten that please you best, and take them away; and the blessing of Heaven go with you.'

"I chose ten of the camels, and after turning them back, I put them in the road to follow mine. I did not think the dervish would have allowed himself to be so easily persuaded. This increased my cupidity, and I flattered myself I should have but little trouble in obtaining ten camels more.

"In fact, instead of thanking the dervish for the rich present he had just made me, I said again, 'Brother, from the concern I take in your peace, I cannot determine to quit you without beseeching you to consider once more how difficult it is to manage thirty laden camels, particularly for a man like you, unaccustomed to this sort of work. You would find it much better to repeat the favour you have just conferred upon me. What I say, you see, is not so much for my own sake and for my own advantage, as for your satisfaction. Think of yourself, therefore, and turn over these other ten camels to a person like me, to whom it will be no more trouble to take the care of a hundred than of a single one.'

"What I said had just the effect I wished; and the dervish gave up to me, without any objection, the ten camels I demanded; so that there remained with him no more than twenty, while I possessed for my share sixty, all laden with a burden the value of which exceeded the wealth of many princes. After this I think I ought to have been contented. But, like a person in a dropsy, who grows the more thirsty the more he drinks, I became still more earnest than before to obtain the last twenty, of which the dervish yet held possession.

"I redoubled my solicitations, my entreaties, and my importunity to induce the dervish to give me up ten of those twenty. He readily consented; and when only ten remained in his care, I embraced him, and conjured him with all the address I was able not to refuse me these, the gift of which would complete the eternal obligation I owed him, and I was overjoyed at hearing him say he consented. 'Make a proper use of them, O my brother,' added he, 'and remember that Allah can take away riches from us as he bestows them upon us, if we do not employ our goods in the service of the poor, whom He is pleased to leave in poverty for the express purpose of giving the rich an opportunity, by their alms, of meriting a greater recompense in another world.'

"My blindness was so great that I was quite unable to reap advantage from this good advice. I was not satisfied with finding myself once more in possession of my fourscore camels, and with the knowledge that they were laden with a treasure so valuable that I ought to have been the happiest of men. It came into my mind that the little box of ointment which the dervish had taken, and which he had shown me, might be something more precious than all the wealth which he had bestowed upon me. 'The place from which the dervish took it,' said I to myself, 'and the solicitude which he showed to gain possession of it, makes me assured that there is contained in it something of a mysterious nature.' This determined me to make an attempt to obtain it. I had just embraced the dervish, and said farewell; but I now went up to him again, and said: 'I have just recollected to ask you what you mean to do with that little box of ointment? It seems to me such a trifle that it is hardly worth your trouble in carrying it away; pray make me a present of it. Besides, a dervish like you, who has renounced the vanities of the world, can have no occasion for ointment.'

"Would to Heaven that he had refused me this box! But if he had been so disposed, I was no longer master of myself: I was the stronger, and thoroughly resolved to take it from him by force; for I had made up my mind that he should not take away the smallest part of the treasure, greatly as I had been indebted to him.

"Far from refusing me the box, the dervish immediately took it from his bosom, and presented it to me with the best grace. 'There, my brother,' said he, 'take it; you are welcome to this also. If I can do more for you, you have only to ask, and you shall be satisfied.'

"When I had the box in my hand, I opened it and looked at the ointment. 'Since,' said I, 'you are so very friendly, and are never tired of obliging me, do, I beseech you, tell me the particular use of this ointment.' 'The use of it is surprising and marvellous,' replied the dervish. 'If you apply a little of this ointment round the left eye, and upon the eye-lid, all the treasures concealed within the bosom of the earth will appear to your view; but if you make the same application to the right eye you will become blind.'

"I wished myself to experience this wonderful effect. 'Take the box,' said I, holding it out to him, 'and do you apply this ointment to my left eye: you understand the matter better than I do. I am impatient to make trial of a thing which appears to me incredible.'

"The dervish very readily undertook to gratify me. He made me shut my left eye, and applied the ointment. When he had done, I opened my eye, and found that he had told me the truth. In fact, I saw an infinite number of places, filled with riches so prodigious, and in such variety, that it would be impossible for me to particularise them. But I was obliged to keep my right eye shut with my hand. This fatigued me, and I begged the dervish to apply some ointment round that eye also. 'I am ready to do so,' said the dervish, 'but you must remember that I told you if you put any ointment upon the right eye, you would instantly become blind. Such is the power of this ointment, and I warn you accordingly.'

"Far from being satisfied that the dervish had told me the truth, I imagined on the contrary that there was some new mystery, which he wished to conceal from me. 'O my brother,' said I, smiling, 'I well know you mean to impose upon me; for I cannot believe that the same ointment should have two such opposite effects.' 'But I am telling you the truth,' replied the dervish, 'as I call upon Allah to witness; and you may believe me, for I do not disguise the truth.'

"I would not take his word, though he spoke honestly; the unconquerable desire I had to view at my ease all the treasures of the earth, and perhaps to possess them if I should choose to have that satisfaction, made me deaf to his remonstrances; nor could I be persuaded of a thing which nevertheless was but too true, as I very soon experienced to my great misfortune.

"Under this strong delusion, I felt convinced that if this ointment had the power of enabling me to see all the treasures of the earth by applying it to my left eye, it might perhaps have the power of giving me the disposal of them if it were applied to my right. Under this impression, I persevered in entreating the dervish to apply it himself round my right eye; but he constantly refused. 'After I have conferred on you wealth and substance,' said he, 'I cannot resolve to do you so great a mischief: consider well with yourself what misery it is to be deprived of sight, and do not reduce me to the sad necessity of complying with your request, and of doing to you what you will repent as long as you live.'

"But my obstinacy was not to be overcome. 'Brother,' said I, with great firmness, 'I beseech you, make no further difficulty on the subject. You have hitherto consented very generously to every request I have made: would you wish me to part from you dissatisfied on a point of so little consequence? In Heaven's name, grant me this last favour; whatever may be the result, I shall never blame you—the fault will be entirely my own.'

"The dervish made every possible objection, but seeing that it was in my power to compel him to compliance, he said: 'Since you are absolutely determined upon the matter, I shall proceed to satisfy you.' He then took a little of this fatal ointment, and applied it to my right eye, which I held closed. But alas! when I came to open it, I perceived nothing with either of my eyes. Intense darkness was around me, and I was blind, as I have continued ever since, and as you now see me.

"'Ah, ill-omened dervish!' cried I at the moment, 'what you foretold is indeed come to pass! Fatal curiosity,' added I, 'insatiable desire of riches, into what an abyss of misery have you plunged me! Too well do I know that I have brought all this upon myself; but, my dear brother,' I cried piteously to the dervish, 'charitable and beneficent as you are, among the many wonderful secrets with which you are acquainted, know you not one by which my sight may be restored?'

"'Thou unhappy wretch!' replied the dervish, 'hadst thou taken my advice thou wouldst have avoided this misfortune: thou hast thy deserts, and the blindness of thy heart has brought upon thee this blindness of thine eyes. It is true I am in possession of secrets—this thou must have learnt even in the short time that I have been with thee; but I have not one by which I can restore to thee thy sight. Address thy prayers to Allah if thou thinkest there is any such remedy; He only can bestow it on thee. He had given thee riches, of which thou wert unworthy. He hath taken them away from thee, and is going to give them by my hands to those who will not be so ungrateful as thou art.'

"The dervish said no more to me, and I had nothing to reply. He left me alone, covered with confusion and overwhelmed with inexpressible grief. He proceeded to collect my fourscore camels, and led them away, and pursued his journey to Balsora.

"I entreated him not to leave me in this miserable situation, and to help me at least so that I might join the next caravan; but he was deaf to my cries and prayers. Thus, deprived of sight and of everything I possessed in the world, I should have died of

THE LAST TOUCH.

grief and hunger if, the next day, a caravan returning from Balsora had not been moved by charity to take me up, and bring me back to Bagdad.

"Thus, from a position equal to that of princes, if not in power and might, at least in wealth and magnificence, I saw myself at once reduced to abject want and beggary. I could do nothing but ask alms, and this has been my employment to the present hour;

but to expiate my crime towards Heaven, I have imposed upon myself the punishment of a blow from every charitable person who shall have compassion on my misery.

"You see, then, O Commander of the Faithful, the motive of the conduct that yesterday appeared to your majesty so strange, and that must have incurred your displeasure. I again ask your pardon as your slave, and submit myself to any punishment you think I have deserved. And if your majesty will deign to judge of the penance I have imposed upon myself, I feel assured you will think it too light, and much below my crime."

"When the blind man had finished his history, the caliph said to him : 'Baba Abdalla, your sin is great, but Allah be praised that you are sensible of its enormity, and have submitted to this public penance to the present time. You have suffered enough ; but you must for the future continue to ask pardon of Allah in each of those prayers which your religion obliges you daily to offer; and that you may not be interrupted in this duty by the necessity of begging for subsistence, I shall supply you with a daily pension during your life of four drachms of silver, which my grand vizier shall pay you : do not, therefore, depart till he has executed my orders.'

"At these words Baba Abdalla threw himself prostrate at the throne of the caliph ; and as he rose he made his acknowledgments, and invoked every kind of happiness and prosperity on the generous Commander of the Faithful.

"The caliph Haroun Alraschid, satisfied with the history of Baba Abdalla and the dervish, now spoke to the young man whom he had seen treat his mare so ill, and asked him his name. The young man prostrated himself, and replied that he was called Sidi Nouman.

"'O Sidi Nouman,' said the caliph to him, 'I have seen horses exercised all my life, and have often exercised them myself, but never before did I see any used in so cruel a manner as the poor mare you rode yesterday in the square full of people, to the great offence of the spectators, who loudly complained of your cruelty; I was not less offended at it than they were, and was very nearly discovering myself, contrary to my design, in order to put a stop to this wantonness. By your appearance, however, I should not consider you savage and cruel, and I am willing to believe you did not behave thus without some reason, the more so as I understand that it is not the first time you have done this, but that for a good while past you have daily thus ill-treated your mare. I would know what the reason of this conduct is, and I have ordered you to come hither that you may inform me of it. Be sure you tell me exactly the state of the case, and disguise nothing.'

"Sidi Nouman readily understood what the caliph required of him, and showed signs of great uneasiness. He changed colour many times, and notwithstanding his endeavours to preserve an outward calmness, could not help showing a very great degree of embarrassment. It was, however, necessary that he should resolve on giving an account of the matter. Therefore he prostrated himself on his face before the throne of the caliph, and then rising, endeavoured to speak ; but he remained silent, less awed by the majesty of the caliph in whose presence he was, than affected by the nature of the recital he had to make.

"Though the caliph was accustomed to have his every command promptly and implicitly obeyed, he manifested no displeasure at the silence of Sidi Nouman. He saw clearly that the courage of the man seemed to fail him in his presence, or that he had been intimidated by the tone which the caliph had used towards him, or, in short, that in what he had to say there might be something which he was very desirous of concealing.

"Accordingly the caliph, to give him courage, said, 'Sidi Nouman, endeavour to recover yourself, and suppose that it is not to me that you are to relate what I require of you, but to one of your friends who requests you to do so. If there is anything in the narrative which you think will call for punishment, and at which you suppose I may take offence, I forgive you from this moment. Therefore, dismiss all your anxiety, speak to me with sincerity, and be as frank with me as you would be with one of your best friends.'

"Sidi Nouman, taking courage at these last words of the caliph's, then prepared to begin his narrative: 'Commander of the Faithful,' said he, 'whatever emotion mortals must experience when they approach your throne, I feel, nevertheless, strength sufficient to believe that this emotion of respect will not so prevent my speaking that I should fail in the obedience I owe to your majesty, in giving you satisfaction upon every point of the history you now require me to relate. I dare not say I am the most perfect of men, yet I am not wicked enough to have committed, nor even to have had the wish to commit, anything contrary to the laws, so as to have occasion to dread their severity. But though my intentions have always been good, I acknowledge that I am not free from sins of ignorance. To ignorance must be attributed any wrong I may have committed; but I do not say that I rely upon the pardon your majesty has been pleased to grant before you have heard me. I submit, on the contrary, to your justice, and am ready to be punished if I have deserved it. I confess that the manner in which I have for some time treated my mare, as your majesty has witnessed, is strange, barbarous, and of very mischievous example; but I hope you will find the motive for it justifiable, and that you will think me more worthy of compassion than punishment. But I must not keep your majesty longer in suspense by a tiresome preface. This, then, is my story:

## The History of Sidi Nouman.

MY family is in no respect distinguished; therefore, I need not trouble your majesty with particulars concerning it. My parents, by their good management, left me as much property as was sufficient to support me in a creditable way; not indeed in luxury, but entirely in independence.

"With these advantages, the only thing I required in order to render my happiness complete was to meet with an amiable wife, on whom I could lavish my tenderest affection, and who, loving me in return, would be willing to make my happiness hers; but this blessing Heaven was not pleased to grant me. On the contrary, I married a wife who, the very day after our marriage, began to exercise my patience in a manner not to be conceived except by those who have been exposed to a similar trial.

"As the custom is, that our marriages take place without our seeing or knowing the woman we are to espouse, your majesty must be aware that a husband has no right to complain, unless he finds that the wife who has fallen to his lot is frightfully ugly or an absolute cheat; and that he must be ready to let her good manners, her sense, and her amiability compensate for any slight imperfection of person.

"The first time I saw my wife without her veil, after she had been brought home to me with the usual ceremonies, I rejoiced to find that I had not been deceived in the account which had been given me of her beauty. She suited my taste, and I was delighted with her.

"The day after our marriage we had a dinner of several dishes. I came into the room where the table was set out, and as I did not see my wife there I desired she might be called. After having made me wait some time she came. I dissembled my impatience, and we sat down together at the table. I began my meal with some rice, which I took in the common way, with a spoon. My wife, on the contrary, instead of eating with a spoon as every one does, drew from a case which she had in her pocket a sort of bodkin, wherewith she began to pick up grains of rice, carrying them to her mouth one by one as she speared them on the bodkin.

"Surprised at this manner of eating, I said, 'Aminè,' for that was her name, 'is this the way you have learnt to eat rice in your family? Do you act thus because your appetite is small? Or perhaps you wish to count the grains, that you may not eat more at one time than at another? If you do this from a principle of saving, and to teach me not to be extravagant, you have nothing to fear on this score; I can assure you we shall not be ruined by our table. We have enough, thank Allah, to live at our ease, and need not stint ourselves in necessaries. Be under no constraint, my dear Aminè, but eat as freely as you see me eat.' The conciliating manner in which I made these remonstrances would, I supposed, have drawn from her some obliging answer; but without giving me a single word, she went on eating just as before, and, as it would appear, to vex me the more, she took these single grains of rice at even longer intervals; and instead of eating of the other dishes with me, she only carried to her mouth in the most deliberate manner small crumbs of bread scarcely enough to satisfy a sparrow.

"I was offended at her obstinacy. I imagined nevertheless, kindly making excuses for her, that she had not been accustomed to eat in the presence of men, and certainly not to dine with a husband, before whom she had perhaps been told to show a degree of restraint, which from ignorance she carried too far.

"I supposed, too, she might have eaten something just before dinner; or if not, that she reserved her appetite till she could eat alone and more at her ease. These considerations prevented my saying anything further to her which might frighten her, or let her see that I was dissatisfied. After dinner, I parted from her with as much cordiality as if I had found no reason to be displeased at her extraordinary behaviour, and left her quite alone.

"The same thing happened again at supper. The next day, and every time we ate together, she behaved just as on the first day. I saw clearly that it was not possible a woman could live on the very little sustenance she took, and that there must be some mystery in the matter which I could not fathom. This made me resolve to dissemble. I pretended to take no notice of her conduct, hoping that in time she would accustom herself to eat with me in the manner I wished. My hopes were vain, and in a very short time I was convinced of it.

"One night when Aminè thought me fast asleep, she rose very softly; and I observed that she dressed herself carefully, so as not to make the least noise, for fear she should awaken me. I could not conceive the reason why she abandoned her rest, and my curiosity to know what was the meaning of this made me pretend a sound sleep. She finished dressing herself, and the next moment walked out of the room without making the least noise.

"The instant she had left the room I rose; and, throwing my cloak across my shoulders, I had just time to see, through a window which looked into the court, that she opened the street door and went out. I ran immediately to the door, which she had left ajar; and favoured by the light of the moon, I followed her till I saw her go into a burying-place near our house. I then crept along under the shadow of a wall which reached to the burying-place, and, taking care to keep out of sight myself, I perceived Aminè with a ghoule.

"Your majesty knows that ghoules are demons which wander about the fields. They commonly inhabit ruinous buildings, whence they issue suddenly and surprise passengers, whom they kill and devour. If they fail thus to capture travellers, they go by night into burying-places, to dig up dead bodies and feed upon them. I was surprised and horrified when I saw my wife with this ghoule. Together they dug up a dead body which had been buried that very day, and the ghoule several times tore off pieces of the flesh, which they both ate as they sat upon the edge of the grave. They conversed together with great composure during their savage and inhuman repast; but I was so far off that it was impossible for me to hear what they said. No doubt their conversation was as wicked as their food, at the recollection of which I still shudder.

"When they had finished their horrid meal, they threw the remains of the carcase into the grave, which they filled again with the earth they had scooped up. I left them thus employed, and returned to my house with all speed. I went in, but left the door partly open as I had found it; and when I reached my chamber, I lay down and pretended to be asleep.

"In a short time Aminè came in without making the least noise. She undressed herself and came to bed again, very well pleased, I make no doubt, at having succeeded in eluding my observation. With my mind full of the idea of the savage and abominable deed which I had just witnessed, and shocked at finding myself married to a woman who had been concerned in it, I could not get to sleep again for a long time. I did, however, sleep again, or rather I dozed in so light and restless a manner, that the first call to public prayers at daybreak awoke me: I dressed myself and went to the mosque.

"When prayers were ended, I went out of the town and passed the morning walking in the gardens, and considering what means I should adopt to make my wife change her manner of living. I rejected every violent method which occurred to my mind, and resolved to employ only gentle means to wean her from the wretched inclination she had manifested. Still pursuing this train of thought, I returned to my own house, which I entered just at the hour of dinner.

SIDI NOUMAN TRANSFORMED INTO A DOG.

"When Aminè saw me, she ordered dinner, and we sat down at the table; but I found she still persisted in taking the rice up grain by grain. 'Aminè,' said I, in a perfectly composed voice, 'you know what reason I had to be surprised the day after our marriage, when I perceived you taking your rice in such small quantities, and in a way that would have offended any husband but myself. You know, too, that I very calmly pointed out the uneasiness it occasioned me, entreating you to eat of the other dishes at table, and that care was taken there should be a variety of food, that your taste might be consulted. Ever since, you have seen our table served in the same manner, the dishes being continually varied, that we might not be obliged always to eat the same things. My remonstrances have been, however, to no purpose; and to this hour you have continually behaved in the same manner and given me the same uneasiness. Unwilling to lay you under any constraint, I have kept silence for a time, and should be sorry if what I am now saying should give you the smallest annoyance; but, dear Aminè, I beseech you, tell me are not the dishes on our table better than the flesh of dead men?'

"I had scarcely uttered these last words, when Aminè, who now understood that I had observed her nocturnal proceedings, fell into a most violent passion. Her face was in a flame, her eyes almost started from her head, and she absolutely foamed with rage.

"The horrible expression of her face quite alarmed me. I stood perfectly motionless, unable to defend myself against the dreadful design which she was meditating, and at which your majesty will be astonished. In the height of her fury she took a glass of water which was near her, and, dipping her fingers into it, muttered a few words which I could not understand. Then she threw the water in my face, and cried in a furious tone, 'Wretch! take the punishment of thy curiosity, and become a dog!'

"So soon as Aminè, whom I had never supposed to be a sorceress, had uttered these fiendish words, I found myself suddenly changed into a dog. The surprise and astonishment I felt at a change so sudden and so unexpected at first prevented my running away. This bewilderment of mine gave her an opportunity of taking a stick to beat me; and, in truth, she made use of it upon me with so much violence, that I scarcely know how I escaped being killed on the spot. I thought to elude her rage by running into the court; but she pursued me thither with the same fury; and, nimble as I tried to be, darting from side to side to avoid her strokes, I could not escape them, and she showered them upon me in great abundance. Tired, at last, with pursuing and beating me, and mortified that she had not killed me as she wished to do, she conceived a new method of effecting her object. She partly opened the door into the street, in order to crush me as I ran out to make my escape. Dog though I was, I suspected her malicious design; and, as imminent danger often suggests a thought how to preserve life, I took my opportunity, by observing her eyes and motions so cleverly as to defeat her vigilance, and passed through the door quickly enough to save my life, and escaped her vengeance with no further mischief than having the end of my tail a little squeezed as the door closed behind me.

"The pain I felt made me cry and howl as I ran along the street. This occasioned other dogs to pursue and worry me. To avoid them, I ran into the shop of a man who dressed and sold sheep's heads, tongues, and feet, and there I got shelter.

"My host took my part very compassionately, driving away the dogs which were following me up, and which even attempted to come quite into his house. For my part, I had at first no other object than to steal into some corner and get out of their sight. Nevertheless, I did not find in this man's house all the refuge and protection I expected. He was one of those exceedingly superstitious people who consider dogs such unclean animals, that water and soap will not purify their garments if by accident a dog has touched them in passing by. After the dogs which had pursued me were driven away, he did all he could, many times in the course of the day, to drive me out; but I hid myself, and baffled his attempts. So, in spite of him, I passed the night within the shop; and, indeed, I had much need of a little rest to recover from the ill-treatment Aminè had inflicted upon me.

"That I may not tire your majesty with circumstances of little importance, I will not stay to particularise the sad reflections which I made upon my metamorphosis. I will at once proceed to state, that the next day my host went out before daylight to make his purchases. He returned laden with sheep's heads, tongues, and feet; and, after he had opened his shop, and while he was exposing his goods to view, I stole out of my corner, and was going away, when I saw a great many dogs of the neighbourhood, attracted by the smell of the meat, collected round the shop of my host, waiting till he threw them something. I joined them, and stood waiting, as they did, in a suppliant posture.

"My host, as it seemed to me, considering that I had not eaten anything since I had taken refuge with him, favoured me by throwing to me larger pieces and more frequently than to the other dogs. When he had ceased distributing his bounty, I was desirous of returning to his shop; looking up at him and wagging my tail in a way to make him understand that I again requested admission. But he was not to be prevailed upon to let me in: with a stick in his hand he forbade my entrance, showing not the least mark of compassion for me, so that I was forced to take to my heels.

"After passing a few houses, I stopped at a baker's shop. This baker, unlike the morose dealer in sheep's heads, seemed of a lively and merry disposition. He was then at breakfast, and though I showed no signs that I wanted to eat, he nevertheless threw me a piece of bread. I did not instantly and greedily seize it, as dogs commonly do, but looked up to him with an expression of countenance and a movement of my tail, expressive of my gratitude. He took my civil behaviour in good part, and smiled. I was not hungry; however, as I thought it would please him, I took the piece of bread, and ate it very slowly, to intimate that I did so out of compliment to him. He observed all this, and allowed me to remain near his shop. There I continued sitting; and turned frequently towards the shop, to signify to him that at present I wanted only his protection. This he afforded me, and took such notice of me besides that I quickly began to hope he would let me into his house. I made him understand that I would not come in without his permission. He did not take this amiss; on the contrary, he showed me a place where I might lie without being at all in his way; and I took possession of the spot, and retained it all the time I was in his house.

"I was extremely well treated there, and he never breakfasted, dined, or supped, without giving me as much as I wanted; and I, on my part, showed him all the attachment and fidelity which he could expect from my gratitude. My eyes were constantly fixed upon him, and he never stirred about the house, but I was always ready to follow. I accompanied him whenever he went on business into the city. I was the more exact in this matter because I saw my attentions pleased him; and often when he was going out, without my having observed his intention, he called me to him by the name which he had given me. On hearing my name, I darted immediately from my kennel into the street; I ran, and leaped, and gambolled before the door. I never ceased dancing and leaping till he came out; and then I was his constant companion, either following or running before him, and from time to time looking at him, to show him how happy I was.

"I had been in this house some time, when one day a woman came to buy bread. In payment for her purchase she gave my host, among some good money, one bad piece. The baker, who noticed the bad piece of money, gave it back to the woman, and asked her to change it. She refused to take it back, and declared it was good. My host maintained the contrary; and in the dispute he said to the woman, 'The piece of money is so visibly counterfeit that I am sure my dog, who is but a brute, would know it. Come here,' said he, calling me by my name. Hearing his voice, I immediately leaped nimbly upon the counter, and the baker, throwing before me the pieces of money, exclaimed, 'See if there is a bad piece of money among these.' I looked over all the pieces, and putting my foot upon the bad one, I separated it from the rest, looking in my master's face, as if to show it him.

"The baker, who had referred the matter to my judgment without much thought, and merely as a jest, was extremely surprised to see that I could recognise bad money. The woman, knowing it to be bad, had nothing to say, and was obliged to give another instead of it. As soon as she was gone, my master called some of his neighbours, and telling them what had happened, enlarged much on my cleverness. The neighbours wished to see the feat performed, and of all the pieces of false money which they showed me mixed with others, there was not one on which I did not put my foot, to separate it from the good coins.

"The woman, on her part, did not fail to relate to every one of her acquaintances whom she met in her way the marvel she had just witnessed. Their reports of my ability in distinguishing false money spread in a short time, not only throughout the neighbourhood, but through every part of the city. The whole day I had plenty of employment. I was obliged to satisfy the curiosity of all who came to buy bread of my master, and to let them see what I could do. A general interest was excited, and people came from the most distant parts of the town to see proofs of my cleverness. My reputation procured my master so much business that he could hardly get through it. This state of things lasted a long time, and my master could not help confessing to his neighbours and friends that he had found a treasure in me.

"My prowess did not fail to excite envy among my master's neighbours. They laid snares to draw me away, and he was obliged to keep me always in his sight. One day a woman, attracted by my fame, came, as others had done, to buy bread. My place was now usually on the counter. She threw down six pieces of money before me, amongst which there was one bad. I drew it away from the rest, and putting my foot on it, I looked at her, as if to ask her if that was not the bad coin. 'Yes,' said this woman, looking at me, 'you are not mistaken, that is the false coin.' She paid for the bread she had just bought, and as she was going out of the shop, unperceived by the baker she made a sign for me to follow. I was always on the watch for the means of delivering myself from the terrible condition I was in. I had remarked the attention with which this woman had looked at me. I imagined she might possibly have some knowledge of my misfortune, and of the wretched state to which I was reduced; and I was not mistaken. I let her go, however, and contented myself with looking after her. She had gone but a few steps before she returned, and seeing that I only looked at her without stirring from my place, she again made a sign for me to follow her. Then, without further deliberation, as I saw the baker was busy cleaning his oven, and that he paid no attention to me, I leaped from the counter, and followed the woman, who appeared to be much pleased at having lured me away.

"After going some distance, she arrived at her house. She opened the door, and when she entered she said, 'Come in; you shall have no reason to repent having followed me.' When I was in the house, she shut the door and led me to her apartment, where I saw a beautiful young lady, who sat at work embroidering. This was the daughter of the charitable woman who had brought me hither, and she was skilful and experienced in the art of magic, as I afterwards found.

"'O my daughter,' said the mother, 'I have brought you the baker's famous dog, who so well knows how to distinguish false money from good. On the first report that was spread about him, you know I told you my idea that he was a man who had been changed into a dog's shape by some wicked enchantment. To-day I took it into my head to go and buy some bread at this baker's. I have convinced myself of the truth of what has been reported, and I have had the art to make this astonishing dog, which has been the wonder of all Bagdad, follow me. What say you, daughter—am I deceived in my conjecture?' 'You are not deceived, mother,' replied the daughter, 'as I shall very soon convince you.'

"The young lady rose from her seat, and took a vessel full of water, into which she dipped her hand. Then, throwing some of the water on me, she said, 'If thou wert born a dog, remain a dog; but if thou wert born a man, resume the form of a man by virtue of this water.' Immediately the enchantment was broken: I quitted the form of a dog, and became once more a man.

"Filled with gratitude for the great service she had done me, I threw myself at the feet of the young lady, and after having kissed the hem of her garment, I cried, 'My dear deliverer, I feel so strongly the excess of your goodness towards an unknown person like myself, that I conjure you to tell me what I can do to show the extent of my gratitude, or rather, dispose of me as of a slave to whom you have an undoubted right. I am no longer my own master—I belong to you; and that you may know how your slave came to the condition from which you have released him, I will give you my history in a few words.'

"Then, after having told who I was, I gave her an account of my marriage with Aminè. I spoke to her of my compliance and patience in supporting my wife's ill-

SIDI NOUMAN'S VENGEANCE ON HIS WIFE.

humour. I recounted the extraordinary indignity with which she had treated me through inconceivable malice; and I concluded by thanking the mother for the inexpressible happiness she had just procured me.

"'Sidi Nouman,' said the daughter, 'talk no more of the obligation you assert you are under to me. Is not the consciousness of having served a worthy man, as you seem to be, a sufficient recompense? Let us talk of Aminè, your wife. I knew her before her marriage. I knew she was a magician, and she also was not ignorant that I had some knowledge of the same art, since we were taught by the same mistress. We even often met at the bath; but as we were of very different tempers, I took particular care to avoid every occasion that might lead to any connection with her; and I found this easy, as I soon saw that, for some reason, she on her part avoided all intercourse with me. I am not surprised at her wickedness. But to return to what immediately concerns you. What I have just done for you is not sufficient; I will finish the work I have begun. It is not enough that I have broken the enchantment by which she had so cruelly excluded you from the society of men; you must punish her for it as she deserves, by returning home and resuming the authority that belongs to you. I will enable you to do so. Remain here and converse with my mother; I shall soon return.'

"My deliverer went into a closet; and whilst she remained there I had time again to express to the mother my sense of the obligation she as well as her daughter had laid me under. 'My daughter,' said she, 'as you see, is not less skilful in the magic art than is Aminè, but she makes such a noble use of her power that you would be astonished did you know the good she does, and has almost every day an opportunity of doing, by the knowledge she possesses. It is for this reason alone that I have suffered, and still suffer, her to practise the art. I would never have permitted her to do this if I had perceived that in the most trifling instance she had made a bad use of her knowledge.'

"The mother had begun to relate to me some of the wonderful things she had witnessed, when her daughter entered with a little bottle in her hand. 'Sidi Nouman,' said she, 'my books, which I have just been consulting, inform me that Aminè is not at this moment at home, but will return presently. From them I also learn, that the dissembler appeared before your servants to be very uneasy at your absence, and made them believe that whilst you were at dinner you recollected some business which obliged you to go out directly. She further declared to them that in going out you had left the door open, and a dog had run in, and had even come into the room where she was finishing her dinner, and that she had driven him out with a stick. Return, therefore, to your house, without loss of time, with this little bottle which I give you. When you have gained admittance, wait in your chamber till Aminè returns; she will not keep you long. When she comes back, go down into the court, and appear before her. Her surprise will be so great at seeing you again, contrary to her expectation, that she will turn to fly from you. Then throw upon her some of this water, which you will hold ready for that purpose, and as you throw it, boldly pronounce these words, *Receive the punishment of thy wickedness*. I need not tell you any more, for you will see what happens.'

"After these words of my benefactress, which I did not forget, I took leave of her and of her mother with every expression of gratitude, and vowing eternally to remember the obligation they had conferred on me, and I immediately returned to my house.

"Everything occurred exactly as the young enchantress had foretold. It was not long before Aminè appeared. As she advanced, I appeared before her with the water in my hand, ready to throw it upon her. She uttered a loud shriek, and as she turned round to gain the door, I threw the water upon her, pronouncing the words the enchantress had taught me. Instantly she was changed into a mare, the same your majesty saw yesterday.

"Immediately profiting by the surprise which had seized her, I took her by the mane, and led her to the stable. I put a halter on her, and after I had tied her up, reproaching her all the time for her crimes and wickedness, I punished her by whipping her so long that fatigue at last obliged me to desist. But I determined every day to inflict the same punishment upon her.

"'And now, O Commander of the Faithful,' added Sidi Nouman, as he concluded his history, 'I dare flatter myself your majesty will not disapprove my conduct, and that you will confess that so wicked and infamous a woman is treated with more indulgence than she deserves.'

"When the caliph saw that Sidi Nouman had nothing more to relate, he said, 'Your history is singular, and the wickedness of your wife admits of no excuse. For this reason I do not absolutely condemn the chastisement you have hitherto inflicted on her, but I would have you consider how great her punishment is in being reduced to the level of the beasts, and I wish you would content yourself with leaving her unmolested now she is in this degraded state. I would even command you to go and solicit the young enchantress who has caused this metamorphosis to disenchant her, if I did not know so well the obstinacy and incorrigible hard-heartedness of magicians, that I should fear the effects of her vengeance against you might be more cruel than they were in the first instance.'

"The caliph, who was by nature gentle and compassionate towards those who suffered, although they might have deserved their misfortunes, after having thus declared his will to Sidi Nouman, addressed himself to the third person whom the grand vizier Giafar had brought. 'Cogia Hassan,' said he, 'when I passed your house yesterday, it appeared so magnificent, that I had the curiosity to inquire to whom it belonged. I was told that you had built it, after you had followed a trade the profits of which were hardly sufficient to support you. I also heard that you had not forgotten your former condition; that you make a good use of the wealth which Heaven has given you; and that your neighbours speak well of you. This account pleases me; and I feel sure that the means by which it has pleased Providence to bestow its gifts must be very extraordinary. I am curious to learn your history from yourself, and it is to obtain this information that I have sent for you. Speak to me, then, without reserve, that I may from my own knowledge have the pleasure of partaking of your happiness; and that no suspicions may arise in your mind from my curiosity, and that you may not think I have any object in wishing to learn your history but what I have just told you, I declare to you, that far from wishing to interfere with you, I give you my protection, and you may enjoy your wealth in security.'

"Upon these assurances from the caliph, Cogia Hassan prostrated himself before the throne, touched with his forehead the carpet with which it was covered, and after he had risen, said, 'O Commander of the Faithful, any one who did not feel his conscience as pure and as clear as I feel mine, would have been alarmed at receiving the order to appear before the throne of your majesty; but as I have never had towards you any sentiments but those of respect and veneration, and as I have not done anything contrary to the obedience I owe to you and the laws which could draw your indignation upon me, the only thing which troubles me is the natural awe I feel at the aspect of the splendour which surrounds you. Nevertheless, the public report of the goodness with which your majesty receives and listens to the most inconsiderable of your subjects encourages me, and I feel certain that that knowledge will give me sufficient confidence to impart to your majesty the information you require of me.'

"After speaking this little compliment to conciliate the favour and attention of the caliph, and after remaining some moments silent, to recollect what he had to say, Cogia Hassan began his history in these terms:

## The History of Cogia Hassan Alhabbal.

N order that your majesty may comprehend the means by which I arrived at the great wealth I now enjoy, I must begin by speaking of two intimate friends, citizens of this very town of Bagdad, who are still living, and who can bear witness to the truth of what I relate: to them I am indebted for it, under Heaven, the first author of all good and of all happiness. Of these two friends, one is named Saadi, and the other Saad. Saadi, who is immensely rich, has always been of opinion that a man cannot be happy in this world without such a fortune and such great wealth as shall enable him to live independent of every one. Saad thinks differently: he allows that a fortune sufficient for the necessaries of life is necessary, but he maintains that virtue ought to constitute the happiness of men, without any more attachment to the good things of this world than in proportion to our real wants, and as they give us the power of doing charitable actions. Saad is of the number of the fortunate, and he lives happily and contentedly in the situation in which he is placed. Thus, though Saadi is infinitely richer, their friendship for each other is nevertheless very sincere, and he who is the most wealthy does not look upon himself as superior to his friend. They have never had any dispute but upon this subject; in everything else their union has been uninterrupted.

"One day, as they were debating this point, as they themselves afterwards told me, Saadi asserted that the poor were not really poor, except when they were born in poverty, or, being born rich, they had lost their fortunes by debauchery, or by some of those unlooked-for misfortunes which sometimes overtake the most prudent. 'My opinion is,' said he, 'that the poor are poor only because they cannot command a sum of money sufficiently large to rescue them from their low position by enabling them to exert their industry to improve it; and my idea is, that if they could once have a capital to commence with, and would make a proper use of their money, they would not only prosper, but in time would be very rich.'

"Saad was not convinced by the reasoning of Saadi. 'The means you propose to make a poor man become rich,' he said, 'do not appear to me to be so certain as you think them. Your thoughts on this matter are very vague, and I could support my opinion against yours by many good arguments; but these would only prolong the discussion. I think that, at least, a poor man may become rich by many other means, as well as by the gift of a sum of money. Accident will often open to men the means of making a larger and more surprising fortune than they can acquire by the use of such a sum of money as you talk of, whatever good management and economy they may exert to increase it.'

"'O Saad,' replied Saadi, 'I perceive I shall not gain any advantage over you by persisting in supporting my opinion against yours; I wish to convince you by making an experiment. For example, I will give such a sum as I think necessary to one of those workmen who have been poor from father to son, and who live by daily labour, and die as poor as they are born. If I do not succeed we will then try your plan.'

"Some days after this conversation had occurred, it happened that the two friends, in walking through the streets, passed through that part of the town where I was at work at my business of ropemaking, the craft to which I had been brought up by my father, who had himself been taught it by my grandfather; for it had descended to us from our ancestors. My appearance and dress sufficiently bespoke my poverty.

"Saad, who remembered Saadi's plan, said to him, 'If you have not forgotten the proposal you lately made to me, there is a man,' and he pointed at me, 'whom I have a long time seen working at his trade as a ropemaker, and who always appears in the same state of poverty. He is a man worthy of your liberality, and quite suited to be the subject of the experiment of which we spoke the other day.' 'I perfectly remember what was said,' replied Saadi, 'and I will now make the experiment: I only waited for an opportunity when we should be together, that you might witness my proceedings. Let us accost this man, and hear if he is really as poor as he appears to be.'

"The two friends came to me, and as I saw they wished to speak with me, I left off working. They both gave me the usual salutation, 'Peace be with you,' and Saadi asked me my name. I returned their greeting, and answered the question of Saadi by saying, 'O my master, my name is Hassan, and because of my employment I am commonly known by the name of Hassan Alhabbal, or the ropemaker.' 'Hassan,' returned Saadi, 'as there is not any trade which does not support its master, I do not doubt that yours maintains you in comfort; and I am astonished, considering the length of time you have been engaged in it, that you have not saved something, and have not bought a good stock of hemp to increase your business, as well for yourself as for the people you have hired to assist you, so that you might by degrees deal in a larger way.'

THE KITE DARTS UPON THE MEAT.

"'Sir,' I replied, 'you will cease to be surprised that I do not save money, and that I do not take the means you mention to become rich, when I tell you that, though I work hard from morning till night, I can scarcely manage to earn enough to procure bread and vegetables for myself and family. I have a wife and five children, and not one of the young ones is old enough to give me the least assistance. I must feed and clothe them; and in a family, be it ever so small, there are always a thousand things that are indispensable, and that must be paid for. Although hemp is not an expensive thing, money is nevertheless required to purchase it, and that money I am obliged to save out of the sale of my goods, otherwise I should not be able to maintain my family. Judge then for yourself,' I added, 'whether it is possible for me to save, and thus better myself and my family. It is sufficient that we are contented with the little it pleases Heaven to give us, and that we do not hanker after what is unattainable. So long as we have enough to live on in the way we are accustomed to, and are not under the necessity of begging, we feel no desire to possess more.'

"When I had given this account of myself to Saadi, he replied: 'O Hassan, my wonder has ceased, and I comprehend all the reasons which induce you to be contented with the situation in which you are; but, if I made you a present of a purse with two hundred pieces of gold, would you make a good use of it? and do you not think that with this sum you would soon become as rich as the principal people in your business?' 'Worthy sir,' I replied, 'you appear to me to be so worthy a man, that I am convinced you are not jesting at my expense, and that you are serious in the offer you make me. I dare then affirm without presumption, that a much smaller sum would be sufficient not only to make me as rich as the principal people in my business, but that in a little time I might even become richer than any of my fellow ropemakers in this great city of Bagdad, large and populous as it is.'

"The generous Saadi convinced me immediately that he was in earnest in the offer he had made. He drew a purse from his bosom, and put it into my hand. 'Take it,' said he, 'there is the purse, and you will find in it exactly two hundred pieces of gold; I pray Allah to make it prosper in your keeping, to bless you with it, and to give you grace to make the use of it I wish; and be assured that my friend Saad here, as well as myself, will have the greatest pleasure in hearing that this sum has contributed to make you more prosperous than you now are.'

"When I had received the purse and had put it into my bosom, I was so transported with joy and overwhelmed with gratitude that I could not speak; and I could only manifest my feelings to my benefactor by putting out my hand to seize the border of his robe to kiss it; but he instantly withdrew, and the friends continued their walk.

"When I returned to my work after they were gone, the first thought that occurred to me was to devise a place of safety where I might put the purse. In my poor little house I had neither box nor chest with a lock, nor any place where I could be sure the money would not be discovered if I concealed it. As I had been used, like other poor people in my way of life, to hide the little money I had in the folds of my turban, I left my work, and went into my house pretending to mend my turban. I took my measures so well that, without my wife and children perceiving what I was about, I drew out of the purse ten pieces of gold, which I put aside for the most pressing wants, and wrapped up the remainder in the folds of the linen which surrounded my cap. The principal expense of that day was to buy a good stock of hemp; then, as I had had no meat in my house for a long time, I went to the market and bought some for supper.

"As I wended my way home, I held the meat in my hand. Suddenly a half-starved kite, before I was aware of its intention, darted upon the meat, and would have snatched it out of my hand had I not clutched it firmly. But, alas! I should have done far better to have let it go; for then I should not have lost my purse. The more resistance the kite found, the more determined he was to get the meat. He dragged me from one side to the other, whilst he kept fluttering in the air without quitting his hold; and it happened, unfortunately, that in the efforts I made to resist him my turban fell to the ground.

"Immediately the kite let go the meat, and seizing my turban before I had time to take it up, he flew away with it. I uttered such piercing cries, that the men, women, and children in the neighbourhood were alarmed, and joined their voices with mine, yelling and screaming to make the kite quit his hold.

"By this method they sometimes succeed in frightening these voracious birds into dropping the prey they have seized; but our outcries did not alarm the kite. He carried my turban so far that we quite lost sight of him; so it was useless for me to give myself the trouble of running after him to recover it.

"I returned home very melancholy at the misfortune I had just undergone in the loss of my turban and my money. I was obliged to buy another, which caused a further diminution in the ten pieces of gold I had taken out of the purse. I had already laid out part of it in buying hemp, and what remained was by no means sufficient to realise the great hopes I had conceived.

"But my chief uneasiness was caused by the thought of the chagrin my benefactor would feel when he should find how his liberal donation had been lost. When he should hear of my disaster he would, perhaps, think my story incredible, and would therefore only look upon it as a frivolous excuse.

"Whilst the few pieces of gold which I had saved lasted, we felt the benefit of it; but I soon fell back into my former position, as totally unable to improve my standing as ever. I did not murmur, however. 'Allah,' said I, 'has thought proper to try me, by giving me wealth at the time I least expected it: He has taken it from me almost at the same instant, because it pleased Him to do so, and it was His. Praise be to His name alway! As I then praised Allah for the blessings He thought fit to bestow, whatever it now pleases Him to do, I submit to His will.'

"These sentiments comforted me in my misfortune; but my wife, to whom I could not help communicating the loss I had just met with and the way in which it had happened, was inconsolable. While my loss was fresh in my mind, I accidentally mentioned before some of my neighbours, that in losing my turban I had lost a hundred and ninety pieces of gold; but as my poverty was well known to them, and as they could not believe it possible that I could have earned so large a sum by my labour, they only laughed, and the children laughed more than my neighbours.

"About six months after the kite had caused this misfortune, the two friends passed through the streets, not far from the place in which I lived. This circumstance naturally brought me to the recollection of Saad. He said to Saadi: 'We are not far from the street in which Hassan Alhabbal lives: let us go to his house, and see if the two hundred pieces of gold that you gave him have in any degree contributed to put him in a better situation than that in which we found him.' 'With all my heart,' replied Saadi; 'I have thought of him for some days past, and I promised to myself great pleasure from the opportunity I should have of showing you the success of my scheme. You may prepare to see a great alteration in him; and I question whether we shall know him again.'

"The two friends had turned the corner and entered the street while Saadi was still speaking. Saad, who first saw me at a distance, said to his friend: 'It seems to me that you promise yourself more than you will enjoy. I see Hassan Alhabbal, but there does not appear to me to be any alteration in his appearance. He is as poorly dressed as he was when we first accosted him. The only difference I can discover is, that his turban is not quite so dirty as it was: see if I am mistaken.'

"As they drew near, Saadi, who now also perceived me, saw that Saad was right; and he knew not how to account for the indications of poverty he saw in my appearance. He was so much astonished, that it was his friend who spoke when they came up to me.

"Saad saluted me in the usual way, and said, 'Well, Hassan, we do not ask you how your affairs have gone on since we saw you; the two hundred pieces of gold must have contributed to make them much more prosperous.' 'O my masters,' replied I, addressing them both, 'I am much mortified at being obliged to inform you that your wishes, your expectations, and your hopes have failed, like mine, of the success you had reason to expect, and which I had promised myself. You will hardly believe the extraordinary adventure which has happened to me. I assure you, nevertheless, on the word of an honest man, and of one who never told a lie, that what you are going to hear is the plain and open truth.' I then told them my adventure, with all the circumstances which I have just related.

"Saadi gave no credit to my story. 'O Hassan,' said he, 'you make a jest of me, and you wish to deceive me. What you tell is quite incredible. Kites do not attack turbans, they only seek for prey to satisfy their hunger. You have done as people in your situation generally do. If they gain an extraordinary advantage, or any good fortune unexpectedly happens to them, they leave their work, they amuse themselves, they take their pleasure, and live well so long as the money lasts; and when it is gone, they find themselves in the same miserable situation, from which the money, well applied, would have rescued them. You remain thus distressed, because you deserve to be so, and you show yourself unworthy of the benefits conferred on you.' 'Worthy sir,' I replied, 'I suffer patiently all these reproaches, and I am ready to bear still more cruel words, if you can find it in your heart to utter them; but I hear them with the greater patience, because I am conscious I do not deserve them. The circumstance, strange as it is, is so well known in this place, that there is not one of my neighbours who will not bear witness to it. If you choose to inquire, you will find I have not imposed upon you. I confess I have never myself heard that kites would carry off turbans; but the thing has happened to me, like many other events which have never before occurred, but may nevertheless happen every day.'

"Saad took my part, and related to Saadi so many stories of kites, some of which he had himself known, not less surprising than mine, that the latter again drew his purse out of his bosom. He counted two hundred pieces of gold into my hand, which I soon put into my bosom for want of a purse. When Saadi had bestowed this second gift upon me, he said: 'O Hassan, I wish once more to make you a present of two hundred pieces of gold; but take care to put them in a safe place, that you may not lose them so unfortunately as you lost the others; and mind that they procure you the benefits which the others ought to have procured.' I acknowledged that the gratitude I owed him for this second favour was still greater than for the first, as I did not deserve a repetition of his great liberality after what had befallen me, and I promised to use every precaution to prevent a recurrence of my former misfortune. I would have continued speaking, but he did not give me time. He quitted me, and proceeded on his way with his friend.

"After they were gone I returned to my work. I then went into my house, my wife and children being at that time from home. I once more took ten pieces of gold out of the two hundred, and wrapped the hundred and ninety pieces in a strip of linen, and tied it up. It was necessary to hide the linen in a safe place; so, after considering for a long time what I should do with the gold, I determined to put it at the bottom of a large earthern pot full of bran which stood in a corner, where I supposed neither my wife nor children would be likely to find it. My wife returned soon after; and as I had but little hemp left, I told her I was going out to buy some, without telling her I had seen the two friends.

"I went out; but whilst I was gone to make this purchase, a man who sells fullers' earth, such as women make use of in the bath, happened to pass through the street, and cried it for sale.

"My wife, who had not any of this earth, called to the man; and as she had no money, she asked him if he would take a pot of bran in exchange for some fullers' earth. He asked to see the bran. My wife showed him the jar, and the bargain was struck. She received the fullers' earth, and he carried away the pot of bran.

"I returned laden with as much hemp as I could carry, followed by five porters laden like myself with the same commodity, with which I filled a little room that I had set apart as a storehouse. I paid the porters for their trouble, and when they were gone I sat down to rest myself after my fatigues. I then cast my eyes towards the place where I had left the jar of bran, and saw it was not there!

"I cannot express to your majesty my surprise, or the effect this discovery had upon me at the moment. I hastily asked my wife what was become of the bran, and she told me, boasting of the bargain she had made as a thing by which she thought herself a great gainer. 'O wretched woman!' I cried, 'you know not the mischief you have done to me, to yourself, and to your children, in making a bargain which has ruined us without remedy. You thought you had only sold some bran, and in giving him this bran you have enriched your seller of fullers' earth with a hundred and ninety pieces of gold, which Saadi, accompanied by his friend, had just given me as a second present.'

"My wife was in despair when she understood the great fault she had through ignorance committed. She lamented, she beat her breast, and tore her hair and clothes. 'Wretch that I am!' cried she, 'I am unworthy to live after making such a cruel mistake. Where can I find the man who sold the fullers' earth? I know him not: he has never before passed through our street, and probably I shall never see him again. Alas! my husband,' added she, 'you have done very wrong; why did you keep an affair of such importance secret from me? This misfortune would not have happened if you had but placed some confidence in me.' I should never conclude if I were to repeat to your majesty everything her grief made her say. You are well aware how eloquent women are in their afflictions.

"'My dear wife,' said I, 'be composed. You do not consider that you will draw all the neighbours about us by your cries and tears: it is not necessary that they should be made acquainted with our distress. Far from sympathising in our misfortune, or giving us consolation, they will take a pleasure in laughing at your simplicity and mine. The best thing we can do is to conceal our loss, and support it patiently in such a way that it may not be suspected: let us submit to the will of Allah. So far from murmuring, let us bless Him, that of the two hundred pieces of gold He has given us, he has withdrawn only a hundred and ninety, and that He has in His goodness left us ten, which, as I have just employed them, will bring us some relief.'

"However strong my arguments might be, my wife was at first but little disposed to relish them. But time, which softens the greatest and most harrowing evils, made her listen at length to my reasonings.

"'We live poorly, it is true,' said I to her, 'but what have the rich that we have not? Do we not breathe the same air that sustains them? Do we not enjoy from the sun the same light and warmth by which they are refreshed? The comforts and conveniences they have might make us envy their happiness, if they did not die as we do. To take things in their best light, while we possess the fear of Allah, which we ought to cherish above all things, the advantages the rich have over us are so trifling that we ought not to think of them.'

"I will not tire your majesty any longer with my moral reflections. My wife and I were consoled, and I continued my work with as calm and tranquil a mind as if I had not met with the mortifying losses which had fallen on me in succession.

"The only thing that vexed me, and which often disturbed me, was the thought how I could support the presence of Saadi when he should come to inquire how I had employed his two hundred pieces of gold, and to what degree I had bettered my circumstances through his liberality; and I saw no other remedy than the resolve to submit to the confusion I must feel on the occasion, although I had not brought this misfortune upon myself by any fault of mine, any more than in the first instance.

"The two friends were longer in returning to inquire into my situation than they had been before. Saad had often proposed to Saadi a visit to my house, but the latter contrived always to defer it. 'The longer we put off going to him,' said he, 'the more wealthy Hassan will have grown, and the more satisfaction I shall feel in witnessing his prosperity.'

"Saad had not the same opinion of the effects of his friend's liberality. 'You think,' he said, 'that your second present will have been better employed by Hassan than your first. I advise you not to be too sanguine, for you will feel proportionately mortified if the contrary should have happened.' 'But,' replied Saadi, 'it does not happen every day that a kite carries away a turban. Hassan has been caught once: he will be very careful a second time.' 'I do not doubt that,' returned Saad; 'but some other accident, which neither you nor I can foresee, may have happened. I say once more, moderate your expectations, and do not be too much taken up with the idea of his great fortune. To tell you what I think, and what I have always thought, however angry you mav be at knowing my opinion, I have a presentiment that you will be disappointed, and that I shall succeed better than you have done, in proving that a poor man can sooner become rich by any other means than by the gift of money.'

"At last, one day when Saad and Saadi were together, the latter said, after a long dispute on this subject, 'I can bear this suspense no longer. I will this very day inform myself how it is. Let us immediately go and see which of us is in the right.' The two friends set out, and I soon saw them coming. I was much affected, and was on the point of quitting my work and running to hide myself, that I might not appear before them. I pretended to be intent on my work, and not to see them, and I never raised my eyes to look at them till they were so near that they gave me the salutation, 'Peace be with you.' I could not then in civility avoid answering them. I immediately cast my eyes on the ground; and relating to them my last misfortune, with its circumstances, I let them know the reason why they found me as poor as at the first time they saw me.

"'You may say,' I added, in conclusion, 'that I ought to have hidden the hundred and ninety pieces of gold in a safer place than in a jar of bran, which might that very day be taken out of my house. But this vessel had stood there and had never been moved for many years; and whenever my wife sold her bran, which she did when it was full, the jar always remained in its old position. How could I foresee that on that very day, in my absence, a man who sold fullers' earth should pass at the very time when my wife was without money, and that she should make such an exchange with him? You will perhaps tell me I ought to have told my wife where I had hidden the money; but I can never believe that such prudent people as I am sure you are would have given me such advice. Had I hidden the money in any other place, what certainty could I have had that it would have been in greater safety there? O my worthy benefactor,' said I, addressing myself to Saadi in particular, 'by one of His impenetrable secrets, which we ought not to attempt to fathom, it has pleased Allah that I should not be enriched by your liberality. He will have me poor, and not rich. I shall always feel the same obligation to you as if your generosity had had the entire effect you wished it to have.'

"I ceased speaking, and Saadi, who took up the conversation, said to me: 'Though I would gladly be convinced that all you have just told us is as true as you intend to make us believe it is, and that you have not invented this extraordinary tale to conceal your debaucheries or bad economy, I must nevertheless be cautious how I proceed in obstinately making an experiment which might in the end ruin me. I do not regret the four hundred pieces of gold I have lost in endeavouring to rescue you from your poverty. I have done it for the love of Allah, without expecting any other recompense than the pleasure of having served you. If anything could make me repent what I have done, it would be, that I have chosen you rather than another person, who would perhaps have derived more advantage from my gifts.' Then, turning towards his friend, he continued, 'O Saad, you may know by what I have just said, that I do not entirely give up the point to you. You are, however, at liberty to make the trial of the theory that you have so long maintained in opposition to me. Convince me that there are other means than the bestowal of money which can make the fortune of a poor man in the way I intended, and take Hassan for your subject. Whatever you can give him, I cannot believe that he will become more rich than he might have become with four hundred pieces of gold.'

"Saad held a piece of lead in his hand, which he showed to Saadi, and then spoke thus: 'You have seen me pick up this bit of lead, which lay at my feet: I am going to give it to Hassan, and you will see how valuable it will be to him.' Saadi burst into a violent fit of laughter, and turned Saad's proposal into ridicule. 'A piece of lead!' cried he: 'and of what value can the sixth part of a farthing be to Hassan? What will he do with it?' But Saad gave me the piece of lead, and said to me, 'Let Saadi laugh, and do not refuse to take it. You will one day tell us what good fortune it has brought you.'

"I thought that Saad could not be in earnest, and that he was only jesting. However, I took the piece of lead, and thanked him for it; and, to satisfy him, I put it carelessly into my bosom. The two friends took leave of me and continued their walk, and I went on with my work.

"At night, when I undressed myself to go to bed, and took off my sash, the piece of lead Saadi had given me, and which I had never thought of since, fell to the ground; I took it up, and put it into the first place that came handy.

"That very night it happened that one of my neighbours, a fisherman, in preparing his nets, found that he wanted a piece of lead. He had not any to supply the place of a missing piece, and at that hour he could not buy any, as the shops were all shut. It was, however, absolutely necessary that he should get some, that he might procure food for the next day for himself and his family, by going to fish two hours before daylight.

THE FISHERMAN GIVES THE FISH TO COGIA HASSAN.

He expressed his vexation to his wife, and sent her to ask his neighbours to furnish him with a bit of lead.

"The wife started on her errand. She went from door to door on both sides of the street, but could not get any lead. She carried back this answer to her husband, who asked her, naming many of his neighbours, if she had knocked at the door of each. She said she had. 'And at Hassan Alhabbal's?' added he. 'I will lay a wager you have not been there.' 'You are right,' replied the wife, 'I have not been there, because it is so far off; and if I had taken the trouble of going there, do you think I should have found what you require? I know by experience his house is exactly the place to which you should go when you want nothing.' 'That does not signify,' said the fisherman: 'you are a lazy creature; I wish you to go there. Though you have been a hundred times without obtaining what you went in search of, you will now perhaps find the lead that I want. I desire you, therefore, to go again.'

"The fisherman's wife went out grumbling and scolding, and came and knocked at my door. I had been some time asleep, but I awoke, and asked what she wanted. 'O Hassan Alhabbal!' said the woman, raising her voice, 'my husband wants a little bit of lead to mend his nets, and if by chance you have any, he begs you will give him a piece.'

"The piece of lead that Saad had given me was so fresh in my memory, especially after what had happened to me in undressing, that I thought of it at once. I answered my neighbour that I had what she wanted, and if she would wait a moment, my wife should bring it her. My wife, who had awoke while we were speaking, rose, and groping about, found the lead in the place where I told her I had put it. She half opened the door, and gave it to her neighbour.

"The fisherman's wife was delighted that she had not come so far in vain. 'My good neighbour,' said she to my wife, 'the service you have done my husband and me is so great, that I promise you all the fish my husband catches in the first throw of his nets, and I assure you he will make good my words.'

"The fisherman, equally delighted at having obtained the lead he so much wanted, approved the promise his wife had made us. 'It was quite right of you,' said he; 'you have done just as I should.' He finished mending his nets, and went to fish two hours before daylight. In the first throw of his nets he caught only one fish, but it was more than a foot long, and thick in proportion: he had afterwards many other draughts, which were all successful, but the fish were much smaller than the first he caught—there was not one that came near it in point of size.

"When the fisherman had done fishing and had returned home, his first care was to redeem his wife's promise to me, and I was extremely surprised, as I was at work, to see him come towards me, bringing this fish. 'Neighbour,' said he, 'my wife promised you last night all the fish that I caught in the first throw of my nets, as an acknowledgment of the service you have done us, and I approved her promise. Heaven sent me only this one for you, and I beg you to accept it: if Allah had been pleased to fill my nets, all I caught would in like manner have been yours. Take it, I entreat you, such as it is, as kindly as if the gift had been more considerable.'

"'My good neighbour,' replied I, 'the piece of lead I sent you is so mere a trifle, that it does not deserve such a return. Neighbours ought to assist each other. I have only done for you what I should suppose you would do for me on a like occasion. I should, therefore, refuse your present if I were not certain you derive a pleasure from making it. I even think you would be offended if I were to refuse your gift. I take it, then, since you wish me to do so, and I thank you for it.'

"I bade farewell to the fisherman, and carried the fish to my wife. 'Take this fish,' said I, 'which our neighbour the fisherman has just brought me in return for the piece of lead that he borrowed last night. It is, I believe, all the advantage we have to hope for from the present Saad made me yesterday, though he promised me it would bring me good luck.' I then told her I had again seen the two friends, and repeated what had passed between them and me.

"My wife was embarrassed by the size of the fish I brought her. 'What would you have me do with it?' said she. 'Our gridiron is only fit to broil small fish, and we have not anything large enough to boil this in.'

"As she was cleaning the fish, my wife took from its entrails a large diamond, which she supposed to be glass. She had heard of diamonds, but even if she had seen or handled them she would not have had sufficient knowledge of the matter to know them at sight. She gave the diamond to the youngest of our children as a plaything; and the child's brothers and sisters, who wished to see it and handle it by turns, gave it to one another, that all might admire its beauty and brilliancy.

"At night, when the lamp was lighted, our children, who continued their sport of handing the diamond about to look at it by turns, perceived that it became brighter in proportion as my wife hid the light of the lamp by carrying it about as she moved to and fro in preparing the supper, and this made the children snatch it from one another to try the experiment. But the little ones cried when the elder ones did not give them so much

THE JEW EXAMINES THE DIAMOND.

time to look at it as they wished, and the elder children were obliged to let them have it to appease them.

"As the merest trifles will amuse children, and cause disputes amongst them, which often happen, neither my wife nor I paid any attention to this noise and bustle amongst our little ones, with which they almost stunned us. It ceased at last when the elder children were placed at table to sup with us, and my wife had given the little ones their share.

"After supper the children got together, and the same noise and disturbance began again. I then inquired what they were disputing about: I called the eldest to me, and asked him what was the reason they made so much noise. 'Father,' said he, 'it is all about a piece of glass, which shines brightest when we turn our backs to the lamp.' I made him bring it me, and tried the experiment myself. This brilliancy appeared to me to be very extraordinary, and led me to ask my wife what this piece of glass was. 'I don't know,' said she; 'it is a piece I took out of the belly of the fish in cleaning it.'

"I did not imagine, any more than did my wife, that it was anything but a piece of glass. I nevertheless carried my experiment a little farther. I bade my wife hide the lamp in the chimney. She did so, and the supposed piece of glass gave so great a light that we could have done without the lamp to go to bed by. I had the lamp extinguished altogether, and placed the piece of glass at the edge of the chimney to give us light. 'Here,' said I, 'is another advantage that the piece of lead my friend Saad gave me will procure us. It will save us the expense of oil.'

"When my children saw that I had extinguished the lamp, and that the piece of glass supplied the place of it, this marvel excited so much admiration amongst them that they shouted so loud as to be heard throughout the neighbourhood. My wife and I increased the noise in our efforts to make them hold their tongues, and we could not entirely carry our point till they were in bed and asleep, after having entertained themselves a considerable time by watching the wonderful light of the piece of glass.

"My wife and I went to bed soon after them, and I sallied forth to my work as usual early the next morning, without thinking any more of the piece of glass. This indifference of mine will be easily accounted for when it is remembered that I was accustomed to see glass, and had never seen diamonds, and if I had seen them, I did not know enough about them to be acquainted with their value.

"I must here inform your majesty that between my house and that of my next neighbour there was only a very slight partition of lath and plaster, which separated us. This house belonged to a very rich Jew, a jeweller by trade, and the room in which he and his wife slept was close to the partition. They were already in bed and asleep, when the great noise made by my children awoke them, and it was a long time before they could get to sleep again.

"The next day the Jew's wife came, as much in her husband's name as her own, to complain to my wife how much their first sleep had been disturbed. 'My good Rachael,' said my wife, 'I am very sorry for what has happened, and I hope you will excuse it. You know what children are: a trifle will make them laugh, and a trifle will make them cry. Come in, and I will show you the cause of the disturbance of which you complain.'

"The Jewess complied, and my wife took up the diamond; for indeed it was one, and of a very rare kind. It was still on the chimney-piece. My wife took it down and showed it to the Jewess. 'See here,' said she, 'it was this piece of glass which caused all the noise you heard last night.' Whilst the Jewess, who was a judge of all sorts of stones, was examining this diamond with admiration, my wife told her how she had found it in the belly of a fish, and related everything that had happened respecting it.

"When my wife had done speaking, the Jewess, who knew her name, said, as she returned the diamond to her, 'O Aishach, I think with you that it is nothing but glass; but as it is better glass than the common kind, and as I have a piece which very much resembles it, which I sometimes wear, and which will match with it, I will buy it of you if you will sell it.' My children, directly they heard there was a talk of selling their plaything, broke in upon the conversation by crying out and begging their mother to keep it; and to pacify them she was forced to promise not to part with it.

"The Jewess, obliged to go away, went out; and before she took leave of my wife, who accompanied her to the door, she begged her in a low voice, if she intended selling the piece of glass, not to let anybody see it without first letting her know.

"Early in the morning the Jew went to his shop, which was in the quarter of the town set apart for jewellers. His wife went to him, and told him of the discovery she had just made. She gave him an account of the size, the beauty, the fine water, and the brightness of the diamond, made a guess at its weight, and above all praised the singular property which, according to my wife's account, it had of shining in the night. The Jew sent back his wife, commissioning her to treat with mine for the purchase of the diamond, and directing her to offer at first such a trifling sum as she might judge proper, and to augment her offer in proportion to the difficulties she found, but at any rate to purchase the diamond, let the price be what it would.

"Following her husband's directions, the Jewess spoke to my wife in private, without waiting to know whether she was determined to sell the diamond, and asked her whether she would take twenty pieces of gold for it. For a piece of glass, as she supposed it to be, my wife thought this a considerable sum. She would not, however, give the Jewess an answer, but only told her she could not listen to her proposal till she had first spoken to me.

"While this transaction was proceeding, I left work, and came home to dinner whilst they were talking at the door. My wife called to me, and asked if I would consent to sell the piece of glass she found in the belly of the fish for twenty pieces of gold, which the Jewess our neighbour had offered for it. I did not give an immediate answer: I reflected on the certainty with which Saad, when he gave me the piece of lead, had promised that it would make my fortune. And as the Jewess thought my silence arose from the contempt in which I held the sum she had offered, she hastened to say, 'Neighbour, I will give you fifty pieces for it; will that satisfy you?'

"As I saw the Jewess so quickly raised the sum from twenty to fifty pieces of gold, I kept firm, and told her she was far below the price for which I expected to sell it. 'My good neighbour,' replied she, 'take a hundred pieces of gold; it is a great deal of money. I do not even know whether my husband will approve my offering so much.' At this new advance, I told her I would have a hundred thousand pieces of gold for the jewel; that I saw the diamond was worth more, but to please her and her husband, who were our neighbours, I would be contented with the sum I had named, which I would certainly have for it; and that if they refused to take it at that price, other jewellers would give me more.

"The Jewess herself confirmed me in my determination by the haste she showed to conclude the bargain by offering repeatedly as far as fifty thousand pieces of gold, which I refused. Then she said, 'I dare not offer more without my husband's leave: he will return to-night, and I shall take it as a favour if you will have patience to wait till he has spoken to you and seen the diamond.' I promised her I would wait.

"At night when the Jew came home, he learned from his wife the failure of the embassy she had undertaken. She told him of the offer of the fifty thousand pieces of gold with which she had tempted us, and how she had asked me to keep the diamond till he saw it. The Jew watched the time when I left work, and came into my house. 'Neighbour Hassan,' said he, approaching me, 'will you be kind enough to show me the diamond that your wife showed to mine.' I desired him to come in, and brought out the diamond.

"As it was almost dark, and the lamp not yet lighted, the Jew knew immediately by the light the diamond gave, and by its great brightness in the palm of my hand, which was illuminated by it, that his wife had given him a true account. He took it from me, and after examining it a long time, and constantly admiring it, he said, 'Well, neighbour, my wife tells me she has offered you fifty thousand pieces of gold; but that you may be satisfied, I offer you twenty thousand more.' 'Neighbour,' replied I, 'your wife might have told you that the price I have set upon it is a hundred thousand; you must give me that or I shall keep the diamond, for I can abate nothing.' He bargained a long time, in hopes I should take something less for it, but he could not succeed; and the fear that I should show it to other jewellers, as indeed I should have done, made him resolve not to leave me till the bargain was concluded at my own price. He told me he had not a hundred thousand pieces of gold in his house, but that the next day at the same hour he would deposit the whole sum; and he brought me that very day two bags of a thousand pieces each to secure the bargain.

"Whether the Jew borrowed money of his friends, or whether he was one of a company of jewellers, I know not: be that as it may, on the morrow he paid me the sum of a hundred thousand pieces of gold, which he brought me at the time appointed, and I delivered up the diamond to him.

"The sale of the diamond having thus made me rich, infinitely beyond my hopes, I returned thanks to Allah for His goodness and bounty. I should have gone and thrown myself at the feet of Saad to testify my gratitude, had I known where my benefactor lived. I should have done the same with respect to Saadi, to whom in the first instance I was indebted for my happiness, although his good intentions towards me had not been immediately successful.

"I thought afterwards of the use I ought to make of so considerable a sum of money. My wife, whose head was already filled with the vanity natural to her sex, wished me directly to buy handsome clothes for herself and children, to purchase a house, and to furnish it elegantly. 'O my good wife,' said I, 'we ought not to begin by extravagant expenditure of this kind: trust to me, and in time you shall have what you ask. Although money is intended to be spent, we must nevertheless proceed in such a way that we may have a fund from which we may draw without the fear of its being exhausted. I will think this matter over, and to-morrow I shall set about establishing this fund.'

"I employed the whole of the following day in going to a set of good workmen in my own trade, whose circumstances were better than mine had hitherto been, and giving them money in advance, I engaged them to work for me in different kinds of rope-making, each according to his ability and power, with a promise not to make them wait, but to be punctual in paying them for their labour, according to the work they did for me. The day after, I made the same engagement with other ropemakers to work for me; and since that time all the ropemakers in Bagdad are employed by me, and are well satisfied with my exactitude in performing my promise.

"As this great number of workmen must produce work in proportion, I hired warehouses in different places, and in each I placed a clerk to receive the work and to sell it by wholesale and retail; and soon by this method my profits and revenue were considerable.

"Afterwards, in order to bring together my warehouses, which were much dispersed, I bought a very large house, which occupied a great space of ground, but was in a very ruinous state. I pulled it down, and in its place I built the mansion which your majesty saw yesterday; but however grand it may appear, it contains only warehouses, which are a necessity in my trade, and a few apartments which I want for myself and my family.

"Some time after I had left my former small house to establish myself in this new building, Saadi and Saad, who had not thought of me till then, remembered me, and agreed to inquire after me. One day, passing in their walk through the street where they had formerly seen me, they were much astonished not to find me engaged in my small trade of ropemaking as they had before seen me. They asked what was become of me, and whether I was living or dead. Their wonder increased when they heard that the man they inquired after was become a very great merchant, and was no longer called simply Hassan, but Cogia Hassan Alhabbal, that is to say, the Merchant Hassan the Ropemaker, and that he had built, in a street whose name was mentioned, a house which had the appearance of a palace.

"The two friends came into this street in search of me. Saadi could not conceive that the piece of lead Saad had given me was the foundation of so large a fortune as I had evidently made. 'I am extremely happy,' said he to Saad, 'that I have made the fortune of Hassan Alhabbal. But I cannot approve of the two falsehoods he told me, to draw from me four hundred pieces of gold instead of two hundred; for to attribute his wealth to the piece of lead you gave him is ridiculous, and nobody, any more than myself, could suppose that gift the foundation of his great prosperity.'

"That is your idea,' replied Saad, 'but I am of a different opinion, and I do not see why you should do Cogia Hassan the injustice to suppose him a liar. You will permit me to think he told you the truth, and that the piece of lead which I gave him is the sole origin of his good fortune; but this is a matter which Cogia Hassan will soon explain to us.'

"Talking thus, the two friends entered the street in which my house is situated. They asked which it was, and it was shown to them, but in looking at the front they could hardly believe they were not mistaken. They knocked at the door, and my porter opened it. Saadi, who was fearful of being thought rude if he took the house of a man of high rank for the building he was in search of, said to the porter, 'This house has been pointed out to me as that of Cogia Hassan Alhabbal; tell us whether we are mistaken.' 'No, sir, you are not mistaken,' answered the porter, opening the door still wider, 'it is the house of Cogia Hassan Alhabbal. Walk in: he is in his apartment, and you will find among the servants some one to announce you.'

"The two friends were introduced, and I knew them again the moment I saw them. I rose from my seat, ran to them, and would have kissed the border of their robe, but they prevented me, and I was obliged, in spite of myself, to suffer them to embrace me. I begged them to be seated on a large sofa, at the same time pointing to a couch for four people, which was placed near my garden. I requested them to take the upper place, but they wished me to occupy it.

"'O my benefactors,' said I to them, 'I have not forgotten that I am the poor Hassan Alhabbal; and were I a greater man, and had not incurred the obligations to you that I owe, I know what is due to you: I entreat you, therefore, not to overwhelm me with confusion.' They took their proper places, and I took mine opposite to them.

"Saadi then began the conversation, and addressing me, said, 'Cogia Hassan, I cannot express the pleasure I feel in seeing you nearly in the position I wished to place you in when I made you the present (which I do not mention to reproach you) of the two hundred pieces of gold which I gave you twice, and I am convinced that the four hundred pieces have made the wonderful change in your fortune which I see with so much satisfaction. One thing only grieves me, and that is, that I cannot understand what reason you could have had for twice concealing the truth from me, in alleging the losses you met with by accidents, which then appeared, and still appear, incredible to me. When we saw you the last time, had you made so little progress in bettering your circumstances with the two sums that you were ashamed to confess it? I cannot but believe this was the case, and I think you are going to confirm me in my opinion.'

"Saad listened to this conversation with great impatience, not to say indignation, which he expressed by casting down his eyes and shaking his head. He suffered Saadi, however, to finish his speech without opening his lips. When he had done, he said, 'Pardon me, O Saadi, if, before Cogia Hassan answers you, I speak to tell you that I am surprised at your prejudice against his sincerity, and that you persist in refusing credit to the assurances he formerly gave you. I have already told you, and I now repeat my assertion, that I at first believed him upon the plain recital of the two accidents which happened to him; and, say what you will, I am sure his story was true. But let him speak: we shall be informed by himself which of us two has done him justice.'

"After the two friends had spoken, I replied thus, addressing myself to both: 'O my masters, I should condemn myself to perpetual silence concerning the explanation you require of me, if I were not certain that the dispute you have had on my account can never break the tie of friendship which unites your hearts. I will therefore explain my present position, since you desire it; but first I protest to you that it is with the same sincerity that I formerly made known to you what had happened to me.' I then related the circumstances to them exactly as your majesty has heard them, without omitting the most trifling part.

"My protestations made not the least impression on the mind of Saadi, nor did they tend to lessen his prejudices. When I had ceased speaking, he replied: 'Cogia Hassan, the adventure of the fish, and of the diamond found in his belly, appears to me as incredible as the story of the turban that was carried off by the kite, and of the jar of bran that was exchanged for the fullers' earth. But be that as it may, I am not the less convinced that you are no longer poor, but rich; and as my sole intention was that you should become wealthy by my means, I am most sincerely rejoiced at your good fortune.'

"As it grew late they rose to take leave. I got up also, and stopping them, I said to them, 'O my benefactors, suffer me to request a favour of you, and I entreat you not to refuse me; it is, that you will permit me to have the honour of giving you a frugal supper, and afterwards each a bed, so that I may carry you to-morrow, by water, to a small house that I have purchased in the country. From thence I will bring you back by land the same day, furnishing you both with horses from my stable.' 'If Saad has not business which calls him elsewhere,' said Saadi, 'I most readily consent to your proposal.' 'I have nothing to do,' replied Saad, 'that can interfere with enjoying your company. We must, then,' continued he, 'send to your house and to mine, to let our families know that they may not expect us.' I summoned a slave, and whilst they gave him this commission, I ordered supper.

"While supper was preparing, I showed every part of my house to my benefactors, who found it very large, and well adapted to my position. I call them both my benefactors without distinction, as, but for Saadi, Saad would never have given me the piece of lead; and, but for Saad, Saadi would not have addressed himself to me to give me the four hundred pieces of gold, which I consider as the source of my happiness. I led them back to the same room, where they asked me many questions concerning the details of my business; and my answers were such that they appeared satisfied with my conduct.

"We were at length informed that supper was served. As the table was set in another apartment, I conducted them thither. They were much pleased with the manner in which this room was lighted up, with the neatness of the room and the sideboard, and above all with the dishes, which they found entirely to their taste. I treated them with vocal and instrumental music during the repast, and when supper was removed, I introduced a company of dancers of both sexes: endeavouring to show my benefactors, as much as possible, how penetrated I was with gratitude towards them.

"The next day, as I had arranged with Saadi and Saad to set out early in the morning, that we might enjoy the freshness of the day, we were at the waterside before the sun rose. We embarked in a very neat boat spread with carpets, which awaited us; and assisted by six good rowers and the current of the water, in about an hour and a half we arrived at my country house.

"On landing, the two friends stopped; less to behold the beauty of the outside of the building, than to admire its advantageous situation in point of prospect, which was neither too confined nor too extensive, but pleasing and harmonious on every side. I conducted them through the apartments, and made them remark how well the rooms were connected one with another, and with the offices and other conveniences, and they thought the whole arrangement cheerful and pleasant.

"We went afterwards into the garden, where the friends were most pleased with a grove, in which orange and citron trees were planted at equal distances in walks, bearing fruit and flowers which perfumed the air, and each tree watered separately by a perpetual stream of water, conveyed directly from the river. The shade, the freshness which was here found, even in the greatest heat of the sun, the gentle murmur of the water, the harmonious warbling of an infinite number of birds, and many other delightful circumstances, struck them so much, that they stopped at almost every step, sometimes to express their thanks to me for having brought them into so delicious a place, sometimes to congratulate me on the purchase I had made, and to pay me many other obliging compliments.

"I brought them to the end of this grove, which is very long and extensive. Then I pointed out to them a wood of large trees that terminated my garden; thereupon I led them to a small room, open on all sides, but shaded by clumps of palm trees, which did not intercept the prospect. I invited them to enter and repose themselves there on a sofa covered with carpets and cushions.

"Two of my sons, who were living in the house, and whom I had sent to this room with their preceptor some time before for the benefit of the air, quitted us on entering the grove; and as they were looking for birds' nests, they perceived one amongst the branches of a large tree. They were at first tempted to climb this tree, but as they had neither strength nor skill for such an undertaking, they pointed out the nest to a slave I had given them, who always attended on them, and desired him to get it.

"The slave climbed the tree, and when he had reached the nest, he was much astonished to see it was built in a turban. He brought away the nest, just as it was, came down from the tree, and showed the turban to my children; and as he thought I

THE TURBAN CONTAINING THE NEST.

should like to see it also, he told them so, and gave it to my eldest son to bring to me. I saw my boys at a distance running to me, with an expression of pleasure common in children who have found a treasure. My eldest held up the nest to me, and said, 'O father, look at this nest in a turban!' Saadi and Saad were not less surprised than myself at this novelty; but I was much more astonished than they when I recognised the very turban that the kite had carried away from me. In the midst of my wonder, after I had examined it and turned it every way, I asked the two friends if they had any recollection of the turban I wore on the day when they first did me the honour of accosting me.

"'I do not suppose,' replied Saad, 'that Saadi, any more than myself, took particular notice of your turban; but neither he nor I can doubt that this is the same if the hundred and ninety pieces of gold are found in it.' 'O my master,' I replied, 'you need not doubt its being the same turban. Independently of my knowing it again, I perceive also by its weight it cannot be any other, and you will yourself be convinced of this if you will only weigh it in your hand.' I presented it to him, after having taken out the birds, which I gave to my children; he took it in his hands, and gave it to Saadi to feel how heavy it was. 'I am ready to believe it to be your turban,' said Saadi; 'I shall nevertheless be still more convinced when I have seen the hundred and ninety pieces of gold.'

"At least, my friends,' I resumed, when I had taken the turban, 'examine it well, I entreat you, before I touch it, and observe that it has not very lately been placed in the tree, and that the state in which you see both that and the nest, which is so neatly put together without the help of man, are certain proofs that it has been there ever since the kite flew away with it, and that the bird must have let it drop, or placed it on the tree, the branches of which prevented its falling to the ground. Do not be offended that I make this observation, as I have so great an interest in removing every suspicion of deceit on my part.' Saad seconded me in my design. 'Saadi,' said he, 'this concerns you, and not me, for I am perfectly convinced that Cogia Hassan has never imposed upon us.'

"While Saad was speaking, I took off the linen which surrounded the cap in many folds, to form the turban, and I drew from it the purse, which Saadi knew to be the same he had given me. I emptied it on the carpet before the two friends, and I said to them, 'O my masters, here are the pieces of gold: count them yourselves, and see if they do not turn out right.' Saad arranged them in tens, to the number of a hundred and ninety; and then Saadi, who could not reject so manifest a truth, addressed me thus: 'Cogia Hassan, I allow that these hundred and ninety pieces of gold cannot have assisted in enriching you; but the other hundred and ninety which you hid in the jar of bran, at least as you would make me believe, may have contributed to found your fortune.'

"'My friend,' I replied, 'I have told you the truth concerning the last sum of money as well as concerning this. You would not have me retract, and tell you a lie?' 'Cogia Hassan,' said Saad to me, 'let Saadi enjoy his opinion; I consent with all my heart that he should think you indebted to him for the half of your good fortune, provided he will acknowledge that I have contributed the other half by means of the piece of lead I gave you, and that he does not call in question the value of the diamond found in the belly of the fish.' 'Saad,' replied Saadi, 'I will think what you please, provided you will leave me at liberty to believe that money can only be obtained by money.' 'What!' returned Saad, 'if by chance I might find a diamond worth fifty thousand pieces of gold, and can get that sum for it, should I acquire that money by money?'

"The dispute ended here. We rose and went back to the house just as dinner was served, and we sat down to table. After dinner I left my guests, that they might repose during the great heat of the day, and went to give orders to my steward and gardener. I then returned to Saadi and Saad, and we conversed on different subjects till the great heat was over, when we went back to the garden, where we remained in the cool almost till sunset. Then the two friends and I mounted our horses, and, followed by a slave, we arrived at Bagdad by moonlight, about two hours after dark.

"I know not by what negligence of my servants it happened that there was no corn for the horses on my return home. The granaries were shut, and they were distant, and it was too late to get any corn elsewhere.

"In searching about through the neighbourhood, one of my slaves found a jar of bran in a shop. He bought the bran, and brought it in the jar, promising to carry back the vessel the next day. The slave emptied the bran into the manger; and in spreading it about that all the horses might have their share, he felt under his hand a piece of linen tied up and very heavy. He brought me the linen without disturbing it, in the state in which he found it, and presenting it to me, said, that perhaps it was the linen he had often heard me mention when I related my history to my friends.

"Quite overjoyed, I said to my benefactors: 'O kind benefactors, it pleases Allah that we should not separate till you have been fully convinced of the truth which I have never ceased to assure you of. Here,' continued I, addressing myself to Saadi, 'are the other hundred and ninety pieces of gold which I received from your hands: I know it by the linen rag you see here.' I untied the rag, and counted the money before them. I also ordered the jar to be brought to me: I knew that again, and I sent it to my wife to ask her if she knew it, desiring she might not be told what had just happened. She recognised it immediately, and sent me word that it was the very jar that contained the bran she had once exchanged for some fullers' earth.

"Saadi candidly acknowledged his error. He said to Saad, 'I give up my opinion; and I allow, with you, that money is not always a certain means of getting money and becoming rich.'

"When Saadi had finished speaking, I said to him, 'My kind friend, I dare not propose to you to take back the three hundred and eighty pieces of gold, which it has now pleased Heaven to bring to light to do away with the opinion you entertained of my knavery. I am sure you did not make the present with the design of having it returned to you. On my part, I do not wish to take advantage of it, contented as I am with what Allah has bestowed upon me by other means. But I hope you will consent to my distributing this money to-morrow amongst the poor, that Allah may reward us both for our charity.'

"The two friends slept the second night at my house, and the next day they embraced me, and taking leave of me, returned home well satisfied with the reception I had given them, and with the knowledge that I did not make an ill use of the good fortune which, under Heaven, I owed to them.

"I have not failed to go and pay my respects to them separately at each of their houses; and since that time I esteem as a great honour the permission they have given me to continue to see them and to cultivate their friendship."

"The Caliph Haroun Alraschid paid so much attention to Cogia Hassan, that he only perceived by the ropemaker's silence that he had finished his history. He then said to him, 'Cogia Hassan, it is a long time since I have heard anything which has given me so much pleasure as the very wonderful manner by which it has pleased Heaven to render you happy in this world. It now behoves you to continue to show your gratitude to Allah, by the good use you make of the blessings He has bestowed. I wish to inform you, that the diamond which has made your fortune is in my treasury, and for my part I am glad to learn by what means it came there. But as it is possible there may still remain some doubts in the mind of Saadi with respect to the singularity of this diamond, which I look upon as the most precious and costly gem I possess, I wish you to bring Saad and Saadi hither, that my treasurer may show the diamond to the latter, so that he may no longer be incredulous; and that he may know that money is not always a certain means for a poor man to acquire great wealth in a short time, and without any trouble. I command you, also, to relate your history to my treasurer, that he may commit it to writing, and preserve it with the diamond.'

"As he concluded these words, the caliph showed by an inclination of his head to Cogia Hassan, Sidi Nouman, and Baba Abdalla, that he was satisfied with them; thereupon they took their leave by prostrating themselves before his throne, and retired from the caliph's presence."

The Sultana Scheherazade would have begun another story; but the Sultan of the Indies, who perceived that the day was breaking, deferred hearing it till the next morning, when she began the following history:—

## THE HISTORY OF ALI BABA, AND OF THE FORTY ROBBERS WHO WERE KILLED BY ONE SLAVE.

N a certain town of Persia, O great monarch, situated on the very confines of your majesty's dominions, there lived two brothers, one of whom was named Cassim, and the other Ali Baba. Their father at his death left them a very moderate fortune, which they divided equally. It might, therefore, be naturally conjectured that their position would be the same; chance, however, ordered it otherwise.

"Cassim married a woman, who very soon after her nuptials inherited a well-furnished shop, a warehouse filled with good merchandise, and some considerable property in land. Her husband thus found himself suddenly quite a prosperous man, and became one of the richest merchants in the whole town.

"Ali Baba, on the other hand, who had taken to wife a woman no better off for worldly goods than himself, lived in a very poor house, and had no other means of gaining his livelihood, and supporting his wife and children, than by going to cut wood in a neighbouring forest, and carrying it about the town to sell, on three asses, which were his only possession.

Ali Baba went one day to the forest, and had very nearly finished cutting as much wood as his asses could carry, when he perceived a thick cloud of dust, which rose very high into the air, and appeared to come from a point to the right of the spot where he stood. It was advancing towards him. He looked at it very attentively, and was soon able to distinguish a numerous company of men on horseback, who were approaching at a quick pace.

"Although that part of the country had never been spoken of as being infested with robbers, Ali Baba nevertheless conjectured that these horsemen came of that denomination. Therefore, without considering what might become of his asses, his first and only care was to save himself. He instantly climbed up into a large tree, the branches of which, at a very little height from the ground, spread out so close and thick that only one small opening was left. He hid himself among the thick branches, with great hope of safety, as he could see everything that occurred without being observed. The tree itself also grew at the foot of a sort of isolated rock, considerably higher than the tree, and so steep that it could not be easily ascended.

"The men, who appeared stout, powerful, and well mounted, came up to this very rock, and alighted at its foot. Ali Baba counted forty of them, and was very sure, from their appearance and mode of equipment, that they were robbers. Nor was he wrong in his conjecture. They were, in fact, a band of robbers, who abstained from committing any depredations in the neighbourhood, but carried on their system of plunder at a considerable distance, and only had their place of rendezvous at that spot. Presently each horseman took the bridle off his horse, and hung over its head a bag filled with barley, which he had brought with him; and when all had fastened their horses to bushes and trees, they took off their travelling bags, which appeared so heavy that Ali Baba thought they must be filled with gold and silver.

"The robber who was nearest to him, and whom Ali Baba took ror the captain of the band, came with his bag on his shoulder close to the rock, beside the very tree in which Ali Baba had concealed himself. After making his way among some bushes and shrubs that grew there, the robber very deliberately pronounced these words, 'OPEN, SESAME!' which Ali Baba distinctly heard. The captain of the band had no sooner spoken, than a door immediately opened; and after making all his men pass before him, and go in through the door, the chief entered also, and the door closed.

ALI BABA ENTERING THE CAVE

"The robbers continued within the rock for a considerable time; and Ali Baba was compelled to remain in the tree, and wait with patience for their departure, as he was afraid to leave his place of refuge and endeavour to save himself by flight, lest some of the horsemen should come out and discover him. He was nevertheless strongly tempted to creep down, seize two of their horses, mount one and lead the other by the bridle, and thus, driving his three asses before him, attempt his escape. But the peril of the undertaking made him follow the safer method of delay.

"At length the door opened, and the forty robbers came out. The captain, contrary to his former proceeding, made his appearance first. After he had seen all his troops pass out before him, Ali Baba heard him pronounce these words: 'SHUT, SESAME!' Each man then returned to his horse, put on its bridle, fastened his bag, and mounted. When the captain saw that they were all ready to proceed, he put himself at their head, and they departed on the road by which they had come.

"Ali Baba did not immediately come down from the tree, because he thought that the robbers might have forgotten something, and be obliged to come back, and that he should thus thrust himself into danger. He followed them with his eyes till he could see them no longer, and, in order to be more secure, delayed his descent till a considerable time after he had lost sight of them. As he recollected the words the captain of the robbers had used to open and shut the door, he had the curiosity to try if the same effect would be produced by his pronouncing them. He therefore made his way through the bushes till he came to the door, which they concealed. He went up to it, and called out, 'Open, sesame!' and the door instantly flew wide open.

"Ali Baba expected to find only a dark and gloomy cave, and was much astonished at seeing a large, spacious, well-lighted and vaulted room, dug out of the rock, and so high that he could not touch the roof with his hand. It received its light from an opening at the top of the rock. He observed in it a large quantity of provisions, numerous bales of rich merchandise, a store of silk stuffs and brocades, rich and valuable carpets, and besides all this, great quantities of money, both silver and gold, partly piled up in heaps, and partly stored in large leather bags, placed one on another. At the sight of all these things, it seemed to him that this cave must have been used, not only for years, but for centuries, as a retreat for successive generations of robbers.

"Ali Baba did not hesitate long as to the plan he should pursue. He went into the cave, and as soon as he was there the door shut; but as he knew the secret by which to open it, this circumstance gave him no sort of uneasiness. He paid no attention to the silver, but made directly for the gold coin, and particularly that portion which was in the bags. He took up in several journeys as much as he could carry, and when he had got together what he thought sufficient for loading his three asses, he went and collected them together, as they had strayed to some distance. He then brought them as close as he could to the rock, and loaded them; and in order to conceal the sacks, he so covered the whole over with wood, that no one could perceive that his beasts had any other load. When he had finished his task he went up to the door, and pronounced the words, 'Shut, sesame!' The portal instantly closed; for although it shut of itself every time he went in, it remained open on his coming out till he commanded it to close.

"Ali Baba now took the road to the town; and when he got to his own house he drove his asses into a small courtyard, and shut the gate with great care. He threw down the faggots of brushwood that covered the bags, and carried the latter into his house, where he laid them down in a row before his wife, who was sitting upon a sofa.

"His wife felt the sacks to find out what might be their contents; and when she found them to be full of money, she suspected her husband of having stolen them; and when he laid them all before her, she could not help saying, 'Ali Baba, is it possible that you should—?' He immediately interrupted her. 'Peace, my dear wife,' exclaimed he, 'do not alarm yourself: I am not a thief, unless it be robbery to deprive thieves of their plunder. You will change your opinion of me when I have told you my good fortune.' Hereupon he emptied the sacks, the contents of which formed a great heap of gold, that quite dazzled his wife's eyes; and when he had done, he related his whole adventure from beginning to end; and in conclusion he entreated her above all things to keep it secret.

"Recovering from her alarm, his wife began to rejoice with Ali Baba on the good fortune which had befallen them, and was about to count over the money that lay before her piece by piece. 'What are you going to do?' said he. 'You are very foolish, O wife: you would never have done counting this mass. I will immediately dig a pit to bury it in—we have no time to lose.' 'But it is only right,' replied the wife, 'that we should know nearly what quantity there may be. I will go and borrow a small measure from some one of our neighbours, and whilst you are digging the pit I will ascertain how much we have.' 'What you want to do, wife,' replied Ali Baba, 'is of no use; and if you will take my advice, you will give up the intention. However, you shall have your own way; only remember not to betray the secret.'

"Persisting in her design, the wife of Ali Baba set off, and went to her brother-in-law, Cassim, who lived at a short distance from her house. Cassim was from home; so she addressed herself to his wife, whom she begged to lend her a measure for a few minutes. Cassim's wife inquired if she wanted a large or a small one, to which Ali Baba's wife replied that a small one would suit her. 'That I will lend you with pleasure,' said the sister-in-law; 'wait a moment, and I will bring it you.' She went to bring a measure; but, knowing the poverty of Ali Baba, she was curious to know what sort of grain his wife wanted to measure; she bethought herself, therefore, of putting some tallow under the measure, in such a way that it could not be observed. She returned with the vessel, and giving it to the wife of Ali Baba, apologized for having made her wait so long, with the excuse that she had some difficulty in finding what she wanted.

"The wife of Ali Baba returned home, and placing the measure on the heap of gold, filled and emptied it at a little distance on the sofa, till she had measured the whole mass. Her husband having by this time dug the pit for its reception, she informed him how many measures there were, and both rejoiced at the magnitude of the treasure. While Ali Baba was burying the gold, his wife, to prove her exactness and punctuality, carried back the measure to her sister-in-law, without observing that a piece of gold had stuck to the bottom of it. 'Here, sister,' said she, on returning it, 'you see I have not kept your measure long; I am much obliged to you for lending it me.'

"So soon as the wife of Ali Baba had taken her departure, Cassim's wife looked at the bottom of the measure, and was inexpressibly astonished to see a piece of gold sticking to it. Envy instantly took possession of her breast. 'What!' said she to herself, 'has Ali Baba such an abundance of gold that he measures, instead of counting it? Where can that miserable wretch have got it?' Her husband Cassim was from home: he had gone as usual to his shop, from whence he would not return till evening. The time of his absence appeared an age to her, for she was burning with impatience to acquaint him with a circumstance which, she concluded, would surprise him as much as it had astonished her.

"On Cassim's return home, his wife said to him, 'Cassim, you think you are rich, but you are deceived; Ali Baba has infinitely more wealth than you can boast: he does not count his money as you do, he measures it.' Cassim demanded an explanation of this enigma, and his wife unravelled it by acquainting him with the expedient she had used to make this discovery, and showing him the piece of money she had found adhering to the bottom of the measure. The coin was so ancient, that the name engraven on it was unknown to her.

"Far from feeling any pleasure at the good fortune which had rescued his brother from poverty, Cassim conceived an implacable jealousy on this occasion. He could scarcely close his eyes the whole night long. The next morning, before sunrise, he went to Ali Baba. He did not accost him as a brother: that endearing appellation had not passed his lips since his marriage with the rich widow. 'O Ali Baba,' said he, addressing him, 'you are very reserved in your affairs: you pretend to be poor and wretched, and a beggar, and yet you have so much money that you must measure it.' 'O my brother,' replied Ali Baba, 'I do not understand your meaning; pray explain yourself.' 'Do not pretend ignorance,' resumed Cassim; and showing Ali Baba the piece of gold his wife had given him, he continued: 'how many pieces have you like this that my wife found sticking to the bottom of the measure which your wife borrowed of her yesterday?'

"From this speech Ali Baba at once understood that, in consequence of his own wife's obstinacy, Cassim and his wife were already acquainted with the fact he was so anxious to conceal from them; but the discovery was made, and nothing could now be done to remedy the evil. Without showing the slightest sign of surprise or vexation, he frankly owned to his brother the whole affair, and told him by what chance he had found out the retreat of the thieves, and where it was situated; and he offered, if Cassim would agree to keep the secret, to share the treasure with him.

"'This I certainly expect you will do,' replied Cassim in a haughty tone; and he added, 'but I demand to know also the precise spot where this treasure lies concealed, and the marks and signs which may enable me to visit the place myself, should I feel inclined to do so. If you refuse this information I will go and inform the officer of the police of the whole transaction, and on my taking this step you will not only be deprived of all hope of obtaining any more money, but you will even lose that you have already taken; whereas I shall receive my portion for having informed against you.'

"Actuated more by his natural goodness of heart, than intimidated by the insolent menaces of this cruel brother, Ali Baba gave him all the information he demanded, and even told him the words he must pronounce both on entering the cave and on quitting it. Cassim made no further inquiries of Ali Baba: he left him with the determination of being beforehand with him in any further views he might have on the treasure. Full of the hope of possessing himself of the whole mass, he set off the next morning, before break of day, with ten mules furnished with large hampers, which he proposed to fill: moreover, indulging the prospect of taking a much larger number of animals in a second expedition, according to the sums he might find in the cave. He took the road which Ali Baba had pointed out, and arrived at the rock and the tree, which, from description, he knew to be the one that had concealed his brother. He looked for the door, and soon discovered it; and to cause it to open he pronounced the words, 'Open, sesame!' The door obeyed, he entered, and it immediately closed behind him. On examining the cave, he felt the utmost astonishment on seeing so much more wealth than the description of Ali Baba had led him to expect; and his admiration increased as he examined each department separately. Avaricious and fond of money as he was, he could have passed the whole day in feasting his eyes with the sight of so much gold, but he reflected that he had come to load his ten mules with as much treasure as he could collect. He took up a number of sacks, and coming to the door, his mind distracted by a multitude of ideas, found that he had forgotten the important words, and instead of pronouncing 'sesame,' he said, 'Open, barley.' He was thunderstruck on perceiving that the door, instead of flying open, remained closed. He named various other kinds of grain, all but the right description, but the door did not move.

"Cassim was not prepared for an adventure of this kind. Fear took entire possession of his mind. The more he endeavoured to recollect the word *sesame*, the more was his memory confused, and he remained as far from any recollection of it as if he had never heard the word mentioned. He threw to the ground the sacks he had collected, and paced with hasty steps backward and forward in the cave. The riches which surrounded him had no longer any charms for his imagination.

"Towards noon the robbers returned to their cave, and when they were within a short distance of it, and saw the mules belonging to Cassim standing about the rock laden with hampers, they were greatly surprised. They immediately advanced at full speed, and drove away the ten mules, which Cassim had neglected to fasten, and which, therefore, soon fled, and dispersed in the forest. The robbers did not give themselves the trouble to run after the mules, for their chief object was to discover the owner of the beasts. While some were employed in searching the exterior recesses of the rock, the captain, with the rest, alighted, and drawing their sabres, the party went towards the door, pronounced the magic words, and it opened.

"Cassim, who from the inside of the cave had heard the noise of horses trampling on the ground, felt certain that the robbers had arrived, and that his death was inevitable. Resolved, however, to make one effort to escape, and reach some place of safety, he posted himself near the door, ready to run out as soon as it should open. The word 'sesame,' which he had in vain endeavoured to recall to his remembrance, was scarcely pronounced when the portal opened, and he rushed out with such violence that he threw the captain to the ground. He could not, however, avoid the other thieves, who, having their sabres drawn, cut him to pieces on the spot.

"The next proceeding of the robbers after this execution was to enter the cave. They found, near the door, the bags which Cassim, after filling them with gold, had removed there for the convenience of loading his mules; and they put them in their places again without observing the absence of those which Ali Baba had previously carried away Conjecturing and consulting upon this event, they could easily account for Cassim's inability to effect his escape, but they could not in any way imagine how he had been able to enter the cave. They supposed that he might have descended from the top of the cave, but the opening which admitted the light was so high, and the summit of the rock so inaccessible on the outside, besides the absence of any traces of his having adopted

CASSIM FOUND IN THE CAVE.

this mode, that they all agreed such a feat was impossible. They could not suppose he had entered by the door, unless he had discovered the password which caused it to open; but they felt quite secure that they alone were possessed of this secret, for they were ignorant of having been overheard by Ali Baba.

"But as the manner in which this entry had been effected remained a mystery, and their united riches were no longer in safety, they agreed to cut the corpse of Cassim into four quarters, and place them in the cave near the door, two quarters on one side, and two on the other, to frighten away any one who might have the boldness to hazard a similar enterprise; resolving, themselves, not to return to the cave for some time. This determination they put into immediate execution, and when they had nothing further to detain them, they left their place of retreat well secured, mounted their horses, and set off to scour the country, and, as before, to infest the roads most frequented by caravans, which afforded them favourable opportunities of exercising their accustomed dexterity in plundering.

"The wife of Cassim in the meantime began to feel very uneasy when she observed night approach, and yet her husband did not return. She went in the utmost alarm to Ali Baba, and said to him, 'O brother, I believe you are well aware that Cassim is gone to the forest, and for what purpose. He has not yet come back, and night is already approaching: I fear that some accident may have befallen him.'

"Ali Baba suspected his brother's intention after the conversation he had held with him, and for this reason he had abstained from visiting the forest on that day, that he might not offend Cassim. However, without uttering any reproaches that could have given the slightest offence either to her or her husband, he replied that she need not yet feel any uneasiness, for that Cassim most probably thought it prudent not to return to the city until the daylight had entirely vanished. The wife of Cassim felt satisfied with this reason, and was the more easily persuaded of its truth when she considered how important it was that her husband should use the greatest secresy for the accomplishment of his purpose. She returned to her house, and waited patiently till midnight; but after that hour her fears returned with twofold strength, and her grief was the greater, as she could not proclaim it, nor even relieve it by cries, which might have caused suspicion and inquiry in the neighbourhood. She then began to repent of the silly curiosity which, heightened by the most blameable envy, had induced her to endeavour to pry into the private affairs of her brother and sister-in-law. She spent the night in weeping, and at break of day she ran to Ali Baba, and announced the cause of her early visit less by her words than by her tears.

"Ali Baba did not wait till his sister entreated him to go and seek for Cassim. After advising the disconsolate wife to restrain her grief, he immediately set off with his three asses, and went to the forest. As he draw near the rock, he was much astonished on observing that blood had been shed near thed oor, and not having met in his way either his brother or the ten mules, he looked on this as an unfavourable omen. He reached the door, and on his pronouncing the words it opened. He was struck with horror when he discovered the body of his brother cut into four quarters · yet, notwithstanding the small share of fraternal affection he had received from Cassim during his life, he did not hesitate on the course he was to pursue in rendering the last act of duty to his brother's remains. He found materials in the cave wherein to wrap up the body, and making two packets of the four quarters, he placed them on one of his asses, covering them with sticks, to conceal them. The other two asses he expeditiously loaded with sacks of gold, putting wood over them as on the preceding occasion; and having finished all he had to do, and commanded the door to close, he took the road to the city, taking care to wait at the entrance of the forest until night had closed, that he might return without being observed. When he got home he left the two asses that were laden with gold, desiring his wife to take care to unload them; and after telling her in a few words what had happened to Cassim, he led the third ass away to his sister-in-law.

"Ali Baba knocked at the door, which was opened to him by a female slave named Morgiana. This Morgiana was crafty, cunning, and fruitful in inventions to forward the success of the most difficult enterprise, and Ali Baba knew her abilities well. When he had entered the courtyard, he unloaded the wood and the two packages from the ass, and taking the slave aside, he said, 'Morgiana, the first thing I have to request of you is inviolable secresy. You will soon see how necessary this is, not only to me, but to your mistress. These two packets contain the body of your master, and we must endeavour to bury him as if he had died a natural death. Let me speak to your mistress, and take good heed of what I shall say to her.'

"Morgiana went to acquaint her mistress that Ali Baba had returned, and Ali Baba followed her. 'Well, brother,' inquired his sister-in-law, in an impatient tone, 'what news do you bring of my husband? Alas! I perceive no hope of consolation in your countenance.' 'O my sister,' replied Ali Baba, 'I cannot answer you, unless you first promise to listen to me from the beginning to the end of my story without interruption.

It is of no less importance to you than to me, under the present circumstances, to preserve the greatest secresy. Discretion is absolutely necessary for your repose and security.' 'Ah,' cried the sister in a mournful voice, 'this preamble convinces me that my husband is no more; but at the same time I feel the necessity of the secresy you require. I must do violence to my feelings: speak, I hear you.'

"Ali Baba then related to her all that had happened during his journey, until he had brought away the body of Cassim. 'Sister,' added he, 'here is a great and sudden affliction for you, the more distressing as it was unexpected. The evil is without remedy, but nevertheless, if my good offices can afford you consolation, I offer to join the small property Heaven has granted me to yours, by marrying you. I can assure you my wife will not be jealous, and you will live comfortably together. If this proposal meets your approbation, we must contrive to bury my brother as if he had died a natural death; and this is an office which I think you may safely entrust to Morgiana, and I will, on my part, contribute all in my power to assist her.'

"The widow of Cassim reflected that she could not do better than consent to this offer, for Ali Baba now possessed greater riches than she could boast, and besides, by the discovery of the treasure, might increase them considerably. She did not, therefore, refuse his proposal, but, on the contrary, regarded it as a reasonable source of consolation. She wiped away her tears, which had begun to flow abundantly, and suppressed those mournful cries which women are accustomed to utter on the death of their husbands, and by these signs she sufficiently testified to Ali Baba that she accepted his offer.

"Ali Baba left the widow of Cassim in this disposition of mind, and having strongly recommended to Morgiana to use the utmost discretion in the difficult part she was to perform, he returned home with his ass.

"Morgiana did not belie her character for cunning. She went out with Ali Baba, and betook herself to an apothecary who lived in the neighbourhood. She knocked at the shop door, and when it was opened asked for a particular kind of lozenge, supposed to possess great efficacy in dangerous disorders. The apothecary gave her as much as the money she offered would pay for, asking who was ill in her master's family. 'Alas!' exclaimed she, with a deep sigh, 'it is my worthy master Cassim himself. No one can understand his complaint: he can neither speak nor eat.' So saying, she carried off the lozenges, which Cassim would never need more.

"On the following day Morgiana again went to the same apothecary, and with tears in her eyes inquired for an essence which it was customary only to administer when the patient was reduced to the last extremity, and when no other remedy had been left untried. 'Alas!' cried she, as she received it from the hands of the apothecary, and she aptly counterfeited the deepest affliction, 'I fear this remedy will not be of more use than the lozenges. I shall lose my beloved master!'

"Moreover, as Ali Baba and his wife were seen going backwards and forwards to and from the house of Cassim in the course of the day, no one was surprised when, towards evening, the piercing cries of the widow and Morgiana announced the death of Cassim. At a very early hour the next morning, when day began to appear, Morgiana, knowing that a good old cobbler lived some distance off who was one of the first to open his shop, went out to visit him. Coming up to him, she wished him a good day, and put a piece of gold into his hand.

"Baba Mustapha, a man well known throughout all the city, was naturally of a gay turn, and had always something laughable to say. He examined the piece of money, as it was yet scarcely daylight, and seeing that it was gold, he said, 'This is good wage; what is to be done? I am ready to do your bidding.' 'Baba Mustapha,' said Morgiana to him, 'take all your materials for sewing, and come directly with me; but I insist on this condition, that you let me put a bandage over your eyes when we have got to a certain place.' At these words Baba Mustapha began to make objections. 'Oh, ho!' said he, 'you want me to do something against my conscience or my honour.' But Morgiana interrupted him by putting another piece of gold into his hand. 'Allah forbid,' she said, 'that I should require you to do anything that would stain your honour; only come with me, and fear nothing.'

"Baba Mustapha suffered himself to be led by the slave, who, when she had reached the place she had mentioned, bound a handkerchief over his eyes, and brought him to her deceased master's; nor did she remove the bandage until he was in the chamber where the body was deposited, the severed quarters having been put together. Taking off the covering, she said, 'Baba Mustapha, I have brought you hither that you might sew these pieces together. Lose no time; and when you have done I will give you another piece of gold.'

"When Baba Mustapha had finished his work, Morgiana bound his eyes again before he left the chamber, and after giving him the third piece of money, according to her promise, and earnestly recommending him to keep her secret, she conducted him to the place where she had first put on the handkerchief. Here she took the bandage from his eyes, and left him to return to his house, watching him, however, until he was out of sight, lest he should have the curiosity to return and notice her movements.

"Morgiana had heated some water to wash the body of Cassim; and Ali Baba, who entered just as she returned, washed it, perfumed it with incense, and wrapped it in the burying-clothes with the customary ceremonies. The joiner also brought the coffin which Ali Baba had taken care to order. In order that he might not observe anything particular, Morgiana received the coffin at the door, and having paid the man and sent him away, she assisted Ali Baba to put the body into it. When he had nailed down the lid of the coffin, she went to the mosque, to give notice that everything was ready for the funeral. The people belonging to the mosque, whose duty it is to wash the bodies of the dead, offered to come and perform their office, but she told them that all was done and ready.

"Morgiana had scarcely returned before the Iman and the other ministers of the mosque arrived. Four of the neighbours took the coffin on their shoulders, and carried it to the cemetery, following the Iman, who repeated prayers as he went along. Morgiana, as slave to the deceased, walked next, with her head uncovered. She was bathed in tears, and uttered the most piteous cries from time to time, beating her breast and tearing her hair. Ali Baba closed the procession, accompanied by some of the neighbours, who occasionally took the place of the bearers, to relieve them in carrying the coffin, until they reached the cemetery.

"As for the widow of Cassim, she remained at home to lament and weep with the women of the neighbourhood, who, according to the usual custom, had repaired to her house during the ceremony of the burial. Joining their cries to hers, they filled the air with sounds of woe. In this manner the fatal end of Cassim was so well dissembled and concealed by Ali Baba and the rest, that no one in the city had the least suspicion of the manner in which he had come by his death.

"Three or four days after the interment of Cassim, Ali Baba removed the few goods he possessed, together with the money he had taken from the robbers' store, which he conveyed by night into the house of the widow of Cassim, in order to establish himself there, and thus announce his marriage with his sister-in-law: and as such matches are by no means extraordinary in our religion, no one showed any marks of surprise on the occasion.

"Ali Baba had a son who had passed a certain time with a merchant of considerable repute, who had always bestowed the highest commendations on his conduct. To this son he gave the shop of Cassim, with a further promise that if the young man continued to behave with prudence, he would, ere long, marry him advantageously.

"Leaving Ali Baba to enjoy his newly-acquired fortune, we will now return to the forty thieves. They came back to their retreat in the forest when the time they had agreed to be absent had expired; but their astonishment was indescribable when they found the body of Cassim gone, and it was greatly increased on perceiving a visible diminution of their treasure. 'We are discovered,' said the captain, 'and entirely ruined if we are not very careful, or neglect to take immediate measures to remedy the evil: we shall by insensible degrees lose all these riches which our ancestors, as well as we, have amassed with so much trouble and fatigue. All that we can at present judge concerning the loss we have sustained is, that the thief whom we surprised at the fortunate moment, when he was going to make his escape, knew the secret of opening the door. But he was not the only one who possessed that secret: another must have the same knowledge. The removal of his body and the diminution of our treasure are incontestable proofs of the fact. And, as we have no reason to suppose that more than two people are acquainted with the secret, having destroyed one, we must not suffer the other to escape. What say you, my brave comrades? Are you not of my opinion?'

"This proposal of the captain's was thought so reasonable and right by the whole troop, that they all approved it, and agreed that it would be advisable to relinquish every

THE ROBBERS IN COUNCIL.

other enterprise, and occupy themselves solely with this affair, which they should not abandon until they had succeeded in detecting the thief.

"'I expected this decision, from your known courage and bravery,' resumed the captain; 'but the first thing to be done is, that one of you who is bold, courageous, and cunning, should go to the city unarmed and in the dress of a traveller and stranger, and employ all his art to discover if the singular death we inflicted on the culprit whom we destroyed as he deserved is the common topic of conversation. Then he must find out who this man was, and where he lived. It is absolutely necessary we should be acquainted with this, that we may not do anything of which we may have to repent, by making ourselves known in a country where we have been so long forgotten, and where it is so much to our interest to remain undisturbed. But in order to inspire with ardour him who shall undertake this commission, and to prevent his bringing us a false report, which might occasion our total ruin, I propose that he should consent to submit to the penalty of death in case of failure.'

"Without waiting till his companions should speak, one of the robbers said, 'I willingly agree to these terms, and glory in exposing my life in the execution of such a commission. If I should fail, you will at least remember that I have displayed both courage and readiness in my offer to serve the whole troop.'

"Amid the commendations of the captain and his companions, the robber disguised himself in such a way that no one could have suspected him of belonging to the nefarious trade he followed. He set off at night, and managed matters so well that he entered the city just as day was beginning to appear. He went towards the public bazaar, where he saw only one shop open, and that was the shop of Baba Mustapha.

"The jovial cobbler was seated on his stool with his awl in his hand, ready to begin work. The robber went up to him, and wished him a good morning, and perceiving that Mustapha was advanced in years, he said, 'My good man, you rise betimes to your work; how is it possible that an old man like you can see clearly at this early hour? Even if it were broad day, I doubt whether your eyes are good enough to see the stitches you make.'

"'Whoever you are,' replied Baba Mustapha, 'you do not know much about me. Notwithstanding my age, I have excellent eyes; and you would have confessed as much, had you known that not long since I sewed up a dead body in a place where there was not more light than we have here.'

"The robber felt greatly elated at having on his arrival addressed himself to a man who of his own accord entered upon the very subject on which he ardently wished to gain information. 'A dead body!' replied he with feigned astonishment, to induce the other to proceed. 'Why should you want to sew up a dead body? I suppose you mean that you sewed the shroud in which he was buried.' 'No, no,' said Baba Mustapha, 'I know what I mean: you want me to tell you more about it, but you shall not hear another syllable.'

"The robber required no further proof to be fully convinced that he was in the right road to discover what he wished to know. He produced a piece of gold, and putting it into Baba Mustapha's hand, he said, 'I have no desire to cheat you of your secret, although I can assure you I should not divulge it even if you entrusted me with it. The only favour I beg at your hands is that you will have the goodness to direct me to the house where you sewed up the dead body, or that you will come with me, and show me the way.'

"'Should I even feel inclined to grant your request,' replied Baba Mustapha, holding the piece of money in his hand as if ready to return it, 'I assure you that I could not do it, and this you may take my word for. And I will tell you why I must refuse. My employers took me to a particular place, and there they bound my eyes; and from thence I suffered myself to be led to the house; and when I had finished what I had to do I was brought back to my own house in the same manner. You see, therefore, how impossible it is that I should serve you in this matter.' 'But at least,' resumed the robber, 'you must nearly remember the way you went after your eyes were bound. Pray come with me: I will put a bandage over your eyes at the place where you were blindfolded, and we will walk together along the same streets, and follow the same turnings, which you will probably recollect to have taken; and, as all labour deserves a reward, here is another piece of gold. Come, grant me this favour.' And as he spoke he put another piece of money into the cobbler's hand.

"The two pieces of gold were a sore temptation to Baba Mustapha. He looked at them in his hand some time without saying a word, pondering within himself what he should do. At length he drew his purse from his bosom, and putting the gold into it, replied, 'I cannot positively assure you that I remember exactly the way they took me; but since you will have it so, come along; I will do my best to satisfy you.'

"To the great satisfaction of the robber, Baba Mustapha got up to go with him; and without staying to shut up his shop, where there was nothing of consequence to lose, he conducted the robber to the spot where Morgiana had put the bandage over his eyes. 'This is the place,' said he, 'where my eyes were bound; and then my face was turned in this direction.' The robber, who had his handkerchief ready, tied it over Mustapha's eyes, and walked by his side, partly leading him, and partly led by him, till Baba Mustapha stopped.

"'I think,' said he, 'I did not go farther than this;' and he was in fact exactly before the house which had once belonged to Cassim, and where Ali Baba now resided. Before taking the bandage from the cobbler's eyes, the robber quickly made a mark on the door with some chalk he had brought for the purpose; and when he had taken the handkerchief off, he asked Baba Mustapha if he knew to whom the house belonged. The merry cobbler replied that he did not live in that quarter of the town, and therefore could not tell. As the robber found that he could gain no further intelligence from Baba Mustapha, he thanked him for the trouble he had taken; and when he had seen the cobbler turn away to go to his shop, he took the road to the forest, where he felt certain he should be well received.

"Soon after the robber and Baba Mustapha had separated, Morgiana had occasion to go out on some errand; and when she returned she observed the mark which the robber had made on the door of Ali Baba's house. She stopped to examine it. 'What can this mark signify?' thought she. 'Has any one a spite against my master, or has it been made only for diversion? Be the motive what it may, I may as well use precautions against the worst that may happen.' She therefore took some chalk; and as several of the doors on each side of her master's house were of the same appearance, she marked them in the same manner, and then went in, without saying anything of what she had done either to her master or mistress.

"In the meantime the thief made the best of his way back into the forest, where he rejoined his companions at an early hour. He related the success of his journey, dwelling much on the good fortune that had befriended him by bringing him into immediate contact with the very man who could give him the best information on the subject he went about, and which only one could have acquainted him with. They all listened to him with great satisfaction; and the captain, after praising his diligence, thus addressed the rest: 'Comrades,' said he, 'we have no time to lose: let us arm ourselves and depart; and when we have entered the city (whither we had best go separately, not to create suspicion), let us all assemble in the great square, some on one side of it, some on the other; and I will go and find out the house with our companion who has brought us this good news, and then I shall be able to judge what method will be most advantageous to pursue.'

"The robbers all applauded their captain's proposal, and they were very soon equipped for their departure. They went in small parties of two or three together; and, walking at a certain distance from each other, they entered the city without occasioning any suspicion. The captain and the robber who had been there in the morning were the last to enter it; and the latter conducted the captain to the street in which he had marked the house of Ali Baba. When they reached the first door that had been marked by Morgiana, the thief pointed it out, saying that was the one he had marked. But as they continued walking on without stopping, that they might not raise suspicion, the captain perceived that the next door was marked in the same manner, and pointed out this circumstance to his guide, inquiring whether this was the house, or the one they had passed? His guide was quite confused, and knew not what to answer; and his embarrassment increased, when, on proceeding with the captain, he found that four or five doors successively had the same mark. He assured the captain, with an oath, that he had marked but one. 'I cannot conceive,' added he, 'who can have imitated my mark with so much exactness; but I confess that I cannot now distinguish my mark from the others.'

"The captain, who found that his design was frustrated, returned to the great square, where he told the first of his people whom he met to inform the rest that they had lost their labour and made a fruitless expedition, and that now there was nothing to be done but to return to their place of retreat. He set the example, and they all followed in the order in which they had come.

"When the troop had re-assembled in the forest, the captain explained to them the reason why he had ordered them to return. The spy was unanimously declared deserving of death, and he acquiesced in his condemnation, owning that he should have been more cautious in taking his measures; and advancing with a serene countenance, he submitted to the stroke of a companion who was ordered to strike his head from his body.

"As it was necessary, for the safety and preservation of the whole band, that the great injury they had suffered should not pass unavenged, another robber, who flattered himself with hopes of better success than had attended the first, presented himself, and requested the preference. It was granted him. He went to the city, corrupted Baba Mustapha by the same artifice that the first robber had used, and the cobbler led him to the house of Ali Baba with his eyes bound.

"The thief marked the door with red chalk in a place where it would be less noticed; thinking that would be a sure method of distinguishing it from those that were marked with white. But a short time afterwards Morgiana went out as on the preceding day, and on her return the red mark did not escape her piercing eye. She reasoned as before, and immediately made a similar red mark on the neighbouring doors.

"When he returned to his companions in the forest, the thief boasted of the precautions he had taken, which he declared to be infallible, to distinguish the house of Ali Baba from the others. The captain and the rest agreed with him, and all thought themselves sure of success. They repaired to the city in the same order and with as much care as before, armed also in the same way, ready to execute the blow they meditated. The captain and the robber went immediately to the street where Ali Baba resided, but the same difficulty occurred as on the former occasion. The captain was irritated, and the thief as utterly confounded as he who had preceded him in the same business.

"Thus was the captain obliged to return a second time with his comrades, as little satisfied with his expedition as he had been on the preceding day. The robber who was the author of the disappointment underwent the punishment which he had agreed to suffer as the penalty of non-success.

"The captain, seeing his troop diminished by two brave associates, feared it might decrease still more if he continued to trust to others the discovery of the house where Ali Baba resided. Experience convinced him that his companions did not excel in affairs that depended on cunning, as in those in which strength of arm only was required. He therefore undertook the business himself. He went to the city, and with the assistance of Baba Mustapha, who was ready to perform the same service for him which he had rendered to the other two, he found the house of Ali Baba; but, not choosing to trust to the stratagem of making marks on it, which had hitherto proved so fallacious, he imprinted it so thoroughly on his memory, by looking at it attentively and by passing before it several times, that at last he was certain he could not mistake it.

"The captain, satisfied that he had accomplished the object of his journey by obtaining the information he desired, returned to the forest, and when he had reached the cave where the rest of the robbers were waiting his return, he said, addressing them, 'Comrades, nothing now can prevent our taking full revenge of the injury that has been done us. I know with certainty the house of the culprit who is to experience our wrath, and on the road I have meditated a way of quitting scores with him so privately, that no one shall be able to discover the place of our retreat any more than the refuge where our treasure is deposited; for this must be carefully considered in our enterprise, otherwise, instead of being serviceable, it will only prove fatal to us all. I have hit upon a plan to obtain this end, and when I have explained the plan to you, if any one can propose a better expedient, let him speak.' He then told them in what manner he intended to conduct the affair, and as they all gave their approbation, he charged them to divide into small parties, and go into the neighbouring towns and villages, and to buy nineteen mules and thirty-eight large leathern jars for carrying oil, one of which jars must be full, and all the others empty.

ALI BABA AND THE OIL MERCHANT.

"In the course of two or three days the thieves had completed their purchases, and as the empty jars were rather too narrow at the mouth for the purpose to which he intended to apply them, the captain had them enlarged. Then he made one of the men, thoroughly armed and accoutred, enter each jar. He closed the jars, so that they appeared full of oil, leaving, however, that part open which had been unsewed, to admit air for the men to breathe; and the better to carry on the deception, he rubbed the outside of each jar with oil which he took from the full one.

"Things being thus prepared, the mules were laden with the thirty-seven robbers, each concealed in a jar, and with the jar that was filled with oil. Then the captain, as conductor, took the road to the city, at the hour that had been agreed on, and arrived about an hour after sunset, as he proposed. He went straight to the house of Ali Baba, intending to knock and request shelter for the night for himself and his mules. He was, however, spared the trouble of knocking, for he found Ali Baba at the door, enjoying the fresh air after supper. He stopped his mules, and addressing himself to Ali Baba, said, 'My good friend, I have brought the oil which you see here from a great distance, to sell to-morrow in the market, and at this late hour I do not know where to obtain shelter for the night. If it would not occasion you much inconvenience, do me the favour to take me in, and you will confer a great obligation on me.'

"Although in the forest Ali Baba had seen the man who now spoke to him, and had even heard his voice, yet he had no idea that this was the captain of the forty robbers, disguised as an oil merchant. 'You are welcome,' he said, and immediately made room for the visitor and his mules to go in. At the same time Ali Baba called a slave, and ordered him, when the mules were unladen, not only to put them under cover in the stable, but to give them some hay and corn. He also took the trouble of going into the kitchen to desire Morgiana to get supper quickly for a guest who had just arrived, and to prepare him a chamber and a bed.

"Ali Baba went still further in his desire to receive his guest with all possible civility. Observing that, after he had unladen his mules, and they had been taken into the stables as he had wished, the new comer seemed making preparations to pass the night with them, he went to him to beg him to come into the room where he received company, saying that he could not suffer him to think of passing the night in the court. The captain of the robbers endeavoured to excuse himself from accepting the invitation, alleging that he was loth to be troublesome, but in reality that he might have an opportunity of executing his meditated project with more ease; and it was not until Ali Baba had used the most urgent persuasions that he complied with his request.

"Ali Baba not only remained with his perfidious guest, who sought his life in return for his hospitality, until Morgiana had served the supper, but he conversed with him on various subjects which he thought might amuse him, and did not leave him till he had finished the repast provided for him. He then said, 'You are at liberty to do as you please: you have only to ask for whatever you may want, and all I have is at your service.'

"The captain of the robbers rcse at the same time with Ali Baba, and accompanied him to the door; and while Ali Baba went into the kitchen to speak to Morgiana, he went into the court, under the pretext of going to the stable to see after his mules.

"Ali Baba having again enjoined Morgiana to be attentive to his guest, and to take care that he wanted nothing, added, 'I give you notice, that to-morrow before daybreak I shall go to the bath. Take care that my bathing linen is ready, and give it to Abdalla' —this was the name of his slave—'and make me some good broth to take when I return.' After giving these orders he went to bed.

"The captain of the robbers in the meantime, on leaving the stable, went to give his people the necessary orders for what they were to do. Beginning at the first jar, and going through the whole number, he said to the man in each, 'When I throw some pebbles from the chamber where I am to be lodged to-night, do not fail to rip open the jar from top to bottom with the knife you are furnished with, and come out: I shall be with you immediately afterwards.' The knife he spoke of was pointed and sharpened for the purpose of cutting the leathern jars. After giving these directions, he returned, and when he got to the kitchen door, Morgiana took a light and conducted him to the chamber she had prepared for him, and there left him; first asking if he required anything more. Not to create any suspicion, he put out the light a short time after, and lay down in his clothes, to be ready to rise as soon as he had taken his first sleep.

"Morgiana did not forget Ali Baba's orders. She prepared her master's linen for the bath, and gave it to Abdalla, who was not yet gone to bed. Then she put the pot on the fire to make the broth; but while she was skimming it the lamp went out. There was no more oil in the house, and she had not any candle, so she knew not what to do. She wanted a light to see to skim the pot, and mentioned her dilemma to Abdalla. 'Why are you so much disturbed at this?' said he; 'go and take some oil out of one of the jars in the court.'

"Morgiana thanked Abdalla for the hint; and while he retired to bed in the next room to Ali Baba, that he might be ready to go with his master to the bath, she took the oil-can, and went into the court. As she drew near to the jar that stood first in the row, the thief who was concealed within said in a low voice, 'Is it time?'

"Although he spoke softly, Morgiana was nevertheless struck with the sound, which she heard the more distinctly, as the captain, when he unloaded his mules, had opened all the jars, and this amongst the rest, to give a little air to his men, who, though not absolutely deprived of breathing-room, were nevertheless in an uneasy position.

"Any other slave but Morgiana would, in the first moment of surprise at finding a man in the jar instead of the oil she expected, have made a great uproar, which might have produced terrible consequences. But Morgiana was superior to the position she held. She was instantly aware of the importance of secresy and caution, and understood the extreme danger in which Ali Baba and his family, as well as herself, were placed; she also saw the urgent necessity of devising a speedy remedy, that should be silently executed. Her quick invention soon conceived the means. She collected her thoughts, and without showing any emotion, assumed the manner of the captain, and answered, 'Not yet, but presently.' She approached the next jar, and the same question was asked her. She went on to all the vessels in succession, making the same answer to the same question, till she came to the last jar, which was full of oil.

"Morgiana by this means discovered that her master, who supposed he was giving a night's lodging to an oil merchant, had afforded shelter to thirty-eight robbers, and that the pretended merchant was their captain. She quickly filled her oil-can from the last jar, and returned into the kitchen; and after having put some oil in her lamp, and lighted it, she took a large kettle, and went again into the court to fill it with oil from the jar. This kettle she immediately put upon the fire, and made a great blaze under it with a quantity of wood; for the sooner the oil boiled, the sooner her plan for the preservation of the whole family would be executed, and it required the utmost dispatch. At length the oil boiled. She took the kettle, and poured into each jar, from the first to the last, sufficient boiling oil to scald the robbers to death, a purpose she effectually carried out.

"When Morgiana had thus silently, and without disturbing any one, performed this intrepid act exactly as she had conceived it, she returned to the kitchen with the empty kettle, and shut the door. She put out the large fire she had made up for this purpose, and only left enough to finish boiling the broth for Ali Baba. She then blew out the lamp, and remained perfectly silent; determined not to go to bed until, from a window of the kitchen which overlooked the court, she had observed, as well as the obscurity of night would allow her to distinguish, what would ensue.

"Morgiana had scarcely waited a quarter of an hour, when the captain of the robbers awoke. He got up, opened the window, and looked out. All was dark, and a profound silence reigned around: he gave the signal by throwing the pebbles, many of which struck the jars, as the sound plainly proved. He listened, but heard nothing that could lead him to suppose his men obeyed the summons. He became uneasy at this delay, and threw some pebbles a second, and even a third time. They all struck the jars, yet nothing appeared to indicate that the signal was answered. He was at a loss to account for this mystery. In the utmost alarm, he descended into the court, with as little noise as possible; and approaching the first jar, intending to ask if the robber contained in it, and whom he supposed still living, was asleep, he smelt a strong scent of hot and burning oil issuing from the jar. Then he began to suspect that his enterprise against Ali

Baba, to destroy him, pillage his house, and carry off, if possible, all the money which he had taken from him and the community, had failed. He proceeded to the next jar, and to all in succession, and discovered that all his men had shared the same fate; and by the diminution of the oil in the vessel which he had brought full, he guessed the means that had been used to deprive him of the assistance he expected. Mortified at having thus missed his aim, he jumped over the garden gate, which led out of the court; and going from one garden to another by getting over the walls, he made his escape.

"When Morgiana perceived that all was silent and still, and that the captain of the thieves did not return, she suspected the truth; namely, that he had decamped by the gardens, instead of attempting to escape by the house door, which was fastened with double bolts. Fully satisfied he was gone, and overjoyed at having succeeded in securing the safety of the whole family, she at length retired to bed, and soon fell asleep.

"Ali Baba went out before daybreak, and repaired to the bath, followed by his slave, totally ignorant of the surprising event which had taken place in his house during the night; for Morgiana had not thought it necessary to wake him, particularly as she had no time to lose while she was engaged in her perilous enterprise, and it was useless to interrupt his repose after she had averted the danger.

"When he returned from the bath, the sun had risen. Ali Baba was surprised to see the jars of oil still in their places, and to find that the merchant had not taken them to the market, with his mules. He inquired the reason of Morgiana, who let him in, and who had left everything in its original state, that she might convince him of the deceit which had been practised on him, and to impress him with the greater sense of the effort she had made for his preservation.

"'My good master,' said Morgiana to Ali Baba, 'may Heaven preserve you and all your family. You will be better informed of what you wish to know when you have seen what I am going to show you, if you will take the trouble to come with me.' Ali Baba followed Morgiana; and when she had shut the door, she took him to the first jar, and bade him look into it and see if it contained oil. He did as she desired; and perceiving a man in the jar, he hastily drew back and uttered a cry of surprise. 'Do not be afraid,' said she: 'the man you see there will not do you any harm: he has attempted mischief, but he will never hurt either you or any one else again, for he is now a lifeless corpse.' 'Morgiana!' exclaimed Ali Baba, 'what does all this mean? I command you to explain this mystery.' 'I will explain it,' replied Morgiana; 'but moderate your astonishment, and do not awaken the curiosity of your neighbours, or let them hear what is of the utmost importance that you should keep secret and concealed. Look first at all the other jars.'

"Ali Baba examined the jars, one after the other, from the first till he came to the last, which contained the oil; and he remarked that its contents were considerably diminished. When his survey was completed, he stood motionless with astonishment, sometimes casting his eyes on Morgiana, then looking at the jars, but without speaking a word, so great was his surprise. At length, as if speech were suddenly restored to him, he said, 'And what has become of the merchant?'

"'The merchant,' replied Morgiana, 'is no more a merchant than I am. I can tell you who he is and what is become of him. But you will hear the whole history more conveniently in your own chamber; and moreover, it is now time that, for the sake of your health, you should take your broth, after coming out of the bath.' Whilst Ali Baba went into his room, Morgiana returned to the kitchen to get the broth; and when she brought it, before Ali Baba would take it he said, 'Begin to relate this wonderful history, and satisfy the extreme impatience I feel to know all its circumstances.'

"In obedience to Ali Baba's request, Morgiana thus began: 'Last night, O my master, when you had retired to bed, I prepared your linen for the bath, as you had desired, and gave it in charge to Abdalla. After that, I put the pot on the fire, to make your broth; and as I was skimming it, the lamp went out suddenly for want of oil, and there was not a drop in the can. I searched for a light of any kind, but could not find one. Abdalla, seeing me in a dilemma, reminded me of the jars of oil which were in the court; for such he, as well as I, supposed them to be, and so, no doubt, did you. I took my can, and went to the first jar; but as I approached it, I heard a voice coming out of it, saying, "Is it time?" I did not feel terrified, but instantly understanding the treachery intended by the feigned merchant, I replied without hesitation, "Not yet, but presently." I passed on to the next jar, and another voice asked me the same question, to which I made the same answer. I went to all the jars, one after the other, making the same reply to the same inquiry, and did not find any oil till I came to the last, from which I filled my can.

"'When I reflected that there were thirty-seven thieves in your court, intent, perhaps, on murder, and only waiting for the signal of their chief, to whom, supposing him to be a merchant, you had given so hospitable a reception, and on whose account you set

THE ROBBER CAPTAIN ALONE.

the whole household to work, I lost no time, but brought in the can and lighted my lamp; then taking the largest kettle in the kitchen, I went and filled it with oil. I placed it on the fire, and when it boiled, I poured some oil into each of the jars which contained the thieves—as much as I thought necessary to prevent their putting in execution the pernicious design which had brought them hither.

"'The affair being thus terminated in the way I had proposed, I returned into the kitchen, and extinguished my lamp; and before I went to bed, I placed myself at the window, to watch quietly what steps the pretended oil merchant would take. After some time, I heard him throw from his window, as a signal, some little pebbles, which fell on tbe jars. He threw some a second time, and also a third; and as he neither heard nor saw anything stirring, he came down, and I observed him go to every jar till he came to the last; after which the darkness of the night prevented me from distinguishing his movements. I still continued, however, on the watch; but as I found he did not return, I concluded that, mortified at his bad success, he had escaped by way of the garden. Convinced, therefore, that the family were now safe, I went to bed.'

"When she had finished this narrative, Morgiana added, 'This is the detail you required of me; and I am convinced that it is the conclusion of a scheme of which I observed the beginning two or three days ago, but with the particulars of which I did not think it necessary to trouble you. One morning, as I returned from the city at an early hour, I perceived the street door marked with white, and on the following day there was a red mark near the white one; each time, without knowing for what purpose these marks were made, I made the same kind of mark, and in the same part, on the doors of three or four of our neighbours on each side of this house. If you connect that fact with what has happened, you will find that the whole is a scheme, contrived by the thieves of the forest, whose troop, I know not wherefore, seems to be diminished by two. But be that as it may, the band is now reduced to three at most. This proves that the robbers had determined on your death, and you will do right to be on your guard against them so long as you are certain that one still remains. On my part, I will do all in my power towards your safety, over which, indeed, I consider it my duty to watch.'

"When Morgiana ceased speaking, Ali Baba, filled with gratitude for the great obligation he owed her, replied, 'I will recompense you as you deserve before I die. I owe my life to you; and to give you an immediate proof of my feelings on the occasion, I give you your liberty from this moment, and will soon reward you in a more ample manner. I am as thoroughly convinced as you are, that the forty robbers laid this snare for me. Through your means Allah has delivered me from the danger; I hope He will continue to protect me from the malice of these my foes, and that in averting destruction from my head, He will make it recoil with greater certainty on them, and thus deliver the world from so dangerous and accursed a persecution. What we have now to do, is to use the utmost dispatch in burying the bodies of this pest of the human race. Yet we must do so with so much secresy, that no one can entertain the slightest suspicion of their fate; and for this purpose I will instantly go to work with Abdalla.'

"Ali Baba's garden was of considerable size, and terminated in a clump of large trees. He went, without delay, with his slave, to dig under these trees a ditch or grave, of sufficient length and breadth to contain the bodies he had to inter. The ground was soft, and easy to remove, so that they were not long in completing their work. They took the bodies out of the jars, and removed the weapons with which the robbers had furnished themselves. They then carried the bodies to the bottom of the garden, and placed them in the grave, and after having covered them with the earth they had previously removed, they spread about what remained to make the surface of the ground appear even, as it was before. Ali Baba carefully concealed the oil jars and the arms; as for the mules, which he did not then require, he sent them to the market at different times, and disposed of them by means of his slave.

"Whilst Ali Baba was taking these precautions to prevent its being publicly known by what means he had become rich in so short a space of time, the captain of the forty thieves had returned to the forest mortified beyond measure; and in the agitation and confusion which he experienced at having met with such a disaster, so contrary to what he had promised himself, he reached the cavern without coming to any resolution on what he should or should not do respecting Ali Baba.

"The dismal solitude of this gloomy habitation appeared to him insupportable. 'O ye brave companions,' cried he, 'ye partners of my labours and my pains, where are you? What can I accomplish without your assistance? Did I select and assemble you only to see you perish all together, by a fate so cruel and so unworthy of your courage? My regret for your loss would not have been so great had you died with your sabres in your hands, like valiant men. When shall I be able to collect together another troop of intrepid men like you? And even should I wish to assemble a new troop, how could I undertake it, without exposing all our treasures of gold and silver to the mercy of him who has already enriched himself with a part of our possessions? I cannot, I must not, think of such an enterprise until I have put a period to his existence. What I have not been able to accomplish with your assistance, I am determined to perform alone; and when I have secured this immense property from the danger of pillage, I will endeavour to provide owners and heirs for it after my decease, that it may be not only preserved, but augmented, to the latest posterity.' Having formed this resolution, he postponed the consideration of means for its accomplishment, and, filled with the most pleasing hopes, he fell asleep, and passed the rest of the night very quietly.

"The next morning the captain of the robbers awoke at an early hour; and putting on a dress which was suitable to the design he meditated, repaired to the city, where he took a lodging in a khan. As he supposed that the events which had happened in the house of Ali Baba might have become generally known, he asked the host if there were any news stirring; in reply to which the host talked on a variety of subjects, but never mentioned the subject the captain had nearest at heart. By this the latter concluded that the reason why Ali Baba kept the transaction so profoundly secret, was, that he did not wish to divulge the fact of his having access to so immense a treasure, and also that he was apprehensive of his life being in danger on this account. This idea excited the captain to neglect nothing that could hasten his enemy's destruction, which he intended to accomplish by means as secret as those Ali Baba had adopted towards the robbers.

"The captain provided himself with a horse, which he made use of to convey to his lodging several kinds of rich stuffs and fine linens, bringing them from the forest at various times, with all necessary precautions for keeping the place from whence he brought them profoundly concealed. In order to dispose of this merchandise, when he had collected together as much as he thought proper, he sought for a shop. Having found one that suited him, he hired it of the proprietor, stocked it with his goods, and established himself in it. The shop that was exactly opposite to his had belonged to Cassim, and was now occupied by the son of Ali Baba.

"The captain of the robbers, who had assumed the name of Cogia Houssain, took an early opportunity of offering those civilities to the merchants his neighbours which new comers were expected to show. The son of Ali Baba being young and of a pleasing address, and the captain having more frequent occasion to converse with him than with the others, the two men soon formed an intimacy. This friendship the robber soon resolved to cultivate with greater assiduity and care, when, three or four days after he had opened his shop, he recognised Ali Baba, who came to see his son, as he was in the constant habit of doing; and on inquiring of the son after Ali Baba's departure, Cogia Houssain discovered that his foe was the young man's father. He now increased his attentions and caresses to him; he made him several little presents, and also often invited him to his table, where he regaled him very handsomely.

"The son of Ali Baba did not choose to receive so many attentions from Cogia Houssain without returning them; but his lodging was small, and he had no convenience for regaling a guest as he wished. He mentioned his intention to his father; adding, that it was not proper that he should delay any longer to return the favours he had received from Cogia Houssain.

"Ali Baba very willingly undertook to provide an entertainment. 'My son,' said he, 'to-morrow is Friday; and as it is a day on which the most considerable merchants, such as Cogia Houssain and yourself, keep their shops shut, invite him to take a walk with you after dinner. On your return, contrive matters that you may pass my house, and then beg him to come in. It will be better to manage thus, than to invite him in a formal way. I will give orders to Morgiana to prepare a supper and have it ready by the time you come.'

"On the Friday, Cogia Houssain and the son of Ali Baba met in the afternoon to take their walk together, as had been agreed. On their return, Ali Baba's son led Cogia Houssain, as if by accident, through the street in which his father lived; and when they had reached the house, he stopped him, and knocked at the door. 'This,' said he, 'is my father's house. He has desired me to procure him the honour of your acquaintance, when I told him of your friendship for me. I entreat you to add this favour to the many I have received from you.'

"Although Cogia Houssain had now reached the object of his desires, by gaining admission into the house of Ali Baba, and to attempt his life without hazarding his own or creating any suspicion, yet he now endeavoured to excuse himself, and pretended to take leave of the son; but, as the slave of Ali Baba opened the door at that moment, the son took him by the hand in a very obliging manner, and going in first, drew him forward, and forced him to enter the house, though seemingly against his wish.

"Ali Baba received Cogia Houssain in a friendly manner, and gave him as hearty a welcome as he could desire. He thanked him for his kindness to his son, saying, 'The obligation he is under to you, and under which you have laid me also, is so much the more considerable, as he is a young man who has not yet been much in the world; and it is very kind in you to condescend to form his manners.'

"Cogia Houssain was profuse of compliments in reply to Ali Baba's speech, assuring him that, although his son had not acquired the experience of older men, yet that he possessed a fund of good sense, which was of more service to him than experience was to many others.

"After a short conversation on other topics of an indifferent nature, Cogia Houssain was going to take his leave, but Ali Baba stopped him. 'Where are you going?' said he: 'O my friend, I entreat you to do me the honour of staying to sup with me. The humble meal you will partake of is little worthy of the honour you will confer on it; but such as it is, I hope you will accept the offer as frankly as it is made.'

"'O my master,' replied Cogia Houssain, 'I am fully sensible of your kindness; and although I beg you to excuse me, if I take my leave without accepting your obliging invitation, yet I entreat you to believe that I refuse you, not from incivility or pride, but because I have a very strong reason, and one which I am sure you would approve, were it known to you.'

"'What can this reason be?' resumed Ali Baba, 'might I take the liberty of asking you?' 'I do not refuse to tell it,' said Cogia Houssain. 'It is this: I never eat of any dish that has salt in it; judge then what a strange figure I should make at your table.' 'If this is your only reason,' replied Ali Baba, 'it need not deprive me of the honour of your company at supper, unless you have absolutely determined to refuse me. In the first place, the bread which is eaten in my house does not contain salt; and as for the meat and other dishes, I promise you there shall be none in those which are placed before you. I will now go to give orders to that effect. Therefore do me the favour to remain, and I will be with you again in an instant.'

"Ali Baba went into the kitchen, and desired Morgiana not to put any salt to the meat she was going to serve for supper. He also told her to prepare, without any salt, two or three of those dishes he had ordered.

"Morgiana, who was just going to serve the supper, could not refrain from expressing some disapprobation at this new order. 'Who,' said she 'is this fastidious man, that cannot eat salt? Your supper will be entirely spoiled if I delay it any longer.' 'Do not be angry,' replied Ali Baba; 'he is a good man: do as I desire you.'

"Morgiana obeyed, though much against her will. She felt some curiosity to see this man who did not eat salt. When she had finished her preparations, and Abdalla had prepared the table, she assisted him in carrying in the dishes. On looking at Cogia Houssain, she instantly recognised him, notwithstanding his disguise, as the captain of the robbers, and examining him with great attention, she perceived that he had a dagger concealed under his dress. 'I am no longer surprised' said she to herself, 'that this villain will not eat salt with my master. He is his bitterest enemy, and means to murder him; but I will yet prevent him from accomplishing his purpose.'

"When Morgiana had finished bringing up the dishes, and assisting Abdalla, she availed herself of the time while her masters and their guest were at supper, to make the necessary preparations for carrying out an enterprise of the boldest and most intrepid nature; and she had just completed them, when Abdalla came to acquaint her that it

MORGIANA DANCING BEFORE COGIA HOUSSAIN.

was time to serve the fruit. She carried it in; and when Abdalla had taken away the supper, she placed it on the table. Then she put a small table near Ali Baba, with the wine and three cups, and left the room with Abdalla, as if to leave Ali Baba, according to custom, at liberty to converse and enjoy himself with his guest while they drank their wine.

"Cogia Houssain, or rather the captain of the forty thieves, now thought he had achieved a favourable opportunity for revenging himself on Ali Baba by taking his life. 'I will make them both drunk,' thought he, 'and then the son, against whom I bear no malice, will be unable to prevent my plunging my dagger into the heart of his father; and I shall escape by way of the garden, as I did before, while the cook and the slave are at their supper, or perhaps asleep in the kitchen.'

"But instead of going to supper, Morgiana, who had penetrated into the views of the pretended Cogia Houssain, did not allow him time to put his wicked intentions in execution. She dressed herself like a dancing girl, put on a head-dress suitable to the character she assumed, and wore round her waist a girdle of silver gilt, to which she fastened a dagger made of the same metal. Her face was covered by a very handsome mask. When she had thus disguised herself, she said to Abdalla, 'Take your tabor, and let us go and entertain our master's guest, and the friend of his son, by the music and dance we sometimes practise together.'

"Abdalla took his tabor, and began to play as he entered the room, walking before Morgiana. The wily slave followed him, making a low courtesy with a deliberate air to attract notice, as if to request permission to show her skill in dancing to amuse the company. Abdalla perceiving that Ali Baba was going to speak, ceased striking his tabor. 'Come in, Morgiana,' cried Ali Baba: 'Cogia Houssain will judge of your skill, and tell us his opinion. Do not think, however, O my friend,' continued he, addressing Cogia Houssain, 'that I have been at any expense to procure you this entertainment. We have all this skill in the household, and it is only my slave and my cook whom you see. I hope you will find their efforts amusing.'

"Cogia Houssain did not expect Ali Baba to add this entertainment to the supper he had given him; and this new circumstance made him apprehensive that he should not be able to avail himself of the opportunity he thought now presented itself. But he still consoled himself with the hopes of meeting with another chance, if he continued the acquaintance with Ali Baba and his son. Therefore, although he would gladly have dispensed with this addition to the entertainment, he nevertheless pretended to be obliged to his host, and added 'that whatever gave Ali Baba pleasure could not fail of being agreeable to him.'

"When Abdalla perceived that Ali Baba and Cogia Houssain had ceased speaking, he again began to play on his tabor, singing to it an air to the tune of which Morgiana might dance: she, who was equal in skill to any professional dancer, performed her part so admirably, that even a critical spectator who had seen her must have been delighted. But of the present company, perhaps Cogia Houssain was the least attentive to her excellence.

"After she had performed several dances with equal grace and agility, Morgiana at length drew out the dagger, and dancing with it in her hand, she surpassed all she had yet done, in her light and graceful movements, and in the wonderful attitudes which she interspersed in the figure; sometimes presenting the dagger as if ready to strike, and at others holding it to her own bosom, pretending to stab herself.

"At length, apparently out of breath, she took the tabor from Abdalla with her left hand, and holding the dagger in her right, she presented the tabor with the hollow part upwards to Ali Baba, in imitation of the professional dancers, who are accustomed to go round in this way appealing to the liberality of the spectators.

"Ali Baba threw a piece of gold into the tabor. Morgiana then presented it to his son, who followed his father's example. Cogia Houssain, who saw that she was advancing towards him for the same purpose, had already taken his purse from his bosom to contribute his present, and was taking out a piece of money, when Morgiana, with a courage and promptness equal to the resolution she had displayed, plunged the dagger into his heart, so deeply that the life-blood streamed from the wound when she withdrew the weapon.

"Ali Baba and his son, terrified at this action, uttered a loud cry. 'Wretch!" exclaimed Ali Baba, 'what hast thou done? Thou hast ruined me and my family for ever.'

"'What I have done,' replied Morgiana, 'is not for your ruin, but for your safety.' Then opening Cogia Houssain's robe to show Ali Baba the poniard which was concealed under it, she continued: "Behold the cruel enemy you had to deal with! Examine his countenance attentively, and you will recognise the pretended oil merchant and the captain of the forty robbers. Do you not recollect that he refused to eat salt with you? Before I even saw him, from the moment you told me of this peculiarity in your guest, I suspected his design, and you are now convinced that my suspicions were not unfounded.'

"Ali Baba, who now understood the fresh obligation he owed to Morgiana for having thus preserved his life a second time, embraced her, and said, 'Morgiana, I gave you your liberty, and at the same time promised to show you stronger proofs of my gratitude at some future period. This period has now arrived. I present you to my son as his wife.' Then addressing his son, he continued, 'I believe you to be too dutiful a son to take it amiss if I bestow Morgiana upon you without previously consulting your inclinations. Your obligation to her is not less than mine. You plainly see that Cogia Houssain only sought your acquaintance that he might gain an opportunity to carry out his diabolical treachery; and had he sacrificed me to his vengeance, you cannot suppose that you would have been spared. You must further consider that, in marrying Morgiana, you connect yourself with the preserver of my family and the support of yours.'

"Far from showing any symptons of discontent, Ali Baba's son replied that he willingly consented to the marriage, not only because he was desirous of proving his ready obedience to his father's wishes, but also because his own inclination strongly urged him to the union. They then resolved to inter the captain of the robbers by the side of his former companions; and this duty was performed with such secresy that the circumstance was not known till many years had expired, and no one was any longer interested to keep this memorable history concealed.

"A few days after, Ali Baba caused the nuptials of his son and Morgiana to be celebrated with great solemnity. He gave a sumptuous feast, accompanied by dances, exhibitions, and other customary diversions; and he had the satisfaction of observing that the friends and neighbours whom he had invited, who did not know the true reason of the marriage, but were not unacquainted with the good qualities of Morgiana, admired his generosity and applauded his discrimination.

"Ali Baba, who had not revisited the cave since he had brought away the body of his brother Cassim, together with the gold with which that unfortunate man had laden his asses, lest he should meet with any of the thieves and be slain by them, still refrained from going thither, even after the death of the thirty-seven robbers and their captain, as he was ignorant of the fate of the other two, and supposed them to be still alive.

"At the expiration of a year, however, finding that no attempt had been made to disturb his quiet, he had the curiosity to make a journey to the cave, taking all necessary precautions for his safety. He mounted his horse; and when he approached the cave, seeing no traces of either men or horses, he conceived this to be a favourable omen. He dismounted, and fastening his horse that it might not stray, he went up to the door and repeated the words, 'Open, sesame,' which he had not forgotten. The door opened, and he entered. The state in which everything appeared in the cave led him to judge that no one had been in it from the time when the pretended Cogia Houssain had opened his shop in the city; and therefore he concluded that the whole troop of robbers was totally dispersed or exterminated; and that he himself was now the only person in the world who was acquainted with the secret of entering the cave, and that consequently the immense treasure it contained was entirely at his disposal. He had provided himself with a bag, and he filled it with as much gold as his horse could carry, with which he returned to the city.

"From that time Ali Baba and his son, whom he took to the cave and taught the secret of entering it, and after them their posterity, who were also entrusted with the important secret, lived in great splendour, enjoying their riches with moderation, and honoured with the most dignified situations in the city."

On concluding this story, Scheherazade perceived that the day had not yet commenced, therefore she began to relate to the sultan the following history :

## THE HISTORY OF ALI COGIA, A MERCHANT OF BAGDAD.

N the reign of the Caliph Haroun Alraschid there lived at Bagdad a merchant, named Ali Cogia, who belonged neither to the richest nor yet to the poorest order, and who dwelt alone in his paternal house, without either wife or children. He was contented with what his business produced, and lived in perfect freedom, with nothing to control his actions or his will. But it came to pass that he had for three successive nights a dream, in which an old man of venerable aspect, but severe countenance, appeared to him, and reprimanded him for not having yet performed a pilgrimage to Mecca.

"This dream very much troubled Ali Cogia, and occasioned him great disturbance. As a good Mussulman he was aware of the necessity of performing this pilgrimage; but as he was encumbered with a house and furniture, and a shop, he had always considered these as reasons sufficiently weighty to free him from the obligation; and he endeavoured to atone for the neglect by charitable and meritorious actions. But since he had these dreams, his conscience so much disturbed him, and he was so fearful lest some misfortune should happen in consequence, that he resolved no longer to defer this act of duty.

"That he might be ready to start the following year, Ali Cogia began to sell his furniture. He then disposed of his shop, together with the greater part of the merchandise with which it was stocked, reserving only the goods he considered saleable at Mecca; and he found a tenant for his house.

"Having thus made every preparation, he was ready to set out at the time when the caravan for Mecca was to take its departure. The only thing that remained to be done was to find some secure place in which he could leave a sum of a thousand pieces of gold, which remained after deducting the money he had set apart for his pilgrimage, and which would have encumbered him during the journey.

"Ali Cogia procured a jar of considerable size, put the thousand pieces of gold into it, and then filled it up with olives. After he had closed the jar tightly, he took it to a merchant, who was his friend. 'O my brother,' said he to him, 'you are doubtless aware of my intention of setting out on a pilgrimage to Mecca with the caravan which goes in a few days; I beg you will oblige me by taking charge of this jar of olives till my return.' The merchant instantly replied, 'Here, this is the key of my warehouse. Take the jar there yourself, and place it where you think fit; I promise you that you shall find it in the same place when you come for it.'

"The day for the departure of the caravan from Badgad having arrived, Ali Cogia joined the procession with a camel laden with the merchandise he had selected, and which also served him as a sort of saddle to ride on; and he arrived in safety at Mecca. In company with the other pilgrims, he visited the celebrated temple, frequented every year by all the Mussulman nations, who repair thither from all parts of the globe to fulfil the religious ceremonies their religion requires of them; and when Ali Cogia had acquitted himself of the duties of his pilgrimage, he exposed for sale the merchandise he had brought with him.

"Two merchants who were passing by his shop and saw the goods of Ali Cogia, found them so beautiful that they stopped to look at them, although they did not want to purchase them. When they had satisfied their curiosity, one said to the other as he was walking away, 'If this merchant knew what profit he could make on his goods at

Cairo, he would take them there in preference to selling them here, where they are not of so much value.'

"This speech sank into the heart of Ali Cogia; and as he had often heard of the beauties of Egypt, he instantly resolved to avail himself of the opportunity, and to travel to that country. Accordingly, he packed up his bales, and, instead of returning to Bagdad, he took the road to Egypt, and joined the caravan that was starting for Cairo. When he arrived there, he found he had not come on a bootless errand; for he met with so good a market that in a few days he had disposed of all his merchandise with much greater profit than he could possibly have expected. He then purchased other goods, intending to go to Damascus; and while he was waiting for the opportunity of a caravan, which was to go in six weeks, he not only visited everything that was worthy

ALI COGIA PUTS THE MONEY IN THE JAR.

of his curiosity in Cairo, but also went to view the pyramids, extended his journey to some distance up the Nile, and visited the most celebrated cities on its banks.

"On his way to Damascus, as the caravan was to pass through Jerusalem, Ali Cogia did not fail to visit the temple, which is considered by all Mussulmen as the most sacred after that of Mecca, and from which the place itself has obtained the epithet of the Holy City. Ali Cogia found Damascus so delicious a spot, from the abundance of its streams, its meadows, and enchanting gardens, that all the various accounts he had read of its delights appeared to be very far below the truth; and he was tempted to prolong his residence there for a considerable time. As, however, he did not forget that he had to return to Bagdad, he at length took his departure, and went to Aleppo, where he also passed some time; and from thence, after having crossed the Euphrates, he took the road to Moussoul, intending to shorten his journey by sailing down the Tigris.

"But when Ali Cogia had reached Moussoul, the Persian merchants with whom he had travelled from Aleppo, and who had formed an intimacy with him, gained so great an ascendency over his mind, by their obliging manners and agreeable conversation, that they had no difficulty in persuading him to accompany them to Schiraz, from whence they declared it would be easy for him to return to Bagdad, and where he might make considerable profit. They conducted him through the cities of Sultania, Reï, Coam, Caschan, Ispahan, and then to Schiraz, from whence he had the further complaisance to go with them to India, thence returning again to Schiraz.

"In consequence of these journeyings, reckoning also the time Ali Cogia resided in each city, it was now nearly seven years since he had quitted Bagdad; and he now determined to return. Till this period, the friend to whom he had entrusted the jar of olives before he left his native city, had never thought more either of him or his jar. At the very time when Ali Cogia was on his return with a caravan from Schiraz, his friend the merchant was one evening at supper with his family, when the conversation by accident turned upon olives, and the wife expressed a desire of eating some, adding, that it was a long time since any had been seen in her house.

"'Now you speak of olives,' said the merchant, 'you remind me that Ali Cogia, when he went to Mecca seven years since, left me a jar of them, which he himself placed in my warehouse, that he might find them there on his return. But I know not what is become of Ali Cogia. I certainly remember that on the return of the caravan, some one said that he was gone into Egypt. He must have died there, as he has never returned in the course of so many years; so we may surely eat the olives, if they are still good. Give me a dish and a light, and I will go and get some, that we may taste them.'

"'In the name of Heaven,' replied his wife, 'refrain, my dear husband, from committing so disgraceful an action; you well know that nothing is so sacred as a trust of this kind. You say that it is seven years since Ali Cogia went to Mecca, and he has never returned; but you were informed he was gone into Egypt; and how can you ascertain that he is not gone still farther? It is enough that you have received no intelligence of his death: he may return to-morrow or the day after to-morrow. Consider what a disgrace it would be for you, as well as your family, if he were to return, and you could not restore the jar into his hands in the same state in which he entrusted it to your care. For my part, I declare that I neither wish for any of these olives, nor will I eat any of them. What I said was merely in the way of conversation. Besides, do you suppose that, after so long a time, the olives can be good? They must be putrid and spoiled. And if Ali Cogia returns, as I have a sort of foreboding that he will, and he perceives that you have opened the jar, what opinion will he form of your friendship and integrity? I conjure you to abandon your design.'

"Thus the good woman exhausted her arguments; but she saw, by her husband's countenance, that he was bent on his design. In fact, he paid no attention to his wife's good advice, but rose from his place, and taking a light and a dish, went to his warehouse. 'Remember at least,' said the wife, 'that I have no share in what you are going to do; so do not attribute any fault to me, if you have hereafter to repent of the action.'

"The merchant still turned a deaf ear to all she said, and persisted in his purpose. When he got into the warehouse, he opened the jar, and found the olives all spoiled; but wishing to ascertain whether those that were underneath were as bad as the upper layers, he poured some out into the dish he had brought with him, and as he shook the jar to make them fall out the easier, some pieces of gold fell out also. At the sight of this money, the merchant, who was naturally of a sordid and avaricious disposition, looked eagerly into the jar, and perceived that he had emptied almost all the olives into the dish, and that the remaining contents consisted of money, in pieces of gold. He put the olives again into the jar, covered it up, and left the warehouse.

"'You spoke the truth, wife,' said he, when he returned: 'the olives are all spoiled, and I have closed the jar again, so that if Ali Cogia ever comes back, he will not discover that I have touched it.' 'You would have done better to have taken my advice,' returned the wife, 'not to have meddled with it. Heaven grant that no evil may come of it.' The merchant paid as little attention to these last words of his wife as he had vouchsafed to her former remonstrance. He passed almost the whole night in devising some scheme for taking possession of Ali Cogia's money, so that he might enjoy it in security, should the true owner ever return and claim the jar. The next morning very early he went out to buy some olives of that year's growth. He threw away those which had been in Ali Cogia's jar; and taking out the gold, he put it in a place of safety; then filling the jar with the fresh olives he had just bought, he put on the old cover, and replaced the jar in the same spot where Ali Cogia had left it.

"About a month after the merchant had committed this treacherous act, which was eventually to cost him very dear, Ali Cogia arrived at Bagdad, after his long absence from that city. As he had let his own house before his departure, he alighted at a khan, where he took a lodging until he had informed his tenant of his return, and requested him to give up possession.

"The next day, Ali Cogia went to see his friend the merchant, who received him with open arms, testifying the utmost joy at seeing him again, after an absence which had been so prolonged that he declared he had scarcely hoped ever to behold him more.

"After the usual compliments had been exchanged on their meeting, Ali Cogia begged the merchant to return him the jar of olives which he had left in his care; at the same time apologising for the liberty he had taken in troubling him in the matter. 'My dear friend,' replied the merchant, 'do not think of making excuses. Your jar has been no incumbrance to me, and I should have asked the same service of you, had I been situated as you were. Here is the key of my warehouse. Go and take away your jar; you will find it where you put it yourself.'

"Ali Cogia went to the warehouse and took out the jar; and on returning the key to the merchant, he thanked him for the favour he had done him. Thereupon he went back to the khan where he lodged. He opened the jar, and thrusting his hand to the place where he supposed the thousand pieces of gold, which he had concealed therein, might be, he was extremely surprised at not feeling them. He thought he must be deceived, and, to unravel the mystery as soon as possible, he took some of the dishes and other utensils of his travelling kitchen, and emptied out all the olives, without finding one single piece of money. For a time he remained motionless with astonishment; then raising his hands and eyes towards heaven, he cried, 'Is it possible, that a man whom I considered my friend could be capable of so flagrant a breach of trust?'

"Exceedingly alarmed at the idea of having sustained so considerable a loss, Ali Cogia returned to the merchant. 'My good friend,' said he, 'do not be surprised that I return to you so quickly: I confess that I recognised the jar of olives which I just now took out of your warehouse as my own; but I had put a thousand pieces of gold in it with the olives, and these I cannot find: perhaps you have wanted them in your trade, and have made use of them. If that be the case, you are very welcome to the use of them; I only beg of you to relieve my fears, and give me some acknowledgment for the thousand pieces, which you may then return to me whenever it may be most convenient to you.'

"The merchant, who expected Ali Cogia to return to him, had prepared an answer. 'O my friend,' replied he, 'when you brought me the jar of olives, did I touch it? Did I not give you the key of my warehouse? Did you not deposit the jar there yourself, and did you not find it in the same place where you put it, exactly in the same state, and covered in the same manner? If you put money in it, the money must be there still. You told me it contained olives, and I believed you. This is all I know about the matter; you may believe me or not as you please, but I assure you I have not touched it.'

"Ali Cogia used the gentlest means to induce the merchant to tell the truth. 'I love peaceable measures,' said he, 'and I should be sorry to proceed to extremities, which would not place you in a very creditable position in the eyes of the world, and to which I should not have recourse without the utmost reluctance. Consider that we as merchants should abandon all private interest to preserve our reputation. Once more I tell you, that I should be sorry if your obstinacy compelled me to apply to public justice, for I have always preferred losing something of my right, rather than have recourse to those means.'

"'O Ali Cogia,' retorted the merchant, "you confess that you have deposited a jar of olives in my warehouse, that you took possession of it again, and that you carried it away; and now you come to demand of me a thousand pieces of gold. Did you ever tell me that they were deposited in the jar? I do not even know if there were olives in it: you did not show them to me. I am surprised that you do not require pearls and diamonds of me rather than money. Take my advice: go home, and do not assemble a crowd about my door.'

"Some people had already stopped before his shop; and these last words, pronounced in a high and angry tone of voice, not only collected a larger number, but made the neighbouring merchants come out of their shops to inquire the reason of the dispute between him and Ali Cogia, and to try to reconcile them. When Ali Cogia had explained to them the cause of the quarrel, the most earnest in the cause asked the merchant what reply he had to make.

"The merchant owned that he had kept the jar belonging to Ali Cogia in his warehouse, but he denied having touched it, and made oath that he only knew it contained olives because Ali Cogia had told him so, and he called upon all present to bear witness of the insult and affront which had been offered to him in his own house.

"'You have drawn the affront on yourself,' said Ali Cogia, taking him by the arm; 'but since you behave so wickedly, I cite you by the public law. Let us see if you will have the face to repeat your assertion before the cadi.'

"At this summons, which every true Mussulman must obey unless he rebels against his religion, the merchant had not the courage to offer any resistance. 'Come,' said he, 'that is the very thing I wish. We shall see who is wrong, you or I.'

"Ali Cogia brought the merchant before the tribunal of the cadi, where he accused him of having stolen a thousand pieces of gold which had been deposited in his care, relating the fact as it took place. The cadi inquired if he had any witnesses. He replied that he had not taken this precaution, because he supposed the person to whom he had entrusted his money to be his friend, and that till now he had every reason to think him an honest man.

"In his defence the merchant simply repeated the words he had already said to Ali Cogia in the presence of his neighbours, and he concluded by offering to take his oath, not only that he had never taken the thousand pieces of gold, but even that he had never the slightest knowledge of their being in his possession. The cadi accepted the oath, after which the accused merchant was dismissed as innocent.

"Ali Cogia, extremely mortified to find himself condemned to suffer so considerable a loss, protested against the sentence, and declared to the cadi that he would lay his complaint before the Caliph Haroun Alraschid, who would do him justice; but the cadi paid no heed to this threat, and considered it merely as the effect of the resentment natural to all who lose their causes; and he thought he had performed his duty by acquitting a man who was accused without any witnesses to prove the fact.

"While the merchant triumphed in his success over Ali Cogia, and hugged himself with delight at having so cleverly got possession of the thousand pieces of gold, Ali Cogia went to draw up a petition; and the next day, having chosen the time when the caliph would be returning from mid-day prayers, he placed himself in a street which led to the mosque; and when the caliph passed he held out his hand with the petition. An officer, duly appointed to receive petitions, and who was walking before the caliph, instantly left his place, and came to take Ali Cogia's paper, that he might present it to his master.

"As Ali Cogia knew that it was the usual custom of the Caliph Haroun Alraschid, when he returned to his palace, to examine with his own eyes all the petitions that were presented to him in this way, he followed the procession, went into the palace, and waited till the officer who had taken the petition should come out of the apartment of the caliph. When this functionary made his appearance he told Ali Cogia that the caliph had read his petition, and appointed the following day to give him an audience; and having inquired

ALI COGIA ACCUSES THE MERCHANT OF THEFT.

of him where the merchant lived, he sent to give him notice to attend the next day at the appointed hour.

"On the evening of the same day, the caliph, with the grand vizier Giafar, and Mesrour, the chief of the eunuchs, all three disguised as citizens, went forth on one of those excursions into the city which I have already told your majesty it was his custom frequently to take. In passing through a street, the caliph heard a noise. He quickened his pace, and came to a door which opened into a court; and looking through a crevice, he saw ten or twelve children, who had not gone to rest, playing there by moonlight.

"The caliph, who felt some curiosity to know what these children were playing at, sat down on a stone bench, which stood very conveniently near the door; and as he was looking at the party through the crevice, he heard one of the most lively and intelligent among them say to the others, 'Let us play at the cadi. I am the cadi. Bring before me Ali Cogia, and the merchant who stole the thousand pieces of gold from him.'

"These words of the child reminded the caliph of the petition which had been presented to him that day, and which he had read. He therefore redoubled his attention to hear what would be the event of the trial.

"As the affair between Ali Cogia and the merchant was a new thing, and much talked of in the city of Bagdad, even among children, the rest of this youthful company joyfully agreed to the proposal made by the eldest, and each chose the character he would perform. The part of cadi was unanimously relinquished to him who had made choice of it; and when he had taken his seat with all the pomp and gravity of a cadi, another lad, personating the officer that attends the tribunal, presented two others to him, one of whom he introduced as Ali Cogia, and the other as the merchant against whom Ali Cogia preferred his complaint.

"The pretended cadi then addressed the disputants, and gravely interrogating the feigned Ali Cogia, said, 'O Ali Cogia, what do you require of this merchant?' He who personated this character then made a profound obeisance, and informed the cadi of the facts in every point; concluding by beseeching him to be pleased to interpose his authority, to prevent his sustaining so considerable a loss. The feigned cadi, after having listened to Ali Cogia, turned to the merchant, and asked him why he did not return to Ali Cogia the sum demanded of him. This young merchant made use of the same arguments which the real one had alleged before the cadi of Bagdad, and also in the same manner asked permission to swear that what he said was the truth.

"'Not so fast,' replied the pretended cadi. 'Before I receive your oath, I should like to see the jar of olives. Ali Cogia,' said he, addressing the boy who acted his part, 'have you brought the jar with you?' As the latter replied that he had not, he desired him to go and bring it.

"Ali Cogia disappeared for a few moments, and then returning, pretended to bring a jar to the cadi, which he said was the same that had been deposited with the merchant, and was now returned to him. Then proceeding according to the established form, the cadi asked the merchant if he owned it to be the same jar; and the merchant, allowing by his silence that he could not deny it, he ordered it to be opened. The feigned Ali Cogia then went through the action of taking off the cover, and the cadi seemed to be looking into the jar. 'These are fine olives: let me taste them,' said he. Then pretending to take one to taste, he added, 'They are excellent. But,' continued he, 'I think that olives which have been kept seven years would not be so good. Order some olive merchants to be called, and let them give their opinion.' Two boys were then presented to him. 'Are you olive merchants?' he inquired, and they replied in the affirmative. Thereupon he added, 'Tell me, then, if you know how long olives, that are prepared by people who make it their business, can be preserved fit to eat?'

"'O my lord,' replied the feigned merchants, 'whatever care may be taken to preserve them, they are worth nothing after the third year: they lose both their flavour and colour, and are only fit to be thrown away,' 'Say you so?' resumed the young cadi: 'look at this jar, and tell me how long the olives that are in it have been kept.'

"The feigned merchants then pretended to examine and taste the olives, and told the cadi that they were fresh and good. 'You are mistaken,' replied the cadi, 'here is Ali Cogia, who says that he put them into the jar seven years ago.' 'O cadi,' said the merchants, who were reckoned experienced in their business, 'we can assure you that these olives are of this year's growth; and we maintain that there is not a single merchant in Bagdad who will not be of the same way of thinking.' The accused merchant was going to protest against this testimony of the merchants, but the cadi did not allow him time. 'Silence!' said he, 'thou art a thief, and shalt be hanged.' The children then clapped their hands, shouted aloud to testify their joy, and finished their game by seizing the supposed criminal, and carrying him off as if to execution.

"It is impossible to express how much the Caliph Haroun Alraschid admired the wisdom and acuteness of the boy, who had pronounced so just a sentence on the very case which was to be pleaded before him on the morrow. Seeing that the game was ended, he rose, and asked the grand vizier, who had been attending to all that passed, if he had heard the sentence given by the boy, and what he thought of it. 'O Commander of the Faithful,' replied Giafar, 'I am astonished at the wisdom evinced by this boy, at so early an age.'

"'But,' resumed the caliph, 'do you know, that to-morrow I am to give my decision on this very affair, and that the true Ali Cogia has this morning presented a petition to me on the subject?' 'Your majesty has informed me of the fact,' replied the grand vizier. 'Do you think,' said the caliph, 'that I can give a juster sentence than that we have now heard?' 'If the affair is the same,' returned the grand vizier, 'it appears to me that your majesty cannot proceed in a better manner, or give any other judgment.' 'Mark well this house, then,' said the caliph, 'and bring me the boy to-morrow, that he may judge the same cause in my presence. Order the cadi also, who acquitted the merchant, to be at the palace, that he may learn his duty from this child, and correct his deficiencies. I desire, too, that you tell Ali Cogia to bring with him his jar of olives; and see that you procure two olive merchants, to be present at the audience.' The caliph gave these orders as he continued his walk, which he finished without meeting with any other incident that deserved his attention.

"On the morrow the grand vizier repaired to the house where the caliph witnessed the game the children had played at, and he asked to speak to the master of it; but as the proprietor was not at home, he was introduced to the mistress. He asked her if she had any children; she replied that she had three, whom she brought to him. 'My children,' said he to them, 'which of you acted the cadi last night, when you were playing together?' The eldest replied that it was he; and, startled at the question thus suddenly asked of him, he changed colour. 'My child,' said the grand vizier, 'come with me: the Commander of the Faithful wishes to see you.'

"The mother was extremely alarmed when she saw that the vizier was going to take away her son. 'O my lord,' said she, 'has the Commander of the Faithful sent for my son to deprive me of him?' The grand vizier quieted her fears by promising her that her son should be sent back again in less than an hour, and that when he returned she would learn the reason of his being sent for, which would give her great pleasure. 'If that is the case, sir,' replied she, 'permit me to dress him in his best garments, that he may be more fit to appear before the Commander of the Faithful.' And she immediately decked him out in holiday attire.

"The grand vizier conducted the boy to the caliph, and presented him at the time appointed for hearing Ali Cogia and the merchant.

"The caliph, who saw that the child was rather terrified, and who wished to prepare him for what he expected him to do, said to him, 'Come hither, my boy, draw near. Was it you who yesterday passed sentence on the case of Ali Cogia and the merchant who robbed him of his gold? I both saw and heard you, and am very well satisfied with you.' The child began to gain confidence, and modestly replied that it was he. 'My child,' resumed the caliph, 'you shall see the true Ali Cogia and the merchant to-day. Come and sit down by me.'

"The caliph then took the boy by the hand, seated himself on his throne, and having placed him by his side, commanded the men to be brought before him. They advanced, and the name of each was pronounced, as he touched with his forehead the carpet that covered the throne. When they had risen, the caliph said to them, 'Let each of you plead his cause. This child will hear and administer justice to you, and if anything be deficient, I will supply it.'

"Ali Cogia and the merchant each spoke in his turn; and when the merchant requested to be allowed to take the same oath he had taken on his first examination, the boy answered that it was not yet time, that the jar of olives must first be inspected. At these words Ali Cogia produced the jar, placed it at the feet of the caliph, and uncovered it. The caliph looked at the olives, and took one, which he tasted. The jar was then handed to some skilful merchants, who had been ordered to appear, and they reported it as their opinion that the olives were good, and of that year's growth. The boy told them that Ali Cogia assured him they had been in the jar seven years; to which the real merchants returned the same answer which the children, as feigned merchants, had made on the preceding evening.

"Although the accused merchant plainly saw that the two olive merchants had thus pronounced his condemnation, he nevertheless attempted to allege reasons in his justification. The boy, however, did not venture to pronounce sentence on him, and send him to execution. 'O Commander of the Faithful,' said he, 'this is not a game. It is your majesty alone who can condemn to death in earnest. I did it yesterday only in play.'

"The caliph, fully persuaded of the treachery of the merchant, gave him up to the ministers of justice to have him hanged; and this sentence was executed, after he had confessed where the thousand pieces of gold were concealed, which were then returned to Ali Cogia. Then Haroun Alraschid, the great monarch celebrated for his justice and equity, advised the cadi who had passed the first sentence, and who was present, to learn from a child to be more exact in the performance of his office: thereupon he embraced the boy, and sent him home again with a purse containing a hundred pieces of gold, which he ordered to be given him as a proof of his liberality."

Having thus concluded this story, Scheherazade went on to relate many others to the sultan, who took great delight in them, and she began the next as follows:

## THE STORY OF THE ENCHANTED HORSE.

AS your majesty well knows, the Nevrouz, or new day, which is the first of the year and of spring, and is thus called by way of superior distinction, ranks as a festival so solemn and so ancient, throughout the whole extent of Persia (for indeed it takes its origin even from the earliest periods of idolatry), that the only religion of our Prophet, pure and unsullied as it is, and esteemed by those who profess it as the only true one, has nevertheless been hitherto unable to abolish it; although we must confess that it is a custom completely pagan, and that the ceremonies observed on its solemnization are of the most superstitious nature. Not only in the large cities of Persia, but in every town, village, and hamlet, the festival is celebrated with extraordinary rejoicings.

"But the celebrations which take place at court surpass all others by the variety of new and surprising spectacles which are exhibited on the occasion; many foreigners also, from neighbouring as well as from distant nations, are attracted by the liberality of the monarch, who rewards those who excel in industry or produce new inventions; so that nothing that is attempted in other parts of the world can approach or be compared to the sumptuous magnificence of this anniversary.

"At one of these festivals, the most skilful and ingenious persons of the country, together with the foreigners who had repaired to Schiraz, where the court was then assembled, had presented the king and his nobles with all the various spectacles intended for their entertainment; and the monarch had, as usual, distributed his gifts, according to the merit each had displayed in producing extraordinary or pleasing specimens of his genius, with liberality and discrimination, which satisfied the highest expectations of all. At the very moment when he was going to withdraw, and the assembly to disperse, that each might retire to his separate home, an Indian appeared and presented himself at the foot of the throne, leading a horse saddled and bridled, and most richly caparisoned. It was a sculptured horse, but so skilfully carved that at first sight every one supposed it to be a living creature.

"The Indian prostrated himself before the throne; when he had risen, he showed the horse to the king, and thus addressed him: 'O mighty monarch, although I am the last to present myself before your majesty as a candidate for your favour, I can nevertheless assure you, that in this day of feasting and rejoicing you have not seen anything so wonderful and astonishing as this horse, which I entreat you will condescend to notice.' 'I see nothing in this horse,' replied the king, 'but the strong resemblance to nature, which the workman, by means of art and industry, has given it. Another workman might have made one like it, and have brought it to still greater perfection.'

'O great king,' resumed the Indian, 'it is not on account of its exterior construction or its appearance that I wish to attract your majesty's attention to my horse. I would call your majesty's attention to the use I make of it, and the office which every one can make it perform, by means of a secret which I am enabled to communicate. When I mount this horse, in whatever region of the earth I may be, and at whatever distance from any particular spot to which I wish to transport myself through the air, I can accomplish the journey in a very short space of time. In short, O great king, it is in this peculiar property that the wonder of my horse consists: a wonderful power, which no one ever heard of, and of which I am ready to give your majesty any proof that you may require.'

"The King of Persia, who was extremely interested in everything that appeared of a scientific construction, and who in all the different things of this nature which he had seen, heard of, and desired to see, had never met with anything at all resembling this horse, told the Indian that nothing except the proof he had proposed to bring, could convince him of the wonderful power of his horse, and that therefore he was ready to witness the truth of the Indian's assertion.

"The Indian instantly put his foot into the stirrup, and threw himself lightly on the horse; when he had got the other foot in the opposite stirrup, and was seated firmly in his saddle, he asked the King of Persia where he should go.

"At the distance of about three leagues from Schiraz there was a high mountain, easily discernible from the large square before the royal palace where the king and all his court and people were assembled. 'Do you see that mountain?' said the king, pointing it out to the Indian; 'it is there that I wish you to go. The distance is not very great, but is sufficient to give me an opinion of your diligence in going thither and returning. And as it is not possible for my sight to follow you thus far, I propose, as a certain proof of your having been there, that you should bring me a branch from a palm tree which grows at the foot of the mountain.'

"The King of Persia had scarcely declared his wishes in these words, when the Indian turned a small peg, which was placed a little above the pummel of the saddle on the horse's neck. In an instant the horse rose from the ground, and bore the Indian through the air, quick as lightning, to such an immense height, that in a few minutes even those who had the longest and clearest sight could no longer discern him. This proceeding excited the astonishment of the king and his courtiers, and shouts of admiration arose from all the spectators.

"A quarter of an hour had scarcely elapsed from the departure of the Indian, when they perceived him high in air, returning with a palm branch in his hand. He was soon hovering above the square, where he performed several feats amidst the acclamations of the admiring multitude, and then came down immediately before the throne on which the king was sitting, alighting on the same spot from whence he had taken his aërial excursion. He dismounted, and, approaching the throne, prostrated himself, and laid the branch at the feet of the king.

"The monarch, who had witnessed with equal admiration and astonishment the marvellous skill which the Indian had just exhibited, immediately conceived a strong desire to become the possessor of this wonderful horse. As he felt certain he should find no difficulty in treating with the Indian, being resolved to give him whatever sum he might require for it, the king already regarded the marvellous steed as his own, and the most valuable addition to the state treasures, amongst which he intended to place it. 'Judging of your horse by its appearance,' said he to the Indian, 'I did not conceive that it could deserve the high commendation which, as you have just shown me, it justly merits. I thank you for having undeceived me; and that you may know how much I appreciate and value the wonderful horse, I am ready to purchase it, if it is to be disposed of.'

"'O mighty king,' replied the Indian, 'I had no doubt that your majesty, who in knowledge and judgment is said to excel all the kings who now reign over the earth, would bestow on my horse that commendation with which you have honoured it, when you were made acquainted with those of its qualities which deserve your attention. I had also forseen that you would not be satisfied with admiring and praising it, but that you would immediately wish to become the owner of it, as you have now informed me is the case. For my part, O king, although I am as well aware of the value of it as any one can be, and know that the possession of it is alone sufficient to render my name immortal; yet am I not so much attached to it as to refuse to part with the horse, to gratify the noble desire of your majesty. But although I make this declaration, I must also plainly announce the conditions which must be fulfilled before I can consent to let the wonderful horse pass into other hands; and these, perhaps, may not please you.

"'Your majesty,' continued the Indian, 'will allow me to remark, that I did not purchase this horse: I obtained it of the inventor and maker, who would not part with it till I gave him my only daughter in marriage as its price, and he at the same time exacted from me a promise that I would never sell it; and that, if I parted with it to any man, it should only be in exchange for any gift I might think proper.'

"The Indian was going to continue, but the king interupted him when he mentioned the word exchange. 'I am ready,' said he, 'to grant you anything in exchange that you may ask of me. You know that my dominions are extensive, and that they are overspread with powerful, wealthy, and populous cities: I leave you to choose any of these that you like. It shall be yours in full sovereignty and power for the rest of your days.'

"This offer appeared to all the court of Persia as truly royal and worthy of a king; but it was far below the recompense the Indian had proposed to himself: he contemplated receiving a far higher reward. He replied to the king, 'O my lord, I am infinitely obliged to your majesty for the offer you have made me, and I cannot sufficiently thank you for your generosity. I entreat you, however, not to be displeased at my temerity, when I venture to tell you that I cannot deliver my horse into your possession except I receive the hand of the princess your daughter as my wife. I have resolved not to part with it on any other terms.'

"The courtiers who surrounded the King of Persia could not refrain from bursting into a violent fit of laughter at this extravagant request of the Indian. But Prince Firouz Schah, the eldest son of the king and heir to the crown, heard it with the utmost indignation. The king was of a different opinion, and indeed did not feel much hesitation in sacrificing the Princess of Persia to the Indian, to satisfy his desire to possess the horse. He did not answer, however, for some time, considering what mode to pursue.

"Prince Firouz Schah, who saw his father meditating what answer he should give the Indian, was fearful lest the king should grant the extravagant demand—a concession which would in his eyes have been equally injurious to the royal dignity, to the princess his sister, and to himself. He therefore determined to interfere, and addressing the king, exclaimed, 'O my king and father, your majesty will pardon me if I take the liberty of asking you, how you can possibly hesitate a moment on the absolute refusal you ought

THE INDIAN PROSTRATES HIMSELF BEFORE THE KING OF PERSIA.

to make to this insolent proposal, from a man who is nothing better than an ignominious mountebank. I marvel how you can allow him the slightest encouragement to flatter himself with the expectation that he is going to be allied to one of the greatest and most powerful monarchs of the earth. I entreat you to consider not only what you owe to yourself, but what is due to your rank, and to the revered memory of your ancestors.'

"'O my son,' replied the King of Persia, 'I receive your remonstrance without displeasure, and commend you for the zeal you evince in wishing to preserve the nobility and lustre of your birth unsullied and pure as you received it. But you do not sufficiently consider the marvellous excellence of this horse. The Indian, who proposes to me this method of obtaining it, may, if I refuse him, go to some other court, where he will make the same proposition, and his conditions will be accepted; and I confess I should be mortified in the highest degree if any other monarch should boast of having surpassed me in generosity, and of having thus deprived me of the honour and glory of possessing a horse which I esteem as the most singular and admirable thing the world contains. I will not, however, say that I consent to the Indian's demand. Perhaps he does not fully understand how exorbitant are his pretensions, and I may yet be able to make some agreement with him, which shall satisfy him without sacrificing the hand of the princess. But before we conclude the affair, I wish you to examine the horse, and make trial of him yourself, that you may give me your opinion of him. I dare say the owner will have no objection to this proposal.'

"As it is natural for a man to hope that his wishes will be fulfilled, the Indian thought he could perceive from this conversation that the King of Persia had no insuperable objection to receiving him into alliance with the royal family, by purchasing the horse on the terms proposed; and he thought it not impossible that, although the prince now appeared so entirely to oppose his views, he might in time become favourable to them. Instead, therefore, of refusing the wish expressed by the king, he on the contrary seemed rejoiced at it; and as a proof that he consented to the request with pleasure, he went towards the prince with the horse, would have assisted him to mount, and afterwards instructed him in the art of managing and guiding the wonderful steed.

"The prince immediately mounted the horse with great agility, without the assistance of the Indian. He placed his feet in the stirrups, and without waiting for any further directions, he turned the peg, as he had observed the Indian do just before when he mounted. The very instant he touched it, the horse rose with him swift as an arrow shot by the strongest archer; and in a few moments the king, as well as all the numerous assemblage of the people present, entirely lost sight of him.

"Neither the horse nor Prince Firouz Schah reappeared, and the King of Persia in vain strained his eyes to descry him in the air. At length the Indian, alarmed at the thought of the consequences that might ensue, prostrated himself at the foot of the throne, and entreated the king to deign to look on him, and listen to the words he wished to say: he then proceeded as follows: 'Your majesty must have observed that the prince in his impatience did not allow me time to give him the necessary instructions for the management of my horse. He conceived it needless to receive any further advice after he had seen what I did to elevate myself in the air; but he is ignorant of the method he must employ to turn the horse, and make it come back to the place from whence it set off. Therefore, O mighty king, the favour I have to request of your majesty is, that you will not hold me responsible for any accident that may befall the prince your son. I am convinced you are too equitable to impute to me any misfortune that he may encounter.'

"The Indian's speech gave the King of Persia infinite uneasiness. He was now aware of the danger his son had incurred, if what the Indian said was true, that the secret for making the horse return was different from that which made it start off and rise in the air. He asked him why he did not call the prince back at the moment he saw him depart.

"'O great king,' replied the Indian, 'your majesty observed the extreme swiftness with which the horse carried off the prince. The surprise I felt at the moment took from me all power of utterance, and when I was able to speak your son was already so distant that he could not have heard my voice; and even if he had heard it, he could not have managed the horse so as to make it return, as he was unacquainted with the secret, which he would not have the patience to learn from me. But, my lord,' added the Indian, 'there is still some reason to hope that, in the embarrassment he must feel before he has proceeded far, the prince may remark another peg. If he only turns this second peg, the horse will cease to ascend, and will come towards the earth, when the prince may alight in whatever spot he pleases, by guiding the horse by the bridle.

"Notwithstanding this reasoning of the Indian, which had a very plausible appearance, the King of Persia was extremely alarmed at the imminent peril in which his son was placed. 'I will suppose,' said he, 'that the prince perceives the other peg you mention, which nevertheless is scarcely probable, and that he uses it in the proper way; but may not the horse, perhaps, instead of descending gradually to the earth, fall on rocks, or dash headlong with him into the middle of the sea?' 'Great monarch,' resumed the Indian, 'I can dispel your fears on this point, by assuring your majesty that the horse passes over any extent of sea without any danger of falling into it, and that he always carries his rider wherever the latter wishes to go; and you may be assured that, if the prince does but perceive the peg I speak of, the horse will carry him to the place where he wishes to alight; and it is not probable that the prince should attempt to alight in any other than a convenient situation, where he can obtain assistance and make himself known.'

"To these consoling assurances of the Indian the king replied, 'Perhaps you speak the truth; but as I cannot rely on the promises you make me, I now declare to you that your head shall be the forfeit, if, in three months, the prince my son does not return in safety, or if I do not, at least, hear satisfactory accounts of his welfare.' Thereupon he ordered the Indian to be seized and placed in close imprisonment, and returned to his palace in the greatest affliction, lamenting that the feast of the Nevrouz, which was so solemnly observed throughout Persia, should have terminated so mournfully for him and his court.

"Prince Firouz Schah in the meantime was flying through the air with the rapidity we have already described; and in less than an hour he found himself at such an immense height, that he could no longer discern any object on the earth, nor distinguish the mountains from the valleys, which appeared to him one confused mass. At length he began to think of returning to the palace from whence he had departed; and to accomplish this he fancied that he had only to turn the peg the contrary way, turning the bridle at the same time. But his astonishment was inexpressible when he perceived that the horse still rose with the same headlong speed. He turned the peg various ways, but found his efforts had no effect. He now felt most deeply the error he had committed in not procuring from the Indian all the particulars necessary for the management of the horse before he had mounted it. He now understood the peril of his situation, but the conviction of his danger did not lessen his presence of mind. He considered, with all the coolness he was capable of, what was to be done; and examining the head and neck of the horse with the greatest attention, he perceived another peg, smaller and less discernible than the first, near the right ear of the horse. He turned it, and instantly remarked that he was beginning to descend towards the earth, in the same right line by which he had ascended, but less rapidly.

"Night had for more than half an hour veiled the spot over which Prince Firouz Schah found himself at the time he turned the second peg; but as the horse descended with the greatest swiftness, the sun, which was still visible in the higher regions of the air, appeared to him to set with equal rapidity, and he soon found himself enveloped in the duskiness of night; so that, far from being able to make choice of a likely and convenient place on which to alight, he was under the necessity of dropping the reins on the horse's neck, and waiting with patience till he had reached the earth; not without feeling some uneasiness about the place where he should stop, which might prove to be some savage or desolate region, or perhaps a river or the sea.

"It was past midnight when the horse stopped, and Prince Firouz Schah dismounted. He felt much fatigued and weak from want of food, not having tasted any since the morning before he left the palace to be present at the various spectacles exhibited at the festival. The first thing he did, notwithstanding the obscurity that prevailed, was to endeavour to discover what place he was in. He found himself on the terraced roof of a magnificent palace, which had a marble balustrade running round it, breast-high. A close examination showed him the staircase which led to the interior of the palace, the door of which was half open.

"A less enterprising man than Prince Firouz Schah might not perhaps have felt willing to go down the stairs in such profound darkness, ignorant also whether he might meet with friends or enemies; but this consideration had no weight with him, nor did it damp his courage. 'I did not come here to injure any one,' thought he, 'and most probably whatever man I meet, seeing me without any weapon in my hands, will have the humanity to listen to me before he attempts to do me an injury.' He therefore opened the door a little further, without making any noise, and began to descend with the utmost caution, lest he should make any false step, the sound of which might wake some of the inhabitants. He descended in safety, and having reached a landing-place on the stairs, he found a door open, which led into a large room, where there was a light.

"Prince Firouz Schah stopped some time at the door to listen, but he heard nothing but a sound that seemed like the breathing of men sunk in deep sleep. He advanced a few steps into the room, and by the light of a lamp perceived that the sleepers whose snoring he had heard were some black eunuchs, each lying with a drawn sabre near him; and this led him to suppose that they were guarding the apartment of some princess; and in this conjecture he was not mistaken.

"The chamber in which the princess slept was next to the room where the eunuchs were placed, and was easily discernible by the great light which shone through a slight silk hanging that concealed the door. The prince advanced towards this hanging with silent footsteps, and reached it without waking the eunuchs: he drew it aside, and entered the chamber. The royal magnificence of the decorations, which he might have noticed in any other situation, did not attract his attention, which was wholly engaged on what was to him of greater consequence. He observed several beds, one of them raised on a sofa, the others being below it. The women who attended on the princess were lying on the lower beds, to bear her company and fulfil her commands, and the princess herself was on the more elevated couch.

"Guided by these appearances, Prince Firouz Schah could not be mistaken in the choice he should make of the person he might address. He approached the princess's bed without disturbing either her or her women. When he was sufficiently near to observe her distinctly, his eyes beheld in her such an enchanting and wonderful beauty, that he was quite charmed, and instantly felt the flame of love in his heart. 'Oh, heavens!' exclaimed he to himself, 'has my wayward fate led me hither to deprive me of that liberty I have till now so uniformly maintained? Must I not expect inevitable thraldom when those eyes are unclosed, which must add a yet greater lustre and brilliancy to that assemblage of charms? Yet I must be content to submit, since I cannot quit this spot, and necessity compels me to await the decree of my destiny!'

"Occupied by reflections of this nature, and inspired alike by the beauty of the princess and the situation in which he found himself, the prince fell on his knees, and taking hold of the princess's sleeve, which but partly concealed an arm of exquisite form and incomparable whiteness, he gently pulled it. The princess awoke, and, opening her eyes, displayed the utmost astonishment at beholding near her a man of a handsome countenance, noble figure, and elegant garb; the surprise she felt did not, however, betray her into any evident emotions of fear and alarm.

"The prince took advantage of this favourable moment. He bowed his head to the floor, and when he raised it began to speak in these words: 'O illustrious princess, in consequence of an adventure of the most astonishing and surprising nature, you now see at your feet a suppliant prince, the son of the King of Persia, who yesterday morning was present with his father at the celebration of a solemn festival, and who now finds himself in the most imminen danger of perishing, unless you have the goodness and generosity to bestow on him your favour and protection. This protection, most adorable princess, I implore, in the full confidence that you will not refuse it me. I venture to flatter myself that my hopes will be fulfilled, from the conviction that nothing but kindness can take up its abode with such exquisite beauty and such incomparable charms.'

"The lady to whom Prince Firouz Schah had thus passionately addressed himself was the Princess of Bengal, the eldest daughter of the king who reigned over that country, and who had built for her, at a short distance from the capital, this palace, whither she frequently resorted, to enter into the diversions of the country. Having listened to the prince with all the kindness he could possibly desire, she replied to him with great affability. 'O prince,' said she, 'take courage: you are not in a country of barbarians. Hospitality, humanity, and politeness hold their reign in the kingdom of Bengal as in that of Persia. It cannot be said that I grant you as a favour the protection you demand; you are entitled to it, and will experience it, not only in my palace, but also in every part of these dominions. You may believe me, and depend upon my word.'

PRINCE FIROUZ SCHAH BESEECHING THE PROTECTION OF THE PRINCESS OF BENGAL.

"The Prince of Persia was about to express his acknowledgments to the Princess of Bengal for her politeness and the favour she had granted him in so obliging a manner, and had already bowed his head in deep reverence before he began to speak, when she interrupted him by saying, 'I feel the greatest curiosity to learn from your own lips by what wonderful adventure you could have travelled hither in so short a space of time from the capital of Persia, and by what enchantment you could have made your way into my apartment, and presented yourself before me so secretly that you evaded the vigilance of my guards. But as I am certain you must be in want of some refreshment, and as I wish to treat you as a guest who deserves a good welcome, I will restrain my curiosity until to-morrow morning, and at present only give orders to my women to prepare a chamber for your reception, and to provide you with everything necessary. Therefore, I request you to take food and rest, and when you feel sufficiently recovered to be able to satisfy my wishes, I shall be prepared to listen to you.'

"The princess's women had been awakened by the first words which Prince Firouz Schah addressed to their royal mistress, and their astonishment at seeing him on his knees before the bed of the princess was increased by their inability to understand how he had made his way into her chamber, without having disturbed either them or the eunuchs. These women were no sooner informed of the princess's intentions, than they arose and quickly dressed themselves, and were soon ready to execute the commands of their mistress. Each took one of the numerous lighted tapers which illuminated the princess's apartment, and when the prince retired, they walked before him, and conducted him into a very beautiful chamber, where some of them prepared him a bed, while the others went into the kitchen to procure him some refreshment. And although the hour was unseasonable for such occupations, they nevertheless were so diligent that he had not long to wait for his repast. They brought him a great abundance of various dishes: he partook of those he liked best; and when he had satisfied his hunger, they cleared all away, and left him at liberty to go to bed, after first pointing out to him where he could find everything he might require.

"The Princess of Bengal had been so struck with the intelligence, politeness, and other amiable qualities of the Prince of Persia, in the short conversation she had held with him, that her mind was wholly occupied by thoughts of him; and she had not yet been able to close her eyes when her women returned into the chamber to go to bed. She inquired if they had taken care to provide him with everything he wanted; if he appeared satisfied; and, above all, what they thought of his appearance and address.

"The women having given satisfactory answers to the former questions, replied thus to the latter: 'We know not, mighty princess, what opinion you have yourself formed of him; but in our minds we should esteem it a fortunate circumstance if the king your father would bestow on you so amiable a prince in marriage. There is no one at the court of Bengal who can be compared with him, and we have not heard that any of the neighbouring states can produce a prince worthy of you.'

"This flattering speech did not displease the Princess of Bengal; but as she did not choose to reveal her own sentiments, she commanded her attendants to be silent. 'You are idle chatterers!' said she: 'get you to bed, and let me go to sleep again.' The next morning, the first care that engaged the princess after she rose was to perform the duties of the toilet. She had never before taken such pains in adorning herself as on that day, and she passed more time than usual in consulting her mirror. Her women had never before been obliged to exercise so much patience in doing and undoing the same thing several times till she was contented.

"'I could plainly see,' said she to herself, 'that I was not unpleasing to the Prince of Persia when he first beheld me last night; but he shall have a higher opinion of me when I am decorated in all my splendour.' She ornamented her head with the largest and most brilliant diamonds, and put on a necklace, and bracelets, and girdle sparkling with an infinity of jewels, all of inestimable value; and the dress she wore was composed of the richest silk that India could produce, a fabric wrought only for kings, princes, or princesses of the highest rank, and of a colour that displayed her beauty to the greatest advantage. When she had repeatedly consulted her mirror, and had asked her women separately if anything was wanting to complete the magnificence of her appearance, she sent to inquire if the Prince of Persia was awake and at leisure; and concluding that he would ask permission to present himself before her, she desired him to be informed that she was coming to him, and that she had particular reasons for acting thus.

"The Prince of Persia, being now perfectly recovered from his fatiguing journey, had just finished dressing himself when he received a message from the Princess of Bengal, by one of her women, to inquire how he had passed the night.

"Without waiting for the princess's woman to deliver her message, the prince immediately inquired if her mistress was ready to receive his respects. But when the woman had executed the commission she had received, he said, 'The princess is mistress here, and I am in her palace only to obey her commands.'

"When the princess was informed that the Prince of Persia was ready to receive her, she went to his apartment. Many compliments were exchanged between them, the prince apologizing for having awakened the princess out of her sleep, for which he entreated her pardon; and she inquiring how he had passed the night, and whether he now felt recovered from his fatigue. The princess then seated herself on the sofa, and Prince Firouz Schah followed her example, placing himself, however, at some distance. to show his respect.

"The princess then began the conversation. 'O prince,' said she, 'I might have received you in the chamber where you found me last night; but as the chief of my eunuchs has the privilege of going there, and as he never enters this place without my express permission, I preferred this as being less exposed to interruption. I feel the utmost impatience to become acquainted with the circumstances of the extraordinary adventure which procures me the happiness of seeing you; I therefore entreat you to oblige me with the details which I am so anxious to know.'

"In order to give the princess full information on every point relating to himself, Prince Firouz Schah began by giving her an account of the festival of Nevrouz which was annually celebrated throughout the dominions of Persia, together with a description of all the remarkable exhibitions which had contributed to the amusement of the court of Persia, and delighted the whole city of Schiraz. He then mentioned the enchanted horse, the description of which, with all the feats performed on it by the Indian before the immense assemblage of people, convinced the princess that nothing in the world could exceed its wonderful mechanism.

"'You may easily imagine, beautiful princess,' continued Prince Firouz Schah, 'that the king my father, who spares no expense to increase his collection of the most rare and curious productions that can be obtained, felt an anxious desire to add to it a horse of so extraordinary a nature, and that he did not long hesitate to ask the Indian at what sum he estimated its value.

"'The Indian's reply was the most extravagant you can can conceive. He said that he had not purchased the horse, but had acquired it in exchange for his only daughter; and that, as he could not consent to part with it except on similar terms, he would not resign it to my father except on condition that the latter consented to give him the princess my sister in marriage.

"'The crowd of courtiers who surrounded my father's throne, and heard this extravagant proposition, laughed aloud at the absurdity of it; for my part, I felt such violent indignation, that I could not dissemble my emotion, and I felt the more angry because I found the king wavering as to the answer he should make. In fact, I firmly believe that he was on the point of granting the rascal Indian his request, if I had not represented to him, in the most forcible terms, the stain with which such an alliance would tarnish his glory. My remonstrances, however, were not sufficiently effectual to make him entirely abandon all intention of sacrificing the princess to this despicable wretch. He supposed I might accede to his wishes, if I could but acquire the same opinion of the inestimable value of the horse which he had conceived. With this view he desired me to examine and mount it, and make a trial of it myself.

"'To please the king my father, I complied, and mounted the horse; and as soon as I was in the saddle, having seen the Indian turn a peg, whose movement occasioned the horse to rise with him, I did the same thing, without waiting for any further instructions from him; and in an instant I rose in the air with a swiftness far surpassing that of an arrow shot by the strongest archer.

"'In a short time I was at such a distance from the earth, that I could no longer distinguish any object on its surface, and I appeared to be approaching so near the vault of heaven, that I began to be apprehensive that I should strike against it. The rapidity of the motion with which I ascended for some time deprived me of my presence of mind, and rendered me insensible of the danger to which I was on all sides exposed. At length

I attempted to turn the peg in a contrary direction, supposing I should by that means descend; but the effect did not answer my expectation. The horse continued to bear me still higher and farther from the earth. After some time I discovered another peg: I turned it, and soon perceived that the horse, instead of rising, began to descend; and as I soon found myself involved in the shades of night, and it was not possible to guide the horse to any place of safety, I loosened the reins and resigned myself to the will of Heaven, to dispose of me as it thought best.

"'The horse at last touched the ground, and I dismounted. I examined the place where I was, and discovered it to be the terrace of this palace. I found the door of the staircase half open, and I went down without making any noise. Presently I came to an open door from which a faint light glimmered. I looked in, and saw the eunuchs asleep, and beyond, a very bright light, which shone through a heavy curtain. Notwithstanding the hazard I ran if the eunuchs awoke, the pressing necessity of my situation inspired me with courage, not to say temerity; and I advanced towards the second door as silently as possible.

"'There is no occasion, mighty princess, to describe what followed; you know it already. Nothing remains but to thank you for your kindness and generosity, and to entreat you to tell me by what means I can evince my gratitude in a way that will be acceptable to you. As, according to the rights of mankind, I am now your slave, and cannot therefore offer you my personal service, I have nothing left to lay at your feet except my heart. But what do I say, lovely princess? This heart is no longer mine; you have stolen it from me by your charms; and far from asking you to return it to me, I resign it entirely to you. Permit me, therefore, to declare that in you I acknowledge the mistress not only of my heart, but of my every hope for the future.'

"These last words were pronounced by Prince Firouz Schah with a tone and air which fully convinced the Princess of Bengal that she had succeeded in producing the effect she had been so anxious to create. She was not displeased with this sudden declaration of the Prince of Persia, and the blushes which overspread her cheeks heightened her beauty and rendered her still more interesting in his eyes.

"When he had finished speaking, she replied: 'O gracious prince, the pleasure you afforded me by your account of all the wonderful and surprising things which you first described, was much lessened by the terror I felt when my imagination pictured you careering through the highest regions of the air; and although I have now the happiness of seeing you before me in perfect safety, yet my agitation did not cease till you told me that the Indian's horse was come to alight on the terrace of my palace. The descent of the enchanted horse might have happened in any one of a thousand different places; and I am delighted that chance should have given me the preference, and at the same time afforded me the opportunity of telling you, that although you might have been guided to some other spot, you would never have been received with more pleasure, or experienced a more heart-felt welcome than shall be yours here.

"'I should therefore feel hurt and offended, prince, if I believed that you seriously considered yourself in the light of my slave, as you just now represented yourself. I attribute that expression to your politeness, rather than to your sincerity; and the reception you met with on your arrival ought to convince you that you are as free and unfettered here as in the midst of the Persian court.

"'Concerning your heart,' added the princess, in a tone which denoted nothing but pleasure and affection, 'as I am fully persuaded that you have not reserved the disposal of it till the present time, and that, doubtless, you have made choice of a princess who deserves your regard, I should be sorry to be the cause of your inconstancy to her.'

"Prince Firouz Schah was going to make the most solemn protestations to the Princess of Bengal that no object had yet occupied his heart; but at the instant when he was beginning to speak, one of the princess's attendants came to acquaint them that dinner was served. This interruption relieved the prince and princess from the necessity of an explanation which would have been equally embarrassing to both. The princess retained a perfect conviction of the sincerity of the prince; and although she had not

PRINCE FIROUZ SCHAH DECLARES HIS LOVE FOR THE PRINCESS OF BENGAL.

explained herself, he nevertheless judged, from the nature of her answer and the favourable manner in which she had listened to him, that he had every reason to be satisfied with his prospect of success.

"The woman who had announced the dinner held the door open, that they might pass through. The princess, as she rose from her seat, said to Firouz Schah, who followed her example, that she did not usually dine at so early an hour, but as she feared he had made but a bad supper, she had ordered the meal to be served sooner than was customary. With these words she conducted him into a magnificent saloon, where a table stood ready, covered with great abundance of excellent dishes. They took their places, and as soon as they had seated themselves, a number of the female slaves belonging to the princess, most richly dressed and of great beauty, began a delightful concert of instrumental and vocal music, which continued during the whole of the repast.

"As the music was soft and sweet, and was managed so as not to interrupt any conversation between the prince and princess, they passed a great part of the repast, the lady in helping the prince and inviting him to eat, and he on his part in serving the princess with whatever he thought the best. He endeavoured to ingratiate himself by his words and actions, and his civilities drew fresh smiles and compliments from the princess; and in this reciprocal commerce of attention and civilities, love made much greater progress than if the interview had been premeditated.

"At length they rose from the table, and the Princess of Bengal led Prince Firouz Schah into a grand and magnificent room, superbly embellished with gold and azure, and furnished in the richest style of elegance. They sat on a sofa, which faced the garden of the palace, the beauty of which struck Prince Firouz Schah, from the uncommon variety of the flowers, shrubs, and trees, all different from those that grow in Persia, yet not inferior to them. Availing himself of the opportunity which this subject afforded him of beginning a conversation with the princess, he said, 'Till now I supposed that no country in the world, except Persia, could boast of superb palaces and beautiful gardens worthy of the majesty of kings. But I now perceive, that wherever there are great and powerful monarchs, they build themselves habitations in character with their grandeur and power; and although these palaces may differ in the construction and decorations, they resemble each other in splendour and magnificence.'

"'O gracious prince,' replied the Princess of Bengal, 'as I have no idea of the palaces in Persia, I can form no judgment of the comparison you make between those and mine, and cannot therefore deliver my opinion; but however sincere you may be, I can scarcely persuade myself that your assertion is just: you must allow me to suppose that politeness has some share in what you say. I will not lessen my palace in your estimation; you have too much taste and discernment not to judge of it as it deserves; but I assure you I think little of its splendour, when I compare it with that of the king my father, which infinitely surpasses it in beauty, richness, and grandeur. You will tell me your opinion of my father's palace when you have seen it. As chance has brought you so far as the capital of this kingdom, I doubt not you will wish to see the king my father, and pay your compliments to him, that he may have an opportunity of showing you those attentions which are due to a prince of your rank and merit.'

"By exciting in the Prince of Persia a degree of curiosity to see the palace of Bengal and to be introduced to the king her father, the princess flattered herself that her father might, when he saw a prince of so elegant an appearance, so clever, and so accomplished in every estimable quality, be induced to propose an alliance by offering her to him in marriage; and as she felt quite certain that she was not indifferent to the prince, and that such an alliance would bring happiness to herself, she hoped by these means to attain the completion of her wishes, still preserving that decorum of conduct necessary in a princess who was desirous of appearing submissive to the commands of her father. But the Prince of Persia did not make that reply to this proposal which she expected from him.

"'Beautiful princess,' he said, 'the preference you have just given to the palace of the King of Bengal over your own, and the manner in which you deliver your opinion, convince me of the sincerity of your words. With regard to the proposal you make me of paying my respects to the king your father, I must reply, that it would be not only a great pleasure to me, but an honour also, to acquit myself of what I should conceive my duty. But,' added he, 'I leave you to judge, fair princess, whether it would be advisable for me to present myself before the throne of so great a monarch, in the guise of a mere chance traveller, without any attendants or equipage suitable to my rank.'

"'Let not that circumstance occasion you a moment's uneasiness,' replied the princess. 'You have only to give utterance to your wishes, and money shall not be wanting to procure you whatever train of attendants you may desire, and I will furnish you with whatever sum you may want. There are many merchants here of your nation; you may therefore procure anything you may judge necessary to make an appearance that will do you credit, and be in character with your situation in life.'

"Prince Firouz Schah easily divined the intention of the princess, and the undoubted proof of her affection which she by these means evinced augmented the love he felt for her; but notwithstanding the increasing violence of his passion, he did not give way to it so as to forget the line of conduct he ought to observe. He replied without the least hesitation, 'My beautiful princess, I should most willingly accept the obliging offer you have made me, and for which I cannot sufficiently express my gratitude, were I not sensible that the anxiety the king my father must feel at my absence, requires my immediate return. I should be unworthy of the tenderness and affection he has always shown towards me, if I did not go back to him immediately, to remove the apprehensions he must naturally feel for my safety. I know his character well; and I feel convinced that while I have the happiness of enjoying the society of the most amiable of princesses, he is plunged in the deepest affliction, without any hope of ever seeing me more. I trust you will do me the justice to allow that I cannot, without being guilty of the blackest ingratitude, for a moment defer the duty of returning to him, to restore him to happiness and perhaps life, of which a protracted absence might deprive him. After that, too lovely princess,' continued he, 'if you should esteem me worthy of becoming your husband, as the king my father has always declared that he would not oppose my choice of a wife, I shall have no difficulty in obtaining his consent to come back again, not as an unknown wanderer, but as the Prince of Persia, bearing a proposal from my father to contract an alliance with the King of Bengal, by means of our union. I am convinced the king my father will readily accede to my wishes, when I have informed him of the generous manner in which you received me in my misfortunes.'

"When the prince had thus explained his sentiments, the Princess of Bengal was too fully satisfied with the justice of them to insist any further on his staying for an introduction to her father, or to propose anything that might be inconsistent with his duty and honour; she was nevertheless alarmed at the idea of the sudden departure he seemed to meditate, and she feared that, if he left her so soon, absence might efface from his memory the impression her beauty had made, and he would forget to fulfil his promise.

"To avert this intention, therefore, she said to him, 'In making you a proposal, prince, to contribute whatever might be necessary to place you in a position suited to your rank, as a preparative to your introduction to my father, I did not mean to oppose so reasonable an excuse as that you have just alleged, and which I had not considered. I should indeed be an accomplice in the error you would commit, could I entertain such a wish; yet I cannot give my approbation to your intention of returning to your own country so soon as you propose. At least grant one favour to my earnest entreaties: allow yourself time to become in some degree acquainted with this country; and since my good fortune has decreed that you have alighted in the kingdom of Bengal, in preference to descending in a desert, or on the summit of some steep rock, from whence you could not have reached the habitable world, I request you to remain here a sufficient time, that you may carry away with you to the court of Persia an accurate account of the country we inhabit.'

"The Princess of Bengal gave this turn to her discourse, that the prince might be persuaded to continue with her for some time; for she hoped that, becoming by insensible degrees more passionately attached to her person and charms, the strong desire he entertained of returning to Persia might decrease, and that then he would determine to appear in public, and be presented to the King of Bengal. He could not refuse the favour she requested, after the kind reception he had met with from her. He consented, and the princess had now no desire but to render his residence with her as agreeable as possible, by all the variety of amusements she could devise.

"For several days nothing was thought of but entertainments, balls, concerts, magnificent feasts, parties of pleasure in the gardens, and hunting expeditions in the park belonging to the palace, where there were all sorts of animals to furnish that diversion, such as stags, hinds, roebucks, and other kinds of creatures peculiar to the country of Bengal, which were not savage enough to render the chase so dangerous that the princess could not join in it.

"When the hunt was over, the prince and princess met in some beautiful spot in the park, where a large carpet was spread for them, with cushions placed on it, that they might sit more commodiously. There resting from their fatigue, and enjoying themselves after the violent exercise they had taken, they conversed upon various subjects. The Princess of Bengal always endeavoured to lead the topic to the greatness, the power, and the riches of the kingdom of Persia, that she might, in reply to the assertions of Prince Firouz Schah, enlarge on the advantages possessed by the kingdom of Bengal, and thus persuade him to remain; but the event turned out contrary both to her wishes and expectation.

"Speaking simply and truly, and without the least exaggeration, the Prince of Persia gave her such an advantageous account of the power, the magnificence, and opulence that reigned in his father's dominions—such a picture of its military force, of its commerce, extending both by sea and land to the most distant countries—such a view of the multitude of its large cities, all nearly as populous as that in which he had fixed his residence, containing palaces, richly furnished, and ready for his immediate reception, according to the different seasons of the year, so that he might enjoy a perpetual spring—in short, he related so many wonders of his native country, that before he had concluded, the princess began to consider the kingdom of Bengal as infinitely inferior to that of Persia in almost every point. And when he requested her in return to speak of the riches of her father's kingdom, she could not be prevailed on for a considerable time to comply.

"At length, however, she consented to gratify the curiosity of Prince Firouz Schah, but without sufficiently enlarging on the superiority which Bengal in some instances possessed over Persia. She so plainly evinced by her conversation that she should feel no reluctance to accompany him, that he concluded she would consent to the first proposal of that nature which he should make to her. He did not, however, think it proper to mention such a thing until he had remained with her long enough, that he might cast the blame on her if she expressed a wish to detain him still longer, and endeavoured to prevent his fulfilling the manifest duty of returning to the king his father.

"For two whole months Prince Firouz Schah entirely devoted himself to the wishes of the princess. He took part in all the amusements she so amply provided for him, with as much eagerness as if he had been destined to pass his whole life with her in the same round of diversion. But when the two months had elapsed, he took an opportunity of declaring to her in the most serious terms that he had too long neglected his duty, and begged her to grant him permission to follow the dictates of filial affection, at the same time repeating his promise that he would return immediately with a retinue worthy of his dignity and of hers, to demand her in marriage, according to the usual forms, of the King of Bengal.

"'Beautiful princess,' added he, 'perhaps, from the request I have made, you are inclined to doubt my promises, and already place me in the list of those false lovers who, when no longer present, dismiss the object of their affection from their hearts; but as a certain proof of the strong and sincere love I feel for you, and of my wish to escape the unhappiness of prolonged absence from so amiable a princess as yourself, I would fain ask the favour of conducting you with me, did I not fear that such a proposal might offend you and meet a refusal.'

"Prince Firouz Schah perceived that the princess blushed at the last words he uttered, and that, without showing any symptoms of anger, she hesitated what answer to make. He therefore continued to urge his request. 'Beloved princess,' said he, 'if you have any doubt of my father's consent to our union, and of the satisfaction which he will feel at

THE JOURNEY OF PRINCE FIROUZ SCHAH AND THE PRINCESS OF BENGAL.

the prospect of my alliance with you, allow me to dispel them. As for the King of Bengal, after all the proofs of affection, tenderness, and regard he has always shown and still continues to show towards you, he would not be the kind father you have described to me—indeed, he would be the enemy of your happiness and peace—if he did not receive with kindness and good-will the embassy my father will send him to obtain his approbation and consent to our marriage.'

"The Princess of Bengal made no reply to the Prince of Persia; but her silence and her downcast eyes convinced him, more than the most formal declaration, that she was not opposed to his proposal, and consented to accompany him into Persia. The only difficulty which presented itself to her imagination was the fear that the prince was not sufficiently experienced in the management of his horse; and she was apprehensive of meeting with embarrassments similar to those which had happened to him when he made his first trial. But Prince Firouz Schah soon dissipated all her fears, by assuring her that she might safely trust to him, and that, after what had happened, he defied even the Indian himself to manage the horse with more skill and address. She now, therefore, thought only of taking proper measures for her departure; and she made her preparations with so much secresy that no one in the palace had the slightest suspicion of her design.

"The next morning, a little before break of day, while all the inhabitants of the palace were sunk in the most profound repose, she repaired to the terrace with the prince. He turned the horse towards Persia, and placed it in such a position that the princess could easily mount behind him. He mounted first, and when his companion had seated herself conveniently, and taken his hand for greater safety, she gave the signal for departure. He instantly turned the same peg he had made use of in the capital of Persia, and the horse rose at once into the air.

"The horse went with his usual swiftness; and Prince Firouz Schah guided it with so much skill, that in the course of two hours and a half he could discern the capital of Persia. He did not descend in the great square from whence he had departed, nor even in the palace of the king, but in a sort of country house, at a little distance from the city. He led the princess into the most beautiful apartment of the palace, and told her that in order to secure to her those honours and that respect which were due to her rank, he would immediately go to the king his father, and acquaint him with her arrival, and that he would then return again presently; in the meantime he gave orders to the steward of the palace, who was present, to furnish everything that the princess could possibly require.

"Having left the princess in this apartment, Prince Firouz Schah desired the steward to get a horse saddled for him. When the horse was produced, he mounted it, and sent the steward to attend on the princess, with express orders to prepare a breakfast of the greatest delicacies he could procure. Then he set off to present himself before his father. As he passed along the road, and the streets which led to the palace, he was received by the people with every demonstration of joy; for they had despaired of ever seeing him again, and had mourned him as dead. The king his father was giving audience, and was surrounded by his council. All the members, as well as the king himself, were in mourning dresses, which they had worn from the time of the prince's disappearance, when he suddenly presented himself before them. His father received him with the most tender embraces, shedding tears of joy and surprise; and immediately inquired, with visible anxiety, what was become of the Indian's horse.

"This question afforded the prince an opportunity of relating to the king all the dangers and perils he had encountered after the horse rose with him into the air. He told how he had escaped, by alighting on the palace of the Princess of Bengal, and the friendly reception he had met with from her. He did not conceal the motives which had induced him to prolong his absence from home for a longer period than was proper, had he consulted his duty alone; and enlarged on the desire the princess had shown in every instance to oblige him, so far as even to consent to accompany him into Persia, after he had given her his solemn promise to marry her. 'And, my honoured father,' continued the prince, as he finished this account, 'I at the same time assured her of your consent to our union; and I have brought her with me on the Indian's horse. I left her in one of the palaces belonging to your majesty, where she is anxiously awaiting my return, to announce to her that I have not reckoned in vain on your kindness and affection.'

"At these words the prince was about to prostrate himself at the feet of the king his father, to prevail on him to grant his request; but the king prevented him, and embracing him a second time, exclaimed, 'My son, I not only give my consent to your marrying the Princess of Bengal, but I will go to visit her myself, and thank her in person for the obligations I am under to her; then I will conduct her to my palace, where your nuptials shall be celebrated this very day.' The king thereupon gave orders to prepare for the arrival of the Princess of Bengal, and commanded that the mourning should be discontinued, and public rejoicings immediately commence, to the sound of drums, trumpets, and other warlike instruments; after which he desired that the Indian should be released from prison and conducted before him.

"His orders were instantly obeyed; and when the Indian appeared, he said to him, 'I had secured thy person, that thy life, which would scarcely have been a sacrifice adequate either to my grief or my rage, might have atoned for that of the prince my son. Return thanks to Heaven for having restored him to me. Go, take thy horse, and never appear again in my sight.'

"When the Indian had left the presence of the King of Persia, he heard from those who had released him from prison that Prince Firouz Schah had returned with a princess, whom he brought with him on the enchanted horse. He was told where the prince had alighted and left the princess, and that the sultan was preparing to go to her, and conduct her to his palace. The Indian did not hesitate to take advantage of this intelligence. Without losing a moment's time, he repaired to the country palace with so much diligence, that he reached it before the King and the Prince of Persia. Addressing himself to the steward of the palace, he told him that he had come by order of the King and the Prince of Persia, to carry the Princess of Bengal on the enchanted horse through the air to the king, who, he said, was waiting to receive her in the great square before his palace, that his whole court and the people of Schiraz might witness the spectacle of her arrival.

"The steward knew the Indian, and was also aware of the fact of his arrest and imprisonment; therefore, seeing him now at liberty, he readily believed his story. He presented him to the princess, who, when she was told that the Indian came by order of the Prince of Persia, at once consented to do what she thought was her lover's wish. The Indian, delighted with the success of his wicked scheme, mounted the horse, and the princess took her place behind him with the assistance of the steward. He turned the peg, and instantly the horse rose with him and the princess to an immense height in the air.

"At this instant, the King of Persia, accompanied by his whole court, came forth out of the palace, to repair to the residence in which the princess had been left; Prince Firouz Schah preceding him, that he might arrive first and prepare the princess for his father's visit. The Indian, to show his scorn of the anger of the king and the prince, and to revenge himself for what he conceived the unjust treatment he had experienced, passed over the city with his victim, in full view of those who were assembled below.

"When the king perceived the Indian's design, which he could not mistake, he remained transfixed at a sight which utterly overwhelmed him with affliction and grief, heightened by the reflection that it would not be possible to make the Indian repent of the flagrant affront he thus publicly offered to the royal dignity. He uttered a thousand imprecations on him; and all who were spectators of this signal insult and unparalleled wickedness sympathised in his anger. The Indian was not much affected by all these maledictions, which he distinctly heard as he pursued his course through the air; and the king was at length obliged to return to his palace, extremely mortified at the injury he had sustained, and at his own utter inability to punish the author of it.

"But the grief of Prince Firouz Schah cannot be described when he beheld the Indian bearing away from him his adored princess, who was the only hope of his life, without being able to rescue her from his power. At this unexpected sight he remained motionless. And whilst he was deliberating whether he should vent his despair in reproaches on the perfidy of the Indian, or in lamentations on the deplorable fate of the princess, or in imprecations on himself for the want of precaution he had shown towards her who had so fully proved the sincerity of her love by resigning herself entirely to his care, the horse continued its progress with inconceivable rapidity, and soon bore them both far out of their view. He knew not what course to adopt. Should he return to the palace of his father, shut himself up in his apartment to give loose to his affliction, and resign all intention of pursuing the ravisher, to deliver the princess from his hands, and punish him as he deserved? His generosity, his courage, his love forbade it. Lost in mournful thought, he bent his way towards the country palace where the princess had been left.

"On the appearance of the prince, the steward, who was by this time aware how credulous he had been, and how he had been deceived by the Indian, presented himself before his master with tears in his eyes, and throwing himself at his feet, began to accuse himself of the crime he had committed, and preparing for the death he expected from the prince's hand.

"'Rise,' said the prince to him: 'I do not impute the loss of my princess to you; I impute it to my own thoughtless imprudence alone. Lose no time, but go instantly to procure me the dress of a dervish, and be careful not to let it be suspected that I have sent you.'

"At a little distance from the country palace, there was a building inhabited by a community of dervishes, whose scheik, or superior, was a friend of the steward's. The steward, therefore, went to him, and pretending to entrust him with a profound secret, informed him that an officer of considerable distinction at court, to whom he was under great obligations, had incurred the displeasure of the king, and that he wished to give him an opportunity of escaping his sovereign's revenge. The steward easily obtained what he required, and returned to the prince with the complete dress of a dervish. Prince Firouz Schah took off his own garments, put on the dervish's habit, and thus disguised, he took with him, to defray the expenses of the journey he was now going to undertake, a box of pearls and diamonds, which he had previously provided as a present for the Princess of Bengal, and left the country palace at the approach of night, uncertain what road to travel, yet fully resolved not to return until he had found his princess.

"Meanwhile the Indian directed the course of the enchanted horse so successfully, that he arrived on the same day, and at an early hour, in a wood adjoining the capital of the kingdom of Cashmere. As he began to feel the pangs of hunger, and supposed that the princess might also be in want of refreshment, he dismounted in this wood, on an open lawn, where he left the princess near a little stream of cool transparent water.

"During the absence of the Indian, the Princess of Bengal, who now found herself in the possession of a worthless robber, whose further proceedings she justly dreaded, conceived the project of making her escape, and seeking a refuge from his power; but as she had eaten a very slight meal that morning on her arrival at the country palace of the King of Persia, she found herself so weak, that she was obliged to relinquish her design of concealing herself, and had no resource but in her courage and fortitude, resolving to suffer death rather than be faithless to Prince Firouz Schah. She did not, therefore, wait for the Indian to give her a second invitation to partake of what he placed before her. She satisfied her hunger, and soon recovered her strength sufficiently to be able to answer with courage and firmness the insolent speeches which he addressed to her towards the end of the repast. At length the menaces of the Indian, who strove to work upon her fears, terrified her to such a pitch that she rose, uttering at the same time loud and repeated cries. Her shrieks immediately drew to the spot a body of horsemen, who surrounded both her and the Indian.

"These horsemen were the Sultan of Cashmere and his attendants, who were returning from hunting, and, fortunately for the Princess of Bengal, passed that way, and were attracted by the sounds they had heard. The sultan addressed himself to the Indian, demanded his name, and what he was doing to the lady who was with him. The Indian boldly replied that she was his wife, and no one had any right to interfere in the quarrel that existed between them.

"The princess, who was ignorant of the rank and quality of the person who so opportunely presented himself for her deliverance, contradicted the Indian's assertion. 'O kind stranger,' said she, 'whoever you may be, whom Heaven sends to my relief, have pity on an unfortunate princess, and do not give credit to the words of an impostor. Heaven preserve me from ever being the wife of so worthless and contemptible a wretch. He is a wicked magician, who has this day forcibly carried me away from the Prince of Persia, to whom I was betrothed; and he has brought me hither on this enchanted horse.'

"The Princess of Bengal had no occasion to say anything more to convince the Sultan of Cashmere that she spoke the truth: her beauty, her majestic demeanour, and her tears were powerful advocates in her favour. She was going to proceed in her petition, but instead of waiting to hear more, the sultan, justly irritated by the insolence of the

THE PEOPLE REJOICING.

Indian, ordered his attendants to surround him, and to cut off his head without delay. This order was executed the more readily as the Indian had carried off the princess immediately after his release from prison, and had therefore no arms about him for his defence.

"The princess, being thus delivered from the persecution of her cruel enemy, was destined to undergo another trial, not less afflicting to her feelings. The sultan ordered her a horse, and conducted her to his palace, where he allotted for her use the most magnificent apartment in the building, excepting that which he himself inhabited. He gave her a number of female slaves to attend upon and serve her, and some eunuchs for a guard. He led her himself to this apartment, and without allowing her time to thank him as she had intended for the favour he had conferred on her, he said, 'O beautiful princess, I doubt not that you must be in want of rest; I therefore leave you to repose:

to-morrow you will be better able to relate to me the circumstances of the singular adventure that has befallen you.' And having spoken these words, he retired.

"The Princess of Bengal felt inexpressible satisfaction at finding herself delivered from the hateful persecutions of a man whom she could not regard but with horror and disgust; and she flattered herself that the Sultan of Cashmere would complete the generous action he had begun, by sending her back to the Prince of Persia, when she should have informed him in what manner she was affianced to Prince Firouz Schah, and requested him to confer this favour on her. But she utterly failed in obtaining the accomplishment of that wish which her delusive hopes presented as certain of fulfilment.

"In fact, the Sultan of Cashmere had determined to marry her on the following day; and he had ordered the usual rejoicings to be announced at the break of day by trumpet, kettle-drums, and other instruments calculated to inspire mirth and joy, which resounded not only in the palace, but throughout the whole city. The princess was awakened by these tumultuous sounds, though she little suspected the true cause of the noise that disturbed her rest. But when the sultan, who had desired to be informed when she would be ready to receive his visit, had paid his compliments and inquired after her health, had begun to acquaint her that the trumpets were flourishing in honour of the nuptials which were to be solemnised, and to which he hoped she would not object, she was seized with such surprise and consternation that she fainted away.

"The princess's women, who were present, ran to her assistance, and the sultan also exerted himself to restore her to life; but she remained for a considerable time quite insensible. At length she began to recover; but being determined to perish rather than be faithless to Prince Firouz Schah, by consenting to the marriage which the sultan had prepared without even consulting her, she pretended that her senses were disordered by the shock she had sustained. She immediately began to say the most extravagant things to the sultan, and even seemed ready to tear him to pieces. This sudden change surprised and afflicted him beyond expression; and as he found she continued in the same state of insanity, he left her with her attendants, whom he desired to pay her every attention, and take the greatest care of her. During the day he sent frequently to inquire after her health, and every time was told either that she continued in the same state, or that the disease increased rather than diminished. Towards evening she grew much worse, so that the Sultan of Cashmere did not pass that night so happily as he had expected.

"Not only on the morrow, but on every succeeding day, the Princess of Bengal continued to show, alike in her conversation and actions, strong symptoms of a disordered mind; the sultan therefore was at last reduced to the necessity of assembling the physicians belonging to the court, to inform them of this unfortunate malady, and ask them if they knew of any remedies that would effect a cure.

"The physicians, after a long consultation among themselves, agreed in replying that there were several kinds and degrees of this malady, some of which, according to their nature, might be overcome, while others were incurable; and they declared that they could not judge to what class the disorder of the Princess of Bengal might belong unless they saw her. The sultan then ordered the eunuchs to conduct the physicians into the chamber of the princess, one at a time, according to their rank.

"The princess had foreseen this circumstance, and was apprehensive that if she suffered the physicians to approach her and feel her pulse, even the most inexperienced of them would soon discover that she was in perfect health, and that her insanity was only feigned. Therefore, as soon as they made their appearance, she began to show such violent marks of aversion, endeavouring to tear their faces if they came near her, that not one had the courage to expose himself to her fury.

"Some who pretended more profound skill in their profession than the rest, and boasted of being able to judge of diseases by only seeing the patient, ordered the princess certain potions, which she made no objection to swallow, as she well knew that it was in her own power to continue her feigned madness as long as she pleased, and while she found it answer her purpose, and that these remedies, therefore, could not do her any material injury.

"When the Sultan of Cashmere found that the physicians belonging to the palace did not effect a cure, he employed certain others who practised in the city, and were very celebrated for their skill and experience; but these were equally unsuccessful. He then sought out men who were renowned for a perfect knowledge of the healing art in the different cities and towns in his kingdom; but the princess did not give them a better reception than she had vouchsafed to the first who presented themselves, and all their prescriptions failed to produce any beneficial effect. At length, the sultan dispatched messengers to all the neighbouring courts and states, with formal invitations to be distributed to the most famous physicians in each, and a promise of paying the expenses of the journey for such as would repair to the capital of Cashmere, and of a princely recompense to him who should effect the cure of the princess. Several physicians undertook the journey, but not one could boast of being more successful than those who had first applied, or of effecting the recovery of the princess; an event which did not depend either on them or their skill, but which was entirely in the power of the princess herself.

"In the meantime, Prince Firouz Schah, disguised under the habit of a dervish, had traversed several provinces, and visited the principal cities in each, searching for his beloved princess. The bodily fatigue he endured was increased by the affliction of his mind, as he was uncertain whether he might not be travelling in a course directly opposite to that which he ought to have taken to obtain the information he sought.

"Listening earnestly to the passing news of the day in each place he visited, he at length arrived at a large city in the Indies, where the general conversation seemed to turn on a Princess of Bengal, who had lost her senses on the very day which the Sultan of Cashmere had appointed for the celebration of his nuptials with her. The name of the Princess of Bengal attracted his notice; and concluding she must be the person he was in search of—which appeared to him the more probable, from his not having heard of there being any other princess at the court of Bengal excepting the one who was betrothed to him—he determined, on the slight information he could obtain concerning her, to bend his way immediately to the capital of the kingdom of Cashmere. On reaching that city he took up his abode in a khan, where he learnt, on the very day of his arrival, the whole story of the Princess of Bengal, and the deservedly tragical end of the criminal Indian who had brought her on the enchanted horse. The latter circumstance fully convinced him that this was the princess he had so anxiously endeavoured to find, and that the sums the sultan expended for her recovery were useless, as he did not doubt her madness to be feigned.

"After obtaining all the necessary information on these various points, the Prince of Persia ordered a physician's dress to be made for him on the next day; and this disguise, which accorded with the long beard he had suffered to grow during his journey, enabled him to pass for a man of that profession as he walked along the streets. The impatience he felt to see his princess would not allow him to defer his appearance at the palace of the sultan, where he asked to speak to one of the officers. He was conducted to the chief of the ushers, and addressing himself to him, remarked that it might possibly be considered as great temerity in him to present himself as a physician who wished to attempt the cure of the princess, after so many had tried without success; but that he flattered himself he might be able, by means of certain specific remedies, the efficacy of which he had experienced, to effect what had hitherto been attempted in vain. The chief of the officers told him he was welcome, and the sultan would receive him with pleasure; adding that if he could succeed in procuring the monarch the satisfaction of seeing the princess in perfect health, he might rely on receiving a recompense worthy of the liberality of the sultan. 'Wait for me here,' added he: 'I will be with you in a moment.'

"Some time had elapsed since any physician had presented himself; and the Sultan of Cashmere, with inexpressible sorrow, found himself deprived of all hopes of seeing the princess restored to the state in which he first beheld her, and of proving to her the faithfulness of his love, by means of the nuptials he was so desirous to solemnize. When the officer, therefore, announced to him the arrival of another physician, he ordered that the stranger should be immediately conducted before him.

"The Prince of Persia was presented to the Sultan of Cashmere under the disguise and appearance of a physician; and the sultan, without wasting any time in preliminary remarks, acquainted him with the disorder of the Princess of Bengal, and that she could not endure the sight of a physician without a return of the violent paroxysms of insanity, which seemed to augment her disease. He then took the prince into a little verandah, or balcony, which looked into her apartment, from whence he could see through the lattice without being perceived.

"When Prince Firouz Schah was in the balcony, he beheld his beloved princess, seated in a negligent posture, and singing, with tears in her eyes, a song in which she deplored her unhappy destiny, which, perhaps, would deprive her for ever of the sight of him she so tenderly loved. Moved with compassion at the unhappy situation in which he found his princess, Prince Firouz Schah wanted no other proof to convince him that her derangement was only feigned, and that she enacted this afflicting part solely on his account. He went down from the closet, and after having spoken to the sultan on the nature of the princess's disorder, and assured him it was not incurable, he added, that to perform a cure it would be necessary that he should converse with her alone and without any witness; and that, so far from showing the violent symptoms she had hitherto given of her insanity when any physician approached her, he undertook to say that she would receive and listen to him with perfect calmness.

"The sultan ordered the door of the princess's chamber to be opened, and Prince Firouz Schah entered the apartment. So soon as the princess perceived him, taking him for a physician, from the dress he wore, she rose from her seat in a rage, using the most threatening and abusive language. This did not prevent him from approaching her; and when he had advanced near enough to be heard, as he wished what he uttered to be for her ear alone, he said to her in a low tone of voice, and with a respectful air, to render his assertion more credible, 'O beautiful princess, I am not a physician: recognise in me the Prince of Persia, who has come to restore you to liberty.'

"At the sound of his voice and the sight of the features of his face, which, notwithstanding the long beard the prince had suffered to grow, she recollected in a moment, the Princess of Bengal began to grow more calm, and immediately her countenance was brightened by the joy naturally created by the sudden appearance of the object she so ardently wished and yet despaired to behold. The agreeable surprise she experienced for some time deprived her of utterance, and allowed Prince Firouz Schah an opportunity of relating to her the despair in which he had been plunged at the moment he saw the Indian carrying her away from him before his very eyes. Then he spoke of the resolution he had immediately formed to abandon every other care, to wander in search of her through every quarter of the globe, and not to cease from his inquiries until he had found and saved her from the power of the miserable Indian. He then told her by what a fortunate accident he had at length, after a painful and fatiguing journey, succeeded in finding her in the palace of the Sultan of Cashmere. When he had concluded his narration, in as concise a manner as he could, he begged the princess to acquaint him with what had passed from the time of her disappearance to the moment when he was enjoying the happiness of speaking to her; saying that it was necessary he should be fully informed of the whole history, that he might take proper measures for releasing her from the tyrannous power of the sultan.

"The Princess of Bengal did not waste many words in her account of herself to the Prince of Persia, since she had only to relate in what manner she had been delivered from the violence of the Indian by the Sultan of Cashmere, as he was returning from the chase; but she added that she had been cruelly treated on the following day by the unexpected declaration the sultan made her, of his solemn intention to marry her on that very day, without having previously shown her any attention that could incline her heart towards him; a course of conduct so violent and tyrannical, that it had instantly caused her to faint away. On her recovery, she said, she saw no mode to adopt, except that

THE PRINCESS OF BENGAL.

which she had hitherto pursued, as the most likely to preserve her affections unmolested, for a prince to whom she had pledged her heart and faith; and she added that, had this scheme failed, she had resolved to die rather than resign herself to the sultan, whom she neither did nor ever could love.

"The princess had nothing more to add; and Prince Firouz Schah inquired if she knew what became of the enchanted horse after the death of the Indian. 'I know not,' replied she, 'what orders the sultan may have given concerning it; but after the wonders I related of it, it is not probable that he neglected to have it properly secured.'

"As Prince Firouz Schah did not doubt that the Sultan of Cashmere had carefully preserved the horse, he communicated to the princess his design of using it to convey them back again to Persia; and then, after consulting upon the measures proper to be pursued for the execution of their design, that nothing might impede its success, they agreed that on the following day the princess should dress herself in more elegant attire than she then wore, and that she should receive the sultan with unusual marks of distinction when Prince Firouz Schah should conduct him to her apartment, nevertheless still preserving her usual silence before him.

"The sultan expressed great pleasure when the Prince of Persia related to him how far his first visit to the princess had operated towards her recovery; and when on the succeeding day the princess received him in a manner which convinced him that the cure was rapidly advancing, he lauded his visitor as the first physician in the universe. Seeing her in this improved state, he told her how delighted he was at observing such indications of returning health; and after having exhorted her to attend implicitly to the directions of her able physician, that what he had so well begun might terminate successfully, he retired, without waiting for any answer from her.

"As the Prince of Persia had accompanied the sultan to the princess's apartment, he left it also with him, and as he went along, he asked the monarch if he might, without being deficient in the respect due to a sovereign ruler, inquire by what adventure a Princess of Bengal happened to be in the kingdom of Cashmere, so far distant from her own dominions, and without any of her family or attendants. He asked this question as if he had been totally ignorant of the whole matter, that he might lead the conversation to the subject of the enchanted horse, and learn from the sultan's lips what was become of it.

"The sultan, who could not penetrate into the motive that induced the prince to make this inquiry, did not make any mystery of the affair. He repeated to his visitor the facts with which the Princess of Bengal had previously made him acquainted, adding that he had ordered the enchanted horse to be conveyed into his treasury as a rare curiosity, although he was ignorant of the secret by which it could be worked.

"'O mighty monarch,' replied the pretended physician, 'the information which your majesty has now imparted to me will furnish me with a method of completing the recovery of the princess. As she was brought here on this horse, which you say is enchanted, she has contracted something of that enchantment, which can only be dissipated by the use of certain perfumes with whose virtues I am acquainted. If your majesty chooses to enjoy, and to present to your court and the inhabitants of your capital, one of the most surprising spectacles that can be exhibited, you have only to order the horse to be brought into the middle of the square before your palace, and to leave the rest to me. I promise to produce to you and the whole assembly, in a few moments, the Princess of Bengal in as perfect mental and bodily health as she ever enjoyed in her life; and that this may be effected with all the pomp such an event requires, it is advisable that the princess should be dressed as magnificently as possible, and decorated with all the most precious jewels your majesty possesses.'

The sultan readily consented to do everything the prince proposed, and would have agreed to comply with more unusual demands to obtain the cure of the princess, which he now considered as near completion.

"On the following day the enchanted horse was by the sultan's orders taken out of the treasury, and placed at an early hour in the great square of the palace. The report was soon circulated through the city that preparations were making for an extraordinary spectacle that was to be exhibited there, and a crowd of beholders assembled from all quarters. The guards belonging to the sultan were ranged round the square to prevent any disorder, and to keep an open space near the horse.

"Presently the Sultan of Cashmere made his appearance; and when he had taken his place on a platform erected for that purpose, where he stood surrounded by the principal nobles and officers of his court, the Princess of Bengal, accompanied by the whole train of ladies whom the sultan had deputed to attend on her, approached the enchanted horse, and, with the assistance of her attendants, mounted it. When she was in the saddle, her foot in the stirrup, and the bridle in her hand, the pretended physician placed round the horse several little vessels full of incense, which he had ordered to be

WEDDING CHEER.

brought; and going round to each, he threw in a perfume composed of a variety of the most exquisite odours. After this, assuming a thoughtful air, with his eyes fixed on the ground, and his hands crossed on his breast, he walked three times round the horse, pretending to pronounce certain words; and at the instant when the vessels all emitted a thick smoke of a delicious fragrance, and the princess was so enveloped in the fumes as, with the horse, to be almost hidden, Prince Firouz Schah bounded on the enchanted steed behind the princess. He bent forward to turn the peg by which the horse was started, and as he mounted with the princess into the air, he pronounced the following words in a loud voice, and so distinctly that the sultan plainly heard them: 'O Sultan of Cashmere, when thou wouldst espouse princesses who implore thy protection, learn first to obtain their consent!'

"By this stratagem did the Prince of Persia deliver the Princess of Bengal from her imprisonment; and he conducted her on the same day, in a very short space of time, to the capital of Persia. But instead of alighting at the country palace, as he had previously done, he went into the middle of the palace, opposite to the king's apartment, where he dismounted. The King of Persia did not defer the solemnization of the nuptials longer than was requisite to make the necessary preparations for the wedding cheer; he then caused the ceremony to be performed with the utmost pomp and magnificence, that he might prove his entire concurrence in the marriage.

"When the number of days allotted for the rejoicings and festivities had elapsed, the king's first care was to prepare and dispatch a sumptuous embassy to the King of Bengal, to inform him of what had taken place, and to request his approbation and ratification of the alliance that he had formed with him by these nuptials. The King of Bengal, when informed of all the circumstances, was proud and happy to express his entire satisfaction."

The Sultana Scheherazade, having thus related the history of the enchanted horse, at once commenced the story of Prince Ahmed and the fairy Pari-Banou, which she told in the following words:

## THE HISTORY OF PRINCE AHMED AND THE FAIRY PARI-BANOU.

SULTAN, one of your majesty's predecessors, and who reigned in peace on the throne of India during many years, had in his old age the satisfaction of beholding around him three princes his sons, the worthy imitators of his virtues, and a princess, his niece, who was the ornament of his court. The eldest of the princes was named Houssain, the second Ali, the youngest Ahmed, and the princess bore the name of Nourounnihar.

"The Princess Nourounnihar was the daughter of a younger brother of the sultan, and her father had settled upon her a very considerable fortune. He died, however, a few years after his marriage, and left her an orphan while she was yet very young. The sultan, in consideration of that perfect brotherly affection which subsisted between them, and the sincere attachment the prince had always shown to his person, took charge of his niece's education, and caused her to be brought up in the palace with the three princes. To the possession of uncommon beauty, and every personal grace and accomplishment, this princess added an excellent understanding; and her kindness and virtue distinguished her among all the princesses of her time.

"The sultan, whose design was to provide a husband for the princess when she was of a proper age, and thus to form an alliance with some neighbouring prince, was very seriously thinking on this subject, when he discovered that all the three princes, his sons, were desperately in love with their fair cousin. This gave him great unhappiness; but his sorrow arose not so much from the fact that their attachment would prevent the alliance he had in contemplation, as from the difficulty he foresaw in effecting an agreement between them, and persuading the two younger to resign their claims to the eldest. He talked to each of the princes in private; and after remarking that it was impossible for one princess to be married to them all, and pointing out the troubles they would occasion by persisting in their passion, he used every argument to persuade them either to submit to the choice which the princess herself might make in favour of one of the three, or

THE SULTAN ADDRESSING HIS SONS.

to relinquish their pretensions, and look out for some other connection, which they should be free to make, and agree among themselves to consent to their cousin's marriage with some foreign prince. But as in each of his sons he had met with an unconquerable obstinacy, he assembled them all three before him, and thus addressed them: 'O my children, since, when I spoke for the advantage and tranquillity of you all, I did **not** succeed in persuading you to think no more about marrying the princess your cousin, and as I am not inclined to use my authority in giving her to one in preference to the other two, I have endeavoured to find a way to satisfy you, and to preserve that union which ought to subsist among you. Therefore attend to me, and listen to what I shall now recommend. I think it advisable that you should go upon your travels each into a different country, so that it shall be impossible for you to meet; and as you know I take great interest in everything that is curious, rare, or singular, I promise the hand of the princess my niece to him who shall bring me the most extraordinary and the most singular rarity: thus, as chance will direct your judgment in estimating the value of the things you shall bring, when you come to compare them fairly together, you will have no difficulty in doing one another justice, and giving the preference where it is due. To defray the expenses of travelling, and for the purchase of the curiosity you are to procure, I will give each of you a sum suitable to the dignity of your birth, but not enough to furnish a great equipage and a numerous retinue, which, by discovering your rank, would deprive you of that freedom which will be necessary to you, not only that you may accomplish the purpose of your journey, but also that you may have leisure to give due attention to whatever is worthy of observation; and, in short, that you may derive the greatest possible advantage from your travels.'

"As the three princes always conformed to the inclinations of the sultan their father, and as each flattered himself that he should be the person whom fortune would most favour, and that he would become the husband of the Princess Nourounnihar, they all testified their readiness to start without delay. The sultan immediately caused the sum he had promised to be paid them, and on that very day orders were given to make preparations for their journey. The princes took leave of the sultan, that they might be in readiness to set off very early the next morning. They went out together at one of the gates of the city, well mounted and equipped, dressed like merchants, each followed by a confidential attendant disguised like a slave, and they kept together till they arrived at the first inn, where the road separated into three, one of which each of them was to take by himself. At night, whilst they were refreshing themselves with the supper they had ordered, they agreed that they would travel during a year, and, after that time, meet again at the same place; and they further resolved that he who came first should wait for the other two, and that the two who met first should wait for the third; so that as they all three took leave of the sultan their father together, they should present themselves to him at once on their return. The next morning at daybreak, after having embraced, and wished one another an agreeable journey, they mounted their horses, and each took one of the three roads, without at all interfering with the other two.

"Prince Houssain, the eldest of the three brothers, who had often heard of the grandeur, strength, riches, and splendour of the kingdom of Bisnagar, took his route towards the Indian Sea; and, after a journey of three months—occasionally joining himself to a caravan—sometimes passing through barren deserts and mountainous tracts—at others, travelling through a country as well peopled, more fruitful, and better cultivated than any other part of the world—he at last arrived at Bisnagar, a city which gives its own name to the country of which it is the capital, and is the usual place of residence of the sovereigns of the land. He took up his abode in a khan appropriated to the reception of foreign merchants; and as he had learnt that there were four principal different divisions of the city, where the merchants of all descriptions had shops for their goods, while in the middle was placed the palace of the king, occupying a large extent of ground, forming as it were the centre of the city, which had three enclosures at least two leagues in length from one gate to the other, he went on the very next day to visit one of the three divisions.

"Prince Houssain could not behold this part without feeling great astonishment. It was of considerable extent, and consisted of streets intersecting each other, all arched over to keep off the heat of the sun; they were, however, very well lighted. The shops were perfectly regular in their architecture, and those belonging to merchants who traded in different kinds of goods were not mingled together, but each sort collected into one street. This was also the case in those streets which were inhabited by artificers or workmen.

"This multitude of shops, each filled with some particular kind of merchandise, such as the finest Indian linens of different sorts, some painted in the most brilliant colours, with figures, landscapes, trees, and flowers, all resembling nature; others with silk stuffs and brocades from Persia, China, and other places; others again with porcelain from Japan and China, and also floor-carpets of every size—all so much surprised him, that he knew not what to admire most. But when he came to the shops belonging to the goldsmiths and jewellers (for these two trades were carried on by the same persons), he was almost in an ecstacy at the profusion of fine works in gold and silver that greeted his view, and completely dazzled by the brilliancy of the diamonds, pearls, rubies, emeralds, sapphires, and other precious stones, which were exposed for sale in large quantities. But if he was so much struck with the riches collected in one part, he was much more surprised when he reflected what must be the wealth of the whole kingdom, as he knew that, except the Brahmins and ministers of the idols, who professed a retired life, free from the vanity of the world, there was not, through its whole extent, one person, either male or female, who had not collars, bracelets, or other ornaments for the feet and arms, made of pearls or other jewels, which produced the greater effect as the wearers were entirely black, a colour which set off these ornaments to great advantage.

"Another circumstance that very much attracted the attention of Prince Houssain, was the multitude of people he saw who sold roses, and who, from their numbers, absolutely crowded the streets. He perceived also that the Indians must be very fond of this flower, as he had not met one who did not either carry a blossom in his hand, or wear a wreath round his head; nor did he observe a merchant who had not several vases filled with them in his shop; so that this division, large and extensive as it was, was entirely perfumed by the fragrance of these beauteous flowers.

"After he had walked through every street in this quarter, meditating upon the immense quantity of riches that he saw, Prince Houssain felt the want of some repose. He expressed his wishes to a merchant, who very civilly invited him to come in and rest himself in his shop. The prince accepted this offer, and had not been long sitting in the merchant's abode, before he saw a crier going about with a carpet, about six feet square, in his hand, which he offered to put up for sale at thirty purses. Prince Houssain called to the crier, and desired to see this carpet, as it seemed to him that the man was demanding a most exorbitant price for it, considering its size and quality. When he had thoroughly examined the carpet, he said to the crier that he could not comprehend the reason why a piece of goods, so small and so indifferently made, should be put up at so high a price.

"The crier, who took Prince Houssain for a merchant, replied, 'O my master, if this sum appears to you unreasonable, you will be more astonished when I shall inform you that I am ordered not to let it go under forty purses, and not to deliver it till the money is paid.' 'Then certainly,' rejoined Prince Houssain, 'there must be some secret quality about the carpet that renders it so valuable.' 'You have guessed right,' said the crier; 'and you will understand the matter when you are informed that by only sitting upon this carpet you may be instantly transported, together with the carpet itself, to whatever place you wish to visit, and will find yourself in the desired spot almost in a moment, without being stopped by any obstacle whatever.'

"The prince, remembering that the principal object of his journey was to procure some extraordinary and especial rarity for the sultan his father, thought that he could not possibly meet with anything with which the sultan would be better pleased. 'If this carpet,' he said to the crier, 'has the power you say it possesses, I not only cease to think it dear, but I will give you the forty purses you demand, and will also make you such a present as shall amply satisfy you.' 'O stranger,' replied the crier, 'I assure you I have told you the truth; and it will be very easy for you to convince yourself of the fact, for as soon as you have determined on the purchase at forty purses, I will show you how to make the experiment. You probably have not the forty purses here, and I must accompany you to the khan, where, as a stranger, you have taken up your abode; therefore if the master of this shop will give us leave, we will retire into the back part of it; I will there spread out my carpet, and when we have both seated ourselves upon it, and you have expressed the wish to be transported to your lodging with me, if we are not instantly conveyed there, the bargain shall not stand, and you shall not be obliged to complete the purchase. With respect to the present you promise me, as the person who sells the carpet pays me for my trouble, I shall receive any gift as a favour which you may please to bestow upon me, and shall feel myself under a great obligation to you for it.'

"The prince believed the words of the crier, and accepted these conditions. He concluded the bargain according to the terms proposed; and then, having obtained the owner's leave, went into the back of the shop. The crier spread out the carpet, and they both seated themselves upon it. The prince had no sooner uttered the wish to be transported to his lodging in the khan, than he found himself with the crier in the very spot he had designated. He had no need of any further proof of the virtue of the carpet; he therefore counted out to the crier the forty purses of gold as the price of the carpet, and added twenty pieces more as a present.

"Great was Prince Houssain's joy at having thus fortunately, almost at the moment of his arrival at Bisnagar, obtained possession of a carpet of such rare and wonderful power, that he had not the least doubt that it would obtain for him the hand of the Princess Nourounnihar. In fact, he thought it impossible for either of his younger brothers to acquire anything in the course of their travels that could at all be put in competition with the rarity he had been fortunate enough to secure. By only sitting down on the carpet, he might have instantly returned to the spot at which the princes had agreed to meet; but he would then have been obliged to wait there a long time for them; and as he was desirous of seeing the King of Bisnagar and his court, and wished to gain some information concerning the strength, laws, customs, religion, and condition of the kingdom, he resolved to employ some months in satisfying his curiosity.

"The King of Bisnagar was accustomed to give an audience once every week to foreign merchants. It was under this character that Prince Houssain, who did not wish to proclaim his real rank, saw the monarch very frequently. And as the prince, besides being handsome and graceful, possessed a brilliant understanding, and was master of a good address and great politeness, he was very much distinguished beyond the other merchants with whom he came into the king's presence. To him, therefore, in preference to others, the king addressed his conversation when he wished to make inquiries about the Sultan of India, and to learn anything concerning the strength, riches, and government of his empire.

"On the other days the prince employed himself in visiting the most remarkable places in the city and in the neighbouring country. Among other things worthy of inspection, he found the temple of idols—a building exceedingly curious in its construction, from being entirely formed of bronze. It was not more than ten cubits square on the inside, and about fifteen high; but the most curious object within it was an idol of massive gold, as large as a man, with eyes formed of single rubies, and so artfully constructed that, on whatever side the spectator stood, they appeared to turn towards him. There was also another temple not less curious. This was built in a village situate in a plain of about ten acres in extent, which formed a delicious garden, filled with roses and other delightful flowers, the whole surrounded by a wall about four feet high, for the purpose of keeping out any animals that came near. In the middle of this plain there was a small terrace raised to about the height of a man, and formed of stones joined together with so much care and skill that the whole looked like one single piece. The temple, in the form of a dome, and erected in the middle of the terrace, was fifty cubits high, and could be seen at the distance of several leagues. The length of it was thirty cubits on one side, and twenty on the other; and the marble of which it was formed was quite red, and very highly polished. The vault of the dome was ornamented with three rows of paintings, finely executed, and in good taste. All the other parts of the temple were so completely filled with pictures, statues, and idols, that there was no vacant space from the top to the bottom where another could be put.

"Every morning and evening some superstitious ceremonies were performed here, followed by different games, instrumental concerts, dances, songs, and other festivities; and the priests belonging to the temple, and the inhabitants of the palace likewise, subsisted solely on the offerings which the pilgrims brought with them, who came in crowds from the most distant parts of the kingdom to fulfil their vows.

"Prince Houssain was also a spectator of a feast which is celebrated once a year at the court of Bisnagar, and to which the governors of provinces, the commanders of fortified places, the rulers and judges of cities, the Brahmins, who are celebrated for

THE MAGIC CARPET.

their tenets and learning, are all obliged to repair, although some of them live at such a distance that their journey does not occupy less than four months. The assembly, thus composed of an innumerable multitude of Indians, was held in a plain of vast extent, where the concourse formed so immense a body, that the eye could scarcely take them all in at once. In the centre of this great plain there was a particular enclosure of considerable extent, bounded on one side by a superb building, forming nine floors or storeys like a scaffold, and supported upon forty columns. This was set apart for the king and his court, and for those strangers whom the monarch honoured with an audience every week. The inside was handsomely ornamented and richly furnished; and the outside was covered with paintings of landscapes, in which were depicted every sort of animal, bird, and insect, even to flies and gnats, all most naturally executed. The other three sides were skirted by buildings four or five storeys high, and painted nearly alike. But the most singular fact concerning these buildings or scaffolds was, that they could be turned, and the different decorations changed from hour to hour.

"On each side of this place, and at a little distance from each other, there were ranged a thousand elephants, all most richly and profusely caparisoned; and upon the back of each was a square tower of gilt wood, containing musicians and buffoons. The trunks of these elephants and the cars were painted both in red and other colours, so that they presented the most grotesque figures.

"But what made Prince Houssain most admire the industry, address, and invention of these Indians was the sight of one of the largest and most powerful of the elephants standing with his feet placed upon four posts, driven perpendicularly into the ground, and about two feet high, and waving his trunk about in exact time with the musical instruments. Nor was he much less surprised at seeing another elephant, not less powerful, standing on the end of a beam, placed across a post ten feet high, with an immense stone fastened to the other end, which served to balance the animal's weight; and thus, sometimes rising in the air, and sometimes descending, the mighty quadruped, in the presence of the king and all his court, by different motions of his body and trunk marked the time and cadence of the music, as well as the other elephant had done. The way the Indians did this was by drawing down to the ground, by the power of men, one end of the beam, after they had fastened the stone as a balance on the other; and then they made the elephant get upon it.

"Had Prince Houssain been able to make a very long stay at the court and in the kingdom of Bisnagar, a variety of other curious things would have agreeably amused him there, until the end of the year, and till the day came on which the princes his brothers and himself had agreed to meet. Fully satisfied, however, with what he had seen, and occupied continually with the thoughts of Nourounnihar, the dear object of his affections, the recollection of whose beauty and charms, since the acquisition he had made of the carpet, every day augmented the violence of his passion, he fancied his mind would be much more at ease, and that he should feel much more happy, if he were only nearer to her. Having first, therefore, paid the master of the khan for the lodging he had occupied, and told him the hour when he might come for the key, which would be left in the door, he went back to his room, without giving any hint by what mode he meant to travel, shut the door, and left the key in it. He then spread out the carpet, and seated himself thereon, with the attendant whom he had brought with him, and having meditated for a moment, he in a very deliberate manner formed the wish to be conveyed to the spot where he and his brothers had agreed to assemble; and he soon perceived that he had arrived there. He resolved to stay where he was, and, without making himself known otherwise than as a merchant, to await the arrival of the two other princes.

"Prince Ali, the next younger brother of Prince Houssain, who intended to travel to Persia, in obedience to the wish of the sultan his father, had set out for that country in company with a caravan, which he had joined on the third day after he had taken leave of his brothers; and after a journey of nearly four months, he at length arrived at Schiraz, which at that time was the capital of the kingdom of Persia. As he had formed a sort of intimacy during the journey with a few merchants, without letting them suppose he was anything more than a jeweller, he took up his abode at the same khan with them.

"The next day, while the merchants were unpacking their bales of merchandise, Prince Ali, who only travelled for his pleasure, and who was encumbered only with the effects absolutely necessary to his comfort, first changed his dress, and then inquired his way to the quarter of the city where jewels, and gold and silver ornaments, brocades, silk stuffs, fine linens, and other kinds of curious and valuable merchandise were sold. This place, which was very spacious and well built, was arched over, and the roof supported by large pillars, round which, as well as along the walls, the shops were all ranged, and also on both sides within and without; and this place at Schiraz was called the Bezestein. Prince Ali examined it in every part, and, from the profusion of rich and costly merchandise exposed for sale, was enabled to judge of the quantity of riches the storehouses must contain. Among the different criers who went about with specimens of various things for sale by auction, he was very much surprised at seeing one man who held an ivory tube in his hand, about a foot long, and not more than an inch thick, which he put up at thirty purses. He imagined the crier must be mad; but in order to be satisfied of the fact, he went to a shop, and pointing the crier out to the merchant, he said, 'Tell me, am I deceived in concluding that yonder crier, who puts up the little ivory tube he has in his hand at thirty purses, is insane?' 'O my friend,' replied the merchant, 'if it be so, he has lost his senses since yesterday. For I can assure you he is one of our best criers, and one of the most employed, as we place the greatest confidence in him, whenever there is anything to be sold of greater value than common. With respect to the ivory tube which he cries at thirty purses, it certainly must be worth as much and even more, however extraordinary the fact may seem from its appearance. He will pass my door in a moment; we will then call him, and you may obtain from him any information you wish. Have the goodness in the meantime to sit down on my sofa, and rest yourself.'

"Prince Ali accepted the obliging offer of the merchant; and he had not been long seated before the crier passed by. The merchant immediately called the man by his name, and when he came up, he pointed to Prince Ali, and said, 'Inform this stranger whether you are in your senses, as, from your putting up that insignificant ivory tube at thirty purses, he has some doubts on the subject. I should myself be astonished at your proceedings, did I not know you to be a prudent, sensible man.' 'O my master,' replied the crier, addressing himself to Prince Ali, 'you are not the only person who supposes I have lost my senses, from the price at which I value this ivory tube; but you shall yourself judge if I am wrong when I have explained its properties to you; and I hope that you will then attend the sale, as several merchants will do who had the same opinion of me that you now have.

"'In the first place,' continued the crier, showing the tube to the prince, 'you will have the goodness to observe that this tube is furnished with a glass at each end; and I must inform you, that when you look through one of these two glasses, whatever you may feel a wish to see you will instantly behold.' 'I am ready to retract my opinion,' cried the prince, 'if you will prove the truth of your assertion.' As he held the tube in his hand, he examined it at both ends, and then added, 'Show me the end through which I must look, that I may be convinced.' The crier immediately did so; and the prince, looking through the tube, formed a wish to see the sultan his father, whom he instantly beheld in perfect health, sitting on his throne in the midst of his council. Then, as no human being, after the sultan, was dearer to him than the Princess Nourounnihar, he silently wished to behold her, and immediately she appeared through the tube seated at her toilet, surrounded by her women, and seemingly in the best health and spirits.

"Prince Ali now felt perfectly convinced that this tube was the most valuable and rare thing, not only in the city of Schiraz, but in the whole world; and he thought that if he neglected to purchase it, he should never again meet with so extraordinary an article, either at Schiraz or anywhere else in his travels, if he spent ten years or more in the search. He then said to the crier, 'I freely retract the bad opinion I had formed of your understanding, and I believe you will be fully satisfied of my sincerity, and of the reparation I am ready to make you, when I inform you that I am willing to purchase your tube. As I should be sorry that any one else should possess it, tell me the exact price the owner has fixed upon it; and then, without giving you the trouble of crying it any longer, or fatiguing yourself by going about with it, if you will accompany me to my lodging, I will count the sum out to you.' The crier assured him that he was ordered not to let the tube go under forty purses, and declared, if the prince had any doubt of the truth of what he said, he was ready to conduct him to the owner. The prince was satisfied with his word, and at once took him to conclude the purchase. When they had arrived at the khan where Prince Ali lodged, he counted out to the crier forty purses of gold, and was placed in possession of the ivory tube.

"When the prince had made this acquisition, he was joyful and triumphant, feeling certain that the princes his brothers could have met with nothing so rare or so deserving of admiration, and that the Princess Nourounnihar would therefore be his reward for the fatigues he had undergone. He now gave himself no further trouble, but spent his time in seeing and contemplating what was going on at the court of Persia, but without discovering his real character. He also visited whatever was curious and worthy of observation in and around Schiraz, until the caravan with which he came was about to return to India. He had almost satisfied his curiosity when the caravan was ready to depart. The prince immediately joined it, and began his journey. No accident disturbed or retarded his progress; and without suffering any other inconvenience than the fatigue inseparable from so long a journey, Prince Ali arrived in safety at the same place where his brother Houssain was waiting for him. The two brothers remained there together, impatiently expecting the arrival of Prince Ahmed.

"This prince had bent his course towards Samarcand; and on the day after his arrival there, he pursued the same plan which his two brothers had followed, and went to the Bezestein. He had hardly entered the place before he saw a crier carrying an artificial apple in his hand, which he put up at thirty-five purses. Prince Ahmed stopped the crier. 'Let me see this apple,' he cried, 'and tell me what particular excellence it possesses, that you should put it up at the very extraordinary price of thirty-five purses.' The crier gave the apple into the prince's hand that he might examine it. 'O stranger,' he said, 'this apple, if you only consider its external appearance, is of very little apparent value; but if you reflect upon its properties, and the great use that can be made of it for the good of mankind, you will confess that it is beyond all price, and that he who possesses it has acquired a true treasure. For there is no disease, however painful or dangerous, whether it be fever, pleurisy, plague, or any disorder whatever, even though the afflicted person be at the point of death, which it will not cure; and the sufferer shall be restored to as perfect a state of health as if he had never been ill during his whole life. And this is effected by the easiest of all possible ways, for you have simply to make the sick person smell at this apple.'

"'If the account you have been giving may be relied upon,' replied Prince Ahmed, 'this apple indeed possesses the most wonderful property, and you may truly call it invaluable; but can I, who really wish to make a purchase of it, be convinced that there is neither deception nor exaggeration in what you have been relating to me?' 'O my lord,' replied the crier, 'the fact is known and can be vouched for by the whole city of Samarcand; and without going a step farther, you have only to ask any of the merchants here, and you will hear what they say on the subject. You will even find some that would not have been alive to-day, as they themselves will declare to you, had it not been for the qualities of this apple. But to make you understand this thing, I must inform you that this wonderful production is the result of the study and long application of a celebrated philospher in this city, who has all his life devoted himself to investigating the virtues of plants and minerals, and who has at length arrived at the knowledge of the composition you now see, by which he has, in this city, performed the most surprising cures, the recollection of which will never be obliterated. An attack so sudden that he had not time to make use of this sovereign remedy, caused his death a short time since; and his widow, whom he has not left very well provided for, and who has several young children, is resolved to put it up for sale, that she and her family may be placed beyond the reach of want.'

"While the crier was giving the prince this account of the artificial apple, many people stopped and listened; and the majority of these confirmed everything he said. One of them presently mentioned that he had a friend who was so dangerously ill that he had given up all hopes of his life, and that this would be a favourable opportunity to try the power of the apple. Thereupon Prince Ahmed told the crier that he would give him forty purses if the smell of the apple cured the sick person. The crier, who had orders to sell it at the price offered by Prince Ahmed, replied, 'Let us go and make the experiment, and the apple shall be yours. I assert this with the greater confidence, because I cannot suppose it will have less efficacy now than it has hitherto possessed, every time it

THE THREE PRINCES AND THEIR TREASURES.

has been employed in rescuing, from the very jaws of death, those who in the extremity of sickness have tried its power.'

"The experiment succeeded, and the prince counted out the forty purses to the crier, who delivered the apple to him. Then he waited with the greatest impatience for the departure of the first caravan that should set out for India. He employed the intermediate time in exploring the city of Samarcand and the neighbouring country, particularly the Valley of Soyda, thus called from a river of the same name which waters it. This valley is reckoned by the Arabs as one of the four earthly paradises, from the beauty of the country, especially in the gardens belonging to the palace, from its universal fertility, and the delightful scenes this favoured region presents in the fine season of the year.

"Prince Ahmed, however, did not lose the opportunity of the very first caravan to return to India. He set out, and, surmounting all the inevitable inconveniences of so long a journey, arrived in perfect health at the place where his brothers Houssain and Ali were waiting for him.

"As Prince Ali had arrived some time before his brother Ahmed, he asked Prince Houssain, who was the first who reached the place of meeting, how long he had been waiting for him. When he learnt that he had been there nearly three months, he said, 'You cannot, then, have been travelling very far.' 'I will tell you nothing at present,' replied Houssain, 'respecting the place where I have been, but I assure you I was more than three months on my journey thither.' 'If that is the case, then,' rejoined Prince Ali, 'you must have made but a very short stay there.' 'You are in error, brother,' said Houssain; 'my residence there was for nearly five months, and if I had been so minded, I could have made it much longer.' 'Then you certainly must have flown back,' resumed Prince Ali: 'I do not at all comprehend how you can otherwise have been here three months, as you wish to make me believe.'

"'I have nevertheless told you the truth,' observed Prince Houssain; 'and this is an enigma which I will not explain to you until the arrival of our brother Ahmed, when I will, at the same time, inform you of the success of my endeavours respecting the object of our journey. I know not how successful you may have been in your search. Perhaps I need scarcely ask, for I see your baggage is not much increased.'

"'Truly,' answered Prince Ali, 'with the exception of a trifling carpet, which lies on your sofa, and which appears as if it belonged to you, I might return you the same compliment. But as you seem to make a mystery of the rarity you have procured, I shall pursue the same course with respect to mine.'

"'I esteem the extraordinary thing I have brought,' replied Houssain, 'so far beyond any other, whatever it may be, that I should have no objection to show it to you, and to make you instantly confess, without the least fear of contradiction, that it is infinitely superior to anything you may have procured; but it is fitting that we should wait for Prince Ahmed, and we may then impart to each other with the greater kindness the good fortune we have each of us encountered.'

"Prince Ali did not wish to enter more at length into the dispute with his brother, concerning the preference which Prince Houssain gave to the rarity he had himself procured. He was perfectly satisfied in his own mind that if the ivory tube he had to show was not the best of all, it at least could not be inferior to any; he, therefore, readily agreed to await the arrival of Prince Ahmed, before exhibiting his acquisition.

"When the latter rejoined the two princes his brothers, and they had mutually embraced and congratulated each other on their happy meeting, and had expressed the pleasure they felt at again seeing each other after their separation, Prince Houssain, being the eldest, began in these words: "We shall have time enough hereafter to entertain each other with the particulars of our different travels. We will now only speak of what is most important to all of us to know; and as I take it for granted that you, as well as myself, remember the principal business that took us from home, we will no longer conceal from each other what we have obtained. And when we have all seen our acquisitions, we will judge in the first instance for ourselves, and see to whom the sultan our father is most likely to give the preference.

"'In order to set you the example,' continued Prince Houssain, 'I must inform you that the rarity I have procured in my travels into the kingdom of Bisnagar is the carpet upon which I am sitting. It appears a common one, and has not much beauty, as you may observe; but when I have told you its qualities, you will be exceedingly astonished, as you have never yet heard of anything like this, and I am sure you will agree with me.

The fact is, that whoever sits upon this carpet, as I now do, and wishes to be transported into any particular place, however distant it may be, will instantly find himself there. I convinced myself of this fact before I counted out the forty purses which the carpet cost me, and which I do not in the least regret. And when I had satisfied my curiosity with seeing everything that was remarkable at the court and in the kingdom of Bisnagar, and wished to return, I made use of no other means of conveyance than this wonderful carpet to bring me and my attendant hither; and he can tell you how short a time we were on our journey. Whenever you wish it, I will give you a proof of its power. I now wait to hear what you have brought that can be put in competition with my carpet.'

"Prince Houssain having finished what he had to say in praise of his carpet, Prince Ali spoke next, and addressed him in these terms: 'I own, brother, that your carpet is one of the most wonderful things in the world, and I do not at all doubt it possesses the property you ascribe to it. But you must, however, acknowledge that there may be other things, I will not say more wonderful than your carpet, but at least equally marvellous, although they may be of a different nature. And to convince you of it,' he went on, 'this ivory tube which I now show you, and which is not more valuable than your carpet in appearance, does not seem a rarity worthy of much attention; I have nevertheless paid as dearly for it as you did for your carpet, nor am I less satisfied with my purchase than you are with yours. Confident, however, as I am of your judgment and candour, you must acknowledge that I have not been mistaken, when you are told, and have had a convincing proof, that by looking through one end of this tube you will behold whatever object you wish to see. I do not expect you to believe this solely upon my word,' added Prince Ali, presenting the tube: 'take it, and see if I impose upon you.'

"Prince Houssain took the ivory tube from Ali; and as he put to his eye that end which his brother had pointed out when he gave it to him, with the intention of seeing the Princess Nourounnihar, and of learning how she was, Prince Ali and his brother Ahmed, who had their eyes fixed upon him, were extremely astonished at seeing him suddenly change countenance, and exhibit not only the greatest surprise, but the greatest concern also. Prince Houssain did not give them time to ask the cause of it. 'O princes,' he exclaimed, 'we have in vain undertaken our painful journey, in the hope of being rewarded with the hand of the charming Nourounnihar: in a very few moments that amiable princess will be no more. I have seen her in her bed, surrounded by her women and eunuchs, who are all in tears, and who seem to expect her decease every moment. Here, look yourselves; behold her pitiable state, and join your tears to mine!'

"Prince Ali took the tube from Prince Houssain. He then looked through it; and having, with the most painful sensations, beheld the sight it had exhibited to his brother, he presented it to Prince Ahmed, that the latter might also see the same melancholy and afflicting sight.

When Prince Ahmed had received the ivory tube from Prince Ali, and had looked through it, and seen the princess apparently at the last gasp, he thus addressed the two princes his brothers: 'The Princess Nourounnihar, my brothers, who is the object of all our desires, is in a condition not far removed from death; but it seems to me that, if we lose no time, her life may still be preserved.'

"Prince Ahmed then drew from his bosom the artificial apple that he had purchased. 'This apple,' said he, showing it to the two princes, 'which you now behold, is not less costly than the carpet and ivory tube which you have brought home from your travels. The occasion that now presents itself to make you witnesses of its wonderful virtues, causes me not in the least to regret the forty purses which the apple cost me. Not to keep you any longer in suspense, I must inform you that it possesses the virtue of restoring a sick person who only smells it to perfect health, though he should be in his last agony. The experience I have had of it leaves no doubt in my mind as to its power, and you may now see the effect of it upon the Princess Nourounnihar, if we hasten to her assistance.'

"'If this be true,' exclaimed Prince Houssain, 'we can make the greatest haste, and be transported in an instant into the chamber of the princess by means of my carpet. Let us then lose no time. Come and seat yourselves by my side; for the carpet is large enough to hold us all without much inconvenience. Let us, however, in the first place, order our attendants to return immediately to the palace, where they will find us.'

When they had given this direction, Prince Ali and Prince Ahmed seated themselves upon the carpet with their brother Prince Houssain; and as they were all three equally interested in the result, they instantly formed the wish to be transported into the apartment of the Princess Nourounnihar. Their desire was fulfilled; and they were conveyed there so quickly, that they seemed at the end of their journey in a single moment.

"The sudden and unexpected presence of the three princes terrified the women and the eunuchs belonging to the princess, as they could not in the least comprehend how these men should thus appear in an instant in the midst of them. They did not at first recognize the princes, and the eunuchs were on the point of attacking them, as persons who had penetrated to a place they were not permitted to approach; they soon, however, discovered their error.

"So soon as Prince Ahmed found himself in the apartment of the princess, and discovered Nourounnihar almost at the point of death, he got up from the carpet, as did also the other two princes, and going up to the bed, applied the wonderful apple to her nose. In a few moments the princess opened her eyes, turned her head first on one side and then on the other, and looking at those who stood near her, raised herself in the bed and desired to be dressed: she did all this with as much composure as if she had just awakened from a long sleep. Her women immediately informed her, that to the princes her cousins, and more particularly to Prince Ahmed, she was indebted for the sudden and complete recovery of her health. She expressed great pleasure at seeing them again, and thanked them all, more especially Prince Ahmed, for their kindness. As she had mentioned her intention of dressing herself, the princes were satisfied with only saying that they were extremely happy at having arrived at a time when they were enabled to contribute to her recovery from the imminent danger in which they had beheld her, and with expressing their most ardent wishes for the preservation of her life; they then immediately retired.

"While Nourounnihar was dressing, the princes went directly from her apartment, to throw themselves at the feet of the sultan their father, and pay him their respects. When they came into his presence, they found that the principal eunuch of the princess had already informed him of their unexpected arrival, and of the manner in which the princess had been by their means perfectly cured. The sultan received and embraced them with the greatest transport, and experienced the greater joy at their return, because their arrival had been the means of the perfect and wonderful recovery of the princess his niece, whom he loved as tenderly as if she had been his own daughter, and whom all the physicians had given over as past cure. After the mutual compliments and inquiries usual on such occasions, each of the princes presented the rarity that he had severally procured: Prince Houssain, the carpet, which he had taken care to bring with him from the apartment of Nourounnihar; Prince Ali, the ivory tube; and Prince Ahmed the artificial apple. And after each of them had spoken in praise of his own acquisition, they delivered them into the hands of the sultan, according to their age, and entreated him to declare to which he gave the preference, and thus determine, according to his promise, on whom he would bestow the Princess Nourounnihar in marriage.

"After listening with the greatest attention and kindness to everything the princes wished to say in behalf of the rarities they brought, without giving them the least interruption, and having also been informed of everything that had passed respecting the cure of the princess, the Sultan of India remained for some time silent, as if he were considering what answer he should make them. He at last broke silence, and addressed them in the following wise and sensible terms: 'O my dear children, I would with the greatest pleasure declare my opinion in favour of one of you, if I could possibly do so with justice; but consider in your own minds whether I can do so. It is indeed true that the princess my niece is indebted to you, Prince Ahmed, for her recovery, which has been effected through your artificial apple; but, I ask you, could it have been thus employed had not the ivory tube of Prince Ali afforded you the opportunity of knowing the danger in which she then was, while the carpet of Prince Houssain procured you the means of instantly coming to her assistance? You, Prince Ali, by means of your ivory tube, had discovered the irreparable loss that you and your brothers were about to experience in the death of the princess your cousin; and it must be acknowledged that she is under a very great obligation to you; but you must also allow that this information would have been inadequate to procure the astonishing recovery that has taken place, without the artificial apple and the carpet. And, my well-beloved Prince Houssain, the Princess Nourounnihar would be ungrateful if she were deficient in gratitude to you for the service

PRINCE AHMED FINDS HIS ARROW.

rendered by your carpet towards the accomplishment of her cure. But you must allow that it would not have been of the smallest use, if you had not become acquainted with her dangerous illness by means of Prince Ali's ivory tube, and if Prince Ahmed had not employed his artificial apple in the cure. Thus, then, as neither the carpet, the ivory tube, nor the artificial apple can be considered as the most useful, but all appear equally rare and excellent, and as I can bestow the Princess Nourounnihar only upon one of you, you must yourselves be aware that the sole advantage you have derived from your travels is the glory of having equally contributed to the saving of her life.

"'And if you acknowledge this,' continued the sultan, 'you must also acknowledge that it is necessary for me to have recourse to some other method to determine me in my choice, and to point out to me on whom I ought to bestow the princess. And as there are still some hours to elapse before the night comes, I wish this affair to be settled to-day. Let each of you, then, go and procure a bow and one arrow, and repair to the great plain without the walls where the horses are exercised; I will go there also. And I now declare that I will give the Princess Nourounnihar in marriage to him who shall shoot his arrow to the greatest distance. I have nothing more to add but to thank every one of you, which I now do most cordially, for the present which each of you has brought me. I have many rarities in my treasury, but I possess nothing that equals in singularity or utility either the carpet, the ivory tube, or the artificial apple, with all of which I shall now enrich my collection. These are three things, each of which will hold a distinguished place, and I will preserve them there most carefully, not from curiosity only, but also for the purpose of making an advantageous use of them whenever the necessity may arise.'

"The three princes had nothing to say in reply to the decision which the sultan had pronounced. When they had left his presence, each of them furnished himself with a bow and arrow, which he gave to one of his attendants, who had all assembled as soon as they heard of their arrival; and they repaired to the plain, followed by an innumerable crowd of people.

"The sultan quickly made his appearance; and as soon as he had arrived, Prince Houssain, as being the eldest, took his bow and made the first shot. Prince Ali then advanced and took his turn, and his arrow fell at a little distance beyond that of Prince Houssain. Prince Ahmed shot last, but the arrow went out of sight, and no one saw it fall. They ran and searched about; but notwithstanding all the pains and diligence of the spectators and of Prince Ahmed himself, the arrow could nowhere be discovered. Although it was most probable that this arrow had been shot to a greater distance than the others, and that Prince Ahmed in consequence deserved the hand of the princess, yet as it was necessary that the arrow should be found to render that fact quite certain, notwithstanding every remonstrance the prince could use with the sultan, the latter did not hesitate to determine in favour of Prince Ali, and at the same time he gave orders to have the preparations made to celebrate the nuptials, which were solemnized in a few days with the greatest magnificence.

"Prince Houssain did not honour the festivities with his presence. As his affection for the princess was very sincere and strong, he had not sufficient fortitude to bear patiently the mortification of beholding the object of his love bestowed upon Prince Ali, who, as he thought, did not deserve her more, nor had shown an affection for her more perfect than his own. His displeasure and disappointment, indeed, were so great that he abandoned the court, renounced his right to the throne, assumed the habit of a dervish, and put himself under the direction of a very famous scheik, who then enjoyed the highest reputation on account of his exemplary mode of life, and who had established his own residence, and that of his numerous disciples, in a pleasant solitude not far from the city.

"Prince Ahmed, actuated by the same motive as that which moved his brother Prince Houssain, did not grace with his presence the nuptials of Prince Ali and the Princess Nourounnihar; but he did not, like his eldest brother, renounce the world. As he could not comprehend how the arrow which he had shot could have thus become invisible, he left his attendants, and resolved to go and search so carefully for it that he should at least be unable to reproach himself with negligence if he failed to find it. He went, therefore, to the spot where the arrows of Prince Houssain and Prince Ali had been found. From this place he walked on straight forward, looking both to the right and left as he went along. He at last wandered away to so great a distance, without discovering what he was in search of, that he thought he was now giving himself only useless trouble. Led on, however, almost in spite of himself, he kept following the same direction, till some very high rocks obliged him to turn aside, if he wished to proceed. These rocks, which were very steep, were situate in a barren place, about four leagues from the spot whence he had set out.

"As he approached these rocks, the prince observed an arrow lying on the ground. He took it up, examined it, and was greatly astonished at discovering it to be the very same that he had shot. 'It certainly is mine,' he exclaimed, 'but neither I nor any other mortal could possibly have strength to send it to such a distance.' And as he had found the arrow lying flat on the ground, and not with the point sticking in the earth, he conjectured also that it must have struck against the rock and rebounded. 'There must be,' he thought, 'something very mysterious in so extraordinary a circumstance; and this mystery may be for my advantage. Fortune, perhaps, while she afflicts me by depriving me of the possession of what I thought would have formed the happiness of my life, has some greater blessing for me.'

"Meditating upon this subject, he entered into a hollow of the rocks, which, by their frequent projections, formed numerous excavations of this sort; and as he turned his eyes from one part to another, he observed an iron door, which seemed to have no latch. He feared it might be fastened from within; but by pushing against it he found it opened inwards, and he saw a gentle declivity without steps, by which he descended with the arrow in his hand. He naturally conjectured that he should be in perfect darkness, but he was immediately surrounded by a light totally different from the sunshine he had left. And on entering a very spacious open place at the distance of fifty or sixty paces, he perceived a magnificent palace, of which he had not time to admire the beautiful style of building; for at that very instant, a lady of most incomparable beauty and of a majestic air, adorned with the richest stuffs and most valuable jewels—decorations which were not at all necessary to increase her natural charms—advanced to the vestibule, accompanied by a band of females, whose mistress he readily conjectured her to be.

"So soon as Prince Ahmed observed the lady, he hastened to advance and pay his respects to her, while the lady, who saw him coming, prevented him by immediately addressing these words to him in a very distinct tone, 'Approach, Prince Ahmed: you are welcome.'

"The prince was very much surprised at hearing his own name in a country of which he himself had not the least knowledge, although it was so near the capital of the sultan his father; and he could not comprehend how he could be known to a lady who was an entire stranger to him. He made his obeisance to her by throwing himself at her feet; and when he arose he said, 'O beautiful lady, I cannot but return you many thanks, on my arrival in a palace into which I was afraid that my curiosity had imprudently led me to penetrate too far, for the assurance you have given me that I am welcome. But may I be permitted to ask, without being guilty of incivility, how it has happened that I am not, as I have understood from yourself, unknown to you, while I myself have not till this moment had the happiness of knowing you, although you reside so near?' 'O prince,' replied the lady, 'let us first go into the saloon; I can then answer your question, and we shall both be more at our ease.'

"She had no sooner said this, than she led the way into the saloon, and Prince Ahmed followed her. This was a room of a most singular description, and the vault of the dome was decorated with gold and azure, which, with the gorgeous furniture, formed altogether so new and grand a sight, that the prince could not help expressing his admiration, and exclaiming that he had never beheld anything so magnificent, and could conceive nothing that could at all equal it. 'I nevertheless assure you,' replied the lady, 'that this saloon is the least worth seeing in my whole palace, as you will yourself own, when I have shown you all the apartments.' She went to the upper end of the saloon, and sat down on a sofa; and when Prince Ahmed at her particular request had taken his place by her side, she said, 'You tell me, prince, that you are surprised that I should know who you are, although you are not at all acquainted with me; but your surprise will cease when I inform you who I am. You are doubtless aware of a fact which your religion teaches you, namely, that the world is inhabited by genii as well as by mortals. I am the daughter of one of these genii, who is among the most powerful and distinguished of his race, and my name is Pari-Banou. Your astonishment at finding me acquainted with your name, as well as that of the sultan your father, the princes your brothers, and the Princess Nourounnihar, will cease when you consider this. I am acquainted with your affection for the princess, and also know of your travels, of all the circumstances of which I can inform you, since I caused the artificial apple which you bought at Samarcand to be exposed for sale, as well as the carpet of Prince Houssain at Bisnagar, and the ivory tube of Prince Ali at Schiraz. Thus you will perceive that I am ignorant of nothing that relates to you. Let me only add one thing more, namely, that you seem to me to be worthy of a better fate than to be united to the Princess Nourounnihar; and in order that you should fulfil your destiny, as I was present when you shot the arrow you now have in your hand, and as I saw that it would not go even beyond Prince Houssain's, I seized it in the air, and gave it sufficient velocity to make it strike against the rocks, near which you found it. It will only depend upon yourself to take advantage of the opportunity which fortune now gives you to secure happiness and prosperity.'

"As the fairy Pari-Banou pronounced these last words in a softened tone of voice, and cast a tender yet modest look upon Prince Ahmed, then blushed, and instantly fixed her eyes upon the ground, the prince had no difficulty in comprehending the sort of happiness she meant. He reflected that the Princess Nourounnihar could never be his, and that the fairy Pari-Banou infinitely surpassed her in beauty and powers of attraction, in intellectual charms, and, as far as he could judge from the magnificence of the palace, in wealth also; and he blessed the moment when the idea had struck him of going a second time to look for his arrow, and rejoiced that he had yielded to the inclination which had seemed to draw him towards this new object that had inflamed his heart. 'O beautiful lady,' he replied, 'if I might but become your slave, and have permission to contemplate and admire your charms for the remainder of my life, I should be the happiest of mortals. Pardon my boldness in making such a request; and do not, by refusing it, disdain to admit within the circle of your court a prince who is entirely devoted to you.'

"'Fair prince,' answered the fairy, 'I have been for a long time, through the kind consent of my parents, mistress of my own wishes and actions. But I wish to admit you into my court, not as a slave, but as the master of my palace and everything that belongs to me; and in pledging your faith to me, and accepting me as your wife, everything will become yours. I trust that you will not form a bad opinion of me from my making this offer. I have already told you that I am mistress of my actions, and I must now add that the custom amongst fairies in matters of marriage is not the same as with women, who never make any advances, and would esteem it a disgrace to do so; but as for us, we consider that the offer should come from us.'

"Prince Ahmed made no answer to this speech. Penetrated with gratitude, he thought he could not show this feeling better than by attempting to kiss the hem of her robe. But the fairy did not allow him to do so; she presented her hand, on which he impressed a fervent kiss. 'Prince Ahmed,' said the fairy, while he held her hand in his own, 'will you now pledge your faith to me, as I do mine most firmly to you?' 'Most beauteous being!' exclaimed he, overcome with excess of joy, 'how can I do otherwise, or what can delight me more? Yes, my sultana, my queen, I give up my whole heart to you, without the least reserve.' 'Then,' said Pari-Banou, 'you are my husband, and I am now wholly yours. Marriages with us are contracted with no other ceremonies; yet they are more lasting and more indissoluble than amongst men, notwithstanding all the forms and protestations the latter are accustomed to employ. In the meantime,' continued the fairy, 'while my servants are making the festive preparations for our nuptials this evening, as you seem to have eaten nothing to-day, they shall bring us a light repast, and I will then show you the different apartments of my palace; and you shall judge whether it be true, as I have before said, that this saloon is the plainest room of all.'

"Some of the attendants who had been in the saloon with Pari-Banou, and understood the intention of their mistress, then went out, and in a short time returned with several dishes and some excellent wine.

"When Prince Ahmed had eaten, and drunk, and refreshed himself, Pari-Banou led him through all the different apartments, where he beheld diamonds, rubies, emeralds, and every sort of precious stone, mingled with pearls, agate, jasper, porphyry, and all the varieties of the most valuable marble, besides furniture of various descriptions and of inestimable value. All these rich materials were employed in so profuse a manner that

THE WEDDING FESTIVITIES.

the prince, who had never seen anything that resembled it, candidly acknowledged to the fairy that nothing in the world could equal this magnificence. 'Beloved prince,' said Pari-Banou, 'if you are so delighted with my palace, which I own possesses great beauties, what would you think of the palaces belonging to the chief of the genii, which are still more rich, spacious, and magnificent? I must also take you to admire the beauty of my garden; but that shall be reserved for another time. Night approaches, and it is time to sit down to table.'

"The hall into which the fairy and Prince Ahmed went, and where the table was set out, was the last apartment that remained for him to see; and he found it not at all inferior to any of the others he had beheld. He was much struck at entering by the appearance of an immense number of lights, all perfumed with amber, which were arranged with so much symmetry that it was a pleasure to look at them. He admired also the large sideboard, covered with golden vases and other vessels, whose elaborate workmanship increased their value. Several groups of females, all superbly dressed and of great beauty, began the most harmonious concert of vocal and instrumental music ever heard. The married pair sat down, and Pari-Banou was very attentive in helping Prince Ahmed to the most delicate of the dishes, all of which she named to him as she requested him to taste them. As these were dishes the prince had never before met with, he gave them all the praise they deserved, and said that the present feast surpassed all he had ever partaken of among mortals. He spoke in the same terms of the excellence of the wines, which both he and the fairy began to drink when the dessert was served, which consisted of fruits, sweetmeats, and other things well suited to give a better flavour to the wine.

"When the repast was finished, Pari-Banou and Prince Ahmed rose from the table, which was instantly removed; and they seated themselves at their ease on a sofa, furnished with cushions of rich silk stuff, delicately embroidered with large flowers in various colours. A great many genii and fairies now entered the hall, and began a very peculiar and graceful dance, which they continued till the fairy and the prince rose from their places. The genii and fairies, still continuing to dance, then went out of the hall, and preceded the newly-married pair until they came to the door of the chamber where the nuptial bed was prepared. On arriving there, they ranged themselves in two ranks, to let the prince and fairy pass on; they then retired, and left them at liberty to go to rest.

"The festive rejoicings attending this marriage continued for several days; and Pari-Banou found no difficulty in diversifying the entertainments by fresh amusements, new feasts, harmonious concerts, and strange dances, with a variety of spectacles, all so grand and wonderful that Prince Ahmed would never have been able even to have conceived them while living with mortals, had his life lasted a thousand years.

"It was the intention of the fairy not only to give the prince the strongest proofs of the sincerity and warmth of her love, but she wished him also to suppose that, as there was nothing at the court of the sultan his father, or anywhere else, that could be put into competition with the splendour of her abode, not to mention her own beauty and charms, so also he would find nothing comparable to the happiness he would enjoy with her; for she wished him to attach himself entirely to her, and never to form a wish to leave her. She completely succeeded in her intentions. The affections of Prince Ahmed did not diminish by the possession of the loved object. His attachment to his fairy wife increased, indeed, to that degree, that it was no longer in his power to control his love, even if he had resolved to conquer it.

"At the end of six months, the prince, who had always felt a great regard and respect for the sultan his father, conceived a strong desire to learn some intelligence of him; and as he could not satisfy his anxiety except by going in person to obtain the information he wished to have, he spoke to Pari-Banou on the subject, and requested her leave to put his design in execution. This speech very much alarmed the fairy, who feared it might be only a pretence for abandoning her. Accordingly, she said to him, 'In what way have I given you cause for discontent, that you request this permission? Is it possible that you have forgotten you have pledged your faith to me, and that you now no longer love me who am so passionately attached to you? You ought to be convinced of my love by the proofs I never cease to give you.'

"'O my queen,' replied Prince Ahmed, 'I am completely convinced of your affection, of which I should be unworthy did I not show my gratitude by a love equally ardent. If you are offended at my request, I beg you will pardon me; and there is no reparation

I am not willing to make for my fault. Yet I have surely done nothing that ought to displease you; for I have only been led to make this request from my respect for the sultan my father, whom I should wish to relieve from the pain he must feel at my long absence. And his affliction must be the greater, as I have reason to believe that he supposes me dead. But since you do not acquiesce in my design to afford him this consolation, I will abandon my intention, for there is nothing in this world I am not ready to do to oblige you.'

"Prince Ahmed, who could not dissemble, and who loved Pari-Banou in his heart as perfectly as he had assured her by his words, ceased from urging his request, and the fairy showed how satisfied she was with his submission. Nevertheless, as he could not entirely abandon the design he had formed, he took an opportunity at different times to converse about the amiable and excellent qualities the Sultan of India possessed, and especially mentioned the marks of affection he had shown towards himself in particular. He did this with the hope that Pari-Banou would at last yield to his wishes.

"Indeed, Prince Ahmed judged rightly concerning the sultan his father; for in the midst of all the rejoicings that accompanied the nuptials of Prince Ali and the Princess Nourounnihar, he was most sensibly afflicted at the absence of his two sons. In a short time he received intelligence of the plan Prince Houssain had adopted to abandon the world, and was informed of the place he had chosen for his retreat. Like a good father, who made a part of his happiness consist in the society of his own children, particularly as they were worthy of his affection, he regretted they had not all remained at court, and attached themselves to his person. As he could not, however, disapprove of Prince Houssain's choice in endeavouring to make himself better and more holy, he bore his absence with fortitude. He made also every possible inquiry after Prince Ahmed. He sent couriers into all the provinces of his dominions, with orders to the governors to detain the prince if he should arrive in any of their cities, and oblige him to return to his court. But all his cares were useless, and his inquiries proved unsuccessful. His affliction, however, instead of lessening, daily increased. He frequently conversed on the subject with his grand vizier. 'O vizier,' he would say, 'you know that of all the princes, Ahmed is the one I love most tenderly, and you are well aware of the means I have taken, but without success, to discover him. The misery I feel is so strong that I shall at length sink under it, unless you have compassion upon me. If you have any interest in my well-being, I conjure you to assist me with your advice.'

"The grand vizier was not less attached to the person of his sovereign than zealous to acquit himself with honour in his administration of the public affairs of the state; and reflecting upon the different methods by which he might lessen the affliction of his master, he remembered to have heard some extraordinary accounts of a certain powerful enchantress. He proposed, therefore, to the sultan to send for and consult her. The sultan consented, and the grand vizier, after having discovered where she was to be found, brought her with him to the court.

"The sultan addressed the enchantress as follows: 'The affliction I have been in since the nuptials of my son Prince Ali with the Princess Nourounnihar, on account of the absence of Prince Ahmed, is so public and well known, that you cannot be ignorant of it. Can you, then, by your skill in magic, inform me what is become of him? Can you tell me whether he be still alive, where he is, and what he is doing? May I expect ever to see him again?' In answer to all the questions of the sultan, the enchantress replied, 'However skilful I may be in my profession, O mighty king, it is nevertheless impossible for me to satisfy your majesty immediately upon the subject of your inquiries; but, if you will allow me till to-morrow, I will give your majesty an answer.' The sultan granted her the required delay, and dismissed her with the promise of a very handsome recompense if her answer was at all in consonance with his wishes.

"The enchantress returned the next morning, and the grand vizier again presented her to the sultan. 'Notwithstanding all the diligence I have used,' said the enchantress, addressing herself to the sultan, 'and all the efforts I have made, according to the rules of my art, in endeavouring to comply with your majesty's wishes, I have only been able to discover one thing; and that is, that Prince Ahmed is not dead. Of this fact your majesty may rest assured. But I have been unable to find out in what place he is.' The Sultan of India was obliged to be satisfied with this answer, which left him almost in the same distressing uncertainty respecting the fate of his son as before.

"In the meantime Prince Ahmed so frequently turned the conversation he had with Pari-Banou towards the sultan his father, though without again mentioning the desire he felt to see him, that this very forbearance made her comprehend his design. As she perceived, therefore, that he refrained from urging his request through the fear he had of displeasing her, after the refusal he had before met with, she concluded that his love for her, of which he did not cease from giving her every possible mark, was very sincere; and judging by her own feelings of the injustice she was guilty of in thus violently opposing the natural affection of a son for his father, and of the unreasonableness of her wish that he should annihilate so natural and so amiable a sentiment, she resolved to grant what she could not but observe he so ardently desired.

"One day, therefore, she said to him, 'Beloved prince, the permission which you requested of me to go and see your father, afforded me reasonable grounds to fear that I might accuse you of inconstancy, and that you sought a pretext to abandon me; and I had no other motive than what arose from this circumstance in refusing your request. But as I am now as fully convinced, from your actions as from your protestations, that I can rely upon your good faith, and upon the strength and fervour of your affection, I have changed my opinion, and grant you the permission you formerly requested; but it must, nevertheless, be upon this condition, that you first promise me your absence shall not be long, but that you will return very soon. This condition ought not to distress you, for it does not arise from any distrust of your love. That is not my motive, because I do not feel any doubt, after the proof you have afforded me of the sincerity of your attachment to me.'

"Prince Ahmed wished to throw himself at the feet of the fairy, to show how much he was penetrated with gratitude, but she prevented him. 'O my sultana,' he exclaimed, 'I know the value of the favour you have granted me, but I lack words to thank you as I wish. Pardon my remissness, I conjure you; and whatever words your affection may suggest, be assured my feelings will be still stronger. You are right in supposing the promise you require of me will not pain me. I give it you the more freely, as it is not possible that I can live long without you. I will now take my departure, and by the diligence with which I shall return you will be convinced that I come back, not from a feeling of honour and a desire to keep my promise, but because I have followed my own wishes, which urge me to pass my whole life with you; and if I sometimes, with your own consent, leave you, I will always, for my own sake as much as yours, avoid the pain of a long absence.'

"Pari-Banou was delighted with these sentiments of Prince Ahmed, which entirely relieved her from the suspicion she had formed, that the eagerness he expressed to see the Sultan of India was merely a specious pretext to break the faith he had pledged to her. 'Depart, prince,' she said, 'whenever you please; but do not take it ill that I first give you some advice upon the precautions you ought to take in connection with your journey. In the first place, I do not think it would be proper for you to mention to the sultan either your marriage, or my rank and situation; either the place in which you reside, or where you have passed your time since you saw him. Beg him to be satisfied with knowing that you are happy, and that your motive in paying him this visit is chiefly to remove the grief and uncertainty he must have felt concerning your fate.' She then gave him twenty horsemen, all well mounted and equipped, to accompany him. When everything was ready, Prince Ahmed took his leave of Pari-Banou, embracing her, and renewing the promise he had made of returning as soon as possible. They brought him a horse which the fairy had ordered to be prepared for him; and which, besides being richly caprisoned, was also much more beautiful and of greater value than any in the sultan's stables. He mounted it very gracefully, and after bidding the fairy farewell, set out on his journey.

"As the road which led to the capital of the sultan was very direct, Prince Ahmed arrived at his journey's end in a very short time. When he entered the city, the people were delighted to see him, and received him with acclamations, and with every token of joy. The majority of them left their business, and accompanied him in crowds till he arrived at the sultan's palace. His father received and embraced him with the greatest enthusiasm; complaining, nevertheless, in a manner which denoted his paternal affection, of the affliction into which Prince Ahmed's long absence had thrown him. 'And this absence,' added the sultan, 'has caused me the greater pain, as, after fate had decided to your disadvantage, in favour of your brother, Prince Ali, I was fearful that your despair had caused you to commit some rash action.'

PRINCE AHMED AND HIS FATHER.

"'My lord and father,' replied Prince Ahmed, 'I will leave it to your majesty to reflect, whether, after having lost the Princess Nourounnihar, who had long been the sole object of my wishes, I could resolve to be a witness of the happiness of Prince Ali. If I had been capable of such spiritless conduct, what would the court and the whole city have thought of my love? What would even your majesty have thought of it? Love is a passion which cannot be subdued at our own pleasure. It completely subjects us—it tyrannizes over us; and a true lover has no longer the use of his reason.

"'Your majesty may remember,' continued the prince, 'that when I drew my bow, the most extraordinary thing happened to me that was ever known. In a plain so large, so level, and so unemcumbered as that in which we made our trial, I still found it impossible to discover the arrow I had shot; in consequence of this I lost the reward which was in justice not less due to my skill than to that of the princes my brothers. Conquered as it seemed by the caprice of fate, I did not pass my time in useless complaints; but, to satisfy my restless and uneasy mind, I separated myself from my attendants, and returned alone to the place where we had shot, in order to look for my lost arrow. I searched for it in every spot I could think of to the right and left of the place where the arrows of Prince Houssain and Prince Ali had been found, and where I thought it most likely that mine had fallen also; but all my endeavours were useless. I did not, however, give up the search, but pursued my investigations, continuing to proceed straight forward in the line I thought it likely my arrow had taken. I had already proceeded more than a league, looking on both sides as I went along, and sometimes even going out of the road if anything appeared at all like an arrow, when at last I began to reflect that it was not possible for mine to have gone so far. I stopped, and asked myself whether I was not insane, to think that I could have strength enough to shoot an arrow to a greater distance than any one of the most ancient heroes, who had been so famous for their strength, could have compassed. I thus reasoned with myself, and was about to abandon my enterprise; but when I was going to turn back, I felt myself led on as it were against my will; and after walking four leagues, I came to a place where the plain was shut in by some steep rocks, and here I perceived an arrow. I ran and took it up, and knew it to be the very same I had shot, but which we had all been unable to find within the period you had named for the completion of the trial.

"'Far, however, from thinking,' continued Prince Ahmed, 'that your majesty had been guilty of injustice in determining in favour of Prince Ali, I interpreted what had happened quite differently; and I did not doubt that there was some mystery attached to this circumstance for my advantage, and concluded that I ought not to neglect anything that would tend to this development. And, in fact, I had no need to seek farther. But I now come to a mystery, concerning which I entreat your majesty not to take it ill if I remain silent, and I request you to be satisfied with knowing from my own lips, that I am happy and contented with my lot. In the midst of my happiness, there was one thing only that troubled me and gave me real uneasiness, and that was the distress I conceived you would experience from your ignorance of what had become of me after I thus disappeared from your court. I therefore thought it my duty to come and free you from this unpleasant doubt. This was my only motive for coming hither; and the only favour I ask of your majesty, in return, is to permit me to come from time to time to pay my respects to you, and inform myself of the state of your health.'

"'O my dear son,' replied the sultan, 'I cannot possibly refuse the permission you request; I should nevertheless have preferred that you had determined to come and live at my court. Tell me, at least, by what means I can gain any intelligence of you whenever you fail to come here yourself, or whenever your presence might be necessary.' 'O my father,' replied Prince Ahmed, 'the information your majesty demands of me forms a part of the mystery I have mentioned; I entreat you, therefore, to suffer me to be silent on this point. I will return so frequently to pay my respects, that I only fear you will think me too importunate, rather than accuse me of negligence in not coming when my presence might be necessary.'

"The Sultan of India did not press Prince Ahmed any more on this subject. 'My son,' said he, 'I do not wish to penetrate any further into your secret. I leave this matter entirely to yourself; but I must say that your presence affords me the greatest pleasure. I have not for a long time past received so much happiness as you now afford me; and you will be truly welcome whenever your own affairs or your inclinations may induce you to come hither.'

"Prince Ahmed remained only three days at the court of the sultan his father. He set out early on the fourth morning, and Pari-Banou saw him return with the greatest joy, as she did not expect to see him so soon; and the haste he had made caused her to blame herself for having suspected him of inconstancy towards her, contrary to his most solemn promise. She did not dissemble the suspicion she had nourished, but frankly confessed her weakness, and requested his pardon. The union of the two lovers was hereafter so perfect, that the one did not breathe a wish that was unreciprocated by the other.

"About a month after the return of Prince Ahmed, the fairy observed that, after having given her an account of his visit, and mentioned the conversation he had had with his father, in which he had stated that he should get permission to come and pay his respects to him very often, the prince was as silent concerning the sultan as if no such person existed, although he had formerly constantly turned the conversation to him; and she concluded that his silence was on her account. She therefore took an opportunity of speaking to him on the subject. 'O my prince,' she said, 'have you forgotten the sultan your father? and do you remember the promise you made him, that you would frequently go and see him? I have not forgotten what you said to me on your return, and I now remind you of it, that you may not any longer delay the performance of your promise.'

"'O my sultana,' replied Prince Ahmed, in the same cheerful tone of voice in which the fairy had spoken. 'I do not feel myself to blame for the negligence and forgetfulness of which you accuse me, because I would rather suffer the reproach you make me, without deserving it, than be exposed to the chance of a refusal, by showing too much haste to obtain what it might give you pain to grant.' 'Beloved prince,' replied the fairy, 'I do not wish you to put a restraint on yourself on my account; and that the same thing may not happen again, as it is now a month since you have seen the sultan your father, I think you never ought to let a longer time than this elapse between your visits to him. Therefore go to him to-morrow, and repeat your visit every month, without troubling yourself either to speak to me on the subject, or to wait till I mention it. I propose this plan very willingly.'

"Prince Ahmed set out the next day, with the same attendants as before, but better equipped, while he himself was more magnificently mounted and dressed than he had been the first time; and he was received by the sultan with the same joy and satisfaction as on his first return. He continued for many months to go regularly and pay his respects, but each time dressed and accompanied in a richer and more magnificent style than before.

"At length, some viziers, who were favourites of the sultan, and who judged of the grandeur and power of Prince Ahmed by the different proofs he thus gave of it, abused the liberty the sultan allowed them of speaking to him, to excite emotions of distrust in the sultan's breast against his son. They represented to him that it would be no more than common prudence in him to wish to know where the prince's place of retreat was; and that he should acertain whence Prince Ahmed derived the means of living at so vast an expense, as the sultan had assigned him no establishment, or fixed revenue, that could enable him to come to court, which they declared he did only as a sort of boast, and to let his father see that he had no occasion for the sultan's liberality to enable him to live like a prince; and that, in short, they were afraid that Prince Ahmed intended to exite a rebellion against his father, and dethrone him.

"The sultan was very far from believing that Prince Ahmed was capable of forming so dreadful a design as that which the favourites attributed to him. 'You are jesting with me,' he replied: 'my son loves me; and I am the more convinced of his affection and fidelity, because I have not given him the least cause to be dissatisfied with me.' Upon this one of the favourites said, 'O my lord, although in the opinion of every sensible man, your majesty could not have taken a better plan than that which you adopted to determine your choice respecting the marriage of the Princess Nourounnihar with one of the princes, yet who can tell whether Prince Ahmed has submitted to the decision of the chance with the resignation which Prince Houssain has exhibited? May not he think that he alone was worthy of her, and that your majesty, in bestowing her upon his elder brother in preference to him, and in suffering the matter to be decided by chance, has been guilty of injustice towards him?

"'Your majesty may perhaps say,' continued this malicious favourite, 'that Prince Ahmed has not shown the least mark of discontent—that our fears are vain, and that we are wrong in suggesting a suspicion of this nature, which may not have the least foundation, against a prince of his rank. But, great monarch, it is possible that these suspicions are well founded. Your majesty must be well aware that in so delicate and important an affair it is necessary to be very careful. You should consider that dissimulation on the part of the prince may be only for the purpose of amusing and deceiving your majesty; and that the danger is the more to be dreaded, inasmuch as Prince Ahmed seems to reside at no great distance from your capital. If your majesty had given the same attention that we have bestowed upon all his movements, you might have observed that, every time the prince comes to visit you, both he and his attendants are quite fresh and gay, and that their dress and the ornaments which they and their horses wear have the same lustre as if they had that instant come out of the hands of the workmen. Even their horses are not in the least fatigued, and appear as if they only came from their exercise. These are evident signs that Prince Ahmed resides in the neighbourhood; and we thought that we should be wanting in our duty if we did not humbly represent these things to your majesty, as well for your own preservation as for the good of the state. It now behoves you to take such steps as you may judge proper.'

"When the favourite had concluded this long speech, the sultan put an end to the conversation by saying, 'However plausible all this may be, I do not believe that my son Prince Ahmed can be so wicked as you wish to persuade me he is. I am nevertheless obliged to you for your advice, and do not doubt that you have spoken with the best intentions.'

"The sultan spoke in this manner to his favourites, that they might not perceive what impression their discourse had made upon his mind. Still, he could not help being very much alarmed, and he resolved to mark the conduct of Prince Ahmed, without even informing his grand vizier. He ordered the enchantress, whom he had once already consulted, to be sent for privately, and had her introduced through a secret door of the palace, and conducted to his apartment. 'You told me the truth,' said the sultan to her, on her entrance, 'when you assured me that my son Prince Ahmed was not dead, and I am much bound to you for having done so; but you must now afford me a further satisfaction. Although I have since discovered him, and he now comes every month to pay me a visit, yet I have not been able to learn from him in what spot he has fixed his residence; and I do not wish to put a restraint upon him, and compel him to tell me against his inclination. I have no doubt, however, that you are skilful enough to satisfy my curiosity, without its being known either to Prince Ahmed or to any one at my court. You know that he is here; and as he is accustomed to depart without taking leave of me or any one else, you must lose no time in taking your measures. Go to-day, and place yourself on the road he takes, and observe him so well that you may find out to what place he goes; and then bring me the information.'

"As the enchantress had been informed concerning the place where Prince Ahmed had found his arrow, she instantly left the palace, and went and concealed herself so carefully among the rocks that no one could perceive her.

"Prince Ahmed set off the next morning according to his usual custom, without taking leave of the sultan his father, or any of the courtiers. The enchantress saw him coming, and followed him with her eyes till she lost sight both of him and his attendants.

"As the rocks formed an insurmountable barrier to mortals either on foot or on horseback, on account of their steepness, the enchantress thought that one of these two things must be the fact—that the prince retired into a cavern, or dwelt in some subterraneous place, where genii and fairies took up their abode. As soon as she supposed that the prince and his attendants would have disappeared, and have gone into the cavern or subterraneous place which she conjectured to be there, she came out of the place in which she had concealed herself, and going into all the recesses as far as she could, she looked about on all sides of her, walking backwards and forwards several times. But notwithstanding all the pains she took, she could not perceive any entrance into the cavern—not even the iron door which Prince Ahmed had discovered on his first visit. In fact, this could be seen only by men, and indeed only by those whom the fairy Pari-Banou wished to receive, and to all women it was invisible.

"The enchantress, who found that she was only giving herself useless trouble, was obliged to be satisfied with the discovery she had already made. She returned, therefore,

THE PRETENDED SICK WOMAN.

to give an account of her proceedings to the sultan; and having related the several steps she had taken, she added, 'Your majesty may easily conjecture, after what I have had the honour of telling you, that it will not be a very difficult matter for me to afford you all the information you can wish respecting the conduct of Prince Ahmed. I will not tell you what I think at present, because I would rather give my information to your majesty in a way that can leave no doubt upon your mind. In order to accomplish this, I only request time and patience, and full permission to follow my own plans, without being obliged to inform you of the means I use.' The sultan agreed to the proposal of the enchantress. 'You shall do as you please,' he said. 'Go: you may use what means you choose, and I will wait with patience to see the effects of your efforts.' In order to give her some encouragement, he presented her with a very valuable diamond, telling her at the same time that it was only the earnest of a greater reward, when she had completed the important service, for the accomplishment of which he relied entirely upon her skill.

"Since Prince Ahmed had obtained permission of the fairy to go to the court of his father, he had never neglected to pay his respects there once a month. And the enchantress was aware of this fact, she waited till the next month had elapsed. A day or two before its conclusion, she did not fail to go on foot to the rocks, and to wait at the very spot where she had lost sight of Prince Ahmed and his attendants. This she did in order to put the scheme she had formed into execution.

"The next morning, when the prince came out as usual from the iron door, with the attendants who always accompanied him, he passed close to the enchantress, whom he did not know, and observing that she was lying down with her head supported against a piece of rock, and that she moaned like a person in great pain, compassion induced him to go to her, and inquire what was the matter with her, and whether he could afford her any assistance. The cunning enchantress, without lifting up her head, but looking at the prince with a pitiful air, so as still more to excite his compassion, replied in broken and interrupted words, as if she spoke and breathed with great difficulty, that she had left her house in the city, and upon the road had been seized with a most violent fever, so that her strength quite failed her; that she had been obliged to stop, and remain in the state they then saw her, in a place so distant from any house, and without the hope of being relieved. 'My good woman,' said Prince Ahmed, 'you are not so bereft of assistance as you may suppose. I am ready to aid you as far as I can, and have you conveyed to a place very near this, where you shall not only have every attention paid you, but shall very soon be cured. You have therefore only to make an effort to rise, and suffer one of my people to take you behind him.'

"On hearing this, the enchantress, who had feigned this illness only for the purpose of discovering Prince Ahmed's abode, how he lived, and what was his position, eagerly accepted the kind offer he so generously made her; and in order to show, rather by her actions than her words, that she accepted it, she made several feigned efforts to rise, pretending all the time that her illness prevented her. Seeing this, two of the attendants assisted her in getting up, and placed her on horseback behind another. While they were remounting, the prince turned back, and went towards the iron door, which was opened by one of the horsemen, who advanced for that purpose. The prince went in, and when he had arrived at the court of Pari-Banou's palace, without dismounting, he sent one of the attendants to say that he wished to speak to her.

"The fairy came very quickly, for she could not conceive what motive had induced the prince to return so suddenly. The latter, without giving her time to ask any questions, said, pointing towards the enchantress, whom two of the attendants had taken from the horse, and were supporting by holding her arms, 'I entreat you, my princess, to have compassion on this poor woman. I found her in the state in which you see her now, and have promised her all the assistance she may require. And I recommend her to your care, as I am well satisfied you will extend your benevolence to her, alike from your own kind consideration, and because it is my request.'

"Pari-Banou, who, during the whole of Prince Ahmed's speech, had not taken her eyes off the pretended sick woman, ordered two of her women to take her from the other attendants, and carry her into an apartment of the palace, and also to take as much care of her as they would of their mistress herself.

"While the two female attendants were executing the orders which the fairy had given them, Pari-Banou went up to Prince Ahmed, and said in a low tone of voice, 'I give you great praise, dear prince, for your compassion: it is worthy of you and your high birth, and I feel great pleasure in aiding your kind wishes. I must, however, tell you, that I am greatly afraid that this good action will meet with but a bad recompense. This woman does not seem to me so ill as she wishes to appear; and unless I am very much deceived, she is employed for the express purpose of carrying out some unpleasant and mortifying proceedings against you. Do not, however, let this grieve you. Be assured that all they may contrive and plan against you shall be of no effect; for I will deliver you from all the snares your enemies may set for you. Go, therefore, and pursue your journey.'

"This speech of Pari-Banou's did not in the least alarm Prince Ahmed. 'As I have no recollection, my princess,' he replied, 'of ever having injured any one, and as I have no intention of committing a wrong, I do not think that any person can have thought of attempting to hurt me. Be this, however, as it may, I will never cease from doing all the good I can, whenever I can see an opportunity.' So saying, he took leave of the fairy, and recommenced his journey, which had been interrupted by meeting with the enchantress; and he soon arrived with his attendants at the court of the sultan his father, who received him with as much of his usual manner as he could assume, endeavouring, as far as possible, to appear as if nothing had happened, and that the conversation which his favourites had held with him had excited no suspicion in his breast.

"In the meantime, the two attendants whom Pari-Banou had ordered to wait upon the pretented sick woman conducted the enchantress into a very beautiful apartment, richly furnished. They at first made her sit down on a sofa, where, while she rested her head on a cushion of gold brocade, they prepared a bed near her on the same sofa, the mattresses of which were made of satin, richly embroidered, while the sheets were of the finest linen, and the counterpane of cloth of gold. They assisted her in getting to bed, for the enchantress still continued to pretend that the fever-fit with which she had been attacked, tormented her so much that she could not assist herself; then one of them went out of the room, and soon came back with a goblet of the finest porcelain in her hand, containing a drink of a certain kind. She presented it to the enchantress, and while the other female assisted her in sitting up, said, 'Take this drink: it is water from the fountain of lions, and is a sovereign remedy for fevers of every kind. You will find the effect of it in less than an hour.'

"To keep up the deception she was practising, the enchantress suffered them to entreat her for a long time, as if she had an insurmountable dislike to drink this liquor. She at last took the goblet, and swallowed its contents, shaking her head at the same time, as if she did the greatest violence to her feelings. When she had lain down once more, the two females covered her closely. 'Remain where you are,' said she who had brought the goblet, 'and even go to sleep if the desire should come upon you. We will now leave you, and hope to find you cured when we return in about an hour.'

"As the enchantress had not undertaken this scheme with any idea of lying in bed for a long time with a pretended illness, but only with the view of discovering the retreat of Prince Ahmed, and to ascertain his motive for abandoning the court of the sultan, and as she was now perfectly satisfied on that point, she would readily have declared that the liquor had cured her at once, because she was desirous of going back and informing the sultan of the fortunate accomplishment of the commission with which she was intrusted; but as they told her that its efficacy was not instantaneous, she was compelled, in spite of herself, to wait for the return of the two attendants.

"They came back at the time they had mentioned, and found the enchantress risen, dressed, and sitting on the sofa, from whence she rose the moment she saw them come in. 'Oh admirable draught!' she exclaimed: 'it has produced its effect much sooner than you told me; and I have been a long time impatiently waiting for you, to entreat you to conduct me to your charitable and excellent mistress, that I may thank her for her great goodness, for which I shall be for ever obliged to her; and that, since I have been so miraculously cured, I may be allowed to proceed on my journey.'

"These two attendants, who, like their mistress, were of the fairy race, after having given evident signs how much they rejoiced at her speedy cure, walked on before, to show her the way; and they conducted her through many beautiful apartments, all of them much more superb than that she had been in, until they came to the most magnificent and richly furnished saloon in the whole palace.

"Here they found Pari-Banou seated on a throne formed of massive gold, enriched with diamonds, rubies, and pearls of extraordinary size; and on each side of her appeared a number of fairies, all extremely handsome and superbly dressed. The enchantress was quite dazzled at the sight of so much magnificence. She could neither utter a word, nor even thank the fairy, as she intended, but remained, after prostrating herself at the foot of the throne, like a person struck motionless. Pari-Banou spared her the trouble of addressing her, by immediately saying, 'I am very happy, my good woman, to have had the opportunity of being of use to you, and that I now find you in a fit state to pursue your journey. I do not wish to detain you; but perhaps it would gratify you to see my palace. Go with my women: they will accompany and show you everything worth seeing.'

"The enchantress, who had not yet recovered from her state of astonishment, could only prostrate herself a second time before the throne, till her face touched the carpet which covered the foot of it. She then took her leave without having the courage to utter a single word, and was conducted through the palace by the two fairies who had before accompanied her. She was shown all the same apartments, one after the other, through which Pari-Banou herself had led Prince Ahmed the first time he presented himself to her; and as she went along, she continually uttered exclamations of astonishment and delight. But when she had examined the whole palace, she was more surprised than ever at what the two fairies told her respecting their mistress; for they asserted that all this was but a small part of Pari-Banou's grandeur and power; and in different parts of her dominions she had other palaces, more than they could tell, all on different plans and of different styles of architecture, and not less superb and magnificent than this. Conversing with the sorceress on these and other subjects, they conducted her to the iron door through which Prince Ahmed had brought her in; they then opened it, and wished her a good journey. She took her leave of them, and thanked them for the trouble they had been at on her account.

"After proceeding a few steps, the enchantress turned round to examine the door, that she might know it again; but she looked in vain for a trace of it. It was now to her as to every other female. She went back to the sultan, well satisfied with the success of her plan, except as to this one circumstance, and was very much elated at having so happily executed the commission which she had been intrusted with. As soon as she got back to the city, she went along the most private streets, and was introduced by the secret door into the palace. The sultan, being informed of her arrival, ordered her into his presence; and as he observed that she had rather a gloomy expression on her countenance, he thought she had not succeeded, and immediately said, 'I conjecture, from your looks, that your journey has been unsuccessful, and that you can give me no information concerning the business I intrusted to your care.' 'Great king,' replied the enchantress, 'your majesty will give me leave to say, that you ought not to judge from my appearance whether I have succeeded in the commission you have honoured me with, but rather from the faithful report I am going to make of what I have done, and of everything that has happened to me. You will find that I have neither forgotten nor neglected anything that could render me worthy of your majesty's approbation. The gloom on my countenance, which you have remarked, arises from a different cause than the want of success, for I trust your majesty will be well satisfied with my diligence and zeal. I will not stop to explain the cause of my gloomy looks, because my relation, if you have the patience to listen to it, will sufficiently show the cause of my fears.'

"The enchantress then related to the Sultan of India how she had pretended illness, and thus excited the compassion of Prince Ahmed, who took her into his subterraneous residence, where he recommended her to the care of the most beautiful fairy that ever was seen, a being such as mortals cannot conceive; and she told how he requested this fairy to see that every attention was paid to her, in order to her recovery. She then informed the sultan with what readiness Pari-Banou gave orders to the two fairies, who attended on and took charge of her, not to leave her till she had quite recovered; and she declared that she was sure all this kindness and consideration could only arise from the desire of a wife to gratify her husband's wishes. The enchantress did not fail to give an even exaggerated account of the surprise she experienced at the sight of the fairy's palace, which she did not believe had its equal in the whole world. She then went on to inform the sultan of their great anxiety, and the attention they had shown her when they had conveyed her to an apartment; she spoke of the liquor they gave her to drink, and the speedy cure that followed; and though the cure in her case was as feigned as the illness itself, yet she declared that she did not in the least doubt the virtue of the liquor. She then proceeded to describe the majestic and splendid appearance of Pari-Banou, seated

THE SULTAN'S REQUEST.

on a throne thickly studded with precious stones, the value of which surpassed all the riches of the kingdom of India, and spoke of the variety and profusion of other superb things that were contained within the great extent of this palace.

"Having finished this account of the success of her commission, the enchantress concluded her discourse in these terms: 'What does your majesty think of these unheard-of riches? Perhaps you will say that you are pleased to hear all this, and that you rejoice at the great fortune which has come to Prince Ahmed, who lives in splendour with the fairy. With respect to myself, I entreat your majesty to pardon me if I take the liberty of saying that I am of a different opinion, and that I am even greatly alarmed when I think of the misfortunes that may in consequence happen to the prince. This was the cause of the uneasiness which your majesty remarked in my countenance, and which I was unable entirely to conceal from you. I am sure that Prince Ahmed is naturally of too good a disposition to undertake anything hostile to your majesty's interest; but who can be sure that the fairy, by her attractions, her caresses, and the influence she has by some means acquired over the mind of her husband, may not inspire him with the horrid wish of supplanting you, and seizing the crown? It therefore behoves your majesty to pay every attention that so important an affair deserves.'

"However satisfied the Sultan of India might be of the excellence of Prince Ahmed's natural disposition, he could not help being disturbed by the speech of the enchantress. 'I am much indebted to you,' he said, as she was about to take her leave, 'both for the trouble you have taken and for your good advice. I am aware of its importance, and I cannot do better than take the opinion of others on this subject.'

"At the very moment when his attendants had come to announce the arrival of the enchantress, the sultan was conversing with the same favourites who had already excited suspicions in his breast against Prince Ahmed. These suspicions were still further increased by the enchantress. He then returned to his favourites, and took her with him. He partly informed these courtiers of what he had heard; and having communicated to them the reason why he was fearful the fairy would alter the disposition of the prince, he asked them by what means they thought he might be enabled to prevent so great an evil.

"One of the favourites then spoke in the name of the rest. 'In order,' he said, 'to counteract this evil, as your majesty knows the person who may bring misfortune upon you, as he is now in the very midst of your court, and as you have the full power to detain him, you ought not to hesitate, but instantly arrest him. I do not say you should take away his life; that perhaps would be going rather too far; but at least it would be advisable to imprison him very closely.' The other favourites were unanimous in applauding this advice.

"The enchantress, however, who thought this mode of proceeding too violent, requested the sultan's leave to say a few words; and when she had obtained permission, she said, 'I am convinced, mighty king, that from the zealous interest these councillors have in your majesty's welfare, they are induced to propose to you the arrest and imprisonment of Prince Ahmed; but I trust they will agree with me in thinking it necessary, when they arrest the prince, to arrest all those who accompany him; but you must reflect that these attendants are genii. Do you think it will be an easy matter to surprise them and put them in bonds? Will they not instantly disappear by means of the power they possess of rendering themselves invisible? Will they not instantly go and inform the fairy of the insult you have offered to her husband? And would not such an insult expose you to the danger of her bitterest revenge? But if, by some other less violent method, the sultan can secure himself from the wicked design that Prince Ahmed may form against him, without the least danger of sullying his glory, or of raising any suspicion that he has any evil design, would it not be right to pursue that method? If his majesty has any confidence in my advice, he will induce Prince Ahmed from filial gratitude to procure him certain advantages through the power of his fairy, under pretence of deriving a considerable benefit from them: genii and fairies can easily accomplish things that are far above the power of mortals. For instance, every time your majesty wishes to take the field, you are obliged to be at a considerable expense, not only for pavilions and tents for yourself and army, but also for camels, mules, and other beasts of burden, only to carry all this apparatus. Now, could you not prevail upon Prince Ahmed, by the great influence he has over the fairy, to procure a pavilion for you, so small that it might be carried in the hand, and yet so large that your whole army might encamp under it? I need not say any more. If the prince should procure you this pavilion, there are many other requests of a similar nature which you can make, till at last he will sink under the difficulty or rather the impossibility of fulfilling them, however fertile the genius and invention of the fairy may be, who has thus taken him from you by her spells and enchantments. He will then be so struck with shame, that he will not dare to appear here again, but will be compelled to pass the remainder of his life with the fairy, excluded from all intercourse with the world; and your majesty will have nothing more to fear from his machinations, nor will you have to reproach yourself with so hateful a crime as that of shedding the blood of a son, or so harsh a measure as that of confining him in perpetual imprisonment.'

"When the enchantress had finished her speech, the sultan asked the favourites if they had any better plan to propose. And as he observed that they kept silence, he determined to follow the advice of the enchantress, as it seemed to him the most rational, and as it also agreed cordially with that mildness of disposition he always exhibited in his general conduct.

"The next day, when Prince Ahmed presented himself before the sultan, who was in council with his favourites, and when he had taken his seat by his father's side, as his presence did not cause any restraint, the conversation continued for some time to turn upon indifferent topics. At last the sultan, addressing himself to Prince Ahmed, said, 'O my son, when you reappeared, and relieved me from the misery in which the great length of your absence had plunged me, you did not inform me concerning the place you had chosen for your retreat. Satisfied with seeing you, and with being told by yourself that you were contented with your situation, I made no attempt to penetrate into your secret, when I found that you wished to be silent. I know not what reason you may have had to pursue this conduct towards a father who has always shown that he took the most lively interest in your happiness. I now know, indeed, in what your happiness consists, and I sincerely rejoice in it with you. I heartily approve the step you have taken, in marrying a fairy so worthy of being beloved, so rich, and so powerful, as my information, which is very good, proclaims your wife to be. Powerful as I am, I should have been unable to provide for you such a connection as this. In the high rank to which you are raised, and which any one but a father like me would envy, I ask you not only that we may continue upon the good terms on which we have hitherto lived, but that you will employ your influence with the fairy to obtain her assistance in anything I may require at your hands, and I shall at once put your influence with her to the test. You cannot but be aware of the very great expense, trouble, and inconvenience which my generals and other officers, as well as myself, suffer from being obliged, every time we take the field during a war, to have pavilions and tents, as well as camels and other beasts of burden, to carry these tents from place to place. If you will consider the pleasure you can afford me, I am sure you will not refuse my request, that you demand of the fairy a pavilion of such a kind that you can hold it in your hand, and that shall yet be sufficiently large to contain my whole army: she will certainly not refuse when you inform her it is for me. The difficulty of providing the thing will not cause you to be refused, for all the world knows that fairies can execute most extraordinary tasks.'

"Prince Ahmed had not the least suspicion that the sultan his father would make such a request of him. It appeared to him not only very difficult of execution, but absolutely impossible; for although he was not entirely ignorant of the great power of genii and fairies, he nevertheless very much doubted whether that power was able to produce such a pavilion as the sultan requested. Besides, he had not hitherto asked anything of Pari-Banou—he was satisfied with the continual proofs she gave of her affection, and he had never neglected anything that might serve to convince her that his regard was equally strong, and that he had every wish to preserve her good opinion. He was, therefore, in the greatest embarrassment about the answer he should make. 'O my father,' he replied, 'if I have made any mystery to your majesty of the adventures that have happened to me, and of the plan I pursued after having found my arrow, my reticence arose from supposing the particulars would possess no interest in your eyes. I am ignorant how this mystery has been revealed to you, but I cannot pretend to deny that you have learned the truth. I am the husband of the fairy you have mentioned: I love her, and am convinced that she returns my affection; but how far the power or influence your majesty supposes me to possess may extend over her I am entirely ignorant. I have not only made no trial of it, but have not even thought about it; and I very much wish you would excuse me from making the attempt, and suffer me to enjoy the happiness of our mutual affection, without the appearance of any interested motive on my part. But the request of a father is a command to a son who makes it his duty to obey his parent in everything. I cannot, however, express how much against my inclination and how repugnant to my feeling this request is. I will, nevertheless, make it to my wife, as your majesty wishes that I should do so; but I cannot promise you that I shall succeed; and if I cease from coming to pay my respects to you, you may consider my absence as a proof of my failure. I therefore now ask you to pardon me, and to consider that you yourself have reduced me to this alternative.'

"'My son,' replied the sultan, 'I should be very sorry if what I ask of you should be the cause of my not seeing you again; but I readily perceive that you are not acquainted with the power which a husband has over a wife. Your fairy will evince but very slight regard for you, if, with all the power which as a fairy she possesses, she refuses to grant you that trifling thing which your regard for me induces you to request. Shake off your fears; they only arise from your not supposing you are so much beloved as you are in reality. Go boldly and make the request, and you will find that the fairy loves you more than you now believe; and remember that our own backwardness in making requests often deprives us of great benefits. Reflect, that you would not refuse anything that she might request, because you love her; neither will she refuse you what you ask, because she certainly loves you.'

"This speech of the sultan's did not convince Prince Ahmed. He would much rather that his father should have required anything else of him, than to expose him to the risk of displeasing Pari-Banou, who was so dear to him; and the vexation he felt from what had passed was so great that he left the court two days sooner than his usual time. As soon as he arrived at Pari-Banou's palace, the fairy, before whom he had hitherto constantly presented himself with an open and contented mien, inquired of him the cause of the change she observed in his countenance. When she found that he asked after her health instead of answering her question, with an air that evidently showed his embarrassment, she replied, 'I will satisfy your inquiries when you have answered mine.' The prince for a long time tried to convince her that nothing had happened; but the more he asserted it, the more she pressed for an explanation. 'I cannot,' she said, 'see you with the face you now wear, without almost insisting upon your declaring the cause of your anxiety, that I may endeavour to dispel it, whatever it may be. It must be something very extraordinary indeed, and nothing less than the death of the sultan your father, if I can find no remedy for it. If that be the cause of your sorrow, time only, in conjunction with my endeavours, can afford you consolation.'

"Prince Ahmed could no longer resist the earnest importunity of the fairy. 'O my love,' he replied, 'may Heaven prolong the life of the sultan my father, and bless him with happiness to the end of his days. I left him in perfect health: this, therefore, is not the cause of the vexation which you perceive I feel. The sultan himself is the cause of it; and I am the more disturbed at it, because he has laid me under the necessity of encroaching upon your kindness. In the first place, you well know the care I have taken, and of which you have yourself approved, to conceal from him the happiness I have in seeing and loving you, and in enjoying in return your good opinion and affection; and I have concealed from him the interchange of our mutual faith. He has, however, discovered the fact, although I am ignorant by what means.'

"Here Pari-Banou interrupted Prince Ahmed. 'I will tell you how it was, she answered. 'Do you recollect what I said to you about the woman whom you thought so ill, and who therefore excited your compassion? It is she who has informed the sultan of what you had concealed from him. I told you that I had an idea she was not so ill as she pretended to be, and she has now confirmed the truth of my suspicions. In fact, after the two females to whose care I recommended her had persuaded her to take a draught of a particular kind of water that is infallible in all sorts of fevers, she pretended, although she had not the least occasion for it, that this water had cured her; and she instantly got up, and was brought to me to take her leave, that she might go as soon as possible to give an account of the success of her enterprise. She was

THE MAGIC PAVILION.

even in such haste, that she would have departed without seeing my palace, if, when I ordered the two females to show it her, I had not made her understand it was well worth the trouble of a visit. But proceed, and let us see the reason of the sultan's wishing to make you troublesome to me; a design in which I assure you he will certainly never succeed.'

"'You may have observed,' resumed Prince Ahmed, 'that I have till now been satisfied with your affection for me, and have never requested any favour of you, but that you would continue to bestow your kind regard upon me. Indeed, after I had gained so amiable a wife, what could I wish for more? Still, I am not unaware of the greatness of your power; but I made it a point not to put it to the proof. Consider, then, I entreat you, that it is not I, but the sultan my father, who makes a request which seems to me very foolish and indiscreet. This request is, that you procure a pavilion which may secure him from the inclemency of the weather when he takes the field. It must be able to contain himself, his court, and all his army, and yet be so small that you may hold it your hand. Once more let me say that it is not I who make the request, but the sultan my father, speaking by my mouth.'

"'Beloved prince,' replied Pari-Banou, with a smile, 'I am really sorry that such a trifle should have caused you the least embarrassment, or have disturbed your mind as it has done. I see clearly that two circumstances have occasioned it. One is the condition you have imposed upon yourself to be satisfied with loving me and being beloved, and abstaining from making any requests that will put my power to the test; the other is, as I have not the least doubt, whatever you may say to the contrary, that you think the demand the sultan has made through you beyond my power of execution. With respect to the first motive, I must both praise and esteem you for it, and, if possible, love you more than ever. As to the second, I shall have no difficulty in convincing you that what the sultan requires is a mere trifle; and if it were necessary, I could execute things infinitely more difficult. Be content, therefore, and do not let this vex you any more: be assured that, far from considering you importunate, I shall always, through my affection for you, have great pleasure in granting you everything you can wish.'

"Hereupon the fairy ordered her female treasurer to appear. When she came, Pari-Banou said to her, 'Nourgihan, bring me the largest pavilion that is in the treasury.' Nourgihan went out, and almost instantly returned with a pavilion that she could not only hold in her hand, but which might be quite hidden if she closed her palm. She presented this pavilion to her mistress, who took it, and then gave it to Prince Ahmed, that he might examine it at his leisure.

"When the prince saw the tiny object the fairy called a pavilion, and which she declared to be the largest that was in her treasury, he thought that she meant to joke with him, and his countenance exhibited evident proofs of his surprise. Pari-Banou, who observed his looks and readily conjectured what he thought, burst into a fit of laughter. 'And do you think, my dear prince,' she exclaimed, 'that I mean to jest with you? You shall immediately see that such is not my intention. Nourgihan,' she said, addressing herself to her attendant as she took the pavilion from the hands of Prince Ahmed, 'go and set it up, that the prince may judge whether the sultan his father will find it smaller than he wishes.'

"The attendant left the palace, and went far enough into the field to put up the pavilion, one end of which, when it was finished, reached quite up to the palace. When it was erected, Prince Ahmed found it, not indeed too small, but so large that even two armies, both as numerous as that of the sultan, could easily be covered by it. 'O my princess,' exclaimed the prince, 'I beg your pardon a thousand times for my incredulity. After the proof you have given me of your power, I do not doubt that you can readily execute whatever you may wish to undertake.' 'You think, then,' replied the fairy, 'that this pavilion is larger than the sultan will ever require; but you must observe also that it has the property of extending or contracting itself to the exact size of what it is wanted to cover.'

"The fairy's attendant took down the pavilion, reduced it to its original form, brought it in, and presented it to the prince. He immediately took it, and without any further delay set out the next morning on horseback, accompanied by his usual attendants, and went to pay his respects to his father.

"The sultan, who was perfectly convinced that such a pavilion as he had demanded was an impossibility, was very much astonished at the prompt reappearance of the prince his son. He received the pavilion at Prince Ahmed's hands, and after having admired its small size, he was thrown into a state of the greatest surprise, from which he did not very soon recover, when he saw it erected in the large plain that has been mentioned before, and when he perceived that two armies quite as large as his own could be very conveniently encamped under it. Lest he should regard this great size as superfluous, and even incommodious, Prince Ahmed did not forget to inform him that the pavilion would always accommodate itself to the size of his army.

"The sultan was profuse in acknowledgments to Prince Ahmed, declaring how much he was obliged to him for this magnificent present, and begging him to return the fairy his most grateful thanks. And to prove the great value he set upon the pavilion, he ordered it to be kept very carefully in his treasury. But in reality he felt still more jealous than when the enchantress and his flatterers first excited that hateful passion in his breast; for now that the fairy had so readily provided this wonderful pavilion, he concluded the prince his son could perform many things infinitely beyond what was in his own power, notwithstanding all his grandeur and riches. More anxious, therefore, than ever to discover some means to ruin Prince Ahmed, he again consulted the enchantress, who advised him to request the prince to bring him some water from the fountain of lions.

"When the sultan had assembled his courtiers in the evening as usual, and Prince Ahmed also was present, he addressed him in these terms: "O my son, I have already expressed to you how much I feel myself obliged for your readiness in procuring the pavilion for me, which I esteem as the most valuable thing in my treasury; but you must also, to prove your regard for me, do another thing which will afford me equal delight. I understand that the fairy, your wife, possesses a certain water from the fountain of lions, which cures all fevers, even the most dangerous kinds. Now, as I am very well assured that my health is dear to you, I do not suppose that you will be unwilling to request some of this water as a gift, and bring it to me, as a sovereign remedy that I may employ whenever I have occasion. I beg you will do me this important service, and thus manifest your tender and filial regard towards a good father.'

"Prince Ahmed, who thought that the sultan would certainly have been very well satisfied with possessing a pavilion so curious and useful as that which he had procured for him, and who never suspected that he would impose a new office upon him, which might injure him in the good opinion of Pari-Banou, remained like a man thunderstruck at this new request of the sultan's, notwithstanding the assurance he had received from the fairy that she would comply with all his wishes, so far as lay in her power. After a silence of some time he thus replied: 'I entreat your majesty to be assured that there is nothing I am not ready to do, to procure what may contribute to prolong your life; but I could wish that the task could be accomplished without an appeal to my wife, as it depends on her power. I dare not promise you to procure this water. All I can do is to assure you that I will make the request; but in doing so, I shall force my own feelings as much as when I begged the pavilion.'

"When Prince Ahmed returned to the fairy the next morning, he gave her a sincere and faithful account of everything that he had done, and of all that had happened at the court of the sultan when he presented the pavilion, for which the sultan had acknowledged himself much obliged to her. Nor did he omit to mention the fresh request that the sultan had charged him to make; and in conclusion he said, 'I mention this to you, my princess, because I would faithfully tell you all that passed between the sultan and myself. But it remains entirely with you, either to comply with or refuse the request as you please; act, therefore, as if I had no interest in this matter, for your wish shall always be mine.'

"'No, no,' replied the fairy; 'I am very well pleased that the Sultan of India knows that you are not indifferent to me. I wish to satisfy him, and whatever advice the enchantress may give him (for I know very well that he attends to what she says), he shall find no lack of readiness either in you or me. There is great malice in what he demands, as you will perceive from the account I am going to give you. The fountain of lions is in the middle of the court of a large castle, the entrance to which is guarded by four very powerful and fierce lions, two of which sleep while the other two watch. But let not this alarm you; I will afford you the means of passing them without any danger.'

"Pari-Banou was at this moment employed with her needle, and as she had several balls of thread by her, she took one and gave it to the prince. 'In the first place,' said she, 'take this ball—I will tell you presently what use you are to make of it. Secondly, order two horses to be got ready. One you must ride and the other you are to lead, for it must be loaded with a sheep, which is to be divided into four quarters, and which we must kill to-day. Thirdly, you must provide yourself with a vessel, or rather I will give you one, to bring the water in to-morrow. Early in the morning you must mount one horse and lead the other; and when you have got beyond the iron door, throw this ball of thread down before you. It will roll on and not stop until it arrives at the gate of the castle. You are to follow it, and when it stops you will see the four lions, as the gate will be open. Those two which are watching with their roaring will awaken the other two that are asleep. Do not, however, be alarmed, but throw to each of them a quarter of the sheep, without dismounting. When you have done this, lose no time, but spur your horse and proceed with the utmost speed to the fountain; fill your vessel as you sit on horseback, and return as quickly as you went. The lions will still be employed in eating the sheep, and will suffer you to come out.'

"Prince Ahmed set out the next morning, at the time the fairy had appointed. He fulfilled every point of his instructions in the manner she had prescribed. He arrived at the gate of the castle, distributed the four quarters of the sheep to the four lions, and after passing intrepidly through the midst of them, he came to the fountain and got the water. Having filled his vessel, he went back, and left the castle unharmed as he had entered. When he had got to a little distance he turned round, and perceived two of the lions following him. Without being at all alarmed, he drew his sabre and prepared to encounter them. But as he observed while he kept moving on that one of them turned out of the road on one side at a little distance from him, and made signs with its head and tail that it was not come for the purpose of doing him any injury, but only to go on before him, while the other followed behind, he returned his sabre to its sheath, and in this manner pursued his journey to the capital of India, which he entered escorted by the two lions, who did not leave him till he arrived at the gate of the sultan's palace. They then suffered him to enter, and went back by the same road by which they had come, not without causing great alarm among the common people and all who saw them; some hiding themselves, others flying on all sides in order to avoid meeting the terrible beasts, while the lions themselves went very quietly along, without showing any marks of ferocity.

"A number of officers, who presented themselves to assist the prince in dismounting, accompanied him to the apartment where the sultan was in conversation with his favourites. Prince Ahmed approached the throne, and setting down the vessel of water at the feet of the sultan, he kissed the rich carpet that covered the footstool; and when he got up he said, 'Here, O honoured father, is the salutary water which your majesty has wished to put among the richest and most curious things in your treasury. I can only pray that your health may be so perfect that you may never have occasion to make use of it.'

"When Prince Ahmed had finished his speech, the sultan made his son take a place on his right hand, and then replied, 'My gratitude to you, O my son, for this present, is proportionate to the danger you have encountered through your regard for me.' For the enchantress had informed him of the peril, as she knew the fountain of lions, and the danger to which every person was liable who went there. 'Do me the favour,' the sultan added, 'to inform me by what art, or rather by what unheard-of power, you have been protected.'

"The prince replied, 'O great king, I cannot assume to myself any part of the compliment which your majesty bestows upon me. It is all due to the fairy my wife; and I attribute to myself no other honour than the credit of having strictly followed her excellent instructions.' He then gave a recital of his journey, and of the methods he had pursued, informing the sultan what the advice of Pari-Banou had been. When he had finished, the sultan, who had listened to him with very evident marks of pleasure, but who nevertheless internally felt his envy and jealousy increase instead of diminishing, rose and retired into the interior of the palace, where he waited alone for the coming of the enchantress, whom he had summoned.

"On her arrival she spared the sultan the trouble of mentioning the prince's return,

SCHAIBAR.

or the success of his expedition, for she had been informed of it by the report that spread over the city; and she said that she was now prepared with a most infallible method to ruin the prince. She informed the sultan what this method was; and the next day in the assembly of the courtiers the sultan addressed Prince Ahmed, who was present, in these words: 'I have now, O my son, but one more petition to urge, after which I will require nothing further either from you or the fairy your wife. My request is, that you procure a man for me, who is not more than a foot and a half high, but whose beard is thirty feet long, and who carries on his shoulders a bar of iron that weighs five hundred pounds, which he makes use of as a quarter-staff, and who can speak.'

"Prince Ahmed, who did not think there existed such a man as the sultan his father had described, desired to be excused; but the sultan persisted in his request, and added that the fairy could fulfil still more difficult requests than this.

"The following day, when Prince Ahmed returned to the subterraneous kingdom of Pari-Banou, and acquainted her with the fresh request of the sultan his father, which he looked upon, he said, as a still more unheard-of thing than the two former had appeared to be, he added, 'I cannot possibly imagine that there can be a man of this kind in any part of the world. Doubtless the sultan wishes to try whether my simplicity will induce me to seek after an impossibility. If, indeed, there should be such a man, it must be my father's intention to kill me; for how can he suppose that I can seize so short a man, who is armed in the way he mentions? What weapons could I make use of to compel him to submit to me? If there be any means to extricate me with honour from this dilemma, I beg you will explain them to me.'

"'Do not alarm yourself, my prince,' replied the fairy; "you ran a considerable risk in procuring the water from the fountain of lions for the sultan your father; but there is no danger in discovering a man like the one he now requires. In fact, my brother Schaibar is just such a man. Although we have the same father, he does not at all resemble me, and he is, moreover, of the most violent disposition. Nothing can prevent him from giving the most sanguinary proofs of this whenever his passions are excited, or he is in the least displeased or offended. Except in this one point, he is the best creature in the world, and he is always ready to oblige me in whatever may be required of him. His appearance is exactly such as the sultan has described, and he carries no other weapon than a bar of iron that weighs five hundred pounds, without which he never stirs; and this serves to make him respected. I will cause him to appear, and you shall judge whether I have not spoken the truth; but, above all things, guard against manifesting any alarm at his extraordinary figure when he presents himself.' 'O my queen,' replied Prince Ahmed, 'do you not say that Schaibar is your brother? However ugly and deformed he may be, so far from being frightened at him, the one circumstance of his relationship to you will alone make me love. honour, and look upon him as one of my nearest kinsmen.'

"The fairy then ordered that a golden vessel in which perfumes are burnt should be brought into the vestibule of the palace, full of fire; and a box of the same metal was likewise brought at her desire. She opened the box, and took out a perfume that was kept there, and as she threw this upon the fire, a thick and dense smoke arose.

"A few moments after this ceremony, Pari-Banou said, 'O my prince, my brother is come; do you not see him?' The prince looked, and perceived Schaibar, who was only a foot and a half high, and who approached in a grave and sedate manner, with the iron bar of five hundred pounds' weight upon his shoulder. His thick and well-grown beard of thirty feet long projected forwards, and did not touch the ground. His moustaches, which were in proportion to his beard, went quite back to his ears, and almost covered his whole face. His little sharp eyes were buried in his head, which was of a most enormous size, and was covered with a pointed cap. To complete the singularity of his appearance, he had a projecting hump both before and behind.

"If the prince had not been previously informed that this was the brother of Pari-Banou, he could not have beheld him without the greatest alarm; encouraged, however, by the knowledge of this fact, he stood perfectly collected by the side of the fairy, and received his strange guest without showing the slightest mark of fear.

"Schaibar, as he advanced, looked up at Prince Ahmed with an eye that would have chilled his very soul, and demanded of Pari-Banou, as he first addressed her, who that man was. 'Brother,' she replied, 'he is my husband. His name is Ahmed, and he is son to the Sultan of India. The reason why I did not invite you to my nuptials, was that I was unwilling to recall you from the expedition in which you were then engaged, and from which I have since learnt with the greatest pleasure that you have returned victorious; and it is on my husband's account that I have now taken the liberty of sending for you.'

"On hearing this speech, Schaibar cast on Prince Ahmed an approving look, which, however, did not in the least lessen his savage and haughty appearance. 'Dear sister, is there anything in which I can be of any service to your husband? He has only to mention it. For me to know that he is your husband is enough to induce me to gratify him in anything he may wish.' 'The sultan his father,' replied Pari-Banou, 'has expressed a curiosity to see you; I therefore beg you will have the goodness to let him be your conductor.' 'Let him set forth as soon as he pleases,' replied Schaibar; 'I am ready to follow him.' 'It is too late, brother,' said Pari-Banou, 'to begin the journey to-day; you had better, therefore, wait till to-morrow morning. In the meantime, as it is no more than right that you should be informed of what has passed between the Sultan of India and Prince Ahmed since our marriage, I will give you an account of everything this evening.'

"The next morning, when Schaibar had been informed of what it was necessary he should know, he began his journey very early, accompanied by Prince Ahmed, who was to present him to the sultan. They arrived at the capital; but so soon as Schaibar appeared at the gate, all who saw him were seized with affright at the appearance of this hideous figure, and many ran and hid themselves in their shops, or in their houses, the doors of which they instantly shut; others took to flight, and communicated the same alarm to those they met, who instantly turned, and ran without once looking behind them. In this manner, as Schaibar and Prince Ahmed advanced at a regular pace, they found a complete solitude in all the streets through which they passed on their way to the palace. When they arrived there, the porters, instead of at least trying to prevent Schaibar from going in, ran off in every direction, and left the entrance quite free. The prince and Schaibar, therefore, advanced without let or hindrance to the council hall, where the sultan was seated on his throne, giving audience. And as all the officers and attendants had abandoned their posts as soon as Schaibar made his appearance, the brothers-in-law entered without the least hindrance.

"With head erect Schaibar haughtily approached the throne, and, without waiting for Prince Ahmed to present him, thus addressed the sultan: 'Thou hast demanded my presence. Behold, here I am. What dost thou require of me?'

"But the sultan, instead of answering, put his hands before his eyes, and turned his head away to avoid the sight of the dreadful object before him. Schaibar was enraged at the uncivil and offensive reception to which he found himself subjected after he had taken the trouble of coming. He therefore lifted up his bar of iron, and exclaiming, 'Wilt thou not speak?' let it fall directly on the sultan's head, and crushed him to the earth. This occured so quickly that Prince Ahmed had no time to interpose to protect his father. It was now as much as he could do to prevent Schaibar from destroying the grand vizier, who was close to the sultan's right hand. And he prevailed upon the angry man only by representing that the advice the vizier always gave the sultan his father was very equitable and excellent. 'Where, then, are those,' exclaimed Schaibar, 'who have given him such execrable advice?' And saying this, he slew all the other viziers, who stood on both sides of the throne, and all the favourites and parasites of the sultan who were the enemies of Prince Ahmed. Death followed upon every blow dealt by his iron bar, and none escaped, except those whose fear was not so powerful as to fix them to the very spot, and who were not too much startled to save their lives by flight.

"After completing this dreadful execution, Schaibar left the hall of audience, and went into the middle of the court, with the bar of iron on his shoulder. 'I know,' he cried, looking at the grand vizier who accompanied Prince Ahmed, to whom he owed his life, 'I know that there dwells here a certain enchantress, who is an enemy to the prince my brother-in-law—a greater enemy than even these infamous favourites, whom I have punished. Let her be brought before me.' The grand vizier immediately sent for the enchantress, and had her brought forth; and when Schaibar, as he raised his bar of iron, said, 'Learn the consequence of giving wicked advice and pretending sickness,' the bar fell, and the enchantress was instantly annihilated on the spot.

"'This is not sufficient,' exclaimed Schaibar: 'I will destroy the whole city, unless Prince Ahmed, my brother-in-law, be instantly acknowledged as Sultan of India.' All those who were present, and who heard this fair speech, immediately made the air resound with cries of 'Long live Sultan Ahmed!' and in a short time the whole city echoed with the same sound. Schaibar next caused the prince to be clothed in the robes of the sultan, and had him instantly installed. After he had paid him homage and taken an oath of fidelity and allegiance, he went for his sister Pari-Banou, conducted her to the city with great pomp, and caused her to be acknowledged as Sultana of India.

"With respect to Prince Ali and the Princess Nourounnihar, as they had taken no part in the conspiracy against Prince Ahmed, who was thus amply revenged, and, indeed, as they were even ignorant of the existence of such a plot, Prince Ahmed gave them for their establishment a very considerable province, with its capital, where they went and passed the remainder of their days. He also sent an officer to Prince Houssain, his eldest brother, to announce the change that had taken place in the government, and offered him the choice of any province in his kingdom, with full sovereignty. But this prince was so happy in his retirement, that he requested the officer to return his sincerest thanks to the sultan, his youngest brother, for Ahmed's good and kind intentions, to assure him of his entire submission and loyalty, and to say that the only favour he requested was permission to pass the remainder of his life in the retreat he had chosen."

Scheherazade, always contriving to interest the sultan by the relation of her different stories, immediately began a new one, and addressed Schahriar in these terms:—

## THE STORY OF THE TWO SISTERS WHO WERE JEALOUS OF THEIR YOUNGER SISTER.

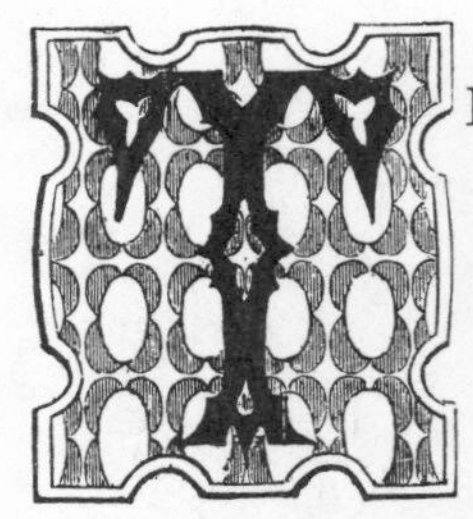

HERE was once a prince of Persia named Khosrouschah, who, when he had come of age, used to amuse himself very frequently by seeking after adventures during the night. He often disguised himself, and, accompanied by one of his confidential attendants, likewise in disguise, visited different parts of the city, and sometimes became acquainted with circumstances of an extraordinary nature, which I will not at present stop to relate to your majesty; but I hope you will derive some pleasure from listening to the account of what happened to him on the first excursion he made a few days after he had ascended the throne of the sultan his father, who, dying at a very advanced age, left him sole heir to the kingdom of Persia.

"After the customary ceremonies on his accession to the crown, and the funeral rites to the memory of his father were performed, the new Sultan Khosrouschah, as much from a feeling of duty as from a desire to inspect what passed in his city, left his palace one night at about two hours after dark, accompanied by his grand vizier, who was disguised like himself. Having strolled into a quarter of the city inhabited by the poorer class of people, he heard, as he passed through a street, some very loud voices, and he approached the house from whence the noise proceeded. Looking through the crevice of a door, he perceived a light, and descried three sisters seated on a sofa, and apparently conversing together after supper. From the words spoken by the eldest, he gathered that the three ladies were talking of their wishes. 'Since we are talking of wishes,' said she, 'mine is that I may have the sultan's baker for a husband; I should then eat as much as I liked of that delicious bread which is called the sultan's bread. Now let us

NUPTIAL CAVALCADE OF THE YOUNGER SISTER.

hear if your taste is as good as mine.' 'My wish,' said the second sister, 'would be to marry the cook in the sultan's kitchen; I should then eat excellent dishes; and as I feel sure that the sultan's bread is in common use in the palace, I should not want for that. You see, sister,' continued she, addressing the elder lady, 'that my taste is quite as good as yours.'

"The youngest sister, who was extremely handsome, and possessed much more wit and readiness than her elder sisters could boast, now spoke in her turn. 'For my part,' said she, 'I do not limit my wishes to so low a standard; I take a higher flight; and since we are about wishing, I should wish to be the wife of the sultan himself. We should have a son, a prince whose hair should be gold on one side and silver on the other; when he cried, the tears that dropped from his eyes should be pearls; and when he smiled, his vermillion lips should appear like an opening rosebud.'

"The wishes of these three sisters, and particularly of the third, appeared to the sultan so singular that he resolved to gratify them. Therefore, without communicating his design to the grand vizier, he desired that officer to take particular notice of the house, that he might come for the three sisters on the following day, and conduct them before the throne.

"The grand vizier, when he executed this order on the morrow, only gave the three sisters time to adorn themselves, without saying anything more to them than that the sultan desired to see them. He took them to the palace, and when he presented them to the sultan, the latter said to them, 'Tell me if you recollect the wishes you expressed yesterday evening, when you were all in such a pleasant humour: do not dissemble, for I must know the truth.'

"At this question of the sultan's, the three sisters, who did not at all expect an address of this nature, exhibited the utmost confusion. They cast down their eyes, and the blushes which overspread their cheeks added a lustre to their beauty, especially to that of the youngest, who now completed her conquest over the heart of the sultan. As their natural modesty, together with the fear of having offended their sovereign by their late conversation, made the ladies silent, the sultan, who perceived their embarrassment, said in an encouraging manner, 'Fear nothing. I have not sent for you to give you pain; and as I see that, contrary to my intention, the question I ask you has confused you, and as I know each of your wishes, I will soon relieve you from your embarrassment. You,' added he, 'who wished to be my wife, shall have your wish fulfilled this very day; and you,' addressing the eldest and the second sister, 'shall also have your wishes gratified, for I will have your nuptials solemnized with my baker and with my chief cook.'

"As soon as the sultan had declared his will, the youngest lady set her sisters an example, by throwing herself at the feet of the sultan, to express her gratitude. 'O mighty king,' said she, 'my wish, since it is known to your majesty, was only expressed in jest and mirth: I am not worthy of the honour you propose to confer upon me, and I entreat your pardon for my boldness and temerity.' The other two sisters wanted also to excuse themselves, but the sultan prevented them. 'No, no,' said he, 'I will hear of no excuses. The wish of each of you shall be gratified.'

"The nuptials of the three sisters were celebrated on that very day as the sultan had decreed, but with far different ceremonies: those of the younger sister were accompanied with all the pomp and rejoicings suitable to the union of a Sultan and Sultana of Persia, while those of the other two sisters were solemnized with no greater festivities than might be expected from the positions of their husbands, the principal baker and the chief cook of the sultan.

"The two elder sisters felt very forcibly the great disproportion between their marriages and their younger sister's. Far from being contented with the good fortune that had befallen them in the fulfilment of their wishes, they felt, through this reflection, in a contrary way, and became excessively jealous, which not only disturbed their own comfort, but also caused very great unhappiness to their younger sister, and was in the end productive of the most mortifying and humiliating affliction to her. The elder sisters had not time at first to communicate to each other their sentiments on the preference which the sultan had given her over them; each had leisure only to prepare for the celebration of her marriage. But when they had an opportunity of meeting some days after at a public bath, where they had made an appointment, the eldest said to the other, 'Tell me, sister, what think you of our youngest sister? Is not she a pretty lady for a sultana?' 'I confess,' replied the other, 'that I do not understand the matter. I cannot conceive what charms the sultan could see in her to fascinate him thus; she is no better than a dressed-up doll, and you know as well as I do the figure we have sometimes seen her. Was it a sufficient reason for the sultan to prefer her to you because her appearance is more youthful than yours? You were worthy of his alliance, and he ought to have done you the justice to give you the preference.'

"'O sister,' replied the eldest, 'we will not speak of me: I should have been content if the sultan had made choice of you; but that he should fix his heart on that silly wench vexes me beyond measure. I will be revenged at all events, and you are as much interested in the business as I am. I therefore propose that you shall join with me, that we may act together in a matter which concerns us equally; and you must communicate to me anything that may occur to you which will be likely to mortify the sultana; while I, on my part, promise to acquaint you with anything my desire to humble her may suggest to me.'

"After this malicious compact the two sisters saw each other frequently, and every time they met their only conversation was on the means they should adopt to interrupt, and if possible destroy, the happiness of the sultana, their younger sister. They proposed several plans, but in deliberating on the execution of each they found such great difficulties that they did not venture to put one in practice. They, however, occasionally visited the sultana together, and with the most cunning and malicious dissimulation they lavished upon her every mark of friendship and affection they could devise, in order to convince her how delighted they were to see a sister raised to so high a rank. The sultana, on her part, always received them with every mark of esteem and affection which they could expect from a sister who was not unduly elated with her newly-acquired dignity, and who still continued to love them with the same cordiality she had shown in old times.

"Some months after her marriage the sultana had hopes of becoming a mother, a circumstance which gave the sultan great pleasure; and universal joy prevailed when the news became known, not only in the palace, but throughout all the Persian dominions. The two sisters came to offer their congratulations, and to entreat their sister to accept them as her attendants. The sultana replied, 'My dear sisters, you may be assured that I should not make choice of any one else, if the matter rested entirely with me; I am infinitely obliged to you for your good wishes to me, but I must submit to whatever the sultan may command. You may, however, use all the interest your husbands possess at court, to have this favour requested of the sultan; and if he speaks to me on the subject, you may be certain that I shall not only express my wish to him that he will confer the favour on me, but shall also thank him most heartily if he makes choice of you.'

"The two husbands each solicited the courtiers who were their patrons, entreating the latter to employ their influence to obtain for their wives the honour they aspired to; and these patrons exerted themselves with so much diligence and success, that the sultan promised to consider the matter. He kept his word; and in a conversation he had with the sultana, he told her that he thought her sisters would be better attendants for her than strangers could be, but that he would not appoint them to that office until he had previously obtained her consent. The sultana, sensible of the deference the sultan thus obligingly paid to her wishes, replied, 'O my lord, I am ready to do whatever your majesty may think right; but since you have had the goodness to turn your thoughts on my sisters, I must thank you for the preference you have given them for my sake; and I will not deny that I shall accept their services with much greater satisfaction than if they were strangers.'

"The Sultan Khosrouschah appointed the sisters of the sultana to attend her; and the sisters in consequence immediately took up their residence in the palace, quite overjoyed at having found so good an opportunity of putting in practice the detestable wickedness which they meditated.

"In due time the sultana became the mother of a prince as beautiful as the morning;

but neither his beauty nor his infant helplessness could soften the obdurate hearts of the two sisters. They wrapped him up very carelessly in some linen clothes, put him into a small basket, and lowered it with him into the current of a canal which flowed under the apartment of the sultana; and they produced a little dead dog, asserting that the sultana had been delivered of it. This unpleasant intelligence was announced to the sultan, who gave way to a violent fit of rage, which might have proved fatal to the sultana if his grand vizier had not represented to him that he could not, without injustice, consider her as responsible for the caprices of nature.

"The basket with the prince in it was carried by the current beyond a wall, which bounded the view from the apartment of the sultana, but did not impede the course of the canal, which crossed the gardens of the palace. By chance the superintendent of the gardens of the sultan, one of the principal and most respected officers in the kingdom, was walking in the garden on the banks of the canal; and he, observing the basket floating on the water, called a gardener who was near. 'Go quickly,' said he, pointing to the floating basket, 'and bring me yonder thing, that I may see what it contains.' The gardener went immediately to the edge of the canal, and with the spade he had in his hand he dexterously drew the basket towards him, and lifted it out of the water.

"The superintendent of the gardens was very much surprised to see in the basket a child wrapped up in linen—a child evidently just born, but nevertheless very beautiful. This officer had been married a considerable time; but, though he was very desirous of having a family, Heaven had not yet granted his wishes. He turned to go home, and desired the gardener to follow him with the basket and child. When he had reached his house, which looked into the garden of the palace, he went immediately to the apartment of his wife. 'My dear wife,' said he, 'we have no children, but here is one that Heaven sends us; and I recommend it to your care. Send for a nurse for this boy as soon as possible, and foster him as if he were our own son: from this moment I adopt him.' The superintendent's wife joyfully took the child, and felt great pleasure in the charge. Her husband did not choose to investigate from whence the child could have come. 'I plainly see,' said he to himself, 'that it is from the apartment of the sultana; but it is not my business to inquire into what passes there, or to cause commotions in a place where peace should reign.'

"The following year the sultana was delivered of another prince. Her unnatural and inhuman sisters felt no more compassion for the second son than they had felt for his elder brother, and they had him exposed in the same way in a basket on the canal, and pretended that the sultana had brought forth a cat. Fortunately for the child, the superintendent of the gardens was near the canal at the time, and had him taken out and carried to his wife, charging her to take the same care of this second child as of the former one; and she readily agreed, not less from inclination than from a wish to comply with the good intentions of her husband.

"The Sultan of Persia felt still more indignant against the sultana for this second disappointment than he had been before; and his anger and resentment would have burst forth had not the grand vizier again made use of the most persuasive remonstrances to appease him.

"The sultana at length became a mother a third time, not of a prince, but of a daughter; but this poor little innocent also shared the fate of the two young princes her brothers. The two sisters, who had resolved not to desist from their detestable design until they succeeded in reducing the sultana to contempt and destitution by making her despised and driving her from her present state, got rid of the little princess by exposing her on the canal. She also was snatched from inevitable death by the charity and compassion of the superintendent, as the two princes her brothers had been, and with them she was nursed and educated.

"To this inhuman action the two sisters added deceit and imposture, as on the former occasions. They showed a piece of wood, which they falsely affirmed to be a mole, of which they declared the sultana had been delivered. The Sultan Khosrouschah could not repress his wrath when he heard of this last extraordinary production. 'This vile woman,' said he, 'will fill my palace with monsters if I suffer her to live any longer. No,' he added, 'this must not be; she is a monster herself, and I will rid the world of her.' He then pronounced the decree for her death, and commanded the grand vizier to see it executed.

"The grand vizier and those of the courtiers who were present threw themselves at the feet of the sultan, entreating him to revoke the sentence. The former addressing him said, 'O dread monarch, will your majesty allow me to represent to you that the laws which condemn evil-doers to death have been established only for the punishment of crimes? The three strange and unexpected misfortunes of the sultana cannot be deemed such. How can she be accused of having done wrong? Many women have met with similar misfortunes, and examples daily occur of such events; they are to be pitied, but

THE INFANT PRINCE SET ADRIFT ON THE CANAL BY THE JEALOUS SISTERS.

they are not punishable. Your majesty may, therefore, desist from seeing the sultana, yet still suffer her to live. The affliction in which she will pass the remainder of her days after having lost your favour will be a sufficient atonement for any offence she may have committed.'

"The Sultan of Persia yielded to these arguments, for he plainly saw the injustice of condemning to death a sultana who had really done no wrong. 'Let her live, then,' cried he; 'but I grant her life only on a condition which will make her wish for death more than once every day. Let there be erected a sort of wooden cage or prison at the gate of the principal mosque, and let one of the windows be always open. She shall be shut up in this cage, dressed in a coarse habit, and every Mussulman who goes to the mosque to say his prayers shall spit in her face as he passes. If any one fails to comply with this order, he shall be subjected to the same punishment. And, that I may be punctually obeyed, I command you, vizier, to appoint proper persons to see this sentence executed.'

"The tone of voice in which the sultan pronounced this inhuman decree silenced the grand vizier. The command was carried into effect, to the great satisfaction of the two jealous sisters. The building was erected. When it was completed, the unfortunate sultana was confined in it as the sultan had commanded, and ignominiously exposed to the contempt and ridicule of the common people. This undeserved humiliation she bore with a firmness and patience that attracted the admiration, and at the same time the compassion, of all those who judged the matter according to the rules of justice.

"Meanwhile the two princes and the princess were brought up with parental tenderness by the superintendent of the gardens and his wife; and this affection was increased as they advanced in age, by the greatness of mind which displayed itself in the brothers as well as the sister, and likewise by the extreme beauty of the latter, who every day unfolded new charms; and still further by the docility of the children, by their inclinations, which were much above the trivial pursuits of children in general, and by a certain air and manner, which plainly indicated their rank. In order to distinguish the two princes according to their age, they named the first Bahman, and the second Perviz, both names of ancient kings of Persia. The princess they called Parizade, also after several of the Persian queens and princesses.

"When the princes were old enough, the superintendent of the gardens provided them with a master to teach them to read and write; and the princess their sister, who was present when they took their lessons, though younger than her brothers, showed so great a desire to learn also, that the superintendent, delighted with the disposition he saw in her to improve herself, gave her the same master. Her vivacity and quick penetration soon excited in her a desire to excel, and in a short time time she became as clever as her brothers.

"From that time the two princes and their sister had the same masters in various branches of learning, such as geography, poetry, and history; and also in the occult sciences. And as they showed wonderful facility in learning, they made so great a progress that their masters were astonished, and soon confessed, without hesitation, that their pupils would in a short time go beyond what they themselves knew. In her hours of recreation, the princess learnt to sing and to play on several instruments. When the princes began to ride on horseback, their sister would not allow them to have even this advantage over her. She took part in their martial exercises, so that she knew the whole art of horsemanship, of archery, of throwing the javelin, and often also excelled them in the race.

"The superintendent, who was highly delighted to see his adopted children so accomplished in every bodily and every mental acquirement, and who considered that they fully recompensed him, even beyond his most sanguine expectations, for the expense he had been at in their education, formed a more extensive plan for their advancement and pleasure. Till then, contented with his residence in the centre of the garden of the palace, he had lived without having a country house: he now purchased one at a little distance from the city, which had a good deal of ground annexed, consisting of fields, meadows, and woods; and as the house did not appear to him sufficiently handsome or convenient, he had it pulled down, and spared no expense in rebuilding it, to render it the most magnificent habitation in the neighbourhood. He went every day, that by his presence he might excite to greater expedition the large number of workmen he employed; and as soon as an apartment was completed for his reception, he passed several days there at a time, indeed spending there all the leisure the functions and duties of his office would allow him. At length, by continued assiduity on his part, the house was finished; and while it was being furnished with equal dispatch in the most elegant style, corresponding with the richness and magnificence of the edifice, he had the garden laid out according to a design which he had himself planned, and in the manner which the nobles of Persia usually adopt. He added to this garden a park of vast extent, which he caused to be enclosed with substantial walls, and stocked with all kinds of animals for the chase, that the princes and their sister might enjoy the diversion of hunting whenever they wished.

"When this house was entirely completed and ready to be inhabited, the superintendent of the gardens threw himself at the feet of the sultan, and after representing to his royal master the length of time he had been in his service and the infirmities of age which were advancing on him, he entreated permission to resign his office into the hands of his majesty. The sultan granted his old servant this favour with much pleasure, for he was well satisfied with the service of the superintendent, who had been in office not only during his own reign, but also while his father was on the throne; and in giving him his dismissal, the sultan asked him what he could do to recompense him. 'O king,' replied the superintendent, 'I am so overwhelmed with the favours I have received from your majesty, as well as from the sultan your father of happy memory, that I have now nothing to desire but that you extend your favour to me until I die.' He then took his leave of the sultan, and removed to the country house he had built, taking with him the two princes Bahman and Perviz, and the Princess Parizade. His wife had been dead some years. He had not enjoyed his retirement here with them longer than five or six months, when he was taken from them by a death so sudden, that he had not even time to acquaint them with the true circumstances of their birth; a thing which, however, he had resolved on doing, as a necessary inducement to them to continue to live, as they had hitherto done, according to their rank and condition, and in conformity with the education he had given them and the natural inclinations they evinced.

"The princes Bahman and Perviz, and their sister Parizade, who knew no other father than the superintendent of the gardens, mourned for him as for a parent, and performed all the duties which filial affection and gratitude required of them. Perfectly satisfied with the possessions bequeathed to them, they continued to live together in the same union which they had hitherto preserved; the princes feeling no ambition to appear at court, or to aspire to those principal offices and dignities which they might easily have acquired.

"One day, when the two brothers were hunting and Parizade had remained at home, an aged female Mussulman devotee presented herself at the gate, and entreated permission to enter and repeat her prayers, as it was the hour of devotion. The princess was asked if she would allow this, and she ordered the applicant to be admitted and shown into the oratory, which had been erected by the superintendent in the house, as there was no mosque in the neighbourhood. The princess also desired that when the devotee had finished her prayers she might be taken over the house and gardens, and then conducted to her.

"The devotee went in and repeated her prayers in the oratory; when she had finished, two of the princess's women, who were waiting for her to come out, invited her to visit the house and gardens. As she declared herself ready to follow them, they took her through all the apartments, in each of which she scanned everything closely, as if she understood the value of the furniture and the proper arrangement of each room. The attendants also went with her into the gardens, the design of which she thought so new and ingenious, that she admired it very much, and observed that whoever had laid them out must have been a great master in the art. She was at last conducted before the princess, who received her in a large saloon, which, in beauty, elegance, and richness, surpassed all that the visitor had seen in the other apartments.

"As soon as the princess saw the devotee enter the saloon, she said, 'O my good mother, come here and sit by me. I am very happy in the opportunity which chance affords me of profiting for some minutes by the experience and conversation of a person like you, who have taken the right path by devoting yourself entirely to Heaven, and whose advice every one that is wise should also follow.'

"The devotee, instead of taking a place upon the sofa, would have seated herself on the ground, but the princess would not suffer her to do so: she rose from her place, and going towards her guest, took the stranger by the hand, and obliged her to sit near her in the place of honour. The devotee was sensible of this civility, and said to her, 'O beautiful lady, I ought not to be treated thus honourably, and I only obey you because you command it, and are mistress in your own house.' When she was seated, before they began to converse, one of the princess's women placed before them a small table, inlaid with mother-of-pearl and ebony, with a basin of porcelain on it containing a variety of cakes, and some smaller dishes with the fruits that were in season, together with sweetmeats, both liquid and dry.

"The princess took one of the cakes and offered it to the devotee. 'Eat this, my good mother,' said she, 'and choose whatever fruit you like: you must want food after the long walk you have had to come here.' 'Lady,' replied the devotee, 'I am not accustomed to eat such delicate things; and if I accept them, it is only because I cannot refuse what Heaven sends me through such liberal hands.' Whilst the devotee was eating, the princess, who also ate something by way of setting her the example, asked her several questions on the devotional exercises she practised, and on the manner in which she lived; to all which the stranger replied with great humility. Led on from one subject to another, the princess at length asked her what she thought of the house they were in, and whether it suited her taste.

"'Bounteous lady,' replied the devotee, 'I should have very bad taste if I found any fault in it. It is elegant, cheerful, and richly furnished, and the decorations are managed with great judgment. It is situated in pleasant grounds, and no one could imagine a garden more delightful than that which belongs to it. But if you will permit me to speak frankly, I must take the liberty to tell you that the house would be incomparable if three things, which in my opinion are wanting, were added to it.' 'My good woman,' replied Parizade, 'what are these three things? I entreat you in the name of Heaven to inform me; I will spare nothing to procure them, if it be possible.'

"'Lady,' returned the devotee, 'the first of these three things is the talking bird. It is a very rare bird, called Bulbulhezar; and it has the power of attracting all the singing birds in the vicinity, which come to accompany its song. The second thing is the singing tree, the leaves of which are so many mouths, that constantly form an harmonious and never-ceasing concert of different voices. The third and last is the golden water, one single drop of which, dropped into a basin made for the purpose in any part of a garden, increases so rapidly, that it immediately fills the vessel, and then rises in the middle in a sort of fountain, which never ceases springing up and falling into the basin without ever running over.'

"'O good mother,' cried the princess, 'how much I am obliged to you for having told me of these things! They are astonishing indeed, and I never heard that the world contained anything so curious and wonderful; but as I am sure that you know the place where they may be found, I hope you will do me the favour to inform me of it.'

"In order to satisfy the princess, the devotee replied, 'I should be unworthy, O beautiful lady, of the hospitality you have so bounteously shown me, if I refused to gratify your curiosity on the subject respecting which you are so desirous of gaining information. Allow me, therefore, to tell you, that the three things I have just mentioned are all to be found in the same place on the confines of this kingdom, and on the side nearest India. The road which leads to this place passes by your house. He whom you send to procure them has only to follow this road for twenty days; and on the twentieth let him ask where the talking bird, the singing tree, and the golden water are to be found, and the first person he meets will point them out to him.' As she finished these words the devotee rose, and having taken her leave, she continued her journey.

"Princess Parizade had her mind so occupied with this information which the Mussulman devotee had given her on the subject of the talking bird, the singing tree, and the golden water, that she did not perceive her visitor was gone until she wanted to ask her some questions to render her instructions more clear. She did not, in fact, think that what she had just heard was sufficiently explanatory to authorise her taking a journey that might be useless. She would not, however, send after the devotee to make her return, but endeavoured to recollect all that she had said, and to impress it on her memory, so that nothing might escape. When she thought that she was perfectly sure

FUNERAL CAVALCADE OF THE SUPERINTENDENT OF THE GARDENS.

of every circumstance, she reflected with the greatest satisfaction on the pleasure she should experience, if she could attain the possession of such wonderful things; but the difficulties that intervened, and the fear of not succeeding in the undertaking, filled her with uneasiness.

"Princess Parizade was absorbed in these considerations when the princes her brothers returned from the chase. They entered the saloon; but instead of finding her with an open countenance and cheerful temper, according to her usual custom, they were surprised to see her brooding and silent, as if some affliction had befallen her. She did not even raise her head to indicate that she was aware of their presence.

"Prince Bahman was the first to speak. 'O sister,' said he, 'where are the cheerfulness and gaiety which have hitherto been your inseparable companions? Are you unwell? Has any misfortune befallen you? Has anything afflicted you? Tell us, that we may participate in your grief, and apply some remedy; or that we may revenge you, if any person has had the temerity to offend a lady like you, to whom every respect is due.'

"The princess remained for some time without making any reply or altering her position. At length she raised her eyes and glanced at the princes her brothers; then looking down again, she replied that nothing ailed her.

"'Dear sister,' replied Prince Bahman, 'you do not tell us the truth: something must be the matter, and even something of a serious nature. It is not possible that in the short time of our absence from you, so great and unexpected a change as that which we observe in you can have happened without a cause. You must not expect us to be content with an answer so far from satisfactory. Do not, therefore, conceal from us what occasions your thoughtfulness, unless you wish us to believe that you desire to end that friendship and union which has till now subsisted among us from our earliest infancy.'

"The princess, who was very far from wishing to quarrel with her brothers, did not choose to let them retain such an opinion. 'When I told you,' she said, 'that nothing ailed me, I meant nothing that affected you; but since you press me to explain the matter, and urge me by the right of friendship and by the affection there is between us, I will tell you all the circumstances.

"'You thought, as I did also, that this house, which our late respected father built for us, was quite complete, and that there was not one single thing wanting in it. I have, however, been informed to-day that there are three things which would set it beyond comparison above every other country house in the whole world. These things are the talking bird, the singing tree, and the golden water.' After having explained to her brothers in what the several excellencies of these three things consisted, she went on and said, 'A devotee of our holy religion is the person who has told me of these things; and she has informed me of the place where they are to be found, and of the way that leads to them. You may think, perhaps, that these things, which are requisite to make our habitation excel all others, are of little consequence, and that our abode will always be esteemed a very handsome one, notwithstanding their absence, and that we can very well do without them. You may think on this subject as you please; but I cannot help telling you that, with respect to myself, I am convinced they are absolutely necessary, and I shall not be satisfied until I see them here. Whether, therefore, you take any interest or not in the things themselves, I request you to assist me with your advice, and point out some one whom I can employ to obtain them.'

"'Dear sister,' replied Prince Bahman, 'nothing that interests you can be indifferent to us. Your anxiety to possess these three things you mention is quite enough to engage us to take the same interest. But beyond what we feel on your account, we are ourselves anxious to possess such rarities. I am well satisfied my brother is of the same opinion with myself. We ought, therefore, to do everything in our power to procure these three things; and, indeed, their singularity and importance fully deserve our endeavours. I, then, will undertake this matter. Only tell me the road I am to go and the place where they are to be found, and I will not defer my journey longer than to-morrow.'

"'Brother,' said Prince Perviz, 'it is not right that you should absent yourself from home for so long a time as this enterprise will require: you are our chief and support; and I must request my sister to join with me in desiring you to relinquish this design, and let me undertake the journey: I will endeavour to acquit myself to your satisfaction, and it will also be much more proper that I should run the risk.' 'I am very well satisfied of your good intentions, brother,' replied Prince Bahman, 'and am sure you would execute the business quite as well as I should; but I have made up my mind I will go, and nothing shall prevent me. You must remain with our sister, whom I need not recommend to your particular care.' The remainder of the day was passed by them in preparations for the journey, and in learning from the princess the different signs and observations that the devotee had given for guidance on the road.

"Very early the next morning Prince Bahman mounted his horse; and Prince Perviz and his sister, who were anxious to see him set off, embraced him and wished him a prosperous journey. At the very instant of their saying farewell, the princess recollected an objection that till now had not struck her. 'Until this moment, my brother,' she exclaimed, 'I did not reflect upon the various accidents to which travellers are exposed in their journeys: who knows whether I shall ever see you again? Dismount, therefore, I conjure you, and do not undertake this journey. I would infinitely rather live without the talking bird, the singing tree, and the golden water, than run the least risk of losing you for ever.'

"'O sister,' replied Prince Bahman, smiling at the sudden alarm of Parizade, 'my resolution is taken; and even were that not the fact, I would take it now, and you should see that I would execute it. The accidents you speak of happen only to the unfortunate. It is true that I may be among that number; but I may also be among the successful, and they form a much more numerous class than the others. But as enterprises of this kind are in their nature uncertain, and as I may fail in my endeavours, all that I can now do is to give you this knife.'

"Prince Bahman then took out a knife, and presented it in its case to the princess. 'Take this,' continued he, 'and occasionally give yourself the trouble to draw it out of its case and examine it. So long as you shall find it clean and bright as it is now, you may be certain that I am alive; but if you ever see any drops of blood fall from it, you may be assured I am no longer living, and may consider me as lost to you.'

"This was the only thing that the princess could obtain from Prince Bahman. He then again took leave of her and his brother; and, being well mounted, armed, and equipped, set out. He proceeded straight forward on his journey, without turning either to the right or left, and continued to traverse the kingdom of Persia. On the twentieth day of his journey he perceived by the side of the road a most hideous old man. The stranger was seated at the foot of a tree, at a little distance from a cottage which served him as a retreat against the inclemency of the weather.

"His eyebrows were like snow, as was also his hair and his beard, and they quite overhung his forehead; his moustaches completely covered his mouth, while his beard, equally white with his hair, descended almost to his feet. The nails of his hands and feet were of an unnatural length; and he wore on his head a sort of large and flat hat that served as an umbrella. The remainder of his dress consisted simply of a mat that was wrapt entirely round him.

"This old man was a dervish, who had for many years retired from the world, and neglected his own concerns, in order to give himself entirely to the duties of devotion; and from disregard of earthly things, he had at last become the figure just described.

"Prince Bahman had been very attentive from the break of day in observing whether he met any one who could describe the place of which he was in search; he stopped, therefore, when he came near the dervish, who was, in fact, the first person he had met, and immediately dismounted, that he might in every particular conform to the instructions the devotee had given the princess. He advanced towards the dervish, holding his horse by the bridle, and addressed him in these words: 'May Heaven, my good father, prolong your days, and grant you the accomplishment of your wishes.'

"The dervish returned the prince's salute, but spoke so unintelligibly that not a single word could be understood. As the prince observed that the obstacle arose from the moustaches of the dervish, which quite covered his mouth, and as he did not wish to proceed without getting the information he wanted, he took a pair of scissors with which he was provided, and after fastening his horse to the branch of a tree, he said to him, 'My good dervish, I have something to say to you, but your moustaches prevent me from understanding your reply. I shall be much obliged to you if you will allow me to cut off both those and your eyebrows, which absolutely disfigure you, and make you look more like a bear than a man.'

"The dervish made no objection to the design of the prince, but suffered him to do as he wished. And as Prince Bahman saw when he had finished the operation that the dervish had a fresh and clear skin, and appeared much younger than he had seemed at first, he said to him, 'If I had a mirror, my good dervish, I would let you see how much younger you appear. You are now a man, but no one could distinguish before what you were.' The compliments of Prince Bahman raised a smile on the countenance of the dervish. 'Whoever you are, sir,' said the dervish to him, 'I am much obliged to you for the good office you have done me; and I am ready to show my gratitude in any way that may be in my power. You would not have dismounted unless you were in want of something: inform me what it is, and I well endeavour to satisfy you if I am able.' 'My good dervish,' replied the prince, 'I come from a considerable distance, and am seeking the talking bird, the singing tree, and the golden water. I know that these three things are somewhere in this neighbourhood, but I am not aware of the precise spot. If you are acquainted with it, I entreat you to show me the way to it, that I may not make a mistake, and thus lose the long journey I have undertaken.'

"As the prince addressed these words to the dervish, he observed that the holy man changed colour, cast his eyes on the ground, and put on a most serious countenance; and then, instead of making any reply, he remained silent. Prince Bahman therefore resumed his speech, and added, 'I think, my good father, that you understand what I say. Tell me, then, whether you can answer me what I ask you, in order that, if you cannot, I may not lose any more time, but go somewhere else for the information.' The dervish at last broke silence. 'O my lord,' said he, 'the road you inquire for is well known to me; but the friendship I conceived for you the instant I beheld you, and which is much increased by the great service you have rendered me, has bred a doubt in me, and makes me uncertain whether I ought to give you the information you require.' 'What motive can hinder you?' asked the prince. 'What difficulty can you have in giving it me?' 'I will tell you,' answered the dervish: 'I am thinking of the danger to which you will be exposed, and which is infinitely greater than you can at all imagine. A great many other persons, and some who did not possess less courage or perseverance than you seem to have, have passed this place, and have asked me the same question which you now put. After I had used all my endeavours and persuasions to prevent them from proceeding, they have nevertheless persisted in carrying out their project. I have at last, although against my inclination, informed them of the road, at their repeated entreaties; and I can assure you that every one of them has perished, and I have not seen one individual return. If, therefore, you have the least regard for your life, and will follow my advice, you will not proceed a step farther, but immediately return home.'

"Prince Bahman, however, persisted in his determination. 'I am willing to believe,' he said to the dervish, 'that your advice is sincere, and I feel obliged to you for this proof of your friendship; but however great the danger may be of which you speak, neither that nor anything else can make me alter my resolution. If any one should attack me, I am well armed to defend myself, and he will not possess greater courage than I.' 'Those, however, who will attack you,' replied the dervish, 'for there are many of them, are invisible. How, then, can you defend yourself from invisible beings?' 'All this is of no consequence,' cried the prince; 'whatever you may say to me, you will not persuade me to act contrary to my duty. Since you are acquainted with the road, I once more entreat you to inform me of it: pray do not refuse me this favour.'

"When the dervish found that he could make no impression upon the mind of Prince Bahman, and that the prince continued obstinately determined to proceed on his journey notwithstanding every dissuasion, he put his hand into a bag that lay by his side, and took out a bowl, which he presented to the prince. 'Since I cannot persuade you,' said the dervish, 'to pay any attention to what I have said, and to profit by my advice, take this bowl; and as soon as you have again mounted your horse, set the bowl rolling

PRINCE BAHMAN AND THE DERVISH.

before you, and follow it until you come to the foot of a mountain, where it will stop. There you must dismount; and you may leave your horse with the bridle over his neck: he will remain in that spot until you come back. As you ascend the mountain you will see both on the right and left of you a great quantity of large black stones, and you will hear on all sides a confusion of voices that will rail at you and say a thousand offensive things in order to discourage you and prevent your reaching the top; but you must be particularly careful not to be alarmed; and above all things be sure not to turn your head to look behind you; for if you do, at that very moment you will be changed into a black stone like those you see about you, which in fact are so many men who, like you, have undertaken this enterprise, and, as I have told you, have failed in the attempt. If you overcome this danger, against which I assure you I cannot warn you in terms sufficiently strong, and on which I would have you reflect very seriously, when you arrive at the top of the mountain you will there find a cage in which is confined the talking bird that you are in search of. As it speaks, you must ask it where the singing tree is, and also the golden water, and it will inform you. I have now nothing more to say: you know what you have to do and what to avoid; but if you are open to good counsel you will follow the advice I have given you, and not expose yourself to the risk of losing your life. Once again, while there still remains an opportunity for you to reflect, consider well what you are undertaking, and that you cannot escape the penalty should you through inadvertence subject yourself to it.'

"'I cannot think of following the advice which you have now repeated, and for which I must ever feel obliged to you,' replied Prince Bahman, after he had taken the bowl; 'but I will endeavour to profit by what you say, and will avoid looking back as I ascend; and I hope you will soon see me return to thank you still more gratefully, laden with the spoils I am in search of.' Having said this, to which the dervish returned no other answer than that he wished him success, and should with great pleasure see him come back, the prince remounted his horse, took leave of the dervish by making a profound reverence with his head, and then threw the bowl before him.

"The bowl continued to roll on with the same celerity with which Prince Bahman first threw it from him; in order, therefore, to follow and not loose sight of it, he was obliged to accommodate the pace of his horse to its motion as it went forward. He continued close behind the bowl; and when it came to the foot of the mountain the dervish mentioned, it stopped, and the prince dismounted. He did not fasten his horse, which, indeed, did not stir from the spot even when he threw the bridle on its neck. When he had cast his eyes over the mountain, as far as he could see, and had observed the black stones, he began to ascend, and had not proceeded more than four or five steps before he heard the voices which the dervish had mentioned, although he could see no one. Some said, 'What is the fool about? Where is he going? What does he want? Don't let him pass.' Others cried, 'Stop him! seize him! murder him!' While a third party, in voices like thunder exclaimed, 'Thief! Assassin! Murderer!' Some, on the contrary, called out in a mocking tone, 'No, no, do not hurt him; let the pretty fellow pass: he is the very person for whom the cage and bird are kept.'

"Never pausing to heed these tiresome and importunate exclamations, Prince Bahman continued for some time to ascend with great fortitude and perseverance. But the voices kept increasing, and the noise became so great, and appeared so nearly surrounding him, that he began to be very much alarmed. His feet and legs trembled under him; he felt faint; and, as soon as he found that his strength began to fail, he forgot the advice of the dervish, and turned round in order to fly, when he was instantly changed into a black stone; a transformation that had happened to many others before him who had attempted the same enterprise. His horse also was changed into stone.

"Ever since Prince Bahman first set out on his expedition, Princess Parizade had constantly wore the knife with its case at her girdle, in order to ascertain, from time to time, whether her brother was alive or dead; nor had she ever omitted to consult it several times during the day. She had in this manner the consolation of learning that Prince Bahman was in perfect health; and she also frequently talked of him with Prince Perviz, who was equally anxious with herself to learn some news of the absent one.

"At length, on the fatal day when Prince Bahman was changed into a black stone, as the prince and princess were as usual conversing about him in the evening, Prince Perviz observed, 'Pray, sister, take the knife out, and let us see how our brother is.' She drew it forth, and, looking at its blade, they saw blood run from the point. Struck with horror at this sight, the princess threw down the knife. 'Alas! my dearest brother,' she exclaimed, 'I, then, have caused you to perish entirely through my own fault! Never shall I see you more. How wretched I am! Why did I mention to you the talking bird, the singing tree, or the golden water? Or rather, what mattered it to me to know the opinion the devotee had formed of this house and grounds, and whether she thought them beautiful or ugly, well or ill furnished? Would to Heaven that she had never thought of addressing herself to me. Hypocritical and deceitful wretch!' she continued, 'is it thus thou hast repaid the reception I afforded thee? Why didst thou speak to me of a bird, of a tree, and of a water which I now believe to have no real existence, but which have yet caused the unfortunate death of my dearest brother? and yet, through thy enchantment, imaginary as they are, I cannot drive them from my mind.'

"Prince Perviz was not less grieved at the loss of his brother than was the princess; but without indulging in useless complaints, and understanding from his sister's lamentations that she still most ardently wished to obtain the talking bird, the singing tree, and the golden water, he interrupted her and said, 'All our sorrow and regret for the death of Prince Bahman are unavailing; neither our tears nor our affliction will restore him to life. It is the will of Heaven, and we ought to submit to it. Let us adore the dispensations of Providence, whether good or ill, and not endeavour to penetrate into the cause of them. Why should we at this moment doubt the words of the devotee, after having hitherto supposed them perfectly just and true? Why should we think she spoke of three things that did not exist, and merely invented them to annoy and deceive you, who, so far from giving her any cause of enmity, have received and entertained her with so much liberality and kindness? Let us rather suppose that the death of my brother arose from his own fault, or from some accident for which we are unable to account. Therefore, my dear sister, let not his death prevent us from pursuing our inquiry. I at first offered to undertake the journey instead of him. I am still willing to do it; and as his example and fate do not in the least make me alter my opinion, I will set out to-morrow morning.'

"The princess did all she could to dissuade Prince Perviz, begging him not to expose himself to the danger, lest, instead of the loss of one brother, she might have to lament the death of two. However, he continued inflexible, notwithstanding all the remonstrances she could make. But before he set out, that she might be informed of the success of his expeditition, as she had been in the instance of Prince Bahman by means of the knife the prince had left her, Prince Perviz gave her a chaplet, consisting of a hundred pearls, for the same purpose. And as he presented it to her he said, 'Tell over this chaplet during my absence, to know my fate; and if, in telling it, it should happen that the pearls are set fast as if they were glued, so that you cannot move them or make them go over each other, it will be a sign that I have experienced the same fate as my brother. But let us hope that this will not happen, and that I shall have the happiness of seeing you again, to our mutual joy.'

"Prince Perviz began his journey, and on the twentieth day he met the dervish, exactly in the same spot where Prince Bahman had found him. He went up to him, and having saluted him, requested information concerning the place where the talking bird, the singing tree, and the golden water were to be found. The dervish made the same difficulties, and urged the same remonstrances, as in the case of Prince Bahman, and even told Prince Perviz that, not long since, a person of the prince's age, and who bore a great likeness to him, had come and asked the road; and that, overcome by the pressing entreaties and importunities of the stranger, he had shown him the way, and had given him a guide, and told him every precaution that he ought to follow in order to succeed but he had never seen the stranger return; and he had therefore no doubt that he had experienced the same fate as those who had gone before.

"'My good dervish,' replied Prince Perviz, 'I know the person you mention very well. He was my elder brother, and I know for a certainty that he is dead. But what was the nature of his death I know not.' 'I can tell you, then,' replied the dervish: 'he has been changed into a black stone, like those I have mentioned to you; and you may expect to undergo the same transformation, unless you follow more accurately than he the advice I have given you—that is, if you persist in proceeding with what I so earnestly exhort you to desist from, and concerning which I still beg you to alter your resolution.'

"'O dervish,' said Prince Perviz, 'I cannot sufficiently prove to you how much I feel indebted for the interest you have taken in the preservation of my life, though I am so much a stranger to you, and have done nothing to deserve your kindness; but I must inform you that I thought very seriously upon the subject before I undertook this expedition, and that I cannot now abandon it. I entreat you, therefore, to extend to me the same favour you showed my brother. I shall perhaps succeed better than he has done in adhering to the advice which I am now waiting to hear from you.' 'Since, then, I cannot accomplish my wishes by persuading you to change your resolution,' said the dervish, 'if my great age did not prevent me rising, I would get up and give you a bowl which would serve you as a guide.'

"Without troubling the dervish to say any more, Prince Perviz dismounted, and as he approached the dervish, the latter took a bowl out of the bag in which there were a great many more, and giving it to the prince, told him how to make use of it, as he had before informed Prince Bahman; and after having warned him to be very careful, and not listen to or be alarmed at the voices he would hear, however threatening they might be, he desired him to continue ascending until he perceived the cage and the bird. The dervish then bade him farewell.

"Prince Perviz thanked the dervish; and as soon as he had mounted his horse, he threw the bowl before him, and rode after it, according to the directions he had received. He at length arrived at the foot of the mountain, and when he saw the bowl stop, he dismounted. Before he began to ascend, he waited a moment to consider and recall to his memory all the advice and precautions the dervish had given him. He then called forth his courage, and went up, quite determined to reach the top of the mountain. He had hardly proceeded five or six paces before he heard a voice close behind him, like that of a man, calling to him in insulting tones. 'Stop, adventurous wretch!' it exclaimed, 'until I punish thy audacity.'

"At this menace Prince Perviz forgot the advice of the dervish, seized his sabre, and drew it. He then turned round to seek his aggressor: he had scarcely time to see that no one followed him before both he and his horse were changed into black stones.

"From the moment when Prince Perviz had set out, Parizade did not omit to put her hand to the chaplet she had received from him the day before his departure, and to count over the pearls with her fingers, whenever she was not otherwise employed; nor did she even part with it during the night. Every evening, when she retired to rest, she put it round her neck; and when she awoke in the morning, the first thing she did was to feel it, in order to know if the different pearls were loose. At length the fatal day and hour arrived when Prince Perviz experienced the same fate as his brother Prince Bahman had encountered, and was changed into a black stone; and as the princess held the chaplet as usual, and began to count it, she suddenly perceived that the pearls could no longer be separated, but seemed fastened together, and she knew too well that the prince her brother was dead.

"As she had already formed her resolution as to the course she intended to take if this unfortunate event happened, she did not waste her time in exclamations of sorrow. She made the greatest efforts to confine her feelings to her own breast; and the next morning, disguised as a man, and well armed and equipped, after first telling her attendants that she should return in a few days, she set out, and pursued the same road the two princes her brothers had taken.

"The princess, who had been very much accustomed to ride on horseback, and had often taken the diversion of hunting, supported the fatigue of the journey much better than most women would have done. As she travelled as quickly as her brothers had done, she also met the dervish on the twentieth day of her journey. As soon as she came up to him, she alighted; and holding her horse by the bridle, she went and sat down close to him. 'Will you allow me, my good dervish,' she said to him, 'to rest myself a little while near you? and will you also do me the favour to inform me whether there is not some place in this neighbourhood where there is a talking bird, a singing tree, and some golden water? 'O lady,' replied the dervish, 'for your voice evidently tells me you are not of our sex, although you are disguised as a man, and therefore I ought to address you as a female, I accept with great pleasure the compliment you pay me. I do know the place where the things are which you mention; but for what reason do you ask this question?' 'I have heard such an extraordinary account of them,' answered the princess, 'that I am anxious beyond measure to possess them.' 'You have been rightly informed, lady,' said the dervish; 'these things are more wonderful and singular than they can even have been described to you; but you probably have not been informed of

PRINCE PERVIZ GIVES A CHAPLET OF PEARLS TO THE PRINCESS.

the difficulties that must be overcome before you can acquire them. You would not, indeed, have engaged in so painful and dangerous an undertaking if you had been better informed. Listen to me, therefore, and do not proceed any farther. Return, and do not request me to contribute to your destruction.'

"'My good father,' replied the princess, 'I have come from a great distance, and I should be exceedingly sorry to return home without having put my design in execution. You tell me of difficulties and dangers; but you do not say in what these difficulties consist, and whence these dangers arise. This is what I wish to know, that I may consider and examine whether I may rely on my own strength and courage, or give up the enterprise.'

"The dervish then related to the princess everything he had before told Prince Bahman and Prince Perviz, and he even exaggerated the difficulties that would beset her in ascending to the top of the mountain where the bird was in its cage, and of which she must take possession, as from the bird she would learn where the tree and golden water were to be found. He mentioned the great noise of dreadful and menacing voices which she would hear on all sides of her, without seeing any one, and also the quantity of black stones she would find scattered around; things which were alone sufficient to alarm and dismay every one who knew that these stones were in fact so many gallant men, who had been thus transformed because they did not strictly observe the principal condition necessary for the success of this enterprise; and again he adjured her not to turn her head nor look back until she had obtained possession of the cage.

"When the dervish had finished his speech, the princess addressed him as follows: 'From what I understand by your instructions, the great difficulty in succeeding in this enterprise arises, in the first place, from the alarm and astonishment excited by the noise and din of different voices, without the appearance of any one, while the traveller ascends the mountain to the spot where the cage is placed; and, in the second place, from the temptation to look round. With respect to this last condition, I trust I shall be sufficiently mistress of myself to observe it most carefully. And in regard to the first, I freely own to you that these voices, as you represent them, are sufficient to alarm the most confident and steady. But as in all enterprises of importance and danger we are not prohibited from making use of any kind of plan or stratagem, I ask you whether I may not adopt some expedient in this instance, which is so very important to me?' 'What do you wish to do?' demanded the dervish. 'It appears to me,' the princess continued, 'that by stopping my ears with cotton, I shall prevent these voices, however loud and alarming they may be, from making any strong impression; and as they will thus also produce a less powerful effect upon my imagination, my mind will be more at ease, and I shall not be so disturbed as to be likely to lose my presence of mind.'

"'O lady,' said the dervish, 'among all those who have hitherto addressed themselves to me, in order to be informed of the road about which you have also inquired, I know not of any one who has made use of the plan you have proposed to me. All I know is, that no one has used such a precaution, and that all have perished. If, then, you persist in your intention, you may try the stratagem, and fortunate will you be if you are successful; but I advise you not to expose yourself to the danger.'

"'My good father,' replied the princess, 'nothing can prevent me from persevering in my design. My heart tells me that my plan will succeed; and I am resolved to make use of the means I mentioned. Nothing now remains, therefore, but that you tell me what road I must take; and this is a favour I must entreat you not to refuse me.' The dervish again exhorted her for the last time to consider well of the enterprise; but as he found she was resolutely fixed on the attempt, he took out a bowl and presented it to her. 'Take this bowl,' he added, 'and when you have remounted your horse, throw it before you. Follow it along all the windings and deviations you observe it to make, for it will roll on towards the mountain that contains what you are in search of, at which place you will find it stop. When this happens, do you also stop. Dismount from your horse, and begin to ascend the mountain. Go: you know the rest; do not neglect to profit by it.'

"Princess Parizade mounted her horse, after having first thanked the dervish and taken leave of him. She then threw the bowl before her, and followed it, as it proceeded along its road, till it came to the foot of the mountain, where it stopped. The princess alighted, and then stuffed her ears with cotton. After considering for a short time what was the path she should pursue in order to arrive at the top of the mountain, she began to ascend with a steady pace and an undaunted mind. She indeed heard the voices, but found that the cotton was of considerable service to her. The farther she advanced, the louder and more numerous did the voices become; but they did not make a sufficient impression to disturb her. She heard various insulting expressions, and satirical remarks derisive of her sex: these, however, she completely despised, and the only effect they had was to excite her laughter. 'Neither your reproaches nor your raillery,' she said to herself, 'offend me. Rail on and say your worst: I shall only think them ridiculous; and you will not prevent me from pursuing my way.' She had at length ascended so high, that she perceived the cage and the bird, which joined its cry to the other voices in the endeavour to intimidate her, calling out in a thundering tone, although it was so small a creature, 'Go back, thou fool: approach not!'

"Animated still more by this sight, the princess redoubled her speed. When she found herself so near the end of her journey, and had gained the top of the mountain, where the ground was level, she ran directly to the cage, and laying her hand upon it, said, 'I have caught thee now, in spite of yourself, and you shall never escape from me.'

"The princess then took the cotton from her ears, and the bird replied to her, 'O brave lady, do not suppose that I wish you any harm, from what I have done, together with those who have made so many efforts to preserve my liberty. Although I am confined within this cage, I am not dissatisfied with my lot; but as I am destined to become a slave, I would rather have you for my mistress, who have obtained me in so worthy and intrepid a manner, than any other person in the world: and from this moment I swear to you the most inviolable fidelity, and an entire submission to your commands. I know who you are, and I can even tell you more about yourself than you know. But the day will come when I shall render you a service which I trust you will candidly acknowledge. That I may immediately give you a mark of my sincerity, tell me what you wish, and I will obey you.'

"The possession of this prize filled the princess with inexpressible joy. She valued the bird the more, as the attempt to acquire it had deprived her of two brothers whom she tenderly loved, and had moreover been productive of so much fatigue and danger to herself; a danger the extent of which she herself was better acquainted with, now it was passed, than when she first undertook the enterprise, notwithstanding everything the dervish had told her. When the bird had finished its speech, the princess said to it, 'It was my intention, O bird, to have informed you that I wished for many things which are of the greatest consequence to me; and I am, therefore, highly pleased that you should have anticipated my inquiries by the evidence you have given of your readiness to oblige me. In the first place, I have understood that there is in this neighbourhood some golden water which possesses most wonderful properties; you must therefore inform me where it is.' The bird described the spot, which was not far distant. The princess went to it, and filled a small silver vessel she had brought with her. She then came back, and said to the bird, 'You must tell me something more: I am in search also of the singing tree;—tell me where that is.' 'Turn round,' replied the bird, 'and you will see behind you a wood; in that wood you will find the tree.' The wood was not far off, and the princess went there. The harmonious sounds she heard made her easily distinguish the tree she sought from all the others; but it was both large and lofty. She came back, and said to the bird, 'I have discovered the singing tree; but I can never take it up by the roots; or even if I could, I am unable to carry it.' 'Nor is it at all necessary,' answered the bird; 'you need only break off the smallest branch, and carry it with you, to plant in your garden. The branch will take root soon after it is planted, and will become in a very short time as beautiful and fine a tree as that which you have just now seen.'

"When the princess held in her hand the three things which the old female devotee had caused her so ardently to desire, she again addressed herself to the bird. 'All that you have yet done for me, O bird,' she said, 'is not sufficient. You have been the cause of the death of my two brothers, who are among the black stones which I saw as I ascended the hill: I must carry them back with me.' The bird seemed very unwilling to satisfy the princess on this point, and raised the greatest difficulty about it. 'Bird! bird!' replied the princess, 'do you remember that you told me you were my slave, as in fact you are, and that your life is at my disposal?' 'I cannot deny it,' answered the bird; 'and although what you request of me is a matter of the greatest difficulty, I will not fail to satisfy you. Cast your eyes around you, and look if you do not see a pitcher.' 'I do,' said the princess. 'Take it, then,' resumed the bird, 'and as you go down, sprinkle a little of the water it contains upon each of the black stones; and this will be the means of discovering your two brothers.'

"Princess Parizade took the pitcher, and at the same time carried the bird in its cage, the silver vessel of water, and the branch of the tree. As she began to descend the hill, she threw a little water from the pitcher upon every stone she passed, and each was directly changed into a man or a horse; and as she did not leave a single stone unsprinkled, all the horses, as well as the princes her brothers and the other persons, resumed their natural forms. She instantly recognized Prince Bahman and his brother, as they also knew her, and ran to embrace her. 'My dear brothers,' she exclaimed, after embracing them in her turn, and expressing her astonishment, 'what have you been doing here?' They replied that they had just awoke from a deep sleep. 'Perhaps so,' she added; 'but your sleep would most likely have continued to the end of the world. Do you not recollect that you went out in search of the talking bird, the singing tree, and the golden water? and that on coming here you beheld a great many black stones lying about this place? Look now, and see if there be one remaining. Those black stones were these gentlemen who stand around us, together with your horses, which are now, as you may observe, waiting for you. And if you wish to know how this miracle has been performed, I must inform you,' she added, showing the pitcher, for which she had now no further occasion, and had therefore set down at the foot of the mountain, 'that it is by virtue of the water with which this pitcher was filled, and some of which I have thrown over each stone. I did not wish to return without you after I had obtained the talking bird, which you may now see in this cage, and found the singing tree, of which this is a branch, and the golden water, of which this vessel is full. Therefore I compelled the bird, by means of the power I have acquired over it, to inform me where this pitcher was, and how I ought to make use of it.'

"Prince Bahman and Prince Perviz thus understood the obligation they were under to their sister: the other gentlemen, who were collected round her, and who had heard her speak, were equally conscious how much they were indebted to her; and so far from envying her the prize she had gained, and to which they had themselves aspired, they thought they could not better show their gratitude for the life she had restored to them than by declaring themselves her slaves, and ready to do whatever she ordered them.

"'My lords,' replied the princess, 'if you had paid any attention to what I said, you might have remarked that my object in what I have done was to recover my two brothers; if, therefore, you have derived any benefit from me, as you say you have, you are not under any obligation. I feel flattered by the compliment you have had the goodness to pay me, and I thank you for it as I ought. I therefore consider you all as being as much at liberty as you were before your misfortune, and I sincerely rejoice with you in the happiness you experience in your freedom. But let us not remain any longer in a place where there is nothing to detain us. Let us mount our horses, and return to that part of the world whence we came.'

"The princess set the example of departure, by taking her horse, which she found in the very spot where she had left it. Prince Bahman, who wished to assist her, went up to her before she mounted, and requested her to permit him to carry the cage. 'O my brother,' replied the princess, 'this bird is my slave, and I wish to carry it myself; but you may, if you please, take charge of the branch of the singing tree. Be so good, however, as to hold the cage while I get on horseback.' When she had mounted, and Prince Bahman had returned the cage to her, she turned towards Prince Perviz, and added, 'You, my brother, shall have the care of the vessel with the golden water in it, if it will not be troublesome to you.' Prince Perviz readily took charge of the silver vessel.

"When the two princes and all the others had mounted their horses, the princess waited for some one of them to put himself at their head and lead the way. The two princes wished, out of civility, that one of the others would do so; and they on the other hand requested the princess to conduct them. As Parizade saw that no one was inclined to assume this honour, but that they all left it to her, she addressed herself to them, and said, 'I am waiting, my lords, for you to proceed.' 'O lady,' replied one of those who were nearest her, in the name of the rest, 'even if we did not acknowledge the deference due to your sex, there is no distinction we should not be ready to bestow upon you, after the great benefits we have derived from you, although your great modesty chooses not to assume it to yourself. We entreat you, therefore, not to deprive us any longer of the happiness of following you.' 'My lords,' replied the princess, 'I by no means deserve the honour you do me, and I accept it only because you wish me to do so.' She immediately began to move forward; while the princes her brothers and all the rest followed without any distinction of rank.

"They all wished to see the dervish as they went on, to thank him for his kindness

THE PRINCESS PARIZADE CARRYING THE SINGING TREE.

and the good advice he had given them, of which they had proved the truth. But they found him no longer alive; nor could they tell whether his death was occasioned by old age, or by the loss of his occupation in pointing out the road which led to the acquisition of the three things which Princess Parizade had thus obtained.

"The company continued their journey; but every day produced a diminution in its numbers, as the different members who composed it had come from different countries. After acknowledging to the princess how much they were indebted to her, and taking leave of her and her brothers, they continued to depart in groups as they approached the different roads by which they had come; while Princess Parizade and the princes her brothers continued their journey until they arrived at their own house.

"When the princess had placed the cage in the garden, on that side of the house on which the saloon was, as the bird began its song a variety of other birds of the country came to accompany it with their notes. With respect to the branch, the Princess Parizade had it planted in her presence, in a particular spot at a little distance from the house. It immediately took root, and soon grew to a large tree, the leaves of which produced as much harmony, and as full a concert, as the tree from which it had been broken. She also ordered a large basin of beautiful marble to be constructed in the midst of a flower-bed; and when it was finished, she poured into it all the golden water the vessel contained. She immediately saw the water increase in volume, and bubble up; and when it had filled the basin up to the edge, it rose in the centre like a large fountain, twenty feet in height, and fell back into the basin without overflowing.

"The news of these wonders was soon spread over the country; and as the doors of the house or garden were never shut against any visitor, a great number of people continued to come and admire the three marvels.

"After a few days, Prince Bahman and Prince Perviz, who had quite recovered from the fatigues of their journey, resumed their former mode of life; and as the chase was their usual diversion, they mounted their horses, and went for the first time since their return, not into their park, but to hunt at the distance of two or three leagues from their house. While they were engaged in their sport, it happened that the Sultan of Persia accidentally came to hunt in the spot they had chosen. As soon, therefore, as they perceived by the great number of horsemen, that the sultan was approaching, they determined to give up their sport and retire, in order to avoid meeting him. But they took the very road by which he came, and thus met him in a part of the way that was so narrow that they could neither turn aside nor retreat without being seen. Their meeting was so sudden that they had only time to dismount, and prostrate themselves to the earth, without even raising their heads to look at the monarch. But the sultan, who saw that they were well mounted, and as handsomely and as properly dressed as if they had belonged to his court, felt some curiosity to see their faces. He stopped, therefore, and ordered them to rise.

"The princes rose, and remained standing before the sultan, in a manner so unrestrained and easy, yet so unassuming and modest, that the sultan was rather surprised. He looked fixedly at them for some time, without speaking. Admiring their open countenances and good manners, he inquired their names, and asked where they lived. Prince Bahman, who took upon himself to answer, replied, 'Mighty monarch, we are the sons of the superintendent of your majesty's gardens—of him who lately died; and we live in a house which he built for us a short time before his death, that we might continue there until we reached an age when we might be of use to your majesty, and request some employment when a proper occasion presented itself.' 'From what I now observe,' said the sultan, 'you seem very fond of hunting.' 'It is our customary amusement,' answered Prince Bahman, 'and a pursuit, moreover, which not one of your majesty's subjects who is destined to bear arms ought to neglect; at least, if he conforms to the ancient customs of the kingdom.' The sultan was delighted with this intelligent answer, and added, 'Since that is the case, I shall be happy to see you hunt. Come with me and choose the sort of hunting you like best.'

"The princes mounted their horses, and followed the sultan. They had not proceeded very far when various kinds of beasts came in view at the same time. Prince Bahman chose a lion as his adversary, and Prince Perviz a bear. They both began the attack with an intrepidity and ardour that astonished the sultan. They encountered their antagonists almost at the same time, and threw their javelins with so much skill that they pierced them through and through, and the sultan saw both the lion and the bear fall dead nearly at the same instant. Without taking any rest, Prince Bahman now pursued a bear, and Prince Perviz a lion, and in a few moments these also were extended lifeless on the ground. The princes still wished to continue the sport, but the sultan prevented them. He called them back, and when they came up to him he said, 'If I were to suffer you to go on, you would soon destroy all my hunting. It is not, however, so much on that account that I restrain you, as for your own sakes; for your lives will, from this time, be very dear to me, because I am convinced that your courage will one day become as useful to me as your society will be agreeable.'

"In fact, the Sultan Khosrouschah felt so strong a regard for the two princes that he invited them to his palace, and even wished them to return with him. 'Gracious sultan,' replied Prince Bahman, 'your majesty heaps honours on us in a manner we do not deserve, and we beg of you to dispense with our attendance.' The sultan could not comprehend what motives the princes could have for refusing the special mark of his

THE PRINCES PROSTRATE THEMSELVES BEFORE THE SULTAN OF PERSIA.

favour he was willing to extend to them; he therefore asked them the reason. 'Great sultan,' answered Prince Bahman, 'we have a sister, who is younger than ourselves, with whom we live in so united and happy a manner that we cannot undertake any plan without first consulting her; especially as she never does anything without asking our advice.' 'I rejoice to hear of this fraternal union,' said the sultan; 'go, then, and consult your sister, and return to-morrow to hunt with me, and bring me back your answer.'

"The two princes returned home. But neither of them thought any more of this adventure of having met the sultan, and of the honour of hunting with him. Accordingly, they omited to tell their sister of his wish that they should go to the palace with him instead of returning home. The next morning, when they were with the sultan, he said to them, 'Have you spoken to your sister? and does she consent to my having the pleasure of enjoying your society in a more agreeable manner?' The princes looked at each other, while the colour rushed into their cheeks. 'Great king,' replied Prince Bahman, 'we entreat your majesty to pardon us; but, in truth, neither my brother nor myself thought of it.' 'Do not, then, forget it again to-day,' answered the sultan, 'and remember to bring me an answer to-morrow.'

"The princes again forgot the sultan's commands; and yet he was not angry with them for their negligence. Instead of reproaching them, he took out three little golden balls which he had in a purse; and putting them into Prince Bahman's bosom, he said, with a smile on his countenance, 'These balls will prevent you from forgetting a third time what my regard for you makes me wish you to remember. The noise these balls will make this evening, in falling out of your clothes, will put you in mind of my injunction if you have not remembered it before.'

"The event turned out exactly as the sultan had predicted: except for the three balls of gold, the princes would again have forgotten to mention the matter to their sister Parizade. But as Prince Bahman took off his girdle, when he was preparing to retire to rest, the balls fell to the ground. He therefore went immediately to Prince Perviz, and they both proceeded to the apartment of their sister, who was not yet gone to bed. They asked the Princess Parizade's pardon for disturbing her at such an unseasonable hour, and then informed her of all the circumstances that had occured in their several meetings with the sultan.

"Princess Parizade was very much alarmed at this intelligence. 'Your accidental meeting with the sultan,' said she to them, 'is both fortunate and honourable for you, and in the end may be very advantageous; but to me it is truly melancholy and distressing. I see very well that it is on my account that you have withstood the wishes of the sultan, and I feel highly obliged to you for your kindness. I am sure, therefore, that your regard for me perfectly equals mine for you. You would rather be guilty of incivility towards the sultan, and refuse his kind invitation, than act in opposition to that fraternal union we have sworn to preserve; for you have supposed that, if you once begin to see and visit him, you will in the end be insensibly obliged to abandon me, and give yourself up entirely to his commands. But do you think it would be so easy a matter absolutely to gainsay the sultan on a point he seems so anxious to obtain? It is dangerous to oppose the wishes of sultans. If, therefore, I were to follow my inclination, and dissuade you from fulfilling what he requires of you, I should only expose you to his resentment, and at the same time make myself miserable. This is my opinion; but before we absolutely determine, let us consult the talking bird, and hear what it will advise. The bird has a great amount of penetration and shrewdness, and has promised his assistance in any difficulties we may encounter.'

"Princess Parizade caused the cage to be brought, and after explaining to the bird in the presence of the princes the embarrassment they were in, she asked what they ought to do in this perplexing situation. To this question the bird thus replied: 'The princes your brothers must comply with the wishes of the sultan; and they must in their turn even invite him to come and see your house.' 'But, bird,' said the princess, 'my brothers and I have such a strong attachment to each other that we are afraid our affectionate union will suffer from this acquiescence.' 'It will not suffer in the least,' answered the bird, 'but will even become stronger,' 'But in this case,' said the princess, 'will not the sultan see me?' 'It is necessary he should see you,' replied the bird; 'and everything will be the better for it.'

"Prince Bahman and Prince Perviz returned to the chase the next morning, and as soon as they were near enough to hear him, the sultan asked them if they had spoken to their sister. Prince Bahman then approached and answered, 'Your majesty may dispose of us as you please; we are ready to obey you. Far from having any difficulty in obtaining our sister's consent, she even chid us for having shown such a deference to her opinion while it was our duty only to attend to your majesty. But she is so worthy of our affection that if we have done wrong we entreat your majesty's pardon.' 'Do not let this matter give you a moment's uneasiness,' replied the sultan; 'so far from being offended at what you have done, I very much approve of it.' The princes were quite confused at the goodness and condecension of the sultan; and they could only answer him by inclining their heads almost to the ground, in order to show him the great respect with which they accepted his kindness.

"Contrary to his usual custom, the sultan soon desisted from the chase; for as he conjectured that the princes possessed cultivated and refined minds combined with their daring and intrepid dispositions, he was impatient to converse with them at his ease, and therefore hastened his return home. As they proceeded towards the capital, he desired them to ride by his side, an honour which excited the jealousy not only of the principal courtiers who accompanied him, but even of the grand vizier himself, who was extremely mortified at seeing strangers thus preferred to honour.

"When the sultan reached his capital, the attention of all the people who lined the streets was entirely taken up in looking at Prince Bahman and Prince Perviz. They asked every one who these strangers were, and whether they were foreigners or natives. 'But be that as it may,' exclaimed some of them, 'would to Heaven the sultan had given us two princes so handsome and gallant as these. They would have been nearly of the age of these men if the sultana who has been suffering so terrible a punishment had not been so unfortunate.'

"The first thing the sultan did when he arrived at the palace was to conduct the princes through the principal apartments, upon the beauty and richness of which they bestowed appropriate praise, as well as on the furniture and ornaments, and on the judgment exhibited in all the arrangements: they spoke without affectation, and like persons possessed of good taste. A very splendid repast was served up, and the sultan made them sit at the same table with himself. They indeed begged to be excused this honour, but at last obeyed the sultan, as he said it was his particular wish that they should dine with him.

"The sultan, who possessed a very good undertsanding, and had made a considerable progress in the different sciences, particularly in history, naturally supposed that the princes, deterred by their modesty or respect, would not take the liberty of beginning any particular conversation with him. To relieve them from this restraint, he accordingly started a subject himself, and continued to converse during the repast. But upon whatever subject he spoke, they showed such a variety of knowledge, wit, discrimination, and judgment, that he was quite astonished at their abilities and acquirements. 'If they had been my own children,' he said to himself, 'and had received all the advantages of the education I could have given them, with such an understanding as they have, they could not be more intelligent or better instructed.' In short, he felt such pleasure in their conversation that, after remaining longer at table than was his custom, he took them into his cabinet, where he again conversed with them for a considerable time. 'I should never have supposed,' said the sultan, addressing them, 'that any young men among my subjects, who resided in the country, possessed so fine an understanding and were so well educated as you. I have never in all my life held a conversation that has afforded me so much pleasure as this has done; but it is time to conclude and let you enjoy some of the amusements of my court; and as nothing is more capable than music of affording relaxation to the mind, we will now go and hear a concert of singers and players, which you will not find at all unpleasant or disagreeable.'

"When he had thus spoken, the musicians, who had already received their orders, came in, and by their skill perfectly answered the expectations that had been excited. This concert was succeeded by the feats of some excellent buffoons, while a performance by troops of dancers of both sexes concluded the entertainment.

"As the two princes observed the evening approaching, they prostrated themselves at the sultan's feet, and requested his leave to retire, after having returned him their thanks for the great condescension and honour with which he had treated them. On taking leave of them, the sultan said, 'I permit you to go; but remember that I have conducted you to the palace myself only to show you the road, that you may for the future come of your own accord. You will always be welcome; and the oftener you come the more pleasure you will afford me.' Before the brothers left the sultan, Prince Bahman thus addressed him: 'O gracious king, if we might be so bold, we would entreat your majesty to do our sister and ourselves the honour, the first time the diversion of hunting leads you into our neighbourhood, to alight and rest yourself at our house. It is not, indeed, worthy of receiving you; but monarchs do not sometimes disdain to repose in a cottage.' 'The house inhabited by such persons as you are,' replied the sultan, 'cannot but be excellent and worthy of yourselves. I shall visit it with great pleasure, and shall be still more rejoiced at being your guest and your sister's; for whom, even now before I see her, I feel a considerable regard, from the account you have given of her good qualities. I will not, therefore, deny myself this satisfaction longer than the day after to-morrow. Early in the morning I will not fail to be at the same spot where I well remember to have first met you: do you, therefore, be present, and become my guides.'

"Prince Bahman and Prince Perviz returned home the same evening, and reported to their sister, on their arrival, the kind and honourable reception the sultan had given them; and they then informed her that they had not neglected to request the monarch to honour their house with his presence whenever he passed near it. They likewise said that he had ot only agreed to come, but had appointed the next day but one for his visit.

"'If that be the case,' answered the princess, 'we must think of preparing a repast that may not be unworthy of his majesty; and in order to do this, I think it will be right to consult the talking bird, who will, perhaps, inform us of some dish which may please the sultan's taste better than any other.' As her brothers agreed to whatever Parizade thought proper to do, the princess went and consulted the bird alone when they had gone to bed. 'O bird,' she said, 'the sultan does us the honour of visiting us the day after to-morrow to see our house, and as we shall have to entertain him, pray tell me in what manner we must acquit ourselves of this duty so as to please him best.' 'My good mistress,' replied the bird, 'you have excellent cooks, who will of course do what they can; but above all things let them prepare a dish of cucumbers with pearl sauce, which must be placed before the sultan in the first course, in preference to every other dish.'

"'Cucumbers dressed with pearls!' exclaimed the princess with astonishment: 'you do not know what you are talking about, O bird: never was such a dish heard of. The sultan, indeed, might admire it from its magnificence, but he sits at table for the purpose of eating, and not to look at pearls. Besides, if I were to use all the pearls I have, there would not be sufficient to make such a dish.' 'My good mistress,' replied the bird, 'be so kind as to do as I say, and do not make yourself uneasy about the event: nothing but good will arise from it. And with respect to the pearls, you have but to go very early to-morrow, and at the foot of the first tree in your park on the right hand, to turn up the earth, and you will find more than you will in any way need.'

"Princess Parizade desired the gardener to be summoned the same evening to hold himself in readiness, and very early the next morning she took him with her, and went to the tree which the bird had pointed out. When the gardener had dug down to a certain depth, he found that his spade struck against a hard substance, and immediately discovered a gold box, about a foot square, which he pointed out to the princess. 'It was for this that I brought you here,' replied the princess: 'dig it up, and take care you no not injure it with your spade.'

"The gardener at last brought out the box and put it into the hands of the princess; and as it was only fastened with small clasps, Parizade easily opened it. She found it quite full of pearls of a moderate and equal size, and very proper for the purpose for which she wanted them. Well satisfied at having found this treasure, she shut the box, put it under her arm, and returned to the house, while the gardener filled up the hole with the earth, and restored it to its former state.

"As Prince Bahman and Prince Perviz had seen the princess in the garden much earlier than usual, while they were dressing in their rooms, they went together to meet her as soon as they were ready. They perceived her in the middle of the garden, and observed at a distance that she was carrying something under her arm. On approaching

PRINCESS PARIZADE WITH THE BOX OF PEARLS.

her, they found it was a small gold box, at which they were very much surprised. 'Dear sister,' said one of the princes in accosting her, 'you carried nothing out with you when we saw you go along followed by the gardener, and now you have a gold box in your hand! Is it a treasure that the gardener has discovered and came to report to you?' 'My dear brothers,' replied the princess, 'you do not guess right. It was I who took the gardener to the spot where the box was, and where, when I had pointed out the place, I made him dig up the earth. And you will be still more astonished at my good luck when you see what this casket contains.'

"The princess then opened the box, and her brothers were greatly surprised when they saw that it was full of pearls, not perhaps very costly from their size, when individually considered, but of great value, both from their quantity and quality. They asked by what accident she had become acquainted with the existence of this treasure. 'If you have no business of any consequence to take you elsewhere,' replied Parizade to her brothers, 'come with me, and I will inform you.' 'What business of importance,' said Prince Perviz, 'could we have, that could prevent us from learning what seems so much to interest you?'

"Princess Parizade then proceeded towards the house with her brothers, one walking on each side; and as she went, she related to them the consultation she had held with the bird; the questions she put, and the answers the bird gave. She spoke of the objection she made to the dish of cucumbers with pearl sauce; of the means the bird had pointed out to procure the pearls; and of the place it had mentioned where she was to go and find the gold box. The princess and her brothers meditated a long time upon these things, and endeavoured to discover the motive of the bird in wishing to have such a dish prepared for the sultan, and in having also pointed out the means of procuring it. But after a great deal of conversation on the subject, they acknowledged they could understand nothing of it; but they determined to follow the advice and directions of the bird in every particular, and not to omit a single point.

"When she went into the house, the princess ordered the chief cook to come to her apartment; and when she had given him all necessary orders for the repast with which she intended to entertain the sultan, she added, 'Besides what I have now ordered, you must prepare one dish for the sultan's particular taste; and no person but you may be employed in its preparation. And this is a dish of cucumbers with pearl sauce.' She then opened the box and showed him the pearls.

"At these words, the chief cook, who had never before heard of such a dish, stepped back two or three paces, and showed by his countenance how much he was astonished. The princess easily conjectured the reason of his surprise. 'I see very well,' she said, 'that you think me very foolish in ordering such a dish, one which you have never heard of before, and which it may be even said has never yet been made. All this is very true, and I know it as well as yourself. But I know what I am about, and am aware of the nature of the order I give you. Do you go, therefore, and execute it. Take the box, and do your best. If there are more pearls than you want, bring me back those that remain.' The chief cook made no answer, but took the box and carried it away. Princess Parizade then went and gave her orders to have everything put in its best state, and properly arranged, both in the house and garden, that she might give the sultan a worthy reception.

"The princes set off rather early the next morning to meet the sultan, and were at the appointed place when he arrived. He then began to hunt, and continued the chase with great eagerness till the heat of the sun, which now approached its highest elevation, obliged him to desist. And then Prince Perviz put himself at the head of the company, to show the way to their house, while Prince Bahman accompanied the sultan. When they came within sight of the house, Prince Perviz rode in advance, in order to announce to Princess Parizade the sultan's arrival; but the attendants of the princess, whom she had placed at some distance on the road for that purpose, had already informed her of his approach, and the prince found her waiting and ready to receive him.

"When the sultan arrived, and had entered the court, where he dismounted close to the vestibule, Princess Parizade came forward and fell at his feet: her brothers, who were present, informed the sultan who she was, and requested him to accept the homage she rendered him. The sultan stooped down and raised the princess, and after looking at her for some time and admiring her beauty, which quite dazzled him, as well as the elegance of her form, and a certain gracefulness of manner which did not at all bespeak the seclu-

PRINCESS PARIZADE SHOWS THE SULTAN THE WONDERS OF HER PALACE.

sion of a country life, he exclaimed, 'Behold here two brothers worthy of their sister, and a sister equally worthy of her brothers: and to judge from what I see, I am no longer surprised that such brothers wish to do nothing without the advice and consent of such a sister; and I hope to become better acquainted with her when I shall have looked over the house.'

"The princess then spoke: 'This, O king, must be considered only as a country house, and suited to such persons as ourselves, who pass our lives at a distance from the great world. It possesses nothing worthy of being compared with the residences in cities, and still less can it challenge comparison with the magnificent palaces belonging to sultans.' 'I cannot,' replied the sultan, in an obliging manner, 'be entirely of your opinion. What I have already seen gives me great expectations of what I am going to view. I will, however, reserve my judgment until you have shown me the whole. Proceed, therefore, and lead the way.'

"The princess, passing by the saloon, took the sultan through all the apartments. After having examined each of them very attentively and admired their variety, he said, 'O beautiful lady, do you call this a country house? The finest and most magnificent cities would be very soon deserted if all country houses resembled yours. I am no longer astonished that you are so well pleased with your position, and despise the city. Let me also see your garden, for I have no doubt it corresponds with the beauty of the house.'

"Princess Parizade then opened the door that led into the garden, where the first thing that attracted the sultan's eyes was the fountain of yellow water, resembling liquid gold. Surprised at so new and unexpected an object, he contemplated it for some time with looks of the greatest admiration. 'Where does this wonderful water come from, with which I am so delighted?' he exclaimed. 'Whence is its source, and by what contrivance does it rise in a way that seems to me more extraordinary than anything in the whole world? I must examine it more nearly.' And as he said this he went forward. The princess continued to conduct him, and at last led him to the place where the singing tree was planted.

"As he approached it, the sultan heard a concert very different from any he was acquainted with. He stopped, and cast his eyes round to see the musicians, but he could not descry any, either far or near; yet he continued to hear a concert that delighted him. 'Where,' he exclaimed, 'are the performers I hear? Are they under the earth, or invisible in the air? With such delightful and charming voices as they possess, they would risk nothing by being seen, but, on the contrary, afford only pleasure.' 'They are not musicians, O great king,' replied the princess, with a smile, 'that give this concert which you hear. The tree which your majesty sees before you produces it; and if you will give yourself the trouble to go three or four steps forward you will be sure of it, as the voices will be more distinct.'

"The sultan went forward, and was so charmed with the sweet harmony of the sounds that he continued listening to them for a long time. He at last recollected that he had seen the golden water not far off; and then he addressed Princess Parizade in these words: 'Tell me, I entreat you, whether you accidentally found this wonderful tree in your garden, whether it was a present that was made you, or whether you have had it brought from any distant country? It must most assuredly come from a considerable distance, otherwise I, who am so curious about natural rarities, should have heard of its fame. By what name is it known?'

"'Great king,' replied the princess, 'this tree is known by no other name than the singing tree, and it does not grow in this country. It would occupy too long a time to relate the adventure through which it came here. Its history is connected with the golden water and the talking bird, both of which were brought here at the same time; and your majesty will see these when you have looked at the golden water as long as you wish. If it is agreeable to you I will have the honour of giving you an account of them when you have rested yourself, and recovered from the labours of the chase and the additional fatigue you have given yourself during the great heat of the sun.'

"'I feel none of the fatigue you mention,' said the sultan, 'so amply am I repaid by the view of the wonderful things you show me. Rather say that I pay no attention to the trouble I give you. Let us finish our inspection, and again go and see the golden water. I am already full of anxiety also to behold and admire the talking bird.'

"When the sultan came to the golden water, he continued to look at it for a long time, particularly at the fountain, which never ceased to rise in the air in a wonderful manner, and again to fall into the basin. 'As you have told me,' said the sultan, addressing Princess Parizade, 'that this water has no source, and comes from no place in the neighbourhood, I must at least conclude that it is foreign, like the singing tree.'

"'Your majesty's conjecture is just,' replied the princess; 'and to prove to you that this water comes from no other place, I must inform you that this basin is made of a single stone, and therefore no water can enter either through the bottom or the sides;

THE PRINCESS AND HER BROTHERS LEARN THEIR EARLY HISTORY.

and what makes this water the more remarkable is, that I only put a very small quantity of it into the basin, and that, through a property which is peculiar to it, the fountain rises up as you see.' The sultan at last left the basin. 'Indeed,' said he, as he went away, 'this is enough for the first time, but I promise myself the pleasure of coming here very often. Take me now to see the talking bird.'

"As they approached the saloon, the sultan perceived a great multitude of birds upon the trees, each of which filled the air with its peculiar song. He inquired on what account the birds thus collected altogether in this place in preference to the other parts of the garden, where he had neither seen nor heard a single one. 'O great king,' replied Princess Parizade, 'the reason is that they all come here to accompany the talking bird. Your majesty may perceive it in its cage upon one of the windows of the saloon into which we are now going. And if you will listen, you will discover also that it sings far more melodiously than all the other birds, not excepting even the nightingale, which does not come near it in excellence.'

"The sultan then went into the saloon, while the bird continued to sing. O my slave,' said the princess, addressing the bird, and raising her voice, 'do you not see the sultan? Pay your homage to him.' The bird immediately ceased singing, on which the other birds were also silent. 'The sultan is welcome,' said the bird, 'and may Heaven cause him to prosper, and prolong his life for many years.' As the repast was served up on a sofa near the window where the bird was, the sultan, on sitting down to the table, replied, 'I thank you, bird, for your good wishes, and am delighted to see in you the sultan and king of birds.'

"The sultan, who perceived near him a dish of cucumbers, which he supposed to be dressed in the usual manner, drew it towards him with his hand, and was astonished to see the garnish of pearls. 'What novelty is this?' he cried. 'Why have a sauce with pearls? They are not fit to eat.' He looked both at the princes and their sister, as if to demand an explanation, but the bird spoke for them. 'Can your majesty be in so great a surprise at seeing cucumbers dressed with pearls, when you could so easily give credit to the account that the sultana your consort gave birth to a dog, a cat, and a piece of wood?' 'I believed it,' replied the sultan, 'because the attending women assured me of the fact.' 'These women,' answered the bird, 'were the sultana's sisters; but they were sisters jealous of the honour and happiness you had bestowed upon her in preference to themselves; and from wicked envy and jealousy they deceived you, O king. They will confess their crime if you question them. The two brothers and the sister whom you behold are your children, whom those wicked sisters abandoned to death, but who were found by the superintendent of your gardens, and who were nursed and educated through his care and kindness.'

"This speech of the bird instantly made the sultan comprehend the whole case. 'O bird,' replied he, 'I understand the whole plot that your speech has discovered to me. The strong inclination that attracted me towards these brothers and this sister, the affection I already feel for them, tell me most plainly they are my offspring. Come, then, my children, and let me embrace you all, and give you the first proof of my tender love as a father.' He rose and embraced them all three, mingling his tears with theirs. 'This is not enough, my children,' he exclaimed: 'you must also embrace each other, not as the offspring of the superintendent of my gardens, to whom I am under an everlasting obligation for having preserved your lives, but as belonging to me, and as having sprung from the blood royal of Persia, of which I am persuaded you will always show yourselves worthy.'

"When the two princes and their sister had mutually embraced each other as the sultan wished, with a new-felt ardour, he sat down to table with them, and pressed them to eat. When he had finished his repast, he said, 'In my person, my children, you behold your father! To-morrow I will bring you the sultana your mother; prepare, therefore, to receive her.'

"The sultan mounted his horse and returned with the utmost diligence to the capital. The first thing he did on dismounting and entering his palace, was to order the grand vizier instantly to draw up an accusation against the two sisters of the sultana. They were arrested, brought from their own houses, and separately interrogated. Their own confession convicted them, and they were condemned to be beheaded and quartered. The sentence was carried out in less than an hour.

"In the meantime Sultan Khosrouschah, followed by his whole court, went on foot to the gate of the great mosque; and after having with his own hand taken the sultana out of the narrow prison in which she had languished for so many years, and suffered so much, embracing her with tears in his eyes at seeing the wretched state she was in, he exclaimed, 'I am come, O my queen, to implore your pardon for the injustice I have done you, and to make you all the reparation that is justly due to you from me. I have already begun it by the punishment of those who deceived me with an abominable imposture; and I hope you will consider my atonement is completed when I shall have presented to you two accomplished princes, and an amiable and charming princess, all of whom are our offspring. Come, then, and resume the rank which belongs to you, with every honour that is your due.'

"This reparation was made before a multitude of people, who had collected in crowds from every part on the first report of what was going forward; for the knowledge of these events was very soon spread all over the city.

"Very early the next morning, the sultan and sultana, the latter of whom had changed the dress of humiliation and affliction which she had worn the preceding day, for a most magnificent robe, such as suited her rank, set out for the house of the children, followed by all the court in regular order. When they arrived, and as soon as they had alighted, the sultan presented the sultana to Prince Bahman, Prince Perviz, and Princess Parizade. 'Behold, O queen,' he exclaimed, 'your two sons and your daughter. Embrace them with the same tenderness and affection I have shown, for they are worthy of us both.' During this affecting introduction, tears of joy fell in abundance from the eyes of all, but most were shed by the sultana, in the tumult of her feelings, at embracing three children who had been the innocent cause of her long and severe distresses.

"The two princes and the princess had prepared a most magnificent repast for the sultan, sultana, and all the court. They then sat down to table, and after the repast was finished, the sultan led the sultana into the garden, where he pointed out to her the singing tree and the golden water. She had already seen the bird in its cage in the saloon, of which the sultan spoke very highly in praise during the repast.

"When nothing remained to detain the sultan any longer, he mounted his horse. Prince Bahman accompanied him, riding on his right, and Prince Perviz on his left, while the sultana, with the princess on her left hand, followed the sultan. In this order, with some of the officers of the court preceding and others following them, each according to his rank, they pursued the road to the capital. As they approached the city, the people came out in crowds, even to some distance from the gates; and they gazed much at the sultana, and rejoiced with her at her happy change, after so long a penance, and then turned to look at the two princes and the princess; and they accompanied them with the loudest acclamations. Their attention was also attracted by the bird in its cage, which the princess carried before her. They could not but admire its singing, by which it attracted all the other birds round it, which kept following it, perching upon the trees in the country, and on the roofs of the houses as they passed along the streets.

"In this magnificent and joyful manner, Prince Bahman, Prince Perviz, and Princess Parizade were all conducted to the palace. In the evening the most brilliant illumination and the greatest rejoicings took place, all of which continued for many days, not only in the palace, but throughout the city."

The Sultan of the Indies could not but admire the astonishing memory of the sultana his consort, whose stock of tales seemed inexhaustible, and who had thus continued to furnish fresh amusement every night for a long period.

A thousand and one nights had passed in this innocent amusement, and the lapse of time had very much tended to diminish the cruel prepossession and prejudice of the sultan against the fidelity of all wives. His mind had become softened, and he was convinced of the great merit and good sense of the Sultana Scheherazade. He well recollected the courage with which she voluntarily exposed herself to destruction, in becoming his queen, without at all dreading the death to which she knew she was destined, like those who had preceded her.

These considerations, added to his experience of the excellent qualities which he found she possessed, at last urged him absolutely to pardon her. "I am well aware," he said, "O amiable Scheherazade, that it is impossible to exhaust your store of those pleasant and amusing tales with which you have so long entertained me. You have at length appeased my anger, and I freely revoke in your favour the cruel law I had promulgated. I receive you entirely into my favour, and wish you to be considered as the preserver of many ladies, who would, but for you, have been sacrificed to my just resentment."

The sultana threw herself at his feet, which she embraced most tenderly, and gave every sign of the most heart-felt and lively gratitude.

The grand vizier heard the delightful intelligence from the sultan himself. It was immediately reported through the city and different provinces; and it brought down upon the heads of Sultan Schahriar and his amiable Sultana Scheherazade, the heart-felt praises and grateful blessings of all the people of the empire of the Indies.